D1513344

THE PENGUIN CLASSICS

EDITED BY E. V. RIEU

LIO

THE
ADVENTURES OF
DON QUIXOTE

BY

Miguel de Cervantes Saavedra

THE
ADVENTURES OF
DON QUIXOTE

BY

Miguel de Cervantes Saavedra

TRANSLATED BY
J. M. COHEN

Published by
Penguin Books, Harmondsworth
Middlesex

Penguin Books Ltd, Harmondsworth, Middlesex

U.S.A.: Penguin Books Inc., 3300 Clipper Mill Road, Baltimore 11, Md
[*Educational Representative:*
D. C. Heath & Co., 285 Columbus Avenue, Boston 16, Mass]

AUSTRALIA: Penguin Books Pty Ltd, 200 Normanby Road,
Melbourne, S.C.5, Victoria

AGENTS IN CANADA: Riverside Books Ltd, 47 Green Street,
Saint Lambert, Montreal, P.Q.

—

Made and printed in Great Britain by
Richard Clay and Company Ltd, Bungay, Suffolk

—

First published 1950
Reprinted 1952

CONTENTS

Translator's Introduction 11

The Adventures of Don Quixote

The Author's Dedication of the First Part 23

THE FIRST PART

Prologue 25
1. The character of the knight 31
2. His first expedition 35
3. He attains knighthood 41
4. An adventure on leaving the inn 46
5. The knight's misfortunes continue 52
6. The inquisition in the library 56
7. His second expedition 63
8. The adventure of the windmills 68
9. The battle with the gallant Basque 75
10. A conversation with Sancho 79
11. His meeting with the goatherds 84
12. The goatherd's story 90
13. The conclusion of the story 95
14. The dead shepherd's verses etc. 104
15. The meeting with the Yanguesans 111
16. The inn which he took for a castle 118
17. More misadventures at the inn 125
18. A second conversation with Sancho, etc. 132
19. The adventure with a corpse 142
20. A tremendous exploit achieved 148
21. The winning of Mambrino's helmet 160
22. The liberation of the galley slaves 171
23. An adventure in the Sierra Morena 181
24. The same adventure continued 191

25. The knight's penitence 199
26. More extravagancies in the Sierra Morena 214
27. The priest and the barber ride out 222
28. Their adventure in the mountains 236
29. They rescue the knight 248
30. The fair Dorothea's trick 258
31. Another conversation with Sancho 268
32. Adventures at the inn 276
33. The Tale of Foolish Curiosity 282
34. The tale continued 299
35. The battle with the wineskins and the end of the tale .. 316
36. Further adventures at the inn 324
37. The princess Micomicona and other matters 332
38. A discourse on arms and learning 342
39. The Captive's tale 345
40. The Captive's tale continued 353
41. The Captive's tale concluded 363
42. Yet more adventures at the inn 381
43. The mule boy and other matters 387
44. Adventures continue at the inn 396
45. The truth about Mambrino's helmet 403
46. Of Sancho's suspicions and other matters 410
47. The knight is enchanted 418
48. The canon on books of chivalry 427
49. Sancho talks with his master 433
50. Don Quixote argues with the canon 440
51. The goatherd's tale 445
52. The last adventure 450

The Author's Dedication of the Second Part 465

THE SECOND PART

Prologue 467
1. The priest, the barber and the knight 471
2. The housekeeper, the niece and the squire 481
3. The knight, the squire and the bachelor 485

4. Sancho answers the bachelor 492
5. Sancho and his wife 497
6. An important chapter 502
7. The knight and his squire 507
8. In search of Dulcinea 514
9. At El Toboso 520
10. Dulcinea enchanted 524
11. The chariot of death 532
12. The Knight of the Mirrors 538
13. The Knight of the Wood and the squires' conversation 544
14. The adventure continued 550
15. The knight's identity revealed 560
16. The gentleman in green 562
17. The adventure of the lions 570
18. A visit to the gentleman in green 580
19. The loving shepherd 587
20. Camacho's wedding 594
21. Camacho's wedding continues 602
22. The cave of Montesinos 607
23. The knight's vision 614
24. Meetings on the road 624
25. The prophesying ape 629
26. The puppet show 638
27. The braying adventure 646
28. Concerning a squire's wages 651
29. The enchanted bark 656
30. The fair huntress 662
31. The squire, the duchess and the waiting-woman 666
32. The knight defends himself 674
33. Sancho talks to the duchess 686
34. The arrival of the enchanters 692
35. How Dulcinea is to be disenchanted 699
36. The Countess Trifaldi and Sancho's letter 706
37. The adventure with the Countess continued 711
38. The Countess's sad story 713
39. The Countess's sad story continued 719

40. The knight's instructions 721
41. The arrival of Clavileño 726
42. The knight's advice to his squire 735
43. Further advice on the government of isles 740
44. Sancho sets out 745
45. Sancho takes possession of his isle 754
46. The alarming cats and bells 760
47. Governor Sancho 764
48. Doña Rodriguez visits the knight 772
49. Sancho makes his rounds 779
50. Teresa receives her presents 789
51. Sancho's progress 797
52. The adventure of Doña Rodriguez 804
53. The end of Sancho's governorship 811
54. Sancho meets Ricote 816
55. Sancho's misadventures 822
56. The knight fights the lackey 829
57. The knight's departure 833
58. Adventures fall thick and fast 837
59. An extraordinary adventure at an inn 847
60. On the road to Barcelona 854
61. The knight enters Barcelona 865
62. The enchanted head 868
63. A visit to the galleys 879
64. The knight's downfall 887
65. The Knight of the Moon revealed 891
66. Sancho's judgment 896
67. The knight chooses the pastoral life 900
68. The adventure with the hogs 905
69. The strangest of all adventures 909
70. Altisidora's last words 914
71. On the way home 920
72. Knight and squire return to their village 926
73. A discussion about omens 930
74. The death of Don Quixote 934

TRANSLATOR'S INTRODUCTION

SOME excuse seems necessary for reintroducing in a fresh translation a book which has been one of the world's best sellers for three centuries, and which already exists in seven or eight English versions. But, for all that, the modern reader would be hard put to it to choose a good Don Quixote. The best and raciest version, Shelton's, being almost contemporary with the original, is the nearest to Cervantes in spirit. It suffers, however, like other seventeenth-century work, from a lack of familiarity with the idiom; many of Shelton's most picturesque touches bear little resemblance to Cervantes' phrases which they purport to translate. The eighteenth-century versions, available in cheap editions, are all of them readable, but none of them appreciably closer to the Spanish than Shelton's, and all prone to omit the passages they do not understand; and what the nineteenth-century translators gained in accuracy they lost in style. So when Mr Rieu offered me an opportunity of producing another version to go before a large public at a reasonable price, I felt that the field was still open, and set about the same task as each of my predecessors, the task of reconciling faithfulness to Cervantes with the writing of contemporary English: with what success it is for the reader to judge.

Don Quixote enjoys a peculiar place among the world's books, as the only well-known representative of a considerable literature; for from the fourteenth to the seventeenth centuries the Spanish was among the great literatures of the world. But although there are other books which deserve to be known, it is in the untranslatable field of poetry and verse drama that Spanish is strongest, and particularly in that most untranslatable of all, the traditional ballad, in which the Spaniards are as rich as ourselves.

It was as a skit on this universally popular poetry that Don Quixote began; and the first seven chapters, which seem to have been modelled on an obscure playlet of the day, are devoted to a crazy gentleman, who sets out to imitate the deeds recorded in the ballads, and ends up by convincing himself that he is the Knight Baldwin; in which character he addresses his neighbour, who is bringing him home on his ass from the first of his misadventures. If the book had gone no further than this *variation on a theme already several times attempted, Don Quixote would have been little more striking than that other madman of Cervantes' invention, the student in one of the* Exemplary Novels *who imagined that he was made of glass, and took precautions accordingly. But, like Fielding's Joseph Andrews, Don Quixote came alive in his author's hands; and if we search for the actual passage in which this miracle happened, it is surely when he turns on this neighbour of his, who protests that he is neither Baldwin nor the Moor Abindarraez, but plain Señor Quixana – Master Lantern-jaws. 'I know who I am,' replies the knight, 'and I know that I am capable of being not only the characters I have named, but all the Twelve Peers of France and all the Nine Worthies as well, for my exploits are far greater than all the deeds they have done, all together and each by himself.' It is with his historic attempt to make good this boast in despite of all the powers of reality that the rest of the book is concerned. While in the process the crazy gentleman is transformed from the victim of other people's horse-play into a dreamer who sometimes succeeds in imposing his vision on those he meets, and even in his most preposterous battles with the sordid forces of here-and-now has always our loving sympathy; though only too often we may have to hold our thumbs for him, as we might for some reckless child who has strayed on to an unrailed roof with a sheer drop to the street. But for all our fears, when he does fall, which he invariably does, he picks himself up, and is only a little the worse for each shaking.*

Cervantes, however, does not come out baldly on the side of the ideal and imaginary against the workaday world. Don Quixote does not live only in his own fantasies, like a Kafka hero. After that first expedition, he is seldom separated from his squire, Sancho Panza, whose peasant common-sense is often near to bringing his master to earth. The adventures of these two are the core of the book; and several modern writers have reminded us that the two of them stand for opposing forces that have been active in Spain ever since the book was written: the spirit of Quixote, living in the mind, oblivious of the successive defeats his country has sustained, master of the huge ramshackle Spanish Empire, whose riches invariably drained into foreign hands, a poor gentleman concerned more with his title to nobility than with the bareness of his larder; and the spirit of Sancho, the shrewd peasant whose simplicity was forever exploited, and whose poverty has never diminished.

Now, once the book got under way with Don Quixote's second ex-

pedition and the introduction of Sancho, Cervantes' irony was turned away from the ballads, which he always quotes with evident pleasure, and on to the romances of chivalry, extravagant adventure stories most popular in Spain at that time, a sort of mannered imitation of the old epics of chivalry which have come down to us in prose in Malory's Morte d'Arthur. *Here Cervantes was on firmer ground than in mocking at the ballads, for just how ridiculous were the many imitations of* 'Amadis of Gaul' *can be seen in the Clavileño episode in the second part of our story. But the book is not just a satire on an exaggerated literary fashion: the romances of chivalry would long ago have been forgotten if Cervantes had not attacked them, and* Don Quixote *would have less readers to-day if his author had not done more than attack Amadis and his brood. For the book is what Don Quixote would have wished it to be, an adventure story. But, unlike most adventure stories it is rich in characters, not only in its principal characters, but in all the many minor personages, some of whom make only a single appearance: the stout innkeeper with his fondness for the stories the reapers used to read in his inn; his wife, kindly enough until any of her property is in danger; their ladylike daughter; the slut Maritornes; the monks on their hired mules; the braggart convict Gines with his half-finished autobiography, and all the rest of them, as lively a bunch as ever Chaucer rode to Canterbury with. And then there are the rather more detailed figures: the priest, the barber, Sampson Carrasco, and that most imaginary of all characters, Don Quixote's version of the brawny Aldonza Lorenzo with the loud voice and the slight moustache, his mistress Dulcinea del Toboso.*

Character and incident come together, then, against the background of the Spain of that day, and Cervantes' eye for detail gives us a shrewd insight into the class structure of the country. On one side we see the Duke and Duchess living in feudal luxury in one of their country houses, and Don Ferdinand's father, a rich landowner, sending for the son of a smaller gentleman, who sees in this unexpected condescension the prospect of a brilliant career for the young man. We see, too, the awe in which these people are held by such prosperous farmers and stock-breeders as Dorothea's father. Yet the middle class contribute not only well-to-do farmers, but such worthies as the Captive's brother, the judge who has picked up a good job in the colonies; and the lady travelling with the Basque squire to join her husband at Seville may well be of the same origin; while the Captive himself shows us another means of livelihood resorted to by the sons of the impoverished gentry, a military career under one of the great captains, the career which Cervantes took up himself as a young man with no conspicuous success. Inset in the first part of the book we have a long account of this captain's captivity in Algiers, culminating in an exciting escape, and describing by the way the battle of Lepanto and other actions at which the author has himself been present. In this digression we get a detailed picture of life in Barbary; while in the second part we get its counterpart, an account of the expulsion of the prosperous Moorish population of Spain, the Moriscos, by Philip III. Then, as for artisans and craftsmen, we are shown the making and printing of books at Barcelona, and the small town administration of that 'isle' in which Sancho enjoyed his brief governorship. Lastly, we get a cross-section of the underworld in the accounts the convicts in the chain gang give of themselves. And every minor figure, from the gentleman whom Sancho observed at court walking with his equerry behind him, to the barber who served two villages and was so unlucky as to put his new brass basin on his head to protect his new hat from the rain, stands out clearly. Only the goatherds and shepherds are sentimentalised; for Cervantes was deeply affected by a convention of his own time, which is as tiresome to us as the extravagancies he himself parodies – I mean the pastoral convention, which involved the pretence that only simple folk had deep and genuine sentiments, and sent the fashionable gentry for a century out into their carefully tended parks in the fancy dress of shepherds and shepherdesses, as Don Quixote found them that day when he and Sancho got entangled in the nets they had stretched among the trees to snare the birds.

These too-eloquent shepherds and goatherds, carving their mistresses' names on the bark of the cork trees and composing poems in their honour, are certainly to our present-day taste the weak spot of the book. And while with Sancho we appreciate the goatherds' good fare, their full wine-skins and their fresh cheese, we find their habit of dying of love neither credible nor poetic, and remain unmoved by the sugar-candy perfection of their shepherdesses, and the artificiality of their sentiments and language. How far Cervantes subscribed to this pastoral convention, or how much he wrote in it to please his readers, is anyone's guess. We know that his first, unsuccessful, book, La Gàlatea, was in this manner, and that he did not choose to write the promised second part.

Another feature of our book which takes the contemporary reader aback is what we may broadly call its sexual morality. This is based on a crude scale of values by which honour is preserved so long as any seduction, however sordid, is covered up by marriage. This very masculine point of view is by no means confined to Cervantes, but is assumed throughout the Spanish literature of the time. But it is difficult for a present-day reader to accept Don Ferdinand's inclusion among the happy bridal couples at the end of the first part. For after seducing Dorothea under promise of marriage, he attempts to steal Lucinda from his best friend, and only after failing is he content to yield himself magnanimously to the loving Dorothea. This highly dubious behaviour, however, in the rich man's son is accepted, and even applauded, by all, including the genial priest; and here we can only assume that Cervantes accepted the conventions of his age without much question. About the 'Tale of Foolish Curiosity' we can hardly be so charitable; for neither its morality nor its psychology bears a moment's examination, and except perhaps for a mild interest in the turn of events, it is difficult to see what amusement the average reader can find in it. My advice to anyone who has found his patience wearing thin, say during Marcela's speech in praise of freedom, is to skip it. Yet we are assured that everyone who heard it thought it a most delightful story, and even the priest approved of it, though with certain reservations.

Nor, despite his frequent shafts of satire against officials and ecclesiastics, can we think of Cervantes as a social critic. If the travelling monks on their sleek mules or the mumbling priests escorting the dead body are figures of fun, the village priest and the canon are both intelligent, charming and broad-minded men. The same rule applies to such public officials as we meet, and as for the Inquisition, which seems to have so far interfered with our author as to make him change Don Quixote's shirt-tail rosary for one of oak-galls, we can discover no protest against its ubiquitous activities, and even find a rather fulsome apology for the combined activities of Church and State in the expulsion of the Moriscos put into the mouth of the Morisco Ricote. It is unnecessary to take this justification for Cervantes' own point of view. But there can be no reason to suppose that he saw the action in the light of history, as an act of arbitrary cruelty which robbed Spain of an industrious and valuable population. The age of the Counter Reformation was not one of social protest, and Cervantes was by no means peculiar in confining himself to satire against individual corruptions rather than against a system which had once and for all suppressed such protestant and bourgeois criticism as had arisen. If we are to deduce Cervantes' ideals from any one character, it must be from the Man in the Green Overcoat, one of those quiet country gentlemen who remained the most enlightened and civilised figures in Europe until well on into the eighteenth century.

But however much we may be delighted and entertained by the rich detail of the social background, it is in the twin figures in the foreground that the true magic lies. It is impossible to lay our fingers on the qualities in the Knight of the Sad Countenance which make him a more and more lovable figure as the book progresses, even though he never becomes any less ridiculous than when he first stood vigil over his arms in the inn yard. How little we should have regretted his violent disillusionment then! Yet by the time of his final overthrow by the Knight of the White Moon we are on his side against all the forces of reason and sanity. For his madness is something we all share, a fantastic protest against the limitations of worldly existence, which makes us lend instant sympathy to the subtlest of all its critics, the comics who take its knocks; to Falstaff, or Charlie Chaplin, or to a more resilient mocker like Groucho Marx.

But if Don Quixote increasingly gains our sympathy as the book progresses, and the sadistic slapstick of the first chapters gives way to the inventive richness of the knight's disquisitions on chivalry, his conversations with his squire, and his magnificently staged penance, Sancho wins our affection by leaps and bounds. A genius seems to develop in the man whose first preoccupations were his belly and his comfort. We watch the coward of the adventure of the fulling mills pull off his first exercise in fiction, the report of his interview with Dulcinea. We see him go from strength to strength, and note the ebb and flow of his credulity, until we have to applaud his consummate skill in passing a peasant girl off on his master as Dulcinea herself, under enchantment. From there to his successful spell as governor of his 'isle' we see his wonder and amazement at his own ingenuity. But we are hardly distressed at his return to the humdrum life of his village. For however much his master's insanity may have drawn him after it into exalted spheres of action, his credulity was never complete and his feet were in reality always well planted on the ground.

There is no doubt at all that the book improves as it progresses; the second part, published some ten years after the first, is by far and away the richer and subtler. It is also more of a unity. For such digressions as there are do not take the form of separate tales, but are incorporated in the main body of the story. These digressions certainly offer an obstacle to the present-day reader; and my advice to anyone who finds himself bogged down by the goatherd's tale in the twelfth chapter is to skip it judiciously, without missing any of Don Quixote's observations, then to read on from the fifteenth chapter, to skip the Cardenio–Lucindo–Dorothea episodes in the twenty-fourth and twenty-eighth, and to cut out the 'Tale of Foolish Curiosity', but to read the Captive's story – which is interesting, though it does not bear on the main theme of the book – and so right on to the end of the first part, leaving out the goatherd's story in chapter fifty-one. For it would be a sad thing indeed if any reader of Don Quixote were to miss the enchantment of Dulcinea, the knight's descent into Montesinos' cave, Master Peter's puppet-show, the adventure of the enchanted bark, or Sancho's spell of government, all in the second part, merely through getting stuck by the pastoral stories in the first. Of the parts devoted to the knight and his squire no one will have any cause to complain, even though Cervantes sometimes drowses – in the rather too sadistic fight with the goatherd at the end of the first part, for instance – and is frequently careless and inconsistent about his detail: the reappearance of the stolen Dapple or the disappearance of the second guard with a firelock in the adventure of the galley-slaves are flagrant examples. The story is leisurely and episodic, being designed no doubt for reading aloud, as the innkeeper tells us the reapers read their stories, in the midday heat; and Cervantes seems never to have made a thorough revision of his book with a view to removing these inconsistencies, which no doubt arose through his making changes in the story as he wrote it.

The author's own life is typical of the all-round activity of the men of his day. Our own Edmund Spenser, Walter Raleigh and Philip Sidney were respectively an administrator, a courtier and adventurer, and a soldier, yet for all that the finest poets of their day. He was born in 1547, the son of a poor doctor, got some education from a schoolmaster who was permeated by the new critical spirit, and at twenty-one took service in Italy. Then, as a regular soldier, he was present at the naval battle of Lepanto (1571), described in the Cap-

tive's story and, though ill of fever, insisted on taking his place on the deck, where he received three wounds, one of which permanently maimed his left hand. After taking part in other engagements also recorded in the Captive's story, the action at Navarino and the failure to relieve the Goletta, he was captured with his brother by pirates on his voyage back to Spain in 1575, *and taken to Algiers, where he became the slave of a renegade Greek, made three unsuccessful attempts to escape, and was finally ransomed in* 1580. *For the rest of his life he was preoccupied with the difficulties of making a living and with unsuccessful attempts to get a good position under the Crown in reward for his services as a soldier. In the early eighties he was writing plays, two of which survive, and a pastoral novel,* La Galatea, *which was a self-confessed failure. In* 1587 *he was employed in the provisioning of the 'Invincible Armada', and incurred excommunication for laying hands on some corn which proved to be ecclesiastical property. This, however, was a less uncommon penalty than it might seem, and he was soon released from the Church's ban. A petition for an important post in America failed in* 1590; *and in the nineties Cervantes was in great poverty and several times in prison, once for failing to produce vouchers for official moneys spent. In* 1592 *he offered to write six plays at fifty ducats apiece, each to be one of the best ever produced in Spain, but no success came to him till the publication of the first part of* Don Quixote *in* 1604, *which brought him instant popularity. Such was the book's success that three pirated editions were produced within a few weeks. How much profit he made by it is not clear; he appeared still to be poor, and in* 1610 *was again hoping for preferment. But his daughter seems to have had some property, which she would not have got from any other source but her father. So his extreme proverty is by no means established. In* 1613 *he published a collection of short stories,* The Exemplary Novels, *an uneven book in which the tales of low life and the satires are as entertaining as the conventional tales of the type of our 'Tale of Foolish Curiosity' are dull. In the preface to the novels he promised a continuation of* Quixote, *and this was hurried on by the publication of Avellaneda's attempt at a sequel, which, from internal evidence, seems to have found Cervantes engaged on his fifty-ninth chapter. It was published in* 1614, *and in the next year Cervantes died, 'old, a soldier, a gentleman and poor', as a French visitor found him. But the book was already famous, and the first part translated into English and French.*

And now for a few words to the reader who has no Spanish and won-ders how much he is missing. There are of course puns and turns of phrase that are untranslatable; there are allusions that a Spaniard would see more readily than an Englishman; but the majority of these are topi-cal and are the subject of long notes in the more ponderous editions of the book. For in this respect Cervantes is as heavily annotated as Shake-peare. The whole of the story is here – or if it is not, the fault is in the translation. The characters' names are best pronounced in the English way. We have grown used to giving Don Quixote our English 'x'; and the guttural Castilian sound was new-fangled in Cervantes' own day, when the x would have been commonly pronounced 'sh', as it is in the French 'Quichotte'. The 'z' in Panza and the 'c' in Rocinante sound right in our ears as the English 'z'; in South American Spanish they are pronounced as 's' and in Castilian as 'th'. The rest of the names I have anglicised where possible – Sampson Carrasco, Dorothea, Lucinda, etc. – and the reader is best advised to pronounce them all in the English way, all the more so because the pronunciation of Spanish has changed since Cervantes' time. My only doubt has been in the case of Roland. For the Roland of our story is often not the paladin of Charlemagne, but the Italian hero of Ariosto's poem 'Orlando Furioso'. I have preferred, however, to give him his English name throughout.

And finally, a word on the translation itself. I have taken as few liberties with the text as possible, and tried to adhere to a modern voca-bulary and modern word order, except in those passages where the ori-ginal language is deliberately archaic. I have had to translate most of Sancho's proverbs, though occasionally I have found an English saying sufficiently close to be able to substitute it. My chief difficulties have been in the pastoral narratives, where the language of the original is frequently stilted, and no amount of adaptation can make the story flow very freely. Some of the oaths and expletives have had to be toned down, as in this respect the richness of our vocabulary has been con-siderably depleted since the seventeenth century, and such a literal ren-dering as 'By God's hand!', or 'Woe is me!' is now merely funny. We have no doubt lost something by reducing our stock of epithets, but the translator must make do with what remain. As to the interpolated poems I cannot pretend to be happy. One or two of the sonnets have dis-tinction, but most of the pieces are not very good. But, since they are put into the mouths of various characters, we must think of them as incidental only to the story, and not as a serious endeavour at poetry-writing by Cervantes. I have generally taken versions from the older translators, often adapting them, particularly when they are Shelton's: for I do not feel any confidence that my own attempts would be better. But the prefatory verses I have left out, and generally produced my own renderings of the ballads, as I feel that the versions in full rhymes usually quoted make them appear more akin to 'The Inchcape Rock', than to 'King Estmere' or 'Chevy Chase', with which they belong. I have put hardly any notes at the bottom of the page. For I feel that the obscurities are few, and no attempts to explain them do much more than pile up indigestible historical references, that prevent the reader from getting along with the book; which is one of the best adventure stories in the world, and contains two of the greatest characters in all fiction.

January 1947.   J. M. C.

THE ADVENTURES OF
DON QUIXOTE

THE FIRST PART

To the Duke of Bejar

Marquis of Gibraleon, Count of Benalcazar and Bañares, Viscount
of the Town of Alcocer, and Lord of the Towns of Capilla,
Curiel and Burguillos

TRUSTING *in the favourable reception and honour your Excellency accords to all kinds of books, as a Prince so well disposed to welcome the liberal arts, more especially those which, out of nobility, are not abased to the service and profit of the vulgar, I have decided to publish the* Ingenious Gentleman Don Quixote de la Mancha *under the shelter of your Excellency's most illustrious name, begging you with the respect I owe to such greatness to receive him graciously under your protection; so that, although naked of that precious adornment of elegance and erudition in which works composed in the houses of the learned usually go clothed, in your shadow he may safely venture to appear before the judgment of some who, undeterred by their own ignorance, are in the habit of condemning the works of others with more rigour than justice. For when your excellency's wisdom takes account of my good intentions, I trust that you will not disdain the poverty of so humble an offering.*

MIGUEL DE CERVANTES SAAVEDRA

The Adventures of Don Quixote

THE FIRST PART

PROLOGUE

IDLE reader, you can believe without any oath of mine that I would wish this book, as the child of my brain, to be the most beautiful, the liveliest and the cleverest imaginable. But I have been unable to transgress the order of nature, by which like gives birth to like. And so, what could my sterile and ill-cultivated genius beget but the story of a lean, shrivelled, whimsical child, full of varied fancies that no one else has ever imagined -- much like one engendered in prison, where every discomfort has its seat and every dismal sound its habitation? Calm, a quiet place, the pleasantness of the fields, the serenity of the skies, the murmuring of streams and the tranquility of the spirit, play a great part in making the most barren muses bear fruit and offer to the world a progeny to fill it with wonder and delight. It may happen that a father has an ugly and ill-favoured child, and that his love for it so blinds his eyes that he cannot see its faults, but takes them rather for talents and beauties, and describes them to his friends as wit and elegance. But I, though in appearance Don Quixote's father, am really his step-father, and so will not drift with the current of custom, nor implore you, almost with tears in my eyes, as others do, dearest reader, to pardon or ignore the faults you see in this child of mine. For you are no relation or friend of his. Your soul is in your own body, and you have free will with the best of them, and are as much a lord in your own house as the King is over his taxes. For you know the old saying: under my cloak a fig for the king -- all of which exempts and frees you from every respect and obligation; and so you can say anything you think fit about this story, without fear of being abused for a bad opinion, or rewarded for a good one.

I would have wished to present it to you naked and unadorned, without the ornament of a prologue or the countless train of customary sonnets, epigrams and eulogies it is the fashion to place at the beginnings of books. For I can tell you that, much toil though it cost me to compose, I found none greater than the making of this preface you are reading. Many times I took up my pen to write it, and many times I put it down, not knowing what to say. And once when I was in this quandary, with the paper before me, my pen in my ear, my elbow on the desk and my hand on my cheek, thinking what to write, a lively and very intelligent friend of mine came in unexpectedly and, seeing me so deep in thought, asked me the reason. I did not conceal it, but said that I was thinking about the prologue I had to make for the history of Don Quixote, and that it so troubled me that I was inclined not to write one, and even not to publish the exploits of that noble knight; 'For how could you expect me not to be worried,' I went on, 'at what that ancient lawgiver they call the public will say when it sees me now, after all these years I have been sleeping in the silence of oblivion, come out with all my years on my back, with a tale as dry as a rush, barren of invention, devoid of style, poor in wit and lacking in all learning and instruction, without quotations in the margins or notes at the end of the book; whereas I see other works, never mind how fabulous and profane, so full of sentences from Aristotle, Plato and the whole herd of philosophers, as to impress their readers and get their authors a reputation for wide reading, erudition and eloquence? And when they quote Holy Scripture! You will be bound to say that they are so many St. Thomases or other doctors of the church, observing such an ingenious solemnity in it all that in one line they will depict a distracted lover and in the next preach a little Christian homily, that is a treat and a pleasure to hear or read. My book will lack all this; for I have nothing to quote in the margin or to note at the end. Nor do I even know what authors I am following in it; and so I cannot set their names at the beginning in alphabetical order, as they all do, starting with Aristotle and ending with Xenophon – and Zoilus or Zeuxis, although one of them was a libeller and the other a painter. My book must go without introductory sonnets as well – or at least sonnets, by dukes, marquises, counts, bishops, great ladies or famous poets; although were I to ask two or three friends in the trade, I know that they would give me them; and such good ones as would be unequalled by the productions of the most highly renowned poets in this Spain of ours. In fact, my dear friend,' I continued, 'I have decided that Don Quixote shall stay buried in the archives of La Mancha till Heaven provides someone to adorn him with all the jewels he lacks; for I find myself incapable of supplying them because of my inadequacy and scanty learning, and because I am too spiritless and lazy by nature to go about looking for authors to say for me what I can say myself without them. That is the cause of the perplexity and abstraction you found me in, for there is reason enough for my mood in what I have just told you.'

When my friend had heard me to the end he slapped his forehead and broke into a loud laugh, saying: 'Good Lord, brother, you have just relieved my mind of an error I have been in ever since I have known you, for I have always thought you were sensible and judicious in all your actions. But I see now that you are as far from being so as the sky is from the earth. How is it possible for matters of so little importance and so easily put right to have the power to perplex and preoccupy as ripe an intelligence as yours, so fitted to break down even greater difficulties and trample them underfoot? This does not spring from any lack of ability, I promise you, but from excess of laziness and poverty of resource. Would you like to be convinced that what I say is true? Then listen to me and you will see me confute all your difficulties in the twinkling of an eye, and set right all the defects which, you say, perplex and frighten you into giving up the publication of the history of your famous Don Quixote, light and mirror of all knight errantry.'

'Tell me,' I replied. 'By what means do you propose to fill the void of my fear and reduce the chaos of my confusion to clarity?'

'Your first stumbling block,' he replied, 'the sonnets, epigrams and eulogies which you lack for your introduction, and which should be by important and titled persons, can be got over by your taking a little trouble and writing them yourself. Afterwards you can baptise them and give them any names you like, fathering them on Prester John of the Indies or the Emperor of Trebizond; who, I have heard it rumoured, were famous poets: and even if they were not, and some pedants and graduates turned up to snap and growl at you behind your back in the name of truth, you need not bother about them a bit; for even if they convict you of a falsehood, they cannot cut off the hand you wrote it with.

'As to quoting in the margins the books and authors from whom you gathered the sentences and sayings you have put in your history, all you have to do is to work in some pat phrases or bits of Latin that you know by heart, or at least that cost you small pains to look out. For example, on the subject of liberty and captivity you might bring in:

'"Non bene pro toto libertas venditur auro."

'And in the margin cite Horace, or whoever said it. Then if you are writing of the power of death, you might make use of:

'"Pallida mors aequo pulsat pede pauperum tabernas
    Regumque turres."

'If you are dealing with friendship and the love God bids you bear to your enemy, come to the point at once with Holy Scripture, which you can do with a little bit of research by quoting the words of no less an authority than God himself: "Ego autem dico vobis: diligite inimicos vestros." If you are on the subject of evil thoughts, make use of the Gospel: "De corde exeunt cogitationes malae."

'On the instability of friendship there is Cato, who will give you his couplet:

'"Donec eris felix, multos numerabis amicos,
    Tempora si fuerint nubila, solus eris."

'With these little bits of Latin and such like, they may even take you for a scholar; and it is no small honour and profit to be one nowadays. As to putting notes at the end of the book, you may safely follow this method: if you mention a giant in the text, see that it is the giant Goliath. And by that alone, which will cost you almost nothing, you have a grand note, since you can write: *The giant Goliath or Golias was a Philistine, whom the shepherd David killed with a sling-shot in the Vale of Terebinth, as is recounted in the Book of Kings* – in whatever chapter you find it is. After that, to show that you are learned in the humanities and in cosmography, contrive to work some mention of the river Tagus into your story, and you will find yourself at once with another famous note: *The river Tagus was so called by a king of Spain; it has its source in such a place and flows into the Ocean, kissing the walls of the famous city of Lisbon. It is reported to have sands of gold, etc.'* If you are writing of thieves I will give you the story of Cacus, which I know by heart; if of prostitutes, there is the Bishop of Mondoñedo, who will assist you with Lamia, Laïs and Flora, and that note will gain you great credit; if of cruel women, Ovid will produce Medea for you; if of witches and sorceresses, Homer has Calypso and Virgil Circe; if of brave commanders, Julius Caesar will lend himself to you in his *Commentaries*, and Plutarch will give you a thousand Alexanders. If you are on the subject of love and have two pennyworth of Italian, you will come across Leon Hebreo, who will give you full measure. But if you do not want to travel into foreign parts, at home you have Fonseca *On the love of God*, which contains everything that you or the cleverest of them could want on the subject. In fact you have nothing more to do but to cite these names in your tale, or touch on the stories I have mentioned, and leave the task of putting in the notes and quotations to me; for I swear I will fill your margins and use up four pages at the end of the book.

'Let us come now to references to authors, which other books contain and yours lacks. The remedy for that is very simple; for you have nothing else to do but look for a book which quotes them all from A to Z, as you say. Then you put this same alphabet into yours. For, granted that the very small need you have to employ them will make your deception transparent, it does not matter a bit; and perhaps there will even be someone silly enough to believe that you have made use of them all in your simple and straightforward story. And if it serves for no other purpose, at least that long catalogue of authors will be useful to lend authority to your book at the outset. Besides, nobody will take the trouble to examine whether you follow your authorities or not, having nothing to gain by it. What is more, if I understand you rightly, this book has no need of any of the things that you say it lacks, for the whole of it is an invective against books of chivalry, which Aristotle never dreamed of, Saint Basil never mentioned, and Cicero never ran across. Nor do the niceties of truth or the calculations of astrology come within the scope of its fabulous narrative; nor is it concerned with geometrical measurements; nor with arguments which can be confuted by rhetoric; nor does it set out to preach to anyone, mingling the human with the divine; which is a kind of motley in which no Christian understanding should be dressed. In what you are writing you have only to make use of imitation, and the more perfect the imitation the better your writing will be. And since this book of yours aims at no more than destroying the authority and influence which books of chivalry have in the world and among the common people, you have no reason to go begging sentences from philosophers, counsel from Holy Writ, fables from poets, speeches from orators, or miracles from saints. You have only to see that your sentences shall come out plain, in expressive, sober and well-ordered language, harmonious and gay, expressing your purpose to the best of your ability, and setting out your ideas without intricacies and obscurities. Be careful too that the reading of your story makes the melancholy laugh and the merry laugh louder; that the simpleton is not confused; that the intelligent admire your invention, the serious do not despise it, nor the prudent withhold their praise. In short, keep your aim steadily fixed on overthrowing the ill-based fabric of these books of chivalry, abhorred by so many yet praised by so many more; for if you achieve that, you will have achieved no small thing.'

I listened in complete silence to my friend's words, and his arguments so impressed themselves on my mind that I accepted them as good without question, and out of them set about framing my prologue. By which, kind reader, you will see his wisdom, and my own good fortune in finding such a counsellor in a time of such need; and yourself be relieved at the straightforward and uncomplicated nature of the history of the famous Don Quixote de la Mancha; who, in the opinion of all the inhabitants of the district around the plain of Montiel, was the chastest lover and the most valiant knight seen in those parts for many a year. I do not want to exaggerate the service I am doing you by introducing to you so notable and honoured a knight. But I do want your thanks for making you acquainted with the famous Sancho Panza, his squire, in whom I think I present to you an epitome of all those squirely humours scattered through the swarm of vain books of chivalry.

And so, God give you health, and may He not forget me.
Farewell.

Chapter 1. *Which treats of the quality and way of life of the famous knight Don Quixote de la Mancha.*

IN a certain village in La Mancha, which I do not wish to name, there lived not long ago a gentleman – one of those who have always a lance in the rack, an ancient shield, a lean hack and a greyhound for coursing. His habitual diet consisted of a stew, more beef than mutton, of hash most nights, boiled bones on Saturdays, lentils on Fridays, and a young pigeon as a Sunday treat; and on this he spent three-quarters of his income. The rest of it went on a fine cloth doublet, velvet breeches and slippers for holidays, and a homespun suit of the best in which he decked himself on weekdays. His household consisted of a housekeeper of rather more than forty, a niece not yet twenty, and a lad for the field and market, who saddled his horse and wielded the pruning-hook.

Our gentleman was verging on fifty, of tough constitution, lean-bodied, thin-faced, a great early riser and a lover of hunting. They say that his surname was Quixada or Quesada – for there is some difference of opinion amongst authors on this point. However, by very reasonable conjecture we may take it that he was called Quexana. But this does not much concern our story; enough that we do not depart by so much as an inch from the truth in the telling of it.

The reader must know, then, that this gentleman, in the times when he had nothing to do – as was the case for most of the year – gave himself up to the reading of books of knight errantry; which he loved and enjoyed so much that he almost entirely forgot his hunting, and even the care of his estate. So odd and foolish, indeed, did he grow on this subject that he sold many acres of corn-land to buy these books of chivalry to read, and in this way brought home every one he could get. And of them all he considered none so good as the works of the famous Feliciano de Silva. For his brilliant style and those complicated sentences seemed to him very pearls, especially when he came upon those love-passages and challenges frequently written in the manner of: 'The reason for the unreason with which you treat my reason, so weakens my reason

31

that with reason I complain of your beauty'; and also when he read: 'The high heavens that with their stars divinely fortify you in your divinity and make you deserving of the desert that your greatness deserves.'

These writings drove the poor knight out of his wits; and he passed sleepless nights trying to understand them and disentangle their meaning, though Aristotle himself would never have unravelled or understood them, even if he had been resurrected for that sole purpose. He did not much like the wounds that Sir Belianis gave and received, for he imagined that his face and his whole body must have been covered with scars and marks, however skilful the surgeons who tended him. But, for all that, he admired the author for ending his book with the promise to continue with that interminable adventure, and often the desire seized him to take up the pen himself, and write the promised sequel for him. No doubt he would have done so, and perhaps successfully, if other greater and more persistent preoccupations had not prevented him.

Often he had arguments with the priest of his village, who was a scholar and a graduate of Siguenza, as to which was the better knight – Palmerin of England or Amadis of Gaul. But Master Nicholas, the barber of that village, said that no one could compare with the Knight of the Sun. Though if anyone could, it was Sir Galaor, brother of Amadis of Gaul. For he had a very accommodating nature, and was not so affected nor such a sniveller as his brother, though he was not a bit behind him in the matter of bravery.

In short, he so buried himself in his books that he spent the nights reading from twilight till daybreak and the days from dawn till dark; and so from little sleep and much reading, his brain dried up and he lost his wits. He filled his mind with all that he read in them, with enchantments, quarrels, battles, challenges, wounds, wooings, loves, torments and other impossible nonsense; and so deeply did he steep his imagination in the belief that all the fanciful stuff he read was true, that to his mind no history in the world was more authentic. He used to say that the Cid Ruy Diaz must have been a very good knight, but that he could not be compared to the Knight of the Burning Sword, who with a single backstroke had cleft a pair of fierce and monstrous giants in two. And he had were to meet with some giant hereabouts, as generally happens to knights errant, and if I were to overthrow him in the encounter, or cut him down the middle or, in short, conquer him and make him surrender, would it not be well to have someone to whom I could send him as a present, so that he could enter and kneel down before my sweet lady and say in tones of humble submission: "Lady, I am the giant Caraculiambro, lord of the island of Malindrania, whom the never-sufficiently-to-be-praised knight, Don Quixote de la Mancha, conquered in single combat and ordered to appear before your Grace, so that your Highness might dispose of me according to your will"?' Oh, how pleased our knight was when he had made up this speech, and even gladder when he found someone whom he could call his lady. It happened, it is believed, in this way: in a village near his there was a very good-looking farm girl, whom he had been taken with at one time, although she is supposed not to have known it or had proof of it. Her name was Aldonza Lorenzo, and she it was he thought fit to call the lady of his fancies; and, casting around for a name which should not be too far away from her own, yet suggest and imply a princess and great lady, he resolved to call her Dulcinea del Toboso – for she was a native of El Toboso –, a name which seemed to him as musical, strange and significant as those others that he had devised for himself and his possessions.

Chapter II. *Which treats of the First Expedition which the ingenious Don Quixote made from his village.*

ONCE these preparations were completed, he was anxious to wait no longer before putting his ideas into effect, impelled to this by the thought of the loss the world suffered by his delay, seeing the grievances there were to redress, the wrongs to right, the injuries to amend, the abuses to correct, and the debts to discharge. So, telling nobody of his intention, and quite unobserved, one morning before dawn – it was on one of those sweltering July days – he armed himself completely, mounted Rocinante, put on his badly-mended headpiece, slung on his shield, seized his lance and went out into the plain through the back gate of his yard, pleased and delighted to see with what ease he had started on his fair design. But scarcely was he

in open country when he was assailed by a thought so terrible that
it almost made him abandon the enterprise he had just begun. For
he suddenly remembered that he had never received the honour of
knighthood, and so, according to the laws of chivalry, he neither
could nor should take arms against any knight, and even if he had
been knighted he was bound, as a novice, to wear plain armour
without a device on his shield until he should gain one by his
prowess. These reflections made him waver in his resolve, but as
his madness outweighed any other argument, he made up his mind
to have himself knighted by the first man he met, in imitation of
many who had done the same, as he had read in the books which
had so influenced him. As to plain armour, he decided to clean his
own, when he had time, till it was whiter than ermine. With this
he quieted his mind and went on his way, taking whatever road his
horse chose, in the belief that in this lay the essence of adventure.

As our brand-new adventurer journeyed along, he talked to
himself, saying: 'Who can doubt that in ages to come, when the
authentic story of my famous deeds comes to light, the sage who
writes of them will say, when he comes to tell of my first expedition
so early in the morning: "Scarce had the ruddy Apollo spread
the golden threads of his lovely hair over the broad and spacious face
of the earth, and scarcely had the forked tongues of the little
painted birds greeted with mellifluous harmony the coming of the
rosy Aurora who, leaving the soft bed of her jealous husband,
showed herself at the doors and balconies of the Manchegan horizon, when the famous knight, Don Quixote de la Mancha, quitting
the slothful down, mounted his famous steed Rocinante and began
to journey across the ancient and celebrated plain of Montiel"?'
That was, in fact, the road that our knight actually took, as he
went on: 'Fortunate the age and fortunate the times in which my
famous deeds shall come to light, deeds worthy to be engraved in
bronze, carved in marble and painted on wood, as a memorial for
posterity. And you, sage enchanter, whoever you may be, to
whose lot it falls to be the chronicler of this strange history, I
beg you not to forget my good Rocinante, my constant companion
on all my rides and journeys!' And presently he cried again, as if
he had really been in love: 'O Princess Dulcinea, mistress of this
captive heart! You did me great injury in dismissing me and in-

flicting on me the cruel rigour of your command not to appear in your beauteous presence. Deign, lady, to be mindful of your captive heart, which suffers such griefs for love of you.'

He went on stringing other nonsense on to this, all after the fashion he had learnt in his reading, and imitating the language of his books at best he could. And all the while he rode so slowly and the sun's heat increased so fast that it would have been enough to turn his brain, if he had had any. Almost all that day he rode without encountering anything of note, which reduced him to despair, for he longed to meet straightway someone against whom he could try the strength of his strong arm.

There are authors who say that the first adventure he met was that of the pass of Lapice. Others say it was the windmills. But what I have been able to discover of the matter and what I have found written in the annals of La Mancha, is that he rode all that day, and that at nightfall his horse and he were weary and dying of hunger. Looking in all directions to see if he could discover any castle or shepherd's hut where he could take shelter and supply his urgent needs, he saw, not far from the road he was travelling on, an inn, which seemed to him like a star to guide him to the gates, if not to the palace, of his redemption. So he hurried on, and reached it just as night was falling. Now there chanced to be standing at the inn door two young women *of easy virtue*, as they are called, who were on the way to Seville with some carriers who happened to have taken up their quarters at the inn that evening. As everything that our adventurer thought, saw or imagined seemed to follow the fashion of his reading, as soon as he saw the inn he convinced himself that it was a fortress with its four towers and pinnacles of shining silver, complete with a drawbridge, a deep moat and all those appurtenances with which such castles are painted. So he approached the inn, which to his mind was a castle, and when still a short distance away reined Rocinante in, expecting some dwarf to mount the battlements and sound a trumpet to announce that a knight was approaching the fortress. But when he saw that there was some delay, and that Rocinante was in a hurry to get to the stable, he went up to the inn door and, seeing the two young women standing there, took them for two beauteous maidens or graceful ladies taking the air at the castle gate. Now at that very moment, as chance would have it, a swineherd was collecting from the stubble a drove of hogs – pardon me for naming them – and blew his horn to call them together. But Don Quixote immediately interpreted this in his own way, as some dwarf giving notice of his approach. So with rare pleasure he rode up, whereupon those ladies, thoroughly frightened at seeing a man come towards them dressed in armour with lance and shield, turned to go back into the inn. But Don Quixote, gathering from their flight that they were afraid, raised his pasteboard visor, partly revealing his lean and dusty face, and addressed them with a charming expression and in a calm voice: 'I beg you, ladies, not to fly, nor to fear any outrage; for it ill fits or suits the order of chivalry which I profess to injure anyone, least of all maidens of such rank as your appearance proclaims you to be.'

The girls stared at him, trying to get a look at his face, which was almost covered by the badly made visor. But when they heard themselves called maidens – a title ill-suited to their profession – they could not help laughing, which stung Don Quixote into replying: 'Civility befits the fair; and laughter arising from trivial causes is, moreover, great folly. I do not say this to offend you nor to incur your displeasure, for I have no other wish than to serve you.'

His language, which was unintelligible to them, and the uncouth figure our knight cut, made the ladies laugh the more. Whereat he flew into a rage, and things would have gone much farther, had not the innkeeper, a very fat man and therefore very peaceable, emerged at this moment. Now when he saw this grotesque figure in his equipment of lance, shield and coat of armour, which sorted so ill with his manner of riding, he was on the point of joining the young women in their demonstrations of amusement. But, fearing such a collection of armaments, he decided to speak politely, and addressed him thus: 'If your worship is looking for lodging, Sir Knight, except for a bed – we have none in this inn – you will find plenty of everything.'

And Don Quixote replied, seeing the humility of the warden of the fortress – for such he took the innkeeper to be: 'For me, Sir Castellan, whatever you have is enough. My ornaments are arms, my rest the bloody fray.'

The host thought that he had called him castellan because he took him for a safe man from Castile, though he was an Andalusian from the Strand of San Lucar, as thievish as Cacus and as tricky as a student or a page. So he replied: 'At that rate, your bed shall be the cruel rock, your sleep to watch till day, and that being so, you can safely dismount here in the certainty that you will find in this house ample reason for lying awake not only for one night but for a whole year.'

As he spoke he went to take Don Quixote's stirrup, and our knight dismounted with great labour and difficulty, as he had fasted all day. He then bade the host take good care of his steed, saying that no better piece of horseflesh munched oats in all the world. The innkeeper stared at the beast, which did not seem as good as Don Quixote said, not by a half. However, he put him up in the stable and, when he came back for his guest's orders, he found that the maidens had made it up with him and were taking off his armour. But although they had got off his breast-plate and back-piece, they had no idea how to get him out of his gorget, nor how to take off his counterfeit head-piece, which was tied with green ribbons that would have to be cut, as they could not undo the knot. But to this he would on no account agree, and so he stayed all that night with his helmet on, cutting the strangest and most ridiculous figure imaginable. And whilst he was being disarmed, imagining that these draggled and loose creatures were illustrious ladies and the mistresses of that castle, he addressed them most gracefully:

> 'Never was there knight
> By ladies so attended
> As was Don Quixote
> When he left his village.
> Maidens waited on him,
> On his horse, princesses –

or Rocinante, which, dear ladies, is the name of my horse, and Don Quixote de la Mancha is mine. For, although I did not wish to reveal myself till deeds done in your service and for your benefit do so for me, the need to adapt this old ballad of Lancelot to the present occasion has betrayed my name to you before the due season. But the time will come when your ladyships may command me and I shall obey; and the valour of my arms will then disclose the desire I have to serve you.'

The girls, who were not used to hearing such high-flown language, did not say a word in reply, but only asked whether he would like anything to eat.

'I would gladly take some food,' replied Don Quixote, 'for I think there is nothing that would come more opportunely.'

That day happened to be a Friday, and there was no food in the inn except some portions of a fish that is called pollack in Castile and cod in Andalusia, in some parts ling and in other troutlet. They asked whether his worship would like some troutlet, as there was no other fish to eat.

'So long as there are plenty of troutlet they may serve me for one trout,' replied Don Quixote, 'for I had just as soon be paid eight separate *reals* as an eight *real* piece. What is more, these troutlet may be like veal, which is better than beef, or kid, which is better than goats' meat. But, however that may be, let me have it now, for the toil and weight of arms cannot be borne without due care for the belly.'

They set the table for him at the inn door for coolness' sake, and the host brought him a portion of badly soaked and worse cooked salt cod with some bread as black and grimy as his armour. It made them laugh a great deal to see him eat because, as he kept his helmet on and his visor up, he could get nothing into his mouth with his own hands, and required someone's assistance to put it in; and so one of those ladies performed this task for him. But to give him anything to drink would have been impossible if the innkeeper had not bored a reed, put one end into his mouth and poured the wine into the other. All this he bore with patience rather than break the ribbons of his helmet.

While they were thus occupied there happened to come to the inn a sow-gelder, and as he arrived he blew his reed whistle four or five times; which finally convinced Don Quixote that he was at some famous castle, that they were entertaining him with music, that the pollack was trout, the black bread of the whitest flour, the whores ladies and the innkeeper warden of the castle. This made him feel that his resolution and his expedition had been to good purpose, but what distressed him most deeply was that he was not yet knighted, for he believed that he could not rightfully embark on any adventure without first receiving the order of knighthood.

Chapter III. *Which tells of the pleasant method by which Don Quixote chose to be knighted.*

So, troubled by these thoughts, he cut short his scanty pothouse supper, and when he was done called the host. Then, shutting the stable door on them both, he fell on his knees before him and said: 'Never will I arise from where I am, valiant knight, till you grant me of your courtesy the boon I am going to beg of you; it is one which will redound to your praise and to the benefit of the human race.'

Seeing his guest at his feet and hearing such language, the innkeeper stared in confusion, not knowing what to do or say, and pressed him to get up; but in vain, for the knight refused to rise until his host had promised to grant him the boon he begged.

'I expected no less from your great magnificence, dear sir,' replied Don Quixote. 'So I will tell you that the boon I begged of you, and you in your generosity granted, is that you will knight me on the morning of to-morrow. This night I will watch my arms in the chapel of this castle of yours, and to-morrow, as I said, my dearest wish will be fulfilled, and I shall have the right to ride through all quarters of the world in search of adventures, for the benefit of the distressed, according to the obligations of knighthood and of knights errant like myself, whose minds are given to such exploits.'

The innkeeper, who, as we have said, was pretty crafty and had already a suspicion that his guest was wrong in the head, was confirmed in his belief when he heard this speech, and, to make some sport for that night, decided to fall in with his humour. So he told him that he was doing a very proper thing in craving the boon he did, and that such a proposal was right and natural in a knight as illustrious as he seemed and his gallant demeanour showed him to be. He added that he, too, in the day of his youth had devoted himself to that honourable profession and travelled in divers parts of the world in search of adventures, not omitting to visit the Fish Market of Malaga, the Isles of Riaran, the Compass of Seville, the Little Market Place at Segovia, the Olive Grove at Valencia, the Circle of Granada, the Strand of San Lucar, the Colt-fountain of Cordova, the Taverns of Toledo and sundry other places, where he had exercised the agility of his heels and the lightness of his fingers, doing many wrongs, wooing many widows, ruining sundry maidens and cheating a few minors – in fact, making himself well-known in almost all the police-courts and law-courts in Spain. Finally he had retired to this castle, where he lived on his own estate and other people's, welcoming all knights errant of whatever quality and condition, only for the great love he bore them – and to take a share of their possessions in payment for his kindness.

He added that there was no chapel in the castle where he could watch his arms, for it had been pulled down to be rebuilt. But he knew that a vigil might be kept in any place whatever in case of need. So that night he might watch his arms in a courtyard of the castle, and in the morning, God willing, the due ceremonies might be performed, and he emerge a full knight, as much a knight as any in the whole world. He asked him if he had any money with him, and Don Quixote replied that he had not a penny, since he had never read in histories concerning knights errant of any knight that had. At this the innkeeper said that he was wrong: for, granted that it was not mentioned in the histories, because their authors could see no need of mentioning anything so obvious and necessary to take with one as money and clean shirts, that was no reason for supposing that knights did not carry them. In fact, he might take it for an established fact that all knights errant, of whom so many histories were stuffed full, carried purses well lined against all eventualities, and also took with them clean shirts and a little box full of ointments to cure the wounds they got. For on the plains and deserts where they fought and got their wounds they had not always someone at hand to cure them, unless of course they had some magician for a friend. A sorcerer, of course, might relieve them at once by bearing through the air on a cloud some maiden or dwarf with a flask of water of such virtue that after tasting a single drop they were immediately cured of their sores and wounds, and it was as if they had never had any injuries. However, in default of this, the knights of old made certain that their squires were provided with money and other necessaries, such as lint and ointment, to dress their wounds. But when such knights chanced to have no squires – there were only a few rare instances – they carried it all themselves on the cruppers of their horses in bags so very thin that they hardly showed, as though they contained something of even more importance. For, except for such purposes, the carrying of bags was not tolerated among knights errant. So he advised Don Quixote – though as his godson, which he was so soon to be, he might even command him – not to travel in future without money and the other requisites he had mentioned, and he would see how useful they would prove when he least expected it.

Don Quixote promised to do exactly as he recommended, and promptly received his instructions as to keeping watch over his armour in a great yard which lay on one side of the inn. He gathered all the pieces together and laid them on a stone trough, which stood beside a well. Then, buckling on his shield, he seized his lance and began to pace jauntily up and down before the trough. And just as he began his watch, night began to fall.

The innkeeper told everyone staying in the inn of his guest's craziness, of the watching of the armour, and of the knighting he was expecting; and, wondering at this strange form of madness, they came out to observe him from a distance, and watched him, sometimes pacing up and down with a peaceful look and sometimes leaning on his lance and gazing on his armour, without taking his eyes off it for a considerable time. Night had now fallen, but the moon was so bright that she might have rivalled the orb that lent her his light; so that whatever the novice knight did was clearly visible to all. Just then it occurred to one of the carriers who was staying at the inn to go and water his mules, and to do this he found it necessary to remove Don Quixote's armour, which lay on the trough. But the knight, seeing him draw near, addressed him in a loud voice: 'You, whoever you are, rash knight, who come to touch the armour of the most valorous errant that ever girt on a sword, take heed what you do. Do not touch it unless you wish to lose your life in payment for your temerity.'

The carrier paid no attention to this speech – it would have been better if he had regarded it, for he would have been regarding his own safety – but, laying hold of the straps, threw the armour some distance from him. At this sight Don Quixote raised his eyes to heaven, and addressing his thoughts, as it seemed, to his lady Dulcinea, cried: 'Assist me, lady, in the first affront offered to this enraptured heart! Let not your favour and protection fail me in this first trial!'

And, uttering these words and others like them, he loosened his shield and, raising his lance in both hands, dealt his adversary a mighty blow on the head with it, which threw him to the ground so injured that, if it had been followed by a second, the carrier would have had no use for a surgeon to cure him. This done, Don Quixote gathered his arms together again and paced up and down once more with the same composure as before.

A little later a second carrier, not knowing what had happened since the first man still lay stunned, came out with the same intention of watering his mules. But, just as he was going to clear the armour from the trough, Don Quixote, without uttering a word or begging anyone's favour, loosened his shield again, once more raised his lance and made more than three pieces of the second carrier's head – for he opened it in four places – without damage to his weapon. At the noise all the people in the inn rushed out, among them the innkeeper. Whereupon Don Quixote buckled on his shield and, putting his hand to his sword, cried: 'O beauteous lady, strength and vigour of this enfeebled heart! Now is the time to turn your illustrious eyes on this your captive knight, who is awaiting so great an adventure.'

With this it seemed to him that he gained so much courage that if all the carriers in the world had attacked him he would not have yielded a foot. When the fellows of the wounded men saw them in that plight they began to shower stones on Don Quixote from some way off. He protected himself from them as best he could with his shield, but dared not leave the trough, for fear of abandoning his armour. And the innkeeper shouted to them to leave him alone, for he had already told them that he was a madman and, being mad, would go scot-free, even though he killed them all.

Don Quixote shouted also, even louder, calling them cowards and traitors, and swearing that the lord of the castle must be a despicable and base-born knight for allowing knights errant to be so treated, and that if he had received the order of knighthood he would have made him sensible of his perfidy.

'But of you, base and vile rabble, I take no account,' he cried. 'Throw stones! Come on, attack! Assail me as hard as you can, and you will see what penalty you have to pay for your insolent folly!'

He spoke with such spirit and boldness that he struck a lively terror into all who heard him; and for that reason, as much as for the innkeeper's persuasions, they stopped pelting him. Then Don Quixote allowed them to remove the wounded, and returned to watch his arms with the same quiet assurance as before.

Now the innkeeper had begun to dislike his guest's pranks, and decided to cut the matter short and give him his wretched order of knighthood immediately, before anything else could go wrong. So he apologized for the insolence with which those low fellows had behaved without his knowledge, adding, however, that they had been soundly punished for their audacity. And seeing, as he had said before, that there was no chapel in that castle, there was no need, he declared, for the rest of the ceremony; for, according to his knowledge of the ceremonial of the order, the whole point of conferring knighthood lay in the blow on the neck and the stroke on the shoulder, and that could be performed in the middle of a field. And Don Quixote had already more than fulfilled the duty of the watching of arms, for he had been more than four hours on vigil, whereas all that was required was a two hours' watch.

Don Quixote believed all this, and said he was ready to obey him. He begged him to conclude the matter as briefly as possible; for if he were again attacked, once knighted, he was resolved to leave no one alive in the castle, except such as he might spare at the castellan's bidding, and out of regard for him.

Forewarned and apprehensive, the castellan then brought out the book in which he used to enter the carriers' accounts for straw and barley. Then, followed by a boy carrying a candle-end and by the two maidens already mentioned, he went up to Don Quixote and ordered him to kneel. Next, reading out of his manual, as if he were reciting some devout prayer, in the middle of his reading he raised his hand and dealt the knight a sound blow on the neck, followed by a handsome stroke on the back with the Don's own sword, all the while muttering in his teeth as if in prayer. When this was over he bade one of the ladies gird on Don Quixote's sword, which she did with great agility and some discretion, no small amount of which was necessary to avoid bursting with laughter at each stage of the ceremony. But what they had already seen of the new knight's prowess kept their mirth within bounds. And as she girt on his sword the good lady said: 'God make your worship a fortunate knight and give you good luck in your battles.'

Don Quixote asked her to tell him her name, as he wished to know in future days to whom he owed the favour received, for he meant to confer on her some part of the honour he was to win by the strength of his arm. She replied very humbly that her name was La Tolosa, and that she was the daughter of a cobbler in Toledo who lived among the stalls of Sancho Bienaya, adding that, wherever she might be, she was at his service and he should be her master. Don Quixote begged her, in reply, as a favour to him, henceforth to take the title of lady and call herself Doña Tolosa, which she promised to do. The other lady then put on his spurs, and his conversation with her was almost the same as with the lady of the sword. He asked her her name, and she replied that she was called La Molinera, and that she was the daughter of an honest miller in Antequera. The Don requested her also to take the title of lady and call herself Doña Molinera, renewing his offers of service and favours.

Now that these unprecedented ceremonies had been hurried through post-haste and at top speed, Don Quixote was impatient to be on horseback and to ride out in search of adventures. So, saddling Rocinante at once, he mounted; then, embracing his host, he thanked him for the favour of knighting him in such extravagant terms that it is impossible to write them down faithfully. The innkeeper, once he saw him safely out of the inn, replied to his speech rather more briefly but in no less high-flown terms and, without even asking him to pay the cost of his lodging, was heartily glad to see him go.

Chapter IV. *What happened to our Knight when he left the Inn.*

IT must have been daybreak when Don Quixote left the inn, so pleased, so gay, so enraptured at being now a knight that his joy seemed likely to burst his horse's girths. But, calling to mind his host's advice about the essential provisions he must carry, especially money and clean shirts, he decided to go home and provide himself with them all, and with a squire as well. He reckoned to take into his service a neighbour of his, a poor labourer who had a large family, but was very suitable for the part of squire in chivalry. With this in mind he turned Rocinante for home, and the horse, as if he smelled his home pastures, began to trot with such zest that his feet seemed not to touch the ground.

He had not gone far when from a thicket on the right he heard a faint voice, raised, so it seemed to him, in complaint; and no sooner did he hear this than he cried: 'I thank Heaven for granting this favour and giving me so prompt an opportunity to perform the duty I owe to my order, and whereby I may be able to gather the fruit of my honourable desires. These cries come no doubt from some man or woman in distress, and in need of my protection and assistance.'

Then, turning his reins, he guided Rocinante towards the place from which the voice seemed to come; and, when he had ridden a little way into the wood, he saw a mare tied to an oak, and tied to another a lad of about fifteen, naked to the waist. It was he who was shouting, and with good reason, for a well-built countryman was flogging him soundly with a belt, and accompanying each blow with mingled scolding and advice, crying: 'Keep your tongue still and your eyes open.'

To which the boy replied: 'I won't do it again, sir. I swear to God I won't do it again. I promise I'll take better care of your sheep in future.'

When Don Quixote saw what was happening he exclaimed in an angry voice: 'Discourteous knight, it is unseemly to attack a defenceless person. Mount your steed, and take your lance' – for the other also had a lance leaning against the oak to which his mare was tied – 'and I will teach you that you are acting like a coward.'

When the countryman saw this figure in full armour come at him brandishing his lance over his head, he gave himself up for dead and answered mildly: 'Sir Knight, this lad I am punishing is my servant. His job is to watch a herd of sheep that I keep around here. But he is so careless that every day I lose one. And because I'm punishing him for his carelessness or his roguery he says I'm doing it through meanness, so as not to have to pay him his due wages. But I swear to God and on my life he's lying.'

'Lying, you say, and in my presence, you wretched boor?' said

Don Quixote. 'By the sun that shines on us, I have a good mind to run you through with this lance. Pay him now and without another word. If you do not, by God who rules us, I will despatch you and annihilate you this very minute. Untie him immediately!'

The farmer bowed his head, and without replying untied his lad, whom Don Quixote asked how much his master owed him. He answered, for nine months at seven *reals* a month. Don Quixote calculated, and found that it came to sixty-three *reals*, whereupon he told the countryman to disburse them immediately, unless he wished to pay with his life. The farmer, in a fright, swore by his present plight and the oath he had taken – though he had not taken any oath – that it did not come to so much, because they must deduct from the reckoning three pairs of shoes he had given him, and a *real* paid for two blood-lettings, when he was sick.

'That is quite right,' Don Quixote answered. 'But set the shoes and the blood-lettings against the undeserved flogging you have given him. For, if he broke the leather of the shoes you gave him, you have broken the skin of his body and, if the barber let his blood when he was sick, you have done the same now, when he is well. So on that score he owes you nothing.'

'The trouble is, Sir Knight, that I have no money here. If Andrew will come home with me I will pay him every *real*.'

'I go home with him?' said the lad. 'Oh Lord, no, sir! Not on your life! Because if I went alone he would flay me like St. Bartholomew.'

'He will do no such thing,' replied Don Quixote. 'I have only to lay my command on him, and he will respect it; and on condition that he gives me his oath on the order of knighthood which he has received, I shall let him go free and will guarantee the payment.'

'Think what you are saying, your worship,' said the lad. 'This master of mine isn't a knight, and hasn't received any order of chivalry. He is the rich John Haldudo, and lives at Quintanar.'

'That is no matter,' replied Don Quixote, 'for there may be knights in the Haldudo family. It is very probable, for every man is the child of his own works.'

'That's quite right,' said Andrew, 'but this master of mine, what works is he the child of, when he refuses me wages for my sweat and labour?'

'I don't refuse them, Andrew my friend,' replied the farmer. 'Do me the favour of coming with me, and I swear by all the orders of chivalry in the world to pay you every single *real*, and perfumed into the bargain.'

'The perfuming I excuse you,' said Don Quixote, 'Give it him in *reals* and I shall be satisfied. But take care that you do what you have sworn, or else, by the same oath, I swear I will come back and look for you and punish you; and I shall find you, even if you hide better than a lizard. And if you wish to know who lays this command on you, so that you may feel the more strictly bound to obey it, know that I am the valorous Don Quixote de la Mancha, the redresser of wrongs and injuries. God be with you, and do not be unmindful of what you have promised under oath, on pain of the penalty pronounced.'

As he spoke he spurred Rocinante, and in a short while had left them. The farmer followed him with his eyes; and when he saw that he had left the wood and was out of sight, returned to his servant and said: 'Come here, my lad. I want to pay you what I owe you, as that redresser of wrongs ordered me to.'

'I swear you will,' said Andrew. 'Indeed you had better comply with that good knight's commands, God bless him! For he is such a brave man and such a fair judge that, by my life, if you don't pay me, he will come back and do what he said.'

'I swear I will, too,' said the countryman, 'but to show you how much I love you, I want to increase the debt, so that I can increase the payment.'

Then, grasping him by the arm, he tied him up once more to the tree and flogged him so soundly that he left him for dead.

'Now, Master Andrew,' said he, 'call on that redresser of wrongs, and he won't redress this one, you'll see. Though I have not finished yet, I think, for I have a mind to flay you alive, as you feared.'

But at last he untied him and gave him leave to go and look for his judge to execute the sentence he had pronounced. Andrew set off in a fury, swearing to go and find the valorous Don Quixote de la Mancha and tell him exactly what had happened. Then his master would have to pay him sevenfold. But for all that, he wept as he went, and his master remained behind laughing; and thus did the valorous Don Quixote redress that wrong.

He rode on, however, highly delighted at what had passed, for it seemed to him that he had made a most happy and glorious beginning in his knight errantry; and, very pleased with himself, he repeated half aloud as he he made his way towards his village: 'Well may you call yourself fortunate above all women living on earth to-day, O Dulcinea del Toboso, more beautiful than all beauties, since it has fallen to your lot to hold as a humble subject to your least desire and pleasure so valiant and famous a knight as is and shall be Don Quixote de la Mancha, who yesterday, as all the world knows, received the order of knighthood and to-day has righted the greatest injury and wrong that injustice could invent or cruelty perpetrate.   To-day he wrested the scourge from the hand of the pitiless enemy who was so undeservedly whipping that delicate infant.'

He now came to a place where the road divided into four, and there immediately leapt into his mind those crossways where knights errant used to stop to consider which of the roads they should take. So, following their example, he halted a moment, and after deep thought let go the reins, submitting his will to Rocinante, who followed his first instinct, which was to take the road towards his stable. When he had gone about two miles Don Quixote sighted a large crowd of people who, as he afterwards learnt, were merchants from Toledo going to buy silks in Murcia. There were six of them, riding beneath their sunshades, with four servants, all on horseback, and three muleteers on foot. As soon as Don Quixote saw them in the distance he imagined this to be matter for some new adventure, and it seemed to him that here was just the right opportunity to make the closest possible imitation of the encounters he had read of in his books. So with a gallant and resolute air he steadied himself in his stirrups, grasped his lance, covered his breast with his shield and, taking up his position in the middle of the road, awaited the arrival of those knights errant; for such he had already decided they were. So when they arrived within sight and earshot Don Quixote raised his voice, and called out in an arrogant tone: 'Let the whole world stand, if the whole world does not confess that there is not in the whole world a more beauteous maiden than the Empress of la Mancha, the peerless Dulcinea del Toboso.'

The merchants stopped when they heard this speech, and saw the strange figure who made it; and both from his appearance and his words they divined that the speaker was mad. But wanting to know more fully what this confession that he required of them really meant, one of them, who was a bit of a joker and very sharp-witted, said: 'Sir Knight, we do not know who this good lady is that you speak of. Show her to us and, if she is as beauteous as you say, we will most willingly and without any pressure acknowledge the truth demanded of us by you.'

'If I were to show her to you,' replied Don Quixote, 'what merit would there be in your confessing so obvious a truth? The essence of the matter is that you must believe, confess, affirm, swear and maintain it without seeing her. If you will not, you must do battle with me, monstrous and proud crew. Now come on! One by one, as the law of chivalry requires, or all together, as is the custom and evil practice of men of your breed. Here I stand and await you, confident in the right which I have on my side.'

'Sir Knight,' replied the merchant, 'I beg your worship in the name of all these princes here present that you will kindly show us a portrait of this lady, even one no bigger than a grain of wheat; because we would not burden our consciences by testifying to something that we have never seen or heard and, what is more, something so detrimental to the Empresses and Queens of Alcarria and Estremadura. For the skein can be judged by the thread, and we shall rest assured and satisfied with this, and your worship will be pleased and content. I even think that we are so far inclined to her side already that supposing your portrait shows us that she squints in one eye and drips vermilion and sulphur from the other, even then, to please you, we will say all that you ask in her favour.'

'Her eyes do not drip, vile scoundrels!' replied Don Quixote in great fury. 'Her eyes do not drip what you say, but ambergris and civet. She is not squinting or humpbacked, but straighter than a spindle of Guadarrama. And you shall pay for the blasphemy you have spoken against such transcendent beauty as my lady's.'

With these words he couched his lance and ran at the man who had spoken with such rage and fury that, if Rocinante had not fortunately stumbled and fallen in the road, things would have gone badly for the rash merchant. Rocinante fell, and his master went rolling some distance over the plain; but when he tried to get up it was in vain, so encumbered was he by his lance, shield, spurs and helmet, together with the weight of his ancient armour. And, whilst he was struggling to get up and could not, he kept shouting: 'Fly not, you coward brood! Stay, you slavish crew! It is not my fault, but my horse's, that I lie here.'

One of their muleteers who was not very good-natured, hearing the arrogant language of the poor man on the ground, could not refrain from dealing him an answer in the ribs; and going up to him, snatched his lance, and broke it in pieces. Then he began to give our Don Quixote such a beating with one of the bits that, in spite of his armour, he pounded him like wheat in a mill. The lad's masters shouted to him not to beat the knight so hard and to let him alone; but he was irritated, and would not give up the game till he had completely vented his rage. So, picking up the other bits of the lance, he broke them all over the poor prostrate knight, who, beneath all that storm of blows which rained on him, never once closed his mouth, but howled continuous threats to heaven and earth against those brigands, as he took them to be. At last the lad tired himself out, and the merchants went on their way with enough to talk about for the rest of the journey on the subject of that poor belaboured gentleman. Now, when Don Quixote found himself alone, he tried once more to see if he could rise. But if he could not do so when he was hale and well, how could he now that he was so pounded and almost destroyed? Yet, for all this, he reckoned himself fortunate. For it seemed to him that this was a disaster peculiar to knights errant, and he attributed it entirely to the fault of his horse. But it was impossible for him to get up, his whole body was so battered.

Chapter v. *Continuing the story of our Knight's Disaster.*

SEEING then that he was in fact unable to stir, it occurred to him to resort to his usual remedy, which was to think of some passage in his books. Whereupon his madness called into his mind that part of the story of the Marquis of Mantua, when Carloto left Baldwin wounded on the mountain, a tale familiar to children, not unknown to youth, and enjoyed and even believed by old men, though for all that no truer than the miracles of Mahomet. It seemed to him to fit his present plight to a T; and so he began to roll about on the ground with every sign of intense pain and to repeat in a languishing voice those words which are attributed to the wounded Knight of the Wood:

> Oh, where are you, my lady,
> That you grieve not for my plight?
> Either you know not of it
> Or else you are faithless and light.

He went on with the ballad in this way till he came to the lines which go:

> O noble Marquis of Mantua,
> My uncle and natural lord!

As chance would have it, when he came to this verse a labourer of his own village, a neighbour of his, passed on his way to take a load of wheat to the mill and, seeing a man lying on the ground, went up and asked him who he was and what it was that made him groan so sadly. Now Don Quixote firmly believed that this was the Marquis of Mantua, his uncle, and so made him no answer, but went on with his quotation, giving an account of his misfortune and of his wife's intrigue with the Emperor's son, all in the words of the ballad. The labourer was astonished at hearing this nonsense and, taking off the knight's visor, which was now battered to pieces from the beating, wiped his dust-covered face and immediately recognized him.

'Master Quixada,' he cried – this must have been his name before he lost his senses and changed himself from a quiet gentleman into a knight errant – 'who has put your worship in this plight?'

But he answered every question by going on with his ballad. Therefore the good man took off his back- and breast-plates, as best he could, to see if he had any wounds. But he saw no blood nor sign of any hurt. Then he tried to get him up from the ground, and with a great effort heaved him on to his own ass, which seemed to him the quieter mount. And gathering up his arms, even to the splinters of his lance, he tied them on Rocinante and, leading him by the bridle and his ass by the halter, took the road for the village,

much concerned to hear the nonsense that Don Quixote was talking. Our knight was no less concerned, being too bruised and
battered to stay on the ass, and from time to time he breathed
groans deep enough to reach heaven, so that his neighbour was
compelled to ask him again what pain he felt. Now it must have
been the Devil himself who put into his mind stories applicable to
his plight; for at that instant he forgot Baldwin and remembered
the Moor Abindarraez, when the governor of Antequera, Rodrigo
de Narvaez, captured him and held him prisoner in his castle. So
that when the labourer asked him once more how he was, and how
he felt, he replied in the very words and phrases in which the
captive Abencerrage answered Rodrigo de Narvaez, as he had read
the story in Jorge Montemayor's *Diana*, applying it so appositely
that the labourer wished himself to the Devil for having to listen
to such a pack of rubbish. Realizing now that his neighbour was
mad, he made haste to the village, to be quit of the nuisance of
listening to Don Quixote's harangue; at the close of which the
knight exclaimed: 'Be it known to your worship, Don Rodrigo de
Narvaez, that this beauteous Xarifa I mentioned is now the fair
Dulcinea del Toboso, for whom I have done, am doing and shall
do the most famous deeds of chivalry that the world has ever seen,
can see or will see.'

To which the labourer replied: 'Look you, your worship, as I am
a sinner, I am not Don Rodrigo de Narvaez, nor the Marquis of
Mantua, but your neighbour Pedro Alonzo. And your worship is
not Baldwin or Abindarraez, but that worthy gentleman Master
Quixada.'

'I know who I am,' replied Don Quixote, 'and I know, too,
that I am capable of being not only the characters I have named,
but all the Twelve Peers of France and all the Nine Worthies as
well, for my exploits are far greater than all the deeds they have
done, all together and each by himself.'

They were deep in such conversation when they reached the
village at nightfall. But the labourer waited till it was rather darker,
so that no one should see the battered gentleman on so shameful a
mount. When he thought it was the proper time he entered the
village, and went to Don Quixote's house, which he found in a
great uproar. The priest was there and the village barber, great

friends of Don Quixote's, and his housekeeper was addressing them at the top of her voice: 'What do you think, Doctor Pero Perez' – for that was the priest's name – 'of my master's misfortune? It is three days now he has not been seen, nor his horse, nor his shield, nor his lance, nor his armour either! Oh dear! Oh dear! What can I think? It is the truth, as sure as I was born to die, that these cursed books of knight errantry of his, that he is always reading, have turned his brain. For now I come to think of it, I have often heard him talking to himself about turning knight errant and going about in those worlds in search of adventures. Satan and Barabbas take all such books for ruining the finest understanding there was in all La Mancha.'

The niece said much the same and something more: 'You know, Master Nicholas,' – for that was the barber's name – 'it has very often happened that dear uncle has gone on reading those soulless books of misadventures for two days and nights on end. Then, when he has finished, he will fling his book down, draw his sword and go slashing the walls; and when he is exhausted he will say that he has killed four giants as tall as towers, and that the sweat that is pouring from him out of exhaustion is blood from the wounds he has got in the battle. Then he will drink a great jug of cold water and lie quiet and easy, saying that the water is a most precious draught which the sage Esquife has brought him, a great magician and a friend of his. But I am to blame for all this, because I did not tell your worships of my dear uncle's follies, so that you could have cured him before he got so far, and burnt all those cursed books. For he has a great many which well deserve to be burnt, just as much as if they were heretics.'

'I agree with that,' said the priest, 'and I swear that to-morrow shall not pass without a public inquisition being held over them. And let them be condemned to the flames, so that they shall not cause others who read them to imitate our good friend.'

The labourer, who with Don Quixote overheard all this, was confirmed in his belief that his neighbour was deranged, and so began to shout: 'Open, your worships, to Sir Baldwin and to the Lord Marquis of Mantua, who comes sore wounded, and to Master Moor Abindarraez, whom the valorous Rodrigo de Narvaez, governor of Antequera, brings captive.'

At this noise they all went out and, recognizing their friend, master and uncle, ran to embrace him, though he had not yet dismounted from his ass, because he could not. But he cried: 'Stop, all of you, for I come sorely wounded through the fault of my steed. Carry me to my bed and, if it is possible, call the wise Urganda to examine and cure my wounds.'

'See, in the name of mischief,' the housekeeper broke in at this point, 'if my heart didn't tell me truly on which leg my master was lame! Come up, your worship. I'm right glad to see you. We'll know how to cure you here, without sending for your Urganda. Oh, confound, confound, confound those books of chivalry which have brought your worship to this pass!'

They took him straight to his bed, but on searching for his wounds could find none. He said that he was bruised all over from taking a grievous fall with his horse Rocinante in a fight with ten of the most monstrous and audacious giants to be found anywhere on earth.

'So ho!' cried the priest. 'So there are giants in the dance? Well, I swear I'll burn them to-morrow before nightfall.'

They asked Don Quixote a great number of questions, but the only reply he would make was to ask them to give him something to eat and to let him sleep; for that was his most urgent need. They did so, and the priest inquired of the labourer at some length how he had found their friend. The peasant told him everything and repeated the nonsense the knight had talked when he discovered him, and as he brought him home. This made the priest more eager to do what he did the next day, which was to call on his friend, master Nicholas the barber, and to go with him to Don Quixote's house.

Chapter VI. *Of the great and pleasant Inquisition held by the Priest and the Barber over our ingenious gentleman's Library.*

THE knight was still asleep when the priest asked the niece for the keys of the room where he kept his books, the authors of the mischief. She was delighted to give them to him. Then they all went in, the housekeeper with them, and found more than a hundred large volumes, very well bound, and some small ones as well. As soon as the housekeeper saw them, she ran out of the room in great haste, and returned presently with a bowl of holy water and a bunch of hyssop. 'Take this, your worship,' she said, 'and sprinkle this room, in case there is some enchanter about, out of all the lot there are in these books, for fear he might put a spell on us, to punish us for the bad turn we're going to deal him by banishing them all out of the world.'

The priest laughed at the housekeeper's simplicity, and bade the barber hand him the books one by one, so that he could see what they were about; for he might find some of them that did not deserve punishment by fire.

'No,' said the niece, 'there is no reason to pardon any of them, for they have all of them caused the trouble. Better throw them out of the windows into the courtyard, and make a pile of them, and set them on fire; or else take them out into the back-yard and have the bonfire there, where the smoke won't be a nuisance.'

The housekeeper agreed, so anxious were they both for the massacre of those innocents; but the priest would not consent without at least reading the titles first. And the first that Master Nicholas handed him was *The Four Books of Amadis of Gaul*. 'This is very curious,' said the priest, 'for, as I have heard tell, this was the first book of chivalries printed in Spain, and all the others took their origin and beginning from it. So it seems to me that, as the first preacher of so pernicious a sect, we must condemn it to the flames without any mercy.'

'No, sir,' said the barber, 'for I have heard that it is the best of all the books of this kind ever written. So, as it is unequalled in its accomplishment, it ought to be pardoned.'

'That is true,' said the priest, 'and therefore let its life be granted for the present. Let us have a look at that other one beside it.'

'That,' said the barber, 'is *The Exploits of Esplandian*, the legitimate son of Amadis of Gaul.'

'In truth,' said the priest, 'the father's goodness shall not help the son. Take him, Mistress Housekeeper. Open that window and throw him into the yard. He shall be the foundation for the bonfire we shall have to make.'

The housekeeper obeyed with great pleasure, and the good Esplandian went flying out into the yard to wait in all patience for the threatened conflagration.

'Let us get on,' said the priest.

'The next,' said the barber, 'is *Amadis of Greece*. In fact, as far as I can see, all these on this side are of the same lineage as *Amadis*.'

'Then into the yard with all of them,' cried the priest, 'for rather than not burn queen Pintiquinestra and the shepherd Darinel with their eclogues and their author's devilish contorted sentences, I would burn the father that begot me as well, if he went about in the shape of a knight errant.'

'I am of the same opinion,' said the barber.

'And I too,' added the niece.

'Since that is so,' said the housekeeper, 'come, into the yard with them!'

They handed them to her and, as there were a great number, to spare herself the stairs she flung them down out of the window.

'What is that huge thing?' asked the priest.

'It is *Don Olivante de Laura*,' answered the barber.

'The author of that book also wrote *The Flower Garden*,' said the priest, 'and to be frank with you, I cannot make out which of the two is the more truthful, or rather the less mendacious. I can only say that for its arrogant nonsense it shall go into the yard.'

'This next is *Florismarte of Hyrcania*,' said the barber.

'What, is Master Florismarte here?' replied the priest. 'Well, he is for a quick end in the yard, I promise you, despite his extraordinary birth and his fantastic adventures. His style is so harsh and dry he deserves nothing better. Into the yard with him and with that other one too, Mistress Housekeeper.'

'With the greatest of pleasure,' she replied, and with much joy she did his bidding.

'Here is *The Knight Platir*,' said the barber.

'That is an old book,' said the priest. 'I can find nothing in it that deserves mercy. Let him join the others without more ado.' And so he did. Then they opened another book, and found its title to be *The Knight of the Cross*.

'For a title as holy as this book has, its ignorance might be pardoned. But they always say "the devil lurks behind the cross". So, to the fire with it.' Then, taking up another book, the barber observed: 'This is *The Mirror of Chivalries*.'

'I know the book well,' said the priest. 'Therein are Lord

Reynald of Montalban with his friends and companions, worse thieves than Cacus; and the Twelve Peers, and that faithful historian Turpin. But I am for condemning them to nothing worse than perpetual banishment, if only because they had a share in inspiring the famous Mateo Boiardo, from whom the Christian poet Ludovico Ariosto also spun his web. If I find him here speaking any language but his own I shall show him no respect. But if he speaks his own tongue, I will wear him next my heart.'

'I have him in Italian,' said the barber, 'but I don't understand him.'

'It would not do you any good if you did,' replied the priest. 'We could have done without the good captain bringing him to Spain and making him a Castilian, for he has robbed him of much of his native value. That is what happens with all authors who translate poetry into other languages. However much care they take, and however much skill they show, they can never make their translations as good as the original. In short, I say that this book and every one we find that deals with these affairs of France, shall be thrown out and deposited in a dry well till we see, after further deliberation, what is to be done with them; excepting one, *Bernardo de Carpio*, which is here somewhere, and another called *Roncesvalles*. For they shall pass straight from my hands into the housekeeper's, and from there into the flames without remission.'

The barber concurred in all this, holding it very fit and proper; for he knew the priest to be too good a Christian and too great a lover of the truth to tell a lie for anything in the world. Opening another book, they saw that it was *Palmerin de Oliva*, and beside it was another called *Palmerin of England*, at the sight of which the priest exclaimed: 'Let that olive be cut to splinters and burnt, so that not so much as the ash remains. But that palm of England, let it be kept and treasured as a rarity, and a casket be made for it, like the one Alexander found among the spoils of Darius and dedicated to the preservation of the works of Homer. This book, my friend, deserves respect for two reasons: one, because it is very good in itself, and the other because it is said to have been written by a wise King of Portugal. All the adventures in the castle of Miraguarda are excellent and very well contrived, and the speeches polished and clear, for they observe and bring out the character of each speaker with great truth and understanding. I say, then, subject to your judgment, Master Nicholas, that this and *Amadis of Gaul* shall be spared the fire, and all the rest perish without any further trial or enquiry.'

'No, my good friend,' replied the barber, 'for the one I have here is the renowned *Sir Belianis*.'

'He too,' said the priest, 'and his second, third and fourth parts, need a little rhubarb to purge their excess of bile. We shall have to cut out all that part too about the Castle of Fame and other nonsense more serious still. So we will allow them time to put in their defence, and as they show signs of amendment, mercy or justice shall be accorded them. Meanwhile, friend, keep them in your house, but let no one read them.'

'With pleasure,' replied the barber. And the priest, not being inclined to tire himself by reading any more books of chivalry, bade the housekeeper take all the big ones and throw them into the yard. His request did not fall on deaf ears, for she would rather have burnt those books than woven the broadest and finest cloth in the world. So, seizing them about eight at a time, she flung them out of the window. And as she took so many together, one fell at the barber's feet; and he, curious to see what it was, found that its title was *History of the Famous Knight Tirante the White*.

'Good heavens!' exclaimed the priest in a loud voice. 'Is *Tirante the White* here? Give it to me, friend, for to my mind that book is a rare treasure of delight and a mine of entertainment. Here is Lord-have-mercy-on-us of Montalban, a valiant knight, and his brother Thomas of Montalban and the knight Fonseca, and the fight the valiant Tirante had with the great mastiff, and the witticisms of the maiden Joy-of-my-life, with the amours and tricks of widow Quiet, and the lady Empress in love with her squire Hippolito. Really, my friend, for its style it is the best book in the world. Here the knights eat and sleep and die in their beds, and make their wills before they die, and other things as well that are left out of all other books of the kind. On that account, the author is a deserving fellow. For he did not commit all those follies deliberately, which might have sent him to the galleys for the rest of his life. Take him home and read him, and you will see that all I have said of him is true.'

ever written in Castilian. They can compare with the most famous in Italy. Let them be preserved as the richest treasures of poetry Spain possesses.'

The priest was too tired to look at any more books, and therefore proposed that the rest should be burnt, contents unknown. But the barber had already opened one called *The Tears of Angelico*.

'I would have shed them myself,' said the priest on hearing the title, 'if I had ordered a book like that to be consigned to the flames. For its author was one of the most famous poets not only in Spain but in the world, and was most happy in translating some of Ovid's fables.'

Chapter VII. *Of the Second Expedition of our good Knight Don Quixote de la Mancha.*

AT this point Don Quixote began to shout at the top of his voice: 'Here, here, valorous knights! Here there is need to show the strength of your valorous arms, for the courtiers are getting the better of the tourney!'

At this frightful noise all rushed upstairs, and the examination of the remaining books proceeded no further. And that is why, so it is believed, *The Carolea* and *The Lion of Spain*, with the *Feats of the Emperor*, compiled by Don Luis de Avila, went on the flames unseen and unheard. For no doubt they must have been among the remaining books, and perhaps if the priest had seen them they would not have suffered so severe a sentence. When they got into Don Quixote's room he was already out of bed, and repeating his shouting and raving, laying about him with his sword in all directions with slashes and back-strokes, as wide awake as if he had never been asleep. They grappled with him, and put him back to bed by main force; and when he had rested quietly a little he started to address the priest, saying:

'Certainly, my Lord Archbishop Turpin, it is a great default in us, who call ourselves the Twelve Peers, to give these courtier knights the victory in this tournament without more ado, seeing that we, the Adventurers, have gained the prize on the three preceding days.'

'Peace, dear comrade,' replied the priest, 'for God may yet grant

us a change of fortune, and what is lost to-day may be won back
to-morrow. But for the present you must mind your health; for
you seem to me to be over-wearied, if not severely wounded.'

'Not wounded,' said Don Quixote, 'but bruised and battered.
There is no doubt of that, for that bastard Roland has pounded me
with the trunk of an oak, and all out of envy, since he knows I am
his only rival in prowess. But let me never be called Reynald of
Montalban again if, when I rise from this bed, I do not pay him
for it despite all his enchantments. But for the present let me be
brought food, for I believe that is what I am in most need of; and
leave me to take care of my revenge.'

They did as he asked, and gave him some food, after which he
went to sleep again, leaving them wondering at his madness.

That same night the housekeeper set light to all the books in the
yard and all those in the whole house as well, and burnt them. Some
that were burnt deserved to be treasured up among the eternal archives, but fate and the laziness of the inquisitor forbade it. And
so in them was fulfilled the saying that the saint sometimes pays for
the sinner.

One of the remedies that the priest and the barber then resorted
to for their friend's complaint was to wall up and close the room
where he had kept his books, so that he should not find them when
he got up. For perhaps if the cause were removed, the effect might
cease; and they might say that an enchanter had carried them off,
room and all.

This was quickly done, and when two days later Don Quixote
got up, the first thing he did was to go and look for his books; and
when he failed to find the room where he had left them he went all
over the house searching for it. Finally he went to the place where
the door used to be, and felt for it with his hands, and ran his eyes
over everything again and again, without saying a word. Then
after a good while he asked his housekeeper whereabouts his book-
closet was, and she, being well primed in her answers, replied:
'What room? Or rather what on earth is your worship looking for?
There is no room and no books in this house now, for the Devil
himself has carried everything off.'

'That was no devil,' put in his niece, 'but an enchanter who
came one night on a cloud, after you went away, and getting down

from the dragon he was riding on, went into the room. I don't know what he did inside, but after a little while he went flying out through the roof, and left the house full of smoke. And when we decided to look and see what he had done, there was no room and not a book to be seen. Only we remember very well, both of us, that as he left, the wicked old man shouted out that we would see later what havoc he had wrought in the house, out of a secret grudge he bore the owner of those books. What's more, he said he was called the sage Muñaton.'

'Freston he must have said,' put in Don Quixote.

'I don't know,' replied the housekeeper, 'whether he was called Freston or Friton. I only know that his name ended in *ton*.'

'That is right,' said Don Quixote. 'He is a learned enchanter, and a great enemy of mine. He bears me malice, for through his arts and spells he knows that in the fullness of time I shall engage a favourite knight of his in single combat, and that I shall conquer him, and he will not be able to prevent it. That is why he tries to serve me every ill-turn he can. But I tell him that he cannot gainsay or avert what Heaven has decreed.'

'Who doubts that?' cried his niece. 'But what concern of yours are these quarrels, my dear uncle? Wouldn't it be better to stay peacefully at home, and not roam about the world seeking better bread than is made of wheat, never considering that many go for wool and come back shorn?'

'Dear niece,' replied Don Quixote, 'you are a long way out in your reckoning! Before they shear me I will pluck out and tear off the beards of all who think to touch so much as the tip of one hair of mine.' And neither of the women cared to make further reply, for they saw that he was getting into a rage.

As it turned out, he stayed fifteen days at home very quietly, showing no sign of any desire to repeat his former strange behaviour; and during that time he had some most pleasant arguments with his two friends, the priest and the barber, on the subject of his statement that the world's greatest need was of knights errant, and that knight errantry should be revived in his person. The priest sometimes contradicted him, and sometimes gave in to him, for if he had not resorted to this trick, he would not have stood a chance of bringing him to reason.

C

All this while Don Quixote was plying a labourer, a neighbour of his and an honest man – if a poor man may be called honest – but without much salt in his brain-pan. In the end, he talked to him so much, persuaded him so hard and gave him such promises that the poor yokel made up his mind to go out with him and serve him as squire. Don Quixote told him, amongst other things, that he ought to feel well disposed to come with him, for some time or another an adventure might occur that would win him in the twinkling of an eye some isle, of which he would leave him governor. These promises and others like them made Sancho Panza – for this was the labourer's name – leave his wife and children and take service as his neighbour's squire. Then Don Quixote set about raising money, and by selling one thing, pawning another, and making a bad bargain each time, he raised a reasonable sum. He also fixed himself up with a shield, which he borrowed from a friend, and patching up his broken helmet as best he could, he gave his squire Sancho notice of the day and the hour on which he proposed to set out, so that he should provide himself with all that was most needful; and he particularly told his squire to bring saddle-bags. Sancho said that he would, and that he was also thinking of bringing a very fine ass he had, for he was not too good at much travelling on foot. At the mention of the ass Don Quixote hesitated a little, racking his brains to remember whether any knight errant ever had a squire mounted on ass-back; but no case came to his memory. But, for all that, he decided to let him take it, intending to provide him with a more proper mount at the earliest opportunity by unhorsing the first discourteous knight he should meet. He provided himself also with shirts and everything else he could, following the advice which the innkeeper had given him. And when all this was arranged and done, without Panza saying goodbye to his wife and children, or Don Quixote taking leave of his housekeeper and niece, they departed from the village one evening, quite unobserved, and rode so far that night that at daybreak they thought they were safe, and that even if anyone came out to search for them they would not be found.

Sancho Panza rode on his ass like a patriarch, with his saddle-bags and his leather bottle, and a great desire to see himself governor of the isle his master had promised him. It chanced that Don

Quixote took the same route and struck the same track across the plain of Montiel as on his first expedition; but he travelled with less discomfort than before, as it was the hour of dawn, and the sun's rays, striking them obliquely, did not annoy them. Then presently Sancho Panza said to his master:

'Mind, your worship, good Sir Knight Errant, that you don't forget about the isle you promised me; for I shall know how to govern it, never mind how big it is.'

To which Don Quixote replied: 'You must know, friend Sancho Panza, that it was a custom much in use among knights errant of old to make their squires governors of the isles or kingdoms they won; and I am determined that, for my part, so beneficial a custom shall not lapse. On the contrary, I intend to improve on it: for they often, perhaps most often, waited till their squires were grown old; and when they were worn out in their service, from bad days and worse nights, they gave them some title of count, or perhaps marquis, of some valley or province of more or less importance. But if you live and I live, it may well be that before six days are gone by I may win some kingdom with others depending upon it, and one of them may prove just right for you to rule. Do not think this any great matter, for adventures befall knights errant in such unheard and unthought-of ways that I might easily be able to bestow on you even more than I promise.'

'At that rate,' said Sancho Panza, 'if by any of those miracles your worship speaks of I were to become king, Juana Gutierrez, my poppet, would be a queen, no less, and my children princes.'

'Well, who doubts it?' answered Don Quixote.

'I doubt it,' replied Sancho Panza, 'for I'm pretty sure that even if God rained kingdoms on the earth, none of them would sit well on Mary Gutierrez' head. As a queen she would not be worth a half-penny, sir. Countess might suit her better, with God's help.'

'Put the matter in God's hands, Sancho,' replied Don Quixote. 'He will give her what is best for her. But do not humble your heart so low as to be content with anything less than to be Captain General.'

'I won't, dear sir,' replied Sancho Panza, 'especially with a master as grand as your worship, who will know how to give me all that will be good for me and that I can bear.'

Chapter VIII. *Of the valorous Don Quixote's success in the dreadful and never before imagined Adventure of the Windmills, with other events worthy of happy record.*

AT that moment they caught sight of some thirty or forty windmills, which stand on that plain, and as soon as Don Quixote saw them he said to his squire: 'Fortune is guiding our affairs better than we could have wished. Look over there, friend Sancho Panza, where more than thirty monstrous giants appear. I intend to do battle with them and take all their lives. With their spoils we will begin to get rich, for this is a fair war, and it is a great service to God to wipe such a wicked brood from the face of the earth.'

'What giants?' asked Sancho Panza.

'Those you see there,' replied his master, 'with their long arms. Some giants have them about six miles long.'

'Take care, your worship,' said Sancho; 'those things over there are not giants but windmills, and what seem to be their arms are the sails, which are whirled round in the wind and make the millstone turn.'

'It is quite clear,' replied Don Quixote, 'that you are not experienced in this matter of adventures. They are giants, and if you are afraid, go away and say your prayers, whilst I advance and engage them in fierce and unequal battle.'

As he spoke, he dug his spurs into his steed Rocinante, paying no attention to his squire's shouted warning that beyond all doubt they were windmills and no giants he was advancing to attack. But he went on, so positive that they were giants that he neither listened to Sancho's cries nor noticed what they were, even when he got near them. Instead he went on shouting in a loud voice: 'Do not fly, cowards, vile creatures, for it is one knight alone who assails you.'

At that moment a slight wind arose, and the great sails began to move. At the sight of which Don Quixote shouted: 'Though you wield more arms than the giant Briareus, you shall pay for it!' Saying this, he commended himself with all his soul to his Lady Dulcinea, beseeching her aid in his great peril. Then, covering himself with his shield and putting his lance in the rest, he urged Rocinante forward at a full gallop and attacked the nearest windmill, thrusting his lance into the sail. But the wind turned it with such violence that it shivered his weapon in pieces, dragging the horse and his rider with it, and sent the knight rolling badly injured across the plain. Sancho Panza rushed to his assistance as fast as his ass could trot, but when he came up he found that the knight could not stir. Such a shock had Rocinante given him in their fall.

'O my goodness!' cried Sancho. 'Didn't I tell your worship to look what you were doing, for they were only windmills? Nobody could mistake them, unless he had windmills on the brain.'

'Silence, friend Sancho,' replied Don Quixote. 'Matters of war are more subject than most to continual change. What is more, I think – and that is the truth – that the same sage Friston who robbed me of my room and my books has turned those giants into windmills, to cheat me of the glory of conquering them. Such is the enmity he bears me; but in the very end his black arts shall avail him little against the goodness of my sword.'

'God send it as He will,' replied Sancho Panza, helping the knight to get up and remount Rocinante, whose shoulders were half dislocated.

As they discussed this last adventure they followed the road to the pass of Lapice where, Don Quixote said, they could not fail to find many and various adventures, as many travellers passed that way. He was much concerned, however, at the loss of his lance, and, speaking of it to his squire, remarked: 'I remember reading that a certain Spanish knight called Diego Perez de Vargas, having broken his sword in battle, tore a great bough or limb from an oak, and performed such deeds with it that day, and pounded so many Moors, that he earned the surname of the Pounder, and thus he and his descendants from that day onwards have been called Vargas y Machuca. I mention this because I propose to tear down just such a limb from the first oak we meet, as big and as good as his; and I intend to do such deeds with it that you may consider yourself most fortunate to have won the right to see them. For you will witness things which will scarcely be credited.'

'With God's help,' replied Sancho, 'and I believe it all as your worship says. But sit a bit more upright, sir, for you seem to be riding lop-sided. It must be from the bruises you got when you fell.'

'That is the truth,' replied Don Quixote. 'And if I do not complain of the pain, it is because a knight errant is not allowed to complain of any wounds, even though his entrails may be dropping out through them.'

'If that's so, I have nothing more to say,' said Sancho, 'but God knows I should be glad if your worship would complain if anything hurt you. I must say, for my part, that I have to cry out at the slightest twinge, unless this business of not complaining extends to knights errants' squires as well.'

Don Quixote could not help smiling at his squire's simplicity, and told him that he could certainly complain how and when he pleased, whether he had any cause or no, for up to that time he had never read anything to the contrary in the law of chivalry.

Sancho reminded him that it was time for dinner, but his master replied that he had need of none, but that his squire might eat whenever he pleased. With this permission Sancho settled himself as comfortably as he could on his ass and, taking out what he had put into the saddle-bags, jogged very leisurely along behind his master, eating all the while; and from time to time he raised the bottle with such relish that the best-fed publican in Malaga might have envied him. Now, as he went along like this, taking repeated gulps, he entirely forgot the promise his master had made him, and reckoned that going in search of adventures, however dangerous, was more like pleasure than hard work.

They passed that night under some trees, from one of which our knight tore down a dead branch to serve him as some sort of lance, and stuck into it the iron head of the one that had been broken. And all night Don Quixote did not sleep but thought about his Lady Dulcinea, to conform to what he had read in his books about knights errant spending many sleepless nights in woodland and desert dwelling on the memory of their ladies. Not so Sancho Panza; for, as his stomach was full, and not of chicory water, he slept right through till morning. And, if his master had not called him, neither the sunbeams, which struck him full on the face, nor the song of the birds, who in great number and very joyfully greeted the dawn of the new day, would have been enough to wake him. As he got up he made a trial of his bottle, and found it rather limper than the night before; whereat his heart sank, for he did not think they were taking the right road to remedy this defect very quickly. Don Quixote wanted no breakfast for, as we have said, he was determined to subsist on savoury memories. Then they turned back on to the road they had been on before, towards the pass of Lapice, which they sighted about three in the afternoon.

'Here,' exclaimed Don Quixote on seeing it, 'here, brother Sancho Panza, we can steep our arms to the elbows in what they call adventures. But take note that though you see me in the greatest danger in the world, you must not put your hand to your sword to defend me, unless you know that my assailants are rabble and common folk; in which case you may come to my aid. But should they be knights, on no account will it be legal or permissible, by the laws of chivalry, for you to assist me until you are yourself knighted.'

'You may be sure, sir,' replied Sancho, 'that I shall obey your worship perfectly there. Especially as I am very peaceable by nature and all against shoving myself into brawls and quarrels. But as to defending myself, sir, I shan't take much notice of those rules, because divine law and human law allow everyone to defend himself against anyone who tries to harm him.'

'I never said otherwise,' replied Don Quixote, 'but in the matter of aiding me against knights, you must restrain your natural impulses.'

'I promise you I will,' replied Sancho, 'and I will observe this rule as strictly as the Sabbath.'

In the middle of this conversation two monks of the order of St. Benedict appeared on the road, mounted on what looked like dromedaries; for the two mules they were riding were quite as big. They were wearing riding-masks against the dust and carrying sunshades. And behind them came a coach, with four or five horsemen escorting it, and two muleteers on foot.

In the coach, as it afterwards turned out, was a Basque lady travelling to Seville to join her husband, who was going out to take up a very important post in the Indies. The monks were not of her company, but merely journeying on the same road.

Now no sooner did Don Quixote see them in the distance than he said to his squire: 'Either I am much mistaken, or this will prove the most famous adventure ever seen. For those dark shapes looming over there must, beyond all doubt, be enchanters bearing off in that coach some princess they have stolen; and it is my duty to redress this wrong with all my might.'

'This will be a worse job than the windmills,' said Sancho. 'Look, sir, those are Benedictine monks, and the coach must belong to some travellers. Listen to me, sir. Be careful what you do, and don't let the Devil deceive you.'

'I have told you,' replied Don Quixote, 'that you know very little of this subject of adventures. What I say is true, and now you will see it.'

So saying, he rode forward and took up his position in the middle of the road along which the monks were coming; and when they got so near that he thought they could hear him, he called out in a loud voice: 'Monstrous and diabolical crew! Release immediately the noble princesses whom you are forcibly carrying off in that coach, or prepare to receive instant death as the just punishment for your misdeeds.'

The monks reined in their mules, and stopped in astonishment at Don Quixote's appearance and at his speech.

'Sir Knight,' they replied, 'we are neither monstrous nor diabolical, but two monks of St Benedict travelling about our business, nor do we know whether there are any princesses being carried off in that coach or not.'

'No fair speeches for me, for I know you, perfidious scoundrels!' cried Don Quixote. Then, without waiting for their reply, he spurred Rocinante and, with his lance lowered, charged at the foremost monk with such vigour and fury that, if he had not slid from his mule, he would have been thrown to the ground and badly hurt, if not killed outright. The second monk, on seeing his companion so treated, struck his heels into his stout mule's flanks and set her galloping over the plain fleeter than the wind itself. When Sancho Panza saw the monk on the ground, he got down lightly from his ass, ran up and started to strip him of his clothes. Upon this, two servants of the monks arrived and asked him why he was stripping their master. Sancho replied that the clothes fell rightly to his share as spoils of the battle which his master, Don Quixote, had won. The lads, who did not get the joke nor understand this talk of spoils and battles, saw that Don Quixote had gone off and was talking with the ladies in the coach, and so fell upon Sancho and knocked him down. And, pulling every hair from his beard, they kicked him mercilessly, and left him stretched on the ground, breathless and stunned. Then, without a moment's hesitation, the monk remounted his mule, trembling, terrified and as white as a sheet; and as soon as he was up he spurred after his comrade, who was waiting for him some distance off, watching to see the upshot of this sudden attack. But without caring to wait for the end of the adventure, they went on their way, crossing themselves more often than if they had had the Devil himself at their backs.

Don Quixote, as we have said, was talking with the lady in the coach: 'Your fair ladyship may now dispose of yourself as you desire, for now the pride of your ravishers lies in the dust, overthrown by this strong arm of mine. And lest you be racked with doubt as to the name of your deliverer, know that I am Don Quixote de la Mancha, knight errant, adventurer and captive to the peerless and beautiful lady, Dulcinea del Toboso. And in requital of the benefit you have received from me, I would ask no more of you than to go to El Toboso and present yourself on my behalf before that lady, telling her what I have done for your deliverance.'

All that Don Quixote said was overheard by one of the squires accompanying the coach, a Basque. And when he saw that the knight would not let them pass, but was talking of their turning back at once to El Toboso, he went up to Don Quixote and, grasping his lance, addressed him in bad Castilian and worse Basque.

'Get along, you ill-gotten knight. By God who made me, if you do not leave coach I kill you, sure as I be Basque.'

Don Quixote understood him very well, and replied with great calm: 'If you were a knight, as you are not, I should have punished your rash insolence by now, you slavish creature.'

'I not gentleman? I swear you liar, as I am a Christian. You throw down lance and draw sword, and you will see you are carrying the water to the cat. Basque on land, gentleman at sea. A gentleman, by the devil, and you lie if you say otherwise!'

' "Now you shall see," said Agrages,' quoted Don Quixote, and threw his lance down on the ground. Then, drawing his sword and grasping his shield, he rushed at his antagonist, determined to take his life. When the Basque saw him coming he would have liked to get down from his mule, as it was a poor sort of hired beast and not to be trusted, but there was nothing for it but to draw his sword. He was, however, lucky enough to be near the coach, from which he was able to snatch a cushion to serve as a shield; whereupon they immediately fell to, as if they had been two mortal enemies. The rest of the party tried to pacify them, but could not; for the Basque swore in his uncouth language that if they did not let him finish the battle, he would himself kill his mistress and all who hindered him.

The lady in the coach, amazed and terrified at the sight, made the coachman drive off a little way, and sat watching the deadly struggle from a distance. In the course of the fight the Basque dealt Don Quixote a mighty blow on one shoulder, thrusting above his shield, and had our knight been without defence he would have been cleft to the waist. When Don Quixote felt the weight of that tremendous stroke he cried out aloud: 'O lady of my soul, Dulcinea, flower of beauty, come to the aid of this your knight, who for the sake of your great goodness is now in this dire peril!'

To speak, to raise his sword, to cover himself with his shield and attack the Basque: all this was the work of a moment. For he had resolved to risk everything upon a single stroke. The Basque, seeing him come on, judged Don Quixote's courage by his daring, and decided to do the same as he. So he covered himself well with his cushion and waited, unable to turn his mule in either direction, for the beast was now dead weary, and not being made for such games, could not budge a step.

Don Quixote, as we have said, rushed at the wary Basque with sword aloft, determined to cleave him to the waist; and the Basque watched, with his sword also raised and well guarded by his cushion; while all the by-standers trembled in terrified suspense, hanging upon the issue of the dreadful blows with which they threatened one another. And the lady of the coach and her waiting-women offered a thousand vows and prayers to all the images and places of devotion in Spain, that God might deliver their squire and them from the great peril they were in.

But the unfortunate thing is that the author of this history left the battle in suspense at this critical point, with the excuse that he could find no more records of Don Quixote's exploits than those related here. It is true that the second author of this work would not believe that such a curious history could have been consigned to oblivion, or that the learned of La Mancha could have been so in- curious as not to have in their archives or in their registries some documents relating to this famous knight. So, strong in this opinion, he did not despair of finding the conclusion of this delightful story and, by the favour of Heaven, found it, as shall be told in our second part.

Chapter IX. *Of the conclusion of the stupendous Battle between the gallant Basque and the valiant Manchegan.*

IN the first part of this history we left the valiant Basque and the famous Don Quixote with naked swords aloft, on the point of dealing two such furious downward strokes as, had they struck true, would have cleft both knights asunder from head to foot, and split them like pomegranates. At this critical point our delightful history stopped short and remained mutilated, our author failing to inform us where to find the missing part. This caused me great annoyance, for my pleasure from the little I had read turned to displeasure at the thought of the small chance there was of finding the rest of this delightful story. For it seemed to me that the greater part was missing. It appeared to my mind impossible, and contrary to all sound custom, that so good a knight should have lacked a sage to undertake the writing of his unparalleled achievements, since there never was one of those knights errant who — as the people say — go out on their adventures, that ever lacked one. For every one of them had one or two sages ready at hand, not only to record their deeds, but to describe their minutest thoughts and most trivial actions, however much concealed; and so good a knight could not have been so unfortunate as to lack what Platir and the like had in such abundance. I really could not bring myself to believe that such a gallant history could have been left maimed and mutilated, and laid the blame on the malice of time, the devourer and consumer of all things, for either concealing or destroying the sequel. On the other hand, I thought that, as there had been found among Don Quixote's books some as modern as *The Unveiling of Jealousy* and *Nymphs and Shepherds of Henares*, his history must be modern too, and that, though it might not be written down, it would be remembered by the people of his village and of the neighbourhood. This thought made me anxious and eager for real and authentic knowledge of the whole life and marvels of our famous Spaniard, Don Quixote de la Mancha, the light and mirror of Manchegan chivalry, and the first man of our times, of these calamitous times of ours, to devote himself to the toils and exercise of knight errantry; to redress wrongs, aid widows and protect maidens, such as roam up-hill and down-dale with their whips and palfreys and their whole virginities about them. For there were virgins in the olden days who, unless ravished by some rogue or by a boor with his steel cap and axe or by some monstrous giant, never slept a night under a roof all their lives, and at the age of eighty went to their graves as spotless virgins as the mothers that bore them. Now I say that for this, and for many other reasons our gallant Quixote deserves continuous and immemorial praise; and even I should have my share, for my toil and pains in searching for the end of this delightful history. Though well I know that if Heaven, chance, and good fortune had not aided me, the world would have remained without the amusement and pleasure which an attentive reader may now enjoy for as much as two hours on end.

This is how the discovery occurred: – One day I was in the Alcana at Toledo, when a lad came to sell some parchments and old papers to a silk merchant. Now as I have a taste for reading even torn papers lying in the streets, I was impelled by my natural inclination to take up one of the parchment books the lad was selling, and saw in it characters which I recognized as Arabic. But though I could recognize them I could not read them, and looked around to see if there was not some Spanish-speaking Moor about, to read them to me; and it was not difficult to find such an interpreter there. For, even if I had wanted one for a better and older language, I should have found one. In short, chance offered me one, to whom I explained what I wanted, placing the book in his hands. He opened it in the middle, and after reading a little began to laugh. I asked him what he was laughing at, and he answered that it was at something written in the margin of the book by way of a note. I asked him to tell me what it was and, still laughing, he answered: 'This is what is written in the margin: "They say that Dulcinea del Toboso, so often mentioned in this history, was the best hand at salting pork of any woman in all La Mancha."'

When I heard the name of Dulcinea del Toboso I was surprised and astonished, for I immediately surmised that these books must contain the story of Don Quixote. With this idea I pressed him to read the beginning, and when he did so, making an extempore translation from the Arabic into Castilian, he said that the heading was: History of Don Quixote de la Mancha, written by Cide Hamete Benengeli, Arabic historian. I needed great caution to conceal the joy I felt when the title of the book reached my ears. Running to the silk merchant, I bought all the lad's parchments and papers for half a *real*, but if he had had any sense and known how much I wanted them, he might very well have demanded and got more than six *reals* from the sale. I then went off with the Moor into the cloister of the cathedral, and asked him to translate for me into Castilian everything in those books that dealt with Don Quixote, adding nothing and omitting nothing; and I offered to pay him whatever he asked. He was satisfied with fifty pounds of raisins and three bushels of wheat, and promised to translate them well, faithfully, and very quickly. But, to make the business easier and not to let such a prize out of my hands, I took him to my house; and there in little more than six weeks he translated it all just as it is set down here.

On the first sheet was a very life-like picture of Don Quixote's fight with the Basque. Both were shown in the very postures the story describes, with swords aloft, the one covered by his shield, the other by his cushion, and the Basque's mule so life-like that you could tell from a mile off that it was a hired one.

At the feet of the Basque was a scroll that read: '*Don Sancho de Azpeitia*', which no doubt was his name: and at Rocinante's was another which read: '*Don Quixote*'. Rocinante was marvellously painted, so long and lank, so hollow and lean, with such a sharp backbone, and so far wasted in consumption that it was quite clear at a glance how wisely and rightly he had been called Rocinante. Beside him stood Sancho Panza, holding his ass by the halter, and at his feet was another label which read: '*Sancho Zancas*'; and according to the picture he must have had a big belly, a short body, and long shanks; which must be what gave him the names of Panza and Zancas, for he is called by both these names at different times in the history. There were some other details to be seen, but they are none of them of great importance, and have no concern with the faithful telling of this story; – and no story is bad if it is truthful.

Now, if any objection can be made against the truth of this history, it can only be that its narrator was an Arab – men of that nation being ready liars, though as they are so much our enemies he might be thought rather to have fallen short of the truth than to have exaggerated. So it seems to me; for when he could and should have let himself go in praise of so worthy a knight he seems deliberately to have passed on in silence; an ill deed and malicious, since historians are bound by right to be exact, truthful, and absolutely unprejudiced, so that neither interest nor fear, dislike nor affection, should make them turn from the path of truth, whose mother is history, rival of time, storehouse of great deeds, witness of the past, example and lesson to the present, warning to the future. In this history I know that you will find all the entertainment you can desire; and if any good quality is missing, I am certain that it is the fault of its dog of an author rather than any default in the subject. To conclude, the second part, according to the translator, began thus:

The trenchant swords of the two valorous and furious combatants, brandished aloft, seemed to threaten the heavens, the earth, and the pit of hell, such was their courageous aspect. The first to strike his blow was the choleric Basque; and he struck with such force and fury that if the edge of his sword had not turned in its descent, that one blow would have been enough to finish the dire conflict and all our knight's adventures. But good fortune was preserving him for greater things, and twisted his enemy's sword, so that, although it struck him on his left shoulder, it did him no other injury than to disarm all that side, taking with it a great piece of his helmet with half an ear, all of which fell to the ground in hideous ruin, leaving our knight in a very evil plight.

God help me, but who is there could worthily describe the rage which now entered the heart of our Manchegan on finding himself thus treated? All that can be said is that he rose once more in his stirrups and, grasping his sword tighter in both his hands, brought it down with such fury full on the Basque's cushion and on his head, that despite that protection he began to spout blood out of his nostrils, his mouth, and his ears, as if a mountain had fallen on him. He looked as if he was going to tumble off his mule, which he would no doubt have done if he had not clung round her neck. But even so he lost his stirrups and then let go with his arms; while the beast, terrified by the weight of the blow, began to gallop about the field, and with a plunge or two threw her master on to the ground.

Don Quixote was looking on most composedly. But, when he saw the squire fall, he jumped down from his horse and, running very nimbly up to him, put the point of his sword between his enemy's eyes, bidding him surrender or he would cut off his head. The Basque was so stunned that he could not answer a word, and things would have gone badly with him, so blind with rage was Don Quixote, if the ladies in the coach, who till then had been watching the fight in dire dismay, had not run to the spot, and begged him very earnestly to do them the great kindness and favour of sparing their squire's life. To which request Don Quixote replied very haughtily and gravely:

'Certainly, fair ladies; I am most willing to do what you ask. But there must be one condition agreed, which is that this knight shall promise me to go to the town of El Toboso, and present himself from me before the peerless Lady Dulcinea, so that she may deal with him according to her pleasure.'

The terrified and distressed ladies did not consider what Don Quixote required nor ask who Dulcinea was, but promised him that the squire should carry out the knight's command.

'Then, upon your word,' said Don Quixote, 'I will do him no other hurt, though he richly deserves it at my hands.'

Chapter X. *Of the Pleasant Conversation between Don Quixote and his Squire Sancho Panza.*

IN the meantime Sancho Panza had got up again after his rough handling by the monks' servants, and had stood watching the battle Don Quixote was fighting, praying to God in his heart to be pleased to grant his master the victory, and that out of it he might gain an isle of which he could be governor, as he had been promised. Then, when he saw that the contest was over and his master about to remount Rocinante, he ran up to hold his stirrup, and, before Don Quixote was up, fell down on his knees before him, seized his hand, kissed it, and said:

'Be so kind, my dear lord Don Quixote, as to make me governor of the isle you have won in this dreadful fight; for however big it is, I feel strong enough to govern it as well as any man who ever governed isles in all the world.'

To this Don Quixote replied: 'Observe, brother Sancho, that this adventure and others of this kind are not adventures of isles but of cross-roads, from which nothing is to be gained but a broken head and the loss of an ear. Be patient, for adventures will occur whereby I shall not only be able to make you governor, but something greater still.'

Sancho thanked him warmly and, once more kissing his hand and the hem of his coat, helped him to mount Rocinante. Then he got on to his ass and began to follow his master, who went off at a brisk trot without taking leave of the ladies in the coach or saying a word more to them, and rode into a near-by wood. Sancho followed him as fast as his ass could go, but Rocinante moved so swiftly that he found himself left behind, and had to shout after his master to wait for him. This Don Quixote did, reining Rocinante in until his weary squire came up, to say as he overtook him:

'I think, sir, that it would be wise for us to retire to some church. For, seeing in what a bad way you left that man you fought with, I shouldn't wonder if they were to report the matter to the Holy Brotherhood and have us arrested; and, my goodness, if they do that, we shall sweat blood before we get out of gaol.'

'Silence!' said Don Quixote. 'Where have you ever heard or read of a knight errant being brought before a judge, however many homicides he may have committed?'

'I don't know anything about your *omecides*,' replied Sancho. 'I have never tried one in my life. I only know that the Holy Brotherhood has something to say to people who fight in the fields, and the other matter's no concern of mine.'

'Do not worry, my friend,' said Don Quixote. 'I will deliver you from the hands of the Chaldeans, let alone the Holy Brotherhood. But tell me, on your oath, have you ever seen a more valorous knight than I am on the whole face of the earth? Have you ever read in histories of one who has or had more spirit in the attack, more wind in the holding out, more art in the wounding, or more skill in the overthrowing?'

'To tell you the truth,' replied Sancho, 'I've never read any histories at all, because I can't read or write. But I'll stake my oath I've never served a braver master than your worship in all the days of my life. Pray God these brave deeds won't be paid for where I just said! But, I beg you, your worship, let me attend to you, for you are losing a lot of blood from that ear, and I've lint here and a little white ointment in the saddle-bag.'

'All that would have been quite needless,' replied Don Quixote, 'if I had remembered to make a flask of the Balsam of Fierabras. One single drop of that would save us both time and medicine.'

'What flask and what balsam is that?' asked Sancho Panza.

'It is a balsam,' replied Don Quixote, 'the recipe for which lies in my memory. With it there is no need to fear death nor so much as to think of dying of any wound. So, when I have made some and given it to you, if ever you see me cut through the middle in some battle – as very often happens – you have only to take the part of my body that has fallen to the ground and place it neatly and cunningly, before the blood congeals, on to the half that is still in the saddle, taking especial care to make them fit exactly. Then you must give me just two drops of this balsam to drink and, you will see, I shall be as sound as an apple.'

'If that's so,' said Panza, 'from now on I renounce the governorship of the promised isle, and all I want in payment for all my good services is for your worship to give me the recipe for that marvellous liquor. For I think it would be worth more than two *reals* an ounce, and I need no more than that to spend the rest of my life in honour and comfort. But I should like to know now whether it costs much to make.'

'For less than three *reals* you can make half a gallon or more,' answered Don Quixote.

'Good Lord!' replied Sancho. 'What's preventing you from making it, sir, and teaching me as well?'

'Hush, friend,' replied Don Quixote. 'I mean to teach you even greater secrets and do you even greater favours. But for the moment let us dress our wounds, for my ear hurts me more than I like.'

Sancho got some lint and ointment out of the saddle-bag. But when Don Quixote saw his helmet he almost went out of his mind. Putting his hand to his sword and raising his eyes to Heaven, he cried, 'I swear on oath, by the Creator of all things, and by the four

Holy Gospels in which they are amply recorded, to lead the life that the great Marquis of Mantua led when he swore to avenge the death of his nephew Baldwin, vowing not to eat bread at table, nor lie with his wife – and some other things, which, though I cannot remember them, I will take as here spoken – until I have exacted entire vengeance on the man who has done me this outrage.'

On hearing which Sancho exclaimed: 'Consider, Don Quixote, that if the knight has complied with your orders and presented himself before my lady Dulcinea del Toboso, he will already have done his duty, and deserves no other punishment unless he commits a new crime.'

'You have spoken well and justly,' replied Don Quixote; 'and so I annul my oath so far as it concerns wreaking fresh vengeance on him. But I swear and confirm anew, that I will lead the life I have vowed to until by force of arms I win from some knight another helmet as good. Do not imagine, Sancho, that I take this oath as a mere bubble. For I know very well what precedent I am following, since exactly similar events occurred in the case of Mambrino's helmet, which cost Sacripante so dear.'

'I wish your worship would send these oaths to the devil, dear master,' replied Sancho, 'for they're very bad for the health and very harmful to the conscience. Besides, tell me now – if perhaps we don't meet a man armed with a helmet for a long time, what shall we do then? Have we got to keep the vow, and put up with all the inconvenience and discomfort of lying in our clothes, and never sleeping in a village, and all those hundreds of penances in that mad old Marquis of Mantua's oath, that your worship's set on reviving? Consider carefully, sir. There aren't any men in armour travelling on any of these roads, but only carriers and carters, who not only don't wear helmets, but have probably never heard of them in all the days of their life.'

'You are wrong about that,' said Don Quixote, 'for we shall not be two hours at these cross-roads before we see more armed men than came to the siege of Albraca to carry off the fair Angelica.'

'Then I agree!' said Sancho. 'And please God we come well out of it, and the time arrives when you win that isle which is costing me so dear – And then let me die!'

'I have told you already, Sancho, not to worry on that account.

For if there is no isle to be had, there is always the Kingdom of Denmark or of Sobradisa, that will fit you like a ring on your finger. What is more, you should like them better, as they are on dry land. But let us leave this to time, and see if you have anything for us to eat in those saddle-bags, because soon we are going in search of a castle where we can lodge to-night and make for ourselves the balsam I spoke of; for I swear to God this ear of mine hurts me exceedingly.'

'I have an onion here and a bit of cheese,' said Sancho, 'and a few hunks of bread. But they are not the victuals for a valiant knight like your worship.'

'How little you understand,' replied Don Quixote. 'I would have you know, Sancho, that it is a point of honour with knights errant not to eat once in a month; and when they do eat to take what they find nearest to hand. You would have realized this if you had read as many histories as I have. For in all the many I have read I have never found more than a passing mention of what knight errants ate, except at those sumptuous banquets they used to be given; for the rest of their days they lived on the flowers of the field. But although it is to be understood that they could not live without eating and satisfying all the other needs of nature – for of course they were men like ourselves – it must be presumed that, as they spent the greater part of their lives roaming through woods and wastes, and without a cook, their most ordinary food would be country fare, like that you are offering me now. So, Sancho, my friend, do not worry about what pleases me, nor seek to build the world anew, nor wrench knight errantry off its hinges.'

'Pardon me, your worship,' said Sancho, 'but since, as I told you before, I can't read or write, I don't know or understand the rules of the profession of knighthood. Still from now on I will fill the saddle-bags with all kinds of dried fruit for your worship, because you are a knight. But for myself, as I am not, I'll provide something more substantial in the way of poultry.'

'I do not say,' replied Don Quixote, 'that knights errant are obliged to eat nothing but the fruit you mention, only that it and certain herbs they used to find in the fields were their ordinary fare.'

'It's a good thing,' replied Sancho, 'to know those herbs, for I'm inclined to think that we may need to make use of that knowledge one day.'

Then he took the good things he had mentioned out of the bag, and the two of them ate their dinner peacefully and companionably. Though, as they were anxious to look for somewhere to lodge that night, they cut their poor dry meal rather short and, mounting at once, made haste to reach some inhabited place before nightfall. But both the sun and their hopes of doing so failed them together near some goatherds' huts; and so they decided to spend the night there. And if it caused Sancho distress not to reach a village, it was a source of satisfaction to his master to sleep beneath the open sky. For it seemed to him that each time he did so he was confirming his title to knighthood by a new act of possession.

Chapter XI. *What passed between Don Quixote and some Goat-herds.*

THE knight was very warmly welcomed by the goatherds, and Sancho did what he could for Rocinante and his ass before following the odour given off by certain pieces of goat's meat, which were boiling in a pot over the fire. He would have liked at that very moment to see if they were ready to be transferred from the pot to the stomach, but refrained, as the goatherds themselves took them off the fire and, spreading some sheepskins on the ground, hurriedly set out their rustic table. Then, with a great show of goodwill, they invited knight and squire to share what they had. Six of them who belonged to that fold begged Don Quixote with rough compliments to sit on a trough which they had set upside down for him, and then seated themselves round on the skins. The knight took this seat, but Sancho remained standing to fill his master's cup, which was a horn one. But when he saw his squire in this posture, Don Quixote said:

'So that you may see, Sancho, the virtue there is in knight errantry, and how speedily those who perform any function in it may attain the honour and estimation of the world, I wish you to sit here beside me in these good people's company, and to be on terms of equality with me, who am your master and natural lord. Eat from my plate and drink from the vessel I drink from; for it can be said of knight errantry as of love: that it puts all things on the same level.'

'I thank you,' said Sancho, 'but I must confess to your worship that so long as I have plenty to eat, I can eat it as well, and better, standing by myself, as seated beside an Emperor. And, to tell you the truth, even if it's only bread and onion that I eat in my corner without bothering about table manners and ceremonies, it tastes to me a great deal better than turkey at other tables where I have to chew slowly, drink little, and wipe my mouth often, and where I can't sneeze and cough when I want to, nor do any of those other things which solitude and freedom allow of. So, dear master, let the honours your worship means to confer on me for being a servant and follower of knight errantry – which being your squire, I am – be exchanged for something of more use and profit to me. For though I acknowledge these honours as received in full, I renounce them from now on and until the end of the world.'

'You must sit down all the same, for whosoever humbleth himself, God doth exalt.' And, seizing him by the arm, Don Quixote compelled Sancho to sit beside him.

The goatherds did not understand this gibberish about squires and knights errant, but just ate in silence and watched their guests, who with a good grace and appetite crammed down lumps as big as their fists. When the meat course was finished they spread a great quantity of shrivelled acorns on the skins, and set beside them half a cheese, which could not have been harder if it had been made of mortar. All this while the horn cup was not idle, for it went the rounds so often, first full and then empty like the bucket at the well, that they easily exhausted one of the two wineskins which hung in sight.

After Don Quixote had sufficiently satisfied his hunger, he took up a handful of acorns and, looking at them intently, gave utterance in the following strain: 'Happy the age and happy the times on which the ancients bestowed the name of golden, not because gold, which in this iron age of ours is rated so highly, was attainable without labour in those fortunate times, but rather because the people of those days did not know those two words *thine* and *mine*. In that blessed age all things were held in common. No man, to gain his common sustenance, needed to make any greater effort than to reach up his hand and pluck it from the strong oaks, which literally invited him to taste their sweet and savoury fruit. Clear springs and running rivers offered him their sweet and limpid water in glorious abundance. In clefts of the rock and hollow trees the careful and provident bees formed their commonwealth, offering to every hand without interest the fertile produce of their fragrant toil. Spontaneously, out of sheer courtesy, the sturdy cork-trees shed their light and broad bark, with which men first covered their houses, supported on rough poles only as a defence against the inclemencies of the heavens. All was peace then, all amity, all concord. The crooked plough had not yet dared to force open and search the kindly bowels of our first mother with its heavy coulter; for without compulsion she yielded from every part of her fertile and broad bosom everything to satisfy, sustain, and delight the children who then possessed her. Then did the simple and lovely shepherdesses go from valley to valley and from hill to hill, with their tresses loose, and without more clothes than were needed to cover modestly what modesty requires, and has always required, to be concealed. Nor were there such ornaments as are in fashion to-day, all trumped up with Tyrian purple and silk in so many contorted shapes. Yet, with only a few green leaves of dock and ivy plaited together, they must have looked as splendid and elegant as our court ladies with the rare and outlandish inventions which idle curiosity has taught them. In those days the soul's amorous fancies were clothed simply and plainly, exactly as they were conceived, without any search for artificial elaborations to enhance them. Nor had fraud, deceit, or malice mingled with truth and sincerity. Justice pursued her own proper purposes, undisturbed and unassailed by favour and interest, which so impair, restrain, and pervert her to-day. The law did not then depend on the judge's nice interpretations, for there were none to judge or to be judged. Maiden modesty roamed, as I have said, wherever she would, single and solitary, without fear of harm from strangers' licence or lascivious assault; and if she was undone it was of her own will and desire.

'But now, in this detestable age of ours, no maiden is safe even though she be hidden in the centre of another Cretan labyrinth; for even there, through some chink or through the air, by dint of its accursed persistence, the plague of love gets in and brings them to ruin despite their seclusion. Therefore, as times rolled on and wickedness increased, the order of knights errant was founded for their protection, to defend maidens, relieve widows, and succour the orphans and the needy. Of this order am I, brother goatherds, whom I thank for the welcome and entertainment which you have given to me and my squire; for although by the law of nature all men are bound to befriend knights errant, yet, as you received and entertained me without knowing of this obligation, I should rightly acknowledge your goodwill with the utmost gratitude.'

Our knight delivered all this harangue, which might well have been spared, only because the acorns they served him reminded him of the golden age. That is why it came into his head to deliver this purposeless discourse to the goatherds, who listened to him in fascination and bewilderment, without answering a word. Sancho was silent too, for he was busy devouring the acorns and making frequent visits to the second wineskin, which they had hung up on a cork-tree to keep the wine cool. Don Quixote devoted more time to talking than to finishing his supper, but finally the meal was over and one of the goatherds said: 'So that you can truly say, Sir Knight Errant, that we have been ready and glad to entertain you, we should like to offer you the pleasure of a song by one of our mates, who will soon be here. He is a clever lad and very much in love; and, what is more, he can read and write, and plays the fiddle as beautifully as can be.'

Scarcely had the goatherd finished speaking when the sound of a fiddle reached their ears, and very soon afterwards the musician came in, a very handsome lad of about twenty-two. His companions asked him if he had had supper, and on his answering Yes, the goatherd who had asked the question said: 'In that case, Antonio, you might do us the favour of a song or two. We want to show this gentleman, our guest, that even in the mountains and woods there are people who know something about music. We have told him of your accomplishments, and we should like you to prove to him that we spoke the truth. So sit down, please, and sing the song about your love, which your uncle the priest composed for you, the one they liked so much in our village.'

'I shall be glad to,' replied the lad; and without waiting to be asked twice, he sat down on the trunk of a fallen oak and tuned his fiddle. Then presently he began to sing most charmingly:

'I know, Olalla, thou dost me adore,
     Though yet to me the same thou hast not said;
Nor shown it once, by one poor glance or more,
     Since love is soonest by such tongues betrayed.

'But as I ever held thee to be wise,
     I am assured thou bearest me good will,
For he is not unfortunate who sees
     That his affections are not taken ill.

'Yet, for all this, Olalla, it is true
     I, by observance, gather to my woe
That thy mind's framed of brass, by art undue,
     And flint thy bosom is, though it seems snow.

'And yet amidst thy rigour's winter face
     And other shifts thou usest to delay me,
Sometimes hope, peeping through, doth promise grace;
     But, woe is me! I fear 'tis to betray me.

'Sweetest, once in the balance of thy mind
     Poise with just weights my faith, which never yet
Diminished, though disfavour it did find;
     Nor can increase more, though thou favouredst it.

'If love be courtesy, as some men say,
     I can expect of your humanity
That my hopes shall, howe'er thou dost delay,
     Reap their reward truly and finally.

'If many services be of esteem
     Or power to render a hard heart benign,
Such things I did for thee as make me deem
     I've gained the match, and that thou shalt be mine.

'For if at any time thou'st taken heed,
     Thou more than once might'st view how I was gay
To honour thee, on Mondays, in the weed
     Which got me credit on God's holiday.

'For love and finery ever must consort
     Together, since they travel the same ways,
Which made me, when I did to thee resort,
     Come always neat and fine beneath thy gaze.

'Here I omit the dances I have done,
     And music I have at thy window given;
When at cock-crow thou listenedst alone,
     And seem'dst, hearing my voice, to be in heaven.

'Neither will I the praises here recount
    Which of thy beauty I've so often sung,
Which, though they all were true, were ever wont
    To cause the envious to judge me wrong.

'When I spoke to the maid of Berocal,
    Teresa, of thy worth and of thy shape,
"You think," she said, "you're in an angel's thrall,
    And yet, for idol, you adore an ape.

'"She to her trinkets thanks may give, and chains,
    False hair and other shifts that she doth use
To mend her beauty, with a thousand pains
    And tricks, which might love's very self abuse."

'Stung by her words, I gave her straight the lie,
    Which did her and her cousin so offend,
He challenged me to fight him presently,
    And well thou knowest how that affair did end.

'I do not seek to buy thy favours cheap,
    And when I court and woo thee to be mine
I swear thy virtue need not fear a trap.
    For purer far than that is my design.

'The church has bonds which do so surely hold
    As no silk cord for strength comes to them near;
To thrust thy neck now in the yoke be bold
    And see if I, to follow thee, will fear.

'If thou wilt not, here solemnly I vow,
    By holiest saint enwrapt in precious shrine,
Never to leave those hills where I dwell now,
    Unless it be to become a Capuchin.'

Here the goatherd ended his song and, although Don Quixote asked him to give them some more, Sancho did not agree. He was more inclined for sleep than for music, and so he said to his master: 'Your worship had better arrange now where you are going to rest to-night. These men work too hard all day long to be able to spend their nights in singing.'

'I understand you, Sancho,' replied Don Quixote. 'It is indeed clear to me that your visits to the wineskin require payment in sleep rather than in music.'

'God be praised, but we all enjoyed the drink,' replied Sancho.

'I do not deny that,' replied Don Quixote. 'So settle where you will; but watching befits men of my profession better than sleep. However, it would be as well if you would dress this ear of mine again, for it is hurting me more than it need.'

Sancho obeyed. But one of the goatherds looked at the wound and told him not to worry, for he would apply a remedy that would easily heal it. Then, taking some leaves of rosemary, which grew plentifully thereabouts, he chewed them and, mixing them with a little salt, applied them to the ear, which he bandaged tightly, assuring the knight that he would need no other remedy; which proved true.

Chapter XII. *Of What a Goatherd told Don Quixote and his Companions.*

MEANWHILE another lad arrived – one of those whose job it was to bring the provisions up from the village.

'Do you know what is happening in our place, fellows?' said he.

'How should we know?' answered one of them.

'Then I'll tell you,' the lad went on. 'The famous shepherd-student Chrysostom died this morning, and the rumour is that he died of love for that devilish Marcela, rich William's daughter, the girl who is always roaming about these parts dressed as a shepherdess.'

'For Marcela, you say?' asked one.

'Yes, I do,' replied the lad; 'and the strange thing is that he has directed in his will that he's to be buried in the fields like a Moor, at the foot of that rock where the spring is, beside the cork-tree, because, the rumour goes – and they say they had it from his own lips – that it was at that spot he saw her for the first time. He has left some other requests as well, such odd ones that the clergy say they mustn't be carried out; and quite right too, because they have a heathenish smack about them. But his great friend Ambrosio the student, who used to go about with him dressed as a shepherd too, answers that everything is to be done exactly as Chrysostom direct-ed. The whole village is in an uproar about it. But, from all they say, they'll end up by doing just as Ambrosio and his friends the shepherds want; and to-morrow they're coming to bring him with

great ceremony to the place I spoke of. It will be a sight worth seeing I can tell you, and I shan't miss it, even if it means I can't get
back to the village to-morrow.'

'We will all see it too,' answered the goatherds, 'and cast lots
which of us is to stay and mind the goats.'

'I agree, Peter,' said one of them, 'though you needn't trouble
about casting lots, for I will stay behind for everybody. And don't
put it down to generosity on my part or think that I don't want to
see what's going on. It's only because of the splinter which stuck
into my foot the other day, so that I can't walk.'

'We thank you all the same,' replied Peter.

Don Quixote requested Peter to tell him who the dead man was,
and who was the shepherdess. Peter replied that all he knew was
that the dead man was a rich gentleman from a village in those
mountains, who had been studying for many years at Salamanca
and had finally returned home with the reputation of being very
learned and well-read. He was especially famous for knowing the
science of the stars, and what the sun and the moon were doing up
in the skies, for he could always give accurate notice of the *clipse*
of the sun and moon.

'*Eclipse* it is called, friend, not *clipse* – the obscuration of those
two great luminaries,' put in Don Quixote.

But Peter took no notice of this trifle, and went on with his story,
saying: 'Also he used to foretell whether the year would be fruitful
or stale.'

'*Sterile* you mean, friend,' put in Don Quixote.

'*Sterile* or *stale*,' replied Peter, 'it comes to the same thing. So
from what he told them, his father and his friends got very
rich, because they believed him and did what he advised. He used
to say: This year sow barley and not wheat, or: Now you can
sow chick-peas and not barley, or: Next year there will be a full
crop of olive-oil, and the three years following there won't be a
drop.'

'That science is called Astrology,' said Don Quixote.

'I don't know its name,' replied Peter, 'but I know that he knew
all that and more too. But to come to the point: one day not many
months after he came from Salamanca, he threw away the long
scholar's gown he used to wear, and appeared all of a sudden

dressed like a shepherd with his crook and sheepskin jacket; and at the same time his great friend Ambrosio, who had been his fellow-student, dressed himself as a shepherd too. I had forgotten to say that poor Chrysostom, the dead man, was a great one at making verses, and was so good at them that he used to write the carols for Christmas Eve and the plays for Corpus Christi, which the boys of our village used to act; and everyone said that they were first-class. When the villagers saw the two students unexpectedly dressed as shepherds they were astonished, and could not guess what had induced them to make such an extraordinary transformation. By this time Chrysostom's father had died, and he inherited considerable property, goods as well as land, and quite large flocks and herds, and a great deal of money. He was left in desolate possession of all this, and indeed he deserved it too, for he was a very good fellow and charitable, and a friend to all good men. And he had a face like a blessing. Afterwards it came out that he had changed his dress only to wander about these wild places after that shepherdess Marcela, whom our lad spoke of a while ago, for poor dead Chrysostom had fallen in love with her. And now I must tell you, for your information, who this young baggage is; for perhaps – no, there is no perhaps about it – you won't hear anything like this in all the days of your life, even if you live longer than Sarna.'

'Say *Sarah*,' replied Don Quixote; who could not bear the goatherd's blunders.

'*Sarna* (the itch) lives long enough too,' replied Peter. 'If you make me correct my words at every turn, sir, we shan't be done in a twelvemonth.'

'Pardon me, friend,' said Don Quixote, 'but there is such a difference between Sarna and Sarah that I had to tell you. However, you answered very rightly, for the itch lives longer than Sarah. So go on with your story, and I will not interrupt you again.'

'I was saying, then, my beloved sir,' said the goatherd, 'that there was a farmer in our village even richer than Chrysostom's father. His name was William and, over and above his many great riches, God gave him a daughter, whose mother, the most respected woman in all these parts, died in giving her birth. I can just see her now, with that face of hers, the sun on one side, as you might say, and the moon on the other. And what a good housewife she was, and such a friend to the poor, and I'm sure that for that alone her soul is this very moment enjoying of God in the other world. Her husband William died of grief at the death of his good wife, leaving his daughter Marcela, young and rich, in the care of one of her uncles, a priest and the parson of our village. The child grew up so beautiful that she used to put us in mind of her mother, who was a great beauty herself, though people thought that the daughter would be even lovelier. So when she was fourteen or fifteen everyone who saw her praised God for giving her such beauty, and most of them fell desperately in love with her. Her uncle kept her very carefully and seldom let her go out. But, all the same, the fame of her great loveliness spread far and wide, and for that reason as much as for her great wealth not only our villagers, but some of the best men for many miles around as well, were begging, persuading and pestering her uncle to give them her hand in marriage. However, he was a really good Christian and, though he would have liked to marry her off soon, since she was of age, would not do so without her consent. Not that he had an eye to the advantage or profit that he would get from managing the girl's estate and putting off her marriage — and that has been remarked in the good priest's favour by more than one circle of village gossips, I can promise you. For I should like you to know, Sir Errant, that in these little places they poke their noses into everything and gossip about everything. You can take my word for it, a parson has to be extraordinarily good to have his parishioners speaking well of him, especially in a village.'

'That is true,' said Don Quixote; 'but go on. It is a very good story, and you, my good Peter, are telling it with a fine grace.'

'May the Lord's grace never fail me: that is the chief thing. To continue, I must tell you that, although her uncle set out and described to his niece the qualities of each one of her many suitors separately, begging her to choose and marry whom she liked, her only answer was that she didn't want to for the present, because, being so young, she did not feel able to bear the responsibilities of matrimony. And as these excuses seemed reasonable to her uncle, he ceased to press her, and waited till she should be somewhat older and know how to choose a companion to her taste. For, he said, and said rightly, parents ought not to settle their children against their will. But, lo and behold, when we least expected it, the modest Marcela suddenly appeared dressed like a shepherdess and, in spite of her uncle and everyone in the village who tried to dissuade her, off she went into the fields with the other village shepherdesses and started to tend her own flock. And once she had appeared in public and her beauty was exposed to all eyes, I couldn't truthfully tell you how many rich youths, gentlemen, and farmers put on the same dress as Chrysostom, and wandered about these fields, courting her. One of them, as I have told you, was our dead man who, they said, no longer loved her, but adored her. Now you mustn't think that because Marcela adopted this free and unconstrained way of life, with little or no privacy, her modesty or her virtue has fallen under any shadow of suspicion. Far from it; she guards her honour so well that not one of her many suitors has boasted — nor has the right to boast — that she has given him the slightest hope of obtaining his desire. For, although she does not avoid the shepherds' company and conversation, but treats them in a friendly and courteous way, if anyone comes to her to reveal his intentions even by a proper and holy proposal of marriage, she flings him off, like a stone from a catapult. And by this kind of behaviour she does more damage in these parts than if the plague had got in, for her easy manner and her beauty win the hearts of all who have to do with her. They court and love her, but her disdain and her plain speaking drive them to the verge of despair. So it is that they don't know what to say to her, but loudly call her cruel and unkind, and by other such names which clearly show her character. If you were to stay here awhile, sir, one day you would hear the hills and valleys echo with the lament of her rejected suitors. Not far from here is a place where there are about two dozen great beeches, and every one of them has Marcela's name cut on its smooth bark. Above it, too, on some of them, there is a crown carved, as if her lover meant to declare in the clearest terms that Marcela wears and deserves the crown of all human beauty. Here one shepherd sighs; there another moans; from the distance you can hear songs of love; from near at hand dirges of despair. There will be one spending all the hours of the night seated at the foot of an oak or of a crag, never closing his tear-dimmed eyes till the sun finds him there next morning, sunken and lost in his thoughts; and there will be another giving no rest or truce to his sighs, but lying stretched on the burning sand in the most sultry heat of a summer afternoon, and sending his complaints up to the merciful heavens; and over every one of them the beautiful Marcela triumphs, free and unconcerned. And all of us who know her are waiting to see how her haughtiness will end, and who will be the lucky man to come and conquer so intractable a nature and enjoy a beauty so perfect. As all that I have told you is well-known fact, I can easily understand that what our lad has said about the cause of Chrysostom's death is the truth as well. So I advise you, sir, to be sure to join us to-morrow at his burial. It will be very well worth seeing, for Chrysostom has many friends; and it's not more than a mile and a half from here to the place where he directed them to bury him.'

'I will certainly be there,' said Don Quixote, 'and I thank you for the pleasure you have given me by telling me such a delightful story.'

'Oh,' replied the goatherd, 'I don't know even half the things that have happened to Marcela's lovers. But maybe to-morrow we shall fall in with some shepherd on the way who may tell us more. But it would be as well for now if you were to go to sleep under cover, for the night dew might hurt your wound, though the ointment they put on it is so good that there's no fear of trouble.'

Sancho Panza also, who already wished the goatherd to the devil with his endless story, begged his master to go and sleep in Peter's hut. This he did and, in imitation of Marcela's lovers, he spent the rest of the night in thoughts of his lady Dulcinea; while Sancho Panza's sleep, as he settled down between Rocinante and his ass, was not that of a rejected lover, but of a soundly kicked human being.

Chapter XIII. *The conclusion of the Tale of Marcela the Shepherdess and Other Matters.*

SCARCELY had day begun to show itself on the balconies of the East when five of the six goatherds got up, and went to wake Don Quixote and to inquire if he still intended to go and see the famous burial of Chrysostom, for if he did they would keep him company. Nothing delighted the knight more, and so he got up and ordered Sancho to saddle the horse and the ass at once. This was quickly done, and with the same despatch they all set off on their way. They had gone less than a mile when they came to a cross road, where they saw approaching them along another track some six shepherds dressed in black skins, with their heads crowned with garlands of cypress and bitter bay. Each of them had a stout holly-stick in his hand, and with them came also two gentlemen on horseback, handsomely equipped for travelling, accompanied by three servants on foot. When the two parties met they exchanged courteous greetings, and on each one asking where the other was going, discovered that they were all bound for the burial-place. So they travelled together.

As they rode on, one of the horsemen observed to his companion: 'I think, Señor Vivaldo, that we can count the hours passed in attending this remarkable funeral time well spent. For, if we are to trust the strange accounts these herdsmen have given us of the dead shepherd and the merciless shepherdess, it cannot fail to be a remarkable event.'

'I agree with you,' replied Vivaldo, 'and I would waste not one day but four rather than miss the sight.'

Don Quixote asked them what they had heard about Marcela and Chrysostom. And the traveller answered that early that morning they had met the shepherds and, seeing them in such mournful attire, had asked them why they were so dressed. Then one of them had explained, and related the strange behaviour and beauty of a shepherdess called Marcela, the loves of her many suitors, and the death of that Chrysostom to whose burial they were going. In short, he had told them all that Peter had told Don Quixote. Here this conversation ceased and another began, the one called Vivaldo asking Don Quixote what made him travel thus armed in so peaceful a country. To which the knight replied: 'The exercise of my profession does not allow or permit me to ride in any other fashion. Ease, luxury, and repose were invented for soft courtiers; but labour, unease, and arms alone were designed and made for those whom the world calls knights errant, of whose number, though unworthy, I am the very least.'

On hearing this, they concluded that he was a madman. But, to make sure of it and to discover what kind of madness his was, Vivaldo went on to ask him what exactly he meant by knights errant.

'Have you not read, sirs,' replied Don Quixote, 'the annals and histories of England, treating of the famous deeds of King Arthur, whom in our Castilian tongue we commonly call King Artus. There is an ancient and widespread tradition concerning him throughout that kingdom of Great Britain, that he did not die, but by magic art was turned into a crow; and they say that in course of time he will come back to reign, and recover his kingdom and sceptre. For which reason no Englishman can be proved ever to have killed a crow, from that day to this. Now in this good king's reign there was instituted that famous order of chivalry, the Knights of the Round Table, and there took place, exactly as they are recorded, the loves of Sir Lancelot of the Lake and Queen Guenevere, in which that honourable Lady Quintañona acted as intermediary and confidante. Whence arose that ballad so widely known and so often sung in modern Spain:

> Never was there knight
> By ladies so attended
> As was Lancelot,
> When he came from Britain.

— with its sweet and charming story of his deeds of love and his bravery. Now, from that time on, this order of chivalry has been gradually growing and spreading through many and various parts of the world. Famous and renowned for their exploits in that order, were the valiant Amadis of Gaul with all his sons and grandsons to the fifth generation, the valorous Felixmarte of Hyrcania, the never sufficiently praised Tirante the White, and that knight whom we have seen and heard and spoken with almost in our own times, the invincible and valorous Sir Belianis of Greece. That, gentlemen, is what it is to be a knight errant, and what I have described to you is the order of chivalry, in which, as I have already said, though a sinner, I have made my profession. What the knights I have told you of professed I profess too; and that is why I am travelling through these wastes and deserts in quest of adventures, with mind resolved to oppose my arms and my person to the greatest perils which fortune may present, in aid of the weak and those in need.'

From these arguments the travellers finally decided that Don Quixote was out of his wits, and realized what form of madness it

D

was that possessed him. And they were as astonished as everyone else had been on first making that discovery. Now Vivaldo was a shrewd and cheerful fellow and, to relieve the boredom of the short journey they had still to take before arriving at the place of burial, he tried to give Don Quixote an opportunity of continuing his wild talk, and consequently observed: 'It seems to me, Sir Knight Errant, that you have adopted one of the strictest professions on earth; and it is my opinion that even the Carthusian monks' is not so severe a calling.'

'The monks' profession may well be as strict,' replied Don Quixote, 'but whether it is as necessary in the world I am within a hair's breadth of doubting. For, truly, the soldier who carries out his captain's orders does no less than the captain who gives the orders. I mean that the religious, in all peace and quiet, pray Heaven for the well-being of the world; but we soldiers and knights carry out what they pray for, defending it with the strength of our arms and the edge of our swords, beneath no roof but the open sky, exposed to the intolerable beams of the sun in summer and the biting frosts in winter. We, therefore, are God's ministers on earth, and the arms by which His justice is executed here. And whereas matters of war and things of that kind cannot be performed without sweat, toil, and labour, it follows that men whose profession is war must, unquestionably, endure more than those who in assured peace and repose are for ever praying God to help the powerless. Far be it from me to say, or even to think, that the state of a knight errant is as good as a cloistered monk's. I only want to argue from my own sufferings that it is most certainly a more painful and belaboured one, hungrier and thirstier, more miserable, ragged and lousy; for there is no doubt that knights errant of old suffered much ill-usage in the course of their lives. And if some of them rose by the valour of their arms to be Emperors, they assuredly paid dearly for it in blood and sweat; and if those who did rise so high had had no enchanters or sages to help them, they would have been defrauded of their desires and cheated of their hopes.'

'I agree with you,' replied the traveller, 'but there is one thing in particular about knights errant that seems wrong to me. That is that when they are on the point of embarking on a great and perilous adventure in which there is manifest danger to their lives, never at the moment of attack do they think of entrusting their souls to God, as every Christian in such peril is bound to do. Instead they commend themselves to their mistresses, with as much fervour and devotion as if these were their God, a practice which seems to me to smack somewhat of paganism.'

'Sir,' replied Don Quixote, 'on no account can it be otherwise, and it would go badly with the knight errant who should act differently. For it is the use and custom of chivalry for the knight errant, in embarking on any great feat of arms, to have his lady before him, and to turn his eyes softly and lovingly upon her, as if thereby begging her favour and protection in the hazardous enterprise that faces him. And even if no one hears him, he is obliged to breathe certain words between his teeth, commending himself to her with all his heart; and of this practice we have innumerable examples in the histories. But it is not to be inferred that they neglect to commend themselves to God; for they have time and opportunity to do so in the course of their task.'

'All the same,' replied the traveller, 'I am still uncertain on one point. I have often read of two knights beginning by bandying words. Then, little by little, their anger begins to kindle, and they turn their horses, make a wide circle in the field, and next, without more ado, charge one another at full speed, commending themselves to their ladies in the midst of the charge; and the usual result of their encounter is that one falls over the cruppers of his horse, speared right through by his opponent's lance; and his opponent too has to cling on to his horse's mane to avoid falling to the ground. Now, I cannot see how the dead man could have had the time to commend himself to God in the course of so very rapid an action. It would have been better if the words spent on commending himself to his lady as he charged had been employed in his duties and obligations as a Christian. What is more, I believe that not all knights errant have ladies to commend themselves to, for they are not all in love.'

'That is impossible,' replied Don Quixote. 'I say that it is impossible that there could be any knight errant without a lady. For it is as right and proper for them to be in love as for the sky to have stars; and I can vouch for it that there has never been a knight errant without a lady in any history whatever. For the very fact of his having no lady would show him to be no legitimate knight, but a bastard who has entered the fortress of chivalry not through the gate but over the fence, like a thief and a robber.'

'Nevertheless,' said the traveller, 'if I remember rightly, I have read that Sir Galaor, brother of the famous Amadis of Gaul, never had a definite lady to commend himself to, and yet was none the worse thought of for that, and was a very valiant and famous knight.'

To which Don Quixote replied: 'Sir, one swallow does not make a summer. Besides, I know that Sir Galaor was secretly very much in love. Indeed, his habit of paying court to any ladies who attracted him was a trait in his nature which he was unable to control. But, to be brief, it is very well authenticated that he had only one lady whom he had made mistress of his heart, and that he commended himself to her very often and secretly, for he prided himself on being a very secretive knight.'

'Then, if it is essential for every knight errant to be in love,' said the traveller, 'it may be fairly presumed that you, your worship, being a professed knight, have also a lady. If, then, you do not pride yourself on your secrecy like Sir Galaor, I beg you most earnestly, on behalf of all this company and of my self, to inform us of the name, the country, the degree, and the beauty of your lady. For she would count herself fortunate to have all the world know that she is loved and served by such a knight as your worship appears to be.'

Here Don Quixote heaved a deep sigh and said: 'I cannot affirm whether my sweet enemy is pleased or not at the whole world's knowing that I serve her. I can only say, in reply to your very polite question, that her name is Dulcinea; her country El Toboso, a village in La Mancha; her degree at least that of Princess, for she is my Queen and mistress; her beauty superhuman, for in her are realized all the impossible and chimerical attributes of beauty which poets give to their ladies; that her hair is gold; her forehead the Elysian fields; her eyebrows rainbows; her eyes suns; her cheeks roses; her lips coral; her teeth pearls; her neck alabaster; her breast marble; her hands ivory; she is white as snow; and those parts which modesty has veiled from human sight are such, I think and believe, that discreet reflection can extol them, but make no comparison.'

'We should like to know her lineage, race, and family,' said Vivaldo.

And Don Quixote replied: 'She is not of the ancient Curtii, Caii, or Scipios of Rome; nor of the modern Colonnas and Orsinis; nor of the Moncadas and Requesenes of Catalonia; nor yet of the Rebellas and Villanovas of Valencia; of the Palafoxes, Nuzas, Rocabertis, Corellas, Lunas, Alagones, Urreas, Fozes, and Gurreas of Aragon; of the Cerdas, Manriques, Mendozas, and Guzmans of Castile; nor of the Alencastres, Pallas, and Meneses of Portugal; but of El Toboso of La Mancha, a lineage which, though modern, may yet give noble birth to the most illustrious families of future ages. Let no one contradict me in this except under the conditions which Cervino put beneath the trophy of Roland's arms:

> Let no one move them
> But one who dares his prowess against Roland.'

'Although I am descended from the Cachopines of Laredo,' replied the traveller, 'I shall not dare to compare my family with the El Tobosos of La Mancha; though, to tell you the truth, such a surname has never reached my ears till now.'

'How not reached you!' exclaimed Don Quixote.

The whole party was listening most attentively to this conversation, and everyone, even the goatherds and shepherds, realized how very much out of his wits Don Quixote was. Only Sancho Panza took all that his master said for truth, knowing who he was and having known him from his birth. But where he rather hesitated was in believing all that about the fair Dulcinea del Toboso, for he had never heard of such a name or such a princess, although he lived near El Toboso. Now, as they went along deep in this talk, they saw coming down through a gap between two high mountains some twenty shepherds, all in skins of black wool and crowned with garlands which, as they made out later, were, some of them, of yew and some of cypress. Six of their number were carrying a bier covered with a great variety of flowers and branches, and at this sight one of the goatherds remarked: 'These men must be bearing Chrysostom's body. The foot of that mountain is the place where he directed them to bury him.'

So they hurried forward, and reached the place just as the new-comers had placed the bier on the ground, and as four of them were beginning to hollow the grave beside a hard rock with their pickaxes. The parties exchanged courteous greetings, and then Don Quixote and his companions immediately went to look at the bier, on which they saw a dead body, dressed like a shepherd and apparently about thirty years old, covered with flowers; and, dead though he was, it was clear that in life he had been a handsome and courtly young man. Around him on the bier were several books and a great number of papers, some open and some sealed; and everyone there, spectators, grave-diggers and the rest, kept a strange silence, till one of the dead man's bearers said to another: 'Look carefully, Ambrosio, and see if this really is the place which Chrysostom meant, since you wish all the directions in his will to be punctiliously observed.'

'This is it, I know,' replied Ambrosio, 'for here my luckless friend often told me the tale of his misfortune. Here, he said, he first saw that mortal enemy of the human race; here it was too that he first declared to her his passion, which was as honourable as it was ardent; here it was that Marcela finally rejected and scorned him, which caused him to put an end to the tragedy of his miserable life; and here in remembrance of so much misfortune he wished to be consigned to the bowels of eternal oblivion.'

Then, turning to Don Quixote and the travellers, he went on: 'This body, gentlemen, which you are gazing on with eyes of pity, was the dwelling-place of a soul in which Heaven had placed an infinite portion of its riches. This is the body of Chrysostom, a man of unique genius, singular courtesy and extreme gentleness, a phoenix in friendship, magnificent beyond measure, grave without arrogance, gay without coarseness; and, in short, first in all the art of goodness, and second to none in all the ways of misfortune. He loved and was hated; adored and was disdained; he courted a savage; he strove to soften marble; he pursued the wind; he cried to the desert; he served ingratitude, whose only reward was to make him the prey of death in the midst of his life's course. For he was brought to his end by a shepherdess whom he strove to render immortal in the memory of mankind, as those papers you are gazing at could well prove, if he had not ordered me to commit them to the flames as we are committing his body to the earth.'

'Then you would be more rigorous and cruel to them than their owner himself,' broke in Vivaldo; 'for it is neither just nor proper to carry out a man's bequests when what he orders exceeds all reason. It would not have been right in Augustus Caesar himself if he had consented to carry out all that the divine Mantuan ordered in his will. Therefore, Ambrosio, although you commit your friend's body to the earth, you should not commit his writings to oblivion; for if he was so wronged as to ask it, you should not be so unwise as to comply, but rather, by granting life to these papers, let Marcela's cruelty live forever and serve as an example to men in times to come, so that they may shun and avoid such pitfalls. For we all know the story of your enamoured and ill-fated friend; and we know of your friendship and the reason for his death, and of the instructions he left in his last hours. From this lamentable tale can be judged the greatness of Marcela's cruelty and of Chrysostom's love, and the sincerity of your friendship. We can learn from it, too, the fate of those who rush recklessly down the path which headlong love opens before their eyes. Last night we heard of Chrysostom's death, and that he was to be buried in this place; and so from curiosity and pity we have turned out of our direct way, and agreed to come and see with our own eyes what moved us to such pity when we heard of it. In return for our compassion and our desire, if it were possible to find a remedy, we pray you, wise Ambrosio – at least I do for my part – that instead of burning these papers you will let me take some of them away.'

Then, without waiting for the shepherd's reply, he stretched out his hand and took some of them that lay nearest him. Seeing which, Ambrosio said: 'Out of courtesy, sir, I will consent to your keeping those you have taken: but it would be vain to think that I shall not burn the rest.'

Vivaldo, who longed to know what was in the papers, opened one immediately, and saw that its title was *A Song of Despair*. On hearing which Ambrosio said: 'That is the last piece the unhappy man wrote; and so that you may see, sir, to what a pass his misfortune brought him, read it aloud. For you will have time enough for that while they are digging his grave.'

'I will do so most gladly,' said Vivaldo; and, as all the bystanders were equally curious, they gathered round him in a circle, as he read in a clear voice the poem which follows.

Chapter XIV. *The Despairing Verses of the Dead Shepherd and other Unexpected Matters.*

'Since you would have me publish, cruel maid,
From tongue to tongue, from one to the other pole,
The efficacy of thy rigour sharp,
I'll constrain hell my grieving soul to aid,
And in my breast infuse a ton of dole,
Whereon my voice, as it is wont, may harp,
And labour, as I wish, at once to carp
And tell my sorrows and thy murdering deed.
The dreadful voice and accents shall agree,
And, with them mixed, for greater torture, be
Lumps of my wretched bowels, which still bleed.
Then listen, and lend thy attentive ear,
Not well-consorted tunes but howling to hear,
That from my bitter bosom's depth takes flight,
And, by constrainèd raving borne away
Issues forth for mine ease and thy despite.

'The lion's roaring, and the dreadful cries
Of ravening wolf, and hissing terrible
Of scaly serpent; and the fearful yell
Of some grim monster; and the ominous crow's
Foreboding, sinister caw; the horrible
Sound on the tossing sea of the blustering gale;
The implacable bellow of the new-conquered bull;
The lonely widowed turtle's sobbing moan,
Most mournful, and the dreary night descant
Of the envious owl, commingled with the plaint
Of all the infernal black battalion;
Let all together cry from my aching soul
United in one sound of such sad dole
That all the senses may confounded be,
For my fierce torment needs a manner new
Wherein I may recount my misery.

'The doleful echoes of such great confusion
Shall not resound o'er father Tagus' sands
Nor touch the olive-watering Betis' ears.
Of my dire pangs I'll only make effusion
'Midst these steep rocks and in the hollow lands,
With my tongue dead, yet with a living cry;
Or in some hidden vale, or on the shy
Shores that no feet of human kind defile,
Or where the sun has never shown his beam,

Or 'midst the venomous crew of beasts unclean
That draw their being from the teeming Nile.
For though amongst those lofty table-lands
The hollow echo indistinctly sounds
Thy matchless rigour and my cruel pain,
Yet, by the privilege of my niggard fates,
It will their force throughout the world proclaim.

  Disdain doth kill; and, whether false or sound
Suspicions will all patience overthrow;
But jealousy with greater rigour slays;
A lengthy absence doth our life confound;
Against fear of oblivion to ensue
Firm hope of best success gives little ease.
Inevitable death lurks in all these.
But I – amazing miracle! – still live,
Jealous, absent, disdained, and certain too
Of the suspicions that my life undo.
Drowned in oblivion, I my fire revive,
And amongst all those pains have never scope
Once to behold the shadow of a hope,
Nor, thus despairing, will I hope allow;
But rather, to exacerbate my wrong,
To live for ever hopeless here I vow.

'At one same time can hope and fear exist?
Or is it reason that they should do so,
Seeing how much more cause there is for fears?
If before me dire jealousy persist,
Shall I then shut my eyes, since it will show
In my soul through a thousand bleeding scars ?
Or who will not the gates unto despair
Fling open wide the moment that he spies
Murdering disdain, and notes each sad suspicion
Confirmed as truth – O bitter transformation! –
Whilst limpid truth is turned to a pack of lies?
O tyrant of love's state, fierce jealousy!
With cruel chains these hands together tie,
With twisted rope couple them, rough disdain!
But, woe is me, with bloody victory
Your memory is by my suffering slain!

'And now I die ; and since all hope I've lost
Ever in life or death, to prosper now,
I obstinate will rest in fantasy,
And say he does the best who loves the most,

And that the soul most liberty doth know
When most enslaved by Love's old tyranny.
I will swear that my constant enemy
In her fair body a fair soul contains,
That her unkindness by my fault arose,
And only by the grievous hurt he does
Can Love his empire in just peace maintain.
And in this fancy, and with this hard knot
I'll hasten my appearance in that court
Where by her bitter scorn I'm forced to come,
And offering to the winds body and soul,
Forfeit the future's laurel wreath and palm.

'Thou that by multiplying wrongs dost show
The reason forcing me to violence
Against this weary life, that's now grown hateful,
Since now by signs notorious thou dost know
From my heart's deepest wound how gladly sense
Doth sacrifice me to thy scorns ungrateful,
Shouldst thou, perchance, my merits find so fruitful
As to dim the clear heaven of your eyes,
And cloud them with my death, yet weep not so.
For I'll yield you no tribute by my woe,
Nor give you my soul's booty as your prize.
But rather, laughing at my funeral sad,
Show how my end begins to make thee glad.
But 'tis a folly to advise thee this,
For I know that in hurrying on my death
Consists my glory and thy chiefest bliss.

'Let Tantalus from the profoundest deeps
Come, for it is high time now, with his thirst;
And Sisyphus with his oppressive stone;
Let Tityus bring his vulture that ne'er sleeps,
Nor Ixion delay with wheel accursed;
Nor the three sisters, ever labouring on;
And let them all at once their mortal pain
Translate into my breast, and scarce aloud
(If funeral rites are granted my despair)
Chant their sad obsequies with doleful air
Over a corpse even denied a shroud.
And the three-faced infernal porter grim,
With thousand monsters and chimaeras come
And swell the mournful descant of despair;
No greater pomp than this, I fear, is due
To any constant lover on his bier.

Despairing song, I beg thee not to grieve
When my sad company thou com'st to leave;
But rather since the course whence thou didst spring
By my misfortune grows more fortunate,
Even in the grave thou must shun sorrowing.'

Chrysostom's song pleased its hearers, though Vivaldo said that it did not seem to him to conform to the account he had heard of Marcela's modesty and goodness. For in it Chrysostom complained of jealousy, suspicions, and neglect, all to the prejudice of Marcela's good name and fame. But Ambrosio answered him out of the knowledge of his friend's most private thoughts: 'To satisfy your doubt, sir, I must tell you that when the unfortunate man wrote this song he had voluntarily banished himself from Marcela to see if absence would have its customary effect upon him. And as there is nothing that does not vex the absent lover, and no fear that does not pursue him, so Chrysostom was tormented by imaginary jealousies and suspicions, as fearful as if they were real. Marcela's goodness, therefore, is as true as fame proclaimed it; for, except for cruelty, some haughtiness, and much scorn, there is no fault that envy itself can rightly find in her.'

'That is true,' replied Vivaldo. And he was going to read another of the papers which he had saved from the fire when he was prevented by a miraculous vision – for such it seemed – which suddenly appeared before their eyes. For on the top of the rock in which they were digging the grave appeared the shepherdess Marcela, looking even more beautiful than she had been described. Those of them who knew her well were just as amazed. But no sooner did Ambrosio catch sight of her than he cried with some show of anger:

'Have you come here, perhaps, fiery basilisk of these mountains, to see if the wounds of this wretch, whom your cruelty killed, will bleed afresh at the sight of you? Or have you come to triumph at your nature's cruel work? Or to gaze from that height, like another pitiless Nero, upon the flames of burning Rome? Or, in your pride, to trample this miserable corpse, as Tarquin's ungrateful daughter did her father's? Tell us quickly why you have come, or what you desire. For, as I know that Chrysostom never failed to be obedient to you during his life, I will take care that even in his death all who call themselves his friends obey you.'

'I have come, Ambrosio, for none of the reasons you give,' replied Marcela, 'but rather to defend myself, and to prove how wrong are those who blame me for their own sufferings and for Chrysostom's death. So I ask all of you here to give me your attention, for it will not take me much time or waste many words to persuade all sensible men of the truth. Heaven made me, you say, so lovely that my beauty makes you love me despite yourselves; and in return for the love you show me, you claim, and even demand, that I should be bound to love you. I know by the natural sense which God has given me that whatever is beautiful is lovable; but I do not understand why, merely because she inspires love, a woman who is loved for her beauty is obliged to love the man who loves her. Besides, it may chance that the man who loves what is beautiful is himself ugly; and, as ugliness is loathsome, it would be absurd for him to say: "I love you for your beauty; love me although I am ugly." But, even supposing that both are equally beautiful, the attraction need not therefore be equal on both sides. For not all beauties inspire love; some only please the eye, but do not subdue the heart. Now if all beauty inspired love and made conquests, the hearts of men would wander confused and astray, not knowing where to alight; for as beauties are infinite, the feelings they inspire must be infinite too. Besides, as I have heard, true love cannot be divided, but must be free and unconstrained. If this is so, as I believe it is, why do you ask me to do violence to my heart, merely because you say you love me? Tell me, if the Heavens had made me ugly instead of beautiful, should I have had the right to complain of your not loving me? What is more, you must consider that I did not choose to be beautiful. My beauty, such as it is, the Heavens gave me freely, without my choice or asking; and just as the viper deserves no blame for the poison which nature gave her, even though she kills with it, I cannot be blamed for being beautiful. For beauty in a modest woman is like distant fire or a sharp sword; the one does not burn nor the other cut the man who does not come near it. Modesty and the virtues are the adornments of the soul, and without them, even if the body is beautiful, it ought not to appear so. Now if modesty is one of the virtues and the fairest adornment of the body and the soul, why must the woman who is loved for her beauty lose it to gratify the desires of a man who, for his pleasure alone, tries with all his strength and ingenuity to rob her of it? I was born free, and to live free I chose the solitude of the fields. The trees on these mountains are my companions; the clear waters of these streams my mirrors; to the trees and the waters I disclose my thoughts and my beauty. I am the distant fire and the far-off sword. Those whom I have attracted with my eyes I have undeceived with my words. If desires are nourished on hope, as I never gave any to Chrysostom or to any other, it may not justly be said that any man's end was my doing, since it was his persistence rather than my cruelties that killed him. And if it is objected that his intentions were honest, and that therefore I was obliged to reciprocate them, my answer is that when he revealed to me the honesty of his intentions on this same spot where now you are digging his grave, I told him that my will was to live in perpetual solitude, and that only the earth would enjoy the fruit of my chastity and the spoils of my beauty. If, despite all this discouragement, he chose to persist against hope and to sail against the wind, is it surprising that he should have drowned in the gulf of his own folly? If I had encouraged him in hope, I should have been false; if I had gratified him, I should have acted against my better feelings and resolutions. He persisted despite discouragement, despaired although not hated. Judge then whether it is right that I should pay the penalty for his sufferings! If I have deceived anyone, let him complain; if I have broken my promise to anyone, let him despair; if I lure anyone on, let him declare it; if I encourage anyone, let him boast of it. But let me not be called cruel or murderous by those whom I have never promised, deceived, lured on, or encouraged. Heaven has not yet fated me to love; and it is folly to think that I shall love out of choice. May this general warning serve for the particular benefit of every man who woos me; and henceforth be it understood that if anyone dies on my account, he will not die out of jealousy or from rejection; for she who loves no man can make no man jealous, and discouragement must not be taken for disdain. If anyone calls me a wild beast and a basilisk, let him shun me as a mischievous and evil thing; if he calls me ungrateful, let him serve me no more; if he calls me strange, know me no more; if cruel, follow me no more; for this wild beast, this basilisk, this ungrateful, strange, and cruel creature will in no way seek, serve, know, or follow him. If Chrysostom's impatience and headstrong passion killed him, why should my modesty and reserve be blamed? If I preserve my purity in the company of the trees, why should he who would have me keep the company of men desire me to lose it? I, as you know, have riches of my own, and covet no one else's. I have a taste for freedom and no wish for subjection. I neither love nor hate any man. I do not deceive one man and encourage another. I do not trifle with one nor keep another in hope. I enjoy the modest company of the village shepherdesses and the care of my goats. My desires are bounded by these mountains; and if they extend beyond them, it is to contemplate the beauty of the sky, a step by which the soul travels to its first abode.'

When she had finished, she turned round without waiting for a reply and plunged into the densest part of the nearby woods, leaving everyone as amazed at her good sense as at her beauty. Some whom the mighty arrow of her fair eyes' gaze had wounded made as if to follow her, heedless of the plain words of discouragement they had just heard. But here Don Quixote, thinking that this was an occasion to exercise his chivalry by the succouring of a maiden in distress, put his hand on his sword-hilt, and loudly and clearly exclaimed:

'Let no man, of whatsoever estate or condition, dare to follow the fair Marcela, under pain of incurring my most furious indignation! She has shown with clear and sufficient argument that she bears little or no blame for Chrysostom's death, and how far she is from yielding to any of her lovers' desires. Wherefore it is right that, instead of being pursued and persecuted, she should be honoured and esteemed by all good men in the world, for she has proved that she is the only woman living with such pure intentions.'

Now whether because of Don Quixote's threats or of Ambrosio's request that they should fulfil the debt they owed to his friend, not one of the shepherds stirred or moved from the place until the grave had been dug, Chrysostom's papers burnt, and his body buried amidst the tears of the spectators.

They sealed the grave with a heavy stone until such time as they should have a tombstone ready, which Ambrosio informed them he intended to have made, and inscribed with the following epitaph:

Here a poor loving swain's
Frozen corpse lies.
He was a shepherd and
Died of disdain.

Died of the cruelty
Of a coy, thankless, fair
Maid, by whom Love's empire
Widens its tyranny.

Then they spread flowers and branches in plenty over the grave, and each of the shepherds, after condoling with his friend Ambrosio, bade him good-bye. Vivaldo and his companions did the same, and Don Quixote said farewell to his hosts and to the travellers, who pressed him to come with them to Seville, which was just the place to strike adventures in, they said, for there are more to be found there, in every street and round every corner, than can be met with in any other place. Don Quixote thanked them for their advice and their evident desire to do him a service, but said that for the present he neither could nor should go to Seville until he had cleared all those mountains of the thieves and robbers who were said to infest them.

In view of this honest purpose, the travellers did not care to press him further. But once more bidding him farewell, they left him and pursued their journey, in the course of which they did not fail to discuss the story of Marcela and Chrysostom as well as the follies of Don Quixote. As for him, he decided to go in search of the shepherdess Marcela and offer her all the service in his power. But things did not turn out as he expected, as will be told in the course of this true story, of which the second part ends here.

Chapter xv. *Of the unfortunate Adventure which befel Don Quixote on his Encounter with some Merciless Yanguesans.*

THE sage Cide Hamete Benengeli relates that as soon as Don Quixote had bidden farewell to his hosts and to everyone who had been present at the shepherd Chrysostom's burial, he and his squire entered that same wood into which they had seen the shepherdess Marcela disappear. And when they had travelled through it for more than two hours, looking for her in vain in all directions, they halted in a meadow, rich in fresh grass, beside which ran a pleasant and refreshing brook, which invited them, or rather induced them, to spend the sultry hours of midday there; for the heat had already become oppressive. Don Quixote and Sancho dismounted and, leaving the ass and Rocinante at large to feed on the abundant grass, they ransacked their saddle-bags. Then, without ceremony, master and man ate the contents in peace and good fellowship. Now Sancho had not troubled to fetter Rocinante, secure in his belief that he was so mild and so little lustful a beast that all the mares in the pastures of Cordova would not provoke him to any impropriety. But as Fate, or the Devil – who is not always sleeping – would have it, there was a herd of Galician mares grazing in that valley. They belonged to some carriers from Yanguas whose habit it is to spend midday with their droves where there is grass and water; and the place where Don Quixote happened to be suited the Yanguesans very well. So it came about that Rocinante was taken with the desire to disport himself with the lady mares and, abandoning his natural pace and habits the moment he smelt them, asked no permission of his master, but set off at a brisk trot to acquaint them of his needs. But they, apparently, preferred the pastures, and gave him such a welcome with their hooves and teeth that in a very short while they had broken his girths and left him stripped of his saddle and naked. But what must have hurt him more was that the carriers, seeing the violence he was offering to their mares, ran up with pack-staves, and laid into him so hard that he was soon on the ground in a very sorry state. At this point Don Quixote and Sancho, who had witnessed Rocinante's beating, ran up panting, the knight saying to his squire:

'From what I can see, friend Sancho, these are no knights, but vile and low-bred men. I say this so that you may freely help me to take due vengeance for the outrage which they have done to Rocinante before our very eyes.'

'How the devil can we take revenge,' replied Sancho, 'when there are more than twenty of them, and we are only two – or perhaps no more than one and a half?'

'I am equal to a hundred,' answered Don Quixote. Then without further discussion he drew his sword and attacked the Yanguesans; and Sancho Panza was spurred on by his master's example to do the same. At the first blow Don Quixote gave one of them a slash, which slit the leather coat he was wearing and cut a great gash in his shoulder. But the Yanguesans, seeing so many of themselves so roughly treated by a mere two men, seized their pack-staves and, surrounding the pair, began to lay into them with might and main. In fact, they stretched Sancho on the ground at their second blow, and the same fate soon befell Don Quixote, his skill and courage availing him nothing; and, as Fate would have it, he fell at the feet of the still prostrate Rocinante. All of which goes to show what hard bruises pack-staves will deal in the hands of angry rustics. Then, seeing the damage they had done, the Yanguesans loaded their beasts as fast as they could and went on their way, leaving the two adventurers in an evil plight and a worse humour.

The first to regain his senses was Sancho Panza who, finding himself beside his master, cried in a weak and piteous voice: 'Don Quixote! Ah, Don Quixote!'

'What is the matter, brother Sancho?' answered Don Quixote in the same faint and plaintive tones.

'Well, sir,' said Sancho Panza, 'I should be glad if your worship could let me have two gulps of that drink of Fair Bras's, if you've got it handy. Perhaps it might be as good for broken bones as it is for wounds.'

'Why,' replied Don Quixote, 'if I had some here, wretch that I am, what more could I want? But I swear to you, Sancho Panza, on my word as a knight errant that, unless fortune ordains otherwise, I will have some in my possession before two days have passed, or it will be no fault of mine.'

'How long does your worship suppose it will be before we shall be able to use our feet?' asked Sancho Panza.

'For myself,' replied the bruised knight Don Quixote, 'I must say that I can see no end to our present plight. But I take the blame for everything upon myself, for I should not have drawn my sword against men who were not dubbed knights, as I am. That is why I believe that the God of battles has permitted me to be so chastised – for breaking the laws of chivalry. So, Sancho Panza, you must be warned by what I am going to say, for it greatly concerns the welfare of us both. It is, that when you see us insulted by such rabble you must not wait for me to draw my sword on them, for I shall on no account do so. But you must draw your own and chastise them at your pleasure. Should any knights come to their aid or defence, I shall know how to protect you and shall attack them with all my strength; and you have already had a thousand signs and proofs of the height to which the valour of this strong arm of mine can reach.' So arrogant was the poor gentleman at his victory over the brave Basque.

But Sancho Panza did not find his master's instructions so good that he could refrain from replying, 'Sir, I am a peaceable, mild, quiet man, and I can overlook any kind of injury, for I have a wife to keep and children to bring up. So let me tell your worship by way of a hint – for it's not my place to give orders – that I shall on no account draw my sword against peasant or against knight, and that from now on, before God, I pardon whatever insults have been, or shall be, done me, whether by person high or low, rich or poor, by gentleman or by commoner, without exception of rank or quality.'

On hearing this, his master replied: 'I wish that I had breath enough to say a few words at my ease, and that the pain I feel in this rib would die down even slightly, so that I could convince you, Sancho Panza, of your error. Listen, wretch! Suppose that the winds of fortune, now so contrary, should turn in our favour, swelling the sails of our desires, and we should reach harbour, safely and unhurt, in one of those isles I promised you – what would become of you if I won it and made you its master? You would ruin everything by not being a knight, nor desiring to be one, having neither the courage nor the resolution to avenge insults and defend your dominions. For you must know that in newly conquered kingdoms and provinces the minds of the natives are never so quiet, or so well disposed to their new lords there, as to leave no fear of their planning some revolt, so as to reverse the state of things once more and, as they say, try their luck again. So the new master must needs have the intelligence to know how to rule, and the courage to take offensive and defensive measures in every emergency.'

'I wish I had had the intelligence and courage you speak of,' replied Sancho, 'when this last thing happened to us; but you must take a poor man's word for it that I'm in greater need of plasters than of sermons. Try, sir, if you can't get up; and we'll see if we can help Rocinante, although he doesn't deserve it, for he was the chief cause of all the knocking about we got. I never thought it of him; for I imagined he was as chaste and peaceable a fellow as I am myself. It is a good saying, after all, that it takes a long time to get to know people, and that there's nothing certain in this life. Who would have said that after all those great sword-thrusts you dealt that wretched knight errant, this great storm of blows would have followed up so fast and burst on our shoulders?'

'Yours,' replied Don Quixote, 'must have been made for such a storm, but as mine were nurtured between cambrics and fine linen, clearly they are more sensitive to the pain of this mishap. If it were not that I imagine – why do I say imagine? – that I most certainly know that all these discomforts are inseparable from the profession of arms, I would be ready to die here of pure vexation.'

To which the squire replied: 'Sir, if these misfortunes are the fruit of chivalry, will your worship tell me if they happen very often, or if they only occur at set times? For it seems to me that after two such crops we should be useless for the third, unless God, of His infinite pity, were to come to our aid.'

'You must know, friend Sancho,' replied Don Quixote, 'that a knight errant's life is subject to countless perils and mischances. Yet he has none the less the potentiality of rising at any moment to become King or Emperor, as experience has demonstrated in the case of many and divers knights whose histories I know in detail. If my pain would let me I could tell you now of some who have climbed, by the valour of their arms alone, to the high degree I mentioned; yet those very knights, both beforehand and afterwards, sustained various calamities and misfortunes. For the valorous Amadis of Gaul was once in the power of his mortal enemy, Arcalaus the enchanter, who, it is well attested, when he held him prisoner, tied him to a pillar in a courtyard and gave him more than two hundred lashes with the reins of his own horse. There is a little-known author too of no small reputation, who says that the Knight of the Sun, being caught in a certain castle by means of a trap-door which gave way beneath his feet, found himself after his fall bound hand and foot in a subterranean cavern; and there they administered to him what is called an enema, of snow-water and sand, which nearly killed him; and if a certain sage who was a great friend of his had not succoured him in his dreadful plight, things would have gone very badly with the poor knight. So I can well afford to suffer in such good company, since they sustained greater affronts than we are suffering now. For I would have you know, Sancho, that wounds dealt with instruments which are accidentally in the hand do not disgrace a man; that is expressly laid down in the law of the duel. So if a shoemaker strikes a man with the last he is holding, even though it is of wood, it shall not therefore be said that the man whom he struck was cudgelled. I say this in case you may suppose that, because we have come out of this struggle soundly bruised, we are disgraced; since the arms which those men carried and pounded us with were no other than their pack-staves; and not one of them, so far as I can remember, carried a rapier, sword, or dagger.'

'They did not give me a chance,' replied Sancho, 'to observe them so closely. For I had no sooner put my hand to my blade than they made so many crosses on my shoulders with their sticks, that they knocked the sight out of my eyes and the strength out of my feet, and laid me out where I'm lying now. I don't care a hang, down here, whether the beating was a disgrace or not, but I do mind a lot about the pain I got from it, and that's likely to stay as deeply in my memory as it bit into my back.'

'For all that, brother Panza,' replied Don Quixote, 'let me tell you that there is no memory which time does not efface, nor any pain that death does not destroy.'

'But what misfortune could be worse,' replied Sancho, 'than one that waits for time to efface it and death to destroy it? If ours were the sort of misfortune that could be cured with a couple of poultices it wouldn't be so bad. But I'm beginning to think that all the plasters in a hospital wouldn't be enough to give it a turn for the better.'

'No more of that, Sancho,' replied Don Quixote, 'but make the best of a bad business, and I shall do the same. Let us see how Rocinante is, for it seems to me that the poor creature got by no means the smallest share of the disaster.'

'There's nothing marvellous about that,' replied Sancho, 'since he's a knight errant too. What does astonish me is that my ass has got off scot-free, while we've got our ribs broken.'

'Fortune always leaves one door open in disasters, to admit a remedy,' said Don Quixote. 'I say this because your little beast will now serve instead of Rocinante to carry me from here to some castle where my wound may be cured. What is more, I shall not consider such a mount a disgrace, for I remember reading how good old Silenus, tutor and guide to the merry god of laughter, rode most gladly on a very handsome ass when he entered the city of the hundred gates.'

'It's very likely he rode as your worship says,' replied Sancho; 'but there's a great deal of difference between riding astride and being laid across like a sack of dung.'

'Wounds received in battle,' answered Don Quixote, 'rather confer honour than take it away. So, friend Panza, give me no more answers, but do as I have told you. Get up as best you can and place me on your ass in any way you like. Then let us depart, before night comes and overtakes us in this wilderness.'

'Yet I have heard your worship say,' said Panza, 'that it is quite the thing for knights errant to sleep in moorland and deserts for the greater part of the year, and to think themselves very fortunate to do so.'

'That is when they cannot help it,' said Don Quixote, 'or when they are in love. In fact there have been knights who have stayed on a rock exposed to sun and shade and all the inclemencies of Heaven for two years, unknown to their ladies; and one of these was Amadis, when he assumed the name of Beltenebros and took up his lodging on the Bare Rock, for eight years, or perhaps eight months – for I am not sure of my reckoning. Suffice it that he was doing penance there for some displeasure the lady Oriana had caused him. But let us leave the matter, before some misfortune like Rocinante's befalls the ass.'

'That would be the devil and all,' observed Sancho. And then, uttering thirty groans, sixty sighs, and a hundred and twenty damns and curses on whoever it was that had got him there, he raised himself, but stopped half-way, bent like a Turkish bow, unable to straighten himself up. However, despite his pain, he harnessed his ass, who had also taken advantage of that day's excess of liberty to stray a little. He then got Rocinante up; and he, if he had had a tongue to complain with, would certainly not have been outdone by squire or master. In the end, Sancho settled Don Quixote on the ass and, tying Rocinante to his tail, led his beast by the halter, making as best he could for the direction in which he thought the highway lay.

And he had not gone more than two miles when Fortune, who was guiding their affairs from good to better, brought him to the road, on which he sighted an inn, which, to his grief and Don Quixote's pleasure, must needs be a castle. Sancho swore that it was an inn, and his master that it was no inn but a castle; and the argument lasted so long that it was not finished when they arrived there, and Sancho entered without further enquiry, followed by his string of beasts.

Chapter XVI. *What happened to the ingenious knight in the Inn that he took for a Castle.*

THE innkeeper, who saw Don Quixote lying across the ass, asked Sancho what was wrong with him. Sancho replied that it was nothing, that he had fallen off a rock and bruised his ribs slightly. Now the innkeeper's wife was a woman of a different sort from the generality of hostesses, for she was kindly by nature and felt for her neighbours' misfortunes. So she immediately set about the cure of Don Quixote and made her young daughter, a very good-looking girl, help her to tend him.

There was an Asturian maid at the inn, broad-faced, flat-nosed, and with a head that seemed to have no back to it; she was blind of one eye and not too sound in the other. But she made up for her other shortcomings by her bodily allurements; she was not more than three feet high from head to toe, and her shoulders, which were rather on the heavy side, made her look down on the ground more than she liked. This charming maid, then, helped her young mistress, and the two of them made a very poor bed for Don Quixote in an attic which had evidently served once, for a long time, as a straw-loft.

There was a carrier lodging in this garret as well. His bed stood a little farther from the door than our knight's; and, although it consisted only of his mule's saddles and blankets, it was a good deal better than Don Quixote's, which was made up of four badly planed boards resting on a pair of not too even trestles; a mattress thin as a quilt and full of lumps, which were as hard as stones to the touch but appeared through various rents in the cover to be wool; two sheets, made of the leather used for shields, and a coverlet whose every thread anyone who wished could have counted without missing a single one.

On this execrable bed Don Quixote lay down, whereupon the hostess and her daughter poulticed him from head to foot, while Maritornes – for this was the Asturian maid's name – held a light.

The hostess, as she plastered him, seeing that parts of his body were covered with weals, remarked that he must have had a beating, not a fall.

'It wasn't a beating,' said Sancho, 'but the rock had a lot of jags and knobs, and each one must have made its mark. And, by the way, if you could be so very kind as to leave a little of that wadding, it might come in handy for someone, for my back's giving me a bit of trouble too.'

'Oh, I see,' replied the hostess; 'you must have had a fall as well.'

'I didn't fall,' said Sancho, 'but I got such a shock from seeing my master tumble that my body aches all over, as if I had been beaten black and blue.'

'That may well be,' said the innkeeper's daughter, 'for very often I've dreamt I fell off a tower and never reached the ground. And when I've woken up I've found myself as bruised and bumped as if I had really tumbled.'

'But here's the point, lady,' replied Sancho Panza. 'I wasn't dreaming. I was more wide awake than I am now, and there I was, almost as bruised as my master Don Quixote.'

'What's the gentleman's name?' asked the Asturian maid.

'Don Quixote de la Mancha,' replied Sancho Panza. 'He's a knight errant. One of the best and bravest the world has seen for a very long time.'

'What's a knight errant?' asked the maid.

'Are you so green that you don't know that?' replied Sancho. 'Then I'll tell you, my girl, that a knight errant – to cut a long story short – is beaten up one day and made Emperor the next. To-day he's the most unfortunate and poverty-stricken creature in the world; to-morrow he'll have two or three kingdoms to give to his squire.'

'Well, seeing that you have such a fine master,' said the hostess, 'how is it you aren't at least a count?'

'There's plenty of time yet,' replied Sancho. 'We've only been out seeking adventures for a month, and up to now we haven't come across anything worth calling one; and sometimes when you're looking for one thing you find another. But I promise you that, if my master Don Quixote recovers from his wound or fall, and I'm not crippled by mine, I won't swap my chances for the noblest title in Spain.'

Here Don Quixote, who had listened very attentively to all this chatter, sat up in bed as best he could and, taking the hostess's hand, addressed her:

'Believe me, beauteous lady, you may count yourself fortunate to have lodging in your castle a person whom I must refrain from praising only because self-praise is said to be a practice unworthy of a gentleman. But my squire will tell you who I am. I will only say that I shall bear the services you have done me eternally inscribed in my memory, so that I may remain grateful to you all the days of my life. Had it not pleased Heaven to keep me in such abject servitude to love's laws and to the eyes of that ungrateful beauty whose name I dare hardly breathe, then the eyes of your beauteous daughter would hold my freedom captive.'

The hostess, her daughter, and the worthy Maritornes were bewildered by the knight errant's words, which might have been Greek so little could they understand them, though they realized that they were all intended as thanks and compliments. But, as they were not used to such language, they stared at him in amazement; for he seemed so very different from the sort of men they were accustomed to. So, thanking him in their innkeepers' language, they left him, and the Asturian maid tended Sancho, who was in no less need of attention than his master.

Now the carrier had arranged with her that they should spend the night together in healthy sport; and she had promised that once the guests were quiet and her master and mistress asleep she would come to him and give him all the pleasure he could desire. And it is told to the credit of this good girl that she never made such promises without fulfilling them, even if she made them far away in the mountains and without any witness at all. For she prided herself on being a maiden of breeding, and did not feel degraded by serving in an inn, because only misfortune and ill-chance, as she said, had brought her to that pass.

Don Quixote's hard, narrow, miserable apology for a bed was the first in this starlit barn; and next beside him Sancho had made his, which consisted only of a rush mat and a horse-blanket, which seemed to be of threadbare canvas rather than of wool. Beyond these two came the carrier's bed, made, as we have said, of the saddles and all the trappings of the two best mules he had. He had twelve glossy, well-covered, splendid beasts, for he was one of the richest muleteers in Arevalo, as the author of this history tells us; and he makes a special mention of this carrier, because he knew him very well, and it is even suggested that he was some relation of his. But, however that may be, Cide Hamete Benengeli was a very exact historian and very precise in all his details, as can be seen by his not passing over these various points, trivial and petty though they may be. He should be an example to those grave historians who give us so short and skimped an account of events that we scarcely taste them, and so the most substantial part of their work, out of carelessness, malice, or ignorance, remains in their ink-horns. A thousand blessings then on the author of *Tablante de Ricamonte* and the writer of that other book which tells us of the deeds of Count Tomillas, for the exhaustiveness with which they describe everything.

But to return to the story. After the carrier had visited his mules and given them their second feed, he stretched himself on his pack-saddles and awaited his most punctual Maritornes. By now Sancho was poulticed and had lain down; but, though he tried to sleep, the pain in his sides would not allow him. Don Quixote, too, with the pain of his ribs was no more able to close his eyes than a hare. The whole inn was in silence, and there was no other light in it but that of a hanging lamp which burnt in the centre of the doorway.

This phenomenal quiet and his habitual preoccupation with the adventures that are related on every page of those books that had been his undoing wrought one of the strangest possible fancies in our knight's imagination. He thought that he had arrived at a famous castle – for, as we have said, every inn where he stayed seemed to him a castle – , and that the innkeeper's daughter was really the daughter of the warden. Overwhelmed by his nobility, she had fallen in love with him and, what is more, she had promised that very night, when her parents were asleep, to come and lie with him awhile. And taking all this fantasy which he had invented for the sober truth, he began to be disturbed and to think of the critical danger to which his honour was exposed, deciding in his heart to commit no treason against the lady Dulcinea del Toboso, even though Queen Guinevere and her lady Quintañona should appear before him.

Whilst he was brooding on this nonsense, unfortunately for him the time arrived for the Asturian maid's visit. She came in her shift, with bare feet and hair done up in a fustian kerchief. With soft and noiseless steps she entered the garret in which the three men were lodged, in search of the carrier. But scarcely had she reached the door when Don Quixote heard her; and, sitting up in bed, despite his plasters and his aching ribs, he stretched out his arms to receive his beauteous maiden. She was gliding modestly and silently, groping with outstretched hands for her lover, when she stumbled into the arms of Don Quixote, who seized her tightly by one wrist and, drawing her to him, she not daring to say a word, forced her to sit on his bed.

Then he felt her shift and, although it was of sackcloth, it seemed to him of the finest, most delicate satin. The glass beads that she wore on her wrist had for him the sheen of rare orient pearls. Her hair, which was coarse as a horse's mane, seemed to him strands of the most glistening gold of Arabia, whose splendour eclipsed the very sun. And her mouth, which, no doubt, reeked of the stale salad of the night before, seemed to him to breathe out a sweet and aromatic odour. In short, he bestowed on her each several feature of that famous princess who came, in the books that he had read, to visit the sore-wounded knight whom she loved so well. In every detail of dress and bearing his imagination copied her exactly. And so blind was the poor knight that neither her touch nor her breath nor anything else about the good maiden revealed his mistake to him, though she would have turned the stomach of anyone but a carrier. Far from it, he imagined that he held in his arms the goddess of beauty and, gripping her tight, in soft, amorous tones he began:

'Would that I could find means, most lovely and high-born lady, with which I could repay the singular favour you have done me in displaying your great beauty. But Fortune, which is never weary of persecuting good men, has laid me on this bed, so bruised and battered that even if I wished to satisfy your desires I could not. And besides that impediment there is another and greater, the pledge of faith I have given to the peerless Dulcinea del Toboso, sole mistress of my most secret thoughts. But were I not prevented in this way, I should not be so simple a knight as to let pass the happy chance you have deigned to offer me.'

Maritornes was bathed in a sweat of anguish at finding herself grasped by Don Quixote and, without understanding or paying the least attention to his protestations, tried silently to break loose. As for the good carrier, whose lusts kept him awake, he had heard his wench from the moment she came in, and had been listening attentively to the knight's every word. Suspecting that the Asturian maid had broken her promise to him in favour of another, he edged nearer and nearer to Don Quixote's bed, silently waiting to see what his incomprehensible speech might lead to. But, when he saw the maid struggling to break loose and Don Quixote trying to hold her, the jest seemed to him to have gone too far. Whereupon he raised his arm and dealt the amorous knight so terrible a blow on his lean jaws that his mouth was filled with blood; and, not content with this, he trod on his ribs and trampled him up and down at a lively rate.

The bed was rather weak and supported on no firm foundations. So, unable to bear the additional weight of the carrier, it gave way with a great crash. This woke the innkeeper, who called for Maritornes and, getting no reply, suspected that she must be the cause of the noise. With this in his mind he got up and, lighting a lamp, made his way towards the scene of the disturbance. The maid, hearing her master coming in and knowing his very bad temper, in fear and alarm climbed into the bed of the still-sleeping Sancho and huddled up in a ball.

At this point the innkeeper entered shouting: 'Where are you, you whore? This is all your doing; I'm sure of it.'

Whereat Sancho, feeling this weight almost on top of him, thought it was a nightmare and began to strike out right and left. A good number of his blows fell on Maritornes, who with the pain of them forgot her modesty and gave him as many in return. This dispelled his dream and, finding himself thus treated and not knowing by whom, he clinched with Maritornes, and the two of them started the most stubborn and comical scuffle in the world. Whereupon the carrier, seeing by the light of the innkeeper's lamp how ill his mistress was faring, left Don Quixote and joined in to give her all necessary help. So did the innkeeper, but with a different purpose: to beat the maid, under the impression that she was the sole cause of all that harmony. And then, as the saying goes, the cat chased the rat, the rat chased the rope, the rope chased the stick. The carrier beat Sancho, Sancho beat the maid, the maid beat him, the innkeeper beat the maid, and they all laid it on so fast that they never took a moment's rest. While, to improve the joke, the innkeeper's lamp went out and left them all in a heap in the dark, lamming out unmercifully and dealing great execution wherever they hit.

It happened that there was staying in the inn that night an officer of the Ancient and Holy Brotherhood of Toledo, who also heard the extraordinary din of the fight and, seizing his wand of office and the tin box with his warrants in it, went into the room in the dark, crying: 'Stop in the name of justice! Stop in the name of the Holy Brotherhood!'

Now the first person he collided with was the poor, trampled knight, lying on his back unconscious amidst the ruins of his bed. And his hand touching the knight's beard as he groped, the officer repeated: 'Help the officers of the Law!' But, seeing that the man he had seized neither struggled nor stirred, he took him for dead and the people in the garret for his murderers; which made him shout even louder: 'Shut the inn door! Let no one go out. There's been a man murdered here!'

This cry alarmed them all, and as soon as they heard it they stopped the brawl. The innkeeper slipped back to his room, the carrier to his pack-saddles, the maid to her corner. Only the unfortunate Don and Sancho were unable to stir from where they lay. At this the officer let go Don Quixote's beard and went out to find a light, with the intention of seeking and arresting the criminals. But he could not find one, because the innkeeper had purposely put out the lamp when he retired to his quarters. So the officer had to go across to the hearth, where, after much time and trouble, he lit another.

Chapter XVII. *Concerning countless more hardships which the brave Don Quixote and his good squire Sancho Panza endured in the Inn which he unfortunately mistook for a Castle.*

B Y this time Don Quixote had recovered from his swoon and, in the same tones in which he had called his squire the day before, when he was lying in the Valley of the Stakes, began to cry: 'Sancho, my friend, are you asleep? Are you asleep, friend Sancho?'

'Sleep, confound it,' replied Sancho in gloom and despair. 'How can I sleep when all the devils in hell must have been at me to-night?'

'You are right about that, for certain,' replied Don Quixote. 'For, if I know anything, this castle is enchanted. You should know ... But what I am going to tell you now you must swear to keep secret till the day of my death.'

' I swear,' replied Sancho.

'You must swear, because I hate to take away anyone's reputation,' continued Don Quixote.

'I do swear, I tell you,' repeated Sancho, 'that I will keep silent to the very last days of your honour's life. And please God I may be free to speak to-morrow.'

'Have I done you such harm, Sancho,' replied Don Quixote, 'that you would have me die so soon?'

'It's not that,' answered Sancho, 'but I hate to keep things long in case they go mouldy from over-keeping.'

'Be that as it may,' said Don Quixote, 'I would trust even greater matters to your love and courtesy. I would have you know that to-night I have encountered one of the strangest adventures imaginable. In short, just now there came to me the daughter of the warden of this castle, the most graceful and beauteous damsel that could be found over the greater part of the world. What could I not tell you of the loveliness of her body? Of her sprightly intelligence? And of those other hidden things that, to keep the faith I owe to my lady Dulcinea del Toboso, I will let pass untouched and unspoken? I will only tell you that, whether because Heaven was envious of the great boon that this adventure had brought me, or perhaps – more probably – because, as I have said, this castle is enchanted, just as I was in sweet and amorous colloquy with her, there came a hand and an arm of some monstrous giant. Where it came from I did not see, nor could I imagine, but it gave me such a blow on the jaws that I was bathed in blood. And after that it pounded me so that I am in worse plight than yesterday, when the carriers did us the injury you know of on account of Rocinante's excess of spirits. From which I conclude that the treasure of that damsel's beauty must be guarded by some Moorish enchanter and is not for me.'

'Nor for me either,' replied Sancho, 'for more than four hundred Moors have mauled me, so that the carriers' beating was tarts and gingerbread in comparison. But tell me, sir, what sort of a fine and rare adventure do you call it that leaves us in this plight? Indeed your worship came off best, for you had in your arms that incomparable beauty you spoke of. But what did I get but the worst beating I ever expect to get in all my life? I wish I had never been born! I am no knight errant and I don't ever expect to be one; but I get the greater share of the misfortunes for all that.'

'Then you got beaten as well?' asked Don Quixote.

'Didn't I say so, devil take it?' Sancho replied.

'Do not worry about that,' said Don Quixote. 'For now I will make up the precious balsam, which will heal us in the twinkling of an eye.'

By then the officer had lit his lamp and come in to view the supposed corpse, and Sancho, seeing an ugly-faced man in his shirt and night-cap with his lamp in his hand, asked his master: 'Will this perhaps be the Moorish enchanter come to give us another hiding, in case there's anywhere he forgot to hit us last time?'

'It cannot be the Moor,' replied Don Quixote, 'for magicians never allow themselves to be seen by anyone.'

'If you can't see them you can certainly feel them,' said Sancho; 'my shoulders can vouch for that.'

'So might mine,' replied Don Quixote; 'but that is not enough to prove that that man is the Moorish enchanter.'

The officer approached. But, seeing them conversing so calmly, he stopped in surprise. Don Quixote, indeed, was still lying on his back, unable to move because of his thrashing and the plasters, when the officer came up to him and said: 'Well, how goes it, my man?'

'I should speak more politely if I were you,' replied Don

Quixote. 'Is it the custom in this country to address knights errant in that way, lout?'

The officer could not suffer this treatment from a wretch of the sorry appearance of Don Quixote and, raising the lamp, which was full of oil, brought it down on the knight's head, leaving him with a fine bruise on his scalp. Then, under cover of darkness, he hurriedly left the room.

'No doubt,' said Sancho Panza, 'that is the Moorish enchanter. He must be keeping the treasure for someone else, and only reserving his beatings and bashings for us.'

'You are right,' replied Don Quixote, 'but there's no point in taking any notice of matters of enchantment, nor in getting angry and enraged about them. For, as these magicians are invisible and supernatural, we shall find no one to take vengeance on, however hard we try. Get up, Sancho, if you can, and call the governor of this fortress, and try to get him to give me a little oil, some wine, some salt, and some rosemary, so that I can make the healing balsam. Indeed, I think that now I am in much need of it, for I am losing a great deal of blood from the wound that apparition gave me.'

Sancho got up with sadly aching bones and went in the dark to find the innkeeper. Running, however, into the officer, who was listening to find out how things were with his enemy, he said:

'Sir, whoever you are, be so very kind as to give us a little rosemary, some oil, some salt, and some wine, for they are needed to heal one of the best knights errant in the world, who is lying on that bed, sorely wounded at the hands of the Moorish enchanter who is in this inn.'

When the officer heard this he thought that Sancho was out of his wits. But, as dawn was breaking by now, he opened the inn door and shouted out to the innkeeper what the poor fellow wanted. The host provided it all, and Sancho took it to Don Quixote, whom he found with his head clasped in his hands, groaning from the pain of his lamp-bashing, which, however, had done him no more harm than to raise a couple of largish bumps; what he took for blood being no more than the sweat which had poured from him in the anguish of the last storm.

In short, he took his ingredients, mixed them and cooked them for some time, till they appeared to be ready. Then he asked for a

flask to put them in. But, as there was none in the inn, he decided to
use a tin oil-can which the innkeeper gave him for nothing. After
that he said eighty Paternosters and as many Ave Marias, Salves, and
Credos over it, and at each word crossed himself by way of benediction. At which ceremony Sancho, the innkeeper, and the officer
were present, but the carrier had by now gone peacefully off and
was looking to his mules.

When this was done Don Quixote was anxious to make an immediate test of the virtue of this precious balsam, as he imagined it to
be, upon himself; and so he drank off more than a pint, which would
not go into the can and was still in the pot he had cooked it in. Now
no sooner had he drunk it than he began to vomit, bringing up
everything that was in his stomach; and with the pain and distress
of his sickness he broke into so copious a sweat that he asked to be
covered up and left alone. This was done, and he slept for more than
three hours; at the end of which time he awoke feeling very much
soothed in his body and so much better from his beating that he
thought himself cured and, verily believing that he had hit upon
the Balsam of Fierabras, he felt that thenceforth, with such a remedy,
he could undertake without fear any assaults, battles, or fights,
however perilous.

Sancho Panza, who also took his master's recovery for a miracle,
begged him for what remained in the pot – and there was a good
deal of it. Don Quixote granted his request; and he, taking the pot
in both hands, with a strong faith and better will, gulped it down,
swallowing almost as much as his master. The fact is, though, that
poor Sancho's stomach was not as delicate as Don Quixote's; and
so, before he was sick, he suffered so many twinges and pangs, so
many sweats and swoons, that he thought his last hour had come in
good earnest; and in his affliction and dismay he cursed the ointment and the scoundrel who had given it to him.

When Don Quixote saw him in such anguish, he observed: 'I
think, Sancho, that all this pain comes from your not being a knight;
for it is my opinion that this liquor cannot be of service to any that
are not.'

'If your worship knew that,' replied Sancho, 'the devil take me
and all my family, why did you let me taste it?'

At this the potion began to work and the poor man to empty

himself at both ends, so violently that soon the rush mat on which he had thrown himself and the coarse blanket that covered him were of no more use. His sweats, his paroxysms, and spasms were such that he, and everyone else as well, thought that he was at the point of death. And this tornado of misery lasted almost two hours, at the end of which time, unlike his master, he was left so battered and broken that he could not stand.

But Don Quixote, as we have said, felt recovered and well, and was anxious to set out immediately in search of adventures. For it seemed to him that every moment he delayed he was depriving the world, and everyone in distress in it, of his favour and protection. And he was encouraged in this feeling by his security and confidence in his balsam. So, urged on by this desire, he saddled Rocinante himself and bridled his squire's ass, helping Sancho to dress himself and climb on his back. Then he mounted his steed and, seeing a javelin in a corner of the inn, seized it to serve as a lance. Everyone in the inn was watching him, and there were more than twenty there. The innkeeper's daughter watched him too, and he did not take his eyes from her, but from time to time heaved a sigh which seemed to be torn from the depths of his bowels, and which every-one thought must be from the pain in his ribs; or so at least thought those who had seen him poulticed the night before.

When the two of them were on horse Don Quixote stopped at the inn door, called the host, and addressed him in very calm and grave tones: 'Many and great are the favours, my lord governor, that I have received in your castle, and I shall remain deeply obliged for them all the days of my life. If I can repay you by taking ven-geance for you on any proud man who may have done you wrong, know that my office is to protect the helpless, to avenge wrongs and to punish treachery. Search your memory and, if you have any-thing of this kind to entrust to me, you have only to say so, and I promise you, by my order of knighthood, to give you reparation and amends to your full satisfaction.'

The innkeeper replied in the same grave tones: 'Sir Knight, I do not need your worship to avenge any injuries, for I know how to take fitting vengeance for all wrongs done me. I only want your worship to pay the score you have run up this night in my inn, for straw and fodder for your two beasts, and for your supper and beds.'

E

'Then this is an inn?' asked Don Quixote.

'Yes, and a very respectable one,' replied the host.

'Then I have been in error till this moment,' answered Don Quixote, 'for I truly thought that it was a castle, and a considerable one too. But, since it is no castle but an inn, there is nothing for it now but for you to excuse my paying, for I cannot contravene the knight errant's rule. I am most certain – and I have never yet read of any case to the contrary – that they never paid for lodging or for anything else at any inn at which they stayed. For they deserve, by privilege and right, whatever hospitality they receive, in repayment for the intolerable hardships they undergo in seeking adventures by night and day, in winter and summer, on foot and horse, in thirst and hunger, in heat and cold, subject to all the inclemencies of the skies and all the discomforts of the earth.'

'That is nothing to do with me,' replied the innkeeper. 'Settle your reckoning, and spare us your tales and your knighthoods. I'm only concerned with getting my money.'

'You are a fool and a vile hosteller,' answered Don Quixote. Then, putting spur to Rocinante and brandishing his javelin, he left the inn without anyone stopping him; and without looking back to see if his squire was following, he rode for some way. When the innkeeper saw him go without paying, he ran to Sancho Panza for his money. But Sancho answered that, as his master had not been willing to pay, he would not either. For, as he was squire to a knight errant, the same rule held for him as for his master, to pay nothing in inns or hostelries. This put the host in a great temper, and he threatened, if he did not pay, to get the money out of him in a way he would not like. But Sancho persisted that by the law of knighthood, which his master had received, he would not pay a single farthing, even if it cost him his life. For he would not be the man to break the good old custom of knights errant, nor should the squires of future knights have to complain and reproach him for violating a privilege so well deserved.

But, as ill fate would have it, among the people in the inn were four wool-combers from Segovia, three needle-makers from the Colt Square in Cordova, and a couple from the Market of Seville, cheerful, well-meaning, playful rogues who, almost of one accord, ran up to Sancho and pulled him from his ass. Then one of them went in for the blanket from the host's bed and threw him on to it. But when they looked up they saw that the roof was rather too low for their purpose, and decided to go out into the back-yard, whose ceiling was the sky; and there, placing Sancho in the centre of the blanket, they began to toss him up and amuse themselves at his expense, as they do with dogs at Shrovetide.

The poor wretch's shouts at his blanket-tossing were loud enough to reach his master's ears, and Don Quixote, stopping to listen carefully, thought that some new adventure was on the way, until he realized that it was only his squire shouting. Whereupon he turned towards the inn at a painful gallop and, finding the door shut, rode round to find somewhere to get in. But no sooner did he get to the walls of the back-yard, which were not very high, than he saw the trick they were playing on his squire. He saw him fall and rise in the air so gracefully and so nimbly that, had it not been for his rage, he would certainly have burst out laughing. He tried to get from his horse on to the thatched wall, but he was so bruised and battered that he could not even dismount. And so from his horse he began to hurl insults and abuse at Sancho's tormentors, so many that it is impossible to record them. But this did not make them stop their tossing and laughter, nor did the flying Sancho cease his lamentations, which were mixed with threats alternating with pleas, though it was all of no use, and they did not give up until they were quite exhausted. Then they brought him his ass, put him on, and threw his greatcoat over his shoulders; and the tender-hearted Maritornes, seeing that he was worn out, thought it right to restore him with a jug of water and, so that it should be really cold, went to the well to draw it. Sancho took it, but just as he was going to put it to his lips he was stopped by his master's shouts.

'My good Sancho,' he cried, 'don't drink it. It will kill you. Look, I have the most holy balsam here' – and he held up the can of liquor. 'Drink two drops of this and you will most certainly be cured.'

At these words Sancho gave his master a sidelong glance and called even louder: 'Has your worship forgotten, by any chance, that I am not a knight, or would you have me bring up such guts as I've still got? Keep your liquor in the devil's name and leave me alone.'

No sooner had he spoken than he began to drink. But, finding at the first draught that it was only water, he would swallow no more, and begged Maritornes to bring him wine, which out of her good nature she did, and paid for it with her own money. For it is said of her that though she was of that trade, there was some shadow and vestige of a Christian about her.

So as soon as he had finished the wine, Sancho dug his heels into his ass's sides and, the inn door being opened for him, went out, very pleased that he had had his way and not paid a penny, though it had been at the cost of his shoulders, which usually went bail for him.

The innkeeper, it is true, remained in possession of his saddle-bags in payment for the reckoning, for Sancho went out in such confusion that he did not miss them. As soon as he was outside, the host wanted to bar the door after him, but the tossers would not agree, for they were the sort of men who would not have cared two straws even if Don Quixote had really been one of the Knights of the Round Table.

Chapter XVIII. *In which are recorded the conversation between Sancho Panza and his master Don Quixote, and other noteworthy adventures.*

SANCHO was so faint and dispirited when he caught his master up, that he could not drive his ass. And, seeing him in that state, Don Quixote said: 'Now I am quite certain, my good Sancho, that that castle or inn is enchanted. For what could those creatures who made such villainous sport with you be but phantoms and creatures of the other world? What makes me positive of it is that, when I was watching the acts of your sad tragedy over the thatched wall of the yard, I could not climb on to it, nor even dismount from Rocinante, for they must have had me under a spell. Because I swear to you on my faith as a Christian that, if I could have climbed on or dismounted, I would have so avenged you that those cowardly scoundrels would have remembered the joke as long as they lived, even if by so doing I had broken the laws of chivalry; which, as I have often told you, do not permit of a knight's striking one who is not a knight except in a case of urgent and extreme necessity, in defence of his own life and person.'

'I would have avenged myself, too, if I could, knight or no knight,' replied Sancho, 'but I couldn't, though it's my opinion that the creatures who amused themselves at my expense were not phantoms or enchanted, as your worship says, but flesh-and-blood men like ourselves. And they had all got names, for I heard them when they were tossing me: one of them was called Pedro Martinez, another Tenorio Hernandez, and I heard them call the innkeeper Juan Palomeque, the left-handed. So it was something different from enchantment that stopped your getting over the yard wall or dismounting from Rocinante. And what I gather from all this is that these adventures which we are always seeking will lead us in the long run to such misadventures that we shan't know our right foot from our left. It would be a good deal better and more proper, my little understanding tells me, for us to go home, now that it's harvest time, and look after our own affairs, and stop wandering from pillar to post, out of the frying-pan into the fire, as they say.'

'How little you understand matters of chivalry, Sancho,' replied Don Quixote. 'Be silent and patient, for the day will come when you will see with your own eyes how honourable it is to follow this profession. Tell me now, what greater pleasure can there be in the world, what joy equal to that of winning a battle and triumphing over an enemy? There can be no doubt of it. None.'

'That may well be,' replied Sancho, 'for all I know. But I do know that since we have been knights errant – or your worship has, for I cannot count myself of that honourable number – we have never won a battle except that one over the Basque, and even from that one your worship came off with the loss of half an ear and half a helmet. But since then it has been nothing but beatings and still more beatings, punches and still more punches, – and I got my tossing into the bargain, and that from persons enchanted, on whom I can't take revenge, and so learn for myself what pleasure there is in conquering an enemy, as your worship says.'

'That is an affliction which I bear and you must bear, Sancho,' replied Don Quixote. 'But from now on I will try to have at hand a sword of such craftsmanship that no kind of enchantment can be worked against its bearer. It is even possible that my fortune may procure me the sword Amadis wore when he was called the *Knight of the Burning Sword*. It was one of the best ever worn by any knight in all the world. For it not only had the virtue I mentioned, but also cut like a razor, and there was no armour, however strong and enchanted, which could stand up to it.'

'Such is my luck,' said Sancho, 'that when this comes about and your worship finds such a sword, it will only be of use and profit to knights, like that balsam. As for squires, they may sup on sorrow.'

'Never fear that,' said Don Quixote, 'for Heaven will deal more kindly with you.'

While Don Quixote and his squire rode on, deep in conversation, our knight saw a great thick cloud of dust approaching them along the road they were taking; and, on seeing it, he turned to Sancho and said: 'This is the day, Sancho, on which shall be seen the good fortune which fate has in store for me. It is on this day, I say, as much as on any other, that the valour of my arm shall be displayed. To-day I shall perform deeds that will remain written in the book of fame for all future ages. Do you see that dust-cloud rising over there, Sancho? It is all churned up by a prodigious army of various and innumerable nations that is marching this way.'

'In that case there must be two armies,' said Sancho, 'for in the opposite direction there is a similar cloud of dust rising as well.'

Don Quixote turned to look and, seeing that Sancho was right, rejoiced exceedingly, being quite certain that there were two armies advancing to the attack, and that they would meet in the middle of that wide plain. For every hour and every minute his mind was always full of those battles, enchantments, adventures, miracles, loves, and challenges which are related in books of chivalry; and everything that he said, thought or did was influenced by his fantasies. As for the dust-cloud he had seen, it was caused by two great flocks of sheep, which were being driven along that road in opposite directions, but owing to the dust they were not visible until they drew near. So emphatically, however, did Don Quixote affirm that they were armies, that Sancho came to believe him and asked: 'Sir, what must we do now?'

'What?' cried Don Quixote. 'Favour and aid those in need and distress. I must tell you, Sancho, that the army which is coming towards us is led and commanded by the great Emperor Alifanfaron, lord of the great island of Taprobana; the other which is marching behind us is the army of his enemy, the King of the Garamantas,

Pentapolin of the Naked Arm, so called because he always rides into battle with his right arm bare.'

'Why do these two lords hate one another, then?' asked Sancho.

'They hate one another,' replied Don Quixote, 'because this Alifanfaron is a furious pagan, and is in love with Pentapolin's daughter, a very lovely and, what is more, a very gracious lady, and a Christian, whose father will not give her to the pagan king unless he first foreswears the faith of his false prophet, Mahomet, and is converted to his own.'

'By my beard,' said Sancho, 'but that Pentapolin is right, and I'll help him all I can.'

'In that you will be doing your duty, Sancho,' said Don Quixote, 'for you do not need to be a knight to take part in battles like this.'

'I can well understand that,' replied Sancho. 'But where shall we put this ass so as to be certain of finding him when the skirmish is over? For I don't think it has ever been the custom to ride into battle on a beast like this.'

'That is true,' said Don Quixote. 'The only thing that you can do is to leave it to chance whether he is lost or not, for we shall have so many horses when we emerge victorious that even Rocinante will be in danger of being exchanged for another. But listen to me and look, for I want to point out the chief knights in these two armies. And so that you may see and note them better, let us retire up that slope, from which we should be able to make out both hosts.'

So they did, and took up their positions on a hillock from which they would have clearly seen both the flocks which Don Quixote had transformed into armies but for the clouds of dust they raised, which obscured and blinded their vision. This, however, did not prevent Don Quixote from imagining what was neither visible nor existing and, raising his voice to say: 'That knight over there in bright yellow armour, with a crowned lion couchant at a damsel's feet on his shield, is the valorous Laurcalco, Lord of the Silver Bridge. The other in the armour flowered with gold, and with three crowns argent on a field azure on his shield, is the redoubtable Micocolembo, Grand Duke of Quirocia. The other, on his right, with gigantic limbs, is the undaunted Brandabarbaran of Boliche, Lord of the three Arabias; he wears a serpent's skin for armour, and has for shield a gate which, report has it, is one of the gates of the temple that Samson pulled down when with his death he avenged himself on his enemies.

'But look in the other direction, and you will see in front, and leading the other army, the ever-victorious, never-vanquished Timonel of Carcajona, Prince of New Biscay; his armour is quartered azure, vert, argent and gold, and on his shield he bears a cat or on a field gules with a scroll inscribed *Miau* – which is the initial of his lady; who, so they say, is the peerless Miaulina, daughter of Duke Alfeñiquen of Algarbe. The other who burdens and oppresses the back of that powerful and spirited war-horse, with armour as white as snow and a white shield without a device, is a new knight of the French nation, called Pierre Papin, Lord of the Baronies of Utrique. That other, pricking with iron heel the flanks of his piebald courser, and bearing for arms the azure cups, is the powerful Duke of Nerbia, Espartafilardo of the Wood, who bears on his shield the device of an asparagus plant, with a motto in Castilian which runs: *Thus trails my fortune.*'

So he went on, naming many imaginary knights in each squadron; for each of whom he improvised armour, colours, devices, and mottoes, carried away by his strangely deluded imagination, and continuing without a pause:

'That squadron in the front is made up of men of various nations: here are drinkers of the sweet waters of the famous Xanthus; mountaineers who tread the Massilian fields; sifters of the pure and fine gold of Arabia Felix; dwellers on the famous cool shores of clear Thermodon; men who in various ways drain golden Pactolus for its precious sand; faithless Numidians; Persians famous for their bows and arrows; Parthians; Medes who fight as they fly; Arabs with no fixed abode; Scythians as cruel as they are fair; Ethiopians with their lips bored; and countless more nations whose visages I see and recognize but whose names I do not remember.

'In that other squadron come drinkers of the crystal waters of olive-bearing Betis; men who burnish and polish their faces with the liquor of the ever-rich and golden Tagus; men who enjoy the health-giving waters of the divine Genil; dwellers in the Tartesian plains with their abundant pastures; men who enjoy the Elysian fields of Jerez; men of La Mancha, rich and crowned with golden corn; men clad in iron, survivors of the ancient Gothic race; bathers in the Pisuerga, famous for its mild current; men who graze their flocks on the broad pastures of the winding Guadiana, famous for its secret bed; men who shiver with the cold of the wooded Pyrenees and among the white snows of the lofty Apennines – in short, all whom Europe contains within its boundaries.'

Good Lord! how many provinces he reeled off, how many nations he enumerated, giving to each one with marvellous readiness its proper attributes, being completely soaked and immersed in all that he had read in his lying books! Sancho Panza hung on his words and said nothing. But from time to time he turned to see if he could distinguish the knights and giants whom his master named. But, as he could not make out one of them, he said: 'Sir, devil a man or a giant, or a knight your worship mentions is to be seen, for all that. At least, I can't see them. Perhaps it's all enchantment, like the apparitions last night.'

'How can you say that?' replied Don Quixote. 'Cannot you hear the horses neighing and the trumpets blaring and the beating of the drums?'

'The only thing that I can hear,' replied Sancho, 'is a great bleating of rams and ewes.' And that was the truth, for the two flocks were getting near.

'It is your fear,' said Don Quixote, 'which prevents your seeing or hearing aright, for one of the effects of fright is to disturb the senses and make things appear as they are not. If you are so afraid, go aside a little and leave me alone, for I am sufficient on my own to ensure victory to the party to which I lend my aid.'

And so saying, he spurred Rocinante, put his lance in its rest and rushed down the little slope like a thunderbolt, with Sancho shouting after him:

'Turn back, Don Quixote, for I swear to God, sir, they are rams and ewes you are going to attack. Turn back! Oh, I wish I had never been born! What madness is it this time? Look, there is not a giant or a knight at all, nor cats, nor arms, nor shields quartered or entire, nor cups azure or bedevilled. What are you doing? Poor sinner that I am!'

But this did not make Don Quixote turn. Instead he went on,

shouting loudly: 'Ho, knights who follow and fight beneath the banner of the valorous Emperor Pentapolin of the Naked Arm, follow me, all of you, and you shall see how easily I will give him his revenge on his enemy Alifanfaron of Taprobana!' With which words he charged into the middle of the squadron of ewes and began to spear them with as much courage and daring as if he were in very truth spearing his mortal enemies. The shepherds and herdsmen who were with the flock shouted to him to stop. But, seeing that this had no effect, they unbuckled their slings and began to salute his ears with stones the size of fists.

Don Quixote took no heed of stones, but galloped all over the place, shouting: 'Where are you, proud Alifanfaron? Come to me. I am a single knight, and desire to prove your valour hand to hand, and to take your life for the wrong you have done the valorous Pentapolin the Garamantan.'

At that moment came a pebble from the brook and, hitting him on the side, buried two of his ribs in his body. Finding himself so battered, he thought that he was certainly killed or badly wounded. So, remembering his balsam, he took out his can, and, putting it to his mouth, began to toss the liquor into his stomach. But before he had managed to swallow what seemed to him sufficient, another sugared almond hit him on the hand and struck the can so fairly that it smashed it in pieces, taking three or four of his teeth out of his mouth on the way and badly bruising two fingers of his hand. So hard was the first blow and so hard the second that the poor knight was knocked from his horse on to the ground. The shepherds then came up to him and, concluding that they had killed him, hurriedly rounded up their flocks, took up the dead sheep, which were about seven in number, and made off without further enquiry.

All this time Sancho stood on the hill and watched his master's strange performance, tearing his beard and cursing the hour and the moment that Fortune had brought them together. But when he saw him lying on the ground and the shepherds gone, he went down the hill to him and found him not stunned but in a very bad way.

'Didn't I tell you, Don Quixote, sir,' he said, 'to turn back, for they were not armies you were going to attack, but flocks of sheep?'

'What a way that scoundrel of an enchanter, my enemy, has of transforming things and making them invisible! You must know, Sancho, that it is a very easy thing for enchanters to give things whatever appearance they please. For this wicked sorcerer, my persecutor, being envious of the glory he saw I was sure to gain from this battle, has turned the hostile squadrons into flocks of sheep. If you do not believe me, Sancho, do one thing, I beg of you, and you will discover that you are mistaken and that I am speaking the truth. Get on your ass, and follow them stealthily. Then you will see that as soon as they get a little way from here they will turn back to their original shapes, and will not be sheep any more but well-built proper men, as I first described them to you. But do not go now, for I have need of your help and service. Come near to me and look how many of my teeth are missing, for I do not think they have left me any in my head.'

Sancho came so near as almost to thrust his eyes into his master's mouth; and that was the very moment when the balsam began to work in Don Quixote's stomach; so that just as Sancho drew close to peer into his mouth the knight threw up what was in him more violently than a shot from a gun, and sent it all over the beard of his compassionate squire.

'Holy Mary!' cried Sancho. 'What has happened to me? Sure, this poor sinner is mortally wounded, since he is vomiting blood.'

But on examining things a little more closely, he realized, from its colour, taste, and smell, that it was not blood but the balsam from the can, which he had seen him drinking; and this so turned his stomach that he threw up his very guts over his master; and the pair of them were then in the same pickle. Sancho ran to his ass to get out of his saddle-bags something with which to clean himself and cure his master, and when he found the bags missing almost went out of his mind. He cursed himself once more, and decided in his heart to leave Don Quixote and return home, even if he were to lose the payment for his services and his hopes of the governorship of the promised isle.

At this the knight got up and, with his left hand to his mouth to prevent the rest of his teeth from falling out, took in the other the reins of the faithful Rocinante, whose disposition was so good and loyal that he had never stirred from his master's side. Then he went over to his squire, who was leaning against his ass with his hand on his cheek, a position expressing great dejection and, seeing his melancholy mood, said to him: 'I tell you, Sancho, that no man is worthier than another unless he does more than another. All these squalls which greet us are signs that the weather will soon clear and things go well with us; for neither good nor evil can last for ever; and so it follows that as evil has lasted a long time, good must now be close at hand. You must not grieve, therefore, at the disasters which befall me, for surely no share of them fell to you.'

'How not?' replied Sancho. 'Wasn't it my father's son who got tossed in the blanket yesterday? And the saddle-bags that I've lost to-day with all my valuables in them, whose were they but mine?'

'What, are your saddle-bags missing, Sancho?' asked Don Quixote.

'Yes, they are,' replied Sancho.

'In that case we have nothing to eat to-day,' said Don Quixote.

'That would be so,' replied Sancho, 'if there were not any of those herbs in the fields, which your worship says you know, and which unfortunate knights errant like yourself use to supply their needs in cases like this.'

'All the same,' replied Don Quixote, 'I would rather have a hunk of bread or a loaf, and a couple of pilchards' heads, than all the herbs in Dioscorides' herbal with all Doctor Laguna's illustrations thrown in. But, anyhow, get on your ass, good Sancho, and follow me. For God, the provider of all things, cannot let us want, especially as we are engaged in His service, since He does not fail the gnats of the air, the worms in the ground, nor the tadpoles in the water, and He is so merciful that He makes the sun rise on the good and the bad, and rains on the just and the unjust.'

'Your worship,' said Sancho, 'would make a better preacher than a knight errant.'

'Knights errant, Sancho, knew – and have to know – about everything,' said Don Quixote; 'for in the olden times a knight errant would be as ready to deliver a sermon or make a speech in the middle of the royal camp as if he were a graduate of the university of Paris; whence it can be inferred that the lance has never blunted the pen, nor the pen the lance.'

'Well, I'll take your worship's word for it,' replied Sancho. 'Let's go on now and try to find somewhere to lodge tonight, and pray God it may be a place where there are no blankets or blanket-tossers, or apparitions, or Moorish enchanters; for if there are, I'll fling meat and hook to the Devil.'

'Ask that of God, son,' said Don Quixote, 'and lead me where you like, for this time I am going to leave the choice of lodging to you. But lend me your hand, and feel with your finger how many teeth are missing from the top jaw on my right side, for that is where I feel the pain. '

Sancho put his fingers in and, as he felt around, asked: 'How many molars used your worship to have on that side?'

'Four,' replied Don Quixote, 'and a wisdom tooth, all sound and whole.'

'Think well what you say, sir,' replied Sancho.

'I say four, or perhaps five,' replied Don Quixote, 'for in all my days I have never had a tooth drawn, nor one fall out, nor destroyed by decay.'

'Well, in this lower jaw,' said Sancho, 'your worship has only two teeth and a half, and on the top not so much as a half, for it is all as smooth as the palm of my hand.'

'Oh, what a misfortune!' exclaimed Don Quixote on hearing his squire's sad news. 'I had rather have lost an arm, provided it were not my sword arm. For I would have you know, Sancho, that a mouth without molars is like a mill without a stone, and a tooth is more precious than a diamond. But we who profess the strict order of chivalry are subject to all such misfortunes. Mount, my friend, and lead on. I will follow at your pace.'

Sancho obeyed, and took the direction in which he thought he might be likely to find lodging, keeping to the highway, which was well beaten in those parts. And as they went along slowly, because the pain in Don Quixote's jaws gave him no rest nor any disposition to hurry, Sancho tried to entertain him and divert his mind by talk. And some of the things he said will be found in the next chapter.

Chapter XIX. *Of the sensible conversation between Sancho Panza and his master, of the Adventure with a Corpse, and other famous happenings.*

'IN my opinion, sir, there isn't a shadow of doubt that all these misfortunes which have happened to us lately have been a punishment for your worship's sinning against the law of chivalry by not fulfiling the oath you took, not to eat bread off a table-cloth nor lie with the queen, and all the rest of the things you swore, until you had got that helmet from Malandrino, or whatever they call the Moor – I can't remember.'

'You are quite right, Sancho,' said Don Quixote, 'but, to tell you the truth, it had slipped my memory. And you can be just as certain that it was for not reminding me of it in time that the affair of the blanket happened to you. But I will make amends; for in the law of chivalry there are ways of compounding for everything.'

'Did I swear something then, by any chance?' asked Sancho.

'It is no matter that you did not swear,' said Don Quixote; 'it is enough that I consider you not very clear of complicity. But whichever way it is, there will be no harm in providing a remedy.'

'If that's so then,' said Sancho, 'take good care, your worship, not to forget that too, like the oath; or perhaps the phantoms may take it into their heads to have their fun with me again, and even with your worship, if they find you so wilful.'

When darkness fell they were still on the high road deep in their conversation, and had not found any place to shelter that night; what was worse, they were dying of hunger, for with their saddlebags they had lost their whole larder and store. And, to complete their misfortunes, there followed an adventure that did not require any contrivance actually to look like one.

The night set in dark, but still they rode on, Sancho thinking that, as they were on the highway, they should by rights find a good inn within six or eight miles. As they continued, then, on their way, the night being dark, the squire hungry and his master more than a little disposed to eat, they saw coming towards them on their road a great number of lights, which looked more like stars in motion than anything else.

Sancho was alarmed at the sight of them, and his master did not altogether like them either. The squire checked his ass, and Don Quixote his horse, and they stopped still, peering attentively to make out what it could be. They saw that the lights were coming near, and the nearer they got the bigger they seemed. At this Sancho began to tremble as if he had taken quicksilver, and the hair of Don Quixote's head stood on end. But the knight gained a little courage and said: 'This, Sancho, beyond a doubt, must be a very great and most perilous adventure, and I shall need to show all my valour and courage.'

'Oh dear me!' replied Sancho. 'If this is an adventure with phantoms, as it seems, where shall I find ribs to endure it?'

'Never mind if they are phantoms,' said Don Quixote. 'I will not let them touch a thread of your garment. If they played the fool with you last time it was because I could not get over the yard wall. But now we are on open ground where I can wield my sword as I please.'

'What if they put a spell on you and cramp you as they did before?' cried Sancho. 'What will it matter if you are on the open ground or not?'

'Nevertheless,' replied Don Quixote, 'I beg you, Sancho, to have courage, for experience will give you proof of mine.'

'I will, if it please God,' replied Sancho. And the pair of them stood a little back from the road, and once more watched carefully to see what those travelling lights might be. Then after a while they made out a number of forms in white surplices, at which frightful vision Sancho Panza's courage absolutely vanished, and his teeth began to chatter as if he had the quartan ague. And his trembling and chattering grew even worse when they distinctly made out what it was; for they saw some twenty horsemen with blazing torches in their hands, and behind them a litter covered in black, followed by six more horsemen swathed in mourning down to their mules' feet – it was evident from their slow pace that they were not horses. The figures in white were muttering to themselves as they came, in low and mournful tones.

This extraordinary spectacle at such an hour and in such a lonely place was quite enough to strike terror into Sancho's heart and even into his master's. The squire's courage was long since exhausted, but it was otherwise with Don Quixote, for by this time his vivid imagination had suggested that this was one of the adventures out of his books. It seemed to him that the litter was a bier on which they were carrying some dead or badly wounded knight, and that the task of avenging him was reserved for himself. So without more ado he couched his lance, steadied himself in the saddle, and with exquisite bearing and courage took up his position in the middle of the road along which the white figures would have to pass. Then, when he saw them approaching, he cried:

'Stop, knights, or whoever you may be, and inform me who you are, where you come from, where you are going, and what it is you are carrying on that bier. For, by all appearances, either you have done or suffered some injustice, and it is proper and needful that I should know it, either to punish you for the wrong you have done, or to avenge the outrage done upon you.'

'We are in a hurry,' replied one of the men in white, 'for the inn is some distance away. We can't stop to answer all your questions.'

Then he spurred his mule and pressed on. But Don Quixote, very indignant at this reply, laid hold of his bridle and said: 'Stop, and be rather more civil. Give me the information that I asked for, or else do battle with me, all of you.'

The mule was timid, and was so frightened at being seized by the bridle that she rose on her hind legs and threw her rider to the ground. A servant who was on foot saw the white-robed figure fall and began to abuse the now furious Don Quixote, who without more ado couched his lance and attacked one of the mourners, throwing him to the ground too, with a severe wound. He then turned on the others, and the speed with which he attacked and routed them was a wonder to see, for Rocinante seemed in that moment to have sprouted wings, so swiftly and proudly did he move. The men in white, a cowardly and unarmed crew, fled from the battle most promptly, and were off in one moment, running across the plain with their flaming torches, looking like nothing so much as masked figures flitting about on a carnival or festival night. As for the mourners, they were so swathed and muffled in their long skirts and gowns that they could not stir, and Don Quixote thrashed them all without the least danger to himself, forcing them to quit the field, much against their will; for they all thought that he was no man, but a devil from Hell come to bear off the corpse which they were carrying on the litter. Sancho looked on at all this, admiring his master's dauntless courage and saying to himself, 'There's no doubt that my master is as valiant and mighty as he says.'

There was a torch burning on the ground beside the first man who had been thrown by his mule, and as soon as Don Quixote saw him by its light he went up to him and poked his lance-point in his face, calling on him to surrender on pain of death. To which the fallen man replied: 'I am surrendered enough already, since I can't move. One of my legs is broken. I beg your worship, if you are a Christian gentleman, not to kill me. You would be committing a great sacrilege, for I am a Master of Arts and have taken my first orders.'

'Then, what the devil brought you here?' cried Don Quixote, 'if you are a churchman?'

'What, sir?' replied the fallen man. 'My bad luck.'

'A still worse fate threatens you,' said Don Quixote, 'if you do not answer satisfactorily all the questions I asked of you in the first place.'

'Your worship shall soon be satisfied,' replied the Master of Arts; 'and I must tell you that although I said before that I was a Master of Arts, I am only a Bachelor. My name is Alonso Lopez, native of Alcobendas. I am on my way from Baeza with eleven other priests – the men with the torches who have run away. We are going to the city of Segovia, escorting a corpse which is lying on that litter. The dead man was a gentleman who died at Baeza, where he was laid, and now, as I say, we are taking his bones to his tomb, which is in Segovia, his native town.'

'And who killed him?' asked Don Quixote.

'God, by means of a pestilent fever which took him,' replied the Bachelor.

'In that case,' said Don Quixote, 'our Lord has relieved me of the task of avenging his death, which I should have taken upon myself, had he fallen by any other hand. But seeing Who it was that killed him, there is nothing for it but to be silent and shrug my shoulders. For I should do the same were He to slay me. But I would have your Reverence know that I am a knight of La Mancha, Don Quixote by name, and that it is my office and profession to roam about the world, righting wrongs and relieving injuries.'

'I don't know what this righting of wrongs may be about,' said the Bachelor; 'for I was all right, and by leaving me with a broken leg which will not be right for all the days of my life you have made me all wrong. The injury you have relieved in me has left me so injured that I shall remain injured for life; and it has been sufficient misadventure to have met on your quest for adventure.'

'You can never tell how things will turn out,' replied Don Quixote. 'The trouble, Sir Bachelor Alonso Lopez, arose from your coming in the night as you did, dressed in those surplices, with your flaming torches, muttering your prayers and swathed in mourning, for you truly looked like some evil things from the other world. I could not therefore refrain from fulfilling my duty by attacking you; and I should have attacked you even if I had known for certain that you were the very devils from Hell which I judged and took you to be.'

'Since my fate would have it so,' said the Bachelor, 'I entreat your worship, Sir Knight Errant, who have done me such arrant mischief, to help me from under this mule, which has caught one of my legs between the stirrup and the saddle.'

'I might have gone on talking till to-morrow,' said Don Quixote. 'How long would you have waited to tell me of your plight?'

Then he shouted for Sancho Panza. But his squire did not choose to come, because he was busy unloading one of the good gentlemen's mules, which carried the stores and was well laden with good things. Sancho made a bag from his overcoat and, cramming all that he could into it, loaded his ass. Which done, he turned to his master's call and helped to get the Bachelor from under the weight of his mule. Then he helped him on and gave him his torch, while Don Quixote bade the poor fellow follow his companions and beg their pardon on his behalf for the injury which he had been unable to avoid doing them. And said Sancho as he departed: 'If by chance these gentlemen wish to know who the valorous knight was that did them such mischief, tell them, your worship, that it was the famous Don Quixote de la Mancha, who also bears the name of The Knight of the Sad Countenance.'

With that the Bachelor rode off, and Don Quixote asked Sancho what had made him call him the Knight of the Sad Countenance at that particular moment.

'I'll tell you,' answered Sancho. 'It's because I was watching you for a while by the light of the torch that poor wretch was carrying, and really your worship has lately got the most dismal face I've ever seen. It must be either from weariness after the battle or from your worship's losing his teeth.'

'It is from neither,' replied Don Quixote, 'but because the sage whose task it is to write the history of my deeds must have thought it right for me to take some title, as all knights did in the olden days. One called himself *The Knight of the Burning Sword*; another *of the Unicorn*; one *of the Damsels*; another *of the Phoenix*; another *The Knight of the Griffin*; and yet another *of Death*; and by these names and devices were they known all round the world. That is why I say that the sage I mentioned has put it into your thoughts and into your mouth to call me now *The Knight of the Sad Countenance*, a name which I intend to use from this day on; and to make it fit me better, I intend to have a very sad countenance painted on my shield when I have an opportunity.'

'There's no need to waste time and money on painting a face,' said Sancho. 'Your worship has only to uncover your own and show it to anyone who looks at you, and they'll call you *The Knight of the Sad Countenance* all right, without any picture or shield, and that's the truth. Believe me, sir – though I'm speaking in fun – hunger and loss of teeth have given you such a dismal face that you can easily do without the sad painting.'

Don Quixote laughed at Sancho's joke; nevertheless he decided to take that name as soon as he could have it painted on his shield or buckler, as he had proposed.

'I fear, Sancho,' he said, 'that I have incurred excommunication for laying violent hands on holy things – *Juxta illud, si quis suadente diabolo*, &c, although I know that I did not lay my hands on them, but this lance; and, what is more, I did not suspect that I was injuring priests or Church property, which, good Catholic and faithful Christian that I am, I respect and adore, for I thought that they were phantoms and spectres from the other world. But if it comes to the worst I remember what happened to the Cid Ruy Diaz, when he broke the chair of that King's Ambassador in the presence of his

Holiness the Pope, who excommunicated him for it; notwithstanding which the good Rodrigo de Vivar bore himself like a very honourable and valiant knight that day.'

By this time the Bachelor had gone, as has been said, without making Don Quixote any reply, and the knight was anxious to see if the body on the litter was a skeleton or not; but Sancho would not agree, saying: 'Sir, your worship has concluded this perilous adventure at less cost to yourself than any that I have seen. But although these people are conquered and defeated, it may occur to them that they were beaten by one man alone; and that may so abash them and shame them that they will pluck up some courage and come back after us; and then we shall have work enough on our hands. The ass is all right; the mountain's near; hunger presses; and we have nothing to do but to beat a graceful retreat and, as the saying is, to the grave with the dead and the living to their bread.' So, driving his ass before him, he begged his master to follow; and Don Quixote, feeling that Sancho was right, did so without another word.

They took their way between two hills, and had not gone far when they found themselves in a wide, secluded valley, where they alighted and Sancho unloaded the ass; and, stretched on the green grass, with hunger for sauce, they took their breakfast, lunch, dinner, and supper all in one, appeasing their hunger from more than one hamper which the dead man's noble clerics – who seldom fail to look after themselves – had brought on their baggage-mule. But another misfortune befell them, and to Sancho this was the worst of all: they had no wine, nor even water, to drink, and were parched with thirst. Sancho, however, saw that the meadow they were in was thick with fresh green grass, and said – what shall be recorded in the following chapter.

Chapter xx. *Of the unparalleled Adventure achieved by the valorous Don Quixote de la Mancha with less peril than any ever achieved by any famous knight in the whole world.*

'To judge from this grass, sir, there must certainly be a spring or a brook about here to keep it moist. So it would be a good idea if we were to go on a little farther, for we might find somewhere to quench this terribly annoying thirst, which is a great deal more distressing than hunger itself.'

This suggestion seemed reasonable to Don Quixote. So he took Rocinante by the rein, and Sancho took his ass by the halter, though not till he had loaded him with what remained from their supper. Then they began to move forward through the meadow, feeling their way, for the night was so dark that they could not see anything. But before they had gone two hundred yards a great noise came to their ears, like the roar of a waterfall tumbling from some huge, high cliff. This sound cheered them enormously. But as they stopped to listen from what direction it came, they heard another loud noise, which drowned the pleasure they got from the sound of the water, especially Sancho's, for he was timid by nature and not at all courageous. What they heard was the sound of regular blows and a sort of clanking of iron and chains which, combined with the furious roaring of the water, would have struck terror into any other heart but Don Quixote's. The night, as has been said, was dark, and they had happened to stray beneath some tall trees, the movements of whose leaves in the soft wind made a gentle but alarming sound; so that, taken all together, the solitude, the locality, the darkness, the roaring of the water and the rustling of the leaves produced a horror and dread, which increased when they found that the blows did not cease, nor the wind die down, nor morning dawn. And to make matters worse, they had no idea where they were. Don Quixote, however, his courage never failing, leapt upon Rocinante, braced his shield, brandished his lance, and cried:

'Sancho, my friend, you must know that, by the will of Heaven, I was born in this iron age of ours to revive the age of gold or, as it is generally called, the golden age. It is for me that are reserved perils, mighty feats, and valorous exploits. It is I, I say once more, who must revive the order of the Round Table, the Twelve Peers of France, and the Nine Worthies, and consign to oblivion the Platirs, Tablantes, Olivantes and Tirantes, the Knights of the Sun and the Belianises, and all that herd of famous knights errant of olden times, by performing in this age in which I live such prodigies, such wonders, and such feats of arms as to eclipse the most famous deeds they ever performed. Observe, loyal and faithful squire, the darkness of this night, its strange silence, the dull, confused sound of these trees, the fearful noise of the water which we came to seek, and which seems to be hurled headlong from the high mountains of the moon, and that ceaseless thumping which wounds and afflicts our ears; which things, taken all together and each by itself, are sufficient to infuse fear, terror, and dread into the breast of Mars himself; and how much more so into one who is unaccustomed to such events and adventures. Yet all that I am describing to you serves only to spur and rouse my courage, and makes my heart bound in my breast with desire to embark on this adventure, however arduous it may prove. Therefore tighten Rocinante's girths a little, and God be with you! Wait for me here three days and no more; at the end of which time, if I should not come back, you may return to our village, and from there, as a favour and service to me, you will go to El Toboso and tell my incomparable lady Dulcinea that her captive knight died attempting deeds which might make him worthy to call himself hers.'

When Sancho heard this speech of his master's, he began to weep most piteously, saying: 'I don't know why your worship wants to start on this frightful adventure. It is night now, and no one can see us here. We can easily turn off the road and get out of danger, even if it means not drinking for three days. And, as there's nobody to see us, no one can call us cowards. What is more, I have heard the priest of our village, whom your worship knows very well, preach that the man who seeks danger perishes in it. So it isn't right to tempt Providence by taking on such a tremendous feat, from which we could only escape by a miracle. Be satisfied with the miracles Heaven has worked for your worship in saving you from the blanket-tossing I got, and bringing you off victorious, safe and sound, from all those enemies there were with that dead man. And, if all this isn't enough to soften that hard heart of yours, perhaps it will be moved by the thought that the very moment your worship has gone from here I'll be sure to give up my soul out of pure fear to anyone who may wish to bear it off. I left my country and forsook my wife and children to come and serve your worship, believing that I should do better and not worse; but as greed burst the bag, so it has rent my hopes; for just as I was most hopefully expecting to get that accursed and unlucky isle your worship has so often promised me, I see that instead you mean to leave me now in this place, far from all human company. In God's name, sir, do me not this wrong. Even if your worship will not altogether give up this exploit, put it off at least till morning. For by the science I learned when I was a shepherd, it can't be more than three hours till dawn, since the muzzle of the Bear is at the top of his head, and at midnight it is in line with the left paw.'

'How can you see, Sancho, where the line is, or the muzzle, or the top of the head you speak of? The night is so dark that there is not a star to be seen in the whole sky.'

'That's true,' said Sancho, 'but fear has many eyes, and can see things underground. So it'll easily see things up above in the sky. Besides, it's reasonable to suppose that it won't be long till dawn.'

'Long or not,' replied Don Quixote, 'it shall never be said of me, now or at any time, that tears and prayers deflected me from my duty as a knight. Therefore, Sancho, pray be silent. For God, who has put it into my heart to embark on this unparalleled adventure, will take care to watch over my safety and to console your grief. All that you have to do is to tighten Rocinante's girths well and wait here, for I will return soon, alive or dead.'

Sancho saw that his master was finally resolved, and that his tears, advice, and prayers had little effect on him. So he decided to use his ingenuity and, if he could, compel his master to wait till day. So, while he was tightening the horse's girths, slyly and unnoticed he tied Rocinante's fore-legs together with the halter of his ass, so that when Don Quixote wanted to start he could not, for his horse could move only by leaps. And when Sancho saw that his trick was successful he exclaimed: 'See, sir, the Heavens are moved by my tears and prayers. They have ordained that Rocinante shall be unable to stir. If you persist in urging, spurring, and striking him, it will be provoking Fortune and, as the saying goes, kicking against the pricks.'

At this Don Quixote grew exceedingly vexed, for the more he spurred his horse the less could he make him go. Therefore, without suspecting the reason, he thought it best to be calm and wait till dawn, or till Rocinante could move, no doubt ascribing the trouble to some cause other than Sancho's ingenuity. And so he said to him: 'Since it is a fact, Sancho, that Rocinante cannot move, I am content to wait here until dawn smiles, although I weep at her delay.'

'There's no need to weep,' replied Sancho, 'for I will entertain your worship and tell you stories from now till daylight, unless you would like to dismount and snatch a little sleep on this green grass, as knights errant do, so that you may be less weary when day comes and it's time to embark on this incomparable adventure that awaits you.'

'Who is it you ask to dismount or to sleep?' asked Don Quixote. 'Am I by chance one of those knights who take their rest amidst dangers? Sleep yourself, for you were born to sleep, or do what you will. I will do what best suits my profession.'

'Don't be annoyed, good master,' replied Sancho. 'I didn't mean to make you angry.' Then he went closer to Don Quixote and put one hand on the pommel of his saddle and the other on the cantle, so that he stood clasping his master's left thigh without daring to stir an inch from him, so frightened was he of the blows which still continued to sound in regular succession. Don Quixote then bade him tell a tale for his entertainment, as he had promised; and Sancho replied that he would, if his dread of the noise would allow him. 'But, for all that,' he said, 'I will endeavour to tell you a story and, if I manage to tell it without interruption, it'll be the best story in the world. Pay good attention, your worship, for I'm going to begin. – Once upon a time; may good befall us all and evil strike the man who seeks it. Notice, your worship, that the ancients didn't begin their stories just as they pleased, but with a sentence by Cato, the Roman censor, who says – "Evil strike the man who seeks it"; and that fits in here like a ring on a finger, meaning that your worship must stay quiet and not go anywhere seeking harm, but that we must turn up some other road, since nobody is making us follow this one, where there are so many terrors to frighten us.'

'Go on with your story, Sancho,' said Don Quixote, 'and leave the road we are to follow to me.'

'I tell you, then,' Sancho resumed, 'that in a village in Estremadura there was once a shepherd – a goatherd I should say, for he kept goats – and this shepherd or goatherd, as my story tells, was called Lope Ruiz. Now this Lope Ruiz fell in love with a shepherdess called Torralba, which shepherdess called Torralba was the daughter of a rich herdsman; and this rich herdsman ...'

'If you tell your story that way, Sancho,' said Don Quixote, 'and repeat everything you have to say twice over, you will not be done in two days. Tell it consequentially, like an intelligent man, or else be quiet.'

'The way I'm telling it,' replied Sancho, 'is the way all stories are told in my country, and I don't know any other way of telling it. It isn't fair for your worship to ask me to get new habits.'

'Tell it as you like,' replied Don Quixote, 'and since it is the will of Fate that I cannot help listening, go on.'

'And so, my dear master,' Sancho went on, 'as I said, this shepherd fell in love with the shepherdess Torralba, who was a plump, high-spirited girl, and rather mannish, for she had a slight moustache – I can almost see her now.'

'Really, did you know her, then?' asked Don Quixote.

'I didn't know her,' replied Sancho, 'but the man who told me this story said that it was so true and authentic that when I told it to anyone else I could swear on my oath that I had seen it all. So, as the days came and the days went, the Devil, who never sleeps and tangles everything up, brought it about that the love which the shepherd had for the shepherdess turned to hatred and ill-will; and the reason was, as evil tongues told, that she caused him a number of little jealousies, such as exceeded the bounds and trespassed on the forbidden; and thenceforth the shepherd loathed her so much that, to avoid her, he decided to leave that country and go where his eyes should never see her again. But when Torralba found that Lope scorned her, she immediately fell to loving him more than she had ever loved him before.'

'That is natural in women,' said Don Quixote, 'to scorn those who love them, and love those who loathe them. Go on, Sancho.'

'It came about that the shepherd put his resolution into effect,' said Sancho, 'and set out driving his goats across the plains of Estremadura to cross into the kingdom of Portugal. Torralba heard of his plan, and followed him at a distance, on foot and bare-legged, with a pilgrim's staff in her hand and a satchel round her neck, which contained, the story goes, a bit of mirror and a broken comb, and some little bottle or other of washes for her face. But whatever it was she carried, I don't mean to set about inquiring now. I'll only say that the story tells how the shepherd came with his flock to cross the Guadiana river, which at that season was swollen and almost overflowing; and at the place he struck it there wasn't a boat of any kind, nor anyone to ferry him or his flock to the other side. This put him very much out, because he saw Torralba coming near, and she was sure to bother him a great deal with her entreaties and tears. He went on looking about him, however, until he saw a fisherman close beside a boat, which was so small that it could only hold one man and one goat. But, all the same, he hailed him and arranged for him to take himself and his three hundred goats across. The fisherman got into the boat and took one goat over, came back and fetched another, and came back once more and took another. Keep an account of the goats which the fisherman is taking over, your worship, for if you lose count of one the story will end, and it won't be possible for me to tell you another word of it. I'll continue now and mention that the landing-place on the other side was very muddy and slippery, which delayed the fisherman a good deal in his journeys backwards and forwards. But, all the same, he came back for another goat, and another, and another.'

'Take it that they are all across,' said Don Quixote, 'and do not go on coming and going like that, or you will never get them all over in a year.'

'How many have got over so far?' asked Sancho.

'How the devil should I know?' replied Don Quixote.

'There now, didn't I tell you to keep a good count? Well, there's an end of the story. God knows there's no going on with it now.'

'How can that be?' replied Don Quixote. 'Is it so essential to the tale to know exactly how many goats have crossed that if you are one out in the number you cannot go on?'

'No, sir, not at all,' answered Sancho. 'But, when I asked your worship to tell me how many goats had got across and you replied that you didn't know, at that very moment everything I had left to say went clean out of my head, though there were some good and amusing things coming, I promise you.'

'So,' said Don Quixote, 'the story is finished, then?'

'As sure as my mother is,' said Sancho.

'Really,' replied Don Quixote, 'you have told me one of the strangest tales – true or false – that anyone could imagine in the whole world; and never in a lifetime was there such a way of telling it or stopping it, although I expected no less from your excellent intelligence. But I am not surprised, for this ceaseless thumping must have disturbed your brains.'

'That may well be,' replied Sancho, 'but I know that so far as my story goes there is nothing more to say, for it just ends where the error begins in counting the goats that cross over.'

'All right, let it end where it will,' said Don Quixote. 'And now let us see if Rocinante can move.' He dug in his spurs once more, and the horse gave a few more leaps. Then he stood stock still, so fast was he tied.

At this point, it seems, either the cold of morning, which was just breaking, or something laxative he had eaten for supper or, as seems more likely, the natural course of things, gave Sancho the inclination and desire to do what no one else could do for him; but so much fear had entered into his heart that he dared not stir a hair's breadth from his master. Yet it was quite impossible even to think of not fulfilling his needs. So what he did was to take a middle course. Very gently he moved his right hand from the crupper of the saddle, and with it neatly and noiselessly loosened the running knot, which was all that kept his breeches up, so that when it was undone they fell down and held him like fetters. After which he hitched up his shirt as best he could, and bared a pair of ample buttocks to the air. This done, which he thought was all he needed to relieve himself of his terrible griping pains, another greater problem confronted him: he was afraid that he could not relieve himself without making some report or noise. So he began to grind his teeth and contract his shoulders, holding his breath as much as he could. But despite all these precautions he was so unfortunate as in the end to make a little noise very different from the din which was causing him so much terror. And when Don Quixote heard it he asked: 'What is that noise, Sancho?'

'I don't know, sir,' he replied. 'It must be something fresh, for these adventures and misadventures never begin for nothing.'

He tried his luck again, and with such success that he relieved himself, without any more noise or disturbance, of the burden which had caused him such discomfort. As Don Quixote's sense of smell, however, was as keen as his hearing, and as Sancho was clinging so closely to him, it was impossible for some of the odour, which ascended almost perpendicularly, not to reach his nose; and no sooner did it get there than he went to the rescue and, holding his nostrils between two fingers, observed in rather snuffling tones: 'You seem to be very frightened, Sancho.'

'Yes, I am,' replied Sancho, 'but how is it that your worship particularly notices it now?'

'Because you smell more now, and not of ambergris,' replied Don Quixote.

'That may be,' said Sancho, 'though it isn't my fault, but your worship's for dragging me out at such unearthly hours into such extraordinary places.'

'Go two or three paces off, friend,' said Don Quixote, without taking his fingers from his nose, 'and pay more attention in future to your person and to the respect that you owe me; for it is my great familiarity with you that has engendered this contempt.'

'I'll bet,' replied Sancho, 'your worship thinks that I have done ... something that I shouldn't with my person.'

'The less said about it the better, friend Sancho,' replied Don Quixote.

Master and servant spent the night in conversation of this sort, and when Sancho saw that morning was fast approaching, he very cautiously unfettered Rocinante and tied up his breeches. And as soon as the horse found himself free, although never very mettlesome by nature, he seemed to revive, and began to paw the ground, for prancing – begging his pardon – was beyond him. Don Quixote took Rocinante's movements as a good omen and a sign for him to attempt that perilous adventure.

Dawn having broken by now and made objects distinctly visible, the knight saw that they were standing beneath some tall chestnut trees, which cast a very deep shadow. He also noticed that the blows had not ceased, though he could not see what the cause of them was. So without more delay he put spur to Rocinante and, turning to take leave of Sancho, told him to wait for him there for three days at most, as he had already bidden him, and if he had not returned by that time, to take it as certain that, by God's will, he had ended his days on that perilous adventure. He once more spoke of Sancho's errand and of the message which he was to take on his behalf to his lady Dulcinea. As for payment for his services, said the knight, his squire need not worry. For, by the will which he had

made before leaving home, Sancho would find himself completely
satisfied in the matter of his wages, which would be duly propor-
tionate to the time he had served. Should God, however, bring him
through this peril safe, sound, and unharmed, his squire might
reckon himself more than certain, he said, of the promised isle.
Sancho burst into fresh tears at again hearing his good master's pitiful words, and determined not to leave him until the final issue and
end of the business.

From these tears and this very honourable resolution the author
of this history concludes that Sancho Panza must have been well
born and at least an *Old Christian*. His master was rather touched by
his feelings, but not sufficiently to show any weakness. On the contrary, concealing it as best he could, he began to ride in the direction
from which the sounds of the water and the blows seemed to come.
Sancho followed him on foot, as usual, leading by the bridle his ass,
his constant companion in good and evil fortune; and when they
had gone some way under those shady chestnut trees, they came out
into a little meadow at the foot of a high cliff, from which fell a great
head of water. Beneath the cliff were a few tumble-down houses,
which looked more like ruins than dwellings, and from them, they
discovered, came the hideous and still unceasing din of the hammering. Rocinante started at the noise of the water and of the thumping, but Don Quixote pacified him, and gradually advanced towards the houses, commending himself to his lady meanwhile with
all his heart, and imploring her to favour him in his formidable task
and enterprise; and on his way he also commended himself to God
that He might not forget him. Sancho did not leave his side, but
craned his neck as far as he could to peer between Rocinante's legs
and to make out the cause of his fears and alarms. They must have
gone another hundred paces when, on their turning a corner, there
appeared, clear and visible, the indubitable cause of that horrific
and, to them, most dreadful sound, which had kept them all that
night in such a state of terror and suspense. It was – do not take it
amiss, good reader! – six fulling-hammers whose regular strokes
made all that din.

Don Quixote was dumbfounded and utterly abashed at this sight
and, when Sancho looked at him, his head hung down on his breast
in confusion. But when Don Quixote looked at Sancho and clearly

saw from his swollen cheeks and his laughing mouth that he was on the point of exploding, despite his own gloom he could not help laughing at the look of him. And as soon as Sancho saw that his master had begun, he let himself go with such violence that he had to hold his sides for fear of bursting. Four times he calmed down, and four times he broke into fresh laughter as violently as before. At this Don Quixote wished him to the devil, especially when he heard him say in mockery: 'You must know, friend Sancho, that I was born by the will of Heaven in this our iron age to revive the age of gold, or the golden age. It is for me that are reserved perils, great exploits, and valorous deeds.' And so he went on, repeating all or most of what his master had said when they first heard that frightful hammering.

When Don Quixote realized that Sancho was making fun of him, he got so furiously angry that he lifted his lance and dealt him two blows which would have relieved the master of the duty of paying his squire's wages, unless perhaps to his heirs, had they caught him on the head instead of on the shoulders. But when Sancho found himself so poorly rewarded for his joke, he was afraid that his master might carry the matter farther, and said to him with great humility: 'Gently, your worship; I was only joking, I swear.'

'You may be joking, but I am not,' replied Don Quixote. 'Come here, master joker. Do you think that if these fulling-hammers had really been some perilous adventure I should not have shown the courage necessary to undertake it and carry it through? Am I, by chance, obliged, being as I am a knight, to recognize and distinguish sounds, and know whether they are fulling-hammers or not? For the case might be – as indeed it is – that I have never seen such things in my life, though you have seen them, wretched peasant that you are, and were born and brought up among them. But turn those six hammers into six giants, and let them beard me one by one or all together, and if I do not lay them all on their backs, make as much fun of me as you will.'

'No more, dear master,' replied Sancho. 'I confess I laughed a little too much. But tell me, your worship, now that we are at peace – and may God bring you as safe and sound through all adventures that befall you as through this one – isn't the awful fright we were in rather a joke, and doesn't it make a good story? At least the fright that I was in, for your worship, I know very well, doesn't so much as know what fear or fright is.'

'I do not deny,' replied Don Quixote, 'that what happened to us is a thing worth laughing at. But it is not worth telling, for not everyone is sufficiently intelligent to be able to see things from the right point of view.'

'At least your worship knew how to point your lance all right when you pointed it at my head but hit my shoulders, thanks to Providence and my prompt ducking. But let that pass. It will all come out in the wash, and I have heard it said, if he makes you weep it is a sure sign he loves you. Besides, when men of quality scold their servants they generally give them a pair of breeches afterwards, though I don't know what they generally give them after a beating, unless perhaps in the case of knights errant it's isles, or kingdoms on dry land.'

'The dice may so fall,' said Don Quixote, 'that every word you say will prove true. Forgive what is past, for you are sensible enough to know that first impulses are outside man's control. But take heed of one thing: you must abstain and refrain from overmuch speech with me in future, for never in any of the countless books of chivalry which I have read have I found a squire who talked to his master as much as you do to yours. In fact I look upon it as a great fault in you and in me: in you for showing me so little respect, and in me for not making myself more respected. We read of Gandalin, the squire of Amadis of Gaul, that though he was Count of the Firm Isle he always spoke to his lord cap in hand, with bowed head and body bent in the Turkish fashion. Then what shall we say of Gasabal, Sir Galaor's squire, who was so quiet that, to inform us of the perfection of his marvellous silence, once only is his name mentioned in the whole of that great and authentic history? From all that I have said, Sancho, you must infer that a distinction must be kept between master and man, between lord and servant, and between knight and squire. So from to-day we must behave with more respect, and not give ourselves rope; since, for whatever reason I may be annoyed with you, it will always be the pitcher that comes off worst. The favours and benefits which I promised you will arrive in due course; and if they do not arrive, your wages at least will not be lost, as I have told you already.'

'What your worship says is all very well,' said Sancho, 'but I should like to know, in case the time for favours never comes and we have to fall back on wages, how much a knight errant's squire earned in those days, and if they contracted by the month, or by the day like builders' labourers.'

'I do not believe that squires ever worked for wages,' replied Don Quixote, 'only for favours; and I have assigned you some now in the sealed will which I have left at home, to provide against accidents; since I do not yet know how chivalry will fare in these calamitous times of ours, and I should not wish my soul to suffer for trifles in the other world. For I would have you know, Sancho, that there is no state more perilous than a knight errant's.'

'That is true,' said Sancho, 'since the mere sound of the hammers of a fulling-mill was enough to alarm and disturb the heart of so valiant a knight errant as your worship. But you may rest assured that henceforth I shall not open my lips to make fun of your worship's business, but shall honour you as my master and natural lord.'

'In that case,' replied Don Quixote, 'your days will be long on the face of the earth, for next to our parents we are bound to honour our masters as we would our fathers.'

Chapter XXI. Of the high Adventure and rich prize of Mambrino's Helmet with other things which befell our invincible Knight.

ABOUT this time it began to rain a little, and Sancho wanted to go into the fulling-mills; but Don Quixote had conceived such a loathing of them, on account of the wretched joke, that he would on no account agree. So, turning to the right, they struck another road, like the one they had ridden on the day before, and had not gone far before Don Quixote caught sight of a man on a horse carrying something on his head which shone like gold; on seeing which he turned to Sancho and said: 'It seems to me, Sancho, that there is no proverb which is not true, for they are all drawn from experience itself, which is the mother of all sciences. This is especially true of the saying: When one door shuts another opens. This I say because if last night Fortune shut the door which we were looking for, and deceived us with the fulling-mills, it is now opening wide to us another, better, and more certain adventure. And if I do not succeed in passing through this one, the fault will be mine, and cannot be attributed to my scanty knowledge of fulling-mills or to the darkness of the night. This I say because, if I am not mistaken, there is someone approaching us bearing on his head that helmet of Mambrino, about which I swore the oath you know of.'

'Take good care what you say, your worship,' said Sancho, 'and even greater care what you do, for I shouldn't like some other fulling-mills to end up by milling and mashing your brains out.'

'The devil take you, fellow,' replied Don Quixote. 'What has a helmet to do with fulling-mills?'

'I've no idea,' replied Sancho, 'but I swear that if I might talk as I used to, I could probably give you some reasons that would make your worship see that you are mistaken.'

'How can I be mistaken, unbelieving traitor?' asked Don Quixote. 'Tell me, can you not see that knight coming towards us on a dapple-grey steed with a gold helmet on his head?'

'What I see and perceive,' replied Sancho, 'is nothing but a man on a grey ass like mine with something glittering on his head.'

'Why, that is Mambrino's helmet,' said Don Quixote. 'Stand aside and leave me to deal with him. You will see how, so as to save time, I shall complete this adventure without uttering a word, and the helmet I have so much desired will be mine.'

'I shall take good care to stand aside,' replied Sancho, 'but pray God it is sweet marjoram, and not fulling-mills.'

'I have told you already, brother, not to remind me again, even by so much as a thought, of those fulling-mills,' said Don Quixote, 'or I swear – and I will say no more – that I will mill your very soul.'

Sancho fell silent, fearing that his master would fulfil the oath he had flung at him so roundly.

Now the truth of this matter of the helmet, the horse, and the horseman that Don Quixote saw is this. There were in that district two villages, one so small that it had neither an apothecary's shop nor a barber, while the other, near-by, had both. So the barber of the bigger place served the smaller, in which there was a sick man who needed bleeding and another fellow who wanted to be shaved; which was why the barber was now on the road carrying a brass

F

basin. Now fate would have it that, as he came along, it began to rain. So, fearing that his hat, which was no doubt a new one, might get spoiled, he put the basin on his head; and, as it was clean, it shone from more than a mile away. He rode, as Sancho said, on a grey ass, and that is the reason why Don Quixote took them for a dapple-grey steed, a knight, and a golden helmet. For everything which he saw he adapted with great facility to his wild, chivalrous and errant fancies. So, when he saw the luckless horseman draw near, without entering into any parley with him, he urged Rocinante into a canter and attacked him with lance couched, intending to run him through and through; and as he got up to him without checking the fury of his career, he cried out: 'Defend yourself, base caitiff creature, or surrender of your own free will what is so rightfully mine.'

The barber, seeing this apparition descending on him so unexpectedly and without warning, had no other means of avoiding his lance but by sliding down from his ass. But, once on the ground, he leapt up lighter than a deer, and began to run across the plain faster than the wind. The basin he left on the ground, and the delighted Don Quixote observed that the pagan had acted most prudently in imitation of the beaver, who, when hard pressed by the hunters, with his own teeth bites off what he knows by his natural instinct to be the object of the chase. So he bade Sancho pick up the helmet. And when he had it in his hands, the squire exclaimed: 'By God, it's a good basin, and worth a *real* if it's worth a farthing.'

He then gave it to his master, who placed it on his head, turning it round and round to find the vizor. But, unable to discover it, he remarked: 'Certainly the pagan to whose measure this famous head-piece was first shaped must have had an enormous head; and the worst of it is that one half of it is missing.'

When Sancho heard the basin called a head-piece he could not restrain his laughter; but suddenly he remembered his master's anger, and stopped short.

'What are you laughing at?' asked Don Quixote.

'It makes me laugh,' he replied, 'to think what a big head that pagan must have had, who owned that head-piece. It's like nothing so much as a barber's basin. Just like it, it is.'

'Do you know what I think, Sancho? This famous piece, this

enchanted helmet, must have fallen by some strange accident into the hands of someone who did not esteem it at its true value. So, not knowing what he was doing, and seeing that it was pure gold, he must have melted down the other half for the sake of the metal, and made from this half what looks like a barber's basin, as you say. But, however that may be, its metamorphosis is of no consequence to me, who know what it really is. For I will have it set right in the first village where there is a smith, and so well that it will not be surpassed or even equalled by the helmet which the god of smithies forged and made for the god of battles. In the meantime, however, I will wear it as best I can, for something is better than nothing; and, besides, it will do very well to defend me from a stoning.'

'So long as they don't shoot with slings,' said Sancho, 'the way they did in that battle between the two armies, when they knocked out your worship's teeth and broke the can which held that most blessed liquor that made me vomit up my guts.'

'Its loss does not trouble me much,' said Don Quixote, 'for, as you know, I have the recipe by heart.'

'So have I,' replied Sancho, 'but if I ever make it up or try it again in all my life, may this be my last hour. What's more, I don't mean to put myself in the way of requiring it, for I intend to use all my five senses to avoid being wounded or wounding anyone. I say nothing about another blanket-tossing, for such misfortunes are difficult to prevent, and if they come there's nothing for it but to hunch your shoulders, hold your breath, close your eyes, and let yourself go where fate and the blanket send you.'

'You are a bad Christian, Sancho,' said Don Quixote; 'you never forget an injury once done you, though you should know that a noble and generous heart sets no store by such trifles. Did you come out with a lame foot or a broken rib or a cracked skull, that you cannot forget that jest? For, when you look at it carefully, it was only a jest and a sport; and if I had not taken it as such, I should long ago have returned there and done more execution to avenge you than the Greeks did for the rape of Helen who, if she had lived in our times, or my Dulcinea in hers, would most certainly not have had such a reputation for beauty as she had.' And here he heaved a sigh that echoed to the clouds.

'Let it pass for a jest, then,' said Sancho, 'since it can't be avenged in earnest. But I know the quality of those jests and earnests, and I know, too, that they won't slip from my memory any more than the feel of them will from my shoulders. But to leave the subject, tell me, your worship, what shall we do with this dapple-grey steed that looks like a grey ass, which that fellow your worship knocked down has left abandoned? For to judge by the dust he kicked up and the way he skipped off he doesn't look as if he will ever come back for it. And I'll be blowed if the dapple is not a good ass.'

'It is not my custom,' said Don Quixote, 'to plunder those whom I conquer, nor is it the usage of chivalry to take their horses and leave them to go on foot, unless the victor has lost his own mount in the fight, in which case it is lawful for him to take the beaten knight's as won in fair combat. Therefore, Sancho, leave the horse, or ass, or whatever you would have it be, for as soon as its master sees that we have gone away he will come back for it.'

'God knows I should like to take it,' replied Sancho, 'or at least to swap it for my own, for it seems a better beast. Really the laws of chivalry are very strict, if they don't even stretch to letting one ass be swapped for another. But I should like to know if I couldn't at least swap the trappings.'

'I am not very certain on that point,' replied Don Quixote; 'but, as it is a doubtful case, until I am better informed I should say that you might make the exchange, if you are in extreme need.'

'So extreme,' replied Sancho, 'that if it were for my own person I couldn't need them more.' So, with this permission, he made an immediate *mutatio capparum*, and put all the finery on his ass, which came off very much the better for the exchange. When this was done they breakfasted off the remains of the provender which they had plundered from the baggage-mule, and drank from the stream which turned the fulling-mills, though without once glancing in their direction, so heartily did they loathe them for the fright they had put them in.

Then, with their anger and even their gloom abated, they mounted, and without deciding what road to take – the custom of knights errant being to leave this matter to chance – they set out in the direction chosen by Rocinante. For his will acted as guide to his masters and to the ass as well, who always followed him in love and good fellowship, wherever he led. But all the same they came back to the highway and followed it at random without any definite plan.

As they were going along Sancho said to his master: 'Sir, will your worship give me permission to say a few words? For since you laid that harsh command of silence upon me several things have been rotting in my stomach, and there's one that I have on the tip of my tongue at the moment and that I shouldn't like to go bad.'

'Tell me,' said Don Quixote, 'and be brief in your arguments, for nothing long is ever pleasing.'

'Well, sir,' replied Sancho, 'for several days lately I've been thinking how little profit is gained from wandering after the adventures which your worship seeks in these wastes and at these cross-roads. For even when the most perilous of them are victoriously concluded, there's no one to see or hear of them; and so they must remain in perpetual oblivion despite your worship's good intentions and their own deserts. So it seems to me that it would be better – with due deference to your worship's better judgment – for us to go and serve an Emperor or some other great Prince who is engaged in some war. In his service your worship might show the valour of your person, your great strength, and greater wisdom. Then, when this lord whom we should serve came to see your worship's qualities, he would be bound to reward us, each according to our deserts; and in that case there couldn't fail to be someone to set down your worship's exploits in writing for everlasting remembrance. About my own I say nothing, because they must not be greater than a squire's should be, although I can say that, if it is customary in chivalry to record the deeds of squires, I don't think that mine will be left out.'

'There is something in what you say, Sancho,' replied Don Quixote, 'but before he gets to that stage a knight must wander through the world, on probation as it were, in pursuit of adventures; so as to gain such a name and reputation, by achieving a few, that, if he goes to the court of some great monarch, he will already be well known by his deeds. Then as soon as the boys see him ride through the city gates, they will all follow him and surround him and shout: "Here is the Knight of the Sun!" – or of the Serpent, or of any other device under which he may have performed his great deeds. "Here," they will cry, "is that knight who in single battle conquered the great giant Brocabruno of mighty strength, the knight who freed the Great Mameluke of Persia from the long enchantment which had held him for almost nine hundred years." Thus from mouth to mouth they will go on proclaiming his deeds, till suddenly, hearing the cries of the boys and the rest of the people, the King of that kingdom will appear at the windows of his royal palace. As soon as he sees the knight, he will recognize him by his armour or by the device on his shield, and then of course he will cry: — "Ho, there, let all the knights of my court ride out to receive the flower of chivalry, who is approaching." All will ride out at his command, and the King himself will come half-way down his staircase, embrace him most warmly, greet him, kiss him on the cheek, and lead him to the chamber of his lady Queen. There the knight will find her with the Princess, her daughter, who is sure to be one of the loveliest and most perfect damsels to be found anywhere, however hard you may search the greater part of the known world. Then immediately afterwards, she will gaze into the knight's eyes, and he into hers, and each will seem to the other rather divine than human; and without knowing how or why, they will be enmeshed and captured in the intricate net of love, and be in great anguish of heart, not knowing in what words to reveal their feelings and desires. From there he will no doubt be taken to some richly furnished room in the palace, where they will strip off his armour and bring him a rich scarlet cloak to wear; and if he is handsome in his armour, he will look still better in the quilted jacket he wears under it. When night falls he will sup with the King, the Queen, and the Princess, never taking his eyes from her, but gazing on her stealthily; and she will do the same with the same caution. For, as I have said, she is a very discreet damsel. The tables will be removed, and suddenly there will enter through the hall door an ugly little dwarf with a beautiful lady following behind him, escorted by two giants, to introduce a certain adventure, so contrived by a most ancient sage that the knight who brings it to a successful conclusion shall be accounted the best in the world.

'Then the King will immediately order all the knights present to attempt it, but none of them will bring it to a victorious conclusion except the stranger knight, to the great enhancement of his fame. At this the Princess will be much delighted, and think herself well rewarded into the bargain, in having firmly set her desires in so exalted a quarter.

'Now it happens, most fortunately, that this King, or Prince, or whatever he is, is engaged in a most stubborn war with another as powerful as himself, and the stranger knight, after some days spent at court, begs for permission to go and serve him in the said war. The King will grant his request with great pleasure, and the knight will kiss his hands most courteously for the favour. Then that night he will take leave of his lady the Princess through the railings of a garden which adjoins her sleeping-chamber; and there it will be that he has spoken with her many times before by the help of a damsel much trusted by the Princess and privy to the whole matter. He will sigh; she will swoon; the damsel will bring water and be much distressed. For it will be nearly morning, and she will fear for her lady's honour that they may be discovered. Finally the Princess will come to herself and put her white hands through the railings for the knight, who will kiss them a thousand, thousand times and bathe them in tears. They will agree how to let one another know their news, good or bad, and the Princess will implore the knight to stay away as short a time as possible, which he will promise with many oaths. Once more he kisses her hands, and bids her farewell with such grief as will come near to ending his life. From there he goes to his chamber, throws himself on the bed, but cannot sleep for the grief of parting. He gets up early in the morning, and goes to take his leave of the King, the Queen, and the Princess. When he has bidden farewell to the royal pair they tell him that the lady Princess is indisposed and cannot receive a visit; the knight concludes that it is from grief at his departure; his heart is pierced and he very nearly betrays his sorrow. The Princess's confidante is present; must observe everything; goes to inform her lady, who receives her with tears, and tells her that one of her greatest griefs is her ignorance of her knight's name, and of whether he is of royal descent or no. The damsel assures her that such courtesy, gentleness, and valour as he displays cannot exist in any but a royal and illustrious person. This consoles the Princess; she endeavours to be calm, so as not to call her parents' attention to herself; and at the end of two days appears in public.

'The knight has already gone off; he fights in the war; conquers the King's enemies; captures many cities; triumphs in many battles; comes back to court, and sees his lady in the place where he had seen her before. They agree that in reward for his services he shall ask her father for her hand in marriage, but the King will not consent, since he does not know who the knight is. Yet, however that may be, either by carrying her off or in some other way, he marries the Princess, and her father in the end considers it a most fortunate affair, for it is revealed that the said knight is the son of a valorous king – of what kingdom I do not know, for I do not think it can be on the map. The father dies; the Princess succeeds him; in fact the knight becomes king. Now comes the time for bestowing favours on his squire, and on all who have helped him to climb to his high estate. He marries his squire to one of the Princess's damsels, no doubt the one who was privy to his love, the daughter of a very important duke.'

'That's what I want, a fair field and no favour,' said Sancho, 'and that is what I expect, for it's all literally bound to turn out like that, since your worship has taken the name of *The Knight of the Sad Countenance*.'

'Most certainly, Sancho,' replied Don Quixote, 'for in that very way, and by the very steps I have described to you, knights errant rise and have risen to be Kings and Emperors. All that we need now is to look out and find some king, Christian or pagan, who is at war and has a beautiful daughter. Though there will be plenty of time to think about that. For, as I have said, we have first to win fame elsewhere before we go to court. And there is something else lacking besides, for even supposing that I find a king at war and with a beautiful daughter, and that I have won incredible fame throughout the whole universe, I do not know how it can be proved that I am of royal blood, or even second cousin to an Emperor; and the King will not want to give me his daughter for a wife until he is perfectly assured on this point, whatever the merits of my famous deeds. So I am afraid that without this proof I shall lose the rich reward of my valour. True it is that I am a gentleman of known family, of possessions, and property, and that my life is worth five hundred pounds fine by the old law; and it may be that the sage who comes to write my history will so establish my parentage and descent that I shall find I am fifth or sixth in descent from a King. For I would have you know, Sancho, that there are two kinds of lineages in the world: those which trace their descent from princes and monarchs, and which little by little time has diminished and reduced to a point, like a pyramid upside down; and others which derive their origin from common folk, and climb step by step till they achieve the dignity of great lords. So that the difference is between those who were and are no longer, and those who are but once were not. It is possible that I may prove to be one of the former, and that, on enquiry, my descent may prove great and noble, which should content the King, my father-in-law to be; but if it does not, the Princess will have to love me so much that, despite her father, she will take me for her lord and husband, even though she clearly knows that I am the son of a water-carrier. And, if she does not, it is a case of stealing her and carrying her off wherever I wish, for time or death must put an end to her parents' displeasure.'

'Yes,' said Sancho, 'it is a case too of Never ask as a favour for what you can take by force, as some good-for-nothings say; although it would suit the situation better to say: A leap over the hedge is better than good men's prayers. This I say because, if the lord King, your worship's father-in-law, shouldn't deign to yield you my lady the Princess, there's nothing for it, as your worship says, but to steal her and hide her. But the trouble is that until peace is made and you can enjoy the kingdom quietly, the poor squire may go whistle for this reward of his, unless the go-between maiden, who is to be his wife, comes away with the Princess, and he shares his misfortunes with her until Heaven ordains otherwise. For it would be quite possible, I think, for his master to give her to him straight off in lawful marriage.'

'There is no one to stop that,' said Don Quixote.

'Well, since that's the case,' replied Sancho, 'we have only to commend ourselves to God and let fortune take what course it will.'

'May God grant it,' replied Don Quixote, 'as I desire and you require and let the man who thinks he is be wretched.'

'So be it, in God's name,' said Sancho, 'for I'm an old Christian, and that is enough ancestry for a count.'

'And more than enough,' said Don Quixote. 'But even if you were not it would not matter, for if I am King I can easily make you noble without either purchase or service on your part; and, if I make you a count, there you are, a gentleman, let them say what they will; for they will have to call you your Lordship, whether they want to or no.'

'You can take it from me that I shall know how to bear my indignity,' said Sancho.

'*Dignity* you should say, not indignity,' put in his master.

'As you will,' replied Sancho Panza, 'I say that I shall know how to carry it off well. For I was once beadle to a brotherhood, and the beadle's gown suited me so nicely that they all said I looked important enough to be the steward of the brotherhood. So what will it be like when I wear a duke's robe on my shoulders, or dress all in gold and pearls, after the fashion of a foreign count? They'll come from hundreds of miles off to see me, I'll be bound.'

'You will look fine,' said Don Quixote, 'but you will need to trim your beard rather often, for you wear it so thick and matted and bushy, that unless you take a razor to it every day at least they will see what you are a gun-shot away.'

'Why,' said Sancho, 'what more have I to do than to get a barber and keep him in the house on wages? And I'll even make him follow me round at a pinch like a grandee's groom.'

'But how do you know,' asked Don Quixote, 'that grandees have their grooms following them?'

'I'll tell you,' replied Sancho. 'Some years ago I spent a month about the court, and there I saw a very little gentleman taking a walk, and they said he was a great grandee. Now wherever he went he had a man following him on horseback, turning everywhere he turned, more like his tail than anything else. I asked why that fellow never caught the other man up but always rode behind him. They told me that he was his groom, and that it was the fashion for grandees to have men like that riding after them. And I've known it ever since, and it's so stuck in my head that I've never forgotten it.'

'You are quite right, I admit,' said Don Quixote, 'and you can take your barber round like that. For customs did not all arise together, nor were they all invented at once, and you may well be the first count to carry your barber round after you. Indeed, trimming a beard is a more intimate duty than saddling a horse.'

'Leave this matter of the barber to me,' said Sancho, 'and let your worship's job be to try and become a King and make me a count.'

'So it shall be,' replied Don Quixote. And, raising his eyes, he saw what shall be told in the next chapter.

Chapter XXII. How Don Quixote set at liberty many unfortunate Creatures who were being borne, much against their will, where they had no wish to go.

CIDE HAMETE BENENGELI, the Arabian and Manchegan author, relates in his most grave, eloquent, meticulous, delightful, and ingenious history that after that conversation between the famous Don Quixote de la Mancha and Sancho Panza, his squire, which is set down at the end of the twenty-first chapter, Don Quixote raised his eyes and saw on the road which he was taking some dozen men on foot, strung by the neck like beads on a great iron chain, and all manacled. With them were two horsemen and two men on foot, the horsemen carrying firelocks,* the footmen javelins and swords. And as soon as Sancho Panza saw them he said: – 'Here's a chain of galley-slaves, men forced by the King, going to serve in the galleys.'

'What! Men forced?' asked Don Quixote. 'It it possible that the King uses force on anyone?'

'I don't say that,' answered Sancho; 'but they are men condemned for their crimes to serve the King in the galleys, and they go perforce.'

'In fact,' replied Don Quixote, 'however you put it, these men are taken, and go by force and not of their own free will.'

'That is so,' said Sancho.

'Then,' said his master, 'this is a case for the exercise of my profession, for the redressing of outrages and the succouring and relieving of the wretched.'

'Consider, your worship,' said Sancho, 'that justice – that is the King himself – is doing no wrong or outrage to such people, but only punishing them for their crimes.'

At this moment the chain of galley-slaves came up, and in most courteous terms Don Quixote begged the guards to be so kind as

* N.B. Only one firelock is accounted for in the subsequent events. The second Cervantes seems to have forgotten.

to inform him of the cause or causes why they were bearing those people off in that fashion. One of the horsemen replied that they were galley-slaves belonging to His Majesty on the way to the galleys, such was the truth of the matter and there was no more to say.

'Nevertheless,' replied Don Quixote, 'I should like to learn from each one of them separately the cause of his misfortune.' He went on in such very polite language to persuade them to give him the information he desired, that the other mounted guard replied: 'Although we have with us here the copies and certificates of the sentences on each of these wretches, there is no time to take them out and read them. But your worship may come and ask them themselves, and they may tell you, if they please – and they will, for they are the sort who not only enjoy acting the villain but boasting of it afterwards too.'

With this permission, which Don Quixote would have taken if it had not been granted, the knight went up to the chain, and asked the first man for what sins he was in that evil plight. He replied that it was for falling in love.

'For no more than that?' cried Don Quixote. 'But if they send men to the galleys for falling in love, I should long since have been rowing there myself.'

'It isn't the kind of love your worship imagines,' said the galley-slave. 'Mine was an over-great affection for a basketful of white linen, which I clasped to me so tight that if the law hadn't wrested it from me by force I shouldn't have let it go of my own free will even to this day. I was taken red-handed; there was no need of the torture; the trial was short; they accommodated my shoulders with a hundred lashes, and three years in the *gurapas* thrown in, and the job was done.'

'What are the *gurapas*?' asked Don Quixote.

'*Gurapas* are galleys,' replied the galley-slave, who was a lad of about twenty-four, and came, as he said, from Piedranita.

Don Quixote asked the same question of the second man, who was too melancholy and dejected to answer a word. But the first man replied for him: 'This man is here for being a canary – I mean a musician and singer.'

'How is that?' asked Don Quixote. 'Do men go to the galleys for being musicians and singers?'

'Yes, sir,' replied the galley-slave: 'for there is nothing worse than singing in anguish.'

'I have always heard the opposite,' said Don Quixote. 'Sing away sorrow, cast away care.'

'Here it's the reverse,' said the galley-slave. 'If you sing once you weep for a lifetime.'

'I do not understand,' said Don Quixote. But one of the guards put in: 'Sir, singing in anguish with these ungodly people means confessing on the rack. They put this sinner to the torture, and he confessed his crime, which was cattle-thieving; and on his confession they sentenced him to six years in the galleys, besides two hundred lashes on the back; and the reason why he is dejected and melancholy is that the rest of the thieves back there, and these marching here, abuse him and bully him, and mock him and despise him, because he confessed and hadn't the courage to say no. For, as they say, *no* takes no longer to say than *yes*, and a crook is in luck if his life depends on his own tongue and not on witnesses and proofs; and I think that they are not far wrong.'

'I agree,' replied Don Quixote. Then, passing to the third man, he asked him the same question as the others, and the man answered very readily and calmly:

'I am going to their ladyships the *gurapas* for five years because I was short of ten ducats.'

'I will give you twenty with pleasure,' said Don Quixote, 'to free you from this distress.'

'That,' replied the galley-slave, 'looks to me like having money when you're in mid-ocean and dying of hunger, and there's nowhere to buy what you need. Because if I had had those twenty ducats your worship now offers me at the right time, I should have greased the clerk's pen with them and livened up my lawyer's wits to such effect that I should have been in the Zocodover square in Toledo to-day, and not dragging along this road like a greyhound on a leash. But God is great. Patience – that's enough.'

Don Quixote went on to the fourth, a man of venerable appearance with a white beard reaching below his chest who, when asked why he was there, began to weep and answered not a word. But the fifth convict lent him a tongue and said: 'This honest fellow is go-

ing to the galleys for four years after parading the town in state and
on horseback.'

'I suppose you mean that he was exposed to public shame,' said
Sancho Panza.

'That's right,' replied the galley-slave, 'and the offence for which
he got his sentence was trafficking in ears, in fact in whole bodies.
What I mean is that this gentleman is here for procuring, and also
for having a touch of the wizard about him.'

'If it had not been for that touch,' said Don Quixote, 'and if it
were merely for procuring, he would not deserve to go and row in
the galleys, but to be their general and command them. For the
office of procurer is no easy one. It requires persons of discretion
and is a most essential office in a well-ordered state. Only men of
good birth should exercise it. Indeed, there ought to be an overseer
and controller of these procurers, as there are of other professions,
and only a certain number should be appointed and recognized, like
brokers on the Exchange. In that way a great many troubles would
be avoided, which are caused through this office getting into the
hands of idiots and people of little intelligence, such as half-witted
servant-maids and little pages and buffoons, raw and inexperienced
folk. Then, at the critical moment, when they have a really important affair to manage, they let the morsel freeze between their
fingers and their mouth, and do not know their right hand from
their left. I should like to go on and explain why it is necessary to
select those who are to hold so necessary a position in the State;
but this is no proper place. But some day I will put the matter before those who can furnish a remedy. Now I can only say that the
grief caused me by the sight of these white hairs and this venerable
countenance in such distress for procuring has been entirely removed by the mention of witchcraft, though I know very well that
there are no wizards in the world capable of affecting or compelling
the affections, as some simple people believe; for our will is free and
there is no drug or spell that can control it. What such simple servant-maids and lying rogues generally do is to make up mixtures
and poisons which drive a man crazy, under the pretence that they
have the power to excite love; whereas, as I have said, it is impossible to compel the affections.'

'That is so,' said the old fellow, 'and really, sir, as to being a wizard, I was not guilty, though I can't deny the procuring. But I never thought that I was doing any harm. All I wanted was for everyone to have a good time and live in peace and quiet, without quarrels or troubles. But the best intentions didn't serve to keep me from going to a place I don't expect to come back from, being stricken in years and having a bladder complaint which never gives me a moment's rest.' Here he burst into tears once more, and Sancho was so sorry for him that he took a *real* from under his shirt and gave it to him out of charity.

Don Quixote passed on and asked another his crime, and this one replied with rather more freedom than the last:

'I am here for having a bit too much fun with two girl cousins of mine, and two other cousins who were not mine. In fact, I had such fun with them all that the result of the joke was an intricate tangle of relationships that is more than any devil of a clerk can make out. It was all proved against me; I had no friends; I had no money; I was within an inch of having my gullet squeezed; they sentenced me to six years on the galleys; I submitted; it's the punishment for my crime. I'm young; if only my life holds out, all may yet come right. But, sir, should your worship have anything about you to give us poor wretches, God will repay you in Heaven, and here on earth we'll be sure to beseech him in our prayers that your worship's life and health may be as long and as prosperous as your good looks deserve.'

The fellow who spoke wore the dress of a student, and one of the guards said that he was a great talker and a very good Latin scholar. Behind the rest came a man of about thirty, of very good appearance except that he squinted when he looked at you. He was fettered in a different way from the others. For he had a chain on his leg so long that it was wound right round his body, and two collars about his neck, one secured to the chain and the other of the kind called a *keep friend* or *friend's foot*. From this two iron bars reached down to his waist, with two manacles attached in which his wrists were secured by a heavy padlock, so that he could neither lift his hands to his mouth nor bend his head down to his hands. Don Quixote asked why this man had so many more fetters than the rest, and the guard replied that it was because he had committed more crimes than all the others put together, and that he was so bold and desperate a criminal that even though he was chained in that way they were not sure of him, but feared he might escape.

'What crimes, then, can he have committed?' asked Don Quixote, 'if they have not earned him a heavier penalty than the galleys?'

'He is going for ten years,' replied the guard, 'which is a sort of civil death. I need tell you no more than that this fellow is the famous Gines de Pasamonte, alias Ginesillo de Parapilla.'

'Not so rough, sergeant,' put in the galley-slave. 'Don't let us be settling names and surnames now. I am called Gines, not Ginesillo, and Pasamonte is my surname, not Parapilla as you say. Let everyone have a good look in his own cupboard, and he'll not be doing too badly.'

'A little less insolence,' replied the sergeant, 'you double-dyed thief, or I may have to shut you up, and then you'll be sorry.'

'You may see,' replied the galley-slave, 'that man proposes and God disposes; but one day somebody may learn whether my name is Ginesillo de Parapilla or not.'

'Isn't that what they call you, then, rogue?' asked the guard.

'Yes, they do,' replied Gines, 'but I'll stop them calling me that or I'll pluck them – but no matter where. If, sir, you have anything to give us, give it us now, and go in God's name; for you weary me with your prying into other men's lives. But if you want to know about mine, I am Gines de Pasamonte, and I have written my life with these very fingers.'

'He is speaking the truth,' put in the sergeant. 'He has written his own story, as fine as you please, and left the book behind at the prison pawned for two hundred *reals*.'

'And I mean to redeem it,' said Gines, 'even if it were pledged for two hundred ducats.'

'Is it as good as that?' said Don Quixote.

'It's so good,' replied Gines, 'that Lazarillo de Tormes will have to look out, and so will everything in that style that has ever been written or ever will be. One thing I can promise you is that it is all the truth, and such well-written, entertaining truth that there is no fiction that can compare with it.'

'And what is the title of the book?' asked Don Quixote.

'*The Life of Gines de Pasamonte*,' replied that hero.

'Is it finished?' asked Don Quixote.

'How can it be finished,' replied the other, 'if my life isn't? What is written begins with my birth and goes down to the point when I was sent to the galleys this last time.'

'Then you have been there before?' said Don Quixote.

'Four years I was there before,' replied Gines, 'in the service of God and the King, and I know the taste of the biscuit and the lash already. I am not greatly grieved at going, for I shall have a chance there to finish my book. I have a lot more to say, and in the Spanish galleys there is more leisure than I shall require, though I shan't need much for what I have to write, because I know it by heart.'

'You seem a clever fellow,' said Don Quixote.

'And an unfortunate one,' replied Gines, 'for misfortunes always pursue men of talent.'

'They pursue rogues,' replied the sergeant.

'I have already requested you to use better language, sergeant,' replied Pasamonte, 'for your superiors did not give you that staff to maltreat us poor devils, but to guide and lead us where his Majesty commands. If you do not, by God – but enough! – perhaps one day the stains that were made at the inn will come out in the wash. And let everyone hold his tongue, live virtuously and speak better. Now let us get along, for this is a bit too much of a joke.'

The sergeant raised his staff to strike Pasamonte in return for his threats. But Don Quixote interposed and begged him not to ill-treat him, for it was no great matter if a man who had his hands tied let his tongue free a little. Then, addressing the whole chain-gang, the knight said:

'From all that you have told me, dearest brethren, I clearly gather that, although it is for your faults they have punished you, the penalties which you are to suffer give you little pleasure. You are going to them, it seems, very reluctantly and much against your wills; and possibly it is only lack of courage under torture in one, shortage of money in another, lack of friends in another – in short, the unfair decisions of the judge – that have been the cause of your undoing and of your failure to receive the justice which was your due. All of which is now so clear in my mind that it bids me, persuades me, and even compels me, to demonstrate on you the purpose for which Heaven has sent me into the world and made me profess therein the order of chivalry which I follow, and the vow I made to succour the needy and those who are oppressed by the strong. Conscious, however, that it is the part of prudence not to do by foul means what can be done by fair, I would beg the gentlemen of the guard and the sergeant to be so good as to release you and let you go in peace, since there will be no lack of men to serve the King out of better motives; for it seems to me a hard case to make slaves of those whom God and nature made free. Furthermore, gentlemen of the guard,' added Don Quixote, 'these poor men have committed no wrong against you. Let everyone answer for his sins in the other world. There is a God in Heaven, who does not neglect to punish the wicked nor to reward the good, and it is not right that honourable men should be executioners of others, having themselves no concern in the matter. I make this request in a calm and gentle manner, so that I may have cause to thank you if you comply; but if you do not do so willingly, then this lance and this sword, together with the valour of my arm, will force you to do so under compulsion.'

'This is fine foolishness,' replied the sergeant. 'It is a good joke he has taken all this time hatching! He would like us to let the King's convicts go, as if we had authority to free them, or he had it to order us to! Get along with you, sir, and good luck to you! Put that basin straight on your head, and don't go about looking for a cat with three legs.'

'You are the cat, the rat, and the rascal!' replied Don Quixote. Then, matching deeds to his words, he attacked him so swiftly that he had dealt him a serious wound with his lance and brought him to the ground before he had a chance to defend himself; and, luckily for Don Quixote, this was the man with the firelock. The rest of the guards were dumbfounded by this unexpected turn of events. They recovered themselves, however, and the horsemen drew their swords, while the men on foot seized their javelins and rushed at Don Quixote, who awaited them in complete calm. And no doubt things would have gone badly for him if the galley-slaves had not seen their chance of gaining their liberty and taken advantage of it to break the chain which linked them together. Such was the confusion, in fact, that the guards ran first to the galley-slaves, who were struggling loose, and then to deal with Don Quixote, who was attacking, and so achieved no good purpose. Sancho, for his part, helped in releasing Gines de Pasamonte, who was the first to leap free and unfettered into the open, where he attacked the fallen sergeant and seized his sword and his firelock. Then, first levelling the gun at one man and then picking on another, without ever firing it he cleared the field of all the guards, who fled from Pasamonte's gun and from the showers of stones, as well, flung by the now liberated galley-slaves.

Sancho was much grieved at this business, for he guessed that the guards who had fled would report the matter to the Holy Brotherhood, who would sound the alarm and come out in pursuit of the criminals. This thought he communicated to his master, begging him that they might clear out immediately and hide in the nearby mountains.

'That is all very well,' said Don Quixote, 'but I know what is right for us to do now.' Then he called all the galley-slaves, who were running about excitedly and had stripped the sergeant to the skin; and when they had gathered around him to hear what his orders might be, he addressed them thus:

'It is a mark of well-born men to show gratitude for benefits received, and ingratitude is one of the sins which most offend God. I say this, gentlemen, because you have already had good experience of benefits received at my hands; as payment for which it is my will that you bear this chain which I have taken from your necks and immediately take the road to the city of El Toboso, there to present yourselves before the Lady Dulcinea del Toboso and tell her that her knight, the Knight of the Sad Countenance, presents his service to her. Then you are to tell her, point by point, every detail of this famous adventure up to the restoration of your long-coveted liberty; and when you have done so you may go wherever you will, and good luck go with you.'

Gino de Pasamonte answered for them all, and said: 'What your worship commands, lord and liberator, is of all impossibilities the most impossible for us to perform, since we cannot appear on the roads together, but must go singly and separately, each one on his own. And we must try to hide in the bowels of the earth for fear of being found by the Holy Brotherhood, for there is no doubt that they will come out in search of us. What your worship can do, and what you should do, is to substitute for this service and tribute to the lady Dulcinea del Toboso some number of Ave Marias and Credos, which we will say for your worship's benefit, this being a thing which can be performed by night and by day, on the run or resting, in peace or in war. But to think of our returning now to the flesh-pots of Egypt, I mean of our taking up our chain and setting out on the road for El Toboso, is to imagine that it is already night when it is not yet ten in the morning, and you can no more ask us for that than you can ask pears from an elm-tree.'

'Then I swear by Heaven,' cried Don Quixote in fury, 'sir son of a whore, Don Ginesillo de Parapillo, or whatever you are called, – that you shall go yourself alone, with your tail between your legs and the whole chain on your back!'

Pasamonte was quite certain from Don Quixote's crazy action in giving them their liberty that he was not right in the head; and being far from long-suffering, when he found himself treated in this way he tipped his companions the wink. They then drew back and began to rain such a shower of stones upon Don Quixote that he could not contrive to cover himself with his shield, and poor Rocinante took no more notice of the spur than if he had been made of brass. Sancho got behind his ass and used him as a defence against the cloud and hailstorm of stones which descended on the pair of them. But Don Quixote could not shield himself well enough, and was hurt by some of the pebbles, which struck him on the body with such force that they knocked him to the ground. The moment he was down the student leapt on him, and seizing the basin from his head, brought it down three or four times on his shoulders, and as many more on the ground, till it was almost smashed to pieces. They also stripped him of a jacket which he wore over his armour, and would have taken off his stockings too if his leg armour had not prevented them. While from Sancho they took his overcoat, and left him in his shirt. Then, dividing the rest of the spoils of battle, they fled, each in a separate direction, more intent on escaping from the dreaded Brotherhood than on loading themselves with the chain and going to present themselves to the lady Dulcinea del Toboso.

All that remained were the ass and Rocinante, Sancho and Don Quixote; the ass pensively hanging his head and shaking his ears now and then, imagining that the storm of stones which had whizzed by his head had not yet ceased; Rocinante prostrate beside his master, for he had also been brought down by a stone; Sancho in his shirt and terrified of the Holy Brotherhood; and Don Quixote much distressed at finding himself so vilely treated by the very men for whom he had done so much.

Chapter XXIII. *Of what happened to the famous Don Quixote in the Sierra Morena, one of the rarest Adventures in the course of this true History.*

FINDING himself in so bad a way, Don Quixote said to his squire: 'I have always heard, Sancho, that doing good to base fellows is like throwing water into the sea. If I had believed what you said to me I should have avoided this trouble. But now that it is done, patience; and let this be a warning for the future.'

'Your worship will take as much warning,' replied Sancho, 'as I'm a Turk. But, as you say that you would have avoided this disaster if you had trusted me, trust me now and you'll avoid even worse. For there's no trying chivalry on the Holy Brotherhood, let me tell you. They don't care a row of pins for all the knights errant in the world; and, believe me, I can hear their arrows whizzing past my ears already.'

'You are a coward by nature, Sancho,' said Don Quixote, 'but I do not want you to say that I am obstinate and never do what you suggest. So this time I am going to take your advice, and retire before the fury which you so much dread. But on one condition: never, in life or death, are you to tell anyone that I retreated and withdrew from this peril out of fear. I do it only to humour your entreaties, and if you say otherwise it will be a lie. Yes, from now till then and from then till now I give you the lie, and say that you lie and will lie every time that you either say it or think it. Do not answer me with another word; for at the mere thought that I am retreating and withdrawing from any peril, particularly from this, which seems to have some faint shadow of danger about it, I am inclined to stay here and await alone, not only the Holy Brotherhood, whose name you speak in terror, but the Brethren of the twelve tribes of Israel, and the seven Maccabees, and Castor and

Pollux, and all the brothers and brotherhoods in the world as well.'

'Sir,' replied Sancho, 'withdrawing is not flight, nor is it prudent to stay when danger outweighs hope. It is a wise man's duty to save himself for to-morrow, and not risk everything on one day. Let me tell you that I've still got some idea of what they call good conduct, although I may be an ignorant peasant. So don't be sorry that you've taken my advice, but climb upon Rocinante if you can – or if you can't I'll help you – and follow me; for my thinking-cap tells me that we've more need of our feet just now than of our hands.'

Don Quixote mounted without another word; and with Sancho leading the way on his ass, they rode into a nearby part of the Sierra Morena, it being Sancho's intention to cross the whole range and come out at Viso or Almodóvar del Campo, and to hide for a few days in that rough country, so as not to be found if the Holy Brotherhood came after them. He was encouraged in this plan by finding that the provisions he carried on the ass's back had escaped from the skirmish with the galley-slaves, which he took as a miracle, considering how much they had taken and how closely they had searched everything.

Now by nightfall they had got into the heart of the Sierra Morena; where Sancho thought it would be well to spend that night, if not some days, or at least as long as the provisions they had with them should last. And so they camped between two crags among a number of cork-trees. But fatal destiny which, according to those who lack the light of true faith, guides, shapes, and disposes everything in its own way, decreed that Gines de Pasamonte, the famous cheat and robber, whom by his valour and madness Don Quixote had delivered from the chain, had decided to hide in those mountains, out of fear of the Holy Brotherhood, which he had good reason to dread. And his luck and fear took him to the spot to which the same motives had brought Don Quixote and Sancho Panza, while it was still light enough for him to recognize them and just as they were falling asleep. Now as the wicked are always ungrateful and necessity drives them to evil deeds, and as present needs outweigh any thought for the future, Gines, who was neither grateful nor well-disposed, decided to steal Sancho Panza's ass, not caring for Rocinante, a security neither pawnable nor saleable. Sancho

Panza slept; Gines stole his ass;* and before morning he was too far off to be found.

Dawn came forth, bringing joy to the earth but grief to Sancho Panza, who missed his Dapple and, when he found himself without him, burst into the saddest and most doleful lament in all the world. So loud was his grief that Don Quixote woke up to hear him cry: 'O child of my bowels, born in my very house, my children's play-mate, my wife's delight, envy of my neighbours, ease of my burdens, and half my means of livelihood besides, for the sixpence halfpenny a day you earned me was the half of my living!'

On seeing his tears and learning the cause Don Quixote consoled his squire with the best reasoning he could, begging him to be patient and promising to give him a bill of exchange entitling him to three of the five ass-foals he had left at home. This comforted Sancho, who dried his tears, controlled his sobs and thanked Don Quixote for this favour. As for the knight, his heart grew glad as they cut into the mountains, for they seemed to him a most suitable scene for the adventures he was seeking. They recalled to his memory the marvellous things which had happened to knights errant in similar wastes and fastnesses; and he rode on with his mind dwelling on such things, and so absorbed and rapt by them that he remembered nothing else. And Sancho's only thought, now that he supposed them out of danger, was of satisfying his stomach with the relics of the clerical booty; so he walked on behind his master, loaded with all that the ass should have carried, taking morsels out of the bag and cramming them into his belly; and while thus employ-ed he would not have given a halfpenny for any other adventure.

While thus engaged, however, he looked up and saw that his master had stopped and with the point of his lance was trying to lift up some bundle lying on the ground. So he hurried on, to catch him up, and help him if necessary; and overtook his master just as he was raising on his lance-point a saddle-cushion with a leather bag at-tached, partly rotten, or rather entirely so and falling to pieces. But it was so heavy that Sancho had to get down and pick it up for him. His master then bade him look what was in the bag. And this he very quickly did. For, although it was secured by a chain and pad-

* The stealing of the ass is another of Cervantes' oversights. Four pages later Sancho is riding him again, and a little later once more without him.

lock, he could see what was inside through the rents and rotten places. There were four shirts of fine cambric, some other fine and fashionable linen, and a considerable pile of gold coins in a hand-kerchief, at the sight of which Sancho cried out: 'Blessed be Heaven for affording us one profitable adventure!' And on a further search he found a little note-book, richly decorated. This Don Quixote asked for, but he told Sancho to take the money for himself and keep it. The squire acknowledged this favour by kissing his master's hands and, rifling the linen, stowed it in their provision bag.

Now when Don Quixote had taken all this in, he observed: 'There seems to me, Sancho, to be no doubt whatever that some traveller must have lost his way in these mountains, and have been attacked by robbers, who must have killed him and brought him to this remote spot to bury him.'

'That can't be so,' replied Sancho, 'for if they had been thieves they wouldn't have left this money here.'

'You are right,' said Don Quixote. 'So I cannot divine or guess what it can be. But wait; let us see if there is not something written in this note-book which will give us a clue.'

He opened it, and the first thing that he saw in it was a beauti-fully written copy of a sonnet, which he read aloud for Sancho to hear. It ran like this:

> Know'st thou, O love, the pangs which I sustain,
> Or, cruel, dost thou view those pangs unmoved?
> Or has some hidden cause its influence proved,
> By all this sad variety of pain?
>
> If Love's a god, then surely he must know,
> And knowing, pity wretchedness like mine.
> From other hands proceeds the fatal blow.
> Is then the deed, unpitying Chloe, thine?
>
> Ah no, a body formed so perfectly
> A soul so merciless can ne'er enclose.
> Nor can it be from Heaven my ruin flows.
> But it's most certain that I soon shall die,
> For when the cause of the complaint's unsure
> 'Twould be a miracle to find a cure.

'We can learn nothing from that poem,' said Sancho, 'unless from that clue we can come to the thread of the matter.'

'What clue do you mean?' asked Don Quixote.

'I thought your worship mentioned a clue?'

'I did not say clue, but Chloe,' replied Don Quixote, 'and that, no doubt, is the name of the lady the author of this sonnet is complaining about. He is a pretty good poet, I am sure, or I am a poor judge of the art!'

'Your worship knows about poetry-writing too, then?' observed Sancho.

'Yes, and better than you think,' replied Don Quixote, 'as you will know when you take a letter written in verse from beginning to end to my lady Dulcinea del Toboso. For I would inform you, Sancho, that all or most knights errant in the olden times were great troubadours and great musicians as well. For these two accomplishments, or rather graces as I should say, belong with love errantry; though it is true that the poems of the knights of old have more spirit than elegance about them.'

'Read some more, your worship,' said Sancho, 'for we may yet find something to satisfy our curiosity.'

Don Quixote turned the page and said, 'This is prose, and looks like a letter.'

'An ordinary letter, sir?' asked Sancho.

'From its opening it looks more like a love-letter,' replied Don Quixote.

'Then read it aloud, your worship,' said Sancho. 'I very much enjoy this love business.'

'With pleasure,' said Don Quixote and, reading it aloud as Sancho had asked him, he found what follows:

'Your false promise and my certain misfortune bear me to a place from which you will sooner hear the news of my death than the sound of my complaining. You have cast me off, ungrateful that you are, for one with more possessions but no more worth than I have. Yet if virtue were esteemed as wealth is, I should envy no man his fortune, nor bewail my own misfortune. What your beauty raised up your deeds have destroyed; from your form I thought you were an angel; from your acts I know you are a woman. Peace be with you, though you cause war in me; and may Heaven grant that your husband's deceptions remain concealed for ever, so that you may not eternally regret what you have done, nor I take a vengeance which I do not desire.'

When he had finished reading the letter Don Quixote observed: 'We can gather less about the writer from this than from the verses, except that he was some scorned lover.' And fingering through the greater part of the little book, he found more verses and letters, some of which he could read and others not. But the contents of all alike were complaints, laments, misgivings, longings and pains, favours and slights – celebrated or deplored. While Don Quixote examined the book, Sancho went through the bag, not leaving a corner of it, or of the saddle-cushion, that he did not search, pry into and explore, nor a seam which he did not rip, nor a tuft of wool that he did not pick, in case anything might be lost out of carelessness or want of diligence; such was the greed aroused in him by the discovery of the money, which amounted to more than a hundred crowns. And although he found no more, still he thought himself well compensated for the blanket-tossing, the vomiting of the balsam, the benedictions of the pack-staves, the blows of the carrier, the loss of the saddle-bags, the stealing of his coat, and all the hunger, thirst, and weariness which he had undergone in his worthy master's service. In fact he counted himself amply repaid for everything by Don Quixote's favour in handing over to him the treasure trove.

Now the Knight of the Sad Countenance had a great desire to know who was the possessor of the bag, guessing from the sonnet and the letter, from the gold coins and the fine quality of the shirts, that he must be a lover of some consequence, whom his lady's scorn and ill-treatment had brought to some desperate end. But as there was likely to be no one in this uninhabited and rugged country who could inform him, he found nothing for it but to ride on, leaving the choice of road to Rocinante – who chose the most passable – labouring under the perpetual illusion that he could not fail to find some extraordinary adventure among those thickets. As he rode on then, with this idea in mind, he saw on the top of a knoll, which showed up straight ahead, a man leaping from rock to rock and from bush to bush with extraordinary agility. He made out that he was half-naked, with a matted black beard, his hair long and tangled, and his legs and feet bare; while his thighs were clad in a pair of breeches, which seemed to be of brown velvet but were so tattered that in many places his skin showed through. His head too was bare; and although he moved swiftly, as has been said, still the Knight of the

Sad Countenance saw and noted all these details. But try as he might, he could not follow him, for it was not given to Rocinante in his weakness to travel over such rough places, he being, besides, slow and sluggish by nature. Then, presently, Don Quixote came to the conclusion that this was the owner of the saddle-cushion and the bag, and he made up his mind to seek him, even though it might mean spending a year among those mountains before he found him. And so he ordered Sancho to dismount from his ass and to cut over one side of the mountains, while he went across the other; as by such measures they might come upon the man who had run away from them so fast.

'I couldn't do that,' replied Sancho, 'for when I leave your worship's side fear springs upon me at once and visits me with all kinds of alarms and visions; and let these words of mine serve as a warning that I won't stir a finger's breadth from your worship's presence from now on.'

'Very well,' said he of the Sad Countenance. 'I am glad that you rely on my courage, which shall never fail you though your soul shall desert your body. Follow me, therefore, slowly or however you can, and use your eyes for lanterns. We will go round this spur, and then perhaps we shall meet the man whom we saw. There can be no doubt that he is none other than the owner of the things we have found.'

To which Sancho replied: 'It would be much better not to look for him. Because if we find him and he happens to be the owner of the money, it is plain that I must give it back; and so it would be better not to take this unnecessary trouble, but for us to keep it faithfully until its real owner turns up in some less strange and laborious way. Perhaps by then I shall have spent it, and then the King's law will acquit me of responsibility.'

'You are wrong on that score,' replied Don Quixote, 'for now that we have a suspicion of who the owner is, and have him almost before our eyes, we are obliged to seek him and restore these things to him; and if we do not seek him, the strong presumption we have of his identity makes us as guilty as if he were really the owner. So, Sancho my friend, you must not let this search grieve you, seeing how much it will relieve my mind to find him.'

Then he pricked Rocinante on, and Sancho followed on foot and loaded, thanks to Ginesillo de Pasamonte. And when they had gone round part of the mountain, they found in a stream bed a dead mule saddled and bridled, half eaten by dogs and picked by crows; all of which confirmed their suspicion that the man who had run away from them was the owner of the mule and of the saddle-cushion.

As they were gazing at it they heard a whistle like that of a shepherd guarding his flock. Then suddenly on their left appeared a great number of goats, and behind them on the mountain top their goatherd, a very old man. Don Quixote shouted to him to come down to them. And he called back to ask who had brought them into that place, which was hardly ever visited except by goats or wolves and other wild beasts which haunted the neighbourhood. Sancho replied that they would explain everything if he would come down, and so he descended, and coming to where Don Quixote was standing, said:

'I'll bet that you are looking at the hired mule, lying dead in that hollow. It has been in that place a good six months, I can tell you. But tell me, have you come across its owner about here?'

'We have met nobody,' replied Don Quixote, 'and seen nothing except a saddle-cushion and a little leather bag, which we found lying not far from here.'

'I found it too,' replied the goatherd, 'but I never liked to pick it up or come near it, for fear of some mishap, or of being charged with stealing it. For the devil's a sly one, and things start up under a man's feet which make him trip and fall, without his knowing how or why.'

'That's just what I say,' replied Sancho. 'I found it too, but wouldn't go within a stone's throw of it. There I left it, and there it is just as it was, for I don't want a dog with a bell.'

'Tell me, my good fellow,' said Don Quixote, 'do you know who is the owner of these articles?'

'All that I can say,' replied the goatherd, 'is that six months ago, more or less, there arrived at a certain shepherd's hut, which will be about nine miles from this spot, a good-looking, well-mannered youth on that same mule that is lying there dead, and with that same saddle-cushion and bag which you say you found and didn't touch. He asked us what part of this range was the roughest and most remote; and we told him that it was where we are now – and that's the truth. For if you were to go on a mile or two more you would possibly never find your way out again; and I am wondering how you were able to reach here, because there's no road or track leading to this place. Well, I tell you, when the youth heard our reply he turned and rode towards the spot we pointed out to him, leaving us all delighted at his handsome appearance, and astonished at his questions and at seeing him ride off so fast in the direction of the mountains. From that time on we did not see him again, until some days ago he appeared on the path in front of one of our goatherds, went up to him without a word and dealt him several punches and kicks. Then he went to our baggage-donkey and took all the bread and the cheese he carried; after which he ran back again into the mountains at an amazing speed. When we heard about this, several of our herdsmen spent almost two days looking for him in the roughest part of this mountain, and finally found him hiding in the hollow of a huge cork-tree. He came out to us, very mild, with his clothes torn and his face disfigured and scorched by the sun, so that we scarcely knew him again. But his clothes, torn as they were, were sufficiently recognizable to convince us that he was the man we were looking for. He greeted us courteously, and in a few polite words begged us not to be surprised to see him wandering about in that state; for he had to do so to fulfil a certain penance which had been laid on him for his many sins. We asked him to tell us who he was, but could not get that out of him. We also begged him to tell us where we could find him, so that we could bring him food when he stood in need of it, for without it he could not exist; and if this was not to his liking, we asked him at least to come and ask for it, and not take it from the herdsmen by force. He thanked us for our offer, asked our pardon for past assaults, and promised for the future to beg for food in God's name, and not do violence to anyone. As to his dwelling-place, he said that he had none but such as chance offered when night overtook him; and he ended his speech with such touching tears that we must have been made of stone if we had not wept too to hear him, considering the change in his appearance since the first time we had seen him. For, as I have said, he was a very charming and handsome young man and, to judge from his courteous and nicely chosen speech, obviously a well-born and very gentlemanly person. For though we that listened to him were country

men, even our simple minds could tell from his good manners what
sort of man he was. But he suddenly fell silent in the middle of his
speech and fixed his eyes on the ground for quite a while. We waited
quietly and expectantly, though in some alarm to see how this fit
would end. He opened his eyes wide and stared fixedly at the ground
for a long while without so much as stirring an eyelid. Then he
closed his eyes, pressed his lips together, and scowled. From all this
we could easily tell that some fit of madness had come upon him.
And he quickly showed us that we were right. For in a great fury he
got up from the ground, where he had thrown himself, and attacked
the man nearest to him with such reckless rage that he would have
punched and bitten him to death, if we hadn't pulled him off. And
all the while he shouted: "Ferdinand, you traitor! You shall pay
here, here, for the wrong you have done me! These hands shall tear
out your heart, which harbours every crime at once, and the greatest
of them all, fraud and deceit!" He went on to abuse that Ferdinand
a great deal more and accused him of treachery and perjury.

'Well, we got our fellow away from him at last with no little
trouble, and he left us without a word and ran off to hide in those
briars and thickets, so that it was impossible for us to follow him.

'So we suppose that he gets fits of madness at times, and that
someone called Ferdinand must have injured him very grievously,
to reduce him to the wretched condition he is in. All this has been
confirmed since, for he will very often come out on to the path,
sometimes to beg the herdsmen for some of their food, and sometimes to take it by force. For when the fit of madness is on him he
will not accept it, even though they offer it gladly, but prefers to
attack them and snatch it from them. Yet when he is in his senses he
asks for it courteously and politely for the love of God, and accepts
it with thanks and sometimes with tears. And, to tell you the truth,
sirs,' the goatherd went on, 'yesterday we decided, I and four herdsmen – two of our fellows and two friends of mine – to search for
him till we find him, and then to take him, willy-nilly, to the town of
Almodovar, which is about twenty-four miles away. There we'll get
him cured, if his disease is curable, or find out who he is when he is
in his senses, and whether he has any relations whom we can inform
of his misfortune. That, gentlemen, is all the answer that I can give
to your questions; and you may be sure that the owner of the

articles which you found is this same man whom you saw run by so naked and so nimble' – for Don Quixote had already told him that they had seen a man leaping among the rocks.

Our knight was amazed at the goatherd's tale, and more anxious than ever to know who the unfortunate madman was. So he decided to carry out a plan which he had already been considering, and to search the whole range for him, leaving no cranny or cave unexplored till he found him. But chance contrived for him better than he hoped or expected. For at that very instant there appeared from a cleft in the mountains, which opened on the place where they were standing, the very youth he was seeking, muttering to himself some words that were unintelligible near-to, let alone at a distance. His clothes were as the goatherd had described them; only when he drew near Don Quixote noticed that the torn leather coat which he wore still smelt of ambergris, from which he concluded that the wearer of such clothes could not be of a very low class. When the youth came up he greeted them in a rough and toneless voice, but very courteously. Don Quixote returned his greetings no less politely and, charmingly and graciously dismounting from Rocinante, advanced to embrace him, and held him for some time clasped in his arms, as if he had known him for a long while. The other, whom we may call the Ragged Knight of the Sorry – as Don Quixote was of the Sad – Countenance, after allowing himself to be embraced drew back a little and, placing his hands on Don Quixote's shoulders, stood gazing at him, as if to see whether he knew him, being no less surprised, perhaps, to see Don Quixote's face, figure, and armour than Don Quixote was to see him. In the end, the first to speak after the embrace was the Ragged Knight, and what he said will be told in the next chapter.

Chapter XXIV. *The Adventure in the Sierra Morena continued.*

THE history tells that Don Quixote listened with the very greatest attention to the ill-starred Knight of the Mountains, who made him the following address:

'Most certainly, sir, whoever you may be – for I do not know you – I thank you for the demonstrations of courtesy you have shown me, and I wish I were in the position to repay you for your gracious reception with more than my good-will. But my luck gives me nothing to offer in return for the kindness you have done me except the desire to respond.'

'My only wish,' replied Don Quixote, 'is to serve you; so much so that I was determined not to leave these mountains till I had discovered you, and learnt from you if there is any sort of remedy to be found for the affliction which your strange way of life shows you to suffer under; and if so, to make every possible effort to find it. But should your misfortune be such as to close all doors to every kind of consolation, it was my intention to join you, as best I could, in your grief and lamentations; for it is still some consolation in sorrows to find someone to grieve for them. If my good intentions, then, deserve to be met by any kind of courtesy, I entreat you, sir, by the great courtesy that is clearly in your nature, and by the person whom in this life you have loved or love best, to tell me who you are, and the cause which has brought you to live and die in these wastes like a brute beast, for your dress and your person show that this is far from being your proper abode. I swear,' added Don Quixote, 'by the order of knighthood which I have received, although an unworthy sinner, and by the profession of knight errant, that if you will oblige me, sir, in this, I will serve you with all the endeavour which it is my duty to exert, either by relieving your misfortune, if any relief is possible, or by joining you in bewailing it, as I have promised.'

When the Knight of the Wood heard the Knight of the Sad Countenance speak in this style, he stared at him in silence, gazing at him again and again, and viewing him from head to foot. Then, when he had gazed his fill, he said: 'If you have anything to give me to eat, for the love of God give it to me; and when I have had some food I will do all that you ask to acknowledge the kind offer you have just made me.'

Then Sancho took from his saddle-bag, and the goatherd from his pouch, enough to satisfy the Ragged Knight's hunger; and he ate what they gave him like a man in a daze, so hurriedly that he did not leave a moment between one mouthful and the next, rather gobbling his meal than eating it; and all the while he ate neither he nor the bystanders said a word. When he had finished he made signs to them to follow him, which they did; and he led them to a little green meadow that lay behind some crags a short way away. When he got there he lay down on the grass, and the others did the same, all in utter silence until the Ragged Knight had made himself comfortable, and began:

'If you wish me to explain to you, gentlemen, the immensity of my misfortunes in a few words, you must promise not to interrupt the thread of my sad tale with any question or remark; for the moment you do so, my narrative will end.'

These words recalled to Don Quixote's mind that tale of his squire's which had been broken off because he had not kept count of the number of goats which had crossed the river. But to return to the Ragged Knight, he went on: 'This warning I give you because I should like to pass briefly over the story of my misfortunes. For to recall them to mind is only to add to them; and the less questions you ask me the quicker I shall come to the end of my tale. Yet I will not leave out anything of importance, as it is my wish to satisfy your curiosity completely.'

Don Quixote promised in the name of the rest not to interrupt him, and with this assurance the Ragged One began: 'My name is Cardenio; my birthplace one of the finest cities here in Andalusia; my family noble; my parents rich; my misfortunes so great that my parents were forced to weep and my relations to grieve for them, being unable to relieve them for all their wealth. For fortune's goods can do little to remedy misfortunes willed by Heaven. There dwelt in this same land a heaven in which Love had placed all the glory I could desire; such is the beauty of Lucinda, a maiden as noble and rich as I but more fortunate, and less firm in her faith than love so honest as mine deserved. This Lucinda I loved, desired, and adored from my tenderest and earliest years, and she loved me with the innocence and seriousness of her youth. Our parents knew of our feelings, and were not disturbed by them, for they clearly saw that their development could lead only to marriage, which the equality of our blood and fortune seemed almost to demand. As we grew older our love grew also, till Lucinda's father thought himself obliged, for prudence' sake, to deny me the house, in this closely imitating the parents of that Thisbe so much sung of by poets. Now this denial added flame to fire and love to love; for although they silenced our tongues, they could not stop our pens, which are

more freely used than tongues to express the heart's secrets to the
beloved; since often the presence of the loved one confuses and
silences the most resolute heart and the boldest tongue. Heavens,
how many letters I wrote her! What delicate and modest replies I
received! How many songs and love-poems I penned, in which my
soul declared and revealed its feelings, painted its warm desires,
went over its memories and refreshed its passion! In the end, my
patience exhausted and my heart consumed with desire to see her, I
determined to put into effect what seemed to me the most suitable
plan for gaining my desired and deserved prize. This was to ask her
father for her hand in lawful marriage, which I did.

'He replied by thanking me for the honour I intended him, and
for wishing to honour myself with his beloved treasure; but that
as my father was alive, it was properly his duty to make this request,
for Lucinda was no woman to be taken or given in an underhand
way without his wish and approval. I thanked him for his kindness,
thinking that he was right in what he said, and that my father would
consent to my proposal as soon as I told him of it. Therefore I immediately went to inform him of my desires. But when I entered the
room where he was, I found him with an open letter in his hand,
which he passed to me before I had uttered a word, saying: "You
will see from this latter, Cardenio, that Duke Richard wishes to do
you a service."

' This Duke Richard, you must know, gentlemen, is a grandee of
Spain, whose estate lies in the richest part of Andalusia. I took and
read the letter, which was so complimentary that even I thought my
father would be wrong not to accept his request that I should be
sent to him immediately. He wanted me as a companion – not
as a servant – for his eldest son, and promised to put me in a
position corresponding to his high opinion of me. I read the letter
and was dumbfounded as I read. But I was even more astonished to
hear my father say: "You will set out the day after to-morrow,
Cardenio, and do as the Duke wishes. Give thanks to God for
opening you a way to the fortune I know you deserve." And he
added some fatherly advice.

'The day came for my departure. I talked one night with Lucinda; I told her all that had happened, and told her father too.
I begged him to wait for a few days and postpone the settling of her

marriage until I saw what Duke Richard wanted of me. He made me a promise, and she confirmed it with innumerable vows, made between fits of fainting. Then at last I reached Duke Richard's, and was so well received and treated that envy soon began to do its work. His old servants considered every sign of favour the Duke made me as prejudicial to themselves. But one person was most delighted at my coming, the Duke's second son Ferdinand, a gay lad with a charming, liberal and amorous disposition. In a very short time he was so eager for my friendship that everyone noticed it; but although his elder brother liked me and was kind to me, he did not show me the same extreme affection and attention as did Ferdinand.

'Now as there are no secrets between friends, and the favour which Ferdinand showed me soon ceased to be favour and turned to friendship, he told me all that was in his mind, and particularly of a love affair which was causing him some little anxiety. He was in love with the daughter of a farmer, a tenant of his father's. Her parents were rich, and she was so beautiful, so modest, discreet, and virtuous that no one of her acquaintance could decide in which of these qualities she was richest. The charms of the fair farmer's daughter reduced Ferdinand to such straits that he decided to gratify his desires and overcome her virtue by a promise of marriage, knowing that it would be impossible to succeed by any other means. Prompted by friendship, I employed the best arguments I knew and warned him as strongly as I could in an endeavour to dissuade him from his purpose. But, finding it was all in vain, I decided to inform his father, the Duke, of the matter. Now Ferdinand was astute and intelligent enough to suspect and fear that; for it was obvious to him that, as a faithful servant, I could not conceal from my Lord the Duke a matter so prejudicial to his honour. So, to put me off the scent, he told me that the only means he could find of getting the beauty who so enthralled him out of his mind was to go away for a few months; and he proposed that we should spend this time together at my father's, and that he should tell the Duke by way of excuse that his journey to my city was to purchase horses, for the best in the world are bred there.

'No sooner had he made this suggestion than my own love prompted me to welcome it as the best imaginable solution, though I should have done so if it had been less good, for I saw what a rare opportunity it gave me of seeing my Lucinda again. So in this frame of mind I approved his scheme and encouraged his plan, advising him to put it into execution at the very earliest opportunity, for absence would certainly have its effect, however strong his affections.

'Now, at the time when he told me this plan, as it came out afterwards, he had already enjoyed the farmer's daughter under promise of marriage, and was waiting for an opportunity of safely divulging the matter. For he was afraid of what the Duke, his father, might do when he came to know of his infatuation. Now, as a lad's love is for the most part not love but lust and, aiming only at gratification, dies when it attains its purpose, what appears to be love then weakening, since it cannot persist beyond its natural limits, which limits do not exist in true love – I mean to say that as soon as Don Ferdinand had enjoyed the farmer's daughter his desires grew calm and his ardour cooled, so that if at first he had pretended that he wanted to go away in order to relieve his passion, now he was really anxious to go to avoid fulfilling his promise.

'The Duke gave him permission and bade me go with him. We came to my city, and my father gave him the reception due to his rank. Presently I visited Lucinda; my passion came to life, although in fact it had been neither dead nor dull and, to my undoing, I spoke of it to Don Ferdinand, for I thought that his great friendship for me forbade my keeping any secrets from him. I praised Lucinda's beauty, her grace and wit, so much so that my praise roused a desire in him to see a maiden endowed with such virtues. To my own misfortune I yielded to him, and let him see her one night by the light of a candle at a window through which it was our habit to talk.

'She was dressed in a loose wrap, looking so beautiful that he forgot all the beauties he had ever seen. He was struck dumb; he lost his senses; he was spellbound; and, in short, fell deeply in love, as you will see in the course of the tale of my misfortunes. And the more to inflame his passions, which he concealed from me but revealed to God in solitude, he chanced one day upon a letter of hers, begging me to ask her father for her hand in marriage, a letter so sensible, so modest, and so full of love, that on reading it he said that in Lucinda alone were united all the charms of beauty and understanding which were the portions of all the other women in the world. It is true, as I confess now, that though I acknowledged the justice of Ferdinand's praise, it vexed me to hear this eulogy from his mouth, and I began to grow fearful and jealous of him; for there was not a moment when he did not want to talk of Lucinda, and he would start the conversation himself, even if he had to drag her in by the hair. This awoke a vague jealousy in me; not that I had any reason to fear a change in Lucinda's faith and virtue, yet, for all that, my fate made me dread the very danger against which she seemed to secure me. Don Ferdinand always tried to read the letters I sent her and her replies. He pretended to derive great pleasure from our turns of phrase. Now Lucinda happened to ask me for a book of chivalry to read, one which she was very fond of. It was *Amadis of Gaul* ...'

No sooner did Don Quixote hear mention of a book of chivalry than he exclaimed: 'If you had told me, sir, at the beginning of your story that the lady Lucinda was fond of books of chivalry, you would have needed no further amplification to convince me of the sublimity of her understanding. For it would not have been as excellent as you, sir, have described it, if she had lacked a taste for such delightful reading. So that there is no need to waste more words in declaring to me her beauty, worth and understanding; for at the mere mention of this passion of hers I pronounce her the loveliest and most intelligent woman in the world. But I could have wished, sir, that you had sent her with *Amadis of Gaul* the good *Sir Rugel of Greece*, for I know that the lady Lucinda would be delighted with Daraida and Garaya, and with the wit of the shepherd Darinel, and with those admirable lines in his bucolics, sung and performed by him with such charm, wit and freedom. But a time may come for remedying this omission. It can be amended whenever you care to come with me to my village, sir. For there I can show you more than three hundred books, which are the treasure of my heart and the delight of my life: — though now it occurs to me that I have none, thanks to the malice of evil and envious enchanters. Pardon me, sir, for having broken our promise not to interrupt your story; but when I hear of matters of chivalry and of knights errant, I can no more prevent myself from talking of them than the sun's rays can help giving heat, or the moon's moisture. So excuse me, and go on, for that is the important thing now.'

Whilst Don Quixote was saying all this, Cardenio let his head fall on his breast, seemingly plunged in deep thought; and although the knight twice asked him to go on with his story, he neither raised his head nor answered a word. But at the end of a good while he looked up and said: 'One thing I cannot get out of my mind, and no one in the world can persuade me or convince me otherwise – indeed, anyone holding the contrary opinion would be an idiot. That arch-scoundrel Master Elisabat was Queen Madasima's lover.'

'That is false, I swear,' replied Don Quixote in great wrath, bursting out in his usual fashion, 'and a most malicious, or rather villainous calumny. Queen Madasima was a very noble lady, and it is not to be supposed that so great a princess would take a quack for a lover. Whoever says otherwise lies like an arrant scoundrel, and I will make him acknowledge it, on foot or horse, armed or unarmed, by night or day, or however he will.'

Cardenio sat staring at him very attentively. For a fit of madness had come on him and he was in no state to continue his tale; nor would Don Quixote have listened if he had, so disgusted was he by what he had heard concerning Madasima. It was extraordinary to see him take her part as though she were in fact his real and natural mistress; such was the power his unholy books had over him.

But, as I said, Cardenio was now mad, and when he heard himself called a liar and a scoundrel and other such names, he took the joke in bad part. In fact he picked up a stone from beside him, and hit Don Quixote so hard on the chest that he knocked him backwards. When Sancho Panza saw his master thus treated, he attacked the madman with clenched fists. But the Ragged Knight gave him such a reception that he had him stretched at his feet at the first blow, after which he got on top of him and trampled his ribs to his heart's content. The goatherd, who tried to defend him, met with the same fate, and after Cardenio had threshed and bruised them all, he left them and retired quietly to his mountain ambush.

Sancho got up and, furious at his undeserved beating, ran to take vengeance on the goatherd, saying that it was all his fault for not having advised them that the man was subject to fits of madness; for had they known it, they would have been prepared to defend themselves. The goatherd replied that he had told them, and it was not his fault if Sancho had not heard. Sancho argued; the goatherd replied; and the dispute ended in their grasping each other's beards and punching each other so hard that they would have thrashed one another to pulp if Don Quixote had not interposed. But Sancho still kept a tight hold on the goatherd as he exclaimed:

'Leave me alone, Sir Knight of the Sad Countenance; for he's a peasant like me and no knight, and I can safely avenge the injury he has done me by fighting him hand to hand, like a man of honour.'

'That is true,' said Don Quixote. 'But I know that he is not to blame for what happened.'

With this he pacified them, and again asked the goatherd if it would be possible to find Cardenio, for he was most anxious to hear the end of his story. The herdsman repeated, as he had done before, that there was no knowing for certain where Cardenio had his lair; but if Don Quixote were to wander much about the district he would not fail to find him, sane or mad.

Chapter XXV. *Of the Strange Things which happened to the valorous Knight of La Mancha in the Sierra Morena, and of his Imitation of the Penance of Beltenebros.*

DON QUIXOTE took leave of the goatherd and, remounting Rocinante bade Sancho follow him, which he did on his ass,* most unwillingly. They then went slowly on into the most desolate part of the mountains. Sancho all the while was dying to talk to his master, but not wishing to disobey his orders, waited for him to start the conversation. At last, however, unable to bear the long silence, he said:

'Don Quixote, please give me your blessing and my liberty, for I want to go back home now to my wife and my children. I shall at least be able to talk to them as much as I like. For your worship's wanting me to ride through these lonely parts day and night and never to speak to you when I've a mind to, is like burying me alive. If nature allowed animals to talk, as they did in Aesop's days, it wouldn't be so bad. Then I could talk to my ass about anything I like, and forget my bad luck that way. For it's hard, and more than patience can bear, to spend all one's life looking for adventures and finding nothing but kicks and blanket-tossings, brick-battings and

---

* The ass is now Sancho's again, and Cervantes has forgotten its theft by Gines.

beatings, and still to have to keep one's mouth tight shut and not dare to say what's in one's heart, just as if one were dumb.'

'I understand you, Sancho,' replied Don Quixote. 'You are dying for me to raise the prohibition I have imposed on your tongue. Consider it raised and say what you will, on condition this licence lasts only so long as we are travelling in these mountains.'

'Very well,' said Sancho. 'Let me talk now, for God knows what will come afterwards; and now, to begin to take advantage of your permission, I should like to ask what made your worship stand up so warmly for that Queen Magimasa, or whatever she's called. What did it matter if that abbot was her friend or not? For if your worship had let it pass, since you were not her judge, I really think that the madman would have gone on with his story, and we should have been spared the stone and the kicks, and more than half a dozen back-handers in the face.'

'I swear, Sancho,' replied Don Quixote, 'that if you knew, as I know, what a great and honourable lady Queen Madasima was, you would certainly say that I showed great patience in not smashing the face that mouthed such blasphemies. For it is great blasphemy to say or to think that a Queen could take a barber-surgeon for a lover. The truth of the story is that this Master Elisabat the madman spoke of was a very wise man and a very good counsellor, and served the Queen as tutor and physician; but to think that she was his lover is a folly deserving the severest punishment. Yet you must see that Cardenio did not know what he was saying; for you must remember that he was already out of his mind when he said it.'

'That's what I say,' answered Sancho, 'and you oughtn't to have taken any notice of what a madman said. What's more, if good luck had not come to your worship's aid, and the stone had struck your head instead of your chest, we should have been in a fine way for standing up for that great lady, God damn her. And just think, Cardenio would have got off scot-free as a madman.'

'Against all men, sane or mad,' said Don Quixote, 'it is every knight errant's duty to defend the honour of all women of whatever rank; particularly of queens as exalted and virtuous as Queen Madasima was. I have a particular regard for her on account of her good qualities; for not only was she very beautiful but prudent too, and very patient in her countless misfortunes; and the advice and company of Master Elisabat were of great advantage and comfort to her, and enabled her to bear her trials with prudence and patience. That is what made the ignorant and malicious rabble say and think that she was his mistress; and they lie, I say again, and two hundred times more I repeat that every one of them who thinks so or says so lies.'

'I don't say so, nor think so,' replied Sancho. 'There let it rest. Let them eat the lie and swallow it with their bread. Whether the two were lovers or no, they'll have accounted to God for it by now. I have my own fish to fry. I know nothing. I'm not one to pry into other people's lives. It's no good lying about the price; your purse always knows better. What's more, I was born naked and naked I am now; I neither lose nor win. Suppose they were lovers, what's that to me? Plenty of people expect to find bacon where there's not so much as a hook to hang it on. Who can hedge in the cuckoo? Especially as God Himself is not spared.'

'Good Lord!' cried Don Quixote, 'what a string of nonsense, Sancho! What have all these proverbs to do with the matter we were discussing? For Heaven's sake be quiet, and in future see you spur your ass and do not interfere with what does not concern you. And get it into your five senses that all my actions, past, present and future, are very well based in reason and conform in every way to the rules of chivalry. For I know these rules better than any knights who have ever professed them in the world.'

'Sir,' replied Sancho, 'is it a good rule of chivalry for us to get lost looking for a madman in these mountains, where there isn't a road or a track? And when we find him, perhaps he'll choose to finish the job he has begun, – not his story, but breaking your head and my ribs till there isn't a whole bone left in our bodies.'

'Once more, Sancho, be quiet,' exclaimed Don Quixote, 'for I would have you know that it is not only my wish to find the madman that draws me to these parts, but my intention of performing a deed here which will gain me perpetual renown and glory throughout all the known world. It shall be such a deed that by it I shall attain the utmost perfection and renown of which a knight errant is capable.'

'And is this deed very perilous?' asked Sancho Panza.

'No,' replied the Knight of the Sad Countenance, 'although the dice may so fall that we throw a blank instead of a double. But everything depends on your diligence.'

'On my diligence?' repeated Sancho.

'Yes,' said Don Quixote, 'because if you come back quickly from the place I mean to send you to, my penance will be soon over and my glory will speedily begin. But it is not right to keep you longer in suspense, hanging on the purport of my words. So I would have you know, Sancho, that the famous Amadis of Gaul was one of the most perfect of knights errant. I was wrong to say *one*; he was the sole, the first, the unique, the prince of all there were in the world in his day. A fig for Sir Belianis and for all who claimed to be in any respect his equal! For I swear they are mistaken. What is more I say that when any painter wishes to win fame in his art, he endeavours to copy the pictures of the most excellent painters he knows; and the same rule obtains for all professions and pursuits of importance that serve to adorn the commonwealth. So what any man who wants a reputation for prudence and patience must do, and does, is to imitate Ulysses, in whose person and labours Homer paints for us a lively picture of prudence and patience; just as Virgil shows us in the person of Aeneas the virtue of a dutiful son and the sagacity of a brave and skilful captain. They do not paint them or describe them as they were, but as they should have been, to serve as examples of their virtues for future generations. In the same way Amadis was the pole-star, the morning star, the sun of all valiant knights and lovers, and all of us who ride beneath the banner of love and chivalry should imitate him. This being the case, Sancho my friend, I conclude that the knight errant who best copies him will attain most nearly to the perfection of chivalry. Now one of the ways in which this knight most clearly showed his wisdom, virtue, valour, patience, steadfastness and love was when, scorned by his lady Oriana, he retired to do penance on the Bare Rock, changing his name to Beltenebros, a name most certainly significant and suitable to the life which he had voluntarily chosen. Therefore, as it is easier for me to imitate him in this way than in cleaving giants, beheading serpents, killing dragons, routing armies, shattering fleets, and breaking spells; and since this place is so fitting for such a purpose, there is no reason for me to let this opportunity pass now that it so conveniently offers me the forelock.'

'What is it then that your worship really means to do in this out-of-the-way place?' asked Sancho.

'Have I not told you,' replied Don Quixote, 'that I intend to imitate Amadis, and to act here the desperate, raving, furious lover; at the same time following the example of the valiant Sir Roland when he found by a spring evidence that the fair Angelica had dishonoured herself with Medoro, for grief at which he turned mad, tore up trees, muddied the waters of the clear springs, killed shepherds, destroyed flocks, fired cottages, pulled down houses, dragged off mares, and performed a hundred thousand extravagant feats, which deserve eternal fame and remembrance? Now although I do not intend to imitate Roland, or Orlando, or Rotolando – for he bore all those names – exactly in all the mad things he did, said and thought, I will sketch them in as best I can, in what appear to me to be their essentials. But perhaps I shall come to be content to imitate Amadis alone, for he attained unrivalled fame by a madness that lay not in wild deeds but in tears and grief.'

'It seems to me,' said Sancho, 'that the knights who did things like that were provoked and had a reason for their follies and penances. But what reason has your worship for going mad? What lady has scorned you, or what evidence have you found that the lady Dulcinea del Toboso has done anything she shouldn't with Moor or Christian?'

'That is the point,' replied Don Quixote, 'and in that lies the beauty of my plan. A knight errant who turns mad for a reason deserves neither merit nor thanks. The thing is to do it without cause; and then my lady can guess what I would do in the wet if I do all this in the dry. What is more, I have sufficient reason in my long absence from my ever supreme mistress Dulcinea del Toboso. For, as you heard that shepherd Ambrosio say the other day, the absent feel and fear every ill. So, friend Sancho, do not waste time advising me to give up so rare, so happy, and so unprecedented an imitation. I am mad, and mad I must be till you come back with the reply to a letter which I intend to send by you to my lady Dulcinea. If it proves such as my fidelity deserves, my raving and my penance will be ended; but if it be unfavourable I shall be mad in earnest, and when I am I shall feel nothing. So, whichever way she replies, I shall be done with the conflict and distress in which you will leave me. For if it is good tidings you bring me, I shall enjoy them in my right mind; and if it is evil, I shall not feel them, being mad. But tell me, Sancho, have you taken good care of Mambrino's helmet? For I saw you pick it up from the ground when that ungrateful wretch tried to destroy it, though he could not do so – and that shows how finely it was tempered.'

To which Sancho replied: 'In God's name, Sir Knight of the Sad Countenance, I cannot endure or bear with patience some of the things your worship says. They make me think that all you tell me about chivalries and winning kingdoms and empires, and giving isles and doing other favours and mighty deeds, as knights errant do, must be just wind and lies, and all friction or fiction or whatever you call it. For to hear your worship say that a barber's basin is Mambrino's helmet, and persist in that error for more than four days, what can one think? Only that a man who persists in saying a thing like that must be cracked in the brain. I have the basin in the bag, all dented, and I'm taking it home to mend it and to use it for shaving, if God is so gracious as to let me live with my wife and children one day.'

'Look you, Sancho, by the same oath as you swore just now, I swear,' said Don Quixote, 'that you have less brains than any squire has or ever had in the whole world. Is it possible that all this while you have been with me you have not discovered that everything to do with knights errant appears to be chimaera, folly and nonsense, and to go all contrariwise? This is not really the case, but there is a crew of enchanters always amongst us who change and alter all our deeds, and transform them according to their pleasure and their desire either to favour us or injure us. So what seems to you to be a barber's basin appears to me to be Mambrino's helmet, and to another as something else. It shows a rare foresight in the sage who is on my side to make what is really and truly Mambrino's helmet seem to everyone a basin. For, as it is of such great value, the whole world would persecute me in order to get it from me. However, as they see that it is nothing more than a barber's basin, they do not trouble about it, as was evident in the case of the wretch who tried to destroy it and left it behind him on the ground; for I promise you that if he had recognized it he would never have left it there. Take care of it, my friend. I do not need it for the present. On the contrary, I must strip off all my armour and be naked as I was born; that is, if I decide to imitate Roland in my penance rather than Amadis.'

Deep in this conversation they came to the foot of a high mountain which stood alone, almost as though it had been cut off from the many which surrounded it. At its foot ran a gentle stream, encircling a meadow so green and luxuriant that it pleased the eyes of all who saw it. There were many woodland trees there, and some shrubs and flowers that made the place pleasant. This site the Knight of the Sad Countenance chose for the performance of his penance, and at the sight of it he began to speak aloud, as if he were out of his wits:

'This is the place, Heavens, where I select and choose to bewail the misfortune into which you yourselves have plunged me. This is the spot where the moisture from my eyes will swell the waters of this little stream, and my deep and incessant sighs perpetually stir the leaves of these mountain trees, in testimony and sign of the grief my tortured heart endures. On you, whoever you may be, rustic deities who have your abode in this inhospitable spot, hear the plaints of this ill-starred lover, whom long absence and some fancied jealousy have brought to mourn among these rugged wastes, and to complain of the cruel nature of that ungrateful beauty, the sum and perfection of all human loveliness! O you, wood-nymphs and dryads, whose custom it is to haunt the mountain thickets, may the swift and sensual satyrs, who love you in vain, never disturb your sweet quiet, that you may aid me to lament my ill fortune, or at least not grow weary of hearing it! O Dulcinea del Toboso, day of my night, glory of my grief, pole-star of my journeys, star of my fate, may Heaven grant you all that you pray for in full measure. Consider now the place and the condition to which your absence has brought me, and grant me in return such reward as my fidelity deserves! O solitary trees, which henceforth must be the companions of my solitude, give me some sign, by the gentle stirring of your branches, that my presence does not offend you! And you, my squire, pleasing companion of my prosperous and adverse fortunes, impress on your memory what you will see me do here, so that you may tell and recite it to the sole cause of it all!'

As he spoke, he dismounted from Rocinante and, stripping him in an instant of bridle and saddle, gave him a slap on the haunches, saying: 'He who lacks liberty bestows it on you, O steed as excellent in your performance as you are unfortunate in your fate! Go where you will; for on your forehead it is written that not Astolfo's Hippogriff, nor yet the famous Frontino which cost Bradamante so dear, was your equal in speed.'

At this Sancho put in: – 'God bless the man who has saved us the trouble of unharnessing Dapple.* He wouldn't have gone short of smacks or speeches in his praise. Though if he were here I would let nobody take off his harness. There would be no reason for it, seeing that the general rules about people in love and in despair were no concern of his, since his master was not one of them. For when it pleased God I was his master. Truly, Sir Knight of the Sad Countenance, if my journey and your worship's madness are going to be in real earnest, it would be a good thing to saddle Rocinante again to serve instead of the ass, for that'll save me time on my double journey. If I do it on foot I don't know when I shall get there or when I shall get back, for I am a very poor walker indeed.'

'Very well, Sancho,' replied Don Quixote, 'it shall be as you wish. Yours does not seem a bad plan to me. And you shall leave in three days' time, for I want you in the interval to observe all that I do and say for her sake. Then you will be able to report everything to her.'

'Well, what more have I to see than I've seen already?' asked Sancho.

'A great deal you know about the story!' replied Don Quixote. 'There still remains the tearing of my garments, the scattering of my arms, the running of my head against the rocks, and other things of the kind which will astonish you.'

'For God's sake,' cried Sancho, 'take care, your worship, how you go hitting your head, for you might strike a rock in such a place that you would put paid to the whole business of this penance with the first blow. But since your worship thinks that these knocks on the head are necessary, and this job can't be done without them, it's my opinion that you ought to be content, since this is all a pretence and a counterfeit and a joke, – you ought to be content, I say, with hitting your head on the water, or on something soft like cot-

* Who is apparently lost again, and remains so until recovered.

ton, and leave the rest to me. For I'll tell my lady that your worship dashed your head against a pointed rock harder than a diamond.'

'I thank you for your kind intentions, friend Sancho,' replied Don Quixote; 'but I would have you know that all these things which I am doing are not in jest, but very much in earnest. Otherwise I should be infringing the laws of chivalry, which bid us tell no lie on pain of degradation; and to do one thing instead of another is the same as a lie. Therefore the blows on the head must be real, hard and efficacious, without any sophistry or deception; and you will have to leave me some lint to heal me since, as ill-luck would have it, we have lost our balsam.'

'Losing the ass was worse,' replied Sancho, 'for with him we lost the lint and all. But please, your worship, don't remind me of that accursed drink, for not only my stomach but my very soul turns over at the mere mention of it. As for the three days allowed me for seeing your mad pranks, please reckon them as already passed. For I take everything you've said for granted and I'll tell wonders to my lady. So write the letter and send me off immediately, for I'm dearly longing to come back and rescue your worship from this purgatory I'm leaving you in.'

'Do you call it purgatory, Sancho?' asked Don Quixote. 'You would do better to call it hell, or even worse, if there is anything worse.'

'For him that's in hell,' replied Sancho, '*nulla est retentio*, as I've heard say.'

'I do not understand what you mean by *retentio*,' said Don Quixote.

'*Retentio*,' answered Sancho, 'means that once a man is in hell he never gets out, and can't. But it'll be the reverse with your worship, or I'll wear out my heels – that is, if I take spurs to liven up Rocinante. Let me once get to El Toboso and into the presence of my lady Dulcinea, and I'll tell her such stories of the follies and mad pranks – for they're all the same – which you have done and are still doing that I'll make her suppler than a glove, even if I find her harder than a cork-tree. Then I'll come back with her sweet and honeyed answer, riding the air like a wizard, and get your worship out of this purgatory, which looks like hell and isn't. For you have a hope of getting out, and that, as I said, people who are in hell haven't got. I don't think your worship will contradict me.'

'That is the truth,' said the Knight of the Sad Countenance, 'but how shall we manage to write the letter?'

'And the bills of asses as well,' added Sancho.

'It will all be included,' said Don Quixote; 'and since there is no paper, it will be as well to write it as the ancients did, on the leaves of trees or on wax tablets; although they would be as difficult to find now as paper. But I have just thought of a good – no, of an excellent – place to write it, and that is in the little note-book which was Cardenio's. Then you can see that it is copied on to paper in a good hand, at the first village you come to in which there is a school-master; or, failing that, a parish clerk will transcribe it for you. But do not give it to a lawyer's clerk to write, for they use a legal hand that Satan himself will not understand.'

'But what's to be done about the signature?' asked Sancho.

'Amadis' letters were never signed,' replied Don Quixote.

'That's all very well,' replied Sancho, 'but the order for the asses must have a signature, or if it is copied they will say that the signature is false, and I shall be left without the ass-colts.'

'The order will be signed in the little note-book itself, so that when my niece sees it she will make no difficulty about complying with it. As for the love-letter, you will put by way of signature: "*Yours till death, The Knight of the Sad Countenance*". It will make no great difference that it is in a strange hand since, as far as I remember, Dulcinea cannot write or read, and she has never seen a letter or writing of mine in all her life. For our love has always been platonic, and never gone farther than a modest glance. And even that so occasionally that I can truly swear that in all the twelve years I have loved her more than the light of these eyes which the earth will one day devour, I have not seen her four times. And perhaps on those four occasions she did not even once notice that I was looking at her; such is the reserve and seclusion in which her father, Lorenzo Corchuelo, and her mother, Aldonza Nogales, have brought her up.'

'Well, well!' exclaimed Sancho. 'So Lorenzo Corchuelo's daughter is the lady Dulcinea del Toboso, otherwise called Aldonza Lorenzo?'

'She is,' said Don Quixote, 'and she it is who deserves to be mistress of all the world.'

'I know her well,' said Sancho, 'and I can tell you that she pitches a bar as well as the strongest lad in the whole village. Praise be to God! She's a brawny girl, well built and tall and sturdy, and she will know how to keep her chin out of the mud with any knight errant who ever has her for his mistress. O the wench, what muscles she's got, and what a pair of lungs! I remember one day she went up the village belfry to call in some of their lads who were working in a fallow field of her father's, and they could hear her as plainly as if they had been at the foot of the tower, although they were nearly two miles away. And the great thing about her is that she's not a bit shy. There's a good deal of the court-lady about her too, for she has a crack with everybody, and makes a joke and a mock of them all. I tell you, Sir Knight of the Sad Countenance, that you're not only quite right to play your mad pranks for her, but you've good reason to despair and hang yourself for her as well. Indeed any one who knows will say you acted better then well, even though the Devil himself should carry you off afterwards. Oh, I wish I were on the road only for the joy of seeing her. I haven't set eyes on her for ever so long. She must be changed, too, for always trudging about the fields in sun and wind greatly spoils a woman's looks. But I must confess to you, Don Quixote, that I have been very much mistaken on one point up to now. I really and truly thought that the lady Dulcinea must be some princess your worship was in love with, or at least a person of quality, to deserve the rich presents you sent her, the Basque and the galley-slaves, for instance, and all the other things you must have won in all the victories your worship must have had before I was your squire. But when you come to think of it, what good is it to the lady Aldonza Lorenzo, I mean the lady Dulcinea del Toboso, to have all the knights you have conquered and sent to her, or all that you ever will send, going down on their knees before her? Just when they arrive she'll very likely be dressing flax or threshing in the barn. Then they'll be confused at seeing her, and she'll burst out laughing and not think much of your present.'

'I have told you very often before now, Sancho,' said Don Quixote, 'that you are a very great babbler. Yet although your wits are blunt your remarks sometimes sting. But just to prove your foolishness and my wisdom, I want you to listen to a little story.

'Once upon a time there was a beautiful widow, young, gay, rich and not a bit prudish, who fell in love with a stout and lusty young lay-brother. His superior heard of it and addressed the good widow one day by way of brotherly reproof: "I am astonished, madam," he said, "and with good reason, that a woman of your quality, beautiful and rich as you are, should have fallen in love with such a coarse, low, ignorant fellow as So-and-So, seeing that we have so many graduates, divinity students, and theologians in this house, and you could pick and choose any of them like pears, and say: I like this one, and not that one." But she answered most gaily and impudently: "You are much mistaken, my dear sir, and very old-fashioned in your ideas, if you think that I have made a bad choice in that fellow, idiot though he may seem, seeing that for all I want of him he knows as much philosophy as Aristotle, and more." So, Sancho, for what I want of Dulcinea del Toboso she is as good as the greatest princess in the land. For not all those poets who praise ladies under names which they choose so freely, really have such mistresses. Do you think that the Amaryllises, the Phyllises, Sylvias, Dianas, Galateas, Phyllidas, and all the rest that books and ballads and barbers' shops and theatres are so full of, were really flesh-and-blood ladies, and the mistresses of the writers who wrote about them? Not a bit of it. Most of them were invented to serve as subjects for verses, and so that the poets might be taken for lovers, or men capable of being so. I am quite satisfied, therefore, to imagine and believe that the good Aldonza Lorenzo is lovely and virtuous; her family does not matter a bit, for no one will inquire into that for the purpose of investing her with any order and, for my part, I think of her as the greatest princess in the world. For you must know, Sancho, if you do not know it already, that two things arouse love more than all others. They are great beauty and a good name; and these two qualities are present in Dulcinea to a surpassing degree; for in beauty she has no rival, and few can equal her in good name. To make an end of the matter, I imagine all I say to be true, neither more nor less, and in my imagination I draw her as I would have her be, both as to her beauty and her rank; unequalled by Helen, unrivalled by Lucretia, or any other famous woman of antiquity, Greek, Barbarian, or Roman. Let anyone say what he likes, for though the ignorant may reproach me for it, men of judgement will not condemn me.'

'What I say is that your worship's always right,' replied Sancho, 'and I'm an ass. But I don't know how that word ass comes to my lips, for one shouldn't talk of halters in the hanged man's house. But give me the letter and good-bye, for I'm off.'

Don Quixote took out the note-book and, drawing a little aside, very calmly set about writing the letter. And when he had finished it he called Sancho, saying that he wanted to read it to him so that he might commit it to memory in case he were to lose it on the way; for with his bad luck anything might happen.

To which Sancho replied: 'Write it two or three times there in the book, your worship, and give it to me. I will carry it very carefully. But it would be mad to think of my learning it by heart, for my memory's so bad that I often forget my own name. Yet read it to me all the same, your worship. I shall enjoy hearing it. It must be as good as a bit of print.'

'Listen; it goes like this,' said Don Quixote:

Don Quixote's letter to Dulcinea del Toboso.

Sovereign and sublime lady,

One stabbed by the dart of absence and pierced to the heart's core wishes you, sweetest Dulcinea del Toboso, the health which he does not himself enjoy. If your beauty scorns me, if your merit acts to my disadvantage, if you disdain my anguish, although inured to suffering I shall be ill able to bear an affliction which is not only severe but of very long duration. My good squire Sancho will give you a full account, O ungrateful beauty and beloved enemy, of the state to which I am reduced for your sake. If it be your pleasure to relieve me, I am yours. If not, do as you will; for by my death I shall have satisfied your cruelty and my passion.

Yours till death,
The Knight of the Sad Countenance.

'God bless my father!' cried Sancho on hearing the letter. 'It's the finest thing I've ever heard! I'll be blowed if your worship doesn't say just what you want to! And how well the *Knight of the*

Sad Countenance fits into the signature. Your worship's the Devil himself, I swear, and there's nothing you don't know.'

'You have to know everything,' replied Don Quixote, 'in the profession I follow.'

'Well, then,' said Sancho, 'put the order for the three colts on the other side of the leaf, sir, and sign it very clearly so that they'll know your hand when they see it.'

'So I will,' answered Don Quixote. And when he had written it, he read it aloud as follows:

'At sight of this my first bill of asses, dear niece, give order that three out of the five which I left at home in your charge be given to Sancho Panza, my squire. Which three colts I order to be delivered in payment for the like amount counted and received of him here; and this with his receipt shall be your discharge. Given in the heart of the Sierra Morena, on the twenty-second of August of the current year.'

'That's right,' said Sancho. 'Please sign it, your worship.'

'There is no need to sign it,' said Don Quixote. 'I need only put my flourish, for that is the same as a signature and will be good enough for three asses, or even for three hundred.'

'I trust your worship,' replied Sancho. 'Now let me go and saddle Rocinante. And get ready, sir, to give me your blessing, for I'm going now. I shan't wait to see the pranks your worship's going to perform, but I'll tell her I saw you do so many that she'll be satisfied.'

'At least I want you to see me naked, Sancho, and performing a dozen wild pranks or so. I will run through them in less than half an hour; and when you have seen them with your own eyes you can safely swear to any others that you may care to add. You will not tell her of as many as I mean to perform, I promise you.'

'For God's sake, dear master, don't make me see you naked. It'll grieve me so that I shan't be able to stop crying, and my head is so bad from the tears I shed last night for Dapple that I'm in no condition for fresh weeping. If your worship wants me to see some of your mad pranks, do some in your clothes – but short ones, and only the most important. Though really I've no need of anything of the sort. For, as I said before, if I go now it'll hasten my return with the news your worship desires and deserves. That I will bring.

Otherwise let the lady Dulcinea look out. For if she doesn't reply as she should, I take my solemn oath that I'll kick and punch a kind answer out of her guts. Wouldn't it be a shame, indeed, for a famous knight errant like your worship to go mad without the least reason in the world, for a – . The lady had better not give me cause to say it or, by God, I'll blurt it out and let her have it wholesale, even though it spoils the market. I'm pretty good at that. She doesn't know me. If she did, I swear she would treat me with proper respect.'

'Really, Sancho,' said Don Quixote, 'as far as I can see, you are no saner than I am.'

'I'm not so mad as you,' replied Sancho, 'but I've a worse temper. But never mind that. What is your worship going to eat till I return? Are you going out on to the road to steal your food from the shepherds like Cardenio?'

'Do not be troubled on that score,' replied Don Quixote, 'for I should not eat anything but the herbs and the fruit which this meadow and these trees provide, even if I had it. The point of this business of mine lies in my fasting and in enduring all such hardships. Farewell, then.'

'But, your worship,' replied Sancho, 'do you know what I'm afraid of? Perhaps I mayn't be able to find my way back to the place I'm leaving you in. It's so out of the way.'

'Observe the landmarks, and I will try to remain near this spot,' said Don Quixote. 'And I will even take the precaution of climbing the highest of these crags to look out for you on your return. But your surest way of not missing me, and not getting lost yourself, will be for you to cut some of the broom that is so plentiful around here. Scatter it at intervals as you go till you get out to open country. The sprigs will serve as landmarks and signs for you to find me by when you come back, just like the thread in Theseus' labyrinth.'

'That's what I'll do,' replied Sancho Panza; and cutting some broom, he asked for his master's blessing and, not without many tears on both sides, took his leave. Then he mounted Rocinante, after receiving an especial charge from Don Quixote to take as good care of him as of his own person, and set out for the plain, scattering the broom sprigs at intervals, as his master had advised. So he rode off, despite Don Quixote's repeated requests that he should stay and watch him perform at least a couple of his wild pranks. But he had not gone above a hundred yards before he turned round and said:

'I think that you were quite right, your worship. It would be as well for me to watch, say, one of your mad pranks, so that I can swear I've seen you doing them with a safe conscience. Though I've seen you doing one very mad thing already, by staying here I mean.'

'Did not I tell you so?' said Don Quixote. 'Wait, Sancho, I will perform several as quickly as you can say a Credo.'

And hurriedly stripping off his breeches, he stood in his skin and his shirt. And then, without more ado, he took two leaps into the air, and twice turned head over heels, revealing such parts of his person as caused Sancho to turn Rocinante's head for fear he might see them a second time. So he departed fully satisfied that he could swear to his master's madness. And so we will leave him pursuing his journey till his return, which was speedy.

Chapter XXVI. *A Continuation of the Refinements practised by Don Quixote to express his love in the Sierra Morena.*

To continue the account of the actions of the Knight of the Sad Countenance once he was alone, our history tells that, after the falls or somersaults performed with his upper parts clothed and his lower parts naked, and after he had seen Sancho depart, unwilling to wait and see any more of his antics, Don Quixote climbed to the top of a high rock, and there turned his thoughts once more to a problem on which he had already pondered many times without reaching any conclusion. This was to decide which was the better and would stand him in the greater stead: to imitate Roland's downright madness or Amadis' melancholy moods. So, communing with himself, he argued: 'If Roland was as good a knight and as valiant as they all say, where is the wonder? since, after all, he was enchanted, and no one could kill him except by stabbing a long pin into the sole of his foot, which was the reason why he always wore shoes with seven iron soles. But these contrivances were of no avail against Bernardo del Carpio, who understood them, and throttled him with his bare hands at Roncesvalles. But, setting his bravery on one side, let us consider his madness, which certainly arose from the evidence he found beside the spring and the news which the shepherd gave him that Angelica had slept more than two afternoons with Medoro, a little curly-haired Moor and page to Agramante. Now if he believed that this was true, and that his lady had done him this foul wrong, it is not surprising that he went mad. But how can I imitate him in his madness without a similar cause? For I dare swear that my Dulcinea del Toboso has never seen a real Moor in his real Moorish dress in all her life, and that she is to-day as her mother bore her; and I should do her a grave injury were I to imagine otherwise and go mad, after the fashion of Roland the Furious.

' On the other hand, I know that Amadis of Gaul achieved an unrivalled reputation as a lover without ever losing his wits or having raving fits. For, as the history tells, on finding himself scorned by his lady Oriana, who had commanded him to appear no more in her presence until it was her pleasure, what he did was merely to retire to the Bare Rock in the company of a hermit; and there he wept his fill and commended himself to God so earnestly that Heaven succoured him in the midst of his greatest tribulation. Now if this is true – and it is – why do I now take pains to strip myself stark naked and give pain to these trees which have done me no harm, and disturb the clear water of these streams, which must give me drink when I am thirsty? All honour then to the memory of Amadis, and let him be the model, so far as it is possible, for Don Quixote de la Mancha, of whom it shall be said, as it was said of that other, that if he did not achieve great things he died attempting them. If I am not cast off and despised by Dulcinea del Toboso, let it suffice, as I have said, that I am absent from her. So now to work! Come into my mind, deeds of Amadis, and teach me where to begin to imitate you. I remember now that most of the time he prayed and commended his soul to God. But what shall I do for a rosary, for I have none?'

At this there came into his head a way of making one. He tore a great strip from the tail of his shirt, which was hanging down, and made eleven knots in it, one fatter than the rest; and this served him for a rosary all the time he was there, during which time he recited a million Ave Marias. But one thing did trouble him a great deal; there was no hermit in the district to hear his confession and administer consolation. He amused himself, however, by pacing about the little meadow, writing and carving in the bark of the trees and tracing on the fine sand a great number of verses, all suited to his sad state, and some of them in praise of Dulcinea. But the only ones which were found complete and could be deciphered afterwards were the following:

> Ye plants, ye herbs, and ye trees,
>   That flourish in this pleasant site
> In lofty and verdant degrees,
>   If my harms do you no delight,
> Hear my holy plaints, which are these.
> And let not my grief you molest,
>   Though it ever so feelingly went,
> Since here for to pay your rest,
> Don Quixote his tears hath addressed,
>   Dulcinea's lack to lament
>   del Toboso.
>
> In this very place doth abide
>   The loyallest lover and true,
> Who himself from his lady did hide,
>   But yet felt his sorrows anew,
> Not knowing whence they might proceed.
> Love doth him cruelly wrest
>   With a passion of evil descent,
> Which robbed Don Quixote of his rest,
> Till a keg with his tears was full pressed,
>   Dulcinea's lack to lament
>   del Toboso.
>
> In search of adventures he pined
>   Among these rough woods and rocks,
> Still cursing his pitiless mind;
>   For a wretch amidst bushes and brakes
> And crags will misfortunes find.
> And Love's whip gave it him hot,
>   Nor did his lashes relent
> Till he'd touched his tenderest spot,
> And drawn tears from poor Don Quixote,
>   Dulcinea's lack to lament
>   del Toboso.

His tacking of *del Toboso* on to Dulcinea's name made the discoverers of the poem laugh heartily. For they supposed Don Quixote must have imagined that the verse would not be understood unless he added del Toboso when he named Dulcinea; and they were right, as he afterwards confessed. He wrote a great number more. But, as has been said, only these three stanzas could be deciphered and were found complete. He passed the time in this writing, and in sighing and calling on the fauns and satyrs of those woods, on the nymphs of the streams and on mournful humid Echo, to listen, reply, and console him. He also searched for herbs to serve as food till Sancho's return. But if he had been away three weeks instead of three days, the Knight of the Sad Countenance would have been so wasted away that he would have been unrecognizable even by the mother who bore him.

But here it will be well to leave him, deep in his sighs and verses, to tell what happened to Sancho Panza on his mission. When he had emerged on to the highway, he set out to find the El Toboso road, and the following day reached the inn where he had suffered his misadventure with the blanket. Now no sooner did he catch sight of it than he felt himself once more sailing through the air; and he had no desire to enter, even though he had come at an hour when he properly should have gone in. For it was dinner-time and he was longing for something hot to eat, since it was a long time since he had eaten anything but cold fare. His inclinations brought him close to the inn, but he was still doubtful whether to enter or not at the moment when two persons came out and presently recognized him.

'Tell me, Master Licentiate,' one of them asked the other, 'isn't that man on the horse Sancho Panza who, so our adventurer's housekeeper told us, went off with her master as his squire?'

'Yes, it is,' replied the Licentiate, 'and that is our Don Quixote's horse.'

They knew him very well, for they were the priest and the barber of his own village, the same men who had performed the trial and general holocaust of the books. And once they were quite certain of Sancho Panza and Rocinante, being anxious for news of Don Quixote, the pair of them went up to him, and the priest called him by name and asked: 'Friend Sancho Panza, where did you leave your master?'

Sancho Panza recognized them at once, and decided not to tell them where his master was, nor to describe the state he had left him in. So he replied that Don Quixote was occupied in a certain place with a certain matter of great importance to him, which he could not reveal for all the eyes in his head.

'No, no, Sancho Panza,' said the barber; 'if you don't tell us where he is, we shall imagine – in fact we already do – that you've killed and robbed him, for here you come riding on his horse. Yes, you'll certainly have to produce the owner of that mount, or it'll be the worse for you.'

'You have no cause to use threats on me. I'm not the man to rob or murder anyone. Let every man die when fate decrees, or when God his Maker calls him. My master's in the heart of these mountains, doing a penance and very much in his element.'

Then he told them right off without stopping of the state he had left his master in, of the adventures which had befallen him, and all about the letter he was taking to the lady Dulcinea del Toboso, the daughter of Lorenzo Corchuelo, and how the knight was up to his ears in love with her. The pair of them were amazed at Sancho's tale. For, although they already knew the nature of Don Quixote's madness, they were astonished afresh every time they had news of him. They then asked Sancho Panza to show them the letter he was taking to the lady Dulcinea del Toboso. He replied that it was written in a note-book, and that his master's orders were that he must have it copied down on paper in the first village he came to. Here the priest asked to see it, and promised to write it out himself in a very good hand. Sancho Panza then felt beneath his shirt for the little book, but could not find it; and he would not have found it if he had searched till this day, because it was still in Don Quixote's possession and had never been given to him. In fact he had not remembered to ask for it.

When Sancho saw that the book was not to be found, he turned pale as death, and felt once more very hurriedly all over his body, only to realize afresh that he could not find it. Without more ado he plunged both hands into his beard and tore half of it out. Then he rapidly dealt himself a dozen blows without stopping, on the face and on the nose, until both were bathed in blood. At this sight the priest and the barber asked him what had happened to make him treat himself so roughly.

'What do you think?' replied Sancho. 'Only that in a single instant I've let three ass-colts slip through my fingers, three ass-colts, each one of them as strong as a castle.'

'How is that?' asked the barber.

'I've lost the note-book,' answered Sancho, 'which had the letter for Dulcinea in it, and a bill signed by my master, ordering his niece to give me three of the four or five ass-colts he has at home.'

Then he told them about the loss of Dapple, and the priest consoled him by promising that when he found his master he would make him renew the order and draw up the bill of exchange in the usual and customary form; for orders drawn in note-books were never honoured or accepted. Sancho was comforted by this, saying that in that case he did not much care about the loss of Dulcinea's letter, for he knew it almost by heart, and so they could take it down where and when they pleased.

'Repeat it to us, then, Sancho,' said the barber, 'and we'll write it down afterwards.'

Sancho Panza stopped and scratched his head to drag the letter up into his memory, standing first on one foot and then on the other. Sometimes he looked down at the ground and sometimes up at the sky. Then, when he had gnawed away half the top of one finger, keeping everyone who was waiting for him to speak in suspense, he burst out after a very long pause: 'God's Truth, Master Licentiate, the devil take all I remember of the letter; though at the beginning it said, *Sublime and suppressed lady.*'

'It wouldn't be suppressed,' said the barber, 'but superhuman or sovereign.'

'That's right,' said Sancho. 'Then, if I remember rightly, it went on ... *He that is oppressed with sleep and wakeful and wounded kisses your hands, ungrateful and most thankless beauty.* Then it said something about the health and sickness which he sent her, and so he went running on till he ended: *Yours till death, the Knight of the Sad Countenance.*'

The pair of them were not a little amused at Sancho's excellent memory and congratulated him warmly upon it. They asked him to recite the letter twice more so that they too might learn it by heart, and write it down when the time came. Sancho said it through three times more, and three times he repeated three thousand comical mistakes. After that he told them more about his master, but he did not say a word about the blanket tossing he had got at the inn, and still refused to enter. He also told them that once he had brought him a favourable despatch from the lady Dulcinea del

Toboso his master was going to set out and try to become Emperor, or at least Monarch, for so they had agreed between them. It was a thing that could be managed very easily, considering the valour of the knight's person and the strength of his arm. And once he had done this, his master was going to find a wife for his squire. For by that time he could not possibly fail to be a widower, and would marry one of the Empress's waiting-women, the heiress to a rich and large estate on dry land – and none of your isles or wiles, for he had no use for them.

Sancho brought all this out with such gravity, wiping his nose from time to time, and so crazily, that the pair of them were astonished afresh at the strength of Don Quixote's madness, since it had carried this poor man's wits along after it. They did not fancy the trouble of dispelling the squire's illusion. In fact it seemed to them better to leave him in it, since it did no harm to his conscience, and particularly as they found it most amusing to listen to his nonsense. So they bade him pray God for his master's health, it being both possible and feasible that he might in the course of time become an Emperor, as he had suggested, or at the least an Archbishop, or something of equal dignity. To which Sancho replied:

'Gentlemen, supposing that by a stroke of fate my master should take it into his head not to be an Emperor but to be an Archbishop, I should like to know here and now what Archbishops are accustomed to give to their squires?'

'Generally,' replied the priest, 'they give them a benefice, or a simple parish, or a sextonship, which brings them in a good tithe besides the altar-gifts, which are usually reckoned at as much again.'

'But for that,' replied Sancho, 'the squire would have to be un-married, and at the very least know how to assist at the Mass. Now if that's so I'm out of luck, because I'm married and don't know the first letter of the A.B.C. What will happen to me if my master gets the idea of being an Archbishop, and not an Emperor as is the use and practice of knights errant?'

'Don't worry, friend Sancho,' said the barber. 'We'll entreat your master and advise him, and even put it to him as a matter of conscience, that he shall be an Emperor and not an Archbishop. It'll be much the easier for him, besides, since he is more of a soldier than a scholar.'

'It has always seemed like that to me,' replied Sancho, 'although I must say that he's clever enough for anything. What I shall do is to pray Our Lord to put him wherever it's best for him, and where he can do me the greatest benefits.'

'You speak like a wise man,' said the priest, 'and you will be acting like a good Christian. But what we have got to do now is to contrive a way of releasing your master from that fruitless penance you say you left him doing. And if we are to think out a means of doing so and get something to eat as well – for it is time – it would be a good idea if we were to go into this inn.'

Sancho answered that they might go in, but that he would wait outside, and tell them afterwards the reason why he was unwilling to enter. But he begged them to bring him out something warm to eat, and some barley too for Rocinante. So they went in and left him outside, and a little later the barber brought him out some food. And afterwards, when they had thoroughly discussed the course to be pursued if they were to achieve their purpose, the priest struck an idea very applicable to Don Quixote's humour, and to the end they had in mind. This was, as he explained to the barber, for him to dress himself up as a damsel errant, and for the barber to make the best show he could of being her squire. Then they would go in that disguise and find Don Quixote – he pretending to be an afflicted damsel in distress – and beg a boon of him. This, as a valorous knight errant, he could not refuse to grant; and the boon which the damsel would ask of him would be to come with her wherever she might lead him, to redress an injury which a wicked knight had done her. She would also beg him not to require her to remove her mask, nor to make any enquiries about her rank, until he had wreaked vengeance for her upon the wicked knight. The priest was quite certain that Don Quixote would consent to anything they might ask him on these terms, and that they could get him away in this way, and take him home to his village, where they would try to find some cure for his strange madness.

Chapter XXVII. *How the Priest and the Barber carried out their plan, and other matters worthy of mention in this great history.*

THE priest's plan did not seem a bad one to the barber – quite the opposite, in fact – and so they set about its immediate execution. They borrowed a dress and a head-dress from the landlady, and left the priest's new cassock for security. Then the barber made himself a long beard from a sorrel and grey ox tail, which the innkeeper kept to hang his comb in. And when the landlady asked them why they wanted all this, the priest told her something about Don Quixote's madness, and said that they needed this disguise to entice him away from the mountains, where he then was. The innkeeper and his wife at once realized that the madman was their guest of the balsam and the master of the blanket-tossed squire, and told the priest the whole story, not omitting the part which Sancho had been so anxious to conceal. In the end the landlady equipped the priest to perfection. She gave him a cloth dress, stiff with black velvet stripes a good eight inches wide, all slashed, and a bodice of green velvet bordered with white satin trimmings, both of which must have been made in the time of King Wamba. The priest would not agree to have his head dressed like a woman's, but put on the little quilted linen cap he generally used for a nightcap, tied one of his black taffeta garters across his forehead, and made a mask with the other, which covered his beard and his face very well. He then put on his broad hat, large enough to serve as a sunshade and, wrapping his cloak around him, mounted his mule side-saddle like a woman, while the barber got up upon his, with his beard reaching to his waist, part sorrel and part white. For, as we have said, it was made from the tail of a pied ox.

They said good-bye to everyone, including the good Maritornes, who promised to recite a whole rosary, sinner though she was, that God might give them success in the very arduous and Christian task they had undertaken. But no sooner were they out of the inn than it struck the priest that he was doing wrong in dressing up in that fashion; for it was indecent for a churchman to appear in such a garb, however deeply he was concerned in the business. This he told the barber, and asked him to change clothes. It would be more fitting, he said, if his friend were to play the distressed maiden and himself be the squire, which part would be less prejudicial to his dignity. And if the barber would not agree he refused to go a step further, even though the devil should run away with Don Quixote. At this point Sancho joined them, and could not help laughing when he saw them in their disguise. In the end the barber gave in to the priest, and they changed their plan. The priest then began to instruct the barber how to act, and what to say to Don Quixote, so as to compel him to come away and cease haunting the place which he had chosen for his fruitless penance. The barber replied that he could carry it off to perfection, without any tuition. But he refused to put on the clothes until they should reach the place where Don Quixote was; and so he folded them up. The priest then stowed away his beard, and they went on their way under the guidance of Sancho Panza, who told them as they went along the story of the madman whom they had found in the mountains. But he kept quiet about the discovery of the leather bag and about its contents; for with all his simplicity he was rather a greedy rascal.

The next day they reached the place where Sancho had strewn the sprigs to guide him to the spot where he had left his master. And when he recognized the place, he told them that this was the way in; and that they had better dress up, if that was necessary for the rescue of his master. For they had already told him that it was of the utmost importance to go thus clothed and disguised, if they were to save Don Quixote from the miserable life that he had chosen; and they had impressed on him that he must not tell his master who they were, or that he knew them. And if Don Quixote were to ask him, as he was bound to, whether he had given Dulcinea the letter, he must reply that he had, but that as she could not read, she had replied by word of mouth, commanding him to come and see her immediately on pain of her displeasure. This, they assured Sancho, was most essential; for in this way, and by means of certain things they intended to say to Don Quixote themselves, they felt certain that they could bring him to a better life, and so contrive it as to put him immediately on the road to becoming an Emperor or a Monarch, for as to his being an Archbishop there was nothing to fear.

Sancho listened to all this and treasured it up in his memory.

He thanked them warmly for their intention of advising his master
to be an Emperor and not an Archbishop, being certain in his own
mind that, so far as bestowing favours on their squires went, Emperors could do more than Archbishops-errant. He also said that
it would be better if he were to go ahead to look for his master and
give him his lady's reply; for that alone might be sufficient to get
him away from the place, without their putting themselves to all
that trouble. They approved Sancho Panza's idea, and so decided to
wait for him to return with the news that he had found his master.
The squire then struck into the mountain clefts, leaving the two of
them in a ravine, which was watered by a little gentle stream and
pleasantly cool from the shade of the rocks and trees surrounding it.
It was a hot day in August, the month when the heat is usually most
intense in those parts; and the time was three o'clock in the afternoon, which made the place even more pleasing. In fact it invited
them to wait there for Sancho's return, which they did. But as the
two of them were lying at their ease in the shade, there came to their
ears a voice singing sweetly and melodiously, though unaccom-
panied by any instrument. Which surprised them not a little, for
this seemed a most unlikely place in which to find so good a singer.
For although report has it that shepherds with excellent voices are to
be found in woods and fields, that is rather poetic exaggeration than
sober truth. They were even more astonished when they heard the
words of his song. For they were not rough shepherd's verses, but
well-turned and courtly, as will be clear from the following lines:

> What turns my happiness to pain?
> > Disdain.
> And greater makes my woe for me?
> > Jealousy.
> What sorest tries my patience?
> > Absence.
> If that be so, then for my wrong
> No remedy may I obtain,
> Since my best hopes I find are slain
> By disdain, jealousy, and absence long.

> Who through my breast this anguish drove?
> > Love.
> Who doth my happiness abate?
> > Fate.

Who consents to this my pain?
          Heaven.
If that be so, I fear 'twill prove
That I must die in this sad plight,
Since for my overthrow unite
The heavens, fate, and love.

Who can better hope bequeath?
          Death.
What are the means to make me free?
          Inconstancy.
And wherein lies the cure for sadness?
          Madness.
If that be so, it's merely silly
To seek my passion's cure,
For there's no remedy that's sure
But death and change and folly.

The time, the season, the solitude, the voice and skill of the singer, all astonished and delighted the two listeners, who waited quietly in the hope of hearing more. But when the silence had continued for rather a long while, they decided to go out and look for this musician with so fine a voice. Just as they were going to do so, however, the same voice came once more to their ears, and kept them motionless throughout the singing of this sonnet:

O sacred friendship that with nimble wing,
Thy phantom leaving here on earth below,
With blessed souls in heaven communing
Up through the empyrean halls dost go.
Thence, at thy pleasure, to us is assigned
Just peace, her features covered with a hood,
But oft, instead of her, Deceit we find
Clad in the garb of virtue and of good.
Leave heaven, friendship, and do not permit
Foul fraud thus openly thy robes to wear
And so all honest purposes defeat.
For if you leave him in your semblance fair
Dark chaos will once more engulf the world
And all to primal anarchy be hurled.

The song ended with a deep sigh, and the pair of them waited attentively to see if he would sing again; but when they heard the music turn to sobs and groans of sorrow, they agreed to go and find out who the unhappy person was who had so excellent a voice and

H

so sorrowing a heart. And they had not gone far when, on coming round the corner of a rock, they saw a man in form and figure resembling Sancho Panza's description of Cardenio. The man did not start at the sight of them, but stayed still, with his head on his breast in a pensive attitude, and did not raise his eyes to look at them again after their first sudden appearance. Now the priest had recognized him from Sancho's account, and consequently knew the cause of his misfortunes; and being a man of ready speech, he went up to him and implored him most persuasively in a few well-chosen words to give up his wretched way of life, and not risk dying in that desolate place, which would be the greatest of all misfortunes. At that time Cardenio was sane, and free from the wild fits which so often drove him out of his mind. Seeing, therefore, the two of them dressed so unlike the usual frequenters of those lonely parts, he could not help being surprised, and was even more so when he heard them speak of his own affairs as if they were common knowledge – for that was the impression he got from the priest's speech. And so he replied:

'I see, gentlemen, whoever you may be, that Heaven, which takes care to succour the good, and often the bad as well, has sent to me, unworthy as I am, even in this remote and desolate spot so far from the traffic of human kind, some persons to show me, by forcible and lively argument, the unreasonable nature of the life I lead, and to endeavour to tempt me away from here to a better place. But not knowing, as I do, that were I to fly from this misery I should fall into a worse, they must take me for a fool, or even worse for a madman. And that would not be surprising. For I am myself aware that the strength of my misery is so intense, and drives me to such distraction, that I am powerless to resist it and am turning to stone, void of all knowledge and feeling. This I realize when I am shown the evidence of the deeds I have done under the mastery of these terrible fits. Then I can only vainly lament and fruitlessly curse my fate, and to excuse my madness tell any who will hear it the story of its cause. For when sensible men learn its cause they will not be surprised at its effects. Though they will be unable to offer me any relief, at least they will not blame me, and their anger at my violence will turn to pity for my misfortunes. If you, sirs, have come with the same intention as the others, I beg you to listen to the story of my misfortunes before you continue with your sensible arguments. For when you have heard it, you will perhaps spare yourselves the trouble of trying to offer consolation for an inconsolable sorrow.'

The pair of them wanted nothing better than to hear the cause of his grief from his own mouth, and begged him to tell them his story, promising to take no measures without his consent either for his relief or for his consolation. Then the unhappy gentleman began his piteous tale, in almost the same words and phrases as he had used in telling it to Don Quixote and the goatherd a few days before, when the story had remained unfinished on account of Master Elisabat and Don Quixote's punctiliousness in defending the dignity of knight errantry. But fortunately this time Cardenio had no fit of madness and was able to tell it to the end. So, when he reached the subject of the letter which Don Ferdinand had found between the leaves of *Amadis of Gaul*, he said that he remembered it perfectly, and that it read as follows:

' "*Lucinda to Cardenio:*

'"*Each day I find in you virtues which oblige and compel me to think more highly of you; and, therefore, if you would relieve me of this debt without prejudice to my honour, you may easily do so. My father knows you and loves me; he will never force me, but he will comply with your just demands, if you value me as you say, and as I believe you do.*"

'This letter moved me, as I have already told you, to ask for Lucinda's hand, and proved her in Don Ferdinand's opinion one of the most discreet and sensible women of her time. And it was this letter which made him determine to ruin me before my design could be put into effect. I told Ferdinand of her father's insistence that mine should make the request, and that I dared not mention the matter to my father for fear that he would not consent. Not that he was ignorant of Lucinda's rank, goodness, virtue and beauty – for he knew that she had virtues enough to ennoble any family in Spain – but because, as I understood, he did not wish me to marry before we knew what Duke Richard might do for me. To be brief, I told him that I dared not ask my father, not only because of this obstacle, but because of other vague apprehensions which made me fear that my desires would never be realized. Ferdinand's reply was that he would speak to my father for me, and make him speak to Lucinda's. O greedy Marius! Cruel Catiline! Criminal Sulla! Crafty Galalon! Treacherous Vellido! Vindictive Julian! Covetous Judas! Cruel, vindictive, crafty traitor! What harm had this poor wretch done you, who so frankly revealed to you the secrets and joys of his heart? How had I offended you? Did I ever say a word, or give you advice, which was not intended for your benefit and honour? But why do I complain, miserable wretch that I am. For it is certain that when the stars in their courses bring disaster, rushing down with fury and violence, no power on earth can stop them, no human ingenuity avert them. Who could have thought that Don Ferdinand, a noble and intelligent gentleman, indebted to me for my services and absolutely certain of success wherever his amorous fancy led him, would be bitten – as they say – with the desire to take from me my one ewe-lamb, who was not even yet mine? But these thoughts are vain and fruitless. Let them rest, and we will take up the broken thread of my unfortunate story.

'Don Ferdinand, then, finding that my presence hindered him from putting his false, wicked plan into practice, decided to send me to his elder brother, on the pretext of borrowing some money from him to pay for six horses, which he had bought on the very day he offered to speak to my father, purposely to provide himself with an excuse for getting me out of the way, the better to carry out his wicked plan. Could I have foreseen this treachery? Could I even have imagined it? No, certainly not. On the contrary, I offered to go immediately with the greatest of pleasure, and was delighted at the good bargain he had made. That night I spoke to Lucinda, told her of my arrangement with Don Ferdinand, and said that we had good reason to hope for a favourable result. She was as unsuspecting as I of Don Ferdinand's treachery, and bade me hurry back, for she was certain that the fulfilment of our desires would be delayed no longer than it would take for my father to speak to hers. I do not know how it was, but as she spoke her eyes filled with tears, and a sudden choking in her throat prevented her speaking another word, though she seemed to have much more to say. This excess of emotion, which I had never seen in her before, surprised me; because on such occasions as my good fortune and my diligence provided, we always talked happily and merrily enough, without mingling tears, sighs, jealousies, suspicions, or fears with our conversation. I would expatiate on my good fortune, thanking Heaven for giving her to me for my mistress, praising her beauty, and extolling her virtue and good sense. She in reply would praise the qualities in me that seemed to her, as my lover, worthy of praise. During these conversations we amused ourselves with a hundred thousand trifles, and gossiped about our neighbours and friends; and the greatest freedom I allowed myself was to take, almost by force, one of her lovely white hands and press it to my lips, as well as the narrowness of the bars between us would allow. But on the night before the sad day of my parting she wept, moaned, and sighed, and then fled, leaving me full of confusion and dread at these new and unusual signs of sorrow and tenderness in Lucinda. But, not to destroy my hopes, I attributed all this to the strength of her love for me, and to the grief which absence always causes true lovers. In short I departed, sad and thoughtful, my mind full of fancies and suspicions, but uncertain what it was I suspected or imagined – all of which clearly presaged the miserable and dark fate which awaited me.

'I came to the town I was sent to, and delivered the letters to Don Ferdinand's brother. I was well received, but not quickly dismissed. For, to my disgust, he bade me wait eight days in a place out of sight of the Duke, his father, since his brother had asked for a certain sum of money to be sent him without his father's knowledge. But all this was a stratagem of the false Don Ferdinand. For his brother was not short of money and might have sent me back with it immediately. I felt much inclined to disobey this order, for it seemed quite impossible to live so long away from Lucinda, especially as I had left her in such a state of distress. But, for all that, like a good servant I obeyed, although I knew it to be to my own detriment. On the fourth day after my arrival, however, a man came after me with a letter which by the address I knew was from Lucinda, for the writing was hers. I opened it in fear and trembling, convinced that it must be something extraordinary which had moved her to write to me in my absence, seeing how seldom she did so when I was near. Before I read it I asked the man who had given it to him, and how long he had been on the road. He told me that as he had happened to be going down one of the city streets about midday, a very beautiful lady had called him from a window, her eyes full of tears, and had said to him very earnestly: 'Brother, if you are a Christian, as you seem to be, I beg you, for the love of God, to carry this letter quickly to the place and the person to whom it is directed – for they are well known. In this you will be performing an act of charity, and that you may not lack the means to do it, take what is wrapped in this handkerchief.' "As she said this," he pursued, "she threw me a handkerchief out of the window; and in it were a hundred *reals*, this gold ring here, and the letter I have given you. Then, without waiting for my reply, she left the window; though first she had seen me take up the letter and the handkerchief, and give her a sign that I would do what she asked. So, seeing how well I was paid for my trouble, and learning from the envelope that the letter was for you, sir, whom I know very well – and moved too by that beautiful lady's tears – I decided not to trust anyone else, but to come myself to deliver it to you; and in the sixteen hours since she gave it to me I have done the journey, which as you know is fifty-four miles." While the kind impromptu messenger was speaking I hung on his words, my legs trembling so that I could scarcely stand. At length I opened the letter and read these words:

'*Don Ferdinand has fulfilled his promise to persuade your father to speak to mine, more to his own satisfaction than to your advantage. I must tell you that he has asked for my hand in marriage, and that, carried away by the advantages he thinks Don Ferdinand has over you, my father has agreed with such eagerness that the betrothal is to take place two days hence, so secretly and privately that the only witnesses will be Heaven, and some of our own household. You can imagine how I feel. Consider whether you should not return. The outcome of the matter will show you whether I love you or not. God grant this may reach your hands before mine are joined to those of a man who keeps his pledged word so ill.*

'These, then, were the contents of the letter, which caused me to set out without waiting for the answer or the money. For now I saw clearly that it was not the purchase of the horses, but the indulgence of his own desires, that had caused Don Ferdinand to send me to his brother. Rage against him and fear of losing the treasure which I had earned by so many years of love and devotion lent wings to my feet, and the next day I reached our town at the most favourable moment for going to speak to Lucinda. I rode in secretly and, leaving my mule at the house of the good man who had brought me the letter, by good luck I found Lucinda posted at the grating which had been the constant witness of our loves. She recognized me immediately, and I her; yet not with our usual joy. But who in the world can boast that he has fathomed and understood the confused mind and changeable nature of a woman? No one, of course. For as soon as Lucinda saw me, she said: "Cardenio, I am dressed for the betrothal. The traitor Don Ferdinand and my greedy father are now waiting for me with the other witnesses in the hall, but they shall rather be witnesses of my death than of my betrothal. Do not be disturbed, my friend, but contrive to be present at this sacrifice. If I cannot prevent it by words, I carry a dagger about me which can oppose the most determined violence by putting an end to my life, and proving the love I bear and have always borne for you."

'I answered her hurriedly and distractedly, for I was afraid that I might lose my opportunity of replying:

' "May your actions, lady, confirm your words. If you have a dagger to secure your honour, I have a sword here to defend you with, or to kill myself with if fortune proves adverse."

'I do not think that she could have listened to all that I said, since I heard them hurriedly call her away. For the bridegroom was waiting. Here the night of my sadness fell; the sun of my happiness set; the light went out of my eyes, the sense from my brain. I could not go into her house nor move in any direction. But when I thought how important my presence was, whatever events might arise, I took better heart and entered. As I knew all the ways in and out, and as the whole household was in a secret bustle, no one noticed me, and I was able to take up my position in the recess formed by a window of the hall itself. This hiding-place was masked by the edges and folds of two pieces of tapestry, between which I could observe everything that happened there without myself being seen. How can I tell you with what alarm my heart beat while I stood there, what thoughts came into my head, what reflections passed through my mind? So many were they, and of such a nature, that they cannot and should not be told. Enough that Don Ferdinand came into the hall, not dressed as a bridegroom but in his usual clothes. His groomsman was a first cousin of Lucinda's, and there was no other person in the whole hall, except the servants. Shortly afterwards Lucinda came out of a dressing-room, accompanied by her mother and two of her maids, adorned as her rank and beauty deserved, and looking the very perfection of fashion and courtly splendour. My distraction and anxiety gave me no opportunity of noting in detail what she wore. I could only mark the colours, which were crimson and white, and the flashing of the jewels and precious stones on her head-dress and all over her clothes. But most beautiful of all was her lovely golden hair, which rivalled her jewels and the light of the great torches which lit the hall, and brought her beauty even more brilliantly before my eyes. O memory, mortal enemy of my peace! To what purpose do you recall to me the incomparable beauty of my beloved enemy? Would it not be better, cruel memory, to picture to me what she did next; so that, under the stress of so flagrant an injury, I may strive, if not to avenge it, at least to lose my life? Do not grow weary, gentlemen, of hearing these digressions of mine; for my grief cannot be told succinctly and methodically, since every circumstance of it seems to me to deserve a long discourse.'

To which the priest replied that not only were they not weary of his tale, but that they were glad to hear the details; since they were not of the sort to be passed over in silence, and deserved the same attention as the main thread of the story.

'Then,' continued Cardenio, 'when they were all in the hall the parish priest came in, and took them each by the hand to perform the ceremony. When he said: "Will you, lady Lucinda, take the lord Don Ferdinand, here present, for your lawful husband, as Holy Mother Church commands?", I stuck my whole head and neck out between the tapestries and listened with straining ears and distracted mind for Lucinda's reply, awaiting from it sentence of death or a fresh lease of life. If only I had then dared to come out and cry: "Lucinda, Lucinda, beware what you do! Consider what you owe me! Remember you are mine, and cannot be another's! Be warned that to say Yes is instantly to end my life. O treacherous Don Ferdinand, thief of my glory, death of my life! What do you want? What claim can you make? Consider that, as a Christian, you cannot achieve your desire, because Lucinda is my wife and I am her husband!" What a madman I am! Now that I am far away from the danger I say what I should have done, but did not do. Now that I have let my dear treasure be stolen I curse the robber, on whom I might have taken vengeance if I had been as prompt to act then as I now am to complain! Then I was a coward and a fool; no wonder that I am dying now, ashamed, repentant, and mad.

'The priest stood waiting for Lucinda's reply, and she did not answer for some time. But when I thought that she was going to draw her dagger in defence of her honour, or raise her voice to utter the truth, or make a protest which might redound to my advantage, I heard her say in weak and fainting tones: "I will". Don Ferdinand pronounced the same words and gave her the ring, and they were tied by an indissoluble bond. But as the bridegroom turned to kiss his bride she put her hand to her heart and fell fainting into her mother's arms.

'It only remains for me to describe my state of mind when I saw in that one Yes my hopes deceived, Lucinda's word and promise broken, and myself for ever powerless to recover all that I had lost in that one instant. I was resourceless. Heaven, it seemed, had abandoned me; sustaining earth had become my enemy; air denied me breath for my sighs, and water moisture for my tears; only fire grew so strong that I seemed to burn all over with rage and jealousy.

'Everyone was thrown into confusion by Lucinda's fainting, and when her mother unlaced her dress to give her air a folded paper was discovered there, which Don Ferdinand immediately snatched and started to read by the light of one of the torches. When he had finished it, he sat down on a chair and put his hand to his cheek, apparently deep in thought, and paying no attention to the attempts which were being made to bring his bride round from her swoon.

'When I saw the whole household in commotion I ventured out, not caring whether I were seen or not, and determined, if I were, to do so desperate a deed that everyone would learn from my punishment of the treacherous Don Ferdinand and from the fickleness of the swooning traitress what just indignation I harboured in my breast. My fate, however, which must be preserving me for worse disasters – if there can possibly be worse – ordained that at that moment I had full use of my reason, which since then I have lacked. So, instead of taking vengeance on my greatest enemies, which would have been easy, since they had no suspicions of my presence,

I resolved to inflict on myself, and with my own hand, the punishment which they deserved — a punishment perhaps more severe than I should have inflicted on them by instant execution. For sudden death swiftly ends all pain, but death which is protracted by torture for ever kills but never puts an end to life.

'At last I left the house, and returned to the place where I had left my mule. I had it saddled, and without saying good-bye to my host I left the city, like another Lot, not daring to look back. When I found myself alone in the fields, concealed by the darkness of the night, its silence invited me to complain without fear of being heard or recognized. I then gave vent to violent curses on Lucinda and Don Ferdinand, as if that were a means of taking vengeance for the wrong they had done me. I called her cruel, faithless, false, ungrateful, but most of all mercenary, since my enemy's riches had blinded the eyes of her love, and made her take her affections from me and transfer them to a man of greater wealth. But in the middle of this storm of reproaches and abuse I found excuses for her. It was not surprising, I cried, that a maiden immured in her parents' house, and always accustomed to obey them, should willingly submit, on their proposing so noble, so rich, and so well-bred a gentleman as her husband. For if she had not accepted him, she would either have been thought senseless or have incurred the suspicion of having engaged her affections elsewhere, which would have seriously prejudiced her honour and good name. Then I thought that, if she had said that I was her husband, they would have realized that she had not made a bad choice and must have excused her. For before Don Ferdinand made his offer they could not themselves reasonably have desired a better match for their daughter than myself. She might easily have declared, I thought, before being finally compelled to give her hand to Don Ferdinand, that I had already given her mine; and I should then have come forward and confirmed any story she might have invented. In fact, I concluded that lack of love, foolishness, ambition and the desire for greatness had made her forget her promise, which had deceived, encouraged, and sustained me in my fervent hopes and honest love.

'With these reflections and in this disquietude I travelled for the rest of the night, and at dawn struck a pass into these mountains, over which I wandered for three days, far from any road or track,

until I stopped in some meadows, on which side of the range I do
not know. There I asked some herdsmen where the wildest parts of
the mountains lay, and they pointed in this direction. Here I came
at once, intending to end my life; and when I reached these crags
my mule fell dead of weariness and hunger, or as I believe, to rid
herself of so useless a burden as myself. So I was left on foot, exhausted and hungry, without so much as a thought of looking for
help. I do not know how long I lay on the ground in this state, but
at length I got up without the feeling of hunger, and found some
goatherds beside me. It must have been they who had satisfied my
needs, for they told me how they had discovered me talking so
wildly that I must clearly have gone out of my mind. And since then
I have been conscious that I am not always well, but sometimes so
weak and deranged that I behave like a madman, tearing my clothes,
shouting in these wastes, cursing my fortune, and vainly repeating
the dear name of my enemy. My only wish and purpose at these
times is to wear out my life in lamentations. And when I recover
my senses, I am so exhausted and bruised that I can hardly move.

'My usual dwelling is a hollow cork-tree large enough to shelter
this wretched body. The cowherds and goatherds who frequent
these parts feed me out of charity. They leave me food by the tracks
and on the rocks, where they expect I may pass and find it. So, even
when my senses are disordered, Nature makes me know my food,
and rouses the instinct in me to take it and eat it. At other times,
they tell me when they find me in my senses, I rush out on to the
tracks and take the food the shepherds bring up from the village to
the sheepcotes. I snatch it by force, they say, even though they
would give it me willingly. So I spend what remains of my miserable life till Heaven shall please to bring it to an end, or to blot
Lucinda's beauty and treachery from my memory, and obliterate
Don Ferdinand's perfidy as well. If Heaven should do so and not
end my life, I will turn my thoughts to some better course. If not I
can only implore God's infinite mercy for my soul. For I feel no
strength or virtue in myself to fetch my body out of this pass into
which I have elected to bring it of my own accord.

'That, sirs, is the bitter story of my misfortunes. Tell me if it
deserves to be told with less emotion than I have shown. Do not
trouble to persuade me or advise me to take some remedy which

your reason may suggest to you. For it will be of no more use to me than a famous doctor's prescription to a patient who will not take it. Without Lucinda I do not desire health; and since it has pleased her to be another's, when she is or should be mine, let me give myself up to misery, since I might have been given up to happiness. She elected by her fickleness to make my perdition permanent, and I choose to comply with her wishes and achieve my final destruction. And it shall be an example to future generations that I alone have lacked what other wretches have in abundance. There is comfort for them in the impossibility of consolation. But for me this is the cause of greater afflictions and evils, which I truly think will not end even with my death.'

Here Cardenio concluded the long recital of his sad love story. But, just as the priest was preparing to offer him some words of consolation, he was prevented by a voice, which came to his ears, uttering in mournful tones what will be related in the fourth part of this narrative. For at this point the wise and judicious historian, Cide Hamete Benengeli, brought his third part to an end.

Chapter XXVIII. Of a Novel and Pleasing Adventure which befell the Priest and the Barber in the same Mountains.

How happy and fortunate was that age in which the boldest of knights, Don Quixote de la Mancha, was born into the world. Since, thanks to his honourable resolution of reviving and restoring to the earth the lost and almost defunct order of knight errantry, we enjoy to-day in our present age, which lacks all pleasant entertainment, not only the delights of his authentic history, but also the tales and episodes set in it. For in some ways these are no less agreeable, ingenious and authentic than the history itself, the thread of which, being carded, twisted, and reeled, may now be resumed. It relates that just as the priest was about to console Cardenio, he was prevented by a voice speaking in mournful tones to this effect:

'O God, is it possible that I have found a spot which will afford a secret grave to the weary burden of my body, which I so unwillingly bear? This will be the place, if the solitude these hills promise does not deceive me. Miserable creature that I am, what company can I have more welcome than these crags and thickets, which will allow me to tell my misery to Heaven, since there is no one on earth from whom I can expect counsel in my perplexities, comfort in my grief, or remedy in my troubles!'

The priest and his companions heard the words distinctly, and got up to look for the speaker, who could not be far away. They had not gone twenty yards, in fact, when from behind a rock they saw a youth dressed like a peasant, who was sitting at the foot of an ash. They could not at first see his face, because his head was bent over a running stream in which he was washing his feet. And so silently did they come up that he did not hear them. For he was busily engaged in washing his feet, which looked like nothing so much as two pieces of pure crystal, lying among the other pebbles of the brook. Their whiteness and beauty astonished the gazers. For they did not seem to be made for breaking clods, nor for following oxen and the plough, as the dress of their owner suggested. So, seeing that they were unobserved, the priest, who was ahead, signed to the other two to crouch behind some near-by fragments of rock; which they did, and watched all that youth's movements attentively.

He was dressed in a short grey double cape, tied round his waist with a white cloth. He wore breeches and leggings of grey cloth and a grey cap on his head. And he had hitched his leggings half-way up his legs, which were as white as alabaster. After washing his lovely feet, he wiped them with a kerchief, which he took from under his cap. And, as he did so, he raised his face, in which the watchers saw such peerless beauty that Cardenio whispered to the priest: 'Since this is not Lucinda it is no human creature. It must be divine.'

The youth took off his cap; and as he shook his head from side to side, there began to fall about his shoulders hair which the sun itself might have envied. By this they realized that here was no peasant lad but a delicate woman, and the most beautiful that two of them had ever seen till then. And Cardenio would have known none lovelier, had he not gazed on Lucinda. For, as he afterwards declared, only Lucinda's beauty could compare with hers. Her long golden hair not only covered her shoulders but fell all round her, hiding her entire body except for her feet. Then she combed it with hands which in contrast to the crystal of her feet seemed to be made of driven snow. All of which increased the astonishment of the three watchers and their desire to know who she was; and so they decided to reveal themselves. But as they moved to get up, the lovely maiden raised her head and, parting her hair from before her eyes with both hands, looked to see who had made the noise. And no sooner did she see them than she got up and, without waiting to put on her shoes or tie up her hair, hurriedly seized a bundle lying beside her, which might have contained clothes, and started to run away in surprise and alarm. But she had not gone six paces when her tender feet were so hurt by the sharp stones that she fell down. At this point the three of them came out, the priest being the first to speak:

'Stop, lady, whoever you are. We only desire to serve you. You have no reason to run away. Besides, it would be of no use. Your feet would not allow it, and we should not permit it.'

She was so astonished and bewildered that she could make no reply. So they went up to her, and the priest, taking her by the hand, continued: 'What your dress, lady, denies, your hair reveals. Clearly you must have had no trivial reason for disguising your beauty in so unsuitable a dress, and coming to so wild a spot, where it has been our good fortune to find you. If we cannot relieve your distress, we can at least advise you. For no evil short of death can be so dire that the sufferer may absolutely refuse to listen to comfort gladly offered. So, dear lady, or dear sir – whichever you prefer – dismiss the fears which our appearance cause you, and tell us of your fortune, good or bad. For in all of us together or each of us separately you will find sympathizers in your distress.'

While the priest was talking, the disguised maiden stood stupefied, gazing at them without moving her lips or saying a single word, like some peasant suddenly confronted with rare treasures never seen before. But when the priest said more to the same effect, she gave a deep sigh and broke her silence:

'Since these lonely mountains cannot hide me, and my hair will not permit my tongue to lie, it would be vain to make a further pretence; which you could accept only out of politeness, and for no other reason. Therefore, gentlemen, I thank you for the offer you have made me, and feel obliged to comply with your request, though I am afraid that the tale of my misfortunes will cause you grief as well as pity. For you can find no remedy nor any consolation to allay them. Nevertheless, so that you may be in no doubt as to my honour, now that you have discovered that I am a woman and seen me, young, alone, and in these clothes – circumstances which singly or all together are enough to destroy any honest reputation – I must tell you what I would rather conceal if I could.'

As she said all this without hesitation, she seemed not only beautiful but eloquent and sweet-voiced as well, which made them admire her good sense no less than her beauty. They once more offered her their help, and begged her to fulfil her promise. Then, after modestly putting on her shoes and tying up her hair, she sat down on a stone without more ado; and the other three sat round her, choking back the tears which sprang to their eyes, as in a calm and clear voice she began the story of her life:

'Here in Andalusia there is a town from which a Duke takes his title, by virtue of which he is a Grandee of Spain. He has two sons, the elder the heir to his estate and, apparently, to his virtues, and the younger, heir to I do not know what, unless it be Vellido's treachery and Galalon's deceit. My parents are tenants of this lord, people of humble birth, but so rich that if their rank were equal to their fortune they could have nothing more to desire. Nor, if that had been so, need I have feared to find myself in my present misfortune; for perhaps my troubles arose only because they were not noble. Not that their rank is shamefully low, but it is not high enough to make me certain that my disaster was not caused by the humbleness of their station. In short they are farmers, simple people without any taint of ignoble blood, and what is generally called "rusty old Christians"; people whose wealth and fine way of life are gradually earning them the name of gentlefolk, or even nobles. But their greatest wealth and nobility in their own eyes lay in having me for their daughter. And, as they had no other heir, and as they were most loving parents, I was the most pampered of children. I was the light of their eyes, the staff of their old age and, save for Heaven, the sole object of their affections – and my wishes never differed from theirs by a jot, such good parents they were. Now just as I was mistress of their affections, I was also mistress of their household. It was I who engaged and dismissed the servants, and the accounts of sowings and crops passed through my hands. The oil-mills, the wine-presses, the stock list and the beehives were under my control. In fact, I kept the complete accounts of a rich farm – for rich my father's was. I was the stewardess and controller, and fulfilled my duties to their absolute satisfaction. Such part of my day as remained after dealing with the overseers, the foremen, and the day-labourers, I spent in occupations proper to young ladies, sewing, lace-making, and often spinning. And if I left these tasks at times to refresh my mind, I turned to some book of devotion or to playing the harp. For experience taught me that music composes disordered thoughts and eases the troubles which are born of the spirit. This, then, is how I lived in my parents' house, and if I have described it in some detail, it has not been out of ostentation, nor to show that I am rich, but to prove how little I am to blame for falling from that happy state into my present misery.

'So it was that I spent my life, busy and in almost monastic seclusion, seen by nobody, as I supposed, but the household servants. For when I went to Mass it was so early in the morning, my mother and I were so surrounded by our servants, and I was so closely veiled and guarded, that my eyes scarcely saw more of the earth than my feet trod. But for all this the eyes of love, or more correctly of idleness, which are keener than a lynx's, discovered me, the eyes of the importunate Don Ferdinand. For that is the name of the Duke's younger son, whom I spoke of.'

No sooner did she mention Don Ferdinand's name than Cardenio's face changed colour, and he began to sweat and to show so much emotion that the priest and the barber looked at him in apprehension, fearing one of those attacks of madness which they had heard he was subject to. But he merely sweated and stayed still, staring hard at the farmer's daughter and reflecting who she might be. She, however, did not notice Cardenio's disturbance, but went on with her story, saying:

'And he had no sooner seen me, as he afterwards declared, than he fell violently in love with me, as his actions soon showed. But, to conclude the tale of my misfortunes quickly, I will pass in silence over the devices Don Ferdinand employed to declare his passion to me. He bribed all the house servants, and offered and gave presents to my relations. Every day was a festival and a holiday in our street; and at night music kept everyone awake. The love-letters which came into my hands – I do not know how – were countless, full of declarations and protestations of passion, and containing more pro-

mises and oaths than syllables. All of which did not soften me. On,
the contrary, they made me harder, as if he were my mortal enemy;
and everything that he did to bend me to his will had quite the
opposite effect. This was not because I disliked Don Ferdinand's
gallantry, or found his wooing excessive. Not at all. I was quite
pleased to be desired and admired by so great a nobleman, and not
at all displeased to read my praises in his letters; for however plain
we women are I think we are always pleased to hear ourselves called
beautiful.

'My modesty, however, resisted, and was backed by the repeated
advice of my parents, who were well aware of Don Ferdinand's
feelings by now, since he did not care if the whole world knew of
them. They told me that they relied on my virtue and goodness
alone, and trusted me with their honour and good name. They bade
me reflect on the difference between Don Ferdinand's rank and
mine, and realize that his plans were directed to his own pleasure
rather than to my advantage, whatever he might say to the contrary.
If I wished to put an end to his wicked suit, they were willing to
marry me then and there to anyone I might choose. I could have
the best man in our own town or in the whole district; for with
their great wealth and my good name anything was possible. With
these promises and the assurance they gave me I strengthened my
resistance, and never gave Don Ferdinand so much as a word of reply which might offer him even a distant hope of achieving his
purpose.

'All my precautions, which he no doubt took for scorn, must have
whetted his lascivious appetite. For that is all I can call his passion
for me, since if it had been what it should have been, you would
never have heard of it: I should have had no occasion to describe it
to you. At length Don Ferdinand learned that my parents were going to make a match for me, so as to put an end to his hopes of possessing me, or at least so that I should have better guards to look
after me; and this intelligence, or suspicion, was the cause of his doing what I shall now tell you. One night I was sitting in my room,
attended by only one serving-maid, with the doors well bolted for
fear that my virtue might be carelessly exposed to any peril, when
suddenly – I could not imagine how – despite all my precautions I
found him standing in front of me in the solitude of my silent re-

treat. The sight of him so disturbed me that my eyes went blind and I was struck dumb. I had no strength to shout; nor do I believe that he would have let me do so. For he came up to me immediately and took me in his arms. I was so confused, as I said, that I had not the strength to defend myself. Then he began to make violent protestations. I do not know how it is possible for the most skilful lying to make such falseness seem true.

'The traitor reinforced his words with tears and his desires with sighs. And I, poor creature, alone in the midst of my own family, and inexperienced in these matters, began – I do not know how – to believe his falsehoods, though his sighs and tears were far from moving me beyond a virtuous compassion. And so, when I had recovered from my first surprise, I began to regain my lost spirits a little, and said with more courage than I had credited myself with: "Sir, if I were in the grasp of a fierce lion, instead of being, as I am, in your arms, and if I could only get free from them by doing or saying something to the prejudice of my honour, it would be no more possible for me to do or say such a thing than it is to alter the past. For, though you hold my body in your arms, my soul is secured by the purity of my thoughts; and how different they are from your evil ones you will see if you violently persist in your plans. I am your tenant, not your slave. Your noble blood can have no right to dishonour and insult my humility. For, peasant and farmer's daughter though I am, I count myself as good as a gentleman and a noble like yourself. Your violence will have no effect on me, nor will your riches. Your words will not deceive me, nor your sighs and tears move me. If I were to find any of your qualities in a man chosen by my parents for my husband, I should bow to his will, and have no other wishes but his. Were it not for my honour, in fact, I would freely yield to you, sir – though without pleasure – what you are trying to gain by force. This I say so that you may not think for a moment that anyone but a lawful husband can gain anything from me.

'"If you are reluctant only on that account, most lovely Dorothea" – for that is this unfortunate woman's name – exclaimed the treacherous gentleman, "here I give you my hand to be yours. May the Heavens, from whom nothing is hidden, be my witness, and this image of Our Lady, that you have here."'

When Cardenio heard her say that her name was Dorothea his agitation returned, and he was confirmed in his first suspicions. He did not choose to interrupt the story, however, being anxious to hear the ending, which he had almost guessed already. And so he only said:

'Then Dorothea is your name, lady? I have heard of another Dorothea whose misfortunes are perhaps similar to yours. Go on, and later I may tell you something which will both astonish you and arouse your pity.'

Struck by Cardenio's words and by his strange and ragged dress, Dorothea asked him to tell her straight away if he knew anything about her affairs. For if misfortune had left her one virtue, it was courage to suffer any possible disaster in the certainty that nothing could worsen her present lot.

'I should not omit to tell you my thoughts, dear lady,' replied Cardenio, 'if what I imagine were true. But so far there has been no occasion to, and it would not profit you to know what is in my mind.'

'Very well,' replied Dorothea. 'To continue my story: Don Ferdinand then took up an image which stood in the room, and called on it to witness our betrothal. He pledged himself with most binding oaths and solemn vows to marry me, even though before he had finished speaking I begged him to think what he was doing, and consider how angry his father would be at finding him married to a peasant girl, one of his own tenants. I implored him not to let my beauty, such as it was, blind him; for it was not sufficient to excuse his error. If he wished to express the love he bore me by doing me a kindness, I begged him to let my fortune take a course befitting my rank, since such unequal marriages are never happy, and do not preserve for long such joy as they begin with. All these arguments I used on him and many more which I do not remember; but they did not deflect him from his purpose. For he was like a man who finds no difficulty in concluding a bargain because he does not intend to pay.

'I thought the matter over briefly at this juncture, saying to myself: "I shall certainly not be the first to rise from low to high estate by marriage, nor will Don Ferdinand be the first whom beauty or blind love – the second is the more likely – have impelled to take a humble bride. Since, therefore, I am doing nothing that has not been done before, it would be as well to accept this honour which fortune offers. For even though his desire may last only until he has had his way, I shall be his wife in the eyes of God all the same. But if I reject him with scorn, I see that he will wickedly force me in the end, and I shall be dishonoured and universally blamed. For who could know how innocently I have come into this predicament? What reasoning could be strong enough to persuade my parents and others that this gentleman has entered my room without my consent?"

'All these reflections I turned over in my mind in a single moment. What is more, Don Ferdinand's oaths, the witnesses he invoked, the tears he shed and, finally, his charm and good looks began to incline me forcibly to a course which proved to be my undoing. For all this together with the many signs of true love he gave me were enough to conquer any heart, even one as independent and modest as mine.

'I called my maid to add her earthly witness to Heaven's. Don Ferdinand repeated and confirmed his oaths, calling on yet more saints, and invoking innumerable curses on himself should he break his promise. The tears came once more to his eyes, and he sighed deeply. He clasped me more firmly in his arms, which had never let me go. Whereafter, when my maid had left the room, I ceased to be a maid and he became a perfidious traitor.

'Day followed on the night of my undoing, but not so fast, I think, as Don Ferdinand desired. For once the appetite is satisfied man's greatest desire is to escape. This I say because Don Ferdinand hurriedly departed with the aid of my maid – it was she who had brought him in – even before it was light in the street. As he took his leave he promised me, though with less ardour than when he came in, that I could rely on his faith and on his oaths; and as further confirmation of his words he took a fine ring from his finger and put it on mine. Finally he left, and I remained, whether sad or glad I do not know. But of one thing I am certain: I was troubled and anxious, and almost beside myself at this strange event. And either I had not the heart, or I forgot, to scold my maid for her treachery in hiding Don Ferdinand in my room; for I had not yet made up my mind if the events of the night had been good or bad.

I told Don Ferdinand, however, as he departed, that he could come
to me on other nights in the same way, until such time as he wished
the marriage to be made public, for I was now his. He came on the
following night, but never again; and for more than a month I tried
in vain to see him in the street or at church, till I grew tired of fruitless waiting; for I knew that he was in the town and on most days
went hunting. He was very fond of the sport.

'Indeed, these were sad, melancholy days for me, and I began to
doubt, even to deny, his fidelity. I remember that I gave my maid
the scolding for her presumption which she had escaped before. I
had to control my tears and compose my looks for fear my parents
might ask me what was making me unhappy, and I be obliged to
invent a lie. But a moment arrived when my caution and delicacy came to an end, when I lost patience and my secret thoughts
escaped me. This was when I heard in the town some days
later that Don Ferdinand had married in the near-by city a young
lady of extreme beauty and very noble family, though not so rich
that her dowry could justify so great a match. Her name was said to
be Lucinda, and various astonishing details were told about the
wedding.'

On hearing Lucinda's name Cardenio only shrugged his shoulders, bowed his head, bit his lips and frowned. But soon a flood of
tears burst from his eyes. Dorothea did not pause in her story, however, but continued:

'When I heard this sad news, so far was my heart from freezing
that in my burning rage I could scarcely prevent myself from rushing into the streets and proclaiming the treacherous wrong he had
done me. But my fury was assuaged for a while by a plan which I
put into effect that very night. I borrowed the dress I am now wearing from a shepherd in my father's service. I told him my troubles,
and asked him to come with me to the city where I heard that my
enemy was. He first took me to task for my rashness and decried
my plan. But when he saw that I was resolved, he offered to accompany me, as he said, to the end of the world. Then I packed some of
my own clothes, some jewels and some money, in a pillow-case –
against any eventuality; and in the silence of the night, without telling my treacherous maid, I left my home with my servant, my mind
full of anxiety, and set out for the city on foot. For, though I could

not prevent what had been done, I was determined at least to demand of Don Ferdinand how his conscience had allowed him to do it.

'I was two and a half days on the way, and when I got to the city I asked for the house of Lucinda's parents. The first man whom I questioned told me more than I wanted to hear. He pointed out the house and informed me of all that had happened at their daughter's betrothal. It was such common knowledge in the city that all the gossips were discussing it. He told me that on the night of the betrothal, after the bride had given her consent, she had fallen into a deep faint, and that when the bridegroom had loosened her dress to give her air, he had found in her breast a letter written in her own hand. It declared that she could not be Don Ferdinand's wife, for she was already married to Cardenio; who, this person told me, was a noble gentleman of that city. If she had said Yes to Don Ferdinand, it continued, it was only so as not to disobey her parents. And the letter concluded by saying that she intended to kill herself at the end of the ceremony, and gave her reasons for ending her life. All this, they say, was confirmed when they found a dagger somewhere in her clothing. Don Ferdinand was so enraged at finding himself deluded, mocked, and slighted that he attacked her before she came out of her faint, trying to stab her with the dagger which they had just found on her; and he would have succeeded if her parents and the witnesses had not prevented him. It was said that Don Ferdinand fled instantly, and that Lucinda did not recover from her faint till the next day, when she told her parents that she was in truth the wife of that Cardenio I spoke of. I learnt too that this Cardenio was said to have been present at the ceremony, and that when he saw her married, which he had never supposed she could be, he had rushed from the city in despair, leaving a letter declaring the wrong Lucinda had done him and his resolution to fly from mankind for ever.

'All this was a matter of public discussions throughout the city. Everyone was talking about it, and they gossiped even more when they heard that Lucinda was missing from her parents' house; that she could not be discovered in the town; that her parents had almost gone out of their minds and did not know what to do to find her. This news gave me some hope. For I was gladder not to have found

Don Ferdinand than to have found him married, since it seemed that all possibility of redress was not yet closed to me. I thought that Heaven might have prevented this second marriage in order to show him his duty to the first and to make him realize that, as a Christian, he was more firmly bound by his conscience than by worldly considerations. I turned all these thoughts over in my mind and got some consolation, though no comfort, from inventing wan and distant hopes to sustain my life, which is now abhorrent to me.

'I was still in the city, and did not know what to do since I could not find Don Ferdinand. Then one day I heard a public crier announcing that a large reward would be paid to anyone finding me, and describing my person and the very clothes I was wearing. I even heard a rumour that I had eloped with the shepherd who had escorted me from home. It stung me to the quick to find my reputation fallen so low. For I had not only lost it by coming away, but, even worse, by my choice of so low and unworthy a companion. The instant I heard the crier I left the city with my servant, who was already showing signs of wavering in his promised fidelity; and that night through fear of being discovered we took refuge in the remotest part of these mountains.

'But one evil calls down another, as they say, and the end of one disaster is often the beginning of a worse. So it was in my case. For, once we were alone in these wilds, my good servant, till then faithful and reliable, tried to take advantage of the opportunity which that wild spot appeared to offer him and, prompted by brutishness rather than by my beauty, lost all respect and made shameless love to me. Then, when I answered him with just contempt, he ceased the entreaties by which he had at first thought to gain his will, and tried to use force. But just Heaven, which seldom or never fails to favour virtue, so favoured mine, that despite my feeble strength I was easily able to force him back over the edge of a precipice. Whether I left him dead or alive I do not know. Then I fled with more speed than might have been expected from my fright and exhaustion, and made my way into these mountains, with no other thought or plan than to hide from my father and anyone he might send to seek me.

'I do not know how many months I had been here when I found.

a herdsman who took me as his servant to a village in the heart of this range. I have worked for him as a shepherd all this time, trying always to keep out in the fields so as to conceal this hair of mine, which you have now so unexpectedly discovered. All my anxieties and precautions, however, were in vain, for my master got to know that I was not a man, and conceived the same wicked idea as my servant. But as fate does not always find an immediate remedy for every ill, I found no precipice or cliff to throw my master down, as I had my servant. And so I thought it would be less unpleasant to leave him and hide in these wilds again, than to try my strength or my protests against him. So, as I said, I took to the mountains once more, to seek a place where I can implore Heaven undisturbed with sighs and tears to take pity on my plight, and to give me grace and strength to escape from it; or else to die among these wastes and leave no memory of this miserable creature, who has so innocently given men cause to speak ill of her, in her own district and abroad.'

Chapter XXIX. *Of the ingenious plan contrived to extricate our enamoured Knight from the very severe Penance he had set himself.*

'THIS, gentlemen, is the true story of my tragedy. Judge for yourselves whether my sighs, my protests and my tears were not more than justified. Now that you know the nature of my misfortune you will see that all consolation is vain, since there is no possible cure. I only beg of you one favour, which you may easily grant: to advise me where I can live in safety, free from my present fears and from the dread of being discovered. For although I know that my parents love me so much that they would give me a kind welcome, I am so overwhelmed by shame at the mere thought of appearing in their presence, so different from the daughter they had supposed me, that I think it would be the lesser evil to banish myself for ever from their sight. Rather that than look them in the face, and know their thoughts. For they will consider that I have lost the honour they had the right to expect of me.'

She fell silent, her blushes clearly showing her grief and shame, and her hearers' minds were filled with pity and wonder at her misfortunes. Then, just as the priest was about to offer her consolation and advice, Cardenio forestalled him by saying:

'Then, lady, you are the fair Dorothea, the only daughter of the rich Clenardo?'

Dorothea was startled to hear her father's name spoken by such a miserable-looking creature – for, as we have already said, Cardenio was in rags.

'Who are you, my friend,' she asked, 'that know my father's name? For I have not mentioned it till now, if I remember rightly, in the whole story of my misfortune.'

'I am that unfortunate Cardenio,' he answered, 'whom, as you said, lady, Lucinda declared to be her husband. I am the hapless Cardenio, reduced to my present state by that same man who brought you to the condition you are in. Ragged, naked, comfortless and, what is worse, out of my mind. For I am sane only in the brief intervals that Heaven grants me. I, Dorothea, was witness of Ferdinand's crime and waited to hear that Yes with which Lucinda declared herself his wife. I had not the courage to see what would come of her fainting, or what became of the letter which was found in her breast. For my heart could not bear to witness so many disasters all together. So I rushed headlong from the house, only leaving a letter with my host to be put into Lucinda's hands. Here I came to these wastes with the intention of bringing my days to an end, for from that moment I loathed life as a mortal enemy. But fate has refused to end my existence and deprived me only of reason, perhaps to preserve me for my good fortune in meeting you. If your story is true, however – as I believe it is – Heaven, perhaps, has in store for us both a better ending to our misfortunes than we suppose. For, since Lucinda is mine and therefore unable to marry Don Ferdinand, as she has so publicly declared, and as he is yours and so also unable to marry, we may yet hope that Heaven will restore to us our own partners; for nothing is irretrievably lost. Since we have this comfort, then, which springs from no very distant hopes or wild imaginings, I beg you, lady, to take fresh courage, as I intend to. Let us adapt ourselves to the expectation of better fortune. For I swear to you, as a Christian gentleman, that I will not forsake you till I see you Don Ferdinand's wife; and if argument cannot bring him to acknowledge his duty to you, I will use my gentleman's privilege and duly challenge him for the wrong he has done you. I will take no account of the injuries he has done me, but leave Heaven to avenge them, whilst I revenge yours here on earth.'

Dorothea was dumbfounded by Cardenio's speech. She did not know how to thank him, and tried to kiss his feet; but Cardenio would not allow her. The priest replied for himself and for her by approving Cardenio's generous determination. But he most earnestly begged, advised and urged them to come to his village, and there provide themselves with all the things they needed. And there too, he said, they could decide on their best course of action : either to search for Don Ferdinand, or to take Dorothea to her parents, or to do anything else which might seem proper. Cardenio and Dorothea thanked him and accepted his offer.

The barber, who had listened in silent amazement to all this, then made a courteous speech, offering no less generously than the priest to do them any service he could. At the same time he told them briefly what had brought the priest and himself there, described Don Quixote's strange madness, and informed them that they were waiting for his squire, who had gone to look for him. Then, like a dream, Cardenio's quarrel with Don Quixote came back into his memory, and he described it to the others, although he could not tell them the cause of the dispute.

At that moment they heard shouts, which they recognized as Sancho Panza's. For he had not found them where he had left them, and was calling out after them at the top of his voice. They went to meet him, and asked him after Don Quixote. He answered that he had found him naked except for his shirt, lean, sallow and half dead with hunger, sighing for his lady Dulcinea. He had told him of her commands that he should leave that place and come to El Toboso, where she was waiting for him. But he had replied that he was determined not to appear in her beauteous presence until he had done deeds worthy of her favour. If that went on much longer, said Sancho, there was a danger that he might never become an Emperor, as he was in honour bound to do, nor even an Archbishop, which was the least he could be. Therefore they must think out a means of getting him away. The priest replied that he had no need to worry, for they would bring him with them, willy-nilly. Then he told Cardenio and Dorothea of the plan they had thought out for curing

Don Quixote, or at least for getting him home. Dorothea then observed that she could play the damsel in distress better than the barber and, what was more, she had a dress with her in which she could do it to the life. They could rely on her to act the part and do all that was necessary. For she had read many books of chivalry, and knew the style in which afflicted maidens were accustomed to beg their boons of knights errant.

'There there is nothing more we need,' said the priest. 'Let us get to work at once. For there is no doubt that luck is in our favour. It has unexpectedly begun to offer you, my friends, a little hope of better things, and made this job of ours easier as well.'

Then Dorothea took a handsome woollen dress and a cloak of fine green cloth out of her bundle, and out of a jewel-box a necklace and other jewels. These she put on, and was instantly transformed into a rich and grand lady. All these things and more, as has already been said, she had brought from home in case she should need them, but had had no use for them till then. Her gracefulness, her elegance, and her loveliness charmed them all, and showed up Don Ferdinand's lack of taste in deserting such a beauty. But most admiring of all was Sancho Panza, who thought that he had never seen so lovely a creature in all the days of his life – and indeed he had not. He asked the priest most insistently to tell him who this beautiful lady was, and what she was looking for in those wild parts.

'This beautiful lady, brother Sancho,' replied the priest, 'is, to be very brief, heiress in the direct male line of the great Kingdom of Micomicon. She has come to seek your master to beg of him a boon, which is to redress a wrong or injury which a wicked giant has done her. For, thanks to your master's reputation as a brave knight throughout all the known world, this princess has come from Guinea in quest of him.'

'She's been lucky to find him,' exclaimed Sancho Panza. 'And she'll be even luckier if my master is so fortunate as to undo that injury, and redress that wrong, and kill that son of a whore – I mean that giant you mentioned, sir. And he'll kill him if he finds him, unless he's a phantom; for my master has no power at all against phantoms. But there's one thing I particularly beg of you, Master Priest. Advise my master to marry this princess right off, sir, so that he doesn't take it into his head to be an Archbishop, as I very much fear he may. Then he'll be incapable of taking Archbishop's orders, and he'll easily come to his Empire, and I shall get everything I want. For I've thought the matter over, and I've figured it out that it won't suit me for my master to be an Archbishop. For I'm no good for the Church, you see, being a married man; and going about getting dispensations to let me hold a church living, seeing that I have a wife and children, would be an endless job. So it all depends on my master marrying this lady straight away, sir – I don't know her name yet, so I can't call her by it.'

'Her name,' replied the priest, 'is Princess Micomicona, as obviously it would be since her kingdom is called Micomicon.'

'Of course,' replied Sancho. 'I've known plenty of men take their titles and surnames from the places they live in – people like Pedro de Alcala, Juan de Ubeda, and Diego de Valladolid. The custom must be the same over there in Guinea, and the queens there take their names from their kingdoms.'

'Yes, you must be right,' said the priest, 'and in this matter of your master's marrying, I will do everything in my power.'

Sancho was content with his assurance; and the priest was amazed at his simplicity, and at the hold these absurdities of his master's had on his imagination. For he seemed seriously to believe that Don Quixote would become an Emperor.

By this time Dorothea had mounted the priest's mule, and the barber had fixed his ox tail beard to his chin. So they told Sancho to guide them to Don Quixote, warning him not to say that he knew the priest or the barber, because the whole matter of his master's becoming an Emperor hung on their not being recognized. Neither Cardenio nor the priest would go with them. For Cardenio was afraid that the sight of him might remind Don Quixote of their quarrel, and the priest did not consider his own presence necessary for the moment. So they let the others ride ahead, and followed slowly on foot. The priest, however, could not forbear instructing Dorothea in the part she had to play. But she said that there was no need for him to worry, for she would conform in every way to the details prescribed in books of chivalry. They had gone little more than two miles when they caught sight of Don Quixote among a maze of rocks, dressed now, but without his armour. Sancho pointed him out to Dorothea, who immediately whipped on her palfrey, followed by the well-bearded barber. When they reached the knight, the squire leapt from his mule to take Dorothea in his arms; and she dismounted with great sprightliness and fell on her knees at Don Quixote's feet. From which position, despite his efforts to raise her, she addressed him in this fashion:

'I will not arise from here, valorous and courageous knight, until your goodness and courtesy grant me a boon, which will redound to the honour and glory of your person and to the advantage of the most disconsolate and wronged damsel beneath the sun. For if the valour of your mighty arm corresponds to the report of your immortal fame, you are obliged to protect this luckless wight who comes from a far country, attracted by the odour of your fame, to seek from you a remedy for her misfortunes.'

'I will not give you a word in answer, beauteous lady,' replied Don Quixote, 'nor hear anything more of your plight till you rise from the ground.'

'I will not rise, sir,' replied the afflicted damsel, 'ere of your courtesy you have granted me the boon I crave.'

'I grant it freely,' replied Don Quixote, 'provided my compliance be not to the disservice or prejudice of my King, my country, or of that lady who holds the key of my heart and liberty.'

'It is not to the disservice or prejudice of any of these, my dear sir,' replied the sorrowing damsel.

At this point Sancho Panza put his lips to his master's ear, and whispered very softly: 'Your worship can easily grant her the boon she begs. It's only a trifle – just to kill a great giant. And the lady herself is the high and mighty princess Micomicona, Queen of the great Kingdom of Micomicon in Ethiopia.'

'Whoever she may be,' replied Don Quixote, 'I shall act as my duty and my conscience dictate, and in obedience to the rules of my profession.' And turning once more to the maiden, he said: 'Fairest lady, arise, for I grant you whatever boon you would ask of me.'

'What I ask,' said the damsel, 'is that, of your magnanimity, you shall come with me instantly where I shall lead you; and that you promise me to engage in no other adventure or enterprise till you have avenged me on a traitor who has usurped my kingdom in despite of all law, human or divine.'

'I repeat that I grant your request,' replied Don Quixote; 'and so, lady, from henceforth you may cast off the melancholy which oppresses you, and allow your fainting hopes to recover new strength and courage. For, with the help of God and my right arm, you shall soon see yourself restored to your kingdom, and seated on the throne of your ancient and high estate, in despite and defiance of all rogues who would oppose it. Now, hands to the wheel! For in delay, it is said, lies danger.'

The distressed damsel struggled persistently to kiss his hands; but Don Quixote, who was in every respect a civil and courteous knight, refused to allow her. On the contrary, he forced her to rise, and embraced her most civilly and courteously. Then he bade Sancho look to Rocinante's girths, and arm him with all speed. The squire took down his armour, which was hanging from a tree like a trophy, looked to the girths and speedily armed his master, who cried as soon as he saw himself in armour: 'Let us go from hence, in God's name, to succour this great lady.'

The barber was still on his knees, taking great care to hide his laughter and to keep his beard from falling off. For their fine plan might miscarry if it fell. But seeing the boon already granted and Don Quixote diligently preparing to fulfil his promise, he got up and took his lady by the other hand, the two of them helping her on to her mule. Then Don Quixote mounted Rocinante, and the barber settled on his mount, leaving Sancho on foot; which made him grieve afresh for the loss of Dapple, whom he now missed. But he bore it all cheerfully, since now his master seemed to be on the way, and just on the very point of becoming Emperor. For Sancho had not the slightest doubt that he would marry the Princess and become at least King of Micomicon. One thought alone distressed him: that this kingdom was in Negro country, and that the people he would have for subjects would all be black. But he at once invented a good remedy for this, saying to himself: 'What do I care if my vassals are black? I've only to put them on board ship and bring them to Spain, where I shall be able to sell them, and be paid in cash. Then with the money I can buy a title or a post on which I can live at my ease for all the days of my life. I've got eyes in my head, and I'm fly enough to sell ten thousand subjects in the winking of an eye – or thirty thousand even. I'll shift 'em, the little ones with big ones, or any other way I can. Never mind how black they start,

I'll turn them into whites or yellows. I think I know how to lick my own fingers.' With these thoughts he trudged on in such good spirits that he forgot the fatigue of going on foot.

Cardenio and the priest had watched all that passed from behind some brambles, and could think of no pretext for joining the company. But the priest, who was a great schemer, presently invented one. With a pair of scissors, which he carried in a case, he hastily cut off Cardenio's beard and dressed him in his own grey jacket and black cape, himself remaining in his breeches and doublet. This so transformed Cardenio's appearance that he would not have known himself if he had looked in a mirror. This done, although the others had gone ahead while they were changing clothes, they had no difficulty in gaining the main road before them. For the thickets and broken paths thereabouts did not allow horsemen to go as quickly as men on foot. In fact they took up their position on the plain, where the pass comes down from the mountains. When Don Quixote and his comrades emerged, the priest stared at the knight for some time, pretending that he was trying to recognize him. Then, after standing for some time gazing at him, he ran up to him with open arms, crying:

'Welcome, mirror of chivalry, my good compatriot Don Quixote de la Mancha, flower and cream of gallantry, protector and aid of the needy, quintessence of knight errantry.'

And as he spoke he clasped Don Quixote's left knee. The knight was alarmed at the man's appearance and at his language, and surveyed him carefully. When he finally recognized him too, he was still amazed to see him, but made a great effort to dismount. The priest, however, would not allow him to, which caused Don Quixote to exclaim:

'Permit me, Master Priest. It is not right that I should be mounted, and so reverend a person as your worship should be on foot.'

'On no account will I allow you,' said the priest. 'Remain mounted, since on horseback it was that your Mightiness performed deeds and exploits unparalleled in our age. I am but an unworthy priest, and it shall be enough for me to ride muleback behind one of those gentlemen of your company, if they are agreeable. And truly I shall count myself mounted on the steed Pegasus, or on the zebra or courser of the famous Moor Muzaraque, who lies to this day beneath a spell on the great hill of Zulema, not far from the grand Compluto ...'

'I did not think of that, my dear Master Priest,' replied Don Quixote; 'but I know that my lady the Princess will be delighted, as a favour to me, to order her squire to give you the saddle of his mule. For he can ride on the crupper if the beast will stand it.'

'Yes, the beast will stand it, I think,' replied the Princess; 'and I am sure that there will be no need to command my squire, for he is too courteous and well-bred to suffer an ecclesiastic to go on foot when he may ride.'

'That's right,' replied the barber. And quickly getting down, he offered the priest the saddle, which he took without much pressing. But unfortunately as the barber was getting up behind, the mule, which was a hired one – and that is as much as to say that it was a bad beast – reared its hind quarters and gave two such kicks, that if they had caught Master Nicholas on the chest or on the head, he would have cursed the day he started rambling after Don Quixote. As it was he fell down in a fright, with so little care for his beard that it came off. Now when he found that he had lost it he could not think what to do except to clasp both hands hurriedly to his face, and cry out that his jaw was broken. Then, seeing all that mass of beard lying without jaws or blood some distance away from the fallen squire's face, Don Quixote exclaimed: 'Good Heavens! This is a great miracle! His beard has been torn as clean from his face as if he had been shaved.'

The priest saw the danger of his plot being discovered. So he instantly ran to the beard and to Master Nicholas, who was still moaning. He quickly clasped the barber's head to his chest, and stuck the beard on in a twinkling, mumbling some words over him, which he said were an infallible charm for refixing beards, as they should see. Then, when it was fixed, he moved away, leaving the squire as well bearded and as sound as before. Don Quixote was vastly amazed at this, and begged the priest to teach him the charm when he had the time. For he was convinced that its efficacy must extend beyond the mere refixing of beards, since clearly the flesh must have been all lacerated and bloody when the beard was torn out. So, as the spell had effected a complete cure it must be good for more than just beards.

'It is,' said the priest, and promised to teach it him at the first opportunity.

They agreed that the priest should ride first, and after him the three of them take turns till they came to the inn, which must have been six miles off. So three of them being now mounted – Don Quixote, the Princess, and the priest – and three on foot – Cardenio, the barber and Sancho Panza – Don Quixote addressed the damsel: 'Lead on, your Highness, in whatever direction you will.'

But before she could reply, the priest put in: 'To what kingdom will your ladyship guide us? Is it perhaps to Micomicon? It must be so surely, or I know very little about kingdoms.'

And Dorothea was quick-witted enough to know that she had to agree, which she did.

'Yes, sir, towards that land my way lies.'

'If that is so,' said the priest, 'we have to pass through my village. From there your worship will take the route for Cartagena, where, if you are fortunate, you may find a ship. Then, if you have a favourable wind, a calm sea and no storms, in less than nine years you will be in sight of the great Meona lake, I mean the Meotis – from which it is little more than a hundred days' journey to your Highness's kingdom.'

'You are mistaken, my good sir,' said she. 'For I left less than two years ago, and have had bad weather all the way. But for all that I am here and have seen the person I so ardently desired to see – that is my lord Don Quixote de la Mancha. His renown came to my ears the moment I set foot in Spain, and impelled me to seek him in order to commend myself to his courtesy and entrust my just cause to the strength of his invincible arm.'

'No more. Cease your praises!' cried Don Quixote at this juncture. 'I hate any kind of flattery and, although this may not be flattery, still such compliments offend my chaste ears. All that I can say, my lady, is that, whether I have valour or no, such as I have or have not shall be employed in your service, even to the death. But leaving this matter till its due time, I beg you to tell me, Master Priest, what has brought you into these parts, alone like this, without attendants, and so thinly clad that you alarm me?'

'I will reply briefly,' answered the priest. 'I must tell you, sir, that I was travelling to Seville with Master Nicholas, our barber and

I

friend, to collect some money sent me by a relative of mine, who settled in the Indies long ago. And it was no small sum either, but more than sixty thousand silver dollars, which is a tidy bit. Now as we were travelling in these parts yesterday we were attacked by four highwaymen, who stripped us to our very beards, so that the barber thought it wise to put on a false one. And as for this young man here' – pointing to Cardenio – 'he was quite transformed. The strange thing is that it is well known about here that the men who robbed us are galley-slaves. They are said to have been set free almost at this very spot, by a man so very valiant that he released them despite the sergeant and the guards. He must either be out of his senses or as great a rogue as they. He can have no soul or conscience to have let the wolf out amongst the sheep, the fox amongst the hens, the fly amidst the honey. For he has deliberately defrauded justice, and rebelled against his King and natural lord, for he acted against his legal authority. He deliberately robbed the galleys of their hands, I tell you, and alarmed the Holy Brotherhood, who have been undisturbed for many years. In short, he has done a deed by which his body will gain nothing and his soul may be lost.'

Sancho had told the priest and the barber the adventure of the galley-slaves, which his master had concluded with so much glory; and the priest laid it on so thick in telling his story to see what Don Quixote would do or say. The knight changed colour at every word, and dared not confess that he had been those good people's liberator.

'Well,' said the priest, 'those were the men who robbed us. May God, in his mercy, pardon the man who prevented their going to the punishment they deserved.'

Chapter XXX. Of the fair Dorothea's cleverness and other pleasant and amusing matters.

SCARCELY had the priest finished when Sancho cried out: 'It was my master, Sir Priest, who did that deed. I swear it was. And not for want of my telling him beforehand. I warned him to look out what he was doing. I said it was a sin to set them at liberty. For they were all going to the galleys because they were very great villains.'

'Blockhead!' broke in Don Quixote. 'It is no concern or duty of knights errant to investigate whether the distressed, chained, and oppressed persons they meet on the roads are brought to that pass, or suffer that anguish, for their crimes or for their whims. Their only task is to succour them because they are in distress, taking account of their sufferings and not of their villainies. I met some mournful, miserable wretches strung together like beads on a rosary, and did for them what my duty requires. The rest is no affair of mine. If anyone objects, saving Master Priest's holy dignity and his reverend person, I say that he knows very little of the matter of chivalry, and that he lies like the son of a whore and a bastard. And I will prove it on him with my sword, which shall answer him at greater length.'

As he said this he steadied himself in his stirrups and pulled down his head-piece. For he carried the barber's basin, which was Mambrino's helmet in his estimation, hanging at his saddle-bow, till such time as the damage which the galley-slaves had done to it could be repaired.

Dorothea was too quick and intelligent not to understand Don Quixote's crazy humour. She saw that everyone except Sancho Panza was making fun of him, and was anxious not to be left out. So, seeing him in such a rage, she said to him:

'Remember, Sir Knight, the boon your worship granted me, and that you are bound by it not to interpose in any other adventure, however urgent it may be. Calm your spirit, therefore. For if the worthy priest had known that it was by that unconquered arm that the galley-slaves were freed, he would have put three stitches through his lips, or even bitten his tongue three times, rather than have uttered a word which might redound to your worship's disparagement.'

'I swear I would,' said the priest. 'I would even have pulled out one of my moustaches.'

'I will be silent, my dear lady,' said Don Quixote, 'and restrain the just anger which has risen in my breast. I will remain quiet and peaceful till I have accomplished the promised boon for you. But, to reward this resolution of mine, I beg you to tell me – if it does not cause you too much pain – the nature of your distress, and the number, names and qualities of the persons on whom I have to take dire, satisfactory and complete revenge.'

'I will do so with all my heart,' replied Dorothea, 'if it will not weary you to hear of griefs and misfortunes.'

'It will not weary me, my lady,' replied Don Quixote.

To which Dorothea replied: 'Since that is so, then give me your attention, your worships.'

With that Cardenio and the barber caught up with her, wishing to hear what sort of story the ingenious Dorothea would invent; and Sancho, who was as much taken in by her as was his master, did the same. Then, settling comfortably into her saddle, after a preliminary cough and other preparatory gestures, she began her story with considerable dash:

'First, gentlemen, you must know that my name is ...' And here she stopped a moment because she had forgotten the name the priest had given her. But he saw what had happened and rushed to her aid, saying:

'It is no wonder, my lady, that your Highness is confused and embarrassed at telling your misfortunes. For affliction often impairs the memory to such an extent that miserable sufferers cannot even remember their own names, as has happened in the case of your exalted Ladyship, who has forgotten that she is the princess Micomicona, lawful heiress to the great Kingdom of Micomicon. Now with this reminder your Highness will be able to call to your distracted memory all that you wish to tell us.'

'You are right,' replied the damsel. 'From now on I think I shall be in no need of prompting, and I shall bring my true story to its proper conclusion. To continue then: My father, King Tinacrio the Sage, was very skilled in what are called the magic arts, and foresaw by his science that my mother, Queen Jaramilla, would die before him, and that very soon afterwards he too would die, and I be left an orphan. But this, he would say, disturbed him less than the certain knowledge that a monstrous giant, ruler of a large island almost bordering on our kingdom, would attack me. This giant bears the name of Pandafilando of the Frowning Eye – for it is a well-known fact that, although his eyes are straight and set in the proper place, he always squints as if he were cross-eyed. This he does out of ill-nature and to strike fear and dread into all on whom he looks. Well, as I told you, my father knew that once this giant heard that I was left an orphan he would invade my kingdom with a powerful army, and take it all from me, not leaving me so much as a little village to retire to. And though he knew that I could avert all this ruin and misfortune by marrying the giant, my father thought it very unlikely that I should ever consent to such an ill-assorted match. He was quite right, for I have never so much as thought of marrying that giant, or any other, however huge and monstrous. My father's counsel was: not to stay after his death nor put up any defence against Pandafilando's invasion of my kingdom, for that would be my ruin; but to leave the kingdom voluntarily to him, if I wished to avoid the death and total destruction of my good and loyal subjects, since I should be unable to defend myself against the giant's hellish power. He bade me instantly set out with some of my subjects for Spain, where I should find a relief for my troubles by meeting a knight errant, whose renown at that time would extend throughout the whole kingdom, and whose name, if I remember rightly, was to be Don Azote or Don Gigote.'

'Don Quixote he must have said,' put in Sancho Panza, 'otherwise called the Knight of the Sad Countenance.'

'You are right,' said Dorothea. 'He also said that he would be a tall, thin-faced man, and that he would have a dark brown mole with hair on it like bristles on his right side under his left shoulder, or somewhere thereabouts.'

Here Don Quixote said to his squire: 'Come, Sancho, help me to strip. I want to see if I am the knight this sage king spoke of in his prophecy.'

'Why should your worship want to take off your clothes?' asked Dorothea.

'To see if I have that mole your father spoke of,' replied Don Quixote.

'There's no reason to strip,' said Sancho. 'I know your worship has a mole just like that in the middle of your spine. It's a sign of strength.'

'That is enough,' said Dorothea; 'for there is no need to look into such trifles among friends, and whether it is on your shoulder or your spine scarcely matters. Enough that you have a mole; wherever it is, it is all the same flesh. No doubt my father was right in all respects. And I am right in commending myself to Don Quixote, for he it is my father meant. That is proved by his features and by the renown he bears not only in Spain but throughout La Mancha. For as soon as we landed at Osuna I heard so many tales of his exploits that my heart told me at once he was the knight I had come to seek.'

'But how, dear lady, did you come to land at Osuna,' asked Don Quixote, 'since it is not a seaport?'

But before Dorothea could reply, the priest put in: 'The lady princess surely means that after she landed at Malaga, the first place where she had news of your worship was Osuna.'

'That is what I meant,' said Dorothea.

'That clears things up,' said the priest. 'Will your Majesty continue?'

'There is no more to say,' replied Dorothea, 'except that finally I have had the good fortune to find the noble Don Quixote, and reckon myself now as good as Queen and Mistress of my whole Kingdom. For, of his courtesy and generosity, he has granted me my boon, and will follow me wherever I conduct him; which shall be into the presence of that Pandafilando of the Frowning Eye, that he may slay him and restore to me what this giant has so wrongfully usurped. All this will come to pass to the letter, for that is the prophecy of my good father, Tinacrio the Sage. He left it recorded too in Chaldean or Greek writing – I cannot read it – that if after beheading the giant this knight of the prophecy should wish to marry me, I should give myself to him without demur as his lawful wife, and grant him possession of my kingdom and my person.'

'What do you think, friend Sancho?' cried Don Quixote at this point. 'Do you hear that? Did I not tell you? See if we have not a kingdom to rule already, and a Queen to marry.'

'I swear you have,' said Sancho. 'Devil take the bastard who wouldn't marry as soon as Sir Pandafilando's windpipe's split! And she isn't a bad bit of goods, the Queen! I wish all the fleas in my bed were as good.'

At that he leapt into the air twice in sign of extreme delight. Then he ran to seize the bridle of Dorothea's mule and, making her stop, fell on his knees before her, beseeching her to give him her hands to kiss, in token that he took her for his Queen and Mistress. And not one of the party could help laughing at the master's madness and the man's simplicity. Dorothea held out her hands to him, and promised to make him a great lord in her kingdom, as soon as she should by the grace of Heaven recover it and enjoy it again. And Sancho thanked her in such language that they all burst out laughing afresh.

'That, gentlemen,' Dorothea went on, 'is my story. It only remains to tell you that of the attendants I brought with me out of my kingdom none but this well-bearded squire survives. All the rest were drowned in a great storm which struck us within sight of harbour. By a miracle he and I got ashore on a couple of planks; and indeed the whole course of my life has been one long miracle and mystery, as you will have noted. And if I have exaggerated in any way, or have not been as exact as I should be, remember what the reverend gentleman said at the beginning of my story. For perpetual and extreme hardships deprive the sufferer even of memory.'

'They will not rob me of mine, exalted and courageous lady,' said Don Quixote, 'however many I may endure in your service, and however great and unprecedented they may be. So once more I confirm the boon I have granted you, and swear to go with you to the end of the world, till I confront your fierce enemy; whose proud head, by the help of God and my strong arm, I mean to cut off with the edge of this ... I will not say good sword, thanks to Gines de Pasamonte, who carried mine off.' These last words he muttered under his breath, and then went on: 'When I have cut off his head and restored to you the peaceful possession of your kingdom, it shall rest with your own choice to dispose of your person in whatever manner you please. For, so long as my memory is engrossed, my heart captive and my mind enthralled by that ... I say no more; it is impossible that I could so much as think of marriage, even with the Phoenix.'

Sancho was so taken aback at his master's last words on the subject of not wishing to marry that he exclaimed in great fury:

'Good God, your worship! You must be out of your mind, I swear! How could there possibly be any doubt about marrying a grand princess like this one? Do you think fortune will offer you a stroke of luck like this round every corner? Can my lady Dulcinea possibly be more beautiful? Of course she isn't, not by half. I should say she isn't good enough to tie this lady's shoes. A poor chance I have of getting my countship if your worship goes fishing for dain-

ties at the bottom of the sea. Marry her! Marry her at once, for the
devil's sake, and lay hold of this kingdom, that's falling into your
hands like a ripe cherry. And when you're a king, make me a marquis or a viceroy, and then to hell with the rest!'

When Don Quixote heard these blasphemies against his lady
Dulcinea he could bear no more. So he raised his lance and, without
word or warning, he dealt Sancho two such blows that he knocked
him down. And if Dorothea had not called out to the knight to stop
he would no doubt have taken his squire's life on the spot.

'Do you think, miserable villain,' asked Don Quixote after a
while, 'that I must always let you pull me by the nose, and that
there is to be nothing but sinning on your side and pardoning on
mine? Do not think that, excommunicate rogue! For that you certainly are, for defaming the peerless Dulcinea. Do not you know,
you clod, you ignominious vagabond, that but for the power she
infuses into my arm I should not have the strength to kill a flea?
Tell me, you viper-tongued villain, who do you think has conquered this kingdom and cut this giant's head off, and made you a
marquis — for I take all this as an accomplished fact — if it is not the
might of Dulcinea, employing my arm as the instrument of her exploits? She fights and conquers through me, and I live and breathe
and have my life and being in her. You villain, you son of a whore!
What ingratitude you show, seeing yourself raised up out of the
dust of the earth to be a titled lord, and your only thanks for such a
benefit is to malign the lady that bestowed it on you!'

Sancho was not too badly hurt to hear his master's reproaches.
He got up rather hurriedly, ran behind Dorothea's palfrey, and addressed his master from there:

'Now think, sir, if your worship's determined not to marry this
great princess, it's plain that the kingdom will not be yours. Now
in that case what favours can you do me? That's what I'm complaining about. Marry this Queen, sir, once for all, now that we have her
here, dropped down from heaven as it were. You can go back to my
lady Dulcinea afterwards; for there have been plenty of kings in the
world who have kept mistresses. As for the matter of beauty, it's no
affair of mine. To tell you the truth, they both seem handsome to
me, though I've never seen the lady Dulcinea.'

'What! You have never seen her, blasphemous traitor?' cried

Don Quixote. 'But have not you just brought me a message from her?'

'I mean that I didn't have time to observe the beauty of her fair features one by one,' said Sancho, 'but she looked all right to me on the whole.'

'Well, I pardon you now,' said Don Quixote, 'and you must forgive me the injury I have done you. For primary impulses are not within man's power to check.'

'So I see,' replied Sancho, 'and in me the need to talk is a primary impulse, and I can't help saying right off what comes to my tongue.'

'All the same,' said Don Quixote, 'watch what you say, Sancho, for the pitcher can go too often to the well ... I say no more.'

'Well, well,' replied Sancho, 'God's in heaven and sees all man's tricks. He'll judge which of us is wickeder, I for my bad words or your worship for your bad actions.'

'No more of that,' said Dorothea. 'Run, Sancho, kiss your master's hand, and beg his pardon. And from now on be more careful with your praises and slanders, and say nothing against this lady Tobosa, of whom all I know is that I am her humble servant. And put your trust in God that he will not fail to bring you to an estate where you can live like a prince.'

Sancho hung his head and begged his master for his hand, which Don Quixote gave him in all gravity. Then, when he had kissed it, the knight gave him his blessing, and bade him come ahead a little, for he had something to ask him and matters of great importance to discuss with him. Sancho obeyed, and once they were slightly in advance of the others Don Quixote said:

'Since your return I have had neither the time nor the opportunity to ask you for many details about the message you took and the answer you brought back. But now that chance has given us both time and opportunity, do not deny me the pleasure that your good news will give me.'

'Ask any questions you like, your worship,' replied Sancho, 'I'll get out of all of them as easily as I got in. But I beseech your worship not to be so vindictive in future.'

'Why do you say that, Sancho?' asked Don Quixote.

'The beating you gave me just now, you know,' replied Sancho, 'was because of the quarrel the Devil raised between us the other

night, and not for what I said against my lady Dulcinea, whom I
reverence like a holy relic. – Of course she's nothing of the sort –
but I love her just because she belongs to your worship.'

'No more of this talk, Sancho, at your peril,' said Don Quixote,
'for it offends me. I pardoned you then, and you know the saying
very well: Fresh sin, fresh penance!'

As they were talking they saw a man on an ass coming down the
road, and when he got nearer they made him out to be a gipsy. But
whenever Sancho Panza saw a donkey he followed it with his eyes
and with his heart, and no sooner did he catch sight of the man than
he knew that he was Gines de Pasamonte. Now this clue of the gipsy
led him to recognize his ass; for it was his own Dapple which Pasamonte was riding. He had put on gipsy dress so as to be able to sell
the ass unrecognized, speaking, as he did, the gipsy language and
many others like a native. But Sancho knew him as soon as he saw
him, and instantly shouted out:

'Gines, you thief! Let go my jewel! Let go my life! Don't rob
me of my comfort! Let go my ass! Let go my treasure! Get out, you
bastard! Get away, you thief! Give up what isn't yours!'

There was no need of all those words or curses, for Gines jumped
down at the first, and took to his heels at a lively trot. In one second,
in fact, he had disappeared from before their eyes. Sancho meanwhile ran up to his Dapple and embraced him, crying:

'How have you been, my dear, my darling Dapple, my darling
companion?'

And all the time he kissed him as if he had been a human being.
The ass stayed quiet and let Sancho caress him without answering a
word. Then the others came up and congratulated the squire on recovering his beast, most of all Don Quixote, who said that he would
not annul the draft for the three colts all the same. Sancho returned
him thanks for this.

Whilst the pair of them were engaged in their conversation, the
priest congratulated Dorothea on her ingenuity in telling her story,
on its brevity and its close resemblance to the tales of knight
errantry. She owned that she had often amused herself by reading
them, but that she did not know where provinces and seaports lay,
and so had said at a venture that she had landed at Osuna.

'I realized that,' said the priest. 'That was why I interrupted as I did, and put everything right. But is it not marvellous to see how easily this poor gentleman believes all these inventions and lies, simply because they are in the same style as the nonsense in his books?'

'It is,' said Cardenio. 'It is so strange and rare that I do not know whether anyone trying to invent such a character in fiction would have the genius to succeed.'

'There is another strange thing about it,' said the priest. 'If you talk to the good gentleman about anything that does not touch on his madness, far from talking nonsense, he speaks very rationally and shows a completely clear and calm understanding. In fact nobody would think him anything but a man of very sound judgement, unless he were to strike him on the subject of chivalries.'

While they were engaged in this conversation Don Quixote continued with his, saying to Sancho: 'Let us let bygones be bygones, friend Panza, and tell me now, forgetting all anger and rancour, where, how, and when did you find Dulcinea? What was she doing? What did you say to her? What did she answer? How did she look when she read my letter? Who copied it for you? Tell me every detail you think I should wish to know about the matter. Do not add or invent anything to please me, and please do not cut the tale short, for that will spoil my pleasure.'

'To tell you the truth, sir,' replied Sancho, 'no one copied the letter for me, because I had no letter with me.'

'Yes, it is just as you say,' replied Don Quixote. 'For I found I had the little note-book I wrote it in still in my possession two days after you had gone. It grieved me deeply, since I did not know what you would do when you found that you had not got the letter. I always thought that you would come back as soon as you missed it.'

'So I should have done,' replied Sancho, 'if I hadn't learnt it by heart when your worship read it to me. So that I repeated it to a parish clerk, who wrote it down exactly from my memory. He said he had never read as nice a letter in all the days of his life, although he had seen and read plenty of letters of excommunication.'

'Do you still remember it now, Sancho?' asked Don Quixote.

'No, sir,' replied Sancho. 'For as soon as I had said it to him, I saw it wouldn't be any more use, and let it out of my mind. If I remember anything at all it's that "*Suppressed*" – I mean "*sovereign-*

lady", and the ending: "*Yours till death, the Knight of the Sad Coun-tenance*". And in between I put more than three hundred "*souls*", "*lives*" and "*dear eyes*".'

Chapter XXXI. *Of the delectable Conversation which passed be-tween Don Quixote and Sancho Panza his squire, and other incidents.*

'ALL this does not displease me at all. Go on,' said Don Quixote. 'You got there; and what was that queen of beauty doing? I am sure that you found her stringing pearls, or embroidering a device with thread of gold for this, her captive knight.'

'No, she wasn't doing that,' replied Sancho, 'but winnowing a couple of bushels of wheat in her back yard.'

'Then you can be certain,' said Don Quixote, 'that the grains of that wheat turned to pearls at the touch of her hand. Did you ob-serve, my friend, whether it was of the white or brown sort?'

'It was neither, but red,' replied Sancho.

'Then I promise you,' said Don Quixote, 'that, winnowed by her hands, it made the finest white bread. There can be no doubt of that. But go on. When you gave her my letter, did she kiss it? Did she put it on her head? Did she perform any ceremony worthy of such a letter? Or what did she do?'

'When I went up to give it to her,' said Sancho, 'she was in the middle of the job with a good lot of wheat in her sieve, and she said: "Put the letter down, friend, on that sack. I can't read it till I've finished sifting what I have here."'

'A wise lady,' said Don Quixote. 'That must have been so that she could read and enjoy it at her leisure. Go on, Sancho. And whilst she was about her task, what speech did she hold with you? What questions did she ask concerning me? And what did you re-ply? Come, tell me everything. Do not leave a drop in the ink-horn.'

'She didn't ask me anything,' said Sancho. 'But I told her how your worship was here doing your penance for her service, naked from the waist up, buried in all these mountains like a savage, sleep-ing on the ground, never eating bread off a table-cloth, nor comb-ing your beard, and weeping and cursing your fate.'

'You spoke wrong in saying that I was cursing my fate,' said Don Quixote. 'On the contrary, I bless it, and shall bless it all the days of my life, for making me worthy of loving so high a lady as Dulcinea del Toboso.'

'So high,' answered Sancho, 'that I swear she's a good hand's breadth taller than I am.'

'How do you know that, Sancho?' asked Don Quixote. 'Did you measure yourself against her?'

'I did,' replied Sancho. 'Like this. I went to help her load a sack of corn on to an ass, and so got we very close together. That's how I noticed she was a good hand's breadth taller than I am.'

'But is it not true,' replied Don Quixote, 'that her great height is accompanied and adorned by a thousand million intellectual graces? One thing you cannot deny me, Sancho. When you stood close to her, did you not smell a spicy odour, an aromatic fragrance, something unutterably sweet to which I cannot give a name? I mean an essence or aroma, as if you were in some rare glover's shop?'

'All that I can say,' answered Sancho, 'is that I got a sniff of something rather mannish. It must have been because she was running with sweat from the hard work.'

'It would not be that,' replied Don Quixote. 'You must have had a cold or have smelt yourself. For well I know the scent of that rose among thorns, that lily of the field, that liquid ambergris.'

'It's quite possible,' replied Sancho, 'for very often there's that same smell about me that seemed to be coming from the lady Dulcinea. But it's not surprising, for one devil is like another.'

'Well, then,' continued Don Quixote, 'she has finished winnowing her corn and sent it to the mill. What did she do when she had read my letter?'

'She didn't read the letter,' said Sancho, 'for she said she couldn't read or write. She tore it up instead, and told me she wouldn't give it to anyone to read, so that her secrets shouldn't be known all over the village. She said it was quite enough that I had told her by word of mouth about your worship's love for her and about the extraordinary penance you had stayed behind to do for her sake. She ended up by telling me to tell your worship that she kissed your hands, and that she had far rather see you than write to you. So she begged and commanded you, at sight hereof, to leave these bushes

and briars and stop doing these mad antics, and set out at once on
the road for El Toboso, if more important business didn't prevent
you; for she was most anxious to see your worship. She laughed a
lot when I told her how you were called *the Knight of the Sad Countenance*. I asked her if that Basque of yours had been there. She said
that he had, and that he was a very decent sort of man. I asked her
about the galley-slaves too, but she said that she hadn't seen any of
them yet.'

'So far so good,' said Don Quixote. 'But tell me, what jewel did
she give you on your departure, in thanks for the news you brought
her of me? For it is an ancient and time-worn custom among
knights errant and their ladies to reward squires, damsels, or dwarfs
who bring them news of their ladies or knights with some rich
jewel in gratitude for their welcome news.'

'That's very likely, and I think it's a good custom. But they must
have done that in the olden times, for nowadays the habit seems to be
just to give them a bit of bread and cheese. That's what my lady Dulcinea gave me, anyhow, over the top of the yard wall when she said
good-bye to me. And what's more, it was a sheep's-milk cheese.'

'She is generous in the extreme,' said Don Quixote; 'and, if she
did not give you a gold jewel, it was no doubt only because she had
not one there at hand to give you. But it is never too late. Gifts are
still good after Easter. I will see her, and all shall be put right. But do
you know what does astonish me, Sancho? You must have gone
and returned through the air. For you have only taken three days
travelling to El Toboso and back, and it is a good ninety miles.
From which I conclude that the sage necromancer, who is my friend
and looks after my affairs – for I certainly have such a friend, or I
should not be a true knight errant – I say that this necromancer
must have assisted you on your journey without your knowing it.
For there are enchanters who have picked up a knight errant asleep
in his bed, and next day, he will not know how or why, but he will
wake up more than a thousand miles from the place where he went
to sleep. If it were not for that, it would be impossible for knights
errant to come to one another's aid in their perils, as they do at
every turn. One of them, perhaps, is fighting in the Armenian
mountains with some dragon or fierce monster, or with another
knight. He is getting the worst of the battle, and is just at the point

of death. Then, when you least expect it, there appears another knight, on a cloud or in a chariot of fire. This friend, who was the moment before in England, comes to his assistance, saves his life, and is back that night in his own lodging, enjoying his supper. Very often the distance from the one place to the other is six or seven thousand miles. Now all this is effected by the skill and wisdom of these sage enchanters who watch over valorous knights. So, friend Sancho, I do not find it difficult to believe that you made the journey to and from El Toboso in so short a time; since, as I have said, some friendly sage must have carried you through the air without your knowing it.'

'That may be so,' said Sancho, 'for certainly Rocinante went like a gipsy's ass with quicksilver in its ears.'

'Quicksilver!' exclaimed Don Quixote. 'And a legion of devils besides, for they are the sort of gentry who travel – and make others travel – tirelessly, as much as they please. But, to leave the subject, what do you think I ought to do about my lady's command to go and see her? For, although I am clearly obliged to fulfil her behests, I find myself prevented by the boon I have granted to the Princess in whose company we are, and the law of chivalry compels me to put my oath before my pleasure. On the one hand I am perplexed and harassed by the desire to see my lady; on the other incited and summoned by my pledged faith and the glory I shall gain in this enterprise. What I propose to do is to press on and get quickly to the place where this giant is. Then, when I get there, I will cut off his head, restore the Princess peacefully to her throne, and instantly return to behold the light which illumines my senses. I will offer her such excuses that she will come to approve my delay. For she will see that it all redounds to her greater glory and fame, since everything which I have achieved, am achieving, and shall achieve by force of arms in this life proceeds wholly from her favour and from my being her knight.'

'Oh dear!' cried Sancho. 'Your worship must be downright crazy! Tell me, sir, do you mean to take the journey for nothing, and let a rich and princely marriage, with a kingdom for dowry, slip through your fingers? They say that her country's more than sixty thousand miles round, and full of everything you want to support human life. I've heard that it's bigger than Portugal and Castile put

together. Don't talk any more, for Heaven's sake. You ought to be
ashamed of what you've said. Take my advice, please, and marry
her straight away, in the first village where there's a priest. Or else
there is our own priest here, who'll do the job a treat. I'm old
enough, mind you, to offer advice, and what I advise you now fits
the case like a glove. For a bird in the hand is worth two in the bush,
and he who had good and chose bad must not be vexed for the ill he
had.'

'Look you, Sancho,' replied Don Quixote, 'if you are advising
me to marry, so that I may be king when I have killed the giant, and
have the means of doing you favours and fulfilling my promise to
you, I would inform you that I can very easily gratify your wishes
without marrying. For I will make it a condition before I go into
the battle that when I come off victorious, they shall give me part
of the kingdom which I can bestow on anyone I will, even though
I do not marry her. And when I get it, whom do you think I shall
give it to but you?'

'That's fair enough,' replied Sancho. 'But take good care, your
worship, to choose a piece on the coast, so that if I don't like the life
I can put my black subjects on board ship, and do what I said with
them. Don't trouble to go and see my lady Dulcinea for the time
being, but go and kill the giant, and let's settle that business. For I
swear to God I think it'll bring us great honour and profit.'

'Yes, Sancho,' said Don Quixote, 'you are in the right, and I will
take your advice about going with the Princess before I visit Dulcinea. But I warn you to say nothing to anyone about what we have
been discussing and arranging, not even to our companions. For
since Dulcinea is so shy that she does not want her feelings known,
it would not be right for me, or for anyone acting for me, to reveal
them.'

'But if that's the case,' said Sancho, 'why, your worship, do you
make everyone you conquer by your mighty arm present himself
to my lady Dulcinea? For that says you love her and that she's
your sweetheart, as clearly as if you'd put your signature to the fact.
And seeing that you force them to go down on their knees in her
presence, and to say that they come from your worship to offer her
their obedience, how can the feelings of the pair of you stay
hidden?'

'Oh, how stupid and simple you are!' exclaimed Don Quixote. 'Do you not see, Sancho, that this all redounds to her greater glory? You must know that in this our state of chivalry it is a great honour for a lady to have many knights errant serving her, with no greater ambition than of serving her for what she is, and without hope of any other reward for their zeal than that she shall be pleased to accept them as her knights.'

'That's the kind of love,' said Sancho, 'I've heard them preach about. They say we ought to love our Lord for Himself alone, without being moved to it by hope of glory or fear of punishment. Though as for me, I'm inclined to love and serve Him for what He can do for me.'

'The devil take you!' said Don Quixote. 'What a peasant you are, and yet what apt things you say at times! One would almost think you had been to school.'

'But I swear I can't read,' replied Sancho.

At this point Master Nicholas called out to them to wait a bit, for the company wanted to stop and drink at a small spring by the roadside. Don Quixote halted, much to Sancho's satisfaction, since by this time he was tired of telling all those lies, and afraid that his master might catch him out. For although he knew that Dulcinea was a peasant girl from El Toboso, he had never seen her in his life. In the meantime Cardenio had put on the clothes which Dorothea was wearing when they met her, and although they were not very good they were a great improvement on his own. They all dismounted at the spring, and with the provisions which the priest had brought from the inn did something to satisfy their great hunger.

And whilst they were thus occupied a lad, who chanced to be passing along the road, stopped and stared at the party, and then, after a moment, rushed up to Don Quixote and clasped him round the legs, most opportunely bursting into tears:

'Oh, my lord,' he cried, 'don't you know me? Take a good look at me. I'm the boy Andrew whom your worship untied from the oak I was bound to.'

Don Quixote recognized him and, taking him by the hand, turned to say to the others: 'To convince you of the importance of having knights errant in the world to redress the outrages and wrongs which are committed here by insolent and wicked men, I

would have your worships know that some days ago, as I was passing by a wood, I heard most piteous shouts and cries, as of someone
afflicted and in distress. Immediately, as was my duty, I hastened in
the direction from which the sad cries seemed to come, and there I
found this lad who is now before you bound to an oak. And now
my soul rejoices at the sight of him, for he shall be my witness and
will not let me stray from the truth in any way. He was tied to a
tree, I tell you, naked to the waist; and a country fellow, who I
learnt afterwards was his master, was lashing him with the reins of
his horse. As soon as I saw him I demanded the reason for this
atrocious flagellation, and the brute replied that he was beating him
because he was his servant and for certain negligences of his which
seemed to spring rather from roguery than from foolishness. At this
the child cried: "Sir, he is only whipping me because I asked him
for my wages." The master answered with some sort of talk and
excuses, which I of course heard but did not admit. To be brief, I
made the peasant untie the boy, and made him swear to take him
and pay him *real* for *real* – and perfumed at that. Now, is not this
all true, Andrew my lad? Did you not note with what authority I
gave my orders, and with what humility he promised to do all that
I commanded and specified and required? Answer; do not be confused or hesitant. Tell these good gentlemen what happened, so that
they may see and reflect how useful it is, as I say, to have knights
errant on the roads.'

'All that your worship has said is quite true,' replied the boy,
'but the end of the business was very much the opposite of what
you suppose.'

'How the opposite?' demanded Don Quixote. 'Did not the
peasant pay you, then?'

'Not only didn't he pay me,' replied the boy, 'but as soon as your
worship was out of the wood and we were alone, he tied me up
again to the same oak and beat me again so hard that I was left
flayed like St. Bartholomew. And at every stroke he gave me, he
mocked and jibed at your worship. So that, if it hadn't been for the
pain, I should have burst out laughing. In fact, he gave me such a
welting that I've been in a hospital ever since, getting cured of the
injuries the wicked wretch did me. And your worship's to blame
for it all. For if you'd gone on your way and not come when you

weren't called, and not interfered with other people's business, my master would have been content to given me a dozen or two lashes. Then he would have let me go and paid me what he owed me. But as your worship abused him so needlessly and called him so many names, he got into a temper, and seeing that he couldn't vent it on you he let fly such a rain of blows on me, once we were alone, that I shall never be a whole man again for the rest of my life.'

'The trouble was,' said Don Quixote, 'that I went away. I should not have gone till I had seen you paid. For, as I ought to have known from long experience, there is never a peasant who keeps his word if he finds it does not suit him. But you remember, Andrew, that I swore I would go and look for him if he did not pay you, and find him too, even if he hid in the whale's belly.'

'That's right,' said Andrew, 'but it wasn't any good.'

'Now you will see if it is any good or not,' exclaimed Don Quixote, getting up very quickly and bidding Sancho bridle Rocinante, who had been browsing during their meal.

Dorothea asked him what what it was he intended to do. He answered that he was going to look for the villain, punish him for his wicked conduct, and see that Andrew was paid to the last farthing, in despite of and in the teeth of every peasant in the world. But she replied by reminding him that he could not. For by the boon he had granted her, he must not engage in any enterprise until hers was accomplished. And as he knew this better than anyone else, he must restrain his anger until his return from her kingdom.

'That is true,' replied Don Quixote, 'and Andrew must be patient till my return, as you say, my lady. But I swear again, and renew my promise, not to rest until I have seen him avenged and paid.'

'I don't believe in these vows,' said Andrew. 'I'd rather have something now to get me on to Seville, than all the vengeance in the world. Give me something to eat and take with me, if you have anything here. Then God bless your worship and all knights errant, and may they be as good errants for themselves as they've been for me.'

Sancho took a piece of bread and some cheese out of his bag and gave it to the lad, saying: 'Take this, brother Andrew, for each of us has a share in your misfortune.'

'Well, what's your share, then?' asked Andrew.

'This share of bread and cheese that I'm giving you,' replied Sancho. 'God knows whether I mayn't need it myself. For I must tell you, my friend, that we squires of knights errant are subject to great hunger and bad luck, and to other things too, which are better felt than told.'

Andrew seized his bread and cheese and, when he saw that no one was going to give him anything more, made his bow and took to the road; though, as he turned to go, he said to Don Quixote:

'For God's sake, Sir Knight Errant, don't come to my help if you meet me again, even though you see me being cut to pieces. But leave me to my troubles, for they can't be so bad that the results of your worship's help won't be worse. And God blast you and every knight errant ever born on the face of the earth!'

Don Quixote started up to punish him; but he ran off so fast that nobody attempted to follow. Our knight was very much abashed at Andrew's story, and the others had much trouble in not completing his discomfiture by laughing outright.

Chapter XXXII. Of what befell Don Quixote and all his company at the inn.

As soon as their excellent meal was over they saddled at once, and arrived next day without any noteworthy incident at that inn which was the dread and terror of Sancho Panza. But although he would rather not have gone in, this time he could not avoid it. And when they saw Don Quixote and Sancho coming, the innkeeper, his wife, their daughter and Maritornes came out to receive them with a great show of pleasure. The knight accepted their welcome with gravity and approbation, and bade them put him up a better bed than they had given him the time before. To which the landlady replied that she would give him one fit for a prince, if he would pay them better than the last time. Don Quixote answered that he would, and so they provided him with a tolerable one in the same loft as before. And there he lay down immediately, for he was severely shaken in body and mind. But no sooner had he shut himself in than the landlady attacked the barber, seizing him by the beard and crying:

'Bless my soul! You shan't use my ox tail for a beard any more.

Give me back my tail, for my husband's what-d'ye-call-it's so kicked about on the floor that it's a shame. I mean his comb that he used to stick into my tail.'

But the barber would not part with it for all her tugging, until the priest told him to give it to her, since they had no more need of disguise. For he could reveal himself in his own shape now, and tell Don Quixote he had fled to that inn after he had been robbed by the galley-slaves. Then, if the knight were to ask after the Princess's squire, they could tell him that she had sent him ahead to inform her subjects that she was on her way, and was bringing their common liberator with her. At this the barber cheerfully returned the landlady her tail, and they gave her back all her property too that she had lent them for Don Quixote's deliverance.

Everyone in the place was struck by Dorothea's beauty, and by the handsomeness of the shepherd Cardenio. The priest ordered them to prepare such food as the inn could provide, and the landlord, in hope of better payment, quickly served them with a tolerable meal. All this while Don Quixote slept, and they agreed not to wake him, since he was in greater need of sleep than of food. The landlord, his wife, his daughter, Maritornes and all the travellers were at the table, and they discussed Don Quixote's strange madness and the state in which they had found him. The landlady told them of his adventures with the carrier. Then she looked to see if Sancho was present and, finding that he was not, told them the tale of his tossing in the blanket, which amused them quite a bit. But when the priest said that it was the books of chivalry which he had read that had turned Don Quixote's brain, the landlord remarked:

'I don't know how that can be, because really I think there's no better reading in the world. I have two or three of them here and some other writings. They've truly put life into me, and not only into me but into plenty of others. For at harvest time a lot of the reapers come in here in the mid-day heat. There's always one of them who can read, and he takes up one of those books. Then as many as thirty of us sit round him, and we enjoy listening so much that it saves us countless grey hairs. At least I can say for myself that when I hear about those furious, terrible blows the knights deal one another, I get the fancy to strike a few myself. And I could go on listening night and day.'

'I agree absolutely,' said the landlady, 'for I never get any peace in my house except when you're listening to the reading. You're so fascinated then that you forget to scold for once.'

'That's right,' said Maritornes. 'I tell you I enjoy hearing them all too. They're very pretty, particularly the parts when some lady or other is lying in her knight's embraces under some orange-trees, and there's a damsel keeping watch for them, dying of envy and frightened to death. It's all as sweet as honey, I say.'

'And you, what do you think about it, young lady?' the priest asked the innkeeper's daughter.

'I don't know, sir, truly I don't,' she answered. 'I listen too, and really, though I don't understand it, I do enjoy it. But I don't like the fighting that pleases my father so much. I prefer the complaints the knights make when they're away from their ladies. Sometimes they actually make me cry, I pity them so much.'

'Then you would give them some relief, young lady,' asked Dorothea, 'if they were weeping for you?'

'I don't know what I'd do,' replied the girl. 'Only I know that some of those ladies are so cruel that their knights call them tigers and lions and lots of other nasty names. And, Jesus, I can't imagine what sort of heartless, conscienceless folk they can be to leave a decent man to die or go mad, rather than look at him. I don't know what's the good of all their coyness — if it's for the sake of their virtue, let 'em marry them, for that's what the gentlemen are after.'

'Be quiet, girl,' said the landlady. 'You seem to know rather much of these matters, and it's not right for young ladies to know or talk so much.'

'But as this gentleman asked me,' she answered, 'I couldn't help answering him.'

'Well, well,' said the priest, 'bring in those books, Master Landlord. I should like to see them.'

'With pleasure,' he replied; and going into his room, brought out a little old trunk, fastened with a small chain, which he undid, revealing three big books and some manuscript papers written in a very fine hand. The first book he opened was *Don Cirongilio of Thrace*, the others *Felixmarte of Hyrcania* and *The History of the Great Captain Gonzalo Hernandez of Cordova* together with the *Life of Diego Garcia de Paredes*.

On reading the titles of the two first, the priest observed to the barber: 'We need our friend's housekeeper here now, and his niece.'

'No, we don't,' replied the barber, 'for I'm just as capable of carrying them to the yard or to the fireplace; and there's a very good fire there now.'

'What,' said the innkeeper, 'does your worship want to burn my books?'

'Only these two,' replied the priest. 'This Don Cirongilio and this Felixmarte.'

'Are my books heretical or phlegmatic, by any chance,' asked the innkeeper, 'that you want to burn them?'

'Schismatic, you mean, my friend,' said the barber, 'not phlegmatic.'

'Yes, yes,' said the innkeeper. 'But if you've a mind to burn any, let it be this one about the Great Captain and Diego Garcia, for I'd rather have one of my children burnt than either of the others.'

'My friend,' pronounced the priest, 'these two books are full of lies and foolishness and vanity. But the one about the Great Captain is true history, and relates the deeds of Gonzalo Hernandez of Cordova, whom the whole world deservedly called The Great Captain, on account of his many great exploits. It is a famous and illustrious name which was earned by none but him. And that Diego Garcia de Paredes too was a noble gentleman, born in the city of Truxillo in Estremadura, a very brave soldier, and of such natural strength that with one finger he stopped a mill-wheel turning at full speed. Once too when he was posted with a two-handed sword at the approaches of a bridge, he prevented a whole vast army from crossing. He did so many other things of that sort too that if instead of his writing them down himself with the modesty of a gentleman who is his own chronicler, a stranger had written a free and dispassionate account of them, his deeds would have cast the exploits of all your Hectors, Achilleses, and Rolands into oblivion.'

'Tell that to my father!' said the innkeeper. 'So that's what astonished you. Just stopping a millwheel! I swear you ought to see what I've read about Felixmarte of Hyrcania. He cut five giants in half with one back-stroke, just as if they'd been so many beans that children make their mannikins of. And another time he attacked a huge and most powerful army of more than one million six hundred thousand soldiers, all in armour from head to foot, and routed them all as if they had been flocks of sheep. I wonder what would you say about the worthy Don Cirongilio of Thrace. He was a valiant and courageous knight, as you may read in the book, where it tells you how once, a fiery serpent came out of the water as he was sailing on a river. As soon as he saw it he rushed at it, got astride its scaly shoulders, and pressed its throat so hard with both his hands that it had no other way of saving itself from being throttled than by diving to the bottom of the river, dragging the knight, who would not leave go, after it. And when they got there, he found himself among such marvellously beautiful palaces and gardens! Then the serpent turned into an old man, and told him such things as were never heard before. Say no more, sir, for if you were to listen to that book you would go mad with pleasure. A fig each for your Great Captain and your Diego Garcia!'

At this Dorothea whispered to Cardenio: 'Our host is not far short of being a second Don Quixote.'

'I agree,' replied Cardenio. 'To judge by what he says, he takes everything in those books for gospel truth, and the barefoot friars themselves wouldn't make him believe otherwise.'

'See here, brother,' began the priest, 'there never were such people in the world as Felixmarte of Hyrcania, or Don Cirongilio of Thrace, or any of the other knights in those books of chivalry. They are all fictions, invented by idle brains who composed them for the very purpose you spoke of, to pass the time as your reapers do in reading them. For I swear to you that really such knights never existed in the world, and all these feats and follies never happened.'

'Try that bone on another dog!' replied the innkeeper. 'As if I didn't know how many beans make five, and where my own shoe pinches! Don't try to feed me with pap, your worship, for I wasn't born yesterday! It's a nice thing for you to try and persuade me that all these fine books say is only nonsense and lies, when they're printed by licence of the Lords of the Privy Council – as if they were people who would allow a pack of lies to be published, and enough battles and enchantments to drive you out of your wits!'

'I have told you already, my friend,' replied the priest, 'that it is done to divert our idle moments. Just as in all well-ruled states such games as chess, tennis, and billiards are permitted for the amusement of men who do not want to work, or do not have to, or cannot; so these books are allowed to be published, in the very reasonable belief that there can be no one so ignorant as to take any of them for true history. If I were permitted now, and my hearers desired it, I would say something about the qualities that books of chivalry require in order to be good. This might perhaps make them useful to some people, and enjoyable too. But I hope that a time will come when I can explain my ideas to those who can turn my criticism to account. In the meantime, Master Landlord, believe what I tell you. Take your books, and decide for yourself whether they are truth or lies, and much good may they do you! But I pray God you never limp on the same foot as your guest Don Quixote.'

'I shan't do that,' replied the innkeeper. 'I shall never be fool enough to turn knight errant. For I see quite well that it's not the fashion now to do as they did in the olden days when they say those famous knights roamed the world.'

Sancho had entered in the middle of this conversation and was much astonished and depressed to hear that knights errant were now out of fashion, and that all books of chivalry were nonsense and lies. And so he decided in his own mind to wait and see how this expedition of his master's turned out; and if the result was not up to his expectations, he resolved to leave Don Quixote and go back to his wife and children and to his usual occupation.

The innkeeper was just taking away the trunk and the books when the priest said to him: 'Wait. I should like to see what is in those papers that are written in such a good hand.' The landlord took them out, and handed them to the priest who found about eight sheets of manuscript, and at the beginning a title in large letters: *The Tale of Foolish Curiosity*. He then read some three or four lines to himself, and said: 'Really, the title of this tale rather takes my fancy, and I have a mind to read it through.'

At which the innkeeper replied: 'Your reverence might do well to read it. Let me tell you that some of my guests who've read it here have enjoyed it very much and have pressed me to give it to them. But I wouldn't let them have it, as I mean to return it to the man who left this trunk behind with all these books and papers. He must have forgotten them, but he may quite likely come this way again some time. Then I'll certainly return him the books, though I know I shall miss them. For I may be an innkeeper, but still I'm a Christian!'

'You are very right, my friend,' said the priest, 'but all the same, if I like the tale you must let me copy it.'

'With the greatest of pleasure,' replied the innkeeper.

Whilst the two of them were talking, Cardenio had picked up the tale and begun to read it. He formed the same opinion of it as the priest had done, and begged him to read it aloud so that they could all hear it.

'I would,' said the priest, 'if it were not better to spend our time in sleeping than in reading.'

'It will be sufficient rest for me,' said Dorothea, 'to pass an hour listening to a story, for my mind is not yet quiet enough to let me sleep.'

'Well, in that case,' said the priest, 'I will read it, if only out of curiosity. Perhaps there will be something pleasant in it.'

Master Nicholas urged him to do so, and Sancho as well. So seeing that it would give them all pleasure, and himself as well, the priest began:

'Well, well! Listen to me, all of you, for this is how the tale begins:

Chapter XXXIII. *The Tale of Foolish Curiosity.*

In Florence, a wealthy and famous Italian city in the province called Tuscany, lived Anselmo and Lothario, two rich and noble gentlemen, and such close friends that everyone who knew them referred to them as *The Two Friends*. They were bachelors, lads of the same age and the same habits, which was sufficient reason for the affection that united them. It is true that Anselmo was rather more inclined to affairs of the heart than was Lothario, who was fonder of hunting. But when the occasion arose, Anselmo would give up his pleasures to take part in Lothario's, and Lothario his to follow Anselmo's. Their minds, in fact, worked in such unison that no clock could keep better time.

Anselmo fell deeply in love with a noble and beautiful damsel of that city. So good was her family and so good was she that he decided, with the approval of his friend Lothario, without which he did nothing, to ask her parents for her hand. And this he did. Lothario himself was the messenger; and it was he who concluded the business so much to his friend's satisfaction that in a short time Anselmo gained the object of his desires. Camilla too was so pleased to have got Anselmo for a husband that she never ceased to thank Heaven and Lothario, the joint agents of her good fortune. For the first few days – which as in all marriages, were spent in feasting – Lothario continued to visit his friend Anselmo's house as usual, striving to do him honour and to entertain and amuse him in every possible way. But once the wedding celebrations were over and the stream of visitors and congratulations had subsided, he began deliberately to visit Anselmo's less often; since it seemed to him, as it should to all reasonable men, that men should not continue to haunt the houses of their married friends as they did when they were bachelors. For though good and true friends should not be in any way suspicious, yet a married man's honour is so delicate that it can be injured even by his own brother. How much more so by his friend.

Anselmo noticed the falling off in Lothario's visits, and made it the subject of loud complaints. He said that he would never have married if he had known that his marriage was going to deprive him of his friend's company. He begged him not to let the charming title of *The Two Friends*, which they had earned by their bachelor harmony, lapse through exaggerated caution. He implored him, in fact, if such a word could rightly be used between them, to treat his house as his own again, and to come and go as before. He assured him that his wife Camilla had no pleasure or desire except such as he wished her to have, and that she was troubled to see Lothario turned so shy, knowing as she did the warmth of their friendship.

Lothario replied to this and to the many arguments Anselmo used to persuade him to come to the house again as he used to do, so prudently, discreetly and judiciously, that Anselmo was satisfied with his friend's decision, and they agreed that Lothario should dine with him twice a week and on feast-days. But although this was settled between the pair of them, Lothario decided to do no more than what seemed best to serve his friend's honour; for he prized Anselmo's good name more than his own. He used to say, and rightly, that a married man on whom Heaven has bestowed a lovely wife has to take as much care of what friends he brings to the house as of what women friends his wife consorts with. For what is not done or arranged in market-places and churches, or at public shows or church-goings – which a husband cannot always deny his wife – is often managed and facilitated at the house of that very woman friend or relative in whom he has most confidence. Lothario used to say too that every married man has need of a friend to warn him of the shortcomings in his behaviour. For it often happens that out of his great love for his wife, a husband does not warn her, for fear of annoying her, that some of her actions may redound either to his honour or to his shame. Though all this could easily be remedied if he had a friend to advise him. But where might a man find a friend as discreet, as loyal, and as faithful as Lothario postulated? Indeed I do not know. Lothario alone was the man, for he guarded his friend's honour with so much care and vigilance that he tried to reduce, shorten, and diminish the agreed times for his visits to the house, for fear that the idle crowd and straying malicious eyes might criticize the visits of a rich, noble, and high-born young man with the attractive qualities which he considered himself to have, to the house of so lovely a woman as Camilla. For even though her goodness and worth might be sufficient to bridle malicious tongues, he did not want to have her good name or his friend's called into question. Therefore he spent most of the days agreed upon in other business and amusements, and pretended that these were unavoidable. So it was that a great part of the hours they spent together passed in complaints on one side and excuses on the other.

Now it happened one day, as the two friends were taking a walk in the fields outside the city, that Anselmo addressed the following remarks to Lothario:

'You may think, friend Lothario, that I am incapable of responding with sufficient gratitude for the favours which God has bestowed on me in making me the son of such parents and in giving me with no mean hand both of nature's and of fortune's goods, and for the greatest blessing of all which He bestowed on me in giving me you for a friend and Camilla for a wife – two treasures which I value as much as I am able, if not as much as I should. Yet with all these blessings, which are commonly the sum with which men should and do live content, I am the most fretful and discontented man in all the world, since for some time now I have been vexed and bothered by a desire so strange and peculiar that I am astonished at myself. I blame and scold myself for it when I am alone, and try to stifle it and to conceal it from my own thoughts. But all this has been of so little use that my whole intention might have been to proclaim it to the world. And since it must come out in the end, I should like it to be kept in the secret archives of your breast. For I am confident that in that way, and through the efforts which you, as my faithful friend, will take to relieve me, I shall be quickly freed from the distress it causes me. Through your sympathy I expect to become as happy as by my own foolishness I am now unhappy.'

This speech of Anselmo's astonished Lothario, for he had no idea where its long preface or preamble was leading to. For although he tried to imagine what desire could possibly be tormenting his friend, he was always wide of the mark. So to rid himself quickly of the distress which this suspense caused him, he answered that Anselmo was doing a clear injustice to their great friendship by searching for round-about ways of telling him his most secret thoughts. For he could count on him either for advice or for help.

'That is true,' replied Anselmo. 'I am confident of that, and I will tell you, friend Lothario, what distresses me. It is the question whether my wife Camilla is as good and perfect as I think. I cannot be sure of the truth except by testing her by an ordeal which shall prove the purity of her virtue, as fire shows the purity of gold. For it is my opinion, my friend, that a woman is good only in proportion to her temptations, and that the only constant woman is one who does not yield to promises, gifts, tears, or the continuous importunities of persistent lovers. What reason has one to thank a woman for being good,' said he, 'if no one has tempted her to be bad? What merit is there in her being reserved and modest, if she has no opportunity of going astray and knows that she has a husband who will kill her if he catches her in her first slip? That is why I do not have the same regard for the woman who is good out of fear or lack of opportunity as for the woman who is wooed and pursued, yet comes off with the crown of victory. So, for these reasons and for many others that I could give you, I want support and confirmation for the opinion I hold. I want my wife Camilla to pass through the ordeal, and be purged and refined in the fire of temptation and solicitation by someone worthy of her. Then, if she comes out, as I believe she will, with the palm of victory, I shall account myself the most fortunate of men. I shall be able to say that the cup of my desires is full. I shall say that I have been fated to possess the virtuous woman of whom the wise man says: *Who shall find her?* And if things should turn out contrary to my expectations, with the satisfaction of having proved the truth I shall bear uncomplainingly the pain that so dearly bought an experiment will cause me. Now it being understood that nothing you say in opposition to my purpose will be of the slightest effect in dissuading me from it, I want you, my friend Lothario, to prepare to be the instrument for carrying this plan of mine into effect. I shall give you an opportunity of doing it, and I shall omit nothing that seems to me necessary, if you are to woo a woman who is chaste, honourable, reserved and in no way mercenary. What most urges me to entrust this arduous enterprise to you is the knowledge that if Camilla is conquered by you, you will not carry your victory to the ultimate extreme, but only do what is necessary by the terms of our agreement. And so I shall be wronged only in the intention, and my injury will remain buried in your virtuous silence; which, I know, will be as eternal as the silence of death, in any concern of mine. Therefore, if you want me to enjoy anything deserving the name of life you must now enter into this conflict of love, not half-heartedly or sluggishly, but with the earnestness and diligence which my plan requires, and with the loyalty our friendship assures me of.'

These were Anselmo's arguments, to which Lothario listened so attentively that he did not open his lips until his friend had finished, except to say the few words here recorded. And then he stared at him for some time as if he were gazing at some dreadful and amazing object, the like of which he had never seen before.

'I cannot persuade myself, friend Anselmo,' he said, 'that what you have just been saying is not a joke. For, if I had thought you were in earnest, I should not have let you go so far. I should not have listened, and that would have cut short your long speech. It is my belief that either you do not know me or I do not know you.

But no, I know very well that you are Anselmo, and you know that I am Lothario. The trouble is that I think you are not the Anselmo you used to be, and you seem to have imagined that I am not the Lothario I ought to be. For what you have just said to me is unworthy of my friend Anselmo, and you should not have made the demands you did of the Lothario you know. Good friends ought to use and prove their friends, as the poet says, *usque ad aras*: I mean that they must not use friendship for purposes offensive to God. And if such was the opinion of a heathen, how much more must a Christian hold to it, knowing as he does that the divine friendship must not be forfeited for a human one? When a friend goes so far as to set aside his duty to God to fulfil that of friendship, it must not be for trifles and trivialities, but for something on which his friend's life and honour depend. Now tell me, Anselmo, is it your life or your honour that is in such danger that I must risk myself to satisfy you, and do the detestable thing you are asking of me? Neither most certainly. On the contrary, as far as I understand, you are asking me to try hard to rob you, and to rob myself of life and honour. For if I take your honour it is clear that I take your life, since a man without honour is worse than dead. If I become the instrument of such an evil as you wish, should I not emerge dishonoured and, consequently, dead? Listen, Anselmo my friend, and have the patience not to answer till I have finished telling you all my thoughts on the subject of this request of yours. There will be time enough after that for you to reply and for me to listen.'

'Most willingly,' said Anselmo. 'Say what you like.'

Then Lothario went on to say: 'You seem to me, Anselmo, to be in the position of the Moors, who cannot be convinced in the error of their sect by quotations from Holy Scripture, nor by arguments drawn from intellectual speculation or based on the canons of faith, but have to have examples, palpable, simple, intelligible, demonstrable and indubitable, with irrefutable mathematical proof, like: *If equals be taken from equals the remainders are equal.* And when they do not understand this in words, as in fact they do not, then you have to show it to them with your hands and put it in front of their eyes. But even then no one can convince them of the truths of our holy faith. Now I shall have to use the same method with you. For this new desire of yours is so extravagant and so far from all shadow of sense that it seems to me it would be waste of time to try and convince you of your foolishness – for that is the only name I can give it at present. Yes, I am even inclined to abandon you to your folly as a punishment for your wickedness. But my friendship for you will not let me treat you so cruelly as to leave you in such obvious danger of destruction. Now, to make the matter clear to you, Anselmo, tell me: did you not ask me to solicit a modest woman? To tempt a chaste one? To bribe an honest one? To woo a prudent one? Yes, that is what you asked. But if you know that you have a modest, chaste, honest, prudent wife, what are you searching to find out? If you believe that she will emerge victorious from all my attacks – as no doubt she will – what titles do you intend to give her afterwards better than those she already has? What more will she be afterwards than she is at present? Either you do not take her for what you say, or you do not know what you are asking. If you do not take her for what you say, why do you want to test her instead of treating her as a bad woman, and punishing her as you think she deserves? But if she is as good as you think, it will be an impertinence to experiment with truth itself, for when the trial is over it cannot have a higher value than it had before. So we must conclude that to attempt things which are more likely to result in harm than in good is the mark of unreasoning and rash minds. All the more so if they attempt such things voluntarily, when it is clear from a mile away that the attempt is sheer madness. Difficult works are attempted for the sake of Heaven, for the world's sake, or for both. The first are tasks undertaken by the saints, who attempt to live the lives of angels in human frames. The second are performed by men who navigate the boundless ocean, and journey through distant countries and changing climates, to acquire what are called the goods of fortune. And those who brave hazardous enterprises for the sake of both God and man are stout soldiers, who no sooner see in the enemy's rampart a breach made by a single cannon-ball than, regardless of all fear and danger, they are borne on the wings of ambition to fight for their faith, their nation, and their king, and rush boldly into the midst of death which awaits them in a thousand shapes.

'Such are the hazards commonly undertaken, and it is honour, glory, and gain to attempt them, however charged they may be with difficulties and danger. But the project you suggest attempting will gain you glory neither from above, nor the goods of fortune, nor renown among men. For, supposing that the result is satisfactory, you will be no happier, no richer, and no more honoured than you are at present; and if you do not succeed, you will be in the greatest imaginable misery. It will do you no good then to think that no one knows your misfortune, for it will be enough to afflict and undo you that you know it yourself. As confirmation I will quote a stanza of the famous poet Luis Tansilo from the end of the first part of his *Tears of St. Peter*, which goes like this:

> In Peter's heart the shame and anguish grew
> As the day broke, and though no man was by
> To see his sin, he knew his own offence
> And blushed deep for his guilt. A noble heart
> Needs no observer to arouse his shame,
> But is abashed at sight of his own guilt,
> Though no one but the heavens and earth can see it.

'So you will not alleviate your grief by secrecy, but will have cause for incessant tears. For even though you may not weep openly, tears of blood will flow from your heart. So wept that simple doctor of whom our poet tells, who made the trial of the cup which the cautious Rinaldo, with greater discretion, declined. Even though that is a poetic fiction, it contains a hidden moral worth observing and following. Moreover, if you will listen to what I am now going to say, you will be finally convinced that it is a great error you now wish to commit. Tell me, Anselmo, if the Heavens or good fortune had made you the owner and lawful possessor of a very fine diamond, and every jewel merchant who saw it was satisfied of its goodness and quality; and if, all together and with one voice, they said that it attained the utmost possible perfection in every respect, and you believed them yourself and had not a suspicion to the contrary – supposing all this, would it be reasonable for you to take it into your head to pick up this stone and put it between the anvil and the hammer, and thus by mere weight of blows and brawn prove whether it was as hard and as fine as they said? Now would it be any more reasonable to put this plan of yours into effect? For supposing that the stone resisted such a stupid trial, would it have any greater value or reputation for that? And if it

K

broke – which well might happen – would not everything be lost? Yes, and its owner would count in the general estimation as a fool.

'Now think of Camilla, Anselmo my friend, as a rare diamond, both in your estimation and others', and consider whether there is any reason for exposing her to the risk of destruction; for even if she remains unbroken, she cannot rise to a greater value than she now has. But, if she fails and does not stand up to the trial, reflect on the state you would be in without her. Think what reason you would have for self-reproach if you were to be the cause of her destruction and your own. For there is no jewel in the world so precious as a chaste and virtuous woman, and the whole honour of women lies in their good reputation. Now, since your wife's virtue is the very highest imaginable, as you know, why should you want to call its truth into question? Look, my friend, woman is an imperfect creature, and you must not put stumbling-blocks in her path, so that she may trip and fall; but rather clear her road of every obstacle, so that she may run free and unburdened to gain the perfection she lacks, which consists in a good life.

'Naturalists tell us that the ermine is a little animal with a fur of extreme whiteness, and that when hunters wish to catch it they use this trick: they find the places it usually passes and frequents, and stop them up with mud; and then, starting their quarry, they drive it that way. Now, when the ermine reaches the mud it stands still and lets itself be seized and caught rather than pass through the dirt, and soil and lose its whiteness, which it values more than its life and liberty. The chaste and virtuous woman is an ermine, and the virtue of chastity is whiter and purer than snow. If man does not wish her to lose it, but to keep and preserve it instead, he must not treat her like the ermine. He must not put mud in front of her – that is to say the gifts and addresses of importunate lovers – for perhaps – no, certainly – she has insufficient virtue and natural strength to trample down and pass through those obstacles on her own. He must remove them from her way, therefore, and set before her the purity of virtue and the beauty which lies in a good name. For a good woman is also like a mirror of clear and shining glass, which is liable to be stained and dimmed by every breath which touches it. A chaste woman must be treated like holy relics, which are to be adored but not touched. A good woman must be guarded and

prized like a beautiful garden full of flowering roses, whose owner
does not allow anyone to walk in it or to touch them; enough that
they enjoy its fragrance and beauty from afar off through its iron
railings. Last of all I want to quote you some verses which have
come into my mind, and which I heard in a modern play; they seem
to me very much to our present point. A shrewd old man is advising
another, the father of a young lady, to look after her, guard her, and
keep her in the house, and among other reasons he adduces these:

> Truly woman's made of glass;
> Therefore no one ought to try her
> Whether she may break or no,
> Seeing all may come to pass.
>
> For the break's the likelier,
> And it's very foolish
> To risk a thing so brittle
> And, once smashed, beyond repair.
>
> So I would have all men dwell
> In this sound opinion;
> For if Danaës abound,
> There are golden showers as well.

'All that I have said to you so far, Anselmo, touches yourself, but
now you must hear something from my side. Forgive me if I am
long-winded, for the labyrinth you are in, and which you want me
to get you out of, makes me so. You count me your friend; yet you
wish to deprive me of that honour, which is against all friendship.
And not only that, but you want me to rob you of your own honour
as well. It is clear that you want to deprive me of mine. For when
Camilla sees me wooing her, as you wish, she is sure to take me for
a man without principles or honour, seeing me attempt something
so contrary to my duty to myself and my friendship to you. There
is no doubt that you wish me to rob you of your own honour. For
when Camilla sees me wooing her she will think that I have detected
some lightness in her, that has made me so bold as to reveal my
wicked desires to her; and when she considers herself dishonoured,
her disgrace will affect you as a part of her. From this arises a well-
known situation: although the husband of an adulterous woman
does not know her guilt, and has never given his wife an excuse for
being what she should not be, or ever had it in his power to prevent

his misfortune, which does not arise from his carelessness or lack of precaution, he is still called by a vile and opprobrious name, and to some extent regarded with eyes of contempt rather than of pity by those who know of his wife's guilt; even though it is not by his fault, but by his guilty partner's will that misfortune has struck him. But I could tell you the reason why the guilty woman's husband is dishonoured, although he does not know of her wickedness, and is not to blame, and has had no hand in it nor ever given her an excuse for her sin. Do not grow tired of listening; it will all serve for your advantage.

'When God created our first father in the earthly paradise, Holy Scripture tells us that He caused a deep sleep to fall on him, and in his sleep took one of the ribs of his left side and created our mother Eve; and when Adam awoke and looked on her, he said: "*This is now bone of my bones and flesh of my flesh.*" And God said: "*Therefore shall a man leave his father and his mother, and they shall be one flesh.*" Then was instituted the divine sacrament of marriage, whose bonds are soluble only by death. This miraculous sacrament has such strength and virtue that it makes two different persons one single flesh; and with happily married couples it does more, for though they have two souls they have only a single will. Hence it arises that, as the flesh of the wife is one with the flesh of the husband, the blemishes which fall on her or the defects she incurs recoil upon the flesh of the husband, although, as I have said, he may be in no respect the cause of the trouble. For, just as the whole body feels the pain of the foot or of any other limb, since they are all one flesh; and the head feels the ankle's pain, although it is not the cause of it; so the husband shares his wife's dishonour, being one with her. Now as all this world's honours and dishonours spring from flesh and blood, and the bad wife's are of this kind, part of them must inevitably fall on the husband; and he must be considered dishonoured, even though he does not know of it. Reflect, then, Anselmo, on the danger you expose yourself to in seeking to disturb your good wife's peace. Consider what vain and foolish curiosity it is that prompts you to stir the passions which now lie quiet in your chaste wife's breast. Be warned that you stand to gain little and to lose so unspeakably much that words fail me to express its value. But, if all that I have said is not enough to deflect you from your wicked plan, you must certainly look for someone else to effect your disgrace and misery. For I do not intend to play the part, even though I lose your friendship by refusing; and that is the greatest loss I can imagine.'

With these words the virtuous and wise Lothario concluded, and left Anselmo so troubled and thoughtful that he could not reply with so much as a word for some time. But at length he said:

'I have listened with attention to all that you have said, Lothario my friend; and your arguments, examples, and comparisons prove your great wisdom and perfect friendship. I see too – and I confess it – that if I do not follow your opinion but my own, I shall be abandoning the good and pursuing the evil. Yet, though I admit this, you must consider that I am now suffering from an illness common in women, which makes them long to eat earth, chalk, coal and other worse things, loathsome to the sight and much more loathsome to the palate. It is necessary, therefore, to find some art to cure me; and this can easily be done, if you will only begin to make up to Camilla, even weakly and hypocritically; for she cannot be so frail that her virtue will fall at the first encounter. I shall be content with just a beginning, and then you will have done what our friendship requires, for not only will you be restoring me my life but convincing me that I retain my honour. This you must do for one reason alone; and that is, that as I am determined to put this plan into practice, you cannot allow me to reveal my obsession to any other person, and so endanger my honour which you are so anxious to save. Even if your own does not stand as high as it should in Camilla's estimation, while you are wooing her, that hardly matters at all: for in a very short time, when we find the integrity in her which we expect, you will be able to tell her the simple truth about our plot; and then you will stand as high in her opinion as before. So since you can give me so much happiness at so little risk to yourself, do not refuse to do as I ask, whatever difficulties it may involve for you. For, as I have said, if you will make only a beginning, I will reckon the matter concluded.'

When Lothario saw Anselmo's resolution, he did not know what further instances to choose, or what fresh arguments to use, in order to dissuade him. Seeing, therefore, that he threatened to divulge his wicked plan to some one else, he resolved to give in to him, to pre-

vent greater mischief, and to do as he wanted; with the sole object
and intention of so managing the business that Anselmo should be
satisfied at no cost to Camilla's peace of mind. So he replied by asking his friend not to tell anyone else of his plan, and promised to
undertake the enterprise and to begin whenever he pleased. Anselmo embraced Lothario tenderly and affectionately, and thanked
him for his offer, as if his friend had done him some great favour.
Then the pair of them agreed that the work should begin on the
very next day. Anselmo would give Lothario time and opportunity
to speak to Camilla alone, and provide him too with money and
jewels to offer her as presents. He advised him to serenade her and to
write verses in her praise; and if he would not, offered to be at the
pains of composing them himself. All this Lothario undertook,
though not with the intention which Anselmo imagined; and with
this understanding they went back to Anselmo's house, where they
found Camilla worried and anxiously awaiting her husband, for he
was later than usual in coming back that day.

Lothario went home, leaving Anselmo contented, but very
puzzled himself as to what line he should take to get out of this
stupid business. But that night he thought of a way of deceiving
Anselmo without offending Camilla; and next day he came to dine
with his friend and was welcomed by Camilla, who always received
him very cordially, knowing how fond her husband was of him.
When they had finished dinner and the table-cloths were removed,
Anselmo asked Lothario to stay with Camilla while he went out on
some urgent business, from which he would be back within an hour
and a half. Camilla begged him not to go, and Lothario offered to
accompany him, but all to no purpose. For Anselmo pressed Lothario all the harder to stay till his return, as he had something of
great importance to discuss with him. Also he told Camilla not to
leave Lothario alone till he got back. In fact, the excuse for his absence was so well sustained that no one could tell it was false.

Anselmo departed, and Camilla remained alone at table with Lothario; for the rest of the household had gone off to dinner. So Lothario found himself engaged in the duel, as his friend desired,
facing an enemy capable of conquering a squadron of armed horsemen with her beauty alone. Indeed, Lothario had reason to fear her!
But all he did was to place his elbow on the arm of his chair and his

hand on his cheek. Then, begging Camilla's pardon for his bad manners, he said that he wanted to take a little rest, till Anselmo's return. Camilla replied that he would rest more comfortably on cushions than in a chair, and begged him therefore to go into the withdrawing room and sleep. But Lothario refused, and stayed there dozing till Anselmo's return. When his friend came back, and found Camilla gone to her room and Lothario sleeping, he concluded that he had been out long enough to give the pair of them time to talk and to sleep as well, and could hardly wait for Lothario to wake, so anxious was he to go out with him and learn what success he had had.

Everything fell out as he wished. Lothario woke up; the pair of them left the house. Then in answer to Anselmo's questions Lothario replied that he had not thought it advisable to reveal himself entirely the first time, and so had merely praised Camilla's beauty, saying that there was no other subject of conversation in the whole city but her loveliness and intelligence. 'This,' he said, 'seemed to me a good way of gaining her confidence and inclining her to listen to me with pleasure next time. It is the method the Devil uses when he wants to deceive the wary. Angel of darkness though he is, he transforms himself into an angel of light, and assumes a cloak of virtue before finally revealing his true character. It is a plan which usually succeeds, unless the deception is discovered at the outset.' This satisfied Anselmo, who said that he would give his friend the same opportunity every day. He would not leave the house, however, but would be so busy there that Camilla would not suspect his plot.

After that came many days on which Lothario never spoke a word to Camilla, but told Anselmo that he had talked to her yet never been able to draw from her the slightest sign of encouragement, or even so much as a shadow of hope. On the contrary, he said, she threatened him that she would have to tell her husband if he did not give up his wicked designs.

'That is good,' said Anselmo. 'Up to now Camilla has resisted words. Now we must see how she resists deeds. To-morrow I will give you two thousand crowns in gold to offer her – no, to give to her – and the same amount to buy jewels to tempt her. For women, particularly beautiful women, are very fond of being well dressed and looking handsome, however chaste they are. If she resists this temptation I shall be satisfied and trouble you no more.'

Lothario answered that, having begun it, he would see the plot through to the end, since he believed that he would come out of it weary and vanquished. The next day he accepted the four thousand crowns in great perplexity, for he did not know what new lie to invent. But, in the end, he made up his mind to tell Anselmo that Camilla was as impervious to gifts and promises as to words, and that there was no purpose in his troubling himself further, since he was wasting his time. But fate guided matters in another way. For when Anselmo had left Lothario and Camilla alone as before, he shut himself into a room and stood at the keyhole, to watch and to listen. And when he saw that Lothario did not throw a single word to Camilla in more than half an hour, and would not have done if he had waited a century, he realized that all his friend had told him about Camilla's replies was nothing but fiction and lies. To make certain of this he came out of the room and, calling Lothario aside, asked him what news he had, and what frame of mind Camilla was in. Lothario answered that he would not budge another step in the business, for she had answered him so sharply and rudely that he had not the courage to speak to her again.

'Oh, Lothario, Lothario,' cried Anselmo, 'how badly you fulfil your duty to me, and my great trust in you! I was watching you just now through the keyhole of that door, and I saw that you did not address a word to Camilla; from which I must infer that you have not said a word yet. If that is so, – and I have no doubt it is, – why are you deceiving me? Why are you trying to deprive me, by this trick of yours, of the only means I can find of obtaining my desire?'

Anselmo said no more, but this was enough to leave Lothario abashed and confused. Being caught in a lie Lothario took almost as a blemish on his honour; and he swore to Anselmo that from that moment he would undertake to satisfy him, and tell no more lies, as his friend would see if he watched carefully. But Anselmo need not put himself to any trouble, because what he now intended to do would satisfy him entirely and free him from all suspicions. His friend believed him and, to give him an opportunity free from interruption, decided to leave his house for a week and go to a friend who lived in a village not far from the city. He arranged with this same friend to send and summon him very urgently, so that he should have an excuse for his departure that would satisfy Camilla.

Unfortunate and ill advised Anselmo, what are you doing? What are you plotting and contriving? See, you are acting against yourself, plotting your own dishonour, and contriving your own undoing. Your wife Camilla is virtuous; in peace and security you possess her; no one interferes with your pleasures; her thoughts do not pass beyond the walls of her house; you are her Heaven upon earth; the goal of her desires; the fulfilment of her joys and the measure by which she rules her will, adapting it in every way to yours and to that of Heaven. Then, since the mine of her honour, beauty, modesty and virtue yields you without any toil all the riches it contains and that you can desire, why must you dig the earth and seek fresh veins of new and unseen treasure? You are taking the risk that everything may collapse, seeing that it is held up only by the feeble props of her frail nature. Remember that by seeking the impossible you may justly be denied the possible or, as a poet has expressed it better:

> In death I seek for life,
> Health in infirmity,
> In jail for liberty;
> I look for rest in strife,
> And faithfulness in treachery.
>
> But envious fate, which still
> Conspires to work my ill,
> With Heaven has decreed
> That easy things shall be denied,
> Since what I crave's the impossible.

Next day Anselmo went to the village, telling Camilla that Lothario would come to look after the house and dine with her while he was away, and that she was to take care to treat him as she would himself. Being a sensible and honest woman, Camilla was distressed at her husband's order, and asked him to consider how wrong it was for anyone to occupy his chair at table while he was away. If this, she said, was because he had no confidence that she could manage the house, let him try for once and learn by experience that she was capable of even greater responsibilities. Anselmo replied that such was his wish, and that she had nothing to do but to bow her head and obey. Camilla acquiesced, though against her will, and Anselmo departed. The next day Lotario came to his house and Camilla gave him an affectionate and modest welcome. She never sat in any room, however, where Lotario might find her alone, but went about surrounded by her men-servants and maids, particularly by her own maid, Leonela, of whom she was very fond. For they had been brought up together from their girlhood in Camilla's parents' house, and she had brought her to Anselmo's when she married him.

For the first three days Lotario did not say a word, though he had an opportunity when the cloth was removed and the household went off to their dinner, which, by Camilla's instructions, was a hurried one. Camilla gave her maid orders to dine before she did and never to leave her side. But the girl had no thought except for her own pleasure, and needed the time for her own affairs. So she did not always comply with her mistresses's orders, but instead left them alone together, as if by instruction. Camilla's modest behaviour and gravity of expression, however, were sufficient to curb Lotario's tongue.

But whatever advantage they gained from Camilla's virtues silencing Lotario's tongue led afterwards to harm for both of them. For, if his tongue was silent, his thoughts ran on; and he had time to contemplate, one by one, all Camilla's perfections of mind and body – and they were enough to inspire love in a marble statue, let alone in a heart of flesh. Lotario gazed at her all the time he should have been speaking to her, thinking how worthy of his love she was; and this reflection began little by little to impinge on his respect for Anselmo. A thousand times he made up his mind to leave the city and go where Anselmo would never see him again, nor he Camilla; but his new-found delight in gazing at her prevented him and kept him back. He struggled and fought with himself to resist the pleasure he felt in looking at her. When he was alone he blamed himself for his madness, calling himself a bad friend, and even a bad Christian. He reasoned, and made comparisons between himself and Anselmo; but he always concluded by saying that Anselmo's folly and over-confidence were greater than his own breach of faith, and that, if he had as good an excuse before God as before men, he would fear no punishment for his crime.

In fine, Camilla's beauty and goodness, combined with the opportunity which the ignorant husband had put in his way, completely overthrew Lothario's loyalty; and when Anselmo had been away three days, during which time he had continuously battled to resist his passion, he began to woo Camilla, without thought for anything but his own gratification. He was so impetuous, in fact, and so warm in his language that Camilla got up shocked, and could think of nothing else to do but retire to her room, without answering so much as a word. But Lothario's hopes were not discouraged by her coldness, for hope is always born with love. On the contrary, he valued Camilla even more highly. She, however, seeing this unexpected side of Lothario's character, did not know what to do. But, as it seemed to her neither safe nor proper to give him an opportunity to speak to her again, she decided to send one of her servants to Anselmo that same night with a letter in which she wrote as follows:

Chapter XXXIV. *The Tale of Foolish Curiosity, continued.*

'IT is generally said that an army looks ill without its general and a castle without its warden, and I say that a young married woman looks even worse without her husband, unless he is detained by the most urgent business. I am so badly off without you, and so powerless to bear your absence, that if you do not come quickly I shall have to go and stay at my parents' house, even though I leave yours unguarded. For the guardian you have left me – if he is here in that character – is more concerned with his own pleasures than with your interest. As you are a wise man I need say no more, and it is as well that I do not.'

When Anselmo received this letter, he realized that Lothario had begun the enterprise, and that Camilla must have responded as he himself would have wished. So, in extreme delight, he sent to Camilla a message in reply, telling her on no account to move from the house, for he would be back in a very short time. Camilla was astonished at this reply, which threw her into greater confusion than ever; she dared not stay at home, and was even more afraid to go to her parents. For by remaining she would endanger her honour, and in going disobey her husband's orders. Finally she resolved on what proved to be the wrong course: which was to stay, and not to avoid Lothario, for fear of giving her servants cause to talk. And now she was sorry that she had written as she had to her husband, and afraid that he might think that some frivolity in her conduct had encouraged Lothario to forget the respect he owed her. But, confident in her virtue, she trusted in God and in her own resolve to answer anything Lothario might say by silence, and to say no more to her husband about the matter; so as not to involve him in any quarrel or unpleasantness. She even thought out ways of excusing Lothario to Anselmo when he should ask her what had prompted her to write him that letter.

Firm in these resolutions, which did more credit to her honour than to her wisdom, Camilla stayed next day to listen to Lothario, and so pressing was he that her steadfastness began to waver; and her virtue had all it could do to guard her eyes, and prevent their showing signs of the compassion which Lothario's tears and arguments had stirred in her breast. All this Lothario observed, and his desire grew the warmer. In the end it seemed to him necessary to take full advantage of the opportunity which Anselmo's absence gave him, and to intensify the siege of the fortress. So he assailed her self-love with praise of her beauty; for there is nothing which reduces and levels the embattled towers of a beautiful woman's vanity so quickly as this same vanity posted upon the tongue of flattery. In fact, he most industriously mined the rock of her integrity with such charges that Camilla would have fallen even if she had been made of brass. Lothario wept, beseeched, promised, flattered and swore, with such ardour and with such signs of real feeling, that he overcame Camilla's chastity and achieved the triumph which he least expected and most desired.

Camilla gave in; she gave in. But what wonder, if Lothario's friendship could not stand its ground? A clear proof that the passion of love can only be conquered by flight, and that it is vain to struggle against so powerful an enemy. For divine force is needed to subdue the power of the flesh. Only Leonela knew of her mistress's failing, for this pair of treacherous lovers could not conceal it from her. Lothario did not tell Camilla of Anselmo's scheme, nor of his having purposely afforded him the chance of doing what he had done. For he was afraid that she might set less store by his love, and think

that it was by chance that he had wooed her, and not by premedita-
tion.

A few days later Anselmo returned, and did not see that the
treasure he had held most lightly, yet valued most, was missing. He
immediately went to see Lothario, found him at home and, when
they had embraced, asked him for the fateful news.

'The news I have for you, friend Anselmo,' said Lothario, 'is
that you have a wife worthy to be called the model and crown of all
good women. The words I spoke to her were wasted on the air;
my promises she scorned; my gifts she refused; my pretended tears
she greeted with open mockery. In fact Camilla is not only the sum
of all beauty, but the treasure-house where modesty resides and
where dwell gentleness, prudence, and all the virtues which make
an honest woman praiseworthy and happy. Take back your money,
my friend. Here it is. I have had no need to touch it. For Camilla's
integrity will not yield to such low things as gifts and promises.
Be content, Anselmo, and make no more trials. You have passed
dryshod over a sea of difficulties and dispelled those suspicions
which men are bound to have on the subject of women. Do not return to the gulf of fresh disquietudes, nor test with another pilot the
goodness and strength of the ship which Heaven has allotted to you,
to bear you over the seas of this world. Consider yourself now safe
in harbour, moor yourself with the anchors of happy thoughts, and
stay until one comes to demand of you the debt which no privilege
of nobility exempts you from paying.'

Anselmo was highly delighted at Lothario's speech, and believed
in it as firmly as if it had been pronounced by an oracle. But he
begged him all the same not to abandon the enterprise, even if it
were for nothing more than curiosity and amusement. Although in
future, he said, he would not use such urgent methods as he had
hitherto. All that he wanted his friend to do was to write some
verses in her praise under the name of Chloris. He would give
Camilla to understand that his friend was in love with a lady to
whom he had given that name, so that he might write of her without
injuring her modesty. And, should Lothario not wish to take the
trouble to write the verses, he would do so himself.

'There will be no need of that,' said Lothario. 'The muses are
not so much my enemies that they do not visit me now and then

during the year. Tell Camilla of this fictitious love affair of mine. I will write the verses; and if they are not as good as the subject deserves, at least they shall be the best I can compose.'

So the foolish husband and his treacherous friend agreed. And when Anselmo returned home he asked Camilla her reason for writing him that letter she had sent him. She was surprised he had not asked before, and replied that Lothario had seemed rather freer in his glances than when her husband was at home, but that she now knew she had been mistaken. It had been merely her imagination, for Lothario had avoided seeing her and being alone with her. Anselmo said that she might well dismiss that suspicion, because he knew that Lothario was in love with a noble maiden of the city, and wrote verses to her under the name of Chloris. But, even if he were not, she had no cause to doubt Lothario's loyalty and his great friendship for them both. Now, if Camilla had not been advised by Lothario that this love of his for Chloris was an invention and that he had himself told Anselmo about it so that he could now and then write poems in Camilla's own praise, she would no doubt have fallen into the desperate snare of jealousy; but as she was forewarned she survived this assault unharmed.

The next day, when the three of them were at table, Anselmo begged Lothario to recite some of the verses he had composed for his beloved Chloris. For, as Camilla did not know her, he could safely say what he pleased.

'Even though she did know her,' replied Lothario, 'I should conceal nothing. For when a lover praises his lady's beauty and taxes her with cruelty he does no harm to her good name. But, however that may be, I will tell you that I wrote a sonnet yesterday on the ingratitude of this Chloris. It runs like this:

'In the dead silence of the peaceful night,
    When others' cares are hushed in soft repose,
    The sad account of my neglected woes
To conscious Heaven and Chloris I recite.
And when the sun with his returning light
    Forth from the east his radiant journey goes,
    With accents such as sorrow only knows
My griefs to tell is all my poor delight.
And when bright Phoebus from his starry throne
    Sends rays direct upon the parched soil,

Still in the mournful tale I persevere;
  Returning night renews my sorrow's toil;
And though from morn to night I weep and moan,
  Nor heaven nor Chloris my complainings hear.'

The sonnet pleased Camilla much, but Anselmo even more. He was loud in its praises, and said that the lady who did not respond to such patent truth was excessively cruel. And Camilla's comment was: 'So everything that these love poets say is true, then?'

'They do not say it as poets,' answered Lothario. 'But as lovers they are both slow to complain and truthful.'

'There is no doubt of that,' replied Anselmo, anxious to support Lothario's opinions before Camilla, who had no suspicion of Anselmo's trick, so deeply was she in love with Lothario.

And so, delighted as she was with anything of his and, moreover, taking it that his feelings and verses were addressed to herself and that she was the real Chloris, she begged him to recite another sonnet or poem, if he had one by heart.

'I have,' replied Lothario, 'but I do not think that it is as good as the first or, to put it better, any less bad. But you can judge, for here it is:

'Fair and ungrateful one, I feel the blow,
  And glory in the near approach of death;
  For when thou seest my corpse devoid of breath,
My constancy and truth thou sure willst know.
Welcome to me Oblivion's shade obscure!
  Welcome the loss of fortune, life, and fame!
  But thy loved features, and thy honoured name,
Deep graven on my heart, shall still endure.
And these, as sacred relics, will I keep
  Till that sad moment when to endless night
  My long-tormented soul shall take her flight.
Alas for him who on the darkened deep
  Floats idly, sport of the tempestuous tide,
  No port to shield him, and no star to guide!'

Anselmo praised this sonnet too, as he had the first; and so he went on adding link on link to the chain in which he was embroiling himself and binding up his own dishonour. For the more Lothario dishonoured him, the more he assured him of his unblemished honour. And so the lower Camilla sank into the abyss of infamy, the higher she rose, in her husband's opinion, towards the peak of virtue and renown. Now once, when Camilla was alone with her maid, she happened to say to her:

'I am ashamed, Leonela, my friend, to see how cheap I have made myself by not making Lothario spend some time purchasing the full possession of what I gave him so quickly and so willingly. I am afraid that he must despise my easiness and lightness, and not realize that he used such violence with me that I could not resist him.'

'Do not worry on that score, my lady,' replied Leonela, 'for it is not worth it. There is no reason why a thing should lose its value because it is easily given, if in fact the gift is a good one and valuable in itself. They even say that he who gives quickly gives twice over.'

'Yes,' said Camilla, 'but they say too that what costs little is little prized.'

'That saying does not apply to you,' replied Leonela, 'because love, I have heard it said, sometimes flies and sometimes walks. With one person it runs, with another creeps; some it cools and some it burns; some it wounds and others it kills; in a single instant it starts on the race of passion, and in the same instant concludes and ends it; in the morning it will besiege a fortress, and by evening it has subdued it, for there is no force that can resist it. That being so, what is it that alarms you and frightens you? For the very same thing must have happened to Lothario, when love took my master's absence as the instrument of your defeat. It was unavoidable that the plan love had determined on should be carried through in that time, and leave no chance of the work's being cut short by Anselmo's return. For love has no better minister to execute its desires than opportunity; it uses opportunity in all its enterprises, but especially in their beginnings. I know all this very well, more by experience than by hearsay, and one day I will tell you, my lady, for I am flesh and blood too, and young blood at that. What is more, lady Camilla, you would never have given yourself over or spoken so soon if you had not first seen Lothario's whole soul in his eyes, in his sighs, in his declarations, his promises, and his gifts; and learnt from its perfection how worthy he was of your love. So, since that is the case, do not let these scruples and prudish thoughts seize hold of your imagination, but be certain that Lothario values you as you value him. Be content and satisfied, since you have fallen into love's snare, that your captor is a worthy and honourable man, who not only possesses the four *S's*, which they say all good lovers should have, but a whole A.B.C. as well. Just listen to me, and you will see that I know it by heart. He is, as I see it, and as far as I can judge, *Amiable, Bountiful, Courteous, Discreet, Enamoured, Firm, Gallant, Honourable, Illustrious, Loyal, Mild, Noble, Open, Prudent, Quiet, Rich* – and the *S's*, according to the saying – and then, *True, Valorous. X* does not fit him because it is a harsh letter; *Y* – yes, I have said it, and *Z* – he is *zealous* of your honour.'

Camilla laughed at her maid's A.B.C., and concluded that she was more practised in matters of love than she said. In fact, she confessed as much by telling Camilla that she was having a love affair with a young gentleman of that city; which disturbed her mistress, who feared that this might endanger her own honour. Camilla pressed to know if their affair had gone farther than mere words, and Leonela quite shamelessly and brazenly replied that it had. For it is certain that the mistress's failings rob their maids of all shame. Since, when they see their ladies trip, girls think nothing of stumbling themselves, and do not care if it is known. Camilla could only beg Leonela not to say anything about her mistress's affairs to the young man she said was her lover, and to manage her own with secrecy, so that they should not come to the notice of Anselmo or Lothario. Leonela agreed, but her way of keeping her promise was enough to confirm Camilla's fears that she would lose her reputation through her maid. For the immoral and brazen Leonela, once she saw that her mistress's behaviour was not what it used to be, had the effrontery to bring her lover into the house and keep him there, confident that her mistress would not dare to expose him, even if she were to see him. This is one of the troubles that mistresses pile up for themselves by their sins. Thus they become the slaves of their own maids, and are obliged to conceal their dishonesties and vices, as happened in Camilla's case. For although she very often knew that Leonela was with her lover in one of the rooms of the house, she not only did not dare to scold her, but gave her the chance to hide him, and removed every obstacle from his path for fear that her husband might see him. But she could not prevent Lothario from observing

him come out on one occasion at daybreak. At first he did not recognize him, but thought that he must be a ghost. But when he saw
him walk away, carefully and cautiously wrapping and muffling
himself up, he abandoned this silly notion for another, which would
have been the ruin of them all if Camilla had not found a remedy.
Lotario did not think that the man whom he had seen leave Anselmo's house at such a strange hour could have gone in for Leonela's sake, for he did not even remember Leonela's existence. He
only thought that Camilla was being just as easy and light with
someone else as she had been with him. For these are the consequences a bad woman's wickedness brings with it: she loses her
reputation for honour with the very man to whose prayers and
entreaties she has yielded; and he believes that she gives herself even
more easily to others, and places implicit credence in any suspicion
that comes into his head.

All Lotario's common sense certainly failed him at this juncture, and all his wise reasonings went out of his mind. For without
so much as a single sound – or even a reasonable thought – impatient
and blind with the jealous rage which gnawed at his entrails, and
dying to take vengeance on Camilla, who had done him no sort of
wrong, he went without more ado to Anselmo, who had not yet got
up, and said:

'I must tell you, Anselmo, that I have been battling with myself for
a long time, and doing myself violence in not telling you something
that it is neither possible nor right for me to conceal any longer.
You must know that Camilla's fortress has now surrendered and is
at my absolute mercy. If I have delayed in revealing this fact to you,
it has only been to see if it was merely a light fancy in her, or if it
was to test me and see whether the love I addressed to her by your
permission was seriously meant. I believed too that, if she were
what she should be and what we both thought her to be she would
already have informed you of my wooing. Seeing, however, that she
has not yet done so, I realize that the promises which she has given
me are in earnest, and that the next time you are away from home
she will speak with me in the closet where you keep your valuables.'
– That in fact was the place where Camilla generally received him.
'I do not want you to rush wildly into taking some sort of vengeance. For the sin so far has been committed only in intention, and

it may be that, between now and the time for action, Camilla will change her mind and repentance will be born instead. So, since you have always followed my advice, either wholly or in part, take the advice I am going to give you now. Then you will be able to satisfy yourself, without any possibility of error, as to the best measures to take. Pretend to go away for two or three days, as you have done before, but contrive to hide in your closet instead. The tapestries there, and other possible coverings, will make this extremely easy. Then you and I will see with our own eyes what Camilla will do; and if she is guilty, which is possible but by no means certain, you may then silently, cautiously, and discreetly avenge your wrongs.'

Anselmo was astonished, amazed, stunned, by Lothario's statements, which caught him at a time when he least expected to hear them. For now he thought of Camilla as triumphant over Lothario's pretended assaults, and was beginning to enjoy the glory of her victory. He was silent for some time, gazing at the ground without so much as moving an eyelash. But finally he said:

'Lothario you have done all that I expected of your friendship. I must follow your advice in everything. Do what you please, and keep this matter secret. That is the only course in this incredible business.'

Lothario promised he would. But by the time he left he had completely repented of what he had said, and realized how stupidly he had acted, since he might have revenged himself on Camilla in a less cruel and dishonourable way. He cursed his stupidity and his feeble resolution. But he was at a loss for a means of undoing what he had done, and could think of no way out. Finally he decided to tell Camilla the whole story and, as there was no lack of opportunity, that same day he found her alone. But as soon as the chance offered it was she who spoke:

'Lothario, my friend, my hearts pains me so that I think it will burst in my breast. It will be a miracle if it does not. Leonela's shamelessness has gone so far that she lets her lover into this house every night, and stays with him till morning. It will greatly harm my reputation, for any one who sees him come out of my house at such an unusual hour will be perfectly free to condemn me. What troubles me is that I cannot punish her or scold her, because her knowledge of our affairs puts a bridle on my tongue, and I must

be silent about her. I am afraid that some harm will come of
this.'

At the beginning of this tale of Camilla's Lothario thought that
it was a trick to make him believe that the young man whom he had
seen come out of the house was Leonela's lover and not hers. But
when he saw her tears and her distress, and when she asked for his
help, he realized the truth, and in that moment was filled with confusion and remorse. But, for all that, he told Camilla not to worry,
for he would contrive a means of stopping Leonela's insolence. He
told her, too, what his furious rage of jealousy had driven him to
say to Anselmo, and how it was agreed that her husband should
hide in the closet and witness her faithlessness to him. He begged
her to forgive him this folly, and to advise him how to remedy it
and find a way out of the tortuous labyrinth his stupidity had put
him into.

Camilla was alarmed at Lothario's story, and turned on him in a
great fury with justifiable reproaches, cursing his wicked suspicions
and the bad and foolish scheme he had contrived. But, as women have
naturally a readier wit for good or for evil than men, although it
fails them when they set about deliberate reasoning, Camilla instantly found a way of remedying this seemingly irremediable business. She told Lothario to try to get Anselmo to hide next day in the
place he had spoken of, for she thought she could turn this hiding
to good purpose. They might, in fact, be able to take their pleasure
together in future without any fear of surprise. She did not tell him
the whole of her plan, but warned him, once Anselmo was hidden, to
be certain to come as soon as Leonela called him, and to answer any
questions she might ask him just as he would if he did not know
that Anselmo was listening. Lothario pressed her to tell him the
whole of her scheme, so that he could do whatever might seem needful with more certainty and caution.

'I assure you,' said Camilla, 'that there are no more precautions
to take. Only answer the questions I shall ask you.'

Camilla did not want to tell him her intentions beforehand because she was afraid that he would not follow this plan, which
seemed so excellent to her, and might think out another which
might not be so good.

At this Lothario went off; and next day Anselmo left the house, making the excuse of a visit to that friend of his in the country. He then came back to hide, which he conveniently could because Camilla and Leonela had deliberately given him the opportunity. Anselmo was now concealed, and his state of anxiety can be imagined; for he expected to see the very heart of his dishonour laid bare before his own eyes. He saw himself, in fact, on the point of losing the supreme treasure which he supposed that he possessed in his beloved Camilla. Then, once Camilla and Leonela were certain that Anselmo was hidden, they went into the closet; and Camilla was no sooner in than she heaved a deep sigh and said:

'Leonela, my friend, before I carry out my intention, which I do not wish you to know for fear you may try to prevent me, would it not be better if you were to take Anselmo's dagger, which I have asked you for, and plunge it into this wicked heart of mine? But do not do it; it would not be right for me to bear the burden of another's sin. First I must know what it is that Lothario's bold, licentious eyes saw in me to give him the courage to reveal his evil designs against his friend and against my honour. Stand at that window, Leonela, and call him; for he is certainly in the street, waiting to carry out his wicked purpose. But first I shall carry out mine, which shall be both cruel and honourable.'

'Oh, my lady,' answered the wily Leonela, who was in the plot, 'what are you going to do with that dagger? Do you perhaps mean to take your own life, or Lothario's? Whichever you do will involve the loss of your honour and good name. Better hide your injury, and not give that wicked man a chance to come into the house now and find us alone. Think, my lady, how weak we women are. He is a man, and resolute. And, being bent on such a villainous purpose, in his blind passion he may possibly do something to you that will be worse than murder, before you have a chance of carrying out your plan. I blame my master Anselmo for making that shameless scoundrel so free of his house. But if you kill him, my lady, as I think you mean to, what shall we do with him when he is dead?'

'What then, my friend?' replied Camilla. 'We will leave him for Anselmo to bury. For he should have the agreeable task of burying his own dishonour. Call him quickly; for every moment I delay in taking due vengeance for my wrong I seem to be failing in the loyalty I owe my husband.'

Anselmo was listening to all this, and at each word that Camilla spoke his mind changed. But when he heard that she was resolved to kill Lothario he decided to emerge and reveal himself, for fear she might do so. But he was restrained by his desire to see where this spirited and virtuous resolution would end. So he decided only to come out just in time to prevent the act.

At this point Camilla fell into a deep swoon; and Leonela, laying her on a bed which was there, began to weep more bitterly, crying: 'Oh, what a misfortune to have, dying here in my arms, the flower of the world's chastity, the crown of pure women, the pattern of virtue!'

And she said so much more in that style that anyone overhearing her would have thought she was the most piteous and faithful maid-servant in the world, and her mistress another persecuted Penelope. Camilla was not long, however, in coming round from her faint, and as she came to, she said:

'Why do you not go, Leonela, and call that most loyal of friends the sun ever saw or the night hid? Be quick, run, hurry, go, or the fire of my anger may be quenched by the delay and the rightful vengeance I desire pass off in threats and curses.'

'I am going to call him now, my lady,' said Leonela. 'But first you must give me that dagger, for fear you may do something with it while I am away, which would leave all of us who love you weeping for the rest of our lives.'

'Do not fear, friend Leonela, I shall not do it,' replied Camilla. 'For though in your eyes I may seem bold and rash for defending my honour, I shall not be as bold as Lucretia. They say she killed herself although she had committed no crime, and without first slaying the cause of her dishonour. I will die, if I must. But my vengeance must be satisfied on the man who has brought me to this pass, in which I weep for his insolence, though it sprang from no fault of mine.'

Leonela required some further entreaties before going out to call Lothario. But at last she went and, whilst awaiting her return, Camilla spoke, as if in soliloquy:

'Heaven help me! Would it not have been better to have sent Lothario away, as I have often done before, and not have allowed him, as I have done now, to think me dishonest and wicked, if only for the little time I must wait before undeceiving him. It would certainly have been better, but then I should not be revenged; nor would my husband's honour be satisfied if he were to escape so neatly and easily from the predicament his wickedness has brought him into. Let the traitor pay for his lecherous desires with his life. Let the world know — if it ever does — that Camilla not only kept faith with her husband, but avenged him on the man who dared to offend him. Yet perhaps it would be better to tell Anselmo of this. Though I have already hinted at it in the letter I sent to him to the country. Seeing that he did not hasten to remedy the trouble I wrote of, I can only imagine that pure goodness and trustfulness prevents his believing that so much as a thought of his dishonour can dwell in the breast of so staunch a friend. I did not believe it myself for a long while, and I should never have believed it if his insolence had not grown so great, and his open bribes, his grand promises, and continual tears had not made it clear to me. But, why all these speeches now? Can a brave resolution have need of any arguments? No, indeed no! Away with you, then, traitors! Now for vengeance! Let the false villain enter; let him come; let him draw near; let him die and be done with, come what may! Pure I came into the possession of the husband Heaven gave me; pure I must go from him, even though I go bathed in my own chaste blood, and in the impure blood of the falsest friend that ever was in all the world.'

As she talked, she paced about the room with the dagger unsheathed, taking such uneven and unsteady strides, and striking such gestures, that she seemed to be out of her wits. She was like no delicate woman, but a desperate ruffian.

All the while Anselmo looked on in utter amazement, concealed behind some tapestries. What he had seen and heard already seemed to him sufficient to refute even graver suspicions, and he would willingly have dispensed with the further proof upon Lothario's arrival; for he was afraid of some sudden disaster. But, as he was on the point of showing himself and emerging to embrace and reassure his wife, he stopped. For Leonela returned leading Lothario by the hand. And as soon as Camilla saw him she drew with the dagger a long line on the floor before her, and said:

'Listen to me, Lothario. If you dare by any chance to pass beyond this line here, or even to approach it, I will plunge this dagger I hold in my hand into my breast, the moment I see you are going to. Now, before you reply by so much as a word, I want you to hear me speak. Afterwards you may answer as you please. Tell me first, Lothario, if you know my husband Anselmo, and what opinion you hold of him. And next, I want to know whether you know me. Answer me. Do not be confused or hesitant in your replies, for these are not riddles that I am asking you.'

Lothario was not so stupid as not to have realized Camilla's plan when she told him to make Anselmo hide. So he fell in with her scheme most cleverly and aptly, and the pair of them made their imposture pass for truer than truth itself. Therefore he answered Camilla in this way, 'I did not think, beauteous Camilla, that you had summoned me to ask me questions so far from the purpose for which I have come. If your intention is to put off granting the favour you promised, you might have postponed it from a greater distance. For the nearer our hopes of possession the more we are tormented by our desires. But, so that you shall not accuse me of not replying to your questions, I will answer that I know your husband Anselmo, and that we have known one another since our tenderest years. Of our friendship I will say nothing. You know all about that, and I do not want to testify against myself. But the wrong I am doing, love — which excuses the greatest of faults — compels me to do. You too I know, and I value you as highly as he does. If that were not so, for lesser charms than yours, I should not have transgressed the holy laws of friendship, which I have now broken and violated at the instigation of that mighty enemy, love.'

'If you confess to that,' replied Camilla, 'mortal enemy of all true love, how can you have the effrontery to appear before the woman whom you know to be his very mirror and reflection? If you would look at yourself in her eyes you would see how little excuse you have for wronging him. But now, poor wretch that I am, I know what has made you break your faith. It must have been some lightness in me. I will not call it immodesty, for it did not spring from deliberate design. It was just one of those indiscretions into which women often carelessly fall when they think that reserve is unnecessary. But tell me, traitor, when did I answer your entreaties with so much as a word or sign that could awaken any shadow of hope in you of accomplishing your wicked desires? When were your words of love not sternly and bitterly and scornfully rejected? When did I accept your presents, or believe in your many promises? But I know that no one can persevere in his wooing unless sustained by some hope. So I will take the blame for your insolence, for no doubt it is my negligence that has made you persist in your suit so long. I will punish myself, therefore, and inflict the penalty of your guilt upon myself. I have brought you here to see that, being so cruel to myself, I could not be anything but cruel to you, and so that you may witness the sacrifice I intend to make to the wounded honour of my most honoured husband. You injured him with the greatest possible deliberation, and I by my lack of precaution in giving you an opportunity – if I did so – of furthering your wicked desires. What troubles me most, I repeat, is my suspicion that some carelessness of mine bred these rash thoughts in you. And that I most fervently desire to blot out with my own hands; for if I were to have any other executioner, my guilt would be more public.

'But before I die, I mean to satisfy my desire for vengeance, and take with me the man who has reduced me to this desperate plight. For when in that other place, wherever it may be, I see the punishment which impartial and unswerving justice will award him, I shall be completely satisfied.'

As she spoke she sprang upon Lothario with incredible strength and swiftness, flourishing the naked dagger; and so determined she appeared to bury it in his heart that even he was almost uncertain whether her demonstrations were false or true. For he had to use all his dexterity to prevent her stabbing him.

So convincingly did she perform her extraordinary act of deceit and fraud that she even shed her own blood to lend it colour. Finding that should could not wound Lothario – or pretending that she could not – she said: 'Though fate denies me complete satisfaction, at least it shall not be so strong as to prevent my attaining it in part.'

At this she wrenched her dagger-hand free from Lothario's grasp and, pointing the knife where it could not wound her deeply, she stabbed herself, burying the weapon above her breast under her left shoulder. She then let herself fall to the ground, as if in a faint.

Leonela and Lothario were speechless with astonishment at this unexpected act, and did not know what to think when they saw

Camilla stretched on the ground and bathed in her own blood. Breathless and shaken with fright, Lotario hurriedly ran to pull out the dagger. But when he saw how small the wound was his fears vanished, and he was amazed afresh at the fair Camilla's ingenuity, coolness, and ready wits. But, to play his part, he broke into a long and doleful lament over her body, just as if she were dead, calling down great curses upon himself and also on the man who had been the cause of the catastrophe. And, knowing that his friend Anselmo was listening, he spoke so that anyone hearing him would have pitied him even more than Camilla, even if he had supposed that she was dead. Leonela took her in her arms and placed her on the bed, begging Lotario to go and find someone to attend to her in secret. She asked him also to advise her what they should say to Anselmo about her mistress's wound, if he were to return before she was healed. He replied that they might say what they pleased, for he was no person to give useful advice. He only told her to try to staunch the blood, for he was going where no man should see him again. Then he left the house with a great show of grief and emotion. But, once he was alone and unobserved, he could not stop crossing himself in amazement at Camilla's ingenuity and Leonela's very apt acting. He reflected how positive Anselmo must be that his wife was a second Portia, and longed to meet him so that they might rejoice together at the most plausible imposture imaginable.

Leonela staunched her mistress's blood as she was told, though there was only just enough to make her performance convincing. Then she washed the wound with a little wine, and bound it up as best she could, making such an outcry as she did so that, even if nothing had been said before, that alone would have been enough to convince Anselmo that in Camilla he possessed the image of chastity. To Leonela's protestations Camilla added others of her own. She reproached herself for cowardice, and for lacking the courage to end her own days at that moment when it was most necessary; for life was abhorrent to her. She asked her maid's advice whether she should tell her beloved husband all that had happened or not, and Leonela advised her not to. For this would compel him to take vengeance on Lotario, which would involve him in great risk to himself. It was a good wife's duty, said the maid, to give her husband no occasion for quarrels, but rather to save him as many as she could. Camilla replied that this was good advice, and that she would follow it; but they would certainly have to find some explanation of her wound, for Anselmo would not fail to see it. Leonela's only reply to this was that she could not tell a lie, even in jest.

'Then how should I, my dear?' asked Camilla. 'I should not dare to invent or brazen out a lie if my whole life depended on it. If we cannot think how to get out of this fix, it would be better to tell him the naked truth than for him to catch us out in a lying tale.'

'Do not worry, my lady,' replied Leonela. 'Between now and to-morrow I will think out something to say. Perhaps you may be able to hide the wound, it being where it is, and he will not see it. Then Heaven may smile on the justice of our case. Be calm, my lady, and try to control your feelings, so that my master shall not find you upset. Leave the rest to me and to God, who always aids good intentions.'

Anselmo had stood listening and watching with rapt attention at this tragedy representing the death of his honour, and performed by the players with such strange and moving passion that they seemed transformed into the very characters they were acting. He longed for night, which would give him an opportunity of slipping out of the house and going to his friend Lothario, to rejoice with him over the pearl which he had found, in the unveiling of his wife's virtue. The pair of them took care to give him an opportunity of getting away; and he took advantage of it to go immediately in search of Lothario. It is impossible to recount how often he embraced him when he found him, what he said in his delight, and how much he praised Camilla. Lothario listened to all this without being able to show any signs of joy, for he could not get out of his mind the thought of how greatly his friend was deceived and how cruelly he had wronged him. But, although Anselmo noticed that Lothario did not show any joy, he supposed that it was because Camilla had been wounded and he had been responsible. So, in the course of their conversation, he told him not to worry about Camilla's accident, for the wound must certainly be a slight one, since they had agreed to hide it from him. Lothario, in fact, had nothing to fear, he said, but should rejoice and be gay with him, since it was through his friend's means and contriving that he had been raised to the highest attainable peak of happiness. What was more, he would have no other pastime from that day on but to write verses in Camilla's praise, to render her memory eternal for future ages. Lothario commended his resolution and promised to assist him in raising so noble an edifice.

From that time on Anselmo was the most deliciously deluded man in the whole world. He himself led home by the hand the man who had completely destroyed his good name, in the firm belief that he had brought him nothing but glory. Camilla received Lothario with seemingly averted glances but with a smiling heart; and this deception lasted for some time, until after many months Fortune turned her wheel, their cunningly concealed wickedness became public, and Anselmo's foolish curiosity cost him his life.

Chapter XXXV. *Of the fierce and monstrous Battle which Don Quixote fought with some Skins of Red Wine, with the conclusion of the Tale of Foolish Curiosity.*

VERY little more of the tale remained to be read when Sancho Panza rushed in alarm from the loft where Don Quixote was lying, shouting at the top of his voice: 'Come quickly, gentlemen, and help my master. I've never seen such a fierce and stubborn battle as he's got himself into. God in Heaven! He's dealt that giant, the lady Princess Micomicona's enemy, such a slash that he's sliced his head clean off like a turnip.'

'What's that you say, brother?' asked the priest, leaving the rest of the tale unread. 'Are you in your senses, Sancho? How the devil can all that be true, seeing that the giant is six thousand miles away?'

Here they heard a tremendous noise in the room and Don Quixote shouting: 'Hold, thief, scoundrel, braggart! Ah, I have you at last. Your scimitar will not help you now.'

And he seemed to be slashing at the walls.

Then Sancho said: 'You shouldn't stand there listening. You ought to go in and get between them, or go to my master's aid. Though there'll be no need now, for the giant's certainly dead by now, and giving an account to God of the wicked life he's led. I saw his blood on the floor, and his head cut off and fallen on one side. It's as big as a great wineskin.'

'Good God!' exclaimed the innkeeper at this point. 'If that

Don Quixote, or Don devil, hasn't been slashing at one of the skins of red wine at the head of his bed! Full they were, and what this fellow takes for blood must be the wine spilt on the floor.'

With that he ran into the room, and the others after him. They found Don Quixote in the strangest outfit in the world. He was in his shirt, which was not long enough in front to cover his thighs completely, and was six inches shorter behind. His legs were very long and thin, covered with hair, and not over-clean. On his head he wore a little greasy red cap which belonged to the innkeeper, and round his left arm he had wound the blanket of the bed – against which Sancho bore a grudge, and very well he knew why. In his right hand was his naked sword, with which he was lamming out in all directions, shouting all the time as if he were really fighting with a giant. The cream of the joke was that his eyes were not open, because he was asleep, and dreaming that he was battling with the giant. For his imagination was so bent on the adventure which he was going to achieve, that it made him dream he had got to the kingdom of Micomicon and was already at grips with his enemy.

What is more, he had slashed the wine-skins so many times, in the belief that he was getting at the giant, that the whole room was flooded with wine. At the sight of this the innkeeper flew into such a fury that he fell on Don Quixote, and began punching him repeatedly with his clenched fists. Indeed if Cardenio and the priest had not pulled him off he would soon have put an end to the war with the giant. But, despite all this, the wretched knight did not wake up until the barber brought a large pitcher of cold water from the well and threw it with a jerk all over his body. This awakened Don Quixote, but not sufficiently for him to realize the state he was in. Seeing how lightly and scantily he was dressed, Dorothea did not care to go in and see the battle between her champion and her adversary; and as for Sancho, he went about looking all over the floor for the giant's head and, not finding it, observed: 'Now I know that everything about this house is enchanted. The last time, right in this very spot where I'm standing, I got a regular punching and beating; yet I never knew who gave it me and never saw anybody at all. And this time the head isn't to be found, though I saw it cut off with my own eyes, and the blood pouring from the body like a fountain.'

'What blood and what fountain are you talking about, enemy of God and His saints?' cried the innkeeper. 'Can't you see, you great thief, that your blood and your fountain are nothing else but these skins here, which are slashed through, and the red wine which this room is swimming in? I should like to see the soul of the man who slashed them swimming in hell.'

'All I know,' replied Sancho, 'is that I'm going to be very unlucky. If I don't find that head, my countship will melt away like salt in water.' For Sancho awake was worse than his master asleep, so obsessed was he with the promises which his master had made him.

The innkeeper was in despair at the imperturbability of the squire and the damage which his master had done, and swore that this time he should not get away without paying, as he had done the time before; and that the privileges of knighthood should not save him from settling both reckonings, down to the very cost of the patches which would have to be stuck on to the torn wine-skins.

The priest was holding Don Quixote down by the hands, when, thinking that he had finished the adventure and was now in the presence of Princess Micomicona, the knight dropped on his knees before him and said: 'Exalted and most famous lady, Your Highness may henceforth live secure from any ill this low-born creature may do you; and, from to-day too, I also am released from the pledge which I gave you. For, by the help of God on high and through the favour of her for whom I live and breathe, I have perfectly fulfilled it.'

'Wasn't that just what I said?' exclaimed Sancho, when he heard this. 'So I wasn't drunk then. It looks as if my master has pickled the giant sure enough. The bulls are all right; I'm sure of my countship.'

Could anyone have kept from laughing at the nonsense of these two, master and servant? Everyone did laugh except the innkeeper, who cursed his luck. At length the barber, Cardenio, and the priest managed, with no little labour, to get Don Quixote into the bed, where he dropped off to sleep in a state of great exhaustion. They left him sleeping and went out to the inn door to console Sancho Panza for not having found the giant's head, although they had more to do to pacify the innkeeper, who was in despair at the sudden death of his wine-skins. The landlady too was shouting and screaming:

'It was an ill wind which blew that knight errant into my house. I wish I'd never set eyes on him, so dear he's cost me! Last time he went off he owed us for the night. Supper and bed for him and his squire, and straw and barley for a horse and an ass. He said that he was a knight adventurer – God send a bad end to his adventures, and the like to all other adventurers in the world! – and that he wasn't supposed to pay anything, that it was written so in the knight errantry regulations. And now, because of him, there comes this other gentleman and takes away my tail, and gives it me back with a pretty pennyworth of damage, with the hair all off, so that it's no good any more for what my husband wants it for. And on top of all that, to burst my wine-skins for me and spill out the wine. I'll see his blood spilt, I will! He shan't get away with it. By my poor father's bones and my blessed mother's grey hairs, if they don't pay me every single penny I'm not called what I am, and I'm not my father's daughter!'

This and more like it the landlady poured out in a great fury, and her good maid Maritornes backed her up; but her daughter kept quiet and smiled from time to time. The priest quietened them down by promising to compensate them for their loss as far as he was able, both for the skins and for the wine, and especially for the damage to the tail, which they made so much of. Dorothea consoled Sancho Panza by promising that, as soon as ever it was certain that his master had cut off the giant's head and once she was in peaceful possession of her kingdom, she would give him the best countship in it. At this Sancho took comfort, vowing that she could be certain that he had seen the giant's head, and, as proof more positive, that the monster had had a beard down to his waist. But, if it did not turn up, it was because everything which happened in that house was bewitched, as he had found the last time he had stayed there. Dorothea said that she believed him, and that he had no need to worry, for all would go well and turn out to his heart's content.

When everyone was quiet the priest expressed a wish to finish reading the tale, for he saw that there was very little left. Cardenio, Dorothea, and all the others begged him to do so and, being anxious to please them all, besides wanting to read it himself, he went on with the story.

'So it came to pass that through the satisfaction which Anselmo took in Camilla's virtue he led a happy and carefree life; and Camilla purposely looked sourly on Lothario, so that Anselmo should take her feelings for him to be the opposite of what they were. And to reinforce this pretence, Lothario asked leave not to come to the house, saying that he could clearly see how much Camilla disliked seeing him. But the deluded Anselmo replied that he would not agree on any account; and thus in a thousand ways Anselmo was the architect of his own dishonour, while he believed that he was making happiness for himself. At this time Leonela's pleasure in finding herself licensed in her love affair reached such a pitch that she pursued it unrestrainedly without any other thought, confident that her mistress would screen her, and even show her how to carry it on without arousing more than slight suspicion. But finally, one night, Anselmo heard steps in Leonela's room and, when he tried to go in and see who it was, found the door barred against him; which made him the more eager to force it. He pushed so hard, in fact, as to prise it open, and broke in just in time to see a man leap out of the window into the street. But when he ran quickly to catch him or see who he was, he could do neither, because Leonela clung to him, crying:

'Calm yourself, my lord, and don't make a disturbance. Don't follow the man who jumped out there. It's my affair; in fact he's my husband.'

Anselmo would not believe her; but blind with rage, drew his dagger and tried to wound her, commanding her to tell him the truth or he would kill her. Then, out of fear, and not knowing what she was saying, she exclaimed: 'Do not kill me, sir, and I will tell something more important than you can imagine.'

'Tell me, then, at once,' said Anselmo. 'If not, you are a dead woman.'

'I can't just now,' said Leonela. 'I'm so upset. Give me till tomorrow, and then I'll tell you something which will amaze you. But I swear to you that the man who jumped out of this window is a young man of this city, who has given me his word that he will marry me.'

Anselmo was satisfied with this, and content to wait the time she asked, for he did not expect to hear anything against Camilla, so absolutely satisfied was he of her virtue. So he went out of the room and left Leonela locked up, saying that she would not be let out till she had told him all that she had promised to reveal.

Then he went straight to Camilla and told her all that had passed between him and her maid, and of her promise to tell him something great and important. There is no need to say whether Camilla was alarmed or not. For so great was her fright, believing as she did and had good reason to, that Leonela was going to tell Anselmo all that she knew about her unfaithfulness, that she had not the courage to wait and see whether her suspicions were justified or not. That same night, when she thought that Anselmo was asleep, collecting her finest jewels and some money, she left the house unobserved and went to Lothario's. Once there, she told him what had happened, and begged him to find a hiding-place for her, or to take her away somewhere where they would both be safe from Anselmo. Lothario was thrown into such confusion that he could not answer a single word, still less make up his mind what to do. In the end he decided to take Camilla to a nunnery of which one of his sisters was prioress. Camilla agreed to this, and with the swiftness which the situation demanded Lothario took her and left her at the nunnery, then himself immediately quitted the city, informing no one of his departure.

When the day broke, so eager was Anselmo to learn what Leonela was going to tell him that he did not notice Camilla's absence from his side, but got up and went to the room where he had left the maid locked up. He opened the door and went in, but could not see Leonela. All he found were some sheets knotted to the window-bars – evidence that she had climbed down and fled. Then he returned at once rather sorrowfully to tell Camilla, and was astounded not to find her in bed or anywhere in the house. He asked the servants where she was, but no one could answer his question. Then, by chance, as he was searching for her, he noticed that her boxes were open and most of her jewels missing. From this he began to realize his disaster, and that Leonela was not the cause of his trouble. So, just as he was, without troubling to finish dressing, he went sadly and dejectedly to tell his friend Lothario of his misfortune. But when he found him gone, and his servants told him that their

L

master had departed that night and had taken all the money he had
with him, he thought he would go out of his mind. And on top of
all this, when he got back to his house he found not one of the men
or maid-servants there, and the house silent and deserted.

He did not know what to think or say or do, but little by little
his wits seemed to be returning to him. He reflected; and saw himself at one blow wifeless, friendless, and servantless, seemingly
abandoned by the Heavens above and, worst of all, robbed of his
honour. For in Camilla's flight he saw his own damnation. Finally,
after a long while, he resolved to go to his friend in the country,
with whom he had stayed when he had given them their opportunity of contriving the whole disaster. He locked the doors of his
house, mounted his horse, and with failing heart set out on the road.
But he had gone no more than half-way when, harassed by his
thoughts, he was compelled to dismount and tie his horse to a tree,
at the foot of which he lay down, heaving piteous and sorrowful
sighs. There he stayed almost till nightfall, when he saw a man
coming on horseback from the city, of whom, after greeting him,
he asked what news there was in Florence.

'The strangest news that we've heard there for many a long day,'
replied the townsman. 'It's publicly reported that Lothario, Anselmo's great friend, the rich man who used to live at San Giovanni,
carried off Anselmo's wife Camilla last night, and that Anselmo
himself is also missing. All this was revealed by a servant of
Camilla's, whom the Governor found, last night also, letting herself
down from the window of Anselmo's house by a sheet. I don't
know, indeed, exactly what happened. I only know that the whole
city is amazed at the business, for such a thing was most unexpected,
considering the great and intimate friendship between these two. It
was so remarkable that they're supposed to have been called *the Two
Friends*.'

'Do you know by any chance,' asked Anselmo, 'what road Lothario and Camilla have taken?'

'I've no idea,' replied the townsman, 'although the Governor has
been very active in looking for them.'

'God be with you, sir,' said Anselmo.

'And with you,' replied the townsman and rode off.

At this disastrous news Anselmo was not merely on the point of

going out of his mind, but on the verge of putting an end to his life.
He got up as best he could, and reached the house of his friend, who
had not yet heard of his misfortune. But when he saw him come in,
pale, exhausted, and haggard, he realized that some serious misfortune had befallen him. Anselmo begged them at once to help
him to bed and give him some writing materials, which they did,
and left him alone in bed with the door locked, just as he asked.
Once alone, he was so overwhelmed by the thought of his disaster
that he clearly saw his life was drawing to a close. So he decided to
leave an account of the cause of his strange death. He began to write.
But before he had finished setting down all he wished his breath
failed him, and he yielded up his life into the hands of that grief
which his foolish curiosity had brought upon him. The master of
the house, seeing that it was late and Anselmo had not called out,
decided to go in and find out if he was any worse. He discovered
him lying on his face, with half of his body on the bed and the other
half on the desk, and with the paper he had written unsealed and the
pen still in his hand. But, seeing that he did not respond and finding
him cold, he realized that he was dead. Amazed and deeply grieved,
he called his household to see the disastrous end that had befallen
Anselmo and, later, read the paper on which he recognized Anselmo's hand. It said:

'*A foolish and ill-judged craving has cost me my life. If the news of
my death should come to Camilla's ears, let her know that I pardon
her. For she was not obliged to perform miracles nor did I need to ask
her to. So, since I was the contriver of my own dishonour, there is no
reason why ...*'

Anselmo had written only so far, and it was clear that his life
had ended before he could finish his sentence. The next day his
friends advised Anselmo's relations of his death. They already knew
of his misfortune and of Camilla's retreat to the nunnery, where she
was almost in a state to accompany her husband on his inevitable
journey; not because of the news of his death, but from what she
had heard of her absent lover. It was said that, although she was
now a widow, she would not leave the nunnery, nor even less take
nun's vows. But not many days later news reached her that Lothario had been killed in a battle, which took place just then between

Monsieur de Lautrec and the great Captain Gonzalo Hernandez de Cordoba, in the kingdom of Naples where Anselmo's friend had retired, repentant too late. When Camilla heard this news she made her profession as a nun, and not long afterwards yielded her life into the cruel hands of sorrow and melancholy. This then was the end of these three, arising from such foolish beginnings.'

'I like the tale,' said the priest, 'but there is something unconvincing about it. If the author invented it he did it badly, for it is impossible to believe that there could be a husband so stupid as to want to make the costly experiment Anselmo did. If it were a case of a lover and his mistress it might pass; but between husband and wife there is something impossible about it. Though as for the manner of its telling, that does not displease me at all.'

Chapter XXXVI. *Of other strange events at the Inn.*

JUST then the landlord, who was standing at the inn door, called out: 'Here's a fine troop of guests coming. If they stop here we can sing "Praise the Lord".'

'What sort of people?' asked Cardenio.

'Four men on horseback,' replied the innkeeper, 'riding with short stirrups, with lances and shields, and all in black travelling-masks. There's a woman dressed in white with them riding side-saddle, with her face covered too, and two others, servants, on foot.'

'Are they very near?' asked the priest.

'So near,' replied the landlord, 'that they are here already.'

Hearing this, Dorothea veiled her face, and Cardenio went into Don Quixote's room; but they had hardly had time to do this when the whole party the host had described came into the inn. The four horsemen, who had a very well-bred appearance and bearing, dismounted and helped the lady down from her side-saddle. Then one of them took her in his arms and seated her in a chair, which stood at the entrance of the room where Cardenio had hidden. All this time neither she nor they had taken off their masks, nor said a word. Only, as she sat down, the lady in the chair heaved a deep sigh, and let her arms fall, as if she were ill or in a faint. The servants then led the horses to the stable.

The priest looked on and, wishing to know who these people were, so strangely dressed and so silent, went over to the servants and asked one of them. His answer was: 'Indeed, sir, I can't tell you who they are. All I know is that they seem to be important people, especially the man you just saw take the lady in his arms. Why I think so is because all the others pay him respect, and do nothing but obey his orders and directions.'

'And who is the lady?' asked the priest.

'I couldn't say either,' answered the servant, 'for I haven't set eyes on her face the whole way. I have only heard her sigh very often and moan as if she were ready to give up the ghost. It's not surprising that we don't know more than we've told you, because my mate and I have only been with them for the last two days. We met them on the road, and they begged and persuaded us to come with them as far as Andalusia, and offered to pay us very well.'

'Have you heard the name of any of them?' asked the priest.

'No, I haven't,' answered the servant. 'They all ride in perfect silence. It's very queer. The only sound we hear from any of them is the poor lady's sighs and sobs, which make us feel sorry for her. It's our firm belief that she's being forced to go wherever it is she's going and, as far as we can gather from her dress, she's a nun, or is going to become one more likely. Perhaps it's because she isn't taking the veil of her own free choice that she looks so sad.'

'That is very possible,' said the priest, and left them, to join Dorothea, whose natural pity was so stirred by the sighs and groans of the lady in disguise, that she went up to her and asked:

'What is your trouble, dear lady? If it is anything that it is in a woman's power to relieve, I would most willingly help you.'

The sorrowful lady made no reply and, although Dorothea repeated her offer, she remained silent till the masked horseman – the one whom the servant had said the others obeyed – came up and said to Dorothea:

'Do not weary yourself, lady, by showing this woman any courtesy, for she is always most ungrateful for whatever is done for her; and do not press her to reply if you do not want to hear her tell you some lie.'

'I have never told one,' exclaimed the lady, breaking her silence at this point. 'It is because I have been so truthful and so guileless that I am in my present unhappy plight. I call you as a witness to that, since it is the pure truth in me which shows you up as a false liar.'

Cardenio heard these words clearly and distinctly, as he was extremely near the speaker, only the door of Don Quixote's room being between them; and directly they came to his ears he cried out: 'Good God! What is that I hear? What voice is that?'

The lady turned her head in alarm at these cries and, not seeing who it was that spoke, rose to her feet and made to go into the room. But the gentleman immediately held her back and would not let her move a step. In her disturbance and agitation, however, her mask fell off, revealing a face of marvellous and incomparable beauty, though pale and frightened. For her eyes searched every spot within sight in such distress that she seemed to be out of her mind; and Dorothea, and all who saw her, were filled with pity for her, though they did not understand the reason for her behaviour. The gentleman held her firmly by the shoulder, but was so busy keeping his grip that he could not manage to hold up his mask, which in the end fell off. So when Dorothea, who had caught the lady in her arms, looked up, she saw that the man who was also holding her was her husband, Don Ferdinand; and the moment she recognized him she fell back senseless, uttering a deep and heartfelt groan. In fact if the barber had not been close by and caught her in his arms, she would have fallen to the ground. The priest at once hastened to take off her veil and throw water in her face; and as soon as he uncovered it, Don Ferdinand – for he it was who was holding the other lady in his arms – recognized her and was almost struck dead at the sight. Nevertheless he did not let go of Lucinda – for she it was – who was struggling to get free from his arms, having recognized Cardenio by his cry, as he had recognized her. Cardenio also heard Dorothea's moan as she fell fainting and, thinking that it was Lucinda's, rushed terrified out of his room. The first person he saw, however, was Don Ferdinand, holding Lucinda in his arms; and as Don Ferdinand also recognized Cardenio at once, all three, Lucinda, Cardenio, and Dorothea, were struck dumb with amazement, hardly knowing what had happened to them.

They all gazed at one another in silence, Dorothea at Don Ferdinand, Don Ferdinand at Cardenio, Cardenio at Lucinda, Lucinda at Cardenio. But the first to break the silence was Lucinda, who addressed Don Ferdinand:

'Leave me, Don Ferdinand, out of regard for yourself if for no other reason. Let me cling to the wall of which I am the ivy, to the prop from which neither your persistence, your threats, your promises, nor your bribes have been able to part me. See how Heaven, by ways strange and mysterious to us, has brought me to my true husband; and well you know by a thousand costly proofs that only death can blot him from my memory. So let this plain declaration tell you — since you have no alternative — to turn your love to rage, your affection to hatred, and put an end to my life. Yet, as I shall die before the eyes of my dear husband, I shall account my life well lost. For it may be that he will be convinced by my death that I have kept faith with him to the last act of my life.'

During this time Dorothea had come to herself, and had been listening to the whole of Lucinda's speech, from which she had realized who she was. Then, seeing that Don Ferdinand still did not let her go or reply to her words, she summoned up all the strength she could, got up, and threw herself on her knees at his feet. Then, bursting into a flood of lovely and piteous tears, she began to speak:

'If, my dear lord, the rays of that sun which you are holding in eclipse within your arms have not dimmed and darkened the light of your eyes, you will have seen that she who kneels at your feet is, as long as you will have it so, the luckless and unhappy Dorothea. I am that humble country girl, whom you chose, out of your kindness or for your pleasure, to raise to the height where she could call herself yours. I lived a contented life, enclosed within the bounds of virtue until, at the voice of your persistent and seemingly genuine and loving affection, I opened the gates of my modesty and entrusted the keys of my liberty to you: a gift which you appreciated very little, as is clearly shown by my being forced to hide in the place where you find me now, and by my seeing you as I do now. But, for all that, I would not have you think for one moment that I have come here along the road of dishonour; grief alone has brought me here, and sorrow at seeing myself deserted by you. It was your wish that I should be yours; and you wished it to such effect that, although now you would not have it so, it will be impossible for you ever to cease to be mine. Think, my lord, that the matchless love I have for you may be a compensation for the beauty and nobility of her for whom you are deserting me. You cannot be the fair Lucinda's, because you are mine; nor can she be yours, because she is Cardenio's. It will be easier, if you will think a moment, to make your heart love the woman who loves you, than to force into loving you a woman who loathes you. You pursued my innocence; you wore down my integrity with your prayers; you were not ignorant of my rank; well you know how completely I gave myself up to your will; you have no ground or reason to plead deception. If that is the truth, as it is, and you are a Christian and a gentleman, why do you put off with all these evasions, making me as happy at the end as you did at the beginning? If you do not want me for what I am, your true and lawful wife, desire me at least and have me for your slave. For if I am in your possession I shall count myself happy and fortunate. Do not leave me and abandon me so that my shame becomes the subject of gossip, or cause my parents a miserable old age. For they have given your parents loyal tenant's service and do not deserve such treatment. If you think that your blood will be debased by mixing with mine, reflect that there is little or no nobility in the world which has not travelled the same road, and that descent on the woman's side is not what counts in the most distinguished lineage. Moreover true nobility lies in virtue and, if you forfeit that by denying me my just rights, I shall be left with higher claims to it than you. Finally, sir, my last word is that I am still your wife, whether you like it or not. Your own promise is a witness which must not and cannot speak falsely, if you pride yourself on possessing what you despise me for lacking. Let your own signature testify, and Heaven, which you invoked to bear testimony to your promise. Should all these fail, your own conscience cannot but whisper in the midst of your joys, repeating the truth I have just spoken to disturb your greatest pleasures and delights.'

The unhappy Dorothea said this, and more like it, with such feeling and tears that everyone present sympathized with her, including even the men who had come with Don Ferdinand. That gentleman himself listened without answering a word till she finished speaking, and broke into such sobbing and sighing that only a heart of bronze would not have been melted by signs of such distress. Lucinda

stood gazing at her, pitying her grief and admiring her good sense
and her beauty. But, although she wanted to go and say something
to comfort Dorothea, Don Ferdinand still held her tight in his
arms and prevented her. Though, after gazing fixedly at Dorothea
for some time, he was overwhelmed with shame and horror, and
opened his arms to let Lucinda go.

'You have conquered, fair Dorothea,' he said. 'You have conquered. I cannot possibly have the heart to deny a combination of
so many truths.'

When Don Ferdinand released her, Lucinda almost fell down
from the faintness that had seized her. But Cardenio was close by,
having taken up his position behind Don Ferdinand so as not to be
recognized – and, setting fear aside, he defied all danger, ran up to
catch her, and clasped her in his arms.

'If merciful Heaven,' he cried, 'be pleased to grant you some rest
at last, my loyal, steadfast and lovely lady, nowhere, I believe, will
you find it more securely than in these arms which clasp you now
as they clasped you once before, when Fortune was pleased to let
me call you mine.'

At these words Lucinda, who had first begun to recognize him
by his voice, fixed her gaze on Cardenio and, assuring herself with
her eyes that it was he, almost beside herself and regardless of the
proprieties, threw her arms round his neck. Then, putting her face
close to his, she said: 'Yes, my dear lord, you are the true master of
this slave of yours, however much adverse fortune may oppose us
and threaten this life of mine, which depends on yours.'

This was a strange spectacle for Don Ferdinand, and for all the
rest, who were astonished at such unforeseen happenings. Dorothea, however, seeing Don Ferdinand change colour and move his
hand in the direction of his sword, imagined that he intended to
take his revenge on Cardenio, and instantly, with extraordinary
quickness, clasped him round the knees, kissing them and holding
them so fast that he could not move. Then, without ceasing her
tears, she said:

'What is it you mean to do, you who are my only refuge in this
unexpected crisis? Here at your feet is your wife, and the woman
you desire is in her husband's arms. Reflect whether it will be right
or possible for you to undo what Heaven has done; or whether it

will not be better to decide to raise to your level one who stands
before you, steadfast in her faith and constancy despite all obstacles,
and bathing her true husband's face and breast in loving tears. For
God's sake, and your own, I beg you not to let this public exposure
increase your anger, but rather to allay it; so that you may be able
calmly and peacefully to suffer these two lovers to live all the days
that Heaven allows them, without any hindrance from you. In that
way you will show the generosity of your illustrious and noble soul,
and the world will see that reason has more power over you than
passion.'

While Dorothea was speaking Cardenio did not take his eyes
from Don Ferdinand, even though he held Lucinda in his arms.
For he was determined, if he saw him make any hostile movement,
to defend himself, and to resist any attack to the uttermost, even at
the cost of his life. But at this point Don Ferdinand's friends – with
the priest and the barber, who had been present all the time, and
even honest Sancho Panza – all surrounded Don Ferdinand, imploring him to be moved by Dorothea's tears and, if she was speaking the truth, as they believed she was, not to suffer her to be defrauded of her just expectations. They begged him to reflect that it
was not by chance, as it appeared, but by a special providence of
Heaven, that they had all come together in such an unexpected
place. The priest warned him, too, that only death could part
Lucinda and Cardenio, and that they would joyfully accept their
death, even if they were sundered by the sword's edge. In these
irremediable circumstances, he said, it would be wisdom to restrain
and conquer himself, and to show a generous heart by allowing
these two, of his own free will, to enjoy the good fortune which
Heaven had granted them. If he would turn his gaze on Dorothea's
beauty, he would see that few or none could equal her, much less
excel her. And besides her beauty he should consider her humility,
and her very great love for him. Above all, he must remember that,
if he counted himself a gentleman and a Christian, he could not fail
to honour his promises, and in doing so he would be doing his duty
to God and be applauded by all men of good sense. For they know
and recognize that it is the prerogative of beauty, even though in a
humble subject, to rise equal to any dignity. For so long as it is
united with virtue, it casts no shadow of reflection on the man who

raises it to his own level. For where the strong laws of passion obtain, so long as there is no sin no man can be blamed for obeying them.

In short, he added so many compelling arguments that Don Ferdinand's valorous heart – which was, after all, nurtured by generous blood – softened, and allowed itself to be conquered by the truth, which he could not deny if he would. And the sign he gave of his surrender and acceptance of the priest's good advice, was to stoop down and embrace Dorothea, saying:

'Rise, my lady! The woman I hold in my heart must not kneel at my feet. If I have given no proof of what I say till now, perhaps it has been by Heaven's decree, that by seeing how faithfully you love me I might know how to value you as you deserve. What I beg of you is not to upbraid me for my misconduct and my neglect, for the same compelling reason which moved me to win you for mine drove me to struggle against being yours. For proof that this is true, turn and look into the eyes of the now happy Lucinda. There you will find an excuse for all my errors. Now, since she has obtained her desires, and I have found my fulfilment in you, I wish her a long and peaceful life, safe and happy with her Cardenio, and I pray Heaven to grant me the same happiness with my Dorothea.'

With these words he embraced her once more, pressing his face to hers with such tender feeling that it was all he could do not to burst into tears in true sign of his love and repentance. But Lucinda, Cardenio, and almost all the rest of the company as well, showed no such restraint, and began to shed so many tears, some for their own happiness and some for others', that it might have been thought some grievous disaster had befallen them all. Even Sancho Panza wept, though he said afterwards that he was only crying at finding that Dorothea was not, as he had believed, that Queen Micomicona from whom he had expected such benefits. It was some time before the general weeping and amazement calmed down; and then Cardenio and Lucinda went down on their knees before Don Ferdinand, and thanked him so courteously for the kindness he had shown them that he did not know how to reply. So he raised them up and embraced them with every mark of politeness and affection.

Then he asked Dorothea to tell him how she had come to that place so far from her home. She told him, briefly and sensibly, all that she had previously told Cardenio; and Don Ferdinand and his companions were so delighted with her story that they would have liked it to last longer, so charmingly did she tell the tale of her misfortunes. As soon as she had finished, Don Ferdinand related what had happened to him in the city, after he had found the paper in Lucinda's breast in which she had declared that she was Cardenio's wife and could not be his. He said that he had wanted to kill her, and would have done so if her parents had not prevented him. Then he had left the house angry and ashamed, and determined to take his revenge on a more convenient occasion. On the next day he had learnt that Lucinda had left her parents' house and that no one could say where she had gone; and finally, after some months, he had discovered that she was in a nunnery and intended to spend the rest of her life there, if she could not spend it with Cardenio. As soon as he had learnt of this he had chosen those three gentlemen for his companions and gone to the place where she was. But he would not speak with her for fear that, if they knew he was there, the convent would be better guarded. So he had waited for a day when the porter's lodge was open, and left two of his companions to secure the door, while he and the third had gone into the nunnery to look for Lucinda, whom they had found in the cloisters talking to a nun. Then they had snatched her up without giving her a chance to resist, and taken her to a place where they provided themselves with everything necessary for her abduction. All this they had been able to do in perfect safety as the nunnery was in the country, a good way outside the town. He said that when Lucinda found herself in his power she lost all consciousness, and when she came to herself did nothing but weep and moan, and never spoke a single word. So, to the accompaniment of silence and tears, they had reached the inn, which to him was like reaching Heaven, where all the ills of the earth are over and done with.

Chapter XXXVII. *A continuation of the History of the renowned Princess Micomicona, and other pleasant Adventures.*

To all this Sancho listened in no small distress of mind, seeing that his hopes of a title were disappearing and going up in smoke, since the lovely Princess Micomicona had turned into Dorothea, and the giant into Don Ferdinand; while there was his master sound asleep and quite oblivious of all that had happened. Dorothea could not feel certain that her happiness was not a dream. Cardenio was in the same state, and Lucinda's thoughts ran a similar course. Don Ferdinand gave thanks to Heaven for favours received, and for extricating him from the intricate labyrinth in which he had been within an ace of losing his honour and his soul. And everyone at the inn was pleased and delighted too, at the happy turn which this difficult and desperate situation had taken. The priest, like a man of sense, set everything in its true light, and congratulated everyone on what each had gained. But the most joyful and contented person in the inn was the landlady, because of the promise which Cardenio and the priest had made her to pay her all the cost and damage she had suffered on Don Quixote's account. Only Sancho, as we have said, felt wretched, disappointed, and sad; and so, with a melancholy expression, he went in to his master, who was just then waking up, and said:

'You can sleep soundly for as long as you like, Sir Sad Countenance, and not trouble about killing any giant or restoring the Princess to her kingdom. For it's all done and finished already.'

'I believe you,' replied Don Quixote, 'for I have fought the most monstrous and outrageous battle with that giant that I ever expect to fight in all the days of my life. With one back stroke – whack! – I slashed his head to the ground; and so much blood poured from him that it ran in streams along the earth, just like water.'

'More like red wine, you might say,' answered Sancho; 'for I would have your worship know, if you don't already, that the dead giant is a slashed wine-skin, and his blood the twelve gallons of red wine it had in its belly, and the head you cut off is ... my bitch of a mother – and the devil take the lot!'

'What is that you say?' retorted Don Quixote. 'You must be crazy, man!'

'If your worship will get up,' said Sancho, 'you'll see what a fine job you've done, and what we shall have to pay. And you'll see the Queen turned into an ordinary lady called Dorothea, and other things which will make you wonder, when you get the hang of them.'

'I should marvel at nothing of that sort,' replied Don Quixote.

'Last time we were here, if you remember rightly, I told you that everything which happened in this place was by way of enchantment. So it would not be surprising if it were the same this time.'

'I should believe it all,' answered Sancho, 'if my blanket-tossing had been that sort of thing. But it wasn't. It was real and true enough. I saw this innkeeper, who is here to-day, holding one end of the blanket, bouncing me up and down in fine trim, and laughing for all he was worth. I may be a simpleton and a sinner, yet it's my opinion that where you start recognizing people there's no enchantment about it, but plenty of bruising and bad luck.'

'Well, God will remedy that,' said Don Quixote. 'Give me my clothes and let me go out there. I want to see these changes and transformations you speak of.'

Sancho handed him his clothes; and while he was dressing, the priest told Don Ferdinand and the others of Don Quixote's madness, and of the trick they had played to get him away from the Bare Rock where, as he imagined, his lady's disdain had brought him. He told them too almost all the adventures which Sancho had described to him, at which they wondered and laughed quite a bit, thinking, like everyone else, that it was the strangest kind of madness that ever attacked a distraught mind. The priest said also that, since the lady Dorothea's good fortune would prevent their going on with their scheme, they would have to invent and work out another way of bringing him home to his village. Cardenio, however, offered to carry on with the original plan, and suggested that Lucinda should take over and play the part of Dorothea.

'No,' cried Don Ferdinand, 'that must not be. I wish Dorothea to carry on the scheme herself. This good knight's village cannot be very far away, and I shall be very glad to see him cured.'

'It is not more than two days' journey from here.'

'Even if it were more I should be glad to make the journey for such a good purpose.'

At this moment Don Quixote came out, armed with all his gear: with Mambrino's helmet, bashed in as it was, on his head; grasping his shield, and leaning on his tree-branch, or lance. Don Ferdinand and the others were astounded at his extraordinary appearance, and gazed upon his face, half a mile long, shrivelled and sallow, his miscellaneous weapons and his grave bearing in attentive silence until, staring very solemnly and intently on the fair Dorothea, the knight pronounced:

'I am informed, beauteous lady, by this squire of mine that your greatness has been cast down and your very being destroyed, since from the Queen and great lady that you were you have turned into a humble maiden. If this has been by command of the necromancer King, your father, out of his fear that I shall not give you due and necessary aid, I say that he has never known, and does not know, the half of his art, and that he has very little acquaintance with histories of chivalry. For, had he read them and studied them as attentively and as much at his leisure as I have, he would have found at every step how other knights, of less renown than I, have achieved things much more difficult. For it is no great matter to kill a paltry giant, however arrogant he may be. Not very long ago, in fact, I fought with him myself and ... I prefer to be silent, in case I may be accused of falsehood. But time, which unveils all mysteries, will reveal this one when we least expect it.'

'It wasn't a giant you fought, but two wine-skins,' put in the inn-keeper at this point. But Don Ferdinand told him to be quiet and on no account to interrupt Don Quixote's remarks. Then the knight went on:

'Indeed, as I say, exalted and disinherited lady, if for the reasons I have stated your father has performed this metamorphosis in your person, you should put no trust in him at all. For there is no peril on earth through which my sword cannot cleave a way, and in the shortest time I can cast your enemy's head to the earth and place the crown of your country upon yours.'

Don Quixote said no more, but waited for the Princess's reply; and she, knowing that Don Ferdinand intended to continue the deception until they had brought Don Quixote home, answered very gracefully and gravely: 'Whoever told you, valorous Knight of the Sad Countenance, that I have altered and transformed myself, did not tell you the truth, for I am the same to-day as I was yesterday. It is true that certain strokes of good fortune have worked some change in me, by giving me the desire nearest to my heart. But, for all that, I have not ceased to be the person I was before, nor to have the same intention as I have always had, of availing myself of the

might of your valorous and invincible arm. Therefore, dear sir, of
your grace, restore his honour to the father who begot me; and think
of him as a man far-seeing and wise, in that he found by his science
such an easy and certain way of remedying my misfortune. I believe, sir, that if it were not for you, I should never have succeeded
in gaining the happiness I have; and in this I speak nothing but the
truth, as most of these gentlemen here will bear witness. All that remains is for us to set out on our way to-morrow, for we shall not
be able to travel far to-day. And the rest of the good fortune that I
expect, I will leave to God and the valour of your heart.'

So spoke the subtle Dorothea and, when he had heard her, Don
Quixote turned to Sancho, and said with signs of great indignation:

'Now I tell you, miserable Sancho, that you are the most despicable rogue in Spain. Tell me, you vagabond thief, did not you say
just now that this Princess had turned into a damsel called Dorothea, and that the head, which, as I believe, I cut off a giant, was the
bitch that bore you, and all sorts of other nonsense that put me into
the greatest perplexity I have ever known in all the days of my life?
I swear ...' – he looked up to Heaven and gritted his teeth – 'that
I have a mind to work such havoc on you as will put salt into the
brainpans of all the lying squires of knights errant in the whole
world, from now till the end of time.'

'Please be calm, my dear master,' replied Sancho. 'It's very possible that I was mistaken in the matter of the lady Princess Micomicona's transformation. But as for the giant's head, or rather the
piercing of the skins, and the blood being red wine, I swear to God
I'm not mistaken. For there the skins lie slashed at the head of your
worship's bed, and the red wine has turned the room into a lake. If
you don't believe me, you'll see it when the eggs are fried – I mean
when his honour the innkeeper here asks you to pay for all the
damage. As for the rest, my heart rejoices that the lady Queen is
the same as she always was, for I shall get my share and so will
every neighbour's child.'

'Now really, Sancho,' said Don Quixote, 'you are a loon, forgive
the expression. And now let us drop the subject.'

'Enough,' said Don Ferdinand. 'Let no more be said of the matter and, since the lady Princess says that we must ride on to-morrow because it is too late to-day, let us do so. We shall be able to

spend the night in pleasant conversation till daybreak. Then we will all bear Don Quixote company, for we are anxious to witness the valorous and incredible exploits he is to perform in the course of this great enterprise which he has undertaken.'

'It is I who shall serve you and bear you company,' replied Don Quixote, 'and I am very grateful for the favour you have done me and the high opinion you have of me, which I shall try to justify, or it shall cost me my life – and even more, if that is possible.'

Many compliments and offers of service passed between Don Quixote and Don Ferdinand. But they were all cut short by a traveller who entered the inn at that moment, a man who by his dress seemed to be a Christian newly arrived from the land of the Moors. He wore a short blue cloth cape with half sleeves and no collar, his breeches were of linen and blue also, and he wore a cap of the same colour. He had long boots, date-brown, and a Moorish short sword slung on a strap across his breast. Behind him on an ass came a wo-man dressed in Moorish fashion, with her face covered and a veil on her head, wearing a little cap of gold brocade, and swathed in a cloak which enveloped her from her shoulders to her feet. The man was of a robust and pleasant appearance, a little more than forty, rather dark-skinned, with long moustaches and a very well-trimmed beard. It was obvious, in fact, from his appearance that if he had been well dressed he would have passed for a person of birth and quality.

On entering he asked for a room, and seemed annoyed when he heard that there was not one to be had in the inn; but going up to his companion, who seemed from her dress to be Moorish, he lifted her down. Lucinda, Dorothea, the landlady, her daughter, and Maritornes were attracted by the novelty of her dress, which was strange to them, and gathered round the Moorish lady; and Doro-thea, who was always charming, courteous, and sensible, seeing that both she and her escort were troubled at there being no room, said to her:

'Do not be concerned, dear lady, at the lack of accommodation here, for it is the way of inns to have none. But, all the same, if you would care to lodge with us' – pointing to Lucinda – 'perhaps you would find your reception better than some you may have met with in the course of your journey.'

The veiled lady made no answer, but simply got up from her seat and, crossing her hands on her breast and bowing her head, inclined her body from the waist in token of thanks. From her silence they concluded that she must certainly be a Moor and not know the Christian tongue. Presently the gentleman who up to then had been busy with other things, drew near and, seeing that they were all grouped round his companion and that she did not reply to anything they said, remarked:

'Ladies, this young woman can hardly understand our language, and can only speak the tongue of her own country. She has not replied to your questions because she cannot.'

'The only thing we have asked her,' replied Lucinda, 'is whether she will accept our company for to-night and share our sleeping-room, where she shall have as much comfort as the accommodation will allow. We will do her every kindness, for we are bound to serve all strangers who are in need, and women most of all.'

'On her behalf and mine,' replied he, 'I kiss your hands, my lady, and value your offer as highly as it deserves. For on an occasion like this, and from such people as your appearance shows me you are, it is clearly a great favour.'

'Tell me, sir,' said Dorothea, 'is this lady a Christian or a Moor? For her dress and her silence make us think that she is what we hope she is not.'

'Moorish she is in body and dress; but in her soul she is a very good Christian, for she has the greatest desire to become one.'

'Then she is not baptised?' asked Lucinda.

'There has been no opportunity,' replied he, 'since we left Algiers, her country and her home; and up to now she has not been in such instant peril of death as to be obliged to receive baptism without first being instructed in all the ceremonies our Mother, the Holy Church, requires. But, please God, she will soon be baptised with the formalities due to her rank, which is greater than her dress or mine shows.'

This answer roused the curiosity of all the party to know who the Moorish lady and the gentleman were. But no one cared to ask just then, for at that time of night it was clearly better to help them get some rest than to ask them questions about their lives. Dorothea took the Moorish lady by the hand, made her sit down beside her, and asked her to take off her veil. But the stranger looked towards her escort, as if to ask him what they were saying and what she should do. He told her in Arabic that they were asking her to take off her veil; which she did, revealing a face so lovely that Dorothea thought her more beautiful than Lucinda, and Lucinda judged her lovelier than Dorothea, while the others were of the opinion that if any woman was the equal of those two in looks it was the Moorish lady; and some of them thought that in some ways she was the loveliest of the three. Now as it is the privilege of beauty to win over all hearts and attract all minds, everyone yielded instantly to the desire of waiting on the lovely Moor.

Don Ferdinand asked her escort for her name, and he replied that it was Lela Zoraida; but when she heard his answer, understanding what the Christian had asked, she broke in hastily and charmingly, though in some dismay:

'No, no, Zoraida: Maria, Maria' – giving them to understand that her name was not Zoraida but Maria.

Her words and the feeling with which she spoke drew tears from some of her hearers, especially from the women, who were naturally tender-hearted. Lucinda embraced her most warmly and said: 'Yes, yes, Maria, Maria.'

And the Moorish lady replied: 'Yes, yes, Maria – Zoraida "*macange*" ' – that is to say, not Zoraida at all.

Meanwhile night had fallen, and under the supervision of Don Ferdinand's companions the innkeeper had taken considerable pains to provide the best supper he could. So, when the time came, they all sat down together at a long refectory table, for there was not a round or a square one in the inn. They gave the most important seat at the head to Don Quixote, though he repeatedly declined it. And he asked the lady Micomicona to sit beside him, since he was her protector. Next Lucinda and Zoraida took their places, and opposite them Don Fernando and Cardenio; beside them the newcomer and the rest of the gentlemen, and next to the ladies the priest and the barber. So they ate their supper with great pleasure, which grew still greater when they saw Don Quixote leave off eating and, moved by the same spirit that had prompted his long speech when he supped with the goatherds, prepare to address them: –

'Most truly, gentlemen, if the matter be deeply considered, great and most extraordinary are the experiences of those who profess the order of knight errantry. For who is there of all men living upon earth who would judge us and know us for what we really are, if he were to come in now through the gate of this castle and see us as we appear at present? Who would be able to guess that this lady at my side is the great queen we all know her to be, and that I am that Knight of the Sad Countenance, so trumpeted by the mouth of Fame? Now there is no doubt that this art and exercise is greater than any discovered by man, and must be the more highly valued the more perils it is subject to. Away with those who say that Letters have the advantage over Arms. For I will tell them that they do not know what they are saying, whoever they are. The argument which such people generally use, and on which they most rely, is that the labours of the spirit are greater than those of the body, and that Arms is only an exercise of the body; as if the practice of it were mere labourer's work for which nothing is needed but sheer bodily strength; or as if the pursuit of what we, who follow it, call the profession of arms, did not entail acts of courage that require great intelligence to carry them through; or as if a warrior commanding an army or defending a besieged city does not labour with his mind as well as with his body. Let it be shown, then, how by mere bodily strength he can come to guess at and know the enemy's intentions, plans, stratagems, and traps, and how foresee what dangers are impending; for all these are activities of the mind, in which the body plays no part. Seeing, therefore, that Arms, like Letters, require intelligence, let us consider now which of the two performs the greater mental labour, the man of letters or the man of war; for this will be decided by the end and object at which each is aiming – since the purpose which has the noblest end in view must be the more highly valued. The end and object of learning – I am not speaking now of theology, whose goal is to aid souls on the way to Heaven; for no other aim can be compared to a purpose so infinite as that – I am speaking of the humanities, whose aim is to maintain impartial justice, to give every man his rights, to make good laws, and to see that they are kept. That is certainly a lofty and generous aim, and highly praiseworthy, though not so much so as the profession of Arms, whose aim and object is peace, the greatest good which men can desire in this life. For the first good news the world and mankind received was proclaimed by the angels on that night which was our day, when they sang in the sky: *"Glory to God in the highest and peace on earth to men of good will"*; and the greeting which the best Master on earth or in Heaven taught His favoured disciples to give when they entered a house was: *"Peace be to this house."* And many other times He would say: *"My peace I give unto you; my peace I leave with you; peace be with you"*; which, given and bequeathed by such a hand, was a jewel and a treasure; indeed such a jewel that there can be no happiness on earth or in Heaven without it. This peace is the true aim of war; for Arms and war are all one. Admitting then this truth, that the aims of war are peace, and that thereby it excels the art of Letters, let us come now to the bodily hardships of the scholar and of the man whose profession is Arms, and see which are the greater.'

Don Quixote pursued his discourse so rationally and in such well-chosen language that none of his hearers could possibly take him for a madman just then. On the contrary, as most of them were gentlemen connected with the profession of Arms, they listened with great pleasure, as he went on speaking:

'I say then that the hardships of the student are these: first of all, poverty – not because they are all poor, but to put the case as strongly as possible – and when I say that they suffer poverty I do not think that there is anything more to say about their misery; for the poor man lacks everything that is good. This poverty they suffer in various forms: sometimes hunger, sometimes cold, sometimes nakedness, sometimes all of them together. But, all the same, things are not so bad that they do not eat, although it may be a little later than they are used to, or from the leavings of the rich man's table; for what students call *"going on the soup"*, or begging for their supper, is their worst misery. And moreover they do share someone's brazier or hearth, which may not warm them but at least takes the edge off the cold; and, last of all, they sleep under cover at night. I do not want to go into other details – lack of shirts, for instance, and shortage of shoes, or scanty and threadbare clothing – or to describe their way of stuffing themselves over-eagerly when Fortune sends them a feast. But by the rough and difficult path which I have indicated, stumbling at times and falling, getting up and falling once more, they do acquire the degree they desire. And when they have got it, I have seen many of them, once passed through those shoals, those Scyllas and Charybdises, as if borne on the wings of Fortune's favour; — I say that we have seen them command and govern the world from an armchair, their hunger exchanged for a full stomach, their cold for a pleasant coolness, their nakedness for fine clothes, and their sleep on a mat for comfortable rest on fine linen and damask: the justly merited rewards of their virtue. But if we set their hardships against those of the militant soldier and compare them, they are left far and away behind, as I shall now explain.'

Chapter XXXVIII. *Don Quixote's curious Discourse on Arms and Letters.*

DON QUIXOTE then went on: 'Since we began in the case of the student by dealing with his poverty and its circumstances, let us consider whether the soldier is any richer. We shall see that he is the poorest of the poor. For he is limited to his wretched pay, which comes either late or never, or to what he can loot with his own hands, at considerable risk to his life and his conscience. Sometimes too he is so naked that a slashed doublet serves him both for uniform and for shirt, and in the open field in the depth of winter he has nothing to warm him against the inclemencies of heaven but the breath of his mouth which, coming out of an empty place, must certainly come out cold, against all the laws of nature. But wait till night-fall; for then he can rest from his discomforts in the bed which awaits him, and which, except by his own fault, will not sin by being too narrow. For he can measure out as many feet as he likes on the earth, and roll about to his heart's content without fear of the sheets rumpling up. Then, at last, comes the day and the hour for him to receive his degree in his art: the day of battle dawns, when they will put on him a doctor's cap made of lint, to heal some bullet wound which may have pierced his temples or left him maimed in arm or leg. And if this does not happen, but merciful Heaven preserves him and keeps him whole and alive, he will very likely remain in the same poverty as before; and there must needs be one skirmish after another and one battle after another, and he must come out victorious from every one, before he has any success at all; but such miracles rarely occur. Now tell me, gentlemen, if you have ever considered it, how many more perish by war than profit by it? Unquestionably your reply will be that there is no comparison. For there is no counting the dead, and those who have benefited by war and survived can be reckoned in three figures.

'It is quite the reverse with scholars; for by their salaries – I will not say by their perquisites – they have all enough to make do, so that although a soldier's hardships are greater, his rewards are less. But you may reply that it is easier to reward two thousand scholars than thirty thousand soldiers; because scholars are rewarded by the gift of posts given to men of their profession, but soldiers cannot be recompensed except out of the very property of the lord they serve. This impossibility makes my argument even stronger.

'Leaving this on one side, however, for it is a very difficult labyrinth to find a way out of, let us come back to the pre-eminence of Arms over Letters, – a question which remains still to be resolved, since each side puts up so many arguments on its own behalf. Besides those which I have given, the scholars say that without them arms could not survive. For war too has its laws and is subject to them, and laws fall within the province of letters and learning. But to this Arms reply that laws could not survive without them; because by Arms states are defended, kingdoms preserved, cities guarded, the roads kept safe, and the seas swept free of pirates. In short, if it were not for them, states, kingdoms, monarchies, cities, and the highways on land and sea, would be subject to the savagery and confusion which war entails, so long as it lasts and is free to exercise its privileges and powers.

'What is more, it is a well-known truth that what costs most is, and should be, the most highly valued. Now to attain eminence in the learned professions costs a man time, nights of study, hunger, nakedness, headaches, indigestion, and other such things, some of which I have mentioned already. But to reach the point of being a good soldier, requires all that it requires to be a student, but to so much greater a degree that there is no comparison; for the soldier is in peril of losing his life at every step. What fear of poverty or want that can befall or afflict a student can compare with the fear a soldier knows when he is besieged in a fortress, on watch or guard in some redoubt or strongpoint, knowing that his enemies are mining towards the spot where he is, and that he may on no account leave his

post, or run away from the danger which threatens him so closely?
The only thing which he can do is to inform his captain of what is
happening, in the hope that he will meet the situation with a coun-
ter-mine; and he must stand calmly, though in fear and expectation
of suddenly rising to the clouds without wings and sinking again to
the depths against his will. If this seems a small danger, let us see if
it is equalled or surpassed in the head-on collision of two galleys in
the midst of the high seas. For when ships are locked and grappled
together, the soldier has no more space left him than two feet of
plank on the beak-head. But though he sees in front of him countless pieces of artillery threatening from the enemy's side, each a
minister of death, and no more than a spear's length from his body;
and though he knows that at his first careless step he will go down
to visit the deep bosom of Neptune, nevertheless with undaunted
heart, sustained by the honour which spurs him on, he exposes himself as a mark for all their shot, and endeavours to pass along that
narrow causeway into the enemy's ship. And, most amazing of all,
no sooner does one man fall, never to rise again this side of Doomsday, than another takes his place; and if he, in his turn, falls into the
sea, which lies in wait for him like an enemy, another, and yet another, takes his place, without a moment passing between their
deaths: the greatest display of valour and daring to be found in all
the hazards of war. Blessed were the times which lacked the dreadful fury of those diabolical engines, the artillery, whose inventor I
firmly believe is now receiving the reward for his devilish invention
in hell; an invention which allows a base and cowardly hand to take
the life of a brave knight, in such a way that, without his knowing
how or why, when his valiant heart is fullest of furious courage,
there comes some random shot – discharged perhaps by a man who
fled in terror from the flash the accursed machine made in firing –
and puts an end in a moment to the consciousness of one who deserved to enjoy life for many an age. And when I think of that, I am
tempted to say that it grieves me to the heart to have adopted this
profession of knight errantry in such a detestable age as we now
live in. For although no danger frightens me, still it causes me misgivings to think that powder and lead may deprive me of the chance
of winning fame and renown by the strength of my arm and the
edge of my sword, over all the known earth. But let Heaven do

what it will. If I achieve my purpose, I shall be the more highly esteemed for having faced greater dangers than did the knights errant of past ages.'

All this long rigmarole Don Quixote spoke whilst the others were eating their supper, forgetting to put a mouthful into his mouth although Sancho Panza urged him several times to eat, with the remark that he would have time to say all he wanted to after-wards. His hearers were moved once more to pity at seeing a man, apparently of such sound intelligence and with such understanding of everything he spoke of, lose it so entirely on the subject of his foul and accursed chivalry. The priest said that there was much justice in all that he had said in favour of arms, and that he was of the very same opinion himself, although a scholar and a graduate.

Then, their supper finished, the table-cloths were removed, and whilst the landlady, her daughter, and Maritornes were clearing up Don Quixote de la Mancha's attic, where they had decided that the women should be lodged by themselves that night, Don Ferdinand asked the newcomer to tell them his life's story. For, from so much as they had gathered by his coming in Zoraida's company, it could not fail to be strange and enjoyable. He replied that he would most gladly comply, only he feared that his story would not give them as much pleasure as he would like. But he would tell it all the same, rather than appear disobliging. The priest and all the others thanked him and pressed him to begin; and when he found them all so urgent he assured them that there was no need of entreaties, for their mere request was enough.

'Listen then, gentlemen, and you will hear a true story, and I doubt whether you will find its equal in the most detailed and careful fiction ever written.'

At these words they all sat down in perfect silence; and when he saw them quiet and waiting for him to speak, he began in a smooth and pleasant voice:

Chapter XXXIX. *The Captive tells the story of his Life and Adventures.*

'MY family had its origin in a village among the mountains of Leon; and nature was kinder and more generous to them than fortune was,

although in those very poor villages my father had the reputation
of being rich; and indeed he would have been if he had been as good
at keeping his money as he was at spending it. This liberal and waste-
ful disposition of his came from his having been a soldier in the days
of his youth. The soldier's trade is a school in which the mean
man learns to be liberal and the liberal man prodigal; for if there are
sometimes soldiers who are misers, they are, like monsters, rarely
seen. My father passed the bounds of liberality and verged on those
of prodigality, a quality which is no advantage to a married man,
with children to inherit his name and station. My father had three,
all sons and all of an age to choose their professions. So, seeing that
he could not, as he said, bridle his nature, he decided to deprive himself of the cause and means which made him a prodigal and a spendthrift; in other words, to give up his estate, without which Alexander himself would have been reckoned a miser. So, calling us all
three one day into a room alone, he addressed us in some such way
as this:

"'My sons, to assure you that I love you, it is quite enough to say
that you are my sons; and to convince you that I do not love you,
it is enough to say that I do not control myself in order to preserve
your fortune. But so that you may know in future that I love you
like a father and do not want to ruin you like a stepfather, I intend
to do something for you, which I have been thinking over for a long
time, and have decided on after mature consideration. You are of an
age to take up a calling, or at least to choose some profession that
will bring you honour and profit when you are older. My plan is to
divide my estate into four parts. Three of them I will give you, an
absolutely equal portion for each, and I shall live on the fourth part
for as long as Heaven is pleased to preserve my life. But I want each
one of you, once you have received your share of the estate, to follow one of the paths which I shall indicate. There is a proverb in
this Spain of ours – a very good one I think, as all of them are, for
they are brief maxims collected from long and deep experience. The
one I am thinking of is: *The Church, the Sea, or the King's Palace.*
The meaning of that is: if you want to be powerful and rich, follow
the Church, or go to sea and practise the merchant's calling, or take
service with kings in their palaces. For it is said: *Better the King's
crumb than the lord's favour.* I mean by all this that I wish one of you

to pursue learning, another commerce, and the third to serve the King in his wars, as it is difficult to get a place in his household; for although war does not bring much riches, it generally brings great fame and renown. Within a week I will give you each your share in money, to the last farthing, as you will see. Tell me then if you are willing to follow my counsel and take the advice I have offered you."

'He called on me, as the eldest, to answer, and I entreated him not to part with his fortune, but to spend it as freely as he liked, for we were young enough to be able to win one ourselves. But in the end, I said that I would obey his wishes and that my choice would be to follow the profession of arms, thereby serving God and my King. My younger brother protested to the same effect, and then elected to go the Indies and invest his portion in merchandise. The youngest, and I think the wisest of us, said that he would follow the Church and go and complete his studies at Salamanca.

'So when the agreement was made and we had each chosen our profession, our father embraced us all, and carried out his promise just as quickly as he had said he would; giving us each, as I remember, three thousand ducats in money, an uncle of ours having bought the estate so that it should not go out of the family, and paid for it in cash. We all three bade our dear father good-bye on the same day. But it seemed to me inhuman to leave so old a man with so little means, and I made him take two thousand of my three thousand ducats, the rest being sufficient to provide me with all that a soldier needs. My two brothers followed my example, and each gave him a thousand ducats; so that he was left with four thousand ducats in money and three thousand more, the value of his share of the estate, which he was unwilling to sell but had kept in land. Well, as I said, we took our leave of him and of this uncle of ours, with great emotion and tears on all sides, they insisting that we should let them have news of us, good or bad, at any favourable opportunity. We promised to do so, embraced them, and received our father's blessing. Then one of us took the road for Salamanca, one for Seville, and I for Alicante, where I had heard that there was a Genoese ship loading with wool for Genoa.

'It is now twenty-two years since I left my father's house, and for all that time I have heard nothing of him or of my brothers, although I have written several letters; and what I have gone through in the interval I will tell you briefly. I went aboard at Alicante, arrived after a prosperous voyage at Genoa, went from there to Milan, where I bought arms and some military clothing, and from there decided to go and enlist in Piedmont. But as I was on the road to Alessandria I got news that the great Duke of Alva was marching into Flanders. So I changed my plans, went with him, and served him in all his campaigns, being present at the deaths of Counts Egmont and Horn. I rose to be an ensign under a famous captain from Guadalajara by the name of Diego de Urbina. After some time news came to Flanders of the alliance his Holiness Pope Pius V, of happy memory, had made with Venice and Spain against the common enemy, the Turk, whose fleet had just then taken the famous island of Cyprus, which had been under the rule of the Venetians: a lamentable and disastrous loss. It was known for certain that the commander of this alliance would be Don John of Austria, the natural brother of our good King Don Philip; and news was abroad of the great preparations which were being made for the war. All this aroused in me a great desire to take part in the expected campaign. So, although I had hopes and almost certain prospects of being promoted to a captaincy as soon as occasion offered, I decided to give it all up and go to Italy, which I did. As my luck would have it, Don John of Austria had just arrived at Genoa on his way to Naples to join up with the Venetian fleet, which he afterwards did at Messina. So, to be brief, I was present at that most glorious battle, being by that time a captain of infantry, to which honourable rank I was promoted rather by luck than merit. On that day, so fortunate for Christendom, since then the world and all the nations learnt how wrong they were in supposing that the Turks were invincible on the sea – on that day I say, when the insolent pride of the Ottomans was broken for ever, among all the fortunate men there – for the Christians who died there were more fortunate than those who survived victorious – I alone was unlucky. For in place of some naval crown, which I might have expected in the days of ancient Rome, I found myself on the night following that famous day with chains on my feet and handcuffs on my hands.

'This is how it happened: Aluch Ali, King of Algiers, a bold and successful pirate, had attacked and beaten the Maltese flagship; and only three knights were left alive in her, and those three badly wounded. Then Juan Andrea's flagship, aboard which I was with my company, came to the rescue, and, doing what was my duty in the circumstances, I jumped aboard the enemy's galley; which then disengaged from our ship, that had grappled her, and thus prevented my men from following me. So I found myself alone among my enemies, unable to resist as they were so many. In fact they took me prisoner, covered with wounds. Now, as you will have heard, gentlemen, Aluch Ali escaped with his whole squadron; and I remained a prisoner in his power, being the only sad man among so many that rejoiced, the only prisoner among all those set free. For there were fifteen thousand Christians rowing that Turkish fleet who that day gained their coveted liberty.

'They took me to Constantinople, where the Grand Turk Selim made my master Commander of the Sea – for doing his duty in that battle and bearing off the standard of the Knights of Malta, as a proof of his valour. The next year – that was 'seventy-two – I was at Navarino, rowing in the admiral's flagship, and witnessed the opportunity of catching the Turkish fleet in harbour which was then lost. For every Turkish sailor and janissary aboard was quite certain that they would be attacked in the port itself, and had his clothes and his *"passamaques"* – which are their shoes – ready, to escape at once by land without waiting to fight; such terror had our navy inspired in them. But Heaven ordained otherwise, through no fault or neglect of our commander but for the sins of Christendom, and because God ordains that there shall always be some scourge to chastise us. In the end Aluch Ali took refuge in Modon, an island close to Navarino and, putting his men ashore, fortified the entrance to the port and stayed there quietly till Don John had retired. In this expedition the galley called "The Prize" was taken. Her captain was a son of the famous pirate Barbarossa. The flagship of Naples, "The She-Wolf", took her, under the command of that thunderbolt of war and father to his soldiers, that fortunate and unbeaten captain, Don Alvaro de Bazan, Marquis of Santa Cruz.

'I do not want to leave out what happened at the capture of "The Prize". The son of Barbarossa was so cruel, and treated his slaves so badly, that as soon as the rowers saw the "She-Wolf" galley nearing them and about to board, they all dropped their oars at once and seized hold of him, where he stood at his station shouting at them to row hard. Then they tossed him from bench to bench, from stern to prow, biting him again and again, so that he had hardly gone farther than the mast before his soul had passed into hell; so cruelly did he treat them, as I said, and so bitterly did they hate him.

'We returned to Constantinople, and the next year – that was 'seventy-three – the news came that Don John had conquered Tunis, wresting that kingdom from the Turks and giving it to Muley Hamet; which deprived Muley Hamida, the cruellest and bravest Moor in the whole world, of his hopes of recovering the throne. The Grand Turk felt this loss very severely and, with the cunning natural to all his house, made peace with the Venetians, who wanted it much more than he. Then the following year, which was 'seventy-four, he attacked the Goletta, and the fort near Tunis which Don John had left half constructed. In all these actions I was at the oar, without any hope of liberty – at least I had no hope of getting it by ransom, for I was resolved not to send the news of my misfortunes to my father.

'In the end the Goletta was lost, and the fort as well. Attacking these places were seventy-five thousand Turkish regular soldiers, and more than four hundred thousand Moors and Arabs from all over Africa. This vast host was supplied with such a quantity of ammunition and material, and with so many sappers, that they could have buried the Goletta and the fortress deep in earth with their bare hands alone. The Goletta, which had been considered impregnable till then, was the first to fall. It was through no fault of its garrison, who defended it to the best of their power and ability, but because, as experience showed, earthworks could be thrown up very easily in that sandy desert; for though water used to be found about 16 inches down, the Turks did not strike it now at six foot. So with a great quantity of sandbags they raised their works high enough to command the walls of the fort and fired from above, so that no one could stay there to put up a defence.

'It was generally thought that our men should not have shut themselves up in the Goletta, but should have opposed the landing in open country. But the people who say that speak from a distance and with little experience of such matters. For as there were hardly seven thousand soldiers in the Goletta and the fort together, how could so small a number, however resolute, have taken the field, as well as held the forts against the enemy's great numbers? And how is it possible not to lose a fort which is not relieved, particularly when it is besieged by such a host of determined enemies and in their own country? Many, however, were of the opinion – as I was myself – that Heaven bestowed a special grace and mercy on Spain by permitting the demolition of that breeding-place and cloak of iniquities: that glutton, sponge, and sink of the infinite money which was wasted there to no advantage, to serve no other purpose than to preserve the memory of its conquest – the auspicious memory of the most invincible Charles V – as if that tract of earth were needed to make his name eternal, as it is and ever will be.

'The fort fell as well. But the Turks had to win it foot by foot. For the soldiers defending it fought so bravely and fiercely that they killed more than twenty-five thousand of the enemy in the twenty-two general assaults they made. Not one of the three hundred survivors was taken unwounded, a clear and manifest proof of their fierceness and bravery and of how well they defended and maintained their positions. A small fort or tower in the middle of the lake, under the command of Don Juan Zanoguera, a Valencian gentleman and a famous soldier, surrendered on terms. They captured Don Pedro Puertocarrero, the commander of the Goletta, who had done everything he could to defend his post, and felt its loss so much that he died of grief on the way to Constantinople, where they were taking him as a prisoner. They also captured the commander of the fort, Gabriel Cervellon by name, a Milanese gentleman, a great engineer and a most courageous soldier. In those two fortresses died many people of note, one of whom was Pagan Doria, a Knight of the Order of St. John, a man of generous character, as was shown by his very liberal treatment of his brother, the famous John Andrew Doria. What made his death even more deplorable was that he fell at the hands of some Arabs in whom he had trusted when he saw that the fortress was lost. They had offered to take him, disguised as a Moor, to Tabarca, a small seaport or station on that coast held by the Genoese, who are engaged in coral-fishing. These Arabs cut off his head and took it to the commander of the Turkish fleet, who proved on them the the truth of our Spanish proverb that though the treason pleases, we abhor the traitor. For they say that the general ordered the men who brought him the present to be hanged for not bringing him alive.

'Among the Christians captured in the fort was one Don Pedro de Aguilar, who came from somewhere in Andalusia. He had been an ensign in the garrison, and was a soldier of great repute and rare intelligence; and he had a remarkable gift for what they call poetry. I mention him because it was his lot to come to my bench in my galley, and to be slave to my own master, and before we left that port this gentleman composed two sonnets by way of epitaphs, one on the Goletta and the other on the fort. And I must really repeat them, for I know them by heart and I think you will probably like them.'

The moment the Captive named Don Pedro de Aguilar Don Ferdinand glanced at his comrades, and all three smiled; then, at the mention of the sonnets, one of them said:

'Before you go any further, sir, please tell me what became of this Don Pedro de Aguilar you spoke of.'

'All I know,' answered the Captive, 'is that after he had been two years in Constantinople he escaped, disguised as an Albanian, with a Greek spy. I do not know whether he got his liberty, but I suppose he did, for I saw that Greek a year later in Constantinople, though I could not ask him whether the escape had been successful.'

'It was,' replied the gentleman. 'That Don Pedro is my brother, and he is at our home now, well and rich, and married with three children.'

'God be praised,' said the Captive, 'for all the mercies He did him; for there is no joy on earth in my opinion so good as regaining one's liberty.'

'What is more,' the gentleman went on, 'I know those sonnets my brother wrote.'

'Then recite them to us, sir,' said the Captive, 'for you will be able to do it better than I.'

'With pleasure,' replied the gentleman, 'the one on the Goletta went like this:

Chapter XL. *The Captive's Story continued.*

'Blest souls, discharged of life's oppressive weight,
  Whose virtue proved your passport to the skies,
You there procured a more propitious fate,
  When for your faith you bravely fell to rise.
When pious rage, diffused through every vein,
  On that ungrateful shore inflamed your blood,
Each drop you lost was bought with crowds of slain,
  Whose vital purple swelled the neighbouring flood.
Though crushed by ruins and by odds, you claim
That perfect glory, that immortal fame
  Which, like true heroes, nobly you pursued;
On these you seized, even when of life deprived,
For still your courage even your lives survived,
  And sure 'tis conquest thus to be subdued.'

'Yes, those are the words that I know,' said the Captive.

'And the one on the fort, if my memory is right,' said the gentleman, 'goes like this:

'Amidst these barren fields and ruined towers,
  The bed of honour of the falling brave,
Three thousand champions of the Christian powers
  Found a new life and triumph in the grave.
Long did their arms their haughty foes repel,
  Yet strewed the fields with slaughtered hopes in vain;
O'ercome by toils the pious heroes fell,
  Or but survived more nobly to be slain.
This dismal soil, so famed in ills of old,
In every age was fatal to the bold,
  The seat of horror and the warrior's tomb!
Yet hence to Heaven more work was ne'er resigned
Than these displayed; nor has the earth combined
  Resumed more noble bodies in her womb.'

The sonnets were much appreciated, and the Captive went on with his tale, delighted with the news they had given him of his comrade:

'Then, when the Goletta and the fort surrendered, the Turks gave orders for the Goletta to be dismantled. But the fortress was in such a state that there was nothing left to demolish. And to save time and labour they mined it in three places. But none of the mines could blow up what appeared its weakest part; which was the old walls, although all that was still standing of the new fortifications,

M

built by El Fratin, came down most easily. Finally the fleet returned to Constantinople, triumphant and victorious, and several months later my master Aluch Ali died. They used to call him *Uchali Fartax*, which means in Turkish "the scabby renegade", which he was. For it is a custom among the Turks to name people by any defect, or by any good quality, they may have. That is because they have only four surnames among them, and those belong to families of Ottoman descent. The rest, as I have said, take their names and surnames either from their bodily defects or from their characters. This Scabby was at the oar as a slave of the Great Turk for fourteen years, and when he was over thirty-four turned renegade, in his fury at a Turk who had given him a slap on the face while he was rowing. In fact he renounced his faith to get his revenge. He had such character too that he came to be king of Algiers and, afterwards, Commander of the Sea – which is the third post in their empire – without resorting to the base methods by which most of the Great Turk's favourites rise. He was a Calabrian by birth, a good moral man, and treated his prisoners with great humanity. In the end he had three thousand of them, who were divided after his death, in accordance with his will, between the Grand Turk – who is reckoned a son and heir of all who die and takes his share with the rest of the dead man's sons – and his renegades. I fell to the share of a Venetian renegade, who had been a ship's cabin-boy when Aluch Ali captured him, for whom his master had such a liking that he was one of his most pampered favourites. He proved to be one of the cruellest renegades ever seen. He was called Hassan Aga and became very rich, eventually rising to be King of Algiers. With him I came from Constantinople, rather pleased to be so near to Spain; not because I thought of writing to tell anyone of my unhappy fate, but because I meant to see if Fortune would not be kinder to me in Algiers than in Constantinople, where I had attempted a thousand ways of escape, but had had no luck with any of them. I thought that in Algiers I would find other means of getting what I so much desired. For I never gave up hope of gaining my liberty, and when the result did not shape with my design in such plans as I contrived, worked out and put in practice, I never gave up, but immediately devised some new hope, never mind how slender and weak, to keep me going.

'So I passed my life, shut up in a prison-house, called by the Turks a *bagnio*, where they keep their Christian prisoners: those belonging to the King and those belonging to private people, and also those who are called the slaves of the *Almazen* – that is to say, of the township – who are employed in the public works of the city and in other communal employment. Slaves of this last kind have great difficulty in gaining their liberty because, as they belong to the community and have no master of their own, there is no one with whom to bargain for their ransom, even if they have the money. To these *bagnios*, as I have said, some private people of the city take their prisoners, particularly when they are waiting to be redeemed. For they are kept here in idleness and safety until their ransom comes. The King's captives, if they are to be ransomed, do not go out to work with the rest of the gang either, except if their ransom is delayed; in which case, to spur them to write more urgently for it, they make them work and fetch firewood with the others, which is no light job.

'I was one of those put on ransom. For as it was known that I was a captain, nothing could prevent their putting me on the list of gentlemen to be redeemed, although I pleaded that I had small means and no property. They put a chain on me, more as a sign that I was to be ransomed than for my safe keeping; and so I spent my life in that *bagnio* with many more gentlemen and men of quality chosen to be held for ransom. And although hunger and lack of clothes distressed us at times – in fact almost always – nothing disturbed us so much as to hear and witness, wherever we went, the unparalleled and incredible cruelty which my master practised on Christians. Every day he hanged someone, impaled another, and cut off the ears of a third; and this on the slightest excuse or on none at all, so that even the Turks acknowledged that he did it only for the sake of doing it, and because it was in his nature to be the murderer of the entire human race. The only one who held his own with him was a Spanish soldier, called something de Saavedra; for his master never so much as struck him, nor bade anyone else strike him, nor even spoke a rough word to him, though he did things which those people will remember for many years, all in efforts to recover his liberty; and the rest of us were afraid that his least actions would be punished by impaling, as he himself feared they would be more than once. And if it were not for lack of time I would tell you something about that soldier's deeds, which you would find much more entertaining and surprising than this story of mine.

'Now, overlooking the courtyard of our prison were the windows of the house of a rich and important Moor, which, as is usual in Moorish houses, were more like loopholes than windows, and even so were covered by thick and close lattices. And I happened one day to be on a flat roof in our prison with three companions, trying to wile away the time by seeing how far we could jump in our chains. We were on our own because all the other Christians had gone out to work. It was by the merest chance that I looked up, and when I did I saw a cane with a handkerchief tied to the end of it appear through one of those little closed windows I spoke of. It was being waved and jerked up and down, as though it were summoning us to go and take it. We stared at it; and one of my companions went and placed himself just below it to see if it would be dropped, or what else would happen; but no sooner did he get there than the cane was raised and jerked from side to side, as if someone were shaking his head to say no. The Christian came back, and again the cane was let down, to make the same movements as before. Another of my companions went up, but with the same result as the first. Last of all the third went, and was treated in the same manner as the first and the second. At this I was tempted to try my luck, and as soon as I got there and stood below the cane, it was let fall, and dropped into the prison just at my feet. I ran up at once to untie the handkerchief, in which I found a knot and in it ten *ʒianies*, which are coins of gold alloy that the Moors use, each worth ten of our *reals*. There is no need to tell you whether I was pleased at this windfall; I was delighted and astonished, but I could not think who could have directed this present, especially to me; since the refusal to drop the cane to anyone else was a clear sign that it was for me the favour was meant. I took my precious money; I broke the cane; I returned to the little roof; I looked up at the window, and saw the whitest of hands emerge to open and shut it very quickly. By this we learnt, or guessed, that it was a woman living in that house who had done us this kindness and, to show our thanks, we made *salaams* after the Moorish fashion, bowing our heads, bending our bodies, and laying our hands on our breasts. Somewhat later a little cross made of cane was put out of the same window and immediately drawn in again. This signal convinced us that there must be a Christian woman slave in the house, and that it was she who had given us the present; but the whiteness of her hand and the bracelets we saw on it contradicted this idea. Then we imagined that she must be a renegade Christian; for often the Moors are glad to marry slaves of this sort, whom they value more highly than women of their own people.

'In all our surmises we were very far from the truth. Our sole occupation from that day on, however, was watching, and the window where our star had appeared was the pole by which we steered. But a good fortnight went by before we saw any further sign. And although in that time we made every effort to find out who lived in the house, and if there was any renegade Christian woman there, no one could tell us anything except that a rich and important Moor called Hadji Murad lived there, and that he had been the governor of Bata, which is one of their most important posts. But when we least expected it to rain more *zianies*, we saw the cane suddenly appear with another handkerchief on the end, tied in another, bigger knot; and this, as before, was at a time when the prison was empty and deserted. We made the customary experiment, each one of the three going before me; but the cane was delivered to none but me, and was dropped as soon as I got there. When I undid the knot I found forty Spanish crowns in gold and a paper written in Arabic, and at the end of the writing there was drawn a large cross. I kissed the cross, took the crowns, and returned to the roof. Then we made our *salaams* and, the hand appearing again, I promised by signs to read the letter; at which the window was closed. We were all astonished and delighted at events. But, as none of us could understand Arabic, our curiosity to know what was in the paper was great and our difficulty in finding anyone to read it to us even greater. In the end I decided to confide in a Murcian renegade, who professed to be a good friend of mine and had exchanged pledges with me which bound him to keep any secret I might entrust him with. For there is a custom among some renegades, when they have a mind to return to Christian lands, to carry with them certificates from important prisoners, testifying, in such form as they can, that

such and such a renegade is an honest man, has always behaved well
to Christians, and proposes to escape at the first possible opportunity. Some of them procure these testimonials with honest intentions; others want them for an emergency, meaning to produce
them should they happen to be shipwrecked or taken prisoner on a
plundering expedition in Christian lands, and to use those certificates as evidence that their purpose in coming is to stay behind on
Christian soil, and that this is their only reason for coming on a raid
with the Turks. In that way they escape the first violence of their
captors, and safely make their peace with the Church; and when
they see their chance, they return to Barbary to be what they were
before. There are others, though, who make proper use of these
papers and get them with the honest intention of remaining in
Christian lands. One such renegade was this friend of mine, who
had testimonials from all our comrades in which we vouched for
him in the highest possible terms; and if the Moors had found these
papers on him they would have burnt him alive. I was aware that
he knew Arabic very well, and could not only speak but write it;
but before taking him completely into my confidence, I asked him
to read me the paper, saying that I had found it by chance in a hole
in my cell. He unfolded it, and spent some time examining it and
spelling it over, muttering under his breath. I asked him if he understood it. Perfectly, he said, and if I would give him pen and ink, he
would give me an exact translation. We instantly supplied him with
what he asked, and he wrote down a literal translation, observing,
when he had finished:

' "I have translated this Moorish letter into Spanish for you word
for word, but you must note that where it says Lela Marien it means
Our Lady the Virgin Mary."

'We read the paper, and this is how it ran: "When I was a girl
my father had a woman slave, who taught me the Christian prayers
in my own tongue, and spoke to me often about Lela Marien. This
Christian died, and I know that she did not go to the fire but to
Allah. For I saw her twice afterwards, and she told me to go to
Christian lands and see Lela Marien, who loved me very much. I do
not know how to go. I have seen many Christians out of this window, but none of them except you has seemed a gentleman. I am
young and very beautiful, and have much money to take with me.

See if you cannot find a way for us to go; and you shall be my husband, if you will; and if you will not I do not mind, for Lela Marien will find me someone to marry. I wrote this; be careful to whom you give it to read. Do not trust any Moor; they are all deceitful. That worries me very much. I do not want you to take anyone into your confidence, because if my father finds out he will immediately throw me down a well and cover me with stones. On to the cane I will fasten a thread. Tie your reply to it. But if you have no one who can write Arabic for you, tell me your answer by signs; Lela Marien will help me to understand you. May she and Allah protect you – and this cross, which I often kiss as my slave told me to."

'Consider, sirs, whether we had not reason to be surprised and delighted at the contents of this letter. Indeed, our feelings were so great that the renegade realized we had not found the paper by chance, but that it was really written to one of us. So he implored us, if his suspicions were correct, to take him into our confidence and tell him the truth, for he would risk his life for our liberty. As he spoke, he took a metal crucifix from under his shirt, and swore with tears in his eyes by the God, whose image it was and in whom he, wicked sinner though he was, truly and faithfully believed, and promised to be loyal to us and to keep anything we might reveal to him secret. For he could almost foretell that he and all of us would gain our liberty with the help of the woman who had written that letter, and that he would gain what he so much desired, re-admission to the body of the Holy Mother Church, from whom he had been severed as a rotten limb, cut off by his ignorance and sin. The renegade spoke with such tears of repentance that we all agreed with one accord to tell him the truth of the matter; and so we told him the whole story, concealing nothing. We showed him the little window out of which the cane had appeared, and by that he noted the house, and promised to take great and special care to find out who lived there. We agreed at the same time that it would be as well to reply to the Moorish lady's letter, since we had someone there who could do it; and the renegade at once wrote, straight off, to my dictation. I can give you the exact words, for I have not forgotten a single material detail of that adventure; nor shall I forget one as long as I live. So this is what I replied to the Moorish lady:

'"The true Allah keep you, dear lady, and the blessed Marien,

who is the true Mother of God and who has put it into your heart
to go to a Christian land, for she loves you well. Pray to her to be
pleased to teach you how you can put her commands into practice;
for she is so kind that she will certainly do so. On behalf of myself
and all my Christian companions, I promise that we will do everything we can for you, even unto death. Do not fail to write and inform me of what you intend to do. I shall always reply; for the
great Allah has given us a Christian prisoner who can speak and
write your language well, as you can judge from this letter. So you
need have no fear, and can tell us anything you wish. As to your saying that you would be my wife if you were to reach Christian soil,
I promise you as a good Christian that this shall be so. And remember that Christians carry out their promises better than Moors.
Allah and Marien His mother protect you, dear lady."

'When this letter was written and sealed I waited two days till
the *bagnio* was deserted as usual, and then I went to the usual place
on the little flat roof to see if the cane would appear; which it did
not take long in doing. As soon as I saw it, although I could not see
who was holding it, I held up the paper as a signal for her to tie on
the thread; but I found that it was already on the cane, and attached
the letter to it. Then, a little while later, our star appeared once
more with the white flag of peace, the knotted handkerchief, tied
to it. It was dropped and, on picking it up, I found inside more
than fifty crowns in all kinds of silver and gold coins; which multi-
plied our joy fifty times more and strengthened our hopes of gaining
our liberty. That very night our renegade returned with the news
that he had found out that the Moor we had been told of before did
live in that house; that he was called Hadji Murad; that he was exceedingly rich, and had an only daughter, the heiress to all his fortune. It was the general opinion, he said, throughout the city that
she was the loveliest woman in all Barbary, and many of the Vice-
roys who came there had asked for her hand; but she would never
consent to marry. He had also found out that she had once a Christian slave, who was now dead—all of which agreed with the contents
of the letter.

'We then consulted the renegade as to any possible plan for
carrying off the Moorish lady and all of us escaping on to Christian
soil. But in the end we agreed to wait, for the time being, for a

second letter from Zoraida – for that was her name, though she now wishes to be called Maria – since it was quite clear to us that she, and she only, would be able to find a solution of all our difficulties. After we had agreed on that, the renegade told us not to worry; for he would either set us at liberty or lose his life in the attempt. The *bagnio* was full of people for the next four days, which meant that for four days the cane did not appear; at the end of that time, when the prison was once more empty as usual, it appeared with a big handkerchief which promised a happy delivery. The cane with its burden pointed to me, and I found in it another letter and a hundred crowns all in gold. The renegade was there, and when we had returned to our cell we gave him the paper to read. He translated it like this:

'"I do not know, dear sir, how to arrange for our going to Spain. Lela Marien has not told me, although I have asked her. What I can do is to pass you a great deal of money through this window. You can then ransom yourself and your friends; and one of you can go to a Christian country, buy a ship, and come back for the others. I can be found in my father's country house at the Babazoun gate, beside the seashore, where I shall be all this summer with my father and servants. You will be able to carry me off from there by night without risk, and take me to the ship. Remember that you must marry me, or I will pray to Marien to punish you. If there is no one you can trust to go for the ship, ransom yourself and go. For I know that you are more certain to return than anyone else, because you are a gentleman and a Christian. Try to find our country house, and when you come on to the roof I shall know that the *bagnio* is empty and give you large sums of money. Allah preserve you, dear sir."

'Those were the words of the second letter; and when we had all seen it, each one said he was willing to be the man ransomed, and promised to go and to return with all speed; and I offered myself as well. But the renegade was totally opposed to this plan, and said that he would on no account agree to anyone getting his liberty till we all did so together; because experience had shown him how badly men fulfil the promises which they have made as prisoners once they are free. For very often prisoners of consequence had tried the expedient of ransoming someone to go to Valencia or

Majorca with money to equip a boat and return for the men who
had ransomed them; but they had never come back; for the fear of
losing their new-found liberty had expunged every obligation in
the world from their memories. To confirm the truth of this, he
briefly told us a case which had happened very recently indeed to
some Christian gentlemen, the most extraordinary affair that had
ever occurred in those parts, where astonishing and marvellous
things happen every day. He concluded by suggesting what should
be done with the money intended for the ransom of one of us. We
were to give it to him to buy a ship with, there in Algiers, on the pretence that he intended to set up as a merchant to trade with Tetuan
and along the coast. Once he was owner of the boat, he would easily
contrive a way of getting us out of the *bagnio* and of taking us all
on board. Besides, if the Moorish lady were to give us enough
money to ransom us all, as she promised, we should be free; and
then it would be extremely easy to get us aboard, even in the middle
of the day. Our greatest difficulty was the fact that the Moors do
not allow a renegade to buy or own a ship, unless it is a large ship
to go on a pirate expedition; for they are afraid that his only reason
for buying a small ship, particularly if he is a Spaniard, is to escape
on to Christian soil. Our renegade would get over this difficulty,
however, by taking a Tagarine Moor as his partner in the purchase
of the craft, and in the trading profits. By this subterfuge he would
become master of the ship; and once he had got that, he reckoned
that the rest would follow. Now, although both my companions
and I thought it a better plan to send to Majorca for the ship, as the
Moorish lady suggested, we dared not contradict him, for fear that
he might betray us if we did not do what he said, and so put us in
danger of execution; especially if he were to report the part played
by Zoraida, for whose life we would all willingly have sacrificed our
own. So we decided to put ourselves in the hands of God and the
renegade and, at that juncture, replied to Zoraida that we would
follow her suggestions, for she had advised us as well as if Lela
Marien had instructed her; and that it rested with her alone whether
the plan should be delayed or put into execution at once. I repeated
my promise to marry her, and then the *bagnio* happening to be
empty, at various times during the next day she gave us two thousand crowns in gold by means of the cane and handkerchief, to-

gether with a letter in which she said that she was going to her father's country house on the next *Juma*, – that is Friday, – and that she would give us some more money before she went. But if that was not enough, we were to let her know; and she would give us as much as we required, for her father had so much that he would not miss it, especially as she had the keys of everything.

'We immediately gave the renegade five hundred crowns to buy the ship, and with eight hundred I redeemed myself, giving the money to a Valencian merchant who was in Algiers at the time. He ransomed me from the King by giving his word that he would pay the money on the arrival of the first ship from Valencia. For if he had paid it down, it would have made the King suspicious that my ransom had been in Algiers for some time, and that the merchant had concealed it for his own profit. In fact, my master was so full of suspicion, he said, that I dared not on any account pay out the money at once. On the Thursday before the Friday on which the fair Zoraida was to go to the country house, she gave us another thousand crowns, and advised us of her departure; asking me, if I ransomed myself, to discover her father's estate at once, and at all costs to find some opportunity of going to see her there. I replied briefly that I would do so, and that she must be sure to commend us to Lela Marien by all the prayers which the slave woman had taught her. After this we set about getting our three companions ransomed, to make it easier for us to leave the *bagnio*; and in case, seeing me ransomed and themselves not – though we had the money – they might get alarmed, and the Devil might put it into their heads to do something which would endanger Zoraida. For although their characters might have relieved me of that fear, yet I did not wish to put the matter to any risk. So I had them ransomed in the same way as I had ransomed myself, delivering the whole sum into the hands of the merchant, so that he might the more confidently and safely go surety for us. But we never revealed our plan or our secret to him, for that would have been too dangerous.

Chapter XLI. *A further continuation of the Captive's story.*

'BEFORE a fortnight had gone by our renegade had bought a very good ship, capable of taking more than thirty people; and to lend

colour to his design and ensure its success, he proposed to make a
trip to a place called Cherchel, which is seventy-two miles from Algiers in the direction of Oran, where there is a great trade in dried
figs. This he did, and made two or three trips in the company of the
Tagarine I mentioned. In Barbary they call the Moors of Aragon
Tagarines, and those of Granada Mudejares; and in the Kingdom of
Fez they call the Mudajares Elches – those are the people the
King makes most use of in war. To proceed: each time he passed in
his ship she anchored in a cove not two bow-shots from the country house where Zoraida was waiting; and there, very deliberately,
the renegade would take up his position with the young Moors who
rowed for him, sometimes to say his prayers and sometimes to re-
hearse his plan. So he would go to Zoraida's estate and beg for fruit,
which her father would give him without recognizing him. But although he tried to speak with Zoraida, as he afterwards told me, and
tell her she might be happy and confident, for he was the man who
was to carry her away to the Christian country by my instructions,
it was never possible; because Moorish ladies never let themselves
be seen by any Moor or Turk, unless by the orders of their husbands or fathers, though they let Christian slaves be with them and
converse to them, even more than is proper. Indeed, it would have
displeased me if he had talked to her, since it might have alarmed
her to find her affairs entrusted to the mouth of a renegade. But God
decreed otherwise, and did not give this fellow a chance of carrying
out his plan. He saw, however, how safely he could go backwards
and forwards to Cherchel; that he could anchor when and how and
where he chose; and that his Tagarine partner had no will of his
own but obeyed him entirely. So seeing that I was ransomed and
that all that was left to do was to find some Christians to row, he
told me to look out for the men I intended to take with me, in addition to the ransomed men, and to arrange with them for next Friday,
which he had fixed on for our start. Thereupon I spoke to a dozen
Spaniards, all strong oarsmen and men who could readily leave the
city. It was no small matter to find so many at that moment. For
there were twenty ships out privateering, and they had taken all the
oarsmen with them. These men would not have been available if it
had not been that their master had stayed behind that summer to
complete a small galley he had on the stocks. I gave them all the

same instructions, that the next Friday evening they should creep out one by one, and make their way to Hadji Murad's estate and wait for me there. I gave these directions to each one separately, and told them all that, should they see other Christians there, they were to say nothing except that I had told them to wait for me.

'This part of the business settled, I had still to do one more thing of the greatest importance to me. That was to advise Zoraida how the matter had progressed, so that she might be prepared and on the watch, and not be alarmed if we rushed upon her suddenly before she imagined the Christian's ship would be back. So I decided to go to the garden, and see if I could speak to her; and I went there one day before our departure on the pretence of gathering herbs. The first person I met was her father, who spoke to me in the language that is spoken between slaves and Moors all over Barbary, and even in Constantinople: it is neither Moorish nor Castilian, nor the tongue of any other country, but a mixture of every language, in which we can all understand one another. Well, as I say, he asked me in this tongue what I was looking for in his garden and whose man I was. I answered that I was a slave of Arnaut Mami – this, because I knew for certain that this man was a very great friend of his – and that I was looking for herbs to make a salad. After that he asked me if I was for ransom or not, and how much my master wanted for me. Whilst we were engaged in this conversation the fair Zoraida, who had not seen me now for a long time, came out of the house; and since Moorish women, as I have said, are not at all shy of showing themselves to Christians, and not in the least bashful with them, she made nothing of coming to where her father stood talking to me. Indeed, when he saw her approaching rather slowly, he called to her to come right up.

'It would be too much to describe to you now Zoraida's great beauty and grace, or the rich and gay dress in which she then appeared. I will only say that more pearls hung from her lovely neck, her ears, and her hair than she had hairs on her head. On her ankles which, in the Moorish fashion, were bare, she had two *carcajes* – that is the Moorish word for rings and bracelets for the feet – of purest gold, set with so many diamonds that she told me afterwards her father valued them at ten thousand dollars; and those she wore on her wrists were worth as much. The pearls were in great numbers and very good. For fine and seed pearls are the chief pride and adornment of Moorish women – which is why there are more pearls among the Moors than among all other nations – and Zoraida's father was famous for having some of the best in Algiers, and also for possessing more than two hundred thousand Spanish crowns, of all of which she was mistress, who is now mine. Judge how lovely she must have looked in all her finery from so much of her beauty as remains after all her troubles.

'Women's beauty, as we know, has its days and times, and varies according to accidents; and it is natural enough for the emotions to increase it or diminish it, though most often they destroy it. But I will be brief, and say that she was then so magnificently attired and so surpassingly lovely that she seemed to me the most perfect creature I had ever seen; and more than that, when I remembered my indebtedness to her, she seemed to me a heavenly goddess come down to earth to bring me happiness and relief.

'As soon as she approached, her father told her in their language that I was a slave of his friend Arnaut Mami, and had come to pick a salad. She broke in to ask me in that mixture of languages whether I was a gentleman, and why I did not ransom myself. I replied that I was already ransomed, and the price would show her how highly my master valued me. For I had given fifteen hundred *sultanies* for myself. To which she replied:

'"If you belonged to my father I would certainly see that he did not part with you for twice as much, because you Christians always lie and make yourselves out poor to cheat us Moors."

'"That may be so, lady," I answered, "but I assure you that I have dealt honestly with my master, as I do with everyone in the whole world, and always shall."

'"When do you go then?" asked Zoraida.

'"To-morrow, I think," said I, "for there is a ship here from France which is sailing in the morning, and I intend to go in her."

'"Would it not be better," asked Zoraida, "to wait until one comes from Spain, and go in that instead of with the French, for they are not your friends?"

'"No," I replied, "although if it is true, as I hear, that there is a ship coming from Spain, I might wait longer for her, but it is more likely that I shall start to-morrow. For I am so eager to be home and with the people I love that I cannot bear to wait even for a better opportunity, should it mean delay."

'"Then no doubt you are married in your own country," asked Zoraida, "and you want to go and see your wife."

'"No, I am not married," I replied, "but I have given my word to marry when I get home."

'"Is the lady whom you have promised to marry beautiful?" asked Zoraida.

'"She is so beautiful," I replied, "that, to tell you the truth about her beauty, she is much like you."

'At this her father laughed heartily and cried: "By Allah, Christian, she must be very beautiful if she is like my daughter, who is the most beautiful woman in the whole kingdom. Look at her well, and you will see I am telling you the truth."

'Zoraida's father, as the better linguist, acted as interpreter for the greater part of this conversation; for although she spoke the bastard language which, as I have said, is in use there, she expressed her meaning more by gestures than by words. Now whilst we were engaged in this conversation a Moor came running up and shouted out that four Turks had jumped over the fence, or the wall, of the garden and were picking the fruit, although it was not yet ripe. The old man got alarmed, and Zoraida too; for the Moors' fear of the Turks is widespread, and second nature to them: especially their terror of soldiers, who are so overbearing and so tyrannical towards the Moors, their subjects, that they treat them worse than slaves. Therefore it was that Zoraida's father said to her: "Go back to the house, daughter, and shut yourself in, while I go and speak to these dogs. And you, Christian, pick your herbs and go on your ways in peace. May Allah bear you safely to your own country."

'I bowed, and he went off to look for the Turks, leaving me alone with Zoraida, who began to make a show of going off as her father had bidden her. But no sooner had she got under the shade of the garden trees, than she turned to me with her eyes full of tears and said:

'"*Tameji*, Christian, *tameji?*" – which means: "Are you going away, Christian, are you going away?"

'"Yes, lady," I replied, "but on no account without you. Expect me next *Juma*, and do not be alarmed when you see us, for we shall most certainly go to Christian lands."

'I said this in such a way that she now perfectly understood all our previous conversation; and putting her arm round my neck, she began to walk towards the house with trembling steps. As Fortune would have it – and things might have gone very badly with us if Heaven had not decreed otherwise – whilst we two were walking in the manner I have described, with her arm round my neck, her father returned from packing the Turks off, and saw us in this compromising situation; and we saw that he had seen us. But Zoraida was resourceful and self-possessed, and did not take her arm from my neck; but drawing closer to me instead, leant her head on her breast, went limp at the knees, and made as if she were fainting, while I acted as if I were forced to hold her up. Then her father came running to us and, seeing his daughter in this condition, asked her what was the matter. But as she made no answer, he said:

'"No doubt she has fainted with fright at those dogs coming into the garden." And taking her from my breast, he rested her against his. Then she heaved a sigh, and with her eyes not yet dry from their tears, spoke again "*Ameji*, Christian, *Ameji*" – ("Go away, Christian, go away"). To which her father replied:

'"There is no need for the Christian to go. He has done you no harm, and the Turks are gone now. Do not be at all alarmed, for there is nothing to frighten you. The Turks, I tell you, went when I asked them to, by the same way as they came in."

'"It was they who alarmed her, sir, as you said," I observed to her father; "but seeing that she tells me to go I do not want to annoy her. Peace be with you, and with your permission I will come to this garden again for herbs, if they are needed; for my master says that nobody has better salad herbs than you."

'"Come as often as you like," answered Hadji Murad. "My daughter did not tell you to go out of annoyance with you or with any other Christian, but probably mistook you for the Turks, or thought it was time for you to pick your herbs."

'At this I took immediate leave of both of them, and she went off with her father, looking as if her heart were torn. Then I wandered all about the garden at my pleasure, pretending to gather herbs, and took a good look at all the ways in and out, at the defences of the house, and at everything we might make use of for the furtherance of our plan.

'When I had done, I returned and gave the renegade and my companions an account of all that had happened, saying how I longed for the moment when I could enjoy undisturbed the happiness which Fortune offered me in the fair and beautiful Zoraida. Now the time passed; at last the longed-for day arrived; and by following the plan which we had settled on after mature consideration and many long arguments, we achieved the success we had hoped for. On the Friday after the day when I had spoken to Zoraida in the garden, our renegade anchored at nightfall with his boat almost opposite the place where the fair Moor lived. The Christians who were to row were already warned, and hidden in different places in the neighbourhood. They were all anxiously and excitedly waiting for me, and longing to seize the ship, which lay before their eyes. For they did not know the renegade's plan, but thought that they would have to gain their liberty by force of arms and by killing all the Moors aboard. So as soon as my companions and I showed ourselves, all the rest came out of their hiding-places. It was already the time when the city gates are shut, and there was no one to be seen over that whole countryside. But once we were all together, we were uncertain whether it would be better first to go for Zoraida or to overpower the Bagarine Moorish oarsmen. While we were in this quandary our renegade came up to us and asked why we were waiting, for it was already time, and his Moors were off their guard and most of them asleep. We told him the reason for our delay, and he said that the most important thing was to get control of the ship first, which could be done most easily and at no risk at all. Then we could go for Zoraida afterwards. We all thought his advice good, and so went to the boat, under his guidance, without further delay. He was the first to jump in and, putting his hand on his cutlass, cried out in Moorish: "Do not move from where you are, not one of you, unless he wants to be killed." By this time almost all the Christians were aboard. The Moors were a poor-spirited lot, and terror-stricken at hearing such a threat from their captain. So without a single one of them drawing a weapon – few or hardly any of them had one – they let the Christians handcuff them without a word. This was very quickly done, the captain threatening the Moors that they would all be put to the sword immediately if they raised any sort of alarm.

'When this was done, half of our number stayed on guard, and the rest of us, still under the renegade's leadership, went to Hadji Murad's garden; and, as good luck would have it, when we came to open the door it gave as easily as if it had not been locked; and so, in absolute calm and silence, we reached the house unnoticed. The lovely Zoraida was watching for us at the window, and as soon as she heard people moving, asked in a whisper if we were "*Niza-rani*" – that is to say, Christians. I replied Yes, and bade her come down. When she recognized me, she did not delay an instant, but without a word of reply came in a flash and opened the door, revealing herself to us in all her beauty, and so richly dressed that I cannot attempt to describe her. As soon as I saw her I took her hand and began to kiss it; the renegade and my two companions did the same; and the others, who did not understand the situation, imitated us, thinking that we were giving her thanks for our freedom. The renegade then asked her in Moorish if her father was in the house. She replied that he was, and asleep.

'"Then we shall have to wake him," said the renegade, "and take him with us, and everything of value in this lovely place."

'"No," she replied, "my father must on no account be touched. There is nothing in the house except what I am bringing with me. That will be quite enough to make you all rich and happy. Wait a moment and you shall see."

'With these words she went back into the house, saying that she would return in a moment, and that we must keep still and make no noise. I asked the renegade what conversation had passed between them; and when he told me I said that Zoraida's wishes must be obeyed in every way. She then came back, bringing a small box full of gold crowns, so heavy that she could hardly carry it. But as ill luck would have it, her father had woken up in the meantime, and heard the noise going on in the garden. He had looked out of the window and, seeing that all the men there were Christians, had started to shout loudly and wildly in Arabic: "Christians, Christians! Thieves, thieves!" These cries threw us all into the greatest confusion and alarm. But, seeing our danger and the importance of getting our plan through before we were detected, the renegade rushed up the steps to Hadji Murad's room, and some of our party with him. As for me, I dared not let go of Zoraida, who had fallen

fainting into my arms. To be brief, the men who went into the
house managed so well that the next moment they brought Hadji
Murad down, with his hands tied and a handkerchief stuffed into his
mouth, which prevented his uttering a word – and they threatened
him that if he did cry out it would cost him his life. When she saw
him, she covered her eyes to avoid the sight; while he was frightened
to death, not knowing how very willingly she had put herself into
our hands. But at that point all we needed was our legs, and we got
aboard ship with all caution and speed. For those on board were
already expecting us, and were afraid that we had met with disaster.

'Some two hours of the night must have passed before we were
all on the ship, where we untied Zoraida's father's hands and took
the gag out of his mouth, though the renegade repeated his threat
to kill him if he uttered so much as a word. When he saw his
daughter there, however, he began to sigh very deeply; and he
groaned when he saw how tightly I was clasping her and that she
made no attempt to resist or complain or fight shy, but stayed quiet.
Yet, for all that, he remained silent out of fear that the renegade's
fierce threats might be put into effect. Then, when Zoraida was on
board and saw that we were going to start rowing, looking at her
father there and the other Moors, all tied up, she bade the renegade
ask me to do her the favour of releasing the Moors and granting her
father his liberty. She pleaded that she would rather fling herself into
the sea than see her father, who loved her so well, carried off before
her eyes, a prisoner on her account. The renegade translated her request and I replied that I would gladly agree, but he objected that it
was impossible. For, if we left them there, they would immediately
raise the country and give the alarm in the city, which would bring
the Unbelievers out after us in light frigates, to cut us off by sea and
by land, so that we could not escape. What we could do was to set
them free at the first Christian port we touched. We were all agreed
on this, and Zoraida also was satisfied when she was told of our
decision and of our reasons for not immediately complying with her
request. Then, in joyful silence, happily and vigorously, every one
of our valiant rowers took his oar and, commending ourselves to
God with all our hearts, we began to steer towards the Balearic
Islands, which are the nearest point of Christian land. But because
a slight north wind began to blow and the sea got rather rough, it

was impossible for us to hold our course for Majorca; and we were forced to keep along the shore in the direction of Oran, in considerable fear of being observed from the town of Cherchel, which is about seventy miles along the coast from Algiers. We were also afraid of meeting one of those small galleys which are engaged in bringing goods from Tetuan; though each one for himself, and all of us jointly, felt confident that if we were to meet a merchant galley, so long as it was not armed for piracy, we not only would not be taken, but would capture a ship in which we could finish our voyage in greater safety. And all the while we rowed, Zoraida lay with her head in my arms to avoid seeing her father. I felt that she was calling on Lela Marien to aid us.

'We must have rowed a good thirty miles when dawn found us about three gunshots from the shore, which we saw to be desert without any inhabitants to observe us. But, for all that, we rowed as hard as we could to get farther out to sea. It was now a little smoother; and when we had got about six miles off, the order was given that only every fourth man should row; so that we might have something to eat, for the ship was well provided with stores. But the rowers said that this was no time to rest, and that those who were not rowing could feed them, as they certainly did not mean to let the oars out of their hands. We did feed them. But at that time a stiff breeze began to blow, obliging us to hoist a sail and stop rowing, and to steer for Oran, for it was impossible to make any other course. All this was done with great speed; and so we sailed at more than eight knots, without any other fear than that of meeting some ship which might prove to be a pirate. We gave our Tagarine Moors food, and the renegade comforted them by saying that they were not prisoners, but would be given their freedom at the first opportunity. He gave the same assurance to Zoraida's father, who replied:

'"I could expect and believe anything else of your generosity and liberality, Christians, but do not think me so simple as to imagine that you will grant me my liberty. You did not put yourselves to the danger of robbing me of it, only to return it to me so freely, particularly since you know who I am and how much you stand to gain by a bargain. If you would name the sum, I offer you here and now as much as you want for myself and for this unhappy daughter of mine; or failing that, for her alone, who is the greater and better part of my soul."

'At these words he began to weep so bitterly that we were all moved to pity, and Zoraida was compelled to look in his direction; and she was so melted at the sight of the old man weeping that she got up from my feet and went over to embrace him. Then, as she put her face to his, they both burst into tears of such affection that many of us did the same. But when he saw that she was in her finest clothes and wearing all those jewels, he asked her in their tongue:

'"What is this, my daughter? Last night, before our present terrible misfortune overtook us, I saw you in your ordinary houseclothes; and now, though you have not had the time to dress yourself up, nor any good news to celebrate by adorning and beautifying yourself, I find you decked out in the best clothes I was able to give you when Fortune was kindest to us. Answer my question, for this is more surprising and alarming to me even than my present misfortune."

'The renegade translated to us all that the Moor said to his daughter, but she did not answer a word. However, when he saw on one side of the ship the little box in which she kept her jewels, and which he was certain he had left at Algiers and not taken to their country house, he was even more disturbed, and asked her how the box had come into our hands, and what was inside it. To which the renegade answered, without waiting for Zoraida to reply:

'"Do not trouble yourself, sir, to ask your daughter Zoraida so many questions, for I can reply to all of them in one word. Let me tell you that she is a Christian; it is she who has been the file to our chains and the key to our captivity. She is with us of her own free will; as glad, I imagine, to be where she is, as a man coming out of darkness into light, out of death into life, out of pain into glory."

'"Is it true, what he says, daughter?" asked the Moor.

'"It is," replied Zoraida.

'"That, in fact, you are a Christian," asked the old man, "and it is you who has put your father into his enemies' power?"

'To which Zoraida replied: "I am a Christian, but it is not I that brought you to this pass, for it was never my wish to leave you or to do you any harm. I only wished to do myself a benefit."

'"And what benefit have you done yourself, daughter?"

' "That," she replied, "you must ask Lela Marien, for she will be able to tell you better than I."

'No sooner did the Moor hear this than he threw himself with incredible agility head foremost into the sea, and no doubt would have drowned if the long and cumbrous clothes he wore had not kept him just above water. Zoraida cried out for us to rescue him; whereat we all instantly went to his aid and, grasping him by his long robes, pulled him out, half drowned and unconscious. And so distressed was Zoraida that she burst into a tender and sorrowful lament over him, as if he were really dead. We turned him face downwards, at which he brought up a great deal of water, and after two hours came to. During this time the wind changed and drove us back towards the land, and we had to row hard to avoid running aground. But by good luck we made a little cove beside a small promontory or cape, which is called by the Moors the Cape of the *"Cava Rumia"*; which means in our language the wicked Christian woman. For there is a tradition among the Moors that it is the place where that *"Cava"* lies buried, through whom Spain was lost; for *"cava"* in their tongue means wicked woman and *"rumia"* Christian. They even look on it as a bad omen to have to anchor there, if necessity drives them to – and otherwise they never do so. But for us it was no wicked woman's shelter, but a secure haven of refuge, as the sea was running high. We posted our sentries on shore and, without dropping our oars, ate the renegade's provisions, and fervently prayed God and Our Lady to aid and favour us with a happy ending to our adventure which had begun so prosperously. At Zoraida's entreaty I gave orders that her father and the other Moors, who were still bound, should be put ashore; for her courage failed her, and her tender heart grieved at the sight of her father bound and those countrymen of hers prisoners. We promised her to free them at the moment of our departure, since we should incur no danger by leaving them in that uninhabited spot. Our prayers were not in vain, for Heaven answered them. The wind presently changed in our favour, and the sea grew calm, inviting us to resume our voyage with joyful hearts. At this we unbound the Moors and put them ashore one by one, to their great astonishment. But when we came to land Zoraida's father, who had entirely regained consciousness, he said:

'"Why do you think, Christians, that this wicked woman is glad you have set me free? Do you think that it is out of pity for me? Not at all. But because my presence would hinder her in the gratification of her wicked desires. Do not imagine that she has been moved to change her faith out of a belief that your religion is better than ours. No, it is because she knows that immorality is more freely practised in your country than in ours."

'And turning to Zoraida, with myself and another Christian holding him by both arms in case he might do something desperate, he cried: "Infamous and misguided girl! Where are you going in your blind frenzy, in the power of these dogs, our natural enemies? Accursed be the hour in which I engendered you, and accursed the pleasure and delight in which I brought you up!"

'But when I saw that he was not likely to end quickly, I hurriedly put him ashore; and from there he went on calling out his curses and lamentations, praying to Mahomet to beseech Allah to destroy us, confound us, and annihilate us. And when we had hoisted sail and could no longer hear his words, we saw his actions, and watched him plucking his beard, tearing his hair, and rolling on the ground. Once indeed he strained his voice so loud that we could hear him cry: "Come back, beloved daughter – come back to land! I forgive you everything! Give those men the money, for it is theirs; and come and comfort this wretched father of yours, who will lose his life in the sands of this desert if you forsake him."

'Zoraida listened to all this, and felt it all, and wept, not knowing what else to say in reply but: "May it please Allah, dear father, that Lela Marien, who has been the cause of my becoming a Christian, may console you in your grief. Allah well knows that I could have done nothing but what I did, and that these Christians owe me nothing for my goodwill. For even if I had wanted not to come with them, but to stay at home, it would have been impossible. So fast did my soul hurry me towards a deed which I know to be good, beloved father, though it appears wicked to you."

'This she said at a time when her father could not hear it, and we could no longer see him. I comforted Zoraida, and we all attended to our ship, which was so speeded by a favourable wind that we fervently expected to be on the Spanish coast at dawn next day.

'But as good seldom or never comes pure and unadulterated, accompanied or followed by no alarming evil, our fortune, or perhaps the curses the Moor cast on his daughter – for a father's curses are always to be feared – so willed it, I say, that when we were well out to sea, and almost three hours of the night had gone by, just as we were scudding before the wind under full sail with oars shipped – for the favourable wind relieved us of the labour of using them – we made out, by the light of a clear moon, a square-rigged ship close by us, with her sails spread, steering with the wind on her quarter and standing across our bows. She was so near that we had to lower our sail so as not to collide with her, and they had to put their helm hard up to give us room to pass. They had gathered on the deck to ask us who we were, where we came from, and where we were sailing for. But as they asked us in French, our renegade said: "Do not reply. They are no doubt some of those French pirates who take everything as a prize."

'At this warning no one said a word. But when we had got a little ahead and the ship was already on our lee, they suddenly let off two cannon, both loaded, it appeared, with chainshot, for with one shot they cut our mast in half and blew it and our sail overboard. A moment later they fired off another, and the ball hit us amidships, laying the vessel's side entirely open, though it did no other damage at all. But we saw that we were sinking, and all began to shout for help, imploring the men in the ship to take us aboard, for we were drowning. Then they put to, and launched their skiff or ship's boat; and a full dozen well-armed Frenchmen got in, with their arquebuses, and their matches lighted, and drew alongside us. Then, seeing how few we were and that our ship was sinking, they picked us up, saying that they had served us in that way for our discourtesy in not replying to them. Meanwhile our renegade took the box with Zoraida's treasures and threw it into the sea, without anyone noticing what he was doing.

'Finally we got aboard among the Frenchmen, who when they had found out all they wanted to about us, robbed us of everything we possessed, as if they were our mortal enemies, stripping Zoraida even of the anklets on her feet. But I was not so much disturbed at Zoraida's distress as at my own fear that, after they had stolen her rich and precious jewels, they would proceed to rob her of the most valuable of all, which she prized the most highly. But these people's desires do not extend beyond money, though of this their lust is insatiable; and on that occasion it was so extreme that they would have stripped us even of our slave's uniforms, if these had been of any use to them. Some of them even wanted to throw us all into the sea, wrapped in a sail, for they meant to pretend to be Bretons and to trade with some Spanish ports; and if they were to take us into harbour, their robbery would be discovered and they would be punished. But the captain – it was he who had robbed my beloved Zoraida – said that he was content with the booty he had, and that he did not want to touch at a Spanish port; but to slip through the Straits of Gibraltar by night, or in any way he could, and make for La Rochelle, which was the place they had sailed from. So they agreed to let us have their ship's boat and all that was necessary for the short voyage we had still to make. This they did next day, close to the Spanish coast, the sight of which made us forget all our troubles and hardships so completely that they might never have occurred: such is man's joy at regaining lost liberty.

'It must have been about midday when they put us into the boat, giving us two barrels of water and some ship's biscuit. And just as the lovely Zoraida was going, the captain was seized with some sort of pity and gave her some forty crowns; and he refused to let his men rob her of the clothes which she is wearing now. We got into the boat, thanking them for this last kindness and displaying gratitude rather than resentment. They then stood out to sea on a course for the Straits, and we set about rowing most vigorously without looking to any guiding star but the shore, which we could see ahead; and at sunset we were so near that we thought we might make land before the night was far spent. But as there was no moon and the sky looked black, it did not seem safe to us to make for the coast, not knowing just where we were. Yet many of us wished to, even though it were among the rocks and far from any inhabited spot. For, as we said, in that case we need have no fear of the Tetuan pirates, who leave Barbary at night and are on the Spanish coast by dawn, where they generally pick up a prize and have got back home by nightfall. But after a great deal of discussion we decided to approach the land slowly, if the sea was calm enough to allow it, and to put ashore wherever we could. This we did; and it must have been a little before midnight when we arrived at the foot of a great hill, which stood back sufficiently from the sea to leave a little space suitable for our landing. We grounded on the beach, leapt ashore, and kissed the earth. With tears of the greatest joy we gave thanks to the Lord God for His incomparable goodness to us. Then, taking out of the boat such provisions as were in it, we dragged it ashore and climbed a good way up the hillside. But although we stood on Christian soil, we could not assure ourselves or really believe that it was so.

'Dawn came, I thought, more slowly than we could have wished. We climbed the hill to the top to see if we could make out a village or shepherd's huts. But though we strained our eyes, we could see no house or person, no path or road. So we decided to push on inland, for we could hardly fail to find someone soon who could tell us where we were. What distressed me most was to see Zoraida on foot in this rough country. For though at times I carried her on my shoulders, she was too distressed by my weariness to be refreshed by the rest it gave her. So she made me put her down and walked patiently on with a great show of cheerfulness, holding me by the hand. We must have gone something less than a mile when the tinkle of a little sheep-bell came to our ears, a sure sign that there was a flock somewhere near. We all looked carefully round to find it, and saw a shepherd lad at the foot of a cork-tree, comfortably and idly whittling a stick with his knife. When we called, he looked up and got briskly to his feet. But, as we afterwards learnt, the first of us he caught sight of were the renegade and Zoraida; and at the sight of their Moorish dress he thought that all the hosts of Barbary were upon him and, running at a surprising speed towards the wood ahead of us he began to bawl at the top of his voice: "Moors! The Moors are ashore! Moors! Moors! To arms! To arms!"

'We were all bewildered by this outcry, and did not know what to do. But realizing that the shepherd's cries would rouse the countryside, and that the mounted coastguards would soon come to see what was the matter, we decided that the renegade should take off his Turkish robes and put on a jacket, or slave's coat; which one of our party gave him at once, though it left him in his shirt. So, commending ourselves to God, we took the path we had seen the shepherd take, expecting every moment that the coastguards would be upon us. And we were not wrong. For two hours had not gone by when, as we left the heath for the plain, we saw about fifty horsemen riding towards us at a very fast half-gallop. At the sight of them we halted and waited. But when they came up and saw a group of wretched Christians instead of the Moors they were expecting, they were puzzled; and one of them asked us if we by chance were the cause of the shepherd's hue and cry. I answered Yes. But as I was going to tell him my story and who we were, one of the Christians in our party recognized the horseman who had asked us the question and, without giving me a chance to speak, cried out: "Thanks be to God, gentlemen, for bringing us to so good a place. For, if I am not deceived, the soil we are treading is close to Velez Malaga. And if my years of captivity have not blotted your image from my mind, you, sir, who are asking us who we are, are my uncle, Pedro de Bustamante."

'The Christian prisoner had no sooner spoken than the horseman jumped from his mount and ran to embrace the young man, crying: "My beloved nephew, I do recognize you now. We mourned you for dead, I and my sister – your mother – and all your family, who are still living. For God has been pleased to spare our lives to enjoy the sight of you. We had learnt that you were at Algiers and, to judge by your clothes and the clothes of your whole party, you have had a miraculous deliverance."

'"That is so," replied the young man, "and we shall have time enough to tell you the whole story."

'Immediately the horsemen realized that we were Christian captives they dismounted, and each one of them offered us his horse to ride to the city of Velez Malaga, which was about four and a half miles away. We told them where we had left the boat, and some of them turned back to get it and bring it along to the city. Others took us up behind them, and Zoraida rode behind our Christian's uncle. The whole town came out to greet us. For they had already had the news of our arrival from one of the guards, who had ridden ahead. They were not at all surprised at seeing escaped slaves or captured Moors, because all the people of that coast are used to seeing both; but they were astonished at Zoraida's beauty, which was at its height at that moment, by reason of the exertion of the journey and of her joy at finding herself on Christian soil, with no more to fear. This had brought such colour to her cheeks that, unless I was then much deceived by my love, I dare swear that there was no more beautiful creature in the world; at least none that I had ever seen.

'We went straight to the church to thank God for mercies received; and the moment Zoraida went in, she exclaimed that there were faces there which looked like Lela Marien's. We told her that those were her images, and the renegade made her understand, as best he could, what they signified, and that she could worship them as she would the true Lela Marien who had spoken to her. She has a good intelligence and an easy and clear intuition, and so she understood what he said about the images at once. They took us from there, and divided us among several houses in the town, but our companion from that place took the renegade, Zoraida, and myself to the house of his parents, who were tolerably well provided with this world's goods, and treated us with as much affection as they did their son.

'We stayed in Velez six days, at the end of which the renegade, having lodged his statement in due form, went off to the city of Granada, to be reconciled to the bosom of Mother Church by means of the Holy Inquisition. The rest of the freed captives went each where he pleased. Only Zoraida and I remained with nothing but the crowns which the Frenchman in his kindness had given her. With these I bought the beast she rides. So I am travelling with her as her father and squire, but not as her husband, with the object of learning whether my father is alive, or if either of my brothers has had better fortune than I; though as Heaven has given me Zoraida as a companion, I do not think that the best lot that can befall me will seem better. Zoraida's patience in bearing the discomforts of poverty, and her desire to become a Christian, fill me with admiration, and bind me to serve her all the days of my life. But my happiness in knowing that I am hers and she is mine is troubled and spoilt by my uncertainty whether I shall find any corner of my country to shelter her. For I fear that time and death may have worked such changes in the fortunes and lives of my father and brothers that, failing them, I shall scarcely find anyone who knows me.

'There is no more of my story to tell you, gentlemen. I leave it to you to judge whether it is strange and entertaining. I can only say that I wish I had told it you more briefly, though fear of boring you has caused me to omit a great number of details.'

Chapter XLII. *Of further events at the Inn, and many other note-*
    worthy matters.

THE Captive was silent after telling his tale, and Don Ferdinand
observed: 'I assure you, Captain, that the way in which you have
told your strange adventure has been as remarkable as the strangeness and novelty of the events themselves. It is a curious tale and
full of astonishing incidents. In fact we have enjoyed listening so
much that we should be glad to have it all over again, even if it took
till tomorrow morning to tell it.'

On his saying this, Cardenio and all the others offered him their
utmost services, in such warm and sincere language that the captain
was thoroughly convinced of their goodwill. Don Ferdinand, in
particular, offered to make his brother the Marquis stand godfather
at Zoraida's baptism if he would return with him, and himself to
provide him with enough money to appear in his own country with
suitable dignity and decency. The Captive thanked him courteously
for all this, but would not accept any of his generous offers.

By this time night had fallen, and when it was quite dark a coach
came up to the inn with some men on horseback, who asked for
accommodation. But the landlady answered that there was not an
inch unoccupied in the whole inn.

'However that may be,' said one of the horsemen, who had come
in, 'room must be found for my lord Judge, who is approaching.'

At this title the landlady grew confused, and said: 'Sir, the
trouble is this: I have no beds. If his worship the Judge brings one
with him, as I suppose he does, let him come in and welcome. My
husband and I will give up our room to accommodate his worship.'

'That will do,' said the squire.

By this time there had alighted from the coach a man whose dress
proclaimed his high office; for his long robe with ruffled sleeves
proved that he was a judge, as his servant had said. He led by the
hand a young lady of about sixteen in travelling dress, so gay,
striking, and beautiful that the sight of her impressed them all; and
so vividly that, if they had not already seen Dorothea, Lucinda, and
Zoraida at that inn, they would have doubted whether she had her
match for beauty.

Don Quixote was present at the entrance of the judge and the young lady; and as soon as he saw them, he said: 'Your worship may certainly enter and take your ease in this castle. For, though it is narrow and uncomfortable, there is no place in the world so narrow and uncomfortable that it does not allow room for arms and learning. Especially if arms and letters bring beauty as their pilot and guide, as your worship's learning does in the person of this fair maiden, before whom not only should castles open and reveal themselves, but rocks split and mountains cleave and bow down to give her entertainment. Come into this paradise, I say, your worship, for here there are stars and suns to attend the heaven your worship brings with you. Here you will find arms at their zenith and beauty in its prime.'

The judge was astounded at Don Quixote's speech, and after gazing at him attentively, was no less astounded at his appearance. But finding no words with which to reply, he fell into a fresh amazement at the sight of Lucinda, Dorothea, and Zoraida, who had heard of the new guests and of the young lady's beauty from the landlady, and had come out to see her and welcome her. Don Ferdinand, Cardenio, and the priest, however, gave the judge a simpler and more courteous greeting. That dignitary was indeed confused, both at what he saw and at what he heard, but the beauties of the inn made the lovely girl welcome. Presently the judge perceived that all the people there were people of quality, though he was bewildered at Don Quixote's figure, face, and air. But when they had all exchanged polite greetings and carefully considered the accommodation of the inn, everything was arranged as before. All the women were to share the attic already described, and the men to stay outside, on guard as it were. So the judge was satisfied that his daughter – for such the young lady was – should lodge with the other ladies, which she was delighted to do; and with part of the landlord's narrow bed and half of the one the judge had brought, they managed better that night than they had expected.

Now the first moment he saw the judge the captive felt his heart leap with the idea that this was his brother. So he asked one of the servants to tell him his master's name, and the district he came from, if he knew it. The squire replied that he was the Licentiate Juan Perez de Viedma, and that he had heard that he came from a little place in the mountains of Leon. This information, together with what he had seen, finally confirmed him in the belief that this was his brother who by their father's advice had followed the profession of learning. The excited and delighted Captive then called Don Ferdinand, Cardenio and the priest aside to tell them, assuring them that the judge really was his brother. What is more, the servant had told him that he was going to take up the post of judge in the Indies, in the High Court of Mexico; also that the young lady was his daughter, whose mother had died at her birth, and that he had become very rich from the dowry left him with the child. The captain asked them to advise him how to reveal himself, or how to find out first whether his brother would be ashamed to discover him poor, or would acknowledge him with open arms, were he to do so.

'Leave it to me to make the experiment,' said the priest. 'I will gladly do so, for there is no reason to think that you will not be very well received, Captain. Your brother shows every sign of goodness and good sense, and his behaviour does not suggest that he is arrogant or ungrateful, or does not know how to assess the accidents of fortune at their true value.'

'All the same,' said the captain, 'I should like to reveal myself in a roundabout way, and not suddenly.'

'I promise you,' said the priest, 'that I will manage it in such a way that we shall all be satisfied.'

By this time supper was ready, and all sat down to table except the captain and the ladies, who were supping on their own in their room. Then in the middle of the meal the priest remarked: 'I had a comrade of your name, Sir Judge, at Constantinople, where I was a slave for several years. That man was one of the bravest commanders in all the Spanish infantry; but, brave and enterprising as he was, he was unfortunate.'

'What was this captain's name, sir?' asked the judge.

'His name,' replied the priest, 'was Ruiz Perez de Viedma, and he came from a place in the mountains of Leon. He told me of an incident that had happened to him and his brothers, which I should have taken for an old wives' tale told over a winter fire, if it had not been related by so truthful a man. What he told me was that his father had divided his property among his three sons, and had given them some advice which was better than Cato's. By his father's advice, anyhow, he went into the army; and in a few years, by his cour-

age and application, he rose to be an infantry captain, by his own
merits alone, and was on the way to be a colonel very soon. But fortune went against him. For when he might have expected things to
be good his luck broke, and he lost his liberty as well, on that most
happy day when many recovered theirs, at the battle of Lepanto. I
lost mine at the Goletta, and afterwards, by various accidents, we
found ourselves comrades in Constantinople. From there he went to
Algiers, where, as I learnt, one of the strangest accidents in the
world happened to him.'

From there the priest went on, and briefly told him the story of
Zoraida and his brother, which the judge heard with greater attention than he had ever given to a case before. The priest stopped at
the point when the French robbed the Christians in the boat, and
ended with a description of the poverty in which they had left his
comrade and the fair Moorish lady. He said that he had not heard
what had become of them since, whether they had reached Spain or
if the Frenchmen had carried them off to France.

The captain listened to all that the priest said, standing some way
off and noting all his brother's movements. And when he saw that
the priest had come to the end of his tale, the judge gave a deep
sigh and exclaimed, with his eyes filling with tears, 'Oh, sir, if you
knew what news you had given me, and how nearly it touches me!
But I cannot help showing it by the tears which spring to my eyes
in spite of all my fortitude and self-control! This brave captain you
speak of is my eldest brother. He was stronger and more courageous than my other brother or I, and chose the honourable and
worthy profession of arms – one of the three courses our father
proposed to us, as your comrade told you in that tale of his which
you thought was a fiction. I followed the career of learning, in
which God and my own hard work have raised me to the rank you
see. My younger brother is in Peru, and so rich that, with what he
has sent to my father and me, he has more than made up for the
capital he took away. He has even given my father enough to satisfy
his natural prodigality; and thanks to him, I have been able to follow my studies in a very fitting and creditable fashion, and to reach
my present position. My father is still alive, though dying with desire for news of his eldest son, and praying God night and day not
to let death close his eyes before he has seen him alive. I am aston-

ished that such a sensible fellow could have failed to send my father news in his great troubles and afflictions, or in his times of prosperity. Had our father or either of us been informed, he would not have had to wait for that miraculous cane to get his ransom. But it troubles me now not to know whether those Frenchmen set him free or killed him to cover up their robbery; and for that reason I shall not continue my journey joyfully as I began it, but in sadness and melancholy. Oh, my dear brother, who can tell where you are now? How gladly I would seek you and relieve you of your hardships, even at the cost of hardships to myself! Who will bear the news to our father that you are still alive, though perhaps in the deepest dungeons of Barbary? But even from there his riches, my brother's, and mine will rescue you. Oh lovely, generous Zoraida, who could ever repay you the good you have done my brother? Who will be present at your soul's rebirth, and at that wedding which would give us all such happiness?'

These were the judge's words, and he said more to the same effect, full of emotion at this news of his brother; and all the rest of the party too showed their compassion for his anxiety. The priest, however, seeing that he had succeeded by his trick in carrying out the captain's wishes, did not want to keep them any longer in sadness. So, getting up from the table and going into the room where Zoraida was, he led her out by the hand, followed by Lucinda, Dorothea, and the judge's daughter. The captain stood waiting to see what the priest would do; and what he did was to take him by the other hand, and lead them both up to the place where the judge and the rest of the gentlemen were sitting.

'Cease your tears, Sir Judge,' said he, 'and your wish shall be crowned with all happiness. For here you have your dear brother and your dear sister-in-law before you. Here is Captain Viedma, and this is the lovely Moorish lady, his benefactress. The Frenchmen, as I told you, reduced them to their present plight only so that you might show them the generosity of your noble heart.'

The captain started forward to embrace his brother, but the judge held him off awhile, with his arms on his shoulders, to look at him from a little farther off. Once he had recognized him, however, he embraced him so warmly and shed such tender tears of happiness, that most of the company had to weep as well. The words the two

N

brothers uttered and the feelings they displayed can hardly be conceived, still less written down. First they exchanged brief accounts of their adventures; then they displayed the warmth of brotherly love; next the judge embraced Zoraida; then he offered her all his possessions; then he made her embrace his daughter; then the lovely Christian girl and the most lovely Moor moved everyone to fresh tears. And there stood Don Quixote, listening and speechless, pondering on these extraordinary events and attributing them all to the chimaeras of knight errantry.

Soon they arranged that the captain and Zoraida should return with his brother to Seville and advise their father of his finding and deliverance, so that the old man might be able to come and be present at Zoraida's marriage and baptism. For it was not possible for the judge to abandon his present voyage, as he had news that the fleet was leaving Seville in a month's time for New Spain, and it would be most inconvenient for him to lose his passage.

The whole company was more than delighted at the captain's good fortune; and as by now almost two-thirds of the night was gone, they agreed to retire and spend the rest of it in sleep. Don Quixote took it on himself to mount guard over the castle, in case they might be attacked by some giant or unscrupulous villain, greedy for the great treasure of beauty which lay therein. Those who knew him thanked him, and gave the judge an account of the knight's strange humour, which delighted him more than a little. Only Sancho Panza was annoyed at the delay in going to bed; and he made himself more comfortable than any of them, throwing himself down on his ass's harness – which cost him very dear, as shall be told by and by. The ladies then having retired to their apartment, and the others accommodating themselves with the least discomfort possible, Don Quixote went out of the inn to be sentinel of the castle, as he had promised.

Now a little before dawn there reached the ears of the ladies a voice so sweet and musical that it compelled them all to listen, especially Dorothea, who was awake, though Doña Clara de Viedma – for this was the name of the judge's daughter – was asleep at her side. No one could imagine who it could be that sang so well; it was a single voice without instrumental accompaniment. At times it sounded as if the singing came from the yard, at times from the stable; and, while they were listening thus undecided, Cardenio came to the door of the room and said:

'If anyone is awake, listen and you will hear a mule-lad singing. As he chants, he enchants.'

'We can hear him, sir,' replied Dorothea. At which Cardenio departed, and Dorothea, listening with great attention, heard the words that he was singing. They were these:

Chapter XLIII. *The charming story of the Mule Lad, with other strange happenings at the Inn.*

> I am a mariner of love,
> And in his depths profound
> Sail on, although without a hope
> Ever to come to ground.
>
> My eyes are on a distant star,
> Which serves me for a guide,
> More beautiful and bright than all
> That Palinurus spied.
>
> I know not where it's leading me;
> And so, confused, I steer,
> My heart intent on watching it,
> Careless, yet full of care.
>
> And her unkindly shyness,
> And too much modesty
> Are clouds that shroud her from my eyes,
> Whom most I long to see.
>
> My Clara, clear and shining star,
> I fade beneath thy light,
> And when you hide your beams from me
> For me it's darkest night.

When the singer had reached this point in his song, Dorothea thought it would be a pity if Clara did not hear such a lovely voice, and so she shook her until she woke her up, saying:

'Forgive my waking you, child. But I want you to enjoy the finest voice you will ever hear in all your life.'

Clara woke up very drowsy, and did not understand at first what Dorothea was saying, but asked her to tell her again. She then repeated her words, upon which Clara began to listen. But scarcely had she heard two verses of the song than she was seized with a violent trembling, as if she had been taken with a serious attack of the quartan ague, and hugged Dorothea tightly, crying:

'Oh, my dear, dear lady, why did you wake me up? For the greatest good that Fortune could do me now would be to keep my eyes and ears shut, so that I should neither see nor hear that unhappy musician.'

'What is that you say, girl? They tell me that the singer is a mulelad.'

'No, he is not,' replied Clara, 'but a lord of many estates, and one he holds in my heart so firmly that, unless he wishes to quit his tenure, it will be his for ever.'

Surprised at the girl's passionate words, which seemed to her much in advance of her apparent youth, Dorothea then said: 'You speak so obscurely that I cannot understand you. Explain yourself more clearly. Tell me what you mean by heart and estates, and about this singer whose song disturbs you so. But do not tell me anything now. I do not want your transports to rob me of the pleasure of hearing the singer, for I think he is going to sing again, with new words and to a new tune.'

'Let him by all means,' replied Clara. But she put her hands over both her ears to avoid hearing him, which surprised Dorothea once more. But she listened to the song, which ran like this:

> Sweet hope of mine,
> That break'st impossibilities and briars,
> And down that path dost run
> Which thou thyself didst make for thy desires,
> Be not dismayed to see
> At every step thyself nigh death to be.
>
> Sluggards do not deserve
> The glory of triumphs or of victory;
> Good luck will never serve
> Those who resist not fortune manfully,
> But weakly fall to ground,
> And in soft sloth their senses all confound.
>
> That love his glories holds
> At a high rate is reasonable and best;
> No precious stones nor gold
> Excel those pledges by love's hand impressed;
> And 'tis a thing most clear,
> Nothing is worth esteem that costs not dear.

An amorous persistence
Will often win things most impossible;
So though I find resistance
To my soul's deep desires, in her stern will,
There's not a fear denies
That I shall climb from earth to her fair skies.

Here the voice ceased, and Clara broke into fresh sobs; all of
which excited Dorothea's desire to know the cause of the sweet
singing and the mournful tears. So once more she asked Clara
what it was she had meant to say before. Then, out of fear that
Lucinda might hear her, Clara hugged Dorothea tightly and put
her mouth so close to her ear that she could safely speak without
being overheard:

'The singer, my lady,' she said, 'is the son of a gentleman of the
Kingdom of Aragon, the lord of two villages, who used to live
opposite my father's house in Madrid. And although my father has
the windows of his house covered with canvas in the winter and
with blinds in summer, I do not know how it was, but this young
student saw me, either in church or somewhere else. He fell in love
with me, in fact, and gave me to understand so from the windows
of his house, so emphatically and with such tears that I had to believe him, and love him too, though I did not know what it was he
wanted of me. One of the gestures he made me was to clasp his two
hands together as a sign that he wanted to marry me; and although
I should have been very glad for that to be, as I was alone and
motherless I did not know whom to tell about it. So I let things be,
and showed him no favour; though, when my father was out of the
house and his father too, I did lift the curtain or the blind a little and
let him see all of me; and he was so enraptured that he seemed almost
beside himself. Then the time came for my father's departure; and
he learnt of it, though not from me, for I could never tell him. He
fell ill of grief, I understand, and so on the day we left I could not
see him to say good-bye, not even by a glance. But when we had
been two days on the road, as we were riding into an inn in a village
a day's journey from here, I saw him at the door of the house,
dressed as a mule-lad; and so much like one that if I had not borne
his portrait in my heart, I should have found it impossible to recognize him. I knew him; I was amazed; I was delighted. He stole a

look at me, undetected by my father, from whom he always hides his face when he passes in front of us on the roads, and as we come to the inns. But knowing who he is, and reflecting that it is for love of me that he travels on foot and endures all these hardships, I am dying of grief, and I follow his every step with my eyes. I do not know his purpose in coming, nor how he managed to escape his father, who loves him extremely, both because he has no other heir and because he deserves it; as you will find when you see him. What is more, let me tell you that all that he sings comes out of his own head, for I have heard that he is a very great scholar and poet. And there is another thing: each time I see him or hear him sing, I tremble all over, for fear my father will recognize him and come to know of our feelings. I have never spoken a word to him in my life, but, all the same, I love him so much that I cannot live without him. That is all that I can tell you, dear lady, about the musician whose voice has pleased you so; but from that alone you can clearly tell that he is no mule-lad, as you say, but a lord of hearts and lands, as I have told you.'

'Say no more, dear Doña Clara,' said Dorothea at this point, kissing her countless times. 'Say no more, I tell you, but wait till the day dawns. For I hope, with God's help, to set your affairs on the way towards the happy ending such a good beginning deserves.'

'But what ending can we expect, dear lady,' asked Doña Clara, 'seeing that his father is so rich and important that he will not think me fit to be his son's servant, much less his wife? Then, I would not marry without my father's knowledge for anything in the world. I only want the young man to go back and leave me. Perhaps with not seeing him, and with the great distance we are going to travel, the pain I feel now might grow less; though I must say that I do not think this remedy I am imagining can be of much use to me. I do not know what witchcraft there has been, nor how this love I feel for him has entered into me, since we are both so young – for I really believe we are of the same age, and I am not quite sixteen yet, nor shall be, my father says, till Michaelmas day.'

Dorothea could not prevent herself from laughing at Doña Clara's childish way of talking, and said: 'Let us sleep, dear lady, for a little of the night is still left, I think. God will send us morning, and things will go well if my skill does not fail me.'

With this they fell asleep, and the whole inn lay in deep silence. Only the innkeeper's daughter and her maid Maritornes were not asleep. For, knowing the ideas that possessed Don Quixote, and that he was outside the inn, mounted on guard, the pair of them decided to play him a trick, or at least to get some amusement by listening to his nonsense.

Now there was not a single window in the whole inn that opened on to the fields, but only a hole in a loft, used for throwing out the straw. At this hole the two demi-virgins placed themselves, and espied Don Quixote on his horse, leaning on his lance and, at intervals, heaving such mournful and deep sighs that each one of them seemed to tear out his soul. At the same time they heard him speak in soft, delicate and amorous tones:

'O my lady Dulcinea del Toboso, sum of all beauty, summit and crown of discretion, treasury of grace, store of virtue and, lastly, pattern of all that is beneficent, modest and delightful in the world! What is your grace doing at this monent? Can it be that you are mindful of your captive knight, who has submitted himself freely to so many perils, only to serve you? Let me have news of her, O three-faced luminary, Diana! Perhaps you are gazing on her now in envy of her looks, and see her pacing some gallery of her sumptuous palaces, or leaning with her breast upon some balcony rail, considering how, without danger to her modesty or greatness, she may alleviate the torment my aching heart suffers for her sake; with what glory she may crown my labours; what assuagement she may give to my anxiety; and lastly, what life to my death, and what reward to my services. And you, sun, who must even now be saddling your steeds in haste to rise and see my lady, I pray you, when you see her, salute her from me! But beware, when you gaze on her and salute her, not to kiss her on the face, or I shall be more jealous of her than you were of that wanton and fickle maid who made you sweat and run across the plains of Thessaly, or by the banks of Peneus; – for I do not well remember where you ran them in your jealous passion.'

When Don Quixote had reached this point in his mournful harangue the innkeeper's daughter began to call to him softly: 'Dear sir, come this way, if you please.'

At this sound Don Quixote turned his head, and saw by the light of the moon, which was then at its brightest, that someone was beckoning him from the hole, which seemed to him to be a window, and even to have gilded bars, which are proper to such rich castles as he imagined that inn to be. Instantly he conceived in his wild imagination that once again, as before, that beauteous damsel, the daughter of the warden of that castle, had come, overwhelmed by love of him, to ask for his favours. With this thought, not wishing to show himself discourteous or ungrateful, he turned Rocinante's head and went up to the window. Then, when he saw the two wenches there, he said:

'I pity you, beauteous lady, for fixing your amorous desires where it is impossible for you to find a response befitting your great merit and breeding; for which you must not blame this wretched knight errant, whom love makes incapable of engaging his heart to any but that maiden whom, from the first moment his eyes lighted on her, he made absolute lady of his soul. Pardon me, kind lady, and retire to your room. Please do not reveal your desires to me further, that I may not appear yet more thankless. Though if, of the love you bear me, you can discover in me anything other than love itself by which I may satisfy you, demand it of me; and I swear to you, by that sweet and absent enemy of mine, to bestow it upon you out of hand, even if you should demand of me a lock of Medusa's hair, which was all snakes, or even the very rays of the sun enclosed in a flask.'

'My lady needs none of that, Sir Knight,' put in Maritornes at this juncture.

'What then does she need, discreet lady?' asked Don Quixote.

'Only one of your beautiful hands,' replied Maritornes, 'with which to appease the great desire which has brought her to this window, at such risk to her honour that if my lord, her father, came to know of it, the least slice he would cut off her would be her ear.'

'I should like to see him do that!' answered Don Quixote. 'But he will take good care not to, if he does not wish to come to the most disastrous end that ever a father met in all the world, for laying his hands on the delicate limbs of his enamoured daughter.'

Maritornes had now no doubt that Don Quixote would give her the hand she had asked him for and, turning her plan over in her mind, got down from the hole and went to the stable, from which she fetched the halter of Sancho Panza's ass. Then she hastily returned to the hole, just as Don Quixote was standing up on Rocinante's saddle to reach the barred window at which he imagined the love-lorn lady was standing. And, as he gave her his hand, he said:

'Take this hand, lady, or rather this scourge of the world's malefactors. Take this hand, I say, which no other woman's has touched, not even hers who has complete possession of my whole body. I do not give it to you to kiss, but that you may gaze on the structure of its sinews, the interlacement of its muscles, the width and capacity of its veins; from all of which you may judge what strength must be in the arm to which such a hand belongs.'

'We shall see that presently,' said Maritornes, and making a running knot in the halter, she threw it over his wrist. Then, as she came down from the hole, she tied the other end very firmly to the bolt of the hay-loft door. At which Don Quixote exclaimed, feeling the roughness of the cord on his wrist:

'Your ladyship seems to be grating my hand rather than fondling it. Do not ill-treat it so. It is not to blame for the ill my heart does you, nor is it right that you should avenge your whole displeasure on so small a part of me. Consider, one who loves so well should not take such ill vengeance.'

But no one was listening to this speech of Don Quixote's. For as soon as Maritornes had tied him up the two of them went off, dying of laughter, and left him so secured that it was impossible for him to free himself. He was, as we have said, standing upon Rocinante, with his arm thrust through the hole and attached by the wrist to the bolt of the door, in the greatest fear and anxiety that he would be left hanging by the arm, if Rocinante were to stir to one side or the other. So he dared not make any movement; though, to judge from Rocinante's patience and quietness, he might well have expected him to stand there motionless for a whole century. In the end, finding that he was tied up and that the ladies had vanished, Don Quixote began to imagine that all this was a matter of enchantment, as on the previous occasion when the enchanted Moor of a carrier had mauled him in that same castle. And in his heart he cursed his lack of sense and judgement in venturing to enter it a second time after coming off so badly the first. For it is a rule among knights errant that their having once attempted an adventure and failed in it is a sign that it is not reserved for them but for others, and that they are therefore under no necessity of making a second attempt. However, he pulled his arm to see if he could get free, but he was so fast tied that all his endeavours were in vain. It is true that he pulled cautiously, for fear that Rocinante might move; but though he longed to sit down on the saddle, he could do nothing but remain standing or tug off his hand.

At times he longed for Amadis' sword, which was proof against any kind of enchantment; at others he cursed his fortune; then he dwelt upon the loss the world suffered through lack of him all the while he remained there enchanted, as he had no doubt at all he was. Then once more he remembered his beloved Dulcinea del Toboso; then he started calling for his good squire Sancho Panza, who lay drowned in sleep, stretched on his ass's pack-saddle, and oblivious at that moment even of the mother who bore him; then he called on the sages Lirgandeo and Alquife to help him; then he invoked his good friend Urganda to come to his rescue; and in the end morning found him there, despairing, bewildered and bellowing like a bull. For he had no hope that day would relieve his plight, which he believed to be eternal, since he imagined he was bewitched. This belief was strengthened when he found that Rocinante did not move or stir; from which he concluded that he and his horse would have to remain like that, without eating, drinking, or sleeping, until that malign influence of the stars should pass, or until another more learned enchanter should break the spell.

But in these beliefs he was much mistaken. For it was no sooner dawn than four well-dressed and equipped horsemen rode up to the inn with their firelocks on their saddle-bows. They called and thundered at the inn doors, which were still shut; and when Don Quixote saw them from the position in which he was still on guard, he cried out to them in loud and commanding tones:

'Knights, or squires, or whoever you may be, you have no right to knock on the doors of this castle; for it is abundantly clear that at such an hour those within are either asleep or, at least, unaccustomed to opening their fortress until the sun has covered the whole land. Retire without, and wait till day grows bright, and then we shall see whether it be right or not to open to you.'

'What the devil's this fortress or castle,' cried one of them, 'to keep us standing on these ceremonies? If you're the landlord, have the doors opened for us. We are travellers, and all we want is to bait our horses and ride on, for we are in a hurry.'

'Do I seem to you, knights, to have the air of an innkeeper?' asked Don Quixote.

'I don't know what you look like,' replied the traveller, 'but I know you're talking nonsense when you call this inn a castle.'

'A castle it is,' replied Don Quixote, 'one of the finest in the whole province, and there are people within who have carried a sceptre in their hands and a crown on their heads.'

'It would be better the other way round,' said the traveller; 'a sceptre on their heads and a crown branded on their hands. Though perhaps what you mean is that there's some company of actors inside; they often wear these crowns and sceptres you talk of. For I can't think that people good enough to have crowns and sceptres are lodging in a little inn like this one, and where it's so quiet too.'

'You know little of the world,' replied Don Quixote, 'since you are ignorant of the events which occur in knight errantry.'

The questioner's companions, growing impatient at his conversation with Don Quixote, began to knock furiously again, and so hard that the innkeeper and everyone else in the inn woke up. The host then got up to enquire who was knocking.

In the meanwhile one of the four travellers' horses happened to smell Rocinante, who was standing motionless, melancholy and sad, with drooping ears, bearing up his outstretched master; and being, after all, of flesh and blood, though he seemed of wood, he could not resist showing some feeling and smelling back at the creature who was making these endearing advances. But no sooner did he make the slightest movement than Don Quixote's feet, which were close together, slipped and, sliding from the saddle, would have landed him on the ground, had he not been hanging by his arm, which caused him so much pain that he felt as though his wrist were being cut off or his arm torn from its socket. For he was hanging so near the ground that he could touch it with the tips of his toes; which made his plight worse because, when he felt what a little way the soles of his feet were from the earth, he struggled and stretched his utmost to get them down. In fact, he was very like someone put to the torture of the 'strappado', in which the victim's feet neither quite touch nor quite fail to touch the earth, and so he increases his own agony in his anxiety to stretch himself, in the delusory hope that with a little more stretching he will reach the ground.

Chapter XLIV. Of more extraordinary adventures at the Inn.

FINALLY Don Quixote raised such a clamour that the inn doors were suddenly opened, and the innkeeper came out in a fright to see who it was shouting so loud. Maritornes too was awakened by his cries and, guessing what it was, went to the hay-loft where, unobserved, she untied the halter which held Don Quixote up. The knight then fell to the ground in front of the innkeeper and the travellers, and they went up to him to ask him what it was that made him shout so loud. He did not reply, but slipped the cord from his wrist and rose to his feet. Then, mounting Rocinante, he braced his shield, couched his lance and, making a wide sweep round the field, came back at a canter, exclaiming:

'Should anyone affirm that I have been rightfully enchanted, if I have the leave of my lady, the princess Micomicona, I will give him the lie, and challenge and defy him to single combat.'

The new arrivals were astounded at Don Quixote's speech; but the landlord relieved their surprise by telling them who he was, and that they need pay no attention to him, for he was out of his mind.

They then asked the innkeeper whether a lad of about fifteen, dressed as a mule-lad, had by any chance come to his inn, and gave a description of him which tallied with the appearance of Doña Clara's lover. The landlord answered that there were so many people in the inn that he had not noticed the person they were asking for. But when one of them saw the coach in which the judge had come, he exclaimed:

'He must be here. There can be no doubt of it, for this is the coach they say he was following. Let one of us stay at the door, and the rest go in and look for him. No, it might be as well if one of us were to ride round the inn, in case he should get away over the yard walls.'

'Let's do as you say,' replied another of them. Then two of them went in, one stayed at the door and the fourth started riding round the inn. The landlord watched all this, and could not conceive what they were taking these precautions for, though he knew quite well that they were looking for the lad whom they had described to him.

By now it was broad daylight; and for that reason, and because of the noise Don Quixote had made, everyone was awake and getting up, particularly Doña Clara and Dorothea, who had been able to sleep very little that night; one of them from excitement because her lover was so near, the other from eagerness to see this lad. Now Don Quixote felt near to bursting with rage, anger and fury when he found all four travellers ignoring him, and not one of them replying to his challenge; and could he have found it in his code of chivalry that a knight may lawfully undertake another enterprise despite his plighted word first to complete the one he is pledged to, he would have attacked them all and forced an answer out of them. But as it did not seem to him right or proper to begin a new undertaking till he had established Micomicona on her throne, he had to hold his tongue, keep quiet, and wait to see the result of the travellers' searching. It ended by one of them finding the young gentleman he was looking for sleeping beside a mule-lad, and little dreaming that anyone was looking for him or still less that he was found. The man, however, pulled him by the arm, and said:

'Really, Don Louis, the clothes you are wearing are *most* suitable to your rank, and the bed I find you on accords *in every way* with the luxury your mother brought you up in!'

The lad rubbed his sleepy eyes and, staring for a while at his captor, finally recognized him as a servant of his father's. This gave him such a surprise that for some time he could not manage to speak a word. And so the servant went on: 'There is nothing else for it now, Don Louis, but to be patient, and give in, and come back home, if you don't want your father, my master, to take a journey to the other world. For it's very much to be feared he will, he's so upset at your absence.'

'Why, how did my father know,' asked Don Louis, 'that I had come this way and in this disguise?'

'There was a student you told your plan to, and he was so upset at your father's grief when he missed you that he gave you away. So our master sent off four of us servants to look for you; and here we all are at your service, more delighted than you can think that we can go back so quickly and restore you to the sight of your very loving father.'

'That shall be as I wish, or as Heaven decrees,' replied Don Louis.

'What can you wish or Heaven decree, except that you agree to come back with us? There is no other course possible.'

All these arguments were overheard by the mule-lad lying next to Don Louis, who got up to tell Don Ferdinand, Cardenio, and the rest, who were now dressed, what was happening. He reported that the man was calling the lad '*Don*', and repeated their conversation, saying that the man wanted the boy to go back to his father's house, but that he would not. This and so much as they already knew of him – the fine voice Heaven had blessed him with – made them all most anxious to learn more about him, and even to help him, should the men try to do him any violence. So they went to the spot where he was, and found him still protesting to his servant. At the same moment Dorothea came out of her room, and Doña Clara after her in great alarm. Dorothea called Cardenio aside and told him very briefly the story of the singer and of Doña Clara; and he told her what had happened when his father's servants had come to look for him. But he did not speak quite quietly enough, for Doña Clara overheard him, and got into such a state, that she would have fallen down if Dorothea had not managed to catch her. Then Cardenio told Dorothea to take the girl back to their room, and promised to try and set everything to rights. So back they went.

Now all four of Don Louis' pursuers had entered the inn, and were standing round him, urging him to come back instantly, without losing a moment, and console his father. He replied that on no account could he do so until he had completed a matter on which depended his life, his honour and his heart. The servants then insisted, saying that under no circumstances would they return without him, and that they would take him whether he agreed or not.

'That you will not do,' replied Don Louis, 'unless you take me dead; although whatever way you take me, I shall be lifeless.'

Now by this time everyone else in the inn had come up to hear the argument, in particular Cardenio, Don Ferdinand, his companions, the judge, the priest, the barber and Don Quixote, who now thought that there was no more need to guard the castle. Cardenio, who knew the boy's story already, asked the servants what motive they had for wishing to take the lad against his will.

'Our reason,' replied one of the four, 'is to save his father's life, for he's in danger of losing it through this gentleman's absence.'

To which Don Louis replied: 'There is no reason why I should give an account of my business here. I am free. I shall go back if I please; and if I do not, none of you shall compel me.'

'Reason will compel you to,' replied the man, 'and if that's not enough for your worship, it's enough to make us do our duty, which is what we came for.'

'Let us know what is at the bottom of this,' put in the judge at this point.

But the man, who recognized him as a neighbour, replied: 'Do you not know this gentleman, my Lord Judge? He is your neighbour's son, and he has run away from his father's house in a disguise most unbecoming to his quality, as your worship can see.'

The judge then looked at the lad more closely, recognized him, and embraced him, saying: 'What childishness is this, Don Louis? What mighty reason can you have had for coming out in this fashion, and in a dress so unfitting to your rank?'

Tears came into the lad's eyes, and he could not answer a single word. But the judge told the four servants to rest assured that everything would be all right. Then, taking Don Louis by the hand, he drew him aside and demanded his reasons for coming.

While the judge was asking him various questions, a great uproar was heard at the inn door. The cause of it was that two guests who had stayed the night there had seen that everyone was busy enquiring about these four men, and had tried to get away without paying their reckoning. But the innkeeper was more attentive to his own business than to other people's and, laying hold of them as they were going out of the door, demanded his money. He called them such names, too, for their dirty trick that they were moved to reply with their fists, and had begun to do so with such vigour that the poor innkeeper had to shout for help. The landlady and her daughter could see no one who was not too busy to help him except Don Quixote, and it was to him the daughter shouted: 'Help, Sir Knight, by the power God gave you, help my poor father; for here are two wicked men thrashing him like corn.'

To which Don Quixote replied slowly and with great composure: 'Beauteous damsel, your petition is ill-timed, for I am prevented from embarking on any other adventure until I have brought the one to which I have pledged myself to a successful conclusion. But what I can do to serve you I will inform you now. Run and tell your father that he must hold his own in the battle as best he can, and on no account let himself be conquered, whilst I beg Princess Micomicona's permission to help him in his distress; and if she gives it to me, you may be assured that I shall rescue him.'

'Sure as I'm a sinner,' said Maritornes, who was standing near, 'before your worship gets this permission of yours, my master will be in the other world.'

'Allow me, lady, only to get this permission,' replied Don Quixote. 'For once I have got it, it will matter very little if he is in the other world. I will fetch him out of it, if the whole of that world oppose me. Or, at least, I will wreak such vengeance for you on those who sent him there that you will be more than moderately satisfied.'

Then without another word he went down on his knees in front of Dorothea, begging her in knightly and errant-like words that her Highness would be pleased to give him permission to help and succour the warden of that castle, who was in a grievous pass. The Princess gave it him most readily, and he instantly buckled his shield, grasped his sword, and ran to the inn door, where the two guests were still pounding the landlord. But no sooner did he get there than he wavered and stood still, although Maritornes and the landlady demanded what it was that prevented him from helping their master and husband.

'I delay,' said Don Quixote, 'because it is not lawful for me to draw my sword against squires and the like. Call my squire Sancho here, for this defence and vengeance properly concerns him.'

In the meantime the fight at the inn door was reaching a climax, and the landlord was getting the worst of it, which infuriated the landlady, her daughter and Maritornes, who were beside themselves at the sight of Don Quixote's cowardice and the damage their husband, father, and master was sustaining.

But let us leave him there, for someone is bound to help him; or, if no one does, let him suffer in silence for his rashness in taking on more than his strength warrants; and let us go back fifty paces and see how Don Louis answered the judge, whom we left asking him privately the reason for his travelling on foot in such poor clothes. The boy, then, clasped him tightly with both hands, in sign that his heart was oppressed by some great sorrow and, shedding copious tears, answered: 'My dear sir, the only thing that I can tell you is that from the moment when Heaven fated us to be neighbours and I saw Doña Clara, your daughter and my lady, I made her mistress of my heart; and if your wishes, my true lord and father, do not hinder me, she shall be my wife this very day. For her I left my father's house; for her I put on these clothes, to follow her wherever she went, as the arrow does the mark, or the sailor the pole-star. She knows no more of my passion than she has been able to learn on the few occasions when she has seen from a distance the tears in my eyes. Now you, sir, know that my family is rich and noble, and that I am their only heir. If these seem to you sufficient advantages, venture to make me completely happy and accept me now as your son. For though my father may be intent on other plans of his own, and may not approve the blessing I have found for myself, yet time has more power to undo and alter things than has human will.'

With this the enamoured youth fell silent. The judge was astonished, perturbed and perplexed, as much by Don Louis' sensible way of revealing his feelings as at finding himself in such a predicament. In fact he did not know what line to take in this sudden and unexpected situation. His only reply, therefore, was to ask Don Louis to keep calm for the time being and arrange with his servants not to go back that day. Then he would have time to consider what was best for everybody. At this Don Louis seized and kissed his hands, bathing them with tears, which would have melted a heart of stone, let alone the judge's. As a man of the world, he had already realized how good a match this would be for his daughter; though he hoped it would be possible for it to be concluded with the consent of Don Louis' father who, he knew, was aspiring to get a title for his son.

By this time the guests and the innkeeper had made their peace, for, through Don Quixote's persuasion and fair words rather than by threats, they had paid their full reckoning. Don Louis' servants, too, were waiting quietly for the judge to conclude his speech and for their master to make his decision, when the Devil, who never sleeps, ordained the sudden arrival at the inn of that barber from whom Don Quixote had taken Mambrino's helmet, and Sancho Panza the ass's harness which he had exchanged for his own. As this barber was taking his ass to the stable, he saw Sancho Panza mending some part of the pack-saddle; and as soon as he recognized him, he attacked him boldly, crying: 'I've got you now, master thief! Give me back my basin and my saddle with all the harness you robbed me of.'

Finding himself suddenly attacked, and hearing this abuse poured on him, Sancho grasped the saddle in one hand and gave the barber a punch with the other, which bathed his jaws in blood. But this did not make him leave go of the saddle; instead, he gave such a shout that everyone in the inn hurried towards the noise of this scuffle.

'Help, in the name of the King and of justice!' cried he. 'For I am taking back my property. This thief, this highwayman wants to kill me.'

'You're lying,' answered Sancho. 'I'm no highwayman, for my master Don Quixote won these spoils in fair fight.'

Don Quixote, who had now come up, was delighted to see his squire attacking and defending himself so well, and from then on he thought of him as a man of courage. He decided at that moment in his heart to knight him at the first available opportunity, confident that he was a fitting recipient of the order of chivalry. Now one of the things which the barber said in the course of the fight was:

'Sirs, this saddle is as much mine as the death I owe God. I recognize it as positively as if I had brought it into the world, and there is my ass in the stable who will not let me lie. Try it on him and see; if it doesn't fit just right, call me a liar. What is more, the same day they took it from me they took a new brass basin as well. It had never been used and was worth a good crown.'

Here Don Quixote could not refrain from answering him, and pushing himself between the pair to part them – the pack-saddle being laid on the ground for public inspection until the truth should be cleared up,

'Gentlemen,' he cried, 'you may clearly and manifestly see this good squire's error in calling that a basin which was, is, and shall be Mambrino's helmet, that I won from him in fair fight, thus becoming its legitimate and lawful owner! In the matter of the pack-saddle I will not interfere. All that I can say is that my squire Sancho asked my permission to strip the trappings from the horse of this vanquished coward and to adorn his own with them. I gave it him, and he took them. As for their being changed from horse's harness to pack-saddle, I can give no other explanation than the common one: that these transformations occur in affairs of chivalry. To confirm which, run Sancho my son, and bring the helmet which this good fellow says is a basin.'

'Good Lord, sir,' said Sancho, 'if we've no better proof of our case than what your worship's saying, Malino's helmet is as much a basin as this good fellow's harness is a pack-saddle.'

'Do what I bid you,' replied Don Quixote, 'for it cannot be that everything in this castle is governed by enchantment.'

Sancho went and fetched the basin and, as soon as Don Quixote saw it, he took it in his hands and said: 'Look, your worships, how can this squire have the face to say that this is a basin and not the said helmet? I swear by the order of chivalry, which I profess, that this was the same helmet I took from him, without addition or subtraction.'

'There is no doubt of that,' put in Sancho, 'for from the time my master won it till now he has not fought more than one battle in it, when he freed that unlucky chain-gang. And if it hadn't been for this basin-helmet, things would have gone badly with him that time, for there was a lot of stone-throwing in that engagement.'

Chapter XLV. *In which the question of Mambrino's Helmet and the Pack-saddle is finally cleared up, with other Adventures which most certainly occurred.*

'WHAT do you think about it, sirs,' asked the barber, 'when you hear these gentlemen swearing and insisting that this isn't a basin but a helmet?'

'Whoever says anything to the contrary,' said Don Quixote, 'if he is a knight, I will teach him that he lies, and if he is a squire, that he lies a thousand times.'

Our barber, who was looking on all the while and knew Don

Quixote's idiosyncrasies so well, decided to encourage his craziness and to give them all a laugh by carrying the joke further. So, addressing the other barber, he said:

'Sir barber, or whoever you are, learn that I am also of your profession, and have held a certificate for more than twenty years. I know all the instruments of the barber's art very well, without exception; and, what is more, I was a soldier for a while in my youth, and I also know what is a helmet, and what is a morion, and what is a closed casque, and other things concerning soldiering – I mean the different military arms. And I say, under correction, always submitting myself to better judgement, that this piece before us, which the good gentleman is holding, not only is not a barber's basin, but is as far from being one as black is from white, or the truth from a lie. But I do say that, though this is a helmet, it is not a complete helmet.'

'Certainly not,' said Don Quixote, 'because half of it – that is the beaver – is missing.'

'That is true,' said the priest, who had now grasped his friend the barber's purpose. Then Cardenio, Don Ferdinand and his comrades backed him up, and even the judge would have taken a hand in the joke if he had not been so concerned with the business of Don Louis; but the serious subject of his thoughts held him so engrossed that he paid little or no attention to these pleasantries.

'Good Heavens alive!' exclaimed the poor butt of a barber at this. 'Can so many honourable gentlemen possibly say that this is not a basin but a helmet? That's enough to surprise a whole university, be it ever so wise. Well, if this basin is a helmet, then, this pack-saddle must be a horse's harness as well, as this gentleman said.'

'It looks like a pack-saddle to me,' said Don Quixote, 'but, as I have already said, I am not interfering in that.'

'Whether it is a pack-saddle or a harness,' said the priest, 'Don Quixote has only to say; for in these matters of chivalry all these gentlemen and myself defer to him.'

'By God, sirs,' said Don Quixote, 'so many strange things have befallen me in this castle on the two occasions I have lodged here that I dare not give any positive answer to any question asked me concerning anything in it; for I imagine that whatever goes on here is by way of enchantment. The first time I was much annoyed by a

Moorish enchanter who dwells here, and Sancho fared rather badly at the hands of some henchmen of his; and last night I was suspended by this arm for almost two hours, without knowing either the means or the cause of my misfortunes. So to interfere now in so perplexed a matter and to give my opinion would be to make a rash judgement. Concerning their statement that this is a basin and not a helmet, I have already answered; but as to declaring whether that is a pack-saddle or a harness, I am not so bold as to give a definitive decision, but leave the matter to your worship's better judgement. Perhaps, since none of you are knights, as I am, the spells in this place will have no effect on you, your understanding will be free, and you will be able to judge of the affairs of this castle as they really and truly are, and not as they appear to me.'

'There is no doubt,' Don Ferdinand replied to this, 'that Don Quixote has spoken very wisely to-day in saying that the decision in this case lies with us; and so that it may rest on sounder foundations I will take the votes of these gentlemen in secret, and give you a clear and full account of the result.'

All this caused the greatest amusement to those who knew Don Quixote's idiosyncrasies; but it seemed the greatest nonsense in the world to those who did not, particularly to Don Louis' four servants, and to Don Louis himself, and to three more travellers who had happened to arrive at the inn and appeared to be troopers of the Holy Brotherhood, which indeed they were. But the most perplexed of all was the barber, whose basin had been turned into Mambrino's helmet before his eyes, and whose pack-saddle he fully expected to be transformed into a fine horse-harness. All of them, however, laughed to see Don Ferdinand go from one to another, taking their votes and whispering in their ears that they must declare in secret whether this pretty thing, which had been the subject of such fighting, was a pack-saddle or a harness. Then, after taking the votes of all those who knew Don Quixote, he loudly proclaimed:

'The fact is, my good fellow, that I am tired of taking so many opinions. For I find that everyone I ask declares that it is ridiculous to affirm that this is an ass's pack-saddle, for it is the harness of a horse, and of a thoroughbred horse at that. So you will have to be patient, for in spite of you and your ass, this is a harness and no pack-saddle, and you have stated and proved your case very badly.'

'May I never have a place in Heaven,' cried the poor barber, 'if your worships aren't all wrong; and may my soul as surely appear before God as this appears to me a pack-saddle and no harness. But might is right ... I say no more. But I promise you I'm not drunk, for I haven't broken my fast to-day, unless it be to sin.'

The barber's simple language caused no less laughter than the craziness of Don Quixote's, who remarked at this juncture: 'There is nothing more for it now but for each one to take his belongings, and what God gives may St. Peter bless.'

But one of the four servants observed: 'If this isn't a concerted joke, I can't understand how intelligent men can swear that these things aren't a basin and a pack-saddle. But you all seem intelligent enough, and yet you insist that you're right. So I suppose there must be some mystery about it all, for what you're saying goes clean against obvious truth and good sense, and I swear by' – and here he let out a round oath – 'that this is a barber's basin, and that's an ass's pack-saddle – and the whole world won't convince me to the contrary.'

'It might be a she-ass's,' observed the priest.

'It's all the same,' cried the servant, 'and that isn't the point. Either it's a pack-saddle or, as your worships say, it isn't.'

When he heard this one of the troopers, who had come in and listened to the argument, cried out angrily: 'It's as much a pack-saddle as my father's my father, and any one who says anything else must be drunk.'

'You lie like a base villain,' answered Don Quixote. And, raising his lance, which he had never let out of his hand, he aimed such a blow at the trooper's head that, unless he had dodged it, it would have left him stretched on the ground. The lance broke to pieces on the earth, and when the rest of the troopers saw their comrade assaulted they raised a shout for help for the Holy Brotherhood. The innkeeper, who was one of the fraternity, ran in an instant for his staff and his sword, and took his place beside his fellows. Don Louis' servants gathered round their young master, so that he should not escape in the scuffle. The barber, seeing the house in a turmoil, grasped his pack-saddle once more, and Sancho did the same. Don Quixote drew his sword and fell upon the troopers. Don Louis called to his servants to leave him and help Don Quixote –

and Cardenio and Don Ferdinand, who were on Don Quixote's side. The priest was shouting; the landlady screaming; her daughter wailing; Maritornes weeping; Dorothea was distracted; Lucinda in a flurry; and Doña Clara in a faint. The barber was mauling Sancho; Sancho pounding the barber; and Don Louis, whom one of his servants had been so bold as to seize by the arm to prevent his running away, had dealt the fellow a blow which bathed his jaws in blood; the judge was defending him; Don Ferdinand had one of the officers under his feet, and was trampling his carcass most heartily; and the innkeeper was straining his voice once more, shouting for help for the Holy Brotherhood. So the whole inn was full of tears, shouts, screams, amazement, fear, alarm, dismay, slashings, punches, blows, kicks and effusion of blood.

In the middle of this confused and chaotic tangle, the idea came into Don Quixote's head that he had been plunged head over heels into the discord in Agramante's camp, and so he cried in a voice which thundered through the inn: 'Hold, all! Sheathe your swords, all! Be calm, all! And listen to me, all of you, if all wish to remain alive!'

At this mighty voice they all stopped, and he continued, saying: 'Did I not tell you, gentlemen, that this castle is enchanted, and must be inhabited by some legion of demons? Behold the confirmation of my words, and gaze upon the discord in Agramante's camp transferred here and performed in our midst. See here they are fighting for the sword, yonder for the horse, here for the eagle, there for the helmet; we are all fighting and all at odds. Come then, Sir Judge, and you, Sir Priest; let one of you stand for King Agramante, the other for King Sobrino, and make peace amongst us. For, by God Almighty, it is a great villainy that people of such quality as we are here should slay one another for such trivial causes.'

The troopers, who did not understand Don Quixote's phraseology and found themselves roughly handled by Don Ferdinand, Cardenio and their companions, were unwilling to be pacified; but the barber was willing, for both his beard and the pack-saddle had been torn in the fight. Sancho, like a good servant, obeyed his master's slightest word. Don Louis' four servants grew calm, seeing how little they stood to gain by being otherwise. Only the innkeeper insisted that this madman's insolences must be punished, for he was always upsetting the inn. At last the uproar was quelled for a time, the pack-saddle remained a harness till Judgement Day, and in Don Quixote's imagination the basin remained a helmet and the inn a castle.

When, at the persuasion of the judge and the priest, everyone was pacified and had made friends, Don Louis' servants once more insisted that he must come with them at once; and whilst he was settling with them, the judge consulted Don Ferdinand, Cardenio, and the priest as to what he should do in the matter. He told them what Don Louis had said to him. It was finally agreed that Don Ferdinand should reveal himself to Don Louis' servants and say that it was his wish that Don Louis should come with him to Andalusia, where he would be received by his brother the Marquis in a manner suitable to his quality; for he knew that Don Louis was determined not to return to his father's presence even if they tore him to pieces. When the four of them were aware of Don Ferdinand's rank and Don Louis' obstinacy, they decided amongst themselves that three of them should return and give his father an account of events, and that the fourth should stay and wait on their young master, and not leave him till the others should return for him, or until he should learn what his father's orders were. Thus this tangle of quarrels was resolved by the authority of Agramante and the wisdom of King Sobrino.

However, the enemy of concord and adversary of peace, finding himself slighted and mocked, and seeing how little fruit he had reaped from plunging them all into this labyrinth of confusion, decided to try his hand again and bring some new quarrels and disturbances to life. It arose thus: the troopers calmed down when they overheard the rank of the men they had been fighting, and retired from the combat, it seeming to them that they would get the worst of the battle, whatever happened. But one of them – the one who had been pounded and trampled by Don Ferdinand – remembered suddenly that, among some warrants he was carrying for the arrest of various delinquents, was one for Don Quixote, whose seizure the Holy Brotherhood had ordered for his freeing the galley-slaves, as Sancho had had good reason to fear they would. When this occurred to him he decided to make certain that the description in the warrants tallied with the knight. So, taking a parchment from his breast, he lighted on what he wanted. Then he set himself to read it slowly – for he was no great reader – and at each word he read he clapped his eyes on Don Quixote, comparing the details in his warrant, one by one, with the knight's features, and found that beyond a doubt it was he that the warrant described. As soon as he had made certain of this, he folded up the parchment and, taking the warrant in his left hand, seized Don Quixote so firmly by the collar with his right that he could not breathe. Then he shouted:

'Help for the Holy Brotherhood! And to prove that I'm serious, read this warrant where it's written that this highway robber must be arrested.'

The priest took the warrant, and saw that all that the trooper said was true and that the description tallied with Don Quixote. But the knight was infuriated at finding himself roughly handled by this base scoundrel, and every bone in his body creaked as he clasped the trooper with all his might, with both hands round his throat. And if the fellow had not been rescued by his companions he would have breathed his last there and then, before Don Quixote would have let go his hold. The innkeeper, who was bound to help his fellow troopers, immediately ran to his aid. The landlady, seeing her husband in a fight once more, screamed again, and was instantly joined by Maritornes and her daughter, all three calling on Heaven and the company for help. And Sancho, seeing what was going on, remarked: 'By the Lord, all that my master says about the enchantments in this castle is true, for it's impossible to stay quiet an hour here.'

Don Ferdinand parted the trooper and Don Quixote and, to the relief of both, unlocked their hands which were clenched fast, the trooper's on the knight's collar, and the knight's round his adversary's throat. But, nevertheless, the troopers persisted in claiming their prisoner and the company's help in delivering him bound at their disposal, for such help it was their duty to the King and the Holy Brotherhood to give. So they once more demanded aid and assistance in the arrest of this robber, brigand and highwayman. But Don Quixote laughed at this description and said very calmly:

'Come here, filthy and low-born rabble! Is it highway robbery you call it, freeing the enchained, releasing prisoners, succouring the unfortunate, raising the fallen, relieving the needy? You infamous brood whose low and vile intelligence deserves no revelation from Heaven of that virtue which lies in knight errantry, nor any knowledge of your sin and ignorance in not reverencing the shadow – how much more the actual presence – of a knight errant! Come here, you pack of thieves, for you are no troopers, but highwaymen licensed by the Holy Brotherhood! Tell me, who was the dolt who signed a warrant of arrest against such a knight as I am? Who was it who did not know that knights errant are exempt from all jurisdiction, that their law is their sword, their charters their courage and their statutes their own will? Who was the idiot, I repeat, who does not know that there is no patent of nobility with so many privileges and immunities as a knight errant receives on the day when he is knighted and undertakes the stern practice of chivalry? What knight errant has ever paid tax, duty, queen's patten money, statute money, customs, or toll? What tailor was ever paid by him for a suit of clothes? What warden who received him in his castle ever made him pay his score? What maiden was not in love with him, and did not give herself up to his will and pleasure? And, lastly, what knight errant has there been, is there, or will there ever be in the world, who has not courage enough, on his own, to deal four hundred beatings to four hundred troopers, should they dare confront him?'

Chapter XLVI. *Of the notable Adventure with the Troopers and the great ferocity of our good Knight Don Quixote.**

WHILE Don Quixote was making this proclamation the priest was persuading the troopers that the knight was out of his mind, as they could see by his deeds and his words, and that, therefore, they need carry the matter no farther. For even if they were to arrest him and take him away, they would have to release him as a madman. But the man with the warrant replied that it was not for him to judge of Don Quixote's madness, but to carry out his superior's orders; and that once he was arrested they could let him out three hundred times if they chose.

* This heading is really misplaced, for the adventure is over. The oversight is the author's.

'For all that,' said the priest, 'your must not take him this time; nor, so far as I can see, will he let you.'

In the end the priest thought of so much to say and Don Quixote of so many crazy things to do that the troopers would have to have been madder than he if they had not recognized Don Quixote's infirmity. So they judged it best to be quiet, and even to make the peace between the barber and Sancho Panza, who were still quarrelling with great bitterness. As officers of justice, therefore, they intervened in the case and arbitrated to such purpose that both parties remained, if not entirely content, at least partially satisfied; it being settled that they should exchange pack-saddles, but not girths or headstalls. In the matter of Mambrino's helmet, too, the priest, unknown to Don Quixote, paid eight *reals* for the basin, and the barber wrote him out a receipt, promising not to take action for fraud thenceforth and for ever more, amen.

These two disputes being settled – and they were the most serious and urgent – nothing remained but for Don Louis' servants to agree that three of them should go back, and one stay to accompany their master wherever Don Ferdinand might take him. And as by now good luck had begun to shift obstacles and smooth difficulties in favour of the lovers and the brave folk in the inn, so Fortune was pleased to complete the task and bring everything to a happy ending. For the servants fell in with Don Louis' request, which so delighted Doña Clara that no one who looked into her face at that time could fail to recognize the rejoicing in her heart. As for Zoraida, although she did not very clearly understand everything she had seen, she was sad or gay by turns, according to the expressions she saw on everyone's face; but it was on her Spaniard's that her eyes were always fixed, in absolute dependence. The innkeeper, who had not failed to note the gift in compensation which the priest had given the barber, demanded payment of Don Quixote's account, and for the damage to the wine-skins and his loss of wine, swearing that neither Rocinante nor Sancho's ass should leave the inn until he had been paid to the last farthing. All this the priest peacefully settled, and Don Ferdinand paid although the judge had also very generously offered to do so. And so they all remained in peace and quietness, so that the inn no longer recalled the discord in Agramante's camp, as Don Quixote had said, but the peace and quiet of the times of Octavian. And it was the general opinion that they owed thanks for all this to the priest's good sense and great eloquence and to Don Ferdinand's incomparable generosity.

Don Quixote, then, seeing himself free and quit of all quarrels, both his squire's and his own, thought it would be well to continue the journey he had begun, and complete the great adventure for which he had been called and chosen; and so, firm in his resolution, he went to kneel down before Dorothea, who refused to let him utter a word until he arose. So he obediently got upon his feet and said:

'It is a common proverb, beauteous lady, that diligence is the mother of good fortune; and in many grave matters experience has shown that the solicitude of the suitor brings a doubtful matter to a happy ending. But in no affairs is this truth more evident than in those of war, in which promptness and speed forestall the enemy's designs, and gain the victory before the adversary has established his defences. All this I say, exalted and precious lady, because it seems to me that our sojourn in this castle is now profitless, and may do us very great harm, too, as we may one day discover. For who knows if your enemy the giant has not learnt, by means of secret and diligent spies, that I am on my way to destroy him, and, taking advantage of this delay, may not be fortifying himself in some impregnable castle or fortress against which my endeavours and the might of my untiring arm may avail me little? So, my lady, let us forestall his designs, as I have said, by our diligence, and depart immediately while our fortune is good; for to keep it on our side, as your Highness will desire, you must wait no longer than I delay in facing your adversary.'

Don Quixote fell silent and said no more, but most calmly awaited the beautiful Princess's reply; and she, with a lordly air, adapted to the style of Don Quixote, answered him as follows:

'I thank you, Sir Knight, for the desire you display to aid me in my great distress, like a true knight whose function and concern it is to succour the orphan and the needy. Pray Heaven that your desire and mine may be fulfilled, and that you may learn that there are grateful women in the world. As for my departure, let it be immediate, for I have no other wish than yours. Dispose of me wholly at your will and pleasure, for she who has once entrusted the defence

of her person to you, and put into your hands the restoration of her
domains, must not dare to go contrary to what your wisdom shall
ordain.'

'By God's hand,' cried Don Quixote, 'seeing a lady humble herself before me, I cannot forbear the opportunity of raising her and
placing her on her hereditary throne. Let our departure be immediate; for the saying that there is danger in delay puts spurs to my desire to be on the way. And since Heaven has never created, nor Hell
seen, anyone to daunt or intimidate me, saddle Rocinante, Sancho,
and harness your ass and the Queen's palfrey. Let us take our leave of
the warden and these gentlemen and be away from here immediately.'

But Sancho, who was standing by all the while, shook his head
and answered: 'Oh, sir, sir, there are more tricks done in the
village than make a noise – saving her ladyship's presence.'

'What nastiness can there be in any village, or in all the towns in
the world, which can be noised to my discredit, peasant?'

'If you're getting annoyed, your worship, I'll hold my tongue
and not say what it's a good squire's duty to say, and what a good
servant ought to say to his master.'

'Say what you like,' replied Don Quixote, 'so long as your words
are not intended to strike fear into me; for if you are afraid, you are
acting true to your character, and if I am fearless, I am acting true
to mine.'

'It's not that, I swear to God as I'm a sinner,' replied Sancho, 'but
I'm positively certain that this lady, who calls herself Queen of the
great Kingdom of Micomicon, is no more a queen than my mother;
for if she was what she says she is, she wouldn't go kissing with
somebody in this company every time anyone turns his head, and
round every corner.'

Dorothea blushed at Sancho's remarks, because it was true that
her husband, Don Ferdinand, had sometimes, when no one was
looking, gathered from her lips some of the rewards his love had
earned. This Sancho had seen; and such immodesty had seemed to
him more fitting in a courtesan than in the queen of a great kingdom. But as she could not contradict Sancho, she had to let him go
on with his observations:

'I'm saying this, sir, because if the gentleman who is enjoying
himself in this inn is going to gather the fruit of our labours, when

we've travelled the highways and by-ways and passed bad nights and worse days, I've got no reason to be in a hurry myself about saddling Rocinante, or harnessing my ass, or getting the palfrey ready. It will be better for us to stay quiet – and let every whore spin and us eat.'

Goodness, what a fury Don Quixote flew into when he heard his squire speak with such disrespect! So tremendous was it that, with a trembling voice and stammering tongue, his eyes darting fire, he exclaimed:

'Villainous peasant, unmannerly, disrespectful, ignorant, blasphemous, foul-mouthed, presumptuous, backbiting slanderer! Dare you utter such words in my presence, and in the presence of these illustrious ladies? How have you presumed to breed such infamies and effronteries in your muddled imagination? Begone from my sight, unnatural monster, storehouse of lies, armoury of deceit, sink of knavery, inventor of iniquities, publisher of ravings, foe to the respect due to royal persons! Go, never appear before me again, on pain of my wrath!'

As he spoke, he frowned severely, puffed out his cheeks, glared in all directions, and stamped loudly on the ground with his right foot in sign of the rage pent up in his heart.

His words and his furious gestures so terrified Sancho that he would have been glad if the earth had opened at that instant before his feet and swallowed him; and he could think of no other course but to turn his back and quit his master's furious presence. But the wise Dorothea, who was now so well schooled in Don Quixote's idiosyncrasies, sought to mitigate his wrath by addressing him thus:

'Do not be vexed, Sir Knight of the Sad Countenance, at the idle words which your good squire has spoken, for perhaps he did not speak them without good reason; nor can we suspect his good understanding and Christian conscience of making false accusations against anyone. So we must positively believe that, as everything in this castle happens by way of enchantment, as you yourself say, Sir Knight, – it may be, I say, that Sancho may have seen, by diabolical illusion, what he says he beheld, so much to the prejudice of my honour.'

'By the Almighty God,' cried Don Quixote at this point, 'I swear

your Highness has hit the mark. Some wicked vision has risen before that sinner Sancho's eyes, and shown him what he could not
possibly have seen by any other means than by sorcery. For I know
the poor man's goodness and innocence too well to believe that he
would make false accusations against anyone.'

'That is the truth, and so let it rest,' said Don Ferdinand. 'Therefore your worship must pardon him and receive him once more into
the bosom of your favour "as it was in the beginning", before these
visions distracted his senses.'

Don Quixote replied that he would pardon him, and the priest
went for Sancho, who came in very humbly and, falling on his
knees, begged for his master's hand. The knight gave it him, and
let him kiss it, and then after bestowing a blessing on him, he said:
'Now you will be convinced, Sancho, my son, that what I have so
often told you is true, and that all events in this castle are performed
by way of enchantment.'

'Indeed, I believe it,' said Sancho, 'except for the matter of that
blanket-tossing. That really happened in the ordinary way.'

'Do not you believe that,' replied Don Quixote, 'for if that had
been the case I should have avenged you then, or would do so even
now. But neither then nor now have I been able to take vengeance
for your injury, nor to see anyone on whom I could take it.'

Everyone wanted to know what this business about a blanket
was, and so the innkeeper gave them a circumstantial account of
Sancho Panza's flight through the air, at which they all laughed not
a little; and Sancho would have been not a little ashamed if his
master had not assured him once more that it was enchantment. But
for all that, Sancho's folly never reached such a pitch that he did not
believe it was absolute and certain truth, without any shadow of
illusion, that he had been tossed by creatures of flesh and blood, and
not by any unreal or imaginary phantoms, as his master believed
and affirmed.

Two days had now passed since that illustrious company had
come to the inn; and thinking that the time for departure had come,
they devised a plan which would spare Dorothea and Don Ferdinand the trouble of going back with Don Quixote to his village
under pretence of restoring Queen Micomicona, and allow the priest
and the barber to bear him off, as they wished, and try to get him

cured of his madness at home. And this was the scheme they contrived. They made a bargain with a waggoner, who happened to be passing that way with a team of oxen, to take him in this way: they made a sort of cage of criss-crossed poles, sufficiently large to hold Don Quixote comfortably; then Don Ferdinand and his companions, with Don Louis' servants, the troopers and the innkeeper, all under the orders and directions of the priest, covered their faces and disguised themselves in various ways, so that Don Quixote should take them for different people from those he had seen at the castle. This done, in absolute silence they entered the room where he was asleep, taking his rest after the late conflicts. They went up to where he was sleeping peacefully, with no suspicion of any plot and, grasping him firmly, securely tied his hands and feet, so that when he woke up with a start he could not stir or do anything but gaze in wonder at the strange faces he saw before him. And at once he fell into the illusion his wild imagination was continually suggesting to him, and assumed that those figures were the phantoms of that enchanted castle, and that he was now positively under a spell, since he could neither stir nor defend himself. All this was precisely what the priest, the inventor of the scheme, had expected. Of all those present only Sancho was in his right mind and undisguised; and although he was not far from sharing his master's disease, did not fail to recognize those disguised figures. But he did not dare to open his mouth until he saw what this assault and seizure of his master would lead to, and the knight did not speak a word either, waiting also to see the issue of this disaster.

The issue was that they dragged him to the cage and shut him in, nailing the bars so fast that they could not be knocked down in a hurry. They then took him on their shoulders. But as they left the room they heard a fearful voice, as awful as the barber could make it – not the barber of the pack-saddle but the other one:

'O Knight of the Sad Countenance!' he cried, 'be not grieved at your confinement. It is needful for the speedier conclusion of the adventure to which your great courage has committed you. The which shall be concluded when the furious Manchegan lion shall be united with the white Tobosan dove, and after they have humbled their lofty crests to the soft matrimonial yoke, from which miraculous mating shall issue to the light of the sun brave whelps, who will

emulate the ravaging talons of their valorous father. This shall come
to pass ere the pursuer of the fugitive nymph shall twice in his swift
and natural course have visited the bright constellations. And you,
most noble and obedient squire that ever bore sword in belt, beard
on chin, or smell in nose, be not dismayed or displeased to see the
flower of knight errantry thus borne away before your eyes. For
very speedily, if it please the Artificer of the world, you will find
yourself so exalted and ennobled that you will not know yourself,
nor shall you be defrauded of the reward your good master has promised you. I assure you, on behalf of the sage Mentironiana, that
your wages shall be paid you, as the proof will show. Follow then
in the footsteps of your valorous and enchanted lord, for it is fitting
that you should go to that place where you both will stay. And
now, as it is not lawful for me to say more, God be with you, for
I return, I well know whither.'

Towards the end of this prophecy the barber raised his voice to
such a pitch, and then lowered it to so quiet a tone, that even those
in the joke almost believed in the truth of what they heard. Don
Quixote was much consoled by this prophecy. For he immediately
grasped its whole meaning, and saw that it promised him union in
holy and lawful wedlock with his beloved Dulcinea del Toboso,
from whose happy womb would issue the whelps, his sons, to the
everlasting glory of La Mancha. So, believing all this sincerely and
firmly, he raised his voice and said with a deep sigh:

'You, whoever you may be, who have prognosticated such happiness for me, I pray you, beg in my name that sage enchanter who
has my affairs in his charge not to let me perish in this captivity in
which I am borne off, until I see the fulfilment of the joyful and incomparable promises that have just been made to me. But, however
that may be, I shall account the pains of my prison glory, these
chains which bind me comfort, and this litter upon which I am laid
no hard field of battle, but a soft couch and happy marriage-bed.
And regarding the consolation of my squire Sancho Panza, I trust
in his honesty and good conduct that he will not leave me in good
or evil fortune. For though it should not happen, from his ill luck
or mine, that I shall be able to bestow on him the isle or other
equivalent gift which I have promised him, at least he cannot lose
his wages, since in the will which I have made I have provided for

o

his payment, not in proportion to his many good services, but to my means.'

Sancho bowed his head in deep respect and kissed both his hands, for he could not kiss one alone, since they were tied together. Then the phantoms lifted the cage on to their shoulders and placed it on the ox-cart.

Chapter XLVII. *Of the strange way in which Don Quixote was enchanted, and other matters.*

WHEN Don Quixote himself was thus caged and placed on the cart, he said: 'I have read many serious histories of knights errant; but I have never read, or seen, or heard of enchanted knights being carried in this fashion and at the pace which these slothful and lazy animals promise. For they are generally borne through the air with extraordinary speed, enclosed in some thick and dusky cloud, or on some chariot of fire, or on some hippogriff or other such beast. But to be carried as I now am on an ox-cart, God help me, it puts me to confusion. But perhaps chivalry and magic in our day must follow a different course from that pursued by the men of old; and it may be, too, that as I am a new knight in the world, and the first to resuscitate the long-forgotten profession of knight errantry, they have invented fresh kinds of enchantment and other methods of carrying the enchanted as well. What do you think about it, Sancho, my son?'

'I don't know what to think,' replied Sancho, 'not being so well read as your worship in the errant writings. But, all the same, I'd be prepared to swear that these apparitions here around us are not altogether Catholic.'

'Catholic? Holy father!' replied Don Quixote. 'How should they be Catholic, if they are all demons who have taken fantastic bodies to come and throw me into this state? If you want to convince yourself of that, touch them and feel them, and you will see that their bodies are only air, and are nothing but an outward semblance.'

'By God, sir,' replied Sancho, 'I've touched them already, and this devil bustling about here is plump and tender. He has another property, too, very different from anything that devils are said to have. They all stink of brimstone and other foul odours, but this one smells of ambergris from a mile off.'

This remark of Sancho's referred to Don Ferdinand who, being a gentleman, must have smelt as Sancho said.

'Do not be surprised at that, Sancho my friend,' replied Don Quixote, 'for I would have you know that devils are very crafty. But although they carry smells about them, they do not smell, because they are spirits; and if they do smell, they cannot smell of good things, but only of evil and stinking ones. The reason is that they carry hell with them wherever they are, and can receive no kind of relief from their torments. Now, a good smell is something to delight and please; so it is not possible for them ever to smell sweet; and if this demon of yours seems to you to smell of ambergris, either you are mistaken or he seeks to deceive you and make you think that he is not a devil.'

All this conversation passed between master and servant; and as Don Ferdinand and Cardenio were afraid that Sancho would tumble to the whole of their plot, which he had already come very near to doing, they decided to cut the parting short. So they called the innkeeper aside and ordered him to saddle Rocinante and harness Sancho's ass, which he very quickly did. In the meantime the priest had come to an arrangement with the troopers to escort him to his village for so much a day. Cardenio hung the knight's shield on one side of Rocinante's saddle and the basin on the other. Then in dumb show he bade Sancho mount his ass and take Rocinante by the reins, and posted the troopers with their firelocks on either side of the cart. But before it moved off, the landlady, her daughter and Maritornes came out to say good-bye to Don Quixote, pretending to weep with sorrow at his misfortune; and he said to them:

'Do not weep, good ladies, for all these mischances are incidental to the calling I profess; and if these calamities did not befall me I should not consider myself a famous knight errant. For such things never happen to knights of small name and fame, since there is no one in the world to cast them a thought. But to the brave they do, for many princes and other knights envy them for their virtue and their valour, and seek by evil ways to destroy these good men. But, for all that, virtue is so powerful that of itself alone it will emerge victorious from any trial, despite all the necromancy ever known to

Zoroaster, its first inventor, and will shed its light on the world as the sun does in heaven. Pardon me, fair ladies, if I have inadvertently done you any displeasure, for wilfully and consciously I have never done so to anyone. And pray God to deliver me from these chains, into which some ill-intentioned magician has cast me, for if ever I am free from them I will never forget the favours you have done me in this castle, but shall acknowledge them, requite them, and repay them as they deserve.'

Whilst this passage was taking place between the ladies and Don Quixote, the priest and the barber took leave of Don Ferdinand and his comrades, of the captain and his brother, and of all those happy ladies, of Dorothea and Lucinda in particular. They all embraced, and agreed to send one another their news. Don Ferdinand made a point of telling the priest where to write and let him know Don Quixote's fate. He insisted that nothing would give him more pleasure than to hear, and promised to let the priest have any news that might please him, about his own marriage and Zoraida's baptism, or Don Louis' affairs and Lucinda's homecoming. The priest promised to comply most punctually with his request. Once more they embraced, and once more exchanged compliments. Then the innkeeper went up to the priest and gave him some papers, saying that he had found them in the lining of the trunk in which he had discovered the *Tale of Foolish Curiosity*, and told him that he might take them all with him as its owner had never come that way again. For, as he could not read, he did not want them himself. The priest thanked him and, on opening the manuscript, saw written at the head: *The Tale of Rinconete and Cortadillo*, from which he assumed that this was another story; and he expected that it would be a good one, since *The Tale of Foolish Curiosity* had been, and it was probably by the same author. So he kept it, intending to read it when he had an opportunity.

Then he and his friend the barber, both wearing their masks so that Don Quixote should not recognize them, mounted and set out after the cart. The order of the procession was the following: first went the cart, driven by its owner; on either side, as we have said, went the troopers with their firelocks; then followed Sancho Panza on his ass, leading Rocinante by the rein; last of all came the priest and the barber on their heavy mules, their faces covered as before mentioned, riding with a grave and sober air as fast as the slow pace of the oxen permitted. Don Quixote travelled seated in his cage, with his hands tied and his feet stretched out, leaning against the bars, as silently and patiently as if he had been no flesh-and-blood man, but a stone statue. And so they rode slowly and silently for about six miles, until they came to a valley which the carter thought would be a convenient place for resting and feeding his oxen. He told his thought to the priest, but the barber was of the opinion that they should go on a little farther; for he knew that behind a hill which showed up not far away there was a valley with more and much better grass than there was there, where they wanted to stop. So the barber's advice was taken, and they resumed their way.

At this moment the priest looked round and saw six or seven horsemen behind them, well dressed and mounted, who soon overtook them. For they were not riding at the slow and leisurely pace of oxen, but as people mounted on canons' mules, and anxious to press on and take their siesta at the inn, which could be seen less than three miles ahead. The swift travellers overtook the slow and greeted them courteously. Now, when one of the newcomers, who proved to be a Canon of Toledo and the master of the rest, saw the orderly procession with the cart, the troopers, Sancho, Rocinante, the priest and the barber, and Don Quixote, in particular, imprisoned in his cage, he could not help asking the reason for their carrying a man in that manner; though he had already concluded from seeing the troopers' badges that he must be some habitual highwayman or other malefactor whose punishment was a matter for the Holy Brotherhood. But one of the troopers, to whom he had put the question, replied: 'Sir, we don't know what it all means. The gentleman must tell you himself why he is carried like this.'

Don Quixote heard this question and answer, and replied: 'Are you gentlemen, perhaps, versed and skilled in matters of knight errantry? For, if you are, I will communicate my misfortunes to you. But if you are not, there is no reason for my tiring myself by telling you.'

By this time the priest and the barber had seen that the travellers were in conversation with Don Quixote de la Mancha, and had come up to answer for him, in case their plot might be discovered. But the canon, whom Don Quixote had addressed, replied: 'Truly,

brother, I know more about books of chivalry than about Villal-
pando's Logic. So, if that is all, you can safely tell me whatever you
please.'

'Then, in God's name, I will,' replied Don Quixote. 'I would
have you know, sir, that I am travelling in this cage under a spell,
because of the envy and fraud of evil enchanters; for virtue is persecuted by the wicked more than it is loved by the good. I am a
knight errant – not one of those whose names Fame has never
thought to record in her memory, but one who, in despite and defiance of envy itself, and of all the Magi ever born in Persia, all the
Brahmans of India, all the Gymnosophists of Ethiopia, shall write
his name in the temple of immortality, to serve as a pattern and
example to future ages, wherein knights errant may see what steps
they should follow if they would climb to the honourable summit
and pinnacle of arms.'

'The knight Don Quixote de la Mancha is speaking the truth,'·
put in the priest at this juncture, 'for he is travelling in this cart beneath a spell, not for his own faults and sins, but through the
malignity of those to whom virtue is loathsome and valour odious.
This, sir, is the Knight of the Sad Countenance – if you have ever
heard speak of him at any time – whose valorous achievements and
mighty deeds will be written on stubborn brass and eternal marble,
however tirelessly envy and malice may work to obscure and conceal them.'

When the canon heard both prisoner and free men talk in this
style he almost crossed himself with astonishment, unable to
imagine what had happened; while the same amazement struck all
his companions. At this Sancho Panza, who had drawn near to hear
the conversation, sought to make everything plain by remarking:
'Now, gentlemen, whether you like it or not, the fact of the matter
is that Don Quixote is no more enchanted than my mother. He is in
possession of all his faculties; he eats and drinks and does his business like other men, and just as he did yesterday before they put him
in the cage. As that's the case, how can they expect me to believe
that he's under a spell? For I've often heard it said that people
who've been bewitched don't eat, or sleep, or speak; while my
master will out-talk thirty lawyers, if they'll only let him alone.'
Then, turning to face the priest, he went on: 'Oh, Master Priest,

Master Priest! Do you think I don't recognize you? Do you imagine I don't see what you're up to? Do you think that I don't see through these new enchantments? Of course I know you, even though you've a mask on your face, and understand you, however much you disguise your tricks. In fact, where envy reigns virtue can't exist, and generosity doesn't go with meanness. Damn it all! If it wasn't for your reverence my master would be married to the Princess Micomicona at this very moment, and I should be a count at least, for I could have expected no less, considering the generosity of my master, the Knight of the Sad Countenance, and the greatness of my services. But I see now that it's true, as they say in these parts, that Fortune's wheel goes swifter than a mill wheel, and the man who was at the very top yesterday is on the ground to-day. It's my wife and my children I'm sorry for. For just when they might have expected to see their father come in at the door a governor or vice-roy of some isle or kingdom, they'll see him enter as a stable-boy. I'm saying all this, Master Priest, to urge you to have some conscience about ill-treating my master like this. You take care that God doesn't call you to account in the other life for imprisoning him like this. He'll make you answer for all these succours and benefits my master, Don Quixote, leaves undone all this time he's a prisoner.'

'Tell that to your grandmother!' put in the barber at this point. 'What, Sancho, are you of your master's fraternity, too? I swear to God I'm beginning to think you'll have to keep him company in his cage, and labour under the same spell as he does, for you've caught something of his humour and chivalry. It was an ill moment when you fell with child by his promises, and worse still when you got that isle you're so set on into your brain.'

'I'm not with child by anyone,' replied Sancho; 'and I'm not a man to let anyone get me with child, not the King himself. For though I'm poor, I'm an old Christian, and I owe nothing to any man. If I'm set on isles, other people are set on worse. Every man's the son of his own deeds; and since I'm a man, I can become pope, let alone governor of an isle, especially since my master's capable of winning so many that he may have no one to give them to. Mind how you talk, Master Barber, for shaving beards isn't everything, and there's some difference between Peter and Peter. I say this be-

cause we all know one another, and there's no passing false dice on
me. As to this enchanting of my master, God knows the truth;
so let it rest there, for it won't improve for stirring.'

The barber did not care to answer him, in case Sancho should let
out in his simplicity what the priest and he were trying so hard to
keep hidden. With the same fear in his mind the priest invited the
canon to ride with him a little ahead, promising to reveal the mystery
of the cage and other things which would amuse him. The canon
agreed and, going ahead with his servants, listened attentively to all
that the priest told him about Don Quixote's character, life, madness, and habits, to a brief account of the beginnings and cause of
his distraction, to the whole course of his history up to his confinement in the cage, and finally, to their plan for getting him back to
his own village to see whether they might find any sort of cure for
his madness. The canon and his servants were amazed anew at hearing Don Quixote's strange history, and when it was finished he
said:

'Truly, Sir Priest, my own experience tells me that so-called
books of chivalry are very prejudicial to the commonwealth; and
although, out of idleness and bad taste, I have read the beginnings
of almost all that have been printed, I have never managed to read
one right through. For they all seem to me more or less the same,
and there is no more in one than in another. Besides, in my opinion
this sort of composition falls under the heading of Milesian Fables,
which are extravagant tales, whose purpose is to amaze, and not to
instruct; quite the opposite of Moral Fables, which delight and instruct at the same time. And even though the principal aim of such
books is to delight, I do not know how they can succeed, seeing the
monstrous absurdities they are filled with. For the delight that the
mind conceives must arise from the beauty and harmony it sees, or
contemplates, in things presented to it by the eyes or the imagination; and nothing ugly or ill proportioned can cause us any pleasure.
What beauty can there be, or what harmony between the parts and
the whole, or between the whole and its parts, in a book or story
in which a sixteen-year-old lad deals a giant as tall as a steeple one
blow with his sword, and cuts him in two as if he were made of
marzipan? And when they want to describe a battle, first they tell
us that there are a million fighting men on the enemy's side. But if

the hero of the book is against them, inevitably, whether we like it or not, we have to believe that such and such a knight gained the victory by the valour of his strong arm alone. Then what are we to say of the ease with which a hereditary Queen or Empress throws herself into the arms of an unknown and wandering knight? What mind not totally barbarous and uncultured can get pleasure from reading that a great tower, full of knights, sails out over the sea like a ship before a favourable wind, and that one night it is in Lombardy and by dawn next morning in the land of Prester John of the Indies, or in some other country that Ptolemy never knew nor Marco Polo visited? If you reply that the men who compose such books write them as fiction, and so are not obliged to look into fine points or truths, I should reply that the more it resembles the truth the better the fiction, and the more probable and possible it is, the better it pleases. Fictions have to match the minds of their readers, and to be written in such a way that, by tempering the impossibilities, moderating excesses, and keeping judgement in the balance, they may so astonish, hold, excite, and entertain, that wonder and pleasure go hand in hand. None of this can be achieved by anyone departing from verisimilitude or from that imitation of nature in which lies the perfection of all that is written. I have never seen a book of chivalry with a whole body for a plot, with all its limbs complete, so that the middle corresponds to the beginning, and the end to the beginning and middle; for they are generally made up of so many limbs that they seem intended rather to form a chimaera or a monster than a well-proportioned figure. What is more, their style is hard, their adventures are incredible, their love-affairs lewd, their compliments absurd, their battles long-winded, their speeches stupid, their travels preposterous and, lastly, they are devoid of all art and sense, and therefore deserve to be banished from a Christian commonwealth, as a useless tribe.'

The priest listened to him with great attention, for he found him a man of good sense, and approved all that he said. And so he told him that, being of the same opinion himself, and bearing a grudge against books of chivalry, he had burnt all Don Quixote's large library of them. Then he went on to tell the story of the inquisition he had held over them, and to say which he had condemned to the flames and which he had spared, at which the Canon laughed a great deal. Yet he continued that, for all that he had said against such books, he found one good thing in them: the fact that they offered a good intellect a chance to display itself. For they presented a broad and spacious field through which the pen could run without let or hindrance, describing shipwrecks, tempests, encounters and battles; painting a brave captain with all the features necessary for the part; showing his wisdom in forestalling his enemies' cunning, his eloquence in persuading or dissuading his soldiers, his ripeness in counsel, his prompt resolution, his courage in awaiting or in making an attack; now depicting a tragic and lamentable incident, now a joyful and unexpected event; here a most beautiful lady, chaste, intelligent, and modest; there a Christian knight, valiant, and gentle; in one place a monstrous, barbarous braggart; in another a courteous prince, brave and wise; representing the goodness and loyalty of vassals, and the greatness and generosity of lords. Sometimes the writer might show his knowledge of astrology, or his excellence at cosmography or as a musician, or his wisdom in affairs of state, and he might even have an opportunity of showing his skill in necromancy. He could portray the subtlety of Ulysses, the piety of Aeneas, the valour of Achilles, the misfortunes of Hector, the treachery of Sinon, the friendship of Euryalus, the generosity of Alexander, the courage of Caesar, the clemency and truthfulness of Trajan, the fidelity of Zopyrus, the prudence of Cato and, in fact, all those attributes which constitute the perfect hero, sometimes placing them in one single man, at other times dividing them amongst many. 'Now,' he concluded, 'if all this is done in a pleasant style and with an ingenious plot, as close as possible to the truth, there is no doubt at all that the author will weave a beautiful and variegated fabric, which, when finished, will be perfect enough to achieve the excellent purpose of such works, which is, as I have said, to instruct and delight at the same time. For the loose plan of these books gives the author an opportunity of showing his talent for the epic, the lyric, the tragic and the comic, and all the qualities contained in the most sweet and pleasing sciences of poetry and rhetoric; for the epic may be written in prose as well as in verse.'

Chapter XLVIII. *In which the Canon pursues the subject of Books of Chivalry and other matters worthy of his genius.*

'WHAT you say is true, Sir Canon,' said the priest, 'and for that reason the writers of such books are most blameworthy, since up to now they have paid no attention to good sense or to the art and rules. For if they had been guided by them, they might have become as famous in prose as the two princes of poetry, Greek and Latin, are in verse.'

'For my part,' replied the canon, 'I have been somewhat tempted to write a book of chivalry, observing all the points I have mentioned. To tell you the truth, I have written more than a hundred pages, and to find out whether they came up to my opinion of them, I have shown them to learned and judicious men given to that kind of reading, and to other ignorant men who merely want the pleasure of listening to nonsense, and I gained flattering approval from them all. But, for all that, I have not continued, because it seemed to me a task unfitting to my profession, and because I found the ignorant were more numerous than the wise; and though it is better to be praised by the few wise and mocked by the many fools, I do not want to subject myself to the muddled judgement of the opinionated crowd, who are generally the most given to reading such books. But most instrumental in making me drop the task of finishing it, even from my thoughts, was an argument which I drew from the comedies that are being played nowadays. For I reflected: if those now in fashion, the fictitious ones and the historical as well, are all, or most of them, notorious nonsense, monsters without feet or head; and if, despite that, the crowd enjoy seeing them, and approve of them and reckon them good, when they are so far from being so; and if the authors who write them and the managers who put them on say that they must be good, because the crowd likes them like that and not otherwise, and that the authors who observe a plan and follow the story as the rules of drama require only serve to please the three or four men of sense who understand them, while all the rest are left unsatisfied and cannot fathom their subtlety; and since these managers add that it suits them better to earn their bread from the many than approval from the few – such would have been the fate of my book after I had scorched my eyebrows studying to keep the rules I spoke of: it would have been love's labour lost. Sometimes I have tried to persuade the managers that their judgements are false, and that they would draw a bigger audience and get better reputations by playing comedies that follow the rules, instead of these extravagant pieces; but they are so bound and wedded to their opinion that there is no argument or proof that can move them from it. I remember saying to one of these obstinate fellows one day: "Tell me, do you remember how a few years ago they were playing three tragedies in Spain by a famous native poet? They were so good that they delighted, surprised and amazed everyone who saw them, learned and simple, the best people and the crowd, and those three alone earned the players more money than thirty of the best produced since?"

'The manager I am speaking of replied: "Of course, your worship means *Isabella, Phyllis* and *Alexandra*." "Those it was I meant," I replied. "Now, did not they keep carefully to the rules of drama, and did that prevent their being the successes they were and pleasing everybody? So the fault is not in the public for demanding absurdities, but in people who cannot put anything else on the stage. For there is no absurdity in *Ingratitude Avenged* or in *Numancia*.* You will not find any in *The Merchant Lover*, nor yet in *The Friendly Enemy*, nor in quite a few others written by various good poets, to their own fame and glory, and to the profit of the players." I said a good deal else as well, and I think I left him in some confusion, but not so satisfied or convinced as to retract his mistaken opinions.'

'You have touched on a subject, Sir Canon,' said the priest at this, 'which wakes in me an old grudge I bear against the plays they act to-day. It is as great as my grudge against books of chivalry. For though Drama, according to Tully, should be a mirror to human life, a pattern of manners, and an image of truth, the plays that are performed nowadays are mirrors of absurdity, patterns of foolishness, and images of lewdness. For what greater absurdity can there be in our present subject than for a child to come on in the first scene of the first act in swaddling clothes, and in the second as a grown man with a beard? What could be more ridiculous than to paint us a valiant old man and a young coward, an eloquent servant, a statesmanlike page, a king as a porter, and a princess a scullery-

* By Cervantes himself.

maid? And they pay no more regard to the place or the time in which their action is supposed to occur. I have seen a play whose first act opened in Europe, its second in Asia, and its third ended in Africa. And if there had been four acts, the fourth no doubt would have finished up in America; and so it would have been played in all four quarters of the globe. If imitation is the chief aim of a play, how is it possible to satisfy any average intelligence, when an action pretends to take place in the time of King Pepin and Charlemagne, and yet they make the principal character in it the Emperor Heraclius, who enters Jerusalem bearing the Cross and wins the Holy Sepulchre, like Godfrey de Bouillon, though there was a whole age between the one event and the other? And when the comedy is based on a fictitious story, how can they introduce historical events into it, and mix in incidents that happened to different people at different times; and, even then, with no attempt at verisimilitude, but with obvious errors inexcusable on every count? The worst of it is that there are idiots who say that this stuff is perfect and to look for anything else is to fish for dainties.

'And when we come to sacred drama? What a multitude of false miracles they invent! What apocryphal and unintelligible plots — the miracles of one saint attributed to another! Even in their profane plays they make bold to introduce miracles without any more reason or consideration than because they think that some miracle — or effect, as they call it — will go well, and that the ignorant public will enjoy it and come to the play. But all this is prejudicial to truth, and to the detriment of history. It shames our Spanish wits before foreigners, who observe the rules of drama with great strictness and consider us ignorant barbarians when they see the absurdities and extravagances of the plays we write. It is not sufficient excuse to say that the principal purpose for which well-ordered states allow public plays to be acted is to give the common people a respectable entertainment, and to divert the ill-humours which idleness at times engenders; and that since any play can do that, whether it is good or bad, there is no reason to impose laws or compel writers and actors to compose their plays in the proper way, because, as I have said, they can achieve their purpose with any play at all. To this I should reply that their purpose could be incomparably better achieved by good plays than by bad ones; because the audience would come out from a well-written and well-constructed play entertained by the comic part, instructed by the serious, surprised by the action, enlivened by the speeches, warned by the tricks, wiser for the moral, incensed against vice, and enamoured of virtue. All these effects a good play can work in the mind of an audience, however rough and sluggish; and it is absolutely impossible for a play with all these qualities not to amuse and entertain, satisfy and please, much better than one that lacks them, as most of the pieces generally played nowadays do. It is not the fault of the poets who write them, for some of them know very well where they are wrong and are thoroughly conscious of what they ought to do. But as plays have become a marketable commodity they say, and say truly, that the players would not buy them if they were not of the usual kind. And so the poet tries to adapt himself to the requirements of the manager who pays him for his work. The truth of that can be seen by the infinite number of plays written by one most fertile genius of these kingdoms with so much splendour and so much grace, with such well-turned verses, such choice language, such serious thought, and lastly, with so much eloquence and in so lofty a style, that the world is full of his fame; and yet, because he wishes to suit the taste of the actors, not all his pieces have achieved, as some have, the perfection which art requires. Other authors pay so little attention to their task that when the play is over the actors have to run away and hide, for fear of being punished, as they have often been, for acting scenes offensive to some prince or libelling some family.

'Now, all these evils, and many more of which I will not speak, would cease, if there were some intelligent and judicious person at court to examine all plays before they are performed, not only those that are acted in the capital, but all that are to be played anywhere in Spain. Then no magistrate in any town would allow any play to be performed without this man's approbation, under his hand and seal; and so the comedians would take good care to send their plays to Madrid, and could then act them in safety. The writers, too, would take more pains with their work, out of fear of the rigorous examination they would have to pass at the hands of someone knowing the business. In this way good plays would be produced, and the purpose of such entertainment successfully achieved: which is not only popular amusement, but also the good reputation of Span-

ish genius, the profit and security of the actors, and the avoidance
of the need to punish them. Now, if the same person or some other
were entrusted with the task of examining newly written books of
chivalry, no doubt some would be produced of the perfection your
worship requires, thus enriching our tongue with the charming and
precious treasure of eloquence, and causing the old books to be
eclipsed in the bright presence of the new. They would provide
honest amusement not only for the idle but for the busiest of men;
for it is impossible for the brow to be always bent, nor can our frail
human nature sustain itself without some lawful recreation.'

When the canon and the priest had reached this point in their
conversation the barber rode forward, caught them up, and said to
the priest:

'Here, Master Priest, is the place I told you of. We can take our
siesta here, and the oxen will find plenty of fresh pasture.'

'It looks good to me,' replied the priest, and told their intentions
to the canon, who was attracted by the sight of the lovely valley
before them and decided to stay with them. And so as to enjoy the
scene and the conversation of the priest, for whom he had taken a
liking, and to hear Don Quixote's adventures in greater detail, he
ordered some of his servants to go to the inn, which was not far
away, and bring enough for them all to eat, as he had decided to rest
there that afternoon. One of his servants replied, however, that the
baggage-mule, which must be at the inn already, carried sufficient
provisions, and that they would need nothing from there but barley.

'If that is so,' said the canon, 'take all our mounts there and bring
the baggage-mule back.'

While this was going on Sancho saw an opportunity of talking
to his master without the continual presence of the priest and the
barber, whom he regarded with suspicion. So he went up to the
cage, and said:

'Sir, I want to relieve my conscience, and tell you something
about your enchantment; and that is, that those two with their faces
covered are our village priest and the barber. I think they've played
this trick of carrying you off like this because they're envious of
your worship for beating them in doing famous deeds. Supposing,
then, that I'm right. It follows that you're not under a spell, but
humbugged and fooled. Now, to prove it to you, I want to ask you

one question, and if you answer me as I think you will, you'll put
your finger on this trick and see that you're not enchanted, but
have had your wits turned upside down.'

'Ask what you like, Sancho my son,' replied Don Quixote, 'and
I will satisfy you and answer you to your heart's content. But as to
your saying that the men accompanying us are the priest and the
barber, our friends and fellow-villagers, it may well be that they
look the same, but you must not believe for a minute that they really
and truly are so. What you must believe and understand is that if
they are like them, as you say, it must be because my enchanters
have taken on their likeness and semblance, for it is easy for magicians to take on any appearance they please. And they will have
assumed the likeness of our friends to give you cause to think as you
do, and to put you into a maze of conjectures, from which not even
the clue of Theseus could extricate you. Their intention will also be
to confuse my brain and make me incapable of guessing the cause
of this disaster. For if you tell me, on the one hand, that our village
priest and barber are travelling here beside me, and if, on the other,
I find myself caged and know that only superhuman power could
encage me – for no human strength would be sufficient – what
would you have me say or think, except that the manner of my enchantment is stranger than any I have read of in any history that
treats of the enchantment of knights errant? So do not be disturbed
by supposing that they are whom you say, but rest assured that they
are no more the priest and the barber than I am a Turk. But as for
these questions you wish to ask me, speak, for I will answer you,
even though you go on asking till to-morrow.'

'Holy Mother!' replied Sancho, raising his voice. 'Can you possibly be so thick-skulled and brain-sick, your worship, that you
can't see it's the sober truth I'm telling you, and that there's
more roguery than enchantment about this unfortunate confinement
of yours? Anyhow, I'll clearly prove it to you that you're not enchanted. Now, tell me, as God shall deliver you out of this trouble,
and as you would find yourself in the arms of my lady Dulcinea
when least you expect it –'

'Stop your hocus-pocus,' cried Don Quixote, 'and ask what you
will. I have promised already to reply faithfully.'

'That's what I want,' said Sancho; 'for you to tell me the *whole* truth, without additions or subtractions, as those, like your worship, who make a profession of arms under the title of knights errant are expected to do.'

'I tell you that I will not lie on any matter,' replied Don Quixote. 'Get on with your questions; for really, Sancho, you weary me with all your oaths, your supplications and preambles.'

'Well,' said Sancho, 'I'm confident that my master's a good man and truthful. And so, I'll ask you one question that's very much to the point. Speaking with all respect, your worship, since you've been cooped up and enchanted, as you think, in this cage, have you been taken with any desire or inclination to make either big or little waters, as the saying is?'

'I do not understand what you mean by making waters, Sancho. Be more explicit, if you want me to answer you fully.'

'Is it possible that your worship doesn't understand what making big or little waters is? Why, boys learn that when they go to school. But what I mean is, have you had no mind to do what nobody can do for you?'

'Oh, I understand you now, Sancho. Yes, very often. In fact I want to at this moment. Get me out of my plight, for things are none too clean.'

Chapter XLIX. *Of the shrewd Conversation between Sancho Panza and his master Don Quixote.*

'AH,' said Sancho, 'now I've caught you. I was longing to know that with all my heart and soul. Come now, sir, can you dispute the saying that's in everyone's mouth when some one's in a bad way: "I don't know what's the matter with so and so. He doesn't eat or drink or sleep, or answer straight when you ask him a question; it really looks as if he's bewitched." – From which you may gather that people who don't eat or drink or sleep or perform the natural functions I mentioned are enchanted; but if they have the desire your worship has, and drink when it's given them, and eat when they have something to eat, and answer all the questions they are asked, then they are certainly not bewitched.'

'You are right, Sancho,' replied Don Quixote; 'but I have told you already that there are many kinds of enchantments; and time may have changed the fashion from one kind to another. It may be usual now for people under a spell to do all that I do, although they did not before; so that there is no arguing or drawing conclusions against the customs of the times. I most certainly know that I am enchanted, and that is sufficient to ease my conscience, which would be greatly burdened if I thought that I was not under a spell, and yet remained in this cage like an idler and a coward, defrauding the many distressed and needy of the succour I could give them. For there must be many at this hour in positive and urgent need of my help and protection.'

'But for all that,' replied Sancho, 'for your greater security and satisfaction, it would be well, I think, if your worship were to try to get out of your prison. I promise to help you with all my power, and even to release you. Then you could try to mount once again on your good Rocinante, who seems to be enchanted as well, he's so melancholy and sad. And when you've done that, we can try our luck and look for more adventures. If we don't succeed there'll still be time to come back to the cage. And I promise you, on the faith of a true and loyal squire, I'll shut myself up alongside your worship, if you should chance to prove so unlucky or I so stupid as not to bring off this plan of mine.'

'I am content to do as you say, brother Sancho,' replied Don Quixote, 'and when you see an opportunity of managing my deliverance, I will obey you absolutely. But you will see, Sancho, how mistaken you are in your opinion about my misfortune.'

Our errant knight and ill-errant squire entertained themselves with this conversation until they reached the place where the priest, the canon and the barber had dismounted and were awaiting them. The carter then unyoked his oxen from the cart and turned them loose in that green and pleasant place, whose freshness invited not only enchanted persons like Don Quixote, but also such a rational and sensible creature as his squire. Sancho begged the priest to let his master out of his cage for a while, for otherwise his prison would not be as clean as decency required the accommodation of such a knight as his master to be. The priest understood him, and said that he would gladly oblige him, if it were not for his fear that once Don Quixote found himself at liberty he would play them one of his tricks, and go off and never be seen again.

'I'll go bail for his not running away,' replied Sancho.

'And I, for any sum,' said the canon, 'particularly if he gives me his word as a knight not to leave us without our consent.'

'I give it,' answered Don Quixote, who was listening all the time, 'the more so because anyone enchanted, as I am, is not at liberty to dispose of his person as he will. For his enchanter can make him powerless to stir from one spot for three centuries; and if he were to escape he would be brought back flying through the air.' Since this was the case, he said, they could certainly release him, especially as it would be to everyone's advantage: in fact, if they did not let him out, he protested, he could not refrain from offending their noses, unless they were to retire to some distance.

The canon took him by one of his hands, although they were tied, and on his pledged word, they let him out of his cage, at which he was vastly delighted. The first thing he did was to stretch his whole body, and then he went over to Rocinante and gave him two slaps on the haunches, saying: 'I still trust in God and his blessed Mother, flower and mirror of steeds, that we two shall soon find ourselves in the state our hearts desire: you with your master on your back, and I on top of you, exercising the function for which God sent me into the world.'

After saying this Don Quixote went aside with Sancho Panza to a distant spot, from which he returned much relieved, and still more eager to put his squire's plan into execution.

The canon gazed at him, and wondered at the strangeness of his crazy humour and at the excellent sense he displayed in his conversation and in his answers, only losing his stirrups, as we have said before, on the subject of chivalry. And so, once they were all seated on the green grass waiting for the provisions, the canon was moved by compassion to ask him:

'Can the idle and unsavoury reading of books of chivalry, my good sir, possibly have had such an effect on you as so to turn your brain that you have come to believe that you are under a spell, and other things of that kind, which are as far from being so as falsehood itself is from the truth? How is it possible for human reason to persuade itself of the existence of all those countless Amadises, of that multitude of famous knights, and of so many Emperors of Trebizond? Who could really believe in Felixmarte of Hyrcania, and all those palfreys, all those wandering damsels, all those serpents, all those dragons, all those giants, all those extraordinary adventures, all those varieties of spells, all those battles, all those desperate encounters, all that fine raiment, all those love-lorn princesses, all those squires who became counts, all those facetious dwarfs, all those love letters, all that wooing, all those courageous ladies and, in fact, all those monstrous absurdities contained in books of chivalry? For myself I can say that they give me a certain pleasure when I read them – so long as I do not deliberately reflect that they are all triviality and lies. But when I consider what they are I throw the very best of them against the wall, and I would pitch them into the fire if I had one near at hand. For such a punishment they certainly deserve for being liars and impostors, beyond the realms of common sense, as founders of new sects and new ways of life, and for causing the ignorant crowd to accept all the nonsense they contain as gospel truth. They have even the audacity to confuse the minds of intelligent and well-born gentlemen, as is clear from their effect on your worship, whom they have reduced to the state of being shut in a cage and carried on an ox-cart, as they transport a lion or a tiger from town to town to exhibit it for money. Come, Don Quixote, take pity on yourself; return into the bosom of discretion, and learn to use the generous talents that Heaven has blessed you with, by applying your mind to some other course of study which may redound to the profit of your soul and to the increasing of your honour. But if your natural inclination is so strong that you must read books of adventures and chivalry, read the Book of Judges in Holy Scripture, where you will find grand and authentic exploits, which are both heroic and true. Portugal had its Viriatus, Rome had its Caesar, Carthage its Hannibal, Greece its Alexander, Castile its Count Ferdinand Gonzalez, Valencia its Cid, Andalusia its Gonzalo Fernandez, Estremadura its Diego Garcia de Paredes, Jerez its Garci Perez de Vargas, Toledo its Garcilaso, Seville its Don Manuel de Leon; and their valorous exploits will entertain, instruct, delight, and surprise the highest intelligence that reads them. They are certainly a study worthy of your excellent mind, my dear Don Quixote, and you will rise from reading of them learned in history, enamoured of virtue, instructed in goodness, improved in manners, valiant but not rash, bold and no coward; and all this to the honour of God, your own profit, and the glory of La Mancha, whence, as I have learnt, you derive your birth and origin.'

Don Quixote listened most attentively to the canon's arguments, gazed at him for some time when he saw that he had finished, and said: 'Sir, your discourse was intended, I think, to persuade me that there have never been knights errant in the world, that all books of chivalry are false, lying, hurtful, and unprofitable to the commonwealth, and that I have done wrong to read them, and worse to believe in them, and worst of all to imitate them in setting myself to follow the very hard profession of knight errantry they teach. And, what is more, you deny the existence of either Amadis of Gaul or of Greece, and of all those other knights of whom the writings are full.'

'I meant precisely what you say,' answered the canon at this. To which Don Quixote replied:

'You were pleased to add also that such books have done me much harm, that they have turned my brain, and caused my present imprisonment, and that it would be better for me to make some amendment, and change my reading to other books more truthful, enjoyable and instructive.'

'Just so,' answered the canon.

'Why then, in my opinion it is you,' replied Don Quixote, 'that are deranged and enchanted, for daring to blaspheme against an institution so universally acknowledged and so authenticated, that anyone denying it, as you do, deserves the very punishment you say that you inflict on certain books when you have read them and they displease you. For to attempt to convince anyone that there were no such persons as Amadis and the other knights errant of whom so many records remain, would be like trying to persuade him that the sun does not shine, nor the frost chill, nor earth yield sustenance. For what intellect could there be in the world capable of persuading another that the story of Princess Floripes and Guy of Burgundy was not true? Or the adventure of Fierabras at the Bridge of Mantible, which took place in the time of Charlemagne, and which, I swear, is as true as that it is now daylight? And if that is a lie, then it must follow that there existed no Hector, nor Achilles, nor Trojan War, nor Twelve Peers of France, nor King Arthur of England, who is still wandering about the world to this day transformed into a raven, and is hourly awaited in his kingdom. Yes, they will even say, no doubt, that the history of Guarino Mezquino is false, and the Quest of the Holy Grail as well, and that the loves of Sir Tristan and Queen Iseult, and of Guenevere and Lancelot are apocryphal, although there are persons who almost remember having seen the Lady Quintañona. She was the best wine-server Great Britain ever had, and her existence is so authentic that I remember my grandmother on my father's side saying, when she saw an old lady with a stately head-dress: "My boy, that woman is very like the Lady Quintañona." From which I conclude that she must herself have known her, or must have seen some portrait of her, at least. Then who can deny the truth of the story of Peter and the fair Magalona, since even to this day you can see in the King's armoury the peg with which the brave Peter guided the wooden horse on which he used to ride through the air, and which is a little bigger than the pole of a coach? And near this peg is Babieca's saddle, and at Roncesvalles is Roland's horn, which is the size of a great beam; from which it can be inferred that the Twelve Peers existed, and the Peters, and the Cids and other such knights, of the sort commonly termed adventurers. If that is denied I shall be told it is not true that the brave Lusitanian Juan de Merlo was a knight errant, who went to Burgundy and fought in the city of Arras with the famous Lord of Charny, called Monseigneur Pierre, and after that with Monseigneur Henri de Remestan in the city of Basle, coming off from both exploits victorious and crowned with honour and glory. They will also deny the adventures and challenges also performed in Burgundy by the valiant Spaniards, Pedro Barba and Gutierre Quixada – from whose stock I am descended in the direct male line – when they beat the sons of the Count St. Pol. Nor will they agree that Don Ferdinand de Guevara went to Germany in quest of adventure, and fought there with Messire George, a knight of the Duke of Austria's house. They will say, too, that the jousts of Suero de Quiñones of the Honourable Pass were a fable, and the exploits of Sir Luis de Falces against the Castilian knight Don Gonzalo de Guzman, and all the many deeds performed by Christian knights of these and foreign realms, so authentic and true, I repeat, that anyone denying them must be devoid of all reason and right understanding.'

The canon was amazed to hear Don Quixote so mingling truth and fiction, and at the knowledge he displayed of everything in any way concerning the exploits of his knight errantry. And so he replied: 'I cannot deny, sir, that some of what you say is true, especially what you say of the Spanish knights errant; and I would admit also the existence of the Twelve Peers of France, though I cannot believe that they performed all those deeds that Archbishop Turpin attributes to them. For the truth of it is that they were knights chosen by the Kings of France, and were called peers as being all equal in worth, in rank and in valour; or at least, if they were not, they should have been. They were an order like the present-day order of Santiago, or of Calatrava, whose professing knights are presumed to be, or should be, worthy, valiant and well born; and as we now speak of a Knight of St. John or of Alcantara, so they used to speak in those days of a Knight of the Twelve Peers, because they were twelve equals, chosen to be members of that military order. As for the Cid, there is no doubt about him, and even less about Bernardo del Carpio; but that they performed the deeds attributed to them is a very doubtful matter. As for that other matter you speak of, Count Pierre's peg and its standing near Babieca's saddle in the King's armoury, I must confess that I am so ignorant or so short-sighted that, although I have seen the saddle, I have never noticed the peg, big as you say it is.'

'Yet it is there without a doubt,' replied Don Quixote, 'and what is more, they say that it is kept in an ox-hide sheath, to save it from rusting.'

'That may well be so,' replied the canon, 'but I swear by my holy orders I do not remember having seen it. Though, supposing I grant that it is there, that is no reason for my having to believe the stories of all these Amadises, or of all that multitude of knights we are told about. Nor is it reasonable for a man like yourself, possessed of your understanding, your reputation and your talents, to accept all the extravagant absurdities in these ridiculous books of chivalry as really true.'

Chapter L. *Of the learned Arguments between Don Quixote and the canon, and other matters.*

'THAT is a good joke!' replied Don Quixote. 'Books which are printed by royal licence and with the approval of those to whom they are submitted, and which are read with universal delight and applause by great and small, poor and rich, learned and ignorant, plebeians and gentlefolk – in short, by all kinds of persons of every quality and condition – could they be lies and at the same time appear so much like the truth? For do they not specify the father, the mother, the family, the time, the place, and the actions, detail by detail and day by day, of this or that knight? Be silent, sir, do not speak such blasphemies; and, believe me, if you take my advice you will be acting like a man of sense. Only read these books, and you will see what pleasure you get from them. For, tell me, could there be anything more delightful than to see displayed here and now before our eyes, as we might say, a great lake of pitch, boiling hot, and swimming and writhing about in it a great number of serpents, snakes and lizards, and many other sorts of savage and frightful creatures; and then to hear issuing from the middle of that lake a most dismal voice crying: "You, Knight, whoever you may be, that gaze on this dreadful lake, if you would reach the treasure hidden beneath these black waters, show the valour of your dauntless heart and plunge into the middle of its dark, burning liquor; for if you do not do so, you will not be worthy to see the mighty marvels hidden within the seven castles of the seven witches who dwell beneath this gloomy water." No sooner has the knight heard this dreadful voice than he abandons all thought for himself, and without reflecting on the peril to which he is exposing himself, or even easing himself of the weight of his ponderous armour, he commends himself to God and his lady, dives into the middle of the boiling lake; and then unexpectedly, and when he least knows where he is going, he finds himself amidst flowery meadows, incomparably finer even than the Elysian fields. There the sky seems to him more transparent and the sun to shine with a new brightness. Before his eyes opens a pleasant grove of green and leafy trees whose verdure charms his vision, while his ears are ravished by the sweet, untaught song of innumerable little bright-coloured birds which flit about the interlacing

branches. Here he discovers a small stream, whose fresh waters glide
like liquid crystal over delicate sand and little white stones, which
resemble sifted gold and purest pearl. There he spies a fountain
made of mottled jasper and smooth marble; here another, roughly
fashioned, where tiny mussel shells, mingled with the twisted yellow
and white houses of the snails, lying in disordered order among
pieces of glittering crystal and counterfeit emeralds, form so gracefully varied a composition that art, the imitator of nature, seems
here to surpass herself. Then suddenly there appears in the distance
a strong castle or handsome palace with walls of solid gold, with
turrets of diamonds, and gates of jacinth; so admirably built, in
fact, that though the materials of which it is constructed are nothing
less than diamonds, carbuncles, rubies, pearls, gold and emeralds,
the workmanship is still more precious. And after this, could there
be a finer sight than a lovely troop of maidens coming out of the
castle in such gay and gorgeous attire that, if I were to set out now
to describe them as the stories do, I should never end? And then for
the one who seems the chief of them all to take the bold knight who
plunged into the burning lake by the hand, and silently lead him
into the rich palace or castle, and strip him as naked as his mother
bore him, and bathe him in warm water, and then anoint him all
over with sweet-smelling ointments, and put on him a shirt of finest
samite, all fragrant and perfumed? Then for another maiden to
come and throw over his shoulder a mantle, reputed to be worth a
city, at the very least, or perhaps more? What finer sight, then, than
after all that, to see them take him to another room where the tables
are laid so magnificently that he is speechless with amazement? And
to watch him sprinkle on his hands water all distilled of ambergris
and sweet-smelling flowers? And to see him seated on an ivory
chair? And to see all the maidens serve him, still preserving their
miraculous silence? And bring him such variety of dishes, so deliciously cooked that the appetite is at a loss to know where to direct
the hand? How pleasant it must be to hear the music which sounds
all the while, without his knowing who is singing or whence it
comes? And when the feast is over and the tables are cleared, for the
knight to stay reclining on his chair, perhaps picking his teeth as his
custom is, when suddenly there enters through the door of the hall
another maiden more lovely than any of the first, who sits down be-

side him and begins to tell him what manner of castle it is, and how she lives there under a spell, and other things which surprise the knight and astonish the readers of his story.

'I will enlarge on this no further, for you can gather from what I have said that any passage from any story of knight errantry is bound to delight and amaze a reader. Believe me, sir, I repeat, and read these books. You will see how they drive away the melancholy, and improve your temper if it happens to be bad. I can say of myself that since I became a knight errant I have been valiant, courteous, liberal, well-bred, generous, polite, bold, gentle and patient, and an endurer of toils, imprisonments and enchantments. And although for the last little while I have been imprisoned in a cage like a mad-man, I expect by the valour of my arm, if Heaven favours me and fate is not against me, to find myself in a few days king of some kingdom, in which I can display the gratitude and liberality en-closed in this bosom of mine. For, by my faith, sir, a poor man is incapacitated from showing the virtue of liberality towards anyone, even though he may possess it in the highest degree; and gratitude which consists only of desire is a dead thing, as faith is dead without works. For that reason I could wish that fortune would speedily offer me an opportunity of making myself Emperor, so that I might show my will to do good to my friends, especially to this poor Sancho Panza, my squire, who is the best man in the world; and I should like to give him the countship which I promised him a long while ago, were it not that I am afraid he will not have the capacity to govern his estate.'

At this Sancho, who had overheard these last words of his mas-ter's, exclaimed: 'Set to work, Don Quixote. Get me that countship you've promised me so often and I've waited for so long. I've no lack of capacity to govern, I assure you; and if I had, I've heard of men who take noblemen's estates in farm, giving them so much a year and looking after the management. Then the lord lies with his feet up, enjoying the rent they pay him without a care in the world; and that's what I'll do. I won't haggle over a few pence more or less. I'll give it all up at once, and enjoy my income like a duke. Then let the world go hang.'

'That, brother Sancho,' said the canon, 'applies to the enjoyment of the revenues. But there is the administration of justice, which the lord of the estate must attend to. That is where capacity and a sound judgement come in and, above all, an honest intention to do right; for if that is lacking in the beginning, everything will go wrong in the middle and the end, and Heaven usually assists the good intentions of the simple, and confounds the evil designs of the crafty.'

'I don't understand these philosophies,' replied Sancho Panza. 'I only wish I were as sure of the countship as of my ability to govern. For I've as large a soul as the next man, and as stout a body as the best of them, and I'd be as good a king of my estate as any other King; and being so, I should do as I liked; and doing as I liked, I should take my pleasure; and taking my pleasure, I should be contented; and when one's content, there's nothing more to desire; and when there's nothing more to desire, there's an end of it. So for Heaven's sake let me have the estate, and then we'll see, as one blind man said to the other.'

'These are not bad philosophies, as you say, Sancho,' put in the canon; 'but all the same there is a great deal to be said on this subject of countships.'

But Don Quixote answered his squire: 'I do not know what more there is to say. I am guided solely by the example of the great Amadis of Gaul, who made his squire Count of the Firm Isle. So I need have no scruple of conscience in making Sancho Panza a count, for he is one of the best squires that ever served knight errant.'

The canon was astonished at this well-reasoned nonsense of Don Quixote's, at his description of the adventure of the Knight of the Lake, and at the impression made on him by the deliberate lies in the books he had read. And he marvelled, too, at Sancho's foolishness in so ardently desiring the countship his master had promised him.

By this time the canon's servants, who had gone to the inn for the baggage-mule, had returned. So, making a carpet and the green meadow-grass their table, they sat down in the shade of some trees and took their meal there, so that the carter could profit from the pasture there, as has already been said. Now, whilst they were eating they suddenly heard a considerable noise and the sound of a little bell from some brambles and thick bushes which grew close by; and at the same moment they saw a fine she-goat speckled with black, white and grey, run out of the thicket. After her came a goatherd calling to her in the language they use when they want their beasts to stop and come back to the fold. But the truant goat ran up to the company, scared and trembling, as if for their protection, and there stayed still till the goatherd arrived and, catching her by the horns, addressed her, as if she were capable of speech and reason:

'Oh, wild one, wild one! Speckle, Speckle, how you've gone limping about these days! What wolves have scared you, little one? Won't you tell me what it is, pretty one? But it can only be that you're a woman and can't stay still! The Devil take your moods, and the moods of all like you. Come back, come back, friend! You'll be safer in your fold, or with your companions, even if you're not so happy. For if you, who should guide them and lead them, go unguided and astray, what will become of them?'

The goatherd's words amused his hearers, especially the canon, who said to him: 'Come, come, do not be angry, brother, I beg you, and do not be in such a hurry to drive this goat back to her fold. For since she is a female, as you say, she must follow her natural instinct, despite all your pains to stop her. Take a snack and drink a drop with us; it will soothe you and the goat can rest a while.'

As he said this he handed him the hindquarter of a cold rabbit on the point of a knife. The goatherd took it and thanked him. Then when he had drunk and rested, he said: 'I shouldn't like your worships to take me for a simpleton for talking to this animal so sensibly; for in truth my words are not without some meaning. I'm a peasant, but not so much of one that I don't understand how to converse with men and beasts.'

'I can very well believe that,' answered the priest, 'for I already know by experience that the mountains breed scholars, and sheepcotes contain philosophers.'

'At least, sir,' said the goatherd, 'they house men who have learnt by experience. And to convince you of that, and to give you an example, too – though, being uninvited, I may seem to be obtruding myself – if it doesn't bore you, gentlemen, and you will lend me your attention for a little, I'll tell you a true tale which will confirm that gentleman's words' – pointing to the priest – 'and mine.'

To which Don Quixote answered: 'Seeing that this matter has a

slight tinge of knightly adventure about it, I will listen to you, for
my part, brother; and so will all these gentlemen, who are men of
good sense and fond of the curious, the entertaining and the marvellous, all of which, I have no doubt, your story contains. Begin,
then, friend, and we will all listen.'

'Count me out,' said Sancho. 'I am off to the stream with this pie,
and I'm going to fill myself with enough for three days. For I have
heard my master, Don Quixote, say that a knight errant's squire
must eat his fill when he gets the chance, since they may lose their
way for six days together in some wood that's so thick they can't
find a way out; and if a man doesn't go in with a full belly or a well-
stored haversack, he may very well stay there, as very often he does,
till he is turned into mummy flesh.'

'You are quite right, Sancho,' said Don Quixote. 'Go where you
like and eat what you can; but I am satisfied already. All I need is
refreshment for my mind, which I will now give it by listening to
this good man's story.'

'And so will we all,' said the canon.

But before beginning the promised tale, the goatherd gave the
goat, which he was holding by the horns, a couple of slaps on the
back, and said: 'Lie down beside me, Speckle, for we shall have time
enough to return to our fold.' The creature seemed to understand
him, for when her master sat down, she stretched herself calmly beside him and, looking up into his face, signified that she was listening, as he began the following story:

Chapter LI.   *What the Goatherd told Don Quixote's escort.*

'NINE miles from this valley is a town which, although small, is one
of the richest in all this district. In it there lived a farmer greatly
honoured, both for his native virtue and for the wealth he had acquired, though honour always goes with riches. But his greatest
fortune in his own eyes was the possession of a daughter of such
consummate beauty, rare good sense, charm and virtue, that everyone who knew her, or even set eyes on her, was amazed at the surpassing qualities with which Heaven and nature had endowed her.
As a child she was pretty, and she went on increasing in loveliness
until at the age of sixteen she was exceedingly beautiful. The fame

of her loveliness began to spread among all the near-by villages – but why do I say near-by villages? It reached to distant cities, and even entered the royal palace and came to the ears of many sorts of people, who would come to see her from all parts, as if she were a rare sight or a wonder-working image. Her father guarded her carefully, and she guarded herself; for there are no locks, bolts, or bars which keep a maiden better guarded than does her own modesty. The father's wealth and the daughter's beauty led many, both of their own town and strangers, to ask for her hand. But, having so rich a jewel to dispose of, he was much perplexed and unable to decide upon which of her infinite number of wooers to bestow her. Now, among the multitude who desired her I was one, and I derived very great hopes of success from her father's knowing me and because I was a native of their town, of pure blood, in the flower of my youth, rich in goods, and no less well endowed in mind. But a fellow-townsman with all the same qualifications was also her suitor; and this caused the father to put off his decision and keep things in the balance, for it seemed to him that either of us would be a good match for his daughter. To solve his difficulty, he decided to refer it to Leandra – for that is the name of the rich maid who has plunged me into such misery – thinking that, as we two were equal, it was best to leave it to his beloved daughter to choose according to her own liking, a course that should be imitated by all fathers with children to marry. I do not mean that they should leave them to make a choice among bad or evil persons, but that they should put the good before them, and let them choose among them according to their taste. I do not know what choice Leandra made; I only know that her father put us both off on the score of his daughter's youth, in general terms which neither bound him nor dismissed us. My rival's name is Anselmo, and mine Eugenio – for I would have you know the names of the persons involved in this tragedy, the end of which is still unresolved, though it is clear enough that it is bound to be disastrous.

'At this time there came to our town one Vicente de la Roca, the son of a poor local farmer, which Vicente had returned from Italy and other places where he had been soldiering. He had been carried off from our town as a lad of about twelve by a captain who happened to be passing through with his troop; and now, about twelve

years later, returned as a youth in a soldier's uniform, pranked out
in countless bright colours, and hung with innumerable glass trinkets and fine steel chains. One day he would put on one bit of
finery, the next another, but all of them flimsy, gaudy, weighing
little, and worth less. The country people, who are malicious
by nature – and when idleness gives them an occasion are malice
itself – noted and reckoned up each one of his bits of finery and
trinkets, and found that he had only three suits of different colours,
with stockings and garters to match. But he made so many transformations and variations with them that, if no one had counted
them, one would have sworn that he had shown off more than ten
suits of clothes and more than twenty plumes of feathers. Now, do
not presume that what I am telling you about his clothes is a digression or superfluous, for they play a principal part in my story.

'Now, he used to sit on a bench under a great poplar in our
market-place, and there he would keep us all open-mouthed, hanging on the exploits he described to us. There was no country in the
whole world he had not visited, and no battle he had not taken part
in. He had killed more Turks than there are in Morocco and Tunis,
and engaged in more single combats, according to his own story,
than Gante and Luna, Diego Garcia de Paredes, and a thousand
others whom he named, and from every one of them he had come
off victorious, without losing so much as a drop of blood. Then,
again, he would show us scars of wounds, and although we could
not make them out, he would persuade us that they came from
musket-shots received in various actions and skirmishes. What is
more, he would have the unparalleled effrontery to patronize his
equals, even those who knew him, and say that his right arm was
his father, his deeds his lineage, and that, as a soldier, he owed nothing even to the King himself. In addition to these pretensions he
was something of a musician and plucked the guitar to such effect
that some people said he could make it speak. But his accomplishments did not stop here, for he had also a talent for poetry, and
used to make up a ballad a mile and a half long on every trifling
thing that happened in the town.

'This soldier, then, whom I have just described, this Vicente de
la Roca, this braggart, this swaggerer, this musician, this poet, was
often seen and admired by Leandra from a window of her house

which looked on to the market-place. She was captivated by the bright tinsel of his clothes, enchanted by his ballads – for he would give away twenty copies of every one he composed – the exploits which he attributed to himself came to her ears and, in the end – for so the Devil must have decreed – she fell in love with him before the presumptuous idea of wooing her had come into his head. And as no love affair is more easily brought to fruition than one which is backed by the lady's desire, Leandra and Vicente came to an agreement without any difficulty; and before any one of her many suitors had realized her infatuation she had already satisfied it by running off from her dearly beloved father's house – she has no mother – and eloping from the village with the soldier, who came off from this enterprise more triumphantly than from all the many others he had laid claim to. This event filled the whole place with astonishment, and everyone else who heard of it, too. I was confounded, Anselmo thunderstruck, her father distressed, her relations ashamed, Justice aroused, and the troopers on the watch. They scoured the roads, searched the woods, and everywhere they could, and at the end of three days found the fickle Leandra in a mountain cave, clad only in her shift and without the store of money and the precious jewels which she had brought away with her. They took her back before her unhappy father and questioned her about her plight. And she confessed quite freely that Vicente de la Roca had deceived her, persuading her, under promise of marriage, to leave her father's house, and offering to take her to the richest and most delightful city in all the world – he meant Naples – and that she had been sufficiently ill-advised and deceived to believe him. For after robbing her father she had entrusted herself to him on the same night she had been missed, when he had taken her to a wild mountain and shut her in the cave where they had found her. She also affirmed that the soldier had not robbed her of her honour, though he had taken everything she had before going off and leaving her in the cave; a fact which astonished everyone afresh.

'It was difficult, sir, to believe in the youth's self-restraint, but she vouched for it with such persistence as partly to console her disconsolate father, who set no store by the valuables they had taken so long as his daughter was left in possession of that jewel which, once lost, is beyond all hope of recovery. The very same day that

Leandra appeared her father removed her again from our sight, taking her and shutting her up in a nunnery at a town not far from here, in the hope that time would work off some part of the disgrace she had brought upon herself. Leandra's youth served as some excuse for her wickedness, at least for such as had nothing to gain from proving her good or bad; but those who knew her intelligence and considerable shrewdness attributed her fault not to ignorance, but to frivolity and the failings natural to woman-kind, who are generally ill-balanced and unsteady.

'With Leandra put away, Anselmo's eyes became blind, or at least there was no sight that gave him any pleasure, and my own were in darkness, without a light to guide them towards joy. In Leandra's absence our sorrow increased, our patience diminished, and we cursed the soldier's finery and railed at her father's lack of precaution. In the end he and I agreed to leave the village and come to this valley, where we spend our lives among the trees, he grazing a large flock of his own sheep, and I a large herd of goats, also my own. Here we give vent to our passion, either singing together in praise or dispraise of the lovely Leandra, or sighing separately and alone, and confiding our complaints to Heaven. Many others of Leandra's suitors have followed our example, and come to these wild mountains to follow the same employment; so many that this place seems to have become the pastoral Arcadia, for it is so crammed with shepherds and sheep-folds that there is not a corner in it where you will not hear the fair Leandra's name. One man curses her and calls her fickle, inconstant and immodest; another denounces her as forward and light; yet another absolves and pardons her; one more tries her and condemns her; one celebrates her beauty; another execrates her character; in fact, all disparage her and all adore her; and the madness extends so far that some complain of her disdain without ever having spoken to her, and some bewail their fate and suffer the maddening disease of jealousy, for which she never gave anyone any cause. For, as I have said, her fault was discovered before her infatuation was known. There is not a hollow rock, nor river bank, nor shade of a tree, that is not occupied by some shepherd or other recounting his misfortunes to the winds; and echo repeats Leandra's name wherever it can sound; the hills ring with Leandra, the streams murmur Leandra, and Leandra

P

keeps us all distracted and enchanted, hoping against hope, and fearing without knowing what we fear.

'Among all these distracted men, the one who shows the least but has the most sense is my rival Anselmo who, having so many other things he might complain of, complains only of her absence, and sings his lament in verses which show his excellent talents, to the sound of a fiddle, which he plays admirably. I follow an easier and, in my opinion, a wiser path, which is to curse the fickleness of women, their inconstancy, their double-dealing, their unkept promises, their broken faith and, last of all, the lack of judgement they show in their choice of objects for their desires and affections.

'And that was the reason, gentlemen, for the words I addressed to this goat on my arrival here; for as a female I despise her, although she is the best of all my flock. This is the story I promised to tell you. If I have been tedious in my tale I will make amends. Near here is my cottage, where I have fresh milk and most delicious cheese, and various fruits now in season, no less pleasant to the sight than to the taste.'

Chapter LII. *Of the Quarrel between Don Quixote and the Goatherd, with the rare Adventure of the Penitents, which he successfully achieved by the sweat of his brow.*

THE goatherd's tale much delighted all who heard it, especially the canon, who was particularly interested in the manner of its telling, which made the narrator appear more like a polished courtier than a rustic goatherd. In fact he remarked that the priest was right when he said that the mountains bred scholars. The whole company complimented Eugenio, but Don Quixote showed himself the most liberal of all in this respect, and said:

'I promise you, brother goatherd, that were I in the position to be able to embark on any adventure, I would immediately set about bringing yours to a happy conclusion. I would deliver Leandra from the nunnery, where there can be no doubt she is kept against her will, in despite of the abbess and all who might oppose me. Then I should place her in your hands, to be dealt with according to your will and pleasure – observing, however, the laws of chivalry, which command that no violence be done to a damsel. Yet

I trust in our Lord God that one malicious enchanter may not be so powerful that another better-intentioned enchanter may not prevail over him. And when that time comes I promise you my favour and aid, as I am bound to do by my profession, which is none other than to succour the weak and the distressed.'

The goatherd stared at him and, seeing Don Quixote so ragged and ill-favoured, asked the barber in astonishment who his neighbour was: 'Sir, who is that man who looks so strange and talks so oddly?'

'Why, who should it be,' answered the barber, 'but the famous Don Quixote de la Mancha, the redresser of injuries, the righter of wrongs, the protector of damsels, the terror of giants, and the victor of battles?'

'That sounds to me like the stuff in books about knights-errant,' observed the goatherd. 'They did all these things you say this fellow does, though I take it that either your worship is joking, or the gentlemen must have some of the rooms in his brain vacant.'

'You are a very great rascal,' cried Don Quixote at this point, 'and it is you that is vacant and deficient. For I am a good deal fuller than ever that whore's daughter, the whore that bore you, was.'

As he spoke, he took up a loaf which lay beside him and hit the goatherd full in the face with it, with such force that he flattened his nose. But the goatherd did not see the joke and, finding himself thus damaged in good earnest, took no account of the carpet or the table-cloth or the diners round it, but jumped upon Don Quixote and, grasping him round the neck with both hands, would no doubt have choked him if Sancho Panza had not come up at this point. Seizing him by the shoulders, the squire threw him on to the tablecloth, breaking the plates, smashing the cups, and upsetting and scattering everything on it. Then Don Quixote, finding himself free, rushed to get on top of the goatherd who, with his face covered in blood from Sancho's kicks, was feeling about on all fours for a knife off the cloth to take some bloody vengeance. But this the canon and the priest prevented. However, with some help from the barber, the goatherd managed to get Don Quixote down, and rained such a shower of blows on him that the knight's face poured blood as freely as his. The canon and the priest were bursting with laughter; the troopers danced for joy, and everyone cheered them on, as men do at a dog-fight. Only Sancho Panza was in despair, because he could not get himself loose from one of the canon's servants, who was preventing him from helping his master. In the end when everyone was enjoying the sport except the two combatants, who were worrying one another, they heard the call of a trumpet, so mournful that they turned their faces in the direction from which it seemed to come. But the person was who most excited at the sound was Don Quixote who, although much against his will, lay underneath the goatherd, pretty well bruised and battered.

'Brother Demon,' he cried to his enemy; 'for it is impossible that you can be anything else, since you have the valour and strength to subdue mine – I pray you, let us call a truce, for just one hour. For the dolorous sound of that trumpet which reaches our ears seems to call me to some new adventure.'

The goatherd, who was now tired of pummelling and being pummelled, let him go at once; and Don Quixote stood up, turning his face too in the direction of the sound, and suddenly saw a number of men dressed in white after the fashion of penitents, descending a little hill.

The fact was that in that year the clouds had denied the earth their moisture, and in all the villages of that district they were making processions, rogations and penances, to pray God to vouchsafe His mercy and send them rain. And to this end the people of a village close by were coming in procession to a holy shrine which stood on a hill beside this valley. At the sight of the strange dress of these penitents Don Quixote failed to call to mind the many times he must have seen the like before, but imagined that this was material of adventure, and that it concerned him alone, as a knight errant, to engage in it. And he was confirmed in this idea by mistaking an image they were carrying, swathed in mourning, for some noble lady whom these villainous and unmannerly scoundrels were forcibly abducting. Now, scarcely had this thought come into his head, than he ran very quickly up to Rocinante, who was grazing nearby and, taking off the bridle and shield which hung by the pommel, he had him bitted in a second. Then, calling to Sancho for his sword, he mounted and, bracing on his shield, cried in a loud voice to everyone present:

'Now, valiant company, you will see how important it is to have knights in the world, who profess the order of knight errantry. Now, I say, you will see, by the freeing of this good lady who is being borne off captive, what value should be set on knights errant.'

As he spoke, he dug his heels into Rocinante, for he had no spurs, and at a canter — for we do not hear in all this authentic history that Rocinante ever went at a full gallop — rode to meet the penitents, although the priest, the canon, and the barber tried to stop him. But they could not do so, nor could even Sancho keep him back by calling:

'Where are you going, Don Quixote? What demons have you in your heart that incite you to assault our Catholic faith? Devil take me! Look, it's a procession of penitents, and that lady they're carrying upon the bier is the most blessed image of the spotless Virgin. Look out, sir, what you're doing, for this time you've made a real mistake.'

Sancho laboured in vain, for his master was so set on reaching the sheeted figures and freeing the lady in black, that he did not hear a word; and, if he had heard, he would not have turned back, even at the King's command. Coming up, then, to the procession, he halted Rocinante, who already wanted a little rest, and cried out in a hoarse and angry voice:

'You who, perhaps because you are evil, keep your faces covered, stop and listen to what I am going to say to you.'

The first to stop were the men carrying the image, and one of the four priests who were chanting the litanies, observing Don Quixote's strange appearance, Rocinante's leanness, and other ludicrous details which he noted in our knight, answered him by saying:

'Worthy brother, if you wish to say anything to us, say it quickly, for these brethren of ours are lashing their flesh, and we cannot possibly stop to hear anything, unless it is so brief that you can say it in two words.'

'I will say it in one,' replied Don Quixote, 'and it is this: Now, this very moment, you must set this beautiful lady free, for her mournful appearance and tears clearly show that you are carrying her off against her will, and that you have done her some notable wrong. I, who was born into the world to redress such injuries, will not consent to your advancing one step farther unless you give her the liberty she desires and deserves.'

At this speech all his hearers concluded that Don Quixote must be some madman, and began to laugh most heartily. Their laughter was like gunpowder thrown on to Don Quixote's anger. For, without another word, he drew his sword and attacked the litter. Then one of the bearers left the burden to his companions, and came out to meet the knight, brandishing a forked stick or pole, which they used to prop the litter up while they rested. And though Don Quixote dealt it a heavy sword stroke, which cut it in three, with the remaining third which remained in his hand he dealt the poor knight such a blow on the shoulder of his sword arm that his shield was powerless to protect him against the peasant's attack, and down he came to the ground in a sad state. Now when Sancho Panza, who came panting at his heels, saw him down, he called out to his assailant not to strike another blow, for his master was a knight under a spell and had done no harm to anyone in all the days of his life. But what stopped the countryman, however, was not Sancho's shouts, but his seeing that Don Quixote stirred neither hand nor foot; and so, in the belief that he had killed him, he hastily tucked up his robe into his belt and started to run across the country like a deer.

By this time all Don Quixote's company had reached the place where he lay; but when the men in the procession saw them come running up, and with them the troopers with their cross-bows, they were afraid of some mischief and made a ring round the image. Then raising their hoods and grasping their scourges, while the priests wielded their candlesticks, they awaited the assault, determined to defend themselves and even, if they could, to attack their assailants. But by good luck things turned out better than they expected, for all that Sancho did was to throw himself upon his master's body and break into the most doleful and ridiculous lament in all the world, in the belief that he was dead. Our priest was recognized by another in the procession; and this recognition calmed the apprehensions of both parties. The first priest gave the second a brief account of Don Quixote. Then he and the whole crowd of penitents went to see if the poor knight was dead, and heard Sancho Panza proclaim with tears in his eyes:

'O flower of chivalry, whose well-spent life one single blow of a stick has cut short! O glory of your race, honour and credit to all La Mancha, and to the whole world besides, which, now that you are here no longer, will be overrun by malefactors who will no longer fear chastisement for their iniquities! O liberal beyond all Alexanders, since for only eight months' service you have given me the best isle surrounded and encircled by the sea! O humble to the proud and arrogant to the humble, undertaker of perils, sufferer of affronts, enamoured without reason, imitator of the virtuous, scourge of the wicked, enemy of evildoers, in a word, knight errant, which is the highest that man can desire!'

Sancho's groans and lamentations brought Don Quixote back to consciousness, and the first words he uttered were: 'He who lives absent from you, sweetest Dulcinea, is subject to greater calamities than these. Help me, Sancho my friend, to get up upon the enchanted car, since I am not fit to burden Rocinante's saddle, for all this shoulder of mine is shattered.'

'I will, sir, with the greatest of pleasure,' replied Sancho. 'Let us return to our village with these gentlemen who wish you well, and there we'll plan another expedition, which may bring us more profit and fame.'

'You are right, Sancho,' replied Don Quixote. 'It will be highly prudent to wait till the malign influence of the stars, which now reigns, has passed over us.'

The canon, the priest and the barber commended him for this resolution, and when they had enjoyed Sancho Panza's simplicities to the full, they placed Don Quixote on the cart, as before. Then the procession formed up once more, and went on its way. The goatherd took his leave of the company, and when the troopers declined to go any farther, the priest paid them what he owed them. The canon then begged the priest to let him know what might happen to Don Quixote – whether he was cured of his madness or remained in it – and with this took his leave. Here in fact they all divided and went their several ways, there remaining only the priest and the barber, Don Quixote, Panza and the good Rocinante, who bore himself throughout all this experience as patiently as his master.

The waggoner yoked his oxen and settled Don Quixote on a truss of hay. Then he followed the priest's directions and took the road, travelling at his usual deliberate pace, till at the end of six days they reached Don Quixote's village. There they arrived at midday, and as it happened to be a Sunday all the people were in the market-place when Don Quixote's cart passed through. They all rushed to see what was in it and, when they recognized their fellow-townsman, they stood in amazement. Then a boy ran off to tell the knight's housekeeper and niece the news that their master and uncle had come back, lean and sallow, and lying on a pile of hay on an ox-wagon. It was pitiful to hear the cries that these two good ladies raised, the slaps they gave themselves, and the curses which they launched afresh against his accursed books of knight errantry; all of which were renewed when they saw the knight enter the house.

At the news of Don Quixote's arrival Sancho Panza's wife ran up, for she knew by this time that her husband had gone with him to serve as his squire. And as soon as she saw Sancho her first inquiry was after his ass, to which Sancho replied that he was in a better state of health than his master.

'Thanks be to God,' she replied, 'for His goodness. But tell me now, my friend, what profit have you got out of your squireships? Have you brought me a skirt? Or some pretty shoes for the children?'

'I haven't brought any of that, wife,' said Sancho, 'although I bring other things of greater value and importance.'

'I'm very glad of that,' replied his wife. 'Show me these things of greater value and importance, my friend. The sight of them would be a joy to this heart of mine, for I have been most sad and sorrowful all the ages you have been away.'

'I'll show you them at home, wife,' said Panza. 'Be satisfied for the present. But if God permits us to go on our travels again, in search of adventures, you will soon see me a count or governor of an isle – and not of one of these local isles, but the best that can be found.'

'Heaven grant you may, husband, for we're in great need of it. But tell me, what is this about isles? I don't understand you.'

'Honey is not for the ass's mouth,' replied Sancho. 'You will see in due course, wife, and you'll be surprised when you hear all your vassals calling you "Your Ladyship".'

'What's that you're saying, Sancho, about Ladyships, isles and vassals?' asked Juana Panza, for that was the name of Sancho's wife – not that they were related by blood but because it is usual in La Mancha for wives to take their husband's surnames.

'Don't fret yourself, Juana, and be in such a hurry to know everything. It's enough that I'm telling you the truth, so shut your mouth. But there's one thing I can say to you in passing, that there's nothing so pleasant in the world for an honest man as to be squire to a knight errant, that seeks adventures. It's true that most of them one finds don't turn out as much to one's liking as a man could wish, for out of every hundred you meet ninety-nine generally turn out cross and unlucky. I know it by experience, for I've come off blanket-tossed from some and bruised from others. But, for all that, it's a nice thing to be looking out for incidents, crossing mountains, searching woods, climbing rocks, visiting castles, and lodging in inns at your pleasure, with the devil a farthing to pay.'

While this conversation was taking place between Sancho Panza and Juana Panza his wife, Don Quixote's housekeeper and niece received him, undressed him, and laid him in his ancient bed, where he stared at them with eyes askance and could not understand where he was. The priest charged the niece to look after her uncle very carefully and to keep good watch that he did not escape again, telling her all the trouble they had had in bringing him home. At this, the two women set up their cries anew. Once more they burst out in abuse of his books of knight errantry and implored Heaven to plunge the authors of so many lies and absurdities into the bottomless pit. In fact they were distracted, and frightened that as soon as their master and uncle felt a little better they would find him missing once more. And events fell out as they feared.

But though the author of this history has anxiously and diligently inquired after Don Quixote's exploits on his third expedition, he has been able to discover no account of them, at least from any authentic documents. Though fame has preserved a tradition in La Mancha that the third time Don Quixote left his home he went to Saragossa, and took part in some famous jousts in that city, and that adventures there befell him worthy of his valour and of his sound intelligence. Our author, in fact, would have been able to learn nothing of his mortal end, nor would he even have learnt of it, if good fortune had not thrown an aged doctor in his path. This man had in his possession a leaden box which, so he said, he had found among the ruined foundations of an ancient hermitage, that was being rebuilt. In this box he had found some parchments written in the Gothic script but in Castilian verse, which contained many of the knight's exploits and dwelt upon the beauty of Dulcinea del Toboso, the shape of Rocinante, the fidelity of Sancho Panza, and the burial of this same Don Quixote, together with various epitaphs and eulogies on his life and habits. Such of these as could be read and understood the trustworthy author of this original and matchless history has set down here, and he asks no recompense from his readers for the immense labours it has cost him to search and ransack all the archives of La Mancha in order to drag it into the light. All that he asks is that they shall accord it such credit as intelligent men usually give to those books of chivalry which are so highly valued in the world. With this he will feel both rewarded, and satisfied, and will be encouraged to seek and discover other histories, perhaps less authentic than this one, but at least as ingenious and entertaining.

The first words written on the parchment found in the leaden box were these:

THE ACADEMICIANS OF ARGAMASILLA,
A TOWN OF LA MANCHA, ON THE LIFE AND DEATH OF
THE VALOROUS DON QUIXOTE DE LA MANCHA,
HOC SCRIPSERUNT.

MUMBO JUMBO, ACADEMICIAN OF ARGAMASILLA,
UPON THE TOMB OF DON QUIXOTE

Epitaph

The dunderhead who for La Mancha won
More trophies than did Jason for his Creta,
The wit whose weathercock was over-fine,
When something broad and blunter were far meeter;
The arm which from Cathay to far Gaeta
Broadened the boundaries of his mighty reign;
The Muse, none dreadfuller and none discreeter,
That carved on brazen plate the poet's line;
He that the Amadises far outstripped
And made the gallant Galaor look a fool,
Leaving them both in love and war well whipped,
And made the Belianises to quail,
He who on Rocinante erring went
Lies now beneath this cold stone monument.

THE GOOD COMPANION, ACADEMICIAN OF ARGAMASILLA, IN LAUDEM DULCINEAE DEL TOBOSO

Sonnet

She that you see here, stout and heavy featured,
High-bosomed, with a rather martial mien,
Is Dulcinea, El Toboso's queen,
Of whom the great Don Quixote was enraptured.
    For her it was he travelled far and wide
Over the great Brown Hills to the renowned
Montiel plain, and down to the grass-crowned
Aranjuez gardens, wearily he trod.
    The fault was Rocinante's! O hard doom
Of this Manchegan dame and errant knight
Unconquered! Dying in her beauty's bloom,
    Of tender years, quenched is her beauty's light,
And he whose fame the inscribed marble proves
Could not escape the wrath and wiles of love.

WHIMSICAL WILL, A VERY WITTY ACADEMICIAN OF ARGAMASILLA, IN PRAISE OF ROCINANTE, DON QUIXOTE DE LA MANCHA'S STEED

Sonnet

Upon the lofty throne of adamant
Trodden by mighty Mars's bloody heel,
The mad Manchegan did his standard plant,
Hanging his arms and that sharp blade of steel,
    With which he hacked, wasted and cleft in twain.
New feats of arms, for which art must devise
A style to suit the newest paladin.
And if Gaul prides herself on Amadis,
    Whose brave descendants have ennobled Greece,
And filled it full of triumphs and of fame,
To-day Bellona crowns Don Quixote's brows.
    Let high La Mancha ne'er forget his name,
Who rode on Rocinante, braver far
Than gallant Bayard or steel Brillador.

THE JOKER, ACADEMICIAN OF ARGAMASILLA, TO SANCHO PANZA

Sonnet

Here Sancho Panza lies, in body small,
But yet, strange miracle, in valour great,
As guileless squire and simple, truth to tell,
As in this world, I swear, lived ever yet.
    Of being a count he came within an ace,
Had not this wicked century conspired
Malignantly to harm him; for an ass
Insults and injuries are never spared.
    An ass he rode – it shames me to record –
This meek squire meekly following behind
The mild steed Rocinante and his lord.
    How vain are all the hopes of humankind!
How sweet their promises of quiet seem,
And yet they end in shadows, smoke and dream.

THE HOBGOBLIN, ACADEMICIAN OF ARGAMASILLA, ON DON QUIXOTE'S TOMB

Epitaph

Here lies the knight in death.
Well bruised and ill errant, he
Was borne by Rocinante
O'er road and track and path.
    Beside him Sancho's laid,
The foolish Sancho Panza,
As faithful as e'er man saw
One of the squirish trade.

DING-DONG, ACADEMICIAN OF ARGAMASILLA, ON THE TOMB OF DULCINEA DEL TOBOSO

Epitaph

Here Dulcinea's laid,
Once of flesh so lusty.
Ashes now cold and dusty
By ugly death she's made.

> Of godly parentage
> And fairish stock she came.
> She was great Quixote's flame,
> And glory of her village.

These were such verses as could be deciphered. The rest, as the characters were worm-eaten, were entrusted to a university scholar to guess out their meaning. We are informed that he has done so, at the cost of many nights of study and much labour, and that he intends to publish them, which gives us hope of a third expedition of Don Quixote.

Forse altri cantera con miglior plettro.

END OF THE FIRST PART

THE ADVENTURES OF
DON QUIXOTE

THE SECOND PART

To the Count of Lemos

SOME *days ago, on sending your Excellency my Comedies, printed before they were played, I said, if I remember rightly, that Don Quixote was waiting with his boots ready spurred to go and kiss your Excellency's hands. Now I announce him booted and on the way, and if he arrives I think I shall have done your Excellency some service; for much pressure has been put on me from countless directions to send him out, in order to purge the disgust and nausea caused by another Don Quixote who has been running about the world masquerading as the second part.*

But the personage who has evinced the greatest longing for him is the Emperor of China, who sent me a letter by express a month ago, begging me, or more correctly imploring me, to send the knight to him, for he wanted to found a college for the teaching of Castilian, and intended The History of Don Quixote *to be the textbook used there. Furthermore he informed me that I was to be rector of the college. I asked the bearer whether his Majesty had given him anything for me by way of contribution to my expenses. He answered that His Majesty had not so much as thought of it. 'Then, brother,' I replied, 'you can go back to your China at ten o'clock or twenty o'clock or at whatever hour you can get away, for I am not in good enough health to undertake so long a voyage. What is more, as well as being in ill health, I am very short of money and, Emperor for Emperor and Monarch for Monarch, I hold by the great Count de Lemos in Naples; for, without all these petty diplomas and benefices, he keeps me, shelters me, and does me more favours than I can desire.'*

With this I dismissed him; and with this I take my leave, offering your Excellency The Travels of Persiles and Sigismunda, *a book which I shall finish within four months, Deo volente, and which is sure to be either the worst or the best written of books of entertainment in our tongue – but I must say that I repent of having said the worst. For, according to the opinions of my friends, it will attain the highest possible excellence. Come, your Excellency, with all the health we can wish you; Persiles shall be ready to kiss your hands, and I your feet, as your Excellency's servant, which I am.*

From Madrid.
    The last day of October 1615.
      Your Excellency's servant

MIGUEL DE CERVANTES SAAVEDRA

THE SECOND PART

PROLOGUE

G OD bless me, how eagerly you must now be awaiting this prologue, illustrious, or maybe plebeian reader, in the expectation of finding in it vengeance, wranglings and railings against the author of the second *Don Quixote* – I mean the one said to have been begotten at Tordesillas and born at Tarragona. But, in truth, I am not going to give you that satisfaction, for though injuries awaken anger in the meekest hearts, in mine the rule must admit of an exception. You would like me to call him ass, fool and bully; but I have not even a thought of doing so. Let his sin be his punishment – with his bread let him eat it, and there let it rest. What I cannot help resenting is that he upbraids me for being old and crippled, as if it were in my power to stop the passage of time, or as if the loss of my hand had taken place in some tavern, and not on the greatest occasion which any age, past, present, or future, ever saw or can ever hope to see. If my wounds do not shine in the eyes of such as look on them, they are at least respected by those who know where they were acquired; for a soldier looks better dead in battle than safe in flight. And so firmly am I of this opinion that even if now I could bring about the impossible, I would still rather have taken part in that prodigious action than be at present whole of my wounds without ever having fought there. The wounds a soldier shows on his face and on his breast are stars to guide others to the heaven of honour and to create in them a noble emulation. Let it be remembered that it is not with grey hairs that one writes, but with the mind, which generally ripens with the years. I also resented his calling me envious, and explaining to me, as if I were ignorant, what sort of thing envy is; though, in very truth, of the two kinds of envy, I know only the righteous, noble and well-meaning sort. And that being the case I am not likely to persecute any priest, particularly if he is a familiar of the Holy Office to boot. And if it was on behalf of a certain person that he wrote what he did, he is absolutely mistaken; for I revere that man's genius, and admire his works and his virtuous and unceasing industry. I am indeed grateful, however, to this kind author for saying that my *Novels* are rather satirical than 'exemplary', though they are good – for they could not be good if they were not good in every respect.

You will agree, I think, that I am showing great restraint and keeping well within the bounds of modesty, out of a feeling that one should not heap affliction on the afflicted, and that the affliction from which this gentleman suffers must certainly be a great one, since he dare not appear in the open field and under a clear sky, but hides his name and disguises his country, as if he were guilty of the crime of high treason. If by any chance you come to know him, tell him from me that I do not consider myself aggrieved. For I know very well what the temptations of the Devil are, and that one of his greatest is to put it into a man's head that he can write and print a book, and gain both money and fame by it; to prove which I should like you, in your pleasant and witty way, to tell him this story:

There was a madman in Seville who was taken with the oddest and craziest notion that ever a madman had in all the world. It was this: he made a tube out of a cane, sharpened at the end, and catching a dog, in the street or elsewhere, he would hold down one of its hind legs with one foot and lift the other one up with his hand. Next, fitting his tube to the right place, he would blow into it, as best he could, till he had made the dog as round as a ball. Then, holding it up in this way, he would give it a couple of slaps on the belly and let it go, saying to the bystanders, – and there were always plenty: 'Your worships will perhaps be thinking that it is an easy thing to blow up a dog?' – Does your worship think it is an easy thing to write a book?

And if the story does not suit him, you can tell him this one, friendly reader, which is also about a madman and a dog:

In Cordova there was another madman, whose habit it was to carry on his head a piece of marble slab or a stone of considerable weight; and when he met with an unwary dog, he would go up close behind it and drop the weight plump on top of it. The dog would fly into a panic and bark and yelp up three streets without stopping. Now it happened once that amongst his victims was a hatter's dog, much beloved by its master. The stone came down and struck its head, and the battered beast set up a howl. Its master, however, saw the deed and flew into a great rage. He seized a yard measure, came after the madman, and beat him till he had not a whole bone in his body, crying out at every blow he gave him: 'You dog, you thief! My pointer! Didn't you see, you cruel wretch, that my dog was a pointer?' And with frequent repetitions of the word 'pointer' he sent the madman off beaten to a pulp. The idiot learnt his lesson and went away, and did not show himself in public for more than a month. But at the end of this time he reappeared with an even heavier weight, and would go up to a dog and stare at it most intently. Then, without the will or the pluck to drop his stone he would say: 'It's a pointer. Look out!'

In fact, he called all the dogs he met pointers, whether they were mastiffs or curs; and so he never dropped his stone on one again. Perhaps the same thing may happen to this story-teller. He may never venture again to discharge the load of his wit in the form of a book, for bad books are harder than rocks.

Tell him too that I do not care a straw for his threat to deprive me of my profit by means of his book. For to adapt the words of the famous farce *La Perendenga*, my answer is: Long live my master the alderman, and Christ for us all. Long live the great Count de Lemos, whose Christian charity and famous generosity keep me on my feet despite all the blows of my scant fortune. And long live the supreme beneficence of His Eminence of Toledo, Don Bernardo de Sandoval y Rojas, even though there may be no more printing-presses in the world, and even though more books be printed against me than there are letters in Mingo Revulgo's couplets. These two princes have received no adulation nor other kind of flattery from me, but out of their goodness alone have taken on themselves to do me kindnesses and favours; by which I consider myself happier and richer than if fortune had placed me on her pinnacle by the ordinary means. The poor man may attain to honour, but not the wicked. Poverty can cloud nobility, but not obscure it altogether. Let virtue but show some light of her own, even though it be through the straits and chinks of penury, and it will come to be valued by lofty and noble spirits, and so win favour. Say no more to him, and I will say no more to you, but only ask you to notice that this second part of *Don Quixote*, which I place before you, is cut by the same craftsman and from the same cloth as the first, and that in it I present you with the knight at greater length and, in the end, dead and buried. Let no one, therefore, presume to raise fresh testimonies to him, for the past ones are sufficient. Suffice it that an honest man has told the story of his amusing follies, and has no wish to take the subject up again. For however good things are an abundance brings down the price, and scarcity, even in bad things, confers a certain value.

I forgot to tell you that you may look out for *Persiles*, which I am just finishing, and the second part of *Galatea*.

Chapter I. Of what passed between the Priest and the Barber in the matter of the Knight's illness.

CIDE HAMETE BENENGELI recounts, in the second part of this history concerning Don Quixote's third expedition, that the priest and the barber did not see him for almost a month, for fear of reviving past events and recalling them to his memory. But all the same, they did not give up visiting his niece and his housekeeper, and charged them to be careful to treat him well, and to give him such food as was comforting and good for his heart and his brain, from which organs they had good reason to believe all his misfortunes arose. The two women declared that they were doing so, and would lavish on their master every possible care and kindness, for they had noticed in him occasional signs of returning sanity. The two friends received this news with great satisfaction, for it seemed to prove that they had done right in bringing him back enchanted in the ox-waggon, as is related in the last chapter of the first part of this great and authentic history. So they decided to visit him and test his recovery, though they hardly expected to find him cured, and agreed not to touch in any way on knight-errantry, so as not to run the danger of bursting open wounds which were still so tender.

They paid him a visit at last, and found him sitting up in bed, dressed in a thick green flannel waistcoat with a red Toledo cap, and so lean and withered that he seemed to be nothing but mummy-flesh. They were very well received by him; and on their questioning him about his health, he gave them a most intelligent account of it in very well-chosen language. In the course of their conversation they happened to discuss the principles of statecraft – as they are called – and methods of government, correcting this abuse and condemning that, reforming one custom and abolishing another, each one of the three setting up as a fresh legislator, a modern Lycurgus or a brand-new Solon. To such a degree did they re-fashion the commonwealth that it was as if they had taken it to the forge and brought away a different one. And Don Quixote spoke

with such intelligence on all the subjects they handled that the two
examiners had no doubt whatever that he was quite recovered and
in complete possession of his wits.

His niece and his housekeeper were present at this discussion, and
could not thank God enough on seeing their master so sound in the
head. But the priest changed his first plan, which was not to touch
on the subject of chivalry, and decided to make a thorough test
whether Don Quixote's recovery was real or false. So, gradually, he
worked round to some news which had come from Madrid, and
told the knight among other things that it was considered certain
that the Turk was going to make a descent with a huge fleet, but
that his purpose was obscure, and no one knew where this mighty
storm would burst. All Christendom, he said, was in alarm from
that same dread which almost every year calls us to arms; and His
Majesty had fortified the coasts of Naples, Sicily and the island of
Malta.

'His Majesty has acted like a most prudent warrior,' answered
Don Quixote, 'in fortifying his Estates in time, so that the enemy
may not find him unprepared. But if he were to ask my advice, I
would counsel him to take one precaution which is far from occur-
ring to His Majesty at present.'

And the moment the priest heard this he said to himself: 'God
protect you, my poor Don Quixote; for you seem to me to be
throwing yourself from the high peak of your madness into the deep
abyss of your folly.'

But the barber, who had already had the same thought as the
priest, asked Don Quixote the nature of the precaution which he
proposed they should adopt; for perhaps it was suitable to be added
to the long list of impertinent projects commonly set before princes.

'Mine, Master Shaver,' said Don Quixote, 'will not be impertinent, but most pertinent.'

'I don't say that it is,' replied the barber, 'but experience has
shown that nearly all the plans presented to his Majesty are either
impracticable or ridiculous, or would do positive harm either to the
King or his kingdom.'

'But mine,' answered Don Quixote, 'is neither impracticable nor
ridiculous, but the easiest, the most proper, and the subtlest and
simplest that could occur to any planner's imagination.'

'Your worship is slow in telling it to us, Don Quixote,' said the priest.

'I do not wish to tell it here at present,' said Don Quixote, 'for it to reach the ears of the Lords of the Council to-morrow morning, and for someone else to get the thanks and reward for my pains.'

'For myself,' said the barber, 'I give you my word, here before God, not to repeat what your worship says to King or Rook or earthly man – an oath which I learned from the Ballad of the Priest, who warned the King in the prologue against the thief who had robbed him of a hundred doublons and his ambling mule.'

'I do not know the story,' said Don Quixote, 'but I know that the oath is a good one, because I believe that the barber is an honest man.'

'Even if he were not,' said the priest, 'I will go bail for him, and guarantee that he will no more speak of this matter than if he were dumb, upon pain of whatever penalty the court may provide.'

'And for your worship? Who will vouch for you, Master Priest?' asked Don Quixote.

'My profession,' replied the priest, 'which is to keep secrets.'

'In Heaven's name, then!' exclaimed Don Quixote, 'what more is there for His Majesty to do but to command by public crier all the knights errant who are wandering about Spain to assemble at the capital on a fixed day. For if only half a dozen came, might there not be one amongst them who would be sufficient in himself to destroy all the power of the Turk? Listen, your worships, and follow me. Is it, by any chance, anything new for a single knight errant to slaughter an army of two hundred men, as if the whole lot of them had one single throat or were made of marzipan? Tell me, now, how many histories are there full of such marvels? If there were living to-day – to my misfortune, though I will not say to any one else's – the famous Don Belianis or any of the innumerable descendants of Amadis of Gaul! If a single one of them were alive to-day and were to confront the Turk, the infidel would come off pretty badly, I promise you. But God will take care of His people and send one, who may not be as manly as the knights errant of old, but at least will not be behind them in spirit. God understands me, and I say no more.'

'Oh dear!' cried the niece at this point, 'may I die if my master doesn't want to turn knight errant again.'

To which Don Quixote replied: 'A knight errant I shall die, and let the Turk make his descent or ascent whenever he will, and with whatever power he can. For I say once more, God understands my meaning.'

At this the barber put in: 'Permit me, your worships, to tell you a short tale about something that happened at Seville. It comes so pat to the point that I'm itching to tell it to you.'

Don Quixote and the priest consented, and the others paid attention as he began thus:

'In the madhouse at Seville was a man whose relations had put him there because he had gone out of his mind. He was a graduate in common law of Osuna, but even if he had been of Salamanca, as many think, he would have been just as mad. This graduate, at the end of some years of confinement, persuaded himself that he was sane and in his right mind, and in this conviction wrote to the Archbishop, imploring him earnestly and in well-chosen language to order his release from the misery in which he lived, since by the mercy of God he had recovered his lost wits; for his relations kept him there to enjoy his share of the estate and, despite the clearest evidence, would have him stay mad till his death. The Archbishop was impressed by his many sensible and intelligent letters, and ordered one of his chaplains to find out from the governor of the madhouse whether what the graduate wrote to him was true. He asked him to speak to the madman and, if he appeared to be in his senses, to set him at liberty. The chaplain called, and the governor informed him that the man was still mad; and that, though he often talked like a person of great intelligence, in the end he would break out into wild talk, just as crazy and as persistent as his previous conversation had been sensible. This he would discover by speaking to him. The chaplain decided to do so, and on visiting the madman, talked with him for an hour and more, and in all this time he never said anything crazy or queer. On the contrary, he spoke so soberly that the chaplain was forced to believe that he was sane. Among other things the madman said was that the governor was hostile to him because he did not want to lose the presents his relations made him for saying that he was still mad, though with lucid intervals. His greatest stumbling-block, he said, in his misfortune was his great wealth. For, to enjoy it, his enemies misjudged him, and threw doubt on the mercy our Lord had done him in restoring him from a beast to a man. In fact he spoke in such a way as to throw suspicion on the governor, and to make his relatives appear covetous and inhuman, and himself sane. So the chaplain decided to take him to the Archbishop, so that he could discover the truth of the matter for himself. In all good faith, then, the excellent chaplain begged the governor to give orders for the graduate to be given back the clothes in which he had arrived. But the governor once more bade him take care what he was doing, for there was no doubt at all that the graduate was still mad. However, the governor's warning could not prevail upon the chaplain to leave the madman behind. So, seeing that it was the Archbishop's order, the governor obeyed, and they dressed the madman in his own clothes, which were new and decent. Now, when he found himself stripped of his madman's dress and clothed in the garb of sanity, he begged the chaplain out of charity to let him go and take leave of his mad companions. The chaplain said that he would like to come with him and see the lunatics who were lodged there. So they went upstairs, accompanied by some other people who were about, and the madman went up to a cage in which was a raging lunatic, who was calm and quiet at the time, however, and addressed him thus:

'"My brother, think if you have any commands for me. I am going home. For God in His infinite goodness and mercy has been pleased to restore me to my senses, little though I deserve it. Now I am sane and in my right mind, for to God's power nothing is impossible. Put great hope and trust in Him; for, since He has restored me to my former state, He will restore you too, if you have faith in Him. I will send you some delicacies to eat, and be sure you eat them; since I must tell you that in my opinion our madness arises from our having our stomachs empty and our brains full of wind. Take heart! Take heart, for despondency in our miseries weakens our health and brings on death."

'Another madman in another cage opposite the raging lunatic's overheard all that the graduate said and, getting up from an old mat on which he was lying naked to the skin, asked in a loud voice who this man was who was going away sane and in his right mind.

The graduate replied: "It is I, brother, who am going. I have no need to stay here any more, for which I give infinite thanks to Heaven, which has done me this great favour."

'"Mind what you say, graduate, and don't let the Devil deceive you," answered the madman. "Rest your feet and stay nice and quiet at home, and you'll spare yourself the return journey."

'"I know that I am well," replied the graduate, "and shall not have to travel the rounds again."

'"You well!" cried the madman. "Good! we shall see. God be with you! But I vow to Jupiter, whose majesty I represent on earth, that for the single sin which Seville is committing to-day by releasing you from this house and treating you as a sane man, I shall inflict such punishment on her as shall be remembered to all eternity, Amen. Don't you know, paltry little graduate, that I have the power to do so? For, let me tell you, I am Jupiter Tonans, and hold in my hands the flaming thunderbolts with which I can and do menace and destroy the world. But with one punishment alone I mean to chastise this ignorant city: for three whole years I will not rain on it, nor on all the surrounding districts; which time is to be reckoned from the instant I utter this threat. You free, you sane, you in your right mind, and I mad, and sick, and in chains ...? I would as soon think of raining as hang myself."

'The madman's loud speech called the attention of the bystanders, but our graduate turned to our chaplain and, seizing him by the hands, reassured him: "Do not be concerned, my dear sir. Take no notice of what this madman says. For if he is Jupiter and will not rain, I am Neptune, the father and god of the waters, and I will rain as often as I please, and whenever it is necessary."

'To which the chaplain replied: "All the same, Lord Neptune, it would not be right to annoy Lord Jupiter. Your worship may remain at home, and we will come back for you another day, when we have more time."

'The governor and the bystanders burst out laughing, which made the chaplain rather ashamed. Then they stripped the graduate and he stayed behind. And that is the end of my story.'

'So that, Master Barber,' said Don Quixote, 'is the story which came so pat to the point that you had to tell it? O, Master Shaver, Master Shaver, how blind is the man who cannot see through a hair-sieve! Is it possible that your worship does not know that comparisons between wit and wit, valour and valour, beauty and beauty, birth and birth, are always odious and resented? I, Master Barber, am not Neptune, the God of the waters, and I am not trying to make anyone believe me wise when I am not. I am only at pains to convince the world of its error in not reviving that most happy age in which the order of chivalry flourished. But our depraved times do not deserve to enjoy so great a blessing as did those in which knights errant undertook and carried on their shoulders the defence of kingdoms, the protection of damsels, the succour of orphans and wards, the chastisement of the proud, and the rewarding of the humble. Most of our knights nowadays prefer to rustle in damasks, brocades, and other rich clothes that they wear, than in armoured coats of mail. There are no knights now to sleep in the open, exposed to the rigour of the skies, in full armour from head to foot. There is no one now to snatch a nap, as they say, leaning on his lance and with his feet in the stirrups, as knights errant did of old. There is no one now to come out of a wood and go into the mountains, and from there tramp a waste and desert shore, most often stormy and tempestuous, and to find there on the beach a little boat without oars, sail, mast, or tackle, and with undaunted heart to fling himself in and commit himself to the implacable waves of the deep sea, which sometimes toss him to the sky and sometimes cast him down to the abyss. Then, exposing his breast to the irresistible tempest, he finds himself, when he least dreams of it, more than nine thousand miles from the place where he embarked; and leaping on to a remote and unknown shore, he undergoes experiences worthy to be inscribed not on parchment but on brass. Now sloth triumphs over industry, idleness over labour, vice over virtue, presumption over valour, and theory over the practice of arms, which only lived and flourished in the golden age and among knights errant. If I am not right, tell me, who was more virtuous and more valiant than the renowned Amadis of Gaul? Who was wiser than Palmerin of England? Who more approachable and skilful than Tirante the White? Who more gallant than Lisuarte of Greece? Who gave and received more sword-thrusts than Don Belianis? Who was more dauntless than Perion of Gaul, or readier to face peril than Felixmarte of Hyrcania, or more sincere than Esplandian? Who was more impetuous than Don Cirongilio of Thrace? Who was more fearless than Rodamonte? Who was more prudent than King Sobrino? Who was bolder than Reynald? Who more invincible than Roland? And who gayer and more courteous than Ruggiero, from whom the present-day Dukes of Ferrara are descended, according to Turpin's *cosmography*. All these knights and many others I could mention, Master Priest, were knights errant, the light and glory of chivalry. These, or such as these, I should wish to take part in my project; and, if they did, His Majesty would find himself well served at great saving of expense, and the Turk would be left tearing his beard. Therefore I wish to remain at home, since the chaplain is not taking me out; and if Jupiter, as the barber has said, will not rain, here am I who will rain whenever I please. This I say so that Master Basin may see that I understand him.'

'Really, Don Quixote,' said the barber, 'that wasn't why I told you the tale. I meant well by it, so help me God, and your worship shouldn't take offence.'

'I know best whether I take offence or not,' replied Don Quixote. At which the priest put in: 'Although I have hardly said a word up to now, I should like to relieve myself of a scruple which is gnawing and grating at my conscience, and which arises from Don Quixote's last remarks.'

'Master Priest has a licence for other graver matters,' replied Don Quixote. 'So he can declare his scruple; for it is not pleasant to go about with scruples on your conscience.'

'Well, with your permission,' replied the priest, 'I will reveal my scruple. It is this. I cannot by any means persuade myself, Don Quixote, that all this crowd of knights errant you have referred to have really and truly been people of flesh and blood living in this world. On the contrary, I think that it is all fiction, fable and lies – dreams told by men awake, or rather half asleep.'

'That is another mistake,' replied Don Quixote, 'into which the many have fallen, who do not believe that such knights have ever existed. Often with different people and at different times I have tried to expose this almost universal error to the light of truth. On some occasions I have not succeeded in my purpose; on others I have, by supporting my argument with evidence so infallible that I might say I have seen Amadis of Gaul with my own eyes. He was a man tall of stature and fair of face, with a well-trimmed black beard. His looks were half mild and half severe. He was short of speech, slow to anger, and quickly appeased. Now, in the same way as I have drawn Amadis, I could, I think, depict and describe all the knights errant in all the histories in the world. For my absolute faith in the details of their histories and my knowledge of their deeds and their characters enable me by sound philosophy to deduce their features, their complexions and their stature.'

'How big then, my dear Don Quixote,' asked the barber, 'would the giant Morgante have been in your worship's opinion?'

'About the existence of giants,' replied Don Quixote, 'there are different opinions. But Holy Scripture, which cannot depart from the truth by so much as an inch, proves that they existed, by telling us the story of that great Philistine, Goliath, who was seven cubits and a half tall – a prodigious height. Besides, in the island of Sicily shin-bones and shoulder-blades have been discovered of a size which shows that their owners were giants as tall as great towers; geometry proves it beyond a doubt. But, for all that, I could not say for certain how tall Morgante was, though I imagine that he could not have been very big. My reason for this opinion is that I find in the history particularly devoted to his exploits that he often slept beneath a roof; and since he found houses he could get into, it is clear that his size was not excessive.'

'That is true,' remarked the priest, delighted to hear him talk such nonsense. He then asked him what he felt about the looks of Reynald of Montalban, of Sir Roland and of the other Twelve Peers of France, since they had all been knights errant.

'Of Reynald,' replied Don Quixote, 'I make bold to say that he was broad-faced, red-complexioned, with rolling and rather prominent eyes, exceedingly touchy and irascible, and a friend to thieves and vagabonds. Of Roland, or Rotolando, or Orlando – for histories give him all these names – I am of the positive opinion that he was of middle stature, broad-shouldered, rather bow-legged, dark complexioned, and red-bearded, with a hairy body and a menacing appearance, short of speech but very well-bred and courteous.'

'If Roland was no more of a gentleman than your worship has said,' returned the priest, 'it was no wonder that the lady Angelica the Fair left him for the gaiety, the dash and the grace of the downy-cheeked little Moor to whom she gave herself. She showed good sense in falling in love with Medoro's smoothness rather than with Roland's roughness.'

'That Angelica, Master Priest,' replied Don Quixote, 'was a giddy, roving damsel and somewhat flighty, and left the world as full of her indiscretions as of her famous beauty. She spurned a thousand lords – a thousand brave and wise lords – and contented herself with a pretty little page, with no other wealth or fame than the reputation for gratitude he won by his loyalty to his friend. The great singer of her beauty, the renowned Ariosto, did not dare, or perhaps did not care, to sing of what happened to this lady after her base surrender – for no doubt her conduct was not over-chaste – and left her with these lines:

> "And how Cathaya's sceptre fell to her
> Someone perhaps will sing to a better lyre."

And no doubt that was a kind of prophecy; for poets are also called *vates*, which means diviners. The truth is plain to see, for since then a famous Andalusian poet has wept and sung her tears, and another famous and unique Castilian poet has sung her beauty.'

'Tell me, Don Quixote,' put in the barber, 'hasn't any poet written a satire on this lady Angelica, seeing that so many have praised her?'

'I certainly believe,' replied Don Quixote, 'that if Sacripante or Roland had been a poet, he would have given the maiden a trouncing. For it is proper and natural for poets who have been scorned or refused by their ladies – feigned or actually modelled on those they have chosen as mistresses of their thoughts – to avenge themselves with satires and lampoons, a vengeance most certainly unworthy of generous hearts. But up to now there has come to my notice no defamatory verse against the lady Angelica, who turned the world upside down.'

'A miracle!' exclaimed the priest. But at this point they heard the housekeeper and the niece, who had withdrawn from the conversation, making a great outcry in the front yard; and they all ran out to the noise.

Chapter II. *Of the notable Quarrel between Sancho Panza and Don Quixote's Niece and Housekeeper, with other delightful Incidents.*

OUR story tells that the voices Don Quixote, the priest and the barber heard were the niece and the housekeeper crying out at Sancho Panza, who was struggling to get in and see Don Quixote, while they were holding the door against him.

'What does the little monster want in this house? Go back to your own, brother, for it's you and no other that lead my master astray, and entice him, and take him rambling along the by-roads.'

To which Sancho replied: 'You old devil! It is I that am enticed and led astray and taken rambling over the by-roads, and not your master. It's he who led me all about the wilds, and don't you make any mistake about it. He wheedled me from home with his blarney, promising me an isle, and I'm still waiting for it.'

'May the foul isles choke you,' replied the niece. 'Damn you, Sancho. And what are isles? Are they something to eat, you glutton, you cormorant?'

'They are not anything to eat,' replied Sancho, 'but to govern and rule. They're better than any four cities, and richer than four judgeships at court.'

'You shan't come in here all the same,' said the housekeeper, 'you bundle of mischief, you bag of villainies! Go and govern your house, and till your plot, and give up trying for your isles and islets.'

The priest and the barber were highly delighted to hear this triangular conversation. But Don Quixote feared that Sancho would blurt out a whole pack of mischievous nonsense and touch on matters not wholly to his credit. So he called him, and forced the pair of them to be quiet and let him in. Sancho entered, and the priest and the barber took their leave of Don Quixote, despairing of his sanity, since they saw how fixed he was in his crazy ideas, and how steeped in the idiocy of his wretched knight errantry. And so the priest said to the barber: 'You will see, friend. When we least expect it, our knight will be off once more to range the bush.'

'I've no doubt of that,' replied the barber, 'but I'm less surprised at the knight's madness than at the squire's foolishness in believing

Q

the story of the isle. For I'm afraid that all the disillusionment you can think of won't get it out of his head.'

'God cure them,' said the priest, 'and let us keep our eyes open. We shall see where this precious knight's pack of nonsense will land him, and his squire's too. For the pair of them seem to be cast in one mould, and the master's madness would not be worth a farthing without the squire's foolishness.'

'That's true,' said the barber. 'I should be very glad to know what the two of them are talking about now.'

'His niece and the housekeeper will tell us afterwards, I promise you,' replied the priest, 'for they aren't the sort to refrain from listening.'

In the meantime Don Quixote had shut himself up in his room with Sancho, and when they were alone he said: 'It grieves me deeply, Sancho, to hear you say that it was I who took you from your cottage, when you know that I did not stay at home myself. We set out together, we lived together, and we wandered together. One fortune and one destiny befell us both. If you have been tossed in a blanket once, I have been beaten a hundred times; and that is where I have the advantage of you.'

'That was only right,' replied Sancho, 'for, as your worship says, disasters have more to do with knights errant than with their squires.'

'You are mistaken, Sancho,' said Don Quixote. 'Remember the saying, *quando caput dolet*, etc.'

'I understand no language but my own,' replied Sancho.

'I mean,' said Don Quixote, 'that when the head aches, all the limbs feel pain; and so, as I am your lord and master, I am your head, and you are a part of me, since you are my servant; and for that reason the ill that touches me, or shall touch me, should give pain to you; and yours to me.'

'So it should be,' said Sancho. 'But when they tossed me, the limb, in the blanket, my head was outside the wall, watching me fly through the air and not feeling any pain. But since the limbs have to suffer for the head's pain, the head should also be made to suffer for the limbs.'

'Do you mean to suggest, Sancho,' replied Don Quixote, 'that I felt no pain when they were tossing you? If that is what you say, you are wrong. You should not even think such a thing. For I felt more pain then in my spirit than you did in your body. But let us put that aside for the present, for there will be a time when we can consider the matter and come to a proper conclusion. Now, tell me, Sancho, my friend, what do they say about me in the village? What opinion have the common people of me, and the gentry and the knights? What do they say of my valour, and my deeds and my courtliness? How do they speak of the resolve I have taken to revive and restore to the world the forgotten order of chivalry? In brief, Sancho, I want you to tell me all that has come to your ears on this score. You must answer me without adding to the good or subtracting from the evil in the very slightest. For it is the duty of loyal vassals to tell their lords the truth in its proper shape and essence, without enlarging on it out of flattery or softening it for any idle reason. I would have you know, Sancho, that if the naked truth were to come to the ears of princes, unclothed in flattery, this would be a different age. Other ages would be held to be of iron in comparison with ours, for this in which we live now I reckon to be of gold. Take this warning, Sancho, and bring discreetly and faithfully to my ears the true answer to the questions I have asked you.'

'I'll do so gladly enough, sir,' replied Sancho, 'on condition that your worship does not get annoyed at what I say. For you want me to tell you the naked truth and not dress it in any clothes, except those I found it in.'

'On no account shall I be angry,' replied Don Quixote. 'You can speak freely, Sancho, without any beating about the bush.'

'Then first of all,' said he, 'let me say that the common people take your worship for a very great madman, and they think I'm a great simpleton too. The gentlemen say that you're not content with being a country gentleman, but must turn yourself into a Don and launch forth into knighthood, with no more than a paltry vineyard and two acres of land, and hardly a rag to your back. The knights say that they don't like the petty gentry to set up in competition with them, especially squires who black their own shoes, and mend their black knitted stockings with green silk.'

'That,' said Don Quixote, 'does not apply to me, for I am always well dressed and never patched. Frayed I may be, but frayed rather from my armour than from age.'

'On the subject of your worship's valour,' Sancho went on, 'of your courtliness, your deeds, and your undertaking, there are different opinions. Some call you mad but amusing. Others, valiant but unfortunate. Others, well-mannered but presumptuous. And so they go running on, till they don't leave a whole bone in your worship's body, nor in mine.'

'Observe, Sancho,' said Don Quixote, 'that virtue is persecuted wherever it exists to an outstanding degree. Few or none of the famous heroes of the past escaped the slander of malice. Julius Caesar, a most courageous, most wise and valiant captain, was branded as ambitious, and not over-clean either in his clothes or in his habits. Alexander, whose exploits won for him the title of the Great, was said to have been given to some measure of drunkenness. Hercules, the hero of the many labours, is said to have been lascivious and effeminate. Sir Galaor, the brother of Amadis of Gaul, is criticized for having been over lecherous, and his brother for being a blubberer. So, Sancho, among so much slander against good men, what they say against me may pass, if it is no more than you have told me.'

'Ah, there's the trouble, damn it,' replied Sancho.

'Is there anything more, then?' asked Don Quixote.

'There's still the tail to skin,' said Sancho. 'What I've said so far is tarts and gingerbread. But if your worship wants to know all the slander they speak of you, I'll bring you here presently some one who'll tell you the lot and not spare a crumb. For last night Bartholomew Carrasco's son arrived from studying at Salamanca, where they made him a bachelor. And when I went to welcome him home he told me that your worship's story is already in print under the title of *The Ingenious Gentleman Don Quixote de la Mancha*. He says that I'm mentioned too under my own name of Sancho Panza, and so is the lady Dulcinea del Toboso, and so are other matters which happened to us in private. It made me cross myself in wonder, to think how the story-writer could have learnt all that.'

'You may be certain, Sancho,' said Don Quixote, 'that the author of our history is some sage enchanter.'

'But if the author of this history was a sage enchanter,' answered Sancho, 'how can it be that, according to the bachelor Sampson Carrasco — for that's the man's name — he's called Cide Hamete Aubergine!'

'That is a Moor's name,' observed Don Quixote.

'So it may be,' replied Sancho, 'for I have heard that your Moors, for the most part, are very fond of aubergines.'

'You must be mistaken, Sancho,' said Don Quixote, 'in the surname of this Cide, which in Arabic means Lord.'

'Very likely,' replied Sancho, 'but if you would like to have me bring the Bachelor here, I'll go for him like a shot.'

'That would be doing me a great favour, friend,' said Don Quixote, 'for I am alarmed at what you have told me, and I shall not eat a mouthful that will do me good until I am informed on the whole subject.'

'Then I'll go for him,' replied Sancho. So leaving his master, he went to find the Bachelor, with whom he returned in a short while. And between these three there passed a most entertaining conversation.

Chapter III. *Of the ridiculous Conversation which passed between Don Quixote, Sancho Panza and the Bachelor Sampson Carrasco.*

DON QUIXOTE was very thoughtful as he waited for the Bachelor Carrasco, from whom he expected to hear how he had been put into a book, as Sancho had told him. He could not persuade himself that such a history existed, for the blood of the enemies he had slain was scarcely dry on his own sword-blade. Yet they would have it that his noble deeds of chivalry were already about in print. Nevertheless he imagined that some sage, either friendly or hostile, had given them to the Press by magic art; if a friend, to magnify and extol them above the most renowned actions of any knight errant; and if an enemy, to annihilate them and place them below the basest ever written of any mean squire – although, he admitted to himself, the deeds of squires were never written of. But if it were true that there was such a history, since it was about a knight errant it must perforce be grandiloquent, lofty, remarkable, magnificent and true. With this he was somewhat consoled; but it disturbed him to think that its author was a Moor, as that name of Cide suggested. For he could hope for no truth of the Moors, since they are all cheats, forgers and schemers. He was afraid too that his love affairs might have been treated with indelicacy, which would redound to the disparagement and prejudice of his lady, Dulcinea del Toboso. For he was anxious that it should be declared that he had always preserved his fidelity and reverence towards her, scorning Queens, Empresses, and damsels of all qualities, and curbing the violence of his natural appetites. And so Sancho found him, wrapt and involved in a thousand such fancies when he returned with Carrasco, whom the knight received with great courtesy.

The Bachelor was not very big in body, although his name was Sampson, but a great wag, of poor colour though of great intelligence. He must have been about twenty-four years old, with a round face, a flat nose, and a big mouth – all signs that he was of a mischievous disposition and fond of jokes and japes, as he showed, on seeing Don Quixote, by going down on his knees before him, and saying:

'Give me your hands, your Mightiness, Don Quixote de la Mancha. For by the habit of St. Peter, which I wear – although I have taken no more than the first four orders – your worship is one of the most famous knights errant there has ever been on all the rotundity of the earth. Blessed be Cide Hamete Benengeli, who has left us the history of your great deeds recorded, and thrice blessed the man of taste who took the pains to have it translated out of the Arabic into our vulgar Castilian, for the universal entertainment of mankind!'

Don Quixote made him get up and said: 'So it is true, then, that there is a history of me, and that he was a Moor and a sage who composed it?'

'So true is it,' said Sampson, 'that it is my opinion there are more than twelve thousand copies of this history in print to-day. If not, let Portugal, Barcelona and Valencia speak; for there they were printed. There is even a report that it is being printed at Antwerp too. In fact, I am pretty sure that there cannot be any nation into whose tongue it will not be translated.'

'One of the things,' said Don Quixote at this, 'which must give the greatest pleasure to a virtuous and eminent man is to see himself, in his life-time, printed and in the Press, and with a good name on peoples' tongues. I said a good name because, were it the opposite, no death could be so bad.'

'If it is a question of a good reputation and a good name,' said the Bachelor, 'your worship alone bears away the palm from all knights errant. For the Moor in his language, and the Christian in his, have carefully and accurately depicted for us your worship's gallantry, your great courage in confronting perils, your patience in adversity, your fortitude too under misfortune and wounds, and the chastity and continence of the most platonic loves of your worship and my lady, Doña Dulcinea del Toboso.'

'Never,' Sancho Panza broke in at this point, 'have I heard my lady Dulcinea called Doña, but simply The Lady Dulcinea del Toboso. There the history's wrong.'

'That is not an important objection,' replied Carrasco.

'No, surely,' replied Don Quixote; 'but tell me, Master Bachelor, which of my exploits are most highly praised in this history?'

'About that,' replied the Bachelor, 'there are different opinions, as there are different tastes. Some favour the adventure of the windmills which seemed to your worship Briareuses and giants. Others the adventure of the fulling mills. One man is for the description of the two armies, which proved afterwards to be two flocks of sheep. Another thinks most highly of the tale of the corpse which they were taking to Segovia for burial. Another says that the best of all is the freeing of the galley-slaves. And yet another that there is nothing equal to the two Benedictine giants and the combat with the valorous Basque.'

'Tell me, Master Bachelor,' put in Sancho, 'does the adventure with the Yanguesans come in, when our good Rocinante had a fancy to look for dainties at the bottom of the sea?'

'The sage left nothing in his ink-horn,' replied Sampson. 'He tells us everything and dwells on every point, even to the capers Sancho cut on the blanket.'

'I cut no capers on the blanket,' replied Sancho. 'But in the air I did, and more than I liked.'

'In my opinion,' said Don Quixote, 'there is no human history in the world which has not got its ups and downs, particularly those that treat of knight errantry. They can never be full of fortunate incidents.'

'For all that,' replied the Bachelor, 'some who have read your history say that they would have been glad if the authors had left out a few of the countless beatings which Don Quixote received in various encounters.'

'That's where the truth of the story comes in,' said Sancho.

'Yet they might in fairness have kept quiet about them,' said Don Quixote, 'for there is no reason to record those actions which do not change or affect the truth of the story, if they redound to the discredit of the hero. Aeneas was not as pious as Virgil paints him, I promise you, nor Ulysses as prudent as Homer describes him.'

'That is true,' replied Sampson; 'but it is one thing to write as a poet, and another as a historian. The poet can relate and sing things, not as they were but as they should have been, without in any way affecting the truth of the matter.'

'Well, if it's telling the truth this Moor's after,' said Sancho, 'and my master's beatings are all set down, then mine will be found amongst them. For they never took the measure of his worship's shoulders without taking it of my whole body. But that's not to be wondered at, for this same master of mine says the limbs have to take a share in the head's pain.'

'You are a sly fellow, Sancho,' answered Don Quixote. 'I swear your memory does not fail you when you want to remember anything.'

'Even if I'd a mind to forget the thrashings I got,' said Sancho, 'the marks wouldn't let me, for they're still fresh on my ribs.'

'Be quiet, Sancho,' said Don Quixote, 'and do not interrupt the Bachelor, whom I beg to proceed and tell me what is said of me in this history of his.'

'And of me,' said Sancho, 'for they say I'm one of the principal presonages in it.'

'Personages, not *presonages*, Sancho my friend,' said Sampson.

'So we have another vocabulary corrector!' said Sancho. 'If it goes on like this we shall never be done in this life.'

'Hang me, Sancho,' answered the Bachelor, 'if you are not the second person in the history. And there are some who think the parts where you talk are the best bits in the story; though there are others who say that you were excessively credulous in believing in the governorship of that isle Don Quixote here promised you.'

'There is still sun on the thatch,' said Don Quixote, 'and all the while Sancho is getting older. With the experience that years bring he will become more competent and fitter to be a governor than he is now.'

'By God, sir,' said Sancho, 'any isle I can't govern at my present age I shall never govern if I live to be as old as Methusaleh. The trouble is that this isle of yours is hidden away, I don't know where, and not that I haven't the brains to govern it.'

'Leave it to God, Sancho,' said Don Quixote, 'and all will be well. Perhaps better than you think, for not a leaf stirs on a tree without God's will.'

'That is the truth,' said Sampson; 'for if God wills, Sancho will not lack a thousand isles to govern, let alone one.'

'I have seen governors about here,' said Sancho, 'who, to my thinking, don't come up to the sole of my shoe. Yet for all that they're called *your worship*, and served off silver.'

'Those are not governors of isles,' answered Sampson, 'but of more manageable territories. Governors of isles must at least be grammarians.'

'The *"gram"* I can easily manage,' said Sancho, 'but the *"marians"* I pass, for I don't understand them. But leaving this matter of a governorship in God's hands – and may He place me where I may serve Him best – let me say, Master Bachelor Sampson Carrasco, that I'm extraordinarily glad that the author of this history has spoken of me so nicely that what he says gives no offence. For, as I'm a good squire, if he'd said things about me unbefitting the old Christian I am, the deaf would be hearing of it.'

'That would be working miracles,' said Sampson.

'Miracles or no miracles,' said Sancho, 'let everyone mind how he speaks or writes about *presons*, and not put down helter-skelter the first thing that come into his head.'

'One of the faults they find in this history,' said the Bachelor, 'is that the author inserted a novel called *The Tale of Foolish Curiosity* – not that it is bad or badly told, but because it is out of place and has nothing to do with the story of his worship Don Quixote.'

'I'll bet the son of a dog has made a fine mix-up of everything,' put in Sancho.

'Now I believe that the author of my story is no sage but an ignorant chatterer,' said Don Quixote, 'and that he set himself to write it down blindly and without any method, and let it turn out anyhow, like Orbaneja, the painter of Ubeda, who, when they asked him what he was painting, used to answer "Whatever it turns out." Sometimes he would paint a cock, in such a fashion and so unlike one that he had to write in Gothic characters beside it: *This is a cock*. And so it must be with my history, which will need a commentary to be understood.'

'No,' replied Sampson, 'for it's so plain that there is nothing in it to raise any difficulty. Children finger it; young people read it; grown men know it by heart, and old men praise it. It is so dog-eared, in fact, and so familiar to all sorts of people that whenever they see a lean horse go by, they cry: "There goes Rocinante." Those who are most given to reading it are pages; there is not a gentleman's antechamber in which you will not find a *Don Quixote*. When one lays it down, another picks it up; some rush at it; others beg for it. In fact, this story is the most delightful and least harmful entertainment ever seen to this day, for nowhere in it is to be found anything even resembling an indelicate expression or an uncatholic thought.'

'To write in any other way,' said Don Quixote, 'would be to write not the truth, but lies; and historians who resort to lies ought to be burnt like coiners of false money. But I do not know what induced the author to make use of novels and irrelevant stories, when he had so much of mine to write about. No doubt he felt bound by the proverb: "With hay or with straw, it is all the same." For really, if he had confined himself to my thoughts, my sighs, my tears, my worthy designs, and my undertakings, he could have made a volume greater than all the works of El Tostado, or at any rate as big. In fact my conclusion is, Master Bachelor, that to compose histories or books of any sort at all you need good judgement and ripe understanding. To be witty and write humorously requires great genius. The cunningest part in a play is the fool's, for a man who wants to be taken for a simpleton must never be one. History is like a sacred writing, for it has to be truthful; and where the truth is, in so far as it is the truth, there God is. But notwithstanding this there are some who compose books and toss them off like fritters.'

'There is no book so bad,' said the Bachelor, 'that there is not something good in it.'

'No doubt of that,' replied Don Quixote, 'but it very often happens that authors who have deservedly reaped and won great fame by their writings have lost it all, or somewhat diminished it, when they have given them to the Press.'

'The cause of that,' said Sampson, 'is that printed books are viewed at leisure, and so their faults are easily seen, and the greater the fame of their authors the more closely are they examined. Renowned men of genius, great poets and famous historians are always, or generally, envied by such as make it their pleasure and particular pastime to judge the writings of others, without having published any of their own.'

'That is not to be wondered at,' said Don Quixote, 'for there are many theologians who are not good in the pulpit, but excellent at recognizing the faults or excesses of those who preach.'

'All that is true, Don Quixote,' said Carrasco, 'but I should be glad if such censors would be more merciful and less scrupulous, and not scold at the specks in the bright sun of the work they review. For, though Homer sometimes nods, let them reflect how long he stayed awake to give us the light of his work with the least possible shadow. And it may well be that what seem faults to them are moles, which at times enhance the beauty of a face. In fact it is my opinion that an author runs a very great risk in printing a book. For it is the greatest of all impossibilities to write one that will satisfy and please every reader.'

'The one which treats of me,' said Don Quixote, 'must have pleased few.'

'Quite the opposite; for as there are an infinite number of fools in the world, an infinite number of people have enjoyed that history. But here are some who have found fault, and taxed the author's memory for forgetting who it was that robbed Sancho of his Dapple. For it is not stated there, but only from the context do we infer that it was stolen. Yet a little farther on we find Sancho riding on this same ass, and are never told how he turned up again. They also say that he forgot to put down what Sancho did with the hundred crowns he found in the leather bag in the Sierra Morena, for they were never mentioned again. Many people want to know what use he made of them, or what he spent them on – that is one of the essential points left out of the work.'

'I'm not prepared now, Master Sampson,' replied Sancho, 'to go into details or accounts, for I've got a stomach-ache, and if I don't cure it with two gulps of the old stuff, it will put me on St. Lucy's thorn. I have a drop at home, and my old woman is waiting for me. I'll come back when I've had my dinner, and answer all your worship's questions, and all the world's besides, whether it's about my losing the ass or spending the hundred crowns.'

Then, waiting for no reply, he went off home without another word. Don Quixote begged and prayed the Bachelor to stop and take pot-luck with him, and he accepted the invitation and stayed to the meal, at which a pair of pigeons were added to the ordinary fare. Over table they talked of knight-errantry, Carrasco following the knight's humour, and when the banquet was ended they slept through the heat of the day, till Sancho came back and their previous discussion was resumed.

Chapter IV. In which Sancho Panza satisfies the Doubts and Questions of the Bachelor Sampson Carrasco, with other matters worthy of being known and related.

SANCHO returned to Don Quixote's house and, resuming the previous conversation, said: 'As to Master Sampson's saying that he wanted to know who stole my ass, and how, and when, I should like to state in reply, that the same night the two of us were running from the Holy Brotherhood in the Sierra Morena, after the luckless adventure of the galley-slaves and the one with the corpse they were carrying to Segovia, my master and I got into a thicket. Don Quixote rested on his lance and I on my Dapple; and, bruised and wearied as we were, from our recent affrays, we settled down to sleep as soundly as if we had been on four feather beds. As for me, I slept so heavily that whoever it was had a chance to come and prop me up on four stakes, which he put under the four corners of my pack-saddle, in such a way that he left me in the air, and took my Dapple from under me without my feeling it.'

'That is an easy trick,' said Don Quixote, 'and nothing new. For the same thing happened to Sacripante at the siege of Albraca, when that famous thief Brunelo took his horse from between his legs by the same device.'

'Dawn broke,' continued Sancho, 'and I had scarcely stretched myself when the stakes gave way and down I came with a great tumble on to the ground. I looked for my ass, and didn't find him. Then tears started to my eyes, and I set up a great wailing. And if the author of our history didn't put that in, you can reckon he left out a good thing. Then, at the end of I don't know how many days, when we were travelling with the lady Princess Micomicona, I recognized my ass, and who should be riding on him but that notorious malefactor Gines de Pasamonte, disguised as a gipsy, the cunning cheat my master and I freed from the galley-chain.'

'The mistake is not there,' replied Sampson, 'but when the author says that Sancho was riding on this same Dapple, before the ass turned up again.'

'I don't know how to answer that,' said Sancho. 'All I can say is that perhaps the history-writer was wrong, or it may have been an error of the printer's.'

'That is it, no doubt,' said Sampson; 'but what became of the hundred crowns? Were they spent?'

'I spent them on myself and on my wife and children. It was because of them that my wife was so patient about my travellings and ramblings in the service of my master Don Quixote. For if I'd come back home at the end of all that time ass-less and penniless, I should have expected a black welcome. Now if there's anything else you want to know, here I am, and I'll answer to the king himself in *preson*, though it's nobody's business to pry into whether I took them or I didn't, and whether I spent them or not. For if the blows I got on that journey were to be paid for in money, even if they were reckoned at no more than four farthings apiece, another hundred crowns wouldn't pay me for half of them. Let every man lay his hand on his heart, and not set himself up to call white black and black white; for everyone is as God made him, and often a good deal worse.'

'I will take care,' said Carrasco, 'to warn the author of this history not to forget what our good Sancho has said should he print it again, for it would improve it by quite a tidy bit.'

'Is there anything else to amend in this legend, Master Bachelor?' asked Don Quixote.

'Yes, no doubt there is,' replied he, 'but nothing as important as the matters mentioned.'

'Does the author,' asked Don Quixote, 'by any chance promise a second part?'

'Yes, he does,' replied Sampson, 'but he says he has not found it, and does not know who has it. And so we are in doubt whether it will come out or not. Indeed, some say that second parts are never any good, and others say that enough has been written about Don Quixote. So it is doubtful whether there will be a second part. Though some, who are more of the jovial sort than the saturnine, cry out: — Let us have more Quixotries. Let Don Quixote charge and Sancho Panza talk, and come what may, we shall be content.'

'What is the author up to, then?' asked Don Quixote.

'What?' replied Sampson. 'As soon as he has found the history which he is taking extraordinary pains to search for, he will give it straight to the Press. For he is keener on the profit he will get from it than for any kind of praise.'

At which Sancho remarked: 'Does the author expect to make money by it? It'll be a marvel if he gets any, for it'll be nothing but hurry, hurry, like a tailor on Easter eve; and work that's done in haste is never finished as perfectly as it ought to be. Let this Master Moor, or whatever he is, take care and look what he is doing, for I and my master will provide him with enough rubble in the way of adventures and different things for him to be able to make up not only a second part but a hundred more. The good man imagines, no doubt, that we're asleep here in the straw; but let him lift up a foot for shoeing, and he'll see whether we're lame. What I mean to say is that, if my master would take my advice, we should be in the field by now, undoing injuries and setting right wrongs, as is the use and custom of good knights errant.'

Sancho had no sooner reached the end of this speech than Rocinante's neighing came to their ears. This Don Quixote took as a good omen, and so he decided to set out on another expedition in three or four days. Then, declaring his intention to the Bachelor, he asked for his advice in what direction to begin his journey. The Bachelor's opinion was they should go towards the city of Saragossa in the Kingdom of Aragon. For there in a few days' time they would be holding most solemn jousts in honour of the feast of St. George, in which, if he were to vanquish all the knights of Aragon, he would acquire an ascendancy over every knight in the world.

He commended Don Quixote's honourable and valiant resolution, yet warned him to be more wary in encountering dangers; for his life was not his own, but belonged to all those who had need of him to protect them and succour them in their misfortunes.

'That's where I cry off, Master Sampson,' said Sancho at this, 'for my master attacks a hundred armed men like a greedy boy falling on half a dozen water-melons. God's truth, Master Bachelor, there are times to attack and times to retreat, and it can't always be *Santiago and at 'em!* Besides, I've heard it said, and by my master himself, if I remember rightly, that between the extremes of cowardice and foolhardiness lies the middle course of bravery. And if that's true, I wouldn't have him run away for no reason, or attack when the odds demand the other thing. But I'd like to warn my master of one thing especially: if he's to take me with him, it must be on condition that he does all the fighting, and that I'm not obliged to do anything except look after his person so far as his cleanliness and his feeding go. There I'll serve him gladly, but if he expects that I'll put hand to sword, even though it's only against base rascals with axe and steel cap, he's imagining the impossible. I'm not thinking of gaining great fame as a fighting man, Master Sampson, but as the best and loyalest squire that ever served knight errant. And if, in return for all my good services, my master Don Quixote should wish to give me some isle of the many which his worship says he's sure to stumble across hereabouts, I shall be much obliged. But, if he shouldn't give me one, I am as I was born, and man mustn't live relying on man but on God. What's more bread will taste as good without a governorship as with one – and perhaps better. How am I to know if the Devil hasn't set a trap for me in these governorships, and if I mightn't trip and fall in and knock out my teeth? Sancho I was born, and Sancho I expect to die. But if, for all that, Heaven should present me with some isle, or something else of the kind, freely and easily and without much trouble or risk, I'm not so foolish as to throw it away. For, as the saying goes, when they give you the heifer run with the halter, and – when a good thing comes take it off home.'

'Brother Sancho,' said Carrasco, 'you have spoken like a professor. But put your trust in God all the same, and in your master, Don Quixote, for he will give you a kingdom – not just an isle.'

'It's all the same to me whichever it is,' replied Sancho, 'although I assure you, Master Carrasco, that my master won't be throwing the kingdom he gives me into a torn sack. For I've felt my own pulse, and I find I've the health to rule kingdoms and govern isles, as I've told my master before now.'

'Look out, Sancho,' said Sampson, 'for honours change manners, and perhaps if you were once a governor, you would not recognize the mother that bore you.'

'That may be true,' replied Sancho, 'of those who are born among the mallows, but not of men that have four inches of old Christian fat on their souls, as I have. Just look at my character, and see whether I could be ungrateful to anyone.'

'God grant you are right,' said Don Quixote. 'We shall see when the governorship comes, for I seem to have it before my eyes already.'

With these words he turned to the Bachelor and begged him, if he were a poet, to do him the favour of composing him some verses on the subject of his intended parting from his lady Dulcinea del Toboso, putting one letter of her name at the beginning of each line, so that when the poem was complete these first letters taken together might read *Dulcinea del Toboso.*

The Bachelor replied that, although he was not one of the most famous poets in Spain – of whom there were said to be no more than three and a half – he would not fail to write the verses. Though he found one very great difficulty in their composition, for the name contained seventeen letters, and if he were to make four stanzas of four lines each, there would be one letter over, and if he were to write five-line stanzas, which go by the name of '*decimas*' or roundelays, there would be three short. But, anyhow, he would try to squeeze one letter, somehow or another, so as to get the name of Dulcinea del Toboso into four stanzas.

'You must get it in, whichever way you do it,' said Don Quixote, 'because if the name is not there, plain and manifest, no woman will believe that the verses have been made for her.'

They agreed on this point, and also that they should set out within eight days. Don Quixote charged the Bachelor to keep his intention secret, especially from the priest and Master Nicholas, and from his niece and his housekeeper, in case they should hinder his honourable and valiant purpose. Carrasco gave his word, and with that took his leave, enjoining Don Quixote to keep him informed of all his successes and reverses, whenever he had an opportunity. And so they parted, and Sancho went to make all necessary preparations for the expedition.

Chapter V. Of the wise and humorous Conversation between Sancho Panza and his wife Teresa Panza, and other matters worthy of happy record.

WHEN the translator of this history comes to write this fifth chapter, he declares that he considers it apocryphal, because in it Sancho's style is much superior to what one would expect of his limited understanding, and his remarks so subtle that they seem beyond the range of his intelligence. But in order to fulfil his duty as a translator he is unwilling to omit it, and so proceeds as follows:

Sancho arrived home so jubilant and cheerful that his wife could observe his joy a bowshot off; so much so that she could not help asking: 'What's the matter with you, Sancho, my friend, that you're so cheerful?'

'If it pleased God,' he replied, 'I should be very glad, wife, not to be as happy as I seem.'

'I don't understand you, husband,' replied she. 'I don't know what you mean about being glad not to be happy, if it pleased God. I may be a fool, but I don't see who can be happy at not being happy.'

'Look, Teresa,' answered Sancho. 'I'm happy because I've decided to take service again with my master, Don Quixote, who is after setting out for a third time to search for adventures. I'm going off with him again, for my poverty demands it. And so does my hope of finding another hundred crowns like those I spent. And this cheers me now, though it makes me sad to have to part from you and the children. If God were pleased to give me food to eat dry-shod and at home, without dragging me over by-paths and cross-roads — which He could do very cheaply by merely wishing to — of course my happiness would be firmer and stronger, for the joy I feel now is mixed with sadness at leaving you. That's why I said truly that I should be glad, if God pleased, not to be happy.'

'See here, Sancho,' replied Teresa. 'Since you've been a limb of a knight errant you talk in such a roundabout way that no one can understand you.'

'It's enough that God understands me, wife,' replied Sancho, 'for He's the understander of all things. Let it rest there. But mind you, woman, you'll have to take good care of Dapple these next three days, so that he's fit to carry arms. Double his feeds, and look out his pack-saddle and the rest of his tackle. For we're not going to a wedding, but to roam the world and play at give-and-take with giants and dragons and hobgoblins, and to hear hissings and roarings, and bellowings and blusterings. And even all that would be flowers of lavender if we hadn't to deal with Yanguesans and enchanted Moors.'

'I can well believe, husband,' replied Teresa, 'that squires errant don't get their bread for nothing, and so I shall pray our Lord without stopping to deliver you quickly from all your misfortunes.'

'I tell you, wife,' replied Sancho, 'that if I didn't expect to be governor of an isle before long I should drop dead here on the spot.'

'Oh, no, husband,' said Teresa, 'don't kill the hen, even if she has got the pip. Live, and to the Devil with all the governorships in the world. Without a governorship you came out of your mother's womb, without a governorship you've lived to this day, and without a governorship you'll go – or they'll take you – to your grave, when it shall please God. There are plenty in the world without a governorship, who don't give up living and being counted in the number of the people for all that! Hunger's the best sauce in the world, and as the poor have no lack of it, they enjoy their food. But, look you, Sancho, if by chance you should come on a governorship, don't forget me and the children. Remember that young Sancho's just fifteen now, and ought to go to school, if his uncle the abbot means to make him a churchman. Don't forget either that your daughter Mari Sancha won't drop down dead if we find a husband for her. For I've a suspicion that she's as anxious to marry as you are to see yourself a governor. And, after all, a daughter's better ill married than well kept.'

'If God lets me have any sort of governorship,' answered Sancho. 'I mean to marry Mari Sancha off all right, wife, so high that no one'll get near her without calling her "*your ladyship*".'

'No, no, Sancho,' replied Teresa. 'Marry her to her equal. That's the best thing. If you raise her from clogs to high-heeled shoes, and from common grey serge to farthingales and silk skirts, and from *Moll* and *you* to *Doña so-and-so* and *your ladyship*, the girl won't know herself. Then she'll come a thousand croppers at every step, and they'll all see she's just coarse and homespun stuff.'

'Be quiet, silly,' said Sancho. 'All she needs is two or three years' practice. Then the grand manner will come to her as if she were born to it. And if not, what does it matter? Let her be *"her ladyship"*, come what may.'

'Keep to your own station, Sancho,' replied Teresa. 'Don't try to raise yourself higher, and remember the proverb: "take your neighbour's son, wipe his nose, and ask him home." It would be a fine thing indeed to marry our Maria to a great count or a fine gentleman. He might take another look at her when the fancy took him, and then call her a peasant, the daughter of clodhoppers and flax-spinners. Not at my time of life, husband! I didn't bring up my child for that. Indeed I didn't. You bring the money, Sancho, and leave marrying her to me. There is Lope Tocho now, Juan Tocho's son, a sound, sturdy lad. We know him, and I can see he doesn't dislike the girl. Now, she'll be well matched with him. He's our equal, and we shall always have her under our eye. Then we shall be all together, parents and children, grand-children and sons-in-law, and peace and God's blessing will go with us all. No, none of your marrying her in those courts and grand palaces of yours, where they won't understand her and she won't understand herself.'

'Come here, beast,' replied Sancho, 'wife of Barabbas. Why do you want to hinder me now, for no reason at all, from marrying my daughter to someone who will give me grandsons who'll be called *"your lordships"*? Look you, Teresa, I've always heard my elders say that anyone who doesn't know how to enjoy good luck when it comes shouldn't complain if it passes him by. And now that it's knocking at our door, it wouldn't be right to shut it out. Let's sail, seeing that there's a fair wind blowing.'

Now it was this turn of speech and Sancho's remarks farther down that made the translator of this history, so he says, regard this chapter as apocryphal.

'Don't you think, creature,' continued Sancho, 'that it'll be a good thing to rig myself out with some profitable government that'll lift our feet out of the mud? Let me choose a husband for Maria Sancha, and see how they'll call you Doña Teresa Panza and give you a seat in church on a rug with pillows and cushions, in spite of all the ladies in the town. No, you had rather stay always the same, neither more nor less, like a figure in a tapestry. Let us talk no more about it, for Sanchicha shall be a countess, whatever you say.'

'How you do go on, husband!' answered Teresa. 'All the same, I'm still afraid that this countessing of my daughter's will be her undoing. But do as you like. Make her a duchess or a princess. But let me tell you that it won't be with my will and consent. I've always been a lover of equality, and I can't bear to see haughtiness with no foundations. Teresa they wrote me down at my baptism, pure and simple without additions or trimmings or ornaments of "*Dons*" or "*Doñas*". Cascajo was my father's name, but as I'm your wife, they call me Teresa Panza, though by rights it should be Teresa Cascajo – but kings act as the laws will. I'm content with my name without having a "*Don*" put on top of it, too heavy for me to carry. I don't want to have people who see me go by dressed up like a countess or a governor's wife crying out: "Look what airs the pig feeder gives herself. Yesterday she wasn't too proud to pull out a lump of flax, and she went to mass with the skirt of her dress over her head for a cloak. And to-day she wears a farthingale and buckles, and she's as proud as if we didn't know her." If God keeps me in my seven, or my five senses, or however many I've got, I don't mean to give them a chance to see me in that scrape. Go off, brother, and be a government or an isle, and give yourself what airs you please. But I swear on my mother's life that neither I nor my daughter will stir a step from our village. An honest woman and a broken leg are best at home, and for an honest girl a job of work's her holiday. Go off on your adventures with your Don Quixote and leave us to our misadventures. God'll send us better luck if we're good. – But I'm sure I don't know who put a Don on him, for his father never had one, nor his grandfather either.'

'You have a devil in that body of yours, I tell you,' replied Sancho. 'Lord bless the woman, what a lot of rubbish you've strung together, one thing on another, without head or tail! What have your Cascajo, your buckles, your proverbs, and your airs to do with what I'm saying? Listen, you silly fool – I've reason enough to call you that, for you don't understand what I say, and go running away from your good fortune – If I'd said that my daughter was to throw herself down from a tower, or go wandering through the world the way Doña Urraca wanted to, you would be right not to agree to my plans. But if in two twos, in less than the twinkling of an eye, I clap a *"Don"* and a ladyship on her shoulders for you, and fetch her out of the stubble and put her under a canopy, on a dais, and in an alcove with more velvet cushions than there were Moors in the Almohada family of Morocco, why won't you consent and fall in with my wishes?'

'Do you know why, husband?' replied Teresa. 'Because of that proverb that says: Who covers you discovers you. Nobody looks very hard at poor people, but they stare at the rich; and if some rich man was poor once, then it's all grumbling and abuse, and you're never done with slanderers, who are as thick in these streets as a swarm of bees.'

'Look here, Teresa,' replied Sancho, 'and listen to what I'm going to say. You'll never have heard the like, perhaps, in all the days of your life. I'm not speaking now just out of my own knowledge, for what I'm going to say is the opinion of the holy father who preach-ed in this village last Lent. He said, if I remember rightly, that what we see present and before our eyes appears, stays and persists in our memories much better and much more vividly than things past.' – This is the second speech of Sancho's, says the translator, that makes him consider this chapter apocryphal, for it is beyond Sancho's capacity. – 'How comes it,' he continued, 'that when we see some-one finely dressed, adorned with rich clothes, and with a train of servants, we seem to be moved and compelled involuntarily to pay him respect, even though at that very moment our memory may recall to us the low condition we once saw him in? For the disgrace of poverty or low birth, once it's in the past, is no more, and the only things which exist are what we see present. So if the man whom Fortune drew out of the obscurity of his low estate – these were the father's very words – to the height of prosperity, is well-bred, generous, and courteous to all, and doesn't set himself up as the equal of people who have been noble since olden times, you may be assured, Teresa, that no one will remember who he was, but everyone will respect what he is — except for the envious — and no good fortune is safe from them.'

'I don't understand you, husband,' replied Teresa. 'Do whatever you like, but don't break my head with your haranguing and fine words. If you are revolved to do what you say ...'

'Resolved you mean, wife,' said Sancho, 'not *revolved*.'

'Don't start arguing with me, husband,' replied Teresa. 'I speak as God would have me speak, and I don't meddle with grand words. What I say is, if you are set on having a governorship, take your son Sancho with you, and teach him how to govern now, for it's a good thing for sons to inherit and learn their fathers' trades.'

'When I get my governorship,' said Sancho, 'I'll send for him post haste, and I'll send you money too, for I shan't be short of it. There's always somebody about who'll make a loan to a governor if he hasn't any. Just you dress him so as to hide what he is and make him look like what he's going to be.'

'You send the money,' said Teresa, 'and I'll dress him like a palm branch in a procession.'

'Then we're agreed,' said Sancho, 'that our daughter is to be a countess.'

'The day I see her a countess,' replied Teresa, 'I shall reckon I'm laying her in her grave. But I say once more, do as you please. For with this burden are women born, to be obedient to their husbands, even if they're dolts.'

And at this she began to cry as bitterly as if she saw little Sancha dead and buried already. Sancho consoled her by saying that though he was bound to make her a countess, he would put it off as long as he could. With this the conversation ended, and Sancho went to visit Don Quixote once more, and to make preparations for their departure.

Chapter VI. *Of what passed between Don Quixote and his Niece and Housekeeper: one of the most important chapters in this whole History.*

Now, whilst Sancho Panza and his wife Teresa were holding the absurd conversation just related, Don Quixote's niece and house-keeper were not idle, for they were beginning to guess from countless signs that their master and uncle was wanting to break away a third time and return to the practice of what was to them his ill-errant chivalry. They tried by all possible means to divert him from so evil a course, but it was like preaching in the wilderness and hammering cold iron. Though amongst the many arguments they used on him was one of the housekeeper's to this effect:

'Really, master, if you don't keep your feet still and stay quiet at home, and give up wandering up hill and down dale like a soul in torment, seeking what they call adventures but I call misfortunes, I'll have to go and make my complaint, and call on God and the King to put a stop to it.'

To which Don Quixote replied: 'I do not know, mistress, what answer God will give to your complaints; or His Majesty either. I only know that if I were King, I should refuse to reply to the num-berless impertinent petitions presented to me every day. For one of the greatest among the many burdens kings bear is to be obliged to listen to everybody and reply to everybody. So I should not want him to be troubled by any affairs of mine.'

To which the housekeeper replied: 'Tell us, sir, are there no knights in His Majesty's court?'

'Yes,' answered Don Quixote, 'there are many. And so there should be, for they enhance the greatness of princes and increase the royal dignity.'

'Then couldn't your worship,' she replied, 'be one of those who serve their Lord and King in comfort as one of his Court?'

'Listen, friend,' answered Don Quixote. 'Not all knights can be courtiers, nor can all courtiers be knights errant, nor should they be. There must be some of all kinds in the world; and although we are all knights, there is a great deal of difference between one and another. For the courtiers do not stir from their rooms or beyond the threshold of their court, but travel over the whole world merely by looking at a map, without a farthing's cost or suffering heat or cold, hunger, or thirst. But we, the true knights errant, measure the whole earth with our own feet, in sun, in cold, and beneath the sky, exposed to the inclemencies of the heavens by night and day, on foot and on horse. We know our enemies, not only from portraits but in their real persons; and in all perils and on all occasions we meet them in fight, without regard for trifling points or for the laws of the duel: whether either party carries a shorter lance or sword or not; whether he has some charm on him or some hidden trickery; whether the sun is to be divided and portioned or not; and other ceremonies of this kind which are observed in single combats between man and man, matters of which I know but you do not. And I must tell you also that a good knight errant may see ten giants whose heads not only touch but overtop the clouds, each of them with two enormous towers for legs, and with arms like the masts of huge and mighty ships, and each eye like a great mill-wheel and blazing more fiercely than a glass furnace, yet he must not be in the least dismayed. But, on the contrary, he must meet them with a brave air and a fearless heart, and attack them and, if it is possible, conquer them and rout them in one brief moment, even though they may be armed with the shells of certain fish which are said to be harder than adamant, and bear instead of swords trenchant knives of Damascus steel or clubs spiked with this same metal, as I have seen them on several occasions. All this I have said, mistress, to prove to you the difference there is between some knights and others. It is only right, then, for every prince to think more highly of this last, or rather of this first species of knight errant. For, as we read in their histories, there have been some amongst them who have been the salvation, not only of one kingdom but of many.'

'Oh, sir,' interposed his niece, 'do remember that all you say about knights errant is fiction and lies. And if their histories aren't burnt, they each deserve to wear a penitent's coat, or a badge by which they can be recognized as infamous corrupters of good manners.'

'By God,' said Don Quixote, 'if you were not my lawful niece, being my own sister's daughter, I should give you such a chastisement for the blasphemy you have uttered that it would resound through the whole world. How is it possible for a young frippet who scarcely knows how to manage a dozen bobbins of lace to dare to disparage and censure the histories of knights errant? What would Sir Amadis say if he were to hear you? He would certainly pardon you, though, for he was the humblest and most courteous knight of his age, and a great protector of maidens as well. But one might have heard you who would have made you sorry: for they are not all courteous and considerate. Some there are that are unmannerly ruffians. Nor are all who style themselves so knights through and through. Some are of gold, others of alloy. All appear to be knights, yet not all can stand the test of the touchstone. There are base fellows who puff themselves up to seem like knights, and there are proud knights who seem to be dying with desire to appear base fellows. The first rise by ambition or by virtue; the second fall from slackness or vice. We need, therefore, to use careful discernment in distinguishing these two kinds of knights, so like in name and so unlike in deeds.'

'Good Heavens!' exclaimed his niece. 'What a lot you know, uncle! Why, at a pinch, you could get up in the pulpit or go and preach in the streets, and yet you're so blind and so palpably foolish that you'd have us think you're valiant when you are old; and strong when you're infirm; that you right wrongs when you're bent by age; and, worst of all, that you're a knight when you aren't, for though a gentleman can be one, a poor man can't!'

'There is much reason in what you say, niece,' replied Don Quixote, 'and I could tell you things about pedigrees that would surprise you. But not choosing to mix the sacred with the profane, I will refrain. Look, friends, and listen to me. All the pedigrees in the world can be reduced to four kinds. The first are those families which from humble beginnings have extended and expanded until they have reached supreme greatness; the second are those of high extraction who have preserved and maintained their original dignity; in the third sort are those who from great beginnings have gradually dwindled and decayed like a pyramid until, like the point of that pyramid, they end in nothingness – for compared with its base or seat, the point of a pyramid is nothing. The last sort – and these are the most numerous – have had neither good beginnings nor a respectable development, and consequently will end up without a name, with no better pedigree than ordinary plebeian folk. Of the first, who have risen from humble origins to their present greatness, let the Ottoman house serve as an example; for, sprung from a lowly and mean shepherd, it stands now at the height we see it. Of the second kind, which had its origins in greatness and preserved its state without increasing it, let many princes serve as example, princes by heredity who maintain their dignities without increasing or diminishing them, containing themselves peacefully within the

limits of their estates. Of those who began great and ended in a
point there are thousands of examples. For all the Pharaohs and
Ptolemies of Egypt, the Caesars of Rome, and all that countless
throng – if one may so call them – of princes, monarchs and lords –
Medes, Assyrians, Persians, Greeks and Barbarians – all those
lineages and lordships have ended in a point and in nothing – like
those who gave them birth. For it would be impossible now to find
any of their descendants, and if we were to find them, it would be
in a low and humble station. Of the plebeian stock all that I can say
is that it only serves to swell the numbers of living men whose
great deeds deserve no other fame or eulogy. From all this I wish
you to infer, my dear sillies, that the subject of genealogies is a most
confused one, and that the only families which have a claim to greatness and fame are those who show it by their virtue, by their riches,
and by the liberality of their members. I said virtues, riches and
liberality, because the great man who is wicked will only be a great
evil-doer, and the rich man who is not liberal will be a miserly
beggar. For the possessor of riches is not rendered fortunate by
having them but by spending them – and not by spending them as
he pleases, but by knowing how to spend well. The poor gentleman
possesses no other way of showing that he is a gentleman except
by virtue; by being affable, well-bred, courteous, polite and accommodating; not haughty, arrogant, or censorious; and above all
by being charitable. For by giving a poor man a halfpenny with a
cheerful heart he will show himself as liberal as the man who gives
alms to the pealing of bells. For there will be no one that sees him
adorned with these virtues I speak of, who will not take him for a
man of good stock, even though he does not know him – and it
would be a wonder if he were not so, since praise has ever been the
prize of virtue, and the virtuous cannot fail to be praised. There are
two roads, my daughters, by which men can come to honour and
riches. One is the way of Letters; the other the way of Arms. For
myself I have more arms than learning, and my inclination is to
Arms, for I was born under the influence of the planet Mars. So I am
almost compelled to follow that road, and must pursue it despite the
whole world; and it will be vain for you to weary yourselves in persuading me to go counter to the heavens' wishes, Fortune's decrees,
reason's demands and, more than that, against my heart's desires.

For knowing as I do the innumerable toils attendant upon knight errantry, I know as well the infinite benefits which can be attained by it. I know that the path of virtue is very narrow, and the road of vice wide and spacious. I know, too, that their final goals are different; for the wide and spacious road of vice ends in death, and the narrow and laborious path of virtue ends in life; and not in life which has an ending, but in life without end. I know, as our great Castilian poet says, that

> By these rough tracks we travel, on our way
> To the high seat of immortality
> Never attained by such as from it stray.'

'Oh dear! Oh dear!' cried his niece; 'my master's a poet too! He knows everything. He can do everything. I'll bet you that, if he chose to turn bricklayer, he would build a house as easily as a bird cage.'

'I promise you, niece,' replied Don Quixote, 'that if these knightly thoughts did not master all my senses there would be nothing I could not do, nor anything rare which my hands could not make, particularly cages and toothpicks.'

Just at that moment there was a knocking at the door, and when Don Quixote asked who was there, Sancho Panza replied that it was he. And no sooner did the housekeeper learn who it was than she ran to hide, so as to avoid seeing him, so much did she loathe him. But the niece opened the door to him, and his master Don Quixote went to receive him with open arms. Then the two of them shut themselves up in his room, where they held another conversation every bit as good as the last.

Chapter VII. *Of a Discussion between Don Quixote and his Squire; with other very notable incidents.*

THE housekeeper no sooner saw Sancho Panza locked in with her master than she began to smell their drift, suspecting that the result of this conference would be a third expedition. So, taking her cloak, she went, full of anxiety and distress, to find the Bachelor Sampson Carrasco, thinking that, as he was a nicely spoken man and her master's new friend, he might be able to persuade him to give up his wild project. She found the Bachelor walking in the courtyard of his house, and on seeing him fell at his feet in a cold sweat of dismay; at the sight of which demonstration of grief and distress Carrasco asked her:

'What is this, Mistress Housekeeper? What has happened to you, that you seem so heartbroken?'

'It's nothing, dear Master Sampson; only that my master is breaking out – breaking out, there's no doubt about it!'

'Where is he breaking out, then, lady?' asked Sampson. 'Has he ruptured any part of his body?'

'He's not breaking out really,' she replied, 'except by way of his madness. I mean, dear Master Bachelor, that he wants to set out again – it will be for the third time – to seek up and down the world what he calls adventures, though I can't understand why he gives them that name. The first time they brought him back to us laid across an ass and beaten black and blue. The second time he came on an ox-cart, sitting shut up in a cage, making believe he was enchanted. And he was in such a state, poor soul, that his own mother wouldn't have known him – thin and sallow, with his eyes sunk right into his skull. It cost me more than six hundred eggs to bring him round to something like himself, as God knows and everybody else too, not counting my hens that won't let me tell a lie.'

'I can well believe that,' replied the Bachelor, 'for they are good, plump and well-bred creatures, and they wouldn't say the wrong thing if they burst for it. But, Mistress Housekeeper, is there nothing else? Has anything awful happened, or is it just that you're afraid of what Don Quixote will be up to next?'

'No, sir,' she replied; 'nothing worse than that.'

'Then don't worry,' said the Bachelor, 'but go home in peace, and get me something warm cooked for breakfast. And on your way recite St. Apollonia's prayer, if you know it. I'll be there very soon, and then you'll see wonders.'

'Oh dear, dear!' replied the housekeeper. 'St. Apollonia's prayer is it your worship says I'm to recite? That would be all right if my master had toothache, but the trouble isn't there but in his brain.'

'I know what I am saying, Mistress Housekeeper. Get along, and don't start arguing with me. You know that I am a Bachelor of Salamanca, and there is no better bacheloring than that,' replied Carrasco. At that the housekeeper went off, and the Bachelor went straight to find the priest and discuss with him a matter which shall be related in due course.

Now, while Don Quixote and Sancho were shut up together, there passed between them a conversation recounted in this history with great precision and in faithful detail. It began by Sancho's saying to his master: 'Sir, I have concerted my wife to let me go with your worship wherever you wish to take me.'

' "*Converted*" you mean, Sancho,' said Don Quixote, 'not "*concerted*".'

'I've implored your worship once or twice, if I remember rightly,' answered Sancho, 'not to correct my words, if you understand what I mean by them, but just to say when you don't understand: *Sancho*, or *Devil*, I don't understand you. And if I don't make myself clear then you can correct me, for I am so *focile*.'

'I do not understand you, Sancho,' replied Don Quixote promptly. 'I do not know what so focile means.'

'So focile,' replied Sancho, 'means I am so – so!'

'Now I understand you even less,' said Don Quixote.

'Well, if you can't understand me,' replied Sancho, 'I don't know how to say it. I can't say any more, God help me.'

'Now, now I have got it!' cried Don Quixote. 'You mean to say that you are so *docile*, pliant and tractable that you will accept what I say to you and act on my instructions.'

'I'll bet you caught my meaning at the very beginning,' said Sancho, 'but you wanted to confuse me so as to hear me make another two hundred blunders.'

'Maybe,' replied Don Quixote. 'Well, now, what does Teresa say?'

'Teresa says,' answered Sancho, 'that I must keep a firm finger on your worship, and let writing speak and beards be silent, since a good bargain doesn't hold up the business, and one gift is worth two promises. But I say a woman's counsel is bad, and he who doesn't take it's mad.'

'And so I say too,' replied Don Quixote. 'Go on, Sancho, my friend, go on; you are speaking pearls to-day.'

'The case is,' replied Sancho, 'as your worship knows, that we are all subject to death, that we are here to-day and gone to-morrow, and the lamb goes as soon as the sheep, and no one can promise himself more hours of life in this world than God is pleased to grant him. For death is deaf, and when it comes to knock on our life's doors it's always in haste, and won't stop for prayers or struggles, or sceptres or mitres, as it's commonly reported, and as they tell us from the pulpits.'

'That is all true,' said Don Quixote; 'but I do not know what you are leading up to.'

'I am leading up,' said Sancho, 'to your worship's settling some fixed wages, which you'll give me each month all the time I serve you, and to this salary being paid out of your estate; because I don't like depending on favours, which come late, or at a bad time, or not at all. May God help me with my own, and I should like to know how much it will be, whether it's much or little, for the hen lays as well on one egg as on several, and many a mickle makes a muckle, and whilst you're earning you're losing nothing. If indeed it should happen (which I neither believe nor expect) that your worship should give me the isle you promised me, I'm not so ungrateful or so particular to a farthing, that I shan't consent to have the rent of the isle reckoned up, and let it be stopped from my wages, cat for quantity.'*

'Sancho, my friend,' replied Don Quixote, 'sometimes a cat is as good as a rat.'

'I see,' said Sancho. 'I'll bet I ought to have said "*rat*" and not "*cat*"; but it doesn't matter, because your worship understood me.'

'Yes, understood you so well,' replied Don Quixote, 'that I have penetrated to the bottom of your thoughts, and I know what target you are aiming at with the countless arrows of your proverbs. Look you, Sancho, I would willingly settle a wage if I had found in any of the histories of knights errant anything to show me what squires used to earn by the month or by the year, or even anything to throw the slightest chink of light on the subject. But I have read all, or the greater part, of these histories, and I never remember reading that any knight errant ever allowed his squire a fixed wage. All I know is that they all served on favour, and when they least expected it, if fortune had gone well with their lords, they found themselves rewarded with an isle, or with something else of equal value, or at the least came off with a title and a lordship. If with these expecta-

---

* He means 'rate for quantity,' *i.e.*, that the revenue from the isle shall be set against his wages.

tions and increments you, Sancho, are pleased to return to my service, come and welcome. But to think that I shall wrench the old customs of knight errantry off their posts and hinges is to imagine the impossible. So, my dear Sancho, go back home and declare my intention to Teresa; and if she is pleased and you are pleased for you to serve me on favour, well and good; but, if not, we are friends as before, for if the dovecot does not lack grain it will not lack pigeons. And remember this, my son, good hopes are better than poor possessions, and a good claim than bad pay. I speak in this way, Sancho, to show you that I can rain down proverbs as well as you. Finally I want to say, and I will say, that if you do not wish to come with me on favour and take the same chances as I take, God be with you and make you a saint, but I shall not be short of squires more obedient and more careful than you, and not so awkward and talkative.'

When Sancho heard his master's firm resolve his sky clouded over and the wings of his heart began to droop, for he had believed that Don Quixote would not go without him for all the treasure in the world. And there he was, confused and thoughtful, when Sampson Carrasco came in, followed by the housekeeper and the niece, who were eager to hear what arguments he would use to persuade their master not to go out again in search of adventures. Then Sampson, the great joker, went up to the knight and, embracing him as before, addressed him in a loud voice: 'O flower of knight errantry! O resplendent light of arms! O honour and mirror of the Spanish nation! May it please almighty God — and so forth as hereinafter set down — that the person or persons placing any impediment or hindrance in the path of your third expedition may find no way out of the labyrinth of their desires, and never accomplish their dearest wishes.'

Then, turning to the housekeeper, he said: 'You may as well give up reciting St. Apollonia's prayer, Mistress Housekeeper, for I know that it is the positive determination of the spheres that Don Quixote shall once more carry out his lofty and novel design, and I should much burden my conscience were I not to advise that knight most forcibly no longer to keep the strength of his mighty arm and the goodness of his most valiant heart under restraint and coercion. For by his delay he defrauds the wronged of their righting, orphans of their protection, maidens of their honour, widows of their consolation, married women of their support, and other things of this kind which touch, belong to, and are part and parcel of, knight errantry. On, then, my good Don Quixote, handsome and brave! Rather to-day than to-morrow should your worshipful Highness take the road; and should any means be lacking for the execution of your resolve, here am I to provide it with my person and from my estate; and were it necessary to serve your Magnificence as your squire, I should count it the greatest of good fortune.'

At which point Don Quixote turned to Sancho and said: 'Did I not tell you, Sancho, that I should have plenty of squires and to spare? See who it is that offers himself for the post! None other than that most rare bachelor Sampson Carrasco, the perpetual entertainer and light of the courts of the Salamantine schools, sound in person, agile of limb, silent, impervious to heat and cold, hunger and thirst, and possessing all the virtues requisite in the squire of a knight errant. But Heaven forbid that this pillar of learning, this repository of science, should be hamstrung and broken for my pleasure, and the lofty palm of the fair and liberal arts be felled. Let this new Sampson stay in his own country, and in honouring it honour the grey hairs of his aged parents as well, for I shall be content with any kind of squire, since Sancho does not deign to come with me.'

'I do deign,' exclaimed Sancho, melted, with his eyes full of tears. 'It shall not be said of me, dear master, the bread eaten, the company forsaken. For I don't come from thankless stock, and all the world knows – especially our villagers – what sort of people my ancestors, the Panzas, were. It's clear to me, besides, from your worship's good deeds and fair speeches how anxious you are to benefit me, and if I went into the question of my wages, how much they were to be, more or less, it was to please my wife. For when once she sets her hand to persuading, there's no mallet so tightens the hoops of a cask as she tightens on to getting her own way. But in the end a man must be a man, and a woman a woman; and since I'm a man anywhere, as I can't deny, I intend to be so in my own house, in despite of everybody. So there's nothing more for it now but for your worship to draw up your will with its codicil, so that it can't be revolted; and then let's get on the road, so that master Sampson's soul shan't suffer. For he says his conscience dictates that he must persuade your worship to go out into the bleak world a third time. And I offer once more to serve you faithfully and loyally, as well as and better than any squire has served knight errant in past or present times.'

The Bachelor was surprised to hear the style and manner of Sancho Panza's speech; for though he had read his master's first history, he had never believed that Sancho was as comical as he was described there. But when he heard him say the will and codicil that cannot be *revolted* instead of the will and codicil that cannot be *revoked*, he believed all that he had read, and set him down as one of the solemnest asses of our age, thinking to himself that two such madmen as master and man could never have been seen in the world before. Finally Don Quixote and Sancho embraced and made friends, and with the advice and approval of the great Carrasco, who was their oracle from that time on, it was decided that their departure should be in three days. In the interval they would have an opportunity of providing for the journey, and of looking for a complete helmet; for this Don Quixote said he must have at all costs. And Sampson offered him one, for he knew that a friend of his had one, and would not refuse it to him, though it was all dingy from rust and mould and had none of the brightness of polished steel.

Countless were the curses which the housekeeper and the niece hurled at the Bachelor. They tore their hair, scratched their faces, and raised such a lament as hired keeners used to, just as if it were their master's death, not his departure, they were mourning. Now the plan which Sampson was following when he persuaded Don Quixote to set out once again involved some action which will be described further on in our history. It was a design formed on the advice of the priest and the barber, with whom he had previously discussed it.

Well, in those three days Don Quixote and Sancho got together what seemed to them necessary. And when Sancho had placated his wife, and Don Quixote his niece and his housekeeper, they set out at nightfall on the road to El Toboso, unobserved by anyone but the Bachelor, who decided to accompany them for a mile or two from the village. Don Quixote jogged along on his good Rocinante, and Sancho on his old Dapple, his saddle-bags stored with

R

food and the like, and his purse with money, which Don Quixote had given him for contingencies. Sampson embraced the knight and begged him to let him know what his luck might be, so that he might either rejoice or mourn, as the laws of friendship required. This Don Quixote promised to do, and Sampson went back to the village, while the two of them took the road to the great city of El Toboso.

Chapter VIII. *In which we learn what happened to Don Quixote on his way to see his Mistress, Dulcinea del Toboso.*

'BLESSED be Allah the mighty,' says Hamete Benengeli at the beginning of this eighth chapter. 'Blessed be Allah!' he repeats three times, and declares that he utters these blessings on finding that he has now got Don Quixote and Sancho Panza into the field, and that the readers of his delightful history may reckon that from this point the exploits and humours of the knight and his squire begin. He begs them to forget the past knight errantries of the Ingenious Gentleman, and fix their eyes on those which are to come and are now beginning on the road to El Toboso, as the others began on the plain of Montiel – and it is not much that he asks, considering how much he promises. And so he goes on to say:

Don Quixote and Sancho were left alone. But scarcely had Sampson gone than Rocinante began to neigh and Dapple to bray, which was taken by both knight and squire for a good sign and a most favourable omen. If the truth be told, however, the snorting and braying of the ass was louder than the horse's neighing, from which Sancho gathered that his luck would surpass and overtop his master's, though whether he based his belief on any judicial astrology he had learnt or not I do not know, for the history does not tell. Though he had been heard to say when he fell or stumbled, that he would be glad if he had never left home, for nothing was to be got from falling and stumbling but a torn shoe or broken ribs; and in that, fool though he was, he was not far out.

'Sancho, my friend,' said Don Quixote, 'the night is coming down faster and darker than it should, if we are to get to El Toboso by daybreak. For I am resolved to go there before undertaking any other adventure. There I shall receive the blessing and the gracious leave of the peerless Dulcinea, with which licence I think that I shall certainly bring to a happy conclusion the most perilous of adventures. For nothing in this life makes knights errant more valiant than the knowledge that they are favoured by their ladies.'

'So I believe,' replied Sancho, 'but I think that it'll be difficult for your worship to get a word with her alone, at least in any place where you can receive her blessing. Though she may throw it to you over the wall of the back-yard, where I saw her the first time, when I took her that letter that told her all about the crazy antics your worship was performing up there in the mountains.'

'Backyard walls did you fancy they were, Sancho,' asked Don Quixote, 'when you gazed over them at her never sufficiently praised grace and beauty? They must certainly have been the galleries, or corridors, or porticoes, or whatever they are called, of rich royal palaces.'

'That may all be so,' replied Sancho, 'but walls they seemed to me, if I remember rightly.'

'However that may be, let us go there, Sancho,' replied Don Quixote. 'For so long as I see her it is all the same to me whether it is over walls or through windows, or chinks or garden grilles. For any ray reaching my eyes from the sun of her beauty will illuminate my understanding and fortify my heart, so that I shall be unique and peerless in wisdom and valour.'

'But really, sir,' replied Sancho, 'when I saw this sun, the lady Dulcinea del Toboso, it wasn't bright enough to cast any rays at all. That must have been because her Grace was winnowing the wheat I told you of, and the great dust she raised must have gathered like a cloud about her face and darkened it.'

'What, do you still persist, Sancho,' cried Don Quixote, 'in saying, thinking, believing, and insisting that my lady Dulcinea was winnowing corn – that being a function and exercise far removed from the common practice of persons of rank, who are constituted and reserved for other employments and amusements, which reveal their quality a bow-shot off! You little remember, Sancho, those verses of our ingenious poet in which he describes to us the tasks which the four nymphs performed in their crystal dwellings, when they raised their heads from their beloved Tagus, and sat in the green meadow to work those rich clothes he there describes, which were all of gold, silk thread and pearls, plaited and interwoven. In such work must my lady have been employed when you saw her, were it not for the envy which some evil enchanter seems to display towards my affairs, in changing and turning everything which might give me pleasure into shapes other than their true ones. And so I am afraid that if the author of that history of my exploits, which they say is now in print, chanced to be some enchanter hostile to me, he has probably changed one thing into another, mingling a thousand lies with one truth, and digressed to narrate actions out of the sequence proper to a faithful history. Oh, envy, root of infinite evil and canker-worm of virtue! All the vices, Sancho, bring with them some manner of delight; but that of envy brings only pain, rancour and furious rage.'

'That's the very thing I say,' replied Sancho. 'And I think that in this legend or history which the Bachelor Carrasco said he had seen about us, my reputation must go jolting topsy-turvy, or helter-skelter, as the saying is. Yet I swear as an honest man I've never spoken ill of any enchanter, and I haven't enough wealth to be envied. True, I have a touch of malice in me and I'm a bit of a rogue, but that's all covered up and hidden under the broad cloak of my simplicity – which is always natural and never artificial. Yet the historians ought to take pity on me and treat me kindly in their writings, if only because I've always believed in God and in all the tenets of the Holy Roman Catholic Church, and because I'm a mortal enemy to the Jews. But let them say what they will; for naked I was born and naked I am now, I neither lose nor gain. And though I chance to be put in books and passed about the world from hand to hand, I don't care a fig – let them say what they like about me.'

'That, Sancho,' said Don Quixote, 'reminds me of what happened to a famous modern poet, who had composed a malicious satire against all courtesans, yet did not include in it the name of a certain lady, for there was some question whether she was one or not. Now, seeing that she was not in the list with the rest, she complained to the poet, asking him what fault he had seen in her that he had not included her with the others, and requesting him to enlarge his satire and put her in the supplement; and if he did not he had better look out for himself. The poet did as she asked, and made her something worse than a character in a waiting-lady's story, and she was satisfied to find herself famous, even if for nothing good. Another story that fits is the one about that shepherd who set on fire and burnt the famous temple of Diana, accounted one of the seven wonders of the world, only so that his name should survive to future ages; and though it was decreed that no one should speak of him, or make any mention of his name by word or in writing, so that he should not achieve his ambition, still it became known that his name was Erostratus. Also to the point is the tale of the great Emperor Charles V and a certain gentleman in Rome. The Emperor wanted to see the Rotunda, a famous temple which in ancient days was called the *Temple of All the Gods*, and is now known by the better name of *all the Saints*. It is the most complete building surviving of all those which heathendom raised in Rome, and the one which best preserves its founders' reputation for grandeur and magnificence. It is in the shape of half an orange, magnificent in the extreme and very well lit, although the only light which enters is through one window, or rather through a round lantern at the top, from which the Emperor was gazing down on the building. With him, standing by his side, was a Roman gentleman, who was pointing out the beauties of this famous masterpiece of architecture. Then, after they had come down from the lantern, he remarked to the Emperor: "A thousand times, most sacred Majesty, the desire seized me to clasp your Majesty and throw myself down from that lantern so that I might win myself eternal fame in the world." "I thank you," replied the Emperor, "for not having put so bad a plan into execution. But henceforth I will give you no further opportunity of putting your loyalty to the proof; and so I command you never to speak to me or to appear where I am." – And with these words he gave him a handsome present. My meaning is, Sancho, that the desire of winning fame is in the highest degree active with us. What was it, do you think, cast Horatius down from the bridge, clothed in his full armour, into the Tiber? What burnt Mutius' arm and hand? What drove Curtius to throw himself into the deep, flaming gulf which opened in the centre of Rome? What made Caesar cross the Rubicon in the face of all the omens which had shown themselves adverse? And, to take more modern examples, what scuttled the ships and left the valiant Spaniards, led by the most courteous Cortes, stranded and isolated in the New World? These and a multitude of other great exploits are the effects of the love of fame, which mortals desire to win by mighty deeds as their portion of immortality. While we, Christians, Catholics and knights errant, have more to expect from future and everlasting glory enjoyed in the ethereal and celestial regions than from the vanity of fame achieved in this present transient life; which fame, however long it lasts, must finally end with the world itself, which has its fixed term. So, Sancho, our works must not transgress the bounds set us by the Christian religion which we profess. It is for us to slay pride by slaying giants; to slay envy by our generosity and nobility; anger by calmness of mind, and serenity of disposition; gluttony, and drowsiness by eating little and watching late into the night; indulgence and lust by preserving our loyalty to those whom we have made ladies of our hearts; and sloth by travelling through all parts of the world in quest of opportunities of becoming famous knights as well as Christians. Such, Sancho, are the means by which we must win that high praise which a good name confers.'

'All that your worship has said to me so far,' said Sancho, 'I've understood very well. Yet I should like you to resorb me one doubt, which has just now come into my head.'

'"*Resolve*", you mean, Sancho,' said Don Quixote. 'Speak up and welcome, for I will answer as well as I can.'

'Tell me, sir,' continued Sancho, 'these Julys and Augusts and all these heroic knights you spoke of, who are now dead, – where are they now?'

'The heathens,' replied Don Quixote, 'are no doubt in Hell. The Christians, if they were good Christians, are either in Purgatory or in Heaven.'

'That's all right,' said Sancho. 'But now tell me this. These tombs where the bodies of these great lords lie – have they silver lamps in front of them, or are the walls of their chapels adorned with crutches, winding-sheets, wigs, legs and wax eyes? If not, how are they adorned?'

'The tombs of the heathens,' replied Don Quixote, 'were for the most part sumptuous temples. The ashes of Julius Caesar were placed in a stone pyramid of extraordinary size, which is now called St. Peter's Needle. The Emperor Hadrian's sepulchre was a castle as big as a fair-sized village and was called *Moles Hadriani*. It is to-day the castle of St. Angelo at Rome. Queen Artemisia buried her husband Mausolus in a tomb which was reckoned one of the seven Wonders of the World. But none of these tombs, nor those many others which the pagans built, were adorned with winding-sheets, nor with any other offerings or signs to show that those buried in them were saints.'

'I'm coming to that,' said Sancho. 'Tell me now, which is the greater thing: to raise a dead man to life or to kill a giant?'

'The answer is obvious,' replied Don Quixote. 'It is a greater thing to bring a dead man to life.'

'I've caught you now,' said Sancho. 'The fame then of those who bring the dead to life, give sight to the blind, cure the lame, and restore the sick to health, before whose tombs lamps burn, and whose chapels are full of devout people kneeling and adoring their relics, will be a better fame, in this life and in the other, than the fame of all the heathen emperors and knights errant in all the world.'

'I grant you that too,' replied Don Quixote.

'Well, this fame,' continued Sancho, 'these favours, these prerogatives, or whatever they're called, rest in the bodies and relics of the saints, who, with the approval and licence of our Holy Mother Church, receive lamps, candles, winding-sheets, crutches, paintings, wigs, eyes, legs, whereby they increase people's devotion and spread abroad their Christian fame. Kings carry the bodies or relics of the saints on their shoulders, kiss the pieces of their bones, and deck and enrich their private chapels and favourite altars with them.'

'What do you mean to infer, Sancho, from all this you are saying?' asked Don Quixote.

'I mean to say,' replied Sancho, 'that we should set about turning saints. Then we shall get the good name we're aiming at rather sooner. Think, sir, yesterday or the day before – it's so lately that we can speak like that – they canonized or beatified two little friars, and now people think it very lucky to kiss and touch the iron chains they bound and tortured their bodies with. They are held in greater veneration, they say, than Roland's sword in our Lord the King's armoury, God bless him! So, dear master, it's better to be a humble little friar, of any order you like, than a valiant and errant knight. A couple of dozen lashings have more effect with God than a couple of thousand lance-thrusts, even against giants, or hobgoblins, or dragons.'

'All that is so,' replied Don Quixote, 'but we cannot all be friars, and many are the ways by which God bears His chosen to heaven. Chivalry is a religion, and there are sainted knights in glory.'

'Yes,' replied Sancho, 'but I have heard it said that there are more friars than knights errant in Heaven.'

'That,' replied Don Quixote, 'is because the number of religious is greater than the number of knights.'

'There are plenty of the errant sort,' said Sancho.

'Many,' replied Don Quixote, 'but few are those deserving the name of knights.'

In this and other such conversations they spent that night and the following day, without meeting with anything worth mentioning, which grieved Don Quixote not a little. Finally, on the next day, at nightfall, they made out the great city of El Toboso, at the sight of which Don Quixote's spirits rose and Sancho's sank, for he did not know which was Dulcinea's house, having never seen it in his life, and no more did his master. So they were both troubled, one with the desire to see her and the other because he had never seen her. And Sancho could not imagine what he should do when his master sent him into El Toboso.

Eventually Don Quixote decided to enter the city once the night had closed in. So until the hour approached they stayed among some oaks which grew around El Toboso, and when the appointed time came they entered the city, where things befell them that were things indeed.

Chapter IX. *The Contents of which will be seen as the Chapter progresses.*

IT was on the stroke of midnight, more or less, that Don Quixote and Sancho left the wooded hill and entered El Toboso. The village lay in a deep silence, for all the inhabitants were asleep, sleeping like logs, as the saying goes. It was a fairly clear night, though Sancho wished it had been quite dark, so that the darkness might cover up his roguery. In the whole village there was no sound to be heard but the barking of dogs, which deafened Don Quixote's ears and alarmed Sancho's heart. From time to time an ass brayed, pigs grunted, and cats mewed; which various-sounding cries were heightened by the stillness of the night. All this the enamoured knight took for a bad omen. But, for all that, he said to Sancho: 'Sancho, my son, lead on to the palace of Dulcinea. It may be that we shall find her awake.'

'Great heavens! what palace am I to lead on to?' asked Sancho. 'For where I saw her Highness was no palace but a very small house.'

'She must have been in retirement then,' replied Don Quixote, 'in some little apartment of her castle, solacing herself alone with her maidens, as is the use and custom of high ladies and princesses.'

'Sir,' said Sancho, 'since your worship will have it, in spite of me, that my Lady Dulcinea's house is a royal castle, is this a likely hour to find the gate open? And would it be right for us to start knocking till they hear us and open for us, and put all the people into uproar and confusion? Is it to our wenches' houses we're going, like their keepers, who come and call and enter at all hours of the day and night?'

'Let us find the castle anyway, first,' replied Don Quixote. 'Then I will tell you what we ought to do, Sancho. But look, either my eyes fail me, or that vast mass of shadow looming up over there must be Dulcinea's palace.'

'Then you lead, your worship,' replied Sancho. 'Perhaps it may be so, though if I were to see it with my eyes and touch it with my hands, I should no more believe it than I'd believe that now it's daylight.'

Don Quixote led on, and when he had gone about two hundred yards forward came to the mass which was throwing the shadow and, seeing a great tower, realized immediately that the building was no royal castle, but the parish church of the place. 'It's the church we have come upon, Sancho,' he said.

'So I see,' replied Sancho, 'and please God we haven't come for our burial. For it's not a good sign to be wandering about grave-yards at this time of night. Besides, if I remember rightly, I told you that the lady's house is in a blind alley.'

'Be damned to you, Sancho, you idiot!' cried Don Quixote. 'Where have you found royal castles and palaces built in blind alleys?'

'Sir,' replied Sancho, 'every land has its own customs. Perhaps it's the custom here in El Toboso to build palaces and great buildings in blind alleys. So I beg your worship to let me search in these streets and alleys here in front of me. I might possibly run across that castle in some corner – and may I see it eaten by dogs for dragging us on such a weary chase!'

'Speak respectfully, Sancho, of what belongs to my lady,' said Don Quixote, 'and let us keep our feast in peace, and not throw away the rope after losing the bucket.'

'I'll control myself, replied Sancho, 'but how can I bear it in patience when your worship wants me, when I've only seen our lady's house once, to recognise it again and find it in the middle of the night? For you can't find it yourself, though you must have seen it thousands of times!'

'You will drive me to despair, Sancho,' cried Don Quixote. 'Look you, heretic, have I not told you a thousand times that I have never seen the peerless Dulcinea in all the days of my life, nor ever crossed the threshold of her palace, and that I am only enamoured of her by hearsay, and because of the great reputation she bears for beauty and wisdom.'

'I hear it now,' replied Sancho, 'and since you say that you have never seen her, neither have I.'

'That cannot be,' said Don Quixote, 'for you told me, at any rate, that you saw her winnowing wheat, when you brought me an answer to the letter I sent to her by you.'

'Don't depend on that, sir,' answered Sancho, 'for I would have you know that my seeing her and the reply I brought back were by hearsay too; for I no more know who the lady Dulcinea is than I can punch the sky.'

'Sancho, Sancho,' cried Don Quixote, 'there are times for joking and times when jokes are out of place and unseemly. Because I say that I have neither seen nor spoken to the lady of my heart there is no reason for you to say that you have not spoken to her or seen her either; the contrary being the case, as well you know.'

While the pair of them were engaged in this argument, they saw a man approaching them with a couple of mules; and from the noise made by the plough, which he was dragging along the ground, they judged that he was a labourer who had got up before daybreak to go to his ploughing, as was the case. The ploughman came along, singing that doleful ballad which runs:

'It was an ill day for Frenchmen,
The rout of Roncesvalles.'

'Hang me, Sancho,' said Don Quixote, as he heard him, 'if we have any good fortune to-night. Do you hear what that peasant is singing?'

'Yes, I can hear,' replied Sancho. 'But what has the rout of Roncesvalles to do with us? He might just as well be singing the ballad of Calainos; it would be all the same so far as our good or ill luck goes.'

At this point the labourer came up, and Don Quixote asked him: 'Could you tell me, my friend – and may God give you good fortune – where hereabouts are the palaces of the peerless princess, Dulcinea del Toboso?'

'Sir,' replied the lad, 'I'm a stranger, and have only been a few days in this place, working in the fields for a rich farmer. In that house in front of you live the village priest and the sacristan, and both or either of them will be able to inform your worship about this princess, for they have a list of all the inhabitants of El Toboso. Though for myself, I don't believe there's any princess living in the whole place, although there are many ladies, and such fine ones that any one of them may be a princess when she's at home.'

'Well, friend,' said Don Quixote, 'among them must be the lady I am asking for.'

'That may be,' replied the youth. 'Good-bye, for the day's breaking now.' And urging on his mules, he waited for no more questions. Then said Sancho, seeing his master perplexed and somewhat out of humour: 'Now, sir, day's coming on apace, and it won't be wise to let the sun find us in the streets. It'll be better for us to go out of the city, and for your worship to hide in some bushes somewhere near. I will return by day and not leave a corner of this whole place unsearched for the house, castle or palace of my lady; and I shall be very unlucky if I don't find it. And when I find it I will speak to her Grace, and tell her where and how your worship is waiting and expecting her to give you orders and instructions how you may see her without damage to her honour and reputation.'

'Sancho,' said Don Quixote, 'you have uttered a thousand words of wisdom in the short space of a few brief sentences. The advice which you have just given me I welcome, and accept with very good will. Come, my son, let us find somewhere for me to hide, and you shall return, as you say, to see and speak with my lady, of whose discretion and courtesy I expect favours more than miraculous.'

Sancho was racked with desire to get his master out of the village, so that he should not detect his lie about the reply he had brought to the Sierra Morena on Dulcinea's behalf. So he hurried their departure, which was immediate. They found, two miles out of the place, a forest or thicket, where Don Quixote hid while Sancho returned to the city to speak with Dulcinea, in which embassy there happened to him things which call for renewed attention and fresh powers of belief.

Chapter X. *In which is related the device Sancho adopted to enchant the Lady Dulcinea, and other incidents as comical as they are true.*

WHEN the author of this great history comes to recount the contents of this chapter, he says that he would have liked to pass it over in silence, through fear of disbelief. For Don Quixote's delusions here reach the greatest imaginable bounds and limits, and even exceed them, great as they are, by two bow-shots. But finally he wrote the deeds down, although with fear and misgivings, just as our knight performed them, without adding or subtracting one atom of truth from the history, or taking into account any accusations of lying that might be laid against him. And he was right, for truth, though it may run thin, never breaks, and always flows over the lie like oil over water. So, continuing his history, he says that as soon as Don Quixote had hidden himself in the thicket, or oak wood, or forest, beside great El Toboso, he ordered Sancho to go back to the city, and not return to his presence without first speaking to his lady on his behalf, and begging her to be so good as to allow herself to be seen by her captive knight, and to deign to bestow her blessing on him, so that he might hope thereby to meet with the highest success in all his encounters and arduous enterprises. Sancho undertook to do as he was commanded, and to bring his master as favourable a reply as he had brought the first time.

'Go, my son,' said Don Quixote, 'and do not be confused when you find yourself before the light of the sun of beauty you are going to seek. How much more fortunate you are than all other squires in the world! Bear in your mind, and let it not escape you, the manner of your reception; whether she changes colour whilst you are delivering her my message; whether she is stirred or troubled on hearing my name; whether she shifts from her cushion, should you, by chance, find her seated on the rich dais of her authority. If she is standing, watch whether she rests first on one foot and then on the other; whether she repeats her reply to you two or three times; whether she changes from mild to harsh, from cruel to amorous; whether she raises her hand to her hair to smooth it, although it is not untidy. In fact, my son, watch all her actions and movements; because, if you relate them to me as they were, I shall deduce what she keeps concealed in the secret places of her heart as far as concerns the matter of my love. For you must know, Sancho, if you do not know already, that between lovers the outward actions and movements they reveal when their loves are under discussion are most certain messengers, bearing news of what is going on in their innermost souls. Go, friend, and may better fortune than mine guide you, and send you better success than I expect, waiting between fear and hope in this bitter solitude where you leave me.'

'I'll go, and come back quickly,' said Sancho. 'Cheer up that little heart of yours, dear master, for it must be no bigger now than a hazel nut. Remember the saying that a stout heart breaks bad luck; and where there are no flitches there are no hooks; and they say, too, where you least expect it, out jumps the hare. This I say because now that it's day I hope to find my lady's palaces or castles where I least expect them, even though we didn't find them last night: and once found, leave me to deal with her alone.'

'Indeed, Sancho,' said Don Quixote, 'you always bring in your proverbs very much to the purpose of our business. May God give me as good luck in my ventures as you have in your sayings.'

At these words Sancho turned away and gave Dapple the stick; and Don Quixote stayed on horseback, resting in his stirrups and leaning on his lance, full of sad and troubled fancies, with which we will leave him and go with Sancho Panza, who parted from his master no less troubled and thoughtful than he. So much so that scarcely had he come out of the wood than he turned round and, seeing that Don Quixote was out of sight, dismounted from his ass. Then, sitting down at the foot of a tree, he began to commune with himself to this effect:

'Now, let us learn, brother Sancho, where your worship is going. Are you going after some ass you have lost? No, certainly not. Then what are you going to look for? I am going to look, as you might say, for nothing, for a Princess, and in her the sun of beauty and all heaven besides. And where do you expect to find this thing you speak of, Sancho? Where? In the great city of El Toboso. Very well, and on whose behalf are you going to seek her? On behalf of the famous knight Don Quixote de la Mancha, who rights wrongs, gives meat to the thirsty, and drink to the hungry. All this is right enough. Now, do you know her house? My master says it will be some royal palace or proud castle. And have you by any chance ever seen her? No, neither I nor my master have ever seen her. And, if the people of El Toboso knew that you are here for the purpose of enticing away their Princesses and disturbing their ladies, do you think it would be right and proper for them to come and give you such a basting as would grind your ribs to powder and not leave you a whole bone in your body? Yes, they would be absolutely in the right, if they did not consider that I am under orders, and that

> You are a messenger, my friend
> And so deserve no blame.

'Don't rely on that, Sancho, for the Manchegans are honest people and very hot-tempered, and they won't stand tickling from anyone. God's truth, if they smell you, you're in for bad luck. Chuck it up, you son of a bitch, and let someone else catch it. No, you won't find me searching for a cat with three legs for someone else's pleasure. What's more, looking for Dulcinea up and down El Toboso will be like looking for little Maria in Ravenna, or the Bachelor in Salamanca. It's the Devil, the Devil himself who has put me into this business. The Devil and no other!'

This colloquy Sancho held with himself, and it led him to the following conclusion: 'Well, now, there's a remedy for everything except death, beneath whose yoke we must all pass, willy-nilly, at the end of our lives. I have seen from countless signs that this master of mine is a raving lunatic who ought to be tied up – and me, I can't be much better, for since I follow him and serve him, I'm more of a fool than he – if the proverb is true that says: tell me what company you keep and I will tell you what you are; and that other one too: not with whom you are born but with whom you feed. Well, he's mad – that he is – and it's the kind of madness that generally mistakes one thing for another, and thinks white black and black white, as was clear when he said that the windmills were giants and the friars' mules dromedaries, and the flocks of sheep hostile armies, and many other things to this tune. So it won't be very difficult to make him believe that the first peasant girl I run across about here is the lady Dulcinea. If he doesn't believe it I'll swear, and if he swears I'll outswear him, and if he sticks to it I shall stick to it harder, so that, come what may, my word shall always stand up to his. Perhaps if I hold out I shall put an end to his sending me on any more of these errands, seeing what poor answers I bring back. Or perhaps he'll think, as I fancy he will, that one of those wicked enchanters who, he says, have a grudge against him, has changed her shape to vex and spite him.'

With these thoughts Sancho quieted his conscience, reckoning the business as good as settled. And there he waited till afternoon, to convince Don Quixote that he had had time to go to El Toboso and back. And so well did everything turn out that when he got up to mount Dapple he saw three peasant girls coming in his direction, riding on three young asses or fillies – our author does not tell us which – though it is more credible that they were she-asses, as these are the ordinary mounts of village women; but as nothing much hangs on it, there is no reason to stop and clear up the point. To continue – as soon as Sancho saw the girls, he went back at a canter to look for his master and found him, sighing and uttering countless amorous lamentations. But as soon as Don Quixote saw him, he cried: 'What luck, Sancho? Shall I mark this day with a white stone or with a black?'

'It'll be better,' replied Sancho, 'for your worship to mark it in red chalk, like college lists, to be plainly seen by all who look.'

'At that rate,' said Don Quixote, 'you bring good news.'

'So good,' answered Sancho, 'that your worship has nothing more to do than to spur Rocinante and go out into the open to see the lady Dulcinea del Toboso, who is coming to meet your worship with two of her damsels.'

'Holy Father! What is that you say, Sancho my friend?' cried Don Quixote. 'See that you do not deceive me, or seek to cheer my real sadness with false joys.'

'What could I gain by deceiving your worship?' replied Sancho. 'Especially as you are so near to discovering the truth of my report. Spur on, sir, come, and you'll see the Princess, our mistress, coming dressed and adorned – to be brief, as befits her. Her maidens and she are one blaze of gold, all ropes of pearls, all diamonds, all rubies, all brocade of more than ten gold strands; their hair loose on their shoulders, like so many sunrays sporting in the wind and, what's more, they are riding on three piebald nackneys, the finest to be seen.'

'Hackneys you mean, Sancho.'

'There is very little difference,' replied Sancho, 'between nackneys and hackneys. But let them come on whatever they may, they are the bravest ladies you could wish for, especially the Princess Dulcinea, my lady, who dazzles the senses.'

'Let us go, Sancho my son,' replied Don Quixote, 'and as a reward for this news, as unexpected as it is welcome, I grant you the best spoil I shall gain in the first adventure that befalls me; and, if that does not content you, I grant you the fillies that my three mares will bear me this year, for you know that I left them to foal on our village common.'

'The fillies for me,' cried Sancho, 'for it's not too certain that the spoils of the first adventure will be good ones.'

At this point they came out of the wood and discovered the three village girls close at hand. Don Quixote cast his eye all along the El Toboso road, and seeing nothing but the three peasant girls, asked Sancho in great perplexity whether he had left the ladies outside the city.

'How outside the city?' he answered. 'Can it be that your worship's eyes are in the back of your head that you don't see that these are they, coming along shining like the very sun at noon?'

'I can see nothing, Sancho,' said Don Quixote, 'but three village girls on three donkeys.'

'Now God deliver me from the Devil,' replied Sancho. 'Is it possible that three hackneys, or whatever they're called, as white as driven snow, look to your worship like asses? Good Lord, if that's the truth, may my beard be plucked out.'

'But I tell you, Sancho my friend,' said Don Quixote, 'that it is as true that they are asses, or she-asses, as that I am Don Quixote and you Sancho Panza. At least, they look so to me.'

'Hush, sir!' said Sancho. 'Don't say such a thing, but wipe those eyes of yours, and come and do homage to the mistress of your thoughts, who is drawing near.'

As he spoke he rode forward to receive the three village girls, and dismounting from Dapple, took one of the girls' asses by the bridle and sank on both knees to the ground, saying: 'Queen and Princess and Duchess of beauty, may your Highness and Mightiness deign to receive into your grace and good liking your captive knight, who stands here, turned to marble stone, all troubled and unnerved at finding himself in your magnificent presence. I am Sancho Panza, his squire, and he is the travel-weary knight, Don Quixote de la Mancha, called also by the name of the Knight of the Sad Countenance.'

By this time Don Quixote had fallen on his knees beside Sancho, and was staring, with his eyes starting out of his head and a puzzled look on his face, at the person whom Sancho called Queen and Lady. And as he could see nothing in her but a country girl, and not a very handsome one at that, she being round-faced and flat-nosed, he was bewildered and amazed, and did not dare to open his lips. The village girls were equally astonished at seeing these two men, so different in appearance, down on their knees and preventing their companion from going forward. But the girl they had stopped broke the silence by crying roughly and angrily: 'Get out of the way, confound you, and let us pass. We're in a hurry.'

To which Sancho replied: 'O Princess and world-famous Lady of El Toboso! How is it that your magnanimous heart is not softened when you see the column and prop of knight errantry kneeling before your sublimated presence?'

On hearing this, one of the two others exclaimed: 'Wait till I get my hands on you, you great ass! See how these petty gentry come and make fun of us village girls, as if we couldn't give them as good as they bring! Get on your way, and let us get on ours. You had better!'

'Rise, Sancho,' said Don Quixote at this; 'for I see that Fortune, unsatisfied with the ill already done me, has closed all roads by which any comfort may come to this wretched soul I bear in my body. And you, O perfection of all desire! Pinnacle of human gentleness! Sole remedy of this afflicted heart, that adores you! Now that the malignant enchanter persecutes me, and has put clouds and cataracts into my eyes, and for them alone, and for no others, has changed and transformed the peerless beauty of your countenance into the semblance of a poor peasant girl, if he has not at the same time turned mine into the appearance of some spectre to make it abominable to your sight, do not refuse to look at me softly and amorously, perceiving in this submission and prostration, which I make before your deformed beauty, the humility with which my soul adores you.'

'Tell that to my grandmother!' replied the girl. 'Do you think I want to listen to that nonsense? Get out of the way and let us go on, and we'll thank you.'

Sancho moved off and let her pass, delighted at having got well out of his fix. And no sooner did the girl who had played the part of Dulcinea find herself free than she prodded her nackney with the point of a stick she carried, and set off at a trot across the field. But when the she-ass felt the point of the stick, which pained her more than usual, she began to plunge so wildly that my lady Dulcinea came off upon the ground. When Don Quixote saw this accident he rushed to pick her up, and Sancho to adjust and strap on the pack-saddle, which had slipped under the ass's belly. But when the saddle was adjusted and Don Quixote was about to lift his enchanted mistress in his arms and place her on her ass, the lady picked herself up from the ground and spared him the trouble. For, stepping back a little, she took a short run, and resting both her hands on the ass's rump, swung her body into the saddle, lighter than a hawk, and sat astride like a man.

At which Sancho exclaimed: 'By St. Roque, the lady, our mistress, is lighter than a falcon, and she could train the nimblest Cordovan or Mexican to mount like a jockey. She was over the crupper of the saddle in one jump, and now without spurs she's making that hackney gallop like a zebra. And her maidens are not much behind her. They're all going like the wind.'

And so they were, for once Dulcinea was mounted, they all

spurred after her and dashed away at full speed, without once looking behind them till they had gone almost two miles. Don Quixote
followed them with his eyes, and, when he saw that they had disappeared, turned to Sancho and said:

'Do you see now what a spite the enchanters have against me,
Sancho? See to what extremes the malice and hatred they bear me
extend, for they have sought to deprive me of the happiness I
should have enjoyed in seeing my mistress in her true person. In
truth, I was born a very pattern for the unfortunate, and to be a
target and mark for the arrows of adversity. You must observe also,
Sancho, that these traitors were not satisfied with changing and
transforming my Dulcinea, but transformed her and changed her
into a figure as low and ugly as that peasant girl's. And they have
deprived her too of something most proper to great ladies, which is
the sweet smell they have from always moving among ambergris
and flowers. For I must tell you, Sancho, that when I went to help
my Dulcinea on to her hackney—as you say it was, though it seemed
a she-ass to me – I got such a whiff of raw garlic as stank me out and
poisoned me to the heart.'

'Oh, the curs!' cried Sancho at this. 'Oh, wretched and spiteful
enchanters! I should like to see you strung up by the gills like pilchards on a reed. Wise you are and powerful – and much evil you
do! It should be enough for you, ruffians, to have changed the
pearls of my lady's eyes into corktree galls, and her hair of purest
gold into red ox tail bristles, and all her features, in fact, from good
to bad, without meddling with her smell. For from that at least we
have gathered what lay concealed beneath that ugly crust. Though,
to tell you the truth, I never saw her ugliness, but only her beauty,
which was enhanced and perfected by a mole she had on her right
lip, like a moustache, with seven or eight red hairs like threads of
gold more than nine inches long.'

'To judge from that mole,' said Don Quixote, 'by the corre-
spondence there is between those on the face and those on the body,
Dulcinea must have another on the fleshy part of her thigh, on the
same side as the one on her face. But hairs of the length you indicate
are very long for moles.'

'But I can assure your worship,' replied Sancho, 'that there they
were, as if they had been born with her.'

'I believe it, friend,' said Don Quixote, 'for nature has put nothing on Dulcinea which is not perfect and well-finished. And so, if she had a hundred moles like the one you speak of on her, they would not be moles, but moons and shining stars. But tell me, Sancho, that which appeared to me to be a pack-saddle and which you set straight – was it a plain saddle or a side-saddle?'

'It was just a lady's saddle,' replied Sancho, 'with an outdoor covering so rich that it was worth half a kingdom.'

'And to think that I did not see all this, Sancho!' cried Don Quixote. 'Now I say once more – and I will repeat it a thousand times – I am the most unfortunate of men.'

And that rascal Sancho had all he could do to hide his amusement on hearing this crazy talk from his master, whom he had so beautifully deceived. In the end, after much further conversation between the pair, they mounted their beasts once more, and followed the road to Saragossa, where they expected to arrive in time to be present at a solemn festival which is held every year in that illustrious city. But before they got there certain things happened to them, so many, so important, and so novel that they deserve to be written down and read, as will be seen hereafter.

Chapter XI. *Of the strange Adventure which befell the valorous Don Quixote with the Car or Waggon of the Parliament of Death.*

VERY much downcast Don Quixote went on his way, pondering on the evil trick the enchanters had played on him in turning his lady Dulcinea into the foul shape of a village girl, and he could think of no remedy he could take to restore her to her original state. These thoughts took him so much out of himself that he gave Rocinante the reins without noticing it. And his horse, feeling the liberty he was given, lingered at each step to browse the green grass, which grew thickly in those fields. But Sancho roused his master from his musing by saying:

'Sir, griefs were not made for beasts but for men. Yet if men feel them too deeply they turn to beasts. Pull yourself together, your worship, and come to your senses and pick up Rocinante's reins. Cheer up and wake up, and show that gay spirit knights errant should have. What the devil is it? What despondency is this? Are we here or in France? Let all the Dulcineas in the world go to Old Nick, for the well-being of a single knight errant is worth more than all the enchantments and transformations on earth.'

'Hush, Sancho,' replied Don Quixote with more spirit than might have been expected. 'Hush, I say, and speak no more blasphemies against that enchanted lady. For I alone am to blame for her misfortune and disaster. From the envy the wicked bear me springs her sad plight.'

'And so say I,' answered Sancho, 'who saw her and can still see her now. What heart is there that would not weep?'

'You may well say that, Sancho,' replied Don Quixote, 'since you saw her in the perfect fullness of her beauty, for the enchantment did not go so far as to disturb your vision or conceal her beauty from you. Against me alone, against my eyes, was directed the power of their venom. But for all that, Sancho, one thing occurs to me: you described her beauty to me badly. For, if I remember rightly, you said that she had eyes like pearls, and eyes like pearls suit a sea-bream better than a lady. According to my belief, Dulcinea's eyes must be green emeralds, full and large, with twin rainbows to serve them for eyebrows. So take these pearls from her eyes and transfer them to her teeth, for no doubt you got mixed up, Sancho, taking her teeth for her eyes.'

'Anything's possible,' replied Sancho, 'for her beauty confused me, as her ugliness did your worship. But let's leave it all in God's hands. For He knows all things that happen in this vale of tears, in this wicked world of ours, where there's hardly anything to be found without a tincture of evil, deceit and roguery in it. But one thing troubles me, dear master, more than all the rest: I can't think what we're to do when your worship conquers a giant or another knight and commands him to go and present himself before the beauteous Dulcinea. Where is he to find her, that poor giant or that poor miserable conquered knight? I seem to see them wandering about El Toboso, gaping like dummies, in search of my lady Dulcinea; and even if they meet her in the middle of the street they won't know her any more than they would my father.'

'Perhaps, Sancho,' answered Don Quixote, 'the enchantment will not extend so far as to deprive vanquished and presented giants

and knights of the power to recognize Dulcinea. But we will make
the experiment with one or two of the first I conquer. We will send
them with orders to return and give me an account of their fortunes
in this respect, and so discover whether they can see her or not.'

'Yes, sir,' said Sancho; 'that seems a good idea to me. By that
trick we shall find out what we want to, and if it proves that she is
only disguised from your worship, the misfortunes will be more
yours than hers. But so long as the lady Dulcinea has her health and
happiness, we in these parts will make shift to put up with it as best
we can. We'll seek our adventures and leave Time to look after
hers; for Time's the best doctor for such ailments and for worse.'

Don Quixote was about to reply to Sancho, but he was interrupted by a waggon, which came out across the road loaded with
some of the strangest shapes imaginable. Driving the mules and acting as carter was an ugly demon, and the waggon itself was open to
the sky, without tilt or hurdle roof. The first figure which presented
itself before Don Quixote's eyes was Death himself with a human
face. Beside him stood an angel with large painted wings. On one
side was an Emperor with a crown on his head, apparently of gold.
At the feet of Death was the God they call Cupid, without his bandage over his eyes, but with his bow, his quiver and his arrows.
There was also a knight in complete armour, except that he wore no
helmet or headpiece, but a hat instead adorned with multi-coloured
plumes. And there were other personages differing in dress and
appearance. The sudden vision of this assembly threw Don Quixote
into some degree of alarm, and struck fear into Sancho's heart. But
soon the knight's spirits mounted with the belief that there was
some new and perilous adventure presenting itself; and with this
idea in his head, and his heart ready to encounter any sort of danger,
he took up his position in front of the cart, and cried in a loud and
threatening voice:

'Carter, coachman, devil, or whatever you may be, tell me instantly who you are, where you are going, and who are the people
you are driving in your coach, which looks more like Charon's bark
than an ordinary cart.'

To which the Devil, stopping the cart, politely replied: 'Sir,
we're players of Angulo El Malo's company. We've been acting
this morning in a village which lies behind that hill – for it's Corpus

Christi week. Our piece is called *The Parliament of Death*; and we have to perform this evening, in that village which you can see over there. So because it's quite near, and to spare ourselves the trouble of taking off our clothes and dressing again, we are travelling in the costumes we act in. That young man there plays Death. The other fellow's the Angel. That lady, who is the manager's wife, is the Queen. This man plays the Soldier. That man's the Emperor. And I'm the Devil and one of the chief characters in the piece, for I play the principal parts in this company. If your worship wants to know anything more about us, ask me. I can tell you every detail, for being the Devil I'm up to everything.'

'On the faith of a knight errant,' answered Don Quixote, 'when I saw this cart I imagined that some great adventure was presenting itself to me. But now I declare that appearances are not always to be trusted. Go, in God's name, good people, and hold your festival; and think whether you have any request to make of me. If I can do you any service I gladly and willingly will do so, for from my boyhood I have been a lover of pantomimes, and in my youth I was always a glutton for comedies.'

Now, whilst they were engaged in this conversation, as Fate would have it, one of the company caught them up, dressed in motley with a lot of bells about him, and carrying three full blown ox-bladders on the end of a stick. When this clown came up to Don Quixote, he began to fence with his stick, to beat the ground with his bladders, and leap into the air to the sound of his bells; and this evil apparition so scared Rocinante that he took the bit between his teeth, and started to gallop across the field with more speed than the bones of his anatomy promised; nor was Don Quixote strong enough to stop him. Then, realizing that his master was in danger of being thrown off, Sancho jumped down from Dapple and ran in all haste to his assistance. But when he got up to him he was already on the ground, and beside him lay Rocinante, who had fallen with his master — for such was the usual upshot of the knight's exploits and Rocinante's high spirits.

But no sooner had Sancho left his own mount to help Don Quixote than the dancing devil jumped on to Dapple, and dealt him a slap with the bladders, whereat, startled by the noise rather than by the pain of the blows, the ass went flying off across country towards the village where the festival was to take place. Sancho watched Dapple's flight and his master's fall, undecided which of the two calls to attend to first. But finally, good squire and good servant that he was, love of his master prevailed over affection for his ass, though each time he saw the bladders rise in the air and fall on his Dapple's rump, he felt the pains and terrors of death, for he would rather have had those blows fall on his own eyeballs than on the least hair of his ass's tail. In this sad state of perplexity he arrived where Don Quixote lay in a great deal worse plight than he cared to see him in and, helping him on to Rocinante, he said: 'Sir, the Devil's carried Dapple off.'

'What Devil?' asked Don Quixote.

'The one with the bladders,' replied Sancho.

'Then I shall get him back,' said Don Quixote, 'even if he were to lock him up in the deepest and darkest dungeons of Hell. Follow me, Sancho. For the waggon goes slowly, and I will take its mules to make up for the loss of Dapple.'

'There's no need to go to that trouble, sir,' said Sancho. 'Cool your anger, your worship, for it looks to me as if the Devil has let Dapple go and is off to his own haunts again.'

And so indeed he was. For when the Devil had given an imitation of Don Quixote and Rocinante by tumbling off Dapple he set off to the village on foot, and the ass came back to his master.

'All the same,' said Don Quixote, 'it will be as well to visit that demon's impoliteness on one of those in the waggon, perhaps on the Emperor himself.'

'Put that thought out of your head, your worship,' answered Sancho. 'Take my advice and never meddle with play-actors, for they're a favoured race. I've seen an actor taken up for a couple of murders and get off scot-free. As they're a merry lot and give pleasure, I would have your worship know that everybody sides with them and protects them, aids them, and esteems them, particularly if they belong to the King's companies and have a charter. And all of them, or most of them, look like princes when they have their costumes and make-up on.'

'For all that,' answered Don Quixote, 'that player devil shall not go away applauding himself, even if the whole human race favours him.'

And as he spoke, he turned towards the waggon, which was now very close to the village, calling out loudly, as he rode: 'Halt! Stop, merry and festive crew! For I would teach you how to treat asses and animals which serve as mounts to the squires of knights errant.'

So loudly did Don Quixote shout that those in the waggon heard and understood him; and judging from his words the purpose of their speaker, Death promptly jumped out of the waggon, and after him the Emperor, the Demon-driver, and the Angel; nor did the Queen or the god Cupid stay behind. Then they all loaded themselves with stones and took up their positions in a row, waiting to receive Don Quixote with the edges of their pebbles. But when he saw them drawn up in so gallant a squadron, with their arms raised in the act of discharging this powerful volley of stones, he reined Rocinante in, and began to consider how to set upon them with least peril to his person. While he was thus checked Sancho came up and, seeing him drawn up to attack that well-ordered squadron, said:

'It would be the height of madness to attempt such an enterprise. Consider, your worship, that there is no defensive armour in the world against the rain of these fellows' bullets, unless you could ram yourself into a brass bell and hide. And you must consider too, master, that it is rashness and not valour for a single man to attack an army with Death in its ranks, Emperors in person fighting in it, and assisted by good and bad angels. What's more, if this isn't reason enough to persuade you to stay quiet, consider that it's a positive fact that although they look like Kings, Princes and Emperors, there isn't a single knight errant among the whole lot of them there.'

'Now, Sancho,' said Don Quixote, 'you have certainly hit on a consideration which should deflect me from my determination. I cannot and must not draw my sword, as I have told you on many occasions before now, against anyone who is not a knight. It rests with you therefore, Sancho, if you wish to take revenge for the injury done to your Dapple; and I will help you from here with words of salutary counsel.'

'There's no reason, sir, to take revenge on anyone,' replied Sancho, 'for it's not right for a good Christian to avenge his injuries. What's more I shall persuade Dapple to leave his cause in my hands, and it's my intention to live peacefully all the days of life that Heaven grants me.'

'Since that is your decision,' answered Don Quixote, 'good Sancho, wise Sancho, Christian Sancho, honest Sancho, let us leave these phantoms and return to our quest for better and more substantial adventures. For I'm sure that this is the sort of country that can't fail to provide us with many and most miraculous ones.'

Then he turned Rocinante, Sancho went to catch his Dapple, and Death and all his flying squadron returned to their waggon and continued their journey. And this was the happy ending of the encounter with the waggon of Death, thanks to the healthy advice which Sancho Panza gave his master, to whom on the next day there came another adventure, with an enamoured knight errant, which proved no less exciting than the last.

Chapter XII. *Of the strange Adventure which befell the valorous Don Quixote with the brave Knight of the Mirrors.*

DON QUIXOTE and his squire passed the night following the day of this encounter with Death beneath some tall and shady trees, where, on Sancho's persuasion, the knight ate some food from the store which Dapple carried. And during their supper Sancho observed to his master: 'Sir, what a fool I should have been if I'd chosen the spoils of your worship's first adventure as my reward, instead of the three mares' foals. Indeed, indeed, a bird in the hand's worth two in the bush.'

'For all that,' replied Don Quixote, 'if you had let me attack, Sancho, as I wanted to, at least the Empress's golden crown and Cupid's painted wings would have fallen to you as spoils, for I should have pulled them off in spite of their struggles, and placed them in your hands.'

'The sceptres and crowns of player-emperors have never been pure gold,' replied Sancho, 'but tinsel or brass foil.'

'That is true,' replied Don Quixote. 'It would not be right for the finery in plays to be real; it should be counterfeit and illusory, as the play is itself. To which plays, Sancho, I would have you favourably disposed, and therefore, to the actors and authors as well, for they are all instrumental in conferring a great benefit on the commonwealth, holding up to us at every step a mirror in which the actions of human life are vividly portrayed. Indeed there is no comparison which presents to us more truly what we are and what we ought to be than the play and the players. Now, tell me, have not you seen a play acted with Kings, Emperors and Popes, knights, ladies and various other personages brought on to the stage? One plays the ruffian, another the cheat; here is a merchant, there is a soldier; one is the wise fool, another the foolish lover. But when the play is over, and they have taken off their dresses, all the actors are equal.'

'Yes, I have indeed,' replied Sancho.

'Now the same thing,' said Don Quixote, 'happens in the comedy and traffic of this world, where some play Emperors, others Popes and, in fact, every part that can be introduced into a play. But when we come to the end, which is when life is over, Death strips them of all the robes that distinguished them, and they are all equals in the grave.'

'A fine comparison,' said Sancho, 'although not so new that I haven't heard it on various occasions before – like the one of the game of chess, where each piece has its particular importance while the game lasts, but when it's over they're all mixed up, thrown together, jumbled, and shoved into a leather bag, which is much like shovelling life away into the grave.'

'Every day, Sancho,' said Don Quixote, 'you grow less simple and wiser.'

'Yes,' replied Sancho, 'for some of your worship's wisdom must stick to me. Since lands of themselves barren and dry, with mucking and tilling come to yield good fruit. I mean that your worship's conversation has been the muck, which has been cast upon the sterile ground of my dry wit, and the time of my service and communion with you has been the tillage. And so I expect to bear fruit of my own, which may be a blessing, and won't disgrace me, I hope, or slither off the paths of good breeding you have beaten in this parched understanding of mine.'

Don Quixote laughed at Sancho's affected language, but what he had said about his improvement seemed to him true. For from time to time he spoke in a way that surprised his master, although on all, or almost all, the occasions when Sancho tried to dispute in a grand

style, his argument ended by tumbling from the heights of simplicity into the depths of ignorance. But where he showed his wit and
his memory to best effect was in his use of proverbs, whether they
applied to the subject or not, as will have been seen and noted in the
course of this history.

In this and suchlike conversation they spent a great part of the
night, till a desire came on Sancho to drop the hatches of his eyes,
as he used to say when he wanted to sleep. So, unharnessing Dapple,
he turned him over to graze freely and abundantly. But he did not
take off Rocinante's saddle, it being his master's express command
that, during such time as they should be in the field or not sleeping
beneath a roof, he should not unsaddle his steed – for it was an ancient custom established and preserved by knights errant, to take
off the bridle and hang it on the saddle-bow; but to unsaddle the
horse – Never! This law Sancho obeyed and gave Rocinante the
same freedom as Dapple. Now the friendship between the pair was
so rare and so strong that there is a tradition handed down from
father to son that the author of this true history devoted some
special chapters to it, but, to preserve the propriety and decorum
proper to so heroic a story, omitted to put them in. Though at
times he forgets this purpose of his, and writes that as soon as the
two beasts were together they would start scratching one another,
and that once they were tired and contented, Rocinante would cross
his neck over Dapple's – and it would stick out by more than half a
yard. Then the two of them would gaze fixedly on the ground and
stand in that position for three days, or at least for so long as they
were left, or hunger did not compel them to seek for sustenance. The
tradition is, I repeat, that the author left in writing a comparison between their friendship and that of Nisus and Euryalus, and of Py-
lades and Orestes. And if this is true, it can be deduced how strong
the friendship between these two pacific animals must have been,
to the wonder of the world and to the shame of humankind, who
are so little able to preserve friendships for one another. Hence the
saying:

> 'There is no friendship between friends ;
> Men's sparring canes are turned to lances'

and that is the reason for that other song:

> 'Twixt friend and friend the bug creeps in.'

But let no one suppose that the author digressed in comparing the friendship of these animals to that of men. For men have received many lessons from the beasts and learnt many important things from them, for example: from storks, the enema; from the dog, vomiting and gratitude; from cranes, vigilance; from ants, thrift; from elephants, chastity, and loyalty from the horse.

At length Sancho fell asleep at the foot of a cork-tree, and Don Quixote into a doze at the foot of a stout oak. But very little time had elapsed before the knight was awoken by a noise which he heard behind him. Thereupon he started up and began to look and to listen whence the noise proceeded. He soon made out two men on horseback, and heard one of them say to the other, as he dropped from his saddle: 'Get down, friend, and unbridle the horses, for this place seems to me both rich in grass for them, and in the silence and solitude my amorous meditations require.'

Saying this and stretching himself on the ground were the action of a moment; and as he threw himself down, the armour he was wearing made a clatter, a clear proof to Don Quixote that he must be a knight errant. So, going up to Sancho, who was still asleep, he pulled him by the arm, and with no little labour brought him to his senses, telling him in a whisper: 'Brother Sancho, we have an adventure.'

'God make it a good one!' answered Sancho. 'And where is she, dear master, her Grace Madam Adventure?'

'Where, Sancho?' replied Don Quixote. 'Turn your eyes and look, and you will see a knight errant lying down over there. It looks to me as if he is not any too cheerful, for I have just watched him leap from his horse and throw himself on the ground with some display of dejection. And when he fell his armour clattered.'

'But how does your worship make out,' asked Sancho, 'that it's an adventure?'

'I do not mean to say,' replied Don Quixote, 'that this is a complete adventure, but the beginning of one. For this is the way adventures start. But listen. It looks as if he is tuning up a lute or a viol, and by the way he is spitting and clearing his throat, he must be getting ready to sing something.'

'Yes indeed, so he is,' replied Sancho. 'Then he must be a knight in love.'

'There is no knight errant who is not,' said Don Quixote. 'Let us listen to him; for, if he does sing, from that thread we shall gain a clue to his thoughts, since out of the abundance of the heart speaks the tongue.'

Sancho was going to reply to his master, but he was prevented by the voice of the Knight of the Wood, which was neither very bad nor very good; and the pair of them listened attentively while he sang the following song:

> Mistress, prescribe a law whereby
>   I may obey your sovereign heart.
> I'll follow it unswervingly
>   And from its precepts ne'er depart.
>
> If you would have me die of pain
>   In silence, then account me dead,
> But if you'd have the ancient strain
>   Ring out, then Love himself shall plead.
>
> Proof against contraries I'm made,
>   Of softest wax and diamond hard.
> Beneath love's rule my heart is laid
>   And for its laws my soul's prepared.
>
> Or soft or hard, my breast is thine.
>   Imprint what characters you will.
> To all eternity, divine
>   Mistress, I'll do your bidding still.

With a sigh, fetched apparently from the depths of his heart, the Knight of the Wood ended his song, and a little later cried in a sad and sorrowful voice:

'O most beautiful and ungrateful woman in all the world! How can it be possible, most serene Casildea de Vandalia, for you to allow your captive knight to be consumed and to perish in perpetual wanderings and in hard and harsh labours? Is it not enough that I have made all the knights of Navarre acknowledge you the most beautiful lady in the world, and all the Knights of Leon, of Tartesia and of Castile, and all the Knights of La Mancha as well?'

'Not so,' remarked Don Quixote at this point, 'for I am of La Mancha, and have acknowledged no such thing. Nor could I, nor should I acknowledge anything so prejudicial to the beauty of my mistress. You can see now, Sancho, that this knight is raving. But let us listen; perhaps he will reveal himself further.'

'Yes, he will,' replied Sancho, 'for he looks the kind to complain for a month on end.'

But it was not so. For, overhearing this talk so near him, the Knight of the Wood proceeded no further with his lamentation, but got on to his feet and called out in loud but courteous tones: 'Who goes there? Who are you? Do you chance to be of the number of the happy or of the afflicted?'

'Of the afflicted,' replied Don Quixote.

'Then come to me,' answered the Knight of the Wood, 'and you will find sorrow and misery itself.'

Then finding himself so delicately and politely answered Don Quixote went over to him, as did Sancho as well, on which the plaintive knight took Don Quixote by the arm and said: 'Sit down here, Sir Knight, for to be assured that you are a knight and profess the order of knight errantry, it is sufficient that I have found you in this spot encompassed by solitude and the dews of night – the natural bed and proper habitation for a knight errant.'

To which Don Quixote replied: 'I am a knight, and of the order you name; and although sorrows, misfortunes, and disasters have their very seat in my soul, the compassion I feel for the misfortunes of others is not therefore banished from my heart. From what you have just sung I gathered that yours are misfortunes of love – I mean of the love you have for that ungrateful beauty whom you named in your lament.'

Now during this conversation they were seated together on the hard ground in peace and comradeship, as if they had not to break each other's heads at break of day.

'Are you, Sir Knight,' the Knight of the Wood asked Don Quixote, 'by any chance in love?'

'By ill chance I am,' replied Don Quixote, 'although the sufferings which arise from well-placed affections should rather be considered benefits than calamities.'

'That is true,' replied the Knight of the Wood, 'if disdain did not confuse the reason and the understanding. For when it is excessive it looks like revenge.'

'I have never been disdained by my mistress,' answered Don Quixote.

'No, certainly not,' said Sancho, who was near them, 'for our lady is as meek as a yearling ewe and softer than butter.'

'Is this your squire?' asked the Knight of the Wood.

'It is,' answered Don Quixote.

'I have never met a squire,' said the Knight of the Wood, 'who dared to speak when his master was speaking. At least there stands that man of mine, who is as big as his father, and it cannot be proved that he ever opened his lips when I was speaking.'

'Well,' said Sancho, 'I've talked right enough, and I can talk before another as ... But let it be; it'll be the worse for stirring.'

Then the Squire of the Wood grasped Sancho's arm and said: 'Let us two go where we can talk squire-like about anything we choose, and let's leave these gentlemen, our masters, to set to and tell one another the stories of their loves. For the morning'll catch them at it, I promise you, and they won't have finished then.'

'That suits me,' said Sancho, 'and I'll tell your worship who I am. Then you'll see whether I can compete with your most talkative of squires.'

At this the two squires drew aside, and the conversation between them was as comical as their masters' was serious.

Chapter XIII. *In which is continued the Adventure of the Knight of the Wood together with the wise, novel and agreeable Conversation between the two Squires.*

THE knights and their squires were separated, the squires telling the stories of their lives, the knights of their loves. But history recounts the servants' conversation first, and then follows the talk between their masters. And so it relates that when they had drawn a little aside the Squire of the Wood said to Sancho: 'It's a wearisome life we have, sir, we that are squires to knights errant. Indeed we eat our bread in the sweat of our brows, which is one of the curses God laid on our first parents.'

'It may be said too,' added Sancho, 'that we eat it in the chill of our bodies, for who suffers the heat and the cold worse than the miserable squires of knight errantry? It wouldn't be so bad if we could eat, for good fare lessens care. Yet sometimes we spend a whole day, or even two, without breaking our fast except on the winds that blow.'

'All that can be borne and put up with,' said the Squire of the Wood, 'seeing what hope we have of reward. For unless the knight errant he is serving is excessively unfortunate a squire will at least find himself rewarded in a little while with the handsome government of some isle, or with a respectable countship.'

'I,' replied Sancho, 'have already told my master that I shall be content with the government of an isle; and so noble and generous is he that he's promised me it on several occasions already.'

'I,' said the Squire of the Wood, 'shall be satisfied with a canonry for my services; and my master has already reserved one for me – and what a one!'

'Then, of course,' said Sancho, 'your worship's master must be a knight in the ecclesiastical line, that he can grant his worthy squire a favour of that kind. But mine is only a layman, though I remember that there was a time when some clever persons – they were rather malicious, I thought – were advising him to try and become an Archbishop. But he was set on becoming an Emperor, though I was trembling at the time for fear he might take it into his head to be a churchman, not feeling myself capable of holding a church benefice. For I would have you know that, though I seem a man, if it's a question of going into the Church I'm a very beast.'

'But indeed your worship is wrong,' said the Squire of the Wood, 'for your insular governments are not all of the right kind. Some are crooked, some poor, and some depressing; and, what's more, the stateliest and best of them brings a heavy load of cares and discomforts with it, and the unlucky man it falls to must bear them on his shoulders. It would be a great deal better for us who profess this accursed service to retire to our homes, and there employ ourselves in more agreeable exercises, as in hunting perhaps or in fishing. For what squire in the world is there so poor that he hasn't a horse and a couple of greyhounds and a fishing-rod to amuse himself with in his own village?'

'I'm not short of any of those things,' answered Sancho, 'though it's true that I haven't a horse. But I have an ass worth twice as much as my master's horse. God send me a bad Easter and may it be

S

the next one, if I would swap with him, even if I got four bushels of barley thrown in. Your worship may think I'm joking when I put that price on my Dapple — for dapple is my ass's colour. But I shan't be short of greyhounds, for there are enough and to spare in my village; and hunting is all the pleasanter when it's at someone else's expense.'

'To tell you the truth, Master Squire,' replied the Squire of the Wood, 'I've made up my mind, and I'm determined to quit the drunken goings-on of these knights of ours, and retire to my village and bring up my children; for I have three of them, lovely as three orient pearls.'

'I have two,' said Sancho, 'fit to be presented to the Pope himself, one girl especially whom I'm bringing up to be a countess, please God — though in spite of her mother.'

'And what's the age of the young lady who is being brought up to be a countess?' asked the Squire of the Wood.

'Fifteen, more or less,' answered Sancho, 'but she's as tall as a lance, as fresh as an April morning, and as strong as a porter.'

'Those are qualities,' said the Squire of the Wood, 'that fit her not only to be a countess, but to be a nymph of the green wood. Oh, the little whore, the whore, what muscles the rogue must have!'

To which Sancho replied rather peevishly: 'She's no whore, nor was her mother, and neither of them ever will be, God willing, whilst I'm alive. Speak rather more politely, for seeing that your worship was brought up amongst knights errant, who are politeness itself, these words of yours don't seem very well chosen.'

'Oh, how little your worship understands the play of compliments, Master Squire,' replied the Squire of the Wood. 'Why, don't you know that when a horseman deals the bull in the square a good lance-thrust, or when anyone does a thing really well the crowd always shout: "Oh, the whore, the little whore, that was nicely done!" And what seems abuse in that term is really notable praise. You should disown, sir, any sons or daughters who don't perform deeds that earn their parents praise like that.'

'Yes, I disown them,' answered Sancho, 'and since you mean so well by it, your worship may clap a whole brothel on top of me, my children and my wife, for everything they do and say is highly deserving of such praise. I'm longing to see them again, and therefore

I pray God to deliver me out of mortal sin – that's to say to deliver me from this perilous office of squire, into which I've run for a second time, through being enticed and deceived by a purse of a hundred ducats which I found one day in the heart of the Sierra Morena. For the Devil's always dangling a bag full of doubloons before my eyes here, there and everywhere. At every step I seem to be laying my hands on it, hugging it, and taking it home, then making investments and settling rents, and living like a prince. And while this runs in my head all the toils I endure with my idiot of a master become light and bearable, though I know he's more of a madman than a knight.'

'That's why they say that greed bursts the bag,' replied the Squire of the Wood. 'But, talking of madmen, there's no greater idiot in the world than my master. There's a proverb that just fits him: other men's cares kill the ass. For to restore another knight his lost wits he's making a madman of himself, and goes about looking for something which may hit him on the snout when he finds it.'

'And is he by any chance in love?'

'Yes,' said the Squire of the Wood, 'with a certain Casildea de Vandalia, the rawest and best-cooked lady to be found in the whole world. But that's not the foot he limps on at present, for there are greater tricks rumbling in his stomach, which he will speak of before many hours have passed.'

'There's no road so smooth,' replied Sancho, 'that it hasn't some obstruction or hole. In other houses they cook beans, but whole cauldrons full in mine. Madness needs more companions and mess-mates than wisdom. But if it's true, as it's commonly said, that to have companions in your troubles generally helps to relieve them, I can draw comfort from your worship since you serve another master as foolish as mine.'

'Foolish but valiant,' said the Squire of the Wood, 'and more of a rogue than either foolish or valiant.'

'That my master isn't,' replied Sancho. 'I mean there's nothing of the rogue in him. His soul is as clean as a pitcher. He can do no harm to anyone, only good to everybody. There's no malice in him. A child might make him believe it's night at noonday. And for that simplicity I love him as dearly as my heart-strings, and can't take to the idea of leaving him for all his wild tricks.'

'All the same, sir and brother,' said the Squire of the Wood, 'if the blind lead the blind, both will be in danger of falling into the ditch. It would be better for us to go back pretty quick and retire to our lairs, for seekers after adventures don't always find good ones.'

All this while Sancho was spitting frequently a kind of dryish gluey saliva; and when the kind Squire of the Wood noticed it, he observed: 'All this talk seems to be making our tongues stick to our palates. I carry a pretty good loosener, though, here hanging at my saddle-bow.'

And, getting up, he came back a moment later with a large leather bottle of wine and a pie half a yard long – which is no exaggeration, for the white rabbit it contained was so large that when Sancho felt it he thought it was a goat, and no kid either. And at this sight our squire exclaimed: 'Do you carry this around with you, sir?'

'Well, what do you think?' replied the other. 'Do I look like a wool and water squire? I carry a better meal on my horse's crupper than a general takes with him when he goes on a march.'

Sancho fell to without invitation and swallowed great shovels-ful in the dark, saying: 'Your worship is certainly a loyal and law-ful squire, good and proper, magnificent and grand, as this banquet shows. For if it hasn't come here by way of enchantment, at least it looks as if it has. You're not like me, poor and unlucky, with only a bit of hard cheese in my saddle bag, that you could break a giant's head with, and four dozen carob beans to bear it company, and about the same number of filberts and nuts. I've my master's mean-ness to thank for that, and his ideas and rules about knights errant keeping body and soul together on nothing but dry fruits and the herbs of the field.'

'My stomach isn't made for your thistles or your wild pears or your forest roots, I promise you, brother,' replied the Squire of the Wood. 'Let our masters have them, with their ideas and their laws of chivalry, and let them eat what they order others to. I carry my panniers and this bottle hanging on my saddle-bow, just in case; and I'm so devoted to it and love it so dearly that seldom an hour passes without my kissing it and hugging it once or twice.'

And so saying, he gave it to Sancho, who tilted it, put it to his mouth and gazed at the stars for a quarter of an hour on end. Then, when he had finished drinking, he let his head fall to one side, and remarked with a deep sigh:

'O the little whore, the rogue! What grand stuff it is!'

'Now see,' said the Squire of the Wood, hearing Sancho's '*little whore*', 'how you praised that wine by calling it a whore.'

'Yes, I confess that it's no dishonour to call anyone a whore, when you mean it for praise,' replied Sancho. 'But, tell me, sir, on your Bible oath, is this wine from Ciudad Real?'

'A rare judge!' answered the Squire of the Wood. 'From no other place, that's a fact, and it's a good few years old too.'

'Trust me for that,' said Sancho. 'Don't suppose that I wasn't up to recognizing its quality. Isn't it good, Sir Squire, that I have such a fine and natural instinct for this wine-judging? You've only to give me a drop to smell and I can hit upon the place, the grape, the savour, and the age; and the changes it'll go through, and every other point to do with wine. But there's nothing surprising in that, for I had in my family, on my father's side, the two best judges of wine that La Mancha has known for many a long year. And to prove it to you I'll tell you a story about them. They gave the pair of them some wine from a cask to try, and asked them their opinion of its condition, its quality, its goodness or badness. One of them tried it on the tip of his tongue, the other did no more than lift it to his nose. The first said that the wine tasted of iron; the second said that it had rather the flavour of leather. The owner said that the cask was clean, and that the wine had no blending from which it could have taken the flavour of iron or of leather. For all that the two famous judges persisted in their opinions. Time went on; the wine was sold; and when they came to clean the cask, they found a little key in it hanging on a leather thong. So your worship can see that a man of a breed like that has a right to give an opinion in such-like cases.'

'That's why I say,' said the Squire of the Wood, 'that we should give up going after adventures, and since we have loaves not seek for cakes, but go back to our cottages, for God will find us there if He wants to.'

'Until my master gets to Saragossa I'll serve him, and after that we'll come to some arrangement.'

At length the two good squires had talked and drunk so much

that they had need of sleep to tie their tongues and allay their thirst, for to quench it would have been impossible. So grasping the almost empty bottle between them, with their meat half chewed in their mouths, they fell asleep; where we will leave them for now, to relate what passed between the Knight of the Wood and the Knight of the Sad Countenance.

Chapter XIV. *In which the Adventure of the Knight of the Wood is continued.*

AMONG the many speeches which passed between Don Quixote and the Knight of the Wood, our history tells us that the latter addressed our knight to this effect:

'To be brief, Sir Knight, I would have you know that my destiny or, to be more exact, my choice led me to fall in love with the peerless Casildea of Vandalia. I call her peerless because she has no equal either in the greatness of her stature or in the perfection of her rank and beauty. Now this Casildea I am telling you of repaid my honest affections and courteous desires by employing me, as his stepmother did Hercules, in many and various labours, promising me at the end of each one that with the conclusion of the next I should attain the goal of my hopes. But in that way my toils have been increased link by link, till they are countless, and I still do not know which is to be the last, and to lead to the fulfilment of my honest desires. Once she commanded me to go and challenge that famous Seville giantess, the Giralda, who is as valiant and strong as if she were of brass, and without stirring from one place, is the most changeable and volatile woman in the world. I came, I saw, I conquered her. I forced her to stay still and keep to one point, for none but the north-wind blew for more than a week. There was a time too when she commanded me to go and weigh those ancient stones, the brave Bulls of Guisando, an exploit fitter to be entrusted to a porter than to a knight. Another time she commanded me to plunge headlong into the cavern of Cabra – a fearful and unheard-of peril – and bring her back a detailed account of what lay concealed in those dark depths. I stayed the motion of La Giralda; I weighed the Bulls of Guisando; I plunged into the cavern and brought to light what lay hidden in its depths; but my hopes are more dead than ever, and her commands and scorn more living. Finally, at long last, she has commanded me to travel through all the provinces of Spain and make all knights errant wandering there confess that she alone surpasses in beauty all ladies to-day living, and that I am the most valiant and the most enamoured knight in the world. In which task I have already travelled through the greater part of Spain, and there conquered many knights who have dared to gainsay me. But the deed I most pride and value myself for is that I vanquished in single battle that most famous knight Don Quixote de la Mancha, and made him confess that my Casildea is more beautiful than his Dulcinea; for by this victory alone I consider that I have conquered all the knights in the world, because this same Don Quixote I speak of has conquered them all; and since I have conquered him, his glory, his fame and his honour are transferred and have passed to my person:

> The victor's honour is increased
> By all his conquered enemy had.

So the innumerable exploits of the said Don Quixote fall to my credit and are mine.'

Don Quixote was amazed to hear the Knight of the Wood, and was a thousand times on the point of telling him that he lied. In fact, he had the word '*liar*' on the very tip of his tongue; but he restrained himself as best he could, so that he might later make him confess out of his own mouth that he lied. And so he calmly replied: 'Of your worship's having conquered most of the knights errant in Spain, Sir Knight, and even in the whole world, I say nothing. But that you have conquered Don Quixote de la Mancha, I beg leave to doubt. It may be that it was some other resembling him, although there are few like him.'

'What?' replied the Knight of the Wood. 'By the heavens above us, I did fight with Don Quixote and conquered him and forced him to yield. He is a man tall of stature, withered of face, lanky and shrivelled of limb, grizzled, with an aquiline and rather crooked nose, and great moustaches, black and drooping. He takes the field under the name of the Knight of the Sad Countenance, and has for his squire a countryman called Sancho Panza. He oppresses the back and guides the reins of a famous steed called Rocinante and, lastly, has for the mistress of his affections a certain Dulcinea del Toboso, formerly called Aldonza Lorenzo – as I call mine, since her name is Casildea and she comes from Andalusia, Casildea de Vandalia. If all these marks are not sufficient to confirm the truth of my words, here is my sword, which shall make incredulity itself give me credence.'

'Calm yourself, Sir Knight,' said Don Quixote, 'and listen to what I shall say. You must know that this Don Quixote you speak of is the best friend I have in this world. So much so that I can say I have the same regard for him as for myself, and by the very exact and precise description of him you have given me I cannot doubt that he is the same whom you conquered. On the other hand, I have the evidence of my eyes and hands that it could not possibly have been the same knight; were it not that he has many enchanters as his enemies – especially one who habitually persecutes him. For one of them may have taken his shape and allowed himself to be defeated so as to defraud him of the renown which his high deeds of chivalry have acquired and reaped for him over the whole known world. And, to confirm this, I would have you also know that it is not two days ago that those enchanters, his adversaries, transformed the shape and person of the fair Dulcinea del Toboso into a base and vile village girl. In just such a way they must have transformed Don Quixote. And if all this is not enough to convince you of the truth of my words, here is Don Quixote himself, who will maintain them with his arms, on foot or on horse or in what manner you please.'

As he spoke he got on to his feet and grasped his sword, awaiting the decision of the Knight of the Wood, who replied in an equally calm voice:

'A good paymaster doesn't worry about sureties. He that could once conquer you, Don Quixote, when you were transformed, may very well hope to overcome you in your proper person. But as it is not becoming for knights to perform their feats of arms in the dark, like highwaymen and ruffians, let us wait for day, so that the sun may look upon our deeds. And it shall be a condition of our battle that the vanquished shall be at the disposal of the victor, to do as he will with him, so long as he commands him to do nothing unbefitting a knight.'

'I am more than satisfied with this condition and I agree,' replied Don Quixote.

At these words they went over to their squires, and found them snoring in the attitudes in which sleep had overcome them. They awoke them and ordered them to get the horses ready, for at sunrise the two knights must engage in bloody and perilous single combat. At which news Sancho was stupefied with amazement, fearing for his master's safety by reason of the Knight of the Wood's valiant deeds, of which he had heard from his squire. But without speaking a word the two squires went to look for their cattle, for by this time all three horses and the ass had smelt one another out and were together. And by the way the Squire of the Wood observed to Sancho: 'You must know, brother, that when fighting men of Andalusia are seconds in any battle, it is not their custom to stand idly with their hands clasped while their principals are in combat. This I say to warn you that, while our masters are battling, we must have a fight as well and shiver one another to splinters.'

'That custom, Sir Squire,' replied Sancho, 'may obtain and hold good amongst the ruffians and fighting men you speak of. But amongst squires of knights errant – not a bit of it! At least I've never heard my master speak of any such custom, and he knows all the rules of knight errantry by heart. But even suppose I agreed that it's true, and that there's an express ordinance that squires must fight when their masters do, I still would not conform to it. I would rather pay such penalty as may be imposed on peaceful squires like myself; for it can't cost me more than two pounds of wax. I'd rather pay that, for I'm sure it will be less expensive than the lint I should need for healing my head, which is as good as split in two at the mere thought of fighting. There's another thing: fighting's quite out of the question, for I haven't a sword and I've never worn one in all my life.'

'I know a good remedy for that,' said the Squire of the Wood; 'I've here two linen bags of the same size. You shall take one and I the other, and we'll fight a pillow fight with equal arms.'

'With those weapons I'll gladly fight,' replied Sancho. 'For that kind of battle's more likely to dust us down than to wound us.'

'No, that shan't be,' answered the other, 'for we'll put in half a dozen nice smooth stones of equal weight. Then the wind won't catch them, and in that way we shall be able to thump one another and do no hurt or damage.'

'Good heavens!' exclaimed Sancho. 'So that's the sort of sable skins or carded cotton balls he's going to put into the bags, to save us bashing our skulls in and grinding our bones to powder! No, I tell you, sir, I'm not fighting, not even if they're filled with silk cocoons. Let our masters fight and good luck to them, but let us drink and eat. For time takes care enough to rob us of our lives, without our going out to look for ways of ending them off before their due time and season. They'll drop off when they're ripe.'

'All the same,' replied the Squire of the Wood, 'we must fight, if only for half an hour.'

'No, no!' answered Sancho. 'I shan't be so discourteous or un-grateful as to begin even the smallest quarrel with a man I've eaten and drunk with. Besides, how could I possibly fight in cold blood, without being provoked to it?'

'I'll provide a sufficient remedy for that,' said the Squire of the Wood. 'Before we begin the fight I'll go up to your worship and deal you three or four neat blows that'll lay you out at my feet. That will rouse your anger, even if it's sleeping sounder than a dormouse.'

'Against that trick,' answered Sancho, 'I know another, every bit as good. I'll take a thick stick, and before your worship starts rous-ing my anger, I'll thrash yours to sleep so soundly that it'll only wake up in the other world, where I'm known as a man who won't allow any one to pull his nose. Let every man look out for his own arrow; although it would be best for everyone to let his anger sleep. For no one knows another man's heart, and some come for wool that go away shorn, and God blessed peace and cursed quarrels. Because if a hunted cat, shut in and hard pressed, turns into a lion, God knows what I, who am a man, might turn into. So, from now on, I give you notice, Sir Squire, that I shall lay all the harm and damage that may result from our quarrel to your account.'

'That's right,' replied the Squire of the Wood. 'God send us day and all will be well.'

And now a thousand kinds of little painted birds began to warble in the trees, and with their various joyful songs seemed to welcome and salute the fresh Dawn, who was now showing her lovely face through the portals and balconies of the East, shaking from her locks an infinite number of liquid pearls, bathed in whose soft liquor the plants seemed also to bud, and to rain their small white pearls. The willows distilled sweet manna, the springs laughed, the brooks murmured, the woods rejoiced, and all the meadows were enriched by her coming.

But no sooner did the light of day allow him to see and distinguish objects than the first thing which presented itself to Sancho Panza's eyes was the nose of the Squire of the Wood, which was so large as almost to overshadow his whole body. The story goes, indeed, that it was of an extraordinary size, bent in the middle, covered with mulberry-coloured warts like an aubergine, and coming down two inches below his mouth. Its size and colour, its warts and its crookedness, made its owner's face so hideous that when Sancho saw it, his hands and feet began to quake like an epileptic child's, and he resolved in his heart to put up with two hundred blows rather than rouse his temper to fight with that demon.

Don Quixote too surveyed his adversary, but found that his helmet was already on with the vizor down, so that he could not see his face. He observed, however, that he was a well-built man, though not very tall in stature. Over his armour he wore a surcoat or cassock, of a material which seemed like finest gold, sprinkled with a great number of little disks of shining looking-glass, which made him appear exceedingly gallant and splendid. Over his helmet waved a great number of green, yellow and white feathers, while his lance, which was leaning against a tree, was very long and thick, and shod with more than a foot of steel.

Don Quixote observed all this and took it in, judging from what he saw, and noted that this knight must be of great strength. However, unlike Sancho Panza, he was not frightened by this, but politely and courageously addressed the Knight of the Mirrors: 'If your eagerness to fight, Sir Knight, has not exhausted your courtesy, I beg you of that courtesy to raise your vizor a little, so that I may see whether the splendour of your face corresponds to that of your carriage.'

'Whether you emerge vanquished or victor from this enterprise, Sir Knight,' replied the Knight of the Mirrors, 'you will have more than enough time and opportunity for gazing on me. And if I do not now satisfy your request, it is because I feel that I should be doing grievous wrong to the fair Casildea de Vandalia by wasting time in stopping to raise my vizor before forcing you to confess what you know I demand.'

'Well, while we are mounting our steeds,' said Don Quixote, 'you might tell me whether I am that Don Quixote whom you said you had conquered.'

'To that we make answer,' replied the knight, 'that you are as like to that knight I conquered as one egg is to another. But as you say that he is persecuted by enchanters I dare not affirm whether you are the aforesaid or not.'

'That is sufficient reason for me to believe you were deceived,' answered Don Quixote. 'However, to deliver you altogether from your error, let our horses be brought. For in less time than you would waste in raising your vizor – if God, my lady and my right arm avail me – I shall see your face, and you shall see that I am not the vanquished Don Quixote you imagine ...'

With that they cut short their speeches and mounted. Then Don Quixote turned Rocinante's rein to take so much of the field as was necessary for running a course with his adversary, while the Knight of the Mirrors did the same. But Don Quixote had not gone twenty paces when he heard the Knight of the Mirrors call him, whereat he returned half way to hear his adversary say: 'Remember, Sir Knight, that the condition of our combat is that the vanquished, as I have said before, must remain at the discretion of the victor.'

'That I know already,' replied Don Quixote, 'but only on condition that what is commanded and imposed on the vanquished does not transgress the bounds of chivalry.'

'That is understood,' replied the Knight of the Mirrors. At this moment the squire's extraordinary nose presented itself to Don Quixote's view, and he was no less astonished at the sight than Sancho. So much so that he judged him some monster, or a new kind of man, uncommon in the world. Sancho saw his master go off to make his charge, and did not care to remain alone with Big Nose. For he feared that with one flick of that nose his own fight would be over, and he would lie stretched on the ground either from the blows or the fright. So he ran after his master, holding on to one of Rocinante's stirrup leathers, and when it seemed to him time for him to turn round, said to him:

'I beseech you, dear master, to help me get up into that cork-tree

before you turn and charge. From there, sir, I shall be able to see
the gallant encounter you are going to have with this knight more
comfortably and better than from the ground.'

'On the contrary, Sancho,' said Don Quixote, 'I think you want
to climb up on to the platform to see the bulls from out of danger.'

'To tell you the truth,' answered Sancho, 'I'm so astounded and
terrified by that squire's monstrous nose that I daren't stay near him.'

'So outrageous is it,' said Don Quixote, 'that, were I not the man
I am, it would frighten me too. So, come, I will help you up into the
spot you suggest.'

While Don Quixote stopped to help Sancho get up into the cork-
tree, the Knight of the Mirrors fetched the circuit of the field that
seemed to him necessary; and supposing that Don Quixote had
done the same, waited for no trumpet sound or other signal to start
them, but turned the head of his horse, which was no swifter nor
better-looking than Rocinante, and rode forward to encounter his
opponent at his full speed, which was a moderate trot. Seeing him,
however, occupied with Sancho's ascent, he checked his rein and
halted in mid-career, for which his horse was most grateful, being
incapable of further movement. But Don Quixote imagined that his
enemy was now flying down on him, and dug his spurs stoutly into
Rocinante's lean flanks, which made him leap forward in such a
fashion that, the history relates, on this single occasion in his life he
went at something like a gallop – for at all other times his pace was a
plain trot; and with this unspeakable fury the knight came down
upon his opponent of the Mirrors, who drove his spurs rowel-deep
into his horse, without being able to make him budge a single inch
from the place where he had come to a halt in his career.

At this fortunate juncture Don Quixote found his adversary embarrassed by his horse and concerned with his lance, which he either
could not, or had not time to, put into its rest. Taking no heed of his
embarrassments, however, Don Quixote attacked the Knight of the
Mirrors, in complete safety and without the slightest risk, and with
such force that, almost unintentionally, he threw him over his horse's
crupper to the ground, giving him such a fall that he moved neither
hand nor foot, but gave every appearance of being dead.

No sooner did Sancho see him down than he slid from the cork-
tree and ran at full speed to his master, who dismounted from Roci-

nante, and stood over the Knight of the Mirrors. Then, unlacing his helmet to see whether he was dead, or to give him air if he was alive, he saw ... Who without striking amazement, wonder and awe into his hearers could say what he saw? He saw, our history relates, the very face, the very physiognomy, the very image, the very picture of the bachelor Sampson Carrasco. And when he saw him he shouted loudly: 'Come here, Sancho, and see what you will not believe when you see it! Quick, my son, and take note what magic can do. Mark what wizards and enchanters are capable of.'

Sancho ran up, and when he saw the face of the Bachelor Sampson Carrasco he began to cross himself and bless himself a thousand times over. All this while the fallen knight showed no signs of life. And so Sancho said to Don Quixote: 'It's my opinion, sir, that your worship should thrust your sword right into this man's mouth, whichever way it is. He certainly looks like the Bachelor Sampson Carrasco, but perhaps if you kill him you'll be killing one of your enemies the enchanters.'

'That is not bad advice,' said Don Quixote, 'for the less enemies the better.' But as he was unsheathing his sword to put Sancho's suggestion into effect, the Mirror Knight's squire ran up, but without the nose which had so disfigured him, and cried out loudly: 'Take care what you're doing, sir. For that man at your feet is your friend the Bachelor Sampson Carrasco, and I'm his squire.'

'And your nose?' cried Sancho, on seeing him without his previous deformity.

And the squire replied: 'I have it here in my pocket.' And putting his hand into his right pocket, he drew out a pasteboard nose, shaped and painted in the manner described. Then, after staring at him more and more attentively, Sancho exclaimed in loud tones of wonder: 'God bless my soul! If it isn't Thomas Cecial, my friend and neighbour!'

'And what if it is?' replied the now un-nosed squire. 'Thomas Cecial I am, Sancho old friend, and I'll tell you presently the means, the tricks, and the schemes that brought me here. Meanwhile, beg and pray his worship your master not to touch, maltreat, wound, or kill the Knight of the Mirrors, who lies at his feet, for beyond any shadow of doubt he's the bold and ill-advised Bachelor Sampson Carrasco, our fellow-countryman.'

At this the Knight of the Mirrors came to himself, and Don Quixote at once put his naked sword point to his face, saying:

'You are dead, knight, if you do not confess that the peerless Dulcinea del Toboso surpasses your Casildea de Vandalia in beauty. What is more, you must promise, if you would survive this combat and defeat, to travel to the city of El Toboso and present yourself before her from me, so that she may do with you what she may best please. Then, if she leaves you to your own devices, you must return to seek me – for the trail of my exploits will serve you for guide and bring you to where I am – and tell me what has passed between her and you; – which conditions, in accordance with those fixed before our combat, do not transgress the rules of knight errantry.'

'I confess,' said the fallen knight, 'that the torn and soiled shoe of the lady Dulcinea del Toboso is worth more than the ill-combed, though clean beard of Casildea; and I promise to go and to return from her presence to yours, and to give you a complete and detailed account of all that you ask.'

'Also you must confess and believe,' added Don Quixote, 'that the knight you conquered was not, and could not have been, Don Quixote de la Mancha, but was another resembling him, as I confess and believe that you, although you resemble the Bachelor Sampson Carrasco, are not he, but another of like appearance, whom my enemies have set before me in his shape, so that I may restrain and moderate the force of my wrath and use the glory of my victory with moderation.'

'All this I acknowledge, hold and think, as you acknowledge, hold and think it,' answered the crippled knight. 'Let me get up, I pray you, if the shock of my fall will allow me, for it has left me in a pretty bad way.'

Don Quixote helped him to rise, with the aid of Thomas Cecial, his squire, from whom Sancho could not take his eyes. He asked him many questions, the replies to which gave him absolute proof that he really was Thomas Cecial, as he said. But the fear which had been aroused in him by his master's story that the enchanters had changed the Knight of the Mirrors into the shape of the Bachelor Carrasco prevented his believing the truth that he saw with his own eyes. In the end both master and man remained in their delusion, and the Knight of the Mirrors and his squire, gloomy and disgruntled, parted with Don Quixote and Sancho, with the intention of looking for a place where the knight's ribs could be plastered and strapped. Don Quixote and Sancho, for their part, resumed their road to Saragossa, where this history leaves them, to give an account of the identity of the Knight of the Mirrors and his big-nosed squire.

Chapter XV. *In which we are told who the Knight of the Mirrors and his Squire were, and given some account of them.*

EXTREMELY joyful, proud and vainglorious Don Quixote was at having subdued so valiant a knight as he imagined the Knight of the Mirrors to be, from whose knightly word he expected to learn whether the enchantment of his mistress still obtained. For the said vanquished knight was obliged to return, under pain of ceasing to be such, and give him an account of what might pass between himself and her. Don Quixote, however, thought one thing and the Knight of the Mirrors another. For, as we have said, he had nothing else in his mind just then but to find somewhere where he might be plastered.

Now our history tells us that when the Bachelor Sampson Carrasco counselled Don Quixote to return to the pursuit of his abandoned chivalries, it was after he had held a conference with the priest and the barber to decide on a means of inducing the knight to stay quietly and safely at home, without exciting himself with his wretched quests for adventures. At this consultation it was decided by unanimous vote, and with the particular approval of Carrasco, that they should let Don Quixote set out, since it seemed impossible to keep him back, and that Sampson should take the road as a knight errant and join battle with him – a pretext would not be lacking – and so vanquish him – which they reckoned an easy matter – and that there should be a covenant and agreement between them that the vanquished should be at the mercy of the victor. So that, Don Quixote being thus overthrown, the Bachelor Knight could command him to return home to his village, and not to leave it for two years, or until he should be commanded otherwise. For it was clear that Don Quixote would indubitably comply with these conditions, in order not to contravene and break the laws of chivalry. And it might so happen that during the time of his seclusion either he would forget his vain notions, or means might be found of curing his madness.

Carrasco accepted this task, and Thomas Cecial, a friend and neighbour of Sancho Panza's and a cheerful, hare-brained fellow, offered to be his squire. Sampson armed himself as has been recorded, and Thomas Cecial fitted over his natural nose the false one mentioned, as a mask, so that he should not be recognized by his friend when they met. So they followed the same road as Don Quixote took, very nearly caught them up during the adventure of the Waggon of Death — and at last lighted on them in the wood — the scene of the action of which the attentive reader has just read. And had it not been for Don Quixote's extraordinary opinions and his belief that the Bachelor was not the Bachelor, that worthy Bachelor would have been for ever incapacitated from proceeding to his Licentiate, all through finding no nests where he expected to find birds. And afterwards, seeing how badly their plans had turned out and the unfortunate end their journey had come to, Thomas Cecial said to the Bachelor:

'We have most certainly got what we deserved, Master Sampson Carrasco. It's easy enough to plan and set about an enterprise, but it's very often difficult to come well out of it. Don Quixote's mad, and we're sane. Yet he gets off sound and smiling, while your worship comes out bruised and sorrowful. So, let's consider now which is the madder, the man who's mad because he can't help it, or the man who's mad by choice?'

To which Sampson replied: 'The difference between these two is that the madman of necessity will be so for ever, but the madman by choice will cease to be so when he will.'

'Very well then,' said Thomas Cecial, 'I was mad by choice when I consented to be your worship's squire, and for that reason I wish to resign the post and go back home.'

'That is all right for you,' replied Sampson, 'but it would be folly to suppose that I shall go back home till I have thrashed Don Quixote. And it will not be the desire to restore him to his senses that will drive me after him, but the desire for revenge; for the pain in my ribs will not allow me to entertain a more charitable purpose.'

The two of them went on talking in this way until they came to a town, where they had the luck to find a bone-setter, who attended to the unfortunate Sampson. Then Thomas Cecial went home, and left the Bachelor behind brooding on his vengeance. Our history will speak of him again when the time comes, but now it must make merry with Don Quixote.

Chapter XVI. *Of Don Quixote's meeting with a Sensible Gentleman of La Mancha.*

JOYFUL, contented and proud, as we have said, Don Quixote pursued his journey, imagining himself from his late victory the most valiant knight errant the world contained in that age, and taking all adventures that might henceforth befall him as already achieved and brought to a successful conclusion. He despised spells and enchanters, and no more remembered the innumerable beatings he had received in the course of his chivalries, nor the stoning which had knocked out half his teeth, nor the ingratitude of the galley-slaves, nor the insolence of the Yanguesans and their shower of stakes. In fact he said to himself that, could he but find an art, means, or device for disenchanting his lady Dulcinea, he would not envy the best of good fortune that the most fortunate knight errant of past ages ever attained or could attain. And he was riding along completely absorbed in these fancies when Sancho addressed him:

'Isn't it odd, sir, that I've still got that monstrous, disproportionate nose of my neighbour, Thomas Cecial, before my eyes?'

'But can you possibly believe, Sancho, that the Knight of the Mirrors was the Bachelor Carrasco, and his squire your neighbour, Thomas Cecial?'

'I don't know what to answer to that,' replied Sancho. 'I can only say that the details he gave me of my house, of my wife and my children no other could have given me but he. And the face, less the nose, was Thomas Cecial's own. I've seen him very often in the village, for there's only a wall between his house and mine. And the tone of his voice was exactly the same.'

'Let us be reasonable, Sancho,' said Don Quixote. 'Think now, how is it conceivable that the Bachelor Sampson Carrasco should have come to fight with me as a knight errant, armed with offensive and defensive arms? Have I ever, by any chance, been his enemy? Have I ever given him reason to bear me a grudge? Am I his rival, or does he make profession of arms, that he should envy the fame that I have won by arms?'

'But what shall we say, sir,' replied Sancho, 'about this knight, whoever he may be, looking so much like the Bachelor Carrasco, and his squire like my neighbour, Thomas Cecial? Now if that's enchantment, as your worship has said, weren't there any other two in the world for them to take the likeness of?'

'It is all an artifice,' answered Don Quixote, 'and a trick of those malign magicians that persecute me. Foreseeing that I should emerge victorious from the combat, they provided that the vanquished knight should reveal the face of my friend the Bachelor, so that the friendship I have for him should come between the edge of my sword and the rigour of my arm, and moderate the just wrath of my heart; by which means he might escape with his life, though he sought by trickery and fraud to rob me of mine. For proof of which, you know, Sancho, from your experience, which will not let you lie or be deceived, how easy it is for enchanters to change one face for another, transforming the beautiful into the ugly and the ugly into the beautiful. Not two days ago you saw with your own eyes the peerless Dulcinea's beauty and grace in all the perfection of their natural proportions, and I saw her in the vile and ugly shape of a coarse country wench, with bleary eyes and a stinking breath in her mouth. So, it is no great matter for the perverse enchanters who dared to make so wicked a transformation to have made another with Sampson Carrasco and your neighbour, to snatch the glory of my victory out of my hands. Even so, however, I am consoled; for, after all, whatever shape he may have taken, I have vanquished my enemy.'

'God knows the truth about everything,' answered Sancho. Though since he knew that Dulcinea's transformation had been his own fraudulent trick, his master's wild theories did not satisfy him. But he did not care to reply, for fear of saying something which would reveal his imposture.

While they were engaged in this conversation they were overtaken by a man who was riding on their road behind them, mounted on a very handsome grey mare, and dressed in a fine green cloth overcoat slashed with tawny velvet, and wearing a hunting cap of the same material. The trappings of his mare were countrified, fit for riding with short stirrups and of the same purple and green colours. He wore a Moorish scimitar, hanging on a broad green and gold sword-belt, and his leggings were of a similar make. His spurs were not gilt but covered with a green lacquer, so glossy and burnished that, since they matched the rest of his dress, they looked better than if they had been pure gold. Now when the traveller caught them up, he greeted them politely and, pricking his mare, was going to pass on ahead, had not Don Quixote addressed him, saying:

'Gallant sir, if your worship is taking the same road as we are, and haste is not important to you, I should esteem it a favour if we could ride together.'

'Really,' replied the man on the mare, 'I should not have pressed on ahead of you if I had not been afraid that your horse would be disturbed by my mare's company.'

'Sir,' broke in Sancho, 'you can safely, very safely, rein in your mare, for our horse is the chastest and best-behaved in the world. He has never done anything unmannerly on such an occasion as this, and the only time he transgressed my master and I paid for it sevenfold. Your worship may pull up, indeed, if it pleases you, for even if your mare were brought him between two plates, our horse wouldn't so much as look her in the face, I assure you.'

The traveller drew in his rein, gazing in astonishment at the figure and the face of Don Quixote, who was riding without his helmet, which Sancho carried like a bag, on the pommel of Dapple's saddle. And the more the man in green stared at Don Quixote, the more did Don Quixote stare at the man in green, who seemed to him a man of substance. His age appeared to be about fifty; his grey hairs few; his face aquiline; his expression between cheerful and grave – in short, from his dress and appearance he gave the impression of a man of good parts. But what the man in green thought of Don Quixote was that he had never seen anyone of that kind or anyone looking like him before. He was amazed at the length of his neck, the tallness of his body, the thinness and sallowness of his face, his armour, his gestures and his carriage – for his was a shape and figure not seen for many a long year in that country. Don Quixote observed the attention with which the traveller gazed at him and from his amazement assumed his curiosity. So, being so courteous and anxious to please everybody, before the other could ask him a question he met him half-way by saying:

'I should not wonder if your worship were surprised at this appearance of mine, for it is both novel and out of the common. But you will cease to be so when I tell you, as I now do, that I am a knight

> Of that breed that, the people say,
> After adventures ride.

I have left my native country; I have pledged my estate; I have given up my comfort and entrusted myself to the arms of Fortune, to take me where she will. I have sought to revive the now extinct order of knight errantry, and for a long while, stumbling here, falling there, flung down in one place and rising up in another, I have been carrying out a great part of my design, succouring widows, protecting maidens, and relieving wives, orphans and wards – which is the proper and natural office of knights errant. So, on account of my many valiant and Christian exploits I have been found worthy to appear in print in almost every country in the world. Thirty thousand volumes of my history have been printed, and it is on the way to be printed thirty thousand thousand times more, if Heaven does not prevent it. In fact, to sum everything up in a few words – or in one only – let me tell you that I am Don Quixote de la Mancha, otherwise called the Knight of the Sad Countenance. And, though praise of self is degrading, I am compelled sometimes to sound my own, though naturally only when there is no one present to sound it for me. So, noble sir, neither this horse, this lance, this shield, nor this squire, nor all these arms together, nor the sallowness of my face, nor my attenuated limbs should henceforth amaze you, now that I have made known to you who I am and the profession I follow.'

After this speech Don Quixote fell silent, and the man in green took a long time to reply, for he seemed unable to find words. But after a while he said: 'You guessed my thoughts, Sir Knight, when you observed my surprise; but you have not succeeded in dispelling my amazement at the sight of you. For though, as you say, sir, knowing who you are should dispel it, it has not done so. On the contrary now that I know, I am the more astounded. What! Is it possible that there are knights errant in the world to-day, and histories printed about real knight errantries? I cannot convince myself that there is anyone on earth to-day who favours widows, protects maidens, honours wives, or succours orphans, and I should not have believed it if I had not seen the proof in your worship with my own eyes. Heaven be praised, for that history of your noble and authentic chivalries, which your worship says is printed, will consign all the innumerable stories of imaginary knights errant, of which the world is full, to oblivion, such harm they do to good manners, and such damage and discredit to genuine history.'

'There is much to be said,' replied Don Quixote, 'on this question of whether the histories of knights errant are fictions or not.'

'But is there anyone,' asked the man in green, 'who doubts their falsehood?'

'I doubt it,' answered Don Quixote, 'but let the matter rest there. For if our journey is long, I trust to God I shall convince your worship that you have done wrong in going with the stream of those who affirm that they are not true.'

From this last speech of Don Quixote's the traveller suspected that he must be an idiot, and waited for some further remarks to confirm his suspicions. But before they could turn to any other subject, Don Quixote begged his fellow-traveller to tell him his name, since he had already told him something of his own condition and way of life.

To which the man in green replied: 'I, Sir Knight of the Sad Countenance, am a gentleman and native of a village where, please God, we shall dine to-day. I am more than moderately rich, and my name is Don Diego de Miranda. I spend my life with my wife, my children and my friends. My pursuits are hunting and fishing, though I keep neither hawk nor hounds, but only a quiet pointer and a good ferret or two. I have about six dozen books, some in Spanish and some in Latin, some historical and some devotional, but books of chivalry have never so much as crossed the threshold of my door. I read profane books more than devotional, since they give me honest entertainment, delighting me by their language, and arresting and startling me by their inventions – though there are very few of this kind in Spain. Sometimes I dine with my neighbours and friends, and very often I entertain them.

My fare is good and well served, and never stinted. I do not enjoy scandal, and do not allow any in my presence. I do not pry into my neighbours' lives, nor do I spy on other men's actions. I hear Mass every day. I share my goods with the poor, without boasting of my good works for fear of letting into my heart hypocrisy and vain-glory, enemies that subtly seize upon the wariest heart. I try to make peace between those I know to be at odds. I am devoted to Our Lady, and always trust in the infinite mercy of our Lord God.'

Sancho listened most attentively to this account of the gentle-man's life and occupations; for it seemed to him that this was a good and holy life, and that the man who led it must be able to work miracles. So, flinging himself off Dapple and hastily seizing his right stirrup, with devout heart and almost in tears he kissed the gentle-man's foot again and again. At which their fellow traveller ex-claimed: 'What are you doing, brother? Why these kisses?'

'Let me kiss you,' answered Sancho, 'for I think your worship's the first saint I've ever seen riding with short stirrups in all the days of my life.'

'I am no saint,' replied the gentleman, 'but a great sinner. Now you, brother, you must be good; your simplicity proves it.'

After this remark, which forced a laugh out of the depths of his master's melancholy and aroused fresh wonder in Don Diego, Sancho climbed once more into the saddle. Don Quixote then asked the man in green how many children he had, and observed that the ancient philosophers, who lacked the true knowledge of God, assumed the highest good to consist in the gifts of nature, in the gifts of Fortune, and in abundance of friends and good children.

'I, Don Quixote,' answered the gentleman, 'have one son and, but for him, perhaps I should count myself more fortunate than I do: not that he is wicked, though, but he is not as good as I should like. He is eighteen years old and has been for six years in Sala-manca studying the Latin and Greek tongues. But when I wished him to pass on to the study of other sciences I found him so soaked in that of Poetry – if it can be called a science – that it is impossible to make him take cheerfully to Law, which I should like him to study, or to the queen of all sciences, Theology. I would have him be an honour to his family, since we live in an age when our princes give high reward to virtuous and deserving scholarship; for learning without virtue is like pearls on a dunghill. He spends the whole day in his criticisms, whether Homer expressed himself well or ill in such a verse of the *Iliad*; whether Martial was indecent or not in some epigram; whether such and such verses of Virgil are to be understood in one way or another. In fact all his conversation is about the books of these poets, and of Horace, Persius, Juvenal and Tibullus; for by modern writers in the vernacular he sets little store. But for all the dislike he seems to have for Spanish poetry, his thoughts are now entirely taken up with making a gloss on four lines they have sent him from Salamanca. It has to do, I think, with some literary competition.'

To all this Don Quixote replied: 'Children, sir, are part of the very bowels of their parents; and so we must love them, whether they are good or bad, as we love the souls that give us life. It is the parents' duty to guide them from childhood along the paths of virtue, of good breeding, and of good and Christian manners, so that when they are grown up, they may be the staff of their parents' old age and a glory to their posterity. But as to forcing them to this or that science, I do not think that it is right, although to persuade them will do no harm; and if they have no need to study to earn their bread – the student being so lucky as to be endowed by Heaven with parents to spare him that – my opinion is that they should be allowed to follow that branch of learning to which they seem most inclined. And although that of Poetry is rather pleasurable than useful, it is not such as generally to do dishonour to its votaries. Poetry, my dear sir, in my opinion is like a tender, young and extremely beautiful maiden, whom other maidens toil to enrich, to polish and adorn. These maidens are the other sciences; and she has to be served by all, while all of them have to justify themselves by her. But this maiden does not care to be handled, or dragged through the streets, nor to be shown at the corners of the market place, or in the antechambers of palaces. She is formed of an alchemy of such virtue that anyone who knows how to treat her will transform her into purest gold of inestimable price. Her possessor must keep her within bounds, not letting her run to base lampoons or impious sonnets. She must be exposed for sale only in the form of heroic poems, piteous tragedies, or gay and artificial comedies. She must not let herself be handled by buffoons, nor by the ignorant vulgar, who are incapable of recognizing or appreciating her treasures. Now do not imagine, sir, that by vulgar I mean only the common and humble people; for all who are ignorant, even if they are lords or princes, can rightfully be included under the name of vulgar. So anyone with the qualities I have named who takes up and handles Poetry will become famous, and his name will be treasured among all the civilized nations of the world. Now as to what you say, sir, about your son not greatly valuing Spanish poetry, I hold that he is wrong there, and the reason is this: great Homer did not write in Latin, because he was a Greek, nor Virgil in Greek, because he was a Latin. In fact all the ancients wrote in the tongues they sucked with their mother's milk, and did not go out to seek strange ones to express the greatness of their conceptions. And, that being so, this custom should rightfully be extended to all nations, and the German poet must not be despised for writing in his language, nor the Castilian, nor even the Basque, for writing in his.

'But your son, sir, as I imagine, does not dislike vernacular poetry, but poets who are merely vernacular and know no other tongues nor sciences to adorn, stimulate and help out their natural inspiration. Yet even in this he may be in error. For, according to true belief, the poet is born – I mean the natural poet comes out of his mother's womb a poet and, with that impulse which Heaven has given him, without further study or art, composes things which prove the truth of the saying: "There is a god in us ..." etcetera. Let me say also that the natural poet who makes use of art will improve himself and be much greater than the poet who relies only on his knowledge of the art. The reason is clear, for art is not better than nature, but perfects her. So nature combined with art, and art with nature, will produce a most perfect poet. To conclude my speech then, my dear sir, you should let your son travel where his star calls him; for if he is as good a scholar as he should be, and if he has successfully mounted the first step of learning, which is that of languages, he will ascend on his own to the summit of humane letters, which are so proper a pursuit for a gentleman of leisure, and adorn, honour and exalt him as mitres do bishops, or robes learned doctors of law. Scold your son, sir, if he writes lampoons to the detriment of other men's honour; punish him and tear them up. But should he write satires after the manner of Horace for the correction of vice in general, and as elegantly as he did, praise him. For a poet may lawfully write against envy, and inveigh against the envious in his verses, and against other vices too, so long as he does not aim at any particular person. Though there are poets who would run the risk of banishment to the Isles of Pontus for the sake of uttering one piece of malice. If the poet, however, is decent in his habits he will be so in his verses too. The pen is the tongue of the soul; and as ideas are there engendered, so will his writings be. And when kings and princes behold the miraculous science of Poetry in some wise, virtuous and grave subject, they honour, esteem and enrich him, and even crown him with the leaves of that tree which the lightning never strikes, as if to show that men whose temples are honoured and adorned by such crowns should be attacked by no one.'

The man in green was lost in amazement at Don Quixote's reasonings, so much so that he had begun to alter his previous opinion that he was an idiot. In the middle of this conversation, however, which was not much to his liking, Sancho had wandered from the road to beg for a little milk from some shepherds who were milking their ewes near by. And just as the gentleman was about to renew the discussion, highly delighted by the knight's sagacity and good sense, Don Quixote raised his head and saw a cart decorated with the King's colours coming along the road by which they were travelling. Believing that this must be some new adventure, he shouted to Sancho to come and bring him his helmet, and Sancho, hearing his name called, left the shepherds, and spurred Dapple hurriedly towards his master, whom a stupendous and desperate adventure now befell.

Chapter XVII. *In which is shown the highest point which Don Quixote's unparalleled Courage ever achieved, with the happy conclusion of the Adventure of the Lions.*

OUR history tells that when Don Quixote shouted to Sancho to bring his helmet he was buying some curds of the shepherds. His master's hurried call perturbed him, and he could neither think what to do with them, nor what to put them in. So in order not to lose them – for he had already paid for them – he decided to tip them into his master's helmet. After taking this precaution he turned back to see what Don Quixote wanted and, on approaching, heard him say: 'Give me that helmet, friend, for either I know very little of adventures, or what I see yonder is one which should, and does, require me to take to arms.'

The man in green heard this, and gazed in all directions without discovering anything but a cart coming towards them hung with two or three small flags, which made him think that it was carrying the King's treasure; and so he told Don Quixote. The knight, however, did not credit it, always firmly imagining that everything which befell him must be adventures and still more adventures. So he replied: 'Forewarned is forearmed. Nothing is lost by taking precautions. For I know by experience that I have enemies visible and invisible, and I do not know when or where, nor at what time or in what shape they will attack me.'

And turning to Sancho, he asked him for his helmet, which, having no opportunity of taking out the curds, the squire was compelled to give him as it was. Don Quixote took it and hurriedly clapped it on his head without noticing what was inside. But as the curds were squeezed and pressed, the whey began to run all over the knight's face and beard, which gave him such a shock that he cried to Sancho:

'What can it be, Sancho? My skull seems to be softening or my brains melting, or else I am bathed in sweat from head to foot. But if I am sweating, indeed it is not out of fear, though I most certainly believe it is a terrible adventure that is now going to befall me. Give me something to wipe myself with, if you have anything; for this copious sweat is blinding my eyes.'

Sancho kept quiet and gave him a cloth, at the same time thanking God that his master had not tumbled to the truth. Don Quixote wiped himself and took off his helmet to see what it was that seemed to be freezing his head. Then seeing the white clots inside his helmet, he put them to his nose and smelt them. At which he cried out: 'By the life of my lady Dulcinea del Toboso, these are curds you have put here, you treacherous, brazen-faced, unmannerly squire!'

To which Sancho replied with great calmness and hypocrisy: 'If

they're curds give them to me, your worship, and I'll eat them.
But let the Devil eat them, for it must be he who put them there!
Should I dare to soil your worship's helmet? You must know who
the villain is! I swear, sir, by the wits God gave me, I must have
enchanters persecuting me too, since I'm your worship's creature
and limb. They must have put that filth there to move your patience
to anger, and make you baste my ribs as you often do. But this
time truly they've leapt wide of the mark; for I trust in my
master's good sense, since he will surely reflect that I've no curds,
nor milk, nor anything of the sort, and that I'd rather put them in
my stomach than in the helmet, if I had.'

'All that may be true,' said Don Quixote. Now the gentleman had
watched this performance with amazement, especially when, after
wiping his head, his face, his beard and the helmet, Don Quixote
put it on again, steadied himself in his stirrups and, reaching for his
sword and grasping his lance, cried: 'Now come what may, for here
I stand ready to do battle against Satan in person.'

At this moment the cart with the flags arrived, and with it was
nobody but the carter on one of the mules, and a man seated in
front. Don Quixote, however, took up his stand before it and called
out: 'Where are you going, brothers? What cart is this? What have
you in it? And what flags are these?'

To which the carter replied: 'The cart's mine. In it are two fierce
lions in a cage, which the General is sending from Oran to the capital as a present for his Majesty. The flags are the King's our master's,
for a sign that there's something of his in my cart.'

'And are the lions big?' asked Don Quixote.

'Very big,' replied the man at the door of the cart. 'There have
never been any so large that have ever crossed from Africa to Spain.
I'm the lion-keeper, and I've brought over others, but none like
these. There's a lioness and a lion. The lion's in this front cage, and
the lioness in the rear one. They're very hungry at present, for
they've had nothing to eat to-day. So will your worship please
stand aside, for we're in a hurry to get to a place where we can feed
them.'

To which Don Quixote replied with a slight smile: 'Lion cubs
to me? To me lion cubs, and at this time of day? Then I swear to
God the gentlemen who have sent them here shall see if I am a man

to be frightened by lions. Get down, my good fellow, and if you are the lion-keeper, open these cages and turn out these beasts for me. For in the middle of this field I will teach them who Don Quixote de la Mancha is, in despite and defiance of the enchanters who have sent them to me.'

'Dear, dear!' muttered the gentleman in green at this juncture. 'Our good knight is giving us a proof of his nature. The curds, no doubt, have softened his skull and ripened his brains.'

At this point Sancho came up to him and cried: 'Sir, for God's sake do something to stop my master fighting with these lions. If he does, they'll tear all of us here to pieces.'

'Is your master so crazy then,' answered the gentleman, 'that you're afraid he will really fight these savage beasts?'

'He's not crazy,' replied Sancho, 'but foolhardy.'

'I will see that he does not,' promised the gentleman. And going up to Don Quixote, who was pressing the keeper to open the cages, he said: 'Sir Knight, knights errant should engage in adventures which offer a prospect of success, and not in such as are altogether desperate. For valour which verges on temerity is more like madness than bravery. What is more, these lions have not come against you, nor do they dream of doing so. They are going to be presented to his Majesty, and it would be wrong to stop them or to hinder their journey.'

'Pray go away, my dear sir, and see to your quiet pointer and your good ferret,' replied Don Quixote, 'and leave every man to do his duty. This is mine, and I know whether they are coming against me or not, these noble lions.' Then, turning once more to the lion-keeper, he said: 'I swear, Sir Ruffian, that if you do not open these cages this very moment I will pin you to your cart with this lance.'

The carter saw the armed phantom's determination, and said: 'Sir, for pity's sake, please let me unyoke the mules, and put myself and them into safety before the lions are let out. For if my beasts are killed I shall be ruined for ever, as I've no other property but my cart and my beasts.'

'O man of little faith!' replied Don Quixote. 'Get down, unyoke them, and do what you will. But you will soon see that you are labouring in vain, and might as well have spared yourself the trouble.'

The carter got down and very hurriedly unyoked, while the lion-keeper cried out loudly: 'Let everyone here be my witness that I'm opening these cages and letting the lions out against my will and under compulsion, and that I protest to this gentleman that all the harm and damage that these beasts may do will fall to his account, and so will my wages and dues. Sirs, take cover before I open, for I'm sure they'll do me no harm.'

Once more the gentleman implored Don Quixote not to do anything so mad, saying that to engage in such a wild freak was to tempt Providence. But Don Quixote replied that he knew what he was doing, and the gentleman warned him once more to look out, for he knew that he was mistaken.

'Now, sir,' replied Don Quixote, 'if you do not want to be a spectator of what in your opinion is going to be a tragedy, spur your grey mare and get into a safe place.'

When Sancho heard this he implored his master with tears in his eyes to desist from this enterprise, compared to which the adventure of the windmills and the fearful one of the fulling-mills and, in fact, every exploit he had attempted in the whole of his life, were tarts and gingerbread.

'Look, sir,' said Sancho, 'here's no enchantment or any such thing, for I've seen the claw of a real lion through the bars and cracks in the cages. And I'm sure that a lion with a claw like that must be bigger than a mountain.'

'Fear, at least,' answered Don Quixote, 'will make it seem bigger to you than half the world. Retire, Sancho, and leave me; and if I die here, you know our old agreement. You will repair to Dulcinea – I say no more.'

And he went on to make further declarations which removed all hope that he would desist from his insane purpose. The man in green would have resisted him, but not being as well armed, he thought it unwise to fight with a madman, for the knight now seemed to him completely mad. Don Quixote then began once more hurrying the lion-keeper and repeating his threats, which gave the gentleman a chance to spur his mare, Sancho to prod Dapple, and the carter his mules, all of them endeavouring to get as far away from the cart as they could before the lions broke loose. Sancho wept for his master's death, for this time he really believed he would perish at the claws of the lions. He cursed his luck and the fatal hour when he first thought of returning to his service. But for all his weeping and lamentations he did not cease from flogging Dapple to get him farther from the cart. Then, when the keeper saw that the fugitives were well away, he repeated his entreaties and warnings to Don Quixote. The knight, however, replied that he heard him, but that he would listen to no more warnings or entreaties, for they would be quite fruitless, and bade him make haste. Now whilst the keeper was opening the first cage, Don Quixote was considering whether it would be better to do battle on foot or on horseback, and finally decided to fight on foot, fearing that Rocinante would take fright at the sight of the lions. Therefore he leapt from his horse, threw away his lance and, buckling his shield and unsheathing his sword, with marvellous bravery and a bold heart took up his position in a leisurely way in front of the cart, commending himself to God with all his soul, and then to his lady Dulcinea.

And here it is to be noted that when the author of our true history came to this passage he exclaimed and cried: 'O brave and incomparably courageous Don Quixote de la Mancha! True mirror to all valiant knights in the world! Thou new and second Don Manuel de Leon — honour and glory of Spanish knights! In what words shall I recount this most fearful exploit, or with what arguments make it credible to future ages? What praises can there be unfitting and unmeet for you, hyperbole upon hyperbole though they be? You on foot, you alone, you bold, you brave-hearted, with only a simple sword and no trenchant Toledo blade, with a shield of not very bright and shining steel, you watching and waiting for the two fiercest lions ever bred in African forests! Let your deeds themselves praise you, valorous Manchegan, for here I leave them in all their glory, lacking words to extol them.'

Here this exclamation of our author's ended, and he went on to knit up the thread of his story, saying:

When the keeper saw Don Quixote firm in his position, and knew that he could not avoid letting the lion out without incurring the displeasure of the bold and angry knight, he flung open the door of the first cage, in which, as we have said, was the beast, which seemed to be of extraordinary size and of a fearful and hideous aspect. The lion's first action, however, was to turn round in his cage, extend his claws, and stretch his full length. Then he opened his mouth and yawned very leisurely, and sticking out almost two foot of tongue, licked the dust out of his eyes and washed his face. This done, he put his head out of his cage and looked in all directions with eyes blazing like live coals, a sight to strike terror into the bravest heart. Alone Don Quixote watched him attentively, hoping that he would now jump out of the cart and come within reach of his hands, for he intended to tear him to pieces. To such a height of extravagance was he transported by his incredible madness. But the noble lion, more courteous than arrogant, took no notice of this childish bravado, and after looking in all directions, as we have said, turned his back and showed Don Quixote his hindquarters. Then he lay down again in his cage with great calmness and composure. At this sight Don Quixote ordered the keeper to beat him and tease him into coming out.

'I won't do that,' answered the keeper, 'for if I excite him I shall be the first to be torn to pieces. Be content, Sir Knight, with the day's work, which is all that could be desired so far as valour goes. Do not seek to tempt Fortune a second time. The lion has his door open. It rests with him whether he comes out or not. But as he has not come out till now, he will not come out the whole day. The greatness of your worship's courage is now proved. No brave champion, as I understand it, is obliged to do more than challenge his enemy and await him in the field. If his opponent does not appear the disgrace lies on him, and the challenger wins the crown of victory.'

'That is true,' replied Don Quixote. 'So shut the door, my friend, and give me a sworn statement of what you have seen me do here, in the best form you can: to wit, that you opened for the lion; that I awaited him; that he did not come out; that I waited for him still; that he still did not come out, but turned and lay down. That is all my duty. Enchantments, away! And God prosper justice and truth and true chivalry. Shut the door, I repeat, while I signal to the fugitive and the absent that they may learn of this exploit from your lips.'

The keeper did as he was told, and putting the cloth with which he had wiped the shower of curds off his face on to the end of his lance, Don Quixote began to call to the others, who had never stopped running away and looking behind them at every step, riding all in a troop driven on by the gentleman in green. But when Sancho chanced to notice the signal of the white cloth, he exclaimed: 'May I die, if my master has not conquered the savage beasts, for he is calling us.'

They all stopped, and seeing that it was Don Quixote making these signals, they lost some part of their fear, and little by little drew nearer, till they could plainly hear him calling them. Finally, they came back to the cart, and when they arrived Don Quixote said to the carter:

'Yoke your mules again, brother, and go on your way; and you, Sancho, give him two gold crowns, for him and for the lion-keeper, in recompense for their having stopped for me.'

'I'll pay them with a very good will,' answered Sancho. 'But what has happened to the lions? Are they dead or alive?'

Thereupon the lion-keeper recounted the result of the encounter, minutely and at his leisure, extolling to the best of his power and skill the valour of Don Quixote, at the sight of whom the cowed lion would not, and dared not, come out of his cage, although he had held the door open for a considerable time. Then when he had told the knight that it would be tempting Providence to excite the lion into going out, as he wished him to, Don Quixote had most grudgingly and unwillingly permitted him to shut the door.

'What do you think of that, Sancho?' asked Don Quixote. 'Do any enchantments prevail against true valour? The enchanters may indeed be able to rob me of good fortune; but of resolution and courage, that is impossible!'

Sancho paid the two crowns; the carter yoked up; the keeper kissed Don Quixote's hands for the favour received, and promised to recount his valorous exploit to the King himself, when he saw him at court.

'If by chance, then, his Majesty should ask who performed it, you will tell him it was "*The Knight of the Lions*", for I am resolved that the title I have hitherto borne of "*The Knight of the Sad Countenance*" shall henceforward be so transformed, altered, varied and changed. And herein I follow the ancient custom of knights errant, who changed their names when they pleased or as the occasion required.'

T

The cart continued on its journey, and Don Quixote, Sancho and the gentleman in the green overcoat continued on theirs. In all this while Don Diego de Miranda had not spoken a word, so carefully was he watching and noting every word and action of Don Quixote, who seemed to him a sane man turned mad or a madman verging on sanity. The first part of this history had not yet come to his notice; for if he had read it he would have ceased to be surprised at the knight's behaviour, since he would then have known the nature of his madness. But as he did not know it, he sometimes took him for sane, sometimes for mad. For Don Quixote's words were consistent, elegant and well put, though his actions were wild, rash and foolish. 'What could be more insane,' he reflected, 'than to put on a helmet full of curds and imagine that the enchanters are softening your skull? And what could be rasher or more idiotic than to insist on fighting with lions?' But from this soliloquy Don Quixote drew him by saying:

'No doubt, Don Diego de Miranda, your worship considers me both foolish and mad. And it would be no marvel if you did, for my deeds testify no less. But, for all that, I wish your worship to take note that I am not so mad or so lacking as I must have seemed to you. It is a brave sight to see a gallant gentleman, beneath the eyes of his King, deliver a well aimed lance-thrust against a brave bull in the midst of a great square. It is a brave sight to see a knight, armed in shining armour, pace the lists in merry jousts before the ladies. And it is a brave sight to see all those knights, in military exercises or the like, entertain, cheer and, if one may say so, grace the courts of their princes. But braver than all these it is to see a knight errant travelling through desert and waste, by cross-roads, forests and mountains, to seek perilous adventures, in order to bring them to a fortunate and happy conclusion only for the sake of glory and lasting renown. It is a braver sight, I say, to see a knight errant succouring a widow in some lonely spot than a courtier knight wooing a maiden in the cities. All knights have their particular offices. Let the courtier serve ladies, lend splendour to the King's court with his liveries, support poor knights at his splendidly appointed table, arrange jousts, maintain at tourneys, and show himself grand, liberal, magnificent and, above all, a good Christian; for in this way he will comply with his precise obligations. But let the knight errant search the corners of the world, penetrate the most intricate labyrinths, at every step encounter the impossible, at midsummer brave the burning rays of the sun on high and desert wastes, and in winter the harsh inclemency of winds and frosts. Let no lions alarm him, nor hobgoblins daunt him, nor dragons affright him; for to seek them, attack them and conquer them all are his chief and proper exercises. I, since it has been my lot to be of the number of knights errant, cannot, then, fail to attempt everything which seems to me to fall within the bounds of my duty. And so to attack these lions whom I just now attacked was my rightful concern, although I knew it to be an excessive temerity. For I well know what valour is – a virtue placed between the two extremes of vice, cowardice and foolhardiness. But it is better for the brave man to rise to the height of rashness than to sink into the depths of cowardice. For just as it is easier for the spendthrift to be liberal than for the miser, so it is easier for the rash than for the cowardly to climb to true valour. And in this matter of encountering adventures, believe me, Don Diego, it is better to lose the game by a card too many than by a card too few, for *such a knight is rash and foolhardy* sounds better in the hearer's ears than *such a knight is timid and cowardly.*'

'I must say, Don Quixote,' answered Don Diego, 'that all that your worship's words and deeds are measured on the scales of reason itself; and I believe that if the ordinances and laws of knight errantry were lost they would be found in your worship's breast, as in their proper repository and archive. But let us hurry on to my village, for it is getting late. At my house your worship can rest from your recent labours. For though they were not of the body, they were of the spirit, and those too sometimes conduce to the body's weariness.'

'I accept your offer as a great favour and kindness, Don Diego,' replied Don Quixote. And spurring on faster than before, at about two o'clock in the afternoon they arrived in the village, at the house of Don Diego, whom Don Quixote called '*The Knight of the Green Coat*'.

Chapter XVIII. *What happened to Don Quixote in the Castle,*
or House of the Knight of the Green Coat, and other very
strange matters.

DON QUIXOTE found Don Diego de Miranda's house spacious
after the country fashion, with his arms, though in coarse stone,
above the street door; the provision store in the front yard; the
wine cellar in the porch, and several earthenware jars around, which,
being of El Toboso make, revived his memories of his enchanted
and transformed Dulcinea. Whereat, regardless of what he said or
before whom he said it, he exclaimed with a sigh:

> 'O lovely pledges, to my woe discovered,
> Joyful and sweet when it was Heaven's will!

O Tobosan jars, how you bring to my memory the sweet pledge of
my great bitterness!'

The student poet, Don Diego's son, who had come out with his
mother to receive the knight, heard him speak these lines. And both
mother and son stood amazed at his strange appearance, as he dismounted from Rocinante and went with great politeness to beg for
her hands to kiss, while Don Diego said: 'Pray, wife, receive Don
Quixote de la Mancha with your usual hospitality. Here he is before
you, a knight errant, and the most valiant and wisest the world contains.'

The lady, whose name was Doña Christina, received him with
marks of great affection and politeness, and Don Quixote greeted
her with an abundance of judicious and polite phrases. He also addressed much the same compliments to the student, who judged
Don Quixote from his speech to be a man of wit and intelligence.

Here the author paints all the details of Don Diego's home, describing the contents of a rich gentleman farmer's house. But it
seems right to the translator of this history to pass over these and
other such particulars in silence, for they do not suit the principal
purpose of this history, which derives its strength rather from truth
than from dull digressions.

They led Don Quixote into a hall, where Sancho took off his
armour, leaving him in his Walloon breeches and chamois leather

jerkin, all stained with the grime of his armour. He wore a Vandyke collar like a student's, unstarched and without lace, date-coloured leggings and waxed shoes. He carried his good sword slung over his shoulders on a sealskin strap, he having, it is believed, a long-standing weakness of the kidneys; and over all this he wore a cloak of good grey cloth. But first of all he had washed his face and head with five or six buckets of water – there is some difference of opin-ion as to the number – the water remaining always the colour of whey, thanks to Sancho's gluttony and his purchase of those foul curds that turned his master so fair. In the garb we have described, and with a charming and gallant air, Don Quixote walked into an-other hall, where the student was waiting to entertain him while the table was being laid; for on the arrival of so noble a guest Doña Christina wanted to show that she knew how to entertain all visi-tors. Now whilst Don Quixote was taking off his armour, Don Lorenzo – for this was the name of Don Diego's son – had an oppor-tunity of saying to his father: 'Who can this knight be, sir, whom you have brought home? For his name, his appearance, and his call-ing himself a knight errant puzzle my mother and me.'

'I don't know what to say, son,' answered Don Diego. 'I can only tell you that I have seen him act like the greatest madman in the world, and yet make such wise speeches as to blot out and efface his deeds. Speak to him yourself and feel the pulse of his under-standing. Then, as you are a shrewd fellow, come to what conclu-sions you can as to his sense or lack of it; though, to tell you the truth, I think he is more mad than sane.'

At this Don Lorenzo went to meet Don Quixote, as has been said, and during their conversation Don Quixote said to him: 'Sir, Don Diego de Miranda, your father, has informed me of your rare abilities and subtle talents and, what is more, that you are a great poet.'

'Poet maybe,' answered Don Lorenzo, 'but by no means a great one. It is true that I am rather given to poetry, and to reading the good poets; but not to such an extent that I can give myself the title of great, as my father does.'

'I do not dislike this humility,' said Don Quixote, 'for there is no poet who is not arrogant, and does not think of himself as the best in the world.'

'There is no rule without exceptions,' answered Don Lorenzo; 'and there may be some who are, and yet do not think so.'

'Few,' said Don Quixote; 'but tell me, sir, what are these verses that you have in hand at present, which your father has told me make you rather restless and thoughtful? If it is a gloss, I understand something of this art of glossing, and I should like to hear them. If they are for a literary competition, try to win the second prize, for the first is always awarded by favour or to some person of quality. The second goes for pure merit. So the third is really the second, and on this reckoning the first should be third. It is just the same with university degrees. Though, for all that, the nominal first cuts a fine figure.'

'Up to now,' said Don Lorenzo to himself, 'I cannot consider you a fool. Let us go on.'

'Sir,' he then said, 'you seem to have frequented the schools. What sciences did you study?'

'Knight errantry,' replied Don Quixote, 'which is as good as poetry, and even two inches better.'

'I do not know what that science is,' observed Lorenzo. 'I have never heard of it till now.'

'It is a science,' replied Don Quixote, 'that comprises all or most of the sciences in the world, since he who professes it must be a jurist and know the laws of justice concerning persons and property, so that he may give to everyone what is his own and his due. He must be a theologian, so that he may give reasons for the Christian rule he professes, clearly and distinctly, wherever he may be asked. He must be a physician, and especially a herbalist, so that he may recognize in the midst of deserts and wildernesses those herbs which have the virtue of healing wounds, for the knight errant cannot go looking at every step for someone to cure him. He must be an astronomer, to know by the stars how many hours of the night are passed, and in what part and climate of the world he is. He must know mathematics, for at any time he may find himself in need of them. Not reckoning that he must be adorned with all the virtues, theological and cardinal, I will descend to other small details and say that he must be able to swim as they say Fish Nicholas or Nicolao did. He must know how to shoe a horse and mend a saddle and bridle. Also, to return to higher matters, he must keep faith with

God and his lady; he must be chaste in his thoughts, straightforward in his words, liberal in his works, valiant in his deeds, patient in his afflictions, charitable towards the needy and, in fact, a maintainer of truth, although its defence may cost him his life. Of all these parts, great and small, a good knight errant is composed. So you may see, Don Lorenzo, whether it is a snivelling science that chivalry teaches those who study and profess it, and whether the loftiest taught in colleges and schools are the equal of it.'

'If that is so,' replied Lorenzo, 'I agree that this science is superior to any.'

'How, if that is so?' demanded Don Quixote.

'What I mean to say,' said Don Lorenzo, 'is that I doubt whether there are, or ever have been, knights errant with so many virtues.'

'What I now say I have said many times before,' replied Don Quixote. 'The majority of people in this world are of the opinion that knights errant have never existed; and I hold that unless Heaven miraculously convinces them to the contrary, any labour undertaken for that purpose must be in vain, as experience has many times shown me. So I will not stop now to deliver your worship from the error you hold in common with the multitude. What I mean to do is to pray Heaven to deliver you from it, and make you see how beneficial and necessary knights errant were to the world in past ages, and how useful they would be in the present, if they were in fashion. But now, for the peoples' sins, sloth, idleness, gluttony and luxury triumph.'

'Our guest has broken out,' said Don Lorenzo to himself at this point. 'But for all that he is a brave madman, and I should be a poor fool not to see that.'

Here their conversation ended, as they were called to dinner. So when Don Diego asked his son what he had made of their guest's wits, he replied: 'All the physicians and authors in the world could not give a clear account of his madness. He is mad in patches, full of lucid streaks.'

They went to dinner, and the food was good, abundant and tasty; it was in fact the fare that Don Diego had said on the road he generally gave to his guests. But what most delighted Don Quixote was the marvellous silence throughout the whole house, which seemed like a Carthusian monastery. So, when the cloths had been removed, a grace said, and their hands washed, he earnestly begged Don Lorenzo to recite to him his verses for the literary competition; to which the young man replied:

'So that I may not seem to be one of those poets who refuse when they are asked to read their verses, but spew them up when they are not asked, I will recite my gloss, for which I expect no prize, as I have written it only to exercise my wits.'

'A wise friend of mine,' said Don Quixote, 'was of the opinion that no one should weary himself by writing glosses; and the reason, he said, was that the gloss could never come near to the text; and that often, or most times, the gloss was a long way from the intention and purpose of the theme set; and, furthermore, that the rules for glossing were too stringent, for they allowed no interrogations, nor "*said he*" nor "*shall say*", nor making verbs of nouns, nor changing the sense; with other restrictions and limitations by which glossers are bound, as your worship must know.'

'In truth, Don Quixote,' said Don Lorenzo, 'I should like to catch your worship out in some serious blunder. But I cannot, for you slip through my hands like an eel.'

'I do not understand what you say, sir,' replied Don Quixote, 'or what you mean about this slipping of mine.'

'I will make myself clear later,' answered Don Lorenzo. 'But, for the present listen, please, to the gloss and to the theme, which go like this:

> If but my 'was' might turn to 'is';
> I look for it, then it comes complete.
> Oh, might I say 'Now, now it is',
> Our after-griefs may be too great.

The Gloss

> As everything passes away,
> So Fortune's goods, that once she gave,
> Passed, and would not with me stay,
> Though she gave once all I could crave.
> Fortune, 'tis long since thou hast seen
> Me at thy feet, long centuries;
> I shall be glad, as I have been,
> If but my 'was' be turned to 'is'.

Unto no glory am I bent,
No prize, honour, or victory,
But to return to my content,
Whose thought afflicts my memory.
If only that you will restore,
Fortune, the vigour of my heat
Is calmed; but let it come before
I look for it, then it comes complete.

Impossible do I desire,
To make the past return, in vain;
No power on earth can so aspire
To call a past state back again.
Time passes on, time runs and flies
Swiftly, and never turns his face.
He is in error then that cries,
'Oh, might I say, "Now, now it is."'

I live in great perplexity,
Sometimes in hope, sometimes in fear,
Which is a death. Better to die
That of my griefs I might get clear;
For me to die were better far.
But fear repeats more soberly:
'Better to go on living, for
Our after griefs may be too great.'

When Don Lorenzo had finished reciting his poem, Don Quixote got upon his feet and grasped the young man's right hand, crying in a loud voice which sounded like a shout:

'Praise be to High Heaven, noble youth, but you are the best
poet in the world, and deserve to be crowned with laurel, not by
Cyprus or Gaeta, as the poet said, whom God forgive, but by the
Academies of Athens, were they surviving to-day, and by those
still in existence at Paris, Bologna and Salamanca. Would to
Heaven that the judges who would deny you the first prize might
be shot to death by the arrows of Phoebus, and that the Muses
might never cross the thresholds of their homes. Read me, sir, if
you will be so good, some of your greater poems; for I should like
to feel the pulse of your admirable genius in all its parts.'

Is it necessary to say that Don Lorenzo was delighted to be
praised by Don Quixote, although he considered him mad? O
power of flattery! How far you extend, and how wide are the fron-

tiers of your pleasing realm! This truth Don Lorenzo proved by
acceding to Don Quixote's request and reciting to him this sonnet
on the legend or story of Pyramus and Thisbe:

Sonnet

The wall was broken by the maiden fair,
Which cleft the gallant heart of Pyramus;
Love flies from Cyprus that he may declare,
Once seen, the narrow breach prodigious.
There only silence speaks; no voice will dare
Into so very strait a strait to pass;
Let their souls speak, Love's nature is so rare
That he makes easy things most arduous.
Desire in her grows violent, and haste
In the rash maid instead of heart's delight
Calls down her death. See now the story's passed:
Both of them in a moment – O strange sight! –
One sword, one sepulchre, one memory
Kills, covers, crowns with immortality.

'Heaven be praised,' cried Don Quixote, when he had heard Don
Lorenzo's sonnet, 'that among an infinite number of rhymers I
have seen one as accomplished as you are, my dear sir!'

Don Quixote was very well entertained at Don Diego's for four
days; at the end of which he asked leave to depart, and thanked his
host for his favours and the kind welcome he had received in his
house. For since it was not right for knights errant to give up many
hours to ease and luxury, he wished to go and fulfil his duty, seeking those adventures with which he was told that land abounded.
In this way he hoped to pass the time till the day of the jousts at
Saragossa, to which he would take the straight road; though first he
must enter the Cave of Montesinos, of which so many amazing
stories were told in those parts, and also investigate and discover
the origin and true source of the seven lagoons commonly called
the Lakes of Ruidera. Don Diego and his son commended his noble
purpose, and bade him take all that he pleased from their house
and farm, for they would most gladly serve him, as they were
bound by his personal worth and his honourable profession to do.

Finally the day of his departure arrived, bringing joy to Don
Quixote but sadness and melancholy to Sancho Panza, who had
very much enjoyed the plenty in Don Diego's house and was loth

to return to the hunger prevalent in forests and deserts, and to the
scantiness of his ill-stored saddle-bags. He did not omit, however,
to stuff them full of everything that seemed to him most necessary.
Then, as he took his leave, Don Quixote said to Don Lorenzo: 'I
do not know whether I have told your worship before, but if I
have I will repeat it, that if you would save labour and pains in
climbing to the inaccessible peak of the temple of Fame, you have
only to quit the rather narrow road of poetry and follow the nar-
rowest path of all, that of knight errantry, which is capable of making you an Emperor in a brace of shakes.'

With these words Don Quixote finally settled the question of his
madness, the more so by adding: 'God knows I should like to take
Don Lorenzo with me to teach him how to spare the humble and
subdue and trample the proud under foot; accomplishments proper
to the profession I follow. But since his youth does not demand it,
nor his praiseworthy pursuits permit of it, I content myself by advising him that, as a poet, he will be able to win fame if he is guided
rather by the opinion of others than by his own. For there is no
father or mother to whom their children seem ugly; and this delusion is even more prevalent in respect of the children of the brain.'

Father and son were once more amazed at Don Quixote's mixture of wise and foolish arguments and at his tenacity in devoting
himself to the search for his luckless adventures, which were the
whole aim and object of his desires. So they repeated their offers and
their compliments; and then, taking leave of the lady of the castle,
Don Quixote and Sancho departed upon Rocinante and the ass.

Chapter XIX. *Of the Adventure of the Enamoured Shepherd,
with other truly pleasant incidents.*

DON QUIXOTE had not left Don Diego's village far behind him
when he met with two men, who seemed to be priests or students,
and two peasants, the four of them riding on four asses. One of the
students was carrying what looked like a piece of fine scarlet cloth
and two pairs of knitted stockings, wrapped up in a piece of green
buckram, which served him for a bag, while the other bore only a
new pair of black fencing-foils with their buttons on. The peasants
were carrying other things which showed that they had been mak-

ing purchases in some big town and were bringing them back to
their village. Now both students and peasants were as astounded
as everyone usually was at the first sight of Don Quixote, and
longed to know who this extraordinary man might be. The knight
greeted them and asked what road they were taking. Then, on
learning that it was the same as his own, he offered them his company, asking them to slacken their pace, for their ass-fillies went
faster than his horse. Next he obligingly gave them a brief account
of himself, his office and his profession of knight errant travelling
in search of adventure in all parts of the world, saying that his proper name was Don Quixote de la Mancha, and his title *The Knight
of the Lions*.

All this was like Greek or gibberish to the two peasants; but not
to the students, who immediately realized that Don Quixote was
weak in the head. But, for all that, they looked at him with wonder
and respect, and one of them said:

'If, Sir Knight, your worship is taking no fixed road, as is the
way of those in search of adventure, come with us, and you will see
as fine and rich a wedding as has ever been celebrated in La Mancha
or for many miles round.'

Don Quixote asked if it was some prince's nuptials, that he spoke
so highly of it.

'No,' answered the student. 'It is the wedding of a farmer and a
farmer's daughter. He is the richest man in the whole country, and
she the most beautiful girl man ever saw. The arrangements they
are making for the wedding are most strange and original, for it is
to take place in a meadow close to the bride's village. She is always
spoken of as Quiteria the fair, and her bridegroom as Camacho the
rich. She is eighteen and he twenty-two, and they are well matched,
although some curious people who know the pedigrees of all the
world by heart are pleased to say that the fair Quiteria's is better
than Camacho's; but we do not take notice of that nowadays, for
riches can solder a great many cracks. To be brief, this Camacho is
generous, and has taken it into his head to have the whole of this
meadow covered in with boughs, so that the sun will have to take
some pains if he wants to get in to visit the green grass which
covers its soil. He has also got up some sword-dances and some
morris dances, for there are many in the village who can jingle and

shake the bells to perfection. Of the shoe-clatterers I say nothing, for he has invited a pack of them. But none of the things I have mentioned, nor many others which I have left out, will make this wedding more memorable than the actions I expect the desperate Basilio will perform there. This Basilio is a shepherd of Quiteria's own village, who has a house next to her parents, where Love took occasion to revive in the world the now-forgotten loves of Pyramus and Thisbe. For Basilio loved Quiteria from his earliest and tenderest years, and she answered his desires with a thousand innocent favours, so much so that the love between the two children, Basilio and Quiteria, was a source of amusement to the village. Now as they grew older, Quiteria's father decided to deny Basilio his former free access to his house and, to save himself from a life of suspicion and mistrust, arranged to marry his daughter to the rich Camacho, as he did not care to match her with Basilio, who is not so well favoured by fortune as by nature. But, to tell you the truth without envy, he is the most active lad we know, a great pitcher of the bar, a fine wrestler and a great ball-player. He runs like a deer, jumps better than a goat, and bowls down the ninepins like magic. He sings like a lark, and when he plays a guitar he almost makes it speak. What is more, he fences with the best of them.'

'For that accomplishment alone,' put in Don Quixote, 'this youth not only deserves to marry the fair Quiteria, but Queen Guenevere herself, if she were alive to-day, in spite of Lancelot and all who might try to stop him.'

'Tell that to my wife!' said Sancho Panza, who had been listening in silence hitherto. 'She doesn't like people marrying any but their equals, sticking to the proverb that says, every ewe to her mate. What I should like is for this good Basilio – I seem to love him already – to marry this lady Quiteria. – And may all those who hinder folks from marrying the ones they love have eternal salvation and sweet repose – I was going to say the opposite.'

'If all lovers were to marry,' said Don Quixote, 'parents would lose their right of marrying their children when and to whom they choose. And if the choice of husband were left to the daughter's pleasure, there would be one who would pick her father's groom, and another some passer-by in the street, whom she might fancy a brave and fine fellow though he might be a debauched swash-

buckler. For love and fancy easily blind the eyes of the understanding, which are so necessary for choosing one's estate. The state of
matrimony is in great danger from errors, and it needs much cir-
cumspection and the particular favour of Heaven to make a good
choice. For if a prudent man wants to take a long journey he seeks
a safe and peaceful companion to go with him, before setting out on
the road. Why then should not he do the same when he has to
travel all his life, right up to the resting-place of death; all the more
so since his companion must be with him at bed and at board and
everywhere, as the wife is with her husband. The companionship of
one's own wife is not merchandise which, once bought, can be returned or bartered or exchanged; for marriage is an inseparable
condition which lasts as long as life endures. It is a noose which becomes a Gordian knot once you put it round your neck, for if
Death's scythe does not cut it, there is no untying it. I could say
much more on this subject, if I were not prevented by my desire to
know whether Master Licentiate has anything more to say about the
story of Basilio.'

To which the student, whether bachelor, or licentiate as Don
Quixote called him, replied: 'There is nothing more to say whatever, except that from the moment Basilio learnt that the fair Quiteria was to marry Camacho the rich he has never been seen to
laugh or talk sensibly. He always goes about thoughtful and sad
and talking to himself – a clear and certain sign that he has lost his
wits. He eats little and sleeps little; and all he does eat is fruit, and
if he does sleep he sleeps in the open, on the hard ground like a wild
animal. From time to time he gazes at the sky, and at other times
fixes his eyes on the earth in such distraction that he looks like nothing so much as a clothed statue with its garments blown about by
the wind. Indeed he shows such signs of a heart torn by passion that
all of us who know him are afraid that to-morrow the fair Quiteria's
Yes will be his sentence of death.'

'God will find a cure,' said Sancho. 'For God, who gives the
wound, gives the remedy. No one knows what's to come. There are
many hours between now and to-morrow, and in one of them –
even in a minute – the house falls. I have seen rain and sunshine together at the same moment. A man lies down sound at night and
next day he can't move. Now, tell me, can there possibly be anyone

who flatters himself that he has put a spoke into the wheel of Fortune? No, of course not. I wouldn't dare to put a pinpoint between a woman's yes and no, for there would be no room. Let them just tell me that Quiteria loves Basilio with all her heart and soul, and I'll give him a bag full of good luck. For love, as I have heard tell, looks through spectacles that make copper seem like gold, poverty like riches, and eye-rheum like pearls.'

'Will you never stop, Sancho, confound you?' exclaimed Don Quixote. 'Once you begin to string proverbs and old tales together, no one but Judas himself – may he take your soul – can follow you. Tell me, animal, what do you know about spokes or wheels or anything else?'

'Oh, if you don't understand me,' replied Sancho, 'it's no marvel my opinions are taken for nonsense. But no matter, I understand myself, and I know there wasn't much foolishness in what I said, though your worship's always such a cricket of my sayings, and of my doings too.'

'Critic, you should say,' said Don Quixote, 'not "*cricket*", you perverter of good language, confound you.'

'Don't turn sour on me, your worship,' replied Sancho. 'You know I wasn't brought up at the Court, and never studied at Salamanca to learn whether I'm putting a letter too many or too few into my words. Good Lord! You mustn't expect a Sayagan to speak like a chap from Toledo, and there may be Toledans who aren't so slick at this business of speaking pretty either.'

'That is so,' said the licentiate. 'Men bred in the tanneries and in Zocodover cannot speak as well as those who spend most of their day strolling in the cloisters of the Cathedral; and yet they are all Toledans. You will find the pure, correct, elegant and clear language among educated people at Court, even though they may have been born at Majalahonda. I said educated because there are many courtiers who are not so, and education is the grammar of good speech, which comes with practice. I, sirs, for my sins have studied canon law at Salamanca, and rather pride myself on expressing my meaning in clear, plain and forcible terms.'

'If you had not prided yourself more on knowing how to manage the foils you carry than your tongue,' said the other student, 'you would have come out first in your degree examination instead of last.'

'Look you, Bachelor Corchuelo,' replied the licentiate, 'if you consider skill in swordsmanship useless you hold the most erroneous opinion possible on the subject.'

'It is no mere opinion of mine,' answered Corchuelo, 'but a well-founded truth. And if you want me to prove it by experiment, you are carrying the swords. Here is a convenient spot. I have muscles and strength, and with my spirit, which is no poor one, I will make you admit that I am not in the wrong. Dismount, and make use of your measured paces, your circles, your angles and your science. Raw and clumsy and unskilled though I am, I hope to make you see stars at noonday. For I trust to God that the man is yet unborn who will make me turn my back, and there is no one on earth I will not force to give ground.'

'As to your turning your back or not,' replied the swordsman, 'it is no affair of mine, although your grave may well open for you on the spot where you first plant your foot – I mean that you will be struck dead there by the skill you despise.'

'We shall see now,' replied Corchuelo. And dismounting briskly from his ass, he snatched one of the swords the licentiate was carrying.

'That is not the way,' broke in Don Quixote. 'For I will be umpire of this duel, and see that this long unsettled question is fairly decided.' Then, alighting from Rocinante and grasping his lance, he took up his position in the middle of the road, at the moment when the licentiate was advancing gracefully and with measured steps against Corchuelo, who rushed at him, his eyes darting fire, as the saying is. The two peasants with them did not dismount from their fillies, but looked on as spectators of the mortal tragedy. Corchuelo's thrusts, lunges, down-strokes, back-strokes and double strokes were innumerable and thicker than hail. He rushed like an angry lion, but was met at full tilt by a blow on the mouth from the button of the licentiate's foil, which stopped him in the midst of his fury. In fact he had to kiss it as if it were a relic, although not with as much devotion as relics generally and rightfully receive. In the end the licentiate's lunges accounted for every one of the buttons of the short cassock his opponent was wearing, and cut his skirts to ribbons like the arms of cuttle-fish. Twice he knocked off his opponent's hat, and so wore him out that, in his vexation, anger and fury, he took his sword by the hilt and flung it into the air with such force that one of the peasant spectators, a clerk, who went for it afterwards, stated on oath that it had travelled a good two miles – which testimony has served, and still serves, to show and prove that, in very truth, brute strength is conquered by skill.

Corchuelo had sat down exhausted, when Sancho approached him and said: 'My goodness, Master Bachelor, if you'll take my advice, you won't challenge anyone to fence after this. Choose wrestling or pitching the bar instead, for you have the youth and strength for that. But as for these crack fighters, I've heard they can put a swordpoint through the eye of a needle.'

'I am satisfied,' replied Corchuelo, 'to have been tumbled off my hobby-horse, and to have learnt by experience a truth I was far from believing.'

So, getting up, he embraced the licentiate, and they remained better friends than before. Then, not caring to wait for the clerk who had gone for the sword, as they thought it would hold them back too long, they decided to push on, so as to arrive in good time at Quiteria's village, to which they all belonged.

During the remainder of the journey the licentiate expatiated on the excellencies of the sword, using such conclusive arguments, and so many instances and mathematical proofs, that they were all convinced of the virtue of the art, and Corchuelo was cured of his obstinacy.

Night was just beginning to fall, but as they arrived the village looked to them all as if it was surrounded by a sky filled with countless shining stars. They heard too the sweet confused sounds of various instruments, such as flutes, little drums, psalteries, recorders, tambourines and timbrels; and when they got near they saw that an arbour of trees, which had been put up by hand at the entrance to the village, was all full of little lights, which the wind did not disturb, for it was blowing so softly just then that it had not the strength to stir the leaves on the trees. The musicians were the merry-makers at the wedding, who were wandering about that pleasant spot in bands, some singing, others dancing, and yet others playing the diversity of instruments named. Indeed, it looked as though joy and gladness themselves were leaping and dancing all over that meadow. There were many others busily raising platforms, from which next day they would be able to see in comfort the plays and dances which were to be performed in that spot, dedicated to the celebration of the rich Camacho's wedding and Basilio's funeral. Don Quixote refused to enter the village, although both the peasant and the student begged him to, giving what seemed to him a most sufficient excuse: that it was the custom of knights errant to sleep in the fields and woods rather than in towns or villages, even though it were under gilded roofs. Therefore he went a little way off the road, much against Sancho's will, for the good lodging he had had in Don Diego's castle or house was still fresh in the squire's memory.

Chapter XX. *A description of the Wedding of Camacho the rich and the Adventure of Basilio the poor.*

SCARCELY had the fair Aurora given shining Phoebus time to dry the liquid pearls of her golden hair with the ardour of his hot rays, when Don Quixote, shaking sloth from his limbs, stood up and called his squire Sancho, who was still snoring. Seeing which, he remarked before waking him:

'O you, fortunate above all who dwell on the face of the earth, for without envy or being envied you sleep with a quiet mind, neither persecuted by enchanters, nor alarmed by enchantments! Sleep, I say again and a hundred times more, sleep; for no jealousy of your lady holds you in perpetual vigil, nor do thoughts of how to pay your debts keep you awake; nor of what you must do to feed yourself and your little straitened family on the morrow. Ambition does not trouble you, nor the vain pomps of the world worry you, for the limits of your desires extend no further than care for your ass. The care of your own person you have laid on my shoulders, a compensatory burden which nature and custom have ever imposed upon masters. The servant sleeps and the master watches, reflecting on means of sustaining, bettering and favouring him. Anguish at seeing the sky turn to brass and shed no needful dew on the earth does not afflict the servant but the master, who in barrenness and famine must support him that served him in festivity and abundance.'

To all this Sancho made no reply, since he was asleep; nor would he have woken so soon if Don Quixote had not brought him to with the butt-end of his lance. In the end he awoke, drowsy and slothful, and looking all around observed: 'There's a good smelling steam coming out of that arbour. If I'm not mistaken it smells more like broiled rashers than thyme and rushes. A wedding that begins with odours like that should be a liberal and generous one, I'll be bound.'

'Stop that, glutton,' said Don Quixote. 'Come, let's go and watch this ceremony, and see what the rejected Basilio does.'

'Let him do what he likes,' answered Sancho. 'He would be poor, and he would marry Quiteria. Isn't it enough not to have a farthing and to want to marry in the clouds? Really, sir, it's my opinion that the poor fellow should be content with what he finds and not go looking for dainties at the bottom of the sea. I'd bet one arm that Camacho could cover Basilio in gold pieces; and if that's so, as it must be, Quiteria would be a fine fool to throw away all the jewels and finery Camacho must have given her, and choose Basilio's bar-pitching and foil-play. They won't give you a pint of wine in a tavern for a good throw of the bar or a clever trick with a sword. Skills and graces that aren't saleable are all right for Count Dirlos, but when these talents fall to someone with good money I'd like to be in his shoes. On a good foundation you can build a good house, and the best foundation and bottom in the world is money.'

'For God's sake, Sancho,' cried Don Quixote at this point, 'be done with this speech of yours. For it is my belief that, if you were left to follow up every idea you start, you would have no time left to eat or sleep. You would waste it all in talking.'

'If your worship had a good memory,' replied Sancho, 'you'd remember the articles of our agreement, made before we left home this last time. One of them was that I should be allowed to talk as much as I pleased, so long as I didn't speak against my neighbour or your worship's authority. And I don't think I've violated that article so far.'

'I do not remember any such article, Sancho,' answered Don Quixote; 'but supposing you are right, I now wish you to be quiet and come. For the instruments we heard last night are once more delighting the valleys, and no doubt the wedding will be celebrated in the freshness of the morning, and not in the afternoon heat.'

Sancho obeyed his master, and saddled Rocinante and Dapple. Then they both mounted and rode leisurely towards the arbour. There the first thing that met Sancho's gaze was a whole steer spitted upon a whole elm, and for the fire over which it was to roast a pretty mountain of wood burning. The six earthen pots which stood around this blaze were not made in the common mould of ordinary pots, but were six medium-sized wine-jars, each one of which could hold a slaughter-house full of meat. Whole sheep were swallowed up in them and vanished from view like so many pigeons. There were numberless skinned hares and plucked chickens too, hanging on the trees, ready for burial in these pots. Countless also were the birds and game of all kinds hanging from the branches to cool in the air. Sancho counted more than sixty wine-skins of more than eight gallons each, and all full, as it afterwards proved, of choice wines. There were also piles of the whitest loaves, heaped up like mountains of wheat on the threshing-floor, and cheeses built up like bricks made a wall, while two cauldrons of oil, larger than dyers' vats, served for frying puddings, which they drew out ready and plunged into another cauldron of warmed honey, which stood alongside. There were more than fifty cooks, male and female, all clean, all busy and all jolly. In the distended belly of the steer were two dozen delicate little sucking-pigs, sewn up inside to make it tasty and tender. The spices of various sorts seemed to have been bought, not by the pound, but by the quarter, and were all displayed in a great chest. To conclude, the provision for the marriage was rustic, but plentiful enough to feed an army.

Sancho Panza gazed at all this, and as he contemplated it he grew to love it. The first things to captivate him and seize on his desires were the pots, from which he would have been glad to take a good dishful. Then the wine-skins captured his fancy, and last the products of the frying-pan, if such bloated vessels could be called pans. And so, unable to bear it any longer, he went up to one of the busy cooks, and in courteous and hungry terms prayed to be allowed to dip a crust of bread into one of the pots. To which the cook answered: 'Thanks to the rich Camacho, brother, hunger holds no sway to-day. Dismount and see if there's a ladle around. Then skim off a hen or two, and may they do you good.'

'I can't see one,' replied Sancho.

'Wait,' said the cook. 'Goodness, what a finnicking faint-hearted fellow you are!' So saying, he took a large cooking-pot and, dipping it into one of the jars, brought out with it three hens and a couple of geese, remarking to Sancho: 'Eat. Take your breakfast off these skimmings, my friend. They'll stay your hunger till dinner time.'

'I've nothing to put them in,' replied Sancho.

'Then take them, ladle and all,' said the cook. 'Camacho's rich enough and generous enough for anything.'

Whilst Sancho was thus occupied Don Quixote was watching the entrance of some dozen peasants on one side of the arbour. All were dressed in their holiday best, and each mounted on a fine mare in rich and splendid country trappings with many bells hanging from the harness. These ran in an orderly troop, not once but many times, up and down the meadow, cheering and shouting: 'Long live Camacho and Quiteria. He is rich and she is fair, the fairest maid in all the world!'

When Don Quixote heard them he said to himself: 'It is clear that they have not seen my Dulcinea del Toboso, for if they had seen her they would be more sparing in their praises of this Quiteria of theirs.'

Shortly afterwards several different teams of dancers began to march into various parts of the arbour, among them a band of sword-dancers, some two dozen shepherds of gallant looks and bearing, all dressed in the finest and whitest of linen, with multi-coloured headdresses worked in fine silk. One of those on horseback asked their leader, a sprightly youth, whether any of the dancers had hurt himself.

'None of us has been hurt, up to now, thank Goodness,' said he. 'We are all fit.' And presently he began to wind his way among his companions, twisting and turning with such skill that, used as Don Quixote was to seeing such dances, this one seemed better than any he had ever beheld.

He was delighted too with a dance performed by a troop of lovely girls of between fourteen and eighteen, all dressed in green. Their hair, which they wore half plaited and half loose, was of such bright gold that their heads, wreathed with jasmine, roses, amaranth and honeysuckle, seemed to rival the very sun. They were

led by a venerable old man and an ancient matron, both more active
and nimbler than might have been expected from their years. They
danced to the sound of a Zamora bagpipe, and with their modest
looks and nimble feet, showed themselves the best dancers in the
world.

After them came another set piece, called a speaking masque. It
was made up of eight nymphs, divided into two files, one of them
led by the god *Love* and the other by *Interest* : *Love* adorned with
wings, a bow, quiver, and arrows, and *Interest* in rich coloured
silks and gold. The nymphs led by *Love* had their names on their
shoulders written in great letters on white parchment. *Poetry* was
the first, *Good Sense* the second, *Good Family* the third, and *Valour*
the fourth. Those that followed *Interest* were distinguished in the
same way. The first was *Liberality*, the second *Gifts*, the third
Treasure, and the fourth *Peaceful Possession*. They were preceded
by a wooden castle drawn by four savages, all clad in ivy and hemp
dyed green, so life-like that for a moment they quite frightened
Sancho. On the front of the castle and on each of its four sides was
written *The Castle of Caution*. Four skilful musicians struck up for
them on the flute and drum. Then *Love* began to dance, and after
two turns he raised his eyes and bent his bow against a maiden
standing on the battlements of the castle, whom he addressed after
this fashion:

> I am the powerful deity
> In Heaven above and earth beneath,
> In sea's and hell's profundity,
> Over all that therein live and breathe.
> What fear is I never knew;
> I can perform all that I will;
> Nothing to me is strange or new;
> I bid, forbid, at pleasure still.

The verse ended, he shot an arrow over the top of the castle and
returned to his position. Then *Interest* came out and made two
turns. The drums stopped and he spoke:

> I am one can do more than Love,
> Yet it is love that is my guide.
> My strain's the greater, for to Jove
> Above I nearest am allied.

> I Interest am, with whom but few
> Perform the honest deeds they should,
> Yet 'twere a miracle to view
> If without me they could do good.

Then *Interest* retired, and *Poetry* came forward and, after doing her turns like the others, fixed her eyes on the maiden in the castle and said:

> Lady, to thee, sweet Poetry
> Her soul in imagery sends,
> Wrapped up in sheaves of sonnetry,
> Whose pleasing strain commends.
> If with my earnestness I then
> Do not annoy, fair damsel, soon
> Your envied fortune shall, by me,
> Mount to the Circle of the Moon.

Poetry retired, and from *Interest's* side *Liberality* danced out and, after her turns, spoke:

> To give is Liberality
> In him that shuns two contraries;
> The one is prodigality,
> The other hateful avarice.
> I'll be profuse in praising thee,
> For though profuseness is a sin,
> It smacks of love and honesty,
> And most in gifts is seen.

In this way all the figures in the two bands came forward and retired, each one making her turns and speaking her verses, some of which were charming and some ridiculous, though Don Quixote only retained in his excellent memory those which have been quoted. Soon they all mingled, making and breaking circles, gaily, easily and gracefully; and when *Love* passed in front of the castle he shot his arrows into the air, but *Interest* broke gilded balls against it. Then, in the end, after a long dance *Interest* took out a big purse, made of a great striped cat-skin, which seemed to be full of money, and flung it at the castle, whose boards fell apart and tumbled down at the shock, leaving the maiden exposed and defenceless. *Interest* then came up with the figures in his train, and throwing a great golden chain around her neck, made show of capturing her and leading her away a prisoner. When *Love* and his party saw this they tried to rescue her, making all their motions to the sound of the drums, they and the musicians playing and dancing in harmony. The savages then pacified the two parties, very speedily setting up and re-fixing the boards of the castle. The maiden shut herself up in it once more, and with this the dance concluded to the great pleasure of the spectators.

Don Quixote asked one of the nymphs who had composed and directed the show, and she replied that it was a clergyman of that village, who was a great hand at these productions.

'I would wager,' said Don Quixote, 'that he is more friendly to Camacho than to Basilio, that bachelor or clergyman, and a better hand at satire than at vespers. How cleverly he introduced Basilio's accomplishments and Camacho's riches into the dance!' Then Sancho Panza, who was listening, put in: 'The King's my cock. I'm for Camacho.'

'Indeed,' said Don Quixote. 'You seem to be the sort of yokel, Sancho, who always shouts "*Long live the conqueror*".'

'I don't know what sort I am,' answered Sancho, 'but I know I shall never get such elegant skimmings from Basilio's pots as I got from Camacho's.' And showing his cooking-pot full of geese and pullets, he pulled one out and began to eat with great zest and appetite, saying: 'Hang Basilio's accomplishments! You're worth as much as you've got, and you get as much as you're worth. There are only two families in the world, my old grandmother used to say, the *Haves* and the *Have-nots*. She was always for the *haves*, and to this very day, my lord Don Quixote, the doctor would rather feel the pulse of a *Have* than a *Know*. An ass covered with gold looks better than a horse with a pack-saddle. So I say again, I'm for Camacho. The skimmings from his pots are geese and pullets, hares, and rabbits in plenty; but Basilio's, if they ever come to hand, will be cask-rinsings.'

'Have you finished your speech, Sancho?' asked Don Quixote.

'I'll get it over,' answered Sancho. 'For I see it offends your worship. But if this hadn't come to interrupt it, I had enough to say to last three days.'

'Pray God, Sancho,' said Don Quixote, 'I may see you dumb before I die.'

'At the rate we're going,' replied Sancho, 'I shall be chewing clay before your worship dies. Then perhaps I shall be so dumb that I shan't speak a word till the end of the world, or at least till Doomsday.'

'Even though that should happen, Sancho,' said Don Quixote, 'your silence would never balance all your talking, past, present and future; especially as in the course of nature I suppose I shall die before you, and so I can never hope to see you dumb, not even when you are drinking or sleeping, which is the least I might have hoped for.'

'Really, sir,' answered Sancho, 'there's no trusting the fleshless woman – I mean Death. She devours the lamb as well as the sheep. And I've heard our priest say that she tramples equally on the high towers of kings and on the humble cottages of the poor. That lady is more powerful than dainty. She's not a bit squeamish. She eats of all and does for all, and fills her bags with all sorts of people, of all ages and conditions. She's no reaper who sleeps in the mid-day heat. She reaps at all hours, and cuts the dry grass as well as the green. She doesn't seem to chew, but gobbles and gulps down everything that's put before her; for she has a dog's appetite and nothing satisfies it. And although she has no belly, she seems to have a dropsy and a thirst to drink the lives of all living beings, as you drink a jug of cold water.'

'No more, Sancho,' Don Quixote broke in. 'Stop your fine phrases, and do not risk a fall. For really, in your country language you have said as much about death as any good preacher could. I tell you, Sancho, if your learning were equal to your natural wits you could take to the pulpit and go about the world preaching the prettiest sermons.'

'He preaches well that lives well,' replied Sancho, 'and I know no other *thologies*.'

'You have no need of them,' said Don Quixote. 'But I have not yet managed to understand or grasp how you know so much, seeing that fear of God is the beginning of wisdom, and you fear a lizard more than you fear Him.'

'Judge of your chivalries, your worship,' answered Sancho, 'and don't meddle with other men's fears or courage, for I've as pretty a fear of God as any neighbour's son. Now leave me to gobble up these skimmings, for all the rest are but idle words, of which we must give account in another life.'

And so saying, he began a fresh assault on his cooking-pot with such appetite as to arouse Don Quixote; and no doubt his master would have helped him, if he had not been hindered by an event which must be told further on.

Chapter XXI. *A continuation of Camacho's wedding, with other delightful Adventures.*

WHILE Don Quixote and Sancho were engaged in the conversation set down in the last chapter they heard loud shouts and a great uproar, which came from the men on horseback, who rode out, galloping and shouting, to meet the bride and bridegroom. The pair were approaching, surrounded by countless different musical instruments and inventions, and accompanied by the priest, the kinsfolk of both, and the most important people from the neighbouring villages, all dressed in their holiday best. And when Sancho saw the bride, he said:

'Well I never! She isn't dressed like a farmer's daughter, but like a fine palace lady! Heavens alive! That necklace of hers looks like fine coral, and she isn't wearing Cuenca cloth but thirty pile velvet! And her trimmings aren't white linen, but I swear they're satin! Then look at her hands! Is it jet rings she's wearing? No, I'll be blowed if they're not gold, and very much so, set with pearls as white as curds, each one of them worth the eye out of my head. Oh, the little whore! And what hair! If it isn't false, I've never seen longer or redder in my life! Then can you find fault with her air or her figure? Wouldn't you say she is like a palm-tree loaded with bunches of dates? For that is what they look like, those jewels she's got hanging from her hair and at her throat. My Lord, she's a fine strapping girl, and could sail through the shoals of Flanders.'

Don Quixote laughed at Sancho Panza's rustic praise; but he thought that, except for his lady Dulcinea del Toboso, he had never seen a more beautiful woman. The fair Quiteria looked rather pale, which might have been from the bad night that brides always have, getting themselves ready for their coming wedding-day. They marched up to a theatre standing on one side of the meadow, decorated with carpets and branches. For there it was the ceremony was to take place, and there they were to sit, looking on at the dances and masques. But just as they arrived at this spot they heard a great outcry behind them, and a voice shouting: 'Wait a little, thoughtless and hasty people!'

At this loud interruption everyone turned round, and saw that the speaker was a man dressed in a black coat, trimmed with crimson patches in the shape of flames. He was crowned, they presently saw, with a wreath of funereal cypress, and carried a stout staff in his hand. When he got closer, everyone recognized him as the gallant Basilio, and all waited in suspense to see what would come of his interruption, fearing some evil consequences from his arriving at such a moment. He came up at last, weary and breathless, and taking up his position in front of the bride and bridegroom, dug his steel-tipped staff into the ground. Then, changing colour and fixing his eyes on Quiteria, he spoke these words, in hoarse and trembling tones:

'Well you know, ungrateful Quiteria, that by the sacred law which binds us, you can take no other husband whilst I live. Nor are you unaware that, while I waited for time and my efforts to increase my fortune, I did not fail to observe the respect due to your honour. But you turn your back on all the obligations you owe my love, and wish to make lord of what is mine another, whose riches not only bring him good fortune but great happiness as well. So, to fill his fortune to the brim – not because I think that he deserves it, but because Heaven has been pleased to give it to him – I will destroy with my own hand such obstacle or impediment as might hinder him, by removing myself from his path. Long life, then, to the rich Camacho with the ungrateful Quiteria! Long and happy years! And let poor Basilio die, for poverty has clipped the wings of his happiness and laid him in his grave.'

And so saying, he grasped his staff, which he had dug into the earth and, breaking it in half on the ground, showed that it served as the sheath for a medium-sized dagger, which was concealed in it. Then, planting what might be called the hilt in the ground, he threw himself nimbly and resolutely upon it, and in an instant the bloody point appeared out of his back with half the steel blade – the unhappy wretch lying stretched on the ground, bathed in his blood,

and transfixed by his own weapon. His friends at once ran up to
help him, appalled at his miserable and piteous plight. Don Quixote
too left Rocinante and, hurrying to his aid, took him in his arms and
found that he had not yet breathed his last. They would have drawn
out the dagger, but the priest, who was present, was of the opinion
that they should not do so till he had made his confession, for he
would certainly die the moment they did. Coming a little to himself, however, Basilio cried in a faint and doleful voice:

'If, cruel Quiteria, in my last and fatal agony you would give me
your hand as my bride, I should think that my rashness had some
excuse, since by it I should attain the bliss of being yours.'

Hearing this, the priest bade him attend to the salvation of his
soul rather than to the pleasures of the body, and earnestly to implore God's pardon for his sins and for his desperate deed. To which
Basilio replied that he would on no account make his confession unless Quiteria would first give him her hand in marriage, for that
happiness would strengthen his heart and give him breath for confession. When Don Quixote heard the wounded man's petition, he
cried aloud that Basilio's request was very just and reasonable and,
what was more, very practicable, and that Sir Camacho would be as
honoured by receiving the lady Quiteria as the widow of the
valorous Basilio as if he were to receive her from her father's
side.

'There is no need of anything more here than one *Yes*,' said he,
'for it can have no sequel, since the bridal bed of this marriage must
be the grave.'

Camacho listened to all this in bewilderment and confusion, not
knowing what to do or say. But so many were the voices of Basilio's friends, beseeching him to permit Quiteria to give him her
hand — so that his soul should not be lost by his desperate end —
that he was moved, or even forced, to say that if Quiteria was willing he was content, since it was only delaying for a moment the fulfilment of his desires. Then they all ran up to Quiteria and, some
with prayers, others with tears, and yet others with persuasive arguments, implored her to give her hand to poor Basilio. But she was
harder than marble and more immovable than a statue, and appeared
to be unable and unwilling to reply with so much as a word. Nor
would she have done so, if the priest had not told her to make up

her mind quickly, for now Basilio's soul was in his teeth, and there was no time to wait for irresolute minds.

The fair Quiteria answered never a word, but seemingly in a fluster of grief moved to where Basilio lay with his eyes turned up, breathing short and painfully, and muttering her name between his teeth, apparently about to die like a heathen and no Christian. At length she reached him, fell on her knees and, rather by signs than by words, besought his hand. Then Basilio opened his eyes and, staring fixedly at her, said: 'Quiteria, you have come to relent at a time when your pity can only serve as a knife to finish off my life. For I have no more strength to bear the honour you are giving me by choosing me as yours, nor will it ease the pain which is so rapidly filming my eyes with the dread shadow of death. I implore of you, my fatal star, not to give me your hand out of mere complaisance nor to deceive me once more, but to confess and declare that you give it to me freely and unconstrainedly, as to your lawful husband; since it would be wrong to deceive me in the condition I am in, or to deal falsely with one who has dealt so truly with you.'

As he was speaking he fainted, and all the bystanders thought that each convulsion would carry his soul away. Then Quiteria, all modest and bashful, took Basilio's right hand in hers, and said: 'No force would be sufficient to constrain my will. With all the freedom in the world I give you my hand as your lawful wife and accept yours, if it is freely given, and your mind is not clouded and changed by the calamity you have rashly brought upon yourself.'

'Yes, I give it,' replied Basilio, 'undisturbed and unchanged, and with the clear understanding that Heaven has granted me. So I give and deliver myself to you as your husband.'

'And I as your wife,' replied Quiteria, 'whether you live many years, or are borne from my arms to the grave.'

'The lad talks a great deal for one so gravely wounded,' remarked Sancho at this point. 'They should make him stop his love-talk and attend to his soul, for to my mind it's nearer to his tongue than to his teeth.'

So Basilio and Quiteria clasped hands, and the priest tenderly and tearfully gave them his benediction, begging God to give good repose to the soul of the bridegroom. But the moment he received the blessing, Basilio jumped briskly to his feet, and with unexpected deftness wrenched out the dagger which was sheathed in his body. All the bystanders were amazed, and some of them, more credulous than curious, began to cry out: 'A miracle, a miracle!'

But Basilio answered: 'No miracle, no miracle; but a trick, a trick!' The priest ran up in confusion and astonishment to feel the wound with both his hands, and found that the knife had not passed through Basilio's flesh and ribs, but through a hollow iron tube, which he had fitted into position, filled with blood so prepared, as it afterwards came out, as not to congeal. In fact the priest, Camacho and all the spectators had been tricked and fooled. The bride, however, showed no signs of resenting the ruse. On the contrary, when she heard that the marriage, being fraudulent, was invalid, she said that she reconfirmed it. From which everyone concluded that the affair had been planned with her agreement and connivance. This so enraged Camacho and his supporters that they took their vengeance into their own hands, and many of them drew their swords and attacked Basilio, in whose defence almost as many swords were unsheathed in an instant. At the head of them Don Quixote on horseback, with his lance on his arm and well covered by his shield, forced everyone to give way before him. But Sancho, who never got any pleasure or solace from such doings, took refuge among the pots from which he had extracted his welcome skimmings, regarding that spot as sacred and certain to be respected. Then Don Quixote cried out in a loud voice:

'Hold, sirs, hold! We have no right to take vengeance for the wrongs love does us. Consider that love and war are one; and as in war it is legitimate and customary to use artifices and stratagems to conquer the enemy, so in contests and rivalries of love deceits and plots practised to attain the desired end are justifiable, so long as they are not to the detriment and dishonour of the loved object. Quiteria was Basilio's, and Basilio Quiteria's, by Heaven's just and favourable decree. Camacho is rich and can buy his pleasure when, where and how he will. Basilio has only this one ewe-lamb, and no one, however powerful, shall take her from him; for whom God hath joined let no man put asunder. And whoever attempts will first have to pass by the point of this lance.' With this he brandished his weapon so stoutly and deftly that he struck fear into all who did not know him.

So deeply did Quiteria's disdain fix itself into Camacho's mind that she was instantly blotted from his memory; and consequently the persuasions of the priest, who was a wise and well-meaning man, prevailed with him, and left him and his partisans appeased and quieted. In sign of which they sheathed their swords, rather blaming Quiteria for her lightness than Basilio for his trick, and Camacho arguing to himself that if Quiteria loved Basilio as a maiden she would still love him after her marriage, and so he must give Heaven greater thanks for losing her than for getting her.

So, Camacho and his supporters being consoled and pacified, all Basilio's party were quiet, and Camacho the rich proved that he did not resent the trick, or take it to heart, by desiring that the entertainment should proceed as if he were really being married. However, neither Basilio nor his wife nor his followers would take part, but went off to Basilio's village. For just as the rich have their flatterers and their train; so even the poor, if virtuous and sensible, have also followers to honour and uphold them.

They took Don Quixote with them, esteeming him a man of worth and valour. Sancho alone was filled with gloom, when he saw himself dragged away from Camacho's splendid feast and entertainment, which lasted till night. Dejectedly and sorrowfully he followed his master, who rode with Basilio's party, and left behind him the flesh-pots of Egypt, though he bore them with him in his heart; their skimmings in the cooking-pot, although almost consumed to the last, representing for him the glory and plenty of the good things he had lost. So, pensive and brooding though hungerless, without alighting from Dapple, he followed in Rocinante's tracks.

Chapter XXII. *Of the great Adventure of Montesinos' Cave in the heart of La Mancha, which the valorous Don Quixote brought to a happy ending.*

MANY and great were the compliments which the newly-married couple paid Don Quixote, being grateful for the readiness he had shown to defend their cause, measuring his wit by his valour, and accounting him a Cid in arms and a Cicero in eloquence. The good Sancho was entertained for three days at the expense of the bridal couple, from whom he learnt that the pretended wounding was not a plot pre-arranged with the fair Quiteria, but a trick of Basilio's, from which he had expected the very result they had witnessed. Though it is true that he confessed he had let some of his friends into his secret, so that they might support his plans and back up his deceptions at the needful moment.

'Deceptions they could not and should not be called,' said Don Quixote, 'seeing that they were designed for a good purpose. For the marriage of two lovers was a project of the highest excellence.' He warned them, however, that love's greatest adversary is hunger and continued poverty. For love is all gaiety, rejoicing and happiness, particularly when the lover is in possession of the beloved, against whom want and poverty are open and declared enemies. All this he said to persuade Basilio to give up practising his arts, for although they brought him fame they earned him no money, and to apply himself to increasing his wealth by lawful and industrious means, which the prudent and hard-working never lack. The poor, honourable man – if it is possible for a poor man to be honourable – in possessing a lovely wife, has such a jewel that if he is robbed of it his honour is lost and slain. The lovely and honourable wife whose husband is poor deserves to be crowned with laurels and palms of victory and triumph. Beauty alone attracts the desires of all who gaze on it and recognize it, and princely eagles and high-soaring birds swoop down upon it as on a dainty lure. But if to this beauty are joined want and necessity, the crows, the kites and all the other birds of prey attack it as well, and the wife who remains constant against all such assaults well deserves to be called her husband's crown.

'Consider, my wise Basilio,' added Don Quixote; 'it was the opinion of I do not remember what sage that there has been only one good woman in the whole world, and he advised everyone to think and believe that his wife was she; for thus would he live content. I am not married myself, nor till now have I had any thought of being so; but, nevertheless, I would be so bold as to give counsel to anyone who might ask me for it as to the way in which he should seek the woman to marry. First I should advise him to consider reputation more than wealth. For the good woman gets a good name not solely by being good, but by appearing so; and looseness and free behaviour in public damage a woman's honour more than secret sinning. If you bring a good woman home it will be easy to preserve her or even increase her in her goodness; but if you bring home a bad one, it will put you to some labour to mend her, for it is not very practicable to pass from one extreme to another. I do not say that it is impossible, but I regard it as difficult.'

Sancho listened to all this, and said to himself: 'When I speak of matters of pith and substance, this master of mine's in the habit of telling me that I ought to take a pulpit in hand and go about the world preaching pretty sermons. But, as for him, it's my opinion that once he begins to string sentences and give advice, it's not only one pulpit he should take in hand, but two on every finger, and go through the markets crying: "Who buys my wares?" The devil take him for a knight errant, so many things he knows. I was thinking to myself that he only knew about these chivalries of his, but there isn't a subject he doesn't pick at and dip his spoon into.'

Sancho muttered this so loud that his master overheard him and asked: 'What are you grumbling at, Sancho?'

'I'm not speaking and I'm not grumbling,' answered Sancho. 'I was only saying to myself that I wish I'd heard what your worship has just said before I got married. Then perhaps I should be saying now that the loosed ox enjoys licking himself.'

'Is your Teresa so bad, Sancho?' asked Don Quixote.

'She's not very bad,' answered Sancho. 'But she's not very good; at least, she's not as good as I should like.'

'You do wrong, Sancho,' said Don Quixote, 'in speaking evil of your wife, for, after all, she is the mother of your children.'

'We owe one another nothing,' answered Sancho, 'for she slanders me when she fancies, especially when she's jealous. And then Satan himself wouldn't be able to bear with her.'

Three days they stayed with the newly married pair, and were regaled and treated like princes. Then Don Quixote asked the skilful licentiate to give him a guide to lead him to the cave of Montesinos, for he had a great desire to explore it and see with his own eyes whether the marvels related about it thereabouts were true. The licentiate suggested a cousin of his, a famous scholar much given to the reading of books of chivalry, who would gladly take him to the mouth of this cave and show him the Ruidera Lagoons, which

U

were also famous throughout La Mancha, or rather throughout the whole of Spain. He went on to say that Don Quixote would enjoy his cousin's company, as he was a lad who knew how to make books for the press and to dedicate them to princes.

By and by the cousin appeared riding an ass in foal, with a pack-saddle covered with a multi-coloured rug or sack-cloth. Sancho saddled Rocinante, bridled Dapple, and filled his saddle-bags, with which the cousin's kept company, being also well provided. Then, after commending themselves to God and bidding everyone fare-well, they set out on their way, taking the road to the famous cave of Montesinos. On the ride Don Quixote asked the cousin the nature or character of his pursuits, his profession and studies. To which he replied that by profession he was a humanist, and that his pursuits and studies were to compose books for the press, all of great profit and entertainment to the commonwealth. One, he said, was entitled *The Book of Liveries*, in which he described seven hundred and three devices with their colours, mottoes and ciphers. From these the gentlemen of the court could extract and use what-ever they pleased at festival times and celebrations, and would then have no need to beg their liveries from anybody, or to rack their brains, as they say, to invent them to suit their desires and purposes.

'For,' said he, 'I give suitable devices to the jealous, the scorned, the forgotten and the absent, and fit them out neat as a new pin. I have another book as well, which I mean to call *Metamorphoses, or the Spanish Ovid*, a new and rare invention. In it, parodying Ovid, I give an account of the Giralda of Seville and the Angel of the Magdalen, the Gutter of Vecinguerra at Cordova and the Bulls of Guisando; the Sierra Morena; the fountains of Leganitos and Lava-pies in Madrid, not omitting those of the Piojo, of the Golden Gutter, and the Priora; all this with such allegories, metaphors, and transformations as will delight, surprise and instruct at the same time. I have another book that I call the *Supplement to Polydore Virgil*, which treats of the invention of things. It is a work of great erudition and research, for I elucidate and set out in an elegant style matters of great importance omitted by Polydore. He forgot to tell us who was the first man in the world to have catarrh, and the first to use ointments to cure himself of the French pox; but all these points I set out with the utmost precision on the testimony of twenty-five authorities. So your worship can judge whether I have not worked well, and whether this book will not be useful to the whole world.'

Then Sancho, who had listened very attentively to the cousin's narrative, inquired of him: 'Tell me, sir – good luck to you with the printing of your books – but can you say – though I know you can, for you know everything – who was the first man to scratch his head? For it's my opinion that it must have been our father Adam.'

'Yes, of course,' replied their guide, 'for there is no doubt Adam had a head and hair; and that being so, and he being the first man in the world, he must sometimes have scratched himself.'

'Yes, so I thought,' answered Sancho; 'but tell me now, who was the first tumbler in the world?'

'Really, brother,' replied their guide, 'I cannot decide that now. I have not gone far enough in my studies. I will look it up when I get back to my books, and satisfy you when we meet again, for this must not be the last time.'

'Now, look you, sir,' answered Sancho. 'Don't put yourself to any trouble about it, for I've hit on the answer to my question. The first tumbler in the world was Lucifer; for when they threw him or flung him out of Heaven, he went tumbling down to the abyss.'

'You are right, my friend,' said their guide.

'That question and answer are not yours, Sancho,' said Don Quixote. 'You have heard them from somebody.'

'Hush, sir,' replied Sancho, 'for if I take to questioning and answering I shan't be done by to-morrow morning, I promise you. Indeed, if it's a matter of asking stupid questions and giving foolish answers I've no need to go looking for help from the neighbours.'

'You have said more than you know, Sancho,' said Don Quixote, 'for there are some who tire themselves out learning and proving things which, once learnt and proved, do not concern either the understanding or the memory a jot.'

That day they spent in such-like pleasant conversations, and at night they lodged in a little village which the scholar told Don Quixote was no more than six miles from Montesinos' cave. If, however, he was resolved to explore it, he would need to provide himself with ropes, by which he might let himself down into its depths. Don Quixote replied that he must see the bottom, even if it reached to the pit of hell. So they bought some hundred and fifty feet of rope, and the next day at two in the afternoon came to the cave, whose mouth is wide and spacious but choked with box-thorn and wild fig-trees, brambles and briars, so thick and intertwined that they entirely mask and cover it. When they found it, the scholar, Sancho and Don Quixote dismounted, and the first two presently tied the knight very firmly with the ropes. And whilst they were swathing and binding him, Sancho said: 'Consider what you are doing, your worship. Don't bury yourself alive, and don't put yourself where you will be like a bottle hung down a well to cool. Indeed, it's no concern of yours, sir, to explore this place. It's probably worse than a dungeon.'

'Bind me and be silent,' answered Don Quixote, 'for such an enterprise as this, Sancho my friend, was reserved for me.'

Then said their guide: 'I beseech your worship, Don Quixote, to be observant and to examine with the eyes of a lynx what lies below. Perhaps there may be things for me to put into my book of transformations.'

'The drum is in hands that knows well how to beat it,' observed Sancho Panza.

When this was said and Don Quixote's fastenings, which went about his doublet and not over his armour, secured, the knight exclaimed: 'We have been careless in not providing ourselves with a little bell to be tied beside me on this rope. For by my sounding it you might have known that I was still descending and still alive. But since that is not possible now, let it be in God's hands to guide me.'

Then he knelt down and said a prayer to Heaven in a low voice, begging God to aid him and give him good fortune in this seemingly novel and perilous adventure. After which he said aloud: 'O mistress of my actions and movements, most illustrious and peerless Dulcinea del Toboso! If it is possible for the prayers and requests of your venturesome lover to reach your ears, I implore you by your incomparable loveliness to listen to them, for their only purpose is to beg you not to deny me your favours and protection now that I have so much need of them. I am about to cast myself, to plunge and bury myself, in the abyss which opens here before me, solely that the world may know that with your favour there is nothing so impossible that I cannot undertake and accomplish it.'

As he said this he drew near to the chasm, and saw that it was not possible to let himself down or make a way to the entrance unless by force of arms or by cutting a way through. So he drew his sword and began to hack and slash at the briars growing at the mouth of the cave. At this frightful clatter a huge number of great crows and jackdaws flew out, so thick and fast that they swept Don Quixote to the ground; and, had he been superstitious, which as a good Catholic he was not, he would have taken them as a bad omen and given up the idea of immuring himself in such a place.

At length he stood up, and seeing no more crows come out, nor any other birds of night, such as bats, which had flown out with the crows, with Sancho and the scholar paying out the rope he let himself down to the bottom of the dreadful cave. And as he descended, Sancho threw him his blessing and made countless signs of the cross over him, saying:

'May God guide you, and the Rock of France, together with the Trinity of Gaeta, O flower, cream, and skimming of knights errant! There you go, braggart of the world, heart of steel, and arm of brass! Once more, God guide you and bring you back, safe, sound and unharmed to the light of this world which you have forsaken to bury yourself in that darkness you're seeking.'

The scholar offered almost the same prayers and entreaties, but Don Quixote went on calling out for rope and more rope, and they paid it out little by little. But when his shouts, which came up from the cave as through a funnel, were heard no more, they had already paid out the hundred and fifty foot and were thinking of hoisting Don Quixote up again, as they could give him no more. Nevertheless they waited for about half an hour, at the end of which they began to hoist the rope, which came easily and without any weight on it, which made them suppose that Don Quixote had stayed below. In this belief Sancho Panza began to weep bitterly and hauled away hurriedly, anxious to learn the truth. But when little more than thirty foot seemed to be left they felt a weight, of which they were extremely glad. Finally at fifteen foot they made Don Quixote out distinctly, and Sancho called to him: 'Welcome back to you, your worship, for we were thinking you had stayed there to found a family.'

But Don Quixote did not reply a word, and when they had drawn him completely out, they saw that his eyes were shut, as if in sleep. They laid him out on the ground and untied him; but for all that he did not wake. Then they turned him over and over, and stirred him and shook him so heartily that after some time he came to himself, stretching his limbs as if waking from a deep sleep. Then gazing in all directions, as if in alarm, he said:

'God pardon you, my friends, for you have robbed me of the sweetest existence and most delightful vision any human being ever enjoyed or beheld. Now, indeed, I positively know that the pleasures of this life pass like a shadow and a dream, and wither like the flowers of the field. Oh, unhappy Montesinos! O gravely wounded Durandarte! O luckless Belerma! O tearful Guadiana, and you, unfortunate daughter of Ruidera, who show by your waters what tears your fair eyes have wept!'

The scholar and Sancho listened most attentively to Don Quixote's words, which he uttered as if wrenching them with immense pain from his bowels. They begged him to explain what he meant, and to tell them what he had seen in that hell.

'Hell you call it?' said Don Quixote. 'Do not call it that. For it does not deserve that name, as you will presently see.'

He begged them for something to eat, for he was very hungry. Then they spread the scholar's saddle-cloth on the green grass and set about emptying the saddle-bags; and all three in love and good fellowship ate their lunch and their supper in one. Then, when the cloth was lifted, Don Quixote de la Mancha said: 'Let no one arise. Listen to me, my sons, all of you!'

Chapter XXIII. *Of the Amazing Things which the consummate Don Quixote related that he had seen in the deep Cave of Montesinos, whose Impossibility and Immensity has caused this Adventure to be considered Apocryphal.*

IT was about four in the afternoon when the sun, obscured by clouds, showed but a dim light, and with his tempered rays gave Don Quixote the opportunity to relate to his two illustrious auditors without heat and discomfort what he had seen in Monte-sinos' cave. He began as follows:

'About eighteen or twenty feet down in the depths of this dungeon, on the right-hand side, there is a concave space capable of containing a large cart with its mules. A little light comes into it from far off through some chinks or holes opening to the earth's surface. This concave space I saw the while I passed, weary and sad at finding myself hanging and dangling by the rope, journeying through that obscure nether region on no assured or charted road; and so I determined to go in there and rest a little. I called out to ask you not to let out any more rope till I bade you, but you could not have heard me. I gathered up the rope you had let down and, rolling it into a coil or pile, sat down on it, most thoughtfully considering how I could reach the bottom without anything to support me. In this perplexed meditation, suddenly and involuntarily I was overcome by a deep sleep, and when I least expected it, not knowing how or why, I woke up to find myself in the middle of the most beautiful, pleasant and delightful meadow nature could create or the liveliest human imagination conceive. I opened and rubbed my eyes, and saw that I was not asleep but really awake. For all that, I felt my head and my bosom to make certain whether it was my very self who was there, or some empty and counterfeit phantom; but touch, feeling and the coherent argument I held with myself assured me that I was there then just as I am here now. Soon there appeared before my eyes a royal and sumptuous palace or castle, whose walls and battlements appeared to be formed of clear transparent crystal; and when two great doors opened in them I saw coming out towards me a venerable old man, in a cloak of purple serge which trailed on the ground. Across his shoulders and breast he wore collegians' bands of green velvet. His head was covered by a black Milan cap, and his hoary beard reached to his waist. He carried no arms at all, but a rosary in his hands of beads larger than fair-sized walnuts, every tenth one the size of an ordinary ostrich egg. His bearing, his gait, his solemnity and his ample presence, each separately and all together, struck me with wonder and admiration. When he came up to me the first thing he did was to embrace me warmly. Then he said:

'"It is many centuries, valorous knight, Don Quixote de la

Mancha, that we who dwell in these enchanted solitudes have been waiting to see you, so that you may inform the world of what is contained here, buried in this deep cave you have entered, which is called Montesinos' cave: an exploit reserved to be attempted only by your invincible heart and your stupendous courage. Come with me, illustrious sir, for I would show you the marvels concealed in this transparent castle, of which I am the governor and perpetual chief warden; for I am Montesinos himself, from whom the cave takes its name."

'Scarcely had he said that he was Montesinos when I asked him whether it was true, as it was reported in the world up here, that he had cut the heart of his great friend Durandarte out of his breast with a little dagger, and carried it to the lady Belerma, as Durandarte had bidden him at the point of death. He replied that the whole story was true, except as regards the dagger, for it was neither a dagger nor small, but a thin stiletto sharper than an awl.'

'That stiletto,' put in Sancho, 'must have been made by Ramon de Hoces of Seville.'

'I do not know,' continued Don Quixote. 'But it could not be that stiletto-maker, because Ramon de Hoces was living yesterday, and the fight at Roncesvalles, where this tragedy occurred, was many years ago. But inquiry into that is of no importance, for it does not disturb or alter the truth and sequence of the history.'

'That is true,' said the scholar. 'Please continue, Don Quixote, for I am listening with all the pleasure in the world.'

'I take no less pleasure in telling my tale,' answered Don Quixote. 'So the venerable Montesinos, I say, brought me into the crystalline palace, where in a low hall of extreme coolness and all of alabaster stood a marble sepulchre made with great craftsmanship, on which I saw a knight lying at full length, wrought not in brass, nor marble, nor carved jasper, as is usual on other tombs, but of pure flesh and bone. He had his right hand – which seemed to me somewhat hairy and muscular, a sign of great strength in its owner – resting beside his heart; and before I could ask Montesinos any question, he saw me gaze with amazement at the figure on the sepulchre, and said:

'"This is my friend Durandarte, flower and mirror of all true lovers and valiant knights of his age. He is kept here enchanted, as

I am, and many more knights and ladies, by Merlin, the French wizard, who, they say, was the Devil's son. Though it is my belief that he was no Devil's son, but knew, as the saying is, one trick more than the Devil. How or why he enchanted us no one knows, but that will be told in the course of time, and before very long now, I imagine. What astonishes me is that I know, as surely as that it is now day, that Durandarte ended his life in my arms, and that after his death I cut out his heart with my own hands. In truth it must have weighed two pounds, and according to natural philosophers a man with a large heart is endowed with greater courage than one with a small. And yet despite my knowing that this knight really died, how is it that ever and anon now he complains and sighs as if he were alive?"

'At those words the wretched Durandarte cried out in a loud voice:

' "Oh, my cousin Montesinos!
It was the last thing I asked you,
That as soon as I was dead
And my spirit had departed,
You should bear my heart to where
Fair Belerma dwelt and waited,
Cutting it from out my chest
With a sword or with a dagger."

'When the venerable Montesinos heard this he threw himself on his knees before the afflicted knight and cried, with tears in his eyes: "Long ago, Sir Durandarte, my dearest cousin – long ago I did what you bade me on that bitter day of our defeat. I tore out your heart as best I could, and left not a fragment of it in your bosom. I wiped it with a lace handkerchief. I set out with it on the road to France, having first laid you in the bosom of the earth, with enough tears to wash my hands clean of the blood-stains they had got from groping in your entrails. And for further proof, beloved cousin, at the first place I came to after leaving Roncesvalles, I threw a little salt on your heart so that it should not smell bad, but should come, if not fresh, at least dry, into the presence of the lady Belerma, whom the sage Merlin has kept here many years enchanted with you and me, your squire Guadiana, Mistress Ruidera, her seven daughters and two nieces, and many others of your acquaintances and friends. Yet, though five hundred years have passed, not one of us has died; only Ruidera, her daughters and nieces are missing, whom out of the compassion he must have had for their tears, Merlin turned into as many lagoons, which are now known in the world of the living and in the province of La Mancha as the Lagoons of Ruidera. The seven belong to the Kings of Spain, and the two nieces to the knights of a most holy order, that of St. John. Guadiana, your squire, also bewailed your sad fate, and was converted into a river called by his name. But when he reached the earth's surface and saw the sun of another sky, so great was his grief at finding he had abandoned you that he plunged into the bowels of the earth. Yet as it is not possible for him to cease flowing in his natural course, from time to time he emerges and shows himself where the sun and mankind may see him. The lagoons I have spoken of minister their waters to him, and with these and many others he enters Portugal in pomp and grandeur. But, for all that, wherever he goes he shows his sorrow and melancholy, and takes no pride in breeding savoury and valuable fish in his waters, but unlike the golden Tagus bears only coarse and tasteless ones. And what I am telling you now, my dear cousin, I have told you many times; but as you do not reply, I imagine either that you do not believe me or do not hear me, which – God knows – pains me greatly. Now, however, I want to give you some news which may not serve to assuage your grief, but will in no way increase it. Learn that you have here in your presence – open your eyes and see him! – that great knight of whom the sage Merlin has prophesied so much, that Don Quixote de la Mancha, I tell you, who has revived and improved on the ancient art of chivalry, which is now forgotten. Through his mediation and favour, too, we ourselves may perhaps be disenchanted, for great deeds are reserved for great men."

'"And if that should not be," replied the afflicted Durandarte in a faint whisper; "if that should not be, cousin, I say: patience and shuffle the cards." And turning upon his side he resumed his customary silence and said not a word more.

'At this moment loud screams and cries were heard, accompanied by deep groans and anguished sobs. I turned my head and saw through the crystal walls a procession of most lovely maidens passing in two files through another hall, all dressed in mourning, with white turbans on their heads after the Turkish fashion. At the tail end of the files came a lady – as by her gravity she seemed – also dressed in black, with a white veil so ample and long that it kissed the ground. Her turban was twice as large as the greatest of the others. She was beetle-browed and somewhat flat-nosed, with a large mouth and red lips. Her teeth, which she sometimes bared, appeared to be few and not very well placed, although they were as white as peeled almonds. She bore in her hands a fine cloth, and in it, as far as could be made out, a heart of mummy flesh; so dry and shrivelled was it. Montesinos told me that all those in the procession were servants of Durandarte and Belerma enchanted there with their master and mistress, and that the last one, carrying in her hands the heart in its cloth, was the lady Belerma, who with her maidens formed that procession on four days in the week, and sang, or rather wept, dirges over his cousin's body and afflicted heart. If she appeared to me somewhat ugly, or not as beautiful as fame reported, he said the reason lay in the bad nights and worse days she spent under that spell, as could be seen from the great rings round her eyes and from her sickly complexion.

'"Do not suppose," he added, "that her sallowness and the rings round her eyes spring from the monthly disorders common to women, for it is many months, or even years, since these have even appeared at her gates. They arise from the grief in her heart for the object she perpetually holds in her hands, which ever renews and brings to her memory the misfortune of her ill-fated lover. For, were it not for this, scarcely would the great Dulcinea del Toboso, so celebrated in all these parts and even throughout the whole world, equal her in beauty, grace and spirit."

'"Not so fast, Sir Montesinos," said I then. "Tell your story properly, sir, for you will know that all comparisons are odious, and so there is no reason to compare anyone with anyone. The peerless Dulcinea is who she is, and the lady Doña Belerma is who she is, and was – and there let it rest."

'To which he replied: "Pardon me, Don Quixote; I confess that I was wrong, and spoke ill in saying that the lady Dulcinea del Toboso would hardly have equalled the lady Belerma. It has been enough for me to learn by certain inductions that your worship is her knight to make me bite my tongue rather than compare her to anything but Heaven itself."

'With this satisfaction which the great Montesinos gave me my heart was quieted from the shock I received at hearing my mistress compared with Belerma.'

'I'm amazed, though,' said Sancho, 'that your worship didn't spring on the old dodderer, and kick his bones to pulp, and pull out his beard till there wasn't a hair left.'

'No, Sancho my friend,' replied Don Quixote, 'it would not have been right in me to do that. For we are all obliged to respect the aged, even if they are not knights, but all the more so when they are such and under enchantment. I know well enough that I was not behind-hand with him in the long conversation which passed between us.'

'I do not know, Don Quixote,' observed the scholar at this point, 'how your worship could have seen so many things and heard and said so much in the short space of time you were down below.'

'How long was I down?' asked Don Quixote.

'A little more than an hour,' answered Sancho.

'That cannot be right,' said Don Quixote, 'for night fell there and morning rose, and three more nights and mornings; so that, by my reckoning, I must have stayed three days in those remote and secret regions.'

'My master should be speaking the truth,' said Sancho, 'for as everything that has happened to him is by way of enchantment, perhaps what seems to us an hour may seem three days and nights down there.'

'That will be right,' answered Don Quixote.

'And did your worship eat anything in all that time, sir?' asked the scholar.

'I did not break my fast with even a mouthful,' answered Don Quixote. 'I had not so much as a thought of hunger.'

'And the enchanted, do they eat?' asked the scholar.

'No, they do not,' answered Don Quixote, 'nor do they defecate, although it is believed that their nails grow, and their beards and hair.'

'And do the enchanted sleep by any chance, sir?' asked Sancho.

'No, certainly not,' answered Don Quixote, 'at least in those three days that I was with them none of them closed an eye, and neither did I.'

'Here's where the proverb fits,' said Sancho; 'tell me what company you keep and I will tell you who you are. Your worship goes about with the enchanted who watch and fast. It's no wonder, then, that you didn't eat or sleep whilst you were in their company. But pardon me if I say, your worship, that of all you have said, God help me – I was going to say the Devil – if I believe one word.'

'Why not?' asked the scholar. 'Would Don Quixote lie? Why, even if he had wanted to he had not time to compose and invent such a multitude of fictions.'

'I don't believe that my master's lying,' answered Sancho.

'Then what do you believe?' asked Don Quixote.

'I believe,' answered Sancho, 'that this Merlin or these enchanters, who bewitched that whole crowd your worship tells us you saw and talked with down below, crammed all that rigmarole you've told us into your head, and what remains to be told as well.'

'All that could be so,' replied Don Quixote, 'but it is not. For what I told you of I saw with my own eyes and touched with my own hands. But what will you say when I tell you now, that among the countless marvellous things that Montesinos showed me – which I shall proceed to tell you of at leisure and in due course during our journey, for they do not all belong here – were three peasant girls, leaping and frisking like she-goats in those pleasant fields, and no sooner did I see them than I realized that one of them was the peerless Dulcinea del Toboso, and the other two those same country girls who were with her when we met them on their way out of El Toboso? I asked Montesinos whether he knew them. He answered no, but that he thought they must be some enchanted ladies of quality, for they had only appeared in those fields a few days before. But I need not be surprised at that, for there were many other ladies of past and present times there, transformed into different strange shapes, and among them he had recognized Queen Guenevere and her attendant Quintañona, who poured out the wine for Lancelot *when from Britain first he came.*'

On hearing this Sancho thought he would go out of his wits or die of laughing. For knowing as he did the truth about Dulcinea's pretended enchantment, and that he had been her enchanter and the inventor of the story, he finally realized, beyond all doubt, that his master was out of his mind and mad on all counts. And so he said to him:

'At an evil time, in a worse season, and on a bitter day did your worship descend to the other world, dear master, and it was an unlucky moment when you met with Sir Montesinos, who has so changed you for us. You were all right up here with your wits whole, as God gave them to you, uttering judgements and offering counsel at every step, and not, as you now are, talking the greatest nonsense imaginable.'

'As I know you, Sancho,' said Don Quixote, 'I take no notice of your words.'

'Nor I of yours either,' answered Sancho, 'though you may beat me or kill me for what I've said, and for what I mean to say, if you don't correct and mend your own. But tell me, your worship, now that we're at peace, how or by what signs did you recognize the lady our mistress? And, if you spoke to her, what did she say and how did you reply?'

'I recognized her,' said Don Quixote, 'because she had on the same clothes as she was wearing when you pointed her out to me. I spoke to her, but she did not answer a word. On the contrary, she turned her back and ran away so fast that an arrow would not have caught her. I made to follow her, and would have done so if Montesinos had not advised me not to tire myself in that way, for it would be in vain; and, what was more, it was high time for me to return out of the cave. He also told me that in course of time he would advise me of a means of disenchanting him, and Belerma and Durandarte and everyone there. But what distressed me most of all I saw and noted was that just as Montesinos was speaking one of the luckless Dulcinea's two companions drew near to my side, without my seeing her come, and with her eyes full of tears said to me in low and troubled tones: "My lady Dulcinea del Toboso kisses your worship's hands and implores you to let her know how you are, and as she is in great want, she also begs your worship most earnestly to be so good as to lend her half a dozen *reals* on this new cotton skirt I have here, – or as many as your worship has about you. She promises to pay you back in a very short time."

'Such an errand surprised and amazed me, and I turned to Montesinos to ask him: "Is it possible, Sir Montesinos, for people of

quality when enchanted to be in want?" to which he replied: "Believe me, Don Quixote, what they call want is usual everywhere,
extends to all regions, reaches everyone, and does not even spare
the enchanted. So, as the lady Dulcinea del Toboso has sent to ask
you for these six *reals*, and the security is apparently good, there
is nothing for it but to give them to her, for no doubt she must be
in some difficulty."

'"A pledge I will not take," I replied, "nor can I give her what
she asks, for all I have got is four *reals*."

'Those I gave her. They were the ones you gave me, Sancho, the
other day to give in alms to any poor we might meet on the roads.
And I said to her:

'"Friend, tell your mistress that I am grieved in the spirit at her
troubles, and that I wish I were Fugger that I might relieve them.
Say that I would have her know that I neither can nor may have
health, lacking her pleasing company and her wise conversation,
and that I beg her with all possible earnestness to be so good as to
allow her captive servant and travel-weary knight to see and address
her. You will say to her also that, when least she expects it, she will
hear that I have made an oath and vow, like that which the Marquis
of Mantua made to avenge his nephew Baldwin when he found him
on the point of death in the midst of the mountains – which was to
eat no bread off table-cloths and sundry additional trifles till he had
obtained his revenge. So too shall I swear; not to rest, and to travel
the seven portions of the earth more diligently than did Don Pedro
of Portugal, until I have released her from her enchantment."

'"All that and more your worship owes my lady," replied the
maiden. And taking the four *reals*, instead of making me a curtsey,
she cut a caper, and leapt two yards, by measure, into the air.'

'Holy Father!' Sancho broke in at this point in a loud voice.
'Are such things possible in the world? Can there be enchanters and
enchantments so strong as to have changed my master's sound wits
into this raving madness? Oh, sir, sir, in God's name, look out for
yourself! Think of your good name, and don't believe in these
bubbles that have spoilt and crazed your wits!'

'It is because you love me, Sancho, that you talk like this,' said
Don Quixote, 'and as you are not experienced in the affairs of this
world, anything that has any difficulty about it seems to you im-

possible. But the time will come, as I have told you already, when I shall relate to you some of the things I saw down there; and they will make you believe what I have said, for their truth admits of no reply or controversy.'

Chapter XXIV. In which a Thousand Trifles are recounted, as nonsensical as they are necessary to the True Understanding of this great History.

THE translator of this great history from the original written by its first author, Cide Hamete Benengeli, says that when he reached the chapter relating the adventure of Montesinos' cave he found written in the margin in the hand of this same Hamete these words:

'I cannot persuade myself that all that is written in the previous chapter literally happened to the valorous Don Quixote. The reason is that all the adventures till now have been feasible and probable, but this one of the cave I can find no way of accepting as true, for it exceeds all reasonable bounds. But I cannot possibly suppose that Don Quixote, who was the most truthful gentleman and the noblest knight of his age, could be lying; for even if he were riddled with arrows he would not tell a lie. Besides, if I consider the minute and circumstantial details he entered into, it seems an even greater impossibility that he could have manufactured such a great mass of extravagance in so short a time. So if this adventure seems apocryphal, it is not I that am to blame, for I write it down without affirming its truth or falsehood. You, judicious reader, must judge for yourself, for I cannot and should not do more. One thing, however, is certain, that finally he retracted it on his death-bed and confessed that he had invented it, since it seemed to him to fit in with the adventures he had read of in his histories.' With that the author continued, saying:

The scholar was astonished alike at Sancho Panza's boldness and at his master's patience, and concluded that the placid disposition he then displayed arose from his pleasure at seeing his lady Dulcinea del Toboso, even though enchanted. For were it not the case, Sancho's speeches and arguments would have earned him a thrashing, since really, thought the scholar, he had been a little too saucy with his master, whom he thus addressed:

'Don Quixote de la Mancha, I reckon this day I have spent with you very well spent, for in it I have gained four things. First, my acquaintance with your worship, which is a great pleasure to me. Secondly, a solution of the secret of Montesinos' cave, of the metamorphoses of Guadiana, and of the lagoons of Ruidera, all of which will serve me for the *Spanish Ovid* I have in hand. Thirdly, to have discovered the antiquity of playing cards, which were in use as far back as the time of the Emperor Charlemagne, as can be deduced from the words you attribute to Durandarte, when, at the end of Montesinos' great speech, he woke up and said: "Patience and shuffle the cards." He cannot have learnt that expression or turn of phrase under a spell, but must have done so before he was enchanted, in France and in the time of the aforesaid emperor. Now this discovery comes just right for the other book I am compiling, which is the *Supplement to Polydore Virgil on the Inventions of Antiquity*, for I believe that he forgot to include the invention of cards, as I shall now do, for it is of great importance, particularly as I shall be able to quote so serious and truthful an informant as Sir Durandarte. Fourthly, to have learnt for certain the source of the river Guadiana, until now unknown to men.'

'You are right,' said Don Quixote, 'but I should like to know to whom you intend to dedicate them – supposing by God's favour you are granted a licence to print these books of yours, which I doubt.'

'There are lords and grandees in Spain to whom they might be dedicated,' replied the scholar.

'Not many,' replied Don Quixote. 'Not because they do not deserve the dedications, but because they do not like to accept them in case they may be under the obligation of making the authors the return to which they are entitled for their labour and courtesy. But I know a prince who can supply the defects of all the rest, with such advantages that if I made bold to mention them I should perhaps awaken the jealousy of more than one generous soul. But let the matter rest here until a more opportune time, and let us go and look for somewhere to lodge to-night.'

'Not far from here,' said their guide, 'is a hermitage where dwells a hermit, who is said to have been a soldier once, and has the reputation of being a good Christian, and very wise and charitable as well. Beside his hermitage he has a little house, which he has built at his own cost; but though it is small, it is big enough to receive guests.'

'Does this hermit happen to keep chickens?' asked Sancho.

'Few hermits are without them,' answered Don Quixote, 'for those you find to-day are not like the anchorites in the Egyptian deserts, who used to wear palm-leaves and eat the roots of the earth. It must not be supposed that because I speak well of the ancients it is at the expense of the hermits of to-day. I only mean to say that present-day penances do not equal the rigours and austerities of olden times; but they are all good, nevertheless. At least I consider them good; and, if the worst comes to the worst, the hypocrite who pretends to be good does less harm than the public sinner.'

Whilst they were talking they saw a man on foot overtaking them, walking fast and prodding with his stick a mule loaded with lances and halberds. On coming up he greeted them and passed. Don Quixote, however, called out: 'Stop, my good fellow! You seem to be going faster than your mule wants to.'

'I can't stop, sir,' replied the man, 'for these weapons you see me carrying are needed for to-morrow. So I'm compelled to press on. Good-bye. But if you want to know the reason why I'm carrying these things, I mean to put up to-night at the inn beyond the hermitage. If you're travelling the same way you'll find me there, and I'll tell you some wonders. So good-bye once more.'

And he prodded his mule on so fast that Don Quixote had no time to ask him what wonders he had to tell them. But as he was rather curious and always possessed by the desire to learn something new, he decided that they should press on that moment so as to spend the night at the inn, and not stop at the hermitage where the scholar wanted them to stay. So all three mounted and took the straight road to the inn, which they reached a little before nightfall. On the way the scholar suggested to Don Quixote that they should call at the hermitage to get a drop to drink; and when Sancho heard him he turned Dapple in that direction, Don Quixote and the scholar taking the same way. But, as Sancho's ill-luck would have it, the hermit was not at home, as they were told by an under-hermitess, whom they found in the hermitage. They asked for a drop of the real stuff, but she replied that her master did not keep it,

though if they would like water for nothing, she would give it them
with pleasure.

'If I had a water thirst,' replied Sancho, 'there are wells on the
road where I could have quenched it. O, Camacho's wedding and
the plenty at Don Diego's, how often I miss you!'

Now they left the hermitage and spurred towards the inn, and a
little farther on they fell in with a lad, who was strolling along in
front of them at so slow a pace that they overtook him. He was
carrying a sword on his shoulder and, slung on it, a bundle or pack-
age, apparently containing clothes, his breeches, cloak and shirt
probably, for he had on a short velvet jacket, in places rubbed shiny
as satin, and his shirt hung out. His stockings were silk and his shoes
square-toed after the court fashion. He must have been eighteen or
nineteen, and he had a merry face and an agile-looking body. As he
went along he sang scraps of songs to relieve the tediousness of the
road, and when they caught him up he had just ended one, which
the scholar got by heart, and which went:

> To the wars I am driven by lack of pence,
> If I had them, nothing would get me hence.

The first to speak to him was Don Quixote, who said: 'You
travel very light, Sir Gallant. Whither bound? Tell us, if you
please.'

To which the lad replied: 'Heat and poverty are my reasons of
my travelling so light, and it's the wars I am bound for.'

'How poverty?' asked Don Quixote. 'Heat is a likely enough
reason.'

'Sir,' replied the lad, 'in this bundle I have a pair of velvet
breeches, the fellows to this jacket. If I wear them out on the road,
I shan't be able to cut a dash in them in the city, and I've no money
to buy others. So, for that reason and to cool myself, I'm travelling
like this until I catch up with some companies of infantry, which are
less than forty miles from here. I shall enlist with them, and there'll
be no lack of baggage-wagons to travel on from there to the port of
embarkation, which is said to be Cartagena. For I'd rather have the
King for my lord and master and serve him in the wars than some
frayed fellow at Court.'

'Do you get an allowance by any chance?' asked the scholar.

'If I'd served a grandee of Spain or an important personage,' replied the lad, 'I should most certainly have one, for that is what comes of serving good masters. Their men generally rise from the servants' hall to be ensigns or captains, or to some other good appointment. But I, poor wretch, have always served adventurers and hangers-on whose pay and rations were so miserably short that they'd be half spent on starching one ruff. It'd be a miracle indeed for a page to an adventurer to get a stroke of luck.'

'But tell me honestly,' asked Don Quixote, 'is it possible that in all the years you served you were not even able to lay hands on a livery?'

'I've had two given me,' answered the page, 'but just as, if a man leaves a monastery without taking his vows they strip him of his habit and give him back his clothes, so my masters returned me mine. For when the business they came to Court for was done they returned home and took back the liveries, which they had only given out for show.'

'A notable *spilorceria*, as the Italians say,' remarked Don Quixote, 'but count yourself lucky, all the same, to be coming away from Court with so laudable an intention. For there is nothing on earth more honourable or more profitable than to serve God first, and then your king and natural lord, especially in the profession of Arms, which may not gain you more riches than Letters, but wins you more honour, as I have very often said. For though Letters may have been the foundation of more estates than Arms, still soldiers have an indefinable superiority over men of letters, and a certain splendour about them which puts them above everybody. Bear in mind what I am now going to say to you, for it will be of great profit and comfort to you in your hardships. It is that you should dismiss from your mind all thought of possible disasters, for the worst of them is death; and to die an honourable death is the best fortune of all. The brave Roman emperor, Julius Caesar, when asked which was the best death, replied the unexpected, the sudden and the unforeseen; and although this was the reply of a heathen, ignorant of the true God, yet considering human infirmity, he was right. For supposing you are killed in the first engagement or skirmish, or by a cannon shot or the springing of a mine, what does it matter? It is but death and there is an end. And, as Terence says, a soldier looks better slain in battle than alive and safe in flight, and the more obedient he is to his captains and commanders the higher does the good soldier rise in fame. Mark, my son, that gunpowder is a more pleasing smell to a soldier than civet; and if old age overtakes you in this honourable profession, though you may be full of wounds, crippled and lamed, at least it will not find you without honour, and honour such as poverty will not be able to diminish. What is more, it is now being enacted that old and crippled soldiers are to be maintained and relieved, for it is not right that they should be treated like blacks, whose masters release them and grant them their liberty when they are old and cannot work, and by casting them out of the house with the title of free men make them the slaves of hunger from whom they can only hope to be freed by death. I will say no more for the present. But get you up on the haunches of this steed of mine as far as the inn. There you will dine with me and continue your journey to-morrow. And may God speed you according to your merit.'

The page refused his invitation to ride behind, but he accepted the supper at the inn, and Sancho is said to have muttered to himself at this point: 'God bless you, what a master he is! Is it possible for a man who can say all the good things he's just said, to swear that he saw all the absurd impossibilities he has told us about Montesinos' cave? Well, well, we shall see!'

At this they reached the inn, just as night was falling; and it was no small pleasure to Sancho to find that his master took it for a real inn and not, as usual, for a castle. And no sooner had they gone in than Don Quixote asked the innkeeper for the man with the lances and halberds; and he replied that he was in the stable attending to his mule. The scholar and Sancho then looked to their asses, and Sancho gave Rocinante the best rack and the best stall in the stable.

Chapter XXV. *Of the adventure of the Braying and the Entertaining Meeting with the Puppet-Showman, together with the memorable Prediction of the Prophetic Ape.*

DON QUIXOTE stood upon thorns, as the saying is, to hear the wonders which had been promised him by the arms-carrier. So he went to the stable to look for him, and on finding him demanded

that he should immediately give them the promised answer to their
questions on the road.

'I can't tell you the tale of my wonders, standing up,' replied the
man, 'I must have leisure. Let me finish giving my beast his fodder,
good sir, and I'll tell you something that will astonish you.'

'Do not let that hinder you,' answered Don Quixote, 'for I will
help you.'

And so he did, sifting the barley and cleaning out the rack, a
humble service which induced the man the more willingly to tell
him what he wanted to hear. So, sitting down on a stone bench with
Don Quixote beside him, and with the scholar, the page, Sancho
Panza and the innkeeper for senate and audience, he began after
this fashion:

'Your worships must know that in a place about fourteen miles
from this inn it happened that an alderman lost an ass, through a
deceitful trick of a servant-maid of his – but that's a long story –
and although this alderman made every possible effort to find him,
he could not. A fortnight must have gone by, so the story goes,
since the ass was missed, when, as the unfortunate alderman was
standing in the market-place, another alderman of the same town
came up to him and said: "Reward me for my good news, friend.
Your ass has turned up."

'"That I will and gladly, friend," replied the other, "but tell me
where he's turned up."

'"I saw him this morning on the mountain," answered the finder,
"without a pack-saddle or gear of any kind, and so lean that he was
a pitiful sight. I wanted to catch him and bring him to you; but he
is so wild and shy now that when I got up to him he ran off into the
thickest part of the wood. We'll go back together to look for him,
if you like. Just let me take this she-ass home, and I'll come straight
back."

'"That will be doing me a great kindness," said the man who had
lost his ass. "I'll try to repay you in the same coin."

'Everybody who knows the truth of the matter tells the story
with these details, just as I'm telling it to you now. To be brief, the
two aldermen went off to the mountain on foot and hand in hand,
but when they got to the exact spot where they expected to see the
ass they couldn't see him, and they couldn't discover him anywhere

in those parts for all their searching. Seeing, then, that he was not to be found, the alderman who had seen him said to the other:

'"Look, my friend, I've just thought of a plan, by which we shall certainly discover the animal, even if he's hidden in the bowels of the earth, not to mention the mountain, and it's this: I can bray to perfection, and you can do a little in that line. Why, it's as good as done."

'"A little, you say, friend?" said the other. "Goodness me, I'll take odds of nobody, not even of the asses themselves."

'"Now we'll see," replied the second alderman, "for my plan is that you shall take one side of the mountain and I the other. We'll make a complete circuit of it, and every few yards you'll bray and I'll bray. The ass can't fail to hear us and answer us if he is on the mountain."

'"I think that's an excellent plan," replied the owner of the ass, "and worthy of your great mind."

'Then they separated, as agreed and, as chance would have it, both brayed almost at the same time. Now each of them was taken in by the other's bray, and ran to look, thinking that the ass had just turned up. But when they met, the owner of the lost beast said: "Is it possible, friend, that it wasn't my ass that brayed?"

'"It was only I," answered the other.

'"Then let me tell you, friend," said the owner of the beast, "that in the matter of braying there's nothing to choose between you and an ass; for I've never seen or heard anything more natural in my life."

'"Such praise and such compliments," replied the inventor of the plan, "apply more fittingly to you than to me, friend. For, by God my Maker, you can give odds of two brays to the best and most skilled brayer in the world. Your tone's loud, your time correct, your note well sustained and your cadences thick and fast. In fact I acknowledge myself beaten, hand you the palm and award you the colours for this rare accomplishment."

'"I declare," replied the owner, "that I shall think more highly of myself from now on, and reckon I know a thing or two, seeing that I have a talent; for though I thought that I could bray well, I never supposed that I did it as perfectly as you say."

'"Let me tell you, too," said the other, "that there are rare talents in this world wasted on the wrong men, who don't know how to make use of them."

'"Ours," replied the owner, "are not of much service to us except in such a case as we now have on our hands; but now, please God, they may come in useful."

'At which they separated once more and resumed their braying, but at every pace they made a fresh mistake and came back to one another, until finally they agreed on a counter-sign and uttered their brays two at a time, so that each might know that it was the other and not the ass. In this way, giving a double bray at every step, they made a complete circuit of the mountain without the lost ass replying by so much as a sign. But how could the poor ill-fated beast have replied? For they found him in the thickest part of the wood, eaten by wolves. And at the sight of him, his master exclaimed:

'"I was astonished myself that he did not reply. For, had he been alive, he would have brayed if he'd heard us, or he would have been no ass. But I'm well rewarded for my labours in looking for him, even though I found him dead, by hearing you bray so gracefully, friend."

'"We're a fine pair," replied the other, "for if the abbot sings well the little monk isn't far behind."

'With this they returned to their village, disconsolate and hoarse; and there they told their friends, their neighbours and acquaintances their adventures in search of the ass, each exaggerating the other's gift for braying; and the story leaked out and spread to the neighbouring villages. Now the Devil, who never sleeps, and loves to sow heart-burnings and discord broadcast, raising calumnies on the wind and grand chimaeras out of nothing, so ordered it that the people of the other villages, at the sight of anyone from ours, would immediately begin to bray as if to throw our alderman's notable accomplishment in our faces. When the boys took to it all the demons in hell seemed to have joined in the sport, for the braying went on spreading from one village to another, till now the natives of our braying village are as well known and as easily distinguished as Negroes from whites. And this unlucky jest has gone so far that very often the mocked have gone forth with arms in their hands and in regular formation to do battle with the mockers, and King or

Rook, fear nor shame, has been strong enough to prevent it. To-morrow or the next day, I believe, the people of my village, the brayers, are to take the field against another village about six miles from ours, one of our worst persecutors; and to be well prepared for them, I have bought the lances and halberds you saw. These are the marvels I promised to tell you, and if they don't seem wonderful to you, I know no others.'

With that the good fellow ended his tale, and just then there came through the outer door of the inn a man all dressed in chamois-leather, hose, breeches and doublet, crying in a loud voice: 'Master landlord, have you any room? For here come the fortune-telling ape and the puppet show, "The Releasing of Melisendra."'

'Good Heavens!' exclaimed the landlord. 'Here's Master Peter. We shall have a great night of it.'

(I forgot to say that this Master Peter had his left eye and almost half his cheek covered with a green silk patch, which showed that there was something wrong with all that side of his face.)

'Your worship is welcome, Master Peter,' the innkeeper went on to say. 'But where are the ape and the puppets? I don't see them.'

'They're not far off,' replied the man in chamois leather, 'but I came ahead to find out if there was room.'

'I would turn out the Duke of Alba himself to make room for Master Peter,' said the innkeeper. 'Bring the ape and the puppets, for there are people in the inn to-night who'll pay to see the show, and the ape's talents as well.'

'Very good,' answered the man with the patch. 'I'll reduce the price and be content with my bare expenses. And now I'll go back and bring in the cart with the ape and the show in it.'

Then Don Quixote enquired of the innkeeper who this Master Peter was, and what the show and the ape were he brought with him. And the landlord replied: 'He's a very famous puppet-player, and he's been travelling about this Aragonese side of La Mancha for some time, showing a play about the releasing of Melisendra by the renowned Sir Gaiferos. It is one of the finest and best acted shows we've seen in this part of the kingdom for many a year. He has an ape with him too, with the rarest talents an ape ever had or man imagined. If you ask him anything he listens to what you say and then jumps on to his master's shoulder and tells him the answer in his ear, and Master Peter repeats it at once. He says more about what's happened than about what's to come; and although he isn't always right in everything, in most cases he's not mistaken; which makes us believe he has the Devil inside him. He charges two *reals* a question, if the ape replies – I mean if his master replies for him, after he's whispered in his ear. So Master Peter's generally supposed to be extremely rich. He's a gallant man, as they say in Italy, and a boon companion, and he leads the grandest life in the world. He talks more than six men and drinks more than twelve, all at the expense of his tongue, his ape and his puppet show.'

At this moment Master Peter came back, and in the cart came the show and the ape, which was big and tailless with buttocks like felt, but not ugly in the face. As soon as Don Quixote saw him, he asked: 'Tell me, you, Master Fortune-teller, what fish do we catch? And what is to become of us? See, here are my two *reals*.'

And he bade Sancho give them to Master Peter, who replied for the ape: 'Sir, this animal doesn't answer or give information about things to come. About the past he knows something, and about the present a little.'

'I swear I wouldn't give a farthing to be told what's happened to me in the past,' cried Sancho. 'For who could know it better than I do myself? And for me to pay to be told what I know already would be mighty foolish. But seeing that he knows the present, here's my two *reals*. Tell me, excellent ape, what my wife Teresa Panza is now doing, and how she's amusing herself.'

Master Peter refused to take the money, saying: 'I don't want to receive payment till the service has been rendered.'

Then he slapped his left shoulder twice with his right hand, and with one spring the ape jumped up. Next, putting his mouth to his master's ear, he gnashed his teeth very rapidly together, and after keeping up this chattering for the length of a *Credo*, jumped with another spring to the ground. And then without a moment's delay Master Peter hastily threw himself on his knees in front of Don Quixote and embraced his legs, exclaiming:

'I embrace these legs as I would embrace the twin pillars of Hercules, O illustrious reviver of the now-forgotten order of knight errantry! O never sufficiently praised Don Quixote de la Mancha, raiser of the faint-hearted, prop of those about to fall, arm of the fallen, staff and consolation of all the unfortunate!'

Don Quixote was astounded; Sancho bewildered; the scholar amazed; the page astonished; the bray-townsman foxed, and the landlord perplexed. In short, all his hearers were dumbfounded at the words of the puppet-showman, who continued:

'And you, good Sancho Panza, the best squire of the best knight in the world, be of good cheer, for your good wife Teresa is well, and at this very hour she's combing a pound of flax, and to prove what I say, on her left she has a broken-mouthed pot, which holds a good drop of wine to cheer her at her work.'

'I can well believe that,' replied Sancho, 'for she's a blessing and, if she weren't jealous, I wouldn't swap her for the giantess Andandona, who was a very excellent and worthy woman according to my master. My Teresa is of the sort who don't go short of anything, even if their heirs have to pay for it.'

'Now I declare,' exclaimed Don Quixote at this point, 'that he who reads much and travels much, sees much and learns much. What amount of persuasion it would have taken to convince me that there are apes in the world with the power to divine, as I have just seen with my own eyes there are. For I am the same Don Quixote de la Mancha that this good animal has spoken of, though he has been somewhat too liberal in my praise. But whatever I may be, I thank Heaven for endowing me with a mild and compassionate nature, always inclined to do good to all and ill to none.'

'If I had money,' said the page, 'I would ask Master Ape what will happen to me on the journey I am taking.'

To which Master Peter, who had got up from Don Quixote's feet, replied: 'I've already said that this little beast doesn't foretell the future. But if he could, your not having money wouldn't matter, for to serve Don Quixote, who is here present, I would forego all the profit in the world. And now, because I am in his debt, and to give him pleasure, I will set up my puppet-show and give everyone in the inn a performance free of charge.'

The innkeeper was immeasurably delighted at this offer, and pointed out a place for him to set up his show, which he did in a moment. Now Don Quixote was not very satisfied with the ape's prophesyings, for he did not think it right for an ape to divine either future or past events. So, whilst Master Peter was arranging his puppets, he took Sancho aside into a corner of the stable, out of the hearing of the company, and said to him:

'Listen, Sancho. I have thoroughly pondered that ape's extraordinary talents and, as I see it, there is no doubt that this Master Peter, his master, must have made a pact, implicit or explicit, with the Demon.'

'If the pack's explosive and with the Demon,' said Sancho, 'it'll certainly be a very dirty pack. But what's the use of the packs to this Master Peter?'

'You do not understand me, Sancho. I only mean to say that he must have made some bargain with the Devil, who has infused this talent into the ape so that he can gain his living by it; and when he is rich, he will give him his soul; for that is what the universal enemy is after. This I conclude from the fact that the ape only answers questions concerning things past or present, for the Devil's knowledge extends no further; he only knows the future by guesswork, and not always then. For to know the times and the seasons is reserved to God alone; for Him there is no past or future, for all is present. And that being so, as it is, it is clear that this ape speaks in the style of the Devil, and I am astonished that he has not been denounced to the Holy Office, and examined, and had it squeezed out of him by whose virtue he divines. For it is certain that this ape is no astrologer, and neither he nor his master casts, or knows how to cast horoscopes, though they are so fashionable in Spain nowadays that there is not a servant-maid or a page or an old cobbler who does not presume to cast a nativity as easily as pick up a knave of cards from the floor, perverting the amazing truth of the science with their ignorant lying. I know of a lady who asked one of these horoscope-casters whether a little lap-dog bitch she had would fall with pup and bear, and how many pups she would have and of what colour. To which Master Astrologer replied, when he had cast the figure, that the bitch would fall and bear three puppies, one green, one scarlet and one speckled, always providing that she were covered between eleven and twelve o'clock of the day or night, either on a Monday or a Saturday. And what happened was that two days later the bitch died of over-eating, and Master Astrologer gained the reputation in the town of being a very accurate caster of a horoscope, a reputation which they mostly have.'

'All the same,' said Sancho, 'I wish, sir, that you'd ask Master Peter to ask his ape whether it's true what happened to you in Montesinos' cave. For it's my opinion, begging your worship's pardon, that it was all fraud and fictions, or at least that you dreamt it.'

'Everything is possible,' answered Don Quixote. 'I will do as you advise, though I have certain scruples about it.'

Here Master Peter came to look for Don Quixote, and telling him that his puppet-show was now up, begged him to come and see it, for it was worth seeing. Don Quixote informed him of what was in his mind, and begged him first to ask his ape to say whether certain happenings in Montesinos' cave were imaginary or real; for to him they seemed to partake of both.

So without a word Master Peter went to fetch his ape and put him before Don Quixote and Sancho, saying: 'Look you, Master Ape, this gentleman wants to know if certain things which happened in a cave called Montesinos' were false or true.'

Then, at the customary sign, the ape leapt on to his left shoulder and apparently spoke in his ear. Whereupon Master Peter immediately answered: 'The ape says that part of what your worship saw or experienced in the said cave is false and part true, and that's all he knows about this question. But if your worship wants to learn more he'll reply to any inquiries made of him on Friday next. For his virtue is now exhausted, and won't return to him till Friday, as he has said.'

'There now,' exclaimed Sancho, 'Didn't I say you'd never make me believe all you told us about the happenings in that cave, or even a half of it?'

'Events will show, Sancho,' answered Don Quixote; 'for time, which reveals all things, leaves nothing that it does not drag into the light of day, even things hidden in the bosom of the earth. But let this suffice for now, and let us go and see good Master Peter's show, for I think there will be some novelty in it.'

'How "some"?' demanded Master Peter. 'This show of mine contains sixty thousand novelties. I tell your worship, Don Quixote, that it's one of the rarest spectacles in the whole world. But deeds, not words! Let's set to work, for time's drawing on, and we have a great deal to do, to say and to show.'

Don Quixote and Sancho complied and went to the show, which was now set up and uncovered; and they found it looking gay and resplendent, being lit all round by a multitude of wax tapers. On their arrival Master Peter got inside, as it was he who had to work the puppets in the play; and outside stood a boy, Master Peter's servant, to serve as interpreter and announcer of the mysteries of the show, holding in his hand a wand with which he pointed out the figures as they appeared.

When everyone in the inn was in his place, some standing in front of the show, and Don Quixote, Sancho, the page and the scholar in the best positions, the interpreter began to announce what the hearer or the reader of the following chapter will hear or see.

Chapter XXVI. A continuation of the Delightful Adventure of the Puppet-Showman, and other matters sufficiently entertaining.

HERE Tyrians and Trojans, all were silent: that is, all the spectators of the show were hanging on the lips of the interpreter of its wonders, when they heard a number of kettle-drums and trumpets strike up inside the puppet theatre, and a sudden volley of artillery, whose noise as suddenly ceased. Then the boy lifted his voice and announced:

'This true story, here presented to your worships, is taken word for word from the French chronicles and the Spanish ballads, which are in everyone's mouth and sung by the boys about the streets. It treats of the lord Sir Gaiferos' freeing of his wife Melisendra, who was a prisoner in Spain, in the hands of the Moors, in the city of Sansueña, now known under the name of Saragossa. And there you may see Sir Gaiferos playing at backgammon according to the song:

> Gaiferos is playing at the tables,
> and now his Melisendra is forgotten.

And that personage, who appears there with a crown on his head and a sceptre in his hand, is the Emperor Charlemagne, reputed father of the said Melisendra, who is vexed at his son-in-law's idleness and negligence, and comes out to scold him. Notice the vehemence and earnestness with which he rates him. It looks as if he has a mind to deal him a knock or two with his sceptre; and there are even authors who say he did so – good and hard. Then after a long speech in which he said that Sir Gaiferos was imperilling his honour by not rescuing his wife, the emperor went on – so the story goes: "Look to it now, sir: I have said enough." And see, the Emperor, sirs, turn his back and leave Sir Gaiferos in a rage. Now you see him, impatient with anger, flinging away the board and the pieces, calling in haste for his armour and begging his cousin Sir Roland for the loan of his sword Durindana. Sir Roland, however, will not lend it to him, but offers him his company in the difficult enterprise he is undertaking. This the angry warrior refuses, saying that he is capable of rescuing his wife alone, even though she were imprisoned in the deepest bowels of the earth. At that he departs to put on his armour, so that he can set out on his journey immediately. Now turn your eyes, sirs, to that tower yonder, which is supposed to be one of the towers of the castle of Saragossa, now called the Aljaferia. The lady appearing on that balcony dressed in the Moorish fashion is the peerless Melisendra, who has often stood gazing from there down the road to France, solacing herself in her captivity by thinking of Paris and her husband. Now behold a new incident, the like of which you have probably never seen before. Do you observe that Moor stealing up on tiptoe, with his finger to his lips, behind Melisendra's back? Now see him give her a kiss full on the mouth, and see her spit and wipe it from her lips with the white sleeve of her smock. See how she wails and tears her lovely hair in grief, as if she were to blame for his crime. Observe, too, that grave Moor standing in the gallery. He is King Marsilio of Sansueña. Now, when he saw this Moor's insolence, although the man was a relative of his and a great favourite, he had him taken and given two hundred lashes. And here he is led through the chief streets of the city with criers before and officers of justice behind. See, here they come to execute his sentence, almost immediately after his crime, for among the Moors there are no indictments or remands, as there are with us.'

'Boy, boy,' interrupted Don Quixote in a loud voice, 'go straight ahead with your story, and do not go curving off at a tangent; for it requires much proof and corroboration to bring a truth to the light.'

'Boy,' cried Master Peter also, from within, 'don't go in for flourishes, but do what this gentleman says. That'll be best. Go on with your plain-song, and don't stray off into counterpoint, for that's the way the strings get broken.'

'Very good, sir,' answered the boy, and resumed his story. 'This figure here on horseback in a Gascony cloak is this same Sir Gaiferos. And there is his wife, now avenged for the amorous Moor's insolence, better and calmer in demeanour, standing on the battlements of the tower and talking to her husband, whom she takes for a traveller. The words of the conversation that passed between them are given in the ballad:

> Sir knight, if it is to France you are going,
> Ask for Gaiferos when you are there.

'But I will not repeat it now, for prolixity often breeds boredom. Enough to see Sir Gaiferos reveal himself, and Melisendra's joyful looks as she recognizes him. Now we see her let herself down from the balcony to get up on to the crupper of her good husband's horse. But, unlucky lady, see, she is caught by the lace of her skirt on one of the balcony spikes, and is hanging in the air, unable to reach the ground. But see how merciful Heaven sends aid in her sorest need, for Sir Gaiferos comes up and, never pausing to see whether her fine skirt is torn or not, grasps her and brings her forcibly to the ground. Then, in one leap, he sets her on the crupper of his horse, astride like a man. Bidding her hold on tight, he puts her arms over his shoulders and crosses them over his chest, so that she shall not fall; for the lady Melisendra was not used to this manner of riding. Hear too how the horse neighs with delight at the brave and lovely burden he is bearing, his own lord and lady. See how they turn round and leave the city, and happily and joyfully take the road to Paris. Go in peace, O peerless pair of true lovers! May you safely reach the land of your desires, and may Fortune not impede your happy journey! May your friends and relations see you enjoying the remainder of your life in calmness and peace, and may your days be as many as Nestor's!'

Here Master Peter raised his voice once more and cried: 'Plainness, boy! Don't soar so high, for all affectation's bad.'

The announcer made no reply, but went on: 'There was no lack of idle spectators, who pry into everything. They observed Melisendra's descent and her mounting on horseback. They informed King Marsilio, and he ordered the alarm to be sounded immediately. See how quickly it is done. Now the city is drowned in peals of bells ringing from all the towers of the mosques.'

'That is not right,' interrupted Don Quixote. 'In this matter of the bells Master Peter is much mistaken, for they do not use bells among the Moors, but kettle-drums and a kind of trumpet like our clarion; and this about ringing the bells in Sansueña is most certainly complete nonsense.'

When he heard this Master Peter stopped ringing and said: 'Don't worry about trifles, Don Quixote, or expect perfection, for you never find it. Don't they perform countless comedies in these parts almost every day, full of innumerable improbabilities and absurdities? But, for all that, they have a successful run and are greeted, not only with applause but with admiration and all. Go on, boy, and let them speak, for so long as I fill my bag they can act as many improbabilities as there are motes in the sun.'

'That is right,' replied Don Quixote. And the boy went on. 'See what a numerous and resplendent cavalcade rides out of the city in pursuit of the pair of Christian lovers! How many trumpets sound, how many clarions blow, how many drums and kettle-drums beat! I am afraid they will catch them and bring them back tied to their own horse's tail. That would be a dreadful spectacle.'

Now seeing this pack of Moors and hearing such an alarm, Don Quixote thought it only right to help the fugitives. So, rising to his feet, he cried aloud:

'Never while I live shall I permit an outrage to be done in my presence on so famous a knight and so bold a lover as Sir Gaiferos! Stop, low-born rabble! Neither follow nor molest him, or you must do battle with me.'

Matching his actions to his words, he unsheathed his sword, and at a single bound planted himself in front of the show. Then with swift and unparalleled fury he began to rain blows upon the puppet-heathenry, knocking down some, beheading others, maim-

x

ing one, and destroying another; and, among other thrusts, he delivered one down-stroke that would have sliced off Master Peter's head as easily as if it had been made of marzipan, had he not ducked and crouched and made himself small.

'Stop, your worship!' he kept shouting. 'Reflect, Don Quixote, that these are not real Moors you're upsetting, demolishing and murdering, but only little pasteboard figures! Look out, you're destroying me, poor sinner that I am, and ruining my whole livelihood!'

But this did not make Don Quixote stop raining down his cuts, his two-handed blows, his forestrokes and his backstrokes. In fact, in less time than it takes to say a couple of *Credos* he had brought the whole show to the ground, and hacked all its fittings and puppets to bits. King Marsilio was gravely wounded, and Charlemagne had his crown and his head cut in two. The crowd of spectators were in an uproar; the ape fled up to the inn roof; the student was frightened; the page in a panic; and even Sancho Panza himself in a terrible alarm. For, as he affirmed after the storm had passed, he had never before seen his master in so outrageous a temper. But when the general destruction of the show was complete, Don Quixote grew rather calmer and said:

'I should like to have before me at this moment all who do not believe, and do not wish to believe that knights errant are useful in the world. Consider what would have happened to the good Sir Gaiferos and the fair Melisendra, if I had not been present here. Assuredly by this hour those dogs would have caught them and wrought them some outrage. When all is done, long live knight errantry, before everything else in the world to-day!'

'A long life and welcome,' put in Master Peter in a weak voice; 'and let me die, for I am so unfortunate that I can say with King Roderick:

> Yesterday I was Lord of Spain,
> But to-day I have not a tower
> That I can say is mine!

Not half an hour ago, indeed not half a minute ago, I was the master of Kings and Emperors. My stables, my coffers and my bags were full of countless horses and fine dresses without number, and now I am desolate and abject, a poor beggar and, worst of all, I've lost my ape, for before I have him in my possession again I shall have to sweat blood for it, I swear. And all because of the inconsiderate fury of this Sir Knight, who is said to protect wards and redress wrongs and perform other works of charity. It's only in my case his generous purpose has come to grief. God bless my soul! He's rightly called the Knight of the Sorrowful Countenance, for he's discountenanced my puppets.'

Sancho Panza was moved by Master Peter's complaint, and said to him: 'Don't weep, Master Peter. Don't moan, or you'll break my heart. I assure you that my master Don Quixote's a good scrupulous Christian and a Catholic, and if he reckons he's done you any wrong he'll admit it and gladly pay you. He'll satisfy you too, and more so.'

'Provided Don Quixote will pay me some part of the damage he has done me I shall be satisfied, and his worship will be quiet in his conscience. For there's no salvation for a man who holds another's property against its owner's will, and does not restore it.'

'That is so,' said Don Quixote, 'but so far I am not aware that I have anything of yours, Master Peter.'

'What?' answered Master Peter. 'Look at these relics lying on this hard and barren ground. How were they scattered and annihilated but by the invincible strength of that powerful arm? And whose were their bodies but mine? And how did I support myself if not by them?'

'Now I am finally convinced,' said Don Quixote at this, 'of what I have very often believed: that these enchanters who persecute me are always placing before my eyes shapes like these, and then changing and transforming them to look like whatever they please. I assure you gentlemen that all that has passed here seemed to me a real occurrence. Melisendra was Melisendra; Sir Gaiferos, Sir Gaiferos; Marsilio, Marsilio; and Charlemagne, Charlemagne. Therefore I was stirred to anger and, to comply with my profession of knight errant, I sought to give aid and protection to the fugitives, with which proper intention I did what you have seen. If things have turned out contrariwise the fault is not mine, but lies with my wicked persecutors. But all the same, I am willing to mulct myself the costs of this error, although it did not arise from malice. Let

Master Peter consider what he wants for the puppets destroyed, and I will pay him for them now in good and current Castilian coin.'

Master Peter bowed and replied: 'I expected no less from the unparalleled Christian spirit of the valorous Don Quixote de la Mancha, true succourer and protector of all needy and distressed vagabonds. Master Landlord here and the great Sancho shall be arbiters and assessors between your worship and myself, as to the probable value of the damaged figures.'

The landlord and Sancho consented to act, and Master Peter then picked up off the ground King Marsilio of Saragossa, less his head, and said: 'Now you can see how impossible it is to restore this king to his former state; and so, to my mind, and subject to your better judgment, I should receive four and a half *reals* for his death, end and extinction.'

'Go on,' said Don Quixote.

'Now for this gash from top to bottom,' Master Peter went on, picking up the cleft Emperor Charlemagne, 'it wouldn't be much if I asked five *reals* and a quarter.'

'That is no small amount,' said Sancho.

'And no great one,' replied the landlord. 'Let's split the difference and say five *reals*.'

'Give him the whole five and a quarter,' said Don Quixote, 'for in such a notable mischance as this we will not stand out for a quarter more or less. But let Master Peter finish quickly, for it's nearly supper time, and I feel certain twinges of hunger.'

'For this figure,' said Master Peter, 'which has lost its nose and one eye and is the fair Melisendra, I want – and I'll be moderate – two *reals* and twelve *maravedis*.'

'Well, the devil is in it,' said Don Quixote, 'if Melisendra and her husband are not over the French border, at least, by now. For the horse they were on seemed to me to fly rather than gallop. So you cannot sell me a cat for a hare by confronting me with a noseless Melisendra when, if all goes well, she is now with her husband in France, taking her pleasure for all she is worth. God help every man to his own, Master Peter. Let us have plain dealing and honest intentions. Now proceed.'

Master Peter saw that Don Quixote was rambling back to his old theme. So, not wanting to let him get away with it, he said: 'It cannot be Melisendra, then, but one of her serving-maids. So if I have sixty *maravedis* for her I shall be well paid and content.'

In this way he went on putting prices on the many other puppets destroyed, and afterwards the two assessors adjusted them to the satisfaction of both parties. The total amounted to forty *reals* and three-quarters; and over and above this sum, which Sancho paid over at once, Master Peter asked two *reals* for the trouble of catching his ape.

'Give them to him, Sancho,' said Don Quixote, 'not to catch his ape but to get a "skinfull". And I would give two hundred more as a gift to anyone who could tell me for certain that the lady Melisendra and her lord Sir Gaiferos were now in France and among their own people.'

'No one could tell us that better than my ape,' said Master Peter, 'but there's no devil could catch him now; though I imagine that affection and hunger will force him to look for me to-night. God will send the morrow and we shall see.'

Finally the storm over the puppet-show died down, and they all supped in peace and amity at the expense of Don Quixote, who was liberal in the extreme.

Before dawn broke the man with the lances and halberds was off, and shortly after daybreak the student and the page came to bid Don Quixote farewell, the one to return home and the other to continue on his way, to help him on which Don Quixote gave him a dozen *reals*. Master Peter did not care to get involved in any more arguments with Don Quixote, for he knew him too well, and so he got up before the sun and, taking up the remains of his show and his ape, also went off to seek adventures. The innkeeper, who did not know Don Quixote, was amazed at his liberality and at his madness, when, last of all, Sancho paid him very well on his master's orders. Then, taking their leave of him, they left the inn at almost eight in the morning and got on their road, where we will leave them, for this is a fitting opportunity for relating other matters pertinent to the telling of this famous history.

*Chapter XXVII. In which we are told who Master Peter and his
Ape were, with Don Quixote's ill-success in the Braying adventure, which did not terminate as he wished or expected.*

CIDE HAMETE, the chronicler of this great history, introduces the
present chapter with these words: '*I swear as a Catholic Christian,*'
on which his translator observes that Cide Hamete's swearing as a
Catholic Christian, he being a Moor, as he doubtless was, meant
only that as a Catholic Christian, when he swears, swears, or should
swear the truth, and observe it in all he says, so he would tell the
truth, as if he had sworn like a Christian Catholic, in writing of Don
Quixote; especially in his statement regarding who Master Peter was,
and about his ape that amazed the whole countryside with its prophesyings. He remarks then that any reader of the first part of this
history will clearly remember Gines de Pasamonte, whom Don
Quixote set free with the other galley-slaves in the Sierra Morena –
a benefit for which he was later ill requited by that malignant and unmannerly crew. That Gines de Pasamonte, whom Don Quixote
called Ginesillo de Parapilla, was the man who stole Dapple from
Sancho Panza; though the time and the manner of the theft having
been omitted from the First Part of this history through the neglect
of the printers, many have attributed the omission to the author's
faulty memory. But, to be brief, Gines stole the ass while Sancho
Panza was asleep on its back, using the cunning method Brunelo
practised when he got Sacripante's steed from between his legs at
the siege of Albraca. And how Sancho recovered his beast has already been related. This Gines, then, was afraid of being discovered
by the officers of the law, who were seeking after him to punish him
for his villainies and crimes, which were so numerous and so hein-
ous that his own account of them filled a large volume. So he decided to cross into the kingdom of Aragon and, putting a patch over
his left eye, took up the trade of puppet-showman, for at this and
at sleight-of-hand he was extremely adept. Later he bought the ape
from some released Christian who had come over from Barbary,
and taught it to jump on to his shoulder at a certain signal, and
whisper, or appear to whisper, in his ear. Thus prepared, before going into a village with his beast and his puppet-show he would collect information in the next place, or from anyone he could, about

local events and the people concerned in them. This he would commit to memory. Then the first thing he would do was to show his
puppet play, sometimes playing one story, sometimes another, but
all gay, amusing and familiar. Then, once the performance was
over, he would announce the ape's accomplishments, telling the
villagers that he could divine all the past and the present, but that
he had no skill in things to come. For an answer to each question he
asked two *reals*, though for some he made it cheaper, according as he
felt the pulse of his questioners. Sometimes he would put up at the
houses of people whose stories he knew, and if he found them unwilling to pay him the price of a question he would merely sign to
his ape, and then say that the beast had told him such and such,
giving an exact account of actual happenings. In this way he gained
an incredible reputation, and everyone followed him. At other
times he was shrewd enough to shape his answers to fit the questions;
and as no one examined him or pressed him to say how his ape did
his divining, he made apes of them all and filled his money bags.
Thus, as soon as he came into the inn he knew Don Quixote and
Sancho, and this made it easy for him to astonish the knight, the
squire and everyone in the place. But it would have cost him dear if
Don Quixote's hand had descended a little lower when he cut off
King Marsilio's head and destroyed all his chivalry, as has been re-
lated in the previous chapter. This is the whole story of Master
Peter and his ape.

But to return to Don Quixote de la Mancha – after he had left the
inn he decided first to view the banks of the river Ebro and all that
district, and then to go on to the city of Saragossa, for there was
enough time for all this before the jousts. With this intention he
pursued his journey and travelled for two days without meeting
with anything worthy of recording. Then on the third day, as he
was mounting a slope, he heard a great din of drums, trumpets and
musketry. At first he thought that a regiment of soldiers was passing
that way, and spurred Rocinante up the hill to get a sight of them.
But when he reached the top he saw below him more than two hundred men, by his reckoning, armed with different sorts of weapons,
such as spears, crossbows, partisans, halberds and pikes, as well as
some muskets and plenty of shields. Then he came down the hillside, and drew so near to the band that he distinctly saw their

banners, distinguished their colours, and made out the devices they bore. One of them in particular, on a standard or pennon of white satin, was a life-like painting of an ass of the little Sardinian breed, with its head up, its mouth open, and its tongue out, in the very act and posture of braying, and round it were written in large letters these two lines:

> They did not bray in vain,
> Our worthy bailiffs twain.

From this device Don Quixote concluded that these must be the people of the braying village, and so he said to Sancho, reading out to him what was written on the standard. He also remarked that the man who had given them an account of the affair had been mistaken in saying that it had been two aldermen who had brayed, because according to the verses on the standard they were bailiffs. To which Sancho Panza replied:

'There's nothing in that, sir. It's perfectly possible that the aldermen who brayed have come in course of time to be bailiffs of their village, and so they can be called by either title. What's more, it doesn't affect the truth of the story whether the brayers were bailiffs or aldermen, since they brayed anyway; for a bailiff's as good a brayer as an alderman.'

In short, they realized that the mocked village was coming out to fight with another, which had mocked it more than was reasonable or neighbourly. Don Quixote rode up to them, to Sancho's no small annoyance; for he was never fond of finding himself mixed up in these affairs. The men in the squadron received him in their midst, thinking that he was one of their party. Don Quixote then raised his vizor with a graceful air and deportment, and went up to the ass-standard, where all the chiefs of their army gathered round to look at him, being struck with the same astonishment that the first sight of him usually excited. And seeing them gaze at him so intently, without anyone speaking or asking him a question, our knight tried to make use of the silence and, breaking his own, raised his voice to say:

'My good sirs, I beg you in all earnestness not to interrupt a speech which I wish to make you, until you find it either annoying or wearisome. But if this happens, at your slightest signal, I will put a seal on my mouth and a gag on my tongue.'

They all bade him say what he would, for they would most gladly listen to him. Then, with their permission, Don Quixote continued:

'I, my dear sirs, am a knight errant, whose exercise is arms and whose profession it is to succour those who need succour and to relieve the distressed. Some days ago I learnt of your misfortune, and the reason which moves you so often to take up arms in order to avenge yourselves on your enemies; and having pondered your affairs in my mind not once but many times, I find that, according to the law of duelling, you are mistaken in regarding yourselves as insulted, for no individual can insult a whole village, except by charging it collectively with treason, not knowing who in particular committed the treason which is the subject of the charge. We have an example of this in Don Diego Ordoñez de Lara, who accused the whole town of Zamora since he did not know that Vellido Dolfos alone had committed the treason of killing his king. So it was that he challenged them all, and the vengeance and the answer concerned all, though it is true that Don Diego went a little too far, and even considerably exceeded the just limits of a challenge, for he had no need to challenge the dead, the waters, the corn, the unborn children, or other objects therein mentioned. But let that pass; for when anger overflows its bed there is no father, governor, or bridle can restrain the tongue. This being so, then, that one man alone cannot insult a kingdom, a province, a city, a commonwealth, or a whole population, there is clearly no need to go out and take up the challenge for such an insult, for it is not one. It would be a fine thing for the people of the *Clock Town* to be perpetually at drawn swords with anyone calling them by that name, or for the *Heretics* either, or the *Aubergine-eaters*, the *Whalers*, the *Soap-boilers*, or others whose names or nicknames are for ever on the tongues of the boys and the riff-raff! It would be a fine thing, indeed, for all these famous towns to be enraged, and take vengeance, and perpetually go about with their swords out like gutting-knives in every petty quarrel. No, no! God does not permit or desire that. Prudent men and well-ordered states must take up arms, unsheathe their swords, and imperil their persons, their lives and their goods for four causes only. Firstly, to defend the Catholic faith; secondly, in self-defence, which is permitted by law natural and divine; thirdly, in defence of honour, family and estates; fourthly, in their king's service in a just war; and if we wish to add a fifth count, which can be reckoned as part of the second, in defence of one's country. To these five principal causes can be added some others which are just and reasonable, and compel one to take up arms. But whoever takes them up for trifles or for matters laughable and amusing rather than insulting is, in my opinion, lacking in all common sense. Besides, the taking of unjust vengeance – and no vengeance can be just – goes directly against the sacred law we profess, by which we are commanded to do good to our enemies and to love those who hate us, a commandment which may seem rather difficult to obey, but which is only so for those who partake less of God than of the world, and more of the flesh than of the spirit. For Jesus Christ – God and true man – who never lied, nor could, nor can lie, being our law-giver, said that His yoke was gentle and His burden light, and therefore He could not have commanded us to do anything impossible to perform. So, my dear sirs, you are bound to keep the peace by law divine and human.'

'The devil take me,' said Sancho to himself at this point, 'if this master of mine isn't a thologian; and if he isn't one, he's as like one as makes no odds.'

Don Quixote took a little breath and, seeing that they were still giving him their attention, decided to go on with his speech. This he would have done, had not Sancho with his usual sharpness interposed and, seeing his master pause, spoken up for him:

'My master, Sir Don Quixote de la Mancha, formerly called *the Knight of the Sad Countenance* and now *The Knight of the Lions*, is a very sensible gentleman who knows both Latin and the vernacular like a Bachelor, and in all he handles or counsels acts like a very good soldier. He has all the laws and ordinances of what they call the duel at his finger-tips, and so there's nothing else for it but to be guided by his advice, and on my head be it if you go astray; the more so since it's said that it's folly to fly into a rage merely at hearing one bray. For I remember that when I was a boy, I brayed whenever I fancied, without any suggestion from anyone, and I did it so gracefully and naturally that when I brayed all the asses in the village brayed too. But I didn't cease on that account to be the son of my parents, who were very honest people; and though quite a

few of the most stuck-up people in my village envied me my talent,
I didn't care a farthing. And to prove that I'm speaking the truth,
wait and listen, for this trick's like swimming, once learnt never forgotten.'

Then, clapping his hand to his nose, he began to bray so stoutly
that all the neighbouring valleys rang. But one of the villagers standing near him thought that he was making fun of them and, raising
the pole he was carrying, dealt him such a blow with it that Sancho
was knocked to the ground unconscious. On seeing his squire so
maltreated, Don Quixote made for his assailant with his lance in his
hand, but so many of them interposed that it was impossible to
avenge him. On the contrary, finding a shower of stones raining
down on him and a thousand levelled crossbows and no less a number of muskets threatening him, he turned Rocinante's head and departed from them as fast as he could gallop, praying to God with all
his heart to deliver him from that peril, and fearing at every step
that a bullet would enter his back and come out through his chest;
and each moment he fetched a breath to see whether he could still
breathe. But the band of villagers were content to see him fly and
did not shoot at him. As for Sancho, they put him on his ass, hardly
yet conscious, and left him to follow his master; not that he had the
sense to guide the beast, but Dapple followed in Rocinante's tracks,
for he could not bear to be separated from him for a moment. When
Don Quixote had gone a considerable distance he turned his head
and saw Sancho coming. Then, finding that he was unpursued, he
waited for him.

The band of villagers stayed there till night, and then, since their
enemies had not come out to battle, went back to their village, rejoicing and happy; and had they known the ancient custom of the
Greeks, there on that spot they would have raised a trophy.

Chapter XXVIII. *Of things which Benengeli says the reader will
learn if he reads them with attention.*

WHEN the valiant man flies it is clear that there is foul play; and
it is a wise man's duty to reserve himself for a better occasion. This
truth was verified in Don Quixote who, yielding before the fury
of the village and the wicked designs of that angry band, could not

be seen for dust. For, oblivious of Sancho and the peril he had left him in, he put himself sufficiently far off to feel safe. Sancho followed him, lying across his ass, as has been said, and caught up with his master at last, having now come to himself. And when he overtook him he let himself fall at Rocinante's feet, sore all over, bruised and beaten, and Don Quixote dismounted to search his wounds; but finding him sound from head to foot, he said to him in some anger:

'It was an evil hour when you learnt to bray, Sancho! For when did you find it a good thing to mention rope in the hanged man's house? What counterpoint but blows could you get to your braying music? Give thanks to God, Sancho, that instead of blessing you with a stick they did not make the sign of the cross over you with a sword.'

'I'm in no state to answer you now,' replied Sancho, 'for my shoulders ache with every word. Let us mount and get away from here, and I'll bray no more. But I can't refrain from saying that knights errant run away and leave their good squire to be ground like privet or wheat at the hands of their enemies.'

'Retreat is not flight,' said Don Quixote. 'For you must know, Sancho, that valour which is not founded upon the basis of prudence is called temerity, and the successes of the rash are rather to be ascribed to good luck than to courage. So I confess that I retired, but I did not fly; and in this I imitated many valiant men who have reserved themselves for better times. History is full of such examples, which I shall not cite now, for they would be of no profit to you and tedious to me.'

By now Sancho had remounted, with the help of Don Quixote, who in his turn climbed on to Rocinante; and at a leisurely pace they made their way towards the shelter of a grove of poplars which was visible as much as a mile away. From time to time Sancho uttered deep sighs and painful groans; and when Don Quixote asked him the cause of his bitter grief he replied that from the base of his spine to the nape of his neck he was in such pain that it was driving him out of his senses.

'The cause of that pain,' said Don Quixote, 'must undoubtedly be that the staff with which they beat you was long and slender, and so caught the whole of your back where the aching parts lie. But if it had caught more of you, the aches would have been worse.'

'Lord love me!' said Sancho. 'Your worship has solved a great mystery and cleared it up most prettily! 'Struth! Was it so difficult, then, to find the cause of my pain, that you must tell me that the aching parts are just the ones the staff hit? If it was my ankles that were sore there might be some doubt about the reason; but that I should ache where they thrashed me – there's not much mystery about that. Honestly, my dear master, another man's hurts are easy to bear; and every day I see more clearly how little I can expect from keeping company with your worship. For since you let me be thrashed this time we shall come back again and again to the blanketings of old and other such pranks; and if it's my back that gets it this time, it'll be my eyes next time. I should do much better – only I am a clod and shan't get any wiser in all the days of my life – I should do better, I say, to go back home and support my wife and bring up my children with whatever God may be pleased to give me than go traipsing after your worship over trackless roads and non-existent paths and rides, drinking poorly and eating worse. Then, take sleeping! Count out seven feet of earth, brother squire, and if you want more, count as many again. Take as much as you like and stretch yourself out to your heart's content. May I see the man who first started knight errantry burning in Hell and ground to dust, or at least the first who was willing to be squire to such a parcel of idiots as the knights errant of old must have been. About present-day ones I say nothing, for since your worship's one of them I hold them in respect, because I'm sure you know a point more than the Devil about all you talk of and think about.'

'I would lay a good bet with you, Sancho,' said Don Quixote, 'that now you are talking without interruption there is no ache in the whole of your body. Say everything that comes into your mind and into your mouth, my son, for if it relieves you of your pain I will willingly control the vexation your impertinences cause me. And if you so much desire to return home to your wife and children, God forbid that I should hinder you. You have money of mine. Reckon how long it is since we left our village on this third expedition, reckon how much is due to you every month, and pay yourself out of hand.'

'When I worked for Thomas Carrasco,' replied Sancho, 'the father of the Bachelor Sampson Carrasco, whom your worship

knows well, I got two ducats a month besides my food. I don't
know what I should earn with your worship, but I know that a
knight errant's squire has more work to do than a farmer's man.
For the fact of the matter is that we who work for farmers have a
stew for supper at night and sleep in our beds, however much we
have to toil by day, and whatever ill may befall us. But I haven't
slept in a bed since I've been in your worship's service. And except
for the short while we stayed at Don Diego de Miranda's, and the
picnic I had with the skimmings from Camacho's pots, and the
time I ate and drank and slept at Basilio's, all the rest of the time I've
slept on the hard ground under the open sky, subject to what they
call the inclemencies of heaven, living on scraps of cheese and crusts
of bread, and drinking water from brooks, or sometimes from the
springs we find in these by-roads we travel.'

'I confess, Sancho,' said Don Quixote, 'that all you say is true.
How much more then do you consider I should give you than
Thomas Carrasco did?'

'I think,' said Sancho, 'if your worship were to give me two *reals*
more a month I should be satisfied. That is so far as wages for my
work go. But in the matter of your solemn promise to grant me the
governorship of an isle, you should rightly add another six *reals* for
compensation, which would make thirty *reals* in all.'

'Very good,' replied Don Quixote. 'Now, to work out the wages
you have allotted to yourself, it is twenty-five days since we left the
village. Reckon proportionately, and see what I owe you. Then pay
yourself, as I have said, from your own pocket.'

'O my Lord!' cried Sancho. 'Your worship's a long way out in
your reckoning; for in the matter of the promised isle you must
count from the day your worship promised it me to this present hour.'

'Well, how long is it since I made the promise, Sancho?' asked
Don Quixote.

'If I remember rightly,' answered Sancho, 'it must be more than
twenty years, to within three days more or less.'

Don Quixote gave himself a great slap on the forehead and began
to laugh very heartily, saying: 'But I hardly travelled for two
months in the Sierra Morena or in the whole course of our expedi-
tions, and you say, Sancho, that it is twenty years since I promised
you the isle? I think you want to absorb all the money of mine

you have in your wages. Though if that is so and it gives you pleasure I grant it you from now on, and much good may it do you; for rather than have so bad a squire I shall be glad to be left poor and penniless. But tell me, perverter of the squirely ordinances of knight errantry, where have you ever seen or read of any knight errant's squire bargaining with his master, with "So much a month you will have to give me for serving you"? Embark, embark, scoundrel, villain, fiend – you seem to be all three – embark I say on the wide seas of their histories, and if you find that any squire has said or thought as you have spoken, you may nail it on my forehead and plant your four fingers in my face to boot. Turn your rein, or your ass's bridle, and go back home, for you shall not take one step further with me. O bread ill-requited! O promises ill-placed! O man more beast than human! Now, when I was intending to establish you in state, and in such a state that they would call you Lord, despite your wife, now do you leave me? Are you going now, when I had come to the firm and mighty resolve to make you lord of the best isle in the world? Well, as you have said again and again, the honey is not ... etcetera. An ass you are, and an ass you must be, and an ass you will end when the course of your life is run. For it is my opinion that it will reach its final term before you realize and acknowledge that you are a beast.'

Sancho looked fixedly at Don Quixote whilst he was uttering these reproaches, and was so stricken with remorse that the tears came into his eyes and he cried in a weak and sorrowful voice: 'Master, I confess that all I need to be a complete ass is a tail. If your worship would care to put one on me, I should reckon I had deserved it, and would serve you as an ass for all the remainder of my life. Pardon me, your worship, take pity on my youth, consider that I know but little, and that if I talk a lot it proceeds rather from weakness than from malice. But who errs and mends, himself to God commends.'

'I should have been surprised, Sancho, if you hadn't mixed some little bit of a proverb into your speech. Well, I pardon you, on condition that you mend your ways and show yourself henceforth not quite so greedy in your own interests, but try instead to broaden your mind, and take courage and spirit to hope for the fulfilment of my promises, for though it may be delayed yet it is not impossible.'

Sancho promised compliance, though it meant drawing strength out of weakness. Then they entered the wood, where Don Quixote settled himself at the foot of an elm and Sancho at the foot of a beech; for such-like trees have feet but no hands. Sancho spent the night in pain, for his beating made itself more felt with the night dew. But Don Quixote passed it in his everlasting meditations, though, for all that, they both closed their eyes in sleep, and when dawn broke pursued their journey in search of the banks of the famous Ebro, where an adventure befell them which will be related in the coming chapter.

Chapter XXIX. *Of the famous Adventure of the Enchanted Boat.*

Two days, by their reckoning, after they left the poplar grove Don Quixote and Sancho came to the river Ebro, the sight of which was a great delight to Don Quixote, as he contemplated and gazed upon the charms of its shores, the clearness of its waters, the smoothness of its stream, and the abundance of its liquid crystal. In fact this cheering sight recalled a thousand amorous thoughts to his mind. Especially he dwelt on his vision in the cave of Montesinos, for although Master Peter's ape had told him that part of it was true and part false, he leaned rather to its being true than false: the very opposite view to Sancho's, who considered it all one great lie. Well, as they were riding along in this way, there hove in sight a little boat without oars or any sort of gear, made fast to the trunk of a tree which grew on the bank. Don Quixote looked in all directions, but could see no one. So without more ado he dismounted from Rocinante, and bade Sancho get down from Dapple and tie the two beasts close together to the trunk of a poplar or willow growing there. And on Sancho's enquiring the reason for this sudden dismounting and tethering, Don Quixote answered:

'I must tell you, Sancho, that this boat, deliberately and beyond all possibility of error, summons me to embark, and travel in it to succour some knight or other person of rank in distress; and he must be in very great trouble. For this, as we read in histories of chivalry, is the practice of the enchanters whose actions and speeches they describe. When a knight is placed in some peril from which he can only be delivered by the hand of another knight, though they may be six or eight thousand, or even more, miles apart, they either snatch the second knight up in a cloud or provide him with a boat to board, and in less than the twinkling of an eye they take him, through the air or over the sea, where they will and where his aid is needed. So, Sancho, this boat is put here for that very purpose, and that is as true as it is now day. But, before this happens, tie Dapple and Rocinante together, and may God's hand guide us, for I would not fail to embark were barefoot friars to entreat me.'

'Well, as it's like that,' replied Sancho, 'and your worship will run at every step into these follies — I don't know what else to call them — there's nothing for it but to obey and bow my head, according to the proverb: Do what your master orders and sit down with him at his table. But for all that, for my conscience' sake I must warn your worship, that I don't think this said boat belongs to any of your enchanted folk, but to some fishermen of this river, for they catch the best shad in the world here.'

This Sancho said as he was tying up the beasts, leaving them to the care and protection of the enchanters, with great grief in his heart. But Don Quixote bade him not to worry about abandoning the animals, for He who was to lead them through such longinquous ways and regions would take care to provide for them.

'I don't understand this logiquous of yours,' said Sancho. 'I have never heard such a word in all the days of my life.'

'*Longinquous*,' replied Don Quixote, 'means remote; and it is no wonder you do not understand it, for you are not obliged to know Latin, like some who claim to know it and do not.'

'Now they're tied up,' said Sancho, 'what have we to do next?'

'What?' answered Don Quixote. 'Cross ourselves and weigh anchor. I mean embark and cut the ropes by which this boat is fastened.' Then, jumping in, with Sancho after him, he cut the boat adrift, and it was carried little by little from the bank. When Sancho found himself some two yards off shore he began to tremble, fearing that he was lost; and nothing caused him more pain than to hear Dapple braying and to see Rocinante struggling to break loose.

'The ass is braying,' he said to his master, 'for grief at being deserted, and Rocinante's trying to get free to rush after us. O my dearest friends, stay there in peace, and may the madness that takes us from you turn to disappointment and bring us back to your company!'

At this he began to weep so bitterly that Don Quixote asked peevishly and testily: 'What are you afraid of, cowardly beast? What are you weeping at, butter-heart? Who is pursuing you or harassing you, soul of a town mouse? What do you lack, always in need amidst the bowels of abundance? Are you perchance travelling barefoot over the Riphaean mountains? No, you are sitting on a bench, like an archduke, on the calm current of this delightful river, from which we shall emerge in a short while into the wide sea. But we must have come out already and have travelled at least two thousand miles – or more. If I had only an astrolabe here with which I could take the height of the pole, I would tell you how far we have gone; though if I know anything we have passed, or soon shall pass, the equinoctial line which divides and cuts the opposing poles at equal distance.'

'And when we get to this noxious line your worship speaks of,' asked Sancho, 'how far shall we have gone?'

'A long way,' replied Don Quixote, 'for we shall have covered the half of the three hundred and sixty degrees of earth and water the globe contains according to the computation of Ptolemy, who was the best cosmographer known, when we come to the line I mentioned.'

'By God,' said Sancho, 'but your worship has got me a pretty fellow for a witness of what you say, this same Tolmy or whatever you call him, with his amputation.'

Don Quixote burst out laughing at the interpretation Sancho had put on the name, the computation and the reckoning of the cosmographer Ptolemy, and said:

'You must learn, Sancho, that according to the Spaniards and those who embark at Cadiz to go to the East Indies, one of the signs by which they know that they have passed the equinoctial line I mentioned is that the lice die on everyone aboard ship. Not one remains alive, and you could not find one in the whole vessel if you were to be paid its weight in gold. So, you might pass a hand over your thigh; if you catch anything living, we shall have no doubts on that score; and if not, then we have passed.'

'I don't believe a word of that,' answered Sancho, 'but I'll do what your worship orders all the same, though I don't know why we need to make these experiments, for I can see with my own eyes that we haven't moved more than five yards from the bank. We haven't drawn two yards off from where the animals are, for there are Rocinante and Dapple in the very place we left them; and, taking our bearings as I do now, I swear we aren't stirring or moving at an ant's pace.'

'Make the investigation I asked of you, Sancho, and do not worry about any others, for you know nothing about the colures, lines, parallels, zodiacs, ecliptics, poles, solstices, equinoxes, planets, signs of the zodiac and points, which are the measures of which the celestial and terrestrial spheres are composed. But if you had that knowledge, or part of it, you would clearly see how many parallels we have cut, how many signs seen, and what constellations we have left behind and are now leaving. Once more I ask you, feel and fish, for I believe you are as clean as a sheet of smooth white paper.'

Sancho felt himself and, reaching his hand gently and cautiously behind his left knee, raised his head and looked at his master, saying: 'Either the test's false or we haven't got where your worship says, not by many a long mile.'

'Well, why?' asked Don Quixote. 'Have you found anything?'

'More than somewhat,' answered Sancho. And shaking his fingers, he washed his whole hand in the river, down which the boat was softly gliding in midstream, without any occult intelligence to move it, or any hidden enchanter, but only the current of the water, which was calm there and smooth.

At that moment they caught sight of two great water-mills in the middle of the river, and no sooner did Don Quixote view them than he exclaimed to Sancho in a loud voice: 'Do you see? There, my friend, stands the city, castle, or fortress. In it must lie the persecuted knight, or the Queen or Princess in distress, for whose succour I have been brought here.'

'What the devil does your worship mean by city, fortress, or castle?' asked Sancho. 'Can't you see that those buildings in the river are water-mills, where they grind the corn?'

'Hush, Sancho!' said Don Quixote. 'They may seem to be water-mills, but they are not. I have already told you that spells transform all things and change them from their natural shapes. I do not mean that they actually change them, but they appear to, as we learnt by experience in the transformation of Dulcinea, sole refuge of my hopes.'

By this time the boat had got into the middle of the stream and had begun to travel rather less slowly than before. And when the millers saw it drifting down the river and on the point of being dragged under by the mill-stream, a number of them rushed hurriedly out with long poles to stop it. And when they came, all floury, with their faces and clothes covered with meal, they presented an ugly appearance, as they shouted out: 'Where are you going, you devils? Are you out of your senses? What are you after? Do you want to drown or be dashed to pieces on these wheels?'

'Did I not tell you, Sancho,' exclaimed Don Quixote at this, 'that we had reached a place where I have to show the strength of my arm? Look what scoundrelly villains have come out to encounter me! Look what fiends are opposing me! Look at those ugly faces grimacing at us! Now then, you shall see, rogues!'

And standing up in the boat he began to threaten the millers, crying out loudly: 'Ugly and ill-advised rabble, set free and deliver him whom you keep under duress in this fortress or prison of yours, be he of high or low or of whatever degree! For I am Don Quixote de la Mancha, otherwise called *the Knight of the Lions*, for whom by Heaven's high destiny the happy accomplishment of this adventure is reserved.'

As he spoke he grasped his sword, and began to make passes in the air against the millers who, hearing but not understanding these ravings, wielded their poles to stop the boat, which was now entering into the rapids of the mill-race. Sancho went down on his knees, devoutly praying Heaven to rescue him from his imminent peril; which it did, thanks to the prompt efforts of the millers, who planted their poles against the boat and stopped it, but not so skilfully as to prevent its overturning and throwing Don Quixote and Sancho head over heels into the water. Fortunately for the knight, he could swim like a duck, though the weight of his armour took him twice to the bottom; and if it had not been for the millers, who plunged into the water and dragged them both out bodily, it would have been good-bye to the pair of them. Then, when they were brought to land, drenched and far from dying of thirst, Sancho went down on his knees and, with hands joined and eyes fixed to Heaven, implored God in a long and devout prayer to deliver him from all his master's rash plans and enterprises in future.

By this time the fishermen had arrived, who owned the boat, which had been broken to pieces by the mill-wheels; and when they saw it smashed, they set about stripping Sancho and demanding payment of Don Quixote, who told the millers and the fishermen very calmly, as if nothing had happened, that he would pay for the boat with the best will in the world, providing they would set free the person or persons who were oppressed in that castle, without ransom.

'What persons and what castle are you talking of, madman?' asked one of the millers. 'Can it be the people who come to this mill to have their corn ground that you want to carry off?'

'Enough,' said Don Quixote to himself. 'It would be preaching in the wilderness to try and induce this rabble by prayers to do any virtuous act. Two powerful enchanters must have met in opposition in this adventure, the one frustrating the other's designs. One provided me with the boat, and the other threw me out. God help us, but this whole world is tricks and devices, one against the other. I can do no more.' And raising his voice, he went on, gazing all the while at the water-mills: 'Friends, whoever you are, who lie locked up in this prison, pardon me. For unfortunately for myself and for you, I cannot deliver you from your affliction. This adventure must remain reserved for another knight.'

Saying this, he compounded with the fishermen, and paid them fifty *reals* for the boat, and Sancho handed the money over with very ill grace, saying:

'Two boat trips like this will sink our whole fortune to the bottom.'

The fishermen and the millers gazed in astonishment at those two figures, so unlike other men, and were quite unable to make out what Don Quixote was driving at. But, concluding that both knight and squire were mad, they left them, the millers returning to their mill and the fishermen to their huts. Don Quixote and Sancho went back to their beasts, and to their beast-like existence; and such was the end of the adventure of the enchanted boat.

Chapter XXX. *Don Quixote's meeting with a fair Huntress.*

KNIGHT and squire were sufficiently depressed and out of humour when they reached their animals – especially Sancho. Indeed it grieved him to the soul to have touched their stock of money, for with every penny taken he seemed to be robbed of his very eyeballs. At length they mounted in silence and left the famous river, Don Quixote deep in thoughts of his love, and Sancho of his preferment, which at that time seemed to him very far from his grasp. For, fool though he was, he was well enough aware that all, or most, of the knight's actions were extravagant, and he was looking for an opportunity of escaping and going home without entering into any reckonings or farewells with his master. But Fortune was kinder to him than he had feared.

It fell out, then, that the next day at sunset, as they were emerging from a wood, Don Quixote cast his eyes about a green meadow, and saw some people on the further side, whom, when he drew near, he recognized to be a hawking party. He rode closer, and saw among them a gallant lady on a palfrey or milk-white hack decked with green trappings and with a silver side-saddle. The lady herself was in green, so bravely and richly attired that she looked the very soul of bravery. On her left wrist she bore a hawk, from which Don Quixote concluded that she was a great lady, and probably the mistress of all the hunters, as was the fact; and so he said to Sancho:

'Run, Sancho my son, and tell that lady with a hawk on the palfrey that I, the *Knight of the Lions*, salute her great beauty, and that if Her Magnificence gives me leave, I will go and kiss her hands, and serve her to the uttermost of my strength in all that her Highness may command me. And mind, Sancho, how you speak. Take care not to mix any of your proverbs into your embassage.'

'What sort of mixer do you take me for!' answered Sancho. 'To tell me that! As if this was the first time in my life I've taken messages to high and mighty ladies.'

'Except for the one you took to the lady Dulcinea,' replied Don Quixote, 'I do not know of any you have ever carried, at least in my service.'

'That's right,' answered Sancho, 'but a good paymaster doesn't worry about sureties, and in a well-stocked house the supper's soon cooked. I mean that there's no need to tell me anything or give me any sort of advice, for I'm ready for anything and I can manage a bit of everything.'

'Indeed I believe you,' said Don Quixote. 'Go then and God guide you!'

Sancho went off at a trot, urging Dapple out of his usual pace and, coming up to the fair huntress, dismounted and went down on his knees before her, saying: 'Beautiful lady, that knight you see yonder, the *Knight of the Lions* by name, is my master, and I am one of his squires, called at home Sancho Panza. This same *Knight of the Lions*, who was known not long ago as the *Knight of the Sad Countenance*, sends by me to ask for your Highness's permission to come, with your approval, goodwill and consent, and put his desire into effect; which is no other, as he says and I confirm, than to serve your lofty haughtiness and beauty. In giving your permission your ladyship will be doing something which will redound to your fame, and he will receive a most signal favour and happiness.'

'Indeed, good squire,' answered the lady, 'you have delivered your message with all the ceremony that such messages demand. Rise from the ground; for it is not right for the squire of so great a knight as he of the *Sad Countenance*, of whom we have already heard a great deal here, to remain on his knees. Rise, friend, and tell your master that he is most welcome to come and serve me and the Duke my husband, in a country house of ours near here.'

Sancho got up, impressed alike by the great lady's beauty and by her good breeding and courtesy, but even more so by her saying that she had knowledge of his master, the *Knight of the Sad Countenance* — and if she did not call him the *Knight of the Lions*, it could only be owing to his having taken the name so recently. The Duchess — whose title is unknown — then asked him:

'Tell me, brother squire, about this master of yours. Is he not one about whom a history has been printed called *The Ingenious Gentleman Don Quixote de la Mancha*, and has he not for the lady of his heart a certain Dulcinea del Toboso?'

'That's the man, my lady,' answered Sancho, 'and his squire, Sancho Panza by name, who is, or should be in that history, is myself, unless I was changed in my cradle — I mean changed in the press.'

'All this is most delightful,' said the Duchess. 'Go, brother Panza, and tell your master that he is heartily welcome on my estates, and that nothing would give me greater pleasure than his visit.'

Sancho returned to his master, overjoyed at this most agreeable answer, and repeated all·that the fine lady had said to him, lauding her great beauty, her charm and her courtesy to the skies in his country language. Don Quixote preened himself in his saddle, set his feet firmly in the stirrups, adjusted his vizor, gave the spur to Rocinante, and advanced with a graceful bearing to kiss the Duchess's hands. And she meanwhile called the Duke, her husband, and repeated the whole of Sancho's message to him while Don Quixote was on the way. The pair of them had read the first part of this history, and consequently knew of Don Quixote's extravagances. So they awaited him with the greatest delight and were most anxious to make his acquaintance, their intention being to fall in with his whimsies, to agree with him in all he said, and to treat him like a knight errant for so long as he would stay with them, observing towards him all the ceremonies usual in books of knight errantry, which they had read and were very fond of.

Now Don Quixote rode up with his vizor raised and made as if to dismount, whereat Sancho hurried to hold his stirrup. But the squire was so unlucky as to catch one foot on a cord of the pack-saddle as he was dismounting from Dapple, and was unable to disentangle himself; so that he remained dangling with his face and his chest on the ground. Don Quixote was not accustomed to dismounting without someone to hold his stirrup, and thinking that Sancho had already caught hold of it, threw his body off with a jerk, carrying Rocinante's saddle, which must have been badly girthed, after him, so that he and the saddle fell to the ground together, to his no small discomfiture, and to the accompaniment of a volley of curses which he uttered between his teeth at the unfortunate Sancho, who still had his foot in the noose. The Duke ordered his huntsmen to go to the assistance of the knight and the squire, and they raised Don Quixote, who was in an ill plight from his fall and went limping to kneel as best he could before the Duke and Duchess. But the Duke would on no account permit this; instead he dismounted from his horse and went to embrace Don Quixote, saying:

'I am grieved, Sir Knight of the Sad Countenance, that the first step your worship has taken upon my land has been as unlucky as we have seen; but the carelessness of squires is often the cause of even worse accidents.'

'The moment of my first meeting with you, valorous Prince,' answered Don Quixote, 'could not possibly be unlucky, even had my fall been to the centre of the deep abyss; for even from there the glory of seeing you would have raised and rescued me. My squire – God's curse on him – is better at loosening his tongue to utter malice than at securing a saddle firmly. But wherever I may be, prostrate or upright, on foot or horse, I shall always be at the service of yourself and of my lady the Duchess, your worthy consort, the sovereign mistress of beauty and universal princess of courtesy.'

'Gently, my dear Don Quixote de la Mancha,' said the Duke, 'for where my lady Doña Dulcinea del Toboso is no other beauties should be praised.'

By this time Sancho Panza was free from the noose and, being close at hand, anticipated his master's reply by saying: 'It cannot be denied – in fact it must be declared that my lady Dulcinea del Toboso is very beautiful. But the hare starts up when least you expect it, and I've heard say that what's called Nature is like a potter who makes vessels of clay, and if a man makes one fine pot he can also make two, three or a hundred. This I say because my Lady the Duchess is every bit as fine as the lady Dulcinea del Toboso, I swear.'

Don Quixote turned to the Duchess and said: 'Your Highness can imagine that never in the world has knight errant had a more garrulous or a droller squire than mine, and he will prove my words if your great Sublimity will accept my service for a few days.'

To which the Duchess replied: 'I am most heartily glad that Sancho is droll, for it is a sign that he is wise. Since jokes and humour, Don Quixote, as you very well know, do not go with sluggish wits. So, as the good Sancho is droll and humorous, from now on I'll affirm he is wise.'

'And garrulous,' added Don Quixote.

'So much the better,' said the Duke. 'For much humour cannot be expressed in few words. But let us not waste our time in talk. Come, great Knight of the Sad Countenance ...'

'Of the Lions, your Highness should say,' interrupted Sancho, 'for there's no *Sad Countenance* now.'

'*Of the Lions*, be it,' continued the Duke, 'Come, Sir Knight of the Lions, I say, to a castle of mine not far from here. There you will be entertained as so exalted a personage should be, and as the Duchess and I are accustomed to entertain all knights errant who come here.'

While they were speaking Sancho had adjusted and girthed Rocinante's saddle. So, Don Quixote mounting on him, and the Duke on a fine horse, they put the Duchess between them and took the road for the castle, the Duchess commanding that Sancho should ride beside her, for she found infinite delight in listening to his wise sayings. Sancho did not require pressing, and working his way in among the three of them, made a fourth in the conversation, to the great pleasure of the Duke and Duchess, who counted it great good fortune to receive in their castle such a knight errant and so itinerant a squire.

Chapter XXXI. *Which treats of many great matters.*

GREAT was Sancho's delight at finding himself, as he thought, in the Duchess's favour, for he figured it out that he would find in her castle all that he had found at Don Diego's and Don Basilio's. For he was always fond of good living, and so seized any opportunity of regaling himself by the forelock, whenever it occurred.

Now our history recounts that on their way to the country-house or castle the Duke rode ahead and gave his servants orders as to their behaviour towards Don Quixote. For when he reached the gates of the castle with the Duchess, two lackeys or grooms promptly ran out, clothed down to their feet in what they call morning-dress of finest crimson satin, and almost before he had heard or seen them caught Don Quixote in their arms, saying: 'Go, your Highness, and help my lady the Duchess to dismount.'

Don Quixote did so, and high compliments passed between the two on the subject. But at length the Duchess's insistence triumphed, and she refused to get down from her palfrey except into the Duke's arms, saying that she did not consider herself worthy of laying so useless a burden on so great a knight. In the end the Duke came out to help her down, and as they entered a great courtyard, two beautiful maidens came up and threw a huge mantle of the finest scarlet over Don Quixote's shoulders. Then in an instant all the galleries of the court were crowded with the Duke and Duchess's men and women servants, crying loudly: 'Welcome to the flower and cream of knights errant.' And all, or most of them, sprinkled flasks of scented waters over Don Quixote and the ducal pair, all to the great astonishment of the knight. And this was the first time that he was positively certain of being a true and no imaginary knight errant, since he found himself treated just as he had read these knights were treated in past ages.

Sancho abandoned Dapple and, tacking himself on to the Duchess, went into the castle. But, his conscience pricking him at leaving the ass alone, he went up to a reverent waiting-woman who had come out with the others to receive the Duchess, and said in a low voice: 'Mistress Gonzalez, or whatever your worship's name may be!'

'Doña Rodriguez de Grijalba is my name,' answered the waiting-woman. 'What are your orders, brother?'

To which Sancho replied: 'I wish your worship would be so kind as to go out to the castle gate, where you'll find a dapple ass of mine. Please put him, or have him put, in the stable; for the poor beast is rather nervous, and can't endure being left alone on any account.'

'If the master has no better manners than his man,' answered the waiting-woman, 'we've struck a fine bunch! Get away, fellow, and ill luck to you and the man who brought you here! Look after your own ass, for we waiting-women in this house aren't accustomed to such offices.'

'But indeed,' replied Sancho, 'I've heard my master – and he is a dowser for histories – tell the story of Lancelot:

> When he from Britain rode,
> Ladies attended him
> And waiting-maids his steed;

and as for my ass, I wouldn't change him for Sir Lancelot's horse.'

'Fellow, if you're a jester,' said the waiting-woman, 'keep your jokes for those that like them and will pay you for them. You'll get nothing but a fig from me.'

'Very well,' answered Sancho, 'so long as it's a good ripe one, and if years count for anything you won't lose the trick by a pip too little.'

'Son of a whore!' exclaimed the waiting-woman, now incensed with rage. 'Whether I'm old or not, my account is with God and not with you, you garlic-stuffed rogue.'

She said this so loudly that the Duchess heard her and, turning round to find her waiting-woman so excited and her eyes so furious, asked her with whom she was having words.

'Here,' answered she, 'I'm having them with this good fellow, who has asked me in all seriousness to go and stable an ass of his which is at the castle gates, raking up as example something about some place or other where ladies waited on a certain Lancelot and waiting-women on his horse – and what's more, he ended up by calling me an old woman.'

'That I should consider an insult,' replied the Duchess, 'the greatest possible insult.' Then, taking Sancho aside, she said: 'Take notice, Sancho, that Doña Rodriguez is quite a girl, and that she wears that headdress for authority and out of habit, not on account of her years.'

'Bad luck follow me for the rest of my days,' answered Sancho, 'if I meant any harm. I only spoke because I'm very fond of my ass, and I thought I couldn't entrust him to a kindlier person that the lady Doña Rodriguez.'

Then Don Quixote, who had overheard all this, demanded: 'Is this fit talk, Sancho, for this place?'

'Sir,' answered Sancho, 'everyone must speak of his needs wherever he is. Here I was when I remembered my Dapple, and here I spoke of him; and if I had thought of him in the stable I would have spoken of him there.'

On which the Duke remarked: 'Sancho is very right, and there's no reason to blame him. Dapple shall have as much fodder as he can eat. Sancho need not worry, for the ass shall be treated as well as he would be himself.'

After this conversation, pleasing to all but Don Quixote, they went upstairs and showed the knight into a hall hung with the richest cloth of gold and brocade. Six maids took off his armour and acted as pages, all of them trained in their parts by the Duke and Duchess, and instructed in their behaviour towards Don Quixote, for his hosts were anxious that he should really believe that they were treating him as a knight errant. When the knight's armour was off he was left in his tight-fitting breeches and his chamois leather doublet. Withered, tall and lank, with his jaws that kissed one another inside his mouth, he was a figure at which the maids would have burst out laughing, if they had not been at pains to disguise their smiles – which was one of the special orders they had received from their master. They begged to be allowed to strip him so as to put a clean shirt on him, but he would not consent, saying that modesty was as necessary in a knight errant as valour. He asked them, however, to give the shirt to Sancho and, shutting himself up with him in a room where there was a rich bed, he stripped and put it on. Then, finding himself thus alone with Sancho, he said to him:

'Tell me, you old clown, to-day promoted to jester, do you think it right to dishonour and insult that venerable and dignified waiting-woman? Was this the time to remember Dapple? Are these the gentlemen to leave animals neglected, seeing how grandly they treat their owners? In God's name, Sancho, control yourself. Do not show the yarn you are woven of, or let them see what gross and peasant stuff you are. Reflect, you sinner, that the more honourable and well bred the servant, the higher the master is esteemed, and that one of the greatest advantages of princes over other men is that they are waited on by servants as good as themselves. Do you not see, obstinate fellow that you are and unlucky man that I am, that if they discover that you are a coarse boor or a simple idiot, they will take me for a charlatan or for some swindling knight? No, no, Sancho, my friend, avoid, avoid these pitfalls, for once you fall into being a babbler and a droll, you have only to stumble and you will descend to the state of a disgraced buffoon. Restrain your tongue. Consider and ruminate upon your words before they leave your mouth, and observe that we have now come to a place which, by God's aid and the valour of my arm, we must leave with our fame and wealth increased to the uttermost.'

Sancho promised most earnestly to obey and to sew up his

mouth or bite his tongue before uttering a single unfitting or ill-considered word. He assured Don Quixote that he might rest easy on that score, for their identity should never transpire through him.

Don Quixote then dressed himself, put on his shoulder-strap with his sword, threw the scarlet mantle over his shoulders, put on a green satin hunting-cap which the maids had given him and, thus adorned, walked out into the great hall, where he found the maidens lined up in two equal rows and each one of them holding some requisite for his ablutions, which she handed him with great courtesies and formalities. Next there came forward twelve pages with the butler to take him to dinner, where the Duke and Duchess were already waiting for him. They put him between them and led him with great pomp and majesty into another hall in which a rich table was laid with only four covers. The Duke and Duchess came to the door of the hall to receive him, and with them one of those grave ecclesiastics who rule the houses of princes; of those who, not being born princes themselves, do not succeed in teaching those who are how to behave as such; who would have the greatness of the great measured by the narrowness of their own souls; who, wanting to show those they rule how to be frugal, make them miserly; such a man, I mean, was this grave ecclesiastic who went out with the Duke and Duchess to receive Don Quixote. After exchanging innumerable courtly compliments, they concluded by taking Don Quixote between them and going to take their seats at the table. The Duke invited our knight to take the head, and although he at first refused his host pressed him so hard that he had to give in. The ecclesiastic sat opposite him, and the Duke and Duchess on either side.

Sancho watched all this ceremony, gaping with astonishment to see the honour these princes were paying his master; and when he saw the many compliments and entreaties which passed between the Duke and Don Quixote on the subject of his sitting at the head of the table, he said: 'If your worships will give me leave I will tell you a story of an incident in my town concerning this business of seats.'

The moment Sancho opened his mouth Don Quixote trembled, in fear that his squire would certainly utter some absurdity. But Sancho read his anxiety from his face and said: 'Have no fear, dear master, of my going astray or saying anything off the point, for I haven't forgotten the advice you gave me just now about speaking much or little, well or ill.'

'I remember nothing about it, Sancho,' answered Don Quixote. 'Say what you like so long as you say it quickly.'

'Well, what I want to say,' said Sancho, 'is quite true, for my master, Don Quixote here, won't let me lie.'

'So far as I am concerned, Sancho,' answered Don Quixote, 'lie as much as you like. I shall not stop you. But be careful what you say.'

'I have so considered it and reconsidered it that I am as safe as the man in the tower who sounds the alarm, as you shall see by the tale.'

'It would be as well,' said Don Quixote, 'if your Highnesses would order this fool to be turned out from here, or he will be uttering a thousand idiocies.'

'But they must not take Sancho away, I declare, not by so much as an inch,' exclaimed the Duchess. 'I love him dearly, for I know he is very wise.'

'A wise life to your Holiness,' exclaimed Sancho, 'for your good opinion of me, although I don't deserve it. Now this is my tale: There was a gentleman of my town who sent out an invitation. He was very rich and important, as he came of the Alamos of Medina del Campo, and was married to Doña Mencia de Quiñones, who was the daughter of Don Alonso de Marañon, Knight of the Order of Santiago, who was drowned in the Herradura. It was about him that the quarrel was years ago in our town – and, as far as I can make out, my master Don Quixote took part in it – I mean when young Thomas, the scamp, the son of Balbastro the smith, got wounded. Isn't this all true, master? Say it is, for goodness' sake, or these gentlefolk may take me for a lying babbler.'

'So far,' said the ecclesiastic, 'I think you are a babbler but no liar. Though I do not know what I shall take you for later.'

'You call on so many witnesses, Sancho,' said Don Quixote, 'and cite so many proofs that I cannot help agreeing that you must be speaking the truth. Go on and cut your story short, for at the rate you are going you will not be done in two days.'

'He must not cut it short,' said the Duchess, 'to please me. No, he must tell it in his own way, even if it takes him six days to finish; for even if it took so long, those would be the best days of my life.'

'Well, good sirs,' Sancho proceeded, 'this same gentleman, whom I know as well as my own hands – for it is only a bowshot from my house to his – sent an invitation to a poor but honest farmer.'

'Go on, brother,' said the ecclesiastic at this point. 'At the rate you are going you will not be done with your tale till the next world.'

'I'll stop short of half-way there, please God,' answered Sancho Panza. 'Well, this same farmer arrived at the house of the gentle-man who had invited him – God rest his soul, for he's dead now and, what's more, they say he died an angel's death, though I wasn't there, as I had to go to Tembleque at the time, harvesting ...'

'On your life, son,' broke in the priest, 'do not wait to bury the gentleman but come back quickly from Tembleque, and finish your story, unless you have a mind for more funerals.'

'Well, the fact is,' Sancho resumed, 'that just as the pair of them were going to sit down to table – I seem to see them now better·than ever ...'

The Duke and Duchess greatly enjoyed the good priest's evident disgust at Sancho's prolixity and at the frequent pauses in his story, but Don Quixote was consumed with anger and vexation.

'Well, then,' said Sancho, 'just as the two of them, as I have said, were going to sit down to the meal, the farmer insisted on the gentleman's taking the head of the table, and the gentleman like-wise insisted on the farmer's taking it, for a man's wishes should be obeyed in his own house. But the farmer, who prided himself on his courtesy and good breeding, steadfastly refused, until the gentle-man angrily put his hands on his shoulders and sat him down by force, saying: "Sit down, blockhead, for wherever I sit shall be head of the table for you." Now that's the story, and I really don't think I've brought it in out of place.'

Don Quixote flushed and his brown face was veined with red, while the Duke and Duchess, perceiving Sancho's malice, concealed their smiles for fear that Don Quixote should end by losing his temper. Then, to change the subject and prevent Sancho from proceeding to further impertinences, the Duchess asked Don Quixote what news he had of the Lady Dulcinea, and whether he had sent her any presents of giants or malefactors recently, since he could not have failed to overcome plenty. To which Don Quixote replied: 'My lady, though my misfortunes had a beginning they will never have an end. Giants I have conquered, and rogues and malefactors I have sent her. But where should they find her, seeing that she is enchanted and transformed into the ugliest peasant girl imaginable?'

'I don't know,' said Sancho. 'She seems the loveliest beautiful creature in the world to me. I'm quite sure, at least, that no tumbler could give her odds for nimbleness or frisking. She can spring from the ground on to an ass as sprightly as a cat, I promise you, lady Duchess.'

'Have you seen her enchanted, Sancho?' asked the Duke.

'Have I seen her!' answered Sancho. 'Why, who the devil was it but I that first thought of this enchantment business? She's as much enchanted as my father!'

When the ecclesiastic heard speak of giants, rogues and enchantments, he reckoned that this must be Don Quixote de la Mancha, whose history was the Duke's ordinary reading, for which he had often taken him to task, saying that it was folly to read such follies. And now that he was convinced that his suspicions were correct, he turned on the Duke in great anger:

'Your Excellency, sir, will have to account to our Lord for this good man's doings. This Don Quixote, or Don Fool, or whatever you call him, cannot be such an idiot, I imagine, as your Excellency would have him be, seeing the opportunities you put in his way of carrying on with his fooleries and nonsense.'

Then, turning to address Don Quixote, he said: 'And you, simpleton, who has driven it into your brain that you are a knight errant and conquer giants and capture malefactors? Get along with you, and take my advice: go back to your home, and bring up your children, if you have any. Look after your estate, and stop wandering about the world, swallowing wind and making yourself a laughing-stock to all who know you and even to those who do not. Where, in the name of mischief, have you ever learnt that knights errant exist to-day, or ever did? Where would you find giants in Spain, or malefactors in La Mancha, or your enchanted Dulcineas, or all that pack of nonsense that figures in your story?'

Y

Don Quixote listened attentively to the venerable man's words, and when he saw that he had done, regardless of the Duke and Duchess, he got on to his feet with an angry expression and excitement in his face, and said:

But his reply deserves a chapter to itself.

Chapter XXXII. *Of Don Quixote's Reply to his Censor, and other incidents serious and entertaining.*

So, springing to his feet and trembling from head to foot like a man filled with mercury, Don Quixote stammered out hastily: 'The place where I am, the presence I am in, and the respect I have, and have always had, for the calling your worship professes, hold and tie the hands of my just indignation. And so, for those reasons and because I know, as everyone knows, that the weapons of gownsmen are the same as women's, the tongue, I will enter with the same weapon into equal battle with you, though I might have expected good counsel from you instead of infamous reproaches. Charitable and wholesome reproof requires different behaviour and different language. But harsh and public reproach exceeds the bounds of just censure; for well-meaning rebukes are better uttered with gentleness than with asperity, and it is wrong, without knowledge of the sin, to proclaim the sinner bluntly a blockhead and a fool. Now tell me, your worship, for what follies that you have seen in me do you condemn and reproach me, and tell me to go home and attend to my household, and to my wife and children, though you do not know if I have any or not? Is it enough to enter other men's houses by hook or by crook and rule their owners, and after a narrow upbringing – without more knowledge of the world than the district sixty or seventy miles around – roundly to lay down the law to chivalry and judge of knights errant? Is it, perchance, idleness and waste of time to wander through the world, seeking no pleasures but the austerities by which the virtuous ascend to the seat of immortality? If knights, grandees, noblemen, or the high-born were to consider me a fool, I should take it as an intolerable affront; but that scholars who never entered or trod the paths of chivalry should set me down as a madman does not affect me a jot. A knight I am and a knight I shall die, if it please the Most High. Some travel over the broad field of proud ambition; others by way of base and servile adulation; others again by way of deceitful hypocrisy, and a few by way of the true religion. But beneath the influence of my star I journey along the narrow path of knight errantry, in which exercise I despise wealth, but not honour. I have redressed grievances, set right wrongs, punished insolences, conquered giants, and trampled down fiends. I am in love, only because knights errant are obliged to be so; and, being so, I am not one of those depraved lovers, but of the continent and platonic sort. I always direct my purposes to virtuous ends, and do good to all and ill to none. Whether he who so purposes, whether he who so labours, whether he who so acts, deserves to be called a fool, let your Highnesses decide, excellent Duke and Duchess.'

'By God, that's good!' cried Sancho. 'Say no more for yourself, my dear master. For there's nothing more in the world to be said, thought, or done. Besides, since this gentleman denies the very existence of knights errant, is it surprising that he doesn't know anything of what he is talking about?'

'Are you perhaps, brother,' asked the priest, 'that Sancho Panza they speak of, to whom your master promised an isle?'

'I am,' answered Sancho, 'and I deserve it as much as anyone on earth. I'm one of your – keep company with good men and you'll be one of them – yes, and of your – not with whom you're bred, but with whom you're fed – and of your – lean against a good tree and you'll get good shelter. – I've leant on my good master, and I've been going about in his company for many months and, God willing, I shall come to be like him. And if he lives and I live he'll have no lack of empires to rule, nor I of isles to govern!'

'No, of course not, Sancho my friend,' interposed the Duke, 'for in Don Quixote's name I can offer you the government of an odd one of mine, and no poor one either.'

'Go down on your knees, Sancho,' cried Don Quixote, 'and kiss his Excellency's feet for the favour.'

Sancho obeyed, and at the sight of him the priest got up from table, exclaiming in a great fury: 'By this habit I wear, I must protest that your Excellency is as stupid as these two sinners. They may well be mad if the sane sanction their insanity! Your Excellency may keep them company, but so long as they stop in this house I shall stay in mine, and refrain from reproving what I cannot remedy.'

And without another word or another mouthful he went off, and the Duke and Duchess's entreaties were powerless to stop him; not that the Duke said much to him, for laughter at his foolish burst of anger. But when he had stopped laughing he said to Don Quixote: 'You have answered so nobly for yourself, Sir Knight of the Lions, that you can require no further satisfaction of him; since, though this appears an offence, it is not one at all, for as women cannot give offence, neither can ecclesiastics, as your worship knows better than I.'

'That is true,' answered Don Quixote, 'and the reason is that one who cannot be offended can offend nobody. As women, children and ecclesiastics cannot defend themselves, even if they are attacked, they cannot be affronted. For between an offence and an affront there is this difference, as your Excellency knows better than I. An affront comes from one who is capable of giving it, gives it, and maintains it, but an offence can come from anyone without carrying an affront with it. Let us take an example: a man is standing carelessly in the street; ten men with arms in their hands come up and strike him; he draws his sword and does his duty; but the number of his opponents is against him and prevents his fulfilling his purpose, which is to avenge himself. This man is offended but not affronted. And this can be confirmed by another example. A man's back is turned; another man comes up and strikes him, and after striking him, does not wait, but runs away; the other follows him, but does not catch him. The man who was struck suffered an offence but no affront; for an affront has to be maintained. If the striker, even if he struck foully, had drawn his sword and stayed facing his enemy, the man who was struck would be offended and affronted at the same time; offended because he had been treacherously hit, and affronted because his assailant maintained his action, holding his ground without turning his back. And so, according to the laws of the accursed duel, I may be offended, but am not affronted. For children cannot wound and women do not generally do so, and so they have no call to maintain their position. The same applies to men of religion, for these three classes of people lack arms offensive and defensive; and so, although naturally they are compelled to defend themselves, they have not the power to offend anyone. But although I just said that I might have been aggrieved, now I say no. That is impossible. For one who cannot receive an affront can still less give one. For which reasons I should not resent, and do not resent, what that good man said to me. I only wish he had stayed a little longer, so that I could have convinced him of his error in supposing that knights errant have never existed in the world. For if Amadis had heard him, or one of his countless lineage, it would have gone badly with his worship, I assure you.'

'I'll swear to that,' said Sancho. 'They would have given him a slashing that would have split him from top to toe like a pomegranate or an over-ripe melon. They were fine lads at putting up with such jests! My goodness, I'm sure that if Reynald of Montalban had heard that little man's words, he would have given him a slap on the mouth that would have kept him quiet for more than three years. No, he should have picked a quarrel with them, and seen what he was like when they'd done with him.'

The Duchess was dying with laughter at Sancho's remarks, considering him madder and more entertaining than his master; and there were many at that time who shared her opinion. At last Don Quixote was calm and the meal finished; and as they were removing the table-cloths four maids came in, one with a silver basin, a second with a jug also of silver, a third with two very fine rich towels on her shoulder, and the fourth with her arms bare to the elbow, bearing in her white hands – and white they were indeed – a round ball of Naples soap. The one with the basin went up and, gracefully and without embarrassment, placed it under Don Quixote's chin. He, wondered at the ceremony, but silently assumed that it must be a custom of that country to wash the beard instead of the hands, and stretched his chin out as far as he could. At that same moment the jug began to rain on it, and the maid with the soap to set about it with such vigour that she raised snowflakes – for the lather was as white as snow – not only on his beard, but over the docile knight's whole face and his eyes – so much so that he was forced to shut them. The Duke and the Duchess, who had been informed of none of this, were waiting to see how the extraordinary ablutions would end. Now when the barber-maid had raised a handful of lather she made believe that she had used up the water, and bade the maid with the jug fetch more, for Don Quixote would wait; on which the second maid departed, and Don Quixote remained the strangest and most ludicrous figure imaginable. All the spectators, and they were many, gazed at him and, seeing him with half a yard of neck more than commonly brown, his eyes closed, and his beard full of soap, it was a great wonder that they were discreet enough to conceal their laughter. The maids who were playing this trick kept their eyes lowered and dared not look at their master and mistress, who were moved to anger and laughter at the same time, and did not know what to do, whether to punish the girls' presumption or reward them for the pleasure of seeing Don Quixote in that state. Finally the girl with the jug came back, and they finished washing Don Quixote. The girl with the towels very deliberately wiped him dry and, making him a low obeisance and curtsey, all four of them together were about to leave the hall. But in case Don Quixote should tumble to the joke, the Duke called to the girl with the basin: 'Come and wash me too, and see that you have enough water.'

The maid, who was shrewd enough, came and offered the basin to the Duke as she had done to Don Quixote, and they hastily soaped him and washed him thoroughly, leaving him dry and clean. Then they curtseyed and departed. It came out afterwards that the Duke had sworn to punish their sauciness if they did not wash him as they had Don Quixote, but they cleverly made amends by soaping him in the same manner.

Sancho paid great attention to these ceremonial ablutions, and said to himself: 'Bless me! What if it's the custom in this country to wash squire's beards as well as knights'? For, upon my soul, I've need of it, and if they were to shave me I should take it for a still greater favour.'

'What are you saying to yourself, Sancho?' asked the Duchess.

'I was saying, lady,' answered he, 'that I've always heard how at other princes' courts they give you water for your hands when they clear away the table-cloths, but not lather for your beard. So a long life's a good thing, for you see a great deal. Yet they say too that those who live long have plenty of ill to suffer, though to suffer one of these washings is more like pleasure than pain.'

'Don't you worry, friend Sancho,' said the Duchess. 'I will have my maids wash you, and scrub you if need be.'

'I'll be content if they do my beard,' answered Sancho, 'at least for the present; but for the rest Heaven will provide in due course.'

'Butler,' said the Duchess, 'see what the good Sancho wants, and comply with his wishes in all respects.'

The butler replied that Sancho should be served in every way, and with that went off to dine, taking Sancho with him, while the Duke, the Duchess and Don Quixote remained at table, talking of many different matters, all touching the profession of arms and of knight errantry. The Duchess asked Don Quixote, since he seemed to have a good memory, to delineate and describe the features of the lovely lady Dulcinea del Toboso who, according to fame's report of her charms, should certainly be the most beautiful creature in the world, even in all La Mancha. Don Quixote sighed on hearing the Duchess' request, and said: 'If I could pluck out my heart and place it before your Highness's eyes on this table in a dish, I should relieve my tongue of the toil of expressing what is almost inconceivable, for in it your Excellency would see her completely portrayed. But why should I set out to describe and delineate the beauty of the peerless Dulcinea, exactly and feature by feature? That is a burden fitter for other backs than mine, an enterprise which should occupy the pencils of Parrhasius, of Timanthus and of Apelles, and the chisels of Lysippus, to paint and to carve her on wood, on marble and in bronze. It would require the Ciceronian and Demosthenian rhetoric as well to praise her.'

'What does Demosthenian mean, Don Quixote?' asked the Duchess. 'It is a word I have never heard in all the days of my life.'

'Demosthenian rhetoric,' answered Don Quixote, 'is as much as to say the rhetoric of Demosthenes, as Ciceronian is Cicero's, which two were the greatest rhetoricians in the world.'

'That is so,' said the Duke, 'and you have shown your ignorance by asking such a question. But, all the same, Don Quixote would give us great pleasure if he would paint her for us, for I am sure that even in rough sketch and outline she will come out so fair that the fairest will envy her.'

'I certainly would,' replied Don Quixote, 'if the misfortune which recently befell her had not blotted her from my mind. So bad was it that I am readier to weep her than to describe her. For I would have your Highness know that when I went some days ago to kiss her hands and receive her blessing, consent and licence for this third expedition, I found a different person from the one I sought. I found her enchanted and transformed from a princess into a country-girl, from beauty to ugliness, from angel to devil, from sweet-smelling to pestiferous, from eloquent to rustic, from gentle to skittish, from light to darkness and, to conclude, from Dulcinea del Toboso to a Sayagan peasant girl.'

'God bless me!' exclaimed the Duke in a loud voice at this moment. 'Who can it have been that did the world such wrong? Who was it that robbed it of the beauty which delighted it, of the grace which charmed it, and the modesty which honoured it?'

'Who?' answered Don Quixote. 'Who can it have been but some malign enchanter, one of the many that envy and persecute me? That accursed race, born into the world to obscure and obliterate the exploits of the good, and to light up and exalt the deeds of the wicked. Persecuted I have been by enchanters. Enchanters persecute me, and enchanters will persecute me till they sink me and my high chivalries into the profound abyss of oblivion. They damage and wound me where they see I feel it most. For to rob a knight errant of his lady is to rob him of the eyes with which he sees, of the sun by which he is lighted, and of the prop by which he is sustained. Many other times I have said it, and now I say it again: a knight errant without a lady is like a tree without leaves, a house without foundations, and a shadow without a body to cast it.'

'There is no more to say,' said the Duchess, 'but yet, if we are to give credit to the history of Don Quixote, which has lately been given to the world to the general applause of mankind, we gather from it, if my memory is correct, that your worship never saw the lady Dulcinea, and that this same lady does not exist on earth, but is a fantastic mistress, whom your worship engendered and bore in your mind, and painted with every grace and perfection you desired.'

'There is much to say on that score,' replied Don Quixote. 'God knows whether Dulcinea exists on earth or no, or whether she is fantastic or not fantastic. These are not matters whose verification can be carried out to the full. I neither engendered nor bore my lady, though I contemplate her in her ideal form, as a lady with all the qualities needed to win her fame in all quarters of the world.

These are: spotless beauty, dignity without pride, love with modesty, politeness springing from courtesy, courtesy from good breeding and, lastly, high lineage, for with good blood beauty shines and glows with a degree of perfection impossible in a humbly born beauty.'

'That is true,' said the Duke, 'but Don Quixote must give me permission to say what the history of his exploits, which I have read, compels me to say. For though it is to be inferred that there is a Dulcinea, in El Toboso or out of it, and that she is beautiful in the highest degree, as your worship paints her, even then it does not appear that she compares in the matter of high lineage with the Orianas, the Alastrajareas, the Madasimas and others of that breed of whom the histories your worship knows so well are full.'

'As to that I may say,' answered Don Quixote, 'that Dulcinea is the daughter of her works, that virtues improve blood, and that the virtuous and humble are to be more highly regarded and prized than the wicked and exalted. All the more so since Dulcinea has a vein in her which may raise her to be a queen with a crown and sceptre, for the merit of one lovely and virtuous woman is sufficient to perform even greater miracles; and if not formally, at least virtually, she has greater fortune stored within her.'

'It's my opinion, Don Quixote,' said the Duchess, 'that you proceed with great caution in all you say, and proceed, as they often say, with plummet in hand. Henceforth I shall believe, and make my whole household believe — and my lord the Duke too, if it is necessary — that there is a Dulcinea in El Toboso, and that she lives to-day, and is beautiful, nobly born and deserving that such a knight as Don Quixote should serve her; which is the highest compliment I know how to pay her. But I cannot help entertaining one scruple, and bearing a certain grudge against Sancho Panza. This is my scruple: the aforesaid history relates that the same Sancho Panza, when he took her a letter on your worship's behalf, found the said Dulcinea winnowing a sack of corn and, to be more exact, they say that it was red wheat. Now, that detail makes me doubt the greatness of her lineage.'

To which Don Quixote replied: 'My lady, your Highness should know that all or most of the things which happen to me are out of the ordinary course of things which befall other knights errant, whether they be directed by the inscrutable will of the fates or by the malice of some envious enchanter; it being a thing now proved that of all the famous knights errant, one has the gift of being immune from enchantment and another has flesh so impenetrable that he cannot be wounded; as had the famous Roland, one of the twelve Peers of France, of whom it is told that he could only be wounded on the sole of his left foot, and even so only with the point of a stout pin and with no other kind of weapon at all. So when Bernardo del Carpio killed him at Roncesvalles, seeing that he could not wound him with his sword he lifted him from the ground in his arms and strangled him, thus recalling the death that Hercules dealt Antaeus, the fierce giant who, they said, was a son of Earth. I mean to infer from what I say that I might possibly have one of these gifts, not of invulnerability, for experience has often taught me that my flesh is soft and by no means impenetrable; nor of immunity from enchantment, for I have known myself to be put into a cage, in which the whole world would not have been strong enough to imprison me had it not been by virtue of enchantment. But since I freed myself from that spell I am inclined to believe that there is no other which can harm me. So that these enchanters, seeing that they cannot use their evil practices on me, avenge themselves on the objects I love best, and seek to take my life by ill-treating Dulcinea by whom I live. So, therefore, I believe that when my squire bore her my message they turned her into a peasant girl employed in the mean occupation of winnowing wheat, though I have affirmed that this wheat was neither red nor wheat, but grains of orient pearl. And to prove the truth of this, I should like to tell your Highness that, coming a little while since by El Toboso, I could never find Dulcinea's palace, and the other day, though Sancho my squire saw her in her proper shape, which is the most beautiful in the world, she appeared to me as a coarse and ugly peasant girl and not at all well spoken, though she is the world's paragon of wisdom. Now, since I am not enchanted and cannot be, according to sound judgment, it is she who is enchanted, injured, changed, altered and transformed. Through her my enemies have avenged themselves upon me, and for her I shall live in perpetual tears till I see her in her pristine state.

  'All this I have told you so that no one may heed Sancho's words about Dulcinea's sifting or winnowing. For since they transformed her for me, it is no wonder that they changed her for him. Dulcinea is noble and well-born, springing from one of El Toboso's gentle-manly families, which are many, old and most noble; and no doubt the peerless Dulcinea has no small share of their blood, for through her her town will be famous and memorable in future ages, as Troy has been for Helen and Spain for La Cava, though hers will be a worthier title to fame.

'On the other hand, I would have your Lordships understand that Sancho Panza is one of the drollest squires that ever served knight errant. Sometimes his simplicities are so shrewd that it gives me no small pleasure to consider whether it is simplicity or shrewd-ness that prevails. Some rogueries in him convict him of knavery, and his indiscretions confirm him a fool. He doubts everything and believes everything. When I think he is going to tumble into folly he comes out with clever sayings which exalt him to the sky. In fact I would not exchange him for any other squire, even if I were to receive a city to boot; and therefore I am in doubt whether it would be right to send him to that governorship with which your High-ness has favoured him, although I see in him a certain aptitude for this governing business, and with a slight trimming of his under-standing he would do as well with some governorship as the King with his taxes. Particularly as we know now through long experi-ence that there is no need of great ability or much learning to be a governor, for there are a hundred round here who can scarcely read, and yet govern like so many goshawks. The whole point is to have good intentions and to desire to do right in everything. For they will never lack some one to advise and guide them in their actions, like those unlettered military governors who have an assessor to pronounce sentence. I would advise him not to take bribes or for-sake justice, and on certain other little matters which are lying on my chest and will come off in due course for Sancho's benefit and to the advantage of the isle he will govern.'

The Duke, the Duchess and Don Quixote had arrived at this point in their conversation when they heard many voices and a great noise of people in the palace. And suddenly Sancho came into the hall in a great scare with a linen-strainer for a bib, and after him a number of lads, or rather kitchen-boys and other underlings, one of whom was carrying a little bowl of water, which from its colour and uncleanliness appeared to be dish-water. The boy with the bowl was following him, and teasing him by trying most persistently to push it right beneath his beard, which another boy made as if to wash.

'What is this, fellows?' asked the Duchess. 'What is this? What are you trying to do to this good man? What, do you not realize that he is a governor elect?'

To which the barber-scullion replied: 'This gentleman won't let himself be washed, as the custom is and as the Duke, my master, was washed and the gentleman, his master.'

'Yes, I will,' answered Sancho, in a great rage, 'but I should like it to be done with cleaner towels, with whiter soap, and less dirty hands; for there's not so much difference between me and my master that he should be washed with angel's water and I with devil's lye. The customs of countries and princes' palaces are only good so long as they give no offence, but the washing custom here in use is worse than the flogging penitents'. My beard's clean, and I've no need of such refreshings. And if anyone comes to wash or touch a hair of my head — I mean of my beard — speaking with all due respect, I'll give him such a punch as will leave my fist embedded in his skull, for these *cirimonies* and soapings seem to me more like practical jokes than hospitable civilities.'

The Duchess was dying with laughter at Sancho's angry protest. But it did not give Don Quixote much pleasure to see him so illadorned in a streaked towel and surrounded by so many of the kitchen underlings. Making a deep bow, therefore, to the Duke and Duchess, as if asking for permission to speak, he calmly addressed the rabble: 'Ho there, knights and gentlemen! Leave this lad alone and go back whence you came, or wherever else you please! For my squire is as clean as another, and these bowls are no more fitting for him than your little narrow-mouthed drinking cups. Take my advice and leave him, for neither he nor I will abide this jesting business.'

But Sancho caught his words out of his mouth and went on: 'No, let them come and make a mock of the stupid yokel! I'll stand for it, as sure as it's now night! Let them bring a comb here, or what ever they like, and curry this beard of mine, and if they get anything out of it which offends against cleanliness let them give me a convict's crop.'

Here the Duchess remarked, still laughing: 'Sancho Panza is absolutely right, and will speak nothing but the truth. He is clean and, as he says, has no need to wash. And if our custom does not please him, his soul is his own. What is more, you ministers of cleanliness have been exceedingly remiss and careless – I do not know whether I should not say presumptuous – in bringing before such a personage and such a beard your wooden troughs and bowls and your dish cloths, instead of jugs and basins of pure gold and holland towels. But, indeed, you are a sorry low-born crew and, like the scoundrels you are, cannot help showing the envy you bear to knight errant's squires.'

The roguish servants, and even the butler who was with them, thought that the Duchess was speaking seriously. So they took the strainer off Sancho's chest, and slunk away abashed and left him. Whereat seeing himself relieved from what had seemed to him extreme peril, he threw himself on his knees before the Duchess, crying: 'Great ladies can do great kindnesses, and I don't know how to repay the one your Highness has just done me except by having myself knighted, so that I may spend all the days of my life in the service of so exalted a lady. I'm a peasant; Sancho Panza is my name; I'm married; I have children and serve as a squire. If in any respect I may serve your Highness, I shall be no slower in obeying than your ladyship in commanding.'

'It is evident, Sancho,' replied the Duchess, 'that you have learnt to be courteous in the school of courtesy itself. It is evident, I mean, that you have been reared in Don Quixote's bosom, who must needs be the cream of courtesy and the flower of ceremonies, or "*cirimonies*" as you call them. Good luck to such a master and such a servant, one the pole-star of knight errantry and the other the star of squirely fidelity. Arise, Sancho my friend, for I will reward your courtesy by making the Duke, my lord, fulfil his promise to favour you with a governorship as speedily as he can.'

With this the conversation ceased, and Don Quixote retired to take his siesta. But the Duchess begged Sancho, if he had no great desire for sleep, to come and spend the afternoon with her and her maidens in a very cool room. Sancho replied that, although it was true that it was his custom to sleep for four or five hours on summer afternoons, he would, to serve her Excellency, try with all his might to take no sleep at all that day, and would come in obedience to her command; and so he left the hall.

Then the Duke renewed his orders to his servants to treat Don Quixote as a knight errant, and to adhere scrupulously to the style in which it is recorded that the knights of old were entertained.

Chapter XXXIII. Of the Delightful Conversation between the Duchess, her Maidens and Sancho Panza, which deserves to be both read and noted.

WELL, the story goes that Sancho did not sleep that afternoon, but kept his promise, and went after dinner to visit the Duchess, who for the pleasure of listening to him made him sit beside her on a low chair, although Sancho was so well bred that he was reluctant to sit down. But the Duchess bade him seat himself like a governor and talk like a squire, because under either head he deserved the very throne of the Cid Ruy Diaz, the Campeador. Sancho shrugged his shoulders, obeyed and sat down, and all the Duchess's maids and waiting-women surrounded him eagerly, keeping perfect silence to hear what he would say. But it was the Duchess who spoke first, saying:

'Now that we are alone and no one can overhear us here, I should like the noble governor to resolve certain doubts of mine arising from the history of the great Don Quixote, now in print. One of these doubts is this: since the good Sancho never saw Dulcinea, I mean the lady Dulcinea del Toboso, nor took her Don Quixote's letter, for it was left in the note-book in the Sierra Morena, how did he venture to forge her reply and all that story about finding her sifting wheat, since it was all a mock and a lie, prejudicial to the peerless Dulcinea's reputation and ill-suited to the quality and fidelity of a good squire?'

At these words Sancho got up from his chair and, without a word of reply, quietly made a circuit of the room, his body bent and one finger on his lips, lifting up the hangings as he went. Then, when he had done, he returned to his seat and said:

'Now, my lady, that I'm sure that nobody's eavesdropping and that only these ladies can hear me, I will reply to your question without fear or alarm, and to anything more I may be asked. Now the first thing I say is that I reckon my master Don Quixote's stark crazy, although sometimes he will talk in a way which, to my thinking and in the opinion of all who hear him, is so wise and leads down so good a track that Satan himself could not speak better. But, all the same, to my mind he's really and truly a madman, an idiot. So, seeing that I've tumbled to that, I don't mind making him believe things without rhyme or reason in them, like that about the reply to his letter, and the business six or eight days ago which I'd like you to know though it's not in the history: the matter of my lady Dulcinea's enchantment. For I made him believe that she's enchanted, which is no more true than the moon's a green cheese.'

The Duchess begged him to tell her about this enchantment or trick, and Sancho related it all just as it had happened, to the no small pleasure of his hearers. Then, pursuing her remarks, the Duchess observed:

'From what the good Sancho has told me there is a doubt leaping up in my mind, and a little whisper comes to my ears and says to me: "Since Don Quixote de la Mancha is a crazy fool and a madman, and Sancho Panza, his squire, knows it, yet, for all that, serves and follows him, and hangs on these empty promises of his, there can be no doubt that he is more of a madman and a fool than his master; and that being so, as it is, you will be criticized, lady Duchess, if you give the said Sancho Panza an isle to govern; for if a man cannot govern himself, how will he know how to govern others?"'

'By God, lady,' said Sancho, 'but this doubt was born in the nick of time. Tell it, your worship, to speak clearly or any way it will, for I know it speaks the truth and that I should have left my master days ago if I had been wise. But that was my lot and my ill-luck. I can do nothing else; I have to follow him; we're of the same village; I've eaten his bread; I love him dearly; I'm grateful to him; he gave me his ass-colts; and, what is more, I'm faithful; and so it's impossible for anything to part us except the man with the pick and shovel. And if your Highness doesn't wish them to give me the promised governorship, God made me without it, and perhaps my not getting it may redound to the good of my conscience. For though I'm a fool, I understand the proverb which says: for his own hurt the ant sprouted wings. And it may well be that Squire Sancho may get to Heaven quicker than Governor Sancho. They bake as good bread here as in France; and in the night all cats are grey; and a man's pretty unlucky if he hasn't broken his fast by two in the afternoon; and there's no stomach a hand's breadth bigger than another, that can be filled, as the saying goes, with straw and hay; and the little birds of the field have God to provide for them and feed them; and four yards of Cuenca shoddy will warm you more than any four of Segovia broadcloth; and when we leave this world and go into the ground below the prince's path is as narrow as the labourer's, and the Pope's body takes up no more feet of earth than the sexton's, though one's higher than the other; for when we go down the pit we all have to shrink and fit, or they make us shrink and fit whether we like it or not – and good night! And I say once more that if your ladyship doesn't wish to give me the isle because I'm a fool, I shall be wise enough not to care. And I've heard say that behind the cross lurks the devil; and all is not gold that glitters; and from among oxen, ploughs and yokes they took Wamba to be King of Spain; and from among silks, entertainments and riches they took Roderick to be eaten by snakes, if the verses of the old ballads don't lie.'

'How not lie!' put in the waiting-woman Doña Rodriguez at this point, she being one of the listeners. 'For there's a ballad that says that they put King Roderick, all alive, into a tomb with toads, snakes and lizards, and that two days later the King cried from inside this tomb in low and doleful tones:

> Now they eat me, now they eat me
> In the part where most I sinned.

and, according to that, this gentleman's quite right when he says that he would rather be a peasant than a king, if he is to be eaten by reptiles.'

The Duchess could not restrain her laughter at her waiting-woman's simplicity, or withhold her astonishment at Sancho's reasonings and proverbs; and she said to him: 'Now the good Sancho knows that once a knight makes a promise he tries to fulfil it, even if it costs him his life. The Duke, my lord and master, although he is no knight errant, is none the less a knight, and so he will keep his word about the promised isle, despite the envy and malice of the world. Let Sancho be of good heart, for when he least expects it he will find himself seated on the throne of his isle, invested in his dignity, and grasping his governorship, which he will fling aside in time for another of brocade three inches thick. But I charge him particularly to look to the government of his vassals, remembering that they are all loyal and well born.'

'About the matter of governing them well,' answered Sancho, 'there's no need to urge me, for I'm charitable by nature and have compassion on the poor; and from him who cooks and kneads you must not steal his bread, and I swear they shan't throw me false dice. I'm an old dog and understand their calls, and I can snuff myself at the right time, and won't let them put cobwebs over my eyes, because I know where the shoe pinches. I mean to say that the good shall have entrance and inflammation with me, and the wicked neither foot nor fellowship. And I think that in this matter of a governorship the beginning's everything, and that, maybe, when I have been governor a fortnight I shall take to it like a duck to water, and know more about it than about the field-work I was brought up in.'

'You are right, Sancho,' said the Duchess, 'for no one is born with knowledge, and bishops are made from men, not from stones. But to come back to the conversation we were having just now about the lady Dulcinea's enchantment, I consider it absolutely certain and proved beyond a doubt that Sancho's scheme of tricking his master and making him believe that the peasant girl was Dulcinea, and that if his master did not recognize her it was because she was enchanted – that all that, I say, was the invention of one of those enchanters who persecute Don Quixote. Because I know that the peasant girl who skipped on to the she-ass really and truly was and is Dulcinea del Toboso, and that it was the good Sancho who was deceived, though he may think he is the deceiver; and there is no more doubt about that than about anything else we have never seen. And I would have Master Sancho know that we also have enchanters here who love us well and tell us what is happening in the world, plainly and simply, without tricks and tangles. And believe me, Sancho, the frisky peasant girl was and is Dulcinea del Toboso, and she is as enchanted as the mother that bore her; and when least we expect to we shall see her in her proper shape, and then Sancho will be disabused of the delusion under which he labours.'

'All that may well be,' said Sancho Panza, 'and now I'm prepared to believe my master's story about his vision in Montesinos' cave; where he says he saw the lady Dulcinea del Toboso in the same dress and looking just as I said I had seen her when I enchanted her just for my own amusement. But it must all have been contrariwise, as your worship says, my lady, because it can't and mustn't be presumed that I could invent such a shrewd trick on the spur of the moment with my poor wits, and I don't believe that my master's so mad as to accept anything so far beyond all the bounds of probability on such weak and feeble persuasion as mine. But you shouldn't reckon me ill-natured on that score, my lady, because a stupid like me isn't bound to tumble to all the malicious plots of these vile enchanters. I made that story up to escape my master Don Quixote's scoldings, and not meaning to harm him; and if things have turned out otherwise, God's in Heaven and judges our hearts.'

'That is true,' said the Duchess; 'but tell me now, Sancho, what is this you say about the cave of Montesinos? I should like to hear about it.'

Then Sancho Panza told her, detail by detail, all that has already been related about this adventure. And when she had heard it the Duchess said: 'Now since the great Don Quixote says he saw the same peasant girl there that Sancho saw on the way out of El Toboso, there is no doubt that we must infer from this incident that it is Dulcinea, and that there are some very active and exceedingly meddling enchanters about here.'

'I agree,' said Sancho Panza, 'but if my lady Dulcinea del Toboso's enchanted, so much the worse for her; for I don't have to take on my master's enemies, who must be plentiful and wicked. The truth may be that it was a peasant girl I saw. I took her for a peasant girl, and a peasant girl I judged her to be. But if it was Dulcinea it can't be laid to my account; they can't run to me about it, or start a scrap with me on the subject. No, I won't have them coming to me every moment with their argy-bargying: "*Sancho said it, Sancho did it, Sancho went, and Sancho came*", as if Sancho were some what's-his-name, and not the same Sancho Panza who is going all about the world now in books, as Sampson Carrasco told me. For he's a person bachelored by Salamanca, at the very least, and the likes of him can't lie excepting only when they've a fancy to, or when it's greatly to their advantage. So there's no reason for anyone to blame me; and since I have a good reputation and, as I have heard my master say, a good name is worth more than great riches, let them fit this governorship on me and they'll see marvels; for one who has been a good squire will be a good governor.'

'All that the good Sancho has just said,' observed the Duchess, 'are Catonian sentences, or at the least drawn from the very heart of Michael Verino himself – *florentibus occidit annis*. Well, well, to speak in Sancho's own fashion, beneath a bad cloak there is often a good drinker.'

'Really, my lady,' replied Sancho, 'I've never drunk out of vice in my life. Out of thirst very possibly, for there's nothing of the hypocrite about me. I drink when I've a fancy, and when I haven't and I'm offered drink, I take it so as not to seem finicky or ill-bred. For a toast to a friend – what marble heart is there that won't pledge a friend? But although I wear shoes I don't soil them, especially as the squires of knights errant almost always drink water, because they're for ever travelling through forests, woods and meadows, by mountains and crags, without finding a merciful drop of wine, even if they'd give one eye for it.'

'So I believe,' answered the Duchess. 'And now let Sancho go and rest. By-and-by we will talk at greater length, and we will give orders for him to be fitted, as he put it, with this governorship.'

Once more Sancho kissed the Duchess's hands, and begged her to be so kind as to see that good care was taken of his Dapple, who was the light of his eyes.

'What Dapple is this?' asked the Duchess.

'My ass,' answered Sancho, 'for not to call him by that name I generally call him Dapple. I asked this waiting-woman here to take care of him when I entered the castle, and she couldn't have got angrier if I'd called her old or ugly, though it should be more proper and natural for waiting-women to look after asses than to lord it in halls. Good Heavens, what a dislike a certain gentleman of my village had for these ladies.'

'He must have been a yokel,' said Doña Rodriguez the waiting-woman, 'for if he were a well-born gentleman he would rate them higher than the horn of the moon.'

'Now, now!' said the Duchess. 'Let us have no more of that. Be quiet, Doña Rodriguez, and be calm, Master Panza, and leave me to see that Dapple is looked after. For if he is a jewel of Sancho's I will place him in the apple of my eye.'

'It will be all right if he's in the stable,' answered Sancho, 'for in the apple of your Highness's eye neither he nor I are worthy to stay for a single moment; and I would no more consent to that than to stab myself all over. For although my master says that in courtesies one should rather lose by a card too many than a card too few, in matters of donkeys and asses you have to go with compass in hand and warily.'

'Let Sancho take him to his government,' said the Duchess. 'There he can tend him as he will and even exempt him from labour.'

'Don't think, lady Duchess, that your Grace has said anything remarkable,' said Sancho, 'for I've seen more than a few asses go to governorships, and my taking mine will be no novelty.'

Sancho's words started the Duchess laughing with delight once more; and sending him to rest, she went to give the Duke an account of her conversation with him. Then, between the two of them, they planned and arranged a new trick to play on Don Quixote, a rare one and well suited to his style of chivalry. And indeed they invented many of that kind, which were both ingenious and appropriate, and are some of the best adventures contained in this great history.

Chapter XXXIV. *Of the Instructions received for the Disenchantment of the peerless Dulcinea del Toboso, which is one of the most famous Adventures in this Book.*

GREAT was the pleasure the Duke and Duchess received from their conversation with Don Quixote and Sancho Panza; and being resolved in their intention of playing some tricks on them which should bear some appearance or semblance of adventures, they took an idea from Don Quixote's account of the cave of Montesinos, and from it prepared a famous one. What most astonished the Duchess, however, was the greatness of Sancho's simplicity. For he had now come to believe that Dulcinea's enchantment was the infallible truth, although he had himself been the enchanter and the trickster in that business. So, having given their servants directions as to their behaviour, some six days later they took Don Quixote on a hunting-party with an array of huntsmen and beaters worthy of a crowned king. They gave him a hunting-suit, and Sancho another of the finest green cloth. But Don Quixote refused to put his on, with the excuse that he had to return next day to the stern exercise of arms, and that he could not carry wardrobes or stores with him. Sancho, however, took what they gave him, with the intention of selling it at the first possible opportunity.

Then, when the appointed day came, Don Quixote put on his armour and Sancho his new suit and, the squire riding on Dapple, whom he would not leave behind even though they offered him a horse, joined the troop of beaters. The Duchess came out magnificently dressed, and Don Quixote, out of pure courtesy and good manners, took the rein of her palfrey, although the Duke tried to prevent him. After some time they reached a wood lying between two very high hills, where they took up their positions, laid their ambushes, arranged their beats, and distributed the huntsmen to their various stations. Then the hunt began with such a great noise of shouting and hallooing that, what with the barking of the dogs and the sound of the horns, they could not hear one another speak.

The Duchess dismounted and took up her station with a sharp spear in her hands in an ambush where she knew the wild boar generally passed. The Duke and Don Quixote also dismounted and placed themselves on either side of her, while Sancho assumed a position at the extreme rear, without getting off his Dapple, whom he dared not abandon for fear that some accident might befall the beast. But scarcely had they alighted and put themselves in a line with a great number of their servants, when they saw a huge wild boar rushing towards them, hard pressed by the hounds and pursued by the huntsmen, gnashing its teeth and tusks, and spraying foam from its mouth. At which sight Don Quixote braced his shield and advanced to encounter it, sword in hand. The Duke also advanced with his spear, but the Duchess would have been ahead of them all if her husband had not prevented her. Only Sancho, at the sight of the valiant beast, abandoned Dapple and started running as fast as he could. He tried to climb a tall oak, but could not; for when he was half way up, as his ill-luck would have it, a bough which he had grasped in his endeavour to get to the top broke and, falling to the ground, left him in the air, caught on a fork of the oak and unable to get down. Finding himself in this plight with his green suit tearing, and thinking that if the fierce beast were to come that way it would be able to reach him, he began to shout so loud and persistently for help that everyone who heard him but did not see him supposed that some wild animal was devouring him. At last the tusked boar was run through by the many javelin points which the hunters levelled against him; and Don Quixote, turning his head at the shouts, which he had already recognized for Sancho's, saw him hanging head down from the oak, and beside him Dapple, who did not abandon him in his calamity – and Cide Hamete says that he seldom saw Sancho without seeing Dapple, or Dapple without seeing Sancho: such was the friendship and loyalty between them. Don Quixote went up and released Sancho who, once free and on the ground, looked at the tear in his hunting-suit and grieved in his soul, for he thought that in that suit he possessed an inheritance.

Meanwhile they laid the mighty boar on a baggage-mule and, covering it with sprigs of rosemary and branches of myrtle, bore it away as the spoils of victory to some large field-tents, which were pitched in the middle of the wood. There they found the tables set and a dinner prepared, a grand and sumptuous spread which clearly displayed the greatness and magnificence of the host. And as Sancho showed the Duchess the rents in his torn coat, he observed: 'If this had been a hunting of the hare or of small birds, my coat would have been in no danger of getting into this state. I don't know what pleasure's to be got from lying in wait for an animal who can kill you, if he catches you on his tusk. I remember hearing an old ballad once which says:

> By the bears you may be eat,
> As was Favila the great.'

'That was a Gothic King,' said Don Quixote, 'who went out hunting and was eaten by a bear.'

'What I mean,' replied Sancho, 'is that I wouldn't have princes and kings putting themselves in such-like perils for the sake of a pleasure that should really not be a pleasure, for it consists in killing an animal which has not committed any offence.'

'But you are quite mistaken,' answered the Duke, 'for the exercise of hunting is the most essential of all sports for kings and princes. Hunting is war on a small scale; in it there are stratagems, artifices and ambushes for the safe conquest of the enemy. In hunting one suffers extremes of cold and intolerable heats; idleness and sleep are cut short; the bodily strength is increased; the hunter's limbs are made nimble. In short, it is an exercise which can be followed without prejudice to anyone and with pleasure to many; and the best thing about it is that it is not for everyone, as other kinds of sport are, except for hawking which is also reserved for kings and great lords. So, Sancho, you must change your mind, and when you are a governor follow the chase. You will see that you will be a hundred times the better for it.'

'No, indeed,' answered Sancho, 'a good governor and a broken leg are best at home. It would be a fine thing if people came wearied out to look for him on some business, and he was amusing himself in the forest. The government would go to the devil at that rate. Indeed, sir, hunting and pastimes are better suited to idlers than to governors. The way I mean to take my pleasure is in a game of cards at Easter, and skittles on Sundays and holidays; for these huntings and the like don't go with my temper or my conscience.'

'Pray God, Sancho, that you prove as good as your word,' said the Duke, 'though there's a gap indeed 'twixt word and deed.'

'Be that as it may,' replied Sancho, 'a good paymaster doesn't worry about sureties; and God's help's better than early rising; and belly carries legs and not legs belly. I mean that if God helps me and I do my duty with a good heart, there's no doubt that I shall govern better than a goshawk. So let them put a finger in my mouth and see if I bite or not.'

'God and all His saints confound you, Sancho you wretch!' cried Don Quixote. 'When will the day come, as I have often asked before, when I shall hear you utter a continuous and connected sentence without proverbs? Let this fool be, your Highnesses, for he will grind your souls, not only between two but between two thousand proverbs, dragged in as fittingly and as much to the point as — God bless him, and me too, if I have patience to listen to them!'

'There may be more of Sancho Panza's proverbs,' said the Duchess, 'than the Greek Commander's, yet they are no less valuable for the pithiness of their expression. I can say for myself that they give me more pleasure than others that are better applied and more seasonably introduced.'

With this and similar entertaining talk they left the tent for the wood, and passed the day visiting the hunters' posts and ambushes. Here they were overtaken by night, which was neither so clear nor so calm as was usual at that season of the year, it being about midsummer. But a certain half-light that obtained was of great assistance to the plans of the Duke and Duchess. For as soon as it was dusk and night was beginning to fall, it suddenly appeared as if the whole wood in all directions was burning, and presently they heard from here, there and everywhere, countless trumpets and other martial instruments, as if several troops of cavalry were passing through the forest. The light of the fires and the sound of warlike instruments almost blinded the eyes and deafened the ears of the spectators, and of everyone in the wood as well. Presently they heard a great shouting of *Lelili*, which is the Moors' battle-cry. Trumpets and clarions blared, kettle-drums rattled, fifes shrilled, almost all together and so continuously and rapidly that any one with any senses at all must have lost them at the confused din of all those instruments. The Duke was struck dumb, the Duchess astonished, Don Quixote amazed, and Sancho trembling; in fact even those who were in the secret were seized with alarm. Fear held them silent when a postilion dressed as a demon passed in front of them, blowing instead of a bugle a huge hollow ox-horn, which emitted a hoarse and fearful sound.

'Hie, there, brother courier!' cried the Duke. 'Who are you? Where do you come from? And what men of war are these who appear to be passing through this wood?'

To which the courier replied in bold and horrific tones: 'I am the Devil. I have come to seek Don Quixote de la Mancha. The people approaching are six troops of enchanters, bearing the peerless Dulcinea del Toboso on a triumphal car. Here she comes enchanted, with the gay Frenchman Montesinos, to give Don Quixote instructions how the said lady is to be disenchanted.'

'If you were the Devil, as you say you are and as your appearance suggests, you would have recognized the said knight Don Quixote de la Mancha, for you have him before you.'

'By God and my conscience,' answered the Devil, 'I was not looking at him; for my mind is distracted by so many matters that I was forgetting the principal purpose I had come for.'

'This Devil must certainly be an honest fellow,' said Sancho, 'and a good Christian. For if he weren't he wouldn't swear by God and his conscience. So I suppose that there must be some good people even in Hell.'

Then the Demon, without dismounting, directed his gaze on Don Quixote and said: 'To you, Knight of the Lions – and may I see you between their claws – I am sent by the unhappy but valiant knight Montesinos, who commanded me to bid you on his behalf await him on the spot where I should meet you, since he brings with him her whom they call Dulcinea del Toboso, for the purpose of giving you instructions as to her disenchantment, and as my coming here was for no other reason I need stay no longer. May demons like myself have you in their keeping, and the good angels preserve this noble pair.' Then, when he had spoken, he blew his enormous horn, turned his back and departed without waiting for a reply.

This produced further amazement in everyone, especially in Sancho and Don Quixote; in Sancho at their insistence, in defiance of the truth, that Dulcinea was enchanted; and in Don Quixote since he could not be certain whether what had happened in Montesinos' cave was true or not. But while he was deep in these thoughts, the Duke asked: 'Does your worship intend to wait, Don Quixote?'

'Why not?' answered he. 'I shall stay here, fearless and strong, though all Hell should come to assail me.'

'But if I see another devil and hear another horn like the last one I'll no more stay here than I'd stay in Flanders,' said Sancho.

By this time the night had grown darker, and numerous lights began to flit about the wood, much as the dry exhalations of the earth flit about the sky and appear to our vision as shooting stars. At the same time a frightful noise was heard, like the rumbling of the ponderous wheels of ox-waggons, from whose harsh and continuous creaking wolves and bears, if there are any around, are said to fly. The turmoil, however, continued to increase, and it actually sounded as if four separate skirmishes or battles were being fought in the four quarters of the wood. Close by there pealed the harsh thunder of dreadful artillery; further off countless musket-shots rang out; almost at hand resounded the shouts of the combatants; afar off the Moslem war cries were repeated; in fact the cornets, horns, bugles, clarions, trumpets, drums, cannons and guns, and, above them all, the fearful creakings of the waggons, made together so confused and horrible a din that Don Quixote had to avail himself of all his courage to endure it. But Sancho's heart fell into his boots and sent him fainting to the skirts of the Duchess, who received him in them, and promptly ordered water to be thrown in his face. This was done, and he returned to his senses just as the waggon with the creaking wheels came up to where they stood. It was drawn by four ponderous oxen, all swathed in black trappings, with a flaming wax torch tied to each horn. On top of the waggon was placed a high seat, on which was seated a venerable old man, dressed in a long robe of black glazed buckram, with a beard whiter than snow and so long that it fell below his waist; for the waggon was full of lights and it was easy to distinguish everything in it. It was driven by two ugly demons dressed in the same buckram, with such hideous faces that once Sancho had seen them he closed his eyes for fear of seeing them again. Then, when the waggon came up opposite the place where they were standing, the venerable old man rose from his high seat and, standing up, called in a loud voice: 'I am the sage Lirgandeo.' Then the waggon passed on without another word. Behind it came another of the same kind, with another old man on a throne, who made the waggon stop and in a voice no less solemn than the first cried: 'I am the sage Alquipe, close friend of Urganda the Unknown.' He passed on, and immediately yet another waggon of the same kind appeared, though the man seated on the throne was not old like the others, but a very stout fellow of an evil appearance who, on coming up, arose like the others, and proclaimed in harsher and more devilish tones: 'I am Arcalaus the enchanter, the mortal enemy of Amadis of Gaul and all his kin'; and passed on. The three waggons halted a little way off, and the deafening din of their wheels ceased. After that there was no further noise but the sound of soft and harmonious music, which delighted

Sancho, who took it for a good omen, and said to the Duchess, from whom he had not stirred by so much as an inch: 'Lady, where there's music there can be no mischief.'

'Nor where there are lights and brightness,' replied the Duchess.

To which Sancho answered: 'Flame may give light and bonfires brightness, as we can see, but they may very well scorch us. But music is always a sign of feasting and merriment.'

'That remains to be seen,' said Don Quixote, who was listening. And he was right, as the following chapter will show.

Chapter XXXV. *A Continuation of Don Quixote's Instructions for the Disenchantment of Dulcinea, and other wonderful things.*

IN time to the delightful music they saw a triumphal car approaching, drawn by six grey mules and covered in white linen; and on each beast rode a penitent, also dressed in white, with a great lighted wax torch in his hand. This waggon was twice, or even three times, bigger than the previous ones. On the front of it and at the side were twelve other penitents, white as snow, all with their torches alight, a sight both marvellous and terrifying. On a raised throne was seated a nymph swathed in countless veils of gold tissue, which made her appear, if not richly, at least gorgeously apparelled. Her face was covered with a delicate and transparent veil, in such a way that its folds did not prevent them from making the features of a lovely maiden; and the multitude of lights made it possible to distinguish her beauty and her youth, for she seemed to be neither more than twenty nor less than seventeen. Beside her came a figure swathed to the feet in a trailing robe which brushed the ground, with his head covered by a black veil. At the moment when the waggon arrived opposite the Duke and Duchess and Don Quixote the music of the oboes ceased, and soon the harps and lutes which were being played in the waggon ceased also. Then, rising to his feet, the figure in the robe threw its folds aside and, stripping the veil from his face, revealed plainly the very shape of Death, fleshless and hideous, which caused Don Quixote some disturbance and Sancho some alarm, while the Duke and Duchess assumed an appearance of fear.

This living Death rose upon his feet, and began to speak in a drowsy voice and with a sleepy articulation, after this manner:

> I Merlin am who, as the histories say,
> Had for my father even the Devil himself
> (A lie by lapse of time now authorized),
> Prince of the Magic Art, repository
> And monarch of the Zoroastrian science.
> Jealous I am of ages and of times
> Which seek to cloak the exploits of the brave
> Knights errant, whom I loved in ancient days,
> And still do love with deep affection.
> Although the nature of enchanters and
> Those that are wizards and magicians is
> Perpetually hard and harsh and stern,
> Yet mine is tender, soft and amorous,
> Loving to do good deeds to one and all.
>
> Into the murky caverns of black Dis,
> Where my soul was, fast occupied in drawing
> Certain rhomboids and mystic characters,
> There came the piteous voice of that fair maid,
> The peerless Dulcinea del Toboso.
> I learnt of her enchantment and mischance,
> And transformation from a highborn lady
> Into a rustic village wench. I grieved,
> And caged my spirit in the hollow shell
> Of this most dreadful and fierce skeleton.
> But after searching through ten thousand books
> Of this, my devilish and my vile craft,
> I come to bring the fitting remedy
> To such a grief and to so great an ill.
>
> O you, glory and pride of all who wear
> The coat of steel and hardest adamant,
> O Light, O lantern, path, pole-star and guide
> Of those who, casting off their sluggish sleep
> And feather beds, make themselves strong to endure
> The intolerable use and exercise
> Of sanguinary and laborious arms,
> To you I say, great Hero never praised
> Enough, yet ever praised, most valiant
> And at the same time most wise Don Quixote,
> La Mancha's splendour and the star of Spain,
> That to restore into her pristine state
> The peerless Dulcinea del Toboso,
> Needful it is that your squire, Sancho Panza,

> Shall deal himself three thousand and three hundred
> Lashes upon his two most ample buttocks,
> Both to the air exposed, and in such sort
> That they shall smart, and sting and vex him sorely.
> This is the universal resolution
> Of all the authors of her sad misfortunes;
> And therefore, lords and ladies, have I come.

'My goodness!' exclaimed Sancho. 'Three thousand lashes! But I'd as soon give myself three stabs as three lashes. The devil take this way of disenchanting! I don't see what my buttocks have got to do with these enchantments. By God, if Master Merlin doesn't find another way of disenchanting the lady Dulcinea del Toboso, she may go enchanted to her grave!'

'I will take you,' said Don Quixote, 'Don Yokel, stuffed with garlic, and I will bind you to a tree, naked as your mother bore you, and not only will I give you three thousand three hundred, but six thousand six hundred lashes, so well laid on that it will take more than three thousand three hundred tugs to pull them off. Do not answer me a word, or I will tear your soul out.'

But on hearing this Merlin observed: 'It must not be done that way. The lashes the good Sancho is to get must not be applied by force, but must be of his own free will; and at such time as he pleases, for there is no date fixed. But it is permitted him, if he wishes to cut this whipping down by half, to receive it at the hand of another, though it must be a fairly weighty hand.'

'At no one else's, nor at my own. Nor shall it be a weighty one, nor one that can be weighed,' replied Sancho. 'No hand whatever shall touch me. Was it I that bore the lady Dulcinea del Toboso, that my buttocks shall pay for the sins of her eyes? My master, now, he's a part of her; for every moment he's calling her *his life* and *his soul* – his support and his prop. He can whip himself for her – and he should – and do all that's needful for her disenchantment. But me whip myself? I bernounce.'

Scarcely had Sancho finished speaking when the silvery nymph who rode beside Merlin rose to her feet and, flinging the thin veil from her face, revealed a countenance which seemed to all excessively lovely. Then, with a masculine assurance and in no very lady-like tones, she addressed Sancho Panza directly: 'O wretched squire with no more soul than a pitcher, with heart of cork, and bowels of flint and pebble! If you were commanded, shameless thief, to cast yourself to the ground off a huge tower; if they bade you, enemy of the human race, to eat a dozen toads, two dozen lizards and three dozen snakes; if they entreated you to kill your wife and children with a fierce and sharp scimitar, it would be no wonder were you to appear squeamish and reluctant. But to make a to-do about three thousand three hundred lashes, when the most wretched charity scholar gets as many every month; that amazes, astonishes and affrights the compassionate bowels of all who hear of it, and of everyone too who may come, in the course of time, to hear of it. Cast, you miserable, hard-hearted animal, cast, I say, those startled owl's eyes of yours upon these pupils of mine, which have been compared to glittering stars, and see them weep thread by thread and skein by skein, making furrows, tracks and channels down the fair fields of my cheeks. Let it move you, knavish and malevolent monster, that my blooming youth – for I am still in my teens: I am nineteen and not yet twenty – is being consumed and withered beneath the skin of a rustic peasant girl; and if I do not look like one now, that is a particular favour that the lord Merlin, here present, has done me, solely in order that my features may soften you; that the tears of a distressed beauty may turn rocks into cotton and tigers into sheep. Lash, lash that thick hide of yours, you great untamed beast; raise up from sloth that spirit which inclines you to eating and still more eating, and set at liberty the smoothness of my skin, the meekness of my temper and the beauty of my countenance. But if you will not relent for me or submit to any reasonable terms, do so for the sake of that poor knight there at your side; for your master, I say, whose soul I can now see stuck in his throat, not ten inches from his lips, only awaiting your answer, harsh or kind, to issue through his mouth or return to his breast.'

On hearing this, Don Quixote felt his throat and said, turning to the Duke: 'By God, sir, Dulcinea has spoken the truth, for here is my soul sticking in my throat like the nut of a crossbow.'

'What do you say to that, Sancho?' asked the Duchess.

'I say, lady,' replied Sancho, 'what I've said already, that as for the lashes I bernounce them.'

'*Renounce* you should say, Sancho, and not what you said,' observed the Duke.

'Let me alone, your Highness, I'm in no state now to look into subtleties or to consider a letter or two more or less; for these lashes I'm to get, or I'm to give myself, have so upset me that I don't know what I'm saying or doing. But I should like to hear from the lady, from my lady Doña Dulcinea del Toboso, where she learnt her way of begging. She comes to ask me to tear my flesh open with lashes and calls me *pitcher-soul* and *great untamed beast,* and a string of other bad names — may the Devil bear them! Is my flesh, by chance, brass? And does it matter to me whether she's disenchanted or not? What hamper of fine linen, shirts, kerchiefs and socks — though I don't wear them — does she bring with her to soften me? None, but just one piece of abuse on top of another, though she knows the local proverb, that an ass loaded with gold goes lightly up a mountain; and that gifts break rocks; and praying God and wielding the hammer; and a bird in the hand is worth two in the bush. Then my lord and master, who should be stroking my neck and wheedling me to make myself soft as wool or carded cotton, says that if he catches me he'll bind me naked to a tree and double the dose of lashes. These compassionate gentlemen should consider that they're not just asking a squire to whip himself, but a governor, which is, as you might say, gilding the lily. Let them learn, let them learn — the devil take them — how to ask, and how to beg, and how to show their breeding; for all times are not the same, and men are not always in a good humour. Now I'm ready to burst with grief because of the tear in my green coat, and they come and ask me to whip myself of my own free will, which I'd as soon do as turn Red Indian.'

'Then, truly, friend Sancho,' said the Duke, 'if you do not get yourself softer than a ripe fig, you shall not set a hand on the government. It would be a fine thing if I were to send my islesmen a cruel governor with bowels of flint, who would not bow to the tears of distressed maidens nor to the petitions of wise, haughty and ancient enchanters and sages. To be brief, Sancho, either you shall be whipped, or you shall whip yourself, or you shall not be governor.'

'Sir,' answered Sancho, 'won't they give me two days to consider what is best for me?'

'No, on no account,' said Merlin. 'Here, at this instant and on this spot the issue of this business must be settled. Either Dulcinea shall return to the cave of Montesinos and to her former state of peasant girl, or she shall be carried in her present shape to the Elysian fields, where she will wait till the number of lashes is complete.'

'Come, good Sancho,' said the Duchess, 'be of good heart, and show your gratitude to Don Quixote for his bread that you have eaten, for we are all bound to serve him and to please him for his worthy character and his high chivalry. Accept this lashing, my son, and let the devil go to the devil and fear to the faint-hearted, for a good heart breaks bad luck, as you well know.'

To this advice Sancho replied by addressing Merlin with an inquiry well off the point: 'Tell me, your worship, Sir Merlin; when the courier-devil came here, he gave my master a message from Sir Montesinos, bidding him wait for him here, since he was going to give him instructions for the disenchantment of the lady Doña Dulcinea del Toboso. Yet so far we haven't seen Montesinos or anyone like him.'

To which Merlin replied: 'The Devil, friend Sancho, is an ass and a very great scamp. I sent him to seek your master with a message not from Montesinos but from me. For Montesinos is in his cave awaiting his disenchantment, or rather hoping for it, for there is still the tail to skin. If he owes you anything, or you have any business to do with him, I will bring him to you, and put him wherever you like. But now make up your mind to accept this penance and, believe me, it will be of great advantage to you, both to your soul and to your body; to your soul because of the charity with which you do it, and to your body because you are of a sanguine temperament, I know, and it can do you no harm to lose a little blood.'

'Many doctors there are in the world – even enchanters are doctors,' replied Sancho, 'but since they all tell me so – though I don't see it myself – I agree to give myself the three thousand three hundred lashes, on condition that I can do it whenever I choose, without any fixing of times and seasons. I'll try to wipe off the debt as soon as possible, so that the world may enjoy the beauty of the lady Doña Dulcinea del Toboso, for it appears that she's really beautiful, though I never thought she was. But there must be one other condition, that I shan't be obliged to draw blood with this whipping, and if any of the lashes are only fly-teasers they must be reckoned in. Also if I make a mistake in the number Sir Merlin, since he knows everything, shall take care to keep count and advise me of the number too many or too few.'

'There will be no need to advise you of any too many,' answered Merlin. 'For the lady Dulcinea will be disenchanted at the very moment when you reach the exact number, and will come in gratitude to look for the good Sancho to give him thanks and a reward too for his good deed. So there is no need to be scrupulous about a few lashes too many or too few, and Heaven forbid that I should deceive anyone, even by so much as a hair's breadth.'

'Well, then, in God's hands be it!' said Sancho. 'I accept my bad luck ... I say that I agree to the penance with the conditions noted.'

No sooner had Sancho pronounced these last words than the music of the oboes struck up once more, and a great number of muskets were fired. Don Quixote hung on Sancho's neck, giving him countless kisses on his forehead and his cheeks. The Duchess and the Duke and all the spectators showed signs of the greatest satisfaction, and the waggon began to move off. As the fair Dulcinea passed she bowed her head to the Duke and Duchess and made a deep curtsey to Sancho.

And now the gay and smiling dawn came on apace; the little flowers of the fields raised their heads and stood erect; and the liquid crystals of the brooks, murmuring over the white and grey pebbles, went to pay tribute to the expectant rivers. The merry earth, the clear sky, the pure air, the serene light, each and all together gave manifest signs that the day, which came treading on the skirts of the dawn, would be calm and bright. Delighted with the chase and at the skill and success of their plans, the Duke and Duchess returned to their castle with the intention of following up their joke, for nothing promised them greater pleasure.

Z

Chapter XXXVI. *Of the strange and inconceivable Adventure of the Afflicted Waiting-woman, alias the Countess Trifaldi, with a letter which Sancho Panza wrote to his wife, Teresa Panza.*

It was a steward of the Duke's, a very comical and nimble-witted fellow, who had played the part of Merlin and arranged all the details of the last adventure. He had composed the verses and made a page play Dulcinea, and now with the collaboration of his master and mistress he contrived another plan, the most amusing and the strangest imaginable.

Next day the Duchess enquired of Sancho whether he had begun upon the penance he had undertaken for the disenchanting of Dulcinea; and he replied that he had, for on the night before he had given himself five strokes. But when the Duchess asked with what instrument he replied that it was with his hand.

'That,' said the Duchess, 'is more like a slapping than a whipping. It is my opinion that the sage Merlin will not be content with such softness. The good Sancho will have to get a whip with prickles or a cat o'nine tails, that can be felt; for learning must be beaten in, and the release of a great lady like Dulcinea must not be sold so cheap. Remember, Sancho, that works of charity which are performed feebly and half-heartedly have no merit and are worth nothing.'

To which Sancho replied: 'Give me a whip or a proper rope's end, your ladyship, and I'll use it, so long as it doesn't hurt me too much. For I would have your Grace know that, peasant though I am, my flesh is more like cotton than rushes, and it would not be right for me to destroy myself for someone else's good.'

'Very well,' answered the Duchess. 'To-morrow I will give you a whip which will just suit you, and agree with the tenderness of your flesh like its own sister.'

To which Sancho replied: 'I must tell you, your Highness, dear lady of my heart, that I've written a letter to my wife, Teresa Panza, giving her an account of everything that's happened to me since I left her. I have it here inside my shirt. There's nothing lacking but the signature. I wish that your Wisdom would read it, for I think it's written in a governor's style – I mean in the way that governors should write.'

'And who dictated it?' asked the Duchess.

'Who should have dictated it but myself, poor sinner that I am?' answered Sancho.

'And did you write it yourself?' asked the Duchess.

'Not a bit of it,' answered Sancho, 'for I can't read or write, though I can make my mark.'

'Let us see it,' said the Duchess, 'for no doubt it will display the quality and aptness of your wit.'

On which Sancho drew from his breast an unsealed letter, which the Duchess took, and saw that it ran like this:

Sancho Panza's letter to Teresa Panza, his wife.

If it is a good whipping they gave me it is a fine mount I have now; if I have a good governorship it cost me a good whipping. You will not understand this now, dear Teresa, but one day you will. I must tell you, Teresa, that I am determined you shall ride in a coach, for that is the proper thing; every other way of travelling is like going on all fours. Wife of a governor you are; see if anyone will tread on your heels. I am sending you herewith a green hunts-man's suit, which my lady the Duchess gave me. Turn it into a bodice and skirt for our daughter. Don Quixote, my master, as I have heard tell in these parts, is a sane madman and a droll idiot, and they say I am just as bad. We have been in Montesinos' cave; and the Sage Merlin has got me to help in the disenchantment of Dul-cinea del Toboso, whom you at home call Aldonza Lorenzo. With three thousand three hundred lashes – less five – which I am to give myself, she will be as disenchanted as the mother that bore her. You will tell nobody about this; for take your business to court and some will say it is white and some black. In a few days I shall leave for my governorship, to which I go very anxious to make money, and I am told that all new governors go in the same frame of mind. I will take its pulse and advise you if you are to come with me or no. Dapple is well, and sends his greetings; I do not intend to leave him behind, even if I am taken to be made Grand Turk. My lady the Duchess kisses your hands a thousand times. Send her two thousand kisses in return, for there is nothing that costs less or goes cheaper,

*as my master says, than fair compliments. God has not been pleased
to furnish me with another bag of another hundred crowns like the
last time, but do not let that worry you, Teresa dear, for the man
who sounds the alarm is safe, and it will all come out in the wash — I
mean the governorship. Only one thing troubles me: they say that
once I taste it I shall eat my hands after it, and if that is so I shall
not get off very cheap, although the maimed and handless find begging alms as good as a canonry. So, one way or another, you will be
rich and fortunate. God grant it you, as he can, and preserve me to
serve you. From this castle, the 20th of July 1614.*

Your husband the governor
Sancho Panza.

When she had finished reading the letter, the Duchess said to
Sancho : 'There are two small matters in which the worthy governor
is a little astray. The first is in saying, or leaving it to be understood,
that he has been given this governorship in return for the whipping
he has to take, though he knows, as he cannot deny, that when my
lord the Duke promised it to him no one dreamt that there was such
a thing as a whipping in the world. The other is that he reveals considerable covetousness, and I would not like him to turn out badly,
for covetousness burst the bag, and the greedy governor does ill-
governed justice.'

'I don't mean all that, lady,' answered Sancho ; 'and if your worship thinks that this letter doesn't go as it should, I've only to tear
it up and write a new one, though maybe it'll be a worse one, if it's
left to my poor brain.'

'No, no,' replied the Duchess. 'It is a good one, and I want the
Duke to see it.'

Upon this they went out into a garden, where they were to dine
that day, and the Duchess showed Sancho's letter to the Duke, who
was highly delighted with it. They dined, and when the cloths had
been removed and they had amused themselves for a good while
with Sancho's savoury conversation, they suddenly heard the doleful sound of a fife and the harsh beating of an untuned drum. Everyone seemed disturbed by this confused, warlike and melancholy
music, especially Don Quixote, who could not sit still for pure excitement. Of Sancho it can only be said that fear took him to his ac-

customed refuge, which was at the Duchess's side or in her skirts; for in sober earnest the sound they heard was most doleful and melancholy. Then, while they were all waiting in suspense, they saw coming down the garden before them two men clad in mourning robes so long and flowing that they trailed on the ground; and as they came they beat two great drums also swathed in black. By their side walked the fifer, pitch black like them, and these three were followed by a personage of gigantic size, bemantled rather than clad, in the blackest of cloaks with a monstrously long train. Over his cloak he wore a broad shoulder-strap, black as well, from which hung a huge scimitar with black hilts and sheath. His face was covered by a transparent black veil, through which could be seen a very long and snow-white beard, and he kept step to the drum-beats with great gravity and composure. To be brief, his size, his solemn gait, his blackness and his escort were sufficient to produce the amazement they did in all who saw him and did not know who he was. Thus he approached in slow and ceremonious state and knelt before the Duke, who with everyone else present awaited him standing, and would not allow him to speak until he had risen up. This the prodigious scarecrow did and, once on his feet, raised the mask from his face to reveal the most horrid, long, white, thick beard ever till then beheld by human eyes. Then from his broad and swelling chest he strained and forced out a grave and sonorous voice, fixing his eyes on the Duke as he spoke:

'Most high and powerful lord, my name is Trifaldin of the White Beard. I am squire to the Countess Trifaldi, otherwise called the Afflicted Waiting-woman, on whose behalf I bring your Highness a message. It is that your Magnificence should be pleased to grant her faculty and licence to enter and tell you of her plight, which is one of the strangest and most amazing that any troubled mind in all the world could imagine. But first she wishes to know whether in this castle of yours there is staying the valorous and unconquered knight Don Quixote de la Mancha, to seek whom she has come on foot and fasting from the kingdom of Candaya to this your realm, a journey which should rightfully be reckoned miraculous or performed by force of enchantment. She is waiting at the door of this fortress or country-house, and only awaits your good pleasure to enter. I have spoken.'

Then he coughed and stroked his beard from top to bottom with both hands, in great composure awaiting the Duke's reply, which was: 'Many days ago, good squire Trifaldin of the White Beard, we heard of the distress of my lady Countess Trifaldi, whom enchanters have caused to be called the Afflicted Waiting-woman. You may gladly tell her to enter, stupendous squire, and that the valiant knight Don Quixote de la Mancha is here, from whose generous nature she may safely expect every protection and aid. You may tell her also on my behalf that if she is in need of my help it shall not fail her, for I am bound to aid her by my knighthood, which compels me to favour every sort of women, in particular widowed matrons in distress and affliction – for such her ladyship must be.'

On hearing this Trifaldin bent his knee to the ground and, motioning the fife and drums to strike up, quitted the garden to the same music and at the same pace as he had come in, leaving everyone amazed at his presence and gravity. Then the Duke turned to Don Quixote and said: 'To be sure, renowned knight, neither the darkness of malice nor of ignorance can cover and obscure the light of valour and virtue. This I say because, virtuous sir, you have hardly been six days with us in this castle, and already the sorrowful and afflicted come from far-off and distant lands to seek you; and not in coaches or on dromedaries, but on foot and fasting, confident of finding in that mighty arm the remedy for their distresses and hardships, thanks to your great deeds which cover and circle the whole of the known world.'

'I wish, Sir Duke,' replied Don Quixote, 'that blessed man of religion were here, who showed at table the other day so great a distaste for knights errant and so malignant a grudge against them, so that he might see with his own eyes whether such knights are necessary in the world. He would at least have certain evidence that your extraordinarily afflicted and disconsolate in harsh predicaments and appalling misfortunes do not go to seek their remedy at the houses of scholars, nor at the village sexton's, nor to the knight who has never ventured beyond the boundaries of his town, nor to the slothful courtier, who had rather look for news to tell and repeat than attempt to perform deeds and exploits for others to relate and write down. Remedy for distresses, relief in hardship, succouring of maidens and consoling of widows are nowhere so readily to be obtained as from knights errant. I give infinite thanks to Heaven that I am one, and I do not repine at whatever trouble or hardship may befall me in this most honourable exercise. Let the waiting-woman come in and ask what she will; for I will work her relief by the strength of my arm and the dauntless resolution of my courageous spirit.'

Chapter XXXVII. The famous Adventure of the Afflicted Waiting-woman continued.

THE Duke and Duchess were highly delighted to see how well Don Quixote responded to their plan. But at that point Sancho exclaimed: 'I shouldn't like this lady to lay any stumbling-block in the way of my promised government, for once I heard a Toledo apothecary say – and he talked like a linnet – that where waiting-women meddled no good could come of it. Heavens alive, how that apothecary disliked them! Now since, as far as I can make out, all waiting-women are meddlers and trouble-makers, whatever their quality or condition, what will they be like when they're afflicted, as they say this Countess Three Skirts or Three Tails is? – for in my country skirts and tails, tails and skirts, are all the same.'

'Be quiet, Sancho my friend,' said Don Quixote, 'for since this waiting-lady comes from such distant lands to seek me, she cannot be one of those in the apothecary's reckoning. Particularly since she is a countess; and when countesses serve as waiting-women it will be in the service of Queens and Empresses, for in their own houses they are high ladies, and are served by other waiting-women.'

At which Doña Rodriguez, who was present, spoke up: 'My lady the Duchess has waiting-women in her service who might have been countesses in their own right, if Fortune had been kind. But laws go as kings will. Let no one speak ill of waiting-women, particularly when they are old and unmarried; for though I am not one, yet I can easily see and appreciate the advantage that a maiden waiting-woman has over a widow; and the man who clipped us still has the shears in his hand.'

'All the same,' replied Sancho, 'there's so much to shear in these waiting-women, according to my barber, that it would be better not to stir the rice, even though it cakes.'

'Squires are always our enemies,' replied Doña Rodriguez. 'For, seeing that they are the imps of the antechambers and watch us at every turn, such times as they are not praying – and those are many – they spend in gossiping about us, disinterring our bones and interring our good names. But let me tell those animated logs that we shall live in the world in spite of them – and in the houses of the great – though we die of hunger and cover our bodies, delicate or otherwise, with black weeds like a nun's, as a dung-hill is sometimes covered up with a sheet on the day of a procession. I can assure you that if I were allowed, and the time were right, I would let them know – not only those present but the whole world – that there is no virtue that you will not find in a waiting-woman.'

'I believe,' said the Duchess, 'that my good Doña Rodriguez is right, very right. But she must wait for a fitting time to defend herself and other waiting-women, to refute the bad opinion of that evil apothecary and to uproot it entirely from the breast of the great Sancho Panza.'

To which Sancho replied: 'Since I've had a sniff at a governorship all squirely vapours have left me, and I don't give a wild fig for all the waiting-women in the world.'

They would have continued with the waiting-woman controversy, had they not heard the fife and drums strike up again to announce the approach of the Afflicted One. The Duchess then asked the Duke whether it would be right to go and receive her, since she was a countess and a lady of rank.

'In so far as she's a countess,' observed Sancho, before the Duke could reply, 'I'm for your Highness's going out to receive her; but in so far as she's a waiting-woman I'm of the opinion you shouldn't stir a step.'

'Who asked you to meddle in this, Sancho?' asked Don Quixote.

'Who, sir?' answered Sancho. 'I meddle, and I've a right to meddle, as a squire who has learnt the laws of courtesy in your worship's school. For you're the most courteous and well-bred knight there is in all courtship; and in these matters, as I've heard your worship say, you may lose as much by a card too many as by a card too few, and good ears need few words.'

'It is as Sancho says,' said the Duke. 'We will see the shape of the countess, and measure by that the courtesy due to her.'

At this the drums and fife came in as before – and here the author ended this brief chapter and began the next, pursuing the same adventure, one of the most notable in the story.

Chapter XXXVIII. *The Afflicted Waiting-woman relates her Misfortune.*

BEHIND the melancholy musicians there began to enter the further part of the garden some waiting-women to the number of twelve, divided into two files, all dressed in ample nuns' habits, seemingly of milled serge, with white stoles of fine Indian muslin, so long that only the edge of their habits showed. Behind them came the Countess Trifaldi, whom the squire Trifaldin of the White Beard led by the hand, she clothed in finest black blanket-cloth, unnapped – for had it been napped every grain would have shown up the size of a good Martos chick-pea. Her tail or skirt, or whatever they call it, fell in three trains, which were borne by three pages, also dressed in mourning and forming a handsome mathematical figure with the three acute angles formed by the three trains, whence it was concluded that she got her name of the Countess Trifaldi, as one might say the *Countess with the Three Skirts*. This, Benengeli says, was correct, for her proper title was the Countess *Lobuna*, from the many wolves bred in her country; and if they had been foxes instead of wolves she would have been the Countess *Zorruna*, it being a custom in those parts for owners to take their titles from the thing or things most abundant on their estates; but to celebrate the novelty of her skirt, this countess dropped *Lobuna* and took the name of *Trifaldi*.

The lady and her twelve waiting-women advanced at a processional pace, their faces covered with black veils, which were not transparent like Trifaldin's, but so thick that nothing showed through them. As soon as this squadron of waiting-women appeared, the Duke, the Duchess and Don Quixote stood up, as did everyone else who was watching the slow procession. The twelve waiting-women stopped and made a passage, through the middle of which the Afflicted One advanced without letting go of Trifaldin's hand. At this the Duke, the Duchess and Don Quixote advanced a matter of a dozen paces to receive her. Then, sinking on to her knees on the ground, she cried in a voice rather coarse and rough than subtle and delicate:

'May it please your Highnesses to show less courtesy to this your waiting-man – I should say waiting-woman. For, as I am the Afflicted One, I shall not be able to reply to you as I ought, since my strange and unparalleled misfortune has carried off my wits I know not where, – but it must be a long way, for the more I seek them the less I find them.'

'He would lack wits, lady Countess,' replied the Duke, 'who did not from your person discover your worth, which, without further examination, is deserving of all the cream of courtesy and all the flower of courtly ceremony.'

And, raising her by the hand, he took her to sit in a seat beside the Duchess, who also received her with great politeness. Don Quixote was silent, and Sancho was dying to see the faces of the Countess and of some of her many ladies; but this was not possible till they uncovered themselves of their own will and accord. All were calm and stood in silence, waiting for someone to break it, which the Afflicted Lady did with these words:

'I am confident, most powerful lord, most lovely lady and most wise company, that my extreme affliction will find in your most valiant breasts a reception no less assured than generous and compassionate. For such it is that it could melt marble, soften adamant, and mollify the steel of the most hardened hearts in the world. But, before it is published in your hearings, not to say in your ears, I should like to be made cognizant whether there is in this body, circle and company that most stainless of knights, Don Quixote de la Manchissima, and his most squirely Panza.'

'The Panza,' said Sancho, before any one else could reply, 'is here, and the Don Quixotissimo as wellissimo; and so, most Afflict- ed and most Waiting-ladylike of Ladies, you may say whatever you wishimo, for we are all ready and most prepared to be your servitor- issimos.'

At this Don Quixote got up and, addressing himself to the Afflicted Lady, said: 'If your distresses, anguished lady, can pro- mise you any hope of relief through any valour or prowess of any knight errant, here is my arm which, short and feeble as it is, shall be wholly employed in your service. I am Don Quixote de la Mancha, whose function it is to succour the necessitous of all sorts; and that being so, assuredly you have no need, lady, to sue for favours, nor to hunt for preambles, but only to state your grievances plainly and without circumlocutions, for your hearers will know how, if not to relieve them, at least to commiserate with them.'

At these words the Afflicted Lady seemed about to fling herself at Don Quixote's feet. Indeed she did throw herself down, and struggled to embrace them, saying: 'Before these feet and legs I throw myself, unconquered knight, for they are the bases and pillars of knight errantry. I would kiss these feet, on whose steps hangs and depends the whole remedy of my misfortune. O valorous knight errant, whose veritable deeds outdistance and obscure the fabulous exploits of the Amadises, Esplandians, and Belianises!'

Then, leaving Don Quixote, she turned to Sancho Panza and, seizing him by the hands, exclaimed: 'O loyalest squire that ever served knight errant in ages present or past, whose goodness is greater than the beard of Trifaldin, my attendant here present! Well may you pride yourself that in serving the great Don Quixote you are serving, symbolically, the whole troop of knights who have ever handled arms in all the world. I conjure you by all you owe to your great benevolence and fidelity to be my kind intercessor with your master that he may immediately favour this most humble and most afflicted Countess.'

'As to my goodness, my lady,' answered Sancho, 'being as long and as large as your squire's beard, that means very little to me. Let me have my soul bearded and whiskered when I quit this life: that's what matters. For the beards of this world I care little or nothing. But without these wiles and prayers I will ask my master — and I know he loves me well, especially now that he has need of me in a certain business — to favour and aid your grace in whatever he can. Unload your distress, relate it to us, and leave the rest to us, for we shall all understand one another.'

The Duke and Duchess were bursting with laughter at this passage, and so was everyone else who had taken the measure of the adventure. And in their hearts they praised the shrewdness and cunning of the Trifaldi, who returned to her seat and said: 'Of the

famous kingdom of Candaya, which lies between the great Tapro-
bona and the Southern Sea, six miles beyond Cape Comorin,
Queen Doña Maguncia was mistress. Widow she was of King
Archipiela, her lord and husband, by which marriage they got and
procreated the Princess Antonomasia, heiress of their kingdom.
Which said Princess Antonomasia was bred and grew up under my
tutelage and teaching, since I was her mother's most ancient and
chiefest waiting-lady. It happened then that, in the course of time,
the girl Antonomasia reached the age of fourteen in such perfection
of beauty that nature could not raise her a point higher. Her wits,
too, were far from contemptible. She was as intelligent as she was
lovely. She was the most beautiful creature in the world; and is so
yet, if the envious fairies and hard-hearted Fates have not cut the
thread of her life. But that they will not have done, for Heaven could
not permit such evil to be done on earth, and a cluster from the fairest
vine in the vineyard to be carried off unripe. Her beauty, insuffi-
ciently praised by my dull tongue, caused an infinite number of
princes, both native and foreign, to fall in love with her; and among
those who dared to raise his thoughts to the heaven of so much
loveliness was a knight of low degree there was at court, who relied
on his youth and gallantry, his many accomplishments and graces,
and the ease and brilliance of his wit. And I would have your Highnesses know, if I am not boring you, that he could play a guitar so
well that he made it speak; and, what is more, he was a poet and a
great dancer, and was so good at making bird-cages that he could
have earned his living by their manufacture if he had been in extreme need. Now all these talents and graces would have been
sufficient to move a mountain, let alone a delicate maiden. But all
his graces and charms, all his endowments and accomplishments,
would have been ineffectual against the fortress of my child's
virtue, if the shameless thief had not resorted to the expedient of
winning me first. First the cursed, godless vagabond set about gaining my goodwill and buying my consent to hand over to him,
like a bad custodian, the keys of the fortress I was guarding. In
short he wheedled me and forced my agreement with all manner of
toys and trifles that he gave me. But what chiefly overthrew me and
brought me to the ground were some verses which I heard him sing
one night, from a barred window which gave upon the narrow

street where he was standing. If I remember rightly they ran like this:

> "An ill doth wound me to the soul,
> Struck by my sweetest enemy,
> Yet what most tormenteth me
> Is that my hurt I must conceal."

'The song seemed to me pearls and his voice syrup, and from that time till now, let me tell you, considering the harm I fell into through these and other such verses, I have been of opinion that poets should be banished from good and well ordered states, as Plato counselled; — at least the lewd ones — for the verses they write are not like the poem about the Marquis of Mantua, which delights and brings tears to the eyes of women and children, but are barbed couplets, which like smooth thorns pierce your soul and wound you there like lightning, leaving your clothes untouched.

'Another time he sang:

> "Come death quietly, without pain.
> Let me not thy coming know,
> That the pleasure to die so
> Make me not to live again."

And many other little verses and refrains of this kind, which enchant when sung, and surprise when read. Then what if they stoop to compose a kind of poem which was then in fashion in Candaya called a roundelay? That makes your soul leap up and laughter tickle in your throat; it fills your body with unease and, in short, is like mercury to all the senses. So, I tell you, my lords, such minstrels ought to be exiled to the islands of lizards. It is not they that are to blame, however, but the simpletons who praise them and the foolish women who believe them. If I had been the good waiting-woman I should have been, his stale conceits would not have moved me, and I could not have believed that he was speaking the truth when he said: "*Dying I live, in frost I burn; In fire I tremble; I hope without hope, I go and stay;*" with other impossibilities of that stamp, of which their writings are full. Then, when they promise the Phoenix of Arabia, Ariadne's crown, the horses of the Sun and the pearls of the South, the gold of Tibar, the balsam of Pancaya! That is where they stretch their pens farthest, for it costs them little to promise what they never intend to, nor can perform. But, where am I digressing to? Alas, I am a luckless creature! What madness or what folly leads me to recite the faults of others, having so much to say of my own? O unlucky I am, I repeat, for it was not the verses that conquered me, but my own guilelessness. It was not the music, but my own lightness which seduced me. My great ignorance and lack of foresight opened the road and freed the path for the passage of Don Clavijo – for that is the name of the gentleman I mentioned. And so I was the go-between, and he found his way, not once but many times, to Antonomasia's room, though under the promise of marriage. By me she was beguiled and not by him, for, sinner that I was, I would not have consented to his approaching the edge of her slipper-sole without swearing to be her husband. No, no, not that! Marriage must always be the condition of any business of that kind I manage. There was only one difficulty in this affair, disparity of rank, since Don Clavijo was a private gentleman and Princess Antonomasia the heiress, as I have said, of the kingdom. For some time this intrigue was hidden and cloaked by my cunning precautions, till it became clear to me that it was speedily being revealed by a certain swelling of Antonomasia's belly, fear at which made the three of us take counsel together. And we decided that before the mischief came to light Don Clavijo should ask for Antonomasia's hand before the vicar, on the strength of a written promise of marriage which the Princess had made him, framed by my ingenuity in such strong terms that Samson himself could not have broken it. Our plan was put into effect, and the vicar examined the contract and took the lady's confession. She confessed openly, and he ordered her to be put under the care of a very honourable sergeant of the court.'

'So there are sergeants of the court and poets and roundelays in Candaya too,' interrupted Sancho. 'I swear it makes me think the world's the same everywhere. But pray hurry up, my lady Trifaldi; for it's late, and I'm dying to know the end of your long story.'

'Indeed I will,' answered the Countess.

Chapter XXXIX. *The Trifaldi continues her Stupendous and Memorable Story.*

EVERY word Sancho spoke delighted the Duchess as much as it vexed Don Quixote. But, commanding him to be silent, the Afflicted One went on: 'At length, after a great number of questions and answers, since the Princess persisted in her resolve without departing or wavering from her first declaration, the vicar pronounced in favour of Don Clavijo and entrusted her to him as his lawful wife, which so annoyed the queen, Doña Maguncia, Princess Antonomasia's mother, that within three days we buried her.'

'She'll have died, no doubt,' exclaimed Sancho.

'That is obvious,' replied Trifaldin, 'for in Candaya we do not bury the living but the dead.'

'There have been cases, Sir Squire,' retorted Sancho, 'when they have buried someone who has fainted in the belief that he was dead. And it seemed to me that Queen Maguncia would have done better to swoon than to die, for with life much can be remedied, and the Princess's slip wasn't so great that they had to take it all that hard. Now if this lady had married one of her pages, or some other servant of the house, as many others have done, so I have heard tell, the damage would have been irreparable. But to have married a well-bred and clever knight, as you have just described him to us, really, really, though it was folly, it was not as bad as they think. For according to my master's rule, and he's here and won't let me lie, just as they make bishops of scholars, they can make Kings and Emperors of knights, especially if they're errants.'

'You are right, Sancho,' said Don Quixote, 'for a knight errant, if he has two grains of luck, has every potentiality for becoming the greatest lord in the world. But let the Afflicted Lady continue; for it is evident to me that the bitter part of this story – so far so sweet – remains to tell.'

'Indeed the bitter part is to come,' replied the Countess. 'And so bitter that bitter-apple is sweet and oleander savoury in comparison. The Queen was dead, not fainting, and we buried her. But no sooner had we covered her with earth and said our last farewell to her than – who but must weep to tell such grief? – on top of the Queen's grave appeared the giant Malambruno, mounted on a wooden horse.

He was first cousin to Maguncia, and not only cruel but an enchanter. Then, in revenge for his cousin's death and Don Clavijo's audacity, and to punish Antonomasia's boldness, by his magic arts he put the pair of them under a spell on top of the very grave itself. She was turned into a brass monkey, and he into a dreadful crocodile of an unknown metal; and between them stands a post, also of metal, with some characters written in the Syriac tongue, which, translated into Candayesque and then into Castilian, make up this sentence:

"These two bold lovers will not regain their former shape until the valorous Manchegan comes to fight me in single combat; since for his great valour alone the Fates reserve this unparalleled adventure."

"The enchantment done, he drew from its sheath a broad and tremendous scimitar and, seizing me by the hair, made a feint of cutting my windpipe and shearing off my head at a blow. I was distraught; my voice stuck in my throat; I was terrified in the extreme. But, for all that, I mastered myself as best I could, and in trembling and piteous tones made him such a copious confession that he suspended the execution of that cruel punishment. Finally he had all the waiting-women in the palace brought before him, all these who are now present and, after enlarging on our fault and abusing the characters of our kind, their evil practices and wicked schemings, and loading on all of us the guilt which was mine alone, he said that he would not inflict capital punishment on us, but other protracted pains which would be a perpetual social death. Then the very instant he finished speaking we all felt the pores of our faces open, and a sensation as if we were being pricked all over them with needlepoints. At once we clapped our hands to our cheeks and found ourselves in the state that you will now see.'

Then the Afflicted One and the other waiting-women lifted the veils which covered them and revealed their faces, all thick with beards, some fair, some black, some white and some grizzled, at the sight of which the Duke and Duchess made show of amazement, Don Quixote and Sancho were stupefied, and all the spectators aghast.

'In this way,' the Trifaldi proceeded, 'that wicked and evil-minded Malambruno punished us by covering the softness and smoothness of our skins with the roughness of these bristles. Would to Heaven he had cut off our heads with his enormous scimitar, instead of darkening the light of our faces with this fleece which covers us. For if we examine the matter, dear gentlemen — and what I am going to say now I should say with my eyes running a fountain of tears; though the thought of our misfortune and the seas which they have wept already keep them moistureless and dry as ears of corn, and therefore I shall speak without tears — where, I ask you, can a waiting-woman go with a beard? What mother or father will take pity on her? Who will give her aid? For even when she has a soft skin and tortures her face with a thousand sorts of lotions and cosmetics, she can scarcely find anyone to like her. So what shall she do when she reveals a face like a forest? O waiting-women, my companions, in an unlucky moment were we born; in an evil hour our parents begot us!' And as she spoke she gave a show of fainting.

Chapter XL. *Of Matters touching and pertaining to this Adventure and this memorable History.*

IN very truth, all who enjoy stories like this should show their gratitude to Cide Hamete, its first author, for his meticulousness in recording its minutest details, leaving nothing, however trivial, which he does not bring clearly to light. He depicts thoughts, reveals intentions, answers unspoken questions, clears up doubts, resolves objections; in fact elucidates the slightest points the most captious critic could raise. O most renowned author! O fortunate Don Quixote! O famous Dulcinea! O droll Sancho Panza! May you live, jointly and separately, for infinite ages, to the delight and general amusement of mankind!

The history goes on to tell that when Sancho saw the Afflicted Lady in a faint, he said: 'On the faith of an honest man and the memory of all my ancestors, the Panzas, I swear I've never heard or seen, nor has my master ever related to me, nor so much as imagined, an adventure like this. May a thousand devils take you — I would not abuse you, Malambruno — for the enchanter and giant you are! Could you find no other sort of punishment to inflict on these sinners except bearding them? Wouldn't it have been better and more fitting to their case to have cut off half their noses from the middle upwards, even if it had made them talk with a snuffle, rather than to have clapped beards on them? I'll bet they haven't enough money to pay for being shaved.'

'That is the truth, sir,' replied one of the twelve. 'We have not the means to cleanse ourselves. So, as an economical remedy, some of us have taken to using pitch or sticking plasters, applying them to our faces and pulling them off with a jerk, which makes us as bare and smooth as the bottom of a stone mortar. For although in Candaya there are women who go from house to house removing body-hairs, plucking eyebrows, and mixing various lotions of use to women, we, being my lady's waiting-women, would never let them in, for most of them smell of your go-betweens who have ceased to be principal parties. So, if we are not relieved by Don Quixote, with beards we shall be carried to the grave.'

'I would pluck mine out,' said Don Quixote, 'in the land of the Moors, if I could not relieve you of yours.'

At this point the Trifaldi recovered from her faint and said: 'The tinkling of that pledge, valorous knight, reached my ears in the midst of my swoon, and was instrumental in bringing me round and restoring my senses. So, once more I beg you, illustrious Errant and indomitable Sir, to put your gracious promise into effect.'

'There will be no delay on my account,' replied Don Quixote. 'Think, lady, what it is I am to do. For my courage is very ready to serve you.'

'The case is this,' answered the Afflicted One. 'From here to the Kingdom of Candaya, if you go by land, it is fifteen thousand miles to within half a dozen. But if you go by air and in a straight line it is nine thousand six hundred and eighty-one. You must also know that Malambruno told me that when Fortune should provide me with a knight to deliver us he would send him a mount, much better than your hired hacks, and with less vices; for it will be the same wooden horse on which the valiant Pierres carried off the fair Magalona. Which horse is guided by a peg in his forehead, which serves for a bridle, and he flies through the air with such speed that the devils themselves seem to be moving him. This same horse, according to ancient tradition, was made by the sage Merlin. He lent it to Pierres, who was his friend and made long journeys on him, and as I have said, stole the fair Magalona and bore her on his crupper through the air, leaving all who watched them from the earth staring like fools. He lent him only to those he liked or who paid him best, and from the great Pierres' time till now we know of nobody who has ridden him. Since then Malambruno has captured him by his arts, holds him in his power, and uses him on the voyages which he takes at times through different parts of the world – to-day he is here, to-morrow in France, and the day after in Potosi. And the good thing is that this horse does not eat or sleep or cost anything to shoe, but ambles at such a pace through the air, though he has no wings, that his rider may carry a cup full of water in his hand without spilling a drop, so smoothly and easily does he travel; for which reason the fair Magalona greatly enjoyed riding him.'

'For smooth and easy going,' interrupted Sancho, 'give me my Dapple. True, he does not go through the air, but on land I'll back him against any ambler in the world.'

Everyone laughed, and the Afflicted Lady went on: 'Now this same horse, if Malambruno intends to put an end to our trouble, will be here in our presence within half an hour of nightfall. For he informed me that the sign by which I should know that I had found the knight I was seeking would be his sending me the horse with all convenience and speed to the place where that knight might be.'

'How many, now, does this horse take?' asked Sancho.

'Two persons,' answered the Afflicted One, 'one on the saddle and the other on the crupper. Generally these two are knight and squire, when there is no stolen maiden.'

'I should like to know, Afflicted Lady,' said Sancho, 'what this horse is called.'

'His name,' replied the lady, 'is not that of Bellerophon's horse, who was called Pegasus; nor of Alexander the Great's, Bucephalus; nor of the furious Roland's, whose name was Brillador; nor yet Bayard, who belonged to Reynald of Montalban; nor Frontino like Ruggiero's; nor Bootes, nor Pirithous, which they say were the names of the horses of the Sun. Nor is he called Orelia either, like the horse on which the unfortunate Roderick, last king of the Goths, rode into the battle in which he lost his life and his kingdom.'

'I'll bet,' said Sancho, 'that seeing they haven't given him any of these famous names of well-known horses, they haven't given him the name of my master's mount, Rocinante, either, though it would fit a great deal better than any of those you've mentioned.'

'You are right,' replied the bearded Countess, 'but yet his name suits him well, for he is called Clavileño the Swift, which name fits him because he is wooden, because of the peg he has in his forehead and because of the speed at which he travels. So, as far as his name goes, he can easily compete with the famous Rocinante.'

'I don't dislike the name,' replied Sancho, 'but what sort of bridle or halter do you have to guide him by?'

'I have already told you,' answered the Trifaldi. 'By the peg. For by turning it in one direction or the other the rider can make him go where he will, either through the air, or brushing and, as it were, sweeping the earth, or by a middle course, which is the proper one for all well-ordered actions.'

'I should like to see him,' said Sancho, 'but to imagine that I'll ride him, either on saddle or crupper, is to want pears from an elm-tree. A fine thing indeed for them to ask me, who can scarcely keep on my Dapple and on a pack-saddle softer than silk itself, to get up on a wooden crupper, without so much as a pillow or a cushion. Lord bless me, I don't intend to bruise myself to take off anyone's beard. Let everyone be shaved as best he can. Nor do I propose to accompany my master on this long journey. Besides I've got nothing to do with the shaving of those beards, as I have with the disenchantment of Dulcinea.'

'Oh yes, you have, friend,' replied the Trifaldi, 'so much so that without your presence I understand we shall achieve nothing.'

'In the name of all the saints,' cried Sancho, 'what have squires to do with their master's adventures? Are they to get the renown for their successes and we to bear the burden? Oh no, no! Supposing now the historians were to say: such a knight achieved such and such an adventure, but with the help of so-and-so, his squire, without whom it would have been impossible to complete it. But they write baldly: Don Paralipomenon of the Three Stars brought off the adventure of the six spectres, no more giving the name of his squire who was present all through, than if he hadn't existed. Now, gentlemen, I say once more that my master can go alone, and much good may it do him. But I shall stay here in the company of my lady the Duchess, and maybe when he comes back he'll find the lady

Dulcinea's case in a very much better way. For I intend, in my idle and leisure moments, to give myself a bout of whipping without a stitch to cover me.'

'All the same, good Sancho,' observed the Duchess, 'you must go with him if it is necessary; for they are good people who are asking you, and these ladies' faces must not be left bristly for your idle fears. That would certainly be a shame.'

'In the name of all the saints, once more!' replied Sancho. 'If this charity were to be done for some modest maidens or foundling girls a man might take some risks, but to endure them to rid waiting-women of their beards. Damn it! I would rather see them all bearded, from the tallest to the shortest, from the nicest to the neatest.'

'You are bitter against waiting-women, Sancho my friend,' said the Duchess. 'You are very much of the opinion of that Toledan apothecary. But you are unfair, I promise you. There are waiting-women in my house who might serve as a model to all their sort; for here is my Doña Rodriguez who will not allow me to say otherwise.'

'Say it, your Excellency,' said the Rodriguez, 'for God knows the truth about everything, and good or bad, bearded or beardless though we be, yet our mothers bore us waiting-women like the rest of our sex. Since God cast us into the world, He knows the reason why; and I hold by His mercy and by no one's beard.'

'That is enough, Lady Rodriguez,' said Don Quixote. 'Lady Trifaldi and company, I wait for Heaven to look with kindly eyes on your distresses. Sancho shall do what I bid him. Now let Clavileño come and let me find myself facing Malambruno, for I know there is no razor could shave your graces more easily than my sword will shave Malambruno's head from his shoulders. For God suffers the wicked, but not for ever.'

'Ah,' exclaimed the Afflicted One, 'may all the stars of the celestial regions look down on your greatness with benignant eyes, valorous knight, and infuse into your spirit all prosperity and valour to be a shield and protection to the down-trodden race of waiting-women, abhorred by apothecaries, slandered by squires and tricked by pages! Woe betide the wretch who in the flower of her years did not prefer to be a nun rather than a waiting-woman! What an unhappy lot we waiting-women are, for even though we were descended in the direct male line from Hector of Troy himself, our mistresses would not leave off calling at us *you there* and *you*, as if they thought that made them queens. O giant Malambruno, although you are an enchanter your promise can be relied on. So send us now the peerless Clavileño so that our misfortunes may be ended, for if the heat comes on and these beards of ours remain we shall be out of luck!'

The Trifaldi spoke with such feeling that she drew tears from the eyes of all the spectators, and even filled Sancho's to the brim, so that he resolved in his heart to follow his master to the very ends of the earth, if it depended on that to rid those venerable faces of their fleeces.

Chapter XLI. *Of the coming of Clavileño and the end of this protracted Adventure.*

BY this time night had come on, and with it the moment fixed for the arrival of the famous horse Clavileño, whose failure to appear troubled Don Quixote. For he thought that Malambruno's delay in sending him meant either that he was not the knight for whom that adventure was reserved, or that the giant dared not meet him in single combat. But all of a sudden there entered through the garden four savages, all dressed in green ivy, bearing a great wooden horse on their shoulders. This they put on its feet on the ground, and one of them cried: 'Let the knight who has courage enough climb upon this machine.'

'I shan't mount it then,' said Sancho, 'for I've no courage and I'm no knight.'

But the savage went on to say: 'Let the squire, if there is one, take the crupper and trust the valiant Malambruno, for except by his sword he will be injured by no other, nor by the malice of any other person. There is no more to do than to turn this peg upon the horse's neck, and he will bear them through the air to where Malambruno awaits them. But for fear the height and distance from the earth should cause them giddiness they must keep their eyes covered till the horse neighs, which will be a sign that they have completed their journey.'

This said, they left Clavileño and retired with a graceful movement in the direction they had come from. And at the sight of the horse the Afflicted One said to Don Quixote, almost in tears: 'Valiant Knight, Malambruno has kept his word. The horse is here, our beards are growing, and each one of us implores you by every hair to shave and shear us, for nothing remains to do but for you to mount with your squire and make a happy start on your strange journey.'

'That I will do, lady Countess Trifaldi,' said Don Quixote, 'with a strong and resolute heart. I will not even wait to find a cushion or put on spurs, for fear of delay, such is my desire to see you, lady, and all these waiting-women smooth and clean.'

'That I will not do,' said Sancho, 'neither with good nor ill will, nor in any way. And if this shaving can't be done without my climbing on the crupper, my master may look for another squire to go with him, and these ladies another way of smoothing their faces, for I'm no sorcerer to enjoy travelling through the air. And what will my islesmen say when they learn that their governor goes roaming down the winds? And another thing: it is nine thousand and odd miles from here to Candaya, and supposing the horse should tire or the giant be in a bad mood, we might be half a dozen years before we got back, and then there would be no isle or islesmen in the world to recognize me. Now since the saying is that there's danger in delay, and when they give you the calf run with the halter, with all due respect to these ladies' beards St. Peter's all right at Rome. I mean that I'm all right in this house, where they have done me such favours, and from whose master I expect the great benefit of seeing myself governor.'

Upon which the Duke replied: 'Sancho, my friend, the isle which I have promised you is neither movable nor fugitive. It has such deep roots struck into the abysses of the earth that it will not be tugged or budged from where it is with three pulls. And I am aware, as you must realize, that there is no kind of position of the first rank that is not gained by some sort of bribe, some more, some less. So the price I mean to exact for this governorship is that you shall go with your master Don Quixote to complete and crown this memorable adventure. For whether you return on Clavileño with the speed his swiftness promises, or adverse fortune befalls you and you return on foot like a pilgrim, from tavern to tavern and inn to inn, whenever you return you will find your isle where you left it, and your islesmen longing as they have always been to receive you as their governor. My goodwill also shall be constant. Do not doubt the truth of this, Master Sancho, for that would be grievously to misunderstand my desire to serve you.'

'No more, sir,' cried Sancho. 'I'm a poor squire and can't carry all these favours on my back. Let my master mount; let them bind these eyes of mine, and commend me to God; and let me be informed whether I shall be able to commend myself to our Lord or invoke the angels to favour me, when we pass through those altitudes.'

To which the Trifaldi replied: 'Sancho, you may safely commend yourself to God, or to whom you will; for though Malambruno is an enchanter he is a Christian, and performs his enchantments with great sagacity and caution, meddling with nobody.'

'Well then,' said Sancho, 'God help me, and the Holy Trinity of Gaeta!'

'Since the memorable adventure of the fulling-mills,' said Don Quixote, 'I have never seen Sancho in such a fright as now; and if I were as superstitious as some, his pusillanimity would cause me some tremors of heart. But come here, Sancho, for with these gentlemen's permission I should like to say a word or two to you in private.'

Then, leading Sancho among some of the garden trees and grasping him by both hands, he said: 'Now you see, Sancho, what a long journey awaits us, and God knows when we shall return, or what opportunities or leisure our business will afford us. Therefore I would have you now retire to your room, as if you were going to look for something needed for the journey, and give yourself in a brace of shakes, say five hundred on account of the three thousand and three hundred lashes promised. They will stand to your credit, for a thing well begun is half done.'

'By God,' said Sancho, 'but your worship must be out of your wits. You might just as well say: you see me in difficulties and ask me for a maidenhead. Now that I've to be sitting on a bare board, does your worship want me to flay my bum? Really and truly, it isn't right of you. Let's go now and shave these waiting-women, and when we get back I promise you, upon my soul, I'll be so quick to redeem my debt that your worship'll be content. I say no more.'

'Well, with that promise, good Sancho,' replied Don Quixote, 'I am comforted; for indeed, though you are foolish you are a veracious man.'

'My complexion's not verdigris but brown,' said Sancho, 'but even if I were a mixture I would keep my word.'

With that they came back to mount Clavileño and, as he climbed on, Don Quixote said: 'Blindfold yourself, Sancho, and mount, Sancho! For whoever sends for us from such distant lands will not deceive us, seeing how little glory would redound to him from defrauding one who trusts him. But supposing everything to turn out contrary to my expectation, no malice can obscure the glory of our having undertaken this exploit.'

'Let's go, sir,' said Sancho, 'for these ladies' beards and tears are sticking into my heart, and I shan't get any nourishment out of my food till I see them in their first smoothness. Get on, your worship, and blindfold yourself beforehand, for if I have to go on the crupper it's clear that the rider in the saddle mounts first.'

'That is true,' replied Don Quixote and, taking a handkerchief from his pocket, he begged the Afflicted One to cover his eyes carefully. But after they were bandaged he uncovered them again to say: 'If I remember rightly, I have read in Virgil of the Trojan Palladium, which was the wooden horse the Greeks presented to the goddess Pallas, and which was pregnant with armed knights who afterwards worked the total ruin of all Troy. So first it would be well to see what Clavileño carries in his stomach.'

'There is no need,' said the Afflicted One. 'I will answer for him, for I know that Malambruno has nothing malicious or treacherous about him. You may mount, Don Quixote, without any fear, and on my shoulders be it if any harm befalls you.'

It seemed to Don Quixote that anything he might say in reply concerning his own safety would be to cast a slur on his valour. So, without further discussion, he mounted Clavileño and tried the peg, which turned easily; and as he had no stirrups and his legs hung down, he looked like nothing so much as a figure in a Flemish tapestry, painted or woven, riding in some Roman triumph. Grudgingly and slowly Sancho also managed to get up and, making himself as comfortable as he could on the crupper, found it rather hard and not at all pleasant. So he begged the Duke, if it were possible, to oblige him with a cushion or pillow, even one from his lady the Duchess's couch or from a page's bed; for the crupper of that horse felt more like marble than wood. To which the Trifaldi objected that Clavileño would suffer no sort or kind of trappings on him, but what he could do was to sit side-saddle like a woman, as he would not feel the hardness so much that way. This Sancho did and, taking his farewell, allowed them to bind his eyes, though after they were bound he uncovered them again and, looking tenderly and tearfully on everyone in the garden, begged them to aid him in his peril with a couple of Paternosters and as many Ave Marias, that God might provide someone to say the same for them when they were in a like predicament. On which Don Quixote said:

'Scoundrel, are you on the gallows, perhaps, or at your last gasp, to resort to prayers of this kind? Are you not, soulless and cowardly creature, in the same seat the fair Magalona occupied, and from which she climbed down, not to her grave but to be Queen of France, if the histories do not lie? And I, who am beside you, cannot I compare with the valiant Pierres, who rested on the same spot where now I rest? Blindfold yourself, blindfold yourself, spiritless beast, and do not let the fear which possesses you issue from your mouth, at least not in my presence.'

'Let them blindfold me,' replied Sancho, 'but since they won't let me commend myself or be commended to God, is it surprising that I'm afraid there may be some region of devils hereabouts, who will bear us off to Peralvillo?'

They were now blindfolded, and Don Quixote, feeling that all was in order, touched the peg; and no sooner did he set his fingers on it than the waiting-women and everyone else present raised their voices and cried: 'God guide you, valorous knight!' 'God be with you, dauntless squire!' 'Now you are in the air already, cleaving it more swiftly than an arrow.' 'Now you are beginning to mount and soar to the astonishment of all of us below;' 'Hold on, valorous Sancho, you are swaying. Be careful not to tumble. For your fall would be worse than that rash youth's who sought to drive the chariot of his father the sun.'

Sancho heard their shouts and, pressing closer to his master, with his arms around him, asked: 'Sir, how can they say we're flying so high when their voices reach us here, and they seem to be speaking just beside us?'

'Pay no attention to that, Sancho. For as these matters of flights are out of the ordinary course of things, you will see and hear what you please a thousand miles away. And do not press me so tight or you will upset me. Indeed I do not know what is so troubling and frightening you, for I dare swear that never in all the days of my life have I ridden an easier-paced mount. We seem not to be moving from one spot. Banish fear, my friend; for really this business is going as it should, and we have the wind astern.'

'That's true enough,' replied Sancho. 'On this side there's such a breeze striking me that it might be a thousand bellows blowing.'

And Sancho was right, for they were giving him air from several large bellows. Indeed so well had the Duke, the Duchess and their steward planned the adventure that no detail was lacking to make it perfect. And when he felt the wind blow on him, Don Quixote said: 'There can be no doubt, Sancho, that we have come to the second region of the air, where the hail and snow are born. Thunder, lightning and thunderbolts are engendered in the third region. If we go on climbing at this rate we shall soon strike the region of fire, and I do not know how to manage this peg so as not to mount so high that we shall scorch.'

Here, with some pieces of tow hanging from a stick and easily lit and quenched, they warmed the riders' faces from the distance. At which Sancho, who felt the heat, exclaimed: 'May I die if we're not in the fiery place already, or very near it, for a great piece of my beard has been singed. And, sir, I'm for taking off the bandage and seeing where we are.'

'Do no such thing,' replied Don Quixote. 'Remember the true story of Doctor Torralva, whom the devils took flying through the air riding on a broomstick, with his eyes shut. In twelve hours he reached Rome and got down at the Torre di Nona, which is a street in that city, and saw all the turmoil, and the attack and the death of Bourbon, and by morning he was back in Madrid, where he gave an account of all he had seen. He also said that, as he was going through the air, the Devil bade him open his eyes, which he did and found himself, it seemed to him, so near the body of the moon that he could have taken hold of it with his hands; and he dared not look down to the earth for fear of turning giddy. So, Sancho, there is no need for us to unbind our eyes; for he in whose charge we are will take care of us. Now perhaps we are fetching round and climbing so that we can swoop down on the kingdom of Candaya, like a hawk or a falcon on a heron, to seize it the better for mounting. And although it seems to us not half an hour since we left the garden, believe me, we must have gone a long way.'

'I know nothing about that,' answered Sancho Panza. 'I can only say that if the lady Magallanes or Magalona was happy on this crupper her flesh couldn't have been very tender.'

All this conversation between the two heroes was overheard by the Duke, the Duchess and those in the garden, and gave them extraordinary delight. But, desiring to bring this strange and well-contrived adventure to an end, they set light to Clavileño's tail with some tow, and suddenly the horse, which was stuffed with crackers, flew into the air with a tremendous bang and threw Don Quixote and Sancho Panza to the ground, half scorched.

By this time the whole troop of bearded waiting-women had disappeared from the garden, the Trifaldi and all; and those who remained lay stretched on the earth as if in a faint. Don Quixote and Sancho rose up in a sorry state and, looking in all directions, were surprised to find themselves in the same garden they had started from, and to see such a number of people lying on the ground. But their wonder grew greater when they saw a tall lance planted in one corner of the garden, and hanging from it by two green silk cords a smooth white parchment on which was written in large gold letters: '*By the mere attempting of it the illustrious Don Quixote de la Mancha has finished and achieved the adventure of the Countess Trifaldi, otherwise called the Afflicted Waiting-woman. Malambruno is completely content and satisfied. The chins of the waiting-women are now smooth and clean, and their Majesties Don Clavijo and Antonomasia are in their pristine state. Now once the squirely whipping is completed, the white dove will be free from the pestiferous goshawks which pursue her, and in the arms of her loving mate; for so it is ordained by the sage Merlin, proto-enchanter of enchanters.*'

When Don Quixote read the letters on the parchment, he clearly understood that they referred to Dulcinea's disenchantment, and giving deep thanks to Heaven for the achievement of so great a deed with so little peril, and for restoring to their former bloom the faces of the venerable waiting-women, who were now nowhere to be seen, he approached the Duke and Duchess, who had not yet come to their senses and, grasping the Duke by the hand, said to him:

'Well, my good lord, courage, courage! It is all nothing. The adventure is achieved, with no harm to anyone, as the words on that parchment clearly show.'

The Duke came to himself gradually, like someone waking from a heavy sleep, and so did the Duchess and all the others who were lying about the garden; and with such signs of wonder and alarm as almost to convince one that what they had learnt so well to act in jest had happened in earnest. The Duke read the scroll with his eyes half closed, and then went with open arms to embrace Don Quixote, telling him that he was the bravest knight ever seen in any age. Meanwhile Sancho went to look for the Afflicted One, to see what her face was like without her beard and whether she was as beautiful without it as her brave appearance promised. But they told him that as soon as Clavileño came down burning through the air and struck the ground, the whole troop of waiting-women, and the Trifaldi with them, had disappeared, and that they had gone shaved clean and without their bristles. The Duchess asked Sancho how he had fared in that long journey, and he replied:

'I felt, lady, that we were going, as my master said, flying through the region of fire, and I wanted to uncover my eyes a bit. But when I asked my master's leave to take off the bandage he wouldn't allow me. But as I have some sparks of curiosity in me, and want to know what is forbidden and denied me, softly and stealthily I pushed the handkerchief that covered my eyes just a little bit up up on my nose and looked down towards the earth. And the whole of it looked to me no bigger than a grain of mustard seed, and the men walking on it little bigger than hazel-nuts. So you can see how high we must have been then.'

At which the Duchess remarked: 'Sancho my friend, reflect what you are saying. For seemingly you did not see the earth but the men going about on it, since it is clear that if the earth appeared to you like a grain of mustard seed and each man like a hazel nut, one man alone would have covered the whole earth.'

'That's true,' replied Sancho, 'but, all the same, I looked through one little corner and saw the whole of it.'

'Mind, Sancho,' said the Duchess, 'for we do not see the whole of what we look at from one little corner.'

'I don't understand these lookings,' answered Sancho. 'I only know that your ladyship would do well to realize that as we flew by enchantment, by enchantment I could see the whole earth and all men on it from wherever I looked. And if you don't believe this, your Grace won't believe that when I moved the bandage up by my eyebrows I saw myself so near the sky that there wasn't a hand's breadth and a half between me and it; and I can swear to you, my lady, it was mighty big too. We happened to be going by the place where the seven little she-goats are and, by God, as I was a goat-herd in my country when I was young, as soon as I saw them I felt a longing to play with them for a bit. And if I hadn't done so I think I should have burst. So, quick as a thought, what do I do? Saying nothing to anyone or to my master either, softly and gently I got down from Clavileño and played with the kids – which are sweet as gillyflowers – for almost three-quarters of an hour, and Clavileño didn't stir from the spot nor move on.'

'And while the good Sancho was playing with the goats,' asked the Duchess, 'how was Don Quixote amusing himself?'

To which Don Quixote replied: 'As all these matters and all such happenings are out of the order of nature, it is no wonder Sancho says what he does. I can only answer for myself that I did not slip the bandage either up or down, nor did I see sky, earth, sea or sands. It is true that I felt myself passing through the regions of air, and even touching the region of fire, but that we passed beyond it I am unable to believe. The region of fire being between the atmosphere of the moon and the farthest region of air, we could not have reached the sky, where the seven kids are that Sancho speaks of, without being scorched. So, seeing that we are not burnt, either Sancho is lying or Sancho is dreaming.'

'I'm neither lying nor dreaming,' answered Sancho. 'Just you ask me the marks on those same goats, and you will see by that whether I'm telling the truth or not.'

'Tell me them, then, Sancho,' said the Duchess.

'Two of them,' answered Sancho, 'are green, two scarlet, two blue and one mottled.'

'That is a new kind of goat,' said the Duke, 'for in this our region of the earth such colours are not usual – I mean she-goats of such colours.'

'That's clear enough,' said Sancho, 'for there certainly should be a difference between the she-goats of heaven and of earth.'

'Tell me, Sancho,' asked the Duke, 'did you see any he-goats there amongst the she-goats?'

'No, sir,' answered Sancho. 'But I've heard tell that not one has passed the horns of the moon.'

They were in no mind to ask him anything more about his journey, for Sancho seemed to be in the mood to roam through all the heavens and give an account of everything in them, although he had not stirred from the garden. In fact this was the end of the adventure of the Afflicted Waiting-woman, which gave the Duke and Duchess cause for laughter, not only at the time but for all their lives, and Sancho a subject of talk for ages, if he should live so long.

But Don Quixote went up to Sancho and whispered in his ear: 'Sancho, if you want me to believe what you saw in the sky, I wish you to accept my account of what I saw in the Cave of Montesinos. I say no more.'

Chapter XLII. *Of Don Quixote's advice to Sancho Panza before he went to govern his Isle, and other grave matters.*

THE Duke and Duchess were so delighted with the entertaining results of the adventure of the Afflicted One, that they decided to carry on with their jests, seeing how apt a subject they had to take them in earnest. So having outlined the plot and given their servants and tenants instructions how they were to act towards Sancho in the matter of the governorship of the promised isle, the day after Clavileño's flight the Duke told Sancho to prepare and put himself in readiness to go and be governor, for his islesmen were longing for him as for water in May. Sancho made his bow and said:

'Ever since my journey through the sky, when from its lofty height I gazed on the earth and saw it so small, my very great desire to be a governor has partly cooled. For what greatness is there in governing on a mustard seed? What dignity or power in commanding half a dozen men the size of hazel nuts – for as far as I could see there were no more on the whole earth? If your Lordship would be so kind as to give me ever so small a bit of the sky, even a mile would do, and I would rather have it than the best isle in the world.'

'See here, friend Sancho,' answered the Duke. 'I cannot give anyone a portion of the sky, not even so much as a finger-nail of it, for such favours and rewards are in God's hands alone. What I can give you I will, and that is an isle, right and straight, round and well proportioned, exceedingly fertile and fruitful; and there, if you know how to manage things, from the riches of earth you can gain the riches of heaven.'

'Well now,' replied Sancho, 'let the isle come. For I'll try to be such a governor that I'll get to Heaven, despite all rogues. And it's not out of greed that I want to leave my poor huts and rise to greater things, but from my desire to find out what it tastes like to be a governor.'

'If once you try it, Sancho,' said the Duke, 'you will take to governing like a duck to water, for it is the sweetest thing to give orders and be obeyed. I am pretty sure that when your master comes to be an Emperor – which no doubt he will, by the way his affairs are going – they will not tear his office away from him at their pleasure, and he will be vexed and grieved from the bottom of his heart for the time lost before he became one.'

'Sir,' replied Sancho, 'it's a good thing to command, I imagine, even if it's only a herd of cattle.'

'Let me be buried alongside you, Sancho,' said the Duke; 'you know everything, and I expect you will be just such a governor as your wisdom promises. But here let it rest. Remember that to-morrow, for certain, you are to go to the governorship of the isle, and this evening you shall be fitted with suitable dress and everything necessary for your departure.'

'Let them dress me as they will,' said Sancho, 'for whatever way I go dressed I shall be Sancho Panza.'

'That is true,' said the Duke, 'but clothes have to suit the office or dignity occupied. It would not be right for a lawyer to be dressed like a soldier, nor a soldier like a priest. You will go, Sancho, dressed as part lawyer, part captain, because in the isle I am giving you arms are as necessary as learning and learning as arms.'

'Learning,' answered Sancho, 'I've little of that, for I don't even know my A.B.C., though I have the big Christ-cross in my memory, and that's enough to make me a good governor.'

'With a memory like his,' said the Duke, 'Sancho cannot go wrong.'

At this moment Don Quixote came up, and when he learned what was happening and how soon Sancho was to leave for his governorship, by the Duke's permission he took his squire by the hand and led him to his apartment to give him advice as to his behaviour in office. Then, having entered, he shut the door after him and, almost forcing Sancho to sit down beside him, addressed him with great deliberation:

'I give infinite thanks to Heaven, Sancho my friend, that first and foremost, before I strike any good luck myself, prosperity has come out to meet and receive you. I who had staked the payment for your services on my own success find myself at the beginning of my advancement; while you find yourself rewarded with your heart's desire before your time and contrary to all reasonable expectations. Some bribe, importune, solicit, rise early, entreat, pester, and yet fail to achieve their aims; then there comes another, and without knowing how or why he finds himself with the place and office which many others have sought for. Here the proverb comes in pat, that there is good and bad luck in petitionings. You are, in my opinion, most certainly a dullard. Yet without rising early or working late or putting yourself to great pains, with only the breath of knight errantry which has touched you, you find yourself without more ado governor of an isle, as if that were nothing. I say all this, Sancho, so that you shall not attribute this favour to your own merits, but shall give thanks to God, who disposes things so kindly, and afterwards to the greatness implicit in the profession of knight errantry.

'With your heart disposed to believe my words, be attentive, my son, to this your Cato, who will advise you and be the pole-star and guide to direct you and bring you to a safe port, out of this stormy sea in which you are likely to drown. For offices and great places are nothing but a deep gulf of confusion.

A A

'Firstly, my son, you must fear God; for in fearing Him is wisdom and, being wise, you can make no mistake.

'Secondly, you must consider what you are, seeking to know yourself, which is the most difficult task conceivable. From self-knowledge you will learn not to puff yourself up, like the frog who wanted to be as big as an ox. If you achieve this, the memory that you kept hogs in your own country will come to be like the peacock's ugly feet to the tail of your folly.'

'True enough,' answered Sancho, 'but that was when I was a boy. Afterwards, when I was more of a man, it was geese I kept, not hogs. But this doesn't seem to me to the point, for not all governors come from royal stock.'

'True,' replied Don Quixote, 'and therefore those who are not of noble origin must accompany the gravity of the office they exercise with a mild suavity which, guided by prudence, may save them from malicious slanderers, from whom no station is free.

'Rejoice, Sancho, in the humbleness of your lineage, and do not think it a disgrace to say you come of peasants; for, seeing that you are not ashamed, no one will attempt to shame you. Consider it more meritorious to be virtuous and poor than noble and a sinner. Innumerable men there are, born of low stock, who have mounted to the highest dignities, pontifical and imperial; and of this truth I could weary you with examples.

'Remember, Sancho, that if you take virtue for your means, and pride yourself on performing virtuous deeds, you will have no reason to envy those who were born princes and lords. For blood is inherited but virtue acquired, and virtue has an intrinsic worth, which blood has not.

'This being so, if any of your relations should chance to come and visit you when you are in your isle, do not reject them or insult them. On the contrary, you must receive them, make much of them and entertain them. In that way you will please God, who would have no one disdain His creation; and what is more, you will be complying with your duty to the order of nature.

'If you should take your wife with you – for it is not right that those engaged in government should be for long without wives of their own – instruct her, indoctrinate her and pare her of her native rudeness; for often everything a wise governor gains is lost and wasted by an ill-mannered and foolish wife.

'If you should chance to be widowed – a thing which may happen – and wish to make a better match to suit your office, do not choose a wife to serve you as a bait and a fishing-rod and take bribes in her hood; for I tell you truly that whatever a judge's wife receives her husband will have to account for at the Last Judgment, where he will have to pay fourfold in death for the statutes of which he has taken no account in his lifetime.

'Never be guided by arbitrary law, which has generally great influence with the ignorant who set up to be clever.

'Let the poor man's tears find more compassion in you, but not more justice, than the pleadings of the rich.

'Try to discover the truth behind the rich man's promises and gifts, as well as behind the poor man's sobbings and importunities.

'Where equity may justly temper the rigour of the law do not pile the whole force of it on to the delinquent; for the rigorous judge has no higher reputation than the merciful.

'If you should chance to bend the rod of justice, do not let it be with the weight of a bribe, but with that of pity.

'When you happen to judge the case of some enemy of yours, turn your mind away from your injury and apply it to the truth of the case.

'Do not let personal passion blind you in another's case, for most of the errors you make will be irremediable, and if you should find a remedy it will cost you your reputation, or even your fortune.

'If a beautiful woman comes to beg you for justice, turn your eyes from her tears and your ears from her groans, and consider the substance of her plea at leisure, if you do not want your reason to be drowned in her sobs and your honour in her sighs.

'Do not revile with words the man you must punish with deeds, since the pain of the punishment is sufficient for the wretch without adding ill-language.

'Consider the culprit who comes before you for judgment as a wretched man, subject to the conditions of our depraved nature, and so far as in you lies without injury to the contrary party, show yourself pitiful and lenient; for although all godlike attributes are equal, mercy is more precious and resplendent in our sight than justice.

'If you follow these precepts and rules, Sancho, your days will be long, your fame eternal, your rewards abundant, your happiness indescribable. You will marry your children as you wish to; they and your grandchildren will have titles; you will live in peace and good-will among men, and in your life's last stages you will arrive at the hour of death in a mild and ripe old age, and the tender and delicate hands of your great-grandchildren will close your eyes.

'The instructions I have so far given you are for the embellish-ment of your soul. Listen now to some which will serve you for the adornment of your body.'

Chapter XLIII. *Of Don Quixote's further Advice to Sancho Panza.*

COULD anyone hear this last discourse of Don Quixote's and not take him for a person of singular intelligence and excellent inten-tions? For as has often been said in the course of this great history, he went astray only in the matter of chivalry, but in the rest of his talk showed a clear and unbiassed understanding, so that his acts discredited his judgment and his judgment his acts at every step. But in this matter of the second set of precepts which he gave Sancho, he showed himself possessed of a very nice humour and displayed both his sense and his madness to an exalted degree. Most attentively did Sancho listen to him and endeavour to commit his counsels to memory, resolved to observe them and thereby to bring the pregnancy of his government to a happy delivery. Don Quixote then went on to say:

'So far as concerns the government of your person and your house, Sancho, my first charge to you is to be clean, and to pare your nails and not let them grow as do some, who are ignorantly persuaded that long nails beautify the hands; as if that excrescence and appendage which they omit to cut were merely nail, whereas it is like the claws of a lizard-catching kestrel – a foul and unsightly object.

'Do not go unbelted and loose; for disorderly clothes are the indication of a careless mind, unless this disorderliness and negligence falls under the head of cunning, as it was judged to do in the case of Julius Caesar.

'Discreetly take the measure of your office's value; and if it will allow you to give your servants liveries, let them be modest and useful, not gaudy and grand, and divide them between your servants and the poor – I mean that if you have six pages to dress, dress three of them and three poor men. Then you will have pages both for heaven and earth. Your vainglorious have not attained to this new fashion of giving liveries.

'Do not eat garlic or onions; for their smell will reveal that you are a peasant.

'Walk leisurely and speak with deliberation; but not so as to seem to be listening to yourself, for all affectation is bad.

'Eat little at dinner and less at supper, for the health of the whole body is forged in the stomach's smithy.

'Be temperate in drinking, remembering that excess of wine keeps neither a secret nor a promise.

'Take care, Sancho, not to chew on both sides of your mouth nor to eruct in anyone's presence.'

'This about *eruct* I don't understand,' said Sancho.

'Eruct, Sancho,' said Don Quixote, 'means belch, and that is one of the coarsest words in the Castilian language, though it is very expressive; and so refined people have resorted to Latin, and instead of *belch* say *eruct* and for *belches eructations*; and if some people do not understand these terms it is of little consequence, for they will come into use in time, and then they will be generally understood; for that is the way to enrich the language, which depends upon custom and the common people.'

'Indeed, sir,' said Sancho, 'I shall bear your counsel about belching in mind, for I generally do it very often.'

'*Eructing*, Sancho, not *belching*,' said Don Quixote.

'Eruct I shall say from now on,' replied Sancho, 'and I swear I won't forget.'

'Also, Sancho, you must not interlard your conversation with the great number of proverbs you usually do; for though proverbs are maxims in brief, you often drag them in by the hair, and they seem more like nonsense.'

'Let God look after that,' answered Sancho, 'for I know more proverbs than a book, and so many of them come all together into my mouth when I speak that they fight one another to get out; and the tongue seizes hold of the first it meets with, even though it mayn't be just to the point. But from now on I'll take care to bring in only those that suit the gravity of my office. For in a well-stocked house the supper is soon cooked; and a good bargain doesn't hold up the business; and the man who sounds the alarm is safe; and giving and taking need some sense.'

'Go on, Sancho,' said Don Quixote. 'Cram them in, thread and string your proverbs together; no one will stop you. My mother scolds me and I whip the top. I tell you to refrain from proverbs, and in one moment you have brought out a whole litany of them which have as much to do with what we are discussing as have the hills of Ubeda. Look you, Sancho, I do not find fault with a proverb aptly introduced, but to load and string on proverbs higgledy-piggledy makes your speech mean and vulgar.

'When you are riding horseback do not throw your body all on the crupper, nor carry your legs stiffly stuck out from the horse's belly; and do not go so slackly either, and look as if you were riding Dapple; for horse-riding makes horsemen of some and stable boys of others.

'Be moderate in your sleeping, for he that does not rise with the sun does not enjoy the day; and remember, Sancho, that industry is the mother of good fortune, and slothfulness, its opposite, never yet succeeded in carrying out an honest purpose.

'This final precept I am going to give you does not concern the adornment of the body, but I would have you keep it carefully in your memory, for I believe that it will be of no less service to you than those I have just given you. It is never to engage in disputes about lineage, or at least never to compare one family with another; for one of the two must necessarily be the better, and you will be hated by the one you set lower and get no sort of reward from the one you place higher.

'Let your clothing be full breeches, a long coat and a cloak a little longer; on no account tight-fitting breeches, for they do not suit either gentlemen or governors.

'This, Sancho, is all the advice that occurs to me for the present.

In the course of time my instructions will suit occasions as they arise, if you take care to inform me of your circumstances.'

'Sir,' replied Sancho, 'I can see very well that all you have told me is good, godly and profitable. But of what use will it be to me if I remember none of it? True enough, that about not letting my nails grow, and about marrying a second time if I have a chance, I shan't easily forget. But as for your other bits and pieces, they're already gone out of my head as clean as last year's clouds. So I shall have to have them in writing; for though I can't read or write I can give them to my confessor, and he'll ram them in and refresh my memory in time of need.'

'Oh, sinner that I am!' said Don Quixote. 'How wrong it is for a governor not to be able to read and write! For you must know, Sancho, that for a man to be illiterate or left-handed argues one of two things: either he is the son of exceedingly poor and base parents, or so perverse and wicked himself that neither good example nor good teaching have been able to penetrate him. It is a great defect in you, and so I should like you to learn at least to sign your name.'

'I can sign my name very well,' replied Sancho. 'For when I was warden of a brotherhood in my village I learnt to make some letters, like they put on bales of goods, and they said they spelt my name. But I'll tell you what, I'll pretend that my right hand is paralysed, and have someone else sign for me. For there's a remedy for everything except death, and as I wield the power and the staff I'll do as I like; the more so because he that has the mayor for his father ... And I being a governor, which is higher than a mayor, let them come on and play at bo-peep with me. Let them flout me and slander me; let them come for wool and they'll go away shorn; and whom God loves, his house knows it; and the rich man's foolishness passes for wisdom in the world; and since I shall be rich, and a governor and liberal as well, which I intend to be, no one will see a fault in me. Make yourself honey and the flies will suck you; you're worth as much as you've got, as my old grandmother used to say; and there's no getting revenge on a well-rooted man.'

'Confound you, Sancho!' interrupted Don Quixote. 'Sixty thousand devils take you and your proverbs! You have been string-ing them together for a whole hour and giving me the pangs of torture with each one. Mark my words, those proverbs of yours will bring you to the gallows one day. Your vassals will take away your government for them, or break into revolts. Tell me, nit-wit, where do you find them? And how do you apply them, stupid? For to utter one and apply it well makes me sweat and labour as if I were digging.'

'Goodness me, my dear master,' answered Sancho, 'you complain about very small matters. Why the devil do you fret yourself because I make use of my wealth? For I have no other. My only fortune is proverbs and still more proverbs. Why, four of them occur to me now, that come in slick to the point or like pears in a basket. But I won't say them, for Sage Silence is Sancho's name.'

'You are not that Sancho,' said Don Quixote. 'You are not Sage Silence, but wicked chatter and perverse obstinacy. But all the same I should like to know what four proverbs come to your mind just now so slick to the point; for I have been racking mine – and it is a good one – and I cannot think of one.'

'What better,' said Sancho, 'than – don't put your thumbs between two back teeth, and – "Get out of my house, what do you want with my wife?" admits of no answer – and whether the pot strikes the stone or vice versa, it's a bad look-out for the pot – every one of which fits to a hair. For no one should meddle with his governor nor with those in authority, for he will come off second best, like the man who puts his finger between the back-teeth – and whether they're back-teeth or not doesn't matter so long as they're molars. And there's no answering the governor any more than there's a reply to "Get out of my house! What do you want with my wife?" As to the one about the stone and the pot, a blind man can see that. So he who sees the mote in the other man's eye must see the beam in his own, so that it shan't be said of him that the dead woman was frightened by the one with her throat cut. And your worship's well aware that the fool knows more in his own house than the wise man in another's.'

'No, no, Sancho,' replied Don Quixote, 'the fool knows nothing in his own house nor in anyone else's, since no edifice of wisdom can rest on a foundation of folly. But let us leave the matter here, Sancho, for if you govern badly the fault will be yours, and the shame mine. But it consoles me that I have done my duty in advising you as truly and wisely as I can. For that absolves me of my obligation and my promise. God guide you, Sancho, and govern you in your government, and deliver me from my suspicion that you will turn your whole isle upside down, a thing which I could prevent by informing the Duke of your character, and telling him that all that fat little body of yours is nothing but a sackful of proverbs and mischief.'

'Sir,' answered Sancho, 'if I don't seem to your worship worthy of this governorship, I give it up from this moment. For I love a single black nail's breadth of my soul more than my whole body, and plain Sancho can live just as well on bread and onions as Governor Sancho on partridges and capons. What's more we're all equal while we're asleep, great and small, poor and rich alike; and if your worship reflects, you'll see that it was only you who put this business of governing into my head, for I know no more of governing isles than a vulture; and if anyone thinks that the Devil will get me for being a governor, I had rather go to Heaven plain Sancho than to Hell a governor.'

'By God, Sancho,' said Don Quixote, 'if only for those last words of yours, I consider you worthy to be governor of a thousand isles. You have a good instinct, without which all knowledge is of no avail. Commend yourself to God and try not go astray in your main resolution. I mean that you must always maintain your unshaken purpose and design to do right in whatever business occurs, for Heaven always favours honest intentions. Now let us go to dinner, for I think that my Lord and Lady are waiting for us.'

Chapter XLIV. *How Sancho Panza was taken to his Governorship, and of the strange Adventure which befell Don Quixote in the Castle.*

THEY say that in the real original of this history it states that when Cide Hamete came to write this chapter his interpreter did not translate it as it was written, for it was in the form of a complaint addressed by the Moor to himself for having undertaken so dry and cramped a story; since he seemed always to be restricted to Don Quixote and Sancho, not daring to launch out into digressions and episodes that would have yielded both pleasure and profit. He said that to have his mind, his hand and his pen always confined to a single subject and to so scanty a list of characters was an unbearable hardship, in no way fruitful for the author; and that to avoid this inconvenience in the first part he had resorted to short tales, like 'The Foolish Curiosity' and 'The Captive Captain', which are, in a sense, separate from the story, though the rest of the tales concern the adventures which befel Don Quixote himself, and could not well be omitted. He also thought, as he says, that many would have all their attention engrossed by the claims of Don Quixote's exploits, and would have none left for the tales. In fact they would hurry through them in haste or disgust and fail to notice the delicacy and ingenuity of their construction, which would have shown up well if they had been published on their own and not tied to Don Quixote's craziness and Sancho's fooleries. So he decided not to insert any tales, either detached or connected, in this second part, but to include some similar episodes arising out of the actual happenings themselves; and even these should be sparing and no longer than their bare narration required. So, being confined and enclosed within the narrow limits of the story, though he has the skill, the knowledge and the capacity for dealing with the whole universe, he begs that his pains shall not be under-valued, and that he shall be praised not for what he writes, but for what he has refrained from writing.

The author then goes on to say that after supper on the evening of the day when Sancho received his instructions Don Quixote handed him a written copy, so that he might get someone to read them to him. But no sooner had he given them to Sancho than they fell into the hands of the Duke, who showed them to the Duchess, and the pair of them were again surprised at Don Quixote's madness and good sense. So, to continue with their jest, they sent Sancho that evening with a great escort to the village which was to serve as his isle. Now the man who had charge of the matter happened to be a steward of the Duke's, a very shrewd and humorous fellow – for there can be no humour without shrewdness – and it was he who had played the part of the Countess Trifaldi so gracefully, as has been already described. With this to his credit and carefully coached by his master and mistress as to his conduct towards Sancho, he was miraculously successful in his design.

Though it must be confessed that the moment Sancho set eyes on this steward, he fancied he was gazing on the very countenance of the Trifaldi; and turning to his master, he said: 'Sir, may the Devil fly away with me here where I stand, a true man and a Christian, if your worship doesn't agree that this steward of the Duke's here is exactly like the Afflicted One.'

Don Quixote examined the steward carefully, and said to Sancho after his inspection: 'There is no call for the Devil to fly away with you, Sancho, either as true man or Christian – though I do not know what you mean – for the Afflicted One's face is just like the steward's. Yet for all that the steward is not the Afflicted One, for that would imply a very palpable contradiction. But this is no time to make these investigations, for that would be to plunge ourselves into inextricable labyrinths. But believe me, friend, we must pray very earnestly to our Lord to deliver us from wicked wizards and enchanters.'

'It's no joke, sir,' replied Sancho. 'I heard him speak just now, and I thought it was the very voice of the Trifaldi sounding in my ears. Well, I'll be quiet; but I shall keep my eyes open in future all the same, and see if I can discover any other sign to confirm or dispel my suspicion.'

'So you must, Sancho,' said Don Quixote, 'and inform me of all you discover about the matter, and of everything that befalls you in your government too.'

At length Sancho set out, accompanied by a great number of people, dressed as a lawyer in a very broad overcoat of tawny watered camlet and a hunting-cap of the same material, and riding with short stirrups on a mule. Behind him, by order of the Duke, went Dapple with brand-new harness and silk trappings. From time to time Sancho turned back to gaze on his ass, in whose company he rode so contentedly that he would not have changed places with the Emperor of Germany. On taking leave of the Duke and Duchess he kissed their hands and begged his master for his blessing, which Don Quixote gave him with tears and Sancho received with blubberings.

Let the good Sancho go in peace, amiable reader, and God speed him. Expect two bushels of laughter when you learn how he behaved in his government. Meanwhile mark what befell his master that night, and if you do not laugh at that, at least you will spread your lips in a monkey grin; for Don Quixote's adventures must be honoured either with wonder or with laughter.

The story goes, then, that no sooner had Sancho departed than Don Quixote felt his loneliness and, had it been possible to revoke his squire's commission and take away his governorship, he would have done so. The Duchess observed his melancholy and asked him why he was sad, saying that if it were for Sancho's absence, she had squires, waiting-women and maids in her house who would serve him to his complete satisfaction.

'It is true, my lady,' answered Don Quixote, 'that I grieve for Sancho's absence. But that is not the principal cause of my seeming sad; nor the reason why of the many offers your Excellency makes me I can only accept the goodwill with which they are made. For the rest I entreat your Excellency to give me leave to wait upon myself within my own apartment.'

'Indeed, Don Quixote,' said the Duchess, 'that must not be. You shall be served by four of my maids, as beautiful as flowers.'

'To me,' replied Don Quixote, 'they will not be like flowers, but like thorns pricking me to the soul. They shall no more come into my room, or anywhere near it, than fly. If your Highness will continue your undeserved favours towards me, suffer me to enjoy them alone and to wait on myself within my own doors, so that I may put a wall between my desires and my virtue. I am unwilling to forego this practice for all your Highness's liberality towards me. In fact I would rather sleep in my clothes than allow anyone to undress me.'

'No more, no more, Don Quixote,' replied the Duchess. 'I promise to give orders that not even a fly shall enter your room, let alone a maid. For myself, I am not one to infringe Don Quixote's sense of decency, for, by what I can perceive, the most resplendent of his many virtues is his modesty. You may undress and dress yourself, your worship, alone and in your own fashion, how and when you will, and no one shall hinder you. In your own room you will find all the utensils needed by one sleeping behind locked doors, so that no call of nature will oblige you to open them. May the great Dulcinea del Toboso live a thousand ages, and may her name travel round the whole earth, for meriting the love of so valiant and modest a knight. And may kind Heaven infuse into the heart of our governor Sancho the desire to finish off his whipping speedily, so that the world may once more enjoy the beauty of so great a lady.'

To which Don Quixote made answer: 'Your Highness's words are true to your character; for in the mouths of virtuous ladies there can be no evil. Dulcinea will be the more fortunate and the more famous in the world for your Highness's commending her than for all the praises the most eloquent in the land could bestow on her.'

'Well now, Don Quixote,' replied the Duchess, 'it is supper-time, and the Duke must be waiting. Come, your worship, let us sup, and you shall retire early, for the journey you took yesterday to Candaya was not so short as not to have caused you some chafing.'

'No, I feel none, lady,' answered Don Quixote, 'for I dare swear to your Excellency that never in all my life have I ridden a quieter or better-paced beast than Clavileño. I do not know what could have induced Malambruno to dispose of so swift and mild a crea-ture, and to burn him like that for no reason at all.'

'We may well imagine,' replied the Duchess, 'that repentance for the wrong he had done the Trifaldi and company and other per-sons, and for the crimes he must have committed as sorcerer and enchanter, decided him to destroy all the instruments of his art; and as Clavileño was the chief of them and caused him most disquiet in his wanderings from land to land, he burnt him, so that his ashes and the trophy scroll might immortalize the valour of the great Don Quixote de la Mancha.'

Once more Don Quixote gave thanks to the Duchess, and after supper he retired to his room alone, refusing to allow anyone to come in and wait on him, so great was his fear of encountering temptations which might induce him, or compel him, to forget the proper chastity he reserved for his lady Dulcinea, having ever pre-sent in his imagination the virtue of Amadis, flower and mirror of knights errant. Closing the door behind him then, he undressed by the light of two candles. But as he took off his stockings – oh disaster unworthy of such a personage! – there burst, not sighs, nor anything else to discredit the purity of his breeding, but about two dozen stitches of one of his stockings, which made it look like a window-lattice. The good gentleman was extremely distressed, and would have given an ounce of silver to have there a sixteenth of an ounce of green silk, for his stockings were green. Here Benengeli

exclaims in his writing: 'Oh, poverty, poverty! I do not know why
the great Cordovan poet was moved to call you

Holy and misvalued gift!

For, Moor though I am, I know very well by the commerce I have
had with Christians that holiness lies in charity, humility, faith,
obedience and poverty. But, for all that, I declare that anyone who
grows content with poverty must have much of God in him, unless
it is that kind of poverty of which one of His greatest saints says:
"*Possess all things as if you possessed them not*", and this they call
poverty in spirit. But you, secondary poverty – for it is of you I
speak – why do you chose to break in upon gentlemen and men of
birth rather than upon other people? Why do you compel them to
shine up their shoes, and to have the buttons of their coats some of
silk, some of hair and some of glass? Why must their ruffles be
generally crumpled and not spread in a smooth pattern?' – which
shows the antiquity of starch and smooth ruffs. 'How wretched,' he
went on, 'is the man of birth who is always regaling his honour
with chicken-broth while he dines poorly behind closed doors,
making a hypocrite of his toothpick by going out into the street
with it, though he has eaten nothing which obliges him to clean his
teeth! How miserable is he, I repeat, whose honour is terrified at the
thought that someone may discover from a mile off the patch on his
shoe, the sweat marks on his hat, the threadbareness of his coat, and
the hunger in his stomach!'

All these reflections were revived in Don Quixote by the breaking of his stitches. But he was comforted by seeing that Sancho had
left him some riding-boots, which he decided to put on next day.
At length he lay down again, brooding and dispirited, as much for
lack of Sancho as for the irreparable disaster to his stockings, which
he would have darned up, even though with silk of another colour –
the most expressive token of a gentleman's penury. He put out the
candles, but it was hot and he could not sleep. So he got out of bed
and slightly opened a window with an iron grille which looked out
on a beautiful garden, and as he opened it, he perceived people walking and talking among the greenery. As he set himself to listen
attentively and the voices from below were fairly loud, he heard
these words:

'Do not press me to sing, Emerencia, for you know that from the moment this stranger entered the castle and my eyes fell upon him, I have been unable to sing, and can only weep. Besides, my mistress's sleep is rather light, and I would not have her find us here for all the treasure in the world; and even supposing she slept and did not wake, my singing would be in vain should he sleep and not wake to hear it, this new Aeneas who has come into my land to abandon me in scorn.'

'Do not mind that, friend Altisidora,' came the answer, 'for no doubt the Duchess and everyone in this house are asleep, except for the lord of your heart and disturber of your soul. For I heard him open the window of his apartment just now. So no doubt he is awake. Sing, poor grieved one, softly and gently to the sound of your harp, and if the Duchess hears us we can blame the heat of the night.'

'That is not the point, Emerencia,' replied Altisidora. 'I do not wish my song to reveal my heart, for I should be taken for a light and capricious girl by those ignorant of the mighty force of love. But, come what may, better a shamed face than a sore heart.'

Then someone began to play most softly on the harp, and Don Quixote marvelled as he heard it. For at that instant there arose in his memory an infinity of similar adventures – of windows, bars and gardens, serenades, love-songs and swoonings, which he had read of in his airy books of chivalry. He immediately imagined that one of the Duchess's maidens had fallen in love with him, and that her modesty compelled her to keep her feelings secret. He trembled at the thought that he might yield, but resolved in his mind not to let himself be conquered. Then, commending himself with good heart and will to his lady Dulcinea del Toboso, he decided to listen to the music and, to let them know that he was there, he gave a pretended sneeze, which considerably delighted the maids, for they wanted nothing better than for Don Quixote to hear them. Then, after running over and tuning her harp, Altisidora struck up this ballad:

Thou that in thy bed dost lie
Between the Holland sheets,
Sleeping with thy legs outstretched
All night long till morn,

O thou knight, the valiantest
All La Mancha has produced.
More modest and more blessed, thou,
Than finest gold of Araby.

Hear a damsel sorrowful,
Nurtured well but thriven ill,
Who with light of thy two suns
Feels her soul scorched and ablaze.

Thou thine own adventures seekest,
Other's misadventures findest,
Dealest wounds and yet refusest
To give healing remedy.

Tell me, O thou valiant youth
— May God prosper thy desires! —
Wert thou born in Lybia,
Or in Jaca's mountains?

Whether serpent gave thee suck,
Or perhaps thy nurses were
The uncouth wildness of the woods
And the mountains horrible.

Dulcinea well may boast,
That most plump and healthy maid,
Conquering a tiger's heart
And taming a most savage beast.

For which famous she shall be
From Henares to Jarama,
From Tagus to Manzanares,
From Pisuerga to Arlanza.

If I could but change with her,
I would give a skirt to boot
Of the gayest that I have,
Hung about with golden fringe.

Oh, that I were in thy arms,
Or, if not, beside thy bed,
That I might but scratch thy head
And of dandruff rid thy hair.

Much I ask, but am not worthy
Of a favour so outstanding,
Let me then but stroke thy feet;
That is enough for one so humble.

What fine night-caps I would give thee,
And what silver socks I'd work thee,
Breeches of the finest damask,
And what Holland cloaks as well!

And how many rarest pearls,
Each as big as an oak-gall,
Which, if it had no companions,
Might be called the only pearl.

Gaze not then from thy Tarpeian
Rock upon this fire that burns me.
Manchegan Nero of the world,
Do not revive it with thy harshness.

Young I am, a tender pullet,
My age is not yet past fifteen.
Fourteen I am and three months over,
I swear by God and by my soul.

I do not limp, I am not lame,
Nothing in me is misshapen,
And my hair is like the lilies;
When I stand it sweeps the ground.

Though my mouth is like an eagle's
And my nose is rather flat,
With my topaz teeth my beauty's
Raised as high as Heaven above.

My voice will prove, if thou but listen,
Equal to the very sweetest,
And thou'lt find my form and figure
Something more than middling too.

These and all my other graces
Are the spoils fall to thy quiver,
I am a maiden of this house,
And my name's Altisidora.

Here ended the song of the sore stricken Altisidora, and here began the fright of the courted Don Quixote, who said to himself,
heaving a deep sigh: 'What an unhappy errant I am, that there
is no maiden sets eyes on me but is enamoured! How sad is the fate
of the peerless Dulcinea del Toboso that she cannot be left alone to
enjoy my incomparable constancy! What do you want of her,
Queens? Why do you persecute her, Empresses? Why do you bait

her, fourteen and fifteen-year-old maidens? Leave, leave the miserable lady to triumph, rejoice and glory in the lot which Love has chosen to bestow on her in rendering her my heart and delivering her my soul. Reflect, enamoured crew, that for Dulcinea alone am I dough and sugar paste, but for all others I am flint. For her I am honey, but for you aloes. For me Dulcinea alone is beautiful, wise, modest, gay and well-born, and the rest ugly, stupid, fickle and base-born. To be hers and no other's nature cast me into the world. Let Altisidora weep or sing; let that lady despair for whose sake I was beaten in the castle of the enchanted Moor; for I must be Dulcinea's – roasted or boiled, clean, well-born and chaste – in despite of all the powers of sorcery in the world.'

With this he banged the window to and, fretful and heavy-hearted, as if some great disaster had befallen him, lay down on his bed, where we will leave him for the present, since the great Sancho Panza is calling us, being desirous of making a beginning of his famous government.

Chapter XLV. *Of how the great Sancho Panza took possession of his Isle and of the fashion in which he began to govern.*

O perpetual discoverer of the Antipodes! Torch of the world! Eye of Heaven! Sweet stirrer of wine coolers! Here Thymbrius, there Phoebus, now archer, now physician! Father of Poetry, inventor of Music, you who always rise and – though you seem to – never set! On you I call, sun, by whose aid man engenders man. On you I call to favour me and to light the darkness of my mind, that I may be scrupulous in the narration of the great Sancho Panza's government; for without you I feel myself timid, faint-hearted and confused.

I must tell you then that Sancho Panza with all his escort arrived at a village of about a thousand inhabitants, which was one of the best in the Duke's dominions. They gave him to understand that this was called the Isle Barataria, either because the town's name was *Baratario*, or because of the '*barato*', or low price, at which he had got the government. When they reached the gates of the place, which was walled, the town-council came out to receive him. They rang the bells, and all the inhabitants demonstrated their general rejoicing and conducted him in great pomp to the principal church to give thanks to God. Then with some comical ceremonies they delivered him the keys of the town, and admitted him as perpetual governor of the Isle Barataria. The new governor's apparel, his beard, his fatness and his smallness surprised everyone who was not in the secret, and even those many who were. Next they bore him from the church to the judge's throne and seated him upon it, where the Duke's steward thus addressed him:

'It is an ancient custom in this famous isle, Lord Governor, that everyone who comes to take possession of it is obliged to reply to a question, and this must be a rather intricate and difficult one. By this reply the town touches and feels the pulse of its new governor's understanding and, accordingly, is either glad or grieved at his coming.'

Whilst the steward was thus addressing him, Sancho was gazing at a number of large letters inscribed on the wall facing his seat. Now, as he could not read, he asked what those paintings were on that wall, and the answer came: 'Sir, yonder is written and recorded the day on which your Lordship took possession of this isle, and the inscription says: "*This day, such a date of such a month in such a year, there took possession of the isle the Lord Don Sancho Panza; may he enjoy it for many years.*"'

'Who are they calling Don Sancho Panza?' asked Sancho.

'Your Lordship,' answered the steward, 'for no other Panza has entered this isle but the one seated on that seat.'

'Then take notice, brother,' said Sancho, 'that I'm no Don, and there has never been a Don in my whole family. Plain Sancho Panza's my name, and Sancho my father was called, and Sancho my grandfather, and they were all Panzas without the addition of Dons or Doñas. I fancy there are more Dons than stones in this isle. But enough. God knows my meaning, and perhaps if my government lasts four days I may weed out these Dons, for judging by their numbers they must be as tiresome as gnats. Go on with your question, Master Steward, for I'll reply as best I can, whether the town be sorry or rejoice.'

At this moment two men came into the judgment-hall, one dressed as a labourer and the other as a tailor with scissors in his hand, the latter crying:

'My lord Governor, here's why I and this countryman have come before your worship. That fellow came to my shop yesterday – I, saving your presence, am a licensed tailor, God be praised! – and put a piece of cloth into my hands, and asked me: "Would there be enough here, sir, to make a cap?" I measured the stuff and answered him yes. I suppose he must have suspected that I intended to rob him of part of the cloth, basing his belief on his own roguery and the bad reputation of tailors. And he was quite right. Then he asked me to examine it again and see if there was enough for two. I guessed his drift, and said yes. Then, persisting in his damned idea, he went on adding caps, and I added more yeses till we came to five. And he has just come this very moment for his caps, and I've offered them to him. And he won't pay me for the making, but demands that I shall pay him instead or return him his cloth.'

'Is all this true, brother?' asked Sancho.

'Yes, sir,' answered the fellow, 'but make him show you the five caps he has made me, your worship.'

'With pleasure,' said the tailor.

And taking his hand suddenly from under his cloak, he displayed five caps, one on the tip of each finger, and said: 'Here are the five caps this good man ordered and, by God and my conscience, there wasn't a scrap of cloth over, and I'll submit the work to be examined by the inspectors of the trade.'

Everyone present laughed at the number of caps and the novel nature of the case. But Sancho set himself to consider a little and said: 'There seems to me no need for long delays in this suit; it can be decided on the spot by a wise man's judgment. My sentence, therefore, is that the tailor shall lose his making and the countryman his cloth, the caps to be given to the prisoners in the jail, and let that be an end of the matter.'

This judgment moved the audience to laughter, but the governor's orders were carried out.

Next there came before him two old men, one of them carrying a cane for a walking stick. 'Sir,' said the one without the stick, 'Some time ago I lent this fellow ten crowns in gold, as a favour and a service to him, on condition that he should repay me on demand. I didn't ask him for them for a long time, so as not to put him into greater difficulties through repaying than he was in when I lent him them. But as he didn't seem to me to be troubling about his debt, I asked him for them, not once but many times. Now not only does he not repay me but he denies the debt, saying that I never lent him these ten crowns, or that if I did he has returned them. I have no witnesses of the loan – nor he of the repayment, for he never made it. So I want your worship to put him under oath, and if he swears that he has repaid me I will let him off the debt here, before God.'

'What do you say to this, you fellow with the stick?' asked Sancho.

'I confess that he lent them to me, sir,' answered the old man. 'Hold down your wand of justice, your worship, and since he leaves it to my oath, I'll swear that I really and truly returned them to him.'

The Governor lowered his wand, and at the same time this old man gave his stick, as if it were very much in his way, to the other old man to hold whilst he took his oath. Then he put his hand on the cross of the wand and declared that he had truly borrowed the ten crowns demanded of him, but that he had returned them into the plaintiff's own hands, and that it was only the other man's forgetfulness that made him continually demand them back.

At this the great Governor asked the creditor what answer he had to give to his adversary. For beyond all doubt the debtor must be speaking the truth since, in his opinion, he was an honest man and a good Christian. It must, in fact, have been the plaintiff who had forgotten how and when the money had been returned, and thenceforward he must never ask for repayment again. The debtor took back his stick, bowed and went out of the court. Now when Sancho saw the defendant also depart without more ado and observed the plaintiffs' resignation, he bowed his head on his breast and, placing the first finger of his right hand over his brows and his nose, remained as if in thought for a short while. Then he raised his head and ordered the old man with the stick, who had already left the building, to be recalled; and when he was brought back into his presence, Sancho said: 'Give me that stick, my fellow. I've need of it.'

'With great pleasure,' replied the old man, putting it into Sancho's hand. 'Here it is, sir.' Sancho then took it and, handing it to the other old man, said to him: 'Go, in God's name. You're repaid now.'

'What, sir?' replied the old man. 'Is this stick worth ten gold crowns then?'

'Yes,' said the Governor. 'If it isn't I'm the greatest dolt in the world. And now you'll see whether I haven't the gumption to govern a whole kingdom.'

Then he ordered the cane to be broken open in the presence of everyone; and when this was done they found ten gold crowns inside. Whereupon everyone expressed astonishment, and hailed the governor as a new Solomon. And when asked how he had deduced that the ten crowns were inside the cane, he answered that he had watched the defendant give the stick to the plaintiff whilst he took his oath that he had really and truly returned the money; and when the fellow had completed his oath and asked for the stick back, it had occurred to him that the sum in dispute must be inside. From this, he added, they might see that sometimes God directs the judgments of governors, even if some of them are fools. Besides, he had heard the priest of his village tell of a similar case, and he had so good a memory that, if it weren't that he forgot everything he wanted to remember, there would not be a better in the whole isle. Finally they departed, one abashed and the other satisfied. The audience was flabbergasted, and the secretary who noted down Sancho's words, acts and gestures was unable to decide whether to write him down a wise man or a fool.

But no sooner was this case over than a woman came into the court, stoutly clinging to a man dressed like a rich herdsman, and crying out loudly as she came: 'Justice, Lord Governor! Justice! If I don't find it on earth, I'll go and seek it in Heaven! Sweet governor, this wicked man sprang on me in the middle of a field, and abused my body like a dirty dish-rag and, poor wretch that I am, he robbed me of a treasure I've kept for more than twenty-three years, and defended from Moors and Christians, natives and foreigners. I've always been as resistent as a cork-tree and preserved myself as pure as the salamander in the fire, or as wool on the briars, for this fellow now to come and handle me with his clean hands!'

'We have still to discover whether this fine fellow has clean hands or not,' said Sancho.

Then, turning to the man, he asked him what answer he had to offer to the woman's complaint. And the man replied in great confusion: 'Sirs, I am a poor herdsman with a herd of swine, and this morning I left this place to sell — saving your presence — four pigs, and what with dues and exactions they took from me very nearly their full value. Now as I was coming back to my village I met this good woman on the way, and the Devil, the author of all mischief, made us couple together. I paid her sufficient, but she wasn't content and caught hold of me and wouldn't let me go until she had dragged me to this place. She says I forced her, and that's a lie, as I'll swear on oath; and that's the whole truth, to the last crumb.'

Then the Governor asked him if he had any silver money on him, and he replied he had about twenty ducats inside his shirt in a leather purse. This the governor ordered him to take out and hand over to the plaintiff just as it was. He obeyed trembling, and the woman took it, making a thousand curtseys to the company, and praying God for the life and health of the good governor, who thus looked after needy orphans and maidens. With this she left the court, grasping the purse tightly with both hands, although she looked first to see if the money in it was really silver. Then, no sooner was she gone than Sancho said to the herdsman, who was on the point of tears, for his eyes and his heart yearned after his purse, 'Run after that woman, my good fellow, and take the purse away from her, whether she likes it or not. Then come back here with her.'

It was not a fool or a deaf man he spoke to, for the man dashed out at once like lightning and ran to obey. All the audience were in suspense as they awaited the outcome of the case. Then shortly afterwards the man and woman came back, more closely entwined and locked together than before, she with her skirt tucked up and the purse in the fold, and the man struggling to get it away from her. But it was impossible, so stoutly did she defend it, crying out loudly: 'Justice, in God's name! Justice! See, Lord worshipful Governor, the shamelessness of this bold, godless fellow. In the middle of the town, in the middle of the street, he's been trying to rob me of the purse your worship made him give me.'

'And did he rob you?' asked the Governor.

'How rob me?' replied the woman. 'I had rather lose my life than this purse. A pretty babe I should be! You must set other cats at my chin than this miserable, filthy fellow. Pincers and hammers, mallets and chisels, won't be enough to get it out of my clutches, nor lion's claws either. They shall sooner have my soul from the very heart of my body!'

'She's right,' said the man. 'I'm beaten, I admit, and tired out. I confess I haven't the strength to take it from her. I give up.'

Then the Governor said to the woman: 'Show me that purse, honest and valiant woman.'

She gave it to him at once, and the Governor returned it to the man, saying to the forcible but unforced woman: 'Sister, if you'd shown the same valorous spirit you've displayed in defending that purse, or even half as much, in defending your body, the strength of Hercules couldn't have forced you. Get out, confound you, and ill luck go with you. Don't stay anywhere in this isle, nor within twenty miles of it, under pain of two hundred lashes. Get out at once, I say, you loose-tongued, shameless swindler.'

The woman was thrown into confusion, and went off hanging her head, in high dudgeon, and the Governor said to the man: 'Good fellow, go back home, in God's name, with your money, and in future, if you don't want to lose it, try not to get a fancy for coupling with anyone.'

The man thanked him with the worst possible grace and departed, and the audience were once more astonished at their new governor's judicious decisions. All this, duly recorded by his chronicler, was straightway written down for the Duke, who was most eagerly waiting for news. But here let good Sancho rest. His master is clamouring for our attention, being disturbed by Altisidora's music.

Chapter XLVI. *Of the fearful Fright Don Quixote received from certain Cats and Bells in the course of his Wooing by the enamoured Altisidora.*

WE left the great Don Quixote wrapt in the imaginations aroused in him by the music of the enamoured maiden Altisidora. He carried them with him to bed where, like fleas, they would not let him sleep or rest a moment, but mingled in his brain with thoughts of his torn stockings. However, as time is swift and no barrier will stay it, he rode the hours apace, and the morrow speedily arrived. When he saw the dawn he quitted his soft feather-bed, and, casting aside sloth, dressed himself in his chamois suit, and put on his riding boots to hide the disaster to his stockings. He threw his scarlet cloak over him and put on his head a green velvet cap trimmed with silver lace; hung his sword-belt over his shoulders with its trusty, trenchant blade; picked up a great rosary which he always carried with him, and with great gravity strutted into the antechamber, where the Duke and Duchess, already dressed, appeared to be expecting him. But as he passed through a gallery he found Altisidora there waiting for him with the other maid, her friend. And the moment she saw him she pretended to faint, and dropped into the arms of her companion, who began to unlace her bodice in a great hurry. This Don Quixote observed and, going up to them, said: 'Now I know the cause of these attacks.'

'I'm sure I don't,' replied the friend, 'Altisidora is the healthiest girl in this whole house, and I've never heard her so much as sigh so long as I've known her. Ill luck to all knights errant in the world, if they're all so ungrateful! Now get along, Don Quixote, for this poor girl won't come to herself so long as you stay here.'

To which Don Quixote replied: 'Kindly have a lute put into my room to-night, and I will console this afflicted maiden to the best of my powers. For in the beginnings of love a prompt undeceiving is generally an effective remedy.'

With this he departed for fear of being observed there. But he was no sooner gone than the fainting Altisidora came to her senses and said to her companion: 'We must put a lute there for him indeed. No doubt Don Quixote means to give us some music, and if it is his own it won't be too bad.'

When they related this last incident to the Duchess, and told her of Don Quixote's request for a lute, she was exceedingly delighted, and planned with the Duke and her maids a new trick which would afford them some harmless amusement. So they looked forward with great pleasure to the night, which was not long in falling. But the Duke and Duchess whiled away the interval in delightful conversation with Don Quixote; and it was on this same day that the Duchess actually sent off one of her pages – the one who had played the part of the enchanted Dulcinea in the wood – to Teresa Panza, with her husband Sancho Panza's letter and the bundle of clothes he had left to be forwarded to her; and she sent him off with injunctions to bring back a faithful account of his conversation with her. After this – it was eleven at night by then – Don Quixote found a guitar in his room. He strummed it and opened the window. Then, hearing people moving in the garden, he ran his fingers over the strings, tuned it as well as he knew how, and after spitting and clearing his throat began to sing in a hoarse but not unmusical voice the following ballad which he had composed himself:

> The powerful force of love
> Doth oft unhinge the soul,
> Taking for instrument
> Unthinking idleness.
>
> Sewing and useful work
> And ceaseless occupation
> Are a sure antidote
> To the poison of love's grief.
>
> Modest and prudent maids,
> Whose longing is to wed,
> Chastity is their dower;
> There is no higher praise.
>
> Those that knight errants be
> And those that haunt the court
> Woo the loose sort of maid,
> But wed the modest ones.
>
> Loves in the East arise
> Between a host and guest,
> But they soon reach their West:
> At parting they are done.
>
> Love that's so newly come,
> Now here, to-morrow gone,
> Never leaves images
> Deep printed in the soul.
>
> Picture on picture drawn
> Leaves neither sign nor mark.
> Where there's one beauty, the
> Second won't win the trick.
>
> On my soul's canvas is
> Painted indelibly
> Peerless Dulcinea.
> Nothing can blot her out.

In lovers constancy's
The most prized quality.
Love can work miracles,
And raise up lovers too.

Don Quixote had come to this point in his song, which was heard by the Duke and Duchess, Altisidora and almost all the people in the castle, when suddenly, from a balcony which directly overhung his window, a rope was let down with more than a hundred sheep-bells fastened to it and, immediately afterwards, a great sack, full of cats with smaller bells tied to their tails, was flung after it. The jingling of the bells and the squawking of the cats made such a din that even the Duke and Duchess, who had contrived the joke, were aghast, while Don Quixote was dumbfounded with fear. Now two or three of the cats, as fate would have it, got through the window, and as they rushed about the room it was as if a legion of devils had broken in. They knocked over and put out the candles burning there, and ran about trying to find a way of escape. And all the while the rope with the great sheep-bells on it continued to rise and fall, and the majority of the people of the castle, not being in the secret, remained speechless with astonishment. Finally Don Quixote rose to his feet and, drawing his sword, began to make stabs through the window, crying loudly:

'Avaunt, evil enchanters! Avaunt, crew of sorcerers! For I am Don Quixote de la Mancha, against whom your wicked plots are powerless and of no avail.'

Then, turning round upon the cats, who were running about the room, he dealt them many blows. And all of them rushed to the window and jumped out, except one which, finding itself hard pressed by Don Quixote's sword-thrusts, jumped at his face and dug its claws and teeth into his nose, whereupon Don Quixote began to roar his very loudest in pain. Now when the Duke and Duchess heard him, realizing the probable cause, they ran in great haste to his room and, opening the door with the master-key, found the poor knight struggling with all his might to tear the cat from his face. They went in with lights, and when he saw the unequal struggle the Duke ran up to disengage them, although Don Quixote cried out:

'Let no one pull him off! Leave me to deal with this devil, this wizard, this enchanter, hand to hand. For I will teach him myself what it is to deal with Don Quixote de la Mancha.'

But the cat snarled and held on, heedless of his threats. At last, however, the Duke pulled it off and threw it out of the window, Don Quixote coming off with a scratched face and not too whole a nose. But he was much annoyed at not being left to finish the battle he was fighting so stoutly against that perverse enchanter. Then they sent for oil of Hypericum, and that same Altisidora with her whitest of hands put bandages on all his wounds, saying to him in a soft voice, as she bound them up:

'All these misfortunes befall you, flinty-hearted knight, for your sin of hardness and obstinacy. May it please God that your squire Sancho shall forget to whip himself, so that this beloved Dulcinea of yours may never emerge from her enchantment, and you may never enjoy her nor come to the bridal bed with her, at least while I, who adore you, am alive.'

To all this Don Quixote gave no word of reply, but heaved a deep sigh, and presently lay down on his bed, after thanking the Duke and Duchess for their kindness, not because he had been in any fear of that cattish and bellish rabble of enchanters, but because he realized their good intentions in coming to his rescue. The noble pair left him to rest and went away concerned at the unfortunate result of their joke, for they had not thought the adventure would have proved so tiresome and costly to Don Quixote. But it kept him confined to his room for five days, and there another adventure befell him, more pleasant than the last. His historian will not relate it now, however, having to visit Sancho Panza, who was proceeding very busily and very drolly with his government.

Chapter XLVII. *The account of Sancho Panza's Behaviour in his Government, continued.*

THE history tells that Sancho Panza was taken from the court of justice to a sumptuous palace, where a royal and most spotless table was laid in a great hall. Immediately upon his entrance into this room the clarions sounded and four pages came in to bring him water for his hands, which Sancho received with great gravity. Then the music stopped and he took his seat at the head of the table, for there was no other seat besides and no other place laid. At his side there stood a personage with a little whalebone wand in his hand, who afterwards proved to be a physician. Then they lifted up the very rich white cloth which covered the fruit and a great variety of dishes of different foods. A person looking like a student pronounced the blessing, and a page tucked a lace bib under Sancho's chin, while another, who performed the office of butler, put a plate of fruit in front of him. But scarcely had he eaten a mouthful when the physician touched the dish with his little wand, and it was whisked from in front of him at top speed. The butler, however, brought him another dish of different food, which Sancho was just going to try. But before he could reach it to taste it the wand touched it, and a page whipped it off as quickly as the other had taken the fruit. Sancho was amazed at this performance and, looking at each one of them, asked whether he was supposed to eat his dinner like a conjuring trick. And the man with the wand replied:

'It must merely be eaten, Lord Governor, according to the manner and custom of other isles where there are governors. I, sir, am a physician, and I am salaried to act as doctor to the Governors of this isle. I am much more careful of their health than of my own, studying day and night and sounding the Governor's constitution to find means of curing him if he should fall ill. My principal duty is to be present at his dinners and suppers, to let him eat what seems to me fitting, and to take away from him what I presume may do him harm and be injurious to his stomach. That is why I ordered that dish of fruit to be removed, it being far too moist; and the other dish I had removed because it was too heating, containing many spices which increase the thirst; for one who drinks much kills and consumes the radical humour wherein life consists.'

'At that rate,' said Sancho, 'the dish of roast partridges over there won't do me any harm. They look very tasty to me.'

To which the physician replied: 'The Lord Governor shall never eat of them whilst I live.'

'Why not?' asked Sancho.

'Because our master Hippocrates,' answered the physician, 'the pole-star and light of medicine, says in one of his aphorisms: "*Omnis saturatio mala perdicis autem pessima*"; which means all surfeit is bad, but that of partridges is worst.'

'If that's so,' said Sancho, 'pray see, Master Doctor, which of all the dishes on the table will be most wholesome for me and do me least harm, and let me eat of it without your tapping it. For, by the life of the Governor and in true earnest, I'm dying of hunger, and to deny me my victuals is more likely to rob me of my life than to lengthen it, whatever you may say, Master Doctor.'

'Your worship is right, Lord Governor,' replied the physician, 'and therefore, in my opinion, you should not eat of those stewed rabbits there, for they are a furry food. You might have tried that veal if it had not been roasted with a pickle sauce; but as it is, it is out of the question.'

'That great smoking dish further over,' said Sancho, 'looks to me like a mixed stew, and seeing what a lot of different things there are in these stews, we can't fail to find something in it tasty and wholesome for me.'

'*Absit!*' cried the physician, 'far from us be such an evil thought! There is nothing in the world less nourishing than a mixed stew. Leave your stews for canons or rectors of colleges, or for country weddings. And let them be banished from Governors' tables, at which every delicacy and refinement must preside. And the reason is that always, everywhere, and by everybody, simple medicines are more highly prized than compounds. For in simple ones there is no danger that one may make a mistake, while in the compounds one may err by varying the proportions of the ingredients. But it is my certain opinion that to conserve and improve his health, my Lord Governor should now eat a hundred wafer rolls and some thin slices of quince flesh, which will sustain his stomach and help his digestion.'

When he heard this Sancho leant against the back of the chair and stared intently at the doctor, demanding in grave tones what his name was and where he had studied.

'My name, Lord Governor,' replied the physician, 'is Doctor Pedro Recio de Aguero, and I am a native of a village called Tirteafuera, which lies on the right of the road from Caracuel to Almodovar del Campo; and I hold the degree of doctor from the university of Osuna.'

To which Sancho replied in a great rage: 'Then, Doctor Pedro Recio de Aguero, native of Tirteafuera, which lies on the right of the road from Caracuel to Almodovar del Campo, graduate of Osuna, get out of here at once! Or if you don't, I swear by the sun I'll take a stick and, beginning with you, I'll beat every doctor out of the isle; every one of them at least that I find to be ignorant, though your learned, prudent and sensible physician I'll raise above my head and honour as a god. And I say again, get out of here, Pedro Recio, or if you don't I'll take this chair I'm sitting on and smash it over your head. And let me answer for it at Doomsday. For I will justify myself by swearing it was a good and godly deed to kill a bad doctor. Bad doctors are the curse of the state. Let me have something to eat, or else you can take away my governorship, for a post that won't find a man in food isn't worth two beans.'

The doctor was alarmed at the Governor's violent outburst, and tried to make his get-away. But at that moment a post-horn sounded in the street, and the butler looked out of the window and turned to say: 'Here's a messenger from my master the Duke. He must be bringing some despatch of importance.'

The courier entered, sweating and flurried, and drawing a sealed envelope from under his shirt, placed in in the Governor's hands. Whereat Sancho gave it to the butler, and ordered him to read the address, which ran as follows: 'To Don Sancho Panza, Governor of the Isle Barataria, into his own hands or those of his secretary.'

Hearing which, Sancho asked: 'Who here is my secretary?'

And one of those standing by answered: 'I, sir, for I can read and write, and I'm a Basque.'

'With that last qualification,' said Sancho, 'you could well be secretary to the Emperor himself. Open this envelope and see what it says.'

The newly-made secretary did so and, having read the contents, pronounced that it was a matter to be discussed in private. Sancho then ordered the room to be cleared, and no one to remain but the steward and the butler; on which the doctor and the rest departed. After which the secretary read the letter, which ran as follows:

'*It has come to my knowledge, Don Sancho Panza, that some enemies of mine and of this isle will deliver a furious assault upon it, though on what night is uncertain. You must keep watch and be on the alert for fear of surprise. I have also learnt by trustworthy spies that four per-*

sons have entered the place in disguise to take your life, for they are afraid of your abilities. Keep your eyes open, watch who comes to speak to you and eat nothing that is set before you. I will be sure to aid you if you find yourself in difficulties. Whatever happens I rely on your acting with your accustomed intelligence.

From this place, the sixteenth of August at four in the morning.

Your friend,
The Duke.'

Sancho was astonished, and his companions pretended to be so as well. Then turning to the steward, he said:

'What we must do now – and immediately – is to put Doctor Recio in the lock-up; for if anyone may kill me it will be he, and that by the most lingering and worst of all deaths, hunger.'

'Yet,' said the butler, 'it is my opinion that your worship ought not to eat anything that is on this table, for it has been prepared by nuns and, as the saying goes, behind the cross stands the devil.'

'I don't dispute it,' replied Sancho. 'So for the moment let me have a piece of bread and some four pounds of grapes. There can be no poison in them. For really I can't hold out without eating, and if we have to be ready for these battles they threaten us with we must be well nourished, since guts carry heart and not heart guts. You, secretary, reply to the Duke, my Lord, and say that all his orders shall be carried out exactly and most faithfully. You will salute my lady the Duchess on my behalf, and say that I beg her not to forget to send my letter and my bundle by messenger to my wife, Teresa Panza. Tell her that I shall consider it a great favour, and will be sure to serve her to the uttermost of my power. And, by the way, you can put in a greeting to my master, Don Quixote de la Mancha, that he may see I'm grateful and, being a good secretary and a good Basque, you may add anything you please that's to the point. Now let them clear away the cloth and give me something to eat, and then I'll deal with all the spies and murderers and enchanters that may set upon me or on my isle.'

At this point a page came in and said: 'There's a countryman here on business who wants to speak to your worship on a matter which he says is of great importance.'

'It's very odd,' said Sancho. 'Can these businessmen really be so

stupid that they can't see this is no time to come about their business?
Are we governors and judges not men of flesh and blood? Don't we
need to rest awhile like other men? Or do they expect us to be made
of marble stone? Upon my soul, if this governorship of mine lasts —
and I've an inkling it won't — I'll lay into some of these businessmen. Now tell that fellow to come in; but make sure first that he
isn't one of these spies or one of my murderers.'

'He isn't, sir,' answered the page. 'He seems a harmless sort. Indeed, if I'm not mistaken he's as harmless as a crust of bread.'

'There's nothing to fear,' said the butler, 'for we're all here.'

'Wouldn't it be possible, steward,' asked Sancho, 'for me to eat
something of weight and substance now Doctor Pedro Recio has
gone, even if it were only a bit of bread and an onion?'

'To-night at supper we will make up for the shortcomings of
your dinner, and your Lordship shall be amply satisfied,' declared
the steward.

'God grant it,' replied Sancho.

At this the peasant came in. He was a man of very good appearance, a decent honest soul as you could see from a thousand miles
off, and his first words were: 'Who here is the Lord Governor?'

'Who should it be,' replied the secretary, 'but the one seated in
the chair?'

'Then I humble myself in his presence,' said the countryman.
And going down on his knees, he begged the Governor for his hand
to kiss. But Sancho refused it, and bade him get up and tell him what
he wanted. And the countryman obeyed, saying: 'I'm a labouring
man, sir, a native of Miguelturra, a village six miles from Ciudad
Real.'

'Here's another Tirteafuera!' exclaimed Sancho. 'But go on,
brother, for I can tell you I know Miguelturra very well. It's not
very far from my own village.'

'The matter is this, sir,' continued the countryman. 'I, by the
mercy of God, am married with the licence and blessing of the Holy
Roman Catholic Church. I have two sons, both students, the
younger studying for a bachelor and the elder for a licentiate. I am
a widower, for my wife died, or rather a wicked doctor killed her by
purging her when she was pregnant; and had God allowed her child
to see the light and it had been a boy I would have put him to study

B B

for a doctor, so that he might not be envious of his brothers, the bachelor and the licentiate.'

'So,' said Sancho, 'if your wife hadn't died, or been killed, you wouldn't be a widower now.'

'No, sir, certainly not,' replied the countryman.

'We're getting on famously,' said Sancho. 'Go ahead, brother; this is a time for sleep rather than for business.'

'Let me tell you, then,' said the countryman, 'that this son of mine, who is to be a bachelor, fell in love with a young lady in our village, called Clara Perlerino, daughter of Andrew Perlerino, a very rich farmer; and this name of Perlerino doesn't come to them by descent or ancestry, but because everyone in the family is paralytic and, to make it sound better, they call themselves Perlerinos. Though, to tell you the truth, the young lady seems an orient pearl, and looked at from the right hand side is like a flower of the field. From the left she isn't so good, for she's short of that eye she lost from small-pox. But although she has a great number of large pits in her face, her admirers say that they aren't pits, but graves in which the souls of her lovers lie buried. She's so clean that her nose is cocked right up, as they say, to avoid soiling her face, and looks as if it's running away from her mouth. But she is extremely handsome all the same, and has a big mouth, that would figure among the shapeliest of its kind, if she wasn't short of ten or a dozen teeth. I don't know what to say about her lips, for they're so thin and delicate that they might be wound into a skein, if it were usual to wind lips. They look marvellous, for they are a different colour from the ordinary run of lips, being mottled blue, green and purple. Pardon me, Lord Governor, for painting the young lady's features in such detail, but she'll be my daughter some day, for I like her, and she doesn't seem bad to me.'

'Paint what you like,' said Sancho. 'Your picture refreshes me; and if I had dined this portrait would be the best dessert in the world.'

'I've still to serve you with that,' answered the countryman, 'but the time may come when we may be acquainted if we aren't now. And I tell you, sir, that if I could paint her elegance and the height of her body it would be something to marvel at. Yet that I can't do because she's bent and shrunken, and her knees meet her mouth.

But it's clear enough, all the same, that if she could stand upright
her head would touch the ceiling. She would have given my bachelor her hand in marriage by now, only she can't stretch it out because it's withered; but even then you can tell how fine and shapely
it is from her long furrowed nails.'

'So far, so good,' said Sancho. 'Take it, brother, that you've
painted her from head to foot. What is it you want now? Come to
the point without all these twistings and windings, and trimmings
and additions.'

'I should like your worship to do me a favour,' answered the
countryman, 'and give me a letter of recommendation to the girl's
father, begging him to be so kind as to let this marriage take place,
since we're not unequal in fortune's gifts or in nature's. For, to tell
you the truth, my Lord Governor, my son's bewitched, and not a
day passes that the evil spirits don't torment him three or four times;
and from falling into the fire once, his face is crinkled like parchment
and his eyes are rather moist and running. But he has a temper like
an angel's and, if it weren't that he bangs and punches himself, he
would be a saint.'

'Do you want anything else, my good fellow?' asked Sancho.

'There's one other thing I should like,' said the countryman,
'only I daren't mention it. But let it come out; it mustn't go bad inside me, come what may. So I'll tell you, sir, I'd like your worship
to give me three hundred or six hundred ducats to help towards my
bachelor's dowry. I mean, sir, to help him set up house; for, after
all, they'll have to live on their own, and not be subject to the in-
terference of their parents.'

'Think if there's anything else you'd like,' said Sancho, 'and
don't let shame or bashfulness prevent your mentioning it.'

'No, nothing at all,' answered the countryman.

But no sooner did he answer than the Governor rose to his feet,
and seizing the chair on which he had been sitting, cried out: 'I
swear to God, Don lubberly, boorish Lumpkin, that if you don't
get out of my sight this instant I'll break your head open with this
chair! You villainous son of a whore! You devil's own painter! Is
this the time to come asking me for six hundred ducats? And where
have I got them, stinker? And why should I give them to you, even
if I had them, rogue and idiot? What are Miguelturra and the whole

family of Perlerinos to me? Get out, I say, or if you don't, I swear by the Duke, my master, I'll do as I said. You can never be from Miguelturra; you are some scoundrel sent here by Hell to tempt me. What, you godless wretch? I haven't held the governorship a day and a half, and you expect me to have six hundred ducats, do you?'

The steward signed to the countryman to leave the room, which he did, hanging his head, and apparently terrified that the Governor might carry out his threat; for the rogue was an excellent actor.

But let us leave Sancho in his rage – and peace to the whole company – and return to Don Quixote, whom we left with his face bound up and dressed for his cattish wounds, which took more than a week to heal. And on one of these days there occurred an incident which Cide Hamete promises to recount as truthfully and exactly as he always relates every minutest detail of this history.

Chapter XLVIII. *Of Don Quixote's Adventure with Doña Rodriguez, the Duchess's Waiting-woman, and other incidents worthy of record and of eternal remembrance.*

THE sore-wounded Don Quixote was exceedingly fretful and melancholy, with his face bandaged and marked, not by the hand of God but by the claws of a cat – such are the misfortunes incidental to knight errantry. For six days he did not appear in public, but on one of those nights, lying awake and watchful, brooding on his misfortunes and on Altisidora's persecution, he heard someone opening the door of his room with a key, and immediately imagined that the enamoured maiden was coming to surprise his chastity and overcome the fidelity he owed his lady Dulcinea del Toboso.

'No,' said he, in an audible voice, believing in his imaginary picture, 'the greatest beauty on earth shall not prevail upon me to cease my adoration of the lady I hold engraved and imprinted in the centre of my heart and in my innermost entrails, whether you are transformed, my lady, into an onion-eating country girl or a nymph of the golden Tagus, weaving tissues of twisted silk and gold, or if Merlin or Montesinos holds you where he will; for wherever you may be you are mine, and everywhere I have been or shall be I am yours.'

As he concluded this speech the door opened. He stood up on the bed, enveloped from head to foot in a yellow satin quilt, a nightcap on his head, and his face and moustache in bandages – his face because of his scratches, and his moustaches to keep them from drooping and falling; and in this costume he appeared the strangest phantom imaginable. He riveted his eyes on the door, but where he expected to see the love-lorn and distressed Altisidora come in, he saw a most venerable waiting-woman, with a white pleated veil, so long that it covered and swathed her from head to foot. In the fingers of her left hand she carried a burning half-candle, and with her right she shaded her face to keep the light from her eyes, which were covered by a pair of enormous spectacles. She advanced with noiseless tread, moving her feet very softly. Don Quixote gazed at her from his vantage point and, imagining from her dress and her silence that this was some witch or sorceress coming to do him a mischief, began to cross himself most energetically. The apparition drew nearer, and when it reached the middle of the room it raised its eyes and observed Don Quixote's frantic exercise. Now if he was frightened at the sight of such a figure, she was equally startled by his appearance, for the moment she saw him so tall and yellow, in his quilt and his disfiguring bandages, she screamed out loudly: 'Jesus! What's that?'

With the sudden fright the candle fell from her hands; and finding herself in the dark, she turned to go. But in her alarm she tripped over her skirt and came down with a great thud. Then the terrified Don Quixote began to speak:

'I conjure you, phantom or whatever you are, to tell me your name and to say what you want of me. If you are a soul in torment, say so, and I will do everything in my power for you, for I am a Catholic Christian and love to benefit all mankind. It was with that end I took up the order of knight errantry which I profess, the exercise of which extends even to relieving souls in purgatory.'

The bewildered waiting-woman, hearing herself thus exorcised, judged Don Quixote's fright by her own, and answered in low and plaintive tones: 'Don Quixote – if, perhaps, your worship is Don Quixote – I am no phantom or apparition or soul in purgatory, as your worship seems to think, but Doña Rodriguez, maid-of-honour to my lady the Duchess, and I come to you in such a distress as it is your custom to remedy.'

'Tell me, Doña Rodriguez,' asked Don Quixote, 'do you come to me, perhaps, on a mediation of love? For I must inform you that I am good for no one, thanks to the peerless beauty of my lady Dulcinea del Toboso. To be plain, Doña Rodriguez, if you will omit and lay on one side all love messages you may go and relight your candle and come back. Then we will talk of anything you may ask or desire, saving, as I say, all incitements to love.'

'I bring a message from anyone, sir!' answered the waiting-woman. 'Little does your worship know me. Indeed, I am not so extremely old as to resort to such child's tricks. God be praised, I have my soul in my body and all my teeth and molars in my mouth, except for a few that I have lost to the catarrh, which is so common in this land of Aragon. But wait for me a moment, your worship. I will go out and light my candle, and come quickly back to recount my griefs to the reliever of all griefs in the world.'

And without waiting for a reply, she went out of the room, leaving Don Quixote calmly and thoughtfully awaiting her return. But a thousand thoughts soon crowded into his mind on the subject of this new adventure, and it occurred to him that he had judged and acted improperly in putting himself in danger of breaking his pledged faith to his lady. 'Who knows,' he said to himself, 'whether the Devil, who is subtle and crafty, is not trying to deceive me now with a waiting-woman, though he has not been able to do so with Empresses, Queens, Duchesses, Marchionesses, or Countesses? For I have very often heard very wise men say that, if he can, he will rather give you a flat-nosed than a hawk-nosed woman. And who knows whether this solitude, this opportunity, and this silence may not arouse my sleeping desires and cause me, after all these years, to fall where I have never stumbled? In such cases it is better to fly than to await battle. Yet I cannot be in my senses to be thinking and talking such nonsense; for it is impossible for a white-veiled, fat, bespectacled waiting-woman to move or arouse any lecherous thought in the most depraved breast in the world. Can there possibly be a waiting-woman on earth with wholesome flesh? Is there one of them in the world who is not impertinent, affected and prudish? Avaunt then, you rabble of waiting-women, useless for any human pleasure. How wise was that lady who, they say, had two dummy ones beside her couch, with spectacles and sewing-cushions as if they were working, and found them as good as the real thing for sustaining the dignity of her hall.'

At this he leapt out of bed with the intention of closing the door and preventing Doña Rodriguez' entrance. When he got there, however, to shut it, the lady was already returning with a lighted white wax candle. But when she saw Don Quixote near-to, wrapped in his quilt with his bandages and his night-çap or bonnet, she was once more seized with fright and, retreating two paces, asked: 'Am I safe, Sir Knight? For I do not take it as a sign of modesty that your worship has got out of bed.'

'I would ask you that same question, lady,' replied Don Quixote. 'Tell me whether I shall be safe from assault and ravishment.'

'From whom or of whom do you ask for this assurance, Sir Knight?' asked the waiting-woman.

'From you and of you,' replied Don Quixote, 'for I am not made of marble nor you of brass, nor is it now ten o'clock in the morning, but midnight, or even a little after, I imagine; and besides, we are in a room more close and secret than that cave can have been where the bold, treacherous Aeneas enjoyed the lovely and gentle Dido. But give me your hand, lady, for I desire no greater security than my continence and modesty and the assurance offered by that reverend hood.'

Saying which, he kissed his right hand, and with it seized hers, which she gave him with the same ceremony.

Here Cide Hamete puts in a parenthesis, and swears by Mahomet that he would give the better cloak of two he had to have seen those two walk from the door to the bed, thus entwined and linked.

Finally Don Quixote got into bed, and Doña Rodriguez remained sitting in a chair a little way from his bedside, without taking off her spectacles or putting down her candle. Don Quixote muffled and covered himself completely, leaving no more than his face revealed, and when the two were settled, the first to break the silence was the knight, who said:

'Now, Doña Rodriguez, you may unburden yourself and disclose all the contents of your sorrowful heart and afflicted bowels. It shall be heard by me with chaste ears and remedied by compassionate deeds.'

'That I believe,' replied the waiting-woman, 'for no less Christian an answer could be expected from your worship's gentle and agreeable appearance. The case is, Don Quixote, that although you see me seated in this chair in the middle of the kingdom of Aragon and in the habit of a decayed and forlorn waiting-woman, I am a native of the highlands of Oviedo and of a family which is allied with many of the best in that province. But my ill luck and the improvidence of my parents, which led to their untimely impoverishment, brought me, I do not know how or why, to the Court of Madrid, where, for the sake of peace and to avert greater misfortunes, my parents put me in service as waiting-maid to a noble lady; and I would have your worship know that no one ever surpassed me at back-stitch and plain work in the whole of my life. My parents left me in service and returned to their country, and a few years afterwards they departed this life – it must have been to Heaven, for they were very good people and Catholic Christians. I was left an orphan depending on the miserable salary and scanty favours of such court servants. About that time a squire of the house fell in love with me, without my giving him the least cause for it, a man already advanced in years, bearded and personable and, what is more, as well-born as the king, for he came from the mountains. We did not manage our affair so secretly as to keep it from the notice of my lady who, to save us from scandalmongers, had us married with the licence and approbation of Holy Mother Church, from which marriage was born a daughter, to put an end to my good fortune, such as it was – not that I died in childbed, for I was delivered safely and in due time, but because shortly afterwards my husband died of a shock he received, which would much astonish your worship if I had time now to tell you of it.'

At this she began to weep piteously, and said: 'Pardon me, your worship, Don Quixote, I cannot help it. Every time I remember my unfortunate husband my eyes fill with tears. God help me! With what dignity he used to carry my lady behind him on the crupper of a stout mule, black as jet itself! For they did not use coaches or chairs in those days, as they say is the fashion now, and ladies rode behind their squires. So much at least I cannot refrain from telling you, so that you may be aware of my husband's fine breeding and manners. A judge of the court happened to be coming out of the

Santiago street in Madrid, which is rather narrow, with two of his officers riding before him, and as soon as my good squire saw him, he turned his mule's rein, as if meaning to wait upon him. Then my lady, who was riding behind, whispered in his ear: "What are you doing, you blockhead? Are you forgetting that I am here?"

'The judge, out of politeness, pulled up his horse and said: "Go on your way, sir, for it is I who should wait upon the lady Casilda" – that was my mistress's name.

'However, my husband, cap in hand, insisted on waiting for the judge. At this my mistress, full of rage and spite, drew a stout pin – or I think it was a bodkin – out of its sheath and ran it into his loins, whereupon my husband gave a loud cry and writhed his body so that both he and his mistress fell to the ground. Two of her grooms ran to pick her up, and the judge and his officers ran to her too. The Guadalajara gate was in an uproar – I mean the idlers who were around. My mistress came away on foot, and my husband ran into a barber's shop, crying that his bowels were pierced right through. After that his courteousness became a subject of gossip, so much so that the boys used to chase after him in the street; and for that reason and because he was rather short-sighted my lady dismissed him; and I am perfectly certain that the grief of it brought on his calamitous death. I was left a widow and unprotected, with a daughter on my hands who went on increasing in beauty like the foam of the sea. At length, as I had the reputation of being a fine needle-woman, my lady the Duchess, who had recently married my lord the Duke, offered to bring me with her to this kingdom of Aragon, and my daughter with me. Here in course of time she grew up, with all the graces in the world. She sings like a lark, dances like a thought, capers in the country-dance like a wild thing, reads and writes like a schoolmaster, and reckons like a miser. Of her cleanliness I say nothing, for running water is not cleaner, and now she must be sixteen, five months and three days, more or less, if my memory does not fail me. To be brief, this girl of mine fell in love with the son of a very rich farmer, who lives in one of my master the Duke's villages, not very far from here. In short, I don't know how it happened, but these two came together. He deceived her under the promise of marriage, and now he refuses to keep his word; and although the Duke my master knows it, because I have complained to him not once but many times and implored him to command this farmer to marry my daughter, he turns a deaf ear and will hardly listen to me. And the reason is that this trickster's father is very rich and lends him money and sometimes goes surety for him in his scrapes, and so he does not like to displease him or worry him in any way. So, my dear sir, I should like your worship to undertake the redressing of this wrong, either by entreaty or by arms; for, as all the world says, your worship was born to right wrongs, to redress injuries, and to protect the unfortunate. Reflect on my daughter's orphan state, your worship, her breeding, her youth, and all the virtues I have told you she possesses; for by God and on my conscience, of all my lady's maids there is not one who reaches up to the sole of her shoe. And as for that Altisidora, whom they reckon the liveliest and the freest, if you compare her with my daughter, she doesn't come within six miles of her. For I must say, my dear sir, that all is not gold that glitters; and that Altisidora has more boldness than beauty about her and more freedom than modesty. Besides which she is not very wholesome, for she has a certain taint in her breath, and one cannot bear to be near her for a moment. And even my lady the Duchess ... But I must be silent, for they say that walls have ears.'

'On my life, Doña Rodriguez, what is the matter with my lady the Duchess?' asked Don Quixote.

'Thus pressed,' replied the waiting-woman, 'I cannot refuse to answer your question with the whole truth. Do you observe, Don Quixote, the beauty of my lady the Duchess, the bloom of her complexion, that is like nothing so much as a smooth and burnished sword; those twin cheeks of milk and carmine, which hold the sun in one and the moon in the other, and the graceful way she treads, as if she scorns the ground? Doesn't she seem to dispense health wherever she goes? But let me tell your worship that she may thank God for it in the first place, and in the next two issues that she has, one on each leg, through which she discharges all the ill humours of which the doctors say she is full.'

'Holy Virgin!' exclaimed Don Quixote. 'Can my lady the Duchess possibly have two such drains? I should not have believed it if the barefoot friars had told me; yet since Doña Rodriguez says so, it must be so. But such issues and in such places must distil not humours but liquid ambergris. Truly, I believe that this opening of issues must be an important matter for the health.'

Scarcely had Don Quixote finished this sentence when the doors of the room burst open with a great bang, and with the shock the candle fell out of Doña Rodriguez' hand, leaving the room dark as the wolf's maw, as the saying is. Then the poor waiting-woman felt her throat so tightly gripped by two hands that she could not squawk; and someone else, without a word, very nimbly lifted her skirts and began to give her a pitifully hearty slapping, apparently with a slipper. And though Don Quixote felt this he did not budge from his bed, having no idea what was the matter, but stayed quiet and still, fearing that it might soon be his turn for a beating. It was no idle fear; for leaving the belaboured waiting-woman, who dared not cry out, the silent executioners fell on Don Quixote and, pulling off his sheet and his quilt, pinched him so hard and so often that he was driven to defend himself with his fists; and all this in a bewildering silence. The battle lasted almost half an hour. Then the phantoms departed. Doña Rodriguez gathered up her skirts and went out of the door, bemoaning her disaster, but without saying a word to Don Quixote. He, mournful and pinched, perplexed and thoughtful, remained alone; where we will leave him, longing to know who was the malign enchanter that had dealt him such a trick. But that will be told in good time. For Sancho Panza calls us, and the order of this history demands that we go to him.

Chapter XLIX. *What happened to Sancho Panza on the Rounds of his Isle.*

WE left the great Governor vexed and angry with that portrait-painting rogue of a peasant, who had been tutored by the steward, as the steward was by the Duke, to make sport of him. But he held his own against them all, ignorant, coarse and clumpish though he was, and said to those with him and to Doctor Pedro Recio, who had come back into the hall once the private matter of the Duke's letter had been disposed of:

'I now plainly understand that judges and governors ought to be, and must be, made of brass, to endure the importunities of your men of business, who expect to be listened to and attended to at all

hours and seasons, and are intent only on their own affairs, come
what may. And if the poor judge doesn't hear them and attend to
them, either because he can't or because it isn't the regular time for
giving them audience, they immediately curse him and slander him
and bite at him and even pull his family to pieces. Foolish man of
business, stupid man of business, don't be in such a hurry! Wait for
the proper time and season for your affairs. Don't come at dinner
time, nor at bed time; for judges are flesh and blood and must give
to their nature what nature requires; excepting only me, who give
mine nothing to eat, thanks to the worthy Doctor Pedro Recio
Tirteafuera there, who would have me die of hunger, and declares
that death is life. God give the same fate to him and all his breed –
I'm speaking of quacks, for good doctors deserve palms and laurels.'

All who knew Sancho Panza were amazed to hear him speak so
elegantly, which they could not account for, unless it be that offices
and serious duties quicken some intellects as they deaden others.
Finally Doctor Pedro Aguero of Tirteafuera promised to allow him
some supper that night, even though it might mean transgressing
all the rules of Hippocrates. With this promise the Governor was
satisfied, and looked forward with great impatience to nightfall
and meal-time; and even though time seemed to him to be standing
still, at length the long wished for moment arrived, and they gave
him for his supper a hash of beef and onions and some boiled calves'
feet, rather stale from keeping. But he fell to it all with more pleasure
than if he had been given Milan game, Roman pheasants, Sorrento
veal, Moron partridges, or Lavajos geese; and during his supper he
turned to the doctor and said:

'Look here, Master Doctor, you needn't trouble in future to give
me choice things and delicate dainties, for that would mean wrenching my stomach off its hinges. It's used to kid, beef, bacon, salt
meat, turnips and onions, and if it's given palace food by chance, it
takes it with queasiness and sometimes with loathing. I'd like the
butler to bring me mixed stews – as they call them; and the stronger
they are the higher they smell. He can shove in anything he likes so
long as it's good to eat, and I'll thank him for it, and pay him one
day. But let no one fool me; for either we are or we aren't. Let's all
live and eat in peace and friendship, for when God sends daylight
it's dawn for all. I shall govern this isle without waiving a right or

taking a bribe; and let everyone keep his eyes open and mind his own business; for I would have them know that the devil is loose in Cantillana, and if they give me cause they'll see wonders. Just you make yourselves honey and the flies'll eat you.'

'Truly, Lord Governor,' said the butler, 'your worship is very right in all you say, and I offer in the name of all the islesmen of this isle to serve you with all diligence, love and goodwill; for the mild manner of government which your worship has shown us in these beginnings leaves us no room to do or think anything which may redound to your disservice.'

'I believe you,' answered Sancho, 'and you would be a set of fools if you did or thought otherwise. Let them look after my feeding and my Dapple's, I say once more, which is the main point of the matter, and the most important. And when the time comes let us make the rounds; for I intend to cleanse this isle of every sort of impurity, and of your vagabond, idle and ill-conditioned persons. For I should like you to know, friends, that your vagrant and lazy sort are the same thing in a state as drones are in the hive, eating up the honey the workers make. I intend to favour labouring men, preserve gentlemen's privileges, reward the virtuous, and above all respect religion and honour the clergy. What do you think of that? Am I saying something or cracking my brains for nothing?'

'You are saying so much, Lord Governor,' said the steward, 'that I am amazed to find a man of so little learning as your worship – for I believe you have none – say so many things that are full of judgment and good counsel. For those that sent you here and we that came with you were far from expecting anything of the sort from you. But every day we see something new in the world; jokes are turned to earnest and mockers find themselves mocked.'

Night had now come on, and the Governor, having eaten his supper by leave of Doctor Recio, prepared to make his rounds, accompanied by the steward, the secretary, the butler, the chronicler, whose duty it was to record his deeds, and enough constables and clerks to make up a fair-sized battalion. Sancho walked in the middle with his wand of justice, a grand sight to see. Now when they had patrolled a few of the town streets they heard the clashing of knives and, running to the spot, found no more than two men fighting. These broke off when they saw the law approaching, one of them crying: 'Here, in the name of God and the King! What! Are people to be attacked here and robbed and assaulted in the open streets?'

'Be calm, my good fellow,' said Sancho, 'and tell me the cause of this quarrel, for I'm the Governor.'

At that his adversary put in: 'My Lord Governor, I will tell you very briefly. Your worship must know that this gentleman has just won more than a thousand *reals* here in this gambling house opposite, God knows how. And I, who was a spectator, decided several doubtful throws in his favour, against all the dictates of my conscience. He got up with his winnings, and when I expected him to give me a crown at least as a fee – such as it's usual and customary to pay men of quality like myself, who stand by to judge fair play, and back up malpractice and prevent quarrels – he pocketed his money and left the house. I came after him in a rage, and requested him in fair and civil words to give me some eight *reals*, for he knows that I am an honourable man and have no profession or place, since my parents neither taught me a trade nor bequeathed me a post. But the rogue – he's a greater thief than Cacus and a greater cheat than Andradilla – wouldn't give me more than four *reals*. So you see, my Lord Governor, what a shameless, conscienceless fellow he is. But I swear, if your worship hadn't come, I would have made him cough up his winnings and taught him how to balance accounts.'

'What do you say to this?' asked Sancho.

The other replied that his adversary was speaking the truth but that he had not intended to give him more than four *reals*, because he was continually giving him something; and that men who expect tips must be polite and take what they get with a smile on their faces, and not haggle with winners unless they know for certain that they are sharpers and that their gains are unfairly got. But there was no better proof of his honesty and that he was no thief, as the other suggested, than his refusal to pay; for sharpers must always pay tribute to their accomplices.

'That's right,' said the steward. 'Now consider, my Lord Governor, what should be done with these men.'

'This is what shall be done,' answered Sancho. 'You, master winner, fair, foul, or indifferent, must pay your knifer a hundred *reals* here and now, and disburse thirty more for the poor in the prisons. And you, who have neither place nor profession and go idly about this isle, must take these hundred *reals* at once, and to-morrow and no later get out of this isle for ten years' banishment, on pain of finishing your sentence in the next life if you break the ban; for I'll hang you on a gallows – or at least the hangman shall do it for me – and let no one reply or he shall feel the weight of my hand.'

The one disbursed, the other took the money; the one left the isle, the other went home; and the Governor went on to say: 'Now if I'm good for anything I'll put down these gambling houses, for I strongly suspect that much harm comes of them.'

'This one at least,' said one of the clerks, 'your worship won't be able to put down, because it's kept by a great personage, and his losses at cards every year are incomparably greater than his winnings. Your worship can show your power against other gambling dens of lower degree, for it's those which do the greatest harm and harbour the worst abuses. But the notorious sharpers dare not practise their tricks in gentlemen's and lords' houses. And since the vice of gambling has become a common habit, it's better for it to be practised in houses of quality than at some tradesmen's, where they catch a wretch after midnight and flay him alive.'

'Yes, Master Clerk, I know there's much to be said on that score,' replied Sancho.

At this moment there came up a constable, who had hold of a youth, and he said: 'Lord Governor, this young man was coming our way, but as soon as he spied the law he turned round and began to run like a stag, a sure sign that he's a criminal. I went off after him, but if it hadn't been that he tripped and fell I should never have caught him.'

'Why did you run away, man?' asked Sancho.

'Sir, to avoid answering all those questions the constable asks,' replied the youth.

'What is your trade?'

'A weaver.'

'And what do you weave?'

'Iron heads for lances, so please your worship.'

'So you choose to be funny? Is it a buffoon you are? Very well. And where were you going just now?'

'To take the air, sir.'

'And where do you take the air in this isle?'

'Where it blows.'

'Good, you answer to the point. You're a clever one, my lad, but kindly reckon that I'm the air, and blow astern of you and drive you into jail. Hold him there, and take him away, for I'll make him sleep there to-night out of the air.'

'By God,' said the lad, 'your worship can no more make me sleep in prison than make me king!'

'Well, why can't I make you sleep in prison?' asked Sancho. 'Haven't I power to arrest and discharge you whenever and as often as I please?'

'However much power your worship may have,' said the youth, 'won't be enough to make me sleep in prison.'

'Why not?' demanded Sancho. 'Take him at once where he'll see his mistake with his own eyes, and in case the jailer should use his interested liberality on his behalf, I'll make him go bail for two thousand ducats that he won't let you stir a step out of prison, my man.'

'This is all ridiculous,' answered the youth. 'The point is that no man living shall make me sleep in the jail.'

'Tell me, devil,' demanded Sancho, 'have you an angel to release you and free you from the fetters that I shall have put on you?'

'Now, my Lord Governor,' answered the youth with a charming smile, 'let us reason together and come to the point. Suppose your worship orders me to be taken to prison, and has me loaded with fetters and chains there and put in a cell, laying the jailer under heavy penalties to carry out your orders, and not let me out; all the same if I don't wish to sleep, and stay awake all night without closing an eyelid, will your worship with all your power be able to make me sleep if I don't choose to?'

'No, of course not,' said the secretary, 'the man has made out his case.'

'You would stay awake then,' asked Sancho, 'only because it's your own will, and with no intention of crossing me?'

'None, sir,' said the youth, 'none at all.'

'Then go, in Heaven's name,' said Sancho. 'Go and sleep at home and God give you sound sleep. I don't want to rob you of it. But

I warn you not to make a mock of the law in future, for you may meet someone who'll return you the joke on your skull.'

The youth went off, and the Governor continued his rounds. Then shortly afterwards two constables came up, grasping a man, and said: 'Lord Governor, this person looks like a man but isn't. She's a woman, and no plain one, dressed up in a man's clothes.'

They raised two or three lanterns to her face, and their light revealed the features of a girl of sixteen or so, with her hair gathered into a little net of gold and green silk, and lovely as a thousand pearls. They looked her up and down, and saw that she was wearing flesh-coloured silk stockings with white taffeta garters edged with gold and seed-pearl. Her breeches were of green cloth of gold, her jacket or coat of the same cloth hung loose, and beneath it she wore a doublet of the finest white and gold material. Her shoes were white and like a man's. She wore no sword on her belt but a jewelled dagger, and on her fingers several very fine rings. In short, everyone thought the girl handsome, but not one of them recognized her, the natives of the place saying that they could not think who she was. But most surprised of all were those who were in the secret of the tricks which were being played on Sancho, because this meeting had not been contrived by them, and so they awaited its upshot with some excitement. Sancho was struck by the girl's beauty, and asked her who she was, where she was going, and what reason she had for wearing those clothes. And she answered with honest shame, her eyes fixed on the ground: 'Sir, I cannot reveal in public what it is so important for me to keep secret. One thing I want to be understood is that I am not a thief or a wicked person, but a poor young lady driven by jealousy to forget my modesty.'

Hearing this, the steward said to Sancho: 'Make your attendants retire, my Lord Governor, so that this lady can say what she will with less embarrassment.'

The Governor gave orders to that effect, and everyone drew aside except the steward, the butler and the secretary. Then, when they were alone, the young lady went on to say: 'Gentlemen, I am the daughter of Pedro Perez Mazorca, who farms the wool in this place and often comes to my father's house.'

'That won't pass, lady,' said the steward, 'for I know Pedro Perez very well, and I know that he has no children, male or female.

What's more you say that he's your father, and then add that he often comes to your father's house.'

'I'd already seen that,' said Sancho.

'Indeed, gentlemen, I'm confused and I don't know what I'm saying,' answered the young lady, 'but the truth is that I am the daughter of Diego de la Llana, whom your worships must all know.'

'Now that'll pass,' said the steward, 'for I know Diego de la Llana and I know that he's an important and rich gentleman, and that he has a son and a daughter, and since he has been left a widower there has been no one in this whole place who can say that he has seen his daughter's face, for he keeps her so confined that he doesn't even let the sun look on her. But, for all that, it's rumoured that she's extremely beautiful.'

'That's the truth,' replied the young lady. 'I am that daughter. Whether rumour lies or not about my beauty, you gentlemen will have discovered, for you have seen me.'

At this she began to weep piteously, and at the sight of her tears the secretary put his lips to the butler's ear and said to him very quietly: 'Something serious must certainly have happened to this poor young lady for her to be wandering from her home in this disguise and at such an hour, she being of such quality too.'

'There's no doubt of that,' answered the butler, 'and besides, her tears confirm the suspicion.'

Sancho comforted her with the best arguments he knew, and begged her to tell him what had happened to her without any fear; for they would all try most earnestly to help her in every possible way.

'This is the case, gentlemen,' she replied. 'My father has kept me confined for the last ten years, that is ever since my mother was laid in the earth. Mass is said at home in a fine chapel, and in all that time I've seen nothing but the sun by day and the stars and the moon by night. I don't know the look of streets, or market-places, or churches, or even men, except my father and my one brother, and Pedro Perez, the wool-farmer, who visits the house so often that it came into my head to call him my father so as not to mention my real one. This confinement, and his refusal to let me leave the house even to go to church, have made me very unhappy these many days and months. I longed to see the world, or at least the village where

I was born, and this wish didn't seem to me to infringe the modesty proper to young ladies of my birth. Now when I heard them talk of bull-fighting and cane-throwing and play-acting, I asked my brother, who is a year younger than I, to tell me about it all, and about many other things I hadn't seen; and he explained them to me in the best way he could, but it only inflamed my longing to see them. In the end, to shorten the tale of my undoing, let me say that I begged and entreated my brother – oh, I wish I had never begged and entreated him ...'

And she burst into tears once more. At which the steward said to her: 'Proceed, lady, and finish telling us what happened to you, for your words and your tears are keeping us all on tenterhooks.'

'There's little more to tell,' replied the young lady, 'though there are still many tears to be shed, for there's no other way of atoning for sinful wishes.'

The young lady's beauty had sunk into the butler's very soul, and as he held up his lantern once more to look at her again, it seemed to him that they were not tears she wept but seed-pearl or meadow dew; and he even raised them a point higher and compared them to orient pearls, hoping all the while that her misfortunes were not as great as her tears and sobs suggested. The Governor was out of all patience at the girl's slowness in telling her story, and bade her put them out of their suspense; for it was late and there was much of the town still to cover. Then, between sobs and half-breathed sighs, she went on:

'My misfortune and misery is no other than this: that I entreated my brother to disguise me as a man in one of his suits, and take me out one night to see all the town, while our father was asleep. He gave in to my entreaties, put these clothes on me, and dressed himself in some of mine, which suited him as if he were born for them, for he has no down on his chin and looks like nothing so much as a lovely girl. To-night – it must be an hour or so ago – we left the house, and our young and unruly fancies sent us wandering all round the town. But just as we were going to return home we saw a great troop of people coming, and my brother said to me: "Sister, this must be the watch. Fly like the wind, and follow me. If we are recognized, it'll be the worse for us." And as he spoke he turned round and set off running, though it was more like flying. Before I had gone six paces I fell down from fright, and then the officers of justice came up and brought me before your worships. And here I am shown up for a wicked, capricious girl before all these people.'

'So that's all your trouble, young lady,' said Sancho, 'and it wasn't jealousy that brought you from your home, as you told us at the beginning of your tale?'

'Yes, that's all, and it wasn't jealousy that brought me out, but just a wish to see the world; and that didn't go further than seeing the streets of this place.'

And the truth of the young lady's story was confirmed by the arrival of two constables with her brother as their prisoner, for one of them had caught him when he ran away from his sister. He wore a rich skirt and a blue damask cloak with fine gold lacings; his head had no covering or adornment except his hair, which was as red and curly as rings of gold. The Governor, the steward and the butler took him on one side out of his sister's hearing, and asked him how he came to be so dressed; and he, with no less shame and embarrassment, told the same tale as she had told, to the great pleasure of the love-stricken butler. The Governor, however, addressed them: 'This has been a very childish prank indeed, and there was no need of all this sighing and sobbing over the telling of your rash and stupid escapade. For if you had said, "we are so-and-so and so-and-so and we left our parents' house in this disguise to amuse ourselves, and we only did it out of curiosity and for no other reason," the story would have been done without all this moaning and weeping and the rest of it.'

'That's quite true,' replied the young lady, 'but I must confess, your worships, that I was in such a confusion that I couldn't decide what to do.'

'Nothing has been lost,' said Sancho. 'Let us go and leave you both at your father's house; perhaps he won't have missed you. But don't behave so childishly in future, or be so anxious to see the world; for an honest maid and a broken leg are best at home, a woman and a hen are soon lost by gadding, and the girl who's anxious to see also longs to be seen. I say no more.'

The youth thanked the Governor for the favour he proposed to do them by escorting them home, which was not far. So they set out. On their arrival the brother threw a pebble at a window, whereat a maid-servant who was waiting for them immediately came down and opened the door; and they went in, leaving everyone wondering at their beauty and good breeding, and at their desire to see the world by night without going further than their village. But they put everything down to their tender years.

The butler was left with his heart transfixed, and at once resolved to ask the young lady's father for her hand next day, feeling quite certain that he would not be refused, as he was a servant of the Duke's. The thought even came into Sancho's head of marrying the youth to his daughter Sanchica, and he decided to put his plan into practice at the proper time, believing that no husband could be refused to a governor's daughter.

This was the end of that night's rounds and, within two days, of the governorship, by which end all Sancho's designs were cut short and obliterated, as shall later be seen.

Chapter L. Which reveals who the Enchanters and Executioners were that beat the Waiting-woman and pinched and scratched Don Quixote, with the Adventure of the Page who bore the letter to Teresa Panza, Sancho Panza's wife.

CIDE HAMETE, that most meticulous investigator of every detail of this true history, says that at the moment when Doña Rodriguez left her room to go to Don Quixote's apartment another waiting-woman, who slept with her, heard her; and as all waiting-women are fond of prying, listening and sniffing, she went after her so silently that the good Rodriguez did not notice her. Now as soon as this waiting-woman saw the other enter Don Quixote's room, for fear of failing in the waiting-woman's custom of tale-bearing she went to inform her mistress the Duchess that Doña Rodriguez was in Don Quixote's bedroom. Whereat the Duchess told the Duke, and asked his permission for herself and Altisidora to go and see what that lady wanted with Don Quixote. The Duke agreed, and the two of them very warily and silently crept step by step and took up their position behind the door of the room, so close that they overheard every word spoken inside. And when the Duchess heard the Rodriguez expose the secret of her garden of fountains, neither she nor Altisidora could bear it; and so they burst into the

room, in a great fury and spoiling for revenge, to pinch Don Quixote and slap the waiting-woman in the manner described. For
affronts directed against the beauty and pride of women awake in
them a high degree of anger, and kindle their desire for revenge.
And when the Duchess told the Duke what had happened, he was
greatly amused.

Then, in pursuance of her plan for amusing herself at Don Quixote's expense, the Duchess sent the page who had played the part of
Dulcinea in the performance of her disenchantment – which Sancho
had clean forgotten in his occupation of governing – to his wife,
Teresa Panza, with her husband's letter and another from herself,
also a great string of fine corals as a present.

Now the history tells that this page was very shrewd and sharp,
and out of eagerness to serve his master and mistress set out with a
very good will for Sancho's village. And just as he entered it he saw
a great number of women doing their washing in a stream, and
asked them if they could tell him whether there was a woman called
Teresa Panza living there, the wife of a certain Sancho Panza, squire
to a knight called Don Quixote de la Mancha. And a girl stood up
from her linen and answered him: 'Teresa Panza's my mother, and
Sancho's my father, and the knight's our master.'

'Then come, young lady,' said the page, 'and take me to your
mother. For I bear a letter and a present for her from that father of
yours.'

'That I will, and gladly, my dear sir,' replied the girl, who
seemed to be fourteen or so.

And leaving the clothes she was washing to one of her companions, she did not wait to put on a hat or shoes, for she was bare-
legged and dishevelled, but ran skipping along before the page's
horse, crying: 'Come, your worship, our house is at this end of the
village, and my mother's at home, in a great state because she
hasn't heard from my father for so long.'

'Well, I bring her such good news,' said the page, 'that she'll
have to thank God for it.'

At length, jumping, running and skipping, the girl came to the
village, but before she entered the house she called from the door:
'Come out, mother Teresa, come out, come out! For here's a gentleman bringing letters and other things from my good father!'

At this call her mother, Teresa Panza, came out spinning a bunch of flax, and wearing a grey skirt, so skimpy that it looked as if it had been cut short as a mark of shame, a grey bodice and a shirt. She was not very old, although she looked more than forty, but strong and tough, vigorous and wizened. When she caught sight of her daughter, and the page on horseback, she said: 'What's this, child? Who's this gentleman?'

'A servant of my Lady Teresa Panza,' answered the page. And with these words he leapt from his horse and went up to kneel most humbly before the Lady Teresa, saying: 'Give me your hands, my Lady Doña Teresa, which you are as the lawful and particular wife of the Lord Don Sancho Panza, own Governor of the Isle Barataria.'

'O my dear sir, get up from there. Don't do that,' replied Teresa. 'I'm none of your palace ladies, but a poor working woman, daughter of a ploughman, and wife of a squire-errant and no governor.'

'Your worship,' answered the page, 'is the most worthy wife of a most arch-worthy Governor, and to prove it true, receive this letter and this present.' And he whipped out from his pocket a string of corals with gold beads between them, and threw them round her neck, saying: 'This letter is from the Governor, and another which I bring and these corals are from my lady the Duchess, who has sent me to your worship.' Teresa was thunderstruck, and her daughter no less so.

'May I die if our master Don Quixote isn't in this,' cried the girl. 'He must have given father the governorship or countship he promised him so often.'

'That's right,' answered the page, 'for it is on account of Don Quixote that Lord Sancho is now governor of the Isle Barataria, as can be seen by this letter.'

'Read it me, your worship, Master Gentleman,' said Teresa, 'for although I can spin I can't read a word.'

'No more can I,' put in Sanchica, 'but wait for me here, and I'll go and call someone to read it, either the priest himself or the Bachelor Sampson Carrasco. They'll be very glad to come and have news of my father.'

'There's no need to call anyone,' said the page, 'for though I

can't spin I can read, and I will read it.' And so he read it all, though
it is not printed here, as it has been set down already. Then he took
out another letter, from the Duchess, which went like this:

'*Friend Teresa,*

*Your husband Sancho's excellent qualities of goodness and wit have
moved me to beg my husband the Duke to confer on him the governorship of one of his many isles. I am informed that he governs like a goshawk, at which I am much pleased, as, of course, is my lord, the Duke.
Wherefore I give great thanks to Heaven that I was not mistaken in
choosing him for this governorship. For I would have the Lady Teresa
know that it is hard to find a good governor in the world, and may God
be as good to me as Sancho is in his governing.*

*I send you herewith, my dear, a string of corals with golden beads
between them. I should have been glad if they had been orient pearls, but
one who gives you a bone does not wish you dead. The time will come
when we shall know one another and converse together; and God knows
what will come of that. I send my regards to Sanchica, your daughter.
Tell her from me to be prepared, for I mean to make a fine match for her
when she least expects it.*

*They tell me that there are fat acorns in your village. Send me some
couple of dozen, for I shall value them most highly, coming from your
hand. Write me a long letter, advising me of your health and prosperity,
and if you need anything you have only to open your mouth and it shall
be filled to full measure. God keep you. From this place.*

Your loving friend,
The Duchess.'

'Ah!' cried Teresa, on hearing the letter, 'what a good, simple,
humble lady! Let me be buried with such ladies, I say, and not the
madams we're used to in this place, who think that because they're
gentry the wind mustn't touch them; and go to church in such
finery as if they were real Queens, and seem to think they're de-
meaning themselves by looking at a peasant woman. And here you
see where this good lady calls me friend and treats me like her equal,
although she's a Duchess; and may I see her equal to the highest
steeple in all La Mancha. As to the acorns, my dear sir, I'll send her
ladyship a peck, so fat that people will come from far and near to
admire them. But for the present, Sanchica, mind and make a fuss

of this gentleman. Look after his horse, get some eggs out of the stable, and cut plenty of bacon. Let's give him a dinner fit for a prince; he deserves it for the good news he's brought us and for his handsome face. In the meantime I'll go and tell my neighbours about our good luck, and the Holy Father too, and Master Nicholas the barber. For they're always been such friends to your father.'

'Yes, I'll do that, mother,' answered Sanchica, 'but you'll have to give me half that necklace, mind, for I don't think my lady the Duchess is so silly as to have sent it all to you.'

'It's all for you, daughter,' cried Teresa, 'but let me wear it round my neck for a few days; for truly it seems to make my heart glad.'

'You'll both be glad too,' said the page, 'when you see the parcel I've got in this bag. It's a suit of the finest cloth which the Governor only wore for one day's hunting, and he's sent it all to the lady Sanchica.'

'May he live a thousand years,' exclaimed Sanchica, 'and the bearer no less – and two thousand more if need be.'

At this Teresa left the house with the letters, and with the necklace round her neck, beating the letters as she went along, as if they were tambourines; and chancing to meet the priest and Sampson Carrasco, she began to dance, crying:

'There's no poor relation about us now, I promise you! We've got a little government! And if your gay gentlewomen meddle with me, I'll take them down a peg or two.'

'What's this, Teresa Panza? Are you crazy? What are those papers?'

'I'm not crazy; but these are letters from Duchesses and Governors, and the beads round my neck are fine corals, and the Ave Marias and Paternosters are of beaten gold, and I'm a Governor's lady.'

'Heaven help us, we don't know what you mean, Teresa. What is it you're saying?'

'There, look,' replied Teresa, and gave them the letters. The priest read them aloud to Sampson Carrasco, and they looked at one another in astonishment at the news they read. Then the Bachelor asked who had brought the letters, and Teresa replied that they should come to her house and see the messenger, who was a

youth as handsome as a gold brooch, and had brought another present worth twice as much. The priest took the corals from her neck
and examined them; and being convinced of their value, he wondered afresh, and said: 'By my cloth, I don't know what to make of
these letters and presents. On the one hand I can see and feel that
these are fine corals, and on the other I read that a Duchess sends to
ask for two dozen acorns.'

'Let us strike a balance between the two,' said Carrasco; 'and let
us go now and see the bearer of this packet, for he may solve the
mystery.'

This they did, and Teresa returned with them. They found the
page sifting some barley for his horse, and Sanchica cutting a rasher
to pave it with eggs for the page's dinner. They were both taken by
his looks and his grand appearance, and after they had exchanged
courteous salutations, Sampson asked him for news of Sancho
Panza and Don Quixote, for though they had read Sancho's letter
and the Duchess's they were still perplexed and could not make out
all this about Sancho's governorship, especially about its being an
isle, seeing that nearly all the islands in the Mediterranean sea belong to His Majesty.

'There's not the slightest doubt that Sancho Panza is a governor,'
replied the page. 'But whether it's an isle or not he governs is no
concern of mine. Enough that it's a place of more than a thousand
inhabitants. But as to my lady the Duchess sending to beg for a few
acorns, if you knew how simple and humble she is you wouldn't be
surprised, for she has even on occasions sent to borrow a comb from
a neighbour. Indeed, I would have your worships know that although the ladies of Aragon are as high in rank as the ladies of
Castile, they're not so haughty and ceremonious, but much more
affable with the people.'

While they were in the middle of this conversation Sanchica
burst in with her apron full of eggs and asked the page: 'Tell me, sir,
does my father wear laced breeches since he's a governor?'

'I have not noticed,' answered the page, 'but he certainly should
wear them.'

'Oh, my Lord,' exclaimed Sanchica, 'what a sight it must be to
see my father in tights! Isn't it odd that I have longed to see him in
laced breeches ever since I was born?'

'Well, your Grace will see him in just such clothes if you live,' answered the page. 'If his government lasts two months he'll be wearing a travelling hood, I promise you.'

The priest and the barber clearly saw that the page was pulling their legs; but the quality of the corals and the hunting-suit Sancho had sent – for Teresa had by now shown them the clothes – spoke on the other side. However, they could not forbear laughing at Sanchica's wish, especially when Teresa said: 'Master Priest, inquire about here if there's anyone going to Madrid or Toledo who could buy me a hooped farthingale, a good, proper, fashionable one, and of the best quality; for I must certainly do my husband's government all the credit I can. They may tease me but I'll go to Court, and buy a coach like the rest of them, for she that has a governor for husband can afford to keep a coach.'

'And why not, mother?' said Sanchica. 'And the sooner the better, please God. Though people may call after us when they see me riding in a coach beside my lady mother: "Look at that good-for-nothing, old Garlic Gut's daughter. See her sitting there in that coach leaning back like Pope Joan." But let them tread in the mud, and me ride in my coach with my feet off the ground. Bad luck to every scandalmonger in the world! Let them laugh so long as I go warm! Aren't I right, mother dear?'

'Oh, how right you are, daughter!' answered Teresa. 'All this good fortune, and even better, my good Sancho foretold me. And you'll see that he won't stop till he has made me a Countess, my girl, for with luck it's the beginning that counts; and I've often heard your dear father say – and he's got more proverbs than children – when they give you the calf run with the halter; when they give you a governorship, hold on to it; when they give you a countship, grip it tight; and when they whistle you with something good to give you, gulp it down. Or else sleep on and don't answer, when luck and good things come knocking at your door.'

'And what do I care,' added Sanchica, 'if some of them say: "Look at the dog in linen breeches"? – and all the rest, when they see me stuck-up and high falutin.'

And the priest observed when he heard her: 'I cannot help thinking that every one of this Panza family was born with a sack of proverbs inside him. I have never known one of them who does not spill them out at all times and in every conversation he takes part in.'

'That's the truth,' said the page, 'for Lord Governor Sancho spouts them at every turn, and although many of them are off the point, still they give pleasure, and my lady the Duchess and the Duke are highly delighted with them.'

'But do you still affirm that it's true, sir,' asked the Bachelor, 'this about Sancho's governorship, and that there is really a Duchess who sends him presents and writes to him? Because we can't believe it, even though we've handled the presents and read the letters. We reckon it's one of our neighbour Don Quixote's inventions, for he thinks that everything is done by enchantment. So I'm afraid we shall have to touch you and feel you, to see if you are an imaginary ambassador or a flesh-and-blood man.'

'Sirs,' answered the page. 'All I know of myself is that I'm a real ambassador, that my Lord Sancho Panza is in fact a governor, that my master and mistress, the Duke and Duchess, can give and have given him that government, in which I've heard the said Sancho Panza performs most admirably. Whether there are enchantments in this or not your worships may settle between yourselves; for that's all I know, as I will swear you an oath on the life of my parents, who are now living and whom I love and honour exceedingly.'

'That may be,' replied the Bachelor, 'but "*dubitat Augustinus*".'

'Let him doubt who will,' said the page, 'but I've told you the truth, and truth will always rise above a lie, like oil on water; and if not, "*operibus credite et non verbis*". Let one of you come with me and he shall see with his own eyes what he does not believe when he hears it.'

'That journey's for me,' exclaimed Sanchica. 'Take me on your horse's crupper, sir. I should love to go and see my father.'

'Governors' daughters,' replied the page, 'mustn't travel the highways on their own. They must be attended by coaches and litters and a great crowd of servants.'

'Good Heavens,' replied Sanchica, 'I can go as easily on an ass as in a coach. Do you take me for one of your squeamish ones?'

'Quiet, girl,' said Teresa, 'you don't know what you're saying. This gentleman's right, for circumstances alter cases. When it was

Sancho, it was Sancha; when it's Governor, it is my Lady. Aren't I right, sir?'

'The Lady Teresa says more than she imagines,' said the page. 'Now let me have my dinner and send me off, for I want to get back this evening.'

'Your worship shall come and do penance with me,' said the priest, 'for Lady Teresa has more goodwill than good cheer to welcome so worthy a guest.'

The page declined, but in the end had to give in, to his own advantage; and the priest bore him off, highly delighted at the opportunity of questioning him at his leisure about Don Quixote and his doings.

The Bachelor offered Teresa to write answers to her letters; but she did not want him meddling in her affairs, as she took him for a bit of a joker; and so she gave a roll and a couple of eggs to a young friar who could write, and he penned two letters for her, one to her husband and the other to the Duchess, dictated out of her own head, and by no means the worst quoted in this famous history, as will be seen later.

Chapter LI. Of the progress of Sancho Panza's Government and other matters such as they are.

DAWN broke after the night of the Governor's rounds, which the butler had passed without sleep, his thoughts dwelling on the face, the charm and the beauty of the disguised young lady, while the steward spent what remained of it writing down for his master and mistress all Sancho's sayings and doings, in considerable amazement at both, for his speeches and his actions were such a mixture of shrewdness and simplicity.

At length the Lord Governor rose and, by order of Doctor Pedro Recio, they made him breakfast on a little preserved fruit and four gulps of cold water. Sancho would willingly have exchanged the meal for a bit of bread and a bunch of grapes. But, finding that it was a matter rather of compulsion than of choice, he submitted with much grief of heart and mortification of stomach, Pedro Recio making him believe that scanty and delicate fare sharpened the intellect, as was most necessary for persons appointed to authority and high employment, which required strength of mind rather than bodily vigour. By this sophistry Sancho was induced to bear such keen hunger that in his secret heart he cursed his government and even the giver of it. However, with his hunger and his preserved fruit, he sat in judgment that day; and the first case that came before him was a question submitted by a stranger in the presence of the steward and the rest of the fraternity. It was this:

'Sir, a deep river divides a certain lord's estate into two parts ... Listen carefully, your worship, for the case is an important one and rather difficult. I must tell you, then, that over this river is a bridge, and at one end a gallows and a sort of courthouse, in which four judges sit to administer the law imposed by the owner of the river, the bridge and the estate. It runs like this: "Before anyone crosses this bridge, he must first state on oath where he is going and for what purpose. If he swears truly, he may be allowed to pass; but if he tells a lie, he shall suffer death by hanging on the gallows there displayed, without any hope of mercy." Though they know the law and its rigorous conditions, many people cross the bridge and, as they clearly make true statements the judges let them pass freely. Now it happened that they once put a man on his oath, and he swore that he was going to die on the gallows there – and that was all. After due deliberation the judges pronounced as follows: "If we let this man pass freely he will have sworn a false oath and, according to the law, he must die; but he swore that he was going to die on the gallows, and if we hang him that will be the truth, so by the same law he should go free." We ask your worship, Lord Governor, what the judges ought to do with this man; for they are still perplexed and undecided; and when they heard of your worship's great wisdom and acuteness, they sent me to beg you for your opinion of this intricate and doubtful case.'

'Really these worthy judges who sent you to me might have saved themselves the trouble,' replied Sancho. 'There's a good deal more dullness than acuteness in me. But repeat the matter to me, all the same, so that I may understand it; and then perhaps I shall hit the nail on the head.'

The questioner repeated what he had said at first, and Sancho observed: 'I think I can resolve this business in a brace of shakes. It's like this: The man swears that he is going to die on the gallows, and if he does die his oath was true, and by the law as it stands he deserves to go free and cross the bridge. But if they don't hang him, he swore to a lie and by that same law deserves to be hanged.'

'The Lord Governor is quite correct,' said the messenger, 'and as regards his judgment and his interpretation of the case, there is no more question or doubt.'

'But let me continue,' replied Sancho. 'They must let that part of the man which swore truly cross the bridge, and hang the part that swore to a lie; and in that way the conditions of passage will be fulfilled to the letter.'

'Then, Lord Governor,' said the questioner, 'this man will have to be divided into two parts, the lying part and the truthful part; and if he's divided, he's bound to die. Thus no part of the law's demands is fulfilled, and it's absolutely necessary for us to comply with it.'

'Look here, my good fellow,' replied Sancho, 'either I'm a dolt or there's as much reason for this passenger of yours to die as to live and cross the bridge; for, if the truth saves him, the lie equally condemns him; and this being so, which it is, I think you should tell those gentlemen who sent you to me that since the reasons for condemning him and acquitting him are equally balanced they must let him pass freely, for it's always more commendable to do good than to do ill. This decision I would give signed with my name if I knew how to sign. And in this case I have not spoken out of my own head, for there came to my mind one of the many precepts my master Don Quixote gave me the night before I came to be made Governor of this isle; which was that when justice was in doubt I should incline to the side of mercy; and God has been pleased to bring it to my mind now, for it fits the case to a T.'

'That's so,' said the steward, 'and I don't believe that Lycurgus himself, who gave laws to the Lacedaemonians, could have given a better decision than the great Panza has done. And now let the session be closed for this morning, and I'll order the Governor a dinner that will more than satisfy him.'

'That's what I want, and fair play,' said Sancho. 'If I have some dinner it may rain cases and decisions. I'll polish them off as they fall.'

The steward kept his word, for it weighed on his conscience to be

killing so wise a governor by hunger. Besides, he intended to finish
with him that same night by playing him the last trick he was commissioned to play. So it was that the Governor dined that day in defiance of all Doctor Tirteafuera's rules and aphorisms, and when the
cloths were lifted a courier came in with a letter for him from Don
Quixote. Sancho bade the secretary read it to himself, and then if
there was nothing in it that should be kept secret, to read it aloud.
The secretary obeyed and, after glancing it over, he said: 'It can
certainly be read aloud. What Don Quixote has written to your
worship deserves to be stamped and written in letters of gold. This
is what he says:

> *Letter of Don Quixote de la Mancha to Sancho Panza, Governor*
> *of the Isle Barataria.*

> *Where I expected, friend Sancho, to hear news of your negligence and*
> *folly, I have had accounts of your wise actions, for which I return*
> *especial thanks to Heaven, which can raise the poor from the dunghill*
> *and make wise men of fools. They tell me you govern like a man; yet as*
> *a man you are scarcely more than a brute creature, so humbly do you*
> *behave. But I would have you take note, Sancho, that it is often fitting*
> *and necessary for the authority of office to go counter to the heart's*
> *humility. For the due state of a person appointed to an important office*
> *must conform to the requirements of that office, and not to the modera-*
> *tion natural to his humble disposition. Dress well, for a stick well decor-*
> *ated seems more than a stick. I do not mean that you should wear finery*
> *or trinkets, or that, being a judge, you should clothe yourself as a soldier,*
> *but that you should wear the dress your office requires, so long as it is*
> *clean and neat.*

> *To gain the goodwill of the people you govern you must do two things*
> *amongst others; the first is to be civil to everyone – though I have told*
> *you this once already – and the other, to provide an abundance of the*
> *necessities of life, for there is nothing which distresses the hearts of the*
> *poor more than hunger and want.*

> *Do not make many statutes, but if you make them, try to make good*
> *ones and, particularly, see that they are kept and fulfilled; for if stat-*
> *utes are not kept they might as well not exist. Besides, they show that*
> *though the prince had the wisdom and authority to make them, he had*
> *not the courage to see that they were observed. And laws which threaten*

but are not carried out come to be like that log which was king of the frogs. He frightened them at first; but in time they despised him and climbed upon his back.

Be a father to virtues and a step-father to vices. Do not always be harsh or always mild; choose the mean between the two extremes, for here lies the point of wisdom.

Visit the prisons, the slaughterhouses and the markets, for the governor's presence in such places is of much importance. It comforts the prisoners, who expect a speedy release; it is a bugbear to the butchers, who for a time, have to use accurate weights; and it scares the market-women for the same reason.

Do not show yourself greedy — even if you are so perhaps, which I do not believe — or given to women or gluttony; for if the people and such as have dealings with you discover your dominant inclination they will open battery-fire on you in that quarter, until they bring you down to the depths of perdition. Consider and reconsider, view and review, the counsels and instructions I gave you in writing before you left here for your government, and you will see that you will find in them, if you observe them, an additional help to ease you over the troubles and difficulties which governors meet at every turn.

Write to your Lord and Lady and show them your gratitude; for ingratitude is the daughter of pride and one of the greatest sins known, and the person who is grateful to his benefactors gives assurance that he will be so to God also, who has done him, and continues to do him, so many benefits.

The Duchess has sent off a messenger with your suit and another present to your wife Teresa Panza. We expect an answer at any moment. I have been a little indisposed from a certain cat-clawing that befell me, somewhat at the expense of my nose. But it was nothing, for if there are enchanters who persecute me, there are also some who defend me.

Let me know whether the steward who is with you had anything to do with the business of the Trifaldi, as you suspected; and you should keep me advised of everything which happens to you, for the distance is short; more particularly as I intend soon to leave this idle life I am living at present, for I was not born for it.

There is a matter which has arisen, and which I believe will put me into disgrace with the Duke and Duchess. But though it concerns me much it does not affect my decision at all. For, when it comes to the point,

C C

I must comply with my profession rather than with their pleasure, according to the saying: amicus Plato, sed magis amica veritas. *I give you this in Latin, for I suppose that you have learnt it since you have become Governor.*

So farewell, and God keep you free from all harm.

Your friend,

Don Quixote de la Mancha.

Sancho listened most attentively to the letter, which was praised for its wisdom by all who heard it. He then rose from table and, calling the secretary, shut himself up in his room with him, intending to reply to his master Don Quixote at once and without more delay. So he instructed the secretary to write from his dictation without adding or omitting a word – which he did – and the answering letter was to this effect:

Sancho Panza's Letter to Don Quixote de la Mancha.

The pressure of my business is so great that I have not time to scratch my head, or even to cut my nails, and so I wear them very long, Heaven help me. This I say, beloved master, so that your worship may not be surprised that I have not given you an account till now of my good or ill fortune in this government, in which I suffer from worse hunger than when we two were roaming the woods and wilds.

The Duke my master wrote to me the other day, informing me that certain spies had come into this isle to kill me. But so far the only one of them I have discovered is a certain doctor in this town, who gets a salary for killing all the governors who come here. His name is Doctor Pedro Recio, and he is a native of Tirteafuera. And your worship can see from that name whether I have not reason to fear death at his hands! This same doctor boasts that he does not cure existing maladies, but prevents them from arising. And the remedies he uses are diet, diet, and still more diet, till he has reduced his patient to skin and bone, as if leanness were not a worse evil than fever. In short he is killing me of hunger, and I am dying of annoyance; and instead of coming here, as I expected, to get warm food and cool drink, and to lay my body between holland sheets and on feather pillows, I have come to do penance like a hermit; and as I am not doing it willingly I think that the Devil will get me in the end.

Up to now I have not touched a fee or taken a bribe, and I cannot imagine where this will end; for they have told me here that most of the governors who come to this isle take a great deal of money either in gifts or in loans from the people of the town before entering, and that this is the ordinary custom among newly created governors, and not only here.

Going the rounds the other night, I came across a most lovely young lady in men's clothes, and a brother of hers dressed as a woman. My butler fell in love with the girl, and has thoughts of making her his wife, so he says, and I have chosen the boy for my son-in-law. To-day the two of us are going to make our intentions known to the father of the pair, a certain Don Diego de la Llana, who is as perfect a gentleman and an old Christian as you could desire.

I visit the markets, as your worship advised me, and yesterday I found a market-woman pretending to sell fresh hazel-nuts, and discovered that she had mixed one bushel of fresh nuts with one of old, worthless, rotten ones. I impounded them all for the charity boys, who will know how to pick the good from the bad, and forbade her to enter the market for a fortnight. The people said that was a good sentence, for it is a common opinion in this town, your worship, that there is not a worse sort of people than your market-women. For they are a shameless, godless, brazen lot, as I can well believe from my experience of other places.

I am very glad that my lady the Duchess has written to my wife Teresa Panza and sent her the present your worship speaks of, and I will try to show myself grateful in due course. Kiss her hands on my behalf, your worship, and tell her I say that she has not thrown it into a torn sack, as the end will show. I should not like you to have any unpleasant disputes with my Lord and Lady, sir, for if you quarrel with them I shall certainly suffer for it; and it would not be right, seeing that you gave me the advice to be grateful, not to be grateful yourself for all the favours they have done you and the hospitality they have given you in their castle.

The cat-clawing business I do not understand; but I imagine it must be one of those tricks the wicked enchanters are always playing on your worship. I shall learn about it when we meet.

I should like to send your worship something; but I do not know what to send, unless it is some enema tubes to be used with bladders. They are very curious things, and made in this isle. But if my office lasts I will find something to send you, by hook or by crook.

If my wife Teresa Panza writes to me, please pay the carriage and send me the letter; for I am longing to hear how things are with my house, my wife and my children. And so may God deliver your worship from evilly disposed enchanters, and bring me safe and sound out of this government – which I doubt, for from the way Doctor Pedro Recio is treating me I do not expect to leave with more than my life.

> *Your worship's servant,*
> *Sancho Panza the Governor.*

The secretary sealed the letter and despatched the courier at once, and Sancho's tormentors assembled and planned together the means of making an end of his government. That evening Sancho spent drawing up some ordinances touching the good government of what he supposed to be his isle. He decreed that there must be no cornering of provisions in the state, and that wine could be imported from anywhere at all, on condition that its place of origin was declared, so that it could be priced according to its value, goodness and reputation; and anyone watering it or changing its name should pay for it with his life. He lowered the price of all footwear, especially of shoes, the current price seeming to him exorbitant. He fixed the rate of servants' wages, which were mounting unchecked at a headlong pace. He imposed the heaviest penalties on singers of lewd and disorderly songs, either by night or by day. He decreed that no blind man should sing miracles in rhyme unless he could bring unquestionable evidence that they were true, as most of their tales were, in his opinion, fictitious and brought discredit upon the genuine ones. He created and selected an inspector of the poor, not to persecute them but to examine whether they were genuine; for under the disguise of poverty and counterfeit sores go sturdy thieves and hale drunkards. So good, in fact, were the laws he ordained that they are kept in that place to this day under the name of '*The Constitutions of the great Governor Sancho Panza.*'

Chapter LII. In which is recorded the Adventure of the second dolorous or distressed Waiting-woman, otherwise called Doña Rodriguez.

CIDE HAMETE relates that once Don Quixote was healed of his scratches, the life he led in that castle seemed to him clean contrary to the rule of knighthood which he professed; and so he determined to beg the Duke and Duchess's leave to depart for Saragossa, as the festival was drawing near at which he hoped to win the armour usually jousted for. But as he was at table one day with his hosts, and on the point of carrying out his intention and asking their permission, suddenly there entered through the door of the great hall two women — as they afterwards proved — swathed in mourning from head to foot. One of them ran up to Don Quixote and threw herself flat on the ground with her lips pressed to his feet, uttering all the while the deepest, saddest and most melancholy groans. All the spectators were in a consternation and even the Duke and Duchess, though they suspected that this was some new trick which their servants had prepared for Don Quixote, were puzzled at the earnestness of the lady's demonstrations of grief until the compassionate Don Quixote prevailed upon her to rise from the ground and remove her cloak from her tearful visage. The face revealed, however, was the cause of even greater astonishment, for they beheld the waiting-woman Doña Rodriguez, and the other mourning figure proved to be her daughter who had been deceived by the rich farmer's son. All who knew her were astonished, and the Duke and Duchess most of all, for though they considered her rather a silly creature, they did not think her so far gone as to perform these crazy tricks.

After a while Doña Rodriguez turned to her master and mistress and said: 'May it please your Excellencies to give me leave to retire a little with this knight, for that I must do if I am to escape from a situation into which I have come through the impudence of an ill-conditioned villain.'

The Duke gave her leave to retire with Don Quixote for as long as she pleased; and she then turned her face to that knight, and said: 'Some days ago, valiant knight, I related to you the treacherous wrong a wicked farmer has done to my dear beloved daughter, who is the unfortunate lady here before you; and you promised me to take up her cause and right the injury she has suffered. But now it has come to my knowledge that you desire to leave this castle in search of good ventures — may God send you them! Therefore I wish you to challenge this stubborn rustic before you slip off into the highways, and force him to marry my daughter, in fulfilment of his promise of marriage made previously to his lying with her. For to expect justice from the Duke, my master, is to ask for pears off an elm tree, for the reason I have declared to your worship in private. So, may our Lord give you good health and not leave us unprotected.'

To this plea Don Quixote replied with great gravity and circumstance: 'Good lady, moderate your tears, or rather dry them, and be sparing of your sighs, for I take upon me the charge of seeing your daughter's wrong redressed; though it would have been better for her not to have been so easy in believing lovers' promises, for most of them are quick to promise but very slow to perform. So, by leave of my Lord the Duke, I will set out immediately to search for this profligate young man, and find him, challenge him and kill him, should he refuse to fulfil his pledged word. For the principal purpose of my order is to spare the humble and punish the proud; — I mean to succour the wretched and to destroy the cruel.'

'There is no need,' replied the Duke, 'for your worship to put yourself to the trouble of searching for the rustic of whom this good lady complains, nor have you any need either to ask my permission to challenge him. I grant him duly challenged and take it upon myself to inform him of this defiance and make him accept it, and come to answer for himself at this castle of mine, where I will give you both a fair field, observing all the conditions proper to such affairs, and securing impartial justice to you; for all princes are obliged to grant a free field to those who do battle within the bounds of their dominions.'

'Then with that assurance and your Highness's good leave,' replied Don Quixote, 'I hereby declare that for this occasion I waive my gentry, lower myself to the meanness of the offender, and reduce myself to his level, thus granting him the right of combat with me; and so I defy and challenge him, though absent, by reason of the wrong he did in defrauding this poor girl, who was a maid and now by his fault is one no longer; and he shall fulfil the promise he gave her to be her lawful husband, or he shall die in the ordeal.'

Then, stripping off a glove, he threw it into the middle of the hall, and the Duke picked it up, repeating that he accepted the challenge in his vassal's name, and fixing the date at six days hence, and the place in the castle courtyard, and the arms those customary among knights — lance and shield and complete armour with all the other pieces, without deceit, trickery, or any supernatural charm, inspected and examined by the judges of the lists. 'But first of all,' said the Duke, 'this good lady and this bad maiden must place the right of their cause in the hands of Don Quixote; for in no other manner can anything be done or this same challenge be brought to due execution.'

'Yes, I do place it there,' answered the waiting-woman.

'And I too,' added the daughter, all tearful, ashamed and confused.

These provisions being settled, and the Duke having made the necessary arrangements, the ladies in mourning departed, and the Duchess commanded that henceforth they should not be treated as her servants, but as ladies errant, who had come to her house to sue for justice. So they were given private quarters and waited on like strangers, much to the astonishment of the other servants, who could not imagine where the folly and presumption of Doña Rodriguez and her unfortunate daughter would stop.

At this point, to crown the feast and bring the meal to a fine conclusion, there suddenly entered the hall the page who had taken the letters and presents to Teresa Panza, the wife of Governor Sancho Panza, which arrival delighted the Duke and Duchess, who were longing for news of his journey. The page replied to their questions by saying that he could not answer publicly or briefly, but he begged their Excellencies to wait until they were alone. In the meantime they might amuse themselves with certain letters, two of which he brought out and put in the Duchess's hands. One was headed '*Letter for my lady the Duchess of I do not know where*,' and the other '*To my husband Sancho Panza, Governor of the isle Barataria, whom may God prosper more years than me.*'

The Duchess's cake would not bake, as the saying is, until she had read her letter. She opened it, glanced through it and, finding that she could read it aloud to the Duke and the bystanders, did so, to this effect:

Teresa Panza's Letter to the Duchess.

I was delighted, your Highness, with the letter you wrote me, for truly my dear lady, I had greatly longed for it. The string of corals is very fine, and my husband's hunting-suit is every bit as good. All this village is glad that your ladyship has made my consort Sancho a

governor, *though everyone disbelieves it, particularly the priest, Master
Nicholas the barber, and Sampson Carrasco the Bachelor; but that
does not worry me. So long as it is true – which it is – they can say
what they like; though, to tell you the truth, I should not have believed
it myself but for the coming of the corals and the suit; for they all take
my husband for a dolt in this village, and cannot imagine he can be
fit to govern any thing except a herd of goats. Heaven be his guide, and
put him in the way he should go to suit his children's needs.*

*My dearest lady, I am determined, by your leave, to make hay whilst
the sun shines, and go to Court and lean back in my coach, to spite the
thousands that envy me already. So please, your Excellency, bid my
husband send me a bit of money, and let it be quite a bit, for expenses
are enormous in the capital. It is amazing, but bread costs a real there
and meat thirty* maravedis *a pound. But if he wishes me not to come,
let him advise me in time, for my feet are itching to get on the road. My
friends and neighbours tell me that if my daughter and I cut a grand and
stately figure at Court, my husband will get more honour by me than I
by him, since many people are sure to ask: 'Who are the ladies in that
coach?', and one of my servants will answer: 'The wife and daughter of
Sancho Panza, Governor of the Isle Barataria'; and in this way Sancho
will get known and I shall be highly thought of – and you can get anything in Rome! I am as sorry as can be that they have not harvested
acorns in our village this year. However, I am sending your Highness
about half a peck, which I went to the woods myself to gather and
pick over, one by one. I could find none bigger, though I wish they were
the size of ostrich eggs.*

*Do not forget to write to me, your Pomposity, and I will be sure to
answer and inform you of my health and of all there may be to tell you
about this place, where I remain, praying our Lord to preserve your
Highness and not to forget me. My daughter Sancha and my son kiss
your Grace's hands.*

*Your servant, whose desire is to see your ladyship rather than to
write,*

                                                      Teresa Panza.

Everybody was highly delighted at Teresa Panza's letter, most
of all the Duke and the Duchess, who asked Don Quixote's opinion
whether it would be right to open the letter addressed to the

Governor, which she imagined must be excellent. Don Quixote said that, to please them, he would open it, which he did, and it ran in this fashion:

Teresa Panza's Letter to Sancho Panza her husband.

I received your letter, my beloved Sancho, and I swear to you as a Catholic Christian I was within an inch of going off my head with delight. Yes, indeed, when I learnt that you are a Governor I thought I should fall dead on the spot from pleasure; for they say that sudden gladness kills like a great grief, you know. And your daughter Sanchica wetted herself without noticing it, out of pure joy. I had the suit you sent me before me, and the corals my lady the Duchess sent me round my neck, and the letters in my hands, and the bearer of them standing there; but for all that it really seemed all to be a dream. For who could have thought that a goatherd would come to be a Governor of Isles? You remember, my dear, how my mother used to say that to see much you must live long? I think she was right, for I expect to see more if I live longer, and I do not mean to stop till I see you a rent-farmer or a tax-gatherer, for in those trades you certainly do have and handle money, though the Devil carries off those that abuse them. My lady the Duchess will tell you how I long to go to Court. Consider the matter and let me know your pleasure; for I will try and do you honour there by going about in a coach.

Neither the priest, the barber, the Bachelor, nor even the sexton, can believe that you are a Governor. They say that it is all humbug or a matter of enchantment, like all your master Don Quixote's affairs; and Sampson says that he is going to look for you, and knock the governorship out of your head and the madness out of Don Quixote's skull. But I do nothing but laugh and look at my necklace, and plan how to make up that suit of yours for our daughter. I sent some acorns to my lady the Duchess. I wish they had been gold. Send me some strings of pearls, if they are in fashion in your isle.

The news in this village is that Berrueca has married her daughter to a wretched sort of painter, who came here to do any sort of painting jobs. The council commissioned him to put His Majesty's arms over the doors of the Council House. He asked for two ducats, which they gave him in advance. He worked for eight days, and at the end of that time he had done nothing and said that he could not manage to paint such trumpery. He returned the money, but all the same he posed as a good workman and got married. The truth is he has given up the pencil and taken to the spade, and now he goes to the fields like a gentleman. Pedro de Lobo's son has taken orders and shaved his head, meaning to be a priest. When Minguilla, Mingo Silvato's grand-daughter, heard of it she sued him for breach of promise. Malicious tongues are pleased to say that she is with child by him, but he denies it stoutly.

This year there are no olives, and there is not a drop of vinegar to be found in the whole village. A company of soldiers passed through here, and took three local girls away with them. I will not tell you their names, for they may come back; and they will be sure to find men to marry them, with all their blemishes, good and bad.

Sanchica is making bone-lace; she earns eight clear maravedis a day, which she is putting by in a money-box to help towards her wedding portion. But now that she is a governor's daughter you will give her a dowry without her working for it. The fountain in the market-place has dried up. A thunderbolt fell on the pillory – may they all fall there!

I await an answer to this and a decision about my going to Court; and with this, may God preserve you more years than me – or as many, for I should not like to leave you in this world without me.

> *Your wife,*
>
> *Teresa Panza.*

These letters called forth applause, laughter, approval and wonder; and, to crown everything, the courier arrived bearing Sancho's letter to Don Quixote, which was also read in public and aroused some doubts as to the Governor's foolishness. The Duchess retired to hear from the page what had happened to him in Sancho's village; and he told her in great detail without omitting any relevant circumstance. He gave her the acorns and also a cheese which Teresa had given him, a very good one, and better than those of Tronchon. The Duchess accepted it with the greatest pleasure; and there we will leave her, to tell of the end of the government of the great Sancho Panza, flower and mirror of all Governors of Isles.

Chapter LIII. *Of the troubled conclusion of Sancho Panza's Government.*

'IT is idle to think that things in this life will last for ever in one state. On the contrary, everything seems to go in cycles, or rather round-about. Summer follows on spring, autumn on summer, winter on autumn, and spring on winter, and so time revolves in this con-tinuous wheel. Only human life speeds to its end faster than the wind, without hope of renewal, except in that other life which has no bounds to limit it.' So says Cide Hamete, the Mohammedan philosopher; for many, by the light of nature and without the illu-mination of the faith, have come to understand the brevity and in-stability of our present existence and the everlastingness of the eternal life to come. In this place, however, our author alludes only to the swiftness with which Sancho's government ended, was con-sumed and undone, and vanished into shadow and smoke.

On the seventh night of his governorship he was lying in bed, sated not with bread or wine but with judging, giving opinions, and making laws and decrees, when just as, despite his hunger, sleep was beginning to close his eyes he heard a great noise of bells and shout-ing, which sounded as if the whole isle were foundering. He sat up in bed and listened, trying to make out the cause of this mighty up-roar; but far from his discovering it, his confusion and terror were only augmented by the sound of countless trumpets and drums, which came on top of the din of voices and bells. So, getting up, he put on his slippers, because of the dampness of the floor, and with-out a dressing-gown or anything of that sort went to the door of his room, just in time to see more than twenty persons with lighted torches in their hands and swords unsheathed, some crying at the tops of their voices: 'Arm! Arm! Lord Governor. Arm! for count-less enemies have invaded this isle, and we are lost if your skill and valour do not succour us!'

Raising this tremendous noise they rushed tumultuously to the place where Sancho was standing, stupefied, and fascinated at what he heard and saw. And when they reached him one of them cried: 'Arm yourself at once, your Lordship, if you do not want to be lost and all the isle with you.'

'What have I to do with arming?' replied Sancho. 'What do I

know of arms or succour? It would be better to leave these matters to my master Don Quixote. He will despatch them and put them right in a flash. For, sinner that I am before God, I don't understand anything about these hurly-burlys.'

'Oh, Lord Governor,' cried another, 'what weakness is this? Arm yourself, sir! For here we bring you arms of offence and defence. Come out to the market square, and be our leader and captain; for that is your duty as our Governor.'

'All right, let me be armed,' answered Sancho.

Instantly they brought him two large and ancient shields with which they had come provided, and clamped them over his shirt, without leaving him time to put on any other clothing, one shield in front and the other behind. They pushed his arms through some holes they had made in them, and bound him very tightly with cords, so that he found himself walled in and boarded up, upright as a spindle and unable to bend his knees or stir a step. Then they put a spear into his hand, and he had to lean on it to keep on his feet. When they had got him trussed up they told him to march and lead them, and put courage into them all; for with him as their pole-star, their lantern and light, all would be well.

'How can I march, poor wretch that I am?' answered Sancho. 'I can't bring my knee-joints into play, for these boards which are clamped to my flesh get in my way. What you must do is to take me up in your arms and lay me, crosswise or standing, at some postern, and I will guard it either with this spear or with my body.'

'Go on, Lord Governor,' cried another. 'It's fear, not the boards, that prevents your walking. Hasten and stir yourself, for it's late. Our enemies are increasing, their cries grow louder, and danger presses.'

Thus urged and abused, the poor Governor attempted to move, but came down on the ground with such a bump that he thought he must be broken to bits. He lay like a tortoise enveloped in its shell, or like a side of bacon clapped between two boards for salting, or like a boat upside-down on the beach. But though they saw him fall, those playful rogues had no compassion on him. Instead, they put out their torches, and began to repeat their urgent call to arms, trampling over poor Sancho, and dealing him repeated bangs on his shield. Indeed, if he had not made himself small and shrunk his head in between them things would have gone very badly with the poor governor, who being thus contracted in that narrow space, sweated copiously, and petitioned God with all his heart to deliver him from his danger. Some stumbled and others fell over him; and there was one who stood on top of him for a good while, and from there, as from a watch-tower, directed the armies, shouting loudly: 'Here, you on our side, here! The enemy is pressing harder over here! Guard that postern! Keep that gate shut! Down with those scaling ladders! Bring up the grenades, the pitch and resin, and the kettles of boiling oil! Barricade the streets with mattresses!'

In fact in a fine frenzy he named every appurtenance, implement and weapon of war used for the defence of a city; and the battered Sancho, who heard and suffered it all, said to himself: 'Oh, if only the Lord would be pleased to make an end of my losing this isle, and I might find myself dead, or out of this great affliction!' Heaven heard his petition, and when least he expected it he heard voices crying: 'Victory! Victory! The enemy are beginning to fly! Here, Lord Governor, arise, enjoy your conquest, and divide the spoils taken from the enemy by the valour of your invincible arm!'

'Lift me up,' moaned the sorrowful Sancho in a woe-begone voice. So they helped him up and, once on his feet, he said: 'I would have you nail to my forehead the enemy I conquered. I will divide no spoils of enemies, but I beg some friend, if I have one, to give me a drink of wine, for I am dry, and to wipe off my sweat, for I'm turning to water.'

They wiped him down, brought him his wine, and untied the shields; and when seated on his bed he fainted away, such had been his fatigue, agony and terror.

The jokers were now sorry they had carried things so far, but were consoled on seeing him recover. He asked them the time, and they replied that it was now daybreak. He said no more, but began to put on his clothes, in deep silence, without another word, while everyone gazed at him, waiting to see what this sudden dressing portended. At length, having slowly put on his clothes, for he was bruised and could not move very fast, he went towards the stable, followed by everyone present. And when he came to Dapple he embraced him, giving him the kiss of peace on his forehead, and said to him with moist eyes: 'Come here, dear companion and friend of mine, my fellow-partner in my trials and sorrows. When I went along with you and had no other thought but the mending of your harness and the feeding of your little carcase, happy were my hours, my days and my years! But since I left you and climbed the tower of ambition and pride a thousand miseries have pierced my soul, a thousand troubles and four thousand tribulations.'

And all the while he was speaking he went on saddling his ass, and no one said a word. When Dapple was ready, he mounted him with great pain and difficulty and, addressing himself to the steward, the secretary and the butler, and to Pedro Recio the doctor, and the many others present, said: 'Make way, gentlemen, and let me return to my old freedom. Let me go and seek the life I left, and rise again from this present death. I was not born to be a governor, nor to defend isles or cities from the enemies who choose to attack them. I understand more about ploughing and digging and the pruning and gathering of vine-shoots than of law-giving or defending provinces or kingdoms. St. Peter is well at Rome: I mean that everyone is best practising the trade for which he was born. A reaper's hook comes better to my hand than a governor's sceptre. I prefer stuffing myself with salad to being at the mercy of a meddling doctor who kills me by hunger; and I had rather lie down under the shade of an oak-tree in summer and wrap myself in a shepherd's cloak of two skins in winter, with my liberty, than lie between holland sheets and dress in sable skins under the burden of a governorship. God be with your worships. Tell the Duke my master that naked I was born and naked I am now; I neither lose nor gain. I mean that I came into this government without a farthing, and I leave it without one, contrary to the way of the governors of other isles. Make way for me and let me go and plaster myself, for I believe that all my ribs are broken, thanks to the enemies who have been trampling me this night.'

'You must not do that, Lord Governor,' said Doctor Recio, 'for I will give your worship a potion that is good against falls and bruises, and which will immediately restore you to your former health and vigour. As for your dinners, I promise to reform my ways, and let you eat abundantly of everything you like.'

'Too late,' answered Sancho. 'I would as soon turn Turk as stay. These tricks aren't to be played twice. I swear I'd as soon fly to

Heaven without wings as remain in this government or accept another, even if it were presented to me between two dishes. I am a Panza, and we are all stubborn. If once we cry odds, odds it must be, even though it's evens, and in spite of all the world. Here in this stable I will leave the ant wings that carried me up into the air for the martins and other birds to peck at. Let us come back to earth and steady walking, for if I'm not to look smart in slashed Cordova shoes I shan't be short of rough hemp sandals. Every ewe to her mate, and let no one stretch his leg more than the length of his sheet. Let me go now, for it's getting late.'

To which the steward replied: 'Lord Governor, we will most willingly let your worship go, though we shall be very sorry to lose you, for your wit and Christian behaviour make us love your presence. But it is common knowledge that every governor is obliged to go into residence before absenting himself from the place where he has governed. Do so, your worship, for the ten days you have held the government. Then go, and God's peace be with you.'

'No one can ask an account of me,' answered Sancho, 'except someone appointed by the Duke, my lord. I am going to see him and I shall give him an exact report. Besides, coming out naked as I do, there is no need of any other evidence to prove that I governed like an angel.'

'By God, the great Sancho is right,' cried Doctor Recio, 'and it is my opinion we should let him go, for the Duke will be infinitely glad to see him.'

To this they all agreed, and they allowed him to depart, first offering him their company and anything he might desire for the comfort of his person and the convenience of his journey. Sancho answered that he wanted no more than a little barley for Dapple, and half a cheese and half a loaf for himself; for the journey was short, and he had no need of more or better provisions. They all embraced him, and he embraced them all with tears in his eyes, and left them wondering, both at his words and at his very determined and sensible resolution.

Chapter LIV. *Concerning matters relating to this History and to no other.*

THE Duke and the Duchess were resolved that Don Quixote's challenge to their vassal in the above-mentioned cause should go forward, and as the youth was in Flanders, where he had fled in order to avoid having Doña Rodriguez for his mother-in-law, they arranged to substitute for him a Gascon lackey called Tosilos, first priming him thoroughly in his part. So two days later the Duke told Don Quixote that his opponent would arrive in four days' time, to present himself in the field, armed as a knight, and maintain that the maiden lied by half a beard – or even by a whole beard – if she affirmed that he had given her a promise of marriage. Don Quixote received this news with great satisfaction and flattered himself that he would perform wonders in this business, counting himself most fortunate to have an opportunity of displaying the power of his mighty arm before the Duke and Duchess; and so he waited most contentedly for the four days which, measured by his impatience, seemed like four hundred centuries.

Now letting them pass, as we let other things, let us go and accompany Sancho, who was riding on Dapple between mirth and mourning, in search of his master whose company gave him more pleasure than the governorship of all the isles in the world. Now it happened before he had gone far from the isle of his governorship – he had never set out to discover whether it was an isle, a city, town, or village he was governor of – that he saw coming along the road he was travelling on six pilgrims with staves, foreigners of the sort that sing for alms. Now when they came up to him they spread out in a row and, raising their voices all together, began their song in a language which Sancho could not understand, except for one word which clearly stood for alms; whence he concluded that it was alms they were asking for in their song. And being extremely charitable, as Cide Hamete tells us, he took the half loaf and the half cheese with which he was provided out of his saddlebag and offered it to them, telling them in dumb show that he had nothing else to give. They received his gift most gratefully, but cried: '*Geld! Geld!*'

'I don't understand what you want of me, good people,' answered Sancho.

Then one of them took a purse from under his shirt and held it up, giving Sancho to understand that it was money they were begging for. So, putting his thumb to his throat and extending his hand upwards, he signed to them that he had not a halfpenny; and spurring Dapple, he broke through their ranks. But as he passed, one of them, who had been staring fixedly at him, rushed up and, flinging his arms round his waist, addressed him loudly in Castilian: 'Good Lord! What's this I see? Can it possibly be my good friend here in my arms, my dear neighbour Sancho Panza? Yes, there can be no doubt of it, for I'm not dreaming, and I'm not drunk – as yet.'

Sancho was astonished to hear himself called by his name and to find a foreign pilgrim embracing him, and hard though he stared at him without saying a word he was unable to recognize him. Seeing his puzzlement, however, the pilgrim exclaimed: 'What! Is it possible, brother Sancho Panza, that you don't recognize your neighbour, Ricote the Moor, your village shopkeeper?'

At this Sancho stared at him more intently still, and beginning to recall his features, in the end recognized him perfectly. Then, without dismounting from his ass, he threw his arms round his neck and cried: 'Who the devil could have recognized you, Ricote, in that clown's dress you're wearing? Tell me, who has frenchified you, and how have you dared return to Spain. You'll get very short shrift if they catch you and recognize you.'

'If you don't give me away, Sancho,' answered the pilgrim, 'I'm sure that no one will know me in this dress. But let's go off the road to that poplar grove over there, where my companions intend to dine and rest. You shall eat there with them, for they're very pleasant folk, and I will have a chance of telling you what's happened to me since I left our village in obedience to His Majesty's proclamation, which threatened the unfortunate people of my nation with so much rigour, as you have heard.'

Sancho complied, and after Ricote had spoken to the rest of the pilgrims they went off to the poplar grove, which showed up some distance from the highway. Here they threw down their staves and took off their capes or pilgrim's cloaks, remaining in their jackets. They were all handsome young fellows except for Ricote, who was well on in years. Each carried a haversack, apparently well stored, at least with those spicy foods that call up the thirst from a mile off.

They lay on the ground and, using the grass for tablecloth, spread out on it bread, salt, knives, onions, walnuts, hunks of cheese and clean hambones, which had nothing on them to gnaw yet were not past sucking. They also produced a black dish, which goes by the name of caviare and is made of fishes' roe – a great rouser of thirst. There was no shortage of olives either, though they were dry and without any pickle, yet tasty and pleasant enough. But the chief glory of that banquet-field was six bottles of wine, each of the men fetching his own out of his haversack. Even the worthy Ricote, who had transformed himself from a Moor into a German or a Dutchman, produced his, which could compare with the other five in size. Then they began to eat with great appetite, most leisurely savouring every mouthful, which they took from the point of the knife – a very little of each thing – and then, all together at one moment, they raised their arms and bottles in the air, and put their own mouths to the bottles' mouths, their eyes as firmly fixed on the sky as if they were taking aim at it. And in this way they continued for some time, shaking their heads from side to side to show their pleasure at emptying the bowels of those vessels into their stomachs. Sancho looked on at all this 'and was in no wise grieved'. On the contrary, remembering the familiar proverb – When at Rome, do as the Romans do – he asked Ricote for his bottle and took his aim with the rest, with no less pleasure than they.

Four times the bottles suffered themselves to be tipped, but the fifth time it was impossible, for they were as sapless and dry as a rush, which rather dampened the spirits of the party. From time to time one of them would thrust his right hand into Sancho's and say: '*Spaniard and Dutchman, all one – goot gombanion,*' and Sancho would reply, '*Goot Gompanion, I swear by Gott,*' and burst into a laugh which lasted an hour, forgetting for the time being all that had befallen him in his governorship; for cares have generally but little sway over the time when men are eating and drinking. At length the wine was finished, and such a drowsiness began to seize them all that they fell asleep on the very table-cloth. Only Ricote and our squire stayed awake, for they had eaten more and drunk less. The Moor drew Sancho aside, and they sat down at the foot of a beech, leaving the pilgrims buried in sweet sleep, and without once stumbling into his Moorish jargon, Ricote spoke as follows in pure

Castilian: 'Well, you know, Sancho Panza, my neighbour and friend, what a terror and dismay the proclamation and edict which His Majesty commanded to be published against those of my nation struck into us all. At least it had that effect upon me, so much so that I almost imagined its dreadful penalty already inflicted upon my own family, even before the time allowed us to leave Spain had expired. So I arranged – sensibly I think – as a man does who knows that on a certain date he will lose his home and so provides himself with another to move to – I arranged, I say, to leave my village, alone and without my family, and to go and look for a place to take them to in comfort and without that haste which generally prevailed. For I saw very well, as all our elders saw, that those proclamations were not just threats, as some said, but would certainly be put into effect at the time appointed. I could not help believing this, knowing as I did our people's desperate and foolish intentions; which made me think it was divine inspiration that had moved His Majesty to adopt such wise measures. Not that we were all guilty, for some of us were steadfast and true Christians. But we were so few that we could not make head against those who were not; and it is no good thing to nourish a snake in your bosom and have enemies within your own house. In fact it was with good reason that all of us were punished with exile; a mild and merciful penalty in the opinion of some, though to us it was the most terrible that could be inflicted. Wherever we are we weep for Spain; for, after all, we were born here and this is our native country. Nowhere do we find the reception our misery requires. In Barbary and in all those parts of Africa where we hoped to be received, entertained and welcomed we are worst treated and abused. We did not know our good fortune till we had lost it, and so ardently do almost all of us long to return to Spain that most of those – and there are plenty – who know the language, as I do, return and leave their wives and children over there unprotected; such is our love for Spain. For now I know by experience the truth of the saying, that the love of one's country is sweet.

'I left our village, as I told you, and went to France, but though they made us very welcome there I wanted to see other lands. I crossed into Italy and reached Germany, where it seemed to me I could live in greater freedom, for its inhabitants do not look into fine points: everyone lives as he pleases, and over the greater part of the country there is liberty of conscience. I took a house in a town near Augsburg, but left it to join with these pilgrims, whose custom it is to come to Spain in some numbers each year to visit its holy places, which they regard as their Indies, where they will get a sure harvest and certain profit. They wander over almost the whole country, and there is no village they do not leave with meat and drink, as you would say, and a *real*, at least, in money. And at the end of their journey they come off with more than a hundred crowns over, which they get out of this country into their own in gold coin, hidden either in the hollows of their staves, or in the patches of their cloaks, or by any device they can contrive, despite the guards at the posts or ports where they are searched. Now it is my intention, Sancho, to dig up the treasure which I left buried, for as it is outside the village I can do so without risk; and then to write, or go myself, from Valencia to my wife and daughter, who I know are in Algiers, and contrive a means of bringing them to some port in France, and of getting them from there to Germany, where we shall await whatever God may please to do with us. For, truly, Sancho, I am certain that Ricota, my daughter, and Francisca Ricota, my wife, are Catholic Christians; and though I am not much of one myself, still there is more Christian than Moor in me, and I always pray to God to open the eyes of my understanding and make me know how to serve Him. But what astonishes me, and what I do not understand, is why my wife and daughter went to Barbary rather than to France, where they could live like Christians.'

To which Sancho replied: 'Look you, Ricote, perhaps it wasn't their choice, for Juan Tiopieyo, your wife's brother, took them away; and as he must be a rank Moor, he would go to the safest place for him. And one more thing I can tell you: I think you've come for nothing, if you're seeking your buried hoard, for we had news that they took a large number of pearls and a great deal of gold coin from your brother-in-law and your wife, who had it on them when they were searched.'

'That may well be,' replied Ricote; 'but I know that they did not touch my hoard, Sancho, for I did not tell them where it was, being afraid of some calamity. So, if you'll come with me, and help me get it up and conceal it, I'll give you two hundred crowns, which will relieve your wants; for, as you know, I'm well aware you have plenty.'

'I would do it,' answered Sancho, 'but I'm not at all greedy. If I had been, I laid down a post this morning where I might have lined the walls of my house with gold, and eaten off silver plate before six months were out. So for that reason, and because to my mind it would be treason against my king to favour his enemies, I would not go with you even if you were to give me four hundred crowns down in cash, instead of a promise of two hundred.'

'And what post is it that you left, Sancho?' asked Ricote.

'I gave up the governorship of an isle,' replied Sancho, 'and such an isle that you won't easily find one like it, I swear.'

'And where is this isle?' asked Ricote.

'Where?' replied Sancho. 'Six miles from here, and it's called the Isle Barataria.'

'Nonsense, Sancho!' said Ricote. 'Isles are out at sea. There are no isles on the mainland.'

'How not?' replied Sancho. 'I tell you, Ricote my friend, that I left it this morning, and yesterday I was governing there at my ease like a sagittary; but I gave it up all the same, for a governor's seems to me a dangerous post.'

'And what did you gain from your government?' asked Ricote.

'I gained,' replied Sancho, 'the knowledge that I'm no good at governing anything but a herd of cattle, and that the wealth that's won from such governments is earned at the price of your rest and sleep, and even of your food. For in isles governors may eat very little, especially if they have doctors to look to their health.'

'I don't understand you, Sancho,' said Ricote. 'All you say seems nonsense to me. For who would give you isles to govern? Was the world short of men more capable of being governors than you? Stop talking, man, and come to your senses. Think whether you won't come with me, as I asked you, and help me get up the treasure I left hidden — for really there's so much of it that I can call it a treasure — and I will give you something to live on, as I said.'

'I've already told you, Ricote,' answered Sancho, 'that I won't. Be satisfied that I shan't betray you. Go your way, in God's name, and leave me to go mine. For I know that well-gotten gains may be lost, and ill-gotten gains may bring down the gainer too.'

'I don't want to press you,' said Ricote. 'But tell me, were you in our village when my wife and daughter and brother-in-law left?'

'Yes, I was,' answered Sancho, 'and I can tell you that your daughter looked so beautiful when she went that everyone in the place came out to see her, and they all said she was the loveliest creature in the world. She departed weeping, and embraced all her friends and acquaintances and all who came to see her, begging everyone to commend her to Our Lord and Our Lady His Mother; and all this with such feeling that it brought tears to my eyes, and I'm not generally much of a weeper. There were many in fact who wanted to go out and capture her on the road and hide her away, but fear of breaking the King's decree prevented them. The person who seemed most affected of all was Don Pedro Gregorio – the rich young heir, you know. They say he loved her dearly. He has never appeared in our village again since she went off, and we all think that he followed after her to steal her away, though we've heard nothing more of it till now.'

'I always had a shrewd suspicion,' said Ricote, 'that that gentleman loved my daughter; but I trusted in my Ricota's virtue, and it never worried me to know he wanted her. For you must have heard, Sancho, that Moorish women seldom or never have affairs with Old Christians, and my daughter, who, in my belief, cared more for her religion than for love, would not pay any attention to the young heir's attentions.'

'God grant you're right,' replied Sancho, 'for it would be bad for both of them. Now let me go off, Ricote my friend, for I want to come to-night to the place where Don Quixote my master is.'

'God be with you, brother Sancho, for now my companions are stirring, and it's time to be on our way.'

Then these two embraced. Sancho mounted Dapple, Ricote seized his staff, and they parted.

Chapter LV. Of what happened to Sancho on the road and other matters, the best in the world.

SANCHO's long stay with Ricote prevented his arriving at the Duke's castle that day, though he had got within a mile and a half of it when night overtook him. It was rather dark and cloudy, but as it was summer that did not trouble him much, and he left the road with the intention of waiting till morning. But as his ill luck would have it, just as he was looking for a place where he could settle most comfortably, he and Dapple fell into a deep and very dark pit, which lay amongst some very old buildings. As he fell he commended himself to God with all his heart, thinking that he would not stop short of the bottom of the abyss. But it was not so, for a little more than eighteen feet down Dapple touched ground, and Sancho found himself still on his back, quite unwounded and undamaged. He felt himself all over his body and drew in his breath to see if he was sound or had a hole in any part of him; but finding himself well and whole and sound in health, he could not give the Lord God sufficient thanks for His mercy He had done him; for he had thought that he was most certainly broken into a thousand pieces. He also groped with his hands over the walls of the pit to see if it was possible for him to get out without anyone's aid, but he found them all smooth and offering no hold, which grieved him deeply, especially when he heard Dapple piteously and dolefully lamenting. And it was no wonder, nor was he complaining for nothing, for he was truly in a sad way.

'Oh,' cried Sancho Panza then, 'what unexpected accidents do happen at every turn to those that live in this miserable world! Who would have said that the man who saw himself yesterday enthroned as the Governor of an isle, commanding his servants and his vassals, would find himself to-day buried in a pit without a soul to relieve him, or a servant or vassal to come to his aid? Here we shall perish of hunger, my ass and I, if we don't die before that, he from his bruises and broken bones, and I from grief. At least I shan't be as lucky as my master Don Quixote de la Mancha when he went down into the cave of that enchanted Montesinos, where he found some-one to entertain him better than if he'd been at home: for it seems he found the cloth laid and his bed made. There he saw beautiful and delightful visions, but here I truly believe I shall see toads and snakes. What a poor wretch I am! Look where my follies and fantasies have brought me! They'll dig my bones out of here, clean and white and scraped, when it's Heaven's will that they find me, and my good Dapple's with them – and from them perhaps they'll discover who we are, those at least who have been told that Sancho

Panza never parted from his ass, nor his ass from Sancho Panza. Once more I say, what wretches we are that our ill-luck hasn't allowed us to die in our own country and among our own people. There, if there was no relief to be found for our calamity, at least there would be no lack of someone to bewail it, and to close our eyes in the last hour of our sojourn on earth. O my companion and friend, what ill payment I have given you for your good services! Pardon me, and beg Fortune in the best way you know to get us out of this miserable plight into which we two are cast, and I promise I'll put a laurel crown on your head, like any poet laureate's, and give you double feeds.'

In this fashion Sancho Panza lamented, and his ass listened to him without answering a word, such was the distress and anguish the poor creature was in. At last, when he had spent all that night in piteous complaints and lamentations, the day came, and by its clarity and splendour Sancho saw that it would be the greatest of all impossibilities to get out of that pit without assistance. So he began to wail and shout, to see if anyone could hear; but all his cries were wasted on the wilderness, for in all the country round there was no one within hearing; and so he ended by giving himself up for dead. Dapple was lying on his back, but Sancho did manage to get him upon his feet, though he could hardly stand. Then taking a piece of bread out of the saddle-bags, which had shared their unfortunate fall, he gave it to his ass, who did not dislike it. And his master said to him, as if he could understand: 'Bread is relief for all grief.'

And now Sancho discovered a hole in one side of the pit, capable of containing one person if he stooped and shrank. This he made for, and squeezing himself into it found that it was large and spacious inside, as he could see by a shaft of sunlight which entered through what might be called the roof and lit up everything. He saw also that it opened and widened into another huge vault, and when he had discovered this he went out again to his ass, and began to break away the earth from the hole with a stone, so that in a little while he had made a passage through which the beast could easily enter, which he did. Then, taking him by the halter, he began to travel onwards through that cavern in search of a way out on the other side. Sometimes he went in the dark and sometimes without much light, but never without fear.

'Help me, almighty God!' he muttered. 'This, though a mis-adventure for me, would be an adventure to my master Don Quixote. For he would certainly take these depths and dungeons for flowery gardens and palaces of Galiana, and would expect to emerge from this dark and narrow place into flowering meadows. But poor me, ill-advised and fainthearted, at every step I expect another pit deeper than this one to open and swallow me up. O welcome the evils that come singly!'

Thus he went on, and when he had gone, as he supposed, a little more than a mile and a half, he made out a dim light, which looked like the light of day, entering from somewhere; and this seemed to him a sign of an opening into some road, which he expected to lead into the other world.

Here Cide Hamete Benengeli leaves him, and returns to Don Quixote, who was looking forward with joy and contentment to the time of the battle which he was to fight with the ravisher of the honour of Doña Rodriguez' daughter, for whom he intended to right the wrong and injury so foully done her. Now he happened to be riding out one morning to exercise and practise for the combat in which he expected to be engaged next day; and as he put Rocinante into a charge or short gallop, the horse chanced to plant his feet so near to a hole that if Don Quixote had not tugged hard at the reins he must inevitably have fallen in. He pulled him up, however, and did not fall. Then, approaching rather nearer but not dismounting, he looked into the depths, and as he peered down he heard loud shouts within; and when he listened attentively he was able to distinguish and understand the shouter's words: 'You up there! Is there any Christian can hear me, or any charitable gentleman to take mercy on a sinner buried alive, on an unhappy Governor without a government?'

It seemed to Don Quixote as if he heard Sancho Panza's voice; and this puzzled and amazed him. But raising his own as high as he could, he called: 'Who is that down there? Who is it crying out?'

'Who else could it be crying out,' came the answer, 'but the forlorn Sancho Panza, Governor, for his sins and misfortune, of the Isle Barataria, once squire to that famous knight, Don Quixote de la Mancha?'

When Don Quixote heard this his amazement was redoubled and

his alarm increased, for it occurred to his mind that Sancho Panza must be dead and his soul be there in purgatory. So, prompted by this thought, he cried: 'I conjure you by all that is holy to tell me as a Catholic Christian who you are. And if you are a soul in purgatory tell me what you wish me to do for you. For since it is my profession to favour and aid those in this world who are in need, it shall also be so to aid and relieve the distressed in the other world who cannot help themselves.'

'That sounds as if it's my master Don Quixote de la Mancha speaking,' came the reply, 'for to judge by the voice it can certainly be no one else.'

'Don Quixote I am,' replied Don Quixote, 'whose profession it is to aid and succour in their needs the living and the dead. Therefore tell me who you are, for you hold me rapt with amazement. If you are my squire Sancho Panza and are dead, since the devils have not got you and, by God's mercy, you lie in purgatory, there are ceremonies of our Holy Mother Church capable of delivering you from your torments, and I will intercede with her, for my part, in so far as my wealth will allow. So declare yourself, and say who you are.'

'I vow by all that's holy and by any oath your worship likes, Don Quixote de la Mancha,' replied the voice, 'that I'm your squire Sancho Panza, and that I've never been dead in all the days of my life. But having left my government for matters and causes that it would take a long time to tell you of, I fell last night into a pit where I'm now lying, and Dapple with me, who will not let me lie – for, to prove it to you, here he is with me.'

What is more, it seems as if the ass understood Sancho's words, for at that moment he began to bray so loudly that the whole cave resounded.

'A famous witness!' cried Don Quixote. 'I recognize that bray as if it were my own child, and I know your voice, dear Sancho. Wait for me. I will go to the Duke's castle, which is nearby, and bring someone to get you out of that pit, where your sins must have cast you.'

'Go, your worship,' said Sancho, 'and come back quickly, for God's sake. I can't bear being buried alive here, and I'm dying of fear.'

Don Quixote left him and went to the castle to tell the Duke and
Duchess of Sancho's plight, which astonished them not a little,
though they well understood how he must have fallen, knowing as
they did that the cavern had existed there from time immemorial.
But they could not imagine how he had left his government without
their having advice of his coming. At last, it is said, they brought
ropes and cables, and by dint of many hands and hard work Dapple
and Sancho Panza were dragged out of their darkness into the light
of the sun, where a certain student saw the squire and observed:
'This is the way all bad governors should leave their governments,
just as this sinner comes out of the depths of the abyss, perishing of
hunger, pale and probably without a farthing.'

And Sancho said when he heard him: 'It's eight or ten days,
brother sharp-tongue, since I went to govern the isle they gave me,
and all that while I've never had my belly full even for an hour.
During that time doctors have persecuted me and enemies have
trampled my bones. I've had no chance of taking bribes or of collecting dues, and since that's the case, I don't think I deserved to
come out like this. But man proposes and God disposes; and God
knows what's best and fittest for everyone; and circumstances alter
cases; and let no one say: this water I won't drink; for where you
think there are flitches, there aren't even hooks. God understands
me, and that's enough. I say no more, though I could.'

'Do not be angry, Sancho, or vexed at what you may hear,' said
Don Quixote, 'otherwise you will never be at peace. Come with a
clean conscience, and let them say what they will; for you may as
well try to put doors to an open field as tie up the tongues of slander. If the Governor leaves his government a rich man they say
that he has been a thief; and if he comes away poor that he is a good-
for-nothing and a dolt.'

'Well this time,' answered Sancho, 'they'll surely take me for a
fool, but not for a thief.'

Deep in this conversation they reached the castle, surrounded by
boys and a great number of other people; and there the Duke and
Duchess were waiting for them in a gallery. But Sancho would not
go up to see the Duke without first putting Dapple up in the stable;
for the ass, he said, had passed a very bad night in their lodging.
Then he went up to see his lord and lady, before whom he went

down on his knees and said: 'I, my Lord and Lady, because your Highnesses would have it so and without any merit of mine, went to govern your Isle Barataria, which I entered naked, and naked I am now: I neither lose nor gain. Whether I have governed well or ill, witnesses of my conduct over there will say as they please. I have settled questions and decided lawsuits, perishing of hunger all the time, since Master Pedro Recio – native of Tirteafuera, insular and governmental doctor – would have it so. We were attacked by enemies at night, and though they pressed us very hard the islemen say that we came off free and victorious by the valour of my arm, and may God save them if they speak the truth. In short, during that time I have measured the burdens and obligations that government entails, and find them, by my reckoning, more than my shoulders can carry. They are no load for my ribs nor arrows for my quiver. And so before the government flung me up I decided to fling up the government; and yesterday morning I left the isle as I found it, with the same streets, houses and roofs that it had when I went into it. I have exacted no loans from anyone, nor taken a share in any profits; and although I intended to make some useful laws I didn't make one, for fear they shouldn't be kept; for in that case one might as well not make them. I left the isle, as I said, with no other company than my Dapple. I fell into a pit and crept along it, till this morning, by the light of the sun, I saw a way out, but no easy one; for if Heaven hadn't sent me my master Don Quixote, I should have been there till the end of the world. So, my lord Duke and my lady Duchess, here's your governor, Sancho Panza, who in those eight days that he has held his governorship has gained this knowledge, that he would not give a farthing to be a governor, not just of one isle but even of the whole world. And that being so, embracing your worship's feet and imitating the boys' game which goes "*you jump and give me one*", I give the government a jump and pass into the service of my master Don Quixote. For with him at least I get my bellyful, although I eat my bread in bodily fear; and it's all one to me whether it's carrots or partridge, so long as I'm full.'

With this Sancho brought his long speech to an end, Don Quixote dreading all the while that he would utter thousands of absurdities; and when he heard him finish with so few, he gave thanks to

Heaven in his heart. The Duke embraced Sancho and said that it grieved him to the heart that he had left his government so soon, but that he would soon manage to give him some other less onerous and more profitable post on his estate. And the Duchess embraced him too, and ordered them to look after him well, for he showed signs of having been badly bruised and worse treated.

Chapter LVI. Of the prodigious and unparalleled Battle which took place between Don Quixote de la Mancha and the lackey Tosilos, in defence of the daughter of Doña Rodriguez, the Waiting-woman.

THE Duke and Duchess did not repent of the trick they had played on Sancho Panza by giving him his governorship; especially as the steward came that same day and related to them minutely all the speeches Sancho had made and all the actions he had performed during his term of office. And in conclusion he gave an exaggerated account of the assault on the isle, of Sancho's fear, and of his departure, from all of which they got no small enjoyment. After this our history relates that the time appointed for the battle arrived. Now as the Duke had instructed his lackey Tosilos over and over again how he was to deal with Don Quixote so as to overthrow him without killing or wounding him, he ordered the steel heads to be taken off the lances, telling Don Quixote that his Christian feeling, on which he prided himself, forbade their imperilling their lives in this battle. He was content, he said, to give them a fair field on his ground – although he was breaking a decree of the Holy Council which prohibits such duels – but he did not desire the affair to be carried to the extremity. Don Quixote said that his Excellency might make whatever dispositions in the matter he pleased, and that he would obey him in every detail. So, when on the dreaded day the Duke had ordered a spacious platform to be erected facing the castle square, on which the judges of the lists and the appellants, mother and daughter, might take their places, a countless troop of people came in from all the towns and villages of the neighbourhood to witness this novel battle; for none like it had been seen or heard of in that country within the memory of living man.

The first to enter the lists was the master of ceremonies, who sur-

veyed the ground and paced it all over, in case there might be any
foul play there or any hidden object over which one of them might
stumble and fall. Next entered the waiting-women, who sat down
on their seats, hooded to their eyes and even to their breasts; and
they showed signs of no small concern when Don Quixote appeared
in the lists. A little later, heralded by many trumpets, there appeared
on one side of the square the great lackey Tosilos, with his vizor
down and wholly encased in stout and shining armour. His horse
was clearly a Friesland, huge and grizzled, with a quarter of a hun-
dredweight of hair hanging from each fetlock. The valiant com-
batant came on, well instructed by the Duke his master how to behave towards the valiant Don Quixote de la Mancha, and warned on
no account to kill him, but to try and avoid his first onset for fear of
meeting his death, which he would certainly do if they were to meet
head-on. He paced the square, and when he arrived in front of the
waiting-women stood for a while to look at the lady who sought
him in marriage. Then the marshal of the field called Don Quixote,
who had already presented himself in the lists, and side by side with
Tosilos he addressed the ladies, asking if they consented to Don
Quixote's undertaking their cause. They assented, saying that they
would accept his judgment in the case as right, final and valid. By
this time the Duke and Duchess had taken their places in a gallery
that overlooked the lists, which were swarming with people waiting to see the merciless and unparalleled battle. A condition of the
combat was that if Don Quixote conquered his antagonist must
marry Doña Rodriguez' daughter, and if he were conquered his
opponent was free of the promise exacted of him and need give
no further satisfaction.

The master of ceremonies divided the sun between them, and set
each of them in the place where he was to stand. The drums struck
up, the air was filled with the sound of trumpets, the earth shook
beneath their feet. The hearts of the gazing crowd were in suspense,
hanging on the issue of the affair, some in hope and others in fear.
At length Don Quixote, recommending himself with all his heart to
our Lord God and to the Lady Dulcinea del Toboso, stood waiting
for them to give the agreed signal for the onset. Our lackey, however, had other thoughts; and what preoccupied him I will now tell
you. It seems that as he gazed upon his fair enemy she appeared to

him the most beautiful woman he had seen in all his life; and the little blind boy, who is generally called Love in these parts, could not lose this opportunity of triumphing over a lackeyish soul and placing it upon the list of his trophies. And so, coming up to him softly and unseen, he ran a six foot dart into the poor lackey's left side and pierced his heart through and through; which he could do in safety, for Love is invisible and comes and goes where he will, without anyone calling him to account for his deeds.

So, when the signal for the charge was given, our lackey was in transports at the beauty of the lady whom he had made mistress of his heart. And so he took no notice of the trumpet's sound; unlike Don Quixote, who charged as soon as he heard it, and rushed against his enemy at the utmost speed that Rocinante would permit. And when his good squire Sancho saw him attack, he called out loudly: 'God guide you, cream and flower of knights errant! God give you victory, for the right is on your side!'

Now although Tosilos saw Don Quixote coming at him, he did not stir a step from his position, but instead called loudly to the marshal of the lists; and when that official came up to see what he wanted he asked him: 'Sir, isn't this a battle to decide whether or not I'm to marry that lady?'

'That is so,' was the reply.

'Then,' said the lackey, 'My conscience pricks me, and it would be a sin if I went on with this battle. So I declare myself beaten, and I'm willing to marry the lady at once.'

The marshal of the lists was amazed at Tosilos' speech, and being in the secret of the plot did not know how to reply to him with so much as a word. Don Quixote drew up in mid-career, seeing that his adversary was not attacking. The Duke could not conceive why they were not going on with the battle, but the marshal of the lists went to tell him what the lackey had said, which left him astonished and extremely angry. Whilst this was going on Tosilos went up to where Doña Rodriguez was sitting and said in a loud voice: 'Madam, I wish to marry your daughter, and I do not want to use strife and contentions to gain what I can have in peace and without peril to my life.'

When the valorous Don Quixote heard this, he said: 'Well, in that case I am free and absolved from my promise. Let them marry, and good luck to them! And since the Lord God has given her to him, may Saint Peter bless her.'

The Duke came down to the castle square, and went up to Tosilos to ask him: 'Is it true, knight, that you yield yourself vanquished, and that your timorous conscience prompts you to marry this lady?'

'Yes, sir,' replied Tosilos.

'He's acting very wisely,' put in Sancho Panza at this point, 'for if you give the cat what you have to give the mouse you'll be out of your trouble.'

Tosilos went off to unlace his helmet, begging for prompt assistance since his breath was failing him, and he could not bear being shut up so long in that narrow lodging. They took it off quickly, and the lackey's face was plainly revealed, at which sight Doña Rodriguez and her daughter cried out aloud: 'It's a cheat! It's a cheat! They've put Tosilos, my master the Duke's lackey, in place of my real husband! Justice from God and the King for this trickery – or this villainy rather!'

'Do not be grieved, ladies,' said Don Quixote, 'for it is neither trickery nor villainy. Or if it is, it is not the Duke who is the cause, but those wicked enchanters who persecute me, and who, jealous of my gaining glory from this victory, have transformed your husband's face into this man's, who you say is the Duke's lackey. Take my advice and marry him, despite the malice of my enemies, for there is no doubt that he is really the man you desire for your husband.'

The Duke, who heard this, was on the point of dispersing all his anger in laughter, and said: 'Such extraordinary things happen to Don Quixote that I am inclined to think this is not my lackey. But here is a plan for us: let us put the marriage off a fortnight, if they will, and keep this personage about whom we are doubtful locked up; in which time perhaps he will return to his original shape. For the spite these enchanters entertain against Don Quixote cannot last as long as that, especially as these deceptions and transformations avail them so little.'

'Oh, sir,' cried Sancho, 'it's the usual practice of these malefactors to change anything my master has to do with from one shape into another. A knight he conquered a long while ago, called the Knight of the Mirrors, they turned into the shape of the Bachelor Sampson Carrasco, a native of our village and a great friend of ours, and my lady Dulcinea del Toboso they turned into a rustic peasant-girl; and so I imagine this lackey will die and live a lackey all the days of his life.'

At which the voice of Doña Rodriguez' daughter put in: 'I don't care who he may be that asks for my hand, I'm grateful to him. I had rather be a lackey's lawful wife than a gentleman's cast-off mistress, though my deceiver's no gentleman.'

The final upshot of all this was that Tosilos was locked up, to see what would come of his transformation. Everyone adjudged the victory to Don Quixote, but most of the spectators remained depressed and sad because the long expected combatants had not hacked one another to pieces; much like boys who are sorry when the man they are expecting to be hanged does not appear because he has been pardoned, either by the injured party or the judge. The people went off; the Duke and Duchess returned to the castle; Tosilos was locked up; Doña Rodriguez and her daughter were very glad to know that in one way or another the matter would end in matrimony; and as for Tosilos, he was of a like mind.

Chapter LVII. *Which tells how Don Quixote took leave of the Duke, and of his adventure with the witty and wanton Altisidora, the Duchess's Maid.*

NOW it seemed right to Don Quixote for him to quit the lazy life he was leading in that castle; for he thought himself guilty of a great fault in permitting himself to be shut up in idleness amidst the countless luxuries and delights which the Duke and Duchess lavished on him in his character of knight errant; and it seemed to him that he would have to render a strict account of his indolence and seclusion to Heaven. So one day he asked the Duke and Duchess for permission to depart. This they granted him, though showing their extreme sorrow at his departure. The Duchess gave Sancho Panza his wife's letters, and he shed tears over them, saying: 'Who would have thought that these great hopes the news of my governorship raised in the breast of my wife Teresa Panza would needs end in my

returning to the draggled adventures of my master Don Quixote de
la Mancha? I'm glad all the same to see that my Teresa behaved in
her true character by sending the acorns to the Duchess. For if she
had not sent them she would have shown herself ungrateful, and I
should have been vexed. It comforts me that this gift can't be called
a bribe, because I already had the governorship when she sent
them, and it's right and proper for those who receive a kindness to
show themselves grateful even if only in trifles. After all, naked I
went into the government, and naked I left it; and so I shall be able
to say with a clean conscience, which is no small matter: "Naked I
was born, naked I am now; I neither lose nor gain."'

This Sancho said to himself on the day of their departure; and
Don Quixote, having taken leave of the Duke and Duchess the
night before, presented himself in the morning in the courtyard of
the castle fully armed. All the people of the house gazed on him
from the galleries, and the Lord and Lady came out to see him as
well. Sancho was mounted on Dapple, with his saddle-bags, his
clothes-bag and his provisions, very pleased because the Duke's
steward – the one who had played the Trifaldi – had given him a
little purse with two hundred gold crowns to supply the needs of
the road. Of this Don Quixote as yet knew nothing.

Now whilst everyone was gazing on him, as has been said,
among the Duchess's other waiting-women and maids who were
watching him the witty and wanton Altisidora raised her voice and
began in piteous tones:

> 'Hear then, O you wicked knight,
> Check your reins a little:
> Do not so bestir the flanks
> Of your most ill-governed beast.
> Think, false one, you are not flying
> From some dreadful serpent,
> Only from a lambkin
> Still not grown to sheep.
> Horrid monster, you have tricked
> The most lovely damsel
> Diana on her hills has seen,
> Or Venus looked on in her woods.
>   Cruel Vireno, fugitive Aeneas,
>   Go off and join up with your mate Barabbas.

Wickedly you're bearing off
In your wicked clutching paws
The heartstrings of a humble maid
Tender and enamoured.
Three kerchiefs you have lifted
And some garters, black and white,
From such legs as equal
Marble in their smoothness.
Two thousand sighs you've taken,
Which, if they were fire, could
Set two thousand Troys alight,
If there were two thousand Troys.
 Cruel Vireno, fugitive Aeneas,
  Go off and join up with your mate Barabbas.

Of your squire, that Sancho,
May his bowels grow tough
And hard, that Dulcinea,
Left in her enchantment,
For the crime that you have done
May sadly bear the penalty.
For sometimes in my country
The just for sinners pay.
May your best adventures
Into misadventures turn,
All your pleasures to a dream,
Firmness to forgetfulness.
 Cruel Vireno, fugitive Aeneas,
  Go off and join up with your mate Barabbas.

And may you be known for false
From Seville to Marchena,
From Granada to Loja,
From London into England.
If you ever play at trumps
At piquet or primera,
May you never have a king,
Never see a seven or ace.
When you cut your corns
May the place be bloody,
If they pull your teeth out,
May the stumps remain!
 Cruel Vireno, fugitive Aeneas,
  Go off and join up with your mate Barabbas.'

And all the while the pitiable maid Altisidora was uttering her lament Don Quixote kept his eyes on her. Then, without a word of reply, he turned his face to Sancho and said: 'By the life of your ancestors, Sancho, I conjure you to answer me truly. Tell me, have you by any chance got the three kerchiefs and the garters this love-sick maiden is talking about?'

To which Sancho replied: 'Yes, I have got the three kerchiefs, but the garters – they are over the hills and far away.'

The Duchess was astonished at Altisidora's effrontery. For although she knew that she was bold, merry and not too moral, she would not have thought her so far gone as to proceed to such freedoms; and as she was not informed of this joke her wonder increased.

But the Duke wanted to carry the sport further, and said: 'It seems wrong to me, Sir Knight, that after the hospitable entertainment you have received in this castle of mine you should make bold to carry off at least three kerchiefs belonging to my maid, if not a pair of garters as well. These are indications of a false heart, and ill become your fair name. Return her garters or I defy you to mortal combat, without any fear that your scoundrelly enchanters may change or transform my face, as they did for Tosilos, my lackey, who entered into battle with you.'

'God forbid,' replied Don Quixote, 'that I should unsheathe my sword against your most illustrious person, from whom I have received such favours. The kerchiefs I will return, since Sancho says he has them. As for the garters it is impossible, for I have never had them, nor he either; and if this maid of yours will look in her hiding-places she will find them, I promise you. I, my Lord Duke, have never been a thief, nor do I ever mean to be one as long as I live, unless God lets me out of His care. This maid speaks, as she admits, like one love-sick, for which I am not to blame. And so I have not to ask pardon of her or of your Excellency, whom I implore to have a better opinion of me, and once more to give me leave to pursue my way.'

'May God send you a good journey, Don Quixote,' said the Duchess, 'and may we always have good news of your exploits. Go, and God bless you, for the longer you delay the greater the fire you kindle in the breasts of the maidens who look upon you. As for this maid of mine, I will punish her so that she shall not transgress in future, either in looks or in deeds.'

'Hear only one word more, valorous Don Quixote,' put in Altisidora. 'I beg your pardon for saying that you had stolen my garters for, by God and my soul, I have them on. I have fallen into the error of the man who went searching for the ass he was riding on.'

'Didn't I say so?' exclaimed Sancho. 'A great hand I am at hiding stolen things! For if I had wanted to I should have had a splendid opportunity in my government.'

Don Quixote bowed his head, and made obeisance to the Duke and Duchess and to all the bystanders. Then, turning Rocinante's rein, with Sancho following him on Dapple, he left the castle, taking his way towards Saragossa.

Chapter LVIII. *Of adventures that poured on Don Quixote so thick and fast that they trod upon each other's heels.*

WHEN Don Quixote found himself in open country, free and disembarrassed of Altisidora's attentions, he felt himself in his element, with his spirits reviving for the fresh pursuit of his scheme of chivalries. And, turning to Sancho, he said: 'Liberty, Sancho, is one of the most precious gifts Heaven has bestowed upon man. No treasures the earth contains or the sea conceals can be compared to it. For liberty, as for honour, one can rightfully risk one's life; and, on the other hand, captivity is the worst evil that can befall men. I say this, Sancho, because you have witnessed the luxury and abundance that we have enjoyed in this castle which we are now leaving. Yet in the midst of those highly-spiced banquets and snow-cooled drinks I seemed to be confined within the straits of hunger, since I did not enjoy them with the same liberty as if they had been my own; for obligations to return benefits and favours received are bonds that curb a free spirit. Happy is he to whom Heaven has given a crust of bread, without the obligation of offering thanks for it to any but Heaven itself!'

'For all that your worship says,' answered Sancho, 'it isn't right for us to be ungrateful, on our side, for two hundred gold crowns which the Duke's steward gave me in a little purse that I'm carrying, as a plaster and comforter next to my heart against emergencies. For we shan't always find castles to be entertained in. Sometimes we shall strike inns where they may beat us.'

The knight and squire errant were engaged in such conversations as this when, after riding for more than three miles, they saw about a dozen men dressed like labourers taking their dinner in a little green meadow, and sitting on their cloaks which were spread on the grass. Beside them they had what looked like white sheets, which covered certain objects underneath, some of which stood upright and some of which lay flat at short distances apart. Don Quixote rode up to the diners and, after first saluting them courteously, asked them what lay under their linen covers. To which one of them replied: 'Sir, beneath these sheets are some images, sculptured in relief, for a show we're presenting in our village. We carry them covered up so that they shan't get soiled, and on our shoulders so that they shan't break.'

'If you would be so kind,' said Don Quixote, 'I should like to see them, for images that are carried with such care must certainly be good ones.'

'Yes, that they are,' said the other, 'considering their price, for there's not one of them that didn't cost more than fifty ducats. And to prove that it's true, your worship, wait and see with your own eyes.'

Then, getting up, he left his dinner and went to take the cover off the first image, which proved to be of St. George, mounted on horseback with his lance thrust through the mouth of a serpent, coiled at his feet and represented with all its usual fierceness. The whole image looked a blaze of gold, as they say, and when Don Quixote saw it he said: 'This knight was one of the best errants in all the Heavenly Host. His name was St. George, and he was an especial defender of maidens. Let us see this other one.'

The man uncovered it, and it proved to be St. Martin, mounted on a horse, dividing his cloak with the poor man. And the moment Don Quixote saw him he exclaimed: 'This knight too was one of the Christian adventurers, and I believe he was even more generous than valiant; as you can see, Sancho, by his dividing his cloak with the poor man and giving him half. And no doubt it must have been winter at the time; for if it had not been he would have given him the whole, since he was so charitable.'

'That couldn't have been the reason,' said Sancho. 'He must have been following the old proverb that says, to give and to keep has need of brains.'

Don Quixote laughed and begged them to take off another of the cloths, beneath which was revealed the image of the patron of Spain on horseback with bloody sword, trampling down Moors and treading on their heads. And when he saw him Don Quixote said: 'This is a knight indeed, and of Christ's squadrons. He is called Don Saint James the Moor-killer, one of the most valiant saints and knights the world ever possessed or Heaven possesses now.'

Then they took off another cover, which revealed St. Paul fallen from his horse, with all the details usual in a picture of his conversion. On seeing it so life-like that you might have said that Christ was speaking and St. Paul replying, Don Quixote said: 'This was the greatest enemy our Lord God's church had in his time, and the best defender it will ever have – a knight errant by his life and a peaceful saint in his death, a tireless labourer in the vineyard of the Lord and teacher of the Gentiles. He had Heaven for his school and Jesus Christ Himself for his professor and master.'

There were no more images, and so Don Quixote bade them be covered up again, saying to those who were carrying them: 'I reckon it a good omen, brothers, that I have seen what I have seen, for these saints and knights professed, even as I do, the calling of arms. But the difference between us is that they were saints and fought in the heavenly fashion, and I am a sinner and fight in the human way. They conquered Heaven by force of arms, because Heaven suffers violence, but up till now I do not know what I am conquering by the force of my labours. But should my Dulcinea del Toboso be released from the pains she suffers, my fortune being improved and my mind righted, it may be I shall direct my steps along a better path than I am now following.'

'May God hear you and sin be deaf,' put in Sancho at this point.

The men were as astonished at Don Quixote's appearance as at his words, and did not understand the half of his meaning. They finished their dinner, lifted up their images and, bidding the knight farewell, went on their way. And Sancho was astonished afresh at his master's knowledge, as if he had never known him before, for it seemed to him that there could be no history or event in the world that he had not got written on his nails and imprinted in his memory.

'Truly, my lord and master,' he said to him, 'if what has happened to us to-day can be called an adventure, it has been one of the mildest and sweetest that has befallen us in all the course of our wanderings. For we have come out from it without a beating or bodily fear; and we haven't so much as put hand to sword, or thumped the earth with our bodies, or even been left hungry. Heaven be praised that I have seen all this with my own eyes!'

'You are right, Sancho,' replied Don Quixote, 'but you must consider that times are wont to vary and change their course. And what the common people generally call omens, being founded on no cause in nature, should be taken by a wise man for happy accidents. One of these omen-watchers may get up early one morning, and as he leaves his house meet a friar of the order of the blessed St. Francis; then he will turn round and go back home, as if he had encountered a griffin. Another, a Mendoza, spills the salt on his table, and melancholy spills on his heart, as if nature were obliged to give signs of approaching disasters by things as unimportant as these. The wise Christian should not pry too curiously into the counsels of Heaven. Scipio lands in Africa and stumbles as he leaps ashore; his soldiers take it for a bad omen, but he embraces the ground and cries: "You cannot escape me, Africa, for I have you clasped in my arms." So, Sancho, my meeting with these images has been for me a most happy event.'

'I can well believe it,' answered Sancho, 'and I should like your worship to tell me the reason why Spaniards, when they're going into battle, call on that St. James, the Moor-killer: "*St. James and close, Spain!*" Is Spain perhaps open, that she has to be closed? Or what is this ceremony?'

'You are very simple, Sancho,' answered Don Quixote. 'See here. God has given Spain for her patron and protector this great knight of the Red Cross, especially in those desperate conflicts the Spaniards have fought with the Moors; and so they invoke and call upon him as their defender in all their battles, and often they have seen him there, visibly overthrowing, trampling, destroying and killing the hosts of Hagar, and I could give you many examples of this recorded in authentic Spanish histories.'

Sancho changed the subject, and said to his master: 'I am amazed, sir, at the brazenness of the Duchess's maid, Altisidora. The creature they call Love must have wounded her and pierced her cruelly. They say that he's a little blind boy, and yet though he's blear-eyed, or rather has no sight, if he takes ever such a little heart for his target he hits it and pierces it through with his arrows. I've heard tell too that Love's darts are blunted and dulled by a maiden's reserve and modesty; but in this Altisidora they seem to have been whetted rather than blunted.'

'Take note, Sancho,' said Don Quixote, 'that Love observes no restraints and keeps no rules of reason in his proceedings. He is of the same temper as Death, who attacks the lofty palaces of kings as well as the humble cottages of shepherds; and when he takes possession of a heart the first thing he does is to remove fear and shame from it. And so, being shameless, Altisidora proclaimed her desires, which roused more confusion than pity in my breast.'

'Shocking cruelty!' exclaimed Sancho. 'Monstrous ingratitude! I can say for myself that I should have surrendered and become her vassal at her slightest word of love. The Devil! What a marble heart! What bowels of brass, and what a rough-cast spirit! But I can't think what that maiden can have seen in your worship to make her yield and submit like that. What grace was it, what dash, what charm, what looks? which of all these was it, or was it all of them together that captivated her? For really and truly, often I stop and look at your worship from your feet to the last hair of your head, and I find more about you to scare me than to charm me. And as I've heard too that beauty is the first and principal quality that breeds love, I don't know what the poor creature fell in love with, since your worship has none.'

'Consider, Sancho,' replied Don Quixote, 'that there are two kinds of beauty, one of the soul and the other of the body. The spiritual is displayed and shown in intelligence, in chastity, in good behaviour, in generosity and in good breeding; and all these qualities may fittingly exist in an ill-favoured man. Then when the gaze is fixed on that beauty, and not on the physical, love generally arises with great violence and intensity. I am well aware, Sancho, that I am not handsome; but I also know that I am not deformed; and it is enough for a man of worth not to be a monster for him to be dearly loved, provided he possesses those spiritual endowments I have mentioned.'

Whilst engaged in this talk they strayed into a wood which lay off the road, and suddenly and unexpectedly Don Quixote found himself entangled in some nets of green thread which were stretched from tree to tree; and unable to imagine what they could be he said to Sancho: 'In my opinion, Sancho, the matter of these nets must be one of the strangest adventures imaginable. May I die if the enchanters who persecute me are not trying to enmesh me and stop my journey, as if to revenge the cruelty I showed to Altisidora. But I will teach them that, though these nets were made of hardest adamant instead of green thread, or were stronger than that in which the jealous God of blacksmiths entangled Venus and Mars, I would break them as easily as I would rushes or cotton yarn.'

But as he was trying to push on and break through, there suddenly appeared ahead from between some trees two most lovely shepherdesses. At least they were dressed like shepherdesses, although their jackets and skirts were of fine brocade, and their skirts, I declare, were petticoats of rich watered gold silk. The gold of their hair, too, which was loose on their shoulders, could compete with the rays of the very sun, and they were crowned with garlands of green laurel and red amaranth. In age they appeared not less than fifteen nor more than eighteen. This was a sight to dazzle Sancho, astonish Don Quixote and make the sun stop in its course to watch them; and so all four remained in wondering silence. At length the first to speak was one of the two shepherdesses, who said to Don Quixote: 'Stop, Sir Knight, and do not break these nets, which are not stretched here to hurt you but for our amusement; and since I know that you will ask why they are placed here and who we are, I will tell you in few words. In a village about six miles away live many people of quality, gentlefolk and rich, several of whom have made up a party, of friends, neighbours and relations, to come and take our pleasure at this spot, which is one of the most charming in all the district. Here we have formed amongst ourselves a new pastoral Arcadia, the girls dressing as shepherdesses and the lads as shepherds. We have learnt two eclogues by heart, one by the famous poet Garcilaso and the other by the most excellent Camoens in his own Portuguese tongue, neither of which have we played till now.

Yesterday we came here. We have pitched our tents – field tents they call them – among these saplings on the banks of a flowing stream which waters all these meadows. And last night we stretched these nets among the trees to catch the silly little birds, meaning to drive them into the snare by our noise. If you please, sir, to be our guest you will be liberally and courteously entertained, for no care or sadness shall be of our party.'

She stopped, and said no more. Then Don Quixote replied: 'Truly, fairest lady, Actaeon could have been struck with no greater wonder or amazement when he spied Diana unawares bathing in the waters, than I am at the sight of your beauty. I commend the scheme of your entertainments, and thank you for your invitation; and if I can serve you, you may command me in the certainty of being obeyed. For my profession is no other than to show myself a grateful benefactor to all kinds of people, especially to those of the rank you seem to be; and if these nets, which can occupy only a small space, were to fill the whole rotundity of the globe I would seek new worlds to pass through so as to avoid breaking them. And so that you may give some credence to this hyperbole of mine, learn that it is Don Quixote de la Mancha – no less – who makes you his promise, if by chance this name has reached your ears.'

'Oh, my dear friend,' the other shepherdess then cried, 'what very good luck! Do you see this gentleman here before us? Well, I would have you know that he is the most valiant, the most enamoured and the most courteous knight in the whole world, unless the history of his exploits, which I have read in print, lies and deceives us. I will wager that this good fellow with him is a certain Sancho Panza, his squire, whose drolleries none can equal.'

'That's quite right,' said Sancho, 'I am the droll fellow and the squire your Grace speaks of, and this gentleman's my master, the same Don Quixote de la Mancha historified and aforesaid.'

'Oh!' cried the other shepherdess. 'Let us beg him to stay, dear, for our families will be overjoyed to have him. I have also heard tell of this valour and charm of his. He is especially famous for being the most steadfast and constant lover known, and they say his lady – a certain Dulcinea del Toboso – bears away the palm from all the beauties in Spain.'

'And she has the right to it,' said Don Quixote, 'unless, indeed your peerless beauty may put the matter in doubt. But do not endeavour to detain me, ladies, for the urgent obligations of my profession leave me in no condition to rest.'

At this moment there came up to them the brother of one of the two shepherdesses, also dressed in shepherd-fashion, and every bit as rich and splendid as his sister, who informed him that the gentleman with them was the valorous Don Quixote de la Mancha, and the other his squire Sancho, of whom he would know, since he had read their history. The gay shepherd paid his compliments, and begged the knight to accompany him to their tents; and Don Quixote had to give in and do so. Then the beaters came up, and the nets were filled with different kinds of birds which, deceived by the colour of the meshes, fell into the peril they were trying to avoid. More than thirty people had assembled in that spot, all extravagantly dressed as shepherds and shepherdesses, and in a moment they were informed who Don Quixote and his squire were; and they were no little delighted, for they knew him already from his history. Then they repaired to the tents, where they found the tables richly, abundantly and elegantly laid, and honoured Don Quixote by placing him at the head; and all gazed at him in wonder. At length when the cloth was removed the knight sonorously and very gravely observed: 'Though some say that man's greatest sin is pride, I say that it is ingratitude, and I base my belief on the common saying that Hell is full of the ungrateful. This sin I have endeavoured to avoid, in so far as I have been able, ever since I have had the use of reason; and if I cannot repay the benefits done me with equal benefits, I substitute my desire to repay them, and when that is not enough I proclaim them abroad. For he that declares and proclaims the benefits he receives would likewise repay them if he could, but for the most part receivers have not the resources of givers. Thus God is above us all, for He is a greater giver than any, and man's gifts cannot equal the beneficence of God because of the infinite distance between them. This poverty and deficiency, however, is to some extent compensated for by gratitude. I, therefore, grateful for the favours here done me, and unable to respond in like measure, being restricted by the narrow limits of my means, offer what little is in my power. I, therefore, engage to maintain, for two whole days, in the middle of this high road which leads to

Saragossa, that these two ladies here disguised as shepherdesses are the most beautiful and the most courteous maidens in the world, excepting only the peerless Dulcinea del Toboso, sole mistress of my heart, without offence be it said to all of either sex who hear me.'

At these words Sancho, who had been listening with great attention, cried out loudly: 'Is it possible that anyone in the world could be bold enough to say and swear that this master of mine is mad? Tell me, your worships, gentlemen shepherds, is there a village priest living, though ever so wise and learned, who could speak as my master has just done? Or is there any knight errant, though ever so renowned for bravery, who could make such an offer as he has made?'

Then with a flushed and angry face Don Quixote turned on Sancho and cried: 'Could there possibly be anyone, Sancho, on the whole face of the earth who would not say that you are a dolt, lined with knavery and fringed with unspeakable mischief and roguery? Who set you meddling with my affairs, and enquiring whether I am a man of sense or crazy? Be quiet! Say no more, but saddle Rocinante, if he is unsaddled, and let us go and put my offer into effect, for seeing that right is on my side you can reckon all who dare gainsay me as vanquished already.'

Then with a great demonstration of furious indignation he rose from his seat, leaving the astonished company wondering whether to reckon him mad or sane. They, however, tried to dissuade him from his challenge, protesting that they were sufficiently assured of his grateful nature and that there was no need of fresh demonstrations to prove his valour, for those related in his history were sufficient. But Don Quixote, all the same, persisted in his resolution and, bracing his shield and grasping his lance, took up his position on Rocinante in the middle of a highway, not far from that green meadow. Sancho followed him on Dapple with all the people of the pastoral flock, curious to see the upshot of his arrogant and extraordinary challenge.

Then, planted, as we have said, in the middle of the road, Don Quixote wounded the air with such words as these: 'You, passengers and wayfarers, knights, squires, travellers on foot and horse, passing along this road or about to pass in the next two days! Learn that Don Quixote de la Mancha, knight errant, is posted here to maintain that there is no beauty or courtesy in the world greater than that of the nymphs inhabiting these meadows and woods, setting on one side the mistress of my soul, Dulcinea del Toboso. So let anyone of the contrary opinion come on. I await him here.'

Twice he repeated these same words, and twice they were unheard by any adventurer. But by a stroke of Fortune, which continued to advance his affairs from success to success, there soon appeared on the road a crowd of men on horseback, many of them with lances in their hands, riding all bunched together and at a great pace. And no sooner did they come into view than they turned and got out of the road, perceiving that they might run into danger if they stayed. Only Don Quixote remained still with undaunted heart, while Sancho Panza shielded himself behind Rocinante's hindquarters. The troop of spearmen came up, and one of them who rode somewhat ahead began to bawl at Don Quixote: 'Get out of the way, you silly devil, or these bulls will trample you to pieces.'

'Ho, rabble!' replied Don Quixote. 'I care for no bulls, not for the fiercest ever bred on the banks of Jarama. Confess, scoundrels, the whole lot of you together, that what I have proclaimed is the truth; otherwise, do battle with me.'

The herdsman had no time to answer, nor had Don Quixote a second to get out of the way, even if he had wanted to; and so the troop of wild bulls and tame bullocks, and the crowd of herdsmen and others, who were taking them to a nearby town where they were to be baited next day, passed over Don Quixote and over Sancho, Rocinante and Dapple, overthrowing them all and tumbling them along the ground. Sancho lay there bruised, Don Quixote was stunned, Dapple trampled, and Rocinante not too sound. But at length they all got up, and Don Quixote set off in great haste, stumbling and falling, as he pursued the herd, shouting: 'Halt! Stop, you scoundrelly rabble! For but a single knight awaits you, one who scorns the coward's maxim: build a bridge of silver for a flying enemy!'

But the runaways did not stop for this, and took no more notice of his threats than of last year's clouds. Weariness halted Don Quixote; and more enraged than revenged he sat down on the road, waiting for Sancho, Rocinante and Dapple to come up. They arrived;

master and man remounted; and without turning to take leave of the pretence or counterfeit Arcadia, they went on their way with more shame than satisfaction.

Chapter LIX. *Of an extraordinary accident which befell Don Quixote and might be considered an adventure.*

IN a clear and limpid spring, which they found in a shady clump of trees, Don Quixote and Sancho removed the dirt they had got from the unmannerly behaviour of the bulls; and there beside it the woe-begone pair sat down to rest from their fatigue, leaving Dapple and Rocinante loose without headstall or bridle. Sancho had recourse to the larder in his saddle-bags, and brought out what he was pleased to call his fodder. He rinsed his mouth, and Don Quixote washed his face, from which refreshment their jaded spirits regained some courage. But Don Quixote ate nothing, out of pure vexation, nor, out of pure courtesy, did Sancho venture to touch the food before him, waiting for his master to take the first bit. Seeing him so deep in thought, however, that he forgot to raise the bread to his mouth, the squire silently, and in defiance of all the rules of good breeding, began to cram the bread and cheese into his mouth.

'Eat, Sancho, my friend,' said Don Quixote. 'Sustain life, for you have more need than I; and let me die a victim of my thoughts and of the force of my misfortunes. I was born, Sancho, to live dying, and you to die eating; and to prove the truth of my words gaze upon me. Printed in histories, famous in arms, courteous in my actions, respected by Princes, courted by maidens; yet after all, when I expected palms, triumphs and crowns, earned and merited by my valorous exploits, I have seen myself this morning trampled, kicked and pounded by the feet of unclean and filthy animals. This reflection blunts my teeth, dulls my grinders, numbs my hands, and completely robs me of appetite, so that I think I may let myself die of hunger, the most cruel of all deaths.'

'At that rate,' said Sancho without ceasing his rapid munching, 'your worship will not approve of the proverb which says: — Let Martha die, but die with her belly full. As for me, I'm not thinking of killing myself. I prefer to do like the cobbler, who stretches the leather with his teeth till he makes it reach where he wants. I will lengthen my life with eating till it reaches the end that Heaven has fixed. For I tell you, sir, that there's nothing crazier than to think of dying of despair, as you do. Take my word for it, and have something to eat. Then lie down to sleep a bit on the green cushions of this grass, and you'll find yourself feeling quite a bit soothed when you wake up.'

Don Quixote complied, thinking that Sancho reasoned more like a philosopher than a fool, and remarked: 'If you could do something for me, Sancho, which I will explain to you, my relief would be more certain and my anxieties less great; and it is this: While I follow your advice and sleep go you a little way off from here and, baring your flesh to the air, give yourself three or four hundred lashes with Rocinante's reins on account of those three thousand and odd you have incurred for Dulcinea's disenchantment; for it is no small pity that the poor lady remains enchanted through your forgetfulness and negligence.'

'There's a great deal to be said on that score,' said Sancho. 'Let us sleep, both of us, for the present; and afterwards God knows what will happen. I tell you, your worship, this whipping a man in cold blood is a hard matter, and harder still if the lashes fall upon a body ill-nourished and underfed. Let my lady Dulcinea have patience, and she'll see me riddled with lashes when she least expects it; and till death all is life – I mean that I'm still alive, and still anxious to perform what I have promised.'

Don Quixote thanked him and ate a little, while Sancho ate a good deal; and the two of them threw themselves down to sleep, leaving those two constant companions and friends, Rocinante and Dapple, to graze unrestrained and at their will on the rich grass, which was plentiful in that meadow. And rather late they awoke, remounted, and continued their journey, pressing on to reach an inn which lay in sight, apparently some three miles away. I say that it was an inn because Don Quixote called it one, contrary to his usual habit of calling all inns castles.

When they arrived he asked the landlord if there was lodging, and received the answer that there was, and as comfortable and luxurious as they could find in Saragossa. So they dismounted, and Sancho put his provisions away in a little room of which the host gave him the key. Then he took the beasts to the stable, gave them their fodder, and came out to see what orders Don Quixote had for him. He found him sitting on a stone bench, and gave especial thanks to Heaven that this inn had not seemed to his master a castle. Now when supper time came they retired to their room, and Sancho asked the landlord what he had to give them to eat. The host replied that they could have as much as they could eat of anything they liked to ask for, as the inn was stocked with the birds of the air, the fowls of the woods and the fish of the sea.

'There's no need of all that,' replied Sancho. 'We shall be satisfied with a couple of chickens roasted for us, for my master is weak in the stomach and eats little, and I'm no enormous glutton.'

The landlord replied that he had no chickens, for the kites had devoured them.

'Then, Master Host,' said Sancho, 'have a pullet roasted for us, so long as it's a tender one.'

'A pullet! Good heavens!' replied the landlord. 'Indeed, I sent more than fifty to town only yesterday to be sold. Ask for anything else you like, your worship, but not for pullets.'

'Well,' said Sancho, 'there'll be no shortage of veal or goat, surely.'

'We've none in the house just now,' replied the landlord, 'for they're all finished up, but next week we shall have plenty.'

'That'll do us a lot of good!' replied Sancho. 'But I'll bet you can make up for everything with lashings of bacon and eggs.'

'My Lord!' exclaimed the landlord. 'He's a fine one, this guest of mine. I've just told him I've got no pullets or hens, and he expects me to have eggs! Discuss some other delicacies, if you like, but stop asking for rarities.'

'Let's decide on something, for goodness' sake,' said Sancho. 'Tell me, once and for all, what you have got, Master Host, and stop your discussions.'

'What I have actually got,' said the innkeeper, 'is two cow heels that might be taken for calves' feet, or two calves' feet that are like cow heels. They are stewed with chick-peas, onions and bacon, and at this very minute they're crying out "*Eat me! Eat me!*"'

'I mark them for mine from this moment,' said Sancho, 'and let no one touch them. I'll pay more than anyone else for them, for there's nothing tastier in the world, to my mind. Just give me cow heels and I don't care a fig whether they're like calves' feet or not.'

'No one shall touch them,' said the landlord, 'for the other guests I have, being people of quality, have their own cook and steward and provisions with them.'

'If you go in for quality,' said Sancho, 'there's none better than my master; but the office he professes doesn't allow of larders and butteries. We just stretch out in the middle of a field and stuff ourselves with acorns or medlars.'

Such was Sancho's conversation with the innkeeper, which he now decided to break off, without answering the host's enquiries regarding his master's office or profession.

Supper-time arrived. The host brought in the stew, such as it was, and Don Quixote went to his room and sat down very comfortably to his meal. He seems, however, to have heard some talking in the next room, which was divided from his own by no more than a thin partition: 'I beg you, Don Jeronimo,' exclaimed a voice, 'till they bring in the supper let us read another chapter of the second part of *Don Quixote de la Mancha*.'

The moment Don Quixote heard his name he stood up and listened, all ears, to what they were saying about him. Then he heard this Don Jeronimo, who had been addressed, reply: 'Why, Don Juan, do you want us to read this nonsense? Can anyone who has read the first part of the history of Don Quixote de la Mancha possibly take any pleasure in reading the second?'

'All the same,' said Don Juan, 'it would be well to read it, for there's no book so bad that there isn't something good in it. But what most displeases me in this one is that it depicts Don Quixote out of love with Dulcinea del Toboso.'

On hearing these words Don Quixote was filled with furious indignation, and called out at the top of his voice: 'Whoever says that Don Quixote de la Mancha has forgotten, or can forget, Dulcinea del Toboso, I will teach him with equal arms that he is a long way from the truth; for the peerless Dulcinea del Toboso can never be forgotten, nor is Don Quixote capable of forgetting. His motto is constancy, and his profession to preserve it with gentleness and without violence.'

'Who is it answering us?' came a voice from the other room.

'Who should it be,' answered Sancho, 'but the same Don Quixote de la Mancha, who will make good all he has said now and in the future; for a good paymaster doesn't worry about sureties.'

As soon as Sancho had spoken two gentlemen – for so they appeared – rushed in through the door of the room, and one of them flung his arms round Don Quixote's neck, crying: 'Your presence cannot belie your name, nor can your name do otherwise than give credit to your person. No doubt, sir, you are the real Don Quixote de la Mancha, pole-star and morning star of knight errantry, in despite of him that sought to usurp your name and annihilate your exploits, as the author of this book has done, which I here deliver to you.'

And he put into his hands a book which his companion had been carrying. Don Quixote took it and without a word began to turn over the pages. Then after a while he returned it, saying: 'In the little that I have seen I have found three things in this author deserving rebuke. The first is some words I have read in the prologue; the second that the language is Aragonese, for he often writes without articles; and the third, which most confirms him an ignoramus, is that he stupidly wanders from the truth in the most essential point in the whole history. For he says here that the wife of Sancho Panza, my squire, is called Mari Gutierrez, and that is wrong, for her name is Teresa Panza; and it is much to be feared that anyone who is mistaken on so important a point will be mistaken throughout the history.'

At which Sancho put in: 'A pretty thing in a historian. He must be very well acquainted with our affairs indeed, if he calls my wife Teresa Panza Mari Gutierrez. Take the book again, sir. See if I'm in it, and whether they've changed my name.'

'From your words, friend,' said Don Jeronimo, 'you must certainly be Sancho Panza, Don Quixote's squire.'

'Yes, I am,' answered Sancho, 'and proud of it.'

'Then I will swear,' said the gentleman, 'that this modern author does not treat you with the decency which your appearance seems to deserve. He depicts you as a guzzler and a fool, with no humour at all, very different from the Sancho described in the first part of your master's history.'

'Heaven forgive him,' said Sancho. 'He should have left me forgotten in my corner. For let him play who knows the strings, and St. Peter is well at Rome.'

The two gentlemen begged Don Quixote to come into their room and sup with them, for they were sure that there was no food fit for him in the inn. And the knight, ever polite, acceded to their request and took supper with them, while Sancho remained in supreme and absolute dominion over the stew. He sat at the head of the table, and with him the innkeeper who was no less devoted than Sancho to cow heel and calves' foot.

During the course of the meal Don Juan asked Don Quixote what news he had of the lady Dulcinea del Toboso; whether she had married, whether she had been brought to bed or was pregnant, or whether she was still a virgin and mindful, saving her chastity and good name, of Don Quixote's amorous addresses. To which he replied: 'Dulcinea is a virgin, my desires more constant than ever, our intercourse as fruitless as of old, and her beauty transformed into that of a coarse peasant girl.'

And then he proceeded to relate to them, in great detail, the lady Dulcinea's enchantment, the events in Montesinos' cave, and the instructions of the sage Merlin for her disenchantment – the affair of Sancho's flagellation. Great was the pleasure the two gentlemen received from hearing Don Quixote relate his extraordinary adventures, and they were alike surprised at his extravagancies and at his elegant manner of recounting them. One moment they thought him a man of sense, and the next he slipped into craziness; nor could they decide what degree to assign him between wisdom and folly.

Sancho finished his supper and, leaving the innkeeper sozzled, went to his master's room, saying as he entered: 'Hang me, gentlemen, if the author of that book you've got there has any wish to be on good terms with me. But though he calls me a guzzler, you tell me, I hope he doesn't call me a drunkard.'

'He does,' said Don Jeronimo, 'though I do not remember his exact words. But I know they were ugly ones, and false as well, as I can plainly read on the physiognomy of honest Sancho here before me.'

'Take my word for it, gentlemen,' said Sancho, 'the Sancho and Don Quixote of that history must be different people from those who figure in the one composed by Cide Hamete Benengeli; for they are truly we two: my master valiant, wise and a true lover, and myself, simple, droll, and no guzzler nor a drunkard.'

'I believe you,' said Don Juan, 'and were it possible, there should have been a law that no one should dare to write of the affairs of the great Don Quixote except Cide Hamete, his first historian; just as Alexander decreed that no one should dare paint him except Apelles.'

'Let anyone portray me who will, but let him not abuse me,' said Don Quixote; 'for patience will very often trip when overloaded with injuries.'

'No injury can be done to Don Quixote,' said Don Juan, 'which he cannot avenge, if he does not ward it off with the shield of his patience, which seems to me both strong and great.'

In such conversation they passed a great part of the night, and although Don Juan would have liked Don Quixote to read more of the book to see what subjects it dwelt on, they could not prevail upon him to do so. He said that he took it as read, and concluded that it was all nonsense. What was more, he did not wish its author to flatter himself with the thought that he had read it, even should he chance to learn that he had had it in his hands; for our thoughts should be kept from filthy and obscene subjects, and much more so our eyes.

They asked him in what direction he had decided to travel. He replied to Saragossa, to take part in the jousts for the suit of armour which are held in that city every year.

Don Juan told him that the new history related how Don Quixote – or whoever it was – had been there, running at the ring – of which the author gives a wretched account, barren of invention, poor in style, and miserably poorest in descriptions, though rich in absurdities.

'For that reason,' replied Don Quixote, 'I will not set foot in Saragossa. Thus I will publish this modern historian's lie to the world, and people shall see that I am not the Don Quixote he writes of.'

'You will do wisely in that,' said Don Jeronimo, 'for there are jousts at Barcelona too, in which Don Quixote will be able to prove his valour.'

'That I intend to do,' said Don Quixote, 'but give me leave to retire, for it is time for bed, and be pleased to count me in the number of your best friends and servitors.'

'And me too,' said Sancho; 'for you may find me good for something.'

With this they took their leave, Don Quixote and Sancho retiring to their room and leaving Don Juan and Don Jeronimo amazed at the spectacle of mingled wisdom and folly they had witnessed. But they were now quite certain that these were the authentic Don Quixote and Sancho, and that those the Aragonese author had described were not.

Don Quixote rose early, and rapped at the partition of the next room to bid his new friends farewell. Then Sancho paid the innkeeper munificently, but advised him either to make less boast of the provisions at his inn or to keep it better provided in future.

Chapter LX. Don Quixote's adventure on the way to Barcelona.

THE morning was cool, and the day gave promise of being so too, when Don Quixote rode out of the inn, having first informed himself which was the most direct way to Barcelona, avoiding Saragossa — for he was determined to prove the falsehood of the new history which he understood had so greatly maligned him. Now it chanced that nothing worth recording befell him for more than six days. But at the end of that time he strayed from the road, and night overtook him among some thick trees — oaks or perhaps cork trees, for on this point Cide Hamete does not observe his usual meticulousness. Master and man dismounted and leant against the tree-trunks, where Sancho, who had taken lunch that day, rushed headlong into the arms of sleep. Don Quixote, however, not from hunger but from his restless imagination, was unable to close his eyes, and let his thoughts wander here and there and in a thousand different places. First he imagined himself in Montesinos' cave; then he saw Dulcinea, transformed into a peasant girl, leap upon her ass-colt; then there rang in his ears the sage Merlin's words, repeating to him the conditions to be observed and the means to be taken for Dulcinea's disenchantment. He was in despair at his squire Sancho's negligence and lack of charity; for to his knowledge he had only given himself five lashes, a poor and disproportionate sum compared to the infinite number outstanding. This thought roused him to such grief and rage that he argued thus with himself: 'If the Great Alexander cut the Gordian knot with the sword, to cut is as good as to untie, yet, nevertheless, became universal lord of all Asia, exactly the same might happen now in the disenchantment of Dulcinea, were I to lash Sancho against his will; for if the virtue of this remedy consists in Sancho's receiving the three thousand and odd stripes, what does it matter to me whether he applies them himself or someone else gives him them, since the efficacy lies in his receiving them, from whatever hand they may come?'

With this idea he went up to Sancho, having first taken Rocinante's reins and arranged them for use as a whip, and began to untie his laces – though it is thought that he had only the one, in front, which kept up his breeches. But no sooner did his master approach than Sancho started up wide awake and cried: 'What is it? Who is touching me and pulling at my clothes?'

'It is I,' answered Don Quixote, 'come to make good your negligence and remedy my own troubles. I have come to whip you, Sancho, and to discharge in part the debt to which you are pledged. Dulcinea is perishing; you are living in idleness; I am dying of desire; so pull down your breeches of your own free will, for it is my intention to give you at least two thousand lashes in this lonely spot.'

'Oh no!' said Sancho. 'Keep off, your worship, or I swear by the true God the deaf shall hear us. The lashes I am pledged to must be applied voluntarily and not by force, and at present I've no desire to whip myself. Enough that I gave your worship my word to flog and flap myself as soon as I feel like it.'

'It cannot be left to your good feeling, Sancho,' said Don Quixote, 'for you are a hard-hearted peasant, although your flesh is tender.'

And so he struggled with him and tried to pull his laces loose. Upon which Sancho jumped to his feet, closed with his master and, gripping him by main force, gave him a back trip which threw him face upwards upon the ground. Then setting his right knee on his chest, he held his master's hands down so tightly that he could not stir and could scarcely breathe.

'What, traitor?' cried Don Quixote. 'Do you rebel against your master and natural lord? Do you presume against your bread-giver?'

'I depose no King, I make no King,' answered Sancho, 'but help myself who am my own lord. Promise to let me alone, your worship, and not try and whip me for the present, and I'll let you go free. But if you don't

> Here and now thou diest, traitor,
> Enemy of Doña Sancha.'

Don Quixote passed his word, and swore on his life not to touch a thread of Sancho's clothing and to leave it to his free will and pleasure to whip himself when he would. Sancho then got up and went some distance off, but just as he was going to lean against another tree he felt something touching his head and, putting up his hands, grasped a man's feet in shoes and stockings. He trembled with fear, and ran to another tree, where the same thing happened. Then he shouted to Don Quixote to come to him. This his master did, asking him what was the matter and what he was afraid of; to which Sancho replied that all the trees were full of human feet and legs. Don Quixote felt them and, immediately guessing the cause, he said: 'You have nothing to be frightened of, Sancho. These are no doubt the legs of robbers and bandits who have been hanged on these trees; for in these parts Justice usually hangs them when it catches them, often in batches of twenty or thirty; by which I conclude that I must be in the neighbourhood of Barcelona.' And he was perfectly right, for when the morning dawned they looked up and saw that the clusters in the trees were bandits' bodies.

But if they were alarmed at those dead bandits they were even more terrified at the sight of more than forty live ones, who suddenly surrounded them and commanded them in Catalan to stay still, and not to move till their captain came up. They found Don Quixote on foot, his horse unbridled and his lance resting against a tree; in short, being utterly defenceless, he thought it best to fold his hands, bow his head, and reserve himself for a better occasion. The robbers immediately fell to work upon Dapple, and quickly emptied the saddle-bag and the clothes-bag; and it was a good thing for Sancho that he carried the Duke's ducats, with his own money, tied in a belly-band. But, for all that, these good folks would have stripped him and searched him, even to see what was hidden between his skin and his flesh, if their captain had not come up at that juncture. He was apparently about thirty-four, stout, of more than medium height, of a stern appearance and swarthy complexion. He rode a powerful horse and wore a coat of mail, with four pistols by his side, of the sort known in those parts as petronels. Seeing that his squires – for that is what they call men of that trade – were going to strip Sancho Panza, he commanded them to stop, and was immediately obeyed: and so it was that the belly-band escaped. But he was surprised to see a lance resting against the tree, a shield on the ground, and Don Quixote in armour and deep in thought, with the gloomiest and most melancholy expression that sadness itself could assume. He therefore approached him, and said: 'Don't be so sad, my good fellow, for you have fallen into the hands of no cruel Osiris, but of Roque Guinart, who is more compassionate than cruel.'

'My sadness,' replied Don Quixote, 'is not on account of falling into your power, valorous Roque, whose fame has no bounds on the whole earth, but that I was so negligent as to let your soldiers catch me unbridled, although I am obliged by the order of knight errantry I profess to live continually on the alert and to be at all hours my own sentinel. For I would inform you, great Roque, that if they had found me on my horse with my lance and shield, it would have been no easy task for them to force me to yield, for I am Don Quixote de la Mancha, with whose exploits the whole world resounds.'

Roque Guinart perceived at once that Don Quixote's infirmity was nearer to madness than to valour, but although he had heard him spoken of at times he had never considered his adventures real, nor been able to persuade himself that such a humour could reign in any man's heart. But he was extremely delighted at this meeting, for he could now prove for himself the truth of the stories he had heard. And so he said to him: 'Valorous knight, do not be vexed or account your present fortune sinister. Perhaps by this stumbling your crooked lot will be set straight, for Heaven frequently raises the fallen and enriches the poor in strange, unheard of and circuitous ways, inconceivable by man.'

Don Quixote was just going to thank him when they heard behind them a noise as of a troop of horse, though it proved to be only one, ridden at full gallop by a youth of apparently twenty, dressed in green damask breeches and a loose coat braided with gold, with a hat turned up in the Walloon fashion, tight-fitting boots, and gilt spurs, dagger and sword. He carried a small firelock in his hand and two pistols by his sides. At the noise Roque turned his head and saw this handsome figure, who cried as he drew near to him: 'I was coming to look for you, valorous Roque, to find in you, if not a cure, at least a relief for my affliction. And not to keep you in suspense, for I see that you have not recognized me, I will tell you who I am. I am Claudia Jeronima, daughter of Simon Forte, your particular friend, and the sworn enemy of Clauquel Torrellas, who is also yours, as he is one of the opposite faction. Now you know that this Torrellas has a son called Don Vicente Torrellas, or at least he was so called two hours ago. He, then – to cut short the tale of my misfortunes I will tell you briefly what he has brought upon me – he saw me and courted me; I listened to him and fell in love with him, unknown to my father; for there is no woman, however secluded or reserved, who has not time enough to carry her unruly desires into effect. In short, he promised to be my husband and I gave him my word to be his wife, though we went no further than that. But yesterday I learnt that he had forgotten his obligations to me and was going to marry another, and that the ceremony was to take place this morning. The news confused my senses and I lost all patience. So, as my father was not in town, I found means of putting on the dress you see and, spurring on my horse, overtook Don Vicente about three miles from here. Then without stopping to make him reproaches or to listen to excuses I fired this gun at him and these two pistols into the bargain, and I believe I must have lodged more than two bullets in his body, thus washing my honour clean in his blood. And there I left him surrounded by his servants, who dared not or could not interfere in his defence. Now I have come to ask you to pass me over into France, where I have relations with whom I can live, and also to beg you to defend my father, so that Don Vicente's many friends may not venture to take their cruel revenge on him.'

Struck with the fair Claudia's gallantry and boldness, with her handsome figure and strange story, Roque said: 'Come, lady, and let us see if your enemy is dead. Then afterwards we will see what we can best do for you.'

But Don Quixote, who had been listening eagerly to Claudia's words and Roque Guinart's reply, broke in: 'No one need trouble himself to defend this lady, for I take it upon myself. Give me my horse and my arms, and wait for me here. I will go and seek this knight and, dead or alive, I will make him keep his pledged word to this beauty.'

'Let no one doubt that,' said Sancho, 'My master's a very good hand at match-making, for it's not many days ago that he made another man marry, who'd also refused to keep his promise to a maiden. And if it hadn't been for the enchanters who persecute him, changing his true shape into a lackey's, that maiden would have been one no longer by this time.'

Roque, who was more concerned with the fair Claudia's adventure than with the speeches of master and man, paid no attention to them, but commanded his squires to return to Sancho all that they had taken off Dapple, and to withdraw to the place where they had been quartered the night before. Then he set out with Claudia in great haste to look for the wounded or dead Don Vicente.

They came to the spot where Claudia had met him, but found nothing there but recently spilled blood. Gazing in all directions, however, they made out some people on a hillside, and concluded rightly that this must be Don Vicente, whom his servants were carrying, alive or dead, to cure him or to bury him. They hurried to catch them up; and as the procession was going slowly, they easily did so, finding Don Vicente in the servants' arms, begging them in a weak and weary voice to leave him to die, for the pain of his wounds would not allow of his going any further.

Claudia and Roque jumped down from their horses and went to him. The servants were frightened at Roque's presence, and Claudia was disturbed at the sight of Don Vicente. So that it was half compassionately and half severely that she went up to him and said, taking him by the hands: 'Had you but given me these hands and kept our compact, you would not have come to this pass.'

The wounded gentleman opened his almost closed eyes and, recognizing Claudia, replied: 'Now I see, fair and deluded mistress, that it was you who killed me, a punishment I never deserved nor earned, for neither in my desires nor in my actions have I ever so much as wished to do you wrong.'

'Then it is not true,' cried Claudia, 'that you were going this morning to marry Leonora, rich Balvastro's daughter?'

'No, certainly not,' answered Don Vicente. 'It must have been my ill-luck that brought you that news, so that you might bereave me of my life out of jealousy. But I count my lot fortunate since I die in your arms. And, to prove to you that this is true, hold my hand and take me for your husband, if you will; for I can give you no other satisfaction for the injury you imagine you have received from me.'

Claudia wrung his hand and was herself wrung to the heart, falling in a faint upon Don Vicente's bloody breast, as the death spasm seized him. Roque was perplexed and did not know what to do. The servants ran for water to throw in their faces, and returned to sprinkle them with it. Claudia recovered from her faint, but not Don Vicente from his paroxysm, for his life was done. When Claudia saw this and realized that her sweet husband no longer lived, she rent the air with her sobs, wounded the Heavens with her lamentations, tore her hair, tossing it to the winds, disfigured her face with her hands, and showed all the signs of grief and sorrow that could be expected from a wounded heart.

'Cruel and unthinking woman,' she cried, 'how easily were you moved to carry out your evil purpose! Jealousy, you raging fury, to what a desperate end you bring her that harbours you in her bosom! O my husband, whose luckless fate has brought you from the bridal bed to the grave, because of your pledge to me!'

So piteous, indeed, were Claudia's plaints that they brought tears to Roque's eyes, though he was not used to weeping. The servants wept; Claudia swooned again and again; and all around seemed a scene of grief and misfortune. At length Roque Guinart ordered Don Vicente's servants to take his body to his father's place, which was near, to give him burial. Claudia told Roque that she would retire to a nunnery where an aunt of hers was abbess, and there she meant to end her days in the company of a better and more eternal spouse. Roque commended her pious resolution, offering to accompany her wherever she pleased, and to defend her father from Don Vicente's relations and from all the world, if they should seek to

injure him. Claudia would on no account accept his company, however, but, thanking him for his proposal in the best words she
could find, took her leave of him in tears. Don Vicente's servants
lifted the body, and Roque returned to his men. So ended the loves
of Claudia Jeronima. But was it surprising, seeing that the cruel and
invincible hands of jealousy wove the web of her lamentable
story?

Roque Guinart found his squires where he had ordered them to
be, and Don Quixote among them, mounted on Rocinante and
making them a speech, to persuade them to give up their style of
life, as perilous for the soul as for the body. But as most of them
were Gascons, a wild and unruly people, Don Quixote's address
did not affect them much. When Roque got back he asked Sancho
Panza whether his men had restored to him the jewels and property
they had taken from Dapple. Sancho replied that they had, but that
three kerchiefs were missing, worth three cities.

'What's that you say, man?' cried one of them. 'I have them, and
they're not worth three *reals*.'

'That is right,' said Don Quixote, 'but my squire values them at
the price he said on account of the person who gave me them.'

Roque Guinart ordered them to be immediately restored; then,
commanding his men to form a line, he bade them produce before
him all the clothing, jewels and money, and everything else that
they had stolen since the last share-out. Then, making a quick esti-
mate and reducing whatever could not be divided into its money
value, he shared it all out among his band with such careful impartiality that there was not one of them who got a farthing more
or less than another. And after this share-out, which left everyone
satisfied and pleased, Roque said to Don Quixote: 'If I were not
so scrupulous with these men, it wouldn't be possible to live with
them.'

Whereupon Sancho remarked: 'Well, justice must be a very
good thing, for here I see that it has to be practised even among
thieves.'

Now this remark of his was overheard by one of the squires,
who raised the butt of his gun, and would no doubt have split
Sancho's skull with it if Roque Guinart had not called to him to
stop. Sancho was scared and decided not to open his lips again so

long as he was in that company. At that moment there ran up one or more of the squires who had been posted as sentinels on the roads to observe all travellers and to keep their chief informed of all that passed.

'Sir,' said this scout, 'there's a great troop of people not far away, coming on the Barcelona road.'

'Have you made out whether they are coming to look for us, or whether they're the sort we look for?' asked Roque.

'They're the sort we seek, every one of them,' answered the squire.

'Then out, all of you,' commanded Roque, 'and bring them here to me. Don't let one escape.'

They obeyed, leaving Don Quixote, Sancho and Roque on their own, anxious to see what would follow. And meanwhile Roque said to Don Quixote: 'This life of ours must seem novel to Don Quixote: strange adventures, strange incidents, and all of them perilous. And I don't wonder if it appears so to him, for I truly admit that there's no way of life more disturbed and full of alarms than ours. I was driven to it by certain desires for revenge, powerful enough to disturb the calmest minds. By nature I am compassionate and good-natured; but, as I have said, the thirst to revenge an injury has so overborne all my good resolutions that I continue in this career despite my conscience. And as deep calls to deep and one sin to another, one feud has linked on to the next until I am involved not only in my own but in those of others. But God is so good that, although entangled in the labyrinth of confusions, I have not lost hope of escaping to a safe harbour.'

Don Quixote was surprised to hear this good and sensible statement, for he had not expected to find a man of such understanding among thieves, murderers and highway robbers. 'Sir Roque,' he replied, 'the beginning of health lies in the knowledge of the disease, and in the sick man's willingness to take the medicines the doctor prescribes. You are sick; you know your complaint, and Heaven, or rather God, who is our doctor, will apply medicines to cure you, medicines which generally cure slowly, not suddenly and by a miracle. What is more, wise sinners are nearer to a cure than foolish ones, and since you have shown your good sense in your speech, you have only to keep up your courage, and hope for an improvement in the sickness of your conscience. But if you would shorten the journey and set yourself easily on the path of your salvation, come with me, and I will teach you to be a knight errant, a calling beset with such toils and misfortunes as, taken as a penance, will carry you to Heaven in a twinkling.'

Roque laughed at Don Quixote's advice and, changing the subject, related Claudia Jeronima's tragic adventure, which moved Sancho deeply, for he had been no little attracted by the girl's beauty, boldness and spirit.

By this time the squires had arrived with their capture, bringing with them two gentlemen on horseback, two pilgrims on foot, and a coach full of women, with some half a dozen servants mounted and on foot, who were of their company, and two muleteers, who followed the gentlemen. The squires were all round them, and victors and vanquished alike kept a profound silence, waiting for the great Roque Guinart to speak. First he asked the gentlemen their names, where they were going and what money they were carrying, to which one of them replied: 'Sir, we are two captains in the Spanish infantry. Our companies are at Naples, and we are going to embark on one of four galleys, which are said to be at Barcelona under orders to sail for Sicily. We have two or three hundred crowns with us, and account ourselves rich. For such is the habitual poverty of soldiers that we are content with a little wealth.'

Roque asked the pilgrims the same questions as the captains, and their reply was that they were going to take ship and cross to Rome, and that between the two of them they might have about sixty *reals*. He also desired to learn who was travelling in the coach, to what place, and with what money, and one of the horsemen replied: 'My mistress, Doña Guiomar de Quiñones, wife of the President of the Naples Tribunal, with a small daughter, a maid and a waiting-woman, travel in this coach. There are six of us servants attending her, and our money is six hundred crowns.'

'So,' said Roque Guinart, 'we have here nine hundred crowns and sixty *reals*. My soldiers must be about sixty in number. Reckon out how much this comes to for each, for I am bad at figures.'

On hearing this the robbers raised a shout of: 'Long live Roque Guinart, and to hell with the villains who seek his ruin!'

The captains showed their distress; the President's lady looked sad; and the pilgrims were not too cheerful at seeing their goods confiscated. Roque kept them for a while in suspense, but he had no mind to prolong their suffering, which could be seen from a mile off. So, turning to the captains, he said: 'Have the kindness, Master Captains, to lend me sixty crowns, and you, Lady President, eighty to satisfy this troop that attends me, for the abbot must eat that sings for his meat. And then you can go your ways free and un-molested, with a safe conduct which I will give you so that if you meet another of my bands which are scattered about these parts they may do you no harm; for it is not my desire to injure soldiers, nor ladies, especially no lady of quality.'

The captains were liberal and eloquent in their acknowledgments of Roque's courtesy and generosity, for so they regarded his leaving them their own money. The lady, Doña Guiomar de Quiñones, wanted to jump out of the coach and kiss the great Roque's hands and feet; but he would not allow her to do so on any account. On the contrary, he begged her pardon for the injury he was forced to do her, to comply with the strict obligations of his wicked calling. The President's lady ordered one of her servants to give him at once the eighty crowns which had been assessed as her contribution, and the captains had already paid out their sixty. The pilgrims were go-ing to hand over their little all, but Roque told them to wait, and turned to his men, saying: 'Two of these crowns go to each of you, and there are twenty men. Let ten be given to these pilgrims, and the other ten to this good squire, so that he may be able to speak well of us and our doings.'

Then bringing out writing materials, with which he always kept himself provided, Roque gave them a written safe-conduct for the chiefs of his bands and, taking leave of them, let them go free, all admiring his generosity, his gallant bearing and strange conduct, and regarding him rather as an Alexander the Great than as a notorious robber.

Then one of his squires said in his Catalan dialect: 'This captain of ours is more like a friar than a highwayman. But if he wants to show himself generous in future, let it be with his own possessions, not with ours.'

The unfortunate fellow did not speak softly enough for his words to escape Roque, who drew his sword and almost cut the man's head in two, saying: 'That's how I punish mutinous babblers.'

Everyone was terror-stricken, and no one dared say a word, such was the awe they held him in.

Roque then drew to one side and wrote a letter to one of his friends at Barcelona, informing him that he had with him the famous Don Quixote de la Mancha, the knight errant of whom there had been such reports; and that he was the most entertaining and sensible fellow in the world. In four days' time, he continued, on St. John the Baptist's day, he would present himself in the middle of the city Strand, in full armour, on his horse Rocinante, with his squire Sancho on an ass; and he bade him advise his friends the Niarros of this, so that they might amuse themselves at his expense. But he wanted his enemies the Cadells to miss that pleasure, though that would be impossible because Don Quixote's deeds, both crazy and sensible, and the drolleries of his squire, Sancho Panza, could not fail to afford general amusement to all the world. This letter Roque despatched by one of his squires, who changed his highwayman's dress for a peasant's, and went into Barcelona to deliver it to the person to whom it was addressed.

Chapter LXI. *What happened to Don Quixote on his entering Barcelona, with other matters containing more truth than wisdom.*

THREE days and three nights Don Quixote stayed with Roque, and if it had been three hundred years he would still have found new matter for observation and wonder in his mode of life. They began the day in one place; they dined in another; sometimes they fled and did not know from whom; at other times they waited for whom they knew not. They slept on their feet, interrupting their sleep to move from one spot to another. It was all sending out spies, listening to scouts, and blowing the matches of fire-locks, though they had only a few of these, for almost all of them used flint-locks. Roque would spend the night away from his men, they had no idea where, for the numerous proclamations which the Viceroy of Barcelona had published against him, setting a price on his head, kept him in continual apprehension. He could trust

E E

nobody, and even feared that his own men would kill him or hand him over to justice; a truly miserable and wearisome life.

Finally by unfrequented roads, by cross-ways and secret paths, Roque, Don Quixote and Sancho set out with six squires for Barcelona. They reached the Strand on St. John's Eve at night, and Roque embraced Don Quixote and Sancho – to whom he gave the ten crowns he had promised, but not handed over till then – and left them with countless offers of service made on both sides. Roque turned back, and Don Quixote remained waiting for day, mounted and just as he was; and it was not long before the fair face of dawn began to peep from the balconies of the East, cheering the grass and the flowers. And their ears were regaled at the same instant by the sound of countless oboes and kettledrums, the ringing of morrice-bells, and the 'Tramp, tramp! Make way, make way!' of people, who appeared to be coming from the city. Dawn gave way to the sun, whose face broader than a shield gradually rose from below the horizon. Then Don Quixote and Sancho gazed in all directions, and saw the sea, which they had never seen before. It appeared to them very broad and spacious, and a good deal bigger than the lagoons of Ruidera, which they had seen in La Mancha. They saw the galleys lying off the Strand, which, with their awnings down, appeared decked with streamers and pennants that fluttered in the wind and kissed and swept the water. From on board there rang out clarions, trumpets and oboes which filled the air near and far with sweet martial music. Then they began to move, and carry out a kind of mock skirmish on the calm waters; and a crowd of gentlemen, riding out from the city, on fine horses and magnificently attired, seemed to be carrying out corresponding movements. The soldiers in the galleys fired countless pieces of artillery, to which those on the city walls and in the forts replied, and the heavy artillery rent the air with its dreadful roar, to be answered by the cannon on board the galleys. The cheerful sea, the joyous land, and the sky, clear though sometimes clouded by the smoke of the artillery, seemed to rouse and spread a sudden gaiety among all the people. Sancho could not imagine how those great bulks he saw moving on the sea could have so many feet.

By this time the gaily clad horsemen had galloped up with cries, cheers and shouts to the place where Don Quixote was standing in amazement and stupefaction; and one of them, the recipient of

Roque's letter, addressed the knight in loud tones: 'Welcome to our city, mirror, beacon, star and pole-star of all knight errantry,' – and so on and so forth. 'Welcome, I say, to the valorous Don Quixote de la Mancha! – not the false, not the fictitious, not the apocryphal Don who has lately been shown us in false histories, but the true, the legitimate and genuine knight, described to us by Cide Hamete Benengeli, flower of historians!'

Don Quixote replied never a word, nor did the gentlemen expect him to answer; but, wheeling about with all their followers, they began to execute a complicated curvet around Don Quixote, who turned to Sancho and said: 'These people have clearly recognized us. I will wager they have read our history, and the lately printed Aragonese one as well.'

Then the gentleman who had spoken to Don Quixote addressed him once more: 'Come with us, Don Quixote, for we are all your servants and true friends of Roque Guinart.'

To which Don Quixote replied: 'If courtesies breed courtesies, yours, Sir Knight, is a daughter or a very close relation of the great Roque's. Take me where you please, for I am wholly at your disposal, especially if you wish to employ me in your service.'

The gentleman replied in no less polite terms and, clustering round him, they all set out for the city to the sound of the oboes and kettle-drums. But as they entered the Evil One, who is master of all mischief, and the boys, who are wickeder than the Evil One – or two mischievous, insolent lads at least mingled with the crowd, and one of them lifting Dapple's tail and the other Rocinante's, fastened a bunch of furze to each. The poor animals felt these strange spurs, and by swishing their tails aggravated their pain to such an extent that with a thousand capers they threw their riders to the ground. Insulted and furious, Don Quixote ran to rid his old horse's tail of its plumage, and Sancho did the same for Dapple. Don Quixote's escort had a mind to punish the boys' insolence, but that was impossible, for they had worked themselves in among the thousands who were following. So Don Quixote and Sancho remounted and, amidst the same acclamations and music, reached their guide's house, a large and important one, which proclaimed the wealth of its owner. And there we will leave them for the present, for Cide Hamete would have it so.

Chapter LXII. *The adventure of the Enchanted Head; with other childish matters which cannot be omitted.*

DON QUIXOTE's host was called Don Antonio Moreno, a rich and intelligent gentleman and very fond of honest and decent entertainment. So when he found the Knight in his house he cast about for innocent ways of bringing out his eccentricities, for the jest that wounds is no jest, and amusements are worth less if they involve injury. The first thing he did was to make Don Quixote take off his armour and show himself in his tight chamois-skin doublet – which has been mentioned and described already – on a balcony giving on to one of the principal streets of the city in sight of the populace and the boys, who gazed at him as though he had been a monkey. The horsemen in their gala dress began to career before him once more, as though they had put on their finery for him alone and not to celebrate the festival; and Sancho was highly delighted, imagining that somehow or other he had stumbled on another Camacho's wedding, another house like Don Diego Miranda's, another castle like the Duke's.

Don Antonio had some of his friends dining with him that day, and they all did Don Quixote honour, treating him like a knight errant, at which he was puffed up with vainglory and could not contain himself for pleasure. And such were Sancho's droll sayings that all the servants of the house and everyone who heard him hung on his lips. And when they were at table Don Antonio addressed Sancho: 'We have heard here, honest Sancho, that you are so fond of minced chicken blancmange and forcemeat balls that if you have any left you stuff them into your shirt for another day.'

'No, sir, that's not true,' answered Sancho, 'for I'm more cleanly than greedy, and my master Don Quixote, who is here present, knows very well that the pair of us often go for eight days together on a handful of acorns or nuts. It's true that sometimes if they happen to give me the heifer I run with the rope; I mean to say that I eat what I'm given, and use my opportunities as I find them; but you can take it from me that if anyone says I'm an inordinate and dirty eater he's wide of the mark; and I would say it in another way but for my respect for the honourable beards here at table.'

'I assure you,' said Don Quixote, 'that the frugality and cleanliness with which Sancho eats might be written and engraved on sheets of brass, to remain as an everlasting memorial for future ages. It is true that when he is hungry he appears something of a gobbler, for he eats fast and chews on both sides of his mouth. But in cleanliness he is most punctilious, and at the time when he was governor he learnt to eat delicately; so much so that he used to eat grapes, and even the seeds of the pomegranate, with a fork.'

'What!' exclaimed Don Antonio, 'has Sancho been a governor?'

'Yes,' answered Sancho, 'of an isle called Barataria. Ten days I governed it as well as you could ask, and in that time I lost my rest and learnt to despise all the governorships in the world. I ran away from it, and fell into a cave, where I gave myself up for dead and escaped alive only by a miracle.'

Don Quixote related in detail the whole episode of Sancho's government, which afforded his hearers the greatest amusement. Then, when the cloths were removed, Don Antonio took the knight by the hand and led him into a private room, where there was no other furniture but a table, apparently of jasper, supported on a stand of the same material on which stood a bust, seemingly of bronze, in the style of the heads of Roman emperors. Don Antonio paced up and down the room with Don Quixote, taking several turns round the table, and after some time observed: 'Now that I am certain, Don Quixote, that no one is listening or can hear us, and the door is shut, I will tell you of one of the extraordinary circumstances, or rather wonders, imaginable, on condition that what I shall communicate be deposited in the inmost, secret recesses of your heart.'

'I swear it shall,' replied Don Quixote; 'and I will even throw a flagstone over it, for greater security. Since I would have you know, Don Antonio' – for by now he had learnt his host's name – 'that you are talking to one who, though he has ears to hear, has no tongue to betray. Therefore you may safely convey what lies in your breast into mine, and be assured it is cast into the abysses of silence.'

'Trusting in that pledge,' replied Don Antonio, 'I will at once strike you with amazement, and somewhat relieve myself from the discomfort of having no one to communicate my secrets to; for they are not fit to be entrusted to all.'

Don Quixote waited in bewilderment for the outcome of all these precautions. Then Don Antonio took hold of his hand and passed it over the bronze head, along the table, and down the jasper stand on which it stood, and then said: 'This head, Don Quixote, was made by one of the greatest enchanters and sorcerers the world has ever known. I believe he was a Pole by race and a disciple of the famous Escotillo, of whom so many wonders are told. He was here in my house, and at the price of a thousand crowns constructed this head, which has the virtue and property of answering any questions spoken into its ear. He took the bearings, drew the figures, observed the stars, marked the seconds, and completed his work as we shall see tomorrow. For on Fridays it is silent and, today being Friday, we shall have to wait until tomorrow. During that time you will be able to decide on your questions, and I know by experience that its answers will be the truth.'

Don Quixote was amazed at this description of the head, and inclined to disbelieve Don Antonio; but, seeing how little time he had to wait before making a trial, he preferred to say nothing, but only to thank his host for revealing so great a secret to him. They then left the room, Don Antonio locked the door, and the two of them went into the hall where the other gentlemen were sitting. In the meanwhile Sancho had told them many of the adventures and incidents which had befallen his master.

That afternoon they took Don Quixote through the city, clad not in armour but in street dress, a long overcoat of tawny cloth which would have made the very ice sweat at that season. They gave their servants orders to keep Sancho entertained, and not to let him leave the house. Don Quixote rode, not on Rocinante but on a big, easy-paced mule with very fine trappings, and when they put on him his overcoat they stitched a parchment to his back, without his noticing it, on which they had written in large letters: '*This is Don Quixote de la Mancha.*' Now as soon as they began their tour the scroll attracted general attention, and as a great number of passers by read it Don Quixote was astonished to find that many people recognized him and greeted him by name. So much so that he turned to Don Antonio, who was riding at his side, and observed: 'Great is the prerogative that lies in knight errantry, since it makes its professors known and famous through all the ends of the earth. For look, Don Antonio, even the boys of this city know me, though they have never seen me before.'

'That is so, Don Quixote,' replied Don Antonio, 'for just as fire cannot be hidden and confined, virtue cannot fail to be recognized; and that virtue which is achieved by the profession of arms out-shines and excels all others.'

Now, as Don Quixote was riding along amidst the acclamations described, a certain Castilian happened to read the scroll on his back and exclaimed very loudly: 'The devil take Don Quixote de la Mancha! How have you got here alive after all the beatings you've received? You're a madman. If you had been mad in private and behind closed doors you would have done less harm. But you have the knack of turning everyone who has to do with you into mad-men and dolts. Just look at these gentlemen riding with you! Go back home, idiot, and look after your estate and your wife and children, and quit this nonsense that worm-eats your brain and skims the cream off your intellect.'

'Get along with you, fellow,' said Don Antonio, 'and don't offer advice where it isn't asked for. Don Quixote de la Mancha is a man of good sense, and we that ride with him are no fools. Virtue must be honoured wherever it's found. Go away and bad luck to you, and don't meddle where you aren't wanted.'

'Indeed you're right, your worship,' replied the Castilian, 'for to offer this fellow advice is to kick against the pricks. But it dis-tresses me all the same that this idiot's reputed good sense should waste away along the channel of knight errantry. But bad luck to me and all my descendants if from now on, should I live more years than Methusaleh, I offer advice to anyone, even though he asks me for it.'

The counsellor then departed and the tour continued; but so great was the crush of boys and people reading the scroll that Don Antonio had to take it off, under the pretence of doing some other thing. When night fell they returned to the house, where a ball took place; for Don Antonio's wife, who was a lady of rank, gay, good-looking and intelligent, had invited some of her friends to come and honour her guest and enjoy his strange humours. Quite a few came, and after a splendid supper the dance began about ten o'clock. Among the ladies were two of a roguish and jocose disposition, who, although very modest, were rather free in devising jokes to afford harmless amusement. These two were so insistent on getting Don Quixote out to dance that they tired him out, body and soul. It was a sight indeed to see the knight's form, tall, lanky, lean and sallow, tightly encased in his clothes, so awkward and, even worse, by no means nimble. These ladies made up to him on the sly, and he repulsed them also surreptitiously; but, finding himself hard pressed by their advances, he raised his voice and cried: '*Fugite, partes adversae!* Leave me in peace, unwelcome thoughts. Away, master your desires, ladies, for she that is my queen, the peerless Dulcinea del Toboso, will allow no thoughts but of her to enslave and subdue me!'

So saying, he sat down on the floor in the middle of the room, wearied and shaken by the exercise of so much dancing. Don Antonio had him taken up bodily and carried to bed, and the first to lay hands on him was Sancho, who asked: 'What the devil did you mean by dancing, master? Do you think that all brave men must be dancers, and all knights errant skip around? If so you're much mistaken. I can tell you there are men bolder at killing a giant than at cutting a caper. If you had been for the clog-dance I would have taken your place, for I can do it like a goshawk, but as for dancing I can't work a stitch at it.'

The company were highly amused at Sancho's observations, and he put his master to bed, covering him up with clothes so that he should sweat out the chill he had taken from his dancing.

The next day Don Antonio decided to make the experiment with the enchanted head, and with Don Quixote, Sancho, two other friends and the two ladies who had tormented the knight at the dance and who had stayed that night with Don Antonio's wife – he locked himself up in the room that contained the head. After explaining its properties he pledged them to secrecy, saying that this was the first time the virtue of this enchanted head was to be put to the test. Now only Don Antonio's two friends knew the trick of this enchantment; and if Don Antonio had not first revealed it to them they would have been as astonished as the rest; for it was impossible not to be impressed by so ingenious and cunning a contrivance.

The first who approached the head was Don Antonio himself,

who whispered in its ear, though not so softly as not to be over-heard by everyone: 'Tell me, head, by the virtue inherent in you, what am I thinking of now?'

And the head replied without moving its lips, in a clear and distinct voice: 'I have no knowledge of thoughts.'

These words struck everyone with amazement, the more so as there was no human being in the neighbourhood of the table or in the whole room who could have spoken the reply.

'How many are we here?' asked Don Antonio again.

And the answer came in the same quiet tone: 'There are you and your wife, two friends of yours and two of hers, a famous knight called Don Quixote de la Mancha, and his squire, Sancho Panza by name.'

Here indeed was fresh cause for astonishment, and everyone's hair stood on end in pure horror. Then Don Antonio moved away from the head and said: 'This is enough to convince me that I was not cheated by the man who sold you to me, learned head, talkative head, answering head, wonderful head! Let someone else come and ask his question.'

And as women are generally impatient and inquisitive, the first to go up was one of Don Antonio's wife's two friends, and her question was: 'Tell me, head, what shall I do to be very beautiful?'

And the reply was: 'Be very chaste.'

'I have no more to ask,' said the questioner.

Then her companion went up and said: 'I should like to know, head, if my husband loves me or not.'

And the answer was: 'Think what he does for you, and you will know.'

The married woman moved away, and said, 'I might have spared it that question, for a man's actions certainly proclaim his feelings.'

Then one of Don Antonio's two friends went up and asked: 'Who am I?'

And the reply came: 'You know.'

'That doesn't answer my question,' replied the gentleman. 'I asked you to tell me whether you knew me.'

'Yes, I know you,' answered the voice. 'You are Don Pedro Noriz.'

'I don't want to know any more, for that's enough to convince me, head, that you know everything.'

Then he moved away, and the other friend went up and asked: 'Tell me, head, what are the desires of my son and heir?'

'I have already said,' came the answer, 'that I have no knowledge of wishes; but I can tell you all the same that your son would like to bury you.'

'That,' said the gentleman, 'is only too plain and palpable.' And he asked no more. Then Don Antonio's wife went up and said: 'I don't know what to ask, head. I should only like to learn from you whether I shall enjoy my dear husband for many years.'

And the answer came: 'Yes, you will, for his good health and temperance promise him long years of life, which it is the habit of many to cut short by intemperance.'

Then Don Quixote approached and asked: 'Tell me, you that reply, was it truth or a dream, the account I gave of my experiences in the cave of Montesinos? Will my squire Sancho's whipping be completed? Will Dulcinea's disenchantment come to pass?'

'As for the matter of the cave,' came the answer, 'there is much to say: it has something in it of both. Sancho's whipping will go on slowly. Dulcinea's disenchantment will be duly accomplished.'

'I wish to know no more,' said Don Quixote, 'for when I see Dulcinea disenchanted I shall reckon that all the good fortune I can desire has come to me at one fell swoop.'

The last to ask was Sancho, and his question was: 'Shall I ever get another governorship? Shall I quit this hungry squire's life? Shall I see my wife and children again?'

To which the answer came: 'You will govern in your own house; and if you go home you will see your wife and children; and by giving up service you will cease to be a squire.'

'By God, that's rich!' exclaimed Sancho Panza. 'I could have told myself all that; the prophet Perogrullo couldn't do better.'

'Animal!' cried Don Quixote. 'What answer do you expect? Is not it enough that the replies this head gives correspond to the questions asked it?'

'Yes, it's enough,' answered Sancho. 'But I wish it would be less sparing of its knowledge and tell me more.'

The questions and answers were now at an end, but there was no end to the amazement of everyone except Don Antonio's two friends who were in the secret. But Cide Hamete Benengeli would at once explain the trick for fear that the astonished world might believe that there was some magic or strange mystery in this head. So he declares that Don Antonio Moreno had it devised at home, in imitation of a head he had seen at Madrid, which was manufactured by an engraver for his own amusement and to puzzle the ignorant. Its construction was like this: the top of the table was of wood painted and varnished to look like jasper, and the stand on which it stood was of the same material, with four eagle's claws projecting from it to support the weight more firmly. The head, which looked like a bronze portrait bust of a Roman emperor, was all hollow, and so was the top of the table, into which it fitted so neatly that no sign of a joint could be seen. The stand of the table was also hollow, to correspond with the throat and head of the bust, and the whole was made to communicate with another room beneath the one where the head stood. Through all the hollows in the stand, the table, the throat and breast of the portrait bust described, ran a metal pipe, so well fitted as to be completely concealed. In the room below, corresponding to the one upstairs, stood the man who was to make the answers, with his mouth to this same pipe, so that the voice from above came down and the voice from below sounded up, clearly and articulately as through an ear trumpet, and so it was impossible to discover the trick. The answerer was a nephew of Don Antonio's, a quick and intelligent student; and as his uncle had told him who would come into the room with him that day, it was easy for him to reply promptly and correctly to the first question, and to answer the others by guesswork and, as he was a clever lad, cleverly. And Cide Hamete goes on to say that this oracular machine continued to exist for ten or twelve days, but when the rumour spread through the city that Don Antonio had in his house an enchanted head which answered all questions asked it, he was afraid that its fame might reach the ears of those watchful sentinels of our faith, so he gave an account of the matter to the Inquisitors, who ordered him to dismantle it and use it no further, for fear the ignorant rabble might be corrupted. But in Don Quixote's opinion and Sancho Panza's, the head re-

mained enchanted and oracular, which pleased Don Quixote
more than it did Sancho.

The gentlemen of the city, for Don Antonio's pleasure and to
entertain Don Quixote and give him an opportunity of displaying
his eccentricities, arranged a tilting at the ring for six days later,
but it failed to take place through an accident which shall be
described later.

Don Quixote had a desire to stroll about the city without ceremony and on foot, for he feared that the boys would bother him
if he went on horseback. So he and Sancho went out for a walk
with two servants whom Don Antonio lent him. Now, as they
were going down a street, Don Quixote happened to raise his eyes,
and saw written over a door in very large letters: '*Books printed
here*', which greatly pleased him, for he had never before seen any
printing and longed to know how it was done. So he went in with
all his followers, and saw them drawing off the sheets in one place,
correcting the proofs in another, setting up the type in a third and
revising in yet another – in fact he saw all the processes of a large
printing-house. Don Quixote went up to one compartment and
asked what they were doing there. The workmen explained to him;
and he watched in wonder and passed on. Then he went up to
another man and asked him what he was doing, and the workman
replied: 'Sir, that gentleman you see there –' and he pointed out a
handsome, important looking fellow with a serious air – 'has
translated an Italian book into our Castilian tongue, and I am setting
it up for the press.'

'What is the title of the book?' asked Don Quixote.

'Sir,' replied the author, 'the book in Italian is called "*Le
Bagatelle.*"'

'And what corresponds to *Le Bagatelle* in our Castilian?' asked
Don Quixote.

'*Le Bagatelle,*' said the author, 'is, one might say, *The Trifles*
in Castilian; but though this book is humble in its title it has good
solid things in it.'

'I know a little Italian,' said Don Quixote, 'and pride myself
on singing some of Ariosto's stanzas. But tell me, sir – and I do
not ask because I wish to test your knowledge, but out of simple
curiosity – have you ever found the word "*pignata*" in your reading?'

'Yes, often,' replied the author.

'And how do you translate it into Castilian, sir?' asked Don Quixote.

'How else,' replied the author, 'but by "*stew*"?'

'Good Heavens!' exclaimed Don Quixote, 'how advanced you are in the Italian tongue! I will lay a firm wager that where the Italian has "*piace*" you say in Castilian "*please*", and where it has "*piu*", you say "*more*", and "*su*" you translate "*above*" and "*giu*" "*beneath*".'

'Yes, of course I do,' replied the author, 'for these are their proper equivalents.'

'Yet I dare swear,' said Don Quixote, 'that you are not appreciated by the world, which is always loath to reward intellect and merit. What abilities are lost here! What talents neglected! What virtues unappreciated! But yet it seems to me that translating from one tongue into another, unless it is from those queens of tongues Greek and Latin, is like viewing Flemish tapestries from the wrong side; for although you see the pictures, they are covered with threads which obscure them so that the smoothness and gloss of the fabric are lost; and translating from easy languages argues no talent or power of words, any more than does transcribing or copying one paper from another. By that I do not mean to imply that this exercise of translation is not praiseworthy, for a man might be occupied in worse things and less profitable occupations. I except from this observation two famous translators: the first Doctor Cristobal de Figueroa for his *Pastor Fido*, and the other Don Juan de Jáuregui for his *Aminta*, which leave you in doubt which is the translation and which the original. But tell me, sir, is this book printed on your own account or have you sold the copyright to a bookseller?'

'I am printing it on my own account,' replied the author, 'and I expect to gain a thousand ducats at least from this first edition of two thousand copies. They will sell like hot cakes at six *reals* apiece.'

'You are very good at figures,' said Don Quixote, 'but it is very clear that you do not know the tricks of the printing trade or the arrangements printers make with one another. When you find yourself saddled with two thousand copies of a book you will find

your back so sore that it will frighten you, I promise you, particularly if the book is a little out of the way and not a bit spicy.'

'What then?' exclaimed the author. 'Would you have me give
it to a bookseller, who will pay me three farthings for the copyright and even think he's doing me a kindness by giving me that?
I don't print my books to win fame in the world, for I am already
known by my works. I want profit, for fame isn't worth a bean
without it.'

'God send you good luck,' replied Don Quixote. And he passed
on to another compartment where he found them correcting a sheet
of a book called *Light of the Soul*, on seeing which he said:
'Books like this, numerous though they are, are the kind that ought
to be printed, for there are many sinners nowadays, and there is
need of infinite light for so many in the dark.'

He went on farther and saw them also correcting another book;
and when he asked its title they replied that it was the *Second part
of the Ingenious Gentleman Don Quixote de la Mancha*, composed
by someone or other, native of Tordesillas.

'I have heard of this book already,' said Don Quixote, 'but
truly, on my conscience, I thought it had been burnt by now and
reduced to ashes for its presumption. But it will get its Martinmas
like every hog. Works of invention are only good in so far as they
adhere to truth or verisimilitude; and general history is the better
for being well authenticated.'

With these words he left the printing-house, with some signs of
annoyance. That same day Don Antonio arranged for him to be
taken to see the galleys lying off the Strand, which delighted Sancho
greatly because he had never seen any in all his life. Don Antonio
informed the commodore that he was going to bring him a guest
that afternoon — the famous Don Quixote de la Mancha, of whom
he and all the inhabitants of the city had heard. But what happened
then shall be told in the next chapter.

Chapter LXIII. *Of the Disaster that befell Sancho Panza on his visit to the Galleys, and the strange adventure of the fair Moorish girl.*

PROFOUND were Don Quixote's reflections over the enchanted head's reply, but none of them hit on the trick, and all centred on Dulcinea's promised disenchantment, which he regarded as certain. To that he returned again and again, and rejoiced in his heart in the belief that he would speedily see its accomplishment. As for Sancho, although he loathed being a governor, as has been said, he still longed to rule again and be obeyed; for such are the evil effects of authority, even of mock authority.

That afternoon Don Antonio Moreno, their host, and his two friends accompanied Don Quixote and Sancho to the galleys. The commodore had been warned of their coming, and as soon as the famous pair reached the shore all the galleys struck their awnings and sounded their clarions. Then they immediately launched a pinnace covered with rich carpets and cushions of crimson velvet, and the moment Don Quixote set foot aboard the captain's galley all the rest discharged their midship guns. Then as Don Quixote climbed the starboard ladder, the whole crew saluted him with three cheers, as is the custom when an important person boards a galley. The General, for so we shall call him, who was a Valencian gentleman of quality, gave Don Quixote his hand, and embraced him, saying: 'I shall mark to-day with a white stone – for I do not expect to spend a better one in all my life than this day of my meeting with Don Quixote de la Mancha – as a sign that in him is contained and epitomised all the valour of knight errantry.'

Don Quixote replied to him in no less courteous terms, immeasurably delighted to find himself treated in so lordly a fashion. They all went on to the poop, which was very well decorated, and sat down on the side benches. Then the boatswain passed along the gangway and gave a signal on his whistle for the crew to strip off their shirts, which they did in a second. Sancho was startled to see so many men bare to the skin, and even more so when he saw them set the awning so quickly that it looked to him as if all the devils were at work there. But this was tarts and gingerbread to what came next. Sancho was sitting on the captain's stand, beside the last oarsman on the starboard side, who following his instructions seized Sancho and lifted him up in his arms. Then, all the crew standing ready, starting from the starboard side they sent him flying along from hand to hand and from bench to bench, so fast that poor Sancho lost the sight of his eyes, and imagined no doubt that the devils of hell were bearing him off; and they did not stop until they had sent him up the larboard side and put him down again in the poop. The poor fellow was left battered, panting and all in a sweat, unable to imagine what had happened to him. Don Quixote, who had witnessed Sancho's wingless flight, asked the general if those were the ceremonies usually practised upon persons coming aboard the galleys for the first time; for if they happened to be, he had no desire to be initiated, and would perform no such exercises; and he swore to God that if anyone presumed to lay hold on him to toss him in that manner, he would kick his soul out of his body. And as he spoke he stood up and grasped his sword.

At that very moment they struck the awning and lowered the lateen-yard from the top of the mast to the bottom with a tremendous noise. Sancho thought that the sky was coming off its hinges and was going to fall on his head, which he ducked in great fear and tucked between his legs. Don Quixote did not find it much to his liking either, for he too began to tremble, hunching his shoulders and visibly blanching. The crew hoisted the yard with the same speed and clatter with which they had lowered it, and all this in silence, as if they had neither voice nor breath. The boatswain gave the signal to weigh anchor and, leaping into the middle of the gangway, began to tickle the crew's backs with his whip or hide-strap; and gradually they put out to sea. When Sancho saw so many red feet — for such he thought the oars to be — moving as one, he said to himself: 'Here are things really and truly enchanted, as the things my master talks of are not. What have these wretches done that they flog them so? And how does this single man, who goes about whistling, have the audacity to whip all these people? Surely this is hell, or at least purgatory.'

Seeing with what attention Sancho was watching events, Don Quixote said to him: 'O friend Sancho, how quickly and at how little cost you could strip yourself to the waist, if you would, and take your place among these gentlemen to complete Dulcinea's disenchantment. For with so many companions in torment you would not feel much yourself; besides, the sage Merlin might perhaps reckon each of these lashes, being well laid on, as ten of those you will have to give yourself in the end.'

The General was going to enquire about those lashes and about Dulcinea's disenchantment, when a sailor cried out: 'Montjuich is signalling that there's a vessel with oars on the coast along the western shore.'

When he heard this the General leapt into the gangway and cried: 'Pull, my lads! Don't let it get away! It must be an Algerian pirate brigantine the watch tower is signalling.'

The other three galleys then caught up the flagship for orders. The General commanded two of them to stand out to sea, intending to keep along the coast himself with the third, for then the vessel could not escape them. The crew plied their oars, driving the galleys forward with such fury that they seemed to be flying. When the galleys that had put out to sea were about two miles off, they sighted a vessel which they judged to be of fourteen or fifteen banks or oars – and so it proved. When this vessel made out the galleys she took to flight, in the hope of getting away by her speed. But things went badly for her, as the flagship was one of the fastest craft sailing the seas, and gained on her so rapidly that the crew of the brigantine plainly realised that they could not escape. Therefore their commander would have had his men abandon their oars and surrender, for fear of exasperating the captain commanding the galleys. But Fortune ordained otherwise, and so it was that when the flagship had got near enough for those aboard the pirate ship to hear the shouted summons to surrender, two Toraquis – that is to say two drunken Turks – out of the fourteen in the brigantine fired their muskets and killed two soldiers who were posted on our forecastle. At this sight the General swore not to leave a single man in the vessel alive, but as he began to attack with extreme fury she slipped away under the flagship's oars. The galley shot some distance ahead, and when the pirates saw that they had escaped they made sail while the galley was turning, and once more set off with sail and oar. But this rash attempt only led to their undoing, for the flagship overtook them within little more than half a mile and, clapping her oars on them, caught them all alive. The two other galleys had come up by this time, and all four returned with their prize to the shore, where a vast crowd was waiting for them, eager to see their capture. The General cast anchor near the land, and sent a pinnace for the Viceroy of the city, whom he had recognized on the Strand. Then he ordered the lateen-yard to be lowered so as to hang the commander out of hand, and the rest of the pirates he had caught in the vessel, about thirty-six in number, all stout fellows, and most of them Turkish musketeers. The General asked who was master of the brigantine, and he was answered in Castilian by one of the captives, who afterwards proved to be a Spanish renegade: 'This young man here, sir, is our master.'

And he pointed to a lad who seemed to be hardly twenty, one of the handsomest and gallantest youths imaginable. Then the General questioned him: 'Tell me, rash dog, what made you kill my soldiers, for you saw it was impossible for you to escape. Is this the respect due to a captain's galley? Do you not know that temerity is not valour? Faint hopes should make men bold but not rash.'

The master would have replied, but the General could not for the moment attend to his answer, having to go and receive the Viceroy, who was just coming aboard the galley, and with him some of his attendants and several people of the city.

'It has been a fine chase, Sir General,' said the Viceroy.

'How good,' replied the General, 'your Excellency will presently see hanging on this yard-arm.'

'How so?' asked the Viceroy.

'Because,' replied the General, 'they have killed two soldiers of mine against all law and against all right and usage of war, two of the best soldiers sailing on these galleys; and I have sworn to hang every man I have captured, and this youth in particular, who is master of the brigantine.' And he pointed him out, with his hands tied and the rope round his neck, awaiting death.

The Viceroy looked at him, and when he saw him so handsome, so gallant and so resigned, the youth's beauty gave him an instant letter of recommendation, and the Viceroy felt a great desire to save him from death. 'Tell me, captain,' he asked him, 'are you a Turk by race, or a Moor, or a renegade?' And the youth replied in the same Castilian tongue: 'I am neither Turk, Moor, nor renegade.'

'Then what are you?' asked the Viceroy.

'A Christian woman,' answered the youth.

'A woman, and a Christian? In such a dress, and such a plight? This is marvellous but hardly credible.'

'Suspend my execution, gentlemen,' said the youth, 'for you'll not lose much by deferring your vengeance while I tell you my life's story.'

Could anyone be so hard-hearted as not to be mollified by these words, or as not at least to listen to what that sad, pitiable youth had to tell? The General bade him say what he would, but not hope to be pardoned for his notorious offence. With this permission the youth began to speak as follows: 'I was born of that nation, unhappy and unwise, on which a sea of misfortune has lately fallen. I was born of Moorish parents, and in the course of their misfortune carried to Barbary by two of my uncles. For though I protested that I was a Christian, which indeed I am, and no pretended and feigned one but a true Catholic, it was in vain. It had no influence on the officers responsible for our miserable banishment, nor would my uncles believe it either. They took it for a fiction I had invented so as to stay in the land where I was born; and so against my will they forced me to go with them. I had a Christian mother and a wise and Christian father too. I sucked the Catholic faith with my mother's milk. I was brought up with good principles, and neither in my language nor in my customs, I think, did I show any signs that I was a Moor. And with my virtues, for so I think them to be, grew such beauty as I have; and although I was very reserved and secluded, that was not enough to prevent my being seen by a young gentleman called Don Gaspar Gregorio, the eldest son of a gentleman whose estate adjoins our village. How he saw me, how we conversed, how he lost his heart to me, and I gained very little by him, would be a long story, particularly at this time when I am afraid that the cruel rope which threatens me may cut short my narrative. So I will only tell you that Don Gregorio wished to accompany me in our exile. He mingled with the Moors from other places, for he knew the language very well, and on the journey made friends with my two uncles with whom I was travelling; for my prudent and far-sighted father had left the place as soon as he heard the first proclamation of our banishment, and gone to look for some spot in foreign lands that would receive us. He left a quantity of pearls and stones of great value, with some money in Portuguese coin and gold doubloons, buried in a hiding place known only to me. He ordered me, in the event of our being expelled before his return, on no account to touch the treasure he was leaving. I obeyed him, and with my uncles, as I have said, and other relatives and friends, crossed over to Barbary. The place where we settled was Algiers – and we might as well have chosen Hell itself. The king got news of my beauty, and rumour told him of my wealth, which proved in some ways to my advantage. He summoned me before him, and asked me from what part of Spain I came, and what money and jewels I had with me. I told him the place, and that the jewels and money were still buried there, but could easily be recovered if I were to go back for them myself. All this I said in hopes that his greed might be more effective in blinding him than my beauty. But whilst he was talking to me news reached him that one of the handsomest and most gallant youths imaginable had come with me. I immediately realized that they were speaking of Don Gaspar Gregorio, whose good looks exceed all possible exaggeration. I was alarmed at the thought of Don Gregorio's danger, for among those barbarous Turks a handsome boy or youth is more highly prized than the most beautiful woman. The king immediately commanded him to be brought before him so that he might see him, and asked me whether what they said of this lad was true. Then, inspired as I believe by Heaven, I assented, but informed him that he was no man, but a woman like myself, and I begged him to let me go and dress this girl in her proper garb, so that she might display her full beauty and appear in his presence without embarrassment. He agreed, and deferred till next day the discussion of my return to Spain to bring out the hidden treasure. I talked with Don Gaspar and told him what danger he ran in appearing as a man. Then I dressed him as a Moorish woman, and that same evening brought him into the presence of the king, who was struck with admiration by the sight of him and decided to keep this maiden as a present for the Great Turk; and to avoid the danger she might run in his own women's seraglio, and out of self-distrust, he had her put into the house of some Moorish ladies of rank, who were to guard and wait on her. There they immediately took Don Gregorio. What the pair of us felt – for I cannot deny that I love him – I leave to the imagination of all parted lovers. The king presently devised a scheme for my returning to Spain in this brigantine, accompanied by two Turks – they were the ones that killed your soldiers. This Spanish renegade came with me as well' – she pointed to the man who had first spoken – 'and I know for certain that he is secretly a Christian, and set on remaining in Spain and not returning to Barbary. The rest of the brigantine's crew are Moors and Turks, who are there only to serve at the oars. But so greedy were these insolent Turks that they violated their orders that as soon as we touched Spain this renegade and I should be put ashore in Christian dress – with which we came provided. They decided first to sweep the coast and take a prize, if they could, fearing that if they landed us first we might meet with some accident which would reveal that the brigantine was at sea, and then they might be taken, if there chanced to be any galleys on that coast. Last night we sighted this shore and, not suspecting these four galleys, were discovered: you have seen our fate. The end of it is that Don Gregorio remains in woman's dress among the Moors, in manifest peril of his life, and I am here with my hands bound, expecting, or rather fearing, to lose my life, of which I am already weary. This, gentlemen, is the conclusion of my lamentable story, as true as it is wretched. But I beg of you to let me die like a Christian, since, as I have told you, I am perfectly guiltless of my nation's crime.'

There she ceased, and the tears which filled her lovely eyes drew many from those of her auditors. Then the Viceroy, who was much moved, went up to her without speaking a word, and with his own fingers untied the rope binding the Moorish girl's fair hands.

Now all the while this Christian Moor told her strange story an ancient pilgrim who had boarded the galley with the Viceroy kept his eyes fixed on her; and no sooner did she end her tale than he threw himself at her feet and embraced them, addressing her in words broken by countless sobs and sighs: 'O Anna Felix, my unhappy daughter! I am your father Ricote, returned to seek you, for I cannot live without you, who are my soul.'

At these words Sancho opened his eyes and raised his head, which he had kept lowered, brooding on his unfortunate handling. And when he looked at the pilgrim he recognized that same Ricote whom he had met on the day he left his government, and he was convinced that this was his daughter. For when she was unbound she embraced her father, mingling her tears with his. Then, turning to the General and the Viceroy, the pilgrim said: 'This, gentlemen, is my daughter, less happy in her fate than in her name. She is called Anna Felix, with the surname of Ricote, and is as famous for her beauty as for her father's riches. I left my country to seek some place in foreign parts to shelter us and take us in, and when I found it in Germany I came back in this pilgrim's habit with other Germans, to look for my daughter and dig up the great riches I had left buried. I did not find my daughter, though I did find my treasure, which I have with me. But now by the strange turn you have seen I have found a treasure which makes me still richer, my beloved daughter. If strict justice can allow the gates of mercy to be opened to our guilelessness and our united tears, extend it to us who have never thought of wronging you or in any way partaken of the designs of our people, who have rightly been expelled.'

Then Sancho spoke: 'I know Ricote well, and I'm sure it's quite true that Anna Felix is his daughter. Though as to the tale of his comings and goings and his good or bad intentions I've nothing to say.'

Everyone present was struck by this strange incident, and the General declared: 'Your tears, let me assure you, will prevent my fulfilling my oath. May you live, Anna Felix, all the years which Heaven has allotted you. But the rash and insolent men who committed the crime must pay the penalty.'

Then he immediately ordered the two Turks who had killed his soldiers to be hanged from the yard-arm. But the Viceroy earnestly entreated him not to hang them, for their action arose rather from frenzy than from design. The General acceded to the Viceroy's plea, for cold-blooded vengeance is never good. They then set about devising a plan for delivering Don Gaspar Gregorio from his peril, and Ricote offered to contribute more than two thousand ducats which he had in pearls and jewels. They discussed many schemes, but the best proposal came from the Spanish renegade, who proposed to go back to Algiers in a small vessel of about six banks of oars manned by Christian rowers, for he knew where, how, and when he could disembark, and was also acquainted with the house where Don Gaspar was kept. The General and the Viceroy were doubtful whether to rely on the renegade, or if they dare trust him with a Christian crew. But Anna Felix answered for him, and her father Ricote promised to pay the Christians' ransoms, if by chance they were captured.

When they had agreed on these plans the Viceroy returned on shore, and Don Antonio Moreno bore the Moorish girl and her father off with him, with the Viceroy's injunctions to receive them and make as much of them as he could. And for his own part that dignitary offered anything in his house for their entertainment, such kindness and goodwill did Anna Felix's beauty inspire in his breast.

Chapter LXIV. *Of an adventure which gave Don Quixote more pain than any which had befallen him before.*

OUR HISTORY tells us that Antonio Moreno's wife received Anna Felix into her house with very great pleasure. She welcomed her with considerable kindness, being attracted both by her beauty and her intelligence, for the Moorish girl was remarkable for both; and all the people of the city crowded to see her, as if they had been brought together by the ringing of bells. Don Quixote told Don Antonio that their scheme for rescuing Don Gregorio was not a good one, for there was more danger than advantage in it. It would be better, he thought, for them to put him ashore in Barbary with his horse and his arms, for he would deliver him in spite of the whole breed of Moors, as Don Gaiferos had done his wife Melisendra.

'Consider, your worship,' said Sancho on hearing this, 'that when Don Gaiferos rescued his wife and took her to France it was all done on dry land; but here, if we do perhaps deliver Don Gregorio, we have no way of bringing him to Spain, for there's the sea in between.'

'There is a remedy for everything except death,' replied Don Quixote. 'We only need a vessel off the shore, and the whole world shall not prevent our boarding it.'

'Your worship paints a good picture and makes it sound easy,' said Sancho, 'but there's many a slip 'twixt cup and lip, and I'm all for the renegade. He seems a stout and likely fellow to me.'

Don Antonio replied that if the renegade did not succeed in his plan they would adopt the expedient of the great Don Quixote's passing over into Barbary. Two days later the renegade left in a light vessel of twelve oars with a very resolute crew; and after another two days the galleys sailed for the Levant, the Viceroy having promised the General to send him an account of the fortunes of Don Gregorio and Anna Felix.

Now one morning Don Quixote was riding out to take the air on the Strand, in complete armour — for, as he often said, his ornaments were arms, his rest the bloody fray, and he was never a moment without them — when he saw coming towards him a knight, also in full armour, with a shining moon painted on his shield, who, when he came near enough to be heard, cried in a loud voice, addressing his words to Don Quixote: 'Illustrious knight and never-sufficiently-praised Don Quixote de la Mancha, I am the knight of the White Moon, whose unparalleled deeds may perhaps recall his name to your memory. I have come to do battle with you and to try the strength of your arms, with the purpose of forcing you to acknowledge and confess that my mistress, let her be who she may, is incomparably more beautiful than your Dulcinea del Toboso; which truth, if you confess it fairly, will save you from death, and me from the pains of killing you. But if you fight and I vanquish you I desire no other satisfaction than that you shall forsake arms, abstain from seeking adventures, and withdraw to your own village for the period of a year, which you must pass without putting hand to sword, in profound peace and profitable ease, such as will contribute to the increase of your estate and the profit of your soul. But if you conquer me, my head shall be at your mercy, the spoils of my armour and horse shall be yours, and the renown of my deeds shall be transferred to you. Consider which is your better course, and reply quickly, for to-day is the only day I have for the despatch of this business.'

Don Quixote stood confounded and amazed, as much at the Knight of the White Moon's arrogance as at the reason for his challenge. But he replied calmly and with a severe demeanour: 'Knight of the White Moon, whose exploits have not till now come to my notice, I will make you swear that you have never seen the illustrious Dulcinea. For had you seen her I know you would have taken care not to engage in this enterprise, since the sight of her must have cured you of all belief that there has been or ever could be any beauty comparable with hers. Therefore, without giving you the lie, but merely saying that you are incorrect in your statement, I accept your challenge upon the conditions you have named, here and now, so that we shall not lose the day to which you are confined. I only except from your conditions the transfer of your renown. For I do not know what your deeds may be, and I am content with my own, such as they are. Take, then, whichever side of the field you wish, and I will do the same; and whom Heaven favours may St. Peter bless.'

The Knight of the White Moon had been observed from the city, and the Viceroy was informed that he was in conversation with Don Quixote de la Mancha. That dignitary supposed that this was some new adventure devised by Don Antonio Moreno or by some other gentleman of the city, and so rode at once to the Strand with Don Antonio and other gentlemen in attendance, just as Don Quixote was wheeling Rocinante round to take the necessary ground for his charge. Whereat, seeing that they were both just on the point of turning for the encounter, the Viceroy interposed, demanding the reason for their sudden battle. The Knight of the White Moon replied that it was a matter of pre-eminence in beauty, repeated to him shortly his challenge to Don Quixote, and informed him of the acceptance of the conditions by both parties. The Viceroy then went up to Don Antonio and asked him quietly whether he knew who this Knight of the White Moon was, or if it was some trick they were playing on Don Quixote. Don Antonio replied that he did not know who he was, nor if the challenge was in jest or earnest. This reply left the Viceroy in doubt whether to let them proceed with the battle or not; but he could not persuade himself that it was anything but a joke and so drew aside, saying: 'Sir Knight, if there is nothing else for it but to confess or die, and Don Quixote swears black and the Knight of the White Moon white, in God's hands be it, and fall to!'

The Knight of the White Moon thanked the Viceroy for his licence in polite and well-chosen terms, and Don Quixote did the

same. Then, commending himself to Heaven with all his heart and
to his Dulcinea – as was his custom at the outset of battles – he
wheeled round to take a little more ground, for he saw that his adversary was doing the same. Then, without any sound of trumpet or
other warlike instrument to give them the signal for the charge, they
both turned their horses at the same moment. But as the Knight
of the White Moon was the nimbler, he met Don Quixote two-
thirds down the course and hurtled into him with such tremendous
force that, without touching him with his lance – which he seemed
to be deliberately holding up – he brought Rocinante and Don
Quixote to the ground with a terrible fall. Then immediately
springing upon the knight, he put his lance to his vizor and cried:
'You are vanquished, knight, and if you do not acknowledge the
conditions of our challenge, you die.'

Then, battered and stunned, without lifting his vizor Don
Quixote proclaimed in a low and feeble voice, as if he were speaking
from inside a tomb: 'Dulcinea del Toboso is the most beautiful
woman in the world, and I am the most unfortunate knight on
earth; nor is it just that my weakness should discredit that truth.
Drive your lance home, knight, and rid me of life, since you have
robbed me of honour.'

'That I will not do, I swear,' said the Knight of the White Moon,
'Let the renown of the lady Dulcinea del Toboso's beauty live un-
impaired; for all the satisfaction I ask is that the great Don Quixote
de la Mancha shall retire to his village for a year, or until such time as
I please, as was agreed between us before entering upon this battle.'

The Viceroy and Don Antonio heard all this, and so did many
others who were there; and they also heard Don Quixote reply that,
as his victor asked nothing of him to the prejudice of Dulcinea, he
would comply with all the rest like a true and scrupulous knight.

After this acknowledgment the Knight of the White Moon
turned rein and, bowing his head to the Viceroy, entered the city
at a canter. The Viceroy ordered Don Antonio to go after him and
find out by any means possible who he was. Then they lifted Don
Quixote up and, uncovering his face, found him pale and bathed in
sweat, nor could Rocinante move for some time, so severe was his
fall. Sancho, very sad and downcast, did not know what to say or
do, for all this episode seemed to him to be happening in a dream,

and the whole business to be a matter of enchantment. He saw his master overthrown and bound to lay aside his arms for a year. The glorious light of his exploits seemed to him darkened, and Sancho's own hopes from his recent promises scattered as the wind scatters smoke. He was afraid that Rocinante might be crippled for ever and his master's bones be permanently knocked out of joint, though it would hardly be a pity if his madness had been knocked out of him too. In the end they carried Don Quixote into the city in a sedan-chair, which the Viceroy sent for, and that functionary himself rode back as well, eager to know who this Knight of the White Moon was that had left Don Quixote in so sad a plight.

Chapter LXV. *Which reveals who the Knight of the White Moon was, with Don Gregorio's deliverance and other events.*

DON ANTONIO MORENO followed the Knight of the White Moon; and a great number of boys followed him too, and pestered him until he took refuge in an inn inside the city, which Don Antonio entered also in his anxiety to make his acquaintance. A squire came out to receive and disarm him, and he then shut himself up in a lower room, where Don Antonio followed him, standing upon thorns to know who he was. Then, when the Knight of the White Moon saw that this gentleman would not leave him, he said: 'I know very well, sir, what you have come for: to find out who I am – and as I know no reason to hide my identity from you, while my servant here is taking off my armour I will tell you the whole truth of the matter, omitting nothing. My name, sir, is Bachelor Sampson Carrasco, and I come from the same village as Don Quixote de la Mancha, whose madness and folly have excited the pity of all who know him. I have felt particularly concerned and, believing that his health depends on his resting at home on his own land, I devised a trick to make him stay there. Some three months ago I went out on to the roads after him, disguised as a knight errant, styling myself *The Knight of the Mirrors*, and intending to fight with him and conquer him without hurting him, and to make it a condition of our combat that the vanquished should be at the disposal of the victor. What I intended to require of him – for I had no doubt of my success – was that he should go home and not leave his village for a whole year, during which time he might be cured. But Fate ordained otherwise, for he conquered me and tumbled me off my horse; and so my plan failed. He continued on his way, and I went home, vanquished, ashamed and shaken by my fall, which was rather a severe one. However, I did not relinquish my project of seeking him once more and beating him, as you have seen to-day. And as he is so scrupulous in observing the ordinances of knight errantry there is no doubt that he will keep the conditions I have laid on him, as he has promised. This, sir, is the whole story, and I have nothing more to tell you. I implore you not to give me away or tell Don Quixote who I am, so that my good plan may work, and his understanding be restored to him; for he has an excellent brain, if he can only be freed from the follies of chivalry.'

'Oh, sir,' said Don Antonio, 'may God pardon you the injury you have done the whole world in your attempt to restore the most amusing of all madmen to his senses. Don't you see, sir, that no benefit to be derived from Don Quixote's recovery could outweigh the pleasure afforded by his extravagances? However, I fancy that all the worthy Bachelor's arts will not be sufficient to restore so completely crazy a man to sanity. And if it were not a sin against charity, I should say that I hope Don Quixote may never be cured, for with his recovery we not only should lose his pleasantries but his squire Sancho Panza's as well; and either of them can turn melancholy itself to mirth. I will keep quiet, all the same, and tell him nothing, to see if I prove right in suspecting that all Master Carrasco's efforts will be in vain.'

The Bachelor replied that anyhow the business was now well on the way, and that he hoped for a favourable result. Upon which Don Antonio offered to follow his instructions, and the Bachelor took his leave, had his armour tied on a mule, mounted the horse on which he had done battle and left the city that same day, returning home without any incident worthy of recording in this true history. Don Antonio repeated all that Carrasco had told him to the Viceroy, who was not over pleased, for with Don Quixote's retirement there was an end of all the entertainment his mad exploits afforded everyone who heard of them.

Don Quixote stayed six days in bed, melancholy, sorrowful, brooding and in a bad way, turning over and over in his mind the misfortune of his defeat. Sancho comforted him, however, saying amongst other things: 'Raise up your head, sir, and cheer up, if you can. Thank Heaven that although you were tumbled to the ground you got off without a single rib broken, for there's give and take in everything, you know, and there aren't always flitches where there are hooks. A fig for the doctor; you've no need of him to cure you of this complaint. Let's go back to our homes, and give up wandering in search of adventures in lands and places we don't know. But when you come to think of it, I'm the greater loser by this, although your worship's in the worse state. For though with my government I gave up all desire to be a governor again, I've never lost my longing to be a count. But that will never come to anything, if your worship gives up trying to be a king, and abandons the profession of chivalry. So my hopes are all going up in smoke.'

'Be quiet, Sancho. Do you not see that my seclusion and retirement need last no more than a year? After that I will return to my honourable calling, and I shall not fail to win a kingdom, and a countship to give you.'

'God grant you may,' said Sancho, 'and may sin turn a deaf ear, for I've always heard that a good hope is better than poor possessions.'

Here their conversation was interrupted by Don Antonio, who entered crying out joyfully: 'A reward for good news, Don Quixote! Don Gregorio and the renegade who went for him are in harbour. In harbour, do I say? They're already at the Viceroy's, and will be here in a moment.'

At this Don Quixote was somewhat cheered, and said: 'Indeed I was just going to say that I should have been delighted if everything had turned out otherwise, for then I should have had to cross to Barbary, where by the force of my arm I should have liberated not only Don Gregorio but all the Christian captives in Barbary. But what am I saying, poor wretch? Have not I been conquered? Have not I been overthrown? Am I not forbidden to take up arms for a year? Then what am I promising? What am I boasting of, seeing that I am fitter to handle a distaff than a sword?'

'No more of that, sir,' said Sancho; 'let the hen live, even if she's got the pip. It's your turn to-day, mine to-morrow. There's no need to worry about all these clashes and knocks, for the man who's down to-day may be up to-morrow, unless he prefers to stay in bed; to lose his pluck I mean, instead of gathering fresh courage for fresh fights. Now, get up, your worship, to receive Don Gregorio, for it sounds to me as if everyone's excited, and he must be in the house by now.'

And he was right, for Don Gregorio and the renegade had already given the Viceroy an account of their journey there and back, and in his eagerness to see Anna Felix Don Gregorio had rushed to Don Antonio's with his rescuer. Although he had been in woman's dress when they got him away from Algiers, he had exchanged clothes in the boat with a slave who had escaped with him. But whatever dress he had worn, his appearance would have commanded respect, admiration and envy, for he was exceedingly handsome and apparently about sixteen or seventeen years old. Ricote and his daughter went out to receive him, the father in tears, the daughter blushing, but they did not embrace, for where there is great love there is not usually overmuch freedom. Their beauty was universally admired, and though they did not speak to one another their eyes revealed their modest and joyful thoughts. The renegade recounted his plan and the means he had employed for Don Gregorio's rescue, and Don Gregorio told of the dangers and difficulties he had been in among the women with whom he had stayed, telling no long story, but showing by his brevity that his discretion outran his years. Finally Ricote liberally rewarded the renegade as well as the men who had rowed the rescue boat. The renegade was reconciled and restored to the Church, and from a rotten limb was made clean and sound again through penance and repentance.

Two days later the Viceroy discussed with Don Antonio how permission might be obtained for Anna Felix and her father to stay in Spain; for it did not seem to them unreasonable that so Christian a daughter and a father apparently so right-minded should be allowed to remain. Don Antonio offered to go to the capital to arrange the matter, having necessarily to go on other business, and intimated that many difficulties could be overcome by means of favours and bribes.

'No,' said Ricote, who was present at this conversation. 'There's nothing to hope from favours or bribes, for no prayers, promises, gifts or compassion can avail with the great Don Bernardino de Velasco, Count de Salazar, to whom his Majesty has entrusted our expulsion. For though it is true that he tempers justice with mercy, since he sees that the whole body of our race is contaminated and rotten he applies to it the burning cautery and not the soothing ointment. And so by prudence, sagacity and diligence, as well as by terror, he has borne the weight of his vast project on his strong shoulders to its due execution; and our arts, stratagems, pleadings and frauds have had no power to dazzle his Argus eyes, which are ever on the watch to see that not one of us remains or lies concealed, to sprout like a hidden root in times to come and bear poisoned fruit in Spain, which is now clean and free from the fears with which our numbers inspired her. What an heroic resolve of the great Philip the Third, and what unheard-of wisdom in entrusting its execution to this Don Bernardino de Velasco!'

'At any rate,' said Don Antonio, 'when I am there I will make every possible effort, and leave the rest to Providence. Don Gregorio shall come with me to relieve the anxiety his parents must feel at his absence. Anna Felix shall stay in my house with my wife, or in a nunnery, and I know that the Viceroy will be glad to have the good Ricote staying with him till we see how I manage.'

The Viceroy consented to all that was proposed; but when Don Gregorio heard what had passed he said that on no account could he, or would he, leave Doña Anna Felix. At length, however, he fell in with the arrangements, reflecting that he might contrive to come back for her when he had seen his parents. So Anna Felix stayed with Don Antonio's wife, and Ricote in the Viceroy's house.

The day came for Don Antonio's departure, and two days later for Don Quixote's and Sancho's, for the knight's fall would not allow of his taking the road any sooner. There were tears, there were sighs, sorrowings and sobbings when Anna Felix took her farewell of Don Gregorio, to whom Ricote offered a thousand crowns, if he wanted them. But he would take no more than five, which he borrowed from Don Antonio, promising to repay them in the capital. With this the pair departed, and afterwards Don Quixote and Sancho, as we have said — Don Quixote unarmed and in travelling clothes, and Sancho on foot, for Dapple was loaded with the armour.

Chapter LXVI. *Which treats of what the reader shall see or the listener hear.*

As THEY left Barcelona Don Quixote turned to gaze on the spot where he had fallen and said: 'Here stood Troy. Here my ill-luck, and not my cowardice, despoiled me of the glory I had won. Here Fortune practised her shifts and changes upon me. Here my exploits were eclipsed. Here, in short, my happiness fell, never to rise again.'

Hearing which, Sancho said: 'Great hearts, my dear master, should be patient in misfortune as well as joyful in prosperity. And this I judge from myself. For if I was merry when I was Governor now that I'm a squire on foot I'm not sad, for I've heard tell that Fortune, as they call her, is a drunken and capricious woman and, worse still, blind; and so she doesn't see what she's doing, and doesn't know whom she is casting down or raising up.'

'You are very philosophical, Sancho,' replied Don Quixote, 'and you talk most wisely. I do not know how you have learnt to. All I can tell you is that there is no such thing in the world as Fortune, and that events here, whether good or ill, do not fall out by chance but by a particular providence of Heaven, from which comes the saying that every man is the architect of his own destiny. I have been so of mine, but have failed in the necessary prudence, and so my presumption has brought me to disaster, for I should have reflected that the feeble Rocinante could never withstand the mighty bulk of the White Moon Knight's horse. However, I stood up to him; I did what I could; I was overthrown; and though I lost my honour I did not lose, nor could I lose, the virtue of keeping my word. When I was a knight errant, daring and valiant, my arms brought credit to my exploits, and now that I am a common squire I will bring credit on my words by fulfilling the promise I made. Trudge on then, friend Sancho, and let us go and spend our year of probation in our own land, and in our seclusion we will gather new virtue to return to that profession of arms which I can never forget.'

'Sir,' answered Sancho, 'trudging on foot is not so pleasant a thing that I feel spurred to make long marches. Let us leave these arms hung up on some tree, to dangle like those thieves we saw.

Then, if I'm on Dapple's back with my feet off the ground, we'll make whatever journeys may please and suit your worship; but if you imagine that I can travel long stages on foot you're expecting the impossible.'

'You have spoken well, Sancho,' replied Don Quixote. 'Let my armour be hung up as a trophy, and beneath it, or somewhere near, let us carve on the trees what was written on the trophy of Roland's arms –

> ... Let no one move them
> But one who dares his prowess against Roland.'

'That seems to me very much to the point,' answered Sancho, 'and if it weren't that we should feel the want of Rocinante on the road, it would be a good thing to leave him hanging there as well.'

'No,' replied Don Quixote. 'I would not have him or the armour hung up, for fear they might say: There is a bad reward for good service.'

'Your worship's quite right,' answered Sancho, 'for wise men say that the ass's fault shouldn't be laid on the pack-saddle; and since you are to blame for this business you should punish yourself and not vent your anger upon your armour, which is battered and bloody already, nor upon poor meek Rocinante, nor upon my tender feet, asking them to travel more than is proper.'

All that day they spent in these arguments and discussions, and the next four as well, without anything arising to hinder their journey. But on the fifth day, as they were coming into a village, they found a crowd of people round the inn door amusing themselves, for it was a holiday. And as Don Quixote approached them a countryman raised his voice and said: 'One of these two gentlemen coming this way shall decide our wager, for he doesn't know the parties.'

'That I will, with pleasure,' answered Don Quixote, 'and with complete impartiality, if I can manage to understand it.'

'The case is this, then, good sir,' said the countryman. 'A man of this village, who is so fat that he weighs twenty stone, has challenged a neighbour of his, who only weighs nine, to run a hundred yards' race with him, upon condition that they run at even weights. Now when the challenger was asked how the weights were to be

F F

made even, he said that the challenged man, who weighs nine stone, must carry eleven stone of iron on his back, and so they would both be equal at twenty stone.'

'That's wrong,' broke in Sancho before Don Quixote could reply. 'It's my job to settle this question and give a decision on the whole case, as it is only a few days since I gave up being a governor and a judge, as all the world knows.'

'Do so and welcome, friend Sancho,' said Don Quixote, 'for I am not fit to give crumbs to the cat, my wits are so shaken and shattered.'

With this permission Sancho addressed the countrymen, who were standing round him in mute and open-mouthed expectation of his decision.

'Brothers, the fat man's demand is unreasonable, and has not a shadow of justice in it. For if what they say is true, that the man challenged may choose the weapons, it isn't right for his opponent to choose for him weapons which would hinder him and prevent his gaining the victory. Therefore my decision is that the fat challenger should prune, pare, scrape, trim and shave away eleven stone of his flesh, from whatever part of his body may seem best to him, and so, reduced to nine stone in weight, he will be on level terms with his adversary at nine: and then they will be able to run even.'

'God's truth,' exclaimed one of the countrymen who heard Sancho's decision, 'this gentleman has spoken like a saint and given sentence like a canon! But I'm pretty sure the fat fellow has no mind to part with an ounce of his flesh, let alone eleven stone.'

'The best way will be for them not to run at all,' put in another. 'Then the thin chap won't break down under his load, nor the fat fellow lose his flesh. Let half of the wager go in wine, and let's take these gentlemen to the tavern that has the best. And the blood be on my head.'

'I thank you, gentlemen,' replied Don Quixote, 'but I cannot stop a moment, for sorrowful thoughts and disastrous events force me to appear discourteous and to travel in haste.'

And so, spurring Rocinante, he pressed on, leaving them all astonished at the appearance of this strange figure and at the wisdom of his servant, for such they judged Sancho to be. And another of the countrymen said: 'If the servant is so wise, what must the master be? If they're going to study at Salamanca, I bet they'll be judges at court in a twinkling. It's all a game. A man studies and studies. Then with favour and good luck he finds himself with a wand in his hand or a mitre on his head, when he least expects it.'

That night master and man spent in the open field under the bare and naked sky, and when they pushed on next day they saw a man coming towards them on foot with a haversack round his neck and a javelin or pike in his hand, a foot-courier to the life. Now as this figure drew near to Don Quixote, he quickened his pace and, coming up to him half running, embraced him round the right thigh, for he could reach no higher, and exclaimed with signs of great pleasure: 'Oh, my lord Don Quixote de la Mancha, how glad my lord the Duke, my master, will be, when he hears that your worship is returning to his castle, for he is still there with my lady the Duchess.'

'I do not recognize you, friend,' replied Don Quixote, 'and I shall not know who you are unless you tell me.'

'I am Tosilos, Don Quixote,' replied the courier, 'my lord the Duke's lackey, who would not fight with your worship about marrying Doña Rodriguez' daughter.'

'God defend me!' exclaimed Don Quixote. 'Is it possible that you are the man whom my enemies the enchanters turned into a lackey to defraud me of the honour of that battle?'

'Gently, my good sir,' replied the messenger. 'There was no enchantment nor any transformation. I was as much the lackey Tosilos when I went into the lists as I was Tosilos the lackey when I came out. I meant to marry without fighting, for I liked the look of the girl; but my plan turned out otherwise, for as soon as you left our castle the Duke my master had me given a hundred strokes for disobeying the orders he had given me before going into the battle; and it all ended with the girl turning nun and Doña Rodriguez going back to Castile. Now I'm on my way to Barcelona to deliver a bundle of letters from my master to the Viceroy. If your worship would like a little drink clean though a bit warm, I've a gourd full of good stuff and a few slices of Tronchon cheese, which will serve to raise your thirst if it happens to be sleeping.'

'I like your offer,' said Sancho. 'Drop the rest of the compliment, and pour out, my good Tosilos, and be damned to all the enchanters in the Indies.'

'Truly,' said Don Quixote, 'you are the greatest glutton in the world, and the greatest simpleton on earth if you cannot be persuaded that this courier is enchanted and this Tosilos counterfeit. But stay with him and drink your fill. I will go on slowly, and wait for you to come up with me.'

The lackey burst out laughing, unsheathed the gourd and unpacked the cheese from his haversack. Then he took out a little loaf, and he and Sancho sat down on the green grass, and in peace and good fellowship quickly despatched the haversack's complete contents, with such a hearty appetite that they even licked the packet of letters, only because it smelt of cheese. And after which Tosilos said to Sancho: 'There's no doubt, friend Sancho, that this master of yours ought to be counted a madman.'

'Why ought?' replied Sancho. 'He owes nothing to anyone, for he pays his debts, especially where madness passes for coin. Plainly I see it, and plainly I tell him; but what's the use? Particularly now that he's done for, for he's been conquered by the Knight of the White Moon.'

Tosilos asked him to relate what had happened, but Sancho replied that it would be uncivil to keep his master waiting for him, for there would be time for the story some other day, if they met. So, getting up and shaking the crumbs from his beard and his clothes, he said goodbye to Tosilos and left him. Then, driving Dapple before him, he overtook his master, who was waiting for him in the shade of a tree.

Chapter LXVII. *Of Don Quixote's resolution to turn Shepherd and lead a pastoral life till the year of his pledge had expired, with other incidents truly good and entertaining.*

IF Don Quixote was much troubled in mind before his overthrow he was much more so after it. He was lying in the shade of a tree, as we have said, and there his thoughts, like flies round honey, set upon him and stung him. Some of them dwelt on Dulcinea's disenchantment and others on the life he must lead in his enforced

retirement. Then Sancho came up, loud in his praises of the
lackey Tosilos' liberality.

'Is it possible, Sancho,' asked Don Quixote, 'that you still think
he is a real lackey? You seem to have forgotten how you saw Dulcinea del Toboso converted and transformed into a country girl,
and the Knight of the Mirrors into the Bachelor Carrasco, all the
work of the enchanters who persecute me. But tell me now; did
you ask that Tosilos, as you call him, what has been the fate of
Altisidora; whether she has wept for my absence or already consigned to oblivion those amorous desires which tormented her in
my presence?'

'I was too well employed,' answered Sancho, 'to have time to ask
such silly questions. Heavens alive, sir! Is your worship now in a fit
state to enquire about other people's desires, especially amorous ones?'

'Look you, Sancho,' said Don Quixote, 'there is a great deal of
difference between acts done out of love and those done out of
gratitude. A knight may very well not be in love; but ungrateful,
to speak in all strictness, he must not be. Altisidora, to all appearances, loved me deeply; she gave me the three kerchiefs you know
of; she wept at my departure; she cursed me; she abused me and,
regardless of shame, complained of me publicly: all certain proofs
that she adored me, for lovers' anger usually vents itself in such
maledictions. I had no hopes to offer her, nor treasures to give her,
for my hopes are pledged to Dulcinea, and the treasures of knights
errant are illusory and false as fairy gold. I can only devote to her
the memories I have of her, without prejudice, however, to those I
have of Dulcinea, whom you wrong by your delay in scourging
yourself and castigating that flesh of yours – may I see the wolves
devour it! – which you would rather preserve for the worms than
apply to the relief of that poor lady.'

'Sir,' answered Sancho, 'to tell you the truth, I can't persuade
myself that the flogging of my posterior has anything to do with
the disenchanting of the enchanted. For you might as well say: If
your head aches, anoint your knees. I'm pretty certain, at least,
there isn't a single instance of disenchantment by lashes in all the
histories of knight errantry your worship has read. But whether
there is or not, I'll lash myself when I've a mind to punish myself
and time serves.'

'God grant you may,' replied Don Quixote, 'and Heaven give you grace to recall and acknowledge your obligation to aid my lady, who is yours too since you are my servant.'

Deep in these conversations, they were pursuing their journey when they came to the very spot where they had been trampled by the bulls. Which Don Quixote recognised, saying to Sancho: 'This is the field where we met the gay shepherdesses and gallant shepherds, who here proposed to revive another pastoral Arcadia. The project was both new and ingenious, and if you think well of it, Sancho, we will follow their example and turn shepherds, at least for the time I have to live in retirement. I will buy some sheep and everything needful for the pastoral vocation. I will call myself the shepherd Quixotiz and you the shepherd Panzino, and we will wander through the mountains, woods and meadows, singing here, lamenting there, drinking of the liquid crystals of the springs, or of the limpid streams, or the mighty rivers. The oaks shall give us of their sweetest fruit with generous hands; the trunks of the hard cork-trees shall offer us seats; the willows, shade; the roses, perfume; the broad meadows, carpets of a thousand blended colours; the clear, pure air shall grant us breath; the moon and the stars their light, despite the darkness of the night; song shall afford us delight, and tears gladness; Apollo verses, and love a theme, whereby we shall be able to win eternal fame, not only in the present age but in those to come.'

'God's truth!' exclaimed Sancho. 'But that kind of life squares with me exactly – and corners too. What's more, no sooner will the Bachelor Sampson Carrasco and Master Nicholas the barber get a sight of us than they'll want to follow it too and turn shepherds with us. But God grant it mayn't come into the priest's head to enter the fold as well – he's so gay and fond of his amusements.'

'You have spoken very well,' said Don Quixote, 'and the Bachelor Sampson Carrasco, if he comes into the pastoral company, as no doubt he will, could call himself the shepherd Samsonino or the shepherd Carrascon. Barber Nicholas might call himself Nicholoso, as old Boscan called himself Nemoroso. I do not know what name we could give the priest, unless it be one deriving from his calling, the shepherd Curiambro perhaps. As for the shepherdesses whose lovers we are to be, we can pick and choose their names like pears; and as my lady's name would suit a shepherdess as well as a Princess, there is no need for me to tire myself out seeking another to suit her better. You, Sancho, shall call your shepherdess by whatever name you please.'

'The only name for mine,' replied Sancho, 'will be Teresona, it'll suit her fatness well, and her name's Teresa. It'll sound well when I sing of her in my verses and reveal my chaste desires, for I'm not one to go to other men's houses seeking better bread than is made of wheat. The priest had better not go taking a shepherdess, for good example's sake, but if the Bachelor decides to have one his soul's his own.'

'God bless me,' exclaimed Don Quixote, 'what a life we shall lead, Sancho my friend! What pipes will ring in our ears! What hurdy-gurdies, what tambourines, what timbrels, and what fiddles! Perhaps then all the *albogues* may sound! Then almost all the pastoral instruments will be there.'

'What are *albogues*?' asked Sancho. 'I've never heard of them or seen one in all my life.'

'*Albogues*,' answered Don Quixote, 'are thin brass plates like candlesticks, which are struck against one another on the concave or hollow side, and make a sound which may not be very agreeable or harmonious, but is not unpleasing and blends well with the rustic quality of the hurdy-gurdy and the tambourine. This word *albogue* is Moorish, like all words beginning with *al* in our Castilian language: for instance *almohaza*, *almorzar*, *alhombra*, *alguacil*, *alhucema*, *almacén*, *alcancía* and a few others like them. Our language contains only three words from the Moorish which end in "*í*"; they are *borceguí*, *zaguizamí* and *maravedí*. *Alhelí* and *alfaquí* can be recognised as Arabic both by their initial "*al*" and by their final "*í*". This I mention by the way, since it has come to my mind through my chancing to mention the *albogue*. One circumstance will greatly contribute to make us perfect in our new profession. I am, as you know, something of a poet, and the Bachelor Sampson Carrasco too is a good one. I do not mention the priest; but I will wager he has a smack and touch of the poet about him, and Master Nicholas has it as well, I have no doubt, for all or most barbers are guitarists and rhymers. I will mourn absent beauty; you shall celebrate yourself as the constant lover; the shepherd Carrascon shall complain of scorn, and the priest Curiambro of whatever he likes; and so we shall go on to our hearts' content.'

'But I'm so unlucky, sir,' replied Sancho, 'that I'm afraid I shall never see the time when I can follow this calling. Oh, what smooth spoons I shall make when I'm a shepherd! What fried breadcrumbs and cream cheeses and garlands and shepherds' nick-nacks! They may not win me a reputation for wisdom, but they won't fail to get me a name for cleverness. My daughter Sanchica shall bring us our dinner to the fold. But, mind out! For she's goodlooking, and shepherds are not all simple. There are rogues amongst them, and I wouldn't like her to go for wool and come back shorn. For your lovings and wicked desires are as common in the fields as in the cities, and you find them in shepherds' huts as well as in royal palaces. So take away the opportunity and you take away the sin; and what the eye doesn't see the heart doesn't grieve for; and a leap over the hedge is better than good men's prayers.'

'No more proverbs, Sancho,' said Don Quixote, 'for any one of those you have cited is enough to explain your thought. Often I have advised you not to be so prodigal of proverbs and to restrain yourself from introducing them, but it seems to me like preaching in the desert, and my mother beats me and I whip the top.'

'Your worship reminds me of the saying that the pot called the kettle black. You scold me for quoting proverbs, and string them together in pairs yourself.'

'Observe, Sancho,' answered Don Quixote, 'that I bring my proverbs in to the purpose, and when I quote them they fit like a ring on a finger. But you bring them in by the hair. You drag them instead of guiding them. And if I remember rightly I have told you before that proverbs are brief maxims drawn from the experience and observations of the wise men of old, and a proverb ill applied is not wisdom but stark nonsense. But let us leave the subject and, as darkness is coming on, go a little off the highway to some place where we can spend the night, and God knows what tomorrow will bring.'

They left the road and supped poorly and late, much to the displeasure of Sancho, who was reminded of the hardships of knight errantry suffered among woods and forests, though sometimes plenty reigned in castles and houses, as at Don Diego de Miranda's and at the rich Camacho's wedding, and at Don Antonio Moreno's. But he reflected that neither day nor night could last for ever, and so he spent that night in sleep and his master in watching.

Chapter LXVIII. *Of the bristling adventure which befell Don Quixote.*

THE night was rather dark, for though the moon was in the sky she was in no part where she was visible. For sometimes the lady Diana goes for a trip to the Antipodes and leaves the mountains dark and the valleys gloomy. Don Quixote yielded to nature and slept his first sleep, but he did not give way to a second. It was quite the opposite with Sancho, who had no second because his first lasted him from night till morning, which showed his sound constitution and freedom from care. But Don Quixote's cares kept him so wide awake that he finally roused Sancho by saying: 'I am amazed, Sancho, at the insensibility of your nature. I believe you are made of marble or brass, and have no emotion or feeling in you. I watch while you sleep; I weep while you sing; I faint from fasting while you can hardly move or breathe from pure gluttony. It is the duty of good servants to share their masters' pains and feel their griefs, even if only for appearance's sake. Observe the serenity of this night and the solitude of the place, which invites us to mingle some watching with our slumber. Get up, in Heaven's name! Go a little way off, and with a willing heart and thankful spirit give yourself three or four hundred lashes upon the score of Dulcinea's disenchanting. This I implore you as a favour, for I do not want to come to grips with you as I did last time, since I know you have a heavy hand. When you have done we will spend the rest of the night singing, I of separation, and you of constancy, embarking this moment upon the pastoral calling we are to follow in our village.'

'Sir,' replied Sancho, 'I am no monk to get up and scourge myself in the middle of my sleep, nor do I think it would be an easy matter to suffer the pain of a whipping one moment and to be singing the next. Allow me to sleep, your worship, and don't worry me about this scourging business, or you'll make me swear an oath never to touch a hair of my coat, much less my flesh.'

'Heart of flint,' cried Don Quixote. 'Remorseless squire, un-

grateful for my bread and thankless for my favours past and future!
Through me you became a governor, and through me you are now
in close expectation of being a count, or of getting some equivalent
title. Nor shall the fulfilment be longer delayed than for this one
year, for "*post tenebras spero lucem*" – After darkness I expect light.'

'I don't understand that,' replied Sancho. 'I only know that
while I sleep I have no fear, nor hope, nor trouble, nor glory.
God bless the inventor of sleep, the cloak that covers all man's
thoughts, the food that cures all hunger, the water that quenches all
thirst, the fire that warms the cold, the cold that cools heat; the
common coin, in short, that can purchase all things, the balancing
weight that levels the shepherd with the king and the simple with
the wise. There's only one bad thing about sleep, as I have heard
say, and that is that it looks like death; for there's but little difference between a sleeping man and a dead one.'

'Sancho,' said Don Quixote, 'I have never heard you speak so
eloquently as now; which makes me realise the truth of that proverb you sometimes cite: "Not with whom you are bred but with
whom you are fed." '

'Devil take it, dear master!' exclaimed Sancho. 'It isn't I that am
stringing proverbs this time; for they fall from your worship's
mouth also, two by two, faster than from mine. Only there is this
difference between yours and mine, that yours come in season and
mine out of place; but they're all proverbs all the same.'

They had reached this point when they heard a harsh, deafening
din spreading through all the valleys around. Don Quixote rose to
his feet and put his hand to his sword. Sancho crouched beneath
Dapple, setting the bundle of armour on one side of him and the
ass's pack-saddle on the other, and trembling as much from fear as
Don Quixote from excitement. The din was gradually getting
louder and drawing nearer to the trembling pair, or to one trembler
at least, for the other's valour is well known by now. The cause was
this – some hog-dealers happened to be driving some six hundred
swine or more at that early hour to sell them at a fair; and this herd
made such a noise with their grunting and squeaking that both Don
Quixote and Sancho were deafened, and utterly at a loss to account
for it.

The straggling swine came snorting on pell-mell, and regardless of all respect for Don Quixote's dignity or Sancho's passed over them both, demolishing Sancho's entrenchments, and not only tumbling Don Quixote over but sweeping Rocinante along into the bargain. On went the unclean beasts at headlong speed, over-throwing as they went the pack-saddle, the armour, Dapple, Rocinante, Sancho and Don Quixote.

Sancho got up as best he could, and asked his master for his sword, saying that he would like to kill half a dozen of those unman-nerly and swinish gentry, for now he had realised what they were.

'Let them be, friend,' said Don Quixote, 'for this outrage is the penalty for my sin, and it is Heaven's just chastisement on a con-quered knight errant, that jackals shall devour him, wasps sting him and hogs trample him down.'

'And it's Heaven's chastisement too, I suppose,' replied Sancho, 'that flies shall sting the squires of vanquished knights errant, that lice shall eat them and hunger assail them. If we squires were the sons of the knights we serve or their very close relatives, it would be no great mattter if the penalties for their faults lighted on us unto the fourth generation. But what have the Panzas to do with the Quixotes? Well, let's get ourselves comfortable again, and sleep through what little remains of the night, and God will send us day and perhaps better luck.'

'You may sleep, Sancho,' replied Don Quixote, 'for you were born to sleep; but I was born to watch, and in the little time that is left till day I will give rein to my thoughts and vent them in a little madrigal, which, unknown to you, I have composed in my head to-night.'

'To my mind,' replied Sancho, 'thoughts that yield to verse can't be very troublesome. Rhyme it as much as you please, your worship, and I'll sleep as long as I can.'

Then, taking up as much ground as he wanted, he curled himself up and slept a sound sleep, undisturbed by bonds, debts, or cares. And Don Quixote, leaning against a beech or cork tree – Cide Hamete Benengeli does not specify what tree it was – sang in this strain to the accompaniment of his own sighs:

> Love, when I dwell upon
> The wounds you deal me, terrible and fierce,
> I run to death apace
> In hopes that there my great pains will be gone.

> But when I reach that place,
> The harbour in this sea of my sad ills,
> Such joy my bosom feels
> That life grows stronger and I cannot pass.
>
> And so by life I'm slain,
> Unwelcome state that mingles life and death!
> Living I die, and as my breath
> Dies, death recalls me into life again.

With each line he sighed and shed some tears, groaning as if his heart were pierced through by grief at his overthrow and by his absence from Dulcinea.

And now day appeared, the sun darting his beams full on Sancho's eyes. He uncurled and awoke, shaking and stretching his drowsy limbs. Then, viewing the havoc the hogs had wrought on his stores, he cursed the herd and more besides. At length the pair resumed their journey, and at dusk saw some ten horsemen coming towards them with four or five men on foot. Don Quixote's heart leapt and Sancho's quailed with terror, for the people approaching carried lances and shields and were advancing in very warlike formation. Whereupon Don Quixote turned to Sancho and said: 'Ah, Sancho, if I could use my arms, and my promise had not tied my hands, I should reckon this array coming against us no more than tarts and gingerbread. Perhaps, however, it may not be as we fear.'

By this time the horsemen had come up and, raising their spears, surrounded Don Quixote without a single word, pointing them at his back and breast and threatening him with death. Then one of those on foot, putting a finger to his lips as a sign to him to be silent, seized Rocinante's bridle and led him off the road. The rest of the men on foot followed in the steps of Don Quixote's captors, driving Sancho and Dapple from behind, and all preserving an amazing silence. Two or three times the knight was on the point of asking where they were taking him and what they wanted, but no sooner did he begin to open his lips than they made as if to close them with the points of their spears; and the same thing happened to Sancho, for as soon as he made to open his mouth one of the footmen pricked him with a goad, serving Dapple in the same way, as if he too wanted to speak. Night closed in; they quickened their pace; the fears of the two prisoners increased; all the more so when they heard their captors cry from time to time: 'Get on, Trog-lodytes!' 'Silence, barbarians!' 'Pay up, Anthropophagi!' 'Don't complain, Scythians!' 'Don't open your eyes, murderous Poly-phemuses, man-eating lions!' and many other such names with which they tormented the ears of the wretched master and man. Sancho went along muttering to himself: 'What, call us ortolans! Us, barbers and Andrew popinjays? And silly 'uns and Polly famouses? I don't like any of those names. It's an ill wind blowing this grain. All our troubles are coming together like kicks on a dog, and pray God it may stop at threats, this ill-venturous adventure!'

Don Quixote rode on in a daze, unable to guess the purpose of these abusive epithets addressed to them for all the thought he put to it, though he gathered that he could expect no good from them and must fear much evil. About an hour after dark they arrived at a castle, which Don Quixote recognised as the Duke's where he had been staying a little while ago.

'God bless me!' he exclaimed, as soon as he made out the build-ings. 'What can this be? In this house, indeed, all is courtesy and kindness; but for the vanquished good turns to evil, and evil to worse.'

And when they came into the main court of the castle they saw it decorated and set out in a manner which increased their astonish-ment and redoubled their fears, as will be seen in the following chapter.

Chapter LXIX. *Of the rarest and strangest adventure that befell Don Quixote in the whole course of this great history.*

THE horsemen dismounted, and with those on foot caught Don Quixote and Sancho violently and bodily in their arms and brought them into the courtyard, around which blazed about a hundred torches set in their sconces, while around the galleries of the court were more than five hundred lamps, so that despite the night, which was rather dark, the scene was as bright as day. In the centre of the yard was raised a bier some six foot above the ground, completely covered with a broad canopy of black velvet, around which, ranged along the steps, there burnt more than a hundred white wax tapers in silver candlesticks; and lying on this bier was displayed the corpse of a maiden so lovely that her beauty seemed to make Death itself beautiful. On a brocade pillow lay her head, crowned with a garland woven of various sweet-smelling flowers; her hands were crossed on her breast, and between them was a branch of yellow victor's palm. On one side of the court a stage had been erected with two seats on which were sitting two persons, who by the crowns on their heads and the sceptres in their hands appeared to be kings, either real or pretended. By the side of this stage, which was approached by steps, were two other seats on which their captors seated Don Quixote and Sancho, still in complete silence and giving the pair to understand by signs that they must keep silent too. But they would have done so without any signs, for amazement at what they saw kept their tongues tied. Then there mounted upon the stage two principal personages, whom Don Quixote recognized as the Duke and Duchess, his hosts, and they took their places on two richly ornamented seats beside the pair who appeared to be kings. Who would not have been amazed at this, when, in addition, Don Quixote recognized the corpse lying on the bier as the fair Altisidora's? As the Duke and Duchess mounted the platform Don Quixote and Sancho rose and made them a deep bow, which they returned by a slight nod of the head. Then an officer came across the court and, going up to Sancho, threw over him a robe of black buckram all painted with fiery flames and, snatching off his victim's cap, put on his head a pasteboard mitre like those worn by the penitents of the Inquisition, whispering in his ear that if he opened his lips they would gag him or take his life. Sancho surveyed himself from head to foot and saw that he was ablaze with flames, but as they did not burn him he did not care two pins for them. He took off the mitre and saw that it was painted with devils. Then he put it on again, saying to himself: 'Well, well, the flames don't burn and the devils don't carry me off.'

Don Quixote also gazed at Sancho, and though fear kept his senses numbed he could not forbear smiling at his squire's appearance. And now, apparently from beneath the bier, a soft and pleasant music of flutes began to rise, which sounded soft and amorous, though unbroken by any human voice, for in that place silence itself was mute. Then there suddenly appeared beside the pillow of this seeming corpse a handsome youth in Roman dress, who sang in a sweet and clear voice to the sound of a harp, which he played himself, these two stanzas:

> Until Altisidora shall return
> To life, she that Don Quixote's cruelty slew,
> And all the while that at the fairy court
> In robes of sackcloth the court ladies mourn,
> And whilst my lady clothes her waiting-maids
> In sombre serge and heavy baize of grief,
> So long in sweeter tones than his of Thrace
> Shall I lament her beauty and disgrace.
>
> Nor do I think that at my dying day
> This, my most mournful duty, will be done,
> For still with tongue struck dead and mouth a-cold
> I mean to pay my debt to you in song.
> And when my soul from prison is released
> And led beside the mournful Stygian lake,
> 'Twill celebrate you as it goes, and sing
> Until the waters of oblivion ring.

'No more,' exclaimed one of the two seeming kings at this point; 'No more, divine singer. It would be an endless task to recall to us the death and charms of the peerless Altisidora, not dead, as the ignorant world thinks, but living on the tongues of fame and in the penance which Sancho Panza, here present, must undergo to restore her to the light. Therefore, O Rhadamanthus, you who judge with me in the gloomy caverns of Dis – for you know all that the inscrutable fates have decreed concerning the restoration of this damsel to life – speak and declare it now, so that the happiness we expect from her return may be delayed no longer.'

Scarcely had Minos, his fellow judge, so spoken when Rhadamanthus rose to his feet and said: 'Here, officers of this house, high and low, great and small! Come here, one and all, and mark Sancho's face with twenty-four slaps. Give him a dozen pinches and six pinpricks on his arms and loins, for on this ceremony depends Altisidora's restoration.'

On hearing this Sancho broke his silence and cried out: 'By my life! I'd as soon turn Moor as let my face be marked or my cheeks be fingered. God's truth! What has the handling of my face to do with this young lady's resurrection? The old woman so enjoyed the spinach that she didn't leave any, green or dry. They enchant

Dulcinea and whip me to disenchant her. Altisidora dies of some disease God chose to give her, and to revive her I am to have twenty-four slaps in the face, my body riddled with pins and my arms black and blue with pinches. Try those jokes on your brother-in-law. I'm an old dog and don't answer to every whistle.'

'You shall die,' proclaimed Rhadamanthus in a loud voice. 'Relent, tiger! Humble yourself, proud Nimrod! Suffer in silence, for nothing impossible is asked of you. And do not start raising difficulties in this business. Smacked you must be; pricked you shall be, and pinched till you groan. Ho, there! Officers, obey your orders. Or, on the word of an honest man, you will see what you were born for.'

At this point there appeared some six waiting-women crossing the court in a procession, one behind the other, four of them with spectacles and all with their right hands raised and four inches of wrist bare to make their hands appear longer, as is the present fashion. And the moment Sancho saw them he bellowed like a bull: 'I'd let the whole world handle me, but to be touched by waiting-women – never! Let the cats scratch my face, as they did my master's in this very castle. Let them run me through the body with sharp dagger points. Let them tear my arms with red hot pincers. I'll bear it all in patience to oblige these gentlemen. But the devil may carry me off before I'll consent to be touched by a waiting-woman.'

Then Don Quixote also broke the silence and observed to Sancho: 'Patience, my son. Oblige these gentlemen and render deep thanks to Heaven for having endowed your person with such virtue that by its martyrdom you can disenchant the enchanted and bring the dead to life.'

By this time the waiting-women had drawn close to Sancho and, quietly now and more resigned, he settled himself squarely in his chair, presented his face and beard to the first one, who dealt him a very well placed slap, and then made him a deep curtsey.

'Less courtesy and less paint, Mistress Waiting-woman,' said Sancho, 'for I'll be blowed if your hands don't smell of vinegar wash!'

To be brief, all the waiting-women slapped him, and many others of the household pinched him. But what he could not stand was the pin-pricking, and so he leapt up from his chair in a visible rage and, seizing a lighted torch from beside him, went after the waiting-women and the rest of his tormentors, crying: 'Get away, monsters of hell! Do you suppose that I'm made of brass that I can't feel your damned torments?'

At this Altisidora, who must have been tired from having lain flat so long, turned on her side, at which sight the whole assembly cried almost with one voice: 'Altisidora is alive! Altisidora is living!'

Rhadamanthus then bade Sancho calm his rage, for their purpose was now achieved. Then as soon as Don Quixote saw Altisidora begin to stir he went down on his knees before Sancho, saying: 'Now is the time, son of my loins – no more my squire! – to give yourself some of those lashes to which you are pledged for Dulcinea's disenchantment. Now, I say, is the time when your virtue is seasoned and effective for the working of the good that is expected of you.'

To which Sancho replied: – 'This is more like plot upon plot than honey upon pancakes. A fine thing it would be to have lashes following on pinches, slaps and pricks. After that there'll be nothing for it but to take a great stone and tie it round my neck and throw me down a well – which I wouldn't much mind if I'm to be made the whipping-boy to cure other folks' ailments. Leave me alone or, by God, I'll fling you all out, thirteen at a time, even if it spoils the market.'

Here Altisidora sat up on her bier, and at the same moment the clarions sounded, accompanied by flutes and by a general shout of: 'Long live Altisidora! Long live Altisidora!'

The Duke and Duchess and the kings, Minos and Rhadamanthus, got up and, all in a body, with Don Quixote and Sancho too, went to receive Altisidora and help her down from the bier. And she, pretending to be faint, bowed to the Duke and Duchess and to the kings and, looking across at Don Quixote, addressed him thus: 'God forgive you, loveless knight, for because of your cruelty I have spent more than a thousand years, as it seems to me, in the other world. But you, most compassionate squire in all the world, you I thank for the life which is restored to me. From this day forth, friend Sancho, dispose of six of my smocks which I bequeath

GG

to you to make you six shirts; and if they are not all whole at least they are all clean.'

Sancho kissed her hands for the gift, kneeling on the ground with the mitre in his hand. The Duke ordered that this should be taken from him and his cap returned, and that his overcoat should be put on him in place of the robe of flames. But Sancho begged the Duke to leave him the robe and the mitre, which he would like to take with him to his own country as a keepsake to remind him of that amazing adventure. The Duchess replied that he should certainly keep them, he must know already how dearly she loved him.

Then the Duke ordered the courtyard to be cleared, all the people to retire to their rooms, and Don Quixote and Sancho to be taken to the apartments they knew from of old.

Chapter LXX. *Which follows the sixty-ninth and deals with matters indispensable for the clear understanding of this history.*

SANCHO slept that night on a truckle-bed in the same room with Don Quixote, an honour he would have avoided if he could, for he knew very well that, what with questions and answers, his master would never let him sleep. And he was in no mood for much talking, for he was still smarting from the pain of his recent martyrdom, which paralyzed his tongue. In fact he would rather have slept alone in a hovel than in that rich room in company. His fears and suspicions were only too well-founded, for the moment his master got into bed he demanded: 'What do you think, Sancho, of this night's events? Great and powerful are the effects of love disdained, for with your own eyes you have seen Altisidora dead, slain by no other arrows, by no other sword, by no other war-like weapon or lethal poison than the cruelty and scorn with which I have always treated her.'

'She might have died and welcome, when she liked and how she liked,' replied Sancho, 'and left me alone, for I never enamoured her nor slighted her in all my life. I don't know, and I can't think, what the health of that capricious, silly young lady Altisidora has to do with the torture of Sancho Panza. I've told you that already. Now indeed I do plainly see that there are enchanters and enchantments in the world, from whom may God deliver me, for I can't deliver myself. All the same I beg your worship to let me sleep and ask me no more questions if you don't want me to throw myself out of the window.'

'Sleep, Sancho, my friend,' replied Don Quixote, 'if the pin-pricks and pinches and face-slappings you have received will allow you.'

'No pain,' answered Sancho, 'equals the insult of that face-slapping, if only because I suffered it at the hands of waiting-women, confound them! But I beg your worship once more to let me sleep. Sleep is the remedy for all our waking miseries.'

'So be it,' said Don Quixote, 'and God be with you.'

The two of them fell asleep, and in the interval Cide Hamete, the author of this great history, wishes to relate the Duke and Duchess's reasons for devising the elaborate contrivance just described. He says that the Bachelor Sampson Carrasco, mindful how as the Knight of the Mirrors he was beaten and overthrown by Don Quix-ote – which defeat and overthrow spoilt and undid all his schemes – decided to try his hand again, hoping for better success than the last time. So, having learnt where Don Quixote was from the page who brought the letter and present to Sancho's wife, Teresa Panza, he looked out new armour and a fresh horse, and painted a white moon on his shield, loading it all on a mule which was led by a country man – not by Thomas Cecial, his old squire, for fear Don Quixote or Sancho might recognise him. He came, then, to the Duke's castle, and that nobleman informed him of Don Quixote's departure, of the road he had chosen and of his intention of taking part in the jousts at Saragossa. The Duke also described their jests at the knight's expense and the scheme for Dulcinea's disenchantment at the cost of Sancho's posterior. Last of all he gave him an account of the trick Sancho had played on his master by giving him to un-derstand that Dulcinea was enchanted and transformed into a peasant girl, and how the Duchess, his wife, had convinced Sancho that it was he that was mistaken, and that Dulcinea really was en-chanted. All this considerably amused and surprised the Bachelor, as he pondered on Sancho's cunning and simplicity and on Don Quix-ote's extreme folly. The Duke begged him, should he find the knight, to return that way, whether he beat him or not, and give him an account of events. The Bachelor promised that he would

and departed on his quest, but not finding Don Quixote at Saragossa, went on – with what success we know. Then he returned to
the Duke's castle and told him the whole story with the conditions
of the combat, and said that Don Quixote was already on his way
back to fulfil his pledge like a good knight errant, and retire to his
village for a year, during which time, said the Bachelor, he might
possibly be cured of his madness. It was that in fact which had
caused him to assume his disguise, for it was a pitiful thing that a
gentleman of Don Quixote's intelligence should remain a lunatic.
With this he took leave of the Duke and went back to his village,
to wait there for Don Quixote, who was following him. Hence it
was that the Duke had a chance to play this last trick, such pleasure
did he take in the humours of Sancho and Don Quixote. He posted
a number of his servants, on foot and on horseback, on all the roads
round the castle, far and near, in every direction by which he
thought Don Quixote might return, to bring him to the castle,
willingly or by force, should they find him. And when they did they
advised the Duke, who had already arranged what was to be done.
As soon as he got word of Don Quixote's arrival he had the torches
and the lamps lit in the court, and Altisidora placed on her bier with
all the accessories described, the whole farce so well and convincingly contrived that the play was but little removed from reality.
In fact Cide Hamete says that he considers the mockers were as mad
as their victims, and the Duke and Duchess within a hair's breadth
of appearing fools themselves for taking such pains to play tricks
on a pair of fools.

Day surprised that pair, one of them sleeping soundly and the
other wakefully indulging his unbridled fancies, and with it came
the desire to rise; for the feather-bed of sloth never pleased Don
Quixote, whether victor or vanquished. Then Altisidora – returned
in Don Quixote's opinion from death to life – following up her
master's and mistress's humour, came into Don Quixote's room,
crowned with the same garland she had worn on the bier, and
dressed in a loose gown of white taffeta flowered with gold, her
hair loose on her shoulders, and leaning on a black stick of finest
ebony. Disturbed and abashed by her entrance, Don Quixote
shrank down and almost completely covered himself under the
sheets and quilts of his bed, tongue-tied and unable to offer her a

single word of greeting. So Altisidora sat down in a chair beside the head of his bed, and after heaving a deep sigh said in a tender and feeble voice: 'When women of rank and reserved maidens tread honour under foot and permit their tongues to break down all impediments and give public notice of their hearts' secrets they are indeed in desperate straits. I, Don Quixote de la Mancha, am one of these, distressed, vanquished and love-lorn, yet still patient and modest; so excessively patient and modest indeed that my heart burst for my silence and I lost my life. For two days ago, through grief at your cruel treatment – oh, harder than the marble to my plaints, thou stony-hearted knight! – I lay dead, or at least was held to be so by all who saw me; and were it not that Love took pity on me and entrusted my cure to the sufferings of this good squire, there I should have stayed in the other world.'

'Love might just as well have entrusted it to my ass,' said Sancho. 'I should have thanked him for it. But tell me, lady – and may Heaven fix you up with a kinder lover than my master! – what did you see in the other world? What's it like in Hell? For if you die in despair you're sure to end up there.'

'To tell you the truth,' replied Altisidora, 'I couldn't have been dead outright, for I never went to Hell. Once I had entered there indeed I shouldn't have been able to get out at my pleasure. The truth is that I arrived at the gate, where something like a dozen devils were playing at tennis, all in their breeches and doublets, with their collars trimmed with Flanders lace and with ruffles of the same that served them for cuffs, with four inches of arm bare to make their hands look longer. They were holding rackets of fire, and what most astonished me was that, instead of balls, they used what looked like books stuffed with wind and fluff – a most amazing thing! But that didn't astonish me so much as seeing that all the players were grumbling and snarling and cursing, though it's usual in games for the winners to be gay and the losers gloomy.'

'That's no wonder,' observed Sancho, 'for whether they're players or not, devils can't be content, winning or losing.'

'That's probably so,' replied Altisidora, 'but there's another thing that astonishes me too – I mean, which astonished me then – and that was that after the first volley there wasn't a ball left whole or of any use for the next time; and so they whirled through books old and new at a wonderful rate. One of them they dealt such a whack – a brand-new one it was and smartly bound – that they knocked its guts out and scattered the leaves. Then one devil said to another: "Look what book that is." And his mate replied: "It's the second part of the History of Don Quixote de la Mancha, not composed by Cide Hamete, its original author, but by an Aragonese who styles himself a native of Tordesillas." "Away with it, out of here," cried the other devil. "Throw it into the pit of hell, and never let me set eyes on it again." "Is it so bad?" asked the other. "So bad," replied the first, "that if I were to set myself deliberately to make it worse I couldn't!" They went on with their game, tossing other books about, but as I had heard the name of my beloved and adored Don Quixote I endeavoured to retain this vision in my memory.'

'A vision it must have been, beyond a doubt,' said Don Quixote, 'for there is no other person of that name in the world; and that history is passing from hand to hand even now, though it stays in none, for they all kick it on. But I have not been disturbed to hear of myself passing like a phantom body through the shades of Hell, nor through the light of earth either, for I am not the person this history is concerned with. If it were good, faithful and true it would have centuries of life; but if it is bad, its passage will be short from its birth to its burial.'

Altisidora was on the point of proceeding with her complaint against Don Quixote when the knight addressed her: 'I have told you many times, lady, how distressed I am that you have fixed your affections on me; for I can only acknowledge them, not relieve them. I was born to belong to Dulcinea del Toboso. The Fates, if they exist, have dedicated me to her, and to think that any other beauty can occupy the place she holds in my heart is to imagine the impossible. This should be sufficient to make you retreat within the limits of your chastity, for no one can be bound to perform the impossible.'

At this Altisidora pretended to be angry and upset, crying: 'My God, Don Stock-fish, Brazen Soul, Date Stone, more obstinate and hard-hearted than a peasant courted when he is aiming at the butts, I'll tear your eyes out if I get at you. Do you really imagine, Don Vanquished, Don Cudgelled, that I died for you? All you've seen to-night has been pretence. I'm not the sort of woman to let myself grieve by so much as the dirt in one finger-nail for such a camel, much less to die for one!'

'That I can well believe,' put in Sancho, 'for this dying for love's a joke. They may talk about it, but as for doing it — believe it, Judas!'

While they were deep in this discussion the musician and poet who had sung the two stanzas already noted came in and said to Don Quixote with a deep bow: 'Number me among your most faithful servants, Sir Knight, for I have been deeply devoted to you for a long time, both on account of your fame and of your deeds.'

'Tell me, sir,' Don Quixote replied, 'who you are, that my courtesy may respond to your deserts.' The lad replied that he was the musician and panegyrist of the previous night.

'Truly,' replied Don Quixote, 'you have a perfect voice, though what you sang did not seem much to the purpose to me; for what have Garcilaso's stanzas to do with that lady's dying?'

'Do not wonder at that,' replied the singer, 'for among the un-shorn poets of our age it is the custom for each to write as he will, and to steal from whomever he likes, whether it is much to the point or not; and there is nothing they sing or write so stupid that they do not put it down to poetic licence.'

Don Quixote was about to reply, but he was prevented by a visit from the Duke and Duchess, with whom he had a long and charming conversation, during which Sancho displayed such drollery and such shrewdness that he left his hosts more astonished than ever at his mixture of simplicity and acuteness. Don Quixote begged them for leave to depart that same day, since it was more fitting for a vanquished knight like himself to live in a pigsty than in a royal palace. They gladly granted him his request, and the Duchess asked him whether Altisidora remained in his good graces. 'Madam,' he replied, 'your ladyship must learn that all the evil in that maiden arises from idleness, the remedy for which is honest and continuous occupation. She has just now informed me that they wear lace in Hell, and since she must certainly know how to make it let it never be out of her hands; for when she is busy working the bobbins the image or images of her desires will not work in her imagination. That is the truth, and that is my opinion and advice.'

'And mine too,' added Sancho, 'for never in all my life have I seen a lacemaker who died for love. Maidens who have work to do spend more thought on finishing their jobs than on thinking of their loves. I speak from experience, for while I am digging I don't think of my poppet, I mean my Teresa Panza, though I love her better than my eyelashes.'

'That is well said, Sancho,' exclaimed the Duchess, 'and I will see that my Altisidora is kept busy in future with some kind of needlework, for she does it extremely well.'

'There is no reason, my lady, to resort to that remedy,' said Altisidora, 'for the thought of the cruelty with which this vagabond scoundrel has treated me will blot him from my memory without any other help. And now, with your Highness's permission, I will retire from here, so as no longer to have before my eyes his sad countenance – I mean his ugly, abominable face.'

'That,' said the Duke, 'reminds me of the saying: He that flings insults will soon forgive.'

Altisidora made a pretence of wiping her tears with her handkerchief, and with a curtsey to her master and mistress left the room.

'Poor girl,' exclaimed Sancho. 'It's ill-luck you have, very ill luck, for his soul's as dry as rushes and his heart's as tough as oak. Now if it was me you'd had to deal with your pigs would have been brought to a better market, I promise you.'

The conversation ended. Don Quixote dressed himself, and dined with the Duke and Duchess; and that afternoon he departed.

Chapter LXXI. *Of what befell Don Quixote and Sancho, his Squire, on the way to their village.*

THE vanquished and travel-worn Don Quixote rode along, very melancholy on one score and very cheerful on another. His sadness arose from his defeat, and his gaiety from the consideration of Sancho's virtue, as he had shown it in the resurrection of Altisidora; although it was with some reservations that he convinced himself that the lovelorn maiden had really died. But Sancho was by no means cheerful. He was sad because Altisidora had not kept her promise to give him her smocks. And, turning this over and over in his mind, he said to his master: 'Really, sir, I'm the most unfortunate doctor in the whole world. There are physicians who kill their patients and get paid for their trouble, though they do no more than sign a slip of paper for medicines which the apothecary makes up for them, and the trick's done. Yet though bringing that maiden to life has cost me drops of blood, slaps, pinches, pricks and whippings, I don't get a farthing. I swear here and now, though, that if they put another sick person on my hands they'll have to grease them before I cure him. For the abbot must eat that sings for his meat, and I won't believe that Heaven has endowed me with the virtue I have for me to communicate it to others free, gratis and for nothing.'

'You are right, Sancho my friend,' answered Don Quixote, 'and Altisidora has acted very wrongly in not giving you the promised smocks; though your virtue was given you gratis and has cost you no study, unless it be a study to learn to suffer tortures on your person. For myself I can say that if it is payment you want for your whipping on account of Dulcinea's disenchantment, I would long ago have given you what was fair. But I do not know whether payment will sort well with the cure, and I should not wish the reward to hinder the medicine. All the same I think that nothing would be lost by trying. So consider, Sancho, how much you want and whip yourself presently. You may pay yourself cash down with your own hand, for you carry my money.'

Sancho opened his eyes and ears a foot wider at this offer and, consenting in his heart to take a hearty whipping, said to his master: 'Well now, sir, I'm ready to put myself at your disposal and satisfy your worship's desires, for my own advantage. If I appear mercenary it's my love for my wife and children that makes me so. Tell me, your worship, how much a stroke will you give me?'

'Were I to pay you, Sancho,' replied Don Quixote, 'in proportion to the magnitude and importance of the service, the treasure of Venice or the mines of Potosi would be a small recompense. Reckon up what you have of mine, and put a price upon each stroke.'

'The number,' replied Sancho, 'is three thousand three hundred odd, and I have given myself about five of them. The rest are to come. Let those five count as the odd ones, and let us come to the three thousand three hundred which at a quarter of a *real* apiece –

and I won't take less to oblige anyone – come to three thousand
three hundred quarter *reals*, and that three thousand makes one
thousand five hundred half *reals*, which come to seven hundred and
fifty *reals*; and the three hundred make a hundred and fifty half
reals, which comes to seventy-five *reals*; and adding these to the
seven hundred and fifty, it comes to eight hundred and twenty-five
reals. These I will subtract from the money of your worship's I have,
and I shall go home rich and contented, though soundly whipped,
for you don't catch trout ... I say no more.'

'O blessed Sancho! O kindly Sancho!' cried Don Quixote. 'How
deeply we shall be bound to serve you, Dulcinea and I, all the days
of our lives that Heaven shall grant us. If she is returned to her former state – and it is impossible she should not be – her misfortune
will have proved good fortune, and my defeat a most happy triumph. Now look, Sancho, when will you begin the scourging? For
if you will make it quick, I will add a hundred *reals*.'

'When?' replied Sancho. 'To-night, without fail. See, your worship, that we spend it in the fields, under the open sky, and I will lay
my flesh open.'

At last night came, night for which Don Quixote had longed with
all the impatience in the world, for it seemed to him that the wheels
of Apollo's car had broken and that the day was of more than its
customary length; just as lovers feel, who can never adjust time to
their desires. At length they went in among some pleasant trees
which stood some way off the road; and there, emptying Rocinante's saddle and Dapple's pack-saddle, they lay down on the
green grass and supped off Sancho's stores. Then, making a strong
and flexible whip out of Dapple's halter and headstall, Sancho retired some twenty paces from his master among some beeches.
Whereat Don Quixote remarked, seeing him depart with such spirit
and resolution: 'Mind you do not cut yourself to pieces, friend.
Let there be a pause between the strokes. Do not rush headlong forward and have your breath fail you in the middle. Do not lay it on
so strong, I mean, that your life fails you before you reach the required number. And for fear you lose by a card too many or too
few, I will stand close by and count the lashes on this rosary of
mine. May Heaven favour you as your good purpose deserves!'

'A good payer doesn't worry about sureties,' replied Sancho. 'I mean to lay it on so that it hurts without killing, for that's where the whole point of this miracle lies.'

Then he stripped himself to the waist and, seizing the whip, began to lay it on, while Don Quixote counted the strokes. Now Sancho must have given himself six or eight when the joke began to appear tiresome, and very dear at the price; so stopping awhile, he informed his master that he had made a mistake, for each stroke was worth half a *real*, not a quarter.

'Go on, Sancho my friend, and do not be faint-hearted,' said Don Quixote, 'I will double the stakes.'

'In that case,' replied Sancho, 'in God's hands be it. Let it rain lashes.'

But the rogue gave up lashing his own shoulders, and belaboured the trees, uttering such deep groans from time to time that with each one it sounded as if his spirit were being torn from his body. Don Quixote, being naturally humane, and much afraid besides that Sancho might put an end to his life and he through Sancho's imprudence not attain his purpose, now cried out: 'On your life, friend, let the matter rest here. For this seems a rough sort of physic to me, and it would be well to take it gently. Zamora was not won in an hour. You have given yourself a thousand lashes, if I have not miscounted. Let that do for now, for the ass, to use a homely phrase, will carry a load, but not a double load.'

'No, no, sir,' replied Sancho, 'It must not be said of me – the money paid, the work delayed. Stand aside a little longer, your worship, and let me give myself another thousand lashes at any rate. Then in two such bouts we shall have finished this job, and even have something to spare.'

'Well, since you are so well disposed,' said Don Quixote, 'may Heaven help you. Stick to it, and I will stand aside.'

Sancho returned to his task so furiously that he had soon stripped a number of trees of their bark, so severely did he lash himself. And once, raising his voice and dealing one of the beeches a tremendous stroke, he cried: 'Here dies Sampson and all with him.'

Don Quixote ran up at once at the sound of that piteous cry and the crack of the merciless lash and, seizing the twisted halter which served Sancho for a whip, exclaimed: 'Heaven forbid, Sancho my friend, that you should lose your life for my pleasure, for it must serve to support your wife and children. Let Dulcinea await another opportunity, and I will contain myself within the bounds of proximate hope until you gain new strength to conclude this matter to everyone's satisfaction.'

'As your worship would have it so, master,' replied Sancho, 'I'll stop, and gladly. Throw your cloak over my shoulders, for I'm sweating and don't want to catch cold, which is a danger your new flagellants run.'

Don Quixote did as he was asked and, himself remaining in his doublet, covered Sancho, who slept till the sun woke him. Then they resumed their journey, which they concluded for the day in a village nine miles further on. There they dismounted at an inn, which Don Quixote recognized as such, and did not take for a castle with a deep moat, towers, portcullises and a drawbridge, for since his defeat he spoke on all subjects with a sounder judgment, as will now be shown. They lodged him in a lower room, which was hung with some old painted cloths such as you find in small villages, instead of with leather hangings. On one of them some wretched dauber had depicted the rape of Helen at the moment when the bold guest stole her from Menelaus; and on another was the history of Dido and Aeneas — she on a high tower in the act of signalling with half a sheet to her fugitive guest, who was in full flight over the sea in a frigate or brigantine. One noticeable difference between the two pictures, however, was that Helen went with no very ill grace, for she was slyly smiling to herself, but the fair Dido was shown dropping tears as big as walnuts from her eyes. Now when Don Quixote saw this he observed: 'Those two ladies were most unfortunate not to have been born in the present age, and I even more unfortunate not to have been born in theirs. Had I encountered those gentlemen, Troy would not have been burnt nor Carthage destroyed; for all those calamities would have been avoided simply by my killing Paris.'

'I'll bet,' said Sancho, 'that before long there won't be a wine-shop or tavern, an inn or a barber's shop, where the history of our exploits won't be painted up. But I should like them to be painted by a better hand than painted these.'

'You are right, Sancho,' said Don Quixote, 'for this artist is like Orbaneja, the painter of Ubeda, who used to answer when they asked him what he was painting, "whatever it turns out". And if he happened to paint a cock, he would write under it: "This is a cock", in case anyone might think it was a vixen. That is the sort of person, it seems to me, the painter or writer — for it is all one — must have been who published the history of this new Don Quixote that has come out. Or he must have been like a certain poet who hung about the court years ago, by the name of Mauleon, who used to answer any question he was asked offhand. When someone inquired of him the meaning of "*Deum de Deo*", he replied "*Do as you like*". But enough of that. Tell me, Sancho, if you have a mind to give yourself another bout to-night, and whether you had rather be under a roof or beneath the open sky.'

'Indeed, sir,' Sancho replied, 'for the whipping I intend to give myself a house is as good as the fields. But I should like to be among trees, all the same, for they seem to have a fellow feeling and help me marvellously to bear my troubles.'

'No, no, friend Sancho, that shall not be,' replied Don Quixote. 'You must get your strength back, and we shall have to wait till we get to our own village; for we shall be there the day after to-morrow at the latest.'

Sancho replied that it should be as his master pleased, but that he would like to finish the matter off quickly in warm blood and while the mill was grinding. 'For there is often danger in delay, and pray to God and wield the hammer, and one gift is better than two promises, and a bird in the hand is worth two in the bush.'

'No more proverbs, Sancho, in God's name,' exclaimed Don Quixote. 'You seem to be returning to *as it was in the beginning*. Speak plainly, simply and without complications, as I have often asked you before, and you will see how one loaf becomes as good for you as a hundred.'

'I don't know why I'm so unlucky,' replied Sancho, 'but I can't utter a sentence without a proverb, nor utter a proverb that doesn't seem to the point. Still I'll amend if I can.'

And with that their conversation ended for the time being.

Chapter LXXII. *How Don Quixote and Sancho arrived at their village.*

ALL that day Don Quixote and Sancho stayed in that village, waiting in the inn for night, the one to make an end of his flagellation in open country, and the other to witness its completion and with it the accomplishment of his desires. Meanwhile a traveller arrived at the inn on horseback with three or four servants, one of whom said to the man, who was apparently his master, 'Here, Don Alvaro Tarfe, your worship can pass the heat of to-day. The lodging looks clean and cool.'

And overhearing this remark Don Quixote observed to Sancho: 'If I remember rightly, Sancho, I came upon the name of Don Alvaro Tarfe as I was turning over the pages of that second part of my history.'

'That may be so,' answered Sancho. 'Let's let him dismount, and then we'll ask him.'

The horseman dismounted, and the hostess gave him a room on the ground floor opposite Don Quixote's, hung with more painted cloths like those in the knight's apartment. The new arrival changed into light summer clothes and, strolling to the wide cool porch of the inn, where Don Quixote was pacing up and down, asked him: 'Which way are you travelling, my dear sir?'

'To a village nearby,' replied Don Quixote, 'where I live. And where is your worship bound for?'

'I am going to Granada, sir,' replied the gentleman, 'which is my native district.'

'And a good district!' said Don Quixote, 'But be so courteous as to tell me your name, for I am more concerned to know it, I think, than I can well tell you.'

'My name is Don Alvaro Tarfe,' replied the guest.

'Then I take it,' said Don Quixote, 'that you are no doubt that Don Alvaro Tarfe who features in the second part of the History of Don Quixote de la Mancha, recently printed and published by a modern author.'

'I am he,' replied the gentleman, 'and this same Don Quixote, the principal subject of that same history, was a very great friend of mine. It was I who drew him from his home or, at least, persuaded him to go to some jousts which were being held at Saragossa, where I was going myself. And to tell you the truth, I did him many kindnesses and saved him from having his back tickled by the hangman for his foolhardiness.'

'And tell me, Don Alvaro, do I in any way resemble this Don Quixote you speak of?'

'No, certainly not,' replied the guest, 'not at all.'

'And this Don Quixote,' said our one, 'did he have a squire with him called Sancho Panza?'

'Yes, he had,' replied Don Alvaro, 'and though he had the reputation of being a comical fellow I never heard him say anything at all funny.'

'I can very well believe that,' broke in Sancho Panza, 'for it's not everyone that can say good things, and this Sancho Panza you mention, sir, must be a very great knave and a dolt and a thief, all rolled into one. For I'm the true Sancho Panza, and I have more wit than ever rained from the sky. Only put me to the test, your worship. Walk behind me for a year or so, and you'll see what good things fall from me at every step. So many and so good they are that often when I don't know what I'm saying everyone who hears me bursts out laughing. And the true Don Quixote de la Mancha, the famous, the valiant and the wise, the enamoured, the righter of wrongs, the guardian of minors and orphans, the protector of widows, the slayer of maidens, he that has the peerless Dulcinea for his sole mistress, is this gentleman here, my master. Any other Don Quixote whatsoever, and any other Sancho Panza, are a mockery and a dream.'

'By God, I believe you,' replied Don Alvaro, 'for you've said more good things in the four sentences I've heard you utter than the other Sancho Panza in all I heard him say, which was a great deal. He was more of a guzzler than a wit. In fact there's no doubt in my mind that the enchanters who persecute Don Quixote the Good have been trying to persecute me with Don Quixote the Bad. But I don't know what I'm saying, for I dare swear that I left him shut up in the madhouse at Toledo for treatment, and here starts up another Don Quixote very different from mine.'

'I do not know,' said Don Quixote, 'whether I am good, but I can say that I am not " *the bad* ". And to prove it I would have you know,

Don Alvaro Tarfe, that I have never been in Saragossa in all the days of my life. On the contrary, when I was told that the fictitious Don Quixote had taken part in the jousts in that city I decided not to go there, and so to proclaim his lie to the world. Instead I went openly to Barcelona, the treasure house of courtesy, the refuge of strangers, the hospital of the poor, the country of the valiant, the avenger of the injured, and the abode of firm and reciprocal friendships, unique in its position and its beauty. And although the adventures that befell me there occasioned me no great pleasure, but rather much grief, I bore them the better for having seen that city. In short, Don Alvaro Tarfe, I am Don Quixote de la Mancha, the same of whom fame speaks, and that miserable man who sought to usurp my name and take the credit for my designs is not he. I beg your worship, as you are a gentleman, to be so kind as to make a declaration before the mayor of this place that you have never seen me in all the days of your life till to-day, and that I am not the Don Quixote written of in the second part, nor is this Sancho Panza, my squire, the man your worship knew.'

'I'll do that with very great pleasure,' replied Don Alvaro, 'for it's very surprising to see two Don Quixotes and two Sanchos at the same time, alike in their names yet how different in their deeds. Let me affirm once more that I didn't see what I did see, and that what happened to me didn't happen.'

'No doubt,' said Sancho, 'your worship must be enchanted, like my lady Dulcinea del Toboso. Would to Heaven I could disenchant you by giving myself another three thousand three hundred lashes as I'm doing for her, for I would give them you without interest.'

'I don't understand what you mean by lashes,' said Don Alvaro. Sancho answered that it was a long story, but he would tell it him if they chanced to be going the same way.

By now it was dinner time, and just as Don Quixote and Don Alvaro were eating together the mayor of the village happened to come into the inn with a clerk. Whereupon Don Quixote laid a petition before him, claiming as a matter of right that Don Alvaro Tarfe, the gentleman there present, should declare before him that he did not know Don Quixote de la Mancha, also there present, and that it was not he who was written of in a history entitled *The*

Second Part of the Exploits of Don Quixote de la Mancha, composed by a certain Avellaneda, native of Tordesillas. To be brief, the mayor complied in due form. The declaration was made judicially to the great satisfaction of Don Quixote and Sancho, as if such a declaration were of great importance to them, and the acts and deeds of the two Don Quixotes and the two Sanchos did not clearly show the difference between them. Many civilities and offers of service passed between Don Alvaro and Don Quixote, in which the great Manchegan showed so much good sense that Don Alvaro Tarfe was convinced that he had been deceived. He even suspected that he must have been enchanted, since he had touched two such different Don Quixotes with his own hands. As evening came on they left the village, and after about a mile and a half their two roads diverged, one leading to Don Quixote's village, and the other the way Don Alvaro had to take. In the short interval Don Quixote had told him of his disastrous defeat, and of Dulcinea's enchantment and relief, all of which amazed Don Alvaro afresh. However, he went on his way, first embracing Don Quixote and Sancho, and left Don Quixote to his.

That night they spent among some trees to give Sancho an opportunity of performing his penance, which he did in the same way as on the night before, damaging the beech trees' bark more than his shoulders, of which he took such care that the whipping would not have brushed off a fly, if there had been one there. The deluded knight did not miss a single stroke in the count, and found that with the last night's score they came to three thousand and twenty-nine. The sun seems to have risen early to see the sacrifice, and in its light they continued on their way talking, the two of them, about Don Alvaro's mistake, and what a good idea it had been to take his affidavit in due and authentic form before the justice. That day and that night they spent on the road without anything noteworthy befalling them, except that Sancho completed his task, to the inordinate delight of his master, who longed for daylight and to see whether he might meet his now disenchanted lady Dulcinea on the road. And as he travelled on he went up to every woman he encountered to see if she was not Dulcinea del Toboso, holding infallibly that the sage Merlin's promise could not prove false. So, full of hopes and expectations, they climbed to the top of a hill, and when they made out their village Sancho fell on his knees and cried: 'Open your eyes, my beloved country, and see your son Sancho Panza returning – if not rich yet well beaten. Open your arms and receive your son Don Quixote too, who, though conquered by another, has conquered himself – which, as I have heard him say, is the very best kind of victory. I bring money though, and if it's a good whipping they gave me it's a fine mount I have now.'

'Stop these fooleries,' said Don Quixote, 'and let us enter our village right foot foremost. Once there, we will give play to our imaginations and devise the scheme of the pastoral life we mean to follow.'

With this they rode down the hill and made for home.

Chapter LXXIII. *Of the omens Don Quixote met on entering his village, and other matters which adorn and confirm this great history.*

As they approached, Cide Hamete tells us, Don Quixote saw two boys quarrelling on the village threshing floor, and heard one of them say to the other: 'Don't worry, Periquello, you won't see it in all the days of your life.'

When Don Quixote heard this he said to Sancho; 'Did you not hear, friend, what that boy said: – "You'll never see it again, never."'

'Well,' replied Sancho, 'what does it matter what the boy said?'

'What?' exclaimed Don Quixote, 'Do you not see that if you apply that saying to myself, it means that I shall never see Dulcinea again?'

Sancho was just going to reply when he was prevented by the sight of a hare coursing over the fields followed by a number of greyhounds and hunters, and in her terror she ran to take shelter beneath Dapple's feet. Sancho took her up safe in his hands and presented her to Don Quixote, who immediately cried out: '*Malum signum! Malum signum!* A hare flies; the hounds pursue her; Dulcinea will not appear!'

'You're a strange one, your worship,' said Sancho. 'Let's suppose that this hare is Dulcinea del Toboso, and these hounds chasing her are the vagabond enchanters who transformed her into a peasant girl. She runs away; I pick her up and put her into your worship's charge; and you have her in your arms and caress her. Now, where's the bad sign in that, and what ill omen do you draw from it?'

The two boys who had been quarrelling came up to see the hare, and Sancho asked one of them what they had been wrangling about. The one who had said: *You will never see it again*, answered that he had taken a cage of crickets from the other boy and did not intend to give it back to him so long as he lived. Sancho took four quarter *reals* from his pocket and gave them to the boy in return for the cage, which he placed in Don Quixote's hands, saying: 'Here, sir, are these omens broken and destroyed. They have nothing more to do with our fortunes, to my mind, than last year's clouds. And if I'm not mistaken I have heard our parish priest say that Christians and sensible people should pay no attention to such nonsense. And even your worship has told me so in days gone by, and given me to understand that all Christians who heeded omens were fools. But there's no need to dwell on that; let's go on into the village.'

The hunters came up and demanded their hare, which Don Quixote gave them. Then he and Sancho passed on, and as they drew near the village they came upon the priest and the Bachelor Carrasco at their prayers in a meadow. Now it must be mentioned that Sancho had thrown over Dapple and the bundle of arms, by way of a cover, the buckram robe painted with flames of fire which they had put on him in the Duke's castle on the night when Altisidora rose from death. He had also squeezed the mitre on to Dapple's head, and this adornment transformed her as strangely as ever ass was transformed in all the world. The priest and the Bachelor recognised them immediately, and went up to them with open arms. Don Quixote dismounted and embraced them warmly; whilst the boys, whose lynx eyes nothing can escape, sighted the ass's mitre and rushed up to look at it, calling to one another: 'Come on, boys, and you'll see Sancho Panza's ass finer than Mingo, and Don Quixote's beast leaner than ever.'

At length, surrounded by boys, they entered the village in the company of the priest and the Bachelor and, going to Don Quixote's house, found his housekeeper and niece, whom the news of his coming had already reached. It had also reached Teresa Panza,

Sancho's wife, who ran out to see her husband, dishevelled and half naked, dragging her daughter Sanchica by the hand and, seeing him not so well got up as she thought a governor should be, she asked him: 'How is it you come like this, husband, on foot? You look footsore, too, and more like a misgoverned wretch than a governor.'

'Hush, Teresa,' answered Sancho, 'for often where there are hooks there's no bacon. Let's go home and you shall hear wonders. I bring money – and that's what counts – gained by my own industry and at no cost to anyone.'

'Bring your money, good husband,' said Teresa. 'I don't care where you gained it, for however you got it you won't have started up a new custom in the world.'

Sanchica kissed her father and asked him whether he had anything for her, for she was longing for him as they do for showers in May. Teresa then took him by the hand on one side and Sanchica held him by the belt on the other, at the same time pulling Dapple along behind, and they went to their house, leaving Don Quixote at his, in the care of his niece and his housekeeper and in the company of the priest and the Bachelor.

Then without waiting on time or season, Don Quixote took the priest and the Bachelor aside that very moment, and told them in few words of his defeat and the obligation he was under not to leave his village for a year; which he intended to observe to the letter, without infringing it by an atom, as befitted a knight errant bound by the rules and order of his profession. He told them also how he intended to turn shepherd for the year, and pass his time in the solitude of the fields, where he could give free rein to his amorous thoughts, whilst occupying himself in that pastoral and virtuous calling. He begged them to be his companions, if they had not much to do and were not prevented by more important business, and said he would buy sufficient sheep and stock to give them the name of shepherds. But, he informed them, the principal part of the business was already done, for he had fixed on names for them which would fit them to a T. The priest asked him for them, and Don Quixote replied that he was to call himself the shepherd Quixotiz, the Bachelor the shepherd Carrascon, the priest the shepherd Curiambro and Sancho Panza the shepherd Panzino. They were all astonished at Don Quixote's fresh craze. But to keep him from leaving the village again on his chivalries, in the hope that he could be cured in that year, they gave in to his new project, applauding his folly as wisdom and offering to join him in its pursuit.

'That is excellent,' said Sampson Carrasco, 'for, as all the world knows by now, I am a most famous poet. I will compose pastoral or courtly verses at every turn, or whatever best suits the case, to afford us some amusement in the lonely places where we shall have to wander. But what is most important of all, gentlemen, is for each one of us to choose the name of the shepherdess he means to celebrate in his verses, and not to leave the toughest tree without her name inscribed and cut into it, according to the use and custom of love-stricken shepherds.'

'That is quite right,' replied Don Quixote, 'though for myself I have no need to seek for the name of any imaginary shepherdess, since there is the peerless Dulcinea del Toboso, glory of these banks, ornament of these meadows, the prop of beauty, the cream of grace and, in short, a fitting object for all praise however hyperbolical.'

'That is true,' said the priest, 'but we must look around for accommodating shepherdesses, and trim their angles if they do not fit us square.'

'And if our invention fails,' added Sampson Carrasco, 'we will give them the names we see in print. The world is full of them, Phyllidas, Amaryllises, Dianas, Fleridas, Galateas and Belisardas; for as they sell them in the markets we can easily buy them and keep them for our own. If my lady – my shepherdess I should say – should happen to be called Anna, I will celebrate her under the name of Anarda; if she is Francesca, I will call her Francenia; if she is Lucia, Lucinda; for that is what it all comes to. And if Sancho Panza is to enter our confraternity, he can celebrate his wife Teresa Panza under the name of Teresaina.'

Don Quixote smiled at the application of the name, and the priest bestowed infinite praise on his chaste and honourable resolution, repeating his offer to bear him company for as long as he could spare from his unavoidable duties. With this they took their leave of him, begging him most urgently to take good care of his health and keep to a wholesome diet.

Now, as Fate would have it, his niece and his housekeeper had overheard the conversation of these three, and as soon as the two visitors were gone they both went in to Don Quixote, whom his niece addressed: 'What is this, uncle? Now that we were thinking that you had come back to stay at home and live a quiet and decent life here, you want to embroil yourself in fresh mazes. So now it's to be "*Are you coming, gentle shepherd, dearest shepherd, are you going?*" Really, uncle, that straw's too old to make pipes of."

Whereupon the housekeeper added: 'And will your worship be able to stand the heat of the summer afternoons in the fields, and the night dews of winter, and the howling of the wolves? Of course not. For that's a life for stout men, hardened and reared for the work almost from their swaddling clothes. Of the two evils now, it would be the lesser to be a knight errant than a shepherd. Look, sir, take my advice, which I'm not giving you on a stomach full of bread and wine, but fasting and with the experience of my fifty years: – Stay at home, look after your property, confess frequently, be good to the poor, and on my soul be it if any harm come to you.'

'Be quiet, daughters,' replied Don Quixote. 'I know very well what I must do. Take me to bed, for I do not feel very well, and rest assured that, whether I am a knight errant now or a wandering shepherd, I shall never fail to provide for your needs, as you shall find by experience.'

And his good daughters – for such his niece and his housekeeper were – took him to bed where they gave him some food and what comfort they could.

Chapter LXXIV. *Of how Don Quixote fell ill, of the Will he made, and of his Death.*

As all human things, especially the lives of men, are transitory, being ever on the decline from their beginnings till they reach their final end, and as Don Quixote had no privilege from Heaven exempting him from the common fate, his dissolution and end came when he least expected it. Whether that event was brought on by melancholy occasioned by the contemplation of his defeat or whether it was by divine ordination, a fever seized him and kept him to his bed for six days, during which time he was frequently visited by his friends, the priest, the Bachelor and the barber, and his good squire Sancho Panza never left his bedside.

All of them believed that grief at his overthrow and the disappointment of his hopes for Dulcinea's deliverance and disenchantment had brought him to this state, and tried to cheer him in every possible way. The Bachelor bade him be of good heart, and get up and begin on his pastoral life, for which he had already composed an eclogue, which would knock out every one Sannazaro had ever written. He said that he had bought a couple of fine dogs with his own money from a herdsman from Quintanar to guard the flock, one called Barcino and the other Butron. But Don Quixote's dejection persisted all the same. His friends called in a doctor, who took his pulse and did not offer much comfort, saying that he should certainly attend to the salvation of his soul, for his body's was in danger. Don Quixote heard this with a quiet mind, but not so his housekeeper, his niece and his squire, who began to weep piteously, as if he already lay dead before their eyes. It was the doctor's opinion that melancholy and despondency were bringing him to his end. Don Quixote begged to be left alone, for he wanted to sleep a little. They obeyed him, and he slept for more than six hours, at a stretch as they say; so long, in fact, that his housekeeper and his niece thought that he would pass away in his sleep. But at the end of that time he woke and cried out loudly: 'Blessed be Almighty God, who has vouchsafed me this great blessing! Indeed his mercies are boundless, nor can the sins of men limit or hinder them.'

His niece was listening to her uncle, and these words seeming to her more rational than his general speech, at least during that illness, she asked him: 'What is it you say, sir? Is there anything new? What mercies are these, or what sins of men?'

'The mercies, niece,' answered Don Quixote, 'are those which God has shown me at this moment, mercies to which, as I have said, my sins are no impediment. My judgment is now clear and free from the misty shadows of ignorance with which my ill-starred and continuous reading of those detestable books of chivalry had obscured it. Now I know their absurdities and their deceits, and the only thing that grieves me is that this discovery has come too late, and leaves me no time to make amends by reading other books, which might enlighten my soul. I feel, niece, that I am on the point of death, and I should like to meet it in such a manner as to convince the world that my life has not been so bad as to leave me the character of a madman; for though I have been one, I would not confirm the fact in my death. Call my good friends, my dear, the priest, Bachelor Sampson Carrasco and Master Nicholas the barber, for I want to confess and make my will.'

But his niece was excused this task by the entrance of the three. And the moment Don Quixote saw them he exclaimed: 'Congratulate me, good sirs, for I am Don Quixote de la Mancha no longer, but Alonso Quixano, called for my way of life the Good. Now I am the enemy of Amadis of Gaul and of all the infinite brood of his progeny. Now all profane histories of knight errantry are odious to me. I know my folly now, and the peril I have incurred from the reading of them. Now, by God's mercy, I have learnt from my own bitter experience and I abominate them.'

When the three heard his words they believed that some fresh madness had certainly seized him, and Sampson said to him: 'Must you come out with that, Don Quixote, just now when we have news that the Lady Dulcinea is disenchanted? Now that we are just on the point of turning shepherds to spend our lives singing like any princes, do you want to turn hermit? No more of that, I pray you. Return to your senses and cease your idle tales!'

'Tales?' replied Don Quixote. 'Up to now they have been only too real, to my cost. But, with Heaven's aid, my death shall turn them to my profit. I feel, sirs, that I am rapidly dying. Stop your fooling, and bring me a priest to confess me and a clerk to make my will, for in such extremities as this a man must not jest with his soul. So send for a clerk, I beg of you, while my friend the priest confesses me.'

They looked at one another in amazement at Don Quixote's words and, though in doubt, were inclined to believe him. And one of the signs by which they concluded that he was dying was the ease with which he changed from mad to sane; for he said much more in the vein of his last utterances, so well spoken, so Christian and so connected, that they were finally resolved of all their doubts and convinced that his mind was sound. The priest made everyone leave the room, remained alone with him and confessed him. The Bachelor went for the clerk, and in a short time came back with him and with Sancho Panza, who had had news from Carrasco of his master's state and, finding the housekeeper and the niece in tears, began to blubber and weep himself. When the confession was ended the priest came out, saying: 'Truly he is dying and truly he is sane, Alonso Quixano the Good. We had better go in so that he can make his will.' This news gave a terrible start to the brimming eyes of his housekeeper, his niece and his good squire, Sancho Panza, causing them to break out into fresh tears and groans. For in truth, as has been said before, whether he was plain Alonso Quixano the Good, or Don Quixote de la Mancha, he was always of an amiable disposition and kind in his behaviour, so that he was well beloved, not only by his own household but by everyone who knew him.

The clerk went in with the others and, after he had drawn up the heads of the will, Don Quixote disposed of his soul with all the requisite Christian formalities and came to the bequests, saying:

'*Item, this is my will regarding certain moneys which Sancho Panza, whom in my madness I made my squire, retains, there having been between him and me certain accounts, receipts and disbursements. I wish him not to be charged with them, nor asked to account for them, but if there should be any surplus after he has paid himself what I owe him, the residue is to be his. It will be very little, and may it do him much good. And if when I was mad I was party to giving him the governorship of an isle, now that I am sane I would give him a kingdom, were I able, for the simplicity of his nature and the fidelity of his conduct deserve it.*'

Then, turning to Sancho, he said: 'Pardon me, friend, that I caused you to appear mad, like me, making you fall into the same sort of error as myself, the belief that there were and still are knights errant in the world.'

'Oh, don't die, dear master!' answered Sancho in tears. 'Take my advice and live many years. For the maddest thing a man can do in this life is to let himself die just like that, without anybody killing him, but just finished off by his own melancholy. Don't be lazy, look you, but get out of bed, and let's go out into the fields dressed as shepherds, as we decided to. Perhaps we shall find the lady Dulcinea behind some hedge, disenchanted and as pretty as a picture. If it's from grief at being beaten you're dying, put the blame on me and say you were tumbled off because I girthed Rocinante badly. For your worship must have seen in your books of chivalries that it's a common thing for one knight to overthrow another, and the one that's conquered to-day may be the conqueror to-morrow.'

'That's right,' said Sampson. 'Honest Sancho has hit the truth of the matter.'

'Let us go gently, gentlemen,' said Don Quixote, 'for there are no birds this year in last year's nests. I was mad, but I am sane now. I was Don Quixote de la Mancha, but to-day, as I have said, I am Alonso Quixano the Good. May my sincere repentance restore your former esteem for me. Now let the clerk go on.

'*Item, I bequeath all my estate, without reserve, to Antonia Quixana, my niece, here present, there being first deducted from it in the most convenient way all that is necessary for the fulfilment of my bequests. And the first payment to be made I desire to be the wages due to my housekeeper for the time she has been in my service, and twenty ducats besides for a dress. I leave as my executors Master Priest and Master Sampson Carrasco, here present. Item, it is my wish that, should my niece Antonia Quixana be inclined to wed, she should marry a man of whom she has first had evidence that he does not even know what books of chivalry are; and in case it shall be discovered that he does know, and my niece shall yet wish to marry him, and shall marry him, she shall lose all I have bequeathed her, which my executors may distribute in pious works as they think fit. Item, I beseech the said gentlemen, my executors, that if by good fortune they should come to know the alleged author of a history circulating hereabouts under the title of* The Second Part of the Exploits of Don Quixote de la Mancha, *they shall beg him on my behalf, with the greatest earnestness, to forgive the occasion I unwittingly gave him of publishing so many gross absurdities as are therein written; for I quit this life with an uneasy conscience at having given him an excuse for writing them.*'

With this he concluded his testament and, falling into a faint, lay stretched at full length on the bed. Everyone was alarmed and ran to his assistance, and during the three days that he lived after making his will he fainted very frequently. The house was in a turmoil. However his niece ate, his housekeeper drank and Sancho Panza was cheerful; for legacies tend to dull or moderate in the inheritor the grief that nature claims for the deceased.

At last Don Quixote's end came, after he had received all the sacraments and expressed his horror of books of chivalry in strong and moving terms. The clerk, who happened to be present, said that he had never read in any book of chivalries of a knight errant dying in his bed in so calm and Christian a manner as Don Quixote, who amidst the compassionate tears of all present gave up the ghost — that is to say, died.

When the priest saw that he was no more he desired the clerk to draw up a certificate that Alonso Quixano the Good, commonly called Don Quixote de la Mancha, had passed out of this present life and died a natural death; which testimonial he required in order to deprive any author other than Cide Hamete Benengeli of all excuse for falsely resuscitating him and writing interminable histories of his deeds.

Such was the end of the Ingenious Gentleman of La Mancha, whose dwelling Cide Hamete was unwilling to indicate exactly, so that every town and village of La Mancha might contend for the honour of fathering and possessing him, as the seven cities of Greece did for Homer. The tears of Sancho, of Don Quixote's niece and of his housekeeper are not here recorded, nor are the recent epitaphs upon his tomb; but this is what Sampson Carrasco put there:

> Here lies the gentle knight and stout,
> Who to such height of valour got
> That, if you mark his deeds throughout,
> Death over his life triumphed not
> With bringing of his death about.
>
> The world as nothing he did prize,
> For as a scarecrow in men's eyes
> He lived, and was their bugbear too;
> And had the luck, with much ado,
> To live a fool, and yet die wise.

And said the most prudent Cide Hamete to his pen: 'Here you shall rest, hanging from this rack by this copper wire, my goose-quill. Whether you are well or ill cut I know not, but you shall live long ages there, unless presumptuous and rascally historians take you down to profane you. But before they approach you, warn them as best you are able:

> Beware, beware, you scoundrels,
> I may be touched by none:
> This is a deed, my worthy king,
> Reserved for me alone.

'For me alone Don Quixote was born and I for him. His was the power of action, mine of writing. Only we two are at one, despite that fictitious and Tordillescan scribe who has dared, and may dare again, to pen the deeds of my valorous knight with his coarse and ill-trimmed ostrich feather. This is no weight for his shoulders, no task for his frozen intellect; and should you chance to make his acquaintance, you may tell him to leave Don Quixote's weary and mouldering bones to rest in the grave, nor seek, against all the canons of death, to carry him off to Old Castile, or to bring him out of the tomb, where he most certainly lies, stretched at full length and powerless to make a third journey, or to embark on any new expedition. For the two on which he rode out are enough to make a mockery of all the countless forays undertaken by all the countless knights errant, such has been the delight and approval they have won from all to whose notice they have come, both here and abroad. Thus you will comply with your Christian profession by offering good counsel to one who wishes you ill, and I shall be proud and satisfied to have been the first author to enjoy the pleasure of witnessing the full effect of his own writing. For my sole object has been to arouse men's contempt for all fabulous and absurd stories of knight errantry, whose credit this tale of my genuine Don Quixote has already shaken, and which will, without a doubt, soon tumble to the ground. Farewell.'

A Recent Penguin Classic

CAMOENS
THE LUSIADS

TRANSLATED BY W. C. ATKINSON

L 26

Camoens is the greatest name in Portuguese literature, and *The Lusiads* (1572) ranks by common consent as the noblest epic in any language of the great age of discovery. Camoens himself had followed in the wake of Vasco da Gama and the other pioneers who, opening up the sea route to India, laid the foundations of a new kind of empire that in the space of a few decades stretched from Brazil to China. The imaginative re-creation of that achievement became in his hands an interpretation not merely of Portugal and her people but of that other and vital aspect of the Renaissance, overseas expansion, which revolutionized men's knowledge of the world and provided new fields of experience against which to assay traditional philosophies and beliefs. Instinct always with the spirit of high endeavour against incalculable odds, it is, too, a thrilling narrative of maritime perils and mischances, of hazardous contacts with strange lands and races, and as such has for centuries made a profound appeal to English readers in a succession of verse translations. The present version, the first, it is believed, ever to have been made into English prose, seeks to recapture the interest of that narrative for its own sake.

The translator is Stevenson Professor of Spanish at Glasgow University. He has published *Spain: a Brief History* (1934) and contributed to many learned periodicals.

2s 6d

Again Available

CHAUCER
THE CANTERBURY TALES
TRANSLATED BY NEVILL COGHILL

L 22

The Canterbury Tales is one of the great books of the world and is certainly the liveliest, wisest, wittiest presentation of the human comedy in our language. The passage of time has, however, in the course of five and a half centuries, obscured it a little from us, and what were once the freshest colloquial Chaucerisms seem at times archaic, quaint, and even difficult to understand to-day. Notes and glossaries are necessary, yet they impede the eager reader plunging for pleasure among the tales. And pleasure there is in plenty, whether in the sharp portrayal of a lively and varied human nature that does not seem to have changed much since the fourteenth century, or in the tales that are told; tales that range from noble romances of love and warfare to the ruderies of millers and cooks. Nevill Coghill's translation or modernization, passages from which have been read and later dramatized on the B.B.C.'s Third Programme, has given the easy fluency of a modern conversational idiom to Chaucer's work, while remaining faithful in scholarship to the original texts, without expurgation; readers who have hitherto found Chaucer too difficult will here become easily and happily acquainted with him and the rich legacy he made to them and to England.

'Altogether Mr Coghill's achievement is remarkable. He has been almost consistently successful and his practice carries out his theory and intentions. The bland, humorous, observing, and courtly spirit that informs the original is somehow preserved in a different idiom.' – *The Times Educational Supplement* character of a madman; for though I have been one, I would not confirm the fact in my death. Call my good friends, my dear, the priest, Bachelor Sampson Carrasco and Master Nicholas the barber, for I want to confess and make my will.'

But his niece was excused this task by the entrance of the three. And the moment Don Quixote saw them he exclaimed: 'Con-gratulate me, good sirs, for I am Don Quixote de la Mancha no lon-ger, but Alonso Quixano, called for my way of life the Good. Now I am the enemy of Amadis of Gaul and of all the infinite brood of his progeny. Now all profane histories of knight errantry are odious to me. I know my folly now, and the peril I have incurred from the reading of them. Now, by God's mercy, I have learnt from my own bitter experience and I abominate them.'

When the three heard his words they believed that some fresh madness had certainly seized him, and Sampson said to him: 'Must you come out with that, Don Quixote, just now when we have news that the Lady Dulcinea is disenchanted? Now that we are just on the point of turning shepherds to spend our lives singing like any princes, do you want to turn hermit? No more of that, I pray you. Return to your senses and cease your idle tales!'

'Tales?' replied Don Quixote. 'Up to now they have been only too real, to my cost. But, with Heaven's aid, my death shall turn them to my profit. I feel, sirs, that I am rapidly dying. Stop your fooling, and bring me a priest to confess me and a clerk to make my will, for in such extremities as this a man must not jest with his soul. So send for a clerk, I beg of you, while my friend the priest con-fesses me.'

They looked at one another in amazement at Don Quixote's words and, though in doubt, were inclined to believe him. And one of the signs by which they concluded that he was dying was the ease with which he changed from mad to sane; for he said much more in the vein of his last utterances, so well spoken, so Christian and so connected, that they were finally resolved of all their doubts and convinced that his mind was sound. The priest made everyone leave the room, remained alone with him and confessed him. The Bachelor went for the clerk, and in a short time came back with him and with Sancho Panza, who had had news from Carrasco of his master's state and, finding the housekeeper and the niece in tears,

All of them believed that grief at his overthrow and the disappointment of his hopes for Dulcinea's deliverance and disenchantment had brought him to this state, and tried to cheer him in every possible way. The Bachelor bade him be of good heart, and get up and begin on his pastoral life, for which he had already composed an eclogue, which would knock out every one Sannazaro had ever written. He said that he had bought a couple of fine dogs with his own money from a herdsman from Quintanar to guard the flock, one called Barcino and the other Button. But Don Quixote's dejection persisted all the same. His friends called in a doctor, who took his pulse and did not offer much comfort, saying that he should certainly attend to the salvation of his soul, for his body's was in danger. Don Quixote heard this with a quiet mind, but not so his housekeeper, his niece and his squire, who began to weep piteously, as if he already lay dead before their eyes. It was the doctor's opinion that melancholy and despondency were bringing him to his end. Don Quixote begged to be left alone, for he wanted to sleep a little. They obeyed him, and he slept for more than six hours, at a stretch as they say; so long, in fact, that his housekeeper and his niece thought that he would pass away in his sleep. But at the end of that time he woke and cried out loudly: 'Blessed be Almighty God, who has vouchsafed me this great blessing! Indeed his mercies are boundless, nor can the sins of men limit or hinder them.'

His niece was listening to her uncle, and these words seeming to her more rational than his general speech, at least during that illness, she asked him: 'What is it you say, sir? Is there anything new? What mercies are these, or what sins of men?'

'The mercies, niece,' answered Don Quixote, 'are those which God has shown me at this moment, mercies to which, as I have said, my sins are no impediment. My judgment is now clear and free from the misty shadows of ignorance with which my ill-starred and continuous reading of those detestable books of chivalry had obscured it. Now I know their absurdities and their deceits, and the only thing that grieves me is that this discovery has come too late, and leaves me no time to make amends by reading other books, which might enlighten my soul. I feel, niece, that I am on the point of death, and I should like to meet it in such a manner as to convince the world that my life has not been so bad as to leave me the